Rembrandt

Rembrandt

a novel by

GLADYS SCHMITT

RANDOM HOUSE · NEW YORK

For Simon

Contents

BOOK I

1623

When the miller Harmen Gerritszoon added "van Rijn" to his name, it was not to make himself sound like a person of consequence. He began to use the name of the river because there were so many Harmens and Gerrits, and with new mills springing up in the windy city of Leyden, it became advisable for him to indicate on his sacks that brewers who wanted more of his finely ground malt could depend on getting it from that particular Harmen, son of Gerrit, whose mill was on the bank of the Rhine.

His life had held little promise to begin with. While his mother was still carrying him, it had looked as if anybody who survived the Spanish occupying army would be wiped out by that other implacable enemy, the sea. Like most of the Leydeners, his people were Protestants—psalm-singers, image-breakers, hot partisans of the Prince of Orange—and had lived for months under the general death sentence passed by the Spanish on all their kind. That sentence could be carried out without further accusation or any pretense of a public trial: when they went about what mean business was left to them in the paralyzed city, it was not unusual for them to find the butcher or the baker dangling by a rope in the doorway of his shop or leaning half-charred against a stake in the square. God, pure and simple, was all they had left to rely on; and it was strange that they did not consider themselves God-forsaken when the great storms gathered the ocean into one solid, oily, yellow-brown line of crests and sent it crashing against the dykes from the Flemish coast to the Zuyder Zee. To the sixteen thousand Protestant martyrs and the ten thousand slaughtered in futile battles with the Spaniards, another hundred thousand were added, swallowed up with their houses and cattle and everything but their weather vanes and steeples in the great December flood.

No, he had not lain peaceful in the womb, or known much comfort in his cradle. During his infancy, helpless endurance had been replaced by what had seemed insane defiance; and city after city, slamming its gates against the tyrant, had paid for its foolhardy insolence in rape and murder and fire—everything but the indestructible towers of the Middle Ages turned to cinders and leveled with the depopulated streets. There were times when communication was cut off between town and town, and guesses and rumors intensified the conviction of universal calamity. Trying to reap the remains of his trampled crop on a hillside, a farmer saw the walls of a city below him suddenly filled like a great brazier with leaping flames; looking up from his forbidden Bible on a Sabbath afternoon, a burgher heard a great lamentation carried in on

3

the wind from a neighboring town where thousands were being put to the sword. That Harmen Gerritszoon or any other man should have come alive and whole out of those times was a proof of God's kindness to His little ones; otherwise they would certainly have perished or been warped into Devil's children, taking in fear as they did with every breath and choking on the curdle of fear in their mother's milk.

He was only four years old when the Spanish had come to besiege his own city; and he could never be sure, when he looked back on that protracted agony, what he could take for a real memory and what had come alive for him because he had heard it recounted a hundred times as reason for thanksgiving at a full table. Had he really stood on the walls and seen the country between the battlements and the yellowish water swarming with the ranks of the black-beards, settled as thick as horseflies on a piece of summer meat? Had he heard them shout up that not a sparrow could get in or out of the city now, or had somebody told it to him afterwards, aping their crazy Dutch? He was sure he could remember the taste of the malt-cake that everybody had eaten after the last of the bread was gone: teeth covered with a sticky coating and tongue cleaving to the roof of the mouth were sensations a man was not likely to make up. He probably could not actually recall the rats, the cats, the dogs, the flesh of sick horses, for his mother told them she had never named the meat and had done whatever she could to obliterate the nature of the creature before she put it on the plate. Nettles, plantain, timothy grass, leaves and bark of trees, boiled leather—these too he had eaten, folding his hands over the board while his father, without irony, had invited the Lord to be a guest at the meal and had finished off the grace with a prayer for the coming of the navy of the Prince of Orange, which was rumored to lie just out of sight beyond the wild stretch of dunes outside the westward wall.

Six months that siege had lasted, and he remembered it mostly as a great, tired silence; the recollection came upon him like a sickness whenever he read in Ecclesiastes, "And the mourners go about the streets." Pestilence had come to work hand in hand with starvation, and no man rose from his bed without asking himself which of those he loved had died in the night. There was not even any weeping—nobody had the strength for weeping—and every utterance, from "God rest his soul" to "Go pick up your toys" came out on a sigh. One thing he was sure he could remember: his mother and he and some of the neighbor women and their children—so cadaverously like what hung on the Spanish gibbets that it seemed strange they should be moving about— went to the cemetery, the only place left as yet unstripped, to eat the grass and ivy from the graves. As they ate, they had kept up a strange, psalmlike murmur, half speech, half chanting; and his persistent curiosity to know what they had been saying had driven him to ask his mother about it in later, better days. "Ah, do you remember that?" she said. "We asked them to forgive us for taking what was theirs. We kept

4

it untouched for a long time, that graveyard, and then we could not leave it any more; we had to give the green things to the children. We were begging their forgiveness for robbing their graves."

The dead had had a watery sleep of it in the weeks before the deliverance. The little navy of the Prince of Orange was the sole remaining hope of Leyden, since the army and the Prince's brother Louis had been slaughtered in the mud at the battle of Mookerheyde. There was only one way to bring the fleet up to the battlements: they sallied out by night and smashed their dykes, so that the sea came in upon the land and the ships were borne in over the dunes and villages on the encroaching flood. Those ships had come over drowned crops and farmsteads, past balconies and steeples and floating houses—but they had come. And what had ruined the land had also devoured the invader; for months after the inundation the receding waters had yielded up the corpses of the Spanish veterans—hundreds had been caught before they could make good their flight.

With such a beginning, who would be foolish enough to hanker after more than the good God had provided? That the Spaniard should have marched away, that the sea should have seeped back into its appointed place, that the drowned meadows and villages should have had their resurrection was enough and more than enough. Harmen Gerritszoon considered himself blessed in the possession of a fine mill, a good house, and a kitchen garden flourishing in what had once been waterlogged country outside the city walls. Adding "van Rijn" to his name was only a prudent measure taken for the sake of his customers; to pretend that he had gotten himself knighted by some Papist king in a foreign court was alien to his nature and his history. His cup ran over, goodness and mercy had followed him, and he would have considered it a sacrilege to ask for anything beyond the bounty in his hands.

Not that he saw the world as uniformly benign, washed in the tepid gleam of an easy piety. Nobody could know the fullness of the light without having looked into the shadow; and there were shadows in his own family that neither he nor his wife tried to hide from themselves. Gerrit, the eldest and the handsomest of the children who had stayed with him, was an almost helpless cripple; both his shins had been shattered when he swerved under the weight of a sack of barley and toppled over the side of the stairs. And Gerrit was not one of those whose spirits sweeten with affliction: his face, startlingly out of keeping with the soft and sunny curls around it, was greyed and hollowed, and his lips were as wry as if he had a perpetual bad taste in his mouth. Adriaen was healthy and well-married and solidly set up as a shoemaker in a decent shop; but because his ailing elder brother had been given much by necessity, and his gifted younger brother Rembrandt even more by the parents' choice, he felt himself cheated. Every now and again he let it be known that if *he* had been enrolled at the university he would never have abandoned it to waste time on crayons and paint-pots; he would have stayed there until he was ready to do something worth while, like preach the word of God.

As for the only girl—it was a hard business for a man to judge his daughter. Lysbeth was blond and buxom, with a white skin brightened by the pink spots on her cheeks and her round little chin, and there would have been nothing to keep her from being as sought-after as any girl in the neighborhood if only she had learned to hold her tongue. But scarcely an evening went by with company in the house when she did not make a spectacle of herself. She delivered impassioned speeches whose intent she never knew until she was half-finished; the less familiar she was with a subject, the more she had to say about it; the more distinctly she saw herself put in the wrong, the more she insisted that she was right, right, right, staring at her bewildered opponent with injured, china-blue eyes. So much ardor might have been overlooked in a girl in her teens if there had not been an indefinable falseness about it all: when she was at her hottest, with her face flushed and her ribbons jerking, he felt—and knew that others felt it too—an underlayer of almost repellent cold. Lads still walked with her on the battlements or the dunes, but none of them ever turned up more than five or six times, and there were long and empty waits between them. She was a good girl, his Lysbeth, and it was a pity to see her playfellows all being married around her—such a pity that cousins and friends of the family had taken to buying her gifts by way of consolation. But these, too, she turned into a cause for embarrassment: every scarf, every brooch, every pair of velvet roses for her shoes she accepted as if it were the sign of some special devotion. Which was particularly unfortunate, since Jan Lievens, Rembrandt's former friend back home on a visit from Amsterdam, had brought her a little red Gospel with metal clasps, and big and good-looking as the Lievens boy was—though a little soft for Harmen Gerritszoon's taste—she was bound to get ideas into her head.

Rembrandt and the Lievens boy . . . It was their absence that had brought on the stillness in the springtime house, the tendency to brood on solemn things, the restlessness that kept taking him into the garden to look at the hyacinth and tulip sprouts. They had gone to the mill to carry some sacks up to the drying-floor, and he was not sorry to miss two or three hours of the young Amsterdammer's company: his high-sounding pronouncements and grandiose gestures, impressive at first, seemed affected after a couple of days. But Rembrandt he missed; on the rare occasions when he spent an afternoon in the house, he liked to have Rembrandt sitting at the table with paper or a square of copper, sketching, pondering, holding one of those conversations in which a sentence, suspended to make way for a series of strokes with the crayon or the etching needle, would be finished after a long pause, the coarse mane of reddish hair lifted into sunlight, the blunt face suddenly kin-

6

dled by the eyes, the eyes themselves—vague with speculation a moment before—sharp and aware, shedding a cool grey light.

And now he thought of the painting on the easel in the attic: with the help of an old purple cloak bought from a ragpicker, Rembrandt was doing his brother Gerrit as Saint Bartholomew. For the first time, with that picture to look at, he had been thinking that his youngest might well recompense the family for what they had sacrificed, might even wipe out the memory of his fruitless session at the university or at least turn it into a kind of joke. On that piece of canvas for which, according to Adriaen, a preposterous price had been paid, Gerrit had actually become Saint Bartholomew, the rainy-day aches in his shattered shins changed into foreshadowings of the pains of martyrdom. Thinking of the pale purplish mantle, deep-piled and rubbed in places like actual velvet, thinking of the moisture of pain on the wan forehead, so real that it invited touch, he could imagine his son in a studio of his own on a good Leyden street; he could even see him as respected as his master, the excellent van Swanenburgh, doing portraits of the Regents of the orphanage and commissioned by the Burgomaster to paint some big historical canvas to be hung in the City Hall.

The house was quiet. The late afternoon sun, weak behind a veil of cloud, lay over the empty and orderly back room. Gerrit was in bed with a book, his wife was at the spit in the kitchen, and Lysbeth had gone to the center of town, where he had sent her to invite Heer van Swanenburgh to do them and their guest the honor of dropping in this evening for a little conversation and a mug of beer. It had been a daring thing to issue such an invitation. The master had come twice before to the van Rijn house, as courtesy required, to let them know that he had accepted Rembrandt as his apprentice and to acknowledge with thanks his receipt of the first installment of the fee, and on both those occasions he had shown them all a warm and easy cordiality. But he belonged to the old aristocracy and was worlds above them, and only the fact that young Lievens had once worked in his studio had given Harmen Gerritszoon courage to ask him to the house as though he had been a cousin or a fellow-tradesman or a family friend.

Yes, and the picture had emboldened him too. This morning, while he stood in front of the easel, it had occurred to him that Heer van Swanenburgh, even though his studio drew the best of the Leyden student artists, must have had few apprentices who could do as well and that he might be willing to extend something more than the traditional courtesies for such a promising pupil's sake. But now, since it was growing late and he was sure that Lysbeth would have hurried home if the news had been good, he felt impelled to go up to the loft and have another look for reassurance: were they as real as he remembered them—the crushed places on the old velvet cloak and the sweat standing out on the wan brow?

7

Lysbeth Harmensdochter prided herself on her good sense, a quality which her friends remarked on with increasing frequency. She knew that her father would be anxious about the result of her walk to town and that her mother should be told as soon as possible that not only the master but also his Italian wife—a real honor because Vrouw van Swanenburgh called only on the richest burghers—would pay them a visit tonight. There was herring to chop, beer to cool in a bucket of water, bread to bring from the baker's, a fire to lay in the front room; and the mistress of the house would have to move fast, since the afternoon was almost gone. Her vaunted good sense carried her in a hurry as far as the Pelican Quay, from which she could see the mill, but there it was suddenly lost because it occurred to her that her brother and his visitor might still be inside. Finding all at once that good sense was a barren source of satisfaction, she turned onto the muddy path still marked by the hoofs of the horses that had brought the barley in, and once she was inside, in the warm and familiar shadow with the smell of fermenting grain around her, her sense of urgency was completely gone.

The fact that the boys were nowhere on the ground floor did not discourage her: it was no place to lie on your back and carry on high talk about fame and art—the rats came back almost as quickly as the rat-catcher carried them away. As she crossed to the steep stairs that had been poor Gerrit's undoing, she could feel the boys' presence somewhere in the sun-drenched shadow, and it was hard to suppress the desire to call out the beloved name. "Jan," she said in a whisper, breathing it into the rich-smelling duskiness with yearning and passion, as the poets said. But the last few years had taught her that matters seldom turned out well if she began them in so high a key; and just before she reached the place on the steps where her head would become visible, she stopped and composed herself, wiping the shine from her nose and flicking out the damp curls that came forward over her brow.

"We almost never draw from casts in Lastman's studio. We almost always work from models," said the deep and impressive voice of the guest from Amsterdam.

"Really?" said Rembrandt. "Women, too?"

"We have women in whenever there's need of them. There are plenty in the city who make their living that way."

"Young women? Pretty women?"

"Oh, now you're asking for too much, my friend. No, they're a flabby lot, really—the master says they're held in shape only by the grace of God and their stays. You should see the one we had last month—she had a belly as big as a keg, and—"

Lysbeth coughed out of discretion and went up two more steps into their sight, looking not at them but beyond them at the malt-mash, flattened out like an enormous pancake on the drying-floor. She was glad that her own belly scarcely curved the gathers in her skirt of flowered cloth.

"Oh, Lysbeth," said young Lievens, jumping up from the grain-strewn planks with cosmopolitan courtliness.

"What are you doing here, Puss? Are we wanted?" said Rembrandt, scarcely bothering to lift his head from the pile of empty sacks it rested on.

Why must he use the foolish pet name in Jan's presence? It relegated her to the place of a troublesome little sister, and she was eighteen, a good year older than he. "No," she said, looking with disapproval at his prone and impervious person. "I was just coming back from a walk, and I thought—"

The visitor made it unnecessary for her to finish by waving her to a seat of honor made of two full sacks laid one upon the other, and let himself down a little below her on the drying-floor. Rembrandt stayed on his back, still playing the surly brother, his head at her feet, his trunk, sturdy and muscular, going out at an angle, his feet in their dusty black shoes almost touching the curled edge of the malt-mash. "Of course, casts aren't exactly to be sneered at," he said, as if she had never made her appearance. "I've learned a thing or two from casts, and from the look of that charcoal male nude you showed me yesterday, so have you."

"That wasn't drawn from a cast, my lad. That was from the statue itself; Lastman owns it. There's all the difference on earth between marble and a dead-white plaster cast. The marble looks alive—it's yellowish, you know, and I imagine it's gotten more so from lying in the ground all those centuries."

Rembrandt sat up and clasped his knees with his hands; they were blunt and knotted even though he had done little rough work, and the knobby wrists were covered with reddish hair. "It's a fine statue, no doubt about it. At least I can copy your charcoal—that is, if I may," he said, fixing his imperious grey look on his companion's face.

"Certainly. Anything I brought back is at your service. But it's a pity you should be copying other people's drawings, with *your* talent. It's time you were working from the originals."

The charged stillness that came over the two of them made her wonder whether they had been discussing matters they meant to keep hidden from her. The air was so quiet that the great sails of the windmill were not moving in the least, and the beams of light slanting to the drying-floor were undisturbed except by gilded motes of dust.

"Oh, I work from originals," Rembrandt said at last. "It isn't as if van Swanenburgh didn't have his own authentic things."

Here, she thought, was the time to tell them about the master's forthcoming visit. She opened her mouth and assumed an air of happy anticipation, but Lievens broke in before she could speak. "Yes, I remem-

9

ber," he said with a disparaging smile. "That Medusa head of his for instance—does he still have you draw it twenty different ways? In the couple of years I was with him I got to know every twist in every snake by heart."

"It's months since we've used that Medusa. You wouldn't have seen the fine old Florentine medallions we're working on now; he got those after you were gone."

"Any antiquities?"

"No, no new antiquities . . ."

"Well, Lastman owns at least a dozen. He came back from Italy with five or six, and his friends over there keep sending him more. Besides, it isn't only what's at Lastman's—it's all the things you can get to see. Last Friday I had a day off; and in that one day, between the collections and the auctions, I saw a Michelangelo drawing, a Titian portrait, and a beautiful little nude in oil by Caravaggio. And if you're talking about medallions, old coins, that sort of thing, the wharf is littered with them. Anybody with a few florins in his pocket can buy his own collection straight off the ships."

Her brother did not answer, but his cool grey look had kindled, and though he tried to hide it by letting down his eyelids, she knew that he and his visitor had indeed come over to the mill to talk secrets of their own. What secrets? Surely not a wish on Rembrandt's part to go to Amsterdam, to wound her mother and father by leaving their house, to desert the excellent van Swanenburgh and turn his back on the true-hearted city that had outfaced the Spaniards while the Amsterdammers had kept the peace to save their florins and their skins.

"That's all very well," her brother said, "but how much would you have left after you paid the sort of fee that Lastman charges?"

"You talk as if it were a fortune," said Lievens. "It's something more than van Swanenburgh gets, I'll admit—perhaps a third again as much. But adding up everything I'd say that it was reasonable, especially when you consider that you'd be living in the house of a gentleman."

The house of a gentleman . . . Certainly, thought Lysbeth, that rich and cultivated house had worked wonders on Jan Lievens. What had gone into it raw had come out polished, with all the farmerish gawkiness gone. Staring into one of the dusty shafts of sunlight, she called up an image of her brother changed in the same fashion. She could see him in the gilded salon of some notable Amsterdam collector, standing against a damask curtain as he sometimes stood against the corner cupboard in the kitchen, his reddish mane thrown back, his blunt chin thrust out, his left hand resting jauntily on his hip. A cloak of scarlet velvet hung casually over the tawny satin of his jacket, and a mysterious moonstone such as the City Advocate's wife wore around her neck on a ribbon dangled from his ear, spotting the clear, fine skin of his cheek with a cold and bluish fire . . .

"That kind of living doesn't concern me," said Rembrandt almost roughly. "When I'm painting it makes no difference to me whether I drink my beer out of crockery or Venetian glass."

"There's more to it than drinking out of fine glasses," said Lievens, at once lofty and evasive. "It's something you'd have to be exposed to before you'd understand."

"What's the point of talking about it anyway?" He picked up a sprouted grain of barley, stripped off the shoot, flung it from him, and reclasped his knobby hands. "It's out of the question. We could never afford it, could we, Puss?" He looked at her directly for the first time since she had come into the loft.

"I don't know—there are all those repairs Father talks about. And for me, it's very hard to think of parting—"

"Why talk about parting?" said Lievens. "Give him a year with Lastman, and he'll be ready to start a studio of his own in Amsterdam. He'll need a house-mistress then to keep his rooms and entertain his friends and patrons, and where could he find a more charming one than here?" He turned his body toward her and laid his strong white fingers on her knee.

That touch, brief as it was, conjured up a heady fantasy. She and Jan and Rembrandt—oh, she could see it as if she were actually there—sauntered arm in arm beside the shimmering water of the famous Prinsenhof Canal, under the branches of the limes and lindens. Poets, painters, scholars moved in a merry company around them, plumed and beribboned, delivered forever from provincial cares and responsibilities . . . But what was she thinking about, what was she doing here? "Good heavens, what time do you think it is?" she said.

"Time for supper, Puss, according to my stomach."

"Five at least," Jan Lievens said.

"Then I'm terribly late—"

"But why? We never eat before six."

"I know, but I was supposed to tell Mother that the van Swanenburghs are coming to see us tonight."

She had brought out the announcement awkwardly enough, and it was followed by an awkward silence. Annoyance tightened the corners of her brother's mouth, though she could not tell whether it rose from his own distaste for spending the evening with his master or from his realization that Jan Lievens, now that his tie with van Swanenburgh was severed, would find the situation embarrassing.

"Old Swanenburgh—I haven't seen him in a good two years," said Lievens.

"No, I don't suppose you have," said Rembrandt. "Whose idea was it to ask him over?"

"Father's. He sent me over to the square to invite him. He thought you'd be pleased—he *thought* you'd consider it an honor." That they should care nothing about what her mother and father had planned to give them pleasure, that neither of them should so much as make a

11

show of appreciation was too painful. "Both of them are coming—his lady, too," she said in an inappropriately boastful voice, knowing that her face was flushed and that tears were standing most unbecomingly in her eyes.

"Oh, it's an honor; it's certainly an honor. I'll be delighted to see them both," said Lievens, mustering up an unconvincing smile.

Her brother stared straight before him at one of the reddening slants of sunlight, his face remote and immobile, a faint cloud of trouble obscuring the keenness of his glance. "Well, I must say it was good of Father to think of it," he said after another uneasy silence—a speech which seemed to her a niggardly response to her father's warm-hearted attempt to provide a happy evening for the guest.

She got up and shook out her skirt. "I'm going. I'm late already," she said.

Jan Lievens sprang to his feet and began to brush a few spears of barley from her flowered skirt, first near the hem, then up around the hips. "Oh, we would have a time of it in Amsterdam, we three," he said, and gave her a nudge at the waist with the back of his hand. "Believe me, you would like it—masquerades at Kermis time and French wine at the taverns and music on the Dam—"

Rembrandt got up and turned on him with a cold look. "Don't get any ideas into your head," he said. "I never gave this Amsterdam business a thought until you brought it up this afternoon."

*

It was not true, of course, that he had never thought before of the Amsterdam business. Jan Lievens had sent him five or six letters from the metropolis, only two of which he had answered, since he considered a pen a tool to draw with, not to waste in the scribbling of platitudes, but every time one of these letters had arrived he had felt the magnetic pull of the place. Naturally he wanted to go to Amsterdam; he took it for granted that there was nobody painting in Leyden or Haarlem or Dordt or Groningen who didn't, but never before this afternoon had the desire become strong enough to discredit what he now possessed. The realization of this change was gnawing at him now, making his supper hard in his stomach while he dressed for the visit of his master; and though Lievens and he were sharing the same copper basin and taking turns at the same little mirror, he did not speak and had made it plain that he did not want to be spoken to. The top of the dresser was too small, the easel was in his way, the sloping walls of the room confined him. Leyden, which had always looked to him like an excellent second choice, had become a limitation, an imposition, a frustration scarcely to be borne.

Lievens was at the mirror, spitting on the tips of his fingers and pasting down his eyebrows—a habit at once soft and vulgar. God moved in a mysterious way, not always distributing His favors to the deserving: some went to Amsterdam to learn to paint and some went to Amsterdam to be patted and prodded into a kind of whitish cheese. If *he* were to live in the metropolis and consort with his peers, if *he* could work under a master as famous as Lastman . . . But that was a dream, that was impossible, and it put him in no better humor with his recalcitrant starched collar to know that he was the one who had made it an impossibility. His rightful portion of the family savings—his proper slice of the loaf, as big as that allotted to Gerrit or Adriaen or Lysbeth—he had simply thrown away in that unfortunate venture at the university. That his mother and father, by hoarding and scrimping, should have found him a second piece, that they should have sent him to van Swanenburgh after he had done nothing for a year but sketch scholars in the library and tropical vines and crocodiles in the botanical gardens was already an indulgence; and he could imagine the storm that would break on his head if he came begging for still another year.

"My sash won't lie down properly. Would you have a pin?" said Lievens in a diffident voice.

"Over there, in that box on the chest. Though why you need it, I don't know. Your sash looks flat enough to me."

"This satin is so bulky."

"Then why wear a satin sash?"

"Why wear a sash at all?" said Lievens, aggrieved.

"That's right. Why wear a sash at all?"

Now that he had said it he would have to abandon his intention of wearing the pale blue woolen sash his mother had given him last year for his seventeenth birthday. That was unfortunate, since she would probably conclude that he did not think it fine enough to wear in front of van Swanenburgh, who in her eyes and his father's was a great painter and a true aristocrat. He could not reasonably be angry because they had invited the master and his bizarre woman to the house: they could not be expected to understand how much it would embarrass Lievens now that he had put the provincial studio behind him; they could not guess how little he himself—seeing the master's limitations as sharply as he did tonight—would want to spend an evening playing the role of devoted and respectful pupil. Yet when sounds came up from the kitchen, reminding him that they were hurrying about to prepare for an occasion they would remember for months, the thought of their excitement was so irritating to him that he had to bury it under a surge of exasperation with Lievens, who was still monopolizing the mirror to make a minute inspection of the part in his hair.

It was useless for him to try to get a look at himself over his visitor's shoulder. For a few moments he looked at the *Saint Bartholomew* on the easel—there was a spot on the cloak that he had meant to fix before Jan Lievens' coming, something that he had been itching to get at these last three days. Then he crossed the room and stopped a couple

13

of feet away from the window, where his reflection made its appearance—cut up and warped and rippled—on the blackness of the night beyond the leaded glass . . . black jacket, white shirt, dignified simplicity perfectly suitable for an evening at home, though he wished his nose had been less broad and blunt at the tip.

"What are you doing?" said Lievens.

"Looking out of the window." It was an obvious piece of rudeness. Night had blotted out everything, even the wan ribbon of canal water that had held the light until half an hour ago.

"You're welcome to the mirror if you want it."

"No, thanks. I'm finished."

"I'll be ready myself in five more minutes. Though why I should be taking so much trouble to get myself in shape for poor old Swanenburgh, I don't know."

He did not answer, only frowned into the darkness. If he could not subscribe to his family's uncritical veneration of the master, neither could he accept so condescending a reference to the most notable painter in Leyden, whose father had been a burgomaster, whose household was famous for its hospitality and its open-handed charities, and whose family was one of the few representatives of the ancient aristocracy to have survived the Spanish holocaust. If Amsterdam had taught his guest good manners, it had failed to supply him with the most rudimentary grasp of other people's feelings: "poor old Swanenburgh" was a term that might have been excusable in his own mouth, though he hoped he hadn't used it at the mill this afternoon, but Lievens should have said "the master" or at the very least "your master." Well, there was no account to be taken of Lievens. He could draw a beautiful flowing line, and he had come back with some remarkable ideas about color and the massing of figures, but sooner or later it would show up in his painting—the fact that he was an incorrigible fool.

"Really, this sash is impossible. I think I'll have to undo it and start all over."

"Take your time," he said, turning his back on the flawed image in the window. "If you'll excuse me, I'll go on down to the kitchen. I ought to take a look at what my mother's getting ready for the guests."

The orderly kitchen and those who were in it—his mother and his brother Adriaen, who had stopped in for a short visit—were visible only in the redness of the supper fire: it would be a pity to have the house reek of oil lamps with company coming, and candles were costly, not to be lighted until the final embers had died. But he always loved this shadowiness and what it did to familiar things, and he paused on the threshold, sensing the quiet that comes when hurried tasks are finished a little early, and drinking in a long breath of peace. His mother, standing with her back to the hearth with only an edging of light around her slight figure, looked venerable enough to be painted as the prophetess Hannah, her wise and wrinkled face half lost in the incense-

14

laden air of the Temple at Jerusalem. His brother Adriaen sat at the table with his stern profile jutting into the dark; his eye, keen and half-lidded like an eagle's, was a moist spot of brightness under his shaggy brow. On the board were the prepared dishes: chopped herring salad, sliced bread covered with a napkin, and a large bowl of pears preserved in cinnamon.

"This is beautiful, Mother!" he said, dissatisfied with his voice, which did not seem earnest or loving enough to break the serene silence. "It was good of you to take so much trouble." And her voice, low and quavering for her years, said out of the shadow, "No trouble, dear. No trouble at all."

And suddenly he did not trust his own voice to answer. That he should have been thinking of leaving this house, this table worn by the thousands of meals they had eaten together, these known, loved faces —it made him want to throw his arms around his mother, to take her hand and hold it against a spot of aching emptiness that had opened in his chest.

"I tasted the salad, and it's unusually good," said Adriaen. "If there's any left, I wish you'd put it by for me. I'll be stopping in again tomorrow around noon."

"Why? Aren't you staying?" he asked. "Couldn't you go and get Antje? We'd like to have both of you sit down with us."

"No, I thought I'd go over to the Guild House. There's a meeting tonight."

It occurred to him for the first time that Adriaen and Gerrit might not rejoice in his skills, his triumphs, and his distinguished visitors exactly as if these had been their own. "I wish you could stay. I wish both you and Gerrit could be here," he said with real humility, not quite sure that his brother was returning his look.

"Poor Gerrit meant to," said his mother. "He helped me with the salad. But then his shins began to bother him, and he thought he'd better get back upstairs."

"I must remember to send Lysbeth up with a plate for Gerrit," he said, and immediately blushed at the realization that he was dispensing his parents' bounty as if it were his own.

"Maybe the meeting won't last too long," said Adriaen, getting up and fastening the top button of his jacket. "Maybe I'll be out in time to have a mug of beer with you. One way or another, enjoy yourselves." He touched his brother briefly on the back, settled his cloak around his shoulders, and went out the back door into the velvety spring night.

Now that he was gone, his mother sighed and moved a little on the hearth, making a rustling with her Sunday skirt and petticoat. "You seem a little sad this evening. Is anything the matter, dear?" she said.

"Not sad, not really." He sank into the chair left vacant by his brother. "A little tired, a little flustered. I'd say I'd had a bit too much of Lievens." It somehow eased his heart to complain about his guest.

15

"Ah, but he's such a good boy, so clever, so gifted, with such beautiful manners. But then you've always been used to spending a lot of time by yourself."

That mild observation seemed for the moment to explain away all dissatisfaction, all disloyalty, all the tormenting restlessness. The need for solitude—that was the source of his sick-heartedness. If he had been following the wholesome and seemly course of his days, if he had come from van Swanenburgh's studio to walk on the dunes and do the little errands that broke up the intensity of his concentration—if he had lived these last three days as he had lived all the clean and blessed others, he would not have been obsessed with this business of Amsterdam.

"You're right about that, Mother. And I certainly miss my painting. I get terribly restless when I'm not working on anything."

"That's only natural. God gave you a talent, and I suppose it nags at you when you can't use it. But you ought to be able to enjoy a day off now and then. Where did you leave Jan?"

"Upstairs in my room. He should be down in a minute."

"I hope Heer van Swanenburgh will like the herring."

"I'm sure he will. Nobody makes better herring than you do, Mother." And if the master should loathe it, he would eat a full portion nevertheless. A good man, van Swanenburgh, a good man and a sufficient master. And now, in this familiar shadowy place of peace, it was possible to believe what he had told himself for months: that it was not necessary for a master to be a great painter, that there was little enough to be learned from a master beyond the basic skills, that a person learned the best and the most of it alone, by cleansing his eyes of every borrowed image and by looking without hypocrisy and self-pity into the recesses of his own heart.

*

The little group in the front room did not sustain the sense of peace he had experienced in the kitchen: it was suffering from that curious mixture of apprehension and affectation which precedes the arrival of respected guests. The voices—Jan's and Lysbeth's and even his mother's—were louder and higher than usual, possibly because everybody was so far away from everybody else, seated as they were in the tall chairs of state, studded with brass nails and covered with dark red leather, which had stood as long as he remembered at strict intervals against the yellow wainscoting along the wall. Only his father remained standing, tall against the big tan and red map of the coast of Africa; he was scrubbed and shaved for the occasion, and his lean cheek and bald head showed ruddy in the candlelight. But he, too, for all his casual stance, seemed ill at ease in his dark brown Sunday jacket and his large linen collar: he took no part in the empty conversation, and his son, troubled by the conviction that he had not shown enough enthusiasm

16

over the unfortunate invitation, could not bring himself to meet his eyes. Instead, he watched Lysbeth, who was nervously picking invisible bits of lint from her velvet jacket and her striped skirt; and he knew that she had half convinced herself that the van Swanenburghs would never turn up and that she and hers would be shamed thereby in Lievens' sight.

That, of course, was ridiculous. In the whole time of his apprenticeship—close to the three required years—he had found his master a man of scrupulous honor. Some Leyden painters used their pupils like so many servants and never gave a thought to their sensibilities; but van Swanenburgh treated every one of them, no matter what artisan's house he had come from, like the son of a gentleman. For the first time, Rembrandt pictured the meeting between the former apprentice and the discarded teacher from the teacher's point of view. How must the master feel toward Lievens, who had made it plain to all Leyden that what could be learned in van Swanenburgh's studio was not enough? What would he think if he could guess—and his perceptions were not lacking in subtlety—the sort of talk that had gone on in the mill this afternoon?

He did not have much time for arraigning himself; at exactly eight the awaited knock sounded on the door. There was a momentary crisis: among the well-to-do, a maid went and opened the door while the family sat stiff as dolls in expectation; but what with the expenses for poor Gerrit and the doctor, the maid had been sent away a couple of years ago. Lysbeth looked at her mother, and her mother looked at her, and it was the father, with wry impatience for all such nonsensical pretensions curling his fine thin lips, who went to the door.

The master's wife, the bizarre Neapolitan, was the first to step into the front room, and it was strange to see her corseted and bejeweled and buttoned to the chin, since she usually had a kind of Italian laxness in the studio. Some of Rembrandt's fellow-apprentices thought her very seductive, with her oily black hair and her full, sleepy eyelids: she was on the good side of forty, at least ten years younger than her husband; and her arms were firm and brown, and tapered down beautifully to the wrists. But he did not like the smell of musk that clung about her, he was troubled and constrained by the way she had of looking at him out of her half-closed eyes, and it was disquieting to think what she and the irreproachable Swanenburgh—whose manner was strangely artificial in spite of his cordiality—must do together in their big curtained bed.

Not that van Swanenburgh was old enough to be beyond such matters. There was not one grey hair in his smooth brown locks, which he always parted meticulously and turned over his finger into a neat row of curls. He wore the ruff and the pleated cuffs suitable to his station, and though these and his mouse-grey velvet jacket and wide black breeches gave him the look of carrying somewhat more than he could bear, his slight and spindly figure could not have changed much since

17

his youth. If the wrinkles in his face were unusually pronounced, that was probably because his affability had gotten him into the habit of making grimaces—there was something of the simian in his creased cheeks and flat, kind, melancholy eyes. He smiled at Rembrandt, bent above the hands of the mother and Lysbeth, and embraced Jan Lievens in the French manner, kissing him on both cheeks—a greeting which his wife seemed to consider excessive in the case of a renegade apprentice: she offered the visitor from Amsterdam, with whom she had been familiar enough in the old days, no more than her fingertips.

"What a fine fire!" said van Swanenburgh, standing in front of it and rubbing his hands as though he were really cold. "And isn't this a handsome room, Fioretta?" Since "fioretta" meant "little flower," the apprentices had done considerable speculating as to whether it was really her name or something that he called her out of doting tenderness.

With the first civilities over, there was a momentary silence in which Rembrandt wondered whether wounded pride would make the master put off as long as possible any mention of Lievens' doings in Amsterdam. Perhaps his father had also sensed the danger of embarrassment, for he talked more than was his custom about such safe and general matters as the renewal of Spanish hostilities in the southern provinces and the fabulous dividends being paid to stockholders in the East India Company. Meanwhile they had taken their seats, though there was some difficulty over this, since the room had only four large leather chairs. Three of them went to the ladies and the fourth, after elaborate disclaiming, to the master. Jan and Rembrandt shared the top of the chest which was set to one side of the table, and Harmen Gerritszoon stood as he had stood earlier, with the back of his bald head resting against the map and his lean arms folded across his chest. Once they were seated, the master did not attempt to avoid the inescapable question: he cleared his throat and turned the whole upper part of his body in a sprightly way to Lievens. "Now tell me, Jan, what sort of thing does Pieter Lastman have you painting these days?" he said.

"Oh, a great many things, Heer van Swanenburgh," said Lievens, and it seemed affected and overscrupulous to Rembrandt that he had not simply called him Master. "Those of us who are beyond the first year paint pretty much what we like. I'm doing a *Pilate Washing His Hands*, and the others are doing all sorts of things, many of them not usually painted. For instance, one of my friends, Claas Anthonieszoon from Dordt, is doing *Balaam and the Angel*, though I wouldn't say too much for the way he's rendering the beast."

It was regrettable that Rembrandt's seat on the chest put him directly opposite his master. He saw the grimace freeze for an instant, and the luster drain from the kind brown eyes. The most frequent complaint against van Swanenburgh was that he was too rigid about assigning subjects—always the same old Assumptions, Journeys of the Magi, Nativities and Apostles—subjects all the more pointless because they had originally been intended to ornament cathedrals, and the triumphant Protestants, considering the sacred pictures nothing but distractions and impious attempts to confine divinity, permitted only whitewash on the walls. But whatever suspicion of criticism had made his creased face static, he was quick to recover himself. His look, warm and frank again, settled on Rembrandt, and he sent an authentically merry laugh into the stillness. "Maybe we ought to try the same sort of thing at our place—eh, Rembrandt?" he said. "What do you think? Should we let van Vliet and Hoeven and Schlegel do just anything that comes into their heads?"

The irony had failed to register on Lysbeth. "That sounds like a marvelous idea," she said brightly, clasping and unclasping her rosy little hands. "One gets so tired of seeing the same old things done over and over, and when a person comes to think of it, there must be hundreds of subjects in the Bible nobody has ever touched."

"But my dear young lady"—van Swanenburgh turned in her direction, though his earnest look still sought his favorite apprentice—"do you have any idea why these same old subjects keep coming up? It's precisely because they've been weighed in the balance and never found wanting. They are *the* sacred subjects—I'd go so far as to say they are the only sacred subjects—suited by their nature to our particular art." He shook out the cuffs that hung over his delicate fingers, and smiled at the two young men seated on the chest: when he had an unusually trenchant criticism to make at the studio, it was his habit to soften it with a smile. "Take for instance *Balaam and the Angel,* that very dramatic subject which your friend from Dordt has lighted on. Attractive as it sounds, it presents all sorts of problems—problems in the massing of figures and the building of shapes—difficulties that would be insuperable even for a master painter, to say nothing of a lad in his apprenticeship. How could you deal with it, with Balaam pulling one way and the ass pulling another and the angel floating somewhere on top of the two? Not that it matters, of course: whatever we paint, we learn something, even if it's only that there are certain things we cannot do."

Ah, but the master was wrong about Balaam, so wrong that his favorite apprentice could not return his reasonable glance. Give him two minutes with crayon and paper and he could do it: he could set down the conflict and bring it to a perfect resolution. He saw the beaten beast, its forelegs curled beneath it, a long dark mass pulling toward the left against still darker rocks and trees. He saw the figure of the prophet, a bulky oblong seated on the animal's haunches, balancing the thrust by pulling back toward the right. He saw the taut reins and the extended staff, parallel with each other and sustaining each other, carrying the eye into the brilliant openness above. And then—but for this he needed color, a sun-drenched, rainbow-tinted whiteness—overmastering the two dusky shapes, drawing the eye upward and reconciling the warring

19

masses, in the highest plane of the picture, the angel would be caught in the instant of descent, a figure as sinuous as a flame and as cool as a white flower.

"It could be done," he said thoughtfully; and he had been so absorbed in the imaginary doing of it that he was surprised to find himself speaking in this room.

"Really?" said the master, with an unaccustomed edge to his voice. "And just how would you go about it, my friend?"

Almost daily in the studio, egged on by other apprentices, they had carried on high-hearted arguments; but for the first time in their shared years the words "my friend" were tainted with irony.

"I'd build it in a triangle—Balaam balancing the beast at the base, and the angel back and above in a kind of twisted position—" He drew the swirling outline of the angel in the air before him.

"And you'd expect to make everything right by *twisting* the angel?" The exquisite fingers, half-veiled by the pleated white cuffs, made an exaggerated imitation of his gesture. The voice was shrill, almost shrewish, and in the difference between it and the voice that had been directing him these many peaceful months, he measured the master's sense of disgrace, the master's pain.

"No, not just by *twisting* the angel." He could not help himself, he had to mimic the sharp and womanish emphasis. "It would be a matter of light and shadow, too. Balaam and the beast would be dark—they're earthy, and they and the trees and rocks around them would have to be done in a kind of earthy brown. But the angel would be light, pure light—"

"It's always been my belief," said van Swanenburgh in a flat tone, "that where there is trouble with the line, it's sheer trickery to try to cover it up with color. A flaw is a flaw, and in spite of all the color in the world a flaw will out."

But he was wrong, he was as hidebound and rigid as Jan Lievens had said at the mill this afternoon. There *was* a way to do it, and in his stubbornness and his wounded pride the master refused to listen, refused to understand . . . In the charged silence that followed, Rembrandt raised his eyes from his own hairy knuckles and looked for support, or at least for some measure of comprehension, toward the bald head of his father shining in the candlelight. But he should have foreseen the uselessness of his appeal: Jacob van Swanenburgh was the repository of all wisdom in Harmen Gerritszoon's eyes, and he got nothing for his trouble but a reproving stare, such a stare as one turns upon a child who rattles a pocketful of marbles during the doxology.

"Young people are all alike." It was the mother's quavering voice that came conciliatory into the embarrassing stillness. "They feel their own strength, and they think they can move mountains."

"Ah, yes," said the master, looking back on his own youth and his early accession of power with exactly that mixture of regret and con-

descension which Rembrandt found maddening in those who made it their boast that they were old. "In my day, too, I thought there was nothing too difficult to be attacked." He sighed, settled back against the red leather, crossed his thin legs, and turned to Jan again. "But it's foolish—isn't it?—to spend our precious time worrying about the problems of your friend from Dordt. What sort of work are *you* doing?—that's what I'm interested in. Did you bring anything with you? Fioretta and I would love to have a look."

It was to the credit of the van Rijn household that drawings could be shown in the front room, that art was more significant here than order. As soon as Lievens came back with his folio, the father pushed aside the patterned tablecloth, Lysbeth and her mother brought over the candles from the mantelpiece, and they all gathered around the table. To Rembrandt what was laid out seemed somewhat less impressive than at first, perhaps because Lievens' signal talent, his flowing line, was a virtue that soon wore thin. He was less concerned with the drawings than with the paper, soft and thick and absorbent for the holding of chalk and the drinking up of bister. Such paper was not to be had in Leyden; the best of it was always bought up in Amsterdam.

Preoccupied with such matters, he heard only enough of the master's comment to know that it was superficial and false—as, under the circumstances, it was bound to be. What could he say, poor man, surrounded as he was by "oh's" from Lysbeth and admiring murmurs from the mother, which Vrouw van Swanenburgh felt required to second with artificial smiles? To call attention to a splotchy ink patch or an error in anatomy would be to challenge the great Pieter Lastman and to lay himself open to the suspicion of jealousy. Yet it was embarrassing to hear him say, "Ah, very good!" or, "Yes, that one is excellent!" when what he looked at was only a little better than mediocre; and it was aggravating to watch Lievens while he drank in the contrived compliments, too intoxicated on his spurious glory to realize that it arose from constraint.

"You've certainly changed," said the master, stepping back from the drawings and from an experience that could only have been awkward and painful to him.

"I'm glad you think so," said his former apprentice complacently. "I suppose it's only natural—a change of air will stimulate anybody." He had the effrontery to look significantly at Rembrandt, who could not keep himself from taking in an audibly sharp breath. "Most of the younger men in Amsterdam think a two-year apprenticeship with a single master ought to be the maximum. The third year is usually a waste— I mean, whatever gets taught usually gets taught in the first two years."

"That, I would say, depends not only on the capacity of the teacher to teach, but on the ability of the pupil to learn," said van Swanenburgh, a blush suffusing his forehead to the roots of his carefully parted hair.

"Three years is the usual period, sanctioned by the Saint Lucas Guild, and most people seem to be satisfied with it—I've yet to hear anybody complain. Besides, those of us who are old in the trade eventually get used to the terrible *ennui*"—he plainly used the French word not to exhibit his own cosmopolitanism but in mockery of the Frenchified affectations of young dandies—"the terrible *ennui* that settles down on some of our apprentices in that intolerable third year. The real nature of the boredom, I believe, is clearer to us than it is to those who suffer from it. It comes partly from a slovenly unwillingness to perfect one's skills, and partly from the lack of an audience. By the end of the second year the master is already impressed—provided he's ever going to be—and there's nobody new to stand around and produce the necessary 'Hurrah's!' "

Harmen Gerritszoon, who had carried the candles back to the mantel, moved the tip of his tongue across his lower lip to hide a smile. "How right you are about that, Heer van Swanenburgh!" he said; and the two of them, leagued in their age against the preposterous arrogance of youth, exchanged a conspiratorial glance as the master, exhausted by his brilliant sally, seated himself in a leather chair and left it to the women to fill up the silence with their nonsense about buttons and bows.

"It's made of bombazine," said the mother, holding out her skirt in reply to the first question the lofty Fioretta had asked her this evening. "Lysbeth and I made it. She's very clever with the needle. She makes almost everything she wears."

Rembrandt was helping Jan gather up the drawings, but he could see the classic form bent forward to inspect his mother's black skirt with its design of yellow—a yellow intended to give the illusion of brocading in gold. "Handsome, very handsome," said Fioretta. But he caught the suggestion of a smirk in the corners of the full Italian lips: Vrouw van Swanenburgh, whose tapering arms were loaded with bracelets and who had a three-inch band of gold embroidery at her hem, was not likely to be impressed by a cheap imitation of gold brocade. "Mother," he said, "we mustn't keep Heer van Swanenburgh too late. He has to teach in the morning."

"Yes," she said, "and we do have a little collation. The children can go and bring it in."

The pretentiousness of the word was not mitigated by the quavering voice that uttered it. "It's only beer and herring," he said, blushing. "Sit still, Lysbeth, I can get it myself."

In the kitchen the fire was out, and the candle that he set down revealed the black and gaping hearth. The table, too, with the covered bread plate, the herring salad, and the bowl of pears, was bled of its earlier charm. Food was food, and part of the bruising tyranny of parental love was to be forever transmuting food into something else, to be forever reminding a person of the loving mind that had planned it

22

and the withering hands that had prepared it, forever turning it into a kind of domestic communion. They held him down with a thousand filaments: to want to go to Amsterdam was to sin against the peace of their shared evenings, his mother's labors over the spit and the tub, his father's sweat at the mill.

In anger he put the food and the good tin Sunday plates on one big tray. Somebody else, Lysbeth or Lievens, would have to come out for the mugs and the beer—he was no dray-horse, he couldn't carry everything. He came through the hall with the dishes clanking, and emerging into the brightness, knew with an immediacy that made him awkward in setting down his burden that Heer van Swanenburgh was more aware of his secret longings than his parents, that the master sat so limply in the tall chair, with his delicate hands laid along his spindly thighs, because he realized that his favorite apprentice was poised for flight. His kind brown eyes, reproachful only in their dispiritedness, followed his pupil while he helped his father pass the plates, followed him with a baffled tenderness and regret. It was only when Lievens and Lysbeth came back with the beer that he roused himself and took a morsel of capers and herring, like any peasant, between his finger and thumb. "This looks so delicious, Vrouw van Rijn, you must excuse me if I can't wait for a fork," he said.

After that, with the whole company around the table serving themselves, van Swanenburgh recovered his self-possession enough to talk to his renegade apprentice about other masters in the metropolis: Nicolaas Elias, Claas Moyert, Thomas de Keyser, and Adriaen van Mieulandt. "Are any of them going to Italy this year?" he asked, turning a bright, worn look in Rembrandt's direction.

"Not anybody that I know of, Heer van Swanenburgh," said Lievens.

"I suppose it's hard to pull yourself away with commissions coming in. But surely some of the younger men are going. If I were a beginner and had been trained in what you Amsterdammers call 'the provinces,' if I felt I had to go somewhere, I doubt I'd choose Amsterdam, which after all is nothing but a bigger Dordt or Leyden. I think I'd go to Italy."

It was plain what he was maneuvering at, plain at least to Rembrandt as he listened to him holding forth on the advantages of working in studios that had turned out Tintoretto, Titian, and Caravaggio. To lose an apprentice to Lastman in Amsterdam was something to be ashamed of; to see an apprentice sail for the Mediterranean to learn from resurrected antiquities and work under painters so alien that they could not be considered rivals was no cause for disgrace. But if he talked all night, he would talk to no purpose: there was no spot on earth, with the sole exception of Spain, as hateful to his pupil as Italy. The very landscape as it appeared in the Italian canvases in the master's fine front room was so distasteful to him that it brought on a feeling of nausea. The world they painted there was so different from the flat stretches of meadow, the undulating dunes, and the oily grey curve of the sea that it threatened to discredit the beauty of everything he called his own.

The voice of the master had trailed off into silence. Lievens smiled politely and Rembrandt nodded vaguely; he had not paid attention— why should he listen to stories about a world to which he had closed his heart?

"I beg you, Heer van Swanenburgh," said his mother, "don't be putting any such ideas into my Rembrandt's head. I'd fret myself into my grave if he was as far away as that, and anyway, his father could never afford it."

Lysbeth was making the rounds with the bowl of spiced pears, and her hand, short and white and touched with pink at the knuckles, came for an instant close to Vrouw van Swanenburgh's classical hand. Though one was somewhat coarse and formless and the other was subtly and beautifully molded, he knew where his allegiance lay: he was a Netherlander and a Protestant, the true son of his mother and his father, and though he might wound them by going to Amsterdam he would not repudiate them by going southward.

"Don't worry, Mother. I can't imagine myself ever going to Italy," he said.

And simply because he felt certain that he would never make that longer and less honorable journey, it was easier for him to entertain through the brief remainder of the evening the possibility of the less questionable desertion. As he went to the door with his father to bid the distinguished visitors good night, it seemed to him that his mind had flown like a gull to the wharves of Amsterdam and was hovering there over the great ships laden with fine papers out of China and ancient coins and earth-stained marble busts. He was glad that his father went upstairs at once, that Lysbeth and his mother began promptly to carry the dishes into the kitchen, and that Lievens yawned and announced himself ready to go to sleep. It was a strong and intoxicating dream that had taken hold upon him, and he was grateful that he could carry it in almost unbroken silence to bed.

*

The morning bell had rung twice, and in a minute now her mother, too considerate to ring it rudely again, would come panting upstairs to see what could be the matter. Yet Lysbeth continued to lie in the stored warmth of her comforts and pillows, waiting until she heard her mother's morning cough at the foot of the stairway. "Don't climb the steps, Mother," she called, sitting up and flinging back the covers. "I'm awake."

"Awake, yes. But are you up?"

She got out of the security of her bed—it was a separate world, built into a corner like a cupboard—before she answered. "Yes, I'm up. Honestly, I'll be down in a minute."

From the chest under the window she took the old red skirt and the dark blue jacket she would wear. These last three days it had given her satisfaction to put on almost discarded, threadbare things; it announced how little she cared about her appearance now that Jan was gone to Amsterdam. If Rembrandt had only spoken to her father . . . If she could only say to herself that this empty time was a time of waiting, and that at the end of it she would be mistress of rooms to which the beloved would come almost every day . . . But the hope that her brother would go to Amsterdam and make a place for her there had dwindled. If he had nourished that hope during the painful evening of the van Swanenburghs' visit, he had certainly abandoned it since: any mention of it would have caused a household tempest, and the family had fallen since Jan's departure into a dull and sodden peace. She poured the water from the tin pitcher into the basin and thought how the vaunted courage of the male, once it was put to the test, proved strangely feeble: *she* would not have been afraid to stand up to a mild man like her father if she had been in Rembrandt's place. But then he was not girded like her in the strength of love; he had not spent his days in longing and his nights in feverish dreams; in fact, it was hard to imagine him in love with anybody—him with his precious privacy and his chilly grey eyes.

"Lysbeth!"

"I'm *up,* Mother. I'm washing myself."

"All right, dear. Go see if there's anything you can do for Gerrit."

"Right away." She was quick about splashing her face and dabbling her fingers. Yesterday and today—and they were the only times since the accident at the mill—she had forgotten to go into her elder brother's room to bring him the washing water which he could manage to get for himself only with awkwardness and pain and self-disgust. "Don't get a thing, Gerrit. I'm coming this minute," she called across the hall to him.

"Don't hurry, I can wait."

Even though his voice was scarcely audible through the bedroom door, she knew it well enough to catch the note of bitterness. Dawdle and dream your fill over your healthy young man from Amsterdam— that was what he was thinking; rejoice in his straight limbs and his free gestures, and take your time about it. I'm in no hurry: what do I have to hurry to except my grave?

And suddenly, while she was drying her face and hands, a sharp recollection came upon her, filling her eyes with tears and closing her throat. She remembered how on her seventh birthday Gerrit had taken her to the dunes to teach her to walk on her new pair of stilts—the dunes were the safest place to learn, you could not really hurt yourself on the sand. It had taken her a long time to gain confidence because she fell at the very beginning, but after more than an hour of patient instruction they had stood there on stilts together, had walked side by side over the rolling knolls, had gone out and out until the bottoms of their stilts began to sink into the dampened sand that would soon be lost again under the rising tide. A feeling of mastery, an elation which she had never known since except in her dreams swept over her there at the water's edge: she knew what it was to be a gull, a weather vane, a tower. The clouds had never come so close to her again; she felt that if she would only dare to let go of the stilts she could gather bits of the fleecy whiteness in her hands. And he—how lordly he had looked, standing against the sky half again as tall as she, his cheeks ruddy with the wind, his white teeth flashing, his curls blown back and as bright as newly minted florins in the sun . . .

She wiped the tears out of the corners of her eyes before she went into the hall, but she could not wipe away the memory: the memory pursued her to the foot of the bed, where he hunched against the pillows; and though her mother and father had given him the best bedroom in the house, it seemed to her a wretched confinement for one who had towered against the clouds and been so daringly familiar with the sea. Though he was scrupulously clean with his person and there was no end to the scrubbing done in his room, she noticed every time she came in the stale, clinging smell of sickness, a smell that was, thank heaven, subtle enough to disappear after the first few breaths. By the books heaped on his coverlet and the small residue of oil in his bedside lamp she knew he had spent a restless night. "I'm sorry you didn't sleep," she said.

"Oh, I slept well enough. I wasn't particularly tired."

Plainly it was one of those mornings when he wanted nobody's pity. She gave him the superficial smile he expected, filled his basin, and brought it to the bed. Then, casting about for something to tell him, she said, "Do you know what I was just thinking about?—the time you taught me to walk on stilts down on the dunes. It was on my birthday— I don't suppose you remember . . ."

He looked at her coldly. "Why shouldn't I remember?" he said. "The fact is, I walk on them still." He motioned with his head toward his crutches standing in the corner. "You forgot to bring my towel. I'll hold the basin while you get it. But hurry if you don't want me dripping all over the quilt."

He had done what he could to cover up her miserable blunder; he had turned it into a sour joke about the crutches and had given her an excuse to hide her flaming face. Stupid, unbelievably stupid to make him remember the high-hearted past, to force him to measure the enormity of his loss! There was nothing left for her to do but put his crutches within reach and go downstairs.

She had been so late getting to her upstairs duties that there was next to nothing to be done in the kitchen. The fire had been kindled

26

by her father, whom she saw through the open back door inspecting the hyacinth shoots and rubbing the stiffness of sleep out of his neck and shoulders, and the breakfast table was almost completely spread. While her mother went to the pantry for the butter, she checked the other items: beer, rusks of bread, herring, and the fine Alkmaar cheese that Jan had given them. The sight of the cheese, plump and beautiful though it was, was disheartening because it took something away from her little red Gospel: the Gospel became, like the cheese, less a sign of particular affection than of gratitude for hospitality.

"So," said her father, coming in with a grating show of lively morning spirits, "I see you've got your red skirt on. Could you be thinking of going to the hog market?"

"No, not this morning, Father. Why?"

"Because the last time I said something about that skirt, you said it was only fit to visit pigs in." He sat down at the head of the table, pleased with his joke, his hyacinths, and himself.

She forced herself to turn a sickly smile in his direction. After all, he was an old man, and nobody would expect him to understand the sufferings of love.

Noise broke in upon them, a loud crash sounding above their heads. "Gerrit!" called her mother, rushing in from the pantry, her hands fluttering with fright. "Are you all right, Gerrit? Did you fall?" The father leaped from his chair and went almost at a run to the foot of the stairs.

"No, Mother, it's me," shouted the voice of Rembrandt, rough with exasperation. "It's nothing; I only knocked the easel over."

"The easel?" said the mother. "Oh, my, my, my—has anything happened to your picture? Is it smeared or anything?"

"No, nothing's the matter with my picture, but it's a great wonder. This room is impossible for a person to paint in. Every time you turn around you bump into one accursed thing or another."

When the father came back into the kitchen, his mouth was tight with annoyance. In the last three days Rembrandt had roused the paternal anger several times by making certain lordly and offhand complaints about the smoke from the peat on the hearth or the scarcity of lamplight in his room. "Really, it's a pity about him," said Harmen Gerritszoon. "When I was his age, I shared a loft with two others. We used to take turns in the morning using the only chair."

"But you weren't *painting* in your room, Father. It's different when you're painting."

He did not look at her, and this, more than his angry words, was galling to her love and pride. "Those who don't find their present quarters satisfactory can always get themselves better if they can afford it."

"Ah, now, that's a bit hard, Harmen," said her mother. "That room of his *is* crowded. I never clean it but I bump into something myself."

They fell silent then to listen to the slow clomp of Gerrit's crutches on the stairs. He swung into the kitchen with a curt good morning, got

27

to his chair at the lower end of the table, and dropped his crutches onto the floor. "Why do you always have to be thinking I'm falling, Mother?" he asked. "I wish you would take it for granted I can stay on my feet, such as they are. If I ever fall, I'll call down and tell you so."

The mother's earlier pallor was succeeded by a splotchy blush. "I'm sorry, dear, I'm very sorry. I know I'm foolishly anxious about you," she said, but not without a suggestion that there was something reprehensible in a son who failed to understand a mother's solicitude.

"There's no necessity for treating me like a baby—"

"Let's forget about it, now, Gerrit," said the father, going back to his place. "Come and sit down, Mother. Hurry a bit, Rembrandt"—her brother's tread, lighter than Jan's, was sounding on the stairway—"I haven't got any more time to waste. I can't see why it should take a man almost an hour to get his breakfast. I've got to get over to the mill."

Looking covertly across the table at her younger brother, Lysbeth thought that he might not have put the Amsterdam business behind him after all: his forehead was puckered, his mouth was pale, and there were bluish markings under his eyes. He sat at the table in a defiant position calculated to provoke his father, who was a defender of good old-fashioned manners: his elbows were set on the board, and his hands were closed into fists and supported the blunt wedge of his chin. He might well have received an outright reproof if everybody's attention had not been drawn to Adriaen walking up between the raw brown flowerbeds; his entry diverted them from the charged situation, especially when he flourished a little grey moneybag. "Look what Cornelis Dirkszoon left with me yesterday evening," he said, his moist glance going straight and joyously for his father's face. "He's putting his boy Claas into my shop as an apprentice. He spoke of it weeks ago, but I didn't want to mention it until I was sure, and here it is—the first payment on the fee."

Lysbeth poured him a mug of beer, and they drank to his good fortune all around the table; and when they were finished he came, a little stiffly and ceremoniously, and set the moneybag on his father's wooden plate. "This isn't all of it, mind you," he said. "I took a little out to get Antje a new cape, but there's enough left to settle what you let me have for the third bench and the fittings. I want to thank you for the loan; I know how much interest I'd have had to pay if I'd gone to anyone else."

The bag on her father's plate—she saw Rembrandt eye it and look swiftly away again, his mouth slightly open so that one could catch the gleam of his teeth, and the pucker deepening between his eyebrows.

"That's very good of you, dear, but can you spare it?" said her mother.

"Yes," said Harmen Gerritszoon, "are you sure you can spare it? I don't have to have it now, you know."

"But I want you to have it, and so does Antje. We wouldn't think of anything else."

"Then thanks to you, and God be thanked also," said her father in one of his infrequent bursts of piety. "Heaven knows, I can put it to good use. I've got a loose iron on one of the sails, and that's the sort of thing you can't let go for long."

"Could I bother you for the butter, Gerrit?" said Rembrandt. And she wondered whether it was only to her that this request sounded cold and out of place.

"And to think," said her mother, "that in such a short time you've got yourself a second apprentice! It certainly does show how well you're thought of. The Lord's been very good to all of us, very good indeed—" Her voice quavered off into silence, and her daughter wondered whether she had seen how difficult it was to claim the Lord's goodness in Gerrit's case; but it was plain at once that what had stopped her was not Gerrit's plight but the fact that her youngest, her darling, might feel neglected while his brother was being praised. "We're proud of you, Adriaen—we're proud of *all* our sons," she said. "With you where you are and Rembrandt doing so well with Heer van Swanenburgh—"

"*He* doesn't seem to think he's doing so well with Heer van Swanenburgh," said Harmen Gerritszoon.

"What do you mean, Father?" It was a chillier voice than the one that had asked for the butter. And suddenly it occurred to Lysbeth that, since the departure of Jan Lievens, her father and her brother, who had always been close if somewhat silent companions, were seldom seen in the same room. She swallowed a mouthful of beer and felt her heart begin to race. These three days now, before and after supper, at times when he usually sat in the back room with his father, drawing or working at etching plates, he had hurried off to hide himself in the attic. Why? To brood over a shattered but still unrelinquished dream?

"I mean exactly what I said. You were in a bad temper last night, and you're in a worse one this morning. What's the matter with you? Has your master been stirring you up about going to Italy?"

That speech, unlike the one about the skirt to visit pigs in, was sharpened with real resentment. She could guess by the tone of it how much capacity her brother had to wound him by flights to the attic and curt good mornings and good nights.

Rembrandt was looking at his father over an untouched mug of beer and a plate of half-eaten rusks of bread. "I think I made it perfectly plain when Heer van Swanenburgh did us the great honor of paying us a visit that I couldn't be dragged to Italy."

"Nobody that I know of has been offering to drag you there or any place else."

"Ah, now, Harmen," said the mother, "it's no matter for teasing. You see he hasn't been himself since his friend's gone off and left him. Why don't you let him alone?"

"He's let alone—there's no reason to worry about that, Neeltje—he lives like a hermit up in his attic. Not that anybody's eager for his precious company, but it's a sorry business if a man's not told what's going on in the minds of his own children. These last three days he's acted as if I'd committed a mortal sin against him, though what I'm supposed to have done to him, only God knows."

"You haven't done anything to me, Father."

"Then why are you walking around like somebody in mourning?"

"Because it happens that at the moment I'm not very happy."

"Why not? What are you sulking about?"

"Nothing."

"Nothing! I don't consider that an answer. If you're not hankering after Italy, then it's something else you feel ought to be handed to you, and my own guess would be that it's Pieter Lastman's studio in Amsterdam."

It was a pity, thought Lysbeth, that her brother's delicate skin should so clearly betray him: two spots spread over his cheekbones, sharp against the surrounding whiteness, more orange than red. "Since you ask me outright, yes, I'd like to go to Pieter Lastman," he said, and the cool nobility of the confession was diminished by the fact that it was gratuitous—anybody would have known as much from his face.

Anybody, that is, but his mother, who looked at him with her withered lips parted in total unbelief. "But I always thought you were so happy with Heer van Swanenburgh!" she said.

"Heer van Swanenburgh has his good points, Mother—"

"Does he indeed?" said the father. "I'm glad to hear it. A gentleman, the son of a burgomaster, whose work is good enough for the City Hall —it's a relief to hear you say a word in his favor; I'm sure he's in need of the recommendation of a seventeen-year-old calf!"

"But listen, Father." For the first time since she had argued with him over the smallness of Rembrandt's room, she dared to raise her voice. "The fact that Heer van Swanenburgh is a fine painter doesn't mean that Lastman couldn't be a better one—"

He turned upon her some of the fury roused by her brother. "Really?" he said. "And who told you so?"

"Jan Lievens thinks he's a better painter—"

"Jan Lievens! And who's Jan Lievens? The son of a tapestry-maker, who went to Amsterdam and learned to talk a lot of fancy words and fling his arms around. Another calf, and a silly one, and yet you quote him like a prophet."

Adriaen shifted in his chair and cleared his throat. "If I'm allowed to say something—and it isn't really my business—I don't see that it makes much difference which of them is the better painter," he said. "Doesn't it all come down to how much money you can spend?" His bright, wet glance darted at the bag on his father's plate. "With repairs to be made in the mill and the house, with Lysbeth's dowry not nearly as large as it could be, with"—he looked at Gerrit and looked away again—"with so many other things, it seems to me a question of whether more money ought to be laid down where so much has been spent before—"

Rembrandt, flushed to the temples now, glared down the length of the board at him, and Lysbeth knew that this sudden accession of rage came less from Adriaen's masked statement than from the fact that he had claimed with a look some lasting proprietorship over what he had put on his father's plate. "You'll never forget it, will you, Adriaen?" he said in a voice that vibrated with quiet fury. "You'll never forgive me for getting a chance to go to the university when you couldn't go there yourself."

"Well, and supposing he doesn't ever forget it?" said Harmen Gerritszoon. "I can't say I'd blame him; any way you look at it, he didn't get too much. *You* got the fee for the university, and that came to nothing. You got the fee for Heer van Swanenburgh—and now it seems that's to come to nothing too."

"I don't see how you can say it's come to nothing, Harmen," said the mother in a tearful voice. "Heer van Swanenburgh will tell you himself he never had an apprentice that could come up to him, and as for the business of the university, I've never heard so much fuss made over anything else that was wasted in this house. Heaven knows, everybody has a right to make one mistake."

But Lysbeth knew that her mother could not be counted on as a partisan: she had barely finished when her mouth began to tremble with the realization that whatever she said in her darling's behalf would only rob her of his presence.

"It isn't one mistake—it's two," said the father. "But that's not the point. Adriaen's right; it's a matter of money. There's the repairs, and there's Lysbeth's dowry—"

"And there's the annuity you bought me, and what you're paying out to the doctor, and the fact that I'll never bring anything in," said Gerrit. "All of you sit here thinking it, so why don't you say it?"

"You're wrong there, Gerrit. I wasn't thinking it, and neither was anybody else. So help me God, son, if it took ten times as much, I'd never begrudge a penny of it. The work you did in the mill before—"

"Before I fell like a fool and got myself crippled?"

"The work you did in the mill for all those years put me so far in your debt that we'd never come out even, not if I kept you for the rest of your days."

The earnestness of the speech was marred by its unfortunate conclusion: it was obvious to everybody at the table, and certainly to Gerrit, that somebody—if not his father, then one of his brothers—would have to keep him for the rest of his days.

"It's a pity," said Rembrandt, "that a person can't lift a finger in this house without committing a sin against everybody else. Because you drove me to it—and you *did* drive me to it, Father—I was stupid enough to admit I wanted to go to Amsterdam. And now I'm supposed

31

to have stolen Lysbeth's dowry and used up Adriaen's hard-earned money and thrown it up to Gerrit that he's not working any more. All I can say is, it's too bad that everybody is so sensitive—"

"Oh, come, now," said the father, "you're not exactly thick-skinned yourself."

"At least I don't go around expecting everybody to consider my feelings—"

"No, you don't. All you expect everybody to do is pay your bills."

"Now, Harmen—"

"As far as I remember, Father, I wasn't asking you for anything."

"Weren't you? Then who *were* you asking? Or do you think you can live in Amsterdam for nothing? Are you such a great painter that this Pieter Lastman is going to feed you and teach you for the joy of it? You *might* dream up something as crazy as that—God knows, you've got an exaggerated opinion of yourself."

The orange spots on Rembrandt's cheeks were larger and darker now, like the marks of blows. He pushed back his plate, flung down his napkin, stood up, and glared at his father with icy grey eyes. "As to that," he said in a voice that was almost a whisper, "I'll tell you something: I'm better than you think. What I have is a thing you don't see often in this world. If Pieter Lastman had any idea what I have here"— he raised his hairy hand, clenched, and held it up before his father— "maybe he *would* teach me for nothing. And if you had any idea— which you never will, because not one of you knows anything about it—you might get your mind onto something besides money for a change."

Oh, thought Lysbeth, that was bad strategy, that was the worst imaginable thing to say. Her father was a humble man; an exhibition of arrogance could only repel him. Her father was a man with a vast unlettered awe for learning and skill and he would take an accusation of heedless ignorance like a slap in the face. Money which might have been forthcoming if it had been asked for as an indulgence would never be rendered up if it was claimed as a right. He also had risen, red in the face, a swollen vein standing out on his bald forehead. "Leave the table," he said.

"That's what I'm doing."

"Leave the house while you're about it."

"Don't upset yourself—I will."

"Answer me like that again, and you'll get the beating you've been asking for—"

"Harmen, in the name of Heaven—"

"You stay out of it, Neeltje. You've spoiled him beyond endurance. All I want is for him to get out of my sight."

He complied, but at a leisurely pace and with a coolness that sent chills of fright and admiration down his sister's spine. He brushed a few crumbs from the front of his shirt, ran his hand through his hair while he walked the length of the table, stepped gracefully over his brother's crutches, and actually paused on the threshold to button up his jacket. And watching him out of the corner of her eye, she found it hard to maintain the look of shocked regret she had assumed for her father's sake—it was all she could do to stifle a smile.

*

Where he was going, how long it would take for the churning within him to subside, what he would do with himself in the meantime, he did not know. A day at the studio was unthinkable. If he could scarcely say a decent good morning to Vrouw Baerens, how could he spend hours under the anxious gaze of his master? If the canal, the windmills, the raw and newly turned meadowland blurred and shimmered before his eyes, how could he stare at a glaring copper etching plate? The flat, almost unpeopled way across the canal and battlements and over the strip of farmland—he chose it simply because it put no strain on his pounding heart and presented him with no more neighbors at whom he would be expected to smile.

Other times when he had gone wandering because of family up-heavals—though there had never been any as violent as this—he had turned off this muddy path and taken the road to Zuytbroek. There, in the farmstead that belonged to his mother's people, with company meals forthcoming and little cousins to sketch and play with, he could stay until sundown, long enough to put everybody at home into a fit of anxiety without giving the slightest inconvenience to himself. But this quarrel was different: it had so shaken and bruised him that the thought of the solicitous questions of his aunt and the noisy demands of the children was as intolerable as the thought of the doings at the studio. Besides, what good would it do him to stay away until evening? What he had said over the breakfast table would not be forgotten no matter how long he stayed away: the fabric of his life had been torn past mending, it would never be the same again.

Oh, he had gone too far—now that he was alone here, crossing Aert Jacobszoon's moist and level field, he could let his shoulders sag, he could admit it. Even the undulating expanse of country before him, passing by stages of increasing vagueness into the barely guessed line where land and sea and sky all melted into light-drenched mist, could not ease him of his inward sickness. To say to them, and especially his father, that they knew nothing about the high matters that *he* was concerned with—that had been brutal as well as arrogant, that must have fallen like corroding acid on his father's heart. He stopped at the end of a square of ploughed-up sod and supported himself with shaking hands against a marking stone. Clenched hand, hairy as Esau's, coarse hand of a braggart . . . why had he done it? Because he had been driven to it; because they treated him like a fisherman, a cobbler,

33

a miller—because they treated him as if he were no different from anybody else. And it was intolerable, it was maddening enough to provoke the most shameful outbursts that he should be doomed to creep around the world unknown, unrecognized, that he should be dealt with as if he did not have these dreams, this swollen heart, this glory and this power.

For a little while, walking swift and upright toward the always receding place where the trinity of land and sky and water became a shimmering oneness, he tasted the blessed bread of his greatness and received from it both nourishment and absolution. Being great, he had an intrinsic claim to a double, yes, a triple birthright. Being great and greatly provoked, he ought to be forgiven. Being great . . . he slowed his pace to take in the smell that was carried to him across the wide tangle of cattails between the fields and the wilderness—a smell of water-sodden driftwood, water-logged roots and the dead and living creatures of the sea. Being great . . . but here at the outermost edge of Aert Jacobszoon's field, which was divided from desolation by a grey stone wall as high as his hip, he looked at the stretch of rushy ruin before him and felt his greatness melting away like a holy wafer on his tongue. Great? Was he great? Who was there to say so but himself?

He climbed over the wall, careful by long habit not to break the good black crayon or wrinkle the folds of sketching paper he always carried in his pocket, careful also that the rough stone should do no injury to his right hand. Twenty or thirty yards out from the wall, he could feel his feet begin to suck up the saturated earth. Greatness? What could he bring to a disinterested bar of judgment to prove his greatness? That he was a better painter than his fellow-apprentices van Vliet and Schlegel and Hoeven? But they were nothing, he thought, breaking the coarse stems of the cattails as he thrust them aside—one did them an honor to think they would be competent some day to paint a few oils for the parlors of minor burghers. Was greatness established by the praise of Jacob van Swanenburgh? The twenty or thirty paintings of the master honorably displayed in the better provincial salons of Leyden and Dordt and Haarlem were insipid and feeble: they had outstayed their season; if anybody but an aristocrat had painted them, nobody would cherish them any more. He pushed his way heedlessly through burs, nettles, last autumn's thistles hidden hazardous in the tangle of rushes—no matter, there was no need to coddle his precious right hand.

Stopping halfway through the amphibious growth, which stood here almost as high as his elbow, he undid the top button of his jacket and wiped the sweat from his neck and chin. The work itself—that was the test; the vine is to be judged by the fruit thereof. Covering his eyes with his hand to shield them from the pale glare that rose from the face of the morning waters, he conjured up a series of images of the best work he had ever done. A drawing of Judas knotting the noose, his eyes

34

bulging, his wiry hair rising on his head in fright—oh, that was false, that was the sort of thing that made him retch when he saw it on the stage. A little oil of a bunch of grapes on a wooden platter, winy translucent globes with the frosty bloom upon them—so real, Fioretta had said, that they made her hungry—but anybody, even Hoeven, could do a bunch of grapes: greatness was not to be purchased with an offering of grapes, melons, dead partridges, and such. An etching of Saint John starting up from his rocky seat on Patmos to greet the apocalyptic angel—sensational, pretentious—would he never do anything honestly, out of a humble mind and a contrite heart? Saint Bartholomew—there was real suffering in that, and nobody else could make sweat so convincing that the drops seemed to be swelling while you stared, but that was another tawdry trick, like the rubbed-down pile of the velvet. The suffering was Gerrit's—the sweat and the velvet alone were his, and all he could claim for himself was a despicable capacity to deceive the eye.

Goaded on as he was by self-disgust, it was short work getting through the rest of the barricade of rushes. On the other side of it lay the dunes, white in the early light, their pale, smooth undulations broken now and again by the upward thrust of some frail and futile stalk or the dissolving body of a jellyfish or a tenantless shell. Down here, with the water not more than half a mile in the distance, the sea smell was strong, acrid to the nostrils; and he thought with a shiver of qualmishness of the mass decay of scaly creatures, slowed down and protracted in the heavy solution of the brine. He turned to the right, not wishing to come closer to the water, and walked along slowly in search of a knoll that would be suitable to sit on, one where no snail had left its oily trail and no fine skeleton lay light upon the sand. Having found such a hillock—and they were scarcer than he would have imagined, the sea's encroachment on the beach was almost total—he let himself down onto the yielding sand and set himself to wrestle with the thought that there was no greatness in him, that he was no different from anybody else.

Wrestle? He could not wrestle. That thought, once evoked, came rushing at him out of the watery bleakness. That thought, a hundred times more powerful than the angel that had fallen upon Jacob, unmanned him utterly. Take away his painting, and there was nothing left to fill up the loose and flabby wineskins of his hours. Take away his hope of glory, and he was less than the least, abject among his brothers, an object for mockery, a self-deceiving fool. Where would he hide himself, what would he do with himself, how could he drag himself from one day to another? His dream of greatness, false as it might be to others, was substantial enough within him to perish and fester unless he could bring it to birth. To deny it, to stifle it, to murder it there in the darkness—that, he knew in his heart, could only bring him to an early death.

35

And for the first time in his life he saw death as a certainty, a thing from which there was no escape. Being like anybody else, he carried within him the already sprouted seed of his own mortality: I am flesh, and flesh melts away as inevitably in the coffin under the earth as in the brine; I am bone, and the heavy skeleton dries and breaks and powders like the light one, and the skull lies open on the burial pillow, all the high dreams spilled out, all thought and passion gone . . .

He could not pray—to try to pray was useless. His mother, his father, and Adriaen could pray with simple and unequivocal fervor, but it was as impossible for him to pray as it was for Gerrit, whose heart was encrusted with a rind of bitterness against the touch of God. Out there on the flat horizon the mists were clearing and the foamy line of the inward-washing tide was visible in places: he could see the boats of the fishing flotilla begin to emerge, their sails warmed to a pale yellow by the increasing brightness of the sun. And some two hundred feet away, between himself and the water, a beggar, a dark figure edged with strips of flapping cloth, was looking for what the tide had left to the poor: grounded eels and mussels to carry home and put on the fire.

In the last few years he had drawn a dozen such beggars. They knocked at doors, they haunted the fairs and beaches; and Callot, the great engraver, had drawn them by the score, fantastic in their rags, picturesque in their misery. He leaned forward from his dune to look more closely, to absorb the mute and patient line of the back, the desperate intentness of the head—never before had he felt himself passing out of his own skin into the very person of a beggar. Loneliness, rejection, the imminent threat of mortality—he knew them, he sensed what they could do to flesh and sinew and bone. His little hunger made it possible for him to enter into a great hunger; his heart, slowed to a sluggish pace by his emptiness and his sick meditations, was one with the starved and loveless heart.

He got up then, walked a hundred paces closer, found himself another dune and settled upon it, disregarding a bloated herring and a starfish. From here, with the light growing always stronger, he could make out the essential details—the sag of the cheeks, the swollen line of the belly coming out of the general lankness, the elbow thrusting through the ragged sleeve. Crayon and paper were in his hands before he knew he had taken them out of his pocket. Line was added to line, surely, but not swiftly: one drew one's own misery humbly, without flourish, with devotion and tenderness. The flapping bits of rag, the strips wound around the legs in place of stockings, the old sack put on the head against rheum and the morning cold—all the things that would have tempted him in the past into making teased and fantastic shapes on the paper—these he scarcely allowed himself to suggest. And since he could not see the eyes from such a distance even with peering, he endowed the mussel-gatherer with his own cold but stricken eyes.

36

The drawing was good, better than good, something to be hoarded away for further use. This wretch searching the sand in numb desolation could be transformed into many other wretches—the halt and the blind groping after the healing hand of Christ, the beggar searching for crusts under the rich man's table, the prodigal son looking for food among the swine. The prodigal son—there were a dozen paintings in that story, no matter what Heer van Swanenburgh might choose to think. Sometime, with God's grace, he would do a whole series: the prodigal son blithely crossing his father's threshold on a misty morning; the prodigal son in the arms of harlots, one of whom could easily look like Fioretta; the prodigal son—why should he weep, why should his cheeks be washed with sudden, copious, easy tears?—falling upon his father's neck, feeling his father's arms close around him in an all-forgiving embrace.

It was early still: by the quality of the yellow on the distant sails he could tell that the sun had not been up for more than three hours. He could have gone to the studio—his lateness would be slight and van Swanenburgh would reprove him only gently for it—but he could not think of taking himself back to those rejected rooms. He was hungry, too, and buttermilk and fresh pancakes would be set out for him at Zuytbroek. Quickly, singing an old chorale at the top of his voice, he retraced his steps over the dunes toward the road that would take him to his mother's village; and as he walked he kept his eyes on the shining roofs of Leyden, the sun-warmed battlements, the flashing sails of the windmills: he did not look at what he knew he must be stepping on —the abandoned shells and the bones.

*

That evening at exactly nine, while the throb of the last steeple chimes still sounded in the damp spring air over Leyden, Harmen Gerritszoon had barred his doors and gone upstairs to bed. Not that he was tired—in fact, he knew that it would be hours before he could hope to go to sleep—but he did not mean to be caught again, as he had been caught on a couple of other occasions, sitting anxiously downstairs to welcome the insolent prodigal back home. Tonight there would be no gratifying anxiety, no all-healing welcome; and it gave him real pleasure, while he folded up his clothes and put on his nightshirt, to imagine the arrogant calf trying the front door, trying the back door, and being forced at last to scramble up the wall and fiddle with a window-catch, fearful all the while that a city watchman would step up and ask how he came to be crawling into people's windows at that time of night.

Possibly it was his preoccupation with the business that made him so slow about undressing. Long before he had finished, his wife had betaken herself in her nightgown to the shelter of their bed, built like a doorless cupboard into a corner. She had knelt to say her prayers with

37

her head at least thrust into that privacy, though her soles, bare and dusty, were exposed to the light of the oil lamp burning on the dresser; she had laid herself down without a word, her face to the wall and her back to him and the harsh, uncomprehending world. "Good night, Neeltje," he said, without expecting an answer. All day she had been looking at him accusingly, as if his unwillingness to produce the required sum of money was the cause of her suffering, though she would only have been thrown into a darker fit of grieving if the money had been forthcoming and her darling had been free to depart. And now, resentful because he had summoned her upstairs at nine, unable to forgive him for involving her in his own cold-heartedness, she would keep as far away from him as the good width of their bed permitted. To pat her thin shoulder would be useless: she would act as if she were asleep, she would make a show of jerking away in her pretended dreams.

He sighed and knelt where she had knelt, on a narrow strip of carpeting worn thin by their repeated devotions. He shuttered his face in his hands—even when nobody was looking it seemed indecent to pray with an uncovered face—and began to whisper the Paternoster: "Our Father Who art in Heaven . . ." But since he required himself to say every word with unclouded awareness, it seemed that he would be as long about his praying as he had been about his undressing. His mind, nagged by the stresses of the day, was as wayward as a nervous horse tonight: when he wanted to evoke the vast, glassy radiance of the word "Heaven" he found himself listening to the consciously measured rise and fall of Neeltje's breath; when he meant to ask humbly for tomorrow's daily bread, he found his ears growing hot with the thought of the holiday fare that had probably been set out for his son at the farmstead in Zuytbroek—pancakes and gingerbread—that was the punishment he would get for his arrogance.

Three times he began the "Our Father," but not once could he get any further than "Forgive us our trespasses." Knowing that Neeltje was too stiff-necked in her anger and her sorrow to turn and see what he could be doing there, he sat back on his calloused heels and considered the words; and some nameless and mournful thing, more depressing than the feel of the dead and horny skin of his feet pressing through the linen of his nightshirt, settled cold upon his heart. "Forgive us our trespasses . . ." All the time he had been trying to keep his mind on the Paternoster he had been obsessed by an image of the kitchen as it had been when this house had belonged to his stepfather: he had been seeing the narrow, bearded, diffident face preaching to him across a dish of apples and a crockery pitcher on the table, telling him awkwardly—it was no easy business to give fatherly advice to a dead man's son—that he had better not set his mind on Mathilde Willemsdochter, that she had her eye on another lad with a bigger inheritance, that when he ran after her on the dunes and waited for her after

38

church he only made a fool of himself. "Run after her" and "make a fool of yourself"—those had been the words; his embarrassment and his fury had stamped them, along with the pitcher and the apples, ineradicably on his brain. Granted that they were ill-chosen words, granted that the man who spoke them was so unsure of himself that there was neither warmth nor authority in his firmness—still they had not deserved the answer they had provoked. "Don't try to act like a father to me," he had shouted at the nervous and gentle being whom afterwards he had come to love. "You're not my father, and you know it, and when you try to act like my father *you* make a fool of *yourself*."

And he had never apologized, never asked forgiveness, not because the loss of Mathilde Willemsdochter had been a lasting grief to him but because, callow as he was, he had sensed the shame he had inflicted and had never been able to remind his stepfather of that shame. And now what was there to do but fix his mind on that ancient, unatoned-for wrong while he started in again at "Forgive us our trespasses" and go tomorrow to plant a few more clumps of crocus on an already scrupulously tended grave?

Having made his devotions, more or less, he stood up sighing and brushed his knees. He could not bring himself to quench the lamp that burned on the dresser, since it was the last light left in the house, and he carried it into the hall and set it on top of the chest, where the yellow glow would be visible in the small high window from the darkened and deserted street. "I left a light in the hall, Neeltje," he said, coming back into the room, but she did not answer. Ah, well, it will be different with her tomorrow, he told himself, and climbed stiffly into bed.

Some months ago he had changed places in the bed with Neeltje. On certain nights of late he had been kept awake and even forced to wander around the house by a quick and violent beating of his heart, and it had seemed better for him to lie on the outer side so that he could get up if he liked without crawling across her, though he had long resisted the change and never came to bed these nights without a sense of loss. Since their wedding night the two of them had been lying face to face in each other's arms, and now they were too old to change their sleeping positions: all they could do was lie back to back, and he missed the weight of her head on his shoulder, the stirring of her breath against his neck. Besides, on nights like this, when he had hurt her feelings, there was less chance of a reconciliation because of the change. There was chill, empty space between them, and the bed was unfriendly without their common warmth, and already he could feel an ominous hastening in the rate of his heart.

Nor would the night yield him the assurance that things were well enough outside him, no matter what chaotic doings were going on within. Aert Jacobszoon's hound whined and rattled the chain that bound him to the fence; a pair of drunkards carried a thick-tongued quarrel down the length of the street; late and solitary footsteps kept sounding under the window—not Rembrandt's, they did not pause, they went with a depressing steadiness toward the Pelican Quay or the White Gate. It would have eased him if he could have let his back and haunches rest against Neeltje's, and he reached behind him tentatively and touched her trailing hand. But there was no response, and it was useless to lie here counting his always-hastening pulse and breathing the fatty, oppressive smell of the goose feathers through the ticking. He rose as carefully as he would have risen if she had really been asleep, put his bare feet into his shoes, and walked into the hall to get the lamp.

No lighted crack showed under the closed door of Gerrit's room, and he grieved to find himself thanking God that so young a man was lost in the blankness of sleep. Lysbeth, too, was sleeping, in spite of the temper in which she had flounced upstairs; her door stood wide open, and he could hear her healthy, even breathing. He was drawn to the window, he wanted to look out into the deserted street; but he knew that his shape would be shadowed forth by the lamplight, and he walked the hall instead, trying to count his footsteps, trying to pay no attention to the thumping in his chest. Where could the crazy calf be at such an hour? Could a villainous beggar have fallen upon him on a desolate stretch of the road from Zuytbroek? But that was womanish nonsense; the times were reasonably good and the jail was almost empty and the city watch made hourly inspections. What had he meant, anyway, clenching his hand like that, thrusting his clenched hand into a person's face? "If you had any idea what I have here . . ." But nobody doubted it, nobody had ever shown anything but respect for his talent. Only, it wasn't enough for him to be treated like the archangel Michael; he felt himself slighted if he wasn't treated like God . . . Some strange and debilitating merging of fear and anger made his erratic heart flip like a caught fish against his side. He ought not to be walking like this; he didn't suppose a doctor would advise him to pace the floor with such turmoil going on inside him, and he sat down, leaning forward and taking little shallow breaths, at the bottom of the crooked stairs that led up to the attic.

The spasm passed, and he considered more reasonable possibilities with a calmer mind, inhaling meanwhile the smell of paint and oil that always came down from the room of the prodigal. Could he have stopped at a tavern? Not very likely: he had no taste for brandy and he retreated into sulky silence whenever he found himself in loud-mouthed company. Could he be with a woman? Less likely still: he was chaste, anybody could swear to that. As likely as not, while a person sat worrying about where he was, he stood in the light cast by some yellow window, his crayon and his paper in his hand, drawing a drunken roisterer and utterly unconscious of the ten o'clock chime that was falling just now from Saint Peter's steeple, a chime so slow and even that it emphasized the crazy pace of the heart.

And though it was useless and unwise to climb twelve steep steps in such a state—his son could not possibly have come into the house without making himself heard—he took the lamp and started up the crooked stairs. The boy had carried the smell of the painter's trade so long in his clothes and hair that the strengthening odor gave a growing illusion of his presence, an illusion so real that once he stood on the threshold and cast the pale light into every corner of the little room, he felt an unreasonable disappointment at its foreknown emptiness. There was the bed, depressing in its creaseless whiteness. There was his cloak —he should have taken it with him, the night was moist and edgy. There on the window sill was the heap of copper squares, ready for the etching needle. And here, staring at him from the canvas, startling him like a living presence suddenly picked out of darkness, was the suffering Gerrit in the purple robe of Saint Bartholomew.

It had been days since he had laid eyes on that picture—he was not one to intrude on a self-appointed hermit—and perhaps because of the long absence, perhaps because of the lamplight trained directly upon it by his unsteady hand, what was there on the canvas struck him with more force than ever before. He stared at it with an absolute belief in its actuality that made him see for the first time why it was that the Catholics had set up such an outcry over their shattered images. Those things which had attracted him most when his mind was clear and his heart was steady fell into relative insignificance: the sweat and the velvet were good enough, but they were nothing beside the fact that the man—Bartholomew or some exalted Gerrit—was simply there, there in an almost embarrassing nakedness of spirit, gazing straight out at him with afflicted eyes. The illusion of presence was so strong that it made him keep his distance, impelled him even to step back and lower the light to decrease the intensity of the painted glance.

And while he looked, certain questions, carried on the swift rhythm of the inward beating, kept assailing him. Had Jacob van Swanenburgh, great master that he was, ever painted anything like it? Did the hand that had painted such a thing have good reason for holding itself up clenched in the face of a stupid world? Wasn't it true that Joseph, a just man in the sight of God, had boasted openly in the foolishness of his youth about his upright sheaf standing in the midst of the bowed sheaves of his brothers? How important was it—here, now, under this compelling painted gaze—if he did not use Adriaen's little bag of money to repair the sail but did the work himself?

He started at the expected sounds: rattle of a bolt, rattle of another bolt after a pause, click of a window-latch, thud of feet landing on the floor. Another pause, and then a whistle, a chorale whistled softly but distinctly into the empty darkness that had been meant to rebuke him— fifteen hours away and unforgiven, and the insolence still thriving: no contrition, not even a decent regret. Stifle the anger, remember Joseph boasting of his sheaf, remember that youth with its insolence is a kind of disease. Put down the lamp on the window sill beside the heap of etching plates: it will not do to have him see the light wavering in an unsteady hand. Stand still with arms hanging while the whistle comes nearer, up one flight of stairs and then through the hall toward another. Plan nothing, leave it all in the hand of God, mindful that He has already foreordained whatever is to be said . . .

The whistle died halfway up the stairs, possibly because the boy had sighted the light. He stopped dead on the threshold, his reddish mane blown wild by his walk along the beach, his face white except where the sea wind had stung and spotted his cheeks, plainly amazed and discomfited that it should be the father, the judge, and not the mother, the comforter, who stood waiting for him here. His hands came out from his crumpled cuffs in a feeble gesture of deprecation. "I'm sorry, Father. I was hoping I'd find you up—I wanted to say I was sorry."

"Let's think no more about it." Whatever satisfaction the halting apology might have yielded was reduced to insignificance by the pounding inside.

"I didn't realize how late it was until I heard the chime—"

"I said we'd say no more about it." The shattering beat was interfering with his sight; he had to blink to clear away the purplish mist. And as he opened his eyes again, he was overcome by a sudden lightheadedness: the room seemed to heave and slip, so that he had to put out his hand to steady himself against the sill.

"Father! What's the matter with you, Father?"

It came out so urgently, so fearfully that it fixed the shifting walls. He blinked again and clearly saw the blunt young face; and by what was in the eyes, by the terror and the tenderness, the Lord made him know the measure of his days. "Nothing," he said, sorry to have forced prematurely a knowledge of mortality that would come soon enough in the nature of things. "I have a little pressure here, a little indigestion—" He moved away from the sill to show that he could stand firmly on his feet. "We had pancakes in broth for supper, and they never did agree with me; and I can't say, either, that I ate them in peace."

"Let me go down and get you something—perhaps a little brandy—"

"No, don't be foolish, there's nothing wrong with me. Now that you're here, I may as well go back to bed."

But before he could take a step his son was standing against him, clasping him round the neck, his arrogant head bowed in unwonted humility, his forehead resting against his father's chest. The gesture was so startling that he could not respond to it at once, could only stand rigid, his arms still hanging at his sides. Then the known scent and the warmth melted all constraint, all anger; and he laid his open palms over the bent young back and let the contact tighten into a strong and all-forgiving embrace.

Once they had stepped apart again, they were ashamed: it was years since they had stood lovingly against each other. Avoiding the white and contrite face whose cheeks were marked with tears, he turned toward the scarcely visible Saint Bartholomew. "I was looking at the picture—I was thinking about that business of the money," he said, going back to the window to pick up the light. "It will take a little doing"—he walked to the door and paused in the doorway only long enough to get the rest of the breathy sentence out—"but I think I see a way to manage so that you can go to Amsterdam."

Back in his room, before he knew what he was doing, he found himself kneeling by the bed on the worn strip of carpet. Ah, well, it would do no harm to say the Paternoster one more time; he had not really brought his mind to bear on it before. With the thumping stilled and all the members of the family safely under the roof, it was possible for him to call up each of the accustomed images. The benign head of the Father, the crystal streets of Heaven, the browned and crusty shape of the daily loaf came one after the other into his thoughts, soothing him, making him ready for rest. Without a pause, with nothing but the most fleeting vision of the blond head of Mathilde Willemsdochter, he got through "Forgive us our trespasses as we forgive those who trespass against us," and his heart was beating evenly, though still a little faintly, when he came to the "Amen."

Sleep had come to Neeltje in his absence and taken away her imaginary wounds and her unreal anger. When he stretched himself beside her in the bed warmed by her breathing presence, she sighed and let her body sink backward against him; and he reached behind him and found and held her unresisting hand. Bitterness and coldness she was able to maintain only by watchfulness, and for the time being, at least, her watch was over: sleep had allowed her to slip back into kindness and love.

BOOK II

1623
-
1624

The master-painter Pieter Lastman seldom had reason to regret tha.
he had brought back a male servant from Italy. The gentleman's gentleman, a bizarre and questionable figure ten years ago when Vincenzo
had stepped off the ship behind him, had become an acceptable, even
an enviable item in Amsterdam society. Manners were changing: men
left their women at home more often now in order to enjoy each other's
company; and the little midnight suppers, with their smoke and their
French wines and their free conversation, were more relaxed if they
were not put on under the rigid scrutiny of an old-fashioned, raw-boned,
righteous Dutch shrew.

And if Vincenzo was valuable on company evenings—moving soft-
footed and self-effacing through the splendid salon to replace burnt-
out candles, to fill up tobacco boxes and decanters, to apply salt to the
wine stain on a priceless Persian carpet or to lead a tottering guest into
the back garden for a breath of air—he was downright essential on the
solitary mornings. Pieter Lastman, whose person had been characterized as Olympian by town poets male and female, had remarked to
two or three of his closest friends that he would have looked less like
Jove and more like Silenus if it hadn't been for the ministrations of that
clever devil he had picked up in Capri. By stitching a bit of fringe on
the bottom of a jacket Vincenzo could draw attention away from the
hips; by the proper placing of a knot in a sash he could minimize the
swell of the belly; by the diagonal draping of a scarf he could make
something monumental out of the fatty chest. If the face that looked at
the master out of his morning mirror seemed to be all drooping lines—
the jowls long and sagging, the corners of the mouth pulled down, the
eyelids so heavy that the pale hazel eyes were only little triangles on
either side of a nose which, of all his features, had alone remained aris-
tocratically thin—Vincenzo had a remedy for that. With hot wet towels
and those marvelous kneading hands, a person could present himself
with some dignity to his apprentices, his cook, and any patrons or fellow-
artists who happened to drop in.

This afternoon, with his usual ease in adapting himself to unforeseen
situations, Vincenzo had grasped at once that Vrouw van Hoorn was
no ordinary visitor, nobody to be brought casually into the studio where
her son Allaert and the five other apprentices were sweating away at
their easels under the August sun. He had conducted her instead into
the anteroom reserved for important or intimate conversations; he had
come quietly into the studio to announce her visit; and now that Pieter
Lastman and Allaert had joined her in the little back chamber where

47

the drapes were drawn against the heat, he had disappeared into the kitchen to prepare some delicate indication of hospitality, something that would be neither too plain nor too ostentatious for the occasion.

That the lady had not come to complain, to ask foolish questions, to play the anxious mother solicitous for her son in the first year of his apprenticeship she made plain from the start by saying to the master while she looked with mock ruefulness at Allaert, "Oh, have you brought my monkey along? You needn't have done that—I see him enough, heaven knows. I only came to pay my respects to *you*." That those respects were to be embodied in some sort of gift she also indicated by casting a grey-blue glance at a lumpy package on the carved arm of her chair. The visit was purely social, and she had plainly gone to some trouble to make herself attractive for it: her thin body was encased in beautiful silvery silk; and the slender wrists, the long neck, and the straight blond hair were adorned with garnets and pearls. What she went on to say in her throaty voice was all intended to show her satisfaction: she and Heer van Hoorn had enjoyed their trip to Italy so much more, knowing how happy Allaert was to spend the time in the house of his new master; what a cook Heer Lastman must keep—Allaert had actually rounded out a little and had become downright critical of the van Hoorn dumplings; even her husband, who was so preoccupied with his shipping business that he couldn't tell the difference between a de Keyser canvas and a Nicolaas Elias, could see that Allaert's drawing had improved.

The master had heard without really listening. The young man had come around to stand beside his mother, and in the hazy golden glow that seeped through the weave of the drawn sand-colored drapes the likeness between them was even more striking than it would have been in full light. Mother and son had the same charming and somewhat touching way of holding their heads a little to one side, the same long and flawless white cheeks, the same clear eyes, the same pale, silky hair. The van Hoorn kind of elegance was bred in the bone: the seventeen-year-old Allaert was no less the adolescent cavalier in his dark blue working jacket than he would have been in plumes and velvet. Every now and again his mother looked at him, hiding her surges of affection in a faintly mocking smile. "It's good of you to go to so much trouble with him," she said. "I'm sure it must be quite a trial to take on anybody new."

Looking at him in all his thin-skinned charm, Pieter Lastman thought wistfully that newness was the best of it: Allaert van Hoorn was able to generate such attraction only because he *was* new. After so many years of teaching, the master had come to accept the transitory nature of one's obsession with one's apprentices. Where now, for instance, was what he had felt in the mellow days of another waning summer for Jan Lievens? The pony had turned into the sleek, well-fleshed horse, and Allaert too would put on either softening weight or coarsening muscle.

A beard would mar the clear, long cheek, and the grey-blue eyes would lose their innocence. "Oh, nothing I've done for Allaert has been in the nature of trouble. He's not only gifted but docile, too—and that, I assure you, is a very rare combination," he said.

"He wants to learn; of that at least I'm certain."

The young man, embarrassed to hear himself commended to his face, resorted to a smile very like his mother's. Mild mockery was obviously a useful item in the princely house on the Heerengracht; whenever delight or anger pressed too close to the surface there, they apparently downed it by teasing each other. "Aren't you forgetting what you came for, Mother?" he said.

"Ah, yes!" She took up the package between her veined and delicate hands and held it out to the master. The gesture was deliberately overdramatized: by handing him his present with a flourish she relieved him of the obligation of anything more than formal thanks. "It's nothing, Heer Lastman. For all I know, it may be actually ugly, but it's an authentic antique at any rate. We found it in Verona, Joris and I."

That she should refer to her husband by his first name was even more gratifying than that she should have brought him a gift from Italy: it meant that she intended to be on cordial terms with him, that she would probably have him to supper with the family one of these nights. The possibility of being numbered in the constellation of distinguished guests in that famous salon made him smile while he undid the string and turned the wrappings back, but then he ceased to smile—the little bronze saucer lamp, green with the patina of the centuries, left him wordless under the assault of remembrances. How many such lamps he and his fellow-students had dug out of the black Italian earth! How high-heartedly they had told themselves, every time they filled one of them with oil and let it burn on some wine-anointed table, that they had set up a bond between themselves and the magnificent past!

"I suppose everybody brings them back. I wouldn't be at all surprised if you told me you had a dozen of them," she said.

"No, not at all. In fact, I haven't a single one. It's beautiful, really; I like it very much." But the room remained charged with his insufficient reaction, and he saw that it would be better to explain. "It was only that it reminded me of my student days, when I was working in Rome with Elsheimer—God rest his soul."

And now that he had said the name, it was as if twenty burdensome years had fallen away from his life and fifty pounds of excess fat had fallen away from his body. Free of breathlessness, light on his feet, he was pacing the opulent lawn of a Roman garden with Elsheimer on a late spring evening when the air was an opiate heavy with pine and roses. Elsheimer's narrow face, always burningly intent, gazed at him and beyond him; the silky reddish hair and beard, lighted by the glow of the Southern sunset, looked like fire; the bony hands, ill cared for, cracked at the knuckles, kept gesturing as if to invoke those beings

49

whose names he uttered—nymph of the river and waterfall, dryad of the poplar and sycamore, genius of the moss-covered well. Whatever we see, Elsheimer had said on that magical evening, is, as the ancients were wise enough to know, only a shabby manifestation, a faulty shadowing forth of its own spirit. And he who reaches the spirit-essence through the material veils around it raises himself out of his mortality, makes himself, if only for the instant of revelation, a fellow of the gods.

"It's strange," she said, lowering her voice as if her acute perceptions had warned her to adjust it to some soft and mournful note, "but I don't think I've ever seen one of Elsheimer's pictures, as often as I've heard his name."

"His pictures stayed in Italy. It was his influence that came to the Netherlands."

He thought of the Northern painters who had journeyed by the score from their pallid and foggy homelands to that sun-drenched paradise: Elsheimer had gathered most of them to himself; Elsheimer had been their guide, their master, yes, almost their god. How many of them had gone home unwillingly, to paint only in expectation of an eventual re-union, to ask themselves in front of their every picture, "What would the master think of this?" How many other Germans and Netherlanders, learning from some traveler that the burning glance was quenched, had felt their hands grow slack, had allowed their spirits to be cushioned in more and more layers of fat, their bereaved minds to be drugged by more and more wine?

"It would have been a great satisfaction to him if he could have seen his teachings bear fruit in canvases like yours," she said.

Would it indeed? The question was too melancholy to be considered, and it was fortunate that Vincenzo should come in just then with some wafer-thin cookies and a dish of fresh peaches and pears. On his way out, he paused at the door and turned his large, quick eyes upon his master. "Excuse me, your honor," he said in a voice at once offhand and respectful. "Is van Rijn to go on grinding the azure?"

"Certainly not!" He was appalled to realize that he had forgotten all about the Leydener, that the half-hour punishment he had meant to mete out to him had, through his own absorption with the van Hoorns, stretched out to something like an hour. Impudent as the fellow had been, to set him to grinding pigment had been a little drastic: work with the mortar and pestle was a menial duty usually assigned only to the thick-handed or the pig-headed, and even to them no later than in their first year. "He was only supposed to stay at it for half an hour," he said, looking uneasily at Allaert, who stopped skinning his peach and did not smile.

"Would you like me to tell him he can stop now, your honor?"

He pondered it for an instant—it would be a way of prolonging the delightful visit—but then he dismissed it as unwise. The boy would take it ill that a servant should give him directives, all the more so because of the humble circumstances from which he had come. "No," he said, "I'll take care of it myself."

But he could not take care of it at once. It would be unthinkable to walk out and leave the mother and son nibbling away alone in the anteroom; etiquette required that he should at least make a show of partaking of the little spread. He ate two of the cookies, which were flavored delicately with anise seed, and took the occasion to express his thanks for the gift more elaborately and conventionally by praising the patina and the exquisite simplicity of the shape of the lamp. But his attempts to hide his sense of urgency did not deceive his visitor; before he could begin to excuse himself, she was on her feet. "Don't let me keep you from your business—I've said everything I came to say and much more," she said, brushing the cookie crumbs from her silvery skirt with her blue-veined hand.

"It's nothing, really," he assured her, crossing the room to be near her in case she should offer him her fingertips. "It's only that I have to stop in the studio and give a few directions."

But instead of extending her hand in the gesture of farewell, she slipped her arm through his and gave him a sidelong, pleading glance. "Take me with you," she said. "I've never seen the place where Allaert works, I've never met any of his fellow-apprentices, and naturally I'm curious."

"Well, come along, by all means," he said, unable to respond to the flirtatious look and feeling his arm stiffen under the firm touch. "But I warn you beforehand, you're going to see a very disorderly place—"

"I wouldn't expect a bachelor's studio to be scrubbed like a housewife's kitchen, you know."

"As for Allaert's fellow-apprentices, there's one of them at least that you're going to find in a very glum humor. I've set him to grinding pigment as a disciplinary measure—"

"Oh, have you been having trouble? Then maybe I shouldn't come," she said.

The difficulty was that he couldn't agree that she shouldn't come without admitting that he'd been "having trouble," a term vague enough to leave an impression of dissension where she would naturally want affability and serenity. "No, no, nothing at all serious," he said. "I have another new apprentice, just about Allaert's age, and very gifted, too. But along with all that, he's a little—well, a little stubborn. We had a model in this afternoon, a really colorful old fellow, and I wanted them to emphasize his quaint aspects, his satyr-like qualities. But by the time van Rijn was finished with him, there was nothing quaint about him: he looked like a derelict, like the dreariest beggar in the world."

"What was the matter? Couldn't he get a likeness?" she asked, still holding onto his arm, still regarding him with her grey-blue eyes.

"Oh, the likeness was accurate enough." He closed his eyes for an instant and saw it—a vigorous portrayal of depravity and misery in red chalk, the anatomy faultless, the details beautifully executed, and every-

51

thing brought into unity by the general coarseness. "As a matter of fact, Vrouw van Hoorn, it was horribly, relentlessly accurate. But it was so *material,* so utterly without charm or imagination." He did not want to tell her that if the glory of the painter lay where Elsheimer had put it—in the ability to reach through the fleshly outer layers to the inner spirit-essence—then this Rembrandt van Rijn would get nowhere, for all his skill. The Leydener actually exulted in the material: he made it more material even than it was; his dirt was dirtier than dirt itself.

"And I suppose he lost his temper and didn't accept instruction in the proper spirit. Well, isn't that more or less to be expected of a seventeen-year-old?" She looked at her own mild lamb quizzically, as if she were a little dismayed to find the expected intractability missing there, but the boy did not return her glance—his eyes, remote and noncommittal, were fixed on his master's face.

"Yes, I suppose it is, but I had to do something to discipline him because he got a little out of hand." He wondered whether Allaert would tell her at supper tonight that the boy had said: "And what if I don't see him the way you see him, Master? If I don't put him down the way I see him, it'll be as if I were drawing a lie."

"Well, Allaert, I hope you didn't give the master any trouble." It was a playful admonition, an oblique way of hiding her fondness and her pride.

"Oh, no, Allaert's drawing was charming. I was delighted with it, I really was. Come, let's go over and see."

The studio was dimmer and emptier than he had expected. Working hours were over, and the pestle sounded all the more ominous, grinding away at the far end of the room with a speed and regularity that bespoke controlled rage. Two of the apprentices, Lievens and Haldingen, had already gone to their quarters in the attic to tidy themselves up for supper; and that was a pity, since the two who were left—the thirteen-year-old Hessels, and Larsen, the gangling and surly Dane—were scarcely the sort to divert the lady's attention from the unpleasant business with van Rijn. Allaert had to shout to them that his mother had come in expressly to meet them, before they stopped scrubbing their palettes and came over to make their careless bows. It was only after Vrouw van Hoorn had invited them all to a nameday party to be held next month for Allaert that the talk became sufficiently animated to allow the master to excuse himself and walk down the long room past the clutter of easels and pedestals and screens, glad that so much space and so many objects should lie between the distinguished visitor and the scene he felt certain would take place.

At the marble grinding slab under the last of the windows, the Leydener was still working at the long-since thoroughly pulverized azure. Though he could not have failed to hear the approaching footsteps—all sounds were disturbingly magnified in the large room—he did not stop or lift his head; without slackening his labors, he merely glanced up

52

from under the unruly reddish mane that nodded over his brow. It was always difficult for the master to look this thorny pupil of his in the face, and at the moment it was all the harder because the chilly grey eyes, in spite of the fury in them, were blurred and reddened by tears. "I didn't intend to keep you at the azure all this time," the master said. "Vrouw van Hoorn dropped in, and we were talking, and—well, to tell the truth, I simply forgot about the whole business."

A stiff, short nod was the only answer.

There were clots of ground azure on the frieze jacket and the blunt fingers, a waste of very precious material, but he let it pass. "You can stop now if you like and get ready for supper. Only"—he had glanced at the Leydener's easel and seen nothing there—"what did you do with the drawing you made this afternoon?"

Again there was no answer, unless the sideward swing of the head could be taken as a reply. Looking in the direction indicated by the movement, the master saw a soiled and crumpled piece of drawing paper on the cluttered floor; and he was the more distressed because the conversation at the other end of the studio had trailed off: Allaert's mother might be watching, might think that his apprentices regularly crumpled up their drawings and threw them down, when nothing of the sort had happened here for years.

"Surely you didn't throw away your sketch, van Rijn?"

"Yes, Master." The voice was harsh and pitiful at once. The wet grey eyes stared stubbornly down at the grinding slab.

"Now, that was a very foolish thing for you to do. Nothing I said"—his conviction that she had seen and was judging him impelled him to raise his voice—"nothing I said could have called for such childish behavior, could it?"

"No, Master. I don't suppose so. But after you were finished with it I got to hate it myself."

"Well, I certainly didn't intend to make you hate your drawing. There were a great many fine things about it, as I pointed out. You can leave the azure where it is; we'll get Hessels to put it away tomorrow. Now go and freshen yourself up for supper."

"Thank you, Master," he said in a flat voice, and stepping over the crumpled drawing, he started up the long aisle between the easels for the door. Nobody looked up as he passed, nobody ventured to halt his hurried advance; and Pieter Lastman felt that Vrouw van Hoorn, gracious as she was, would certainly have called the solitary figure into her little group if she had not heard what had passed and sensed that it would be more charitable to let him alone.

Nothing that followed gave Lastman any pleasure, not even walking with the visitor to Allaert's easel, where the face of the old model, obediently transformed into a satyr—but what an innocent satyr, what a guileless old face!—looked out at him from the paper. The words he marshaled up to commend the drawing—"charming," "sensitive," "appealing"—seemed as unconvincing as his response to the gift. He was made uneasy, too, by a certain belligerent look in little Hessels' dark almond-shaped eyes; this runt of the brood, who had taken a fancy to the Leydener, had shown his disapproval of the criticism of his idol by standing close at hand and munching on an apple as loudly as he could. He was young—a bribe might serve the purpose better than a reproof. "Hessels," he said in the first suitable pause in the conversation, "I wonder if you'd be good enough to ask Vincenzo to get some gingerbread for us to have after supper with the grapes." And Hessels responded beautifully: the stiffness went out of his small, spare person; his eyes grew mild in his little heart-shaped face; and he ran off to do his master's pleasurable bidding, his black hair bobbing behind him.

She, too, turned away from Allaert's easel and offered her hand to the master. "You'll remember—won't you?—to save the evening of the twenty-ninth of September for the nameday party," she said, taking her son's arm as if to indicate that there was no need for her host to walk with her to the door. "Not that we don't hope to see you long before then. Come, Allaert, get your hat and gloves, wherever you left them. Thank you again, Heer Lastman. Good night."

Now that he was alone in the studio, he slumped and wandered back to the place where the Leydener's easel stood, looking forlorn in its emptiness; and there it was, the mauled and discarded sketch, lying among the scraps of paint rag and ends of chalk on the floor. Something had to be done about it—he could not walk away and leave it there—and once he had picked it up and straightened it out, he had to look at it again to check himself. But now he could not pass sound judgment on it. The wrinkles, the places where the red chalk had smeared, the rip that started in the right-hand corner and came all the way down into the old male model's face were almost unmanning in their pathos: they somehow altered the drawing, they endowed it with a timeless and melancholy authenticity.

His sense of stress was relieved by Vincenzo, who came in to ask how many guests were expected in the evening. It was cheering to repeat the distinguished names while the servant tallied them off on the tips of his fingers, to review the menu for the midnight supper, to make the proper selection of wine. When he had finished with all that, the crumpled drawing seemed alien to him and remote from the rest of his world. "Take this and put it in the big folio in the anteroom," he said; and as soon as the thing was gone, he could not refrain from rubbing his fingertips on the chestnut-colored velvet of his jacket.

*

By this time he should have learned to feel at home here, Rembrandt told himself, lying on his cot in Heer Lastman's attic and staring at the four big windows whose heavy glass looked blurred and bubbled in the light of the August moon. By now the whitewashed walls, the six cots arranged in one stark row, the chests and hampers and stools set orderly between them, the polished planks of the floor and the slight slope of the ceiling should have begun to intrude as little on his consciousness as the familiar things he slept among back home. But they persisted in asserting themselves, and even the washbasin and clothes peg and cupboard that he used every day never seemed real to him, were as unauthentic as objects in a drawing by an untalented child.

The city, too, lying beyond these walls, with its vast concentric canals catching the moonlight, with its clustered gables and its splendid steeples and its broad tree-lined streets, retained for him in the face of all his attempts to grasp it an intangibility, a ghostliness. Many of the things he had dreamed of doing he had done: he had seen scores of pictures, he had attended several auctions, and he had gone to the wharf and bought himself a little lacquered Japanese box; but these excursions as he remembered them were like things watched from a distance rather than things engaged in. In fact, there were times when it seemed to him that he had engaged in nothing since he left Leyden, that he had been as isolated as a deaf-mute in the studio and here in this upper room, that he had never been so detached, unmoored, alone.

And that inner loneliness might have been more bearable if he could have indulged it, if he had not been forced for the first time to live constantly impinged upon by others. It was not that the apprentices' quarters were crowded; the big top room in the master's house could have accommodated more than the six that were in service; and since Allaert went home before supper now, there was room to spare. Room— but no privacy at all, no cubicle where a person could use a chamber pot or brush the shameful stains of azure from his jacket or kneel to try to say his prayers or even think in peace. He had always been used to thinking, particularly about matters that were painful, in the ample, windy solitude of the dunes; and there had been no opportunity for him to think about what had gone on today between him and the master —neither at supper in the midst of the usual chatter, nor on the walk he took thereafter, since Larsen and Hessels had insisted on tagging along. Even now, when they had gotten into their beds and fallen into what he hoped would be a nightlong silence, he could not get rid of the notion that one or another of them was peering through the darkness to see the expression on his face.

Actually, he doubted that any of them *could* see him: the flawed moonlight, falling through the big glass oblong opposite his bed, had scarcely reached his feet. On his right was Jan Lievens, and that he would have any spirit left for watching was doubtful—Jan was having troubles of his own. Haldingen's cot was empty; he had stolen out as he always did on Wednesdays, slipping past the master's guests at their smoking and drinking in the big salon to keep his assignation with a neighbor's maid. On the far side of Haldingen's unrumpled coverlet

Larsen could be made out vaguely in the shadows, lying naked on top of his sheet. Such nakedness was coarse and unseemly, but mild as the Netherlands summer was, it was still too much for the Dane: his long, loose-jointed body was always drenched with sweat, and even in his dreams he protested against the heat. Now that Allaert was sleeping at home, little Hessels had left his place under the gable and was using the cot to Rembrandt's left because the others complained that he whimpered and talked in his sleep about Mamma and Katie and Dordt; but Rembrandt, too, found his restlessness disturbing, susceptible as he was to this contagious longing for home.

With so many alien bodies around him he had reason to be thankful for the master's obsession with cleanliness. The room was regularly aired, scrubbed, and dusted; and there were weekly baths and daily washings of armpits and faces and hands. The only smells in the place tonight were the scent of the dried lavender sprigs laid in with the stored sheets and the savory odor of the goose being seared in the kitchen for the guests. That crisping goose, like the bursts of laughter that came up through the intervening chambers, only increased his sense of isolation—the master seemed more than ever remote in the midst of the forbidden merriment going on below.

"Rembrandt," said little Hessels in a whisper.

He did not answer.

"Rembrandt"—the voice was still as high as a girl's—"are you asleep?"

"I was, and I'm tired, too. Why did you have to wake me up? Why can't you lie down and keep quiet?" He could see through the velvety darkness that the boy was sitting up with his arms clasped around his knees.

"I tried to, but I can't."

"August's almost gone—that leaves only four months until you'll be going home to Dordt for Christmas."

"It isn't that. It's because I keep thinking you're angry with me."

"What would I have to be angry about?" As soon as it was out, he knew it to be a risky question, the sort he would never have asked if he had had time to think about what had happened this afternoon. Just before supper, while he was washing the redness from his eyes, Larsen had said something about the master's smoothing things over with Hessels by getting the little idiot some gingerbread. And Hessels, childish as he was, might give a childishly honest answer to his question, might say within hearing of the others: "Because I betrayed you, because I made it up with him for a miserable after-supper sweet."

Something of the sort hung unspoken in the moon-washed stillness; then the little apprentice said with touching and unexpected tact, "I'm glad if you're not. I don't feel very good tonight. I wish I hadn't eaten any of the gingerbread."

"Well, it's no wonder if you don't feel good," said the exhausted and sepulchral voice of Larsen. "How could you expect to, after the way you stuffed yourself? It was disgraceful, the amount of cake you ate, especially when the master was only using it to buy you off with. A couple of slices of gingerbread, and you're the master's darling little lamb again. Say, Rembrandt"—the long white body, suddenly vitalized, shot up and sat on the edge of the cot—"I wanted to ask you: What did he say to you after he came back? Allaert's dear mamma was going on so much we couldn't hear a thing."

There was no malice in the question, nothing but idle curiosity. Larsen cared little enough for painting and even less for Lastman; Larsen could not be expected to know that the episode in the studio had left a painful bruise on his heart. "Nothing much," he said, and wished he could have stopped at that, wished that his need to stand high-headed among them hadn't driven him to add: "He said he didn't mean to keep me at the grinding so long. He said he was sorry—he and Vrouw van Hoorn had got to talking, and he simply forgot."

"Maybe so," said Larsen, sighing heavily and wiping his sweaty chest with the sheet. "But he certainly seemed to be handing it out to you today—if it wasn't one thing, it was another. All day long, everything little angel Allaert did was right, and everything you did was wrong."

Whether or not such was the case—the disaffected Larsen often saw grievances where none existed—it was hard to have it dragged out into public view. He was stung bitterly enough to want to say that it was better to be criticized than ignored: the master regularly ignored both Larsen and Haldingen, nodding if what he saw on their easels was tolerable, and merely shrugging at their gross mistakes. But he reminded himself that Larsen was stupid rather than malicious, was even loyal to him in a tepid way because he had once gone to some trouble to explain perspective to him. "I knew I wasn't doing what he wanted. I expected to get a lecture for it," he said.

"Yes, but such a lecture! The way he talked to you, a person would think he actually disliked you."

Actually disliked you . . . the words repeated themselves mournfully until Jan Lievens, roused for the first time out of his sodden passivity, propped his elbow on his pillow and his cheek on his hand, and cleared his throat to call attention to himself. "You're taking the whole affair too seriously, Larsen," he said with a pompousness that had been growing in proportion to the waning of his favor. "I've been here longer than the rest of you, and you can take it from me that it was nothing. If we'd had a different model, it would never have happened. The master saw the old man one way and Rembrandt saw him another, and both of them were too stubborn to give an inch. Tomorrow it'll be as if it never happened. The master has nothing against Rembrandt, nothing at all."

He wished he could believe it. Until this afternoon, it had never oc-

57

curred to him that the master might not have kindly feelings toward him; whatever feelings he could still discern in himself in his present uprooted state were directed toward the mellow, worldly-wise man who carried his fat with so much grace and humor, the inventive painter who transmuted the ordinary into the legendary and the fantastic. Absence of Lastman's affection was as much as he could entertain at the moment; he could not even consider the possibility of hostility.

"He was very pleasant to you at supper, Rembrandt," said little Hessels.

"Naturally," said Lievens, "he was pleasant to him at supper. Why shouldn't he be? He's never had such a talented apprentice—he told me so himself."

But much as he stood in need of comfort, his reason taught him to be wary of any that Lievens might offer. Lievens would want the master to consider him talented; the master had taken him on Lievens' word. Besides, his fellow-townsman was growing more and more adept in the art of self-deception. He could even manage to close his eyes to what was perfectly plain to everybody else: that the days of his favor were over, that van Hoorn was in and he was out. If the master spent an inordinate amount of time at Allaert's easel, with his glance traveling back and forth between Allaert's picture and Allaert's face, it was not—according to Jan—that he was taken with either the art or the artist; it was only because he would naturally show special attention to the only son of a family distinguished enough to receive beautifully printed personal greetings from the Prince of Orange at Easter and Christmas.

"Well, he was a rotten old model anyhow," said Larsen, collapsing back onto his pillow. "How's a person supposed to draw somebody who has the shakes? Even from where I was standing, you could smell the liquor on him. I hope we're going to do still life tomorrow; I'm better at that kind of stuff."

"Tomorrow we're doing life again," said Lievens.

"Who'll be sitting for us?" asked Hessels.

"How would we know?" said Larsen. "I imagine he has to wait to see what turns up."

"It so happens I know whom we're having," said Lievens. "We're having a female model." He was constantly making a point these days of knowing what came next and where such-and-such was stored, and his authoritative air was pitiful as well as exasperating, since its purpose was plainly to remind the others of his seniority and to starch his sagging self-respect.

"Who is she, Jan?" said Hessels.

"Now, who do you think she'd be—the leading lady from the English Company?" said Larsen. It was impossible to mention women in his presence without goading him into a tirade; Haldingen, in whom he had been fool enough to confide, had blabbed to everybody that the Dane had been betrothed in Copenhagen to the daughter of the owner of a fleet of fishing boats, that she had deceived him with a French tailor whom her father had forced her to marry, and that Larsen had felt the loss so acutely in both his heart and his pocketbook that his parents had sent him to Amsterdam to divert him from hanging himself. "Don't get yourself excited, she won't be anything much. She's probably some old whore like the one he dragged in out of the streets last year."

Rembrandt was on the point of asking whether the previous model had really been a whore, but stopped himself because such a question would only give the Dane an opening for a foul-mouthed lecture to the effect that anything in petticoats, no matter how pious and mealy-mouthed, was a whore at heart.

"Her name," said Jan, "is Rinske Dobbels, and for your information, she's a washerwoman, not a prostitute."

"Washerwoman or not," said Larsen, "she can't be decent, not if she'll stand around and let half a dozen of us draw her naked."

"Naked? Are we going to draw her naked?" Hessels' voice, suddenly gone girlish again, squealed the question, and Rembrandt was unnerved to find himself as startled as the thirteen-year-old. He stared at a patch of glowing whitewash on the ceiling and tried to quiet his racing heart.

"And won't that be wonderful?" said Larsen bitterly. "Well, you can have her—bubs, butt, pussy and all."

He had not heard such words since his days in grammar school, when smirking ten-year-olds had scrawled them on walls or whispered them in latrines. No apprentice would have used them in the close little tattle-tale world at Leyden; Gerrit in his most destructive mood would never have breathed them into the pious decency of the paternal house. To dwell on such things in privacy was bad enough, but to mouth them the way Larsen and Haldingen did, to take positive pleasure in saying them in public was beyond imagining.

"I tell you," said Jan insistently, as if his credit with Lastman depended upon it, "she's a perfectly respectable woman. She only does it for money."

"She could always take in more washing, couldn't she?" said Larsen. "But washing isn't as easy as standing around and showing what you've got to anybody that wants to see."

The shameless image called up by that was even more disturbing than the filthy words. "Really, Larsen," he said as soon as he could trust his voice, "I can't see any reason for being so vulgar about it."

"No," said Lievens, "neither can I."

"Can't you, though? Who am I supposed to watch my mouth for? Little angel Allaert isn't sleeping here any more."

"Allaert isn't, but Hessels is," said Rembrandt, acutely aware of the priggishness in his own voice.

"Yes, and so are you," said Larsen. "You never saw a naked woman yourself, no more than Hessels did."

"Pardon me, that's not the case."

59

"No? All right then, tell us, who was it?"

"That isn't any of your business."

"Where did it happen?"

"It happened in Leyden, but I don't intend to talk about it. Anybody halfway decent knows to keep such things to himself."

It seemed all the more unjust that his show of high-mindedness should have silenced the Dane since the person he had spied on in her nakedness was his own sister. He was certain that none of the rest of them, not even Larsen, could ever have descended to such depravity. One Saturday night, when he was about the same age as little Hessels, he had waited in bed—his cheeks flushed, his heart pounding up into his throat, his fingers icy cold—until she would be bathing in the kitchen. As soon as he heard his father's shoes fall in the room below him, he had gone barefoot in his nightshirt down the two flights of steps and out into the foggy October night. He remembered how clever he had considered himself: walking open-eyed and blank-faced down the narrow alley and into the back yard, he had planned to pretend that he was walking in his sleep if he should encounter anyone, but nobody had come; nothing had disturbed him but the rustle of dead sunflower stalks and the thin touch of cobwebs across his face. Standing precariously on two bales of peat moss and gripping the window sill, he had been able to look straight into the kitchen, to see in the light of the embers what he had imagined through hours of feverish wakefulness, to look as much as he liked at what he had never seen before and never since. What he could recall had been blurred by his earnest efforts to erase it from his memory—not for years now had he been able to see it all at once or see it topped with Lysbeth's head—but parts of it had remained. Nothing he had ever imagined had prepared him for the startling division of the girl-body, like a man's, into two legs below, for the provocatively rounded buttocks, for the overwhelming impact of the nothingness masked by the triangle of hair—wet hair that was a darker gold than the hair on her head.

"What about that Rinske—is she going to stand frontwards or backwards?" said little Hessels. He was still sitting up in his cot, his excitement warding off his sleepiness, his arms clasped around his shins and his chin resting on his knees.

"Oh," said Larsen, yawning, "the master'll probably put you behind her, since you're so young and innocent. But I guess you'll be able to sneak around and take a look. Just be careful you don't get too close—"

"Why? Would she be insulted?"

Nobody answered. The door creaked open, and Haldingen came in and stood in the bright and bubbled patch of moonlight at the foot of his unrumpled cot. It was unfortunate that he had come back so early: the others had been on the point of going to sleep, but now all of them, even the high-minded Jan, would rouse themselves to hear of his doings with the neighbor's maid. One couldn't believe half of what he said, but it was impossible to shut it out—impossible, too, to keep from staring at his person, somehow disturbing in spite of its masculine comeliness, or from watching him as he went through his indolent stripping, interrupted every now and again as he rubbed some newly exposed part of himself approvingly. Haldingen's face, clearly visible in the flawed white light, had a masklike smoothness capable of only three expressions: an assumed attentiveness, an exaggerated frown, and a quick smile that showed his teeth for an instant—small teeth, cruel and white, under the pale brown neatly trimmed moustache.

What he had to say about the goings-on in the tool shed was all the more sickening because Rembrandt knew the girl, had seen her often standing at the hedge with a basket on her arm and carrying on lively conversation with Vincenzo—a sallow girl with a hard knot of dark hair on top of her head, a straight stick of a girl whose starched bib-apron obscured every suggestion of breast and belly and thigh. To think of that one lying on the floor of the shed with her secret parts displayed in a confusion of apron, skirt, and petticoat, to think of the half-exposed Haldingen coming into contact with her—oh, it was disgusting—how would he ever be able to sleep?

But when Haldingen was finished with his boasting and his undressing, when Jan had fallen into an uneasy dream and little Hessels had lain down and covered himself and Larsen had turned his naked back to his neighbors and his face to the wall, the silence did not bring the expected relief. The obscene talk had served at least one purpose: it had distracted him from thinking about the master. Now, in the utter silence, that worry surged up again like sourness coming into his throat —the cold and chiding voice, the eyes that would not meet his glance, the forced conciliatory smile. "A person would think he actually disliked you . . ." Maybe so, but why? Because my nose is blunt and common? Because I dress in homemade friezes? Because I am a miller's son?

By now the whole room had been cleansed in the cool wash of the moonlight. Sheet and ceiling absorbed it and glowed with it; pitcher and basin cast long shadows into the airy whiteness of it; wet patches of it, like pools of water, shone on the polished floor. The moonlight, too clean and delicate for the gross beings who talked filthy talk and fornicated in its quiet radiance, helped to calm him, made it possible for him at least to mouth his prayers. But in the middle of the Paternoster he felt the snail-cold trail of two slow tears creeping down his cheeks. Why? Nothing as bad as all that could have happened—certainly nothing bad enough to make him weep.

*

That dream last night had been disastrous. All through breakfast he kept worrying about the servant girl who was tidying the third-floor room. Could she tell which apprentice slept in which cot? She was very young—had she ever seen such a sheet before? Her appearance at the breakfast table, fresh-faced and untroubled, had lessened the sense of stress, but only melancholy had come in its place. The remembered dream, bled of its excitement, had begotten a tremulous sorrow in him —he could not drink his beer, he could not swallow the fresh bread and the excellent fruit. Why had the imaginary Rinske in the dream had the tapering arms and musk-scented hair of Jacob van Swanenburgh's wife, and why should she have come to him in Jacob van Swanenburgh's dining chamber, where he and his Leyden fellow-apprentices had sat on namedays and holidays through many an innocent and good-natured feast? The little portrait of a child by Lucas van Leyden—the one his other master had loved so much—had hung in the dream where it had always hung when he ate his meals at the master's house, its clear lines and pure colors not wavering before him until her dream-fingers had exposed him below and touched him into foredoomed ecstasy, triumph that immediately knew itself for defeat. And, spent as he was, how could he be titillated by the real model, the one that stood before him in the middle of the studio, her thick body still covered by a crimson velvet robe borrowed from the master's wardrobe, the plumes and pearls in her reddish hair made ridiculous by the bunions on her feet? This Rinske Dobbels was nothing but a broad-beamed, flat-nosed washerwoman. The August sun, pouring hot and vibrant through the high windows, was pitiless to her coarseness and hurt his shimmering eyes.

"This morning," said the master, who looked none the worse for the goose and the wine and the midnight laughter, "we're fortunate enough to have a female model, the first we've been able to get for some months. Van Hoorn, van Rijn, Hessels: I believe I'm right in concluding that none of you has ever worked with a female model? Well, *carpe diem,* make the best of your time. We're lucky to have Rinske; she's an unusually good model, well built and able to stand still almost interminably . . ."

Doubtless he intended to pay her a compliment, but the allusion seemed uncomfortable, even in questionable taste. She stood motionless and expressionless while the master smiled upon her, staring with her mud-colored eyes at an empty easel. It would probably have been better if he had behaved as if she were a cast or a statue, not to be reckoned with at all.

"Now, let's not simply *draw* Rinske, let's not just get her down in any fashion," said the master, disregarding the inevitable titter. "Let's exercise our imaginations. And this time"—he did not look at Rembrandt, only examined his large agate ring—"let's all aim more or less at the same goal. Let's consider what we do as a sketch for a Biblical canvas, a big, rich, colorful painting of Susanna and the Elders. Let's try to imagine that clutter of stuff behind her"—he pointed a plump finger at a beautifully arranged group of antiquities—"as the wall of an ancient city. The floor here"—he walked up close to the model and marked an area around her feet with a sweep of the toe of his shoe—"we'll consider that a gleaming pool of water. And here in the foreground"—he took several steps backward and almost collided with Jan's easel—"here you can have rushes, water, grass, a little bank, anything you please. Now, Rinske, you're Susanna."

"Yes, your honor," she said without lifting her eyes or raising her head.

"Drop your robe, if you please."

She dropped it indifferently and stood in front of them in her drab nakedness. Her thighs, just beginning to grow flabby, showed the red indentations of her garters; her belly, big, firm, and grossly muscular, bore the crisscross impression of her lacings. Her breasts were rough-grained like the rind of a drying orange, and the nipples surprised him by their brownness: he had been led to believe that every woman's nipples, like Lysbeth's, were a pale salmon-tinted red. The expected cleft below was indiscernible even at close range, covered as it was with brown hair, unpleasantly coarse and kinky; he wondered whether the thick mat had lost its reddish tone because it was always kept out of the sunlight or had simply faded with the years.

"Now, what we want here, Rinske, is a pose of fright, a gesture of timidity."

"Yes, your honor."

"The Elders have come up behind you to spy on you. Do you know the passage in the Apocrypha?"

"No, your honor. I'm afraid I don't."

"Well, never mind, I'll explain. The Elders, the three evil old men, have come up behind you to watch you bathing, and suddenly you know they're there, you hear them. You're catching up your robe—come, Rinske, catch it up, you're supposed to be frightened—you're a virtuous wife, you're appalled that anybody should see you in your nakedness."

Half stooping, with the crimson velvet robe caught up between her heavy breasts, she cowered convincingly. She knew fear in her blood and bones, that much was certain, though what she was accustomed to shrink from would scarcely be spying and caressing, would more likely be cursing and blows.

He was distracted by a movement on his left: Allaert, in the sweetness of his nature—mindful, probably, of yesterday's shameful scene and eager to show that it in no wise spoiled his kindly intent toward his fellow from Leyden—was moving his easel up very close to Rembrandt's side. "If you don't mind," he said, turning his clear, childish face upon his new neighbor, "I like to see what you're doing, it's always so different—and then up here I get a better view."

He wished he could respond to these subtle little attentions with some turn of phrase that would indicate his pleasure and his sense of indebtedness. But the only thing he could find to say was, "I don't mind at all."

"If you have a little extra time," said the master, "it might be a good idea to sketch the Elders in. Maybe here, and over here, and over here near the wall of the city." He assumed the stations as he named them, surprisingly quick and light on his feet. "They're prurient, they're really very obscene old men, and at the moment they're overwhelmed with desire."

"Oh, those poor Elders," said Allaert in a whisper, making a rueful face. "What dreary lives they must have had if anything like *that* could overwhelm them with desire."

Coming from Haldingen or Larsen or Lievens, it would have been the weakest sort of joke; but issuing from the modest mouth of Allaert van Hoorn, it was both surprising and significant. He could only conclude that it was another overture, another attempt to make up for yesterday. Allaert respected him, might possibly be fond of him; Allaert had even descended to his innocent idea of raw talk to promote their halting fellowship. "It would certainly take more than that to stir me up," he said, slanting his easel to give the newcomer a better view.

"Me, too."

But that was so obvious as to be unintentionally comical. He closed his eyes for an instant against the common body cringing there before him and evoked instead the girls who danced in the princely mansion to which Allaert went home every night—fragile daughters of the wealthy burghers moving to the music of the clavier, the violoncello, and the flute, their flawless faces lifted into the radiance of scores of candles, their fair hair wreathed in violets and held in place by combs that were set with pearls. Such creatures belonged to a different order of being: their buttocks did not, could not look like this.

"Well, come now," said the master, "let's be at it. You, van Hoorn, pick up your chalk, and you, too, Rembrandt."

So, thought Rembrandt, he feels impelled in honor to censure his favorite before he says another word to me; if he snapped at me every hour, he couldn't put me more unquestionably into my lesser place.

"You, there, Hessels, try to liberate your line a bit. Draw bigger than you did yesterday. Don't be afraid of it; see what happens if you draw with a large sweep." He indicated in the air the undulating line which had brought him his fame and which Lievens had so aptly learned to imitate; and in so doing he must have been reminded of the existence of his former favorite, for he turned to him with an ingratiating smile. "Suppose you help Hessels this morning, Jan. You'll be able to show him, you know exactly what I mean," he said; and he walked away, with the complacency of one who has just given himself a good conscience, to take his ease on one of the benches that constituted part of the imaginary city wall.

With the master out of it and Allaert settled obediently down to work, there was nothing to do but apply himself to the business of drawing. He cautioned himself not to repeat yesterday's error, not to disregard the master's most tentative suggestion, not to lay himself open to accusations of unteachability and willfulness. If he was supposed to see her as Susanna, then he had better try to see her as one of those delicate light-footed girls whom he and the other plebeians would encounter at Allaert's nameday party. Staring not at Rinske Dobbels but at a festoon of rose-colored damask close to the beamed ceiling, he managed, in spite of his depletion, to conjure up at least the face of a Susanna: large dark eyes peering fearfully over the crumpled robe, water streaming over the round forehead and the drenched, abundant hair. But having gotten that much down on the painfully brilliant white of the paper, he had to resort to the model for the rest; and the minute he began to draw the body he knew he would have to rub out what he had done at first: the body in front of him in all its gross actuality belied the dreamed-of face.

And as he stared at it that body became absorbing, even engrossing to him. Not, certainly, as an object of desire: if he yearned to set down one harsh and decisive line after another it was because his own flesh was crossed out, obliterated by the thing he saw and by the stale weariness that was the aftermath of last night. Rinske's body was the record of a life, a life that was all the more clearly there to be read because it was not refined by an intellect or obscured by deceptive loveliness. The hard bent neck spoke of endurance under pain and deprivation and dull sorrow; the breasts sagged from the repeated surges of milk that had dried away; the nipples had been coarsened by God knows how many importunate infant mouths pitilessly sucking. The muscles of the back and belly and thighs were strong, but not with the resilient strength of health and youth; theirs was the stiff strength that came from performing the same exhausting movements of bending over the washtub and scrubbing and wringing. The hands were raw with soap and water, and the feet, from standing unflaggingly day after day, were as archless and horny as the feet of an animal.

"Let's remember that Susanna was a gracious lady," said the master from his station on the antique marble bench, "a young and virtuous wife, loving and beloved."

Loving and beloved? He snorted under his breath. Pawed by drunken shiphands and rope-makers in cheap taverns, assaulted by the master or explored by the son of the master on the back stairs, often promised, and seldom given, a five- or six-penny fee. A gracious lady? He drew the harsh record with harsh lines, thinking when he came to the dark mat how life had entered here—blind life, careless, not even cruel, using everything, even her, to keep the agony and the ecstasy unmitigated still—the mourning and the laughter, the lights in peaceful windows, the mortal, heavy breathing in the night.

Van Hoorn made a tentative movement toward him. Unable to take the fever of his obsession out of his eyes, he turned his head over his shoulder and knew that his wild look had startled the gentle burgher. "Did you want anything, Allaert?"

"No . . . I just wanted to look at what you're doing there. It's wonderful—more like her than she is herself, if you know what I mean. But won't you have to—well, tone her down a bit, if she's supposed to be Susanna?"

He had forgotten all about Susanna. The dream-face was still faintly visible on the paper, and it struck him as a kind of treachery against the new, the honestly brutal head that he had drawn. With the rough frieze of his sleeve, he rubbed the blurred lines away completely. "Yes, I suppose I will," he said, knowing that he had passed from looking mad to sounding stupid. "By and by I'll try to fix it up," and he went on drawing exactly as he had been drawing before.

Then, perhaps because he had begun in exhaustion and had been worked upon by the violence of his revelation, he found himself suddenly tired. He put the chalk down on the ledge of the easel, sighed, and closed his eyes. When he opened them again, the studio seemed strange to him, as if it were under water: long staring and excitement—yes, and Allaert's well-meant warning, too—had brought the water stinging into his eyes. Through that glimmering film he looked afresh at his drawing. Tone it down? Not according to Allaert's sense of the word; yet he knew that it called for some transformation, especially in the face. His heart and his mind, chastened as they were by the realization of his own grossness and bruised by the master's displeasure, should be able to do better than that by a suffering Rinske Dobbels. Should and would: he took up the red chalk again and began to work on the tired lips, the heavy lids, the colorless and watery eyes.

Some chime in some steeple—he could not stop to count it, he was too busy with the swollen vein that ran across her temple—fell iron and ponderous into the still, hot August atmosphere. A model never stood for more than an hour, and surely her hour was almost over. Her back and neck were sloping downward more than at first; one of her grained and downy buttocks had begun to twitch, and a look of stony endurance had come into her face. Wiping his sweaty forehead with his sleeve, he stepped back to see what he had done and knew there could be no two ways about it: either it was a little masterpiece whose like had never before been put on paper in Lastman's studio or it was a brutal and tasteless atrocity. Tone it down? Soften the decisive lines, lighten the grotesque dark fuzz of the mat, erase the ridges left by the garters and the lacings? No, not even the concern in the grey-blue eyes of Allaert could make him do it. Besides, it was too late; the master was saying through a yawn, "All right, then, Rinske, you can get into your robe now. Vincenzo will take care of your fee. Thanks very much for your trouble."

Wrapped once more in the incongruous splendor of the crimson robe, Rinske started up the length of the studio toward the door. Instinctively, as she passed his easel, he stepped in front of it to cover his drawing. Why should she see herself as he had seen her? Why should she have that ugliness and devastation to remember when she was straining over the washtub or letting her exhausted body down onto the bed for gratification or sleep? Near the door she stopped for an instant and smiled a false and vacant smile at the fine gentlewoman that Jan Lievens had made out of her; and he knew with an aching mournfulness that she would like anything, even the trash on the easels of Larsen and Haldingen, better than what had issued in travail and pity out of *his* mind and heart.

"What's the matter?" said little Hessels, coming up with his heart-shaped face smeared with brick-red chalk dust. "Why are you hiding it? Aren't you going to let me have a look?"

"Of course. Only, I wouldn't expect you to like it."

"Why not? Why wouldn't I like it?"

"Because nobody's going to like it." He did not believe it, of course; if he had believed it, he would have taken a rope down to Vincenzo's wine cellar and hanged himself, but it relieved his dammed-up feelings to elaborate. "Why should anybody like it?" he said, throwing a defiant look over his shoulder into the puzzled face of the master's favorite. "It isn't in the nature of the human beast—not many of them, anyway—to like the truth."

*

Master Pieter Lastman, having risen from the marble bench, advanced to criticize the assortment of Susannas at a slow and disheartened pace. The moment that was to have been for him the crown of the morning, the moment whose anticipation had infused vitality into his heavy body and wit into his dulled brain, the moment when he was to see what Allaert van Hoorn could make out of a nude woman had been foredoomed for him some time back. The exquisite young burgher, in the foolishness of his charitable heart, had drawn his easel up so close to the Leydener's that it would be impossible to see his drawing untainted by the other's. Ah, well, he thought, tasting the sourness of last night's wine in his mouth, he would save that moment until the last nevertheless. And he walked over to the place where Hessels stood, so close to the spot where the model had taken her pose that the thick August air seemed still to be burdened with the woman-smell of her.

Hessels' drawing, though done with the big sweeps that he had recommended, was grossly, even comically out of proportion—all buttocks and breasts. The lad himself was plainly shaken, a fact which made it less difficult for the master to stifle his amusement: the poor little devil had doubtless never laid eyes on a naked female before, and it was touching to think how much store he had probably set by the promised view and how long it would take him—how many soiled and debilitating nights—to recognize that it was nothing like he had dreamed it would be. So it was easy to be considerate, easy to lay an arm around the slight shoulders, easy to renounce what would have been a really clever discourse on the exaggerations and to make a demonstration with the chalk instead. With a few light strokes that corrected rather than insulted the underlying absurdities, he put some order into the thing. "There, now, that's better. It's only natural that we should go too far when we try to loosen up," he said, smiling into the heart-shaped face.

Larsen and Haldingen were standing together, and he dealt with them together. Mediocre though they were, they might have risen to competence if they had not been lax; and remembering how Elsheimer had raised him from competence to greatness, he gave them, with as much vigor as last night's undigested goose would permit, a long-due lecture on their laxity. A rare opportunity had been given to them in the person of Rinske Dobbels, and what had come of it?—he slashed red chalk across their feeble lines—why, this, and this, and this! No master of any trade, no digger of peat, no winder of hemp, no maker of pots would permit himself such tawdry workmanship. When he turned his back on them he was warmed by the conviction of duty done: no matter now if days went by before he stopped again in the deadening atmosphere around their easels; it was obvious to everybody present that he scorned rather than neglected them, that it was they, not he, who were to blame.

But here was Jan Lievens, waiting with the old eagerness beside an unexceptionable drawing; and for his feelings toward this one—or rather his total lack of feelings—he could offer no excuse. He could not accuse his senior apprentice of being importunate; the young man had long since given up his attempts to attract the master's attention. He could not without self-censure criticize his somewhat flamboyant manners; those manners were only imperfect copies of his own. But he could not behave, either, as if what had died was still alive in him: time would teach Lievens, as it had taught *him,* to bury his dead. Only, time was slow about it, and Jan was looking at him thirstily, and there was nothing to do but stop as if in amazed admiration in front of a piece of work that was only half as good as the expression on his face was making it out to be. "Excellent, excellent!' he said, tracing in the air before him the creditable sweeping line that began at Susanna's neck, flowed down her back, and lost itself in the folds of drapery clutched against her thighs. "Here, Larsen, Haldingen, come and have a look at this. This is what I mean by craftsmanship."

But his maneuvering was getting him nowhere: the empty exclamations of the two pariahs he had called up to relieve him of a solitary exchange with Lievens proved neither distractions nor consolations, and his senior apprentice continued to gaze at him with fixed and somewhat glassy eyes. "If I may, Master," he said with his first essay at irony, "I wanted to take a minute of your time to ask you something important— at least, it seemed important to me."

"Certainly, certainly. I have all the time in the world—you know that."

"This flowing line—do you think I'm overdoing it? I mean, do you think I've been concentrating on it to the detriment of other things?"

"What other things?" He regretted the annoyance in his voice; it went ill with the cordial mask he had made of his face.

"Intensity, profundity—I don't know—"

"Well, suppose you think about it until you're sure you can define it." The eyes did not release him and something—perhaps anger, perhaps pain—stirred under the glazed stillness of their stare. "Let's talk about it tomorrow, Jan. Then you'll have had a chance to think about it, and so will I." The gaze remained unwavering, and the mouth twitched strangely and unbecomingly under the dark down that marred the upper lip. "It'll be better if we discuss it in private. Suppose you hold onto this drawing and bring it over to my anteroom tomorrow night." But even that offer did not satisfy Lievens. He nodded curtly, and the graceless gesture, ill-suited as it was to the rest of his extravagant movements, re-minded one that there was no call to take him so much to heart, that after all he was only the son of a poor Leyden tapestry-maker playing the gentleman.

Taking time to compose himself, the master walked slowly to the place where Allaert and Rembrandt stood. He had intended to dis-charge his obligations to the Leydener first, but now that he stood in the narrow space between their easels he could not wait; he had to turn his back on the thorn and his face to the flower. Sun fell on Allaert's silky head, held a little to one side in charming humility; a few stray hairs, as bright as yellow thread, lay across the paleness of his cheek; and at the part in his hair the pink of his scalp, clean as a loved infant's, showed through. And laying his arm around the lad's slender shoulders, he knew that he could not separate the creation from the creator, could not discount the scent of fine soap and dried lavender, or the deli-cate warmth, or the gentle rise and fall of the breath.

Yet the drawing was delightful, too—exquisite, imaginative, and washed in the sweet waters of innocence. Allaert's mind had taken im-mediate and easy flight from Rinske Dobbels. After one look, Allaert had run back to some fairy-tale world his lady mother must have evoked for him on the wintry evenings of his childhood; one could see a smaller, frailer Allaert sitting in that beautiful old house on the Heer-engracht, stretching against satin pillows and eating sugarplums and inhaling the fragrance of an applewood fire. Rinske Dobbels had become for him the princess in a fairy story, a princess who by some inexplicable and rather amusing accident had been caught with her clothes off. The breasts were there, the haunches were there, even the unmentionable place had been obediently sketched in. But all of it was drawn so delicately, with such naïveté and gratifying detachment that nobody would hesitate to hang the sketch above the bed of a child. "That's charming, Allaert—utterly charming and quite in your style. Lay it by in your folio, won't you? I'd like to see you turn it into a nice little oil," he said.

"I couldn't get around to doing all of the Elders—"

He saw them for the first time, wizard-faces emerging vaguely out of the cloudy foliage, and the attempt to render prurience was so feeble that he had to smile. "Ah, well, we can do without the Elders," he said, permitting his hand to close over the velvet-clad round of the shoulder and shaking it gently. "This sort of sketch would serve for a number of subjects—Bathsheba, Psyche, Diana at the bath . . ." He let his voice trail off, unhappy with the realization that he could not go on shaking the lad forever, that he must turn now and meet the Leydener's grey, enigmatic eyes. But he could at least pick up the piece of blunt chalk that the young burgher had been working with; it still felt moist as he rolled it in his palm, and, counterfeiting absent-mindedness, he allowed himself to drop it into his pocket.

"I suppose she does look more like Psyche," said Allaert, brushing the silky hairs away from his cheek.

"More like Psyche than like Rinske—that much is certain. And now shall we see what Rembrandt's done?" He referred to him by his first name in the hope that his relations with the difficult young man might become less prickly if he could only remember to use the more intimate form of address.

But the sight of the Leydener, when he turned to him, could not have been more upsetting if he had just walked out of a street brawl: his reddish mane was disordered, his collar was undone, and his face was at once drained and wild. He looked worse, if possible, than after yesterday's unfortunate business with the old male model. It was troubling, too, that he should stand in such a way as to half screen what he had done, troubling that it should be necessary to tap him on the elbow, as if he were standing there in his sleep, to get him to step aside. "Excuse me," he said, moving out of the way at last; and his voice was as strange and somnambulistic as his face.

And the picture—the picture—no, never—never anywhere so grossly womanish a woman's body—and there, set crazily on top of it, that maudlin, suffering face! Coarse flesh and raw spirit clashed together there in jarring dissonance. That such suffering should find a habitation in that kind of flesh—it was too much, it was all he could do to stifle an open show of disgust. He had been sorry to see yesterday's old man smudged and wrinkled; but he wanted this crumpled, he wanted it stepped on, he had an almost overpowering impulse to snatch it and crush it himself. "Is that supposed to be Susanna?" he said as soon as he could depend on his own voice; and even then the words came out of him shaken by the pounding of his heart.

"No, Master, I'm afraid I forgot about Susanna."

"Forgot about Susanna? But that was the point of it."

"I know, I'm sorry, I got carried away with the model herself."

That was obvious. One could say he had managed, in some mad way, to rape her on paper and say an orison for her soul before he got out of her bed. Grim though the thought was, it struck him in his exigency as a joke, and he was hard put to it to master a nervous twitching at the corners of his lips. To laugh would be unthinkable—yet humor was probably the only way out of the impasse: he shrugged and scratched the back of his neck in a bearish way, and pulled a wry and rueful face. "Well, Rembrandt," he said, smiling at the young man's forehead and avoiding his eyes, "what I'm supposed to do with you I honestly don't know. Yesterday I gave you a colorful character, a sort of satyr out of the gutter, and you turned him into the most pathetic old wreck I ever saw. And today I give you a strapping washer-wench, and you give me back only God knows what—something with the head of a Mater Dolorosa and the body of a whore."

Everybody had been listening, but nobody laughed, and the master saw that the witty flourish had been a dreadful mistake. An oppressive quiet had settled upon the room; he knew that the look which he did not dare to meet was flickering like heat lightning; and he himself—standing foolishly there with his hand still rubbing at the nape of his neck—felt his heart hastening while he waited for the inevitable blast.

But the fierce reply that he expected did not come. Nothing came but a quick, light, forward lunge of the stocky body, a lunge so sudden and unlooked-for that the master automatically stepped back to avoid it, and was the more ridiculous because it had not been directed at his person—it was not on him, but on the abused drawing, that the Leydener had meant to vent his fury and his pain. The hairy hand, white at the knuckles, caught at the corner of the paper—would have rent, would have crumpled, would have cast it to the floor if Allaert had not intervened. "Don't!" said Allaert, catching at Rembrandt's fingers. "Don't tear it, don't spoil it. If you don't want it, give it to me."

That interposition gave the master time enough to recover himself, time enough to see that his only recourse was to assert his legally established dignity. "*I* will take that drawing," he said, holding out his hand for it. "That drawing, according to the rules of the Saint Lucas Guild, belongs to *me*. You seem to forget, van Rijn, that as long as an apprentice is unlicensed, any work that he does in the master's studio belongs to the master. To destroy your work is as illegal and outrageous as to break one of my vases or hack up one of my paintings. Your work is my property."

The raw hand relinquished the drawing and fell, inert and helpless, at the young man's side. Only now, only because of the defeat that was to be seen in the loose fingers, was Pieter Lastman able to look into his apprentice's eyes.

"I don't know how they do things in Leyden, Rembrandt," he said, adjusting his voice to the fact that he had caught no insolence, only sick hopelessness in the wild grey look. "I don't know how your former master dealt with your outbursts, but I think you had better understand that we simply do not tolerate such displays of temper here. I want peace in my studio, peace and quiet, and I mean to have them—"

"Yes, Master."

"To say 'Yes, Master' after such a scene is not enough."

"I shouldn't have lost my temper. I'm very sorry."

"Very well, then. See that it doesn't happen again." He turned and started up the aisle between the easels with the hated drawing in his hand, looking neither left nor right. The charged quietness remained unbroken, and remembering how none of them had laughed, he wondered what had impelled him to use such an unfortunate word as "whore."

*

Matters standing as they did, Rembrandt was scarcely in a mood to go to anybody's nameday party. The determination to hold his unruly impulses down, to be humble and to learn in spite of himself was a conscious and precarious determination; and every distraction threatened it. Yet as the weeks of his mortification and penance went by, he began to see that on the twenty-ninth of September he would have to carry his spirit, raw as it was, into company. Not because he could not bear a solitary evening in Heer Lastman's attic—he would have liked nothing better than a few hours to work without interruption. Nor was he reluctant to miss a feast in the princely house on the Heerengracht; he was convinced he would wander about there separate and ignored. But since Allaert had made a point of presenting him with two Oriental brushes the day after the unfortunate incident with Lastman, his absence would be an open insult to the gentle young burgher, who did not deserve to be slighted by anybody, and least of all by him to whom he had been subtly and unflaggingly kind.

No, there could be no way out of the nameday party, even though it involved the expense of buying a new jacket: his frieze one was a work jacket, his brown one was going thin at the elbows, and his black one, according to Lievens, was out of the question because it would give everybody the impression that he was in mourning for a member of his family. Lievens had offered to go with him to make the purchase, to take him to "his tailor on the Singel," and Lievens in the role of arbiter of fashion had been as aggravating as he had anticipated. A whole Saturday morning had been consumed in a business that should not have taken more than an hour; nine bolts of cloth had been dragged down from the shelves even though he had made his choice—a piece of mulberry-blue woolen—after seeing the first two; and there had been a great deal of affected chatter about the distinguished minds to be encountered at the van Hoorns', not to speak of the beautiful girls—talk that made him sorry for poor Lysbeth, even though she *was* such a fool.

Now that the purchasing was over and they were strolling at a maddeningly slow pace down the autumnal street, along the shimmering canal which reflected metallic leaves and lordly gables, past purposeful and confident faces that only deepened his own conviction of failure and isolation, his mood grew even grimmer than it had been in the tailor shop. It was all very well for Jan to talk about what a bargain they had come by—Jan had not spent every penny of the money sent him in secret by his mother. Jan could enjoy himself stopping at every tradesman's window to look at plumes and hats and boots; *he* was not haunted by accusing images of Adriaen's moist eye staring at the little moneybag, Lysbeth scrubbing the floor in her old red skirt, his mother panting over the washtub, his father bent almost double under a sack of malt, Gerrit dragging himself upstairs. But his silence did nothing to decrease the effervescence of his companion's spirits; Jan was so ebullient that he even became generous—a rare phenomenon, since it was his way to insist that other people spend their money gaily, lavishly, while he kept a very careful watch on his own. "What do you say to a pancake and a mug of milk?" he asked, stopping in front of what was plainly a genteel eating shop. "Never mind about the money—I know you're short of it after the jacket. I'll pay; it won't be much."

It was a small, clean shop, with a blast of heat and a burnt-butter smell coming into it intermittently from the back door that kept opening and closing on a ruddy and sputtering kitchen. The nine or ten little wooden tables were almost all occupied by chattering young ladies and suavely conversing gallants: it was fashionable to stop about noon to rest from the exhaustions of shopping, and most of the talk—twittered excitedly in high voices or dropped casually in low ones—was about "my lace-maker near the Bourse" or "my boot-maker on the Dam." Sitting down with Jan at an empty table in the corner, he closed his ears against the nonsense, and with tight nerves suddenly loosened by the warmth, contemplated the noonday sunlight pouring in through the doorway and the leaded windows. It was a strong and steady light that showed the sparseness of a newly cultivated beard, brightened the flushed round of a girl's cheek, and made the white plume on a velvet hat almost as evanescent as the smoke floating in the upper atmosphere. Here, he thought, was a scene that could be done best in an etching; and it occurred to him that some of his depression might have risen from the fact that he had been cut off so long from the tonic harshness of the needle and the copper plate. "When do you think the master's going to let us do some etching?" he said.

Jan shrugged. It was obvious that his mind was not on studio matters, surrounded as he was by so many gilded burghers' sons and daughters whom he would have given anything to know. Assuming the pose of the bored artist, puckering his smooth forehead and resting his cheek on his large white hand, he stared dreamily up into the floating veils of smoke. "I never try to predict what the master's going to do any more," he said in a voice loud enough to draw the attention of the gallant and the two young ladies who were sitting at the table on his right. "Heer Lastman is so volatile—half his genius lies in his spontaneity."

There was no use in begging to differ, in pointing out, for instance, that Heer Lastman made innumerable sketches before he touched a brush to canvas, or that if some of his lessons trailed off into nothing, it was never for lack of a solid plan but only because the teacher had given up in the middle out of weariness or disgust. Plainly, the characterization had been offered only as a colorful bid for the attention of the younger of the two girls at the neighboring table, a plump, blond little thing who could not have been more than fifteen and who wore her curls in two objectionable clusters over her ears. "When did you start working on etchings last year?" he asked, hoping to hold his companion down to facts.

"March—April—really, I don't remember. If we do them again this year, I'm going to do a series on myths. By the way, you *did* like my little *Diana Surprised by Actaeon,* didn't you?"

Jan had forced him into a rather lengthy discourse on it several days ago, and he had managed to temper his reservations with carefully worded praise. Now his companion wanted the praise unadulterated, phrased extravagantly enough to identify him as a promising young artist for the benefit of the blond chit with the curls, her scantily bearded escort, and her flat-chested friend. "It's very skillful, Jan, very masterful, as I told you before," he said. "I particularly liked the little temple between the trees . . ." And to avoid the necessity to lie, he went into a discussion of perspective which proved utterly boring to the three on the right, who began to whisper among themselves.

"Ah, well, why should we talk about studio business when we're out on a holiday?" said Jan, pushing back the locks that were nodding over his forehead. "What are you going to eat? Have anything you want, but I can recommend the pancakes. There's only one other place where the pancakes can compare to these—Lotje's Sugar Pot over near the Dam—and there a person meets *everybody,* there it's impossible to carry on a private conversation."

The door to the kitchen swung open again, emitting another ruddy burst of heat, and a dour and angular woman in her fifties came up to take their orders. "Pancakes?" she said with an air of resignation, as if she expected such customers to order pancakes and nothing else— not milk, not tea, not chocolate, and certainly neither spirits nor wine.

"Two pancakes and two mugs of milk," said Jan, but he could not leave it at that, he must show the serving wench and anybody else who cared to listen that he knew exactly what he was about. "And see to it, if you please, that the pancakes aren't overdone—I can't abide the taste of burnt butter, and I don't want any of those little black scallops around the edge."

As she took herself off with the starched tails of her apron flapping behind her, it seemed to Rembrandt that their neighbor, who was saying something behind his hand to the girl with the flat chest, was making fun of the flourish with which the meager order had been given. He could not be sure—the upper half of the sardonic face was almost lost in the shadow of a drooping hat brim, and the listening young ladies did nothing more than smile—but the suspicion rendered him incapable of inventing conversation; and when the waitress returned to serve them and to present herself at the adjoining table, every word of the transaction could be heard. The gentleman wanted a glass of wine and a wing of chicken; the ladies wanted pancakes and tea. "But wait a minute, about those pancakes," said he of the new beard in a drawling voice. "We don't want any black scallops—in fact, we don't want *any* scallops. Tell the cook to draw them with a compass, cut them out with a scissors, and examine them for possible flaws under a magnifying glass." The flat-chested one looked down, shook her head, and made a clucking sound at once deprecatory and appreciative; and the blond one, apparently too young for self-control, went off into trills of laughter and had to bite on her handkerchief to muffle her merriment.

It was embarrassing, to be sure, but not embarrassing enough to account for the unnerving effect it had upon Jan Lievens. His shoulders sagged, his mouth came open, and his big lineless face went rose-pink to the roots of his hair. Pretentious ass that he was, he was also a friend of sorts and a fellow-townsman, and some sharp retort ought to be furnished in his defense. "Some people," he said, "will go to any lengths to show off in front of girls." And though the remark was scarcely as cutting as he would have wished, the voice at least was properly chilly and controlled.

"Oh, the devil with him—who cares about him?" said Lievens. "All I want is to get out of this city, soon, forever. I hate this place, I've hated it for months, all I want to do is pack up and go home." He said it passionately but in a low voice that could not be audible at the next table. "I mean it—I'm sick of this city and everybody in it, especially the master. Everything I turn out he calls exquisite, beautiful—it doesn't mean a thing; half the time he doesn't even see. All he does is put me off—he won't even answer a simple question. It's weeks—months —since we've looked each other in the face."

A fop unmasking himself, a fool exhibiting his sufferings was somehow more unmanning than tragedy, and for a long time he could offer no reply. He bent over his plate and began mechanically to cut up and eat his pancake, but it was difficult to swallow, and the crisped dough yielded him no taste at all. "He did invite you to his anteroom though, didn't he? You did get a chance to talk things over," he said at last, and remembered how Hessels had pointed out that the master had been very pleasant to *him* at supper—cold comfort at best.

"Oh, he invited me to the anteroom all right, and I must say he did his best to put some sort of face on it—served what we used to eat together and had ready-made answers for some of the things I'd been trying to ask him about. He also managed to keep from yawning for almost an hour."

"That's just his manner, Jan. It's his way of being easy with people, acting sleepy and lazy—"

"Is it? Does he look sleepy and lazy to you when he's hanging over Allaert's easel? Look, do me the kindness to face the facts—he's through with me, he's simply through with me."

To protest would be dishonest and futile, and to agree would be cruel. He could only stare with contempt at the three at the next table who had brought on this calamitous taking of inventory.

"No, there's no getting around it for either of us," said his companion, chopping up his pancake. "He's like the Lord God Almighty: he loves whom he loves and he hates whom he hates. He's finished with me, and he's never even going to get started with you."

That, too, left him silent. So he had been put immutably into the category of the rejected . . . So the master did not have and would never have where he was concerned the slightest fondness, the smallest sympathy. Well, time had made him stronger: only three weeks ago that thought had summoned up the snail-cold tears, and now he could see it as an axiom—hard perhaps, but to be accepted with resignation. Regrettable as it was—and it was the more regrettable because he had to admit that it was not his frieze jacket or his parentage but his soul and his skin and his bones that the master could not love—it did not undo him utterly.

"And the worst of it is," said Jan, "that he can't teach you unless he's *fascinated* with you. If he isn't fascinated, he doesn't see either you or what's on your easel; he only waves his hands around and says anything that comes into his head. Since the day he crossed me off, I haven't learned a thing from him—and neither will you, not if you stay with him a hundred years."

It could not be so; he pushed it away with the cold remainder of the pancake. He could not afford to abandon all the dreams for which he had shouted at his father words that could never be retracted, all the dreams for which he had spent the contents of Adriaen's moneybag and robbed his sister of part of her dowry and put a lasting bruise on his mother's heart. "That he'll never be fascinated with me, whatever that is, I'm willing to admit," he said. "But to say I can't learn anything from him unless I'm a second Allaert to him doesn't necessarily follow. I'll learn—I'm learning now."

"I'm damned if I can say the same for myself."

"The more fool you." He smiled to cover the stiffness of his lower lip. "The more fool you to care so much."

"And you—you shrug it off like nothing?"

"No, Jan, I wouldn't say I shrug it off like nothing. Only, I came to learn, and I robbed other people to do it, and there's something to be gotten here, and I can't go home without it, not if it—" The cool eyes of the flat-chested girl, observing him with covert curiosity, made him say "not if it takes me months" instead of "not if it breaks my heart."

Jan abandoned his pancake, laid down his knife, and focused his shifting eyes on his companion's face. "Look, I was the one who brought you here in the first place," he said, "and believe me, I've lived to regret it. I've had to admit to myself, and so should you, that you'd have been better off if I'd let you alone. Suppose you'd never laid eyes on him or his canvases—what would you have lost?"

"A great deal. More than I could afford to lose." It was not only that he wanted to offer Jan a swift absolution. Staring through the floating layers of smoke, he called up an image of Pieter Lastman's canvases, some in ornate frames and some in the studio still unfinished, wonderful even in their half-born state. *Jesus Healing the Sick, Coriolanus Receiving the Ambassadors, David Playing the Harp, The Sacrifice of Juno:* each was like a brilliant scene in a lavish pageant, high gesture caught in its living eloquence. Movement flowed into movement, color merged with color, line carried into line, and all of it was set so high on some radiant and exalted plane, so intricately embellished with drapery and garlands and festoons that one looked and was swept up into the height and the splendor, one looked and one's blood was stirred as by a fanfare of trumpets, a roll of drums. Whatever Lastman was, he could grasp the lofty moments in man's history and set them down for lesser men to see. If he ate too much, drank too much, fell into drowses, loved whom he loved and hated whom he hated, nevertheless he drew the curtain back and presented with pomp and magnificence the drama of the human race.

"Name one thing for me," said Jan persistently. "Just name me a single thing you would have been sorry to miss."

"But how can a person find words for it? It's mostly the way he sees things—for instance, the way he sees the past."

"How does he see it? How do you mean?"

He sighed, partly at his own wearisome difficulty with words and partly at the knowledge that no matter what eloquence was mustered into service here, the young man on the other side of the table would not have the capacity to understand. "Why go into it? I'm learning; that's all I need to know."

"*You're* learning? Learning from Lastman? Let me tell you: right now, this very minute, you're as far beyond him as I'm beyond Larsen and Haldingen. Whatever I've learned since I came back, I've learned from watching you."

77

He avoided his companion's seeking eyes, disregarded the sudden hastening of his heart, stifled the senseless smile that stirred at the corners of his mouth, and said, "What are you talking about?"

"Your greatness—your obvious greatness." The voice had revived, was speaking with the old grandiloquence, was inviting the eyes of others to lift themselves up from chicken and wine and pancakes to behold the blushing great. "That little drawing—the one you tore up—I wouldn't trade it for the biggest of his canvases. I'd gladly throw away the three years I've spent in his studio for six months in any old warehouse in Leyden—without models, without drapes, without antiquities—working alone with you."

He was glad of the false and high-flown manner; it helped him to reject what was said. He sat stiffly, his elbows pressed against his sides, trying to master his face, striving to put down a vision tempting in its very austerity. Any old warehouse in Leyden, cold, with the snow drifting past the windows . . . No models, no drapes, no antiquities—only known faces, known dunes, known steeples . . . No fine-spun sophisticated precepts imposed from the outside—nothing to follow but the sure and wordless dictates of the eyes and the mind and the heart . . . To cease to wait for a love that would never be forthcoming, to come home like the prodigal son, chastened but dear, to sleep among realities in a familiar attic, to wake at dawn to work, to labor until exhaustion canceled out even the possibility of dreams . . . Oh, but it was absurd! If he of the sparse beard had held his tongue, Lievens would never have thought of departure for an instant, would never have pushed a tawdry artificial crown of laurels across the table. "You're out of your mind. He's a master, and I'm an apprentice with everything to learn," he said.

"You say it, but you don't believe it."

He could not answer; he was having too much difficulty with his pounding heart and with the nervous laugh that stirred and tickled in his chest.

"If we went back to Leyden, your father would find a room for us to work in. Your family would sit for us—your parents and Gerrit and Adriaen and Lysbeth—"

He thought for an instant how Lysbeth would look to a man with a broken spirit. But enough was enough, he told himself, pushing back his chair as if to rise. "Forget about it, Jan," he said. "I haven't the slightest intention of going back—and neither did you before we walked in here. You'll stay out your time, and so will I. Anything else would be insanity."

He was surprised and relieved that his companion should relinquish the dream without another word, should push back his chair, reach for the money pouch at his belt, and shrug away the last vestige of regret. "You know your own mind," he said, running his fingers through his hair. "I guess we'd better be getting out of here. Somebody else will be wanting our seats."

The dour waitress darted out of the kitchen and stood close enough to their table to convey the impression that if they were not watched they might slip out without paying their bill. Whether it was her presence, or the mean business of pulling out and counting pennies, or the thought of returning to the studio that depressed him, he did not know; but his collapse was almost as complete as Jan's, and he did not trouble himself to offer the proper thanks for the treat or to continue the conversation on the walk home.

On the broad steps that led up to the door of Heer Lastman's house, the two of them found Allaert waiting. Plainly his parents had just left him there: the rumble of their carriage, one of the finest in Amsterdam, and the hoofbeats of their famous dappled horses were still sounding around the corner. Dressed for the turn of the season in a plumed velvet hat and a royal-blue cloak with a grey squirrel lining, Allaert stood on the topmost step and smiled down at them, with the reflected light of the canal and the quivering shadow of poplar leaves on his face. "Where have you been? Out shopping? Well, that's a pity! It's such a beautiful afternoon I thought we might go walking. And now you're all worn out and won't want to do anything but sprawl."

In spite of his weariness, Rembrandt would have announced himself ready to start out if he had been less heavy-hearted. As it was, he only labored up the steps in an exaggrated pantomime of exhaustion. "We've walked our feet off," said Lievens, coming up behind him. "He ordered himself a jacket from my tailor on the Singel. Wait until you see it; it's the most elegant piece of cloth—a glossy woolen in a beautiful mulberry-blue."

And the ostrich plume in your hat alone, thought Rembrandt, is worth the price of three such jackets. But he thought it without bitterness: whatever finery found its way onto the person of the gentle burgher belonged there by the lawless and inexplicable rights of beauty and grace.

"I bought it for your nameday party," he said. "I hope it will be right."

"Oh, but you shouldn't have done any such thing!" said Allaert. "After all, it's only going to be an artists' party. Your brown one would have been more than good enough. Still, I'm glad you bought it, because now I can be sure you're coming."

If it mattered to him as much as his voice implied, then the money secretly sent from Leyden had not been entirely ill-spent. He looked into the grey-blue eyes and smiled.

"Mother was just telling me to make sure you were going to be there. She didn't really meet you the last time she was here—"

No, she had not really met him. Unintentionally, of course, Allaert had thrust him back into the time when he had walked past her in the studio, looking neither to left nor right, seeing her only as a silvery coolness out there beyond the orbit of his wretchedness. He stiffened to think that she could have remembered the occasion, could have made a point of asking, out of patrician pity, that he be given an opportunity to appear before her in a less deplorable state. "Why should she want to meet me?" he said.

"That's what I was wanting to tell you—she stopped and looked at your little oil of Esther and Haman when she went through the studio this afternoon, and she loved it. She wouldn't leave until the master had brought out everything of yours he could lay his hands on. Believe me, she was enormously impressed."

For several seconds he did not believe it. Then, remembering that Allaert never flattered and never exaggerated, he was forced to accept it as the truth. A line, a thin, living line like the filament of a spider, had been spun out without his knowledge into the life of this woman whose house was a haven for the great; she had bent her pale gold head over his drawings—*his*—and had found them good and told the master so. And this realization was liberating and exhilarating; it was as if he saw for the first time the cool blue sky over the ornate gables and the tremulous tops of the poplars, the delicate wash of golden sunlight on the ancient roofs and cornices, the smoke gliding up from distant chimneys and floating away, light, light as his heart . . . "Well, that was very good of her, Allaert. Thank her for me when you see her next," he said.

"And the master—how did he take to that?" said Lievens.

"Oh, he acted very pleased about it; he has great respect for my mother."

To be in favor with those to whom the master looked up, to stand in a famed salon at the side of that silvery lady, to talk on equal terms with her and the poets and painters and scholars who visited her house, and with the master looking on . . . He even permitted himself a vision of Pieter Lastman coming up behind him and Allaert and laying an arm over each of their shoulders, and thought how good it would be to look for once into his unaverted eyes.

*

The night of the nameday party was the first wild night of that autumn. Gusts came in from the waters, making a dry clatter among the remaining leaves and bringing in moisture and the smell of the sea. Of the five apprentices who set out from Heer Lastman's house, four complained about the weather: it disrupted the results of Haldingen's hourlong dressing, it threatened the voice of the lute slung over Larsen's shoulder, it gave little Hessels a chill, and it took the waves out of Jan Lievens' hair. But Rembrandt reveled in it, let the wind tangle his mane as it would, walked at a stride into every new blast. It was a night for high doings, and as he looked up at the lighted windows in the gables where servants or apprentices were settling down to their evening's rest, he thought of sudden changes in fortune—of woodcutters' sons taken into service by princes, of a fisherman finding in a mean day's catch an oyster secreting a pearl.

The master was not with them; he had been invited to take a light supper at Allaert's house beforehand, which was, in a way, a pity. His most troublesome apprentice knew that tonight he would have found courage to walk beside the opulent presence, that excitement and high expectation would have loosed his halting tongue. No matter, he would show them later what stuff he was made of, with Vrouw van Hoorn and Allaert to draw him out.

"What do you think they'll give us to eat?" said little Hessels.

"Pickled pheasants' asses," said Larsen.

"I'll tell you one thing," said Haldingen sententiously, "once you get there you'd better watch your tongue."

"Yes," said Lievens, "don't use your usual vocabulary around me in there, especially in front of the ladies. If you do, you can expect me to act as if I'd never laid eyes on you before."

The house on the Heerengracht was pointed out across a glimmering stretch of black canal water broken by islands of drifting leaves—a dazzling façade of glass and stone and light. On his way across the arched bridge, he thought of poor Lysbeth: a day might come when he could take her to such a house as this. He whittled her down for the occasion, brushed out her hair and twined it with pearls and gold thread, dressed her in a scarlet jacket with cuffs and neckband of snow-white rabbit skin. "Vrouw van Hoorn, allow me to present my sister . . . And my mother who, you will notice, bears a noble resemblance to the prophetess Hannah . . ."

Through the opened door, as they went up the broad flight of steps, he could see the gilded pilasters, the blue and green draperies shimmering in the light of twenty or thirty candles, the checkerboard marble floor. Mother, son, and father, all dressed in bluish or silvery tones that were at once restrained and festive, stood in a line ready to give their guests a formal welcome, flanked on either side by great iron standing candelabra and set off by a fan of laurel that rose behind them out of a priceless Oriental vase. For an instant their flawless elegance made him conscious of his stinging cheeks and wind-tangled hair, but only for an instant, since the chatelaine took him by both his hands and looked straight into his eyes. "Don't tell me your name—I know it; you're Rembrandt van Rijn, a very promising young painter and my son's good friend. You're to come and talk to me later, if you can spare the time from the younger, prettier ones." And before he could really look at her and see more than that her curls lay smooth and pale against her long white neck and that there was a certain melancholy in her smile, she passed him lightly along to her son, who also held out both his hands.

The warm grasp put a public stamp upon their friendship. It was gratifying, too, that the gentle young burgher should look down at the medallion which hung on a heavy silver chain over the bluish velvet of his jacket. That medallion, the aggregate nameday present of his fellow-apprentices, had been bought on the wharf a week ago by Rembrandt and presented to Allaert only this morning; and it was touching that in these few hours he should have had it to a goldsmith's to be pierced and put on a chain so that he could show his pleasure by wearing it tonight. "You were the one who picked it, I know," he said. "It's beautiful, perfectly beautiful, and Mother says it must be very old."

Heer van Hoorn, dry and hard and angular, turned to them and said that the chain had also come from the wharf and was fifteenth-century Portuguese. In one of those transports of insight which sometimes come in moments of exhilaration, the visitor could see that whereas mother and son were immutably bound together so that each would sense the other's depression or exaltation at the ends of the nerves, the father was alien. He would knock on their doors before he entered, would move through the many rooms of this fine house tentatively, never knowing when he might rend the threads of the exquisite net woven between the other two.

Now that he had gone through the formal business of being greeted, Rembrandt was at a loss as to where he should station himself. There was a small room at the left where Heer Lastman, splendid and monumental in garnet-colored woolen, was conversing with three or four impressive-looking guests, but that was certainly not the place to begin. The other little room on the right was not indicated either: he tried it and was put off by an explosion of giggles—it was filled with girls, most of them doing something to their hair. Vrouw van Hoorn, looking out at him solicitously, lifted her white hand to let him know that what he sought was to be found behind the fan of laurel leaves; and after yielding his cloak to the manservant who had probably been following him about, he suffered himself to be joined by Haldingen and Hessels and found his way into the huge, crowded salon.

It was a room almost blindingly bright with candles, draped from ceiling to floor in lengths of yellow brocade, and everywhere—in the draperies, in the loosened curls, on the white bare throats, on the gesturing fingers—there was the gleam and glitter of gold. With so much to dazzle him, with the multitudinous talk going on all around him, it was not strange that he should stand bewildered, not knowing to which of a dozen chattering groups he should try to attach himself, not certain whether he wished to cling to or be rid of Hessels and Haldingen. The one was so obviously young that he really should have been left at home; but Haldingen, saturnine, mask-faced, and pale in deep-brown velvet, looked much like any of the other gallants on whose arms bejeweled young women were leaning—it was hard to imagine him in the shed with the neighbor's maid. Self-assured, he went at a determined stride toward a group in which the ladies were in the majority; and it was no great comfort to be rescued, together with Hessels, by a rosy old couple who treated them as if they had been grandsons. Their talk was blundering and ridiculous: it was obvious that invitations to artists' parties were issued to those that knew nothing about art. The old couple could not have told the difference between an etching and an engraving, confused Heer Lastman with a certain Heer Lustman who sold fine cheeses, and were finally reduced to trying to figure out exactly how many times in the course of their long lives the canals had been frozen hard enough to skate on. "I broke my leg once, skating," said the old lady with incomprehensible self-satisfaction. "That was forty years ago, but—would you believe it?—every time the first snow comes I feel it like a toothache, right below the knee."

He excused himself to them and Hessels and went resolutely in search of the superior things which must be lying within reach; but the subject matter under discussion in most of the groups was unfamiliar enough to keep him hovering on the margins. At one end of the salon there was a fire burning away in a great, ornate stone chimney place, and in order to find time to re-evaluate the situation and recruit his flagging energies, he moved up close to it and stood before the leaping flames, holding out his hands as if his only interest were in dispelling a chill. Out of the corner of his eye he could see that some of his fellows were swimming in the glittering tide more easily than he: Lievens was holding forth with sweeping gestures to a girl with a garnet tiara, and Larsen and one of the musicians were comparing lutes. He turned around, meaning to start out again, and found there was no need: the chatelaine, her silvery person washed by the pale gold cast of the fire, was standing beside him, had come through the crowd to find him, had really meant her promise in the hall. "Come," she said, slipping her arm through his and giving him a sidelong glance. "Almost everybody has arrived, and those that haven't are so late they don't deserve to be greeted. We'll go and find a little room where we can talk."

The little room they found after a gratifying walk down the length of the salon under everybody's eyes was the one where the girls had been giggling and arranging their hair. Though it was empty now, furs and gloves were still strewn about, the imprint of small feet still showed in the thick pile of the Chinese carpet, and the air still carried the scent of mingled perfumes. She turned back an ermine cape to make room for herself on a double-seat and sat down, arranging her skirt and looking with a shyness that could only be affected at her small veined feet in their grey velvet shoes.

He did not have the courage to sit on the double-seat beside her, yet the chairs seemed too far away, and after an awkward moment he pulled up a velvet-covered stool and sat below her, so that his line of vision ran directly to the beautifully wrought star of pearls and gold that hung on a chain over her somewhat bony chest. Her perfume was drier and more subdued than the other perfumes; she probably scented her clothes with the powdered petals of dead flowers. The smooth curl that hung over her shoulder was silver-streaked, and there were raised veins in her thin hands. "Allaert's fond of you—but I mean he's really very fond of you. He has tremendous respect for the work you're doing, and so do I," she said.

He could not answer at once because he was thinking, not without envy, of the delicate web woven between Allaert and his mother. Were there any such webs in the house in Leyden? He supposed there were, but he knew also that they were made of coarser stuff. This woman, for example, would never refer to food as "a little collation," and one look at her person would put the indolent Fioretta in her proper place. "It's kind of Allaert to think well of me," he said at last, wondering why he could not put more cordiality into his voice. "Heer Lastman, of course, considers him more gifted than I am." He added it after a pause, and was amazed and ashamed that it should have come out with a certain undertone of bitterness.

"I wonder if he really does," she said. "I doubt he could deceive himself as much as all that. If he gives any such impression—if, for instance, he's a little sharper with you than he is with Allaert—it could be because he knows you're completely committed, too much so to be discouraged. And Allaert isn't— Allaert's a very vulnerable kind of person, you know."

He had an unnerving sense of shifting ground: it had never occurred to him that the fortunate, gifted, and charming Allaert could possibly be more vulnerable than himself. "Oh, Allaert's very talented, immensely so," he said with much more warmth, managing to smile at the bejeweled star that rose and fell with her breath.

"Talented, yes. But immensely so? I doubt it. I doubt it, and I'll tell you something"—she bent forward and made an abortive gesture with her fingers as if she half meant to touch him—"at the bottom of my heart I wouldn't really want him to be. He plays at it—surely you know that's what he does: he plays at it. Beautifully, gracefully, aptly, of course, because that's his nature. But it's only playing, and to tell God's truth—though I'd never say so to him—I hope it will always be that way."

She broke off, possibly because she saw that she had kindled anger. And what else could she expect, reducing what was a struggle between Jacob and the angel to the wretched proportions of an elegant parlor game? "It won't give him much satisfaction then," he said, staring sternly at her silk-draped knees. "Not if he does it like that, not if he doesn't paint as well as he can."

"Oh, my dear, he'll paint as well as he can, don't worry. All I mean is: he'll never be able to paint more than very nicely, no matter what our good Heer Lastman thinks. I can see this is appalling to you, but honestly it's a kind of relief to me. You know, you make it hard for a person to talk to you because you simply won't look. Right now, for instance, you think I'm talking lightly, and you'd realize I'm not, you'd see that I'm in dead earnest if only you'd look up—" He forced himself to do so, but only long enough to glimpse a rueful, half-mocking, half-tender smile. "You and Allaert are doing completely different things: it's the difference between trimming little bushes and chopping down enormous trees. He'll go along pleasing everybody and never getting dirt on the front of his shirt. But you—you'll labor greatly and make tremendous gains. Only, before you do, you'll make some terrible mistakes, and you mustn't mind—that's what I wanted to say."

Oh, she was not seeing him as he looked tonight in his mulberry-colored jacket, but as he had come up the aisle in the studio, his face marred by tears of rage, his clothes stained with powdered azure—and he minded the sweat and the ugliness, he minded the blunders that had been committed and those yet to be committed; he minded with all his heart. Nor could he believe she was in earnest when she talked about chopping down trees and trimming bushes: nobody could be detached enough to assign a son to a minor place. It was one of those devices—not quite a lie but not a naked piece of honesty either—that a man must learn to cope with if he ever wandered away from his own uncomplicated kind. "The master's supposed to be the judge," he said, not caring that the words and the tone implied that she was not. "The master's supposed to know, and I'm sure he has no great opinion of me."

"Do you care about that so much?" she asked, and she seemed to be echoing his own statement to Jan in the pancake shop. "Really"—she did reach out now and put her long fingers firmly down on his knee—"you'd be more of a child than I believe you are if you take what he thinks too much to heart. Maybe it's only that he doesn't know what to make of you. When I first looked at your drawings, I was a little put off by them, too—there's bound to be uneasiness, maybe even resentment, when something new and unrecognizable pushes itself into the world. You'd naturally have less trouble with him if you created in his image or in some other one that he knows and loves. But you're creating something entirely your own, and if it's different from the others', that's all to the good: we want dissenters, we need diversity. The more at variance we are down here, the more subtle their work up there is going to be." She took her hand away and laughed lightly at "up there," wherever it was. "Provided, of course, there will be what I like to think —an ultimate resolution."

He did not know what she was talking about, and he doubted that she did, except that she somehow equated painting with religion as one of the ways to go toward God. "Yes, I suppose that's true enough."

"Oh, but who knows what's true?" she said, and sighed.

They had come to an impasse, and it gave him no small satisfaction to see that those who expressed themselves in beautifully pronounced sentences might also find themselves at a loss for words. But he could

not bring himself to rise and let her go until she had given him something more tangible to carry back to Heer Lastman's attic, something to
cherish there as an actuality among all the unrealities. He cleared his
throat and tried to look at her again, focusing his glance on a small, pale
mole on her chin. "Since you were good enough to look at my drawings,
I'd like to know what you thought of them," he said.

"I thought they were promising—very promising. I thought they were
like—like—" She stammered and halted, and he waited for the glorious
names: Dürer, Titian, Michelangelo. "I thought they were like the
world must have been when it was only half-created—rough and
strange and wild—"

He held his mouth in a hard, untrembling line and kept his eyes fixed
on the mole, which seemed to be swimming about like a fleck of cinnamon on milk.

"I think that almost anything could come out of such a beginning.
But not tomorrow, not next month, maybe not for years."

"Thank you," he said, and would have stood up if she had not
stopped him by laying her compelling fingers again on his knee.
"I wanted to ask you, Rembrandt—isn't there something that I—that
we—might do for you? I'd be very happy if there were any way in
which I could help you—"

The shameful blush burned up into the hatefully thin skin of his
forehead and his cheeks. He would rather beg alms at the door of the
Old Church, he would rather ask for a loan from Adriaen. "No, thank
you," he said. "My father's doing very well. He's perfectly capable of
providing for me."

She drew back from him, and a blush—an older woman's blush, pink
and spotty—spread over the skin around the bejeweled star. "You see,
I can make some dreadful mistakes myself," she said in a voice that was
tremulous in spite of its attempt at airiness. "Well, perhaps when you've
established yourself in your own studio, I can come to you to have my
portrait painted."

Propelled in part by his own embarrassment and in part by the embarrassment he thought he had caused her—he could not be sure, because now more than ever it seemed impossible to look into her face—
he started up from the stool and was stopped again by her hand, which
fell lightly and without conviction, but flesh against flesh this time, on
his bare and hairy wrist. "Wait a minute, don't go, not quite yet, unless
you've promised yourself to a dancing partner. There's one more thing
I wanted to ask you. Why do you tear up your drawings?"

"Tear up my drawings?" It was the futile evasion of a child caught
in the act. "I don't tear up my drawings. That is, I've only torn up one
or two of them, so far as I can remember."

"But you shouldn't—really, you shouldn't. If I've learned anything
in the course of my relatively long and stupid life, I've learned there's
no good in that sort of thing. Whatever blunders we make, we can't

erase them—we've got to absorb them somehow into the stuff of our lives. But maybe that's something women have to learn more quickly than men. Maybe I do you no favor, trying to force my woman's knowledge down your throat when it's perfectly clear you'd rather be let alone." Her hand—aging and beautiful, motherly and loverly at once—released but did not relinquish his wrist. To his amazement, she stroked it—reddish hair, coarse skin, and all—and he thought how he would carry this strange and inexplicable thing back through the windy streets with him tonight: that she had touched his flesh with tenderness. "If a girl falls in love, for instance, and is deceived and used, she can't undo it, she can't tear it up and throw it away. She simply has to go on living with the knowledge that she's been deceived and used. If afterwards, out of what she thinks is reason and resignation, she makes a marriage and sees later that it wasn't reasonable and she isn't resigned, she can't blot it out—it's simply there, morning and evening, for the rest of her days." She had succeeded at last, by the power of utter earnestness, in making him look into her eyes; and he knew that she was speaking of herself, and was doing it out of honor because, having looked into the sore and shameful places of *his* heart, she wished to make a fair exchange, to let him see her soreness and her shame.

"So," she said lightly, flirtatiously, rising and drawing him up with her, "you mustn't tear up the things you do for Heer Lastman. And you must stay on good terms with Allaert—he needs a friend in breeches, and he couldn't find a better friend than you. Also, provided that you don't have too dull a time of it here, you must come back to see us all again."

The strange, still exultation remained with him as long as she walked with her arm through his out of their privacy and into the ceremonious and public atmosphere of the salon. But when she had left him, when he had taken himself out of her sight and was alone among the groups that chattered in the reception hall where she had promised him so much in her greeting, he was appalled to think how little of what he had hoped to hear she had actually said. What, he asked himself, avoiding the rosy old couple, was the sum of her stated opinion? That he had promise, that he might go some distance after repeatedly falling into the mud, that some day, when he had learned to paint, he could paint her portrait—all of which was little enough.

Yet in spite of its depressingly meager yield, their talk had been charged enough to make whatever else was at hand seem drab and insignificant. The last thing he wanted to do was go to the trouble of finding a partner in the line of young ladies, and after making a couple of futile journeys into the salon, where a person was deafened by talk and music and might always collide with a dancer, he stationed himself against one of the enormous iron candelabra that had originally flanked his hosts. It was not a felicitous place to stand, since the hall had become a kind of highway, and like an ill-placed piece of statuary he was in the road and constantly attracting more attention than he wanted in his isolation. A very plain woman came up and bored him with an account of her tulip-raising; Lievens sighted him through the doorway and beckoned him to come and dance; and Allaert's father—apparently putting him into the same category as little Hessels—clapped him on the shoulder and told him to be of good cheer because there would soon be something nice to eat. But he went on standing in the midst of the traffic, feeling the sharp edges of the twisted iron pressing into his back, for only from here could he see the other little anteroom, where Heer Lastman and Allaert and three more gentlemen and an ancient lady with a lace shawl on her head were absorbed in earnest talk. Nothing they said could be heard above the noise, but he was certain it was the only important talk now going on under the roof of this great house.

He found he could recognize most of the participants from previous descriptions by Allaert: the old lady was a cousin of the great historian Hooft, herself a collector of lost letters from moldering archives; the heavy man in simple grey with the soft, benign face was the poet Vondel, the greatest man of letters in the Netherlands; the sallow young man in purplish velvet was the eminent German painter Joachim von Sandrart. The fourth, who sat in a high-backed chair cracking his knuckles, he was unable to identify, though he was the most arresting-looking of them all, with dark, dry hair growing far down on his low forehead, prominent brown eyes that were keenly intelligent, dry lips drawn in over the teeth, and a heavy beard chopped into a small tuft on his firm chin. And there among the lot of them, sitting low on a stool, was Allaert, robbed of some of his glitter either by the glory of his companions or by what had passed in the other anteroom. His youth, his vulnerability, and the not too intelligent droop of his open mouth posed the question: If *he* can listen, why not I?

The music stopped; the entrance of the food had put a temporary halt to the dancing. A train of liveried servants, coming the long way around in order to display what they carried, bore a series of kitchen masterpieces—partridge, ham, turkey, steaming breads, pyramids of figs and oranges, quivering puddings—into the salon. He wanted none of it: all of it was only another barrier between him and the glorious six who pursued their high purposes in there, but by the time the table was spread and the dancers were coming up to eat, he saw that he would have to move. Haldingen, adrift between one young woman and another, and Hessels, at loose ends and beginning to yawn, had sighted him and might come toward him, and he could not bear to think of any of the august personages in the anteroom associating him with a gaudy rake and a silly child. Disregarding a thin girl in the doorway who plainly hoped that he or anybody else would take her in, he went into the salon and up to the table alone. With the overzealous help of a manservant, he got a plateful of food he did not intend to eat and stood against a golden curtain, wondering whether this ostentatious plenty, spread out on linen and Delft china and silver plate, could properly be termed "a collation.".

While he was standing there, the only solitary one among many groups of threes and fours, the unidentified man who had been cracking his knuckles came in from the anteroom, also alone, rejected a plate with a careless negative gesture, took instead a beaker of ruby-colored wine, and stood close to Rembrandt, smacking his lips. "Don't eat if you don't want to," he said so abruptly and brusquely that it was hard to believe he was initiating a conversation. "I'm a physician and I know what I'm talking about. Depend on your stomach—it knows what to reject better than you do. When you don't want to eat and you've nothing to do with your hands, try drinking."

Obediently, as though he were following a medical prescription, Rembrandt set the full plate on the table and took a beaker. The wine, lighter and more sour than what he had drunk on festal occasions in Heer van Swanenburgh's house in Leyden, did have a tonic effect; and though it was too astringent for his taste he drank with the conviction that he was imbibing something precious and beneficial to his health.

"I saw you leaning against the candelabra out there," said the doctor. "Could you hear any of that—?"

"No, not a word." He felt like an eavesdropper. "There was too much noise."

"Well, I can't say you missed anything much—it was a lot of high-flown jabber about beauty. It seems there are canons, rules by which a person can measure beauty: von Sandrart seems to have picked up a whole string of them the last time he was in France. By the way, young man, what's your name?"

"Rembrandt van Rijn."

"Mine's Nicolaas Pieterszoon, though they call me Dr. Tulp. I came by that because there happens to be a tulip carved into the gable of my house, not, I assure you, because I have the time or the inclination to cultivate the things. I take it you're one of Allaert's fellow-apprentices over at Lastman's place—I go there every now and again, professionally and otherwise. By the way, don't you shake hands with people when they introduce themselves to you? It's one of the few conventions I subscribe to."

Rembrandt took the dry, ivory-colored fingers and hoped that he was indicating, by the restrained strength of his pressure, that awe, not unwillingness, had made him hesitate.

"Do you know anything about these canons?" said the doctor.

"No, I can't say that I do."

"Well, take them with a grain of salt if they're served up to you. So far as I can gather—and I'll admit I'm ignorant about the arts, though I do have an outsider's passion for certain kinds of painting—they're too neat to fit what goes on in this world. A beautiful figure, according to Herr von Sandrart's canons, measures such and such a number of inches from the ankle to the knee, from the knee to the hip-joint, from the hip-joint to the waist—there happened to be a lady present, so we didn't get the specifications on some of the more interesting things. Now in my capacity as surgeon I've seen a lot of human figures—the women in their shifts and the men mother-naked—and while some of them can be pretty repulsive and some of them peculiarly touching and memorable, I'm damned if I ever saw one that would fit the requirements of our eminent German's Parisian measuring stick."

Listening to these heretical pronouncements and looking into the intelligent and youthful face—the surgeon could have been anything from twenty-five to forty-five—he had an inexplicable sense of identification with this being so different from himself, a strange conviction that they were made of the same stuff, so that even the next question, personal though it was, did not startle him.

"Tell me, why do you people want to stick human beings onto canvas? I've always wondered about that," the doctor said.

"To preserve them, I suppose, to make them immortal." But that was more "beautiful" than true. "To show what they are—their virtues and their vices, their wisdom and their foolishness." But that, too, sounded better than it should. "What I mean is, a person wants to see into them, to find out, to discover. I don't know why it is, but the very act of painting them becomes the best way of seeing them—though I'm not saying at all what I mean . . ."

"You say it well enough. But are you any good? Can you really do it?"

"Well, I'm only a beginner—I can't really tell."

"Can't you, though, really? I'd take it just from looking at you that you're pretty cocky. Beginner or no, I'd swear you're sure you can do anything. And if that's the case, then why don't you say so?—there's nothing wrong with self-respect. Ask me if I'm good, and I'll tell you unequivocally that there's nothing like me in the Netherlands, not in pharmaceutics and not in anatomy. I know the position of every vein in the human body, and I'll reorganize the entire system of drug classification before I'm finished. Very well, then—how good are *you?*"

He remembered the charged and strained silence in the anteroom where he had waited to hear her say the glorious names. He remembered, and knew that wisdom lay in confined claims or careful evasions, yet, under these eyes that had seen the repulsive and the touching in their nakedness, why should *he* be wise? "I'm very good, your honor. Since you ask me, I'm so good that if it turns out I'm only second-best I wouldn't want to paint at all."

"As good as that? Well, I said you were cocky." He lifted his beaker and took a long draught without withdrawing his faintly mocking glance. "And Pieter Lastman—does he know what a lion he's got caged up over there?"

"I'm not my master's favorite apprentice."

"No? Why not?"

"I believe he thinks I'm—well, excessive—even vulgar—"

"Vulgar? Excessive? That's good, that's very good. You're just start-ing out, and I always contend a person should start out with a prodigious cartload of manure; you've really got to if there's to be any left for ferti-lizing the terminal years."

"Are you joking, Doctor?"

"Not in the least." He set down his beaker, passed his arm around Rembrandt's shoulders, and squeezed him through the sleeve of his mulberry-colored jacket, partly as if he was impelled to give vent to a sudden impulse of affection and partly as if he wanted to test the muscle and determine the shape of the bone. "I'm putting it vulgarly, of course, since Pieter Lastman thinks you're vulgar, but I mean every word. Just watch out that you don't end up like poor old Hercules Seghers. I don't imagine there are five people in this room who ever heard of him, and yet this is supposed to be an artists' party and the old man did some wonderful things. He lives in a hole and can't support his children. He drinks too much; he's going to drink himself to death. The only regular patron he's got is a greengrocer—the grocer buys his prints by the heap to wrap his beans and lettuce in. Seghers is one of those people who never manage to get themselves established—fashion just passed him by and left him in the ditch. But I don't know why I'm filling your ears with this morbid stuff. You ought to be enjoying yourself with the girls, and I'd better make myself pleasant to our host, or Louisa van Hoorn will never forgive me."

It was a definite dismissal even if it was a kind one, and Rembrandt walked away from the table toward the chimney place with the con-viction that he had bored his eminent companion, that the doctor had sent him off like a child to play with other children. But there were no young people he could attach himself to; in the wide semicircle that had formed around the fireplace for some entertainment, everybody he knew was occupied. Nobody had any need of him now: Haldingen and a lively red-headed girl were eating, cheek to cheek, out of the same dish of pudding; Lievens was lolling on the floor beside a chair in which the female with the garnets was sitting, his head flung back against her knee; and little Hessels was engaged in a subdued shoving-match with somebody else who should have been left at home in bed, each trying to make the other lose his footing on the slippery floor. As for Larsen— what better example of the inanities of fortune could be found?—it was around that vulgar nobody that the semicircle had formed itself. A horse-faced matron was entreating respectful silence in his behalf, ex-plaining that this young stranger within the gates had graciously con-sented to sing some of the songs of his native land, accompanying him-self on the lute.

He did so, and much more adeptly and movingly than his fellow-apprentice would have dreamed possible. His voice—a clear, sharp tenor—had an intensity and authenticity in song that one could never have imagined from his speech, and whatever was slipshod and gross in his Dutch was lost when he intoned the harder syllables of his native tongue. His crass identity was absorbed into the role of the singer; his gangling body, supporting and embracing the lute, took on a spare and archaic grace; and his fair straight hair falling loose over his forehead suggested that he was more preoccupied with the music than with courting his impressive audience—in fact, he seemed almost unaware of the firelit faces, the earnest eyes fixed upon him, the fitfully lighted smiles.

While he listened, standing solitary at the outskirts of the semicircle, yearnings stirred in him, contradictory, erratic. He wished he were sitting down to bread and beer among his own in the Leyden kitchen; he wished that like Haldingen he were running his hand over a white forearm veiled in lace; he wished some bearded dignitary were saying to him almost casually, "But of course there hasn't been anybody to compare with you since Michelangelo." Then, as the first song ended and Larsen stopped to take breath and shake back his hair, he knew what it was that he really wanted. The surgeon had been a mere distraction, diverting him from the only worthy and courageous line of action. He would go back to the entrance hall, but this time he would not stop there, standing against the candelabra like a lovesick girl. Allaert had shown a certain carelessness about protocol by sitting in one small room all evening instead of making himself pleasant to everybody; and Allaert could not blame him if he, too, showed a fine unconcern for what ought or ought not to be done, if he simply walked into the anteroom and asked his friend to present him to the great.

What he envisioned was a private word with Allaert to begin with, but that was impossible: the five who were occupying the little space were talking with the same absorbed vigor as before; and as he stopped fearfully near them on the threshold he knew that he could not have chosen a more unfortunate moment for asserting the claims of friendship. Allaert had just said something with which the lean and jaundiced painter Herr von Sandrart was begging to differ; Allaert was getting a thorough talking-to; and the little old lady was smiling half playfully, half maliciously at the spectacle. "One should never argue from an analogy," said the German in stiff and pedantic Dutch. "Analogy is acceptable for the purpose of explanation, but to use analogy as a basis for argument is to fly in the face of logic and invite the descent of confusion."

"I'm sorry." A blush spread over the gentle burgher's long, clear face. "I suppose I was thinking of intuition rather than logic." His eyes, lighting on his fellow-apprentice there in the doorway, looked vague and distressed. But the medallion on his chest, bought at the wharf and graciously recognized in the entrance hall where so much had been promised, was a guarantee against disregard, an assurance that there was no need for flight.

"The rules of logic," said Herr von Sandrart, "are not to be taken lightly, even by those whose primary method of reaching conclusions is the way of intuition. Logic schools intuition, tempers it, chastens it, keeps it"—he laughed a dry, short laugh—"from making a crazy fool out of itself."

"Yes, that's very true. If I might interrupt, just for a moment—won't you come in, Rembrandt?—I'd like to present my good friend and fellow-apprentice Rembrandt van Rijn."

He did not come in. The eyes of the master, cold triangles between their drooping lids and the fat of the cheeks, stared at him in affront and amazement: Who did he think he was? How did he dare?

Allaert got up from his stool and stood limply, robbed of his grace, while he made the unavoidable introductions: "The Lady Amalia van Hooft"—was she senile that she should find everything so amusing? "Herr von Sandrart, our eminent visitor from Germany"—cold, cold and sickly. "The greatest of our poets, Joost van den Vondel"—some pity there, some attempt at graciousness in the nod of the round, benign head, some kindness in the small brown eyes that refused to look at another man's embarrassment. "Our master—that's silly—of course you know our master. Won't you come in?"

"No, thank you. I was looking for Jan Lievens."

"Oh, Lievens is out in the salon, listening to the music, where I ought to be myself." His hand, apparently driven by conscience, flew to the medallion on his chest. "I'll be coming in a minute. Do tell Mother so if you happen to see her. And don't think of going; there'll be more dancing later."

"Excuse the interruption. Good night, gentlemen. Good night, Master. Madame"—the French word seemed right, at once icy and sophisticated—"madame, good night."

And this is what comes of overreaching yourself, he thought, crossing the hall again, fixing his hatred on the fan of laurel and the candelabra that had provided a backdrop for their fickle promises. The salon, where Larsen was singing another song more abandoned and grieving than the first—the salon was the place for him to hide his flaming face. Panting like a swimmer emerging from cold water, he stood at the edge of the listening group and looked about and tried to determine what he should do with himself. To leave at once, to walk through the windy streets, venting the anger that churned in his chest, releasing the tears that stung in his eyes—that was the course he wanted to take, but that would be cowardly and would only involve him in further disgrace. Tonight under the sloping ceiling of Heer Lastman's attic—Jesus, how he loathed Heer Lastman's attic!—the others would boast of their achievements; Haldingen and Lievens—oh, poor Lysbeth!—describing the girls they had flirted with, Larsen accepting congratulations on his singing, even little Hessels flaunting his gratification over fine eating and a new-found friend. And he? He had not even danced, though in Leyden he was considered an excellent dancer. In his pursuit of the ultimate he had cheated himself of what every dolt, every mediocrity had taken and enjoyed. He would wait, he would *have* to wait—to go home earlier than the others would be to make himself an object of derision in the attic—he would wait until the singing was over, and then he would find a partner and join in the dance.

Not ten paces away, standing by herself with her little chin tilted, was the girl he selected for himself. She was something he would be able to boast of—small, plump, and pretty; her hair, falling in snaky yellow waves over her shoulders, was adorned with violet-colored ribbons; pearls and some other stones, unidentifiable in the flickering light of the fire, sank into the soft flesh of her throat and wrists. The song was long enough to permit his pulse to grow steady and his blush to subside, and during the burst of applause that followed he went manfully up to her and touched her on the elbow. She started a little affectedly and then smiled politely, expectantly upon him. "Excuse me. May I have the next dance with you?" he said.

"The next dance?" She looked at him, and it seemed to him that he pleased her. "But I'm engaged for the next dance," she said.

"And the one after that?"

Her eyes, small but well set and of a provocatively indefinite color, moved from his face to his hands in curiosity or embarrassment. "I'm terribly sorry," she said with that earnest and cultivated sweetness of which he had had his bellyful tonight. "That one's gone, too. To tell the truth, *all* of them are, even the last. I wish you had asked me earlier —I would have liked to dance with you."

He stood wordless, utterly undone by this second assault of humiliation.

Graciousness—their false and hateful kind of graciousness—held her there while the musicians began to tune their instruments. "You're one of Allaert's fellow-apprentices, aren't you? I'm Allaert's cousin." Why was it his ill luck to fall in with another of that breed? "If you still care to ask me, I'd love to dance with you at the next party."

The next party? A nervous, bitter laugh tickled in his chest as he turned on his heel and walked back into the hall, in search of a servant who could give him his cloak. There would never be a next party. The Netherlands could sink forever under the slimy waters before he would expose himself again to this sort of thing. Nobody was there to say good-bye—not the silky chatelaine, not the faithless Allaert, not even the alien husband to whom they owed their meat and bread. He stood stiff with fury while the servant put his cloak around his shoulders, and did not say a word of thanks, only went out into the windy darkness, making sure that he banged the heavy door.

This much Pieter Lastman had to say for the Leydener: he had—to put it kindly—the courage of his convictions, or—to put it baldly—enough sheer gall to do very well for himself. In the two months gone by since Allaert's nameday party, certain people of consequence had shown a puzzling inclination to ask questions about him. Dr. Tulp, in the midst of the stresses of a minor outbreak of plague, had dropped in one evening for no discernible reason except to look at his drawings; and Allaert's mother, when she had invited the master to supper, had wondered aloud over brandy if it wouldn't be a pleasure as well as a charity to take such a gifted boy to Italy.

Such uncalled-for attention had naturally influenced the master's behavior, though he could not say it had changed his attitude. He had been forbearing, friendly, even outgoing to the Leydener lately, though his apprentice's success at the nameday party had only made him more thorny and solitary and unreachable than before. He seldom talked to Allaert, though the good-hearted little fool still wandered up to beg him for bits of conversation. He and his companion Lievens—malcontents, both of them—had assumed the tragic mask: they scorned the world and forgot to have their linen laundered; one heard them agreeing somberly that the great group portraits in the Military Club and the various houses of charity left them cold; and though the weather had been horrible and everybody else felt safer from the threat of the plague closed in around a rheum-devouring fire, they left the house the moment supper was over and prowled the damp and infectious streets until late at night.

Still, however impossible the young man was, the strangely persistent concern for him could not be disregarded; and it had occurred to Pieter Lastman with a minor shock that although the lad had been with him for close to half a year, he had never invited him into the anteroom. He had moved promptly to rectify that oversight, issuing a cordial invitation for the very next Saturday afternoon. He had even asked Vincenzo, who was usually aware of every apprentice's tastes, what would serve best for a little spread, but for once the Italian had proved useless—he had never seen the Leydener display enthusiasm for any of the dishes that were the pride of his honor's kitchen; the Leydener was so buried in himself that he scarcely noticed what he put into his mouth and could probably have subsisted cheerfully on herring, inferior beer, and black bread.

Still, a little collation had been prepared in the anteroom—a plate of neatly buttered bread, a platter of sliced lamb, and a bowl of figs and apples—a fire had been kindled, and the saffron-colored drapes had been pulled back to let in the thin and wintry light. The master had come fifteen minutes early to the meeting place because the thought of the impending hour had been unpleasant enough to keep him from caring to do anything else, and now, as he stood at the window looking out over the bleak canal with reflections of black and naked trees cutting across it—as if matters were not dreary enough already—the first snow of the year began to fall.

The large flakes—slow in their motion and haphazard in their shapes, dark against the whitish glare of the sky, almost invisible against the pallid stone of the house fronts, startlingly white when they floated past the tree trunks and eddied close to the small leaded panes of the window—the large flakes were downright repellent to him. He had never seen a snowfall without revulsion since his return from Italy. Snow was an affront to the spirit as well as to the flesh; snow somehow robbed whatever he painted of its authenticity. Those radiant canvases of his, steeped in the remembered golden light of the Italian campagna, lived and glowed through spring and summer and fall, but in a somberly lighted room like this, with windows darkened by the desultory dance of flakes, their power over the beholder was utterly lost.

And seeing through the window a poor workman's child swathed in knitted things, his cheeks glowing blatantly, his tongue stuck out to taste the aimless scraps of floating cold, he had an unwelcome flash of insight: was it because he himself had been such a one and wished to forget it, wished to believe that he had no memories save the ones begotten in the everlasting Italian summer, that he felt affronted by the coming on of winter? The world that the snow and ice brought out —the chestnut-roasters crouched over their fires, the collisions and falls and boisterous laughter on the frozen canals, the little front rooms redolent of smoking peat—it was a Dutch world, Dutch and common and thick with the threat of unacceptable remembrances. He had fled that world and all its coarseness in good time; Elsheimer had helped him to reject and obliterate it, and it was a satisfaction to him to think as he watched the downward whirling of the flakes that snow would never fall on Elsheimer's grave. He had seen too many winters, he had been too long in the Lowlands: next winter he would send his apprentices elsewhere and take himself to Italy.

While he gazed and pondered, the Leydener appeared in the white maelstrom, walking up the street along the canal and past the stripped black trees, hatless, his head flung back as if to receive the scurrying snowflakes, an almost beatific smile curving his mouth as though this inimical world, this gross and inclement season were yielding him some secret happiness. Wherever he had gone, he should have come back earlier, should have given himself time to tidy his clothes, brush the flakes and snarls out of his hair, and change his damp shoes. But he did not go upstairs even briefly; though he had had the decency to leave his cloak behind him in the hall, he walked into the anteroom just as he had come from the street.

"Come in, come in," said Lastman, unable to keep himself from looking apprehensively at his Persian carpet as the lad crossed to the fireplace. "Where have you been? To another auction?"

"No, Master. I was just out walking."

The reply could not be called curt, but there was something provocative in the mere announcement that he had seen fit to wander around the streets in a time of plague, for no particular reason. "Where did you walk to?" he said.

"No special place. Just up and down the little alleys that come out on the fish market and the wharf. I often go and look at the houses down there. Some of them must be at least three hundred years old."

He could scarcely be expected to enter into the young man's enthusiasm: these same little alleys and picturesque houses were the chief breeding-ground of the infection. He moved away from his guest in spite of himself, leaving him on the other side of the great chimney place, seeing that he was separated from him by the wholesome blast of the fire. "Aren't you being a bit foolhardy?" he asked, trying to keep the edge of irritation out of his voice. Since the beginning of the recent outbreak of plague, he had been swallowing every specific and scrubbing his person so often that his skin was chapped; and he was hard put to it not to feel the little bag of bitter herbs that hung between his underclothes and his chest. "Even if there weren't the danger of infection, I can't understand why anybody would want to go walking in weather like this. The harder it snows, the uglier it gets. Well, maybe it will be stopping soon."

"I hope not. I hope it piles up." He looked out the window at the slow gyrations of the flakes, and his face wore the same exultant look it had worn outside. "I don't know why, but the minute it starts to snow I want to draw everything I see. On snowy days, especially around suppertime, there's a marvelous mixture of lights—light from the sky and light from the bonfires and light that seems to be coming up from the snow itself—"

He did not answer. The talk made him uneasy, perhaps because of his inability to join it to his own experience: he wondered whether some appalling stupidity or insensitivity had made him miss the wonders described by this Leydener or whether they were merely the inventions of his peculiar brain. "Speaking of light," he said, stepping up to the table and heaping two plates with slices of bread and lamb, "I don't believe we Northerners know anything about it. When I woke up on my first morning in Italy, I simply couldn't believe my eyes—those whites, those blues and purples, those greens, those liquid golds. Once you've had a look at that, you feel as if you'd been living in a cellar. The fact is"—he placed one of the plates in Rembrandt's hands—"the painter who's never been in Italy doesn't know what color is. I swear, before I went to Rome, I never really saw the sun."

"Then I suppose I'm in a pretty sorry way," the young man said. "It looks as if I'll have to get on with dingy color and miserable light as well as I can."

It took him an instant to make sure he had not misheard the speech. Coming as it did to cut him down in his first flight of the afternoon, to mock his eloquence and expose his infatuation with things Italian, it was not only flippant, it was downright insolent. He managed to stifle a sharp retort only by reminding himself that his visitor might merely be trying to cover up bitterness over the poverty that kept such light and color beyond his grasp. "There's no reason for you to be hopeless about it," he said in a more guarded voice. "Chances are bound to come your way eventually. One of these days you'll be making the tour like anybody else."

"No, Master, I don't believe I will." He was staring somberly at the dish of figs.

"Aren't you unnecessarily grim about it? Even if you couldn't find the money yourself, others might find it for you. People of means and influence——" He broke off, startled by a flash from the chilly eyes.

The raw hand laid a choice bit of lamb back on the plate and wiped itself on a napkin: Pilate washing his hands could not have asserted the symbolism of the act more blatantly. "No, Master," he said again, looking him straight in the face. "Even if the wife of the Prince of Orange offered me passage money—which will never happen, because my work isn't what they care for in the great houses—I still wouldn't go to Italy."

He could not help remembering the sort of begging he had had to do in the days of his obscurity. It had been outright, shameless begging: no Vrouw van Hoorn had talked of taking him on a trip to the South, no Dr. Tulp had wanted to look at the halting sketches he had made in his master's studio. "Nobody," he said, avoiding the unblinking eyes and staring authoritatively between the reddish brows, "absolutely nobody opens a successful studio any more unless he's served his year or two in Italy."

"Then I suppose I'll never open a successful studio."

No matter what this insolence sprang from, there was no excuse for it. It was all the more galling because it was not restrained by the hospitality of the spread table or by his attempt, late and dilatory though it was, to stand in the capacity of counselor and friend. "You're young, you're very young," he said, unable to keep the icy superiority out of his voice. "You'll be changing your mind about a great many things."

"Yes, Master, I probably will, but never about Italy."

He managed to shrug and produce a dry little laugh: he was a gentleman, and nobody was going to force him into contention over meat and bread. Yet it was impossible to retreat without stirring up certain muddy currents of doubt in the young man's mind. "To save my life, I can't understand what you have against the poor Italians," he said. "They're Catholics, certainly, but they wouldn't make you go to Mass, they wouldn't ask you to confess. Anyway, from what I've seen of you, I doubt you're much of a Calvinist. It must be something else—some objection to their courtly manners and easy ways, some notion that they must be decadent because they're civilized. I don't believe it's just a matter of religion."

"But it is a matter of religion in a way, though you're right in thinking it hasn't got much to do with Calvinism."

"Excuse me, but I don't quite know what you're talking about."

"I'm sorry—it's a hard thing to explain, I don't even know whether I can get it said. But I never look at an Italian painting without thinking that the painter has gone his own way, turned his back on the real creation. They don't want dealings with what really is. What I'm trying to say is: they reject God's world."

"Reject God's world?" His scorn for the excessive phrase sounded in his voice.

"Yes, God's world, Master, that's the only way I know how to put it. They consider it crude, they consider it ugly. They walk away from it and make up another world, a world of their own. But you're not interested in any of that," he said, turning aside a little, so that his profile showed against the window whitened by the thickening fall of snow. "I suppose you asked me here because there was something you wanted to talk to me about."

"No, no, there was nothing in particular. Only, it seems to me you're not exactly satisfied." He regretted the last word as soon as he had uttered it; why he should be expected to satisfy this miller's son from Leyden, he did not know.

"I suppose I'm hard to satisfy—harder than most. If I'm not satisfied, it's certainly none of your doing."

He bridled; there was an exasperating magnanimity implied in that. "I thought perhaps you had something you wanted to talk to me about, Rembrandt."

"The fact is, I do, Master. I've been wanting to ask you what I can hope for. How much talent do you think I've got?"

But anybody who put such a question was a fool, as much of a fool and a nuisance as a woman who asks, "Why don't you love me?" He crossed the room and stood with his back to his apprentice and his face toward the fire, and the young man followed and stationed himself on the other side of the hearth. "I don't want you to flatter me," he said in a muted voice. "I want you to tell me the truth."

"But you've only been with me five or six months. Wouldn't it be a little early for me to know?"

"That depends." The yellow light of the blaze on the tightening face gave it a melancholy austerity. "I mean, if I were a very bad painter or a very good one, you would have known it almost from the start, wouldn't you?"

"But suppose you didn't happen to be either? Suppose, like most of us, you were something in between?"

"That's the one thing I couldn't be, Master. I couldn't be in between."

"How do you figure that?"

"What I want to do, what I try to do—it's so far outside the ordinary that I'd have to be either great or ridiculous. Either I'm a second Michelangelo or I'm an ass—I couldn't be anything else."

A second Michelangelo? He tried to keep his face inert, but he could not control himself; wit was the only possible answer to the preposterous proposition. "I'd never thought of putting you in either class," he said. "But if you insist on being one or the other, I'll have to tell you you're an ass."

"I thought so." His rigid stance, his unquivering face, his unwavering eyes all emanated unshaken dignity.

"If you thought so, why did you ask me?"

"Because I had to know. I had to know before I could make up my mind to stay or go."

That the choice should be there for the making, that he, the master, had not thrown this presumptuous fellow out of his studio on half a dozen appropriate occasions—it was galling. "And have you found another master who's willing to support you in your unwarranted illusions about yourself?" he said.

"No. All I know is that I can't go on painting here any longer. I've learned a great deal from you, and I could learn a great deal more, but I can't stay on; I can't lay myself open to anybody who won't take my greatness on trust."

"You'll go a long way before you'll find anybody to fill that specification."

"But I won't be looking for another master. I'm going back to Leyden and work by myself."

"And will Lievens be going with you?"

"Yes, I believe he will."

He sighed and felt his anger draining away. Why had he distressed himself? What had he to lose? His malcontents would be departing both at once, and this long winter would go by in peace. "Good luck to you then, whatever ill-advised business you're setting out on," he said.

"Since I'm leaving, I'll be doing it quickly. I may not have another chance to say good-bye to you, Master." Obviously eager to indicate that he did not mean to burden his host with a long farewell, he moved past the scarcely touched table toward the door. "Don't think I'm unaware of what I've learned from you or that I'm not grateful. But I've got to leave; I've got to work it out for myself. And you won't be sorry to see me go—I've been a trial to you, I know."

It struck the master as strange that he was not able to find some pleasant thing to say to cover up the awkward moment, that for all his celebrated ease and grace he should stand wordless there on the hearth. And once the door was shut behind his departing apprentice—the first that had ever left him—he felt a maddening mixture of amusement and rage, relief and regret. He stood for a long while, breathing in the wholesome heat of the fire, before he could bring himself to move; and when he finally bestirred himself it was only to walk to the window and pull the curtain angrily across the leaded panes. He preferred the darkness to the whirling of the snow.

*

That snow heaped up and was followed by rain and then by a mixture of more snow and sleet. It froze, melted and froze again; it turned into an iron-dark casing on the window sills. It was still there, solid and made ugly by the smoke of burned peat, on the evening when Nicolaas Pieterszoon, otherwise known as Dr. Tulp, came to disturb Pieter Lastman's lately won peace.

Because of the doctor's status, his friends were forced to make him welcome even though he regularly visited infected hospital wards and plague-stricken houses. It was not mere thoughtlessness; others beside the master had noticed that he seemed to take a devilish pleasure in reminding his hosts of where he had been and what he might be carrying. "Six deaths today, and probably more tomorrow," he said as he walked down the length of the shadowy studio, making his way between the deserted easels to the end of the room where Lastman had come in his idleness to find an ancient pot in which to plant a hyacinth. "I *did* have a bath, and I smoked myself out, but I wouldn't blame you if you didn't want to shake hands."

By way of explanation his host looked down at the precious piece of late Roman crockery that he held against his chest; his natural solicitude for such a rarity would be enough to excuse him from the amenities. His visitor, stepping into the circle of light cast by the single candle which the master had set on a marble bench behind him, was by no means a reassuring sight: his prominent eyes, his bushy hair, his ivory-colored skin drawn tight over the bones of his face made him look in this scant and fitful illumination like one of the figures in Dürer's *Dance of Death*. "Gloating over your antiquities, Pieter?" he said.

"Not exactly. Vrouw van Hoorn gave me a bulb, and I was looking for something to plant it in." The room, with its paper-cluttered floor, its deserted easels and stools, and its vast expanses of black window glass, had suddenly become intolerable to him. "I'm finished here— shall we go over to the anteroom and have a glass of brandy?" There, at least, there would be a purging fire, and the curtains would be drawn against the bleakness of the night.

101

"No, thanks, I'm on my way to the hospital. The person I really wanted to see was that apprentice of yours, that Rembrandt. I've got a fetus, and I thought maybe he'd draw it for me before it went bad."

"I'm sorry," he said, trying not to envision a decomposing fetus. "The van Rijn boy is gone."

"Gone?"

The question was put grimly enough to remind Pieter Lastman that with the plague spreading as it was, anybody might be gone in a different sense of the word—anybody including himself. "I mean he left last week for Leyden," he said.

"Left for Leyden?" The spare, taut face was stirred by laughter. "Just walked out of your studio and went his way, did he?"

"That's right. It seems he couldn't expose himself to anybody who didn't take his genius for granted, and I wasn't enthusiastic enough. I have another fellow, Larsen—"

"No, never mind. I don't want anybody else."

So the doctor was not primarily concerned about his fetus; what he really wanted was another meeting with the miller's son. "Really, Nicolaas, his presumption was considerably larger than his talent."

"Yes, doubtless, but how large *was* his talent?"

He peered through the darkness at the easel where the Leydener had worked; he must get it out of his sight one of these days. "How could I be expected to tell?" he said. "He was only with me for less than half a year, you know."

"Do you have any of the stuff he did—any paintings, any drawings?"

This one and Vrouw van Hoorn and Allaert and little Hessels—it was incomprehensible and exasperating the way they couldn't get the fellow out of their heads. "Scraps and patches—some sketches like the ones you saw the last time you were here—an unfinished painting—nothing much—"

"I'd like to buy them. No, I'm not joking; I'd really like to buy them. What do you want for them—two florins, three florins? I'll meet your price."

"I'd be cheating you if I charged you more than one."

"Charge me whatever you think."

"But don't you want to look at them first?"

"No, I don't think so. If they're like the ones I saw, they're good enough. Get Vincenzo to wrap them, will you? I'll stop to pick them up on my way back from the hospital tonight."

It was not a cheering prospect. Vincenzo had gone to the theater, and the maids would be in bed; unless he got one of them up it would be he who would have to go to the door, and this time his visitor would be coming without a bath or a smoking-out. "Why should you bother? I'll have one of the boys bring them to you tomorrow," he said.

"No, I want them tonight. I've had a bad day, and it's going to be worse before it's finished. I want to reward myself by looking at them before I go to bed."

"Very well, then, I'll get them ready."

"Don't wait up for me; that would be foolish. Wrap them and set them out in the vestibule; they'll be safe enough in the dark."

Carrying his piece of crockery in one hand and his candle in the other, Lastman lighted his guest to the front door, and as soon as the doctor and the dank blast had been closed out together, he sighed and put the pot on a table near the entrance; he would come back for it later—with unpleasant duties disposed of, he would enjoy the little business of planting more. Back in the studio, he set the candle on one of the stone grinding slabs and opened the huge Venetian chest filled almost to the top with student work that he had been dropping into it for years. An unpleasant odor of must came up from the oldest ones, the ones at the bottom. Rembrandt's things were on the top, together with Lievens'; and he took them out without looking at them—it would have been too difficult to see them anyway in the meager light.

Sleet began to fall as he wrapped them—sharp tappings against the black windows, icy whisperings in the seldom-used chimney place at the other end of the room. By the time he had knotted the cord, the freezing downpour had increased, and when he opened the door he saw the glint of ice on the deserted street. It took him only an instant to set the package down, and once he was inside again he caught himself wiping his fingers on the velvet of his jacket as carefully as if what he had been touching had been the doctor's hand. Why it should be, he did not understand, but he found it strangely appropriate that he should be leaving the last of the Leydener's stuff outside for Dr. Tulp to carry away on his return from his midnight urgencies: the raw and unwanted things were exactly where they belonged, out there in the wintry desolation and the dark.

BOOK III

1630
-
1631

My lord Constantyn Huyghens, private secretary to Prince Frederik Hendrik at The Hague, had not this time come down to Leyden on official business of the House of Orange. The House of Orange, headed now by the relatively cultivated man who had succeeded a stiff-necked soldier brother four years ago, was not greatly concerned with the city of Leyden. The only battles waged there were theological battles— abstruse and shopworn dissensions between rival professors and ministers—and the interests of the House of Orange were no longer theological. They had put a period to their participation in the bitter quarrels between the strict Reformed Church and the liberal dissenters by chopping off the head of one venerable minister of state and sending several of his abettors into exile; and since that particular fracas had soured their consciences and reduced their popularity, they had been leaving godly matters more or less to the preachers and to God. My lord Huyghens had come to Leyden only to remove himself from the stresses at The Hague, to visit an aging aunt, to see again the magnificent, if austerely stripped, interior of old Saint Peter's Church, to play a little music with old friends, and to get a rest.

None of the Leyden dignitaries who saw him at the little dinners in his honor could have guessed that he stood in any need of renewing himself. His small neat body in its impeccable ceremonial black and his lively face between the vertical of his ruff and the slanted brim of his beaver hat emanated vitality. The pointed silky beard lying over the starched white pleats and the brown moustache twisted up at the ends would have given him the look of a dandy if it had not been for his liquid, full-lidded eyes. His talk in the elegant houses he had honored by his presence had been impressive, covering everything from the renewed hostilities with Spain to the most recent innovations in chemistry and harmony; he played the lute for the delectation of the ladies and recited his own translations of the lyrics of John Donne for the edification of the gentlemen; and always, after he left, the dazzled greybeards wondered aloud how a man in his thirties could know so much.

There were good minds and creditable musicians in Leyden, and Huyghens enjoyed himself so much that he scarcely had time to miss his wife. He was almost at the end of his stay when he recalled that he ought in sheer courtesy to bring back something in the way of a gift for Prince Frederik Hendrik, the other lodestar of his days—a folio of drawings or a set of prints if anything of the sort could be found hereabouts, since the Head of the State made a point of cultivating the pictorial arts.

But it turned out that the ground to be covered in such a search was meager. According to the Leyden dignitaries, who could not be accused of understating the resources of their city, there was only one real studio, and even that had suffered a decline some five years ago when a couple of the master's apprentices had run off to get better instruction in Amsterdam. Nevertheless, since it was the only one, he had his servant drop around to ask whether Heer van Swanenburgh—who, according to the aging aunt, was one of the few remaining descendants of the old aristocracy—would be good enough to receive him at eight that night.

It was closer to nine when he got there on that moist, softly snowing February evening. He was still warm with the wine he had taken at the last of the little suppers, still dazzled by the recollection of the muted purplish sunset that had lent charm to the small and select company and poetry to the conversation; and his amorous propensities, strengthened by abstinence, had begun to conjure up, for the first time on this visit, images of his wife coming wet out of her bath or lying half-covered by a velvet spread across their bed. He knew his mood and his nature, and he warned himself as he shook hands with his amiable host not to enhance whatever he might see in this old-fashioned, scrupulously orderly studio with the tremulous sense of affirmation and tenderness which was making a palpable and swollen thing of his heart. As he sat down in a carved chair by the fireplace at the end of the big square room, he reminded himself how one evening, in just such a state, he had been moved to the point of tears by an air of Sweelinck's, only to find later that it was banal and thin. Not that he needed to be niggardly about his florins: his means were so large that he never realized their extent without being slightly startled, and in spite of the fact that he had made open-handed contributions to every Leyden charity and learned society brought to his attention, he had been entertained so hospitably that he had not yet exhausted two-thirds of the money he had taken with him for the trip. But few things were more painful to him than disillusionment after enthusiasm; and more to check himself than to present himself as a cautious collector to the small, mild, monkey-faced gentleman on the other side of the hearth, he began on a rueful note. "You must be lonely here, Heer van Swanenburgh. So far as I can gather, there isn't too much of an artist's life left in Leyden," he said.

The master smiled, not in the resigned way that one expected, but knowingly, as if he were savoring a secret. My lord Huyghens had not encountered another such smile during his stay in Leyden; it did more than the ruff, more than the gold chain over the narrow chest, more than the exquisitely fine ruffles that veiled the small wrinkled hands, to remind him that this man's roots went deeper and rose from more ancient soil than his own. "Naturally it isn't the kind of painters' town it used to be in the days of Lucas van Leyden," he said. "But it isn't

108

exactly defunct, either, though it may well look that way to those who see it from The Hague or Amsterdam. There are one or two things going on hereabouts that are relatively exciting—exciting enough, anyway, to divert me in my declining days."

"Heer van Swanenburgh can scarcely consider himself in anything but the good, ripe days of summer."

"I'm fifty-five, your honor. Fifty-five, and coming to the point where I'm almost willing to close up shop." He turned his head over his shoulder, shaking out the soft, meticulously parted, greying fall of his hair. His eyes, still keen if a little faded, took in the room, which had indeed the air of a place put into a terminal state of order: every easel stood at an exact interval from its neighbor, neat piles of drawings were lined up against the beautiful old wainscoting, and no clutter marred the sheen of the polished floor. "Five more years, I tell my wife, and I'll turn this into a salon where I can display my little collection. It's never been a passion with me, collecting, but I've picked up a few nice things, nevertheless."

My lord Huyghens, who had wandered around in the best salons in the Netherlands, Italy, England, Spain, and France, hoped he would not be asked to examine the said collection. In spite of his courtly training, his face froze and his gestures stiffened when something mediocre was presented for his admiration. He sidestepped the possible dilemma by complimenting van Swanenburgh on the fine woodwork in the room and expressing his hope that the master wasn't really closing up—especially since he had heard there wasn't another creditable studio in the whole town.

The knowing smile came back, deepening the creases in the sallow cheeks. "Oh, there's another good studio, though you'd probably think it a very strange one," he said, tapping gently on the arm of his carved chair. "It's in an old outbuilding near a mill on the river bank. I get over there every now and again, though I haven't been there lately: there's no way of heating the place, and it gets unbearably cold. But the work goes on there winter and summer, day and night. I'd swear if you passed there now you'd find them both still working—Rembrandt van Rijn and Jan Lievens. I don't imagine you've heard of either of them, have you? Well, it's no wonder—Rembrandt is only twenty-three and Lievens can't be more than a year older."

"Apprentices of yours, Heer van Swanenburgh?"

"Not exactly, your honor. They studied with me to begin with, and found me dull or old-fashioned or something of the sort"—he laughed a small dry laugh that made the skin of his cheeks break into a network of fine wrinkles—"and they took themselves off to work with Pieter Lastman in Amsterdam."

"Pieter Lastman? But isn't he out of fashion? I know they're weary of him at The Hague."

"Are they? Well, I wish I had enough Christian grace in me to say

I'm sorry to hear it. I don't believe the lads found him entirely satisfactory either; they came home in short order. And now they're over in that building working by themselves."

Only the most tactful of compliments would serve under the circumstances, and he liked the man well enough to have it ready. "And doubtless you're kind enough to give them the advice they've grown old enough to profit by," he said.

"Scarcely, your honor." He brought his delicate fingers together near his chin and smiled at his visitor over the joined fingertips. "Lievens listens to nobody but Rembrandt, and Rembrandt listens to nobody but God—I'm not a member of that trinity. But I go over there once in a while to see what they're doing, and not a week goes by when one of them doesn't drop in on me. It can't be of the slightest interest to you, my lord, and I wouldn't want to give the impression that it was any obsession with me; I only wanted to disclaim the dubious distinction of having the only creditable studio in town."

But obviously it *was* an obsession, and Constantyn Huyghens had learned in a diplomatic life made up for the most part of short and intense encounters that no stranger could be as interesting as a stranger who was obsessed. "Are they teaching, these two young men? Do they have any regular apprentices?" he said.

"Oh, yes, after a fashion—though you mustn't imagine they're rivals of mine. One of their boys is a fellow named van Vliet that I sent packing because he simply couldn't paint, and the other one's a fellow named Dou, a thirteen-year-old whose father wanted to get him out of the family glass factory before he mutilated himself or set fire to the place. That's as many as they have over there, and as many as they want, so far as I know. They paint like furies, they grudge themselves every minute they're away from their easels. But what can I do for your honor? I'm completely at your service, though it's taken me so long to get around to saying so."

The visitor explained that he wanted a little gift. Nothing ostentatious—a folio of prints, a couple of nicely mounted drawings—no canvases, because to walk into the princely presence lugging a canvas somehow made a person feel like a fool.

"I know exactly what you mean," said Heer van Swanenburgh, rising and going in the direction of the drawings stacked along the wall. "A canvas is a ridiculous thing to carry, though it would be a pity for the artists if everybody thought so." With a creaking of bones he got down on his knees and flipped through one pile after another, but even the scant collection that he finally assembled he laid aside as if he had no intention of showing it. "Really, my lord, there's nothing much here," he said, getting up and brushing imaginary dust from his knees. "However, if you'll excuse me for returning to the subject, I do have something else, though it's a little on the morbid side: six prints of beggars by this Rembrandt van Rijn that I've been going on about."

"After the manner of Callot?"

"Oh, no, by comparison with these, Callot's are Kermis scenes. These are stark poverty—the thing itself; there's nothing picturesque about these." He went to a cabinet and opened a drawer and took out a handful of paint brushes and a large lump of lapis lazuli. "You see, I keep my treasures here, and this folio, in my provincial opinion, is something of a treasure. But we can't see it here—let's step over into the light."

They stood in the glow of a six-branched candelabra set on a bare table and opened the folio. At the sight of that first etching, as elemental as rocks or sods or roots of trees, my lord Huyghens could not keep himself from making a foolish sound of appreciation, a sound about which his wife often teased him, a murmur that came into his throat when words were too poor to serve: Susanna said it sounded like the mating-talk of doves. The drawings had a spare, raw eloquence, and their execution was unbelievably masterful; he had never seen such expressive lines, such transparent shadows, such velvety blacks. Though he realized that what he was looking at would never do for the gift— no prince can be reminded that such misery walks his land unalleviated —he continued to look, and did not know what moved him most: the wounds that the subjects inflicted on his spirit or the delight that the rendering gave his eyes.

"You like them, my lord?"

"But who wouldn't like them?"

"So it seems to me. And yet, at The Hague and in Amsterdam, it's as if this fellow didn't exist."

With the magic of those prints working potently upon him, Huyghens considered the possibility of deception by omission. He could buy the folio at a generous price, keep it for himself, and say nothing about the impossibility of presenting it to the Prince. The money would probably be welcome; any artist who drew destitution with such an authentic touch and worked in an outbuilding without a fireplace must have first-hand knowledge of poverty. Yet a ruse seemed out of keeping, unworthy of the candor of his host, and he cleared his throat and explained the situation manfully—that, unsuitable as they were for the Prince, he would like to purchase the prints for his own collection, which, if he might say so, was as good a place for a beginner to exhibit as anywhere in The Hague.

"But if you're really interested in a set for yourself, your honor, might I suggest that you go over to their studio and buy one directly from the artist? You see, he made me a present of these, and besides, you might find something else in his studio that would be exactly right for a gift."

Both of them looked at the same instant toward the little collection of unexamined drawings that the master had pulled out of the heaps, but neither of them said anything, and there was something conspiratorial about the stillness between them.

"Actually, Heer van Swanenburgh, I was planning to go home tomorrow," he said, closing up the folio. "But on second thought I'll stay over a day and go and visit your young friend. May I count on seeing you there?"

"No, my lord, though I'm sorry to say so. The last time I went I got such a rheum that I did nothing but blow my nose for a week. Besides, I spoil the young men's style; they'll get on much better, I'm sure, if you see them by yourself."

The master, plainly satisfied with the results of the visit, did not try to entice his guest back to the tall chair by the fire; with only the briefest pressure of the hand and another of his knowing smiles, he released the private secretary of Prince Frederik Hendrik as casually as if he had been a neighbor who had dropped in to borrow a book. And even when it occurred to my lord that he had been worked upon, pushed in the direction of the outbuilding on the river bank, he felt no touch of distaste. The street was purplish-dark except for a few palely lighted windows; the air was soft with snow, though no snow fell; and every now and again as he walked through the powdery whiteness, he stopped to shake his head at himself and smile.

*

It was Harmen Gerritszoon who went to the door to take the message from Heer van Swanenburgh's servant. He went slowly, because the noonday meal, light as it had been, somehow lay heavy on his stomach and interfered with his breathing, and he came back without cheerfulness because the message, heartening as it was, had started again the procession of grim thoughts in his brain. Alone in the kitchen—his discomfort and his apathy had kept him there after the others had gone about their business—he found a piece of paper, an oily scrap which the butter had come wrapped in from the market, and spread it out on the table beside the half-eaten apple that he had abandoned almost an hour ago. Reaching into the pocket of his jacket, groping with his fingertips in the chaff and dust and fuzz from the worn woolen, he got hold of the stub with which he marked his sacks, and cursing the oiled spots of the paper that refused to take the crayon, wrote out: "My lord Constantyn Huyghens, secretary of the Prince of Orange. Expect him between eight and nine tonight."

He read it through, dubious as always about his spelling, folded the paper and wrote "Rembrandt" across it. It had been his thought to ask Lysbeth to take it to the outbuilding where the four of them would be working, but he was reluctant to send his daughter over there; and after throwing the apple into the trash bucket and putting his plate and knife into the soapy water in the dish basin, he decided to take the message himself.

His little walk in the sharp wintry air, so light and pure that it should have been a specific against bodily ills, only increased the discomfort in his chest, and he found himself made wearier by the effort of taking cumbered steps in and out of the cracking crust of the snow. He reproved himself for not taking proper satisfaction in the fact that the secretary of the Prince of Orange was coming to his house—but then the princely title had lost much of its stern grandeur during the last twenty years. This was not the old Prince who had come with the fleet to the deliverance of Leyden and had died later by the bullets of a Spanish assassin, asking God to have mercy on his poor soul and his poor people. The heroic days were over, and the new Prince of Orange was a man of compromise and many-stranded purposes, unlikely to invite anybody's bullets but equally unlikely to keep the populace in the churches praying for him day and night. Nevertheless, somebody whose business brought him regularly to the palace at The Hague was going to visit that low, ugly, snow-burdened building which stood on the other side of the stream in the blinding winter sunlight; and he supposed he ought to be grateful, he did his best to care.

He did not go to the door at once; he walked through some of the mounded snow that had slid from the roof and looked through the narrow slit of a window. Though he had long had his doubts that what was going on in there could properly be called by the honorable name of teaching, he had too much respect for teaching of any sort to break rudely in. The room, which had once been a storage place for grain, was so cluttered that he winced to think of its coming under the eyes of an aristocratic visitor. The four easels seemed to be thrusting themselves up out of a rubbish heap; crumpled paper, paint rags, folios of drawings, canvases and panels cluttered the floor. How they could walk around in there without stepping on the things they had been so wildly enthusiastic about last week, he could not understand.

The sight of the artists themselves was no more reassuring. They were intent and quiet enough, but it was disturbing to see what they were intent upon. Dangling on a piece of rope from the ceiling was something they called their manikin—Rembrandt had bought it a month ago on one of his little trips to Amsterdam. It was always repellent to Harmen Gerritszoon in its smooth, jointed, painted wooden nakedness, and its present decoration had not improved it: some gold embroidery floss had been stuck onto its bald pate, dirty gauze had been draped over its trunk, and from its shoulders, in grotesque and impious mockery of the airy messengers of heaven, sprouted two dusty and bedraggled bittern wings.

The cold was troubling him; with every breath the congestion in his chest was thickening, and yet he stayed to look. Rembrandt, unshaven and somber, his chin hidden in the old black muffler that swathed his neck and shoulders, was staring at the manikin and biting the end of his brush-handle. Five years of labor at the easel—a person had to admit that he did not coddle himself, he hurried through his meals, he seldom gave himself more than six hours' sleep—had toughened and thinned him. He looked like a bear coming out of his hiding place at the end of winter—spare and rough and patchy; his hair was a wild, dull mane, and there were red blotches on his face. Lievens, who worked nearly as hard as Rembrandt, looked less seedy for it, perhaps because he relieved the stress periodically by haunting the taverns and getting himself women at the dancing schools—something his son never did, unless he did it in Amsterdam.

As for the other two, if they could be called by the respectable name of painter's apprentices, then he, Harmen Gerritszoon, had grave doubts about the painter's trade. Dou and van Vliet had been taking the noonday meal with the family for two years, and, as he had told Neeltje, it was like having a weasel and an ape in the house: one darted and the other lumbered, and both were forever under a person's feet. Dou, who might have been handsome if he had ever scrubbed himself down to his blond paleness, was little and into everything—telling Lysbeth where to shop and Neeltje how to cook and Adriaen how to make shoes. Van Vliet, big, dark, hairy, and careless about covering his massive chest, was as stolid as his fellow-apprentice was lively. He seldom engaged in conversation; the necessary no's and yes's that were wrested from him sounded more like animal grunts than like human speech, and he had to be shoved or shouted at before he would move out of the way. Well, luckily the apprentices went home for supper and would be off the premises before my lord Huyghens arrived tonight.

But once the miller had opened the door and stepped inside, he experienced again one of those sharp reversals of feeling that had been going on in him ever since the boy had come back from Pieter Lastman's studio. The familiar oily smell hung in the icy air; the pieces of cloth that he and Neeltje had been draped in for their portraits asserted themselves in the general clutter on the floor; and he saw with pity that a cloud of mist was going up in front of Lievens' half-open mouth and that little Dou's fingers were blue from the cold. Nor could his antipathy for the manikin discredit what Rembrandt was making of it with broad strokes of watered ink: the figure that hovered on the paper was an authentic angel borne lightly up on unseen currents of air, the hands uplifted, the face flooded with solemn tenderness. He stepped up to the easel and nodded approvingly at the drawing. "A servant came over from Heer van Swanenburgh," he said.

"Anything important?"

"Yes, I think so." He unfolded the butter-paper, as uncertain of his memory as he was of his spelling. "My lord Constantyn Huyghens. He's the secretary of the Prince of Orange. He's been to see the master, and he's coming over here. You're supposed to expect him between eight and nine tonight."

Lievens gasped and struck the side of his face with the flat of his hand. Dou squealed, and van Vliet stood with his brush held in the air, a frown-mark growing deeper between his thick black brows. But Rembrandt only thrust his chin deeper into his muffler; his pinched and spotted face took on an unbecoming look of unconcern and arrogance. "You can be sure of one thing: he'll come and look and walk out empty-handed. Not that it wasn't kind of Heer van Swanenburgh to send him over," he said.

"My man in the biretta—we'll show him that," said Lievens.

"My boy rolling the hoop—you'll show him that, too, won't you?" said Dou, his brown, rabbitlike eyes shining in his dirty little face.

Van Vliet said nothing. His massive, hairy chest, only half-covered by the grain sack wrapped around his shoulders and knotted at the throat, heaved in an audible sigh.

"Sit down, Father. Here's a stool for you." He swept the stool clear of a fringed scarf and a peacock feather, and turned back to the other three. "The point as I see it," he said, "is to blot the rope out of your mind. The manikin must be seen as floating, not hanging. Something supports it, something buoys it up, like a fish in the water or a milkweed seed on the wind."

It was false, his father thought, that show of unconcern which he was putting on—false like much of what he had done and said ever since he had come back from Pieter Lastman. The waste of money, the green hopes blasted, the need to explain to inquisitive friends and neighbors why this high-flying son of his had come down so fast and hard—these things, bitter though they were, had not been nearly as hard to swallow as the change that had come about in the young man himself. Doubtless he had met with some defeat in Amsterdam, but that was no reason for anybody in his early twenties to reject everything beforehand because it might turn out to be another defeat, no justification for shutting himself away, with these shoddy and ill-assorted three, from the rest of the human race.

"Do sit down, Father. You look tired."

He seated himself on the stool, not because he had any hope of further communication, only because it was true that he was weary, so weary that he could not imagine himself setting out for the house without a little rest. The work went on in silence; to stare at the manikin, moving almost imperceptibly in a draft from the window, made him dizzy; he looked instead at the paintings set against the wall and lying on the floor. And as he stared, something that he had known vaguely for months emerged into his thoughts with fearful, irreversible certainty: there were many of his son's paintings that he simply did not like. Some were actually repellent to him, and the strange thing was that the ones he found it hardest to tolerate were exactly the ones Rembrandt liked best.

Balaam and the Angel—there was no point in trying to deceive himself; it was as sorry a failure as Heer van Swanenburgh had predicted. *The Baptism of the Eunuch, Samson and Delilah, Saint Peter in Prison*

—he was embarrassed to look at them, he could not bear the violent gestures, the clasped hands, the upturned eyes. He twisted the butter-wrapper in his effort to understand his distaste, and came up with something so simple-minded that he would never have dared to say it to Rembrandt or Neeltje or anybody else: In trying to be bigger than life, these pictures of his son's had fallen short of life—they could not possibly do enough because they tried to do too much . . .

"The draperies," said Lievens, "can carry the illusion of floating."

"The draperies should *fortify* the illusion, not carry it. The illusion has to be centered in the body of the angel itself."

The voice of his son was cold, dictatorial, almost hateful. It was better for a man to look the worst of it in the face: perhaps they had ruined him and his painting past all mending in Amsterdam. What was left of him at the end of these five lean years, the pride of the house for whom his parents had deprived the rest? A painter? He had sold a few pieces here and there for a miserable handful of florins. A master? The master of an ape and a weasel in a filthy shambles. A happy being, following wherever his soul would have him go, and to the devil with the profit? *He* happy?—his face was as sour as Gerrit's. The preacher had been to the house to say he might be more at peace with himself if he attended services, but he rejected even the worldly comforts that God provided—food and sleep and the nourishing pleasures of the conjugal bed.

"Be good enough to watch where you're going," he said to van Vliet. "There are three of my oils on the floor behind you."

The big impervious one started, laid down his brush, and stooped to pick up the paintings. Harmen Gerritszoon, breathing less shallowly now because the congestion in his chest had begun to pass, watched the crouching body muffled in the ugly grain sack, and saw in the careful movements of the thick hands a rude gentleness. The three small paintings, still unframed, were all portraits: one of the painter, one of Neeltje, one of himself decked out like a burgher captain with a feather in his cap and a heavy chain across his chest. "Excuse me," he said, abandoning his determination to hold his peace, "can I look at those?" And when van Vliet brought them and laid them at his feet it was as if he were being told that in cutting the loaf unequally he had at least not done injustice in vain. Through the hard and weathered flesh of his own face down there, through Neeltje's finely wrinkled cheeks and shrunken mouth and small all-seeing eyes, through the stern peasant countenance of his son something came up to him, some honorable assertion of what *was,* no more and no less.

"Excuse me, Rembrandt," he said, "but I've been looking at these portraits here; I hope you're going to leave them out for my lord Huyghens to see."

"But they're not paintings, Father. They're only studies." His voice was hard with annoyance, annoyance at the interruption, at parental interference, at the ignorance of those who presume to make suggestions when they know nothing about the trade.

"Still, it seems to me they're very good—very good in their own way, anyhow."

"Why those particular ones, Father? There must be twenty like them lying around."

Twenty like them? He remembered how he had sat in a turban and Neeltje had sat with the Bible and Rembrandt had stood before the mirror making one kind of face after another at himself, and he supposed that it was true. If the five years had yielded twenty like them— the spirit showing through the flesh, the flesh itself painted with all its beauties and infirmities—could it be said of the harvest that it had been blasted? "Yes, I suppose you *have* done a lot of them, now that I think of it. Anyway, *I* like them, and I think you should leave some of them out," he said, rising to go.

"Wait a minute, Father, until I finish this wing, and I'll walk over with you."

"No need. Keep at your work. Only, I hope you're going to clean up the studio."

"Why? Because he's an aristocrat? Because he comes from the court at The Hague? Because—"

"Because it looks like a pigsty and would look like a pigsty to anybody," he said, opening the door and tentatively drawing the first breath of icy air into his sore chest.

"Don't be angry with me, Father."

He looked back over his shoulder and saw that his son had turned away from his easel. His chin and mouth were still buried in the muffler; the unshaven cheeks were pale and pitiful and unlovely with red blotches; and he stared at Harmen Gerritszoon with afflicted eyes.

"I'm not angry. I only thought you might tidy it up a little."

"Very well, I'll clean it. It's got to be cleaned sometime, I suppose. As for those studies—if you think I ought to leave them out for him, I will. But he won't like them, I can tell you that beforehand. Pieter Lastman didn't care for that sort of thing—did he, Jan?—and neither will anybody else."

*

It was half past seven, and the studio was cleaned, and so for the first time in many days was he. If he had taken a steaming bath and washed his hair and pared his nails, it was not because he was concerned about making himself respectable for any fop from the Prince's chambers at The Hague; it was only that putting the studio into decent condition had made him so filthy that he had been unacceptable even to himself. Dou had gone home at five; Lievens had insisted that some rare edibles should be on hand and had left at half past five to ransack the shops for pickled eels and French wine. Only van Vliet, who could not hope to get anything out of my lord's visit, had stayed to help, raking up the accumulated rubbish, lugging the unwanted drawings and paintings and etchings behind the burlap curtain, and scrubbing the splintery floor.

He had been appalled by the amount of trash that had come out of the place. He and van Vliet had carried it out by the barrel and heaped it up in a four-foot mound in the snowy field behind the studio, where the apprentice had set it on fire, keeping watch on it all the while Rembrandt was washing and dressing back at the house. Now, looking out of the studio window, he saw nothing but a flickering glow in the middle of a big black circle: it was a safe fire at last, and van Vliet was gone.

He kindled the oil lamps, looked about him, and found the room strangely depressing in its scrubbed and orderly state. The shadows of the four easels fell long and unbroken across the wet, uncluttered floor, and he sat down on a stool and sighed profoundly. He knew what it was that made him sigh: the room was as it had been when he and Jan Lievens had first set up their easels in it five years ago, and the new austerity forced him to remember the beginning, to take stock of the gain and see and accept the loss.

Yesterday, when he had put the last touches on *Judas Returning the Thirty Pieces of Silver*—it stood on his easel, arresting enough to put anybody, even a Court collector, in his proper place—yesterday he had seen nothing but the gains. The little painting, which he had worked on for months, was a masterpiece fit to evoke the envy of Lastman. The blue robe of the Temple dignitary, the gold-embroidered mantle of the high priest, the sacred books, the rich cover on the table, the thirty pieces of silver—on each of them he had expended unstinted and unhurried care. Yet, beautiful though they were, they were thrown into the background by the figure of Judas himself, a soul-chilling Judas, a Judas issued mad out of a mind that knew what it was to reel on the black edge of madness, a Judas down on his knees, his clothes torn, his face and arms contorted, his whole body in a convulsion of despair. But yesterday the last touches had been put upon it, and today had been one of those empty days between work and work, and with nothing else begun, there were the world, the present, the actualities—his empty pocket, his shabby ménage, the blotches on his face, the raw-edged nervousness that told him that the next time he went to Amsterdam he would go to Pieter-Jacob Street and accept the invitation of one of the whores.

He did not want to think of that—it made him feverish, even though the room was bitter cold. He laid out, open on the table, his folio of *Beggars*, and added two fine drawings of Lievens' and one of Dou's that reminded him of Allaert's things, only Dou had more vitality, more wit. The girls on Pieter-Jacob Street with their loose sickly-sweet smiles and their hands that were willing to help you . . . He shuddered and wondered when Lievens would be coming back with the wine.

Lievens' precious painting, *A Man in a Biretta*, was hard to drag out and scarcely worth the effort. It was tremendous; the single figure was life-size and the fire before which it sat was a full-scale blaze. Part of his distaste for the thing, he supposed, rose from his having been responsible for it: it was the final product of certain studies in various kinds of light that he and Jan had made, but what the two of them had learned together had been so grossly and trickily applied here that he could not look at it without feeling ashamed. Nevertheless, since Jan was proud of it, he set it against the wall where the light of two lamps converged upon it—there was no telling, Huyghens was probably enough of an ass to be taken in. *Balaam and the Angel* he relegated to the dark behind the curtain. *The Baptism of the Eunuch* and *Saint Peter in Prison* he placed, together with a couple of Jan's Biblical things and Dou's painting of the boy with the hoop, against a decently lighted wall. The little portraits he laid out on the floor, not with any hope that the visitor would like them, only because he had given a promise to his father, who had looked so pale and peaked this afternoon, so suddenly grown old.

He ran his fingers through his hair, soft, moist, and strangely alive to his touch after the washing. The room looked repellent in its bareness; what he liked to think of as chaste austerity would doubtless give the impression of pitiable poverty. Taking one of the oil lamps with him, he went to the far end of the room and drew the soiled burlap curtain aside. Behind it, with a heap of pictures, was a shabby trunk overflowing with his treasures—damasks, satins, gorgets, weapons, beads, chains, feathers; it was on these that he had spent the greater part of his miserable earnings—whether or not he sold anything on a trip to Amsterdam, he could not come home with empty hands. And seeing them all together like that, he was forced to do what he could usually avoid: guess their aggregate price. Taken one at a time, each had cost little more than the mugs of beer he had denied himself, but his father could have hired a hand at the mill during the weeks of the busy season for what the heap of them had cost . . .

Well, he told himself, selecting a length of purple velvet, an ostrich plume, and an old chased helmet, if my lord Huyghens buys anything —which he probably won't—whatever he pays can go into the family funds. And cheered by his virtuous resolution, he set about adorning the room. The velvet he draped over van Vliet's empty easel; the helmet he put on a peg in the wall; the plume he stuck into the mug that held his pens and brushes. The two fine Oriental brushes, Allaert's present, were still there; they had worn far better than the mulberry-colored jacket, thin at the elbows and tight and short for him now, which was all he could find to wear tonight. And he was thinking that they could take him or leave him—those who came mincing down from The Hague in their squirrel-lined velvets—when the expected knock sounded on the door.

His first surprise was that the knock should be so unassertive, his second that the person who stood on the snowy threshold should be so slight. For some reason he had imagined Prince Frederik Hendrik's secretary to be as tall and massive as the Prince, and he had to lower his eyes to meet the liquid glance of a man a good inch shorter than himself. "Heer van Rijn?" said the visitor gently. His manner of address was in itself disarming; he had been "Heer van Rijn" to nobody here in the provinces; a prophet in his own country went by the leveling, homespun "Rembrandt Harmenszoon."

"Van Rijn, yes. I take it you're my lord Constantyn Huyghens. Step in, if you please, though I'm afraid it's colder in here than it is outside."

And, still more amazingly, the little gentleman gave him no answer. The little gentleman, severely if expensively dressed in black with an unpretentious white ruff, stepped quickly past him and went, like a moth drawn irresistibly by light, directly to his *Judas*. "Good God—is this yours? Did you do this, at your age?" he said.

He did not answer. He stood open-mouthed, with hope clawing at the iron casing that he had wrought around his heart, while a strange sound of appreciation, embarrassing and profoundly moving at once, issued from the throat of the visitor, a sound like the cooing of doves. He could not withstand it; it was as if the metal bands were snapping in his chest; his mouth began to tremble and tears came into his eyes. "Yes, that's my *Judas*. I finished it yesterday. I thought it was good myself," he said at last.

And what he heard in reply was what he had no longer even permitted himself to dream that he would ever hear: his own intentions assimilated by another man and given back to him in the words after which he had groped in vain. Nothing went unnoticed; everything, from the agony of Judas to the clear blue of the Temple dignitary's robe and the separate rendering of the thirty small pieces of silver, was put into utterance and given authenticity. He stood behind the speaker at a little distance, afraid to move, afraid that a footfall would interrupt the flow of that revitalizing current. And he knew that if the speaker did not turn to address him it was only because he was ashamed to show his own transported face.

Whatever was between them could not have been sustained much longer. If my lord Huyghens had turned away from the easel while the two of them were alone together in the room, the only possible—the unthinkable—conclusion to his rhapsody would have been an embrace. It was probably fortunate that Jan Lievens broke in upon them while the wonderfully articulate sentences were still directed toward the picture rather than toward himself. It was probably fortunate, though at the moment it was enough to make him want to beat his fists against the wall.

The voice trailed into silence, the magnetism between the painting and the slight body was broken, and my lord turned around, a visiting courtier in every respect except his shamefaced smile. "A friend of yours, Heer van Rijn?" he said, looking cordially at Lievens, who was closing the door with his buttocks since he had a bottle of wine in one hand and a package of eels in the other.

"A fellow-painter, my lord. This is Jan Lievens. He and I have been working here together for five years."

"But why here?" said the visitor. Plainly, in spite of the cold, he meant to settle down; he dropped his cloak, his beaver hat, and his gloves carelessly onto the worktable and perched on one of the stools. "Why would you want to bury yourself in a town like this? Not that I haven't been enjoying myself in it thoroughly, but unless I'm grossly misinformed, it's the last place in the world for a painter—"

"There you're more than right, my lord," said Jan Lievens, setting down his little burdens, freeing his large white hands for gesturing. "This is a place for theologians, lawyers, doctors: they're the ones the sun rises and sets on in Leyden. You can imagine what Leyden is if the painter of a work like that"—he flung out his arm toward Rembrandt's *Baptism of the Eunuch*, which became somehow tainted by the theatricality of the presentation—"is forced to work for years without a patron, without a market, in a room like this. Everything you see against that wall over there"—the *Man in a Biretta* was one of the group indicated—"was done under the most deplorable conditions— abominable light and no heat at all."

The eyes of the visitor, having rested with courteous attention on the speaker for the length of the speech, turned back to Rembrandt. They were large and lustrous; some recollection of the earlier magic was in them still. "If everything Heer Lievens says is true, and I can well believe it is, I'm all the more puzzled as to why you stay on here," he said.

But how was he to be answered? Was a person to say: I hid myself away here after a lost battle, like a dog that crawls down under the piles of a dock and licks his wounds? "Leyden is my native town. I tried it for a while in Amsterdam, and so did Lievens, and nothing came of it, so we both came home."

"But no matter how attached you are to your family and your birth-place, eventually you'll have to tear yourself loose and establish yourself elsewhere, you know."

"Yes, I suppose I will, my lord, though I can't see myself doing it very soon—"

"If I were you, I'd do it immediately. From what I see around me, you could have moved out years ago. If you have any doubts about your readiness to take your place among your fellow-artists, those doubts are simply preposterous. That little *Judas* of yours is the work of a master. De Keyser, Elias, Jordaens—any one of them would be proud to have painted it. It would be snatched up at any auction in The Hague or Amsterdam."

"Ah, yes, my lord, provided the name of Jordaens or Elias or de Keyser was down in the corner," Jan Lievens said in a voice vibrant with noble melancholy. "It's by the name they buy, and how can a poor devil working in Leyden—no matter how splendidly he paints—get himself a name? My friend and master here has taken his things to Amsterdam, and he's even been good enough to drag a few of mine along too. They're nothing to compare with his, of course, I'd be the first to admit it, though they're done with the same concept: the two of us burn with a single flame. But who would think of buying what we have to sell, unknowns that we are? Paintings as fine as anything you see in this room have gone to petty shopkeepers and such at a price that scarcely repays us for the frames and the paint and the panels we did them on."

Unable to look at him, Rembrandt had been staring at Lievens' shadow, elongated and gesturing widely into the shadows of the easels on the floor. He was ashamed of the speech; everything in it was colored up and none of it was completely true. Besides, the resonant voice and the large white hands were playing upon my lord Huyghens, and the fact that he had gone directly to the *Judas* and made those unmanning sounds in his throat should have put him beyond manipulation. "Look, now, Jan, it's not quite as bad as you're making it out to be," he said.

"Three florins for your *Philosopher*, five for your beautiful *Vanitas* with the skull and the hourglass and all those marvelously painted books. Four for my *Ganymede* and three for my *Saint Paul in Athens*. Now I ask you, my lord, are those decent prices? For paintings like these, is that enough?"

He could not raise his eyes; Jan Lievens was rubbing the dust from the wings of the moth, was handling and desecrating what was too delicate to touch. Still staring at the scrubbed floor, he saw my lord Huyghens shake his head in a vague negative.

"Nobody of any consequence will buy," said the irrepressible Lievens. "And those who do buy can't pay a decent price."

"Well," said the visitor, getting down from his perch, "perhaps we can do a little something to remedy that. I'm not exactly without consequence, and I have a reputation as a collector of sorts both at The Hague and in Amsterdam. *I'm* going to buy, and I'll start with the *Judas*. I'm prepared to offer you a hundred florins, Heer van Rijn."

A hundred florins? But in his most sanguine moments he had hoped his whole year's earnings might come to a hundred florins. With a hundred florins a man could knock out the middle of the roof and put in glass and have light, abundant light, from morning to evening. With a hundred florins he might indulge himself, he might even buy some paintings . . . But he was no florin snatcher, no manipulator, no Lievens. "A hundred florins is too much, my lord," he said.

"Not in the least, not for what I'm getting." He went back to it again, bent over it, touched the outside edge with timorous care and love. "It's dry enough, isn't it? Good, I'll take it with me. I have a frame-maker at home who'll do it justice. I've brought my money, too, because I was hoping I'd find something here, but nothing like this, certainly nothing like this."

He went to the worktable, took the money pouch from his belt, and began to count out the proper sum in gold. The counting out of the money could have been humiliating: Rembrandt remembered how other buyers had shamed him by handing him much smaller sums, some of them with an insulting flourish, some of them reluctantly, counting over twice or thrice before they put what was theirs into another man's hands. But my lord Constantyn Huyghens paid him, simply paid him; and when all the money was there in one heap he pushed it back out of the light, into the nodding shadow of the ostrich plume. "And now what else have you got to show me? I'm in a buying frame of mind," he said.

He was indeed. He laid down a small heap of florins for the portfolio of *Beggars*; no need to look at it, he said—he had seen it at Heer van Swanenburgh's studio and had made quite enough of a fool of himself over it there. He also took, for five florins, the larger and more detailed of the Lievens drawings—probably out of politeness, Rembrandt thought, since his comments were routine; but how fine a thing it was to care so little about five florins, to spend five florins without a second thought in order to do a young man a courtesy. Appeased by his earnings, Jan dropped the tragic mask and the grand manner and served up the eels and wine. The three of them stood near the table, eating and drinking and talking as easily as if they had been three equals met at an inn; and though their breaths went up in clouds before their faces and the little gentleman often shivered and rubbed his hands, there was no sense of haste: he led them on to speak about where they had studied and how they prepared their etching plates and whom they knew in Amsterdam and why they didn't care to go to Italy. If, toward the end of that delightful half-hour, Rembrandt's high spirits had subsided, it was not because anything was wanting in the cordial attentiveness and sprightly conversation of his guest but because it had suddenly occurred to him that there would be no skylight, no paintings, nothing for himself from the money: he had resolved not an hour ago that whatever my lord Huyghens left behind him was earmarked for the family, and it would be contemptible to withhold any part of the largesse because it had been unexpectedly great.

It was Lievens who got the three of them to move away from the table and toward the wall where the other paintings were on exhibition. He had his reasons: though my lord was warm and outgoing, he had so far given the *Man in a Biretta* only the most cursory glance. Rembrandt, seeing his own paintings over my lord's shoulder, regretted that he had not put them into hiding with *Balaam and the Angel*. Neither was a match for the little *Judas*, and he was hard put to it to keep from disclaiming them, from saying that he had turned his back on them and their like months ago.

"Those two," said the visitor, "must have been done under the influence of Pieter Lastman. I know his work, of course—it was in high fashion for a while in Amsterdam."

"Yes, my lord."

"But you need his influence as little as you need to hide yourself away, if I may say so. Follow the *Judas*; the *Judas* is the thing. Now this large one here, this *Man in a Biretta*—I take it that's yours, Heer Lievens."

"Yes, that's his," said Rembrandt, "and you couldn't possibly see it to advantage with those clashing colors on either side of it." He stepped in front of the other two and turned *Saint Peter* and the *Eunuch* with their faces to the wall.

Whereupon the visitor delivered himself—not, thank God, of the foolish remembered sounds—but of a knowing whistle. Without the others to detract from it, Lievens' painting sprang into life with a startling if vulgar immediacy: the fire in it seemed to offer warmth to their brittle fingers, the man reading before the blaze became a fourth to their company, ready to close his book and speak.

"If it pleases my lord at all," said Jan, his head bent, his eyes fixed modestly on his shoes, "the credit goes to Rembrandt. It was he that gave me the idea for it; it's the last of a series we did to investigate various sorts of light."

My lord walked up to it, peered at it, stepped back from it, whistled again. He commented with vivacity upon a number of things: the remarkable interplay of light and shadow, the warm reds and yellows, the black that was never really black, the way Heer Lievens had used the butt end of his brush to draw a hair over his subject's brow. It was some consolation for Rembrandt that everything which delighted the visitor—and he was delighted, not transported—was present in the accursed picture because *he* had told Jan Lievens to put it there; yet my lord Huyghens had not been on hand to hear him teaching, and he felt the sharp bite of jealousy. "Notice the hand and the book, my lord. It's beautifully done—the contrast between the living flesh and the dry parchment," he said.

"Yes, I can see—it's something quite new, this picture. It's something the like of which has never been seen at Court, I'm sure of that. Prince Frederik Hendrik's taste runs to the Flemish—" There was something faintly disparaging in his dry intonation. "He's fascinated with Rubens at the moment, and naturally everybody around him is given to the same predilection; but this, Dutch though it is, is startling enough to impress anybody."

Still staring at his shoes, Lievens did what he could to keep his mask of modesty intact; but his eyes kindled with hope of fame and florins, and his mouth grew rigid in his effort to stifle a smile.

"I can use it, I'm sure I can use it, though handling it isn't going to be easy," said my lord, touching a bit of fine impasto work with his small fingertip. "And now, as to the price, I'm a little puzzled. It's not worked out as carefully as the *Judas*—and certainly it shouldn't be, it's not at all the same sort of thing—but then, considering the size of it—"

Eighty florins, thought Rembrandt, would be more than generous.

"The price is up to you, my lord," said Lievens, lifting his head and tossing back the fall of hair from his noble white brow. "That *you* should care to have it is reward enough for me."

"A hundred and fifty florins? Does that seem right to you?"

"Munificent—positively munificent, my lord."

He returned to the worktable to count out the money, and, having finished, stood wordless and static for the first time this evening, apparently searching his mind for a way of saying something; and Rembrandt did not know whether it was to him that the visitor wanted to speak or whether he only thought so to relieve his jealousy. "From what you said a little while back, Heer van Rijn, I gather that you used to know Vrouw van Hoorn in Amsterdam," he said at last, setting his fine black beaver on his head at a dapper angle.

"Yes, my lord, though I can scarcely say I really knew her. She was good enough to talk to me at length, and she showed some interest in what I was doing then."

"And when you go back to Amsterdam, you naturally pay her a visit?"

"No, I've never called on her, my lord."

"But isn't that a little foolish? She's a charming woman and a very intelligent one—you wouldn't find it dull, I'm sure. Besides, she knows people who could help you get established, people like Vondel and von Sandrart—they're not to be waved away, you know."

"It's five years since I saw her. I doubt she'd remember me."

"Maybe so and maybe not. You couldn't tell, could you, until you'd tried?"

"I can't see myself trying, my lord."

"No?" He put on his cloak and settled its collar under his little pointed beard. "Well, if you won't follow up your connections in Amsterdam, I'll have to see what I can do for you at The Hague. Now, how am I to get my pictures? I'm leaving early tomorrow."

"I'll have one of the apprentices bring them over to you. You should have them by seven o'clock."

"That will be perfect." Pulling on his elegant black gloves, he stepped over to take one more look at the *Judas*. No sounds rose in his throat, but his face took on a look of utter happiness. "The *Man in a Biretta*," he said, "should do you some good, Heer Lievens, because I mean to use it as a gift to Prince Frederik Hendrik, whose collection is, of course, world-famous. The little *Judas*"—he bent even closer to it, plainly it was painful to him to separate himself from it even for a night—"the little *Judas* I'll keep for myself."

Saying farewell to him on the stoop in the icy air, Rembrandt began to shiver. If his heart was cold in him now, it was not because of the extra fifty florins that were Lievens' portion—all his florins were going to the family anyway. But to have one's work presented to the Prince was no small matter; the Prince, crass as he probably was, was still the first person in the land. A presentation to the Prince was something that could readily be boasted about; but it would be almost sacrilegious to tell anybody how the secretary of the said Prince had murmured over the little *Judas*. He found himself wishing that my lord Huyghens could somehow have given the *Judas* to the Prince of Orange and at the same time kept it; and he was reluctant to go back into the studio, to gather up the little portraits that everybody had forgotten in the excitement, to bear with Jan Lievens' hilarity and submit to Jan Lievens' unacceptable embrace.

*

Though Lysbeth Harmensdochter was still loyal to Rembrandt out of old habit, she found little to say in his defense these days. For three or four months after my lord What's-His-Name had come from The Hague to sow a doomed crop of hopes and leave a long-since-spent heap of florins, her brother had come out of his grim preoccupation with his work, had even found it possible to make visits to Zuytbroek and go to Sunday service, to talk at the supper table instead of sternly chewing on his food and staring at the wall like a man possessed. But whatever gains had been made in spring were lost in summer and forgotten in fall; by winter he was as bad as ever—so short-tempered, so hateful and cold that she was surprised that she should resent his increasingly frequent little trips to Amsterdam.

She supposed he had to go: he took his paintings and sometimes managed to sell them. Usually he stayed overnight with a young man named Uylenburgh who kept an art shop; sometimes—perhaps because he found himself a woman—he didn't turn up at home for two or three days. She was particularly annoyed when he chose the middle of the week to disappear, because it was on Wednesdays that she had to cope with the unwanted guest that her parents had provided for her benefit—it was they, not she, who had extended the perpetual invitation to the carpenter's journeyman Hendrik Isaakszoon.

For a while on this particular Wednesday she had imagined she could escape: her father had had a vomiting fit at the mill and had come home early, and her mother had sent a neighbor's child for the doctor, who had promised to drop in between six and seven. Sorry as she was that her father should be ailing, she had seized upon it as an excuse for calling off the young man's visit—she could wander over to the outbuilding, she would not have to spend all evening inventing foolish sentences to cover up her suitor's still more foolish silences. "Look, Mother," she had said, "since everything's upset here this evening, why

126

don't I just run over and ask Hendrik's sister to tell him not to come? I'm sure he'd understand." But Neeltje Willemsdochter, laying the company cloth on the table and setting out the good tin plates, had made known in her quavering voice that it would be rude to warn Hendrik off at so late an hour, that her father was almost himself again, and that everybody was to stay downstairs during the doctor's visit—it was unnecessary and unseemly for the whole family to stand gaping around a sick man's bed.

So they had had their company and their company supper, though she doubted anybody had gotten much satisfaction out of it. Gerrit had not come down, and the three empty chairs had given a certain bleakness to the table, and neither she nor her mother nor the visitor had shown much appetite for the cheese or the fish or the cold dish of sugared beer and bread. And now, washing the dishes with the assistance of the wordless Hendrik—for her mother had gone upstairs with the doctor whether it was seemly or not—she felt trapped and deserted: her mind, as fitful as the fire that crackled on the kitchen hearth, kept leaping here and there and would give her no repose.

None of this disquiet could be blamed on Hendrik Isaakszoon, who stood on the other side of the copper basin drying whatever wet thing she thrust into his bony, big-knuckled hands. He was nobody to call up uneasiness, though his height was such that his curly head barely cleared the rafters. In the whole length of his body, which he held stooped as though he were ashamed of it, there was not one drop of audacity. Unlike Jan Lievens, he would put in a formal request before he kissed a person; he would never lunge at a girl at the foot of a dark staircase, taking her so tightly to him that thigh seemed to blend with thigh and breast with hard, strong chest. This one's breath, when he came close enough to inflict it on her—which was seldom—smelled of butter and milk, not of tobacco and French wine. His throat was no pillar of living marble; it was raw from close shaving and had an Adam's apple that bobbed between the frayed, clean wings of his collar. And his eyes were the brown eyes of a dog, exasperatingly pleading, infuriatingly kind.

She thrust a yellow bowl in his direction, and he took and held it, staring at the plate of uneaten fish on the kitchen shelf. "I didn't do so well by your mother's fine supper this evening. I hope she didn't take offense," he said.

"Don't worry. She didn't."

"I guess I missed your father—the table isn't the same without him." He was drying the inside of the bowl with irritating thoroughness.

"He'll be up and around again tomorrow."

"I certainly hope he will!"

His fervor was a reproof to her. It reminded her that he loved her father with an immediate, familiar love that made for the doing of carpentry jobs in the house and the mill, the lifting of heavy grain sacks, the cheerful running of errands to any part of town. She reached past him for the battered tin milk pitcher and immersed it in the sudsy water, and while he was staring at her hands in the basin, she looked out the window at the outbuilding where no lights were burning tonight —though why she should want lights there, why it would have been a comfort to her to know that what was unattainable was close to her in space, she did not understand.

"He's been looking tired lately—don't you think?"

"What would you expect when he works the way he does?" She snatched the bowl out of his hands and set it down hard on the shelf. She despised a man who followed a woman around in the kitchen; he made himself ridiculous doing a woman's duties for her. Whenever Jan had stayed in the kitchen with her, he had never cheapened himself by picking up a dishtowel or wiping a table. But it was seldom enough that Jan had looked for ways to be alone with her—not more than a dozen times in the six years he had been back in Leyden. And this at least she had taught herself to see: that he was impelled to come to her only after a search had yielded him nobody else.

Come to her, come to her . . . whatever that might mean. In spite of his worldly ways, he was a blunderer. She did not even know whether she was still a virgin, though she supposed she was, since there had never been any blood. The memories seemed the more shameful with Hendrik's eyes fixed houndlike on her face and the rasping voice of the doctor, no word of his pronouncements intelligible, going on in the bedroom above their heads.

"Will your brother be coming home tonight?"

"I wouldn't have any idea." It was sharper than she had intended, and she tried to soften it with a stiff smile. "There's no telling; he might come home tonight, and then again he might stay until Saturday. Anyhow, don't throw the fish away—if he does come back he'll want something to eat."

"I imagine he'll be upset about your father."

She did not answer; she was staring out the window. A light had just flared up over there in the studio—Jan had come and would probably be working alone there for hours. And there was a kind of gain in that, even though she could not wander over: the squares of yellow light falling on the snowy field on the other side of the water told her that he had not found anybody for the evening, that at least nobody else would be melting under his exploring hands tonight. The doctor's rasping voice continued to sound above her, and Hendrik was staring at her, but still she could not keep herself from remembering. Too much was going on at once—it was as if a flock of wild birds had been let loose in the kitchen and were sweeping from all directions at her head. "I'm dizzy," she said, and had to close her eyes and rest her back against the wall and draw one wet and soapy hand across her brow.

"You'd better sit down," said Hendrik, unable to take even this opportunity to touch her. "Is anything the matter?"

"It's nothing—I told you, I'm just a little dizzy." As she sat down on a stool, the fire and part of the kitchen wall seemed to be moving past her like the rim of a turning wheel; she could stop the nauseating movement only by staring at her hands.

"You sit still. I'll finish up here and put the things in the cupboard."

"Thanks. Don't empty the basin yet. If Rembrandt comes, we'll have to wash the dishes."

"Yes, I know."

She continued to look at her hands: what had once been pink in them had deepened to a dry, rough red; the knuckles were swollen, and the flesh looked puffy at the wrists. The one that lay in the folds of her damp apron cried for a wedding ring; only a wedding ring could dignify its workaday look. And there stood Hendrik Isaakszoon, a carpenter's journeyman who would soon be making a decent living—sturdy and reliable, in love with her, and such a one as would doubtless ask her regularly on Saturday nights if she would permit him to lie with her . . . A full minute passed before he spoke again. "I wonder why he's staying up there so long—the doctor, I mean."

She was wondering about that herself, but she had no time to say so; the back door swung open and Rembrandt came in, letting in the cool draft and the fresh smell of February snow. There was an unaccustomed high-heartedness in his greeting, which could only have come from the fact that he had sold another picture. He actually smiled as he took off his cloak and laid a parcel on the table; doubtless it was filled with the sort of gimcrack things he was always dragging back from Amsterdam. "Good evening," he said to Hendrik, "I hope they fed you well at supper." And even such an offhand bit of courtesy was enough to bring light into the dog's eyes of the carpenter's journeyman, who had learned that what he could usually expect was icy politeness at best.

"Oh, yes, very well," he said, watching her brother take out a length of olive-green damask with gold embroidery, a dagger in a leather sheath, some blue glass beads, and a square of flame-colored silk. "I see you've been making some purchases, Rembrandt Harmenszoon."

Vapid as the remark was, it was taken up by the buyer, who seemed glad tonight to have anybody, even Hendrik Isaakszoon, to serve as an audience. "Yes, Uylenburgh sold my little *Flight into Egypt* for more than I expected, and I got these in the Jewish section for less than nothing. This damask came from Florence—" She watched him shake it out, totally unaware in his obsession with it that neither his mother nor his father was there to welcome him. "You can see the Florentine lilies worked in between the shells."

"Very nice," said her suitor, reaching across the table and fingering the fabric obligingly. "And what are you going to do with it?"

"Paint it," he said, snatching it back with some impatience, as if damask could not possibly be used for any other purpose. "This flame-colored scarf now"—he flipped it out so that it hovered for an instant

129

in the air—"this I can use when I . . . But look, is anything the matter?" He caught the floating silk and crushed it into a ball and looked helplessly around the room. "Why is the place so empty? Where *is* everybody tonight?"

"Father's sick. He came home early this afternoon and went to bed," she told him, wondering why, since she had assured herself that it was nothing, she should make it sound so grim for her brother's benefit.

"Sick?" His face had gone so white that the pink weather-spots on his cheekbones burned bright. "Where is he?" His voice was apprehensive enough to make her heart begin to race.

"Upstairs in bed. Nothing's the matter, he just had a vomiting fit—"

He dropped the scarf onto the soap-spotted table and started for the hall.

"I wouldn't go up just now if I were you. The doctor's up there with him."

"The doctor?"

"Yes. Stay here and I'll get you your supper. You can go up later, when the doctor's through."

"But what do you want me to wait for?" His voice was loud with the senseless anger begotten by fright. "The devil with the doctor. I'm going upstairs."

Since he was going where she had been forbidden to go, she could not repress a smile at hearing him blocked before he got there. The doctor and her mother were coming down just as he started up, and before she could put the tawdry Amsterdam stuff out of sight, all three of them walked into the room.

She found it disturbing to look at the dapper, sandy-haired Dr. Claas Duartszoon, who seated himself on the edge of one of the benches, his hands clasped around his knees. It was not only that his face—small, lineless, and ruddy—was connected with the pains of her childhood and the humiliations of her adolescence; it was also that the expression in his eyes could not be read because the candle flame was reflected in the lenses of his spectacles.

"Is Father all right now?" she said.

"I'd say he was resting comfortably at the moment, Lysbeth Harmensdochter."

Was that ominous or did it only seem so because the flame danced double in his glasses? Did she hate him senselessly for past ministrations or intuitively for something to come?

"What was it, Doctor? Indigestion or something like that?" said Hendrik Isaakszoon.

"When certain symptoms occur, we of the profession say to ourselves: given the manifestation, it may be indigestion and it may be something else. May I ask, Neeltje Willemsdochter—one doesn't like to ask in front of the patient—when your good husband came back from the mill, did you notice his color? Would you say it was livid or ruddy, pale or red?"

"Pale," she said, standing erect in front of the corner cupboard with her arms folded. "Stone-grey, I would call it."

"Good." That was a lie, thought Lysbeth; he did not find it good at all. "A stone-grey color is what we expect in these cases."

These cases—what in the name of God did he mean by "these cases"? "Is it anything serious?" she asked, in spite of her mother's admonishing eyes.

"Ah, now, a pricked finger, a little blow on the head can be serious, Lysbeth Harmensdochter. And a man with such a fever that we don't believe he can live out the night can get up next morning with no fever at all. Serious? Everything's serious—"

"Yes, but what *is* it?" It was her brother, demanding as only a man can demand. The kitchen was beginning its slow turning again, and Rembrandt's face also seemed to her the color of a stone. "Is it his heart?"

"Well, now, it *could* be his heart, as I was telling your mother when we met you on the stairs. I'm not saying it is his heart; I'm saying it could be his heart. And if it is his heart, then I'd be very irresponsible if I said it wasn't serious, though 'serious' doesn't mean 'grave,' and 'grave' doesn't mean 'fatal,' you know."

Hendrik Isaakszoon—she had quite forgotten him sitting there on the other side of the table—reached for her hand over the Amsterdam treasures, and it took all her self-control to keep from snatching it away.

"But then," said Rembrandt wildly, "why does he work the way he does? What is he doing, dragging those heavy sacks up and down the stairs?"

"That," said Dr. Claas Duartszoon, "he certainly shouldn't be doing. If it is his heart, and if he should be foolhardy enough to put such a strain on it, I for one wouldn't want to be responsible. In fact, I'm going to suggest, merely for safety's sake, Neeltje Willemsdochter, that he do nothing whatever for the next two weeks. For the next two weeks at the very least, he should rest quietly in bed."

Lysbeth's hand, lying on top of the flame-colored silk under Hendrik Isaakszoon's hand, clenched in spite of herself. Her father was sick—seriously, gravely, sick beyond curing, sick unto death. Her mother knew it and her brother knew it, and Dr. Claas Duartszoon knew it as he rose and bade them all good night, glad that he had managed to convey the dreadful thing without uttering it, relieved at the prospect of passing out of this doomed house into the fresh and snowy night with his own heart beating soundly in his chest. Hendrik Isaakszoon knew it, and even she had come to know it at last; and the knowledge was like the raging of a great wind through a tree that she had been leaning against all her days, a tree which was torn up by the roots, and where it had been, there was only a hole in the earth.

The tumult subsided and she knew herself to be here in the kitchen, sitting near the table among the other silent ones. The clean draft let in by the doctor still hung in the air, bearing that softness which promises spring and calls up the first thoughts of Easter and the Resurrection. Miracles had been and could be, and she was not even asking for a miracle: her father was not dead, her father was up in his bedroom, living and breathing still and resting comfortably at the moment. He might even be wondering how matters were going down here and whether the connection with Hendrik Isaakszoon that he so plainly wanted was making any progress tonight. And little as she liked the carpenter's journeyman with his bobbing Adam's apple, she would accept him as a rod laid on her sinful flesh by a just God, would perform all that was required of her in atonement if in return for her penance the death that had looked in on them tonight would be turned back from the door.

"One thing's certain—he can't go on with the kind of work he's been doing," Rembrandt said.

"That's true enough," said her mother, looking without malice at the heap of finery on the table and then through the window at the light in the faraway studio. "But who's to do it in his place?"

"All of us will do it." He was twisting his fingers and cracking his knuckles. "I can shovel in the malt and carry the grain sacks. Lysbeth can do the lighter things, like turning the mash and picking out the bad sprouts. And when it gets to be too much for the two of us, I'm sure Adriaen will run over and lend us a hand."

"There are things that I could do, too, Neeltje Willemsdochter," her suitor said. "I could come over almost any evening. And on Sundays when the shop is closed I always have plenty of time."

Her brother said nothing, and his silence left Lysbeth in a strange dilemma: she did not know whether she was relieved or affronted that he did not acknowledge the offer of the carpenter's journeyman, showed no disposition to draw him into the family solidarity.

"That's very kind of you, my dear," said her mother in a voice that was shaken for the first time this evening. "If you do it out of good feeling for my husband, God knows you don't do it without return—my husband's very fond of you."

Hearing it said in her mother's quavering voice was somehow moving —so moving that the frozen surface of her face broke up and tears came surging into her eyes. But her mother, stepping over to the hearth and putting the kettle onto the hook, threw her another warning look. The thin erect body forcing itself to step self-possessed into the quicksands of calamity, the tight wrinkled face keeping its secrets to itself, the withered hands busying themselves with daily tasks—it was as if they

132

wanted no part of her or her grief, wanted only that all should come to pass in seemliness and dignity.

"There's beer and fish and cheese—I'll set it out for you, Rembrandt," her mother said.

"No, thanks, Mother. I don't want anything."

"Maybe later then. Lysbeth, get me a couple of eggs; the doctor said a couple of soft-boiled eggs might do your father good."

"I'll get the eggs, Neeltje Willemsdochter. Lysbeth isn't feeling well; she was dizzy a little while ago," Hendrik Isaakszoon said.

"Dizzy?" The small eyes widened, and a faint spasm of worry passed over the wizened features. She could tell that her mother was counting, telling off the months since she had left her daughter alone downstairs with Jan Lievens. It was a long tally and a safe one, and she sighed. "Well, it wouldn't be a wonder if she was dizzy; she scarcely touched her supper. I'll get the eggs, Hendrik. You get Lysbeth a mug of milk and some bread."

Counting, counting . . . how many years now had her mother been counting? Hate boiled up in her as she watched the wrinkled hands drop the eggs into the kettle. Keep at me, Mother, she thought, and I'll give you something to count about, and with a man of your own choosing, too. Count for me once more, and I'll bring this one down with me on any heap of hay. I owe it to myself at least to see whether I can put up with him for the rest of my life.

The big hands of her suitor set milk and bread before her, pushing the gaudy silk aside to make room for the mug and the plate. She was glad to bend over the rusks, thankful for an excuse to hide her face. To think such thoughts when her father was lying upstairs with his fatal illness upon him! Her mother had rejected her, and God would do likewise, and no great wonder! What could He want with such a one as she?

She sat silent, nor did Hendrik or Rembrandt stir from their places. Her mother was the only one in motion. Like a spider that spins another web when the first is torn, she was doing little duties: folding dishtowels, getting out a tray and a napkin, putting a stool into its proper place. "You'd better be careful about your things from Amsterdam, Rembrandt. Why don't you take them over to the studio before they get something on them?" she said.

He came and gathered up his treasures, a flush spreading over his face as he folded up the length of fabric and pocketed the glass beads. Once he was finished, he stood with his hands ridiculously burdened. "Can I go up?" he asked. "I haven't seen Father for a couple of days."

"The doctor wanted him to take some sleeping drops as soon as he's had something to eat. If many of us go running in and out, we're sure to keep him awake." She took the eggs out of the boiling water and began to break the shells without wincing; her withered fingers had grown insensitive to heat with the years of washing and scrubbing. "I'll give him your love, Rembrandt. You can see him tomorrow. Go over to the studio and get back to your work. I'm going upstairs."

And what about me? thought Lysbeth when her mother and brother were gone. Am I to be penned up in this kitchen with Hendrik Isaakszoon every night, sitting with him when he's finished his charitable duties? Am I supposed to make myself pleasant to him while he has a mug of beer before he leaves? Am I to give him my hand to kiss, on request, before I let him out for the night? Am I never to walk alone on the old walls again, remembering what I want to remember? Am I never to wander over to the studio, never to feed my eyes on what I can no longer touch?

"I'd do anything in the world for your father," said Hendrik into the silence.

"Yes, I know you would," she told him in a flat and weary voice, pushing aside her plate.

"I'll pray for him, too, Lysbeth Harmensdochter."

"Yes, pray by all means." That came out with a little more ardor. If the foolish and the innocent were good for nothing else, their prayers might count for something. The prayers of Hendrik Isaakszoon, as simple-minded as the prayers of little children, might make themselves heard at the throne of God.

*

Harmen Gerritszoon was up and about, after a fashion. His head was light and his ankles were swollen; his feet seemed strangers to him, netted all over with small reddish-purple veins and so plump he could no longer see the bones. Walking about on these alien feet with the strange dizziness swathed around his head, a dizziness akin to holiday drunkenness or exaltation, was no easy matter. So far, he had tried it only in the house, going like a child learning to walk from doorway to doorway and from chair to chair. But this morning the first of the hyacinths were out, and he had ventured into the back garden to see the spikes of bells, white, crimson, and violet, standing upright in the crown of crisp green leaves that divided them from the trash of last winter— old leaves, some of them leathery and curled, some of them lacy as the caterpillars had left them last fall, some of them stripped of all their leafy nature and reduced to mere skeletons.

He directed his heavy feet through the yielding rubble and carried his dizzy head through the pale April sun. The sails of his mill creaked and hummed in the gentle flow of the wind, but he did not turn his head to see the whirling: good children that they were, they did not need him at the mill, they scarcely even came to ask him questions any more. Adriaen labored there three days out of the week, leaving his cobbler's shop in the care of his journeyman, and Lysbeth toiled there with her good young man until nine every evening. Rembrandt put down his brushes at three instead of five and filled the sacks and loaded them onto the wagon; and even the apprentices stayed on a little after their day's assignment was finished, lending a massive shoulder or a set of nimble fingers for carrying the sacks or picking out the sickly sprouts.

Afraid as he was to bend over, he could only imagine the fragrance of the hyacinths. Neeltje would come out and snap off a couple for him if he asked her, and it would have been pleasant to have the sweetness of the spikes close to his face in the kitchen where he sat most of the day on one chair with his feet on another; but it had always seemed wrong to him to gather flowers in their prime. These stems bled a clear, cool blood when a person snapped them off, and all things came to their ends, and there was no use hastening the time . . . Hearing the click of the latch, he looked up and became conscious of a presence coming through the gate. Presences—people, cats, trees—appeared to him suddenly these days because the dizziness hung blurred and radiant out there some twenty feet beyond him, working like a mist to make things nonexistent until they were at hand. This presence, stopping in the clear circle around him, was Heer van Swanenburgh, his face broken up with wrinkles, his hair silvery in the sun. Ah, well, he thought, holding out his hand to his visitor, everybody has to get old . . .

They talked for a while of the slow coming on of spring and the hardiness of hyacinths, and the master went on in his learned way about how the fresh smell of flowers was something nobody had ever succeeded in getting into perfume. "Rich, heavy, overripe—that's what it becomes when you put it in bottles. The Lord never intended us to have that fragrance for longer than the blooming season," he said.

It was Lent, the beginning of Passion Week, when every day had its set series of Gospel readings and solemn matters for meditation. "Yet I was reading just last night how Mary Magdalen broke an alabaster box of precious ointment and poured it on Jesus' head,"said Harmen Gerritszoon. "That must have been perfume."

"You're right, my friend. Perfume it was—Mary of Magdala was a maker of perfumes—so Fioretta tells me." Then, as if he was afraid there might be something offensively Catholic in his wife's odd bit of Romish lore, he brushed the subject away by turning the exquisite lawn cuffs back from his little withered hands. "How's your health these days?" he asked in a cheerful, workaday voice. "You're looking ten times better than when I saw you last Saturday. There's color in your cheeks; you're quite like yourself."

He felt his cheeks in some embarrassment; he was sorely in need of a shave. If there was color in them, it must have come from the wind that kept the iron sails turning and creaking: whenever he bothered to look at himself he always found himself dead-white. "My legs are swollen, that's the worst of it. The pain's all gone, thank God." As he spoke his voice took on the sharpness of his irritation. Mild and peaceable as he had always been, respectful to his superiors and easygoing with his equals, he had lately grown irritable; he even felt that he had been given an inalienable right to irritability. He was irritated with the pastor when he spoke of the godly man's right to live long without labor, enjoying the fullness of his harvest; he was irritated with the doctor, who clapped him on the shoulder and told him that his heart sounded as strong as a drum; he was irritated with Neeltje when she spoke of what the two of them would be doing next autumn, next winter, next spring. What was real were these hyacinths and these dead leaves and his swollen feet set numb among them; and he wished that even Heer van Swanenburgh would take himself off and let him alone.

"I have news of a sort for the lads over in the studio," said the master. By looking down at the silver buttons on his jacket, he seemed to imply that the news was not altogether good.

Harmen Gerritszoon also looked down, his eyes on an early bee that clung to a crimson bell, taking like a lover. There had been a time when he could not have waited until the midday meal to hear what was afoot, when he would have offered to walk over with Heer van Swanenburgh; and knowing that it was not only his heavy feet that held him where he was, he sighed. "Well, don't let me keep you, your honor. You'll find them at work over there," he said.

"Yesterday I had a letter, a very long one, from my lord Constantyn Huyghens—"

He could remember the name—that was the Prince's secretary who had come a year and more ago and raised such high hopes and never been heard from since. Remembrances, like presences, evoked surprise in him these days; time, like space, was confined to a little area by the all-surrounding mist. "Was there anything in it for Rembrandt?" he asked, trying to count the exact number of months through which his son had been waiting.

"Yes, there was. But there was more for Jan Lievens."

More for Lievens? The irritability rose in him again like gall. He need not have learned about it until the noonday meal was on the table.

"Doubtless you remember, Harmen Gerritszoon, how my lord Huyghens bought one of Lievens' paintings for the Prince—"

Remember? How could a person forget it? For months the fool had grinned over it, nourished himself with it, grown sleek on it.

"It seems the Prince didn't keep the picture; he gave it to the English Ambassador." He hurried on, holding his hand suspended, lest malicious hope should take root where there was no soil for it to grow upon. "Some weeks ago, the English Ambassador took it home with him and presented it to his King, and the King was so impressed with it—you may recall that it was a very *show*y piece—the King was so impressed with it that he's inviting Lievens to come over to paint at the English Court. It's a fine appointment, I won't deny, but you and I know that nothing is ever as glorious as it looks."

It was Passion Week and surely no time to wish one's fellow-Christian ill, even if one's fellow-Christian had climbed into the range of King Charles's vision on Rembrandt's shoulders and also had an unfortunate habit of reaching under the table for Lysbeth's knees. It was Passion Week, but the enthusiastic speech the occasion required simply refused to come into his weary brain; the best he could do was nod his strange and dizzy head.

"What I wanted to tell you, Harmen Gerritszoon"—the elegant little hand, veiled by its floating lawn cuff, touched him on the chest through the worn woolen of his jacket—"what I wanted to tell you is that no matter what luck comes Lievens' way, your son Rembrandt is as far beyond him as you and I are beyond the dancing bear at the Kermis. Your son Rembrandt will paint as nobody in the Netherlands ever painted before him. His name will be mentioned with Dürer's and Michelangelo's, and when that day comes it will mean nothing that his imitator was the one who got the invitation to the English Court. Believe me, my good friend"—his finger pressed harder into the miller's pounding chest—"what I say, I say in all honesty, as I hope my sins will be forgiven and my soul will be saved."

But he could not even indicate his gratefulness; too many currents were converging upon him—the sea across which Jan Lievens would be sailing to wealth and glory, the onrush of the years, the crested waves of hope that crashed against his heart, the torrent of his own stirred blood. Perhaps I will die here now, he thought, staring down at the blurred spikes of white and violet and crimson. Perhaps I will fall on my face and the neighbors will come to their windows and the women will come running out of the house, making their senseless hue and cry . . . But the tumult subsided and the waves withdrew and he knew that Heer van Swanenburgh was holding him by the elbow and peering anxiously into his face. "Are you well, Harmen Gerritszoon?" the master said.

"Oh, yes, perfectly well, your honor. I was dizzy, but it's gone again —that's the way it is, it comes and it goes."

"You're not trying to do any work? You're taking your ease completely?"

"Oh, yes, completely. Everything's done for me, they won't allow me to lift a finger."

"That's only as it ought to be."

His house emerged out of the blur, with its clean stoop and its shining windows washed down for Easter. He wished he could find the words to tell the master what a blessed quiet had been established within it, how since his illness had been upon him the Lord had seen fit to impose order upon the world which he was about to leave so that he might go from it without an afterthought. Gerrit, now that he had a companion in pain, seemed to bear his suffering with more hardihood. Rembrandt and Adriaen, with the respect and trust that had been growing between them since the pile of florins had repaid the contents of the moneybag, labored together for the common good. Lysbeth had put behind her whatever foolishness she had contemplated or committed, and would learn in good time how much better it was to be nourished by a reality than to be eaten away by a dream. Even Neeltje would do well enough by and by: she knew that she would be walking to church one of these days in a widow's bonnet; the truth was there at the bottom of her small keen eyes in spite of all her talk about next summer and next winter and next spring. "I'm blessed in my family, Heer van Swanenburgh. They all work together these days, as if they had only one heart among them," he said.

"Since I never had any children, I can't imagine how it would feel to have begotten and fostered greatness—"

Greatness? In the slowness and confusion of his brain, he had almost forgotten about the greatness. "I begot him and fed him and housed him, your honor, but it was you who fostered him—in the spirit, anyway," he said, looking down in embarrassment at the hyacinths.

Their conversation ended as it had begun, with the flowers. Heer van Swanenburgh expressed his wonder that the tulip had become the queen of the bulb varieties; to him there was something cold and over-formal about a tulip—what was a flower without some sort of perfume? Harmen Gerritszoon agreed, and admitted self-consciously that it was because of the scent that he was particularly fond of hyacinths: he regretted that he had not smelled them this year, since stooping over made him a little giddy in the head.

"But that can be easily remedied," said the master, and he bent over before he could be stopped and snapped the largest of the spikes off close to the root. It was the one whose bells were tinged with purple, the Easter color, the color of death and resurrection. The sweetness, at once chaste and intoxicating, came to the miller as he took the flower from his visitor's hand.

And now that he had it, he allowed himself to enjoy it, inhaling its scent in long, deep breaths while Heer van Swanenburgh bade him good morning and good health and made his way toward the outbuilding over the little footbridge that spanned the narrow water. As he took in the poignant freshness, he was reminded of the Gospel text that he had mentioned to Heer van Swanenburgh, the one where the woman —had it really been Mary Magdalen?—had broken an alabaster box and poured the precious ointment on Jesus' head. A waste, the disciples had told her in indignation, a shameful waste, for the ointment might have been sold for much, and with the price of it the poor might have been fed . . . And the text came back to him as he breathed the smell of the sacrificed flower and wiped a trickle of its cold and colorless blood from his wrist: He who had never in His life taken anything for Himself had laid claim to this last fragrance—"For inasmuch as she hath poured this ointment on my body, she did it for my burial."

138

*

It was for his sister's sake that Rembrandt decided to do a little Madonna. The subject, Catholic as it was, had never had much appeal for him, and he could think of half a dozen others that would have lain closer to his sore and heavy heart. In a *Jesus Driving Out the Money Lenders* he could have given vent to the sense of outrage called up in him by my lord Huyghens' long silence and Jan Lievens' preferment. In a *Jacob Blessing His Children* he could have tried to embody some of the peace, at once somber and sublime, that sometimes came upon him when he sat on the stoop with his father, neither of them speaking or looking at each other, their faces lifted to the mild April sun. The family harmony—the sense of all wills and needs melting away before imminent loss—he had tried to get into sketches for a *Last Supper*, but it seemed pointless to begin working on anything that large when so much of his time was taken up with his duties at the mill. So, partly because he had to be painting something and partly because Lysbeth's wretchedness had lately begun to seem even deeper than his own, he asked her to sit with his manikin for a small and sunny *Mother and Child*.

He wondered that nobody else in the house had noticed the change in Lysbeth. Since the news of Lievens' going, her chatter had given way to silence: she worked like a beast on a treadmill, never stopping, seldom looking up; to everybody, including the poor oaf who was trying to woo her, she presented the same set face. There were days when she went to bed in much the same state as she had gotten out of it; she turned to her tasks as soon as her clothes were on, not bothering to wash her face and hands or comb her hair. It was only by convincing her that there would be no picture unless she put down her bucket and scrubbing brush and came out to the studio that he had wrested from her a faltering and resigned consent.

He had his troubles arranging a time for that sitting. He had to choose an afternoon when Lievens would be elsewhere, since it would be no rest for her to sit under his eyes; but fortunately he was busy these days with preparations for his going, and on a certain Monday it turned out that he would be off to Haarlem to get a trunk from his cousin. Piet Janszoon the brewer, one of Harmen Gerritszoon's steadiest customers, was arriving that day at four to pick up a load of malt, but Adriaen had promised to leave his shop and look after the mill. It was weeks since he had had an afternoon to himself to paint in, and he could do it with the better conscience because he would be doing his sister a service while he was about his own business.

When she came in at the appointed hour, he was touched to see how much trouble she had taken with herself. She had washed herself scrupulously and bound back her hair so that it would not interfere with

139

the coif and turban he had told her she would wear; and her face, un-softened by the usual frame of loose curls, looked austere and pale. She had decked herself out in a purple dress that she was wearing for the first time: though she had cut it out in February, she had not found leisure to finish it for the Easter festivities. He did not have the heart to cover it with the lengths of blue satin that he had laid out on the work-table; he consoled himself instead with the thought that the purple would set up a startling harmony with the orange tones of the piece of fox fur he had meant to lay under her feet. "How nice you look, Lys-beth," he said. "I think I'll do you just as you are, except for the coif and turban. And I'll not enthrone you, either"—it would be a mockery to enthrone her in her present state—"I'll set you on a low stool and drape the fox fur over your knees."

While she put on the headdress and came and took the pose, she had nothing to say but "Yes" and "No" to his casual talk, and he won-dered whether she was apprehensive lest he try to draw her out about Jan or Hendrik Isaakszoon. Nothing was further from his inten-tions, and he tried to let her know as much by chattering about mill business and house business. What he guessed concerning her and Lie-vens was more than he wanted to know, and though he could not have told her that he considered the carpenter's journeyman a suitable match for her, he did not want the responsibility of discrediting him, either— he supposed Hendrik Isaakszoon was better than nobody at all. He spread the dry and musky piece of fur over her lap and got the manikin, which little Dou had dressed for him in swaddling bands. "Here—he looks ridiculous, I know, but try not to laugh at him," he said, laying the doll across her knees.

But as soon as he had perched himself on a high stool, ready to make a sketch, he knew that something would have to be done about the pose: she was as lifeless as the manikin. "You've got to hold onto him," he said, speaking as he had learned to speak in these last sad weeks, with every taint of annoyance carefully drained out of his voice. "He looks as if he's going to tumble out of your lap. Put one hand un-der his head and the other one over his feet."

She did as she was bidden, but the pose was scarcely better for it. Her back was stiff; there was no connection between her and the man-ikin; and he had never seen anything more unconvincing than the obedient arrangement of her worn fingertips. "But hold him, you've got to hold him," he said, laughing nervously to cover his exasperation. "You've got to imagine you're his mother. Miserable creature though he is, he's supposed to be your child."

She did not move, except to raise her head a little. "I can't do it," she said. "You should have looked around for somebody else."

"Nonsense. You've held babies before."

"Not the way you want me to, I haven't. My friends' babies—I don't

140

hold them right, either. There's something wrong with me, I suppose —I just don't feel like a mother."

It was an appalling thing that she had said about herself, and he could not gainsay her. She was not interested in calves or nestlings or puppies; if a child tagged after her to market, she felt nothing but irritation. As he crumpled up the first stillborn sketch he thought how their parents were making a mistake if they believed that children would recompense her for dull years in the company of a fool. Men were what she cared for—showy ones like Jan Lievens, and unless it was such a one that had sown the seed it would be a meager draught that any infant would get at her breast. "Could you lean forward a little? Maybe if you just bent forward and looked at him . . ." he said.

She leaned forward, but not in the brooding, tender way he had envisioned. She bowed her back, simply bowed it, as if a weight of sacks had been laid on her shoulders. Her eyes, withdrawn from his—doubtless because he had refused to discuss her lack of motherly feelings—stared vacantly at the floor. And he did not want her angry; he wanted to give her some comfort, some assurance that she was needed, even if he was ruining one good piece of paper after another. "You know, Puss, I'm worried about you," he said, thinking how mournfully inappropriate the old nickname was now that her softness was gone.

"Worried about me? Why should you be worried?"

He could not say: Because you have been shamefully befooled and betrayed. He could not say: Because your beauty, such as it was, is worn away, and because the life you will live seems to me scarcely worth living. He said instead, staring with false preoccupation at his futile lines, "Because you're so tired, because you work so hard."

"Work so hard? That's a blessing. If I didn't work so hard, they'd probably have to lock me up. Take away my broom and my scrubbing brush, and I think I'd go out of my head."

"Because of Father?" It was an artful way of avoiding the issue, and a cruel one. Seeing a spasm twitch her white, loose face, he thought that she had perhaps loved her father even more dearly than he in her emptiness and her loneliness.

"Partly because of Father," she said flatly, "and partly because of other things. But let's not talk about it: there's nothing to be said about Father, and you don't want to hear about the rest."

"If there's anything I can do for you, Lysbeth, I certainly want to—"

"All right. Carry the slops out after supper. The pail's too heavy for me—my back cracks when I lift it."

"Of course. I'd be glad to. Remind me so I don't forget."

Even that limited kindness moved her to gratefulness; he felt with shame and remorse that she was looking at him with kind eyes. "Not that I want to burden you with extra duties," she said. "God knows, you've got enough."

141

He was relieved that he had extricated himself from the sordidness of her inner troubles without losing her good will, so relieved that he crumpled up another piece of paper without regret. "Let's see if I can rearrange you a bit," he said, and came cheerfully over to her and playfully prodded her knee and took her by the chin and changed the angle of her head. This time she gave herself to the position more naturally, and as he added line after line to his sketch, he felt again the old joy of deep absorption. And he could not understand why she should break the pose—it was less than ten minutes ago that the clocks of Leyden had chimed four o'clock—until he turned and saw that Adriaen, harried and abstracted and covered with the fine grey dust of the dried malt, was standing just inside the door. "I'm looking for sacks. Have you got any in here?" his brother said.

"No, not that I know of."

"But I thought you had. I was sure I saw van Vliet walking around with one of them tied around his neck."

"Oh, that must have been months ago."

"If I could just lay my hands on five or six—"

"We *did* take a few sometime early in the winter." It had never occurred to him that there could be anything wrong with commandeering some empty sacks, yet he felt a small shock of guilt when he encountered Adriaen's moist eyes. "I don't remember that we took more than four or five. Anyway, we tore them up and used them for paint rags. There's no use looking; the last of them is gone."

"Well, that's a pity. Somebody will have to go down to the shop and get some. I don't suppose Hendrik Isaakszoon will be here before supper, will he?" It was a muted reproach directed at Lysbeth: Adriaen felt, as their parents did, that so willing a laborer should be invited to sit down at table with the family every night.

"Not today. He was here yesterday, and he'll be here tomorrow. I need an evening now and again to mend my clothes and take a bath," she said.

"I only thought, from the way you were all dressed up, you must be expecting company."

"She put on the dress to sit for me. As soon as I'm finished drawing her, I'll go and buy the sacks and bring them over to you at the mill," Rembrandt said.

"And when are you expecting to finish?"

"At five, as I told you yesterday."

"But five's a bit late; I doubt that three will do. Piet Janszoon's here with his cart, and we're short five or six sacks to make up his load, and I can't exactly tell him to wait until you've finished your sketch. I'd go myself, but I'd have to wash up before I did—there's malt dust all over me, and I wouldn't want to run into my customers looking like this."

Rembrandt turned and laid his drawing down on the worktable behind him. "What I don't understand is why every little thing around here has to be turned into a crisis," he said. "Couldn't you see that the sacks were running out? You didn't have to wait until the last minute to tell me so."

"See?" He flung up his hands, and their downward fall struck two clouds of dust from his baggy breeches. "You're here all day, and I only came a couple of hours ago, and even at that I had to leave my shop like a shambles. You knew as well as I did that Piet Janszoon was due here. I should think you'd be the one to see."

"But he's been busy all day," said poor Lysbeth, instinctively crossing her forearms over the manikin to hide the ridiculous sort of thing he had been busy with. "He hardly ever has any time to work on his own things, and he was counting on this afternoon."

"And what about me?" said Adriaen, and it was frightening to hear him: no such voice had been lifted these last two months to rip their carefully woven peace. "I have a wife, but I never see her. Meals are cooked for me, but I haven't time or stomach to eat them. My journey-man cheats me, and my apprentices go home when they please, and there's nothing I can do to stop it. My business is going to the devil, but who cares about my business?—I have no business but the mill. It's two men's work on one man's shoulders, and I'm not an ox, it's gotten to be more than I can bear. And you stand there and ask me how it is I didn't notice that the sacks were running out. Good God, it seems to me that with nothing to do but paint from morning to night you could make yourself responsible for a little thing like that."

"From morning to night! I'd like to see the day. Before I ever set foot in this place I'm over at the mill to look after the malt-mash—the best hours of my day I waste picking out the bad sprouts. I set up my easel and Mother wants me to empty the washtub. I come back and get my palette ready, and Gerrit needs me to bring him his basin. I never have an hour to myself, I'm over at the mill as much as you are, and you seem to forget I've got apprentices too—"

"Your apprentices!" He laughed a short, derisive laugh. "Your apprentices are a couple of mangy dogs. I'd be ashamed to be seen with either of them in the street."

"Yet van Vliet would be good enough to send after your grain sacks if he happened to be around, wouldn't he?"

"Yes, I suppose he would, and it would be the only useful thing he'd ever do. Somebody's got to go for them, and soon."

"I told you I'd go for them as soon as I'm finished. And I won't be finished any sooner if you stand there shouting at me."

"Don't put yourself out; whenever you finish it'll be too late. I'll simply tell him that we haven't got the sacks—if it's all right with you, it's all right with me: he can get the rest of his load from somebody else. What's it to me what happens at the mill? Why should I concern myself if you don't care? Let them go, one customer after another, and never come back. That wasn't Father's way of doing things, but Father's not running the business any more, and God knows I can't be expected to run it alone."

His face worked crazily as he turned and went out, banging the door. To run after him, to beg to be permitted to do the errand now would be too much; yet to stay, to pick up paper and crayon and start to draw again was impossible.

"Don't you believe him," said Lysbeth, doing her best to resume the pose. "Piet Janszoon will come back. He won't break with us; he's been getting his malt from us for fifteen years."

But if the salt stinging in his eyes made a cloud between him and his sketch, it was not for the possible loss of Piet Janszoon's trade or even for the perfect record marred at the end of fifteen years of mutual satisfaction and trust. It was for the torn serenity that they had fashioned together with infinite tenderness for the sake of the dying one—the hateful will, the brutal assertion of self had come out at last and desecrated that pure peace. His father would not know they had quarreled: Adriaen was no talebearer, Adriaen would behave as though nothing had happened when he saw his father again. Yet something *had* happened, something that worked his own face and drove out his tears so that he had to wipe them away with the back of his hand.

"Don't cry," said Lysbeth, weeping herself. "It's only some sacks. What's there to cry about?"

Everything, everything . . . the flowerbeds in the back yard hoed and turned as straight and neat as the father had always kept them; the oil put into the creaking locks, the putty into the rattling windows, the nails into the sagging floor. Everything . . . the mornings when it was enough to know that the dear voice could still be lifted up, when the bread and the beer were blessed by the fact that he had outlived the night. All the peaceful afternoons when he had sat on the stoop, remembering or pondering, with his work-worn hands turned empty to the sun; and all the evenings when his children had sat together in the kitchen, so aching from their labors that merely to sit was enough.

"Would you rather I'd leave you by yourself?" said Lysbeth.

"No, no. I'll be able to draw in a minute. Don't change the pose, Puss, the pose is fine."

And, strangely, he was able to draw, able to get the drape of the cloth over the relaxed shoulders, the new and gentle curve of the wrist. There was no longer any use hurrying: Piet Janszoon's cart, minus its five or six sacks, had rattled past the window. What he was drawing, he thought, might well deserve to be turned into a life-size painting, a *Holy Family Resting on the Road to Egypt*. He would find somebody to sit for Joseph; he would take the whole thing out into the open under a great, dark tree—the purple of the dress and the tawny tones in the fur would go magnificently with the green. His cheeks were stiff where the tears had dried upon them, but his fingers were marvelously apt, marvelously free. And when the door opened behind him again, he finished the long curved line of the back before he raised his head: it would be Adriaen come back to apologize, and he would be able to deal with him more graciously if he finished what was under his hand.

But it was not Adriaen, it was his mother. The light was all behind her, and he could not see her face; he could see only that she was supporting herself against the door frame with one hand. "Is there something you wanted me to do for you, Mother?" he said.

"Go and tell Adriaen—"

There was that in her breathless utterance which made him wheel around and brought Lysbeth to her feet, so that the fur and the manikin tumbled to the floor. "What's wrong, Mother?" she said in a shrill voice. And she came with her arms held out, as if she meant to throw herself against her mother's breast.

But their mother let go of the door frame and extended both her hands before her to keep her daughter back: it was as if she had just come away from some ultimate embrace and did not wish to submit to any other touch. "He's gone," she said. "Somebody will have to go and tell Gerrit. I found him sitting in the kitchen, just sitting there with his head down on the table. He's dead—my Harmen's dead."

*

The dead had been laid in the grave, and half of the fine spring day, rich in blossoms and alive with bees, was over. The dank earth piled on the church floor had been shoveled in on top of the coffin, and the stone slab had been put—provisionally, because there would be some sinking—into place. Such human obligations as had been invented to keep the mind's ear from hearing the fall of the clods on the wood and the mind's eye from seeing the dead face locked in its eternal darkness had also been fulfilled according to custom. Neighbor and friend and old customer and pastor and doctor had eaten the fresh bread and the cold funeral meats and gone their way; aunt and granduncle and cousin had set out on the long way back to Zuytbroek, going across the dunes and along the blinding noonday brightness of the April sea. Now that the last plates were washed and the last leftovers wrapped and stored, there was nothing to do but sit in the parlor as if it had been a holiday or a Sunday afternoon. Only now there were six where there should have been seven, six knowing that the seventh was not only buried and mourned in the proper fashion, but also irretrievably gone beyond the reach of sight and touch.

There was no empty chair on which their wandering looks could come together. Harmen Gerritszoon had seldom sat down in the parlor; the place that manifested his non-being was the parchment map where the rivers and mountains of Africa had so often been hidden by the broad shoulders and the bald head. It was Adriaen who stood now, not

145

against the map but a little to one side of it, while the others sat stiffly, confined in their mourning clothes: Adriaen's Antje and his mother and Lysbeth and Gerrit and himself.

The window behind the old chest on which he sat opened on the small front garden where the leaves of the lindens still shone in their new gloss and the tulips seemed almost indecent with the flamboyance of their full-blown reds and yellows amid the droning of the bees. Adriaen's Antje, her pale brown hair severe in a net and her blunt nose and full eyelids red with crying, had opened this window and one in every other room, though what her purpose was—whether she was letting death out or entreating life to come back in—he did not know. She was a kind one, Adriaen's Antje; her small rough hand had wandered over and taken hold of Gerrit's. He had not wept at the funeral, and all of them had been waiting with apprehension for the time when he would break down and weep. By sitting beside him and taking his hand, she was warning her husband that some departure from strict decorum was only to be expected. Since Adriaen himself had shattered the resonant dignity of Pastor Appelman's "The Lord is my shepherd" with a gulping sob, he ought not to be embarrassed if Gerrit—whose grief had been hindered by the attention he had to pay to his crutches— should give way at last to a few quiet tears.

They ran down the hollow cheeks with surprising ease, almost as if he had made them well up to oblige Antje and relieve the tension of the others. He did not say what most of them were thinking: that his separation from the dead was bound to be brief, that the next time the diggers dislodged a slab in the church floor, it would probably be to make *his* grave. The mother took a fresh handkerchief out of her pocket and handed it to Lysbeth, who got up and took it over to Gerrit. He wiped his eyes and blew his nose without shame, and all of them sighed.

"He was a good man," said Antje. "It's a comfort to think that such a good man should have lived, if you know what I mean."

"Yes," said the mother in a quavering voice. And Rembrandt remembered that Hendrik Isaakszoon, in much the same words, had said the same thing before he had shaken hands all around and excused himself to go back to the carpenter's shop.

"God has received him, we can be certain of that," said Adriaen in a voice that was still somewhat hoarse with weeping.

"And it isn't as if he didn't have his rewards on earth," their mother said. "I've been thinking he didn't live as long as he might have, but before he went he had so many blessed things."

The remembrance of those blessings carried the threat of tears, and Antje, who had quietly been discharging most of the day's minor responsibilities, took it upon herself to turn their thoughts to other matters. "I never saw so many beautiful dishes brought in to a funeral meal," she said. "That egg and herring salad—the cousins must have spent hours to chop it so fine. And think of carrying it all the way from Zuyt-broek, too!"

"And the dozen fresh loaves from Hendrik Isaakszoon," said her husband, looking at Lysbeth, who made no answer.

"And the pickled beets and eggs from the Baerens family," said Gerrit. Since the Baerenses lived close enough to make short visits, he knew them better than the other guests.

"Yes," said the mother, "and so many things from the customers, too." Courtesies from the customers had always given her an innocent pride. "The Corneliszoons brought enough beer to last us a week, and there's all that gingerbread from the Blickers, not to mention Piet Janszoon's beautiful ham."

Adriaen moved closer to the map and folded his arms across his chest. "About the customers—we'd better be ready to take care of them before the end of the week," he said. "The way I see it, if there's any break in the supply they'll take their trade elsewhere, no matter how good their intentions toward us are."

The end of the week? As soon as that? thought Rembrandt. Today, for all its Sunday serenity, was really Wednesday, and if they were to be ready for customers by Friday, the terrible treadmill would be turning again by tomorrow; and he was so worn with waking and watching and the months of double labor that he did not see how he could lift a hand. This afternoon, which he had been seeing as a brief and blighted prelude to the repose that would come after—this afternoon and this evening were all the rest that he could expect.

"Couldn't you put it off for a week?" said Lysbeth. "It seems to me they might give us a week to get things started."

"You poor children certainly need it—all of you," said the mother.

With his moist eyes fixed on the ceiling Adriaen considered the proposal, but Rembrandt realized that it made little difference whether it was tomorrow or next Wednesday that he would be chained again, like a mute and helpless beast, to a life he could not bear. He had been able to endure these recent months only by telling himself that there would some day be an end to his labors, but all that had come to an end was the life of his father, all that had come to an end was his sole reason for beating down his spirit and dulling his brain; and the prospect was so appalling that he forgot himself. "Start tomorrow or start next week—it's all the same to me," he said with bitterness.

Gerrit's eyes, still wet with their effortless weeping, stared at him. "If this hadn't happened to me," he said, kicking at his crutches, "none of you would have to concern yourselves with the mill. Now I can't even help to divide the burden."

Adriaen shook his head. "Divide it ten ways and it would still be impossible. It's not the kind of work that can be divided. That's been the trouble all along," he said.

"But what else is to be done with it?" asked Lysbeth. "You surely aren't thinking of selling it. We can't—not while—" And the words she did not say hung over them: not while Mother lives.

"No, of course not," said her elder brother. "One of us"—he looked at the ceiling, not at Rembrandt—"will have to do what Father did: give all his time to the mill. If we're to keep it going—and we must, for Gerrit's sake as well as Mother's—one of us will have to give up everything else and take full responsibility."

Give up everything else? Give up the painting? Never, not if he had to break with them before the slab had settled on his father's grave, not if he made himself in their eyes, now and forever, an irresponsible dog. Yet he could not bring himself to speak his protest out; all he could do was tug helplessly, like a chidden ten-year-old, at the metal clasp on the chest.

"I don't imagine you'd want to do that, would you, Rembrandt?"

"No, I certainly wouldn't *want* to do it."

"I didn't think you would."

"I'm a painter, Adriaen; I can't give it up!" He had never felt so exposed, so vulnerable in his shame. He knew himself such a child that it seemed to him only just that his mother should plead his cause.

"Your father wouldn't have wanted you to either, Rembrandt. Your father meant you to be a painter," she said, and pressed her handkerchief against her mouth and began to weep.

"Ah, now, don't cry, Mother," said Antje, looking at her earnestly. "Adriaen didn't mean that Rembrandt *should* take over the mill. All he said was that he didn't think he wanted to—that's all you said, now, wasn't it, dear? Nobody expects any more from Rembrandt and Lysbeth than they've been doing right along. In fact, they should have it easier from now on."

"Yes," said her husband, "we talked it over last night, Antje and I, and there's only one thing to be done as far as we can see. I'll have to sell my cobbler's shop and come over here and take Father's place."

The wild wave of relief that surged up in Rembrandt's chest could not come to a crest; it was dissipated in a backwash of pity and regret. The cobbler's trade was not the art of painting, and Adriaen had gone into it only half-heartedly—he had really wanted to prepare for the ministry. But he had worked conscientiously in his shop and had finally come to draw from it no small measure of pride. Every new lathe and counter and bench, every new customer had been a source of gratification, another step in his hard, slow climb. So the thought of his trade and his tools passing into somebody else's hands was unbearably pathetic; and the pathos was the more painful since there was no release from it, no possibility of embracing and thanking this cold, self-righteous brother who was always self-sacrificing and whom he did not love.

"But you like your shop—you can't want to get rid of it," said Lysbeth, twisting her handkerchief. "When I think how hard you've worked to get it where it is—"

"Don't let it break your heart," he said almost hatefully. "I won't lose money. The business is in good condition; I'll get a good price."

"But it's not the money," said Gerrit. "It's all the years you—"

"The years weren't wasted. We made a living out of it while it lasted." He moved his shoulders in an angry shrug and hurried on. "I'll have to keep the shop going until I find a purchaser, but I have a good prospect, and I can come over here the first thing tomorrow morning and start to get the place in shape."

Only the mother offered something like sufficient thanks. "You're a good son, you've always been good, you're the last one to think about yourself," she said. "God knows, you've got my gratitude, and you would have had your father's."

But not their love, thought Rembrandt, not either of their loves . . .

Possibly it was the shock of just such a thought that made Adriaen draw himself up to his full height against the map, so that the rivers and mountains of Africa were lost behind his faintly grizzled hair. "I hope," he said in his preacherly voice, "that nobody considers it a lack of respect for our dear father that I'm trying to settle these affairs at once. It seems to me that he would have wanted them settled. He was a sensible man, he always wanted good order and just accounts—"

"Certainly, certainly, dear," the mother said.

"Then while we're all together, let's review the whole situation. Gerrit, we'll see that you're provided for, of course."

It was something beneath his much praised goodness, Rembrandt thought, that he should mention the provision for Gerrit. Gerrit would be taken care of for life by an annuity purchased for him a few months after his accident—and it was Harmen Gerritszoon, not Adriaen, who had paid for that annuity. The poor cripple himself seemed to be thinking as much; the sour line of scorn showed between his compressed lips, and he merely nodded.

"As for Lysbeth, I take it she'll soon be married—"

She dropped her handkerchief and bent down to get it. When she straightened, her face was as red as the raw hand with which she pushed back her hair.

"And once she is," he went on, fixing his look on her forehead, "I suppose Antje and I will come over here. We'd like to do that now; there's a lot that Antje could do for Mother and Gerrit, and I'd like to be closer to the mill. But the way things are at the moment, there won't be room—"

"Oh, heavens, Adriaen, I hope you're not making plans on *those* grounds," his sister said, and she let out a hysterical titter, affected and out of place.

"But you are expecting to be married, aren't you?"

"Hendrik Isaakszoon hasn't asked me, if that's what you mean."

"Naturally, he wouldn't have asked you. It shows a consideration on his part that ought to make him all the more acceptable. He sees you're

149

distracted; that's his only reason for biding his time. I'm sure he'll ask you as soon as it's decent—I believe two months is the usual period of mourning. About his devotion to you and your chance for happiness with him, nobody here can have any doubt."

But her father would not have spoken to her like that, thought Rembrandt. Her father, partial though he had been to the carpenter's journeyman, had confined himself to asking him often to sit down at table; though he had hoped for the marriage, he would never have demanded the marriage. "Talk to her about it later. She's in no frame of mind to talk about it now," he said.

But if he imagined he could protest like an equal, he was put promptly in his place. Adriaen's eyes regarded him coldly from beneath their drooping lids, his mouth tightened in an almost imperceptible smile. "All of us are upset, I understand," he said, "but upset or not we're obliged to get the important things clear, and how Lysbeth's to be provided for is one of the important things. Still, it'll probably be a good two months before Hendrik Isaakszoon brings the matter up again—"

"Yes," said Antje, turning a pleading look on her husband, "we can let it rest for the moment; there'll be plenty of time."

"Rembrandt, of course, will go on just the way he did before Harmen took sick," said the mother in a voice that quavered in spite of the determination in her wan and wrinkled face.

"Yes, that's the way I thought it would work out," said Adriaen. "I hope, though, he'll be finding himself more and better apprentices. I suppose it'll be all right for him to go on keeping shop in the outbuilding, though he'll have to take over full responsibility for the place."

"What responsibility?" He felt patronized and managed, and his pain and fury sounded in his voice.

"Things like repairs—if the roof began to leak, for instance—"

"It hasn't leaked in ten years. I don't see why it should start to leak now." He asserted it with chilly assurance, as if the haughtiness of his voice could save his lost position as the darling of the house.

"Well, I hope it won't. That sort of thing can set you back pretty far, especially if you aren't earning much."

"Oh, now," said his mother, "he's earning enough. Harmen and I never thought he'd be earning as much as he does at this point. Antje, dear, I feel a little faint. I wonder if you'd get me a sip of wine."

They stood around her while she drank, trying to act as if nothing had occurred to taint their sense of solidarity. Indulging themselves in the sorrowful pleasure of sharing their remembrances, they recalled how proud he had been of the way he had mended the sail on the windmill, how much he had enjoyed the roast lamb at Easter, how he had ridden with them to Zuytbroek last Christmas night. But Rembrandt, tormented by his shame and anger, could take no consolation in the exchanges, nor could he bring himself to add his portion to the store of recollections. After listening awhile in silence and constraint, he said he would step out and get a breath of air.

More than two hours had gone by since the sun had moved away from the zenith. There was no wind, and suspended all around him were the generative smells of roots and warmed earth and the perfume of blossoming things. He rested his back against a linden and looked at the frail blades of grass and the new dark leaves of the plantain weed, and suddenly it broke upon him that he had lost his shackles, and his heart was high with the release. Even though he had bought his liberation at the cost of shame, he could paint tomorrow and for the rest of his days, and the tears that trickled over his cheeks sprang alike from grief for his father and from joy—joy in spite of the disgrace—that they had set him free.

*

On the canal boat to Amsterdam he had read Uylenburgh's note a dozen times, though the writer had dashed it off so briefly that the re-readings had yielded him nothing more than he could tell at first sight. It said only that he should get to the art dealer's shop by three o'clock on May sixteenth because there was the possibility of an important commission, something so fine that neither a broken leg nor a death in the family should hold him back. Uylenburgh could not have known, of course, that there *had* been a death in the family; and Rembrandt hoped he would not be embarrassed to see the person to whom he had written so lightly turn up in mourning clothes.

From the moment he got out of the canal boat at the Leyden Gate and began to walk across the city, it seemed like a place he had never seen before. It was not only that there was a great deal of demolition and construction going on, so that the air kept sounding with the rasp of saws and the ring of hammers driving piles; some transmutation had also taken place in him since his last visit—long confinement had sharpened his senses and grief had given a peculiar keenness to his eyes. The streets he walked, slowly in spite of his impatience to learn what this important commission might be, were beautiful with their lordly gables and shimmering canals showing through the cloudy green of the new young leaves—so beautiful that he could feel them converging with the dreams he had entertained before he had lived miserably in Lastman's splendid house. Carts laden with flowers or hot loaves or the first garden greens rattled over the paving stones; talk and snatches of music floated from open windows; and his happiness—which he knew to be suspect because so many other promises had come to nothing—was nevertheless so strong that he had to keep reminding himself that his father was dead, that my lord Huyghens had forgotten him, and that he had a studio to work in only by the scornful sufferance of his brother Adriaen.

Uylenburgh was nowhere to be seen when he entered the shop, but he came down from his second-class treasures in the attic almost at once in answer to the jingling of the bell on the door. He was a Frieslander, not long enough in town to have completely lost his provincial look; and though he was elegantly slender and trimly dressed in grey woolen, there was something countrified about his white and pink complexion and his thick, close-cropped blond hair. His eyes, dark blue and candid, kindled at the sight of Rembrandt and then clouded at once at the black in which he was dressed. "Good God, what's happened? Your father? Oh, and that ridiculous note! But certainly you realized I knew nothing about it," he said.

Rembrandt covered the event briefly in a voice that was deliberately flat. His dealings with Uylenburgh had been amiable but not personal; the fact that they had shared a meal and a bedroom and some gossip did not guarantee that the dealer would wish to share his grief—that was not the way things went in Amsterdam. Besides, Uylenburgh, though he was an outlander, came from an excellent Friesian family. His uncle had been with the old Prince of Orange when the assassin's bullet had shot him down; his cousins were installed in distinguished pulpits and in chairs at two universities; and he bore himself with something of the van Hoorn false-familiar ease. Yet as he listened he came off his guard, possibly because he had compromised himself by his note, and his soft lips actually puckered. "You know, strange as it seems, I feel I knew your father just because I handled a couple of etchings you did of him. I suppose I must have hoped I'd meet him. I'm terribly sorry—accept my sincere condolences," he said.

Plainly he did not know how to broach the business of the commission. His sense of decency led him into such devious byways as Rembrandt's mother's health, the sudden heat, the Portuguese Jewish families that were moving into his part of town. "In fact," he said, "I was just going out to ask one of them to lend me a bottle; they're very neighborly and they stock wonderful wines. Dr. Tulp's coming, and I hope we'll be having something to celebrate." He looked at an ornate and unbeautiful clock, on sale at fifteen florins. "He ought to be here in less than half an hour."

"Dr. Tulp?" So it was the surgeon he had talked with at the van Hoorns' . . . He knew by his disappointment that the name he had been waiting to hear was that of Constantyn Huyghens.

"Yes, and I promised not to tell you anything until he gets here. I'd better go out for the wine now; if I stay around much longer I'll let it slip, and he asked me to wait until a few routine matters were settled. Anyway, I think he wants to tell you about it himself."

Therewith he went out, and his visitor vented his excitement by examining the inlaid hilt of an Oriental scimitar. Now that he knew Dr. Tulp was involved in the business, the visions of glory he had been harboring were tainted by recollections of Allaert's nameday party; he saw the falsely cordial faces in the reception hall, saw himself wandering alone among chattering groups in the salon, saw the master—how was it with him now?—and the master's icy eyes. What he had been then he still was: a crude Leydener with no relative in a university chair or a pulpit, his studio an old outbuilding and his apprentices a butt for jokes. He had changed only in a way that nobody at that party would have been concerned with—he was master of his brush, a wizard with light and shadow, and he had attained a spurious dominion, merely by painting what he yearned for, over a splendid world he would never really grasp; and in his confusion and his bitterness he avidly stroked the intricate hilt of the scimitar, feeling the inlaid bits of ebony and mother-of-pearl.

The bell on the door jingled him out of his meditations. It was not Uylenburgh—it was the doctor, changed by the intervening six years. He had only an instant to observe the hard, muscular figure in its dark brown clothes, the dry hair growing far down on the forehead, the expressive hands coming out of the starched cuffs. Then, amazingly, the newcomer descended upon him and closed him in a free and joyous embrace. "You're made, my lad," said the doctor, shoving him back a bit. "The world's in the palm of your hand."

It came out then, unbelievably, but with no doubts or drawbacks. He was to do what no artist of his age had ever done in Amsterdam— paint a Regents' piece, one of those big formal canvases that were the glory of the city, the sort of thing that had made the reputation of Nicolaas Elias and Thomas de Keyser, the sort of thing that would bring a horde of burghers to have their portraits done, to say nothing of the fact that it would pay handsomely in itself. The piece was to be done for the Surgeons' Guild and would hang in their meeting chamber. Yes, it was unusual for an unknown painter to pick up such a commission, and it had taken a bit of convincing: all they knew of the work of Rembrandt van Rijn was what they had seen in a few little things done years ago. But why should he, Dr. Tulp, pretend that the taste of his fellow-surgeons was as good as his? Being head of the Guild and in a position to impose his will in favor of something out of the ordinary, he had simply imposed it. Nobody was going to be sorry, either; now that they had taken the step, they were congratulating themselves on their daring and boasting that they were betting on a new name. "I hope you're not squeamish about dead bodies, because you're going to paint me in the act of dissecting while seven of my colleagues stand around and admire my talents. My face isn't much, I know, but an artist would have to go a long way to find a better pair of hands."

He held them into the sunlight, strong and ivory-white, the nails beautifully cared for; but it was hard for Rembrandt to think of them or of anything except that now he would be out of Adriaen's grasp.

"You know why these things pay so well, don't you?" said the doctor. "Everybody in the picture contributes his fee, and I've seen to it that there'll be no scrimping because you're new at the game. I'd like something more exciting than the usual piece. That *Anatomy Lesson of Doctor Egbertz,* the one Aert Pieterszoon did—it's all right, I suppose, but the doctors look deader than the corpse, and he's got too many faces turned in the same direction, too many ruffs, too many bald heads. You'll have more freedom because there'll be only eight of us, and none of us knows so much about it that he won't be willing to take your suggestions."

He broke off because Uylenburgh had come back. "Have you told him? Is it settled?" he asked, setting the borrowed bottle, veiled with cobwebs, among the objects on the counter.

"All settled," said the doctor, sitting down for the first time on one of the three-legged stools. "Go ahead with the formalities."

Rembrandt also sat down, though he wanted to be moving, pacing, gesticulating. He could not listen closely, even though it was his own glorious business that the other two were talking about, Uylenburgh assuming the role of agent and speaking of sums and contracts and time limits in a manner constrained enough to reveal his uncertainty—he had plainly never dealt with so splendid and complicated an affair before. "I'll raise your price at once, Rembrandt," he said, "and I'll want you to bring everything you have to the shop as soon as you can. When the news of this gets out, there'll be collectors here by the dozen, and we mustn't waste the opportunity. If you'd like a little money in advance, I'd be glad to let you have credit, say, for a thousand florins."

A thousand florins? The very enormity of it made him reject it. "No," he said, "but there's one thing I would like to have—that Oriental scimitar."

"Certainly. Consider it a gift—no, I mean it. This is a great day for me, too; after all, I'm the one who's selling your things. What have you got at home? How many finished canvases?"

Since he had been so fortunate, he felt obligated to deal honorably; he would not sell the *Balaam and the Angel* or the *Saint Peter in Prison.* "I'm working on a *Holy Family Resting on the Road to Egypt.* I ought to have it finished in a week or so."

"The sooner I have it the better. Not, of course, that I want to press you, considering your troubles—"

The doctor, who had been playing absently with Rembrandt's hat on the counter, started back from it, realizing for the first time that there was a mourning band around it. "My God, I didn't notice! Who was it that died?" he said. And the explanations and condolences were less embarrassing because he had said "died," had shown his willingness to deal with the fact of annihilation.

"Your father was a miller—eh?"

"Yes, a malt miller."

Uylenburgh bent down and straightened the buckle on his shoe.

"My father was a farmer," said the doctor. "He made plenty of money in his day, but he was never afraid to dirty his hands. Some of that money went into my schooling; your father must have done as much for you or you would never have gotten to Lastman. He'd be proud if he knew what was going on here today, God rest his soul!"

"God rest his soul!" said Uylenburgh softly, and a faint blush spread up to the line of his silky hair. In his capacity as agent, then, he brought up other matters while he served the wine. Rembrandt must share his quarters whenever he liked: a commission like this would necessitate long stays in Amsterdam. When the two months of mourning were over —traditions like that should be respected—he wanted to give a little supper for those who would be asking for an introduction to the new celebrity. The apprentices in Leyden shouldn't feel put out if their teacher skimped a little on his teaching time, considering the services he would be able to render them later, but it probably wouldn't be wise to sign them up for another year. This was the city for an eminent artist to live in, and the lads who wouldn't follow him eventually to Amsterdam would have to look for somebody else.

The city for an eminent artist to live in . . . When he had shaken hands and started back alone for the Leyden Gate, where he would eat cold beef and wait for the Leyden boat, he found that Uylenburgh's phrase kept running through his head. An eminent artist . . . His heart was so high that he wanted to catch a handful of glossy leaves from a low bough and stopped himself only because he recalled that he was in mourning. Instead, he took a small green leaf from a hedge and put it covertly in his mouth and chewed it, and found it at once bitter and sweet.

*

These days, with the father gone and Gerrit more and more often asking to have his supper brought upstairs, there were few enough of them to sit down in the kitchen for a reading from the Bible. Tonight it was his mother's turn to read, and there were only himself and Lysbeth to listen; and as she drew near the end of the passage he noticed how the June sunset tinted the page of the book rosy pink under her hand and gave the hand itself, as it followed the lines, a cast of red-tinged gold.

"For the Lord thy God bringeth thee into a good land, a land of brooks of water, of fountains and depths that spring out of valleys and hills; a land of wheat and barley, and vines, and fig trees, and pomegranates; a land of oil olive, and honey; a land wherein thou shalt eat bread without scarceness, thou shalt not lack any thing in it; a land whose stones are iron, and out of whose hills thou mayest dig brass. When thou hast eaten and art full, then thou shalt bless the Lord thy God for the good land which He hath given thee."

As she read, he realized that she had not stumbled upon the passage as she had pretended; she must have remembered it from some earlier reading and found it again today while she was in the house alone. It was her manner of saying to him: I know, whether you choose to tell me so or not, that you have set your mind on going. I will not bind you or make your remorse greater than it is. Go, and remember God and me in your new habitation, and prosper, and be blessed.

She closed the Bible and looked at him archly over the rims of her spectacles, proud of herself for finding so apt a passage, wanting his praise for that and for her unselfishness. He reached across the table and stroked her withered hand. "So you're bowing me out, Mother?" he said.

"I know you're going."

"I suppose I'll have to. The last time I was there, I got orders for three portraits, to say nothing of the sketches I still have to do for Dr. Tulp's Regents' piece."

"Yes, but you want to go, too," she said, giving him a playful rap across the fingers. "You really want to—tell yourself the truth."

He looked about him at the familiar dishes in the corner cupboard, at the kettle on the hook and the embers of the supper fire on the hearth, their pink radiance scarcely visible in a patch of sun. He looked also at the chair in which his father used to sit—none of them, not even Adriaen, had yet brought himself to sit down in that chair. "I want to, but you mustn't think I'm glad to. I hope you see the difference," he said.

"Oh, yes, I see the difference." She took off her spectacles, rubbed the bridge of her nose and looked at him slyly, like a flirting girl. When her grieving gave way to anything these days, it was to this pathetic skittishness; it was almost as if her husband's death had made her what she had been to him in the beginning, almost as if, in departing, he had set her back into her youth.

Lysbeth, sitting apart from them on the other side of the table, began to busy herself with the tinware. In front of her she had some knives she had been polishing until the instant the reading had begun, and as the big brass clasp was locked over the worn leather, her hand reached again for the polishing cloth. If Adriaen's coming to look after the mill had taken burdens from her, it certainly had given her no rest: she was forever running from the cellar to the attic, and even when she sat down her hands were never still.

"When do you expect to be going?" said his mother.

"A week—two weeks—I don't know. It will have to be soon."

"And where do you intend to live?"

"At Uylenburgh's place at first, I suppose. Van Vliet will be coming with me—" His sister gave him a surprised and reproachful look, a look that made him wonder whether she could possibly be remembering those old suggestions of Jan's that she go along as his housekeeper. He felt called upon to add that van Vliet would be helpful to him in his studio.

"And how do you mean to live?" his mother asked. "I mean, how does a single person eat and get his clothes washed and ironed and his buttons sewed on?"

"Uylenburgh does it. Thousands of young men in Amsterdam do it," he said, put out by a touch of malice in her bright little eyes—she *wanted* to see him in an ill-ironed shirt with missing buttons.

"What do they do? Hire somebody, some washerwoman?"

"That's what Uylenburgh does."

"But they're terribly hard on clothes, those washerwomen. Your shirts won't last a year with them, you'll see."

He thought it was no great matter how long his shirts held out: with things going as they were, he could buy as many shirts as he wanted. Yet, looking at her thin, dry fingers, he realized that it would be cruel to make light of the tasks she had done so long in his service. "Nothing will be done the way you and Lysbeth did it for me here. I don't expect to be taken care of like that ever again," he said.

There was a little clatter; his sister had dropped one of the knives on the floor. He reached under the table and picked it up for her, but she did not smile and thank him: she looked fixedly, imploring, into his face. "You're sure you wouldn't be better off with a housekeeper?" she said.

"A housekeeper? I'll be doing well, I trust, but not well enough to afford a full-time servant—"

"But suppose"—she tried to make her poor rough face arch and secretive and succeeded only in making it grotesque—"suppose you could have a full-time servant free? I mean, suppose it worked out the way we thought it would a long time ago. If I came with you, I'd do everything—I'd work hard, I'd earn my keep—"

"Lysbeth," said her mother sternly, "excuse me, but are you crazy?"

"No," she said almost in a whisper, "no, I believe I'm sane, though God knows why."

"Then how can you think of going to Amsterdam with him? You couldn't stay there long enough to make it worth his trouble. You'll be married by fall."

She dropped her polishing cloth and clutched the edge of the table. Her eyes, usually watery and vague, darkened and focused sharply on her mother's face. "*I* never said I'd be married in the fall. The rest of you said it, but I never did."

"If he hasn't asked you, it's only out of consideration. I'm sure he's going to—"

"Yes, Mother, and so am I, but that's not the point. There's still the little business of my telling him 'Yes,' and I'm not going to. Don't glare at me, it won't make any difference—"

"You mean you're not going to marry him, after everything he's done—"

"That's what I mean, Mother. I can't abide him, and I'm not tying myself up to what I can't abide, not if I have to stay single the rest of my days."

"But I thought you'd decided, I thought you were willing—"

"The only reason I was willing was to please Father."

"It would have pleased your father, dear—"

"Yes, I suppose so. Only, Father's dead."

With one impulse the two of them turned and looked at the chair standing empty. Then both of them began to weep, his mother meagerly and bitterly, her tears squeezed out of her closed eyes and her hands clasped before her on the board; Lysbeth wildly and with loud sobbing, her tears streaking swiftly over her cheeks, her clenched fists pressing into the hollow between her breasts. And he knew, staring wordless and helpless from one to the other, that it was not only their mutual loss that the two of them were mourning. His mother was weeping because her daughter did not love her and she did not love her daughter —this, more than the empty chair, prolonged the slow succession of her tears. And Lysbeth had given way at last to the fierce assault of self-pity: it was plain to her that they were willing to marry her to any dolt who asked her, that their only concern was to get her out from under their feet.

"I know Father was very fond of Hendrik," he said at last. "But he wouldn't have imposed his will on Lysbeth. He wouldn't have wanted her to marry anybody she wasn't fond of herself."

"That may be true," said the mother, "but I don't believe she knows what a risk she's taking. Anywhere—in Amsterdam or Leyden—it's a miserable thing to be a single woman. It's a sorry life to have no man, no house, no children, nothing you can call your own."

"Do you think I don't know that?" The pale eyes blazed anger at her. "I've had my taste of it already."

"Then shouldn't you take what the good God offers before it's too late?"

"Excuse me, Mother, but I can't see myself going to bed with what the good God offers."

His mother compressed her lips and decided to overlook the impiety. "That isn't everything. There are other things to marriage too," she said.

"But if that's missing, isn't everything else?"

"That depends on the woman. That depends on whether the woman can learn to chasten her rebellious heart."

He gazed at the sky, ruddy and flecked with bits of golden cloud, beyond the open window. Three months ago he had seen himself rejected, forgotten, destined to paint unknown forever, and he had not chastened *his* rebellious heart. "Who can say what's going to happen to her later? She doesn't have to take what she doesn't want. It isn't as if it's the only thing she'll ever get," he said.

"Will she be better off with you in Amsterdam?"

He started a little. He had not been aware that there were only those two alternatives: a life with Hendrik Isaakszoon or a life with him in Amsterdam. But if such was the case, there were advantages as well as drawbacks. He could see her in a dress trimmed with bands of sable—ermine would no longer suit her—welcoming his guests and slicing the chicken as thin as the master's Vincenzo had ever sliced it. Besides, with all the connections he would soon be making in Amsterdam, it was always possible that she would find a better match than Hendrik Isaakszoon. "She wouldn't be any worse off with me, I can say that much. At least she wouldn't lack company, and there would always be things for her to do and see," he said.

He had to think of spoiling her the way she had been spoiled in her early teens—of buying her lace collars, of bringing her chocolate and taking her to the theater—in order to lessen the assault of guilt he felt at her display of gratefulness. She got up, leaving the knives haphazard on the table as if she were about to depart with him at once; she came round to the back of his chair and laid her cheek against his—poor cheek, puffy and wet with tears. "God bless you, God bless you; you'll never be sorry, you'll see," she said, and kissed him on the top of his head and left the room, trying to stifle the strange sound, half sob, half laugh, that rose in her throat.

And now that she was gone it came upon him strangely, like a sudden failing of light—the light had indeed decreased; it had crimsoned, and there was a deep tinge of purple in it—it came upon him that he was leaving his mother, and he felt that imminent departure much more profoundly than when he had set out for the first time, scarcely looking back, hearing nothing but the singing in his own heart. It was not only because this time she was older and closer to death: she had always seemed old and frail to him, even when he was a child. It was probably—to use the words of the book that lay before her—because in the interim he had eaten of the Fruit of the Tree and had gotten knowledge of good and evil: knowledge that there was evil in every good, that the bitter seed waits at the core of the pomegranate, that the dead midge lies crystallized in the honey.

"I hate to leave you. You'll be lonely, with the two of us going."

"There'll still be Gerrit, and Adriaen and Antje will come. Don't worry yourself over me."

Gerrit, Adriaen, Antje: no doubt she had taught herself to mete out to them a just and sufficient measure of her love. She would look to their needs, give them little trouble, speak of them to the neighbors with pride. But the love abounding, the living water that rushed out of the rock, had sprung up out of the depths of her only for him and for his father; and he was going to another city, and his father was in the grave. "Maybe you shouldn't stay here," he said. "Maybe you ought to think of coming to live with me eventually. The way things look now, I can imagine a time when I'll buy a house in Amsterdam."

"Ask me before you do it, and I'll advise you against it. Houses in Amsterdam are for rich burghers and aristocrats, not for the likes of us," she said. "Besides"—she looked at the corner cupboard, which was her husband's handiwork, and laid the palm of her hand on the worn, nicked surface of the table—"I've lived in this house since the day I was married, and I wouldn't want to live anywhere else."

He put down a stinging urge to let her know that both Lastman and de Keyser had sumptuous Amsterdam houses, and thought instead of this room whose floor she had walked for so many years that the boards were worn silky smooth by her feet. He stared at her hand, open and passive on the battered wood, and knew it was only a consoling dream that he would some day call her to him: he, who could envision anything he liked so long as there was the blood of truth in it, could simply not conjure up a picture of her in a fine salon or strolling by a lordly canal or crossing a crowded street between hurrying carts.

"Then I'll come to see you often, Mother."

"Yes, you do that, Rembrandt. Come whenever you can."

He tried to imagine those homecomings, but that was only another effort to elude their mutual pain. And then all remedies receded and left the naked skeleton of truth: that his life in Leyden was over, that he was walking away from the ruins of it, that he was leaving her behind; and when her hand went out across the worn wood to comfort him, he let his face come down upon it and wept freely, without constraint, like a bereaved child.

BOOK IV

1632
-
1633

Lysbeth van Rijn—the old name, scrawled for identification in crayon on the miller's sacks, was taken here in Amsterdam to belong to some aristocratic if provincial family—took her key out of her pocket and opened to herself the little world on the Bloemgracht where she said and did and bought whatever she pleased. It was three o'clock in the afternoon; the trumpeter of the Old Church had just announced the fact by shrilling the tune of "The Earth Is the Lord's" into the icy February air. Nobody would be coming until half past three, and it would be up to her to decide what would go best with the raisin buns she had just bought: hot chocolate or wine flavored with cinnamon. She walked a little apprehensively up the dark stairs—since the first floor of the building was a warehouse stored with fodder, it was not unusual to encounter a mouse—and opened the door at the top into a big square parlor flooded with light. "Everything in order," she said aloud, for the pleasure of this new life was keen enough to call for expression even in solitude, and in the long hours when Rembrandt was at the New Market painting the corpse and the doctors, she had fallen into the habit of voicing her satisfaction in their new possessions—the great oak table, the red damask drapes, and the olive-green velvet cushions.

Behind the parlor were two bedrooms and the kitchen; and in back of these, stretching across the whole length of the building and getting the northwestern light through its broad casements, was the room where Rembrandt painted and taught. Having left her tippet and her velvet bonnet on her bed, she went into the studio and dusted the chair where her friend Margheretha would be sitting as Minerva—a cloaked, half-sorrowful figure with her head and shoulders slanting forward and her pale hands, slight and freckled, laid one over the other on an open, ancient book. Margheretha always washed her hair before a sitting; and it was lovely hair, though it was not, as some people said, the only really beautiful thing about her: it was silky and pale red like new copper, and soft and easy to curl over your finger like the hair of a child. Today it would show to full advantage; by the time Rembrandt got home from the New Market, the area around the chair would be drenched with sun. She blew at the top of Minerva's little round table—nothing there could be touched, not the globe nor the books and scrolls nor the folded scarf whose every loop and turn was right. Where could he find himself a housekeeper who would know his every need as well as she? Who would treat his antiquities and his palette and his brushes as they deserved—who except herself, and possibly Margheretha van Meer?

And wishing to be about some business that would be a compliment to Margheretha when she came, Lysbeth returned to the parlor and took from the writing desk a small book of English poetry and a Dutch prose translation of one of the poems, written for her a week ago on some sheets of letter paper by the delicately freckled hand. Margheretha knew Latin, English, French, and Swedish, and only her profound Protestant piety kept her from mastering Spanish and Italian. Margheretha was something that she had never encountered before—a learned woman; and when the noise of the evening parties had subsided and the beauties had grown frowzy and begun to yawn, Margheretha could be seen, erect and reposeful, talking gravely with a pastor about the works of Erasmus or with a doctor about the drawings in Vesalius. The poet she had translated was also Protestant and pious, though he used Italian titles like *L'Allegro* and *Il Penseroso*. With the book in one hand and the translation in the other she went and settled herself on the window seat among the velvet cushions and tried to capture what Margheretha called "the savor of the English."

> Hence, vain deluding joys,
>   The brood of folly without father bred,
> How little you bestead,
>   Or fill the fixed mind with all your toys.

She was not sure she was really finding it beautiful, though this time, her sixth time through it, she could mark the rhythms and hear the rhymes. Her real unstudied pleasure came from remembering the alien words as they had been uttered for her in the serene contralto voice. How much beauty was lodged in that slender throat encased in its simple white linen collar!—a collar patterned on those of the English Puritans. How much sympathy burned in that somewhat meager breast! And she, Lysbeth Harmensdochter—out of respect for simple collars and militant English divines she could almost have dropped the "van Rijn"—how fortunate she was to have found such a friend! It was almost enough to make up for the miserable portion she had gotten in love.

Having worked her way through the first page of the poem, she went into the kitchen, blew the fire up with the bellows, put the wine and cinnamon bark into the kettle, and arranged the buns on a fine new pewter dish. She was back in the parlor putting out plates and napkins when she heard the expected footfalls on the stair and went and opened the door. Margheretha did not run up the steps—she never ran—but she certainly made haste, taking her hand out of her woolen muff to show that she too was eager for touch. On the threshold between the dark landing and the bright parlor they embraced fully and tenderly, as if they had been apart for weeks instead of three days. The soft curls and the cool lips moved across Lysbeth's cheek; the eyes—large, blue, and perhaps too protrusive for ordinary taste but gaining thereby a wonderful brightness and frankness—looked earnestly into her eyes. "Am I too early, Lysbeth?" Margheretha said.

"You could never be too early." She took her guest's cloak—good but shabby, and the more admirable, the more singularly hers for its shabbiness—and laid it carefully over a chair. "Have you heard anything from your parents?"

"Yes, we finally had a letter. Nothing but dreary news, though it was just what I expected. They'll have to stay through the winter; they'll be lucky if they get home by spring."

"Poor Margheretha, with your grandaunt and your little sister and the house to look after!"

"Poor Mother, with that terrible winter getting into her bones!"

Margheretha's father, a former army officer expert in the building of fortresses and fosses, had been invited by a Swedish iron-maker to sink an ore shaft near Bergen at a salary that he could not bring himself in his poverty to refuse. With her parents gone the young woman was harried with household responsibilities, but she had also gained an unusual degree of freedom; Lysbeth doubted that she would have been sitting even for a Minerva—studious, spiritual, and muffled in a cloak—if her mother had been on hand. Not that there was any self-deception involved; she knew what models were and how her serving as a model would strike her family and the world. But, like Justice with the Scales, she had weighed the artist's need against foolish gossip, had made the proper decision, and had written a full account of her commitment to her family.

"Did they write anything about your posing?"

"No, nothing much. Only that they were sure I'd know how to conduct myself. I don't imagine, though, they knew how long it was going to take; they seemed to assume I'd be finished before I got their reply. I'm glad it didn't work out that way"—she crossed the room and sat down on the window seat—"I'm glad your brother's taking his time. I like to sit: I suppose it's a way of being silent and friendly at once. It's the only way I've ever found of meditating without being lonely."

For the first time Lysbeth wondered whether this honorable friend of hers could be telling the truth. Would she have sat for any painter who asked her merely for the pleasure of meditating without loneliness? Would she have agreed to pose for Rembrandt if there hadn't been something close to tender consideration in his approach to the quiet red-haired girl who had played the flute at Dr. Tulp's musical evening? And now that he had flung himself into the work, now that the one thing he seemed to want of her was to get her down in paint, why was she so ready to come? Was it only the delights of meditation that kept her sitting patient and uncomplaining through the wearing and almost wordless hours? "Well, whatever your reasons are, I'm glad you decided to do it, for Rembrandt's sake as well as mine," said

Lysbeth, sitting down beside her. "The way he paints with you is the way he used to paint back home, really giving himself to what he's doing, not bothering about the impression he's making. He isn't used to talking while he paints, the way he does with Cornelia Pronk."

"Who used to sit for him in Leyden?" The fact that she averted her glance, usually so ready and open, made Lysbeth wonder whether she was afraid some girlish face, fairer if less distinguished than hers, would look up at her if she ever dared to go through the stack of old canvases in the studio.

"Mostly the family. My mother, my father, my brothers, myself once or twice."

"No friends?" Perhaps to show that she was prepared and resigned, she smiled, and it was a beautiful smile, a slow increasing of light in the large, still eyes, a faint indentation growing at the corners of the lips.

"No, no friends. Sometimes van Vliet and Dou—you've seen van Vliet, and Dou was his other apprentice. Those old things back in the studio are mostly Biblical subjects, and even for them he usually used the family. Actually, Margheretha, the only friend he had back home was Lievens. They studied together for years, and now Jan's gone."

"Yes, your brother told me. It must be lonely for him, working by himself."

"It's even lonelier for me." She stared at her own hands, veiled and flattered by the lace cuffs that flowed over them but still ringless, still puffy at the knuckles and the wrists.

"Why? Were you very fond of Heer Lievens, Lysbeth?"

"Fond of him? I was in love with him." Amazingly, that revelation called forth no embarrassment but a look of unstinted and uncritical concern, a look so gratifying to her thirsty heart that she had to go on. "To tell the truth, I thought I'd die of it, I was so much in love with him."

"Ah, really?" It was no question; it was a protest against the depth of her sorrow, the vastness of her loss. The blue eyes continued to gaze at her, and she knew she did not wholly deserve their concern: her connection with Jan had been so sordid that Margheretha would have been shocked to hear the details; and besides, she had been brooding on him less and less since she had moved to Amsterdam. The freckled fingers reached out and touched her knee, and she was ashamed of herself.

"Well, anyway, it's over," she said. "I don't suppose I'll ever see him again, and it's probably better that way."

"But don't you even write each other letters?"

"What would be the good of it? Letters would only prolong our unhappiness. We agreed between us to part and forget." She had no idea why she was doing it, why she should be making herself and Jan Lievens a pair of figures in van Mander's *Bucolics*. And the worst of it was that

166

Margheretha took the tawdry stuff she was spinning out to be the simple truth.

"But what was the matter? Family objections, or something about money?"

"Money, naturally, though I can't say my family ever really approved."

"But now that he's got such a fine place at the English Court won't he—"

"Be sending for me? Scarcely!" She had a conviction that the best way out of the dilemma would be to say: "Forgive me—I made it up. He never cared for me; I was no more to him than any servant girl he caught up with on the back stairs." There was something in the grave presence beside her that made her believe she would be forgiven, but it was a promise she did not dare to trust. "Everything he earns at Court will have to go to his people," she said. "His father is a tapestry-maker, and he's hopelessly in debt. Jan ought to marry a girl with an inheritance, and, as handsome as he is, he probably will."

The thin hand patted her gently on the knee and withdrew, and she was appalled that the Devil should have furnished her with the clever-ness to slide out of the tight place, appalled too that she should have slandered the poor tapestry-maker who boasted that he had never owed anybody a penny. "Anyway, I really don't know why I'm going on about it like this," she said. "Since we've been in Amsterdam, I'm quite happy as I am. I love these rooms, and we have a very busy, cheerful kind of life, and I never dreamed I'd have a friend like you. My brother's the soul of generosity; I don't dare to admire anything in a shop for fear he'll buy it and bring it home for me." And in her relief at having extri-cated herself, she wanted her friend to be as happy as she. "In many ways he reminds me of you," she said. "He's so absorbed in his work, so devoted to the pursuit of more serious things that he hasn't the time for any nonsense like flirtations. Actually, Margheretha, believe it or not, in all the weeks we've been together I've never heard him mention the same young woman twice."

Margheretha said nothing, merely crossed her hands over the dark folds of her skirt and fetched up a small, suppressed sigh. But the ten-sion had gone out of the line of her spare shoulders, and the slow smile was growing again at the corners of her mouth, and Lysbeth wondered whether she hadn't been led into saying too much. What similarity was there, really, between this serene young woman and her tempestu-ous brother? And what assurance was to be had from the fact that he seldom mentioned the girls he was plainly impelled to stare at? "Of course, he never did do much talking about his own affairs," she said.

But this effort at rectification did not make up for what had gone before it. She looked at the book and the sheets of letter paper and wished that she and Margheretha had spent the time reading another poem; the aromatic smell of the wine and the bubbling of the kettle made her realize how far the occasion had fallen short of what she had hoped it would be. The afternoon had been manipulated too much: like a piece of fruit, it had lost its perishable bloom, and she found herself burdened with the talk, merely putting in the time until Rembrandt would come home.

*

That afternoon, for the first time since he was back in Amsterdam, he had no desire to go home and work in his studio, though the *Minerva* was being painted wholly out of the happy impulse of his heart. Today there was no such impulse, and on the outskirts of his neighborhood he thought of turning off—to the devil with the sitting!—and going to the Barrel Tavern, where van Vliet and the new apprentices, Flinck and Bol, would be drinking with others of their kind. There, after three or four mugs of beer or a beaker of something stronger, he might be able to shake off the heavy thoughts that had been disturbing him for the last three hours. But Lysbeth would be worried, and Margheretha would be pained—there was no help for it, he would have to go home.

It had never occurred to him that he would be upset by working from a corpse. A week ago, when Dr. Tulp's servingman had dropped in to announce that the corpse had finally been delivered, he had felt nothing but a fierce excitement, a veritable intellectual passion for exploring the inner recesses of the temple of the body, for seeing the veins and muscles and bones. About the possible smells he had been a little apprehensive: he had a poor stomach even for the smells that came up from the butcher's market under the dissecting room, smells of blood and hacked and portioned flesh of hogs and oxen and sheep. But he had been assured that vinegar would be poured and herbs would be burned to drown out the offense, and he had told himself he had no right to a more delicate nose than de Keyser or Mierveldt or Aert Pieterszoon, all of whom had painted dissections in equally fetid air.

The doctors kept letting him know how lucky he was to have a corpse to paint, and that had been the first thing to disturb him—the thought that another man's hanging should be his own good luck. Corpses were rare; the only bodies that the Medical Guilds could legally claim were the bodies of executed criminals, and sometimes a whole year would come and go without an execution. Adriaen Adriaenszoon, known in criminal records as "The Child," had had a magnificent body; even now, laid out on the dissecting table, it emanated power. The flatness of the belly, the high arch of the ribs, the firm pillar of the throat still flaunted the insolent manliness that had kept him flinging himself in the face of the Law, performing one outrage after another, determined to outdo his predecessors and the Devil and himself. The arrogant smile that had exasperated burgomasters and sheriffs at his trial still drew up his lip and showed the white gleam of his teeth. His body—pull it this way, shove it that way, cut it, paint it, curse it for its smell—still mocked its users: it asserted through its half-closed eyes that nothing they did could make it care.

There had been times when he had been able to see it simply as an object for painting—a pale wedge cleaving the somber oblong surrounding it, a slant of light at the center of dark, a fearful thing to catch and hold the eyes before they traveled to the faces clustered above it. But today had not been one of those days; today he had kept asking himself how The Child had looked in his actual childhood, what mother and father and rooms he had known, what never-to-be-duplicated world had been quenched in his brain when the hangman's rope had finished him. Though he had managed to paint the dissected arm beautifully, getting just the right red-brown into the muscles and the blood to pick up the reddish tone of Dr. Tulp's sock, he had been tormentingly aware of the crafty eyes, the contemptuous and ineradicable smile.

Then, too, the doctors had fallen into a grim kind of joking that had only increased his morbidity. Dr. Hartmanszoon had begun it by teasing him about how much time he was taking, holding them there while the well got sick and the sick got worse and the serious cases died. Dr. Kolkoen had urged him to make haste and get his sitters down while they were there for the getting—back at the beginning of the century Aert Pieterszoon had had a terrible time completing his *Anatomy Lesson of Doctor Egbertz;* most of the doctors were too busy with the plague to be able to sit, and some of the original subscribers had gone to their graves without paying their fees. "Behold," Dr. van Loenen had said, holding up his hands in mockery of the preachers, "all medical flesh is as the grass." And perhaps because the smells, the ones from the corpse and the ones from the meat market, seemed actually to becloud and obfuscate the air around the group, he had seen all of them, the living as well as the dead, as precariously stable entities constantly assailed by decay, holding off by inexplicable forces the destruction that was always encroaching upon them.

To come from such a situation directly to the painting of the *Minerva* would have been possible, he supposed, by a sheer act of will. But he was not to be permitted to take a clean plunge from the one into the other. There would be—he remembered it with annoyance just as he sighted the windows of his studio, golden with the warmthless winter sunlight—the social half-hour made necessary by the fact that his model was not a model. There would be Margheretha and Lysbeth and talk and an afternoon spread when he wanted nobody and no conversation and nothing to eat. And before he could bring himself to go up the stairs he stopped in front of the great iron gate between the warehouse and the canal, and breaking off a long icicle from the grillework, sucked on it as if he could find something purifying in the wetness and the cold.

But up there in the parlor things were not as trying as he had expected: the spread table, lighted by a single early candle, was innocent of meat; the buns were as inoffensive as communion bread, and the cinnamon bark gave a cleansing bite to the wine. Though Margheretha, with her shy, scared ways and her tight little collar and her carefully thought-out sentences, was nobody to put a person into high spirits, he found her company unobjectionable. The talk, mostly about Mierveldt's *Anatomy Lesson,* which she had seen in Delft, was quiet and intelligent—she always put a welcome restraint on Lysbeth's tendency to talk too much. And to his own sick mood there was something pleasurable even in the sight of her, just as to a sick stomach, which finds French brandy abhorrent, there is something gratifying about a cup of herb tea.

No time was lost in the trivial talk that often accompanied their settling down to work; Lysbeth stayed behind in the parlor and Margheretha assumed the pose so exactly that it was as if she had never left it. Yet there was some difference, either in the model or in his own vision: Minerva—or Margheretha—seemed to emanate more compassion, more dignity than on other afternoons. Her face, not really beautiful and shadowed heavily since it was turned away from the sunlight, conveyed a tender melancholy that did not jar with his mood; and he saw again in the slope of her slight shoulders the touching suggestion of mastered weariness that had made him watch her that evening at Dr. Tulp's when she had played the flute. So, once he had laid another layer of paint over the still-moist brightness of her curls, he felt impelled to break their unspoken compact of silence. "Is anything the matter? You look a little sad today," he said.

"Sad? No, I'm not sad." Unlike his other sitters, who used every pretext to break the pose, she moved nothing but her pale, small lips. "If anything, I suppose I'm slightly worried."

He waited to get down a soft line of light on the cloak before he asked her, "What about?"

"My mother and father—my father mostly. I had a letter from him a couple of days ago, and there was something about the handwriting that made me realize he's getting old. Forty-eight isn't old, not really, and yet it's too old for certain things—"

"Like what?" he said, knowing that she had trailed off because she was afraid of interfering with his work.

"Like making new friends in Sweden. Like going back into the army when he comes home. Like looking around for other iron forgers who want shafts. Like going down to see how the digging is coming along, into the damp and the dark and the cold under the ground—"

He thought how everybody must do that eventually, and the stroke he made was too broad, so that he had to scrape it off with his palette knife. "But he won't have to be doing anything for a long time now, will he? Lysbeth tells me he'll bring home a nice sum of money for this."

"Oh, a nice sum of money!" Her frail hands, laid one over the other on the ancient book, made a gesture of disparagement and immediately rearranged themselves. "Not that I'm not grateful to God for it. But no sum of money is ever as large as it looks, and he says himself a good third of it will dwindle away before he gets home. Here we've learned the tricks of living on next to nothing, but in a foreign city the same tricks won't work. And even if he could save more of it, no sum of money lasts forever, you know."

It was a bitter thought, and he could not gainsay it: the greater part of the advance payment on *The Anatomy Lesson* was already gone. True, they lived better than need be, he and Lysbeth; but there were only two of them, and the army officer had five to feed and owned an old house that was hard to heat in the cruel winters and was constantly needing repairs. He himself would already have run into debt if Uylenburgh hadn't gotten him so many portrait commissions; and even as it was, there were months when he had to tell his sister to hide the money for the rent, for fear he would spend it on some canvas of Seghers' or Brouwer's.

"The worst of it is that my father has nobody to help him," she said. "The rest of us are women: my mother, my grandaunt—we don't dare to let her cook any more when she's alone, we're so afraid she'll set herself on fire—and my little sister and myself. I know French and Swedish and English and Latin, and I really know them very well"—she reported it simply and without pride—"and I was wondering if a woman could give lessons. Not to men, of course—they'd never want me—but to young ladies and children."

The nature of that life—its proud and respectable shabbiness, its wan cheerfulness, its sorrowful loyalties—gave rise to a thought that held him static in front of the painting. Womanly weak and diffident as she was, she was more steadfast than he. When the life in Leyden had begun to crumble, he had had only one overmastering desire: to flee the ruin and save himself. But she would never take flight; she would teach and sew and scrub and study between times and watch that the grandaunt's skirt stayed out of the fire, and he felt a strange, unsettling confusion of pity and admiration. "Why shouldn't a man study with you? If I had time to learn a language, I'm sure I couldn't find a better teacher," he said.

She could not suppress her smile. "That's very kind of you, but that would be something different; I'd never let you pay."

"Why not?"

"Because you're my friend—at least I like to think you're my friend—"

"Of course I'm your friend." He remembered with regret occasions when he had been behindhand with his friendship: he had not invited her to go with them on their little trip to Haarlem, and he had quite forgotten her when he wrote down the names of the guests for his last party—it was Lysbeth who had added her to the list. "I've never seen your father," he said, getting to work again. "What is he like?"

"Oh, he's a thin man, still very straight in spite of his age. His hair used to be the same color as mine, but now it's mostly white. There are deep wrinkles around his mouth, but he still looks kind somehow. And your father—I commend his spirit to the living God—what was he like?" she said.

Her eyes, downcast and fixed on the book, got more from him than would have been possible if they had been turned, blue and too prominent, full on his face. "He was an unlettered man, simple, a malt miller in Leyden. The 'van Rijn' in his name—he added that just so there wouldn't be any confusion about where his malt sacks came from," he said. "He lived through the siege, and that toughened him and made him grateful for life itself. To me he was more generous than I deserved."

"So is God to all of us." She said it mildly, as a thing taken for granted: there was no taint of cant in her piety. "Did he look at all like you?"

"No, not a bit. Wait a minute." He put down his brush and his palette and went to the big cupboard and took out of a folio a mounted drawing which he had made of his father just a few days after their quarrel over his going to Lastman. It was an excellent likeness made in red and black chalk washed over with diluted ink, detailed but very animated and free; and recently some impulse had made him clip the edges of it neatly and draw a sort of frame around it and write at the bottom of it, in ink, his father's name. He carried the drawing over to her, remembering how the setting down of that framing line and the name had given him a reasonless happiness, as if he had been undoing his father's mortality. "Here, this is what he looked like, almost exactly," he said, standing behind her and slipping the sketch between the page and her thin hand. The air around her had a certain fresh fragrance, which rose, he supposed, from her new-washed hair.

"He looks like a good man, and a loving one. You must miss him very much," she said.

He went back to his easel, leaving the sketch under her hand and liking to have it there, and began to work on the fur lining of the cloak. "Not as much as I used to back home," he said, wanting to maintain their mutual honesty. "Back home I was always seeing places where I expected him to be and he wasn't: a certain place in the parlor where he used to stand, the flowerbed out in the garden, his kitchen chair. I did a painting of him afterwards, from memory—"

"I'd like to see it."

"No, it's not as real as that drawing. The likeness is good enough, better than I imagined I could make it. But there's something about the eyes—they won't look at you, they're flat, I guess they're dead." He mixed a patch of creamy white, meaning to lighten the page under her fingers. "I suppose we can't hold onto the dead," he said. "I suppose we have to accept the fact that they're gone."

"Oh, do you think so? Well, maybe that's because your work concerns itself so much with bodies, and bodies *are* impermanent, more so even than the images of them you put in your paintings. I suppose if I painted them all day long I'd forget too that they're only the vessels made to hold the essence. But the love they felt for us while they lived —that's part of the essence and can't be taken away with the flesh."

He was grateful that the words had flowed out of her with no motion but the motion of her lips. "And you—have you ever lost anybody close to you?" he said.

"Oh, yes, three times. Two infant sisters and a seven-year-old brother. The babies were so little that they never quite got defined for me; after the second one died, I couldn't remember them separately— it was as if they had become one soul. But it was different with my brother. He had fine, soft hair, and a blue vein that ran across his temple, and very large eyes, and, by the grace of God, nothing of him was taken away from me by his death and his burial—when I walked up the stairs at bedtime I could actually feel him putting his hand into mine."

"But you saw him in the body, didn't you? You saw his eyes, and that vein, and you felt his hand—"

"Yes, you're right, of course. We're in the flesh, and our knowledge is fleshly, no matter how we strive after something purer and more free. I was thinking about that the other night when I was reading Augustine. He tried to conceive of God as pure spirit, and yet he calls on Him to take him by the hand, to breathe upon him, to reveal Himself to him face to face."

He stood immobilized with his brush held up, partly because of the naked intensity of her self-revelation and partly because she seemed inexplicably beautiful with tears standing in her prominent eyes and an innocent smile, half-shamed, half-tender, deepening the corners of her pale lips. No words came to him in answer to hers; nothing would come except a cloudy vision of painted figures, neither flesh nor spirit, hovering between light and dark, essence and body, life and death. He made a movement with the hand that held the palette to indicate his regret for his own inarticulate tongue, and she blinked and shaped her mouth into a more daily smile. "But I'm keeping you from your painting," she said.

"No, not in the least. I was only thinking, you manage to be on better terms with death than I do—"

"Not such good terms, believe me, that I'm not afraid of it—not so much for myself, more for others—" The words trailed off, and she settled back into silence. He was at work now on the intricate folds of cloth over her bosom, trying to shadow forth without exactly revealing the shape of her meager and somewhat childish breasts. But he could not help seeing those breasts in his mind's eye as he suggested them in paint, could not help wondering whether the nipples were pale or dark, whether the flesh was crossed by branching veins, whether the mounds would be cool or warm to the seeking lips. And after that how could he keep from envisioning her in her nakedness? That vision yielded him neither pleasure nor excitement; all assertive impulses were cut off by the guilty sense that he was taking advantage of her in some shameless way, as he had done on that evening when he had climbed up to the kitchen window to look at Lysbeth taking her bath. But why should he accuse himself? The young woman sitting before him was not his sister, and he himself was no longer a child. Was it any fault of his if the wholesome stirrings of the flesh seemed crude and incongruous beside her sensibility? Perhaps there was even something spurious about a spirituality that forced a man to feel ashamed of his powers? "I never read Augustine," he said in a voice that struck him as cold. "But then I almost never read anything except the Bible. I don't believe I've read a book since I left the university."

"Why should you? You're a painter, not a scholar. If I could paint, I suppose I wouldn't read much either. But you'd better get back to your work—I've been distracting you; we'd better not talk any more."

He left the breasts and returned to the cuffs and the collar. He had no desire for further conversation; he was thinking of the girls on Pieter-Jacob Street, the prostitutes. Back in the dissecting chamber, while he was working at the calloused soles of the corpse's feet, it had seemed to him that the only way of breaking out of the oppressive sense of death would be to let his flesh assert its own fierce life, to get himself a girl for the night. But that, it was plain to him now, would be only a temporary cure: death or the living likeness of it would be bound to settle in again —the inevitable alienation, the heavy-hearted self-disgust. If the high-mindedness that excluded the flesh was an equivocal business, the flesh without the spirit was equally so. To take a body without tenderness or compassion—he had guessed it while he stared at the insensate thing that had been The Child—would intensify rather than relieve his sense of mortality. He sighed and laid down the palette and brush and kneaded his suddenly stiff right hand.

"Shall we stop? Are you tired?"

It was strange that she should have been the one to ask the question. Usually the model was shifting and sighing and covertly scratching long before he felt any tension in his fingers, and Margheretha had scarcely stirred since she had taken her place. "Yes, I suppose we'd better stop. I worked a long time today at the New Market."

"How is it going?"

"Very well."

"And when do you want me to sit again? Next Wednesday as usual?"

But on Wednesday Dr. de Witte was giving a little supper party to celebrate the fact that his portrait was the first in the group to be fin-ished. He had commandeered the big room at the Barrel and had told

Rembrandt to bring his sister and his apprentices and anybody else he pleased. For an instant, watching her stand up and drag her hand across the back of her strained and weary neck, he thought of asking *her:* though she was never really merry at a party, she was never a burden either, and he knew that her pleasures must be few.

"No, I'm afraid it can't be Wednesday. We'll be with Dr. de Witte on Wednesday, unfortunately." To offer her an invitation seemed somewhat too pointed now; besides, he did not want the responsibility for making certain that she was not slighted or forgotten among his more raucous companions. "I suppose we'll have to make it Thursday or Friday. Either day would do for me."

"It'll have to be Friday. Thursday I take my sister for her clavier lesson."

"Oh, yes, I forgot about that." A faint annoyance, thoroughly unjustifiable, stirred in him as he thought of the multiplicity and dullness of her obligations. "Friday will do, of course. It's very good of you."

She stepped away from the little table into the sunlight, but he could not shake hands with her because there was paint on his fingers, and he did not follow her back into the parlor since he was in no state of mind to take part in another round of chatter with her and Lysbeth. He stayed where he was, cleaning his brushes, while the two of them exchanged a few words and had another sip of wine; but he was sorry to hear her bid his sister good-bye and felt a sense of loss at the sound of the closing of the door.

*

Lysbeth turned away from the parlor window, where she had been watching the naked poplars blown this way and that in the erratic March gusts, and listened to what was going on in the studio. "I told you to simplify it," said her brother's voice, with the prickle of exasperation in it, "but simplifying doesn't mean vulgarizing, you know."

Van Vliet was the one he was talking to, of course. He would never take such a tone with Bol or Flinck, both of whom, if you compared them with the poor ape from Leyden, were gentlemen. His patience with van Vliet, like certain of his other admirable qualities, was wearing thin these days. He squandered his earnings, skimped his teaching time, broke his appointments, and had actually left a note under Margheretha's door after twelve last night to tell her she needn't come to sit this afternoon. And the lecture he was giving at the moment on the virtues of simplicity would have been more impressive if his sister hadn't been able to imagine how he looked—he in his mouse-colored velvet jacket and his Flemish lace collar, he with his pearl dangling from his ear and his silver medallion on his chest, *he* talking about simplicity!

And the only reason he had gotten himself up like that—and canceled Margheretha's sitting—was that he was expecting a visit from

Uylenburgh. Uylenburgh and some Frieslander cousin of his, some pampered doll named Briskia or something equally affected, were doing him the honor of dropping in at about two this afternoon. The cousin, who had come into town yesterday after dark, could not be expected to make calls in the morning; her delicate constitution would be shattered by the rigors of the coach, and it would be noon before she could be roused out of her beauty sleep. So Margheretha had to be warned off, and the parlor had to be put into impeccable order, and oranges and gingerbread had to be bought, and she herself must put on her dress with the sable bands as if they were receiving the Queen of Portugal. Not that she objected to the extra work: if the cousin had belonged to Dr. Tulp or kind, chubby Master Coppenol, she would have gone about the preparations with a high heart. But Uylenburgh she had never cared for, not from the start—or very nearly from the start.

"I have no more yellow ocher," said Ferdinand Bol. "May I take a little from your palette, Master?"

"No, not now. We'll be stopping in fifteen minutes. I'm expecting guests."

Uylenburgh—a fine guest, a really significant reason for sending the apprentices away early! A pretentious fool who washed his hair in lemon water and polished his nails with powdered pumice! If she had been taken in by him last Christmas it was only because he had made such an elaborate pretense of having a special interest in her, taking her to the theater and bringing her presents now and then. But all you had to do was squeeze his hand once, and he never greeted you again without a frozen face, he was so afraid of getting involved. He knew how to look out for himself, too: the moment he heard that Burgomaster van Pellicorne had laid down an advance payment on a double portrait, he had come asking for a loan of a thousand florins—a preposterous amount, and there was no telling whether he would ever pay it back. He rode on Rembrandt's shoulders more shamelessly than Jan Lievens ever had, and with less right: Jan at least had talent, and this one had nothing but a few eminent relatives to boast about.

On the writing desk behind the tall chair lay the letter from Leyden; when she had cleaned up the parlor she had left it out deliberately, as a kind of reproach, to decrease her brother's pleasure in his visitors. Antje had written it because their mother's hand was too stiff and Adriaen was too wildly busy and Gerrit was too sick, but even through Antje's well-intentioned sentences it was easy to see how ill things were going at home. The malt wasn't what it had been in their father's day, and some of the customers had dropped off—not many, only three or four. Gerrit was abed almost always now; something in his back had slipped, and he seldom tried to walk any more. Mother at least was as sound as a board, and said there was no reason to worry, and sent her love . . . It was a sad letter; she had wept when Rembrandt read it aloud to her, and merely looking at the folded sheets now she felt her eyes fill with tears. Crotchety as Adriaen was, he could have put a thousand florins to better use than Hendrik Uylenburgh, who still managed to give little suppers with imported wine almost every week; and it seemed to her that she would be showing gross disloyalty to her family as well as to her friend Margheretha if she made a great to-do over the guests. Aloofness and icy politeness were what the occasion called for, and she sat erect on the window seat and passed her hand over her hair to make sure that no curl had slipped out of place. When Flinck and van Vliet and Bol came through the parlor on the way out, she could barely bring herself to exchange the civilities.

But she was nervous when the company came up the stairs, diffident and incapable during the flurry of greetings and introductions; and before they had gotten themselves seated in the tall chairs that Rembrandt gallantly set out for them she hated herself for behaving with downright obsequiousness. A person had to admit that the cousin—her name was really Saskia—was not the usual provincial belle. The bovine qualities that Lysbeth had endowed her with beforehand, probably because Friesland was noted for its butter and cheese, were simply not there. Her figure, in spite of its fullness, was somehow slight and elegant: the breasts and hips were womanly rather than plump, and the waistline, girdled by a belt of gilded leather, could easily have been circled by two large hands. The little head above the appealing body was round like a cherub's and framed in short, abundant, honey-colored curls; and the mouth, the wide dark eyes, and the small blunt nose were marked, like a cherub's, with innocent sauciness. But she was not so artless that she hadn't calculated the most becoming way of holding that precious head: she held it up and a little to one side, to show the round and creamy neck to advantage and to set off what would later be a fault but was a charm at the moment—the slightest suggestion of a double chin. There was a sparkle about her, not only in her rings and bracelets and in the chains and brooches that ornamented the deep emerald velvet of her dress, but also in her hair, her eyes, her teeth, and the constant play of her small moist lips.

It was to Rembrandt that she addressed herself as soon as she had settled down, though she had been demonstrative enough to break down his sister's reserve before she turned her attention in a more interesting direction. Sitting in the tall chair, which seemed all the taller because part of its carved back was showing above her shining head, she comported herself with an ease and a merriment that dispelled all stress and made Lysbeth feel hopelessly big in body and dull in brain. "I hope you'll forgive me if I'm chattering too much," she said, shaking her jingling bracelets back over the soft curve of her arm. "It's just that I feel so free—I start to feel like that ten miles outside of Amsterdam, and it never really leaves me until I wake up in Leeuwarden to my stupid life in my own stupid bed. I swear, the air is different here; ours smells all the time of sour milk. And the things that Hendrik's arranged for me

177

to do"—she bent forward and laid her dimpled hand on her cousin's knee—"the supper parties and the concerts and the plays! If I were back home, do you know what I'd be doing night after night? Playing backgammon with my sisters or sitting in church and maybe going to a dance once in a month—and a fine sort of dance it would be, with all the fiddlers out of tune and somebody sure to tread on my feet."

They all looked at her feet, of course—very small and deliciously plump, the insteps rising firm and full in pretty red stockings out of the neat green velvet shoes; and Lysbeth could not help thinking of Margheretha's feet, narrow and decent in their sturdy black leather slippers and well-darned black stockings, and it was enough to make her want to weep. That life in Friesland—opulent enough to pad the little bones with luscious flesh, rich enough to deck her out in gold and jewels and shockingly expensive cloth—what Margheretha would have made of such a life, even if it smelled of sour milk!

Rembrandt crossed the room and sat down beside her on the window seat, not out of any brotherly impulse, since he was plainly annoyed at her silence and her awkwardness, but because it was the best vantage point from which to watch the lively gestures, the pert little grimaces. "And where will you be staying while you're in Amsterdam, Saskia van Uylenburgh? Is Hendrik putting you up?" he said.

She answered him with a burst of musical laughter, mocking but not in the least insulting. "Oh, no, I wouldn't dare to go as far as *that*," she said, somehow managing to suggest, charmingly and quite blamelessly, a whole glittering world of possible naughtiness. "My address, at least, will be irreproachable. I'm staying with my uncle, who's a pastor. And furthermore, my uncle and my aunt are both past fifty. And furthermore again—it's the only cloud over my holiday—they won't go to bed until they've seen me safely tucked in."

They were so occupied imagining her tucked in—that honey-colored head on the goose-feather pillow, those round breasts raising the velvet quilt—that they paid small attention to Hendrik's account of his efforts to enlighten the aging couple who could not understand why a supper party should last beyond eleven.

"Oh, but they're really darlings! We mustn't slander them, they're terribly good to me," she said, touching her cousin again, this time on the wrist.

Oh, yes, I can well imagine, Lysbeth thought. Pat them and smile at them and cock your little head at them, and they'll be letting you do whatever you please.

Her brother gave her to understand with one of his cold grey looks that it was about time she passed the gingerbread and the oranges, and she took them from the table and walked toward the visitors with what she knew to be a sickly-sweet smile. "Oh, how good of you!" said Saskia van Uylenburgh, quite excessively, since after all it wasn't roast pheasant. "No oranges, thank you, not until just before I go, anyway—

I'm so messy with oranges I always need a bath. But what beautiful gingerbread! Did you make it yourself?"

Scarcely, she thought, since he didn't bother to say you were coming until an hour before you got here. "No, unfortunately, though I can recommend it, it's from an excellent baker," she said, despising herself. "I would have liked to make something especially nice for you—I only wish I had known in time."

"Never mind, she'll be coming again," said Rembrandt, "and you can make her one of your currant cakes. Lysbeth makes an excellent currant cake. Last week Dr. Kolkoen and Master Coppenol did away with a tremendous one just between the two of them."

She found the speech offensive on two counts: she was not a servant whose culinary skills he could put at the service of anybody he pleased, and she did not like the way he was naming names. She suspected him of wanting to let this glittering little female know that people of consequence ate under his roof, and the suspicion was the more disquieting because she had never caught him trying to impress anybody else.

She *was* impressed, or at least she pretended to be, wetting her lips with the tip of her tongue and nodding attentively. Dr. Kolkoen, she said, no doubt was one of the famous physicians in the wonderful Regents' piece that Hendrik had been telling her so much about; but Coppenol—Coppenol—her hand grasped after his identity with the quick gesture of someone trying to catch a butterfly—she knew the gentleman was famous, but to save her soul she couldn't remember what for.

"Penmanship," said Rembrandt. "He teaches handwriting."

"Yes," said Hendrik, "as an art."

"Of course, of course! My sister's French teacher in Leeuwarden has his signature in an album—the most beautiful signature I ever saw, all curlicues and flourishes."

And it was impossible to tell, little witch that she was, whether there really was a French teacher or an album or a signature, or whether she had conjured them all up for everybody's gratification.

"Saskia's looking forward to meeting our friends at the little supper I'm giving to celebrate the hanging of your *Anatomy Lesson*," Hendrik said. "Incidentally, now that she's here, we'll have to split the honors: the first two courses will be for your picture and the second two courses for the out-of-town guest."

"I couldn't be more delighted."

Lysbeth, letting herself down again beside him on the window seat, did not dare to look at his face to discern whether he had merely uttered a gallant formula. He was not eating; he had crossed his legs, and his hands were clasped tensely around his knee.

"Dr. Tulp, Dr. Kolkoen, Frans van Pellicorne—he's the Burgomaster's nephew—that's about as far as I've gone with the list," said Hendrik, picking the pulp off a section of orange with his polished fingernails. "You'll come, of course, Lysbeth. As a matter of fact, it looks as if we might be a little short of ladies. Would you care to bring that learned friend of yours, Margheretha What's-Her-Name?"

"Van Meer. Margheretha van Meer. I'll ask her if you want me to, though she's very much engaged these days, and I'd have to let her know in plenty of time."

Poor Margheretha! While the three of them went on in their easy, artificial way about the plays and dances and auctions, Lysbeth sat silent on the window seat, absently consumed a slice of gingerbread and tried to divide her fears from the facts. There was some reassurance to be gotten out of Hendrik's guest list: there were better fish than Rembrandt to be caught in Amsterdam. Dr. Kolkoen was fascinating in a somewhat sinister way, and Frans van Pellicorne was handsome and had a fortune to add to his attractions. The girl was an heiress—her manner more than her jewels made that plain; nobody but an heiress could have such complacency, such complete certainty that everybody in the room would be happier if she smiled or tossed her head. She might be willing to flirt with a newly famous young painter through a few holiday evenings, but her interest would dwindle when she discovered that his money flew out the window as soon as it came in the door. As for him, he was moody and careless and impatient with conventions; it was hard to imagine him making the planned public maneuvers he would have to carry out if he wanted to see this one, as he was constantly seeing Margheretha, by herself.

"Finish your gingerbread, sweetheart," said Hendrik. "We can't stay long; I'll have to look in on the shop."

"And how's your business going this week?" asked Rembrandt automatically, watching Saskia going at her hand like a kitten, licking the crumbs daintily from her little fingertips.

"Oh, nothing to boast of. I sold a set of engravings from Bellini yesterday, but not much else. Well, anyway, your end of it is holding up, you've got nothing to complain about. By the way, would you like to do another portrait?"

"Who's the sitter?"

"Saskia here. You and she can argue about it. It was her idea, not mine."

"Can you—please?" she said, laying her hands together in an impish imitation of the attitude of prayer. "It would be a wonderful experience—for me, I mean. I've never been painted before."

"But, Rembrandt, how could you possibly take on anything else?" said Lysbeth, appalled that she was actually voicing the protest. "What I mean is: you have sittings arranged for weeks ahead. Saskia van Uylenburgh can't stay in town forever just to have her portrait done."

"Well, maybe not forever, but *almost* forever." The brilliant eyes looked at her without displeasure; she plainly couldn't imagine anybody wanting *her* out of the way. "Nobody told me when I was supposed to come back; nobody even asked how long I thought I'd stay. That's the one blessed thing about being an orphan—I come and go as I please."

"I can always find time to do *your* portrait, Saskia van Uylenburgh." If it was overcordial, she had nobody to blame but herself: her brother was constrained to make amends for her discourtesy. She doubted, too, that the idea was the young lady's; Hendrik had probably thought it up as a way of making some return for the loan without unduly inconveniencing himself. "Suppose I bring my crayons to Hendrik's party. I could make a couple of preliminary drawings there if you weren't more happily occupied."

She rose, smiling, and said she couldn't imagine herself more happily occupied; and he looked at her with those keen painter's eyes of his, appraising the swelling breasts, the creamy neck, and the round cherubic head. She knew what he was doing, and she liked it, too; she even arranged to have a dimple deepen in her cheek as she offered her smiling face without embarrassment for his inspection. Margheretha had blushed when he had said, "Come, let me look at you"; Margheretha, out of decent shamefacedness or out of the knowledge that God had not created her without mortal flaws, had found it hard to tilt back her head.

"Oh, come along," said Hendrik. "I can't leave my shop closed all afternoon."

"I'll walk down with you," said Rembrandt, picking up her cloak, a beautiful olive-green one, edged and collared with moleskin. "Let me see you to the door."

The visitor stepped forward, holding out both hands to Lysbeth, and there was an instant when Lysbeth imagined that the moist and mobile lips were about to offer her a kiss. If such had actually been the intention and something in her own stiff bearing had rejected it, she did not care. She listened to their chatter on the stairway, and thought of Margheretha, and hoped that they would see a mouse.

There was a long interval before her brother came back up—long enough for her to have decided that the less said about Saskia van Uylenburgh the better. But when he appeared in the parlor, with his hair disordered and his cheeks turned red by the wind, she had to ask, she could not help herself. "What did you think of the little Frieslander?" she said.

"Oh, there's no lack of self-confidence *there*," he said over his shoulder, and laughed, and took himself off to his studio.

No lack of self-confidence there . . . he was not deploring it; that unabashed complacency had amused and pleased him. Bitterness surged up in her, and she picked up the crumbs around Saskia's chair in something close to rage. Beauty was the only thing worth possessing; beauty excused everything and accomplished everything, no matter what the preachers said. Compassion, self-effacement, learning, modesty —they counted for nothing and could lay claim to nothing, not even to what was in itself not beautiful, for he himself was certainly no Frans van

Pellicorne. The eyes of men were blind to the graces of the spirit. No spirit, however gracious, could undo protruding eyes and freckled hands.

*

When *The Anatomy Lesson of Doctor Tulp* was hung in the main meeting chamber of the Surgeons' Guild, nobody remarked that the young painter was as good as Titian or Dürer or Michelangelo; but none of the other paeans of praise that had haunted his dreams were left unsaid. It was stated and restated that Nicolaas Elias and Thomas de Keyser had never done anything to compare with it, that Joachim von Sandrart would go green with envy when he got back from Germany, that it equaled Frans Hals' best pieces for vigor and surpassed them in depth and dignity. Those who knew what they were talking about spoke of the expert massing of figures and the remarkable use of light; and those who did not, were impressed by what they called "the speaking likenesses," quoting until it became a cliché Burgomaster van Pellicorne's pronouncement that it was "a worthy tribute to those uncelebrated heroes who had contended with the plague face to face."

The actual hanging of the picture could well have been an anticlimax. Hendrik Uylenburgh had gone on about it so much beforehand that there were those in certain established circles who were predisposed—the more so since the art dealer had only a second-rate reputation—to find it less than a masterpiece. But the painting itself, massive and stark and novel, had overridden all malice and shattered all doubt. The day after the official hanging Rembrandt knew what it was to be famous, to be snowed under by congratulatory notes and besieged with invitations and flustered with demands for portraits, to be greeted by Regents and burghers and their ladies, to receive pleased smiles of recognition from strangers in the streets.

On one occasion—he was walking on the Dam, fast but aimlessly, merely to relieve the swollen sensation of happiness in his heart—an aging man whom he had never seen before, a tall man in the red cap that was the mark of the herring-carriers, stepped into his path, raised his work-hardened hand in a kind of salute, called him by name, and embraced him, saying, "I have seen it, it is magnificent!" And when the strong arms had loosed him and the man was gone, he had to stand against the wall of the Bourse, trying to master his tears. It was as if his old life in Leyden had absolved him, as if his father had come back to embrace him whole and exultant, out of the grace.

The only thing that fell short was the note he got from Pieter Lastman. He consoled himself as best he could by recalling that the master was lazy and disliked the business of writing, a fact that could account for his failure to say anything either good or bad about the painting: the whole communication was a three-line sentence congratulating him on his rise to fame. But the minor bruise he felt was healed the next morning by a message from Hendrik Uylenburgh, saying that Allaert van Hoorn had been at the shop inquiring after Master van Rijn's address, and that he had taken the occasion to invite Heer van Hoorn and his bride to the little supper party tomorrow night. Well, Allaert had come to him, and Lastman and my lord Constantyn Huyghens would come eventually. It was a good thing that some blessings should be postponed; his cup was running over, he had more joy than he could hold in his heart. And as he dressed for that party—the first two courses for him and the second two for the little Frieslander—everything seemed beautiful: the room, his clothes, his silver buttons and his silver chain, the patch of watery sunlight on the floor, even himself.

The little Frieslander . . . To say that he had thought of her much would have been inaccurate. He had had no specific thoughts of her in the press and radiance of his success, but she had somehow become commingled with the swift events and the high-heartedness. Her laughter sounded whenever he had occasion for laughing; her small soft lips and her brilliant eyes connected themselves with the heap of congratulatory letters on the desk; and no invitation was extended to him without his imagining, quite irrationally, that he would encounter her at the stated address, would sight beyond the other clustered heads her little round head with its honey-colored curls.

And the thought that he would be seeing her within the hour so exhilarated him that he was not ruffled on the walk to Hendrik's by Lysbeth's sulkiness. Her remoteness had set him wondering lately whether she could be harboring the preposterous notion that his success had made her less useful to him, that he might send her back to Leyden and get a fashionable male servant in her place. He had done what he could to reassure her, had bought her a sable muff and a garnet brooch and had ordered some magnificent damask drapes and cushions for her room. But nothing had dispelled her brooding silence; she walked with her head turned aside, always a step or two behind him; and after a couple of attempts at conversation, he gave up and went at his own lively pace, feeling the crayons in his pocket and whistling to himself.

The huge second-floor room above Uylenburgh's shop was everything at once: sitting room, dining room, kitchen by virtue of a hearth and an array of pots and pans, bedroom by virtue of a big couch covered tonight for the sake of decency and elegance with a length of wine-red velvet and the moth-eaten skin of a bear. On this couch, stretched out at full length with the ease and insouciance that had kept him a contented bachelor into his forty-third year, lay Dr. Matthys Kolkoen, his hands clasped behind his head and his beard thrust into the air—a goatish yet distinguished beard, glossy black with a streak of grey. He was talking at Margheretha, who sat in a prim grey dress on the edge of the couch at his feet. "Earth, air, water, and fire—and fire was the primary element; all the rest were derived from it, according to Heraclitus," he said.

"Fire may be the primary element, but what I need at the moment is water," said Hendrik. "This sauce is thickening too fast." He was on his knees at the opposite end of the room, holding a pan over the fire and stirring what was bound to be a violent and inedible concoction.

And who came to lift the kettle from the hook and pour the water into the oniony stuff? Saskia van Uylenburgh, walking away from a window red-gold with sunset into the deeper, more vivid gold of the fire. If she did not greet the newcomers who stood in the doorway, it was not because she did not see them; either it was sheer impishness that kept her from acknowledging their presence or it was something more stirring still—shame that she should have been watching for them through the window, should have known exactly when they would come through the door.

"Rembrandt! Our Apelles! Here he is!" said Hendrik, handing the pan to Saskia and coming to embrace him. "The crown—what did you do with it, Matthys? Where's the crown?"

"Under the bed," said Kolkoen, reaching down without moving any part of his torso and getting the silly wreath of greens and tossing it halfway across the room.

"Please don't tell me I'm going to have to put that on," said Rembrandt.

"You are indeed," said Hendrik. "We had it specially made up. It's only boxwood; there wasn't any laurel. Get yours, Saskia—it's right up there on the nail with the frying pan—we got one for Saskia too."

And he was able to go through the ridiculous business of crowning himself only because she was his fellow-victim. Margheretha came and took the pan and the kettle out of her hands, and Saskia stood not too close to him but not far from him either, putting the wreath on toward the back of her head, so that the leaves seemed to be growing out of a circle of firelighted curls.

"Do I have it on straight, Lysbeth van Rijn?" she said, smiling trustfully at his sister.

"Straighter than Rembrandt's, anyway," said Lysbeth.

"Yours *is* crooked. You're supposed to be a high-minded god, not Pan or Silenus," she said, and came close, so close that her milky breath moved across his face while she arranged his crown.

Dr. Tulp came in just then, alone because his little daughter had croup and his wife had stayed at home with her. He shook hands all around, asked if Margheretha had brought her flute, and told Kolkoen that it was just a bit early for a man to climb into bed. Then, having tasted the sauce at Hendrik's request, he pronounced it nauseating.

"Come here, Saskia van Uylenburgh," said Kolkoen, sitting up. "You see, I'm no longer in a dangerous position. Here's a little bow I found under the bed; I think it would look nice on your crown."

"Not now," she told him over her shoulder. She hung up the kettle for Margheretha and then went back to her earlier place near the flaming leaded windowpanes. "If you'll behave yourself, I'll come and talk to you after I've seen the sun go down and told Rembrandt van Rijn how beautiful his painting is. I know you've heard it all before, but I really must get it off my mind—I've been practicing since morning."

What she said while they stood together at the window with the red and gold March sunset flaming into their faces was, to tell the truth, pretty much what a dozen others had said. But she looked at him so earnestly with her radiant eyes; she asked so many humble little questions—Could she be right about this? Could she have misunderstood about that?—she lifted her face in such a touching way in order to keep meeting his look, that he found himself talking twice as much as he had ever talked before. How long they stood there he could not tell—long enough for the golden streaks of light to pale above the purpling roofs and the smoking chimneys and the leafless boughs, long enough for Dr. Tulp to have engaged Margheretha in a discussion about the Catholic machinations of Queen Henrietta of England, long enough for his sister to have told Matthys Kolkoen a great deal of embarrassing stuff about how dangerous her brother's new success might be if it made him abandon his simple ways. What went on in the room seemed far off, much farther off than the darkening vista on the other side of the window; and he knew that it was Saskia van Uylenburgh that made it so. He talked of his picture, of his lean years in Leyden, of the canvases he was painting now and the canvases he meant to paint; and she listened, with her lovely face grown immobile at last, as if there were no sound but the sound of his voice in all the world.

The new voice that was greeting the host from the doorway was unquestionably Allaert's, though it was deeper and more resonant than in the old days. Uneasy, even apprehensive, Rembrandt turned from the bewitching face before him and saw what was almost a stranger's face—the skin darkened and hardened, the long cheekbone sharper, a silky blond moustache and beard on the lip and chin. But the grey-blue eyes greeted him with unclouded pleasure, so that an embrace was possible though he himself could not quite meet the look: he felt a surprising surge of guilt and pain that so much transformation of mind and body should have taken place without his ever having stopped at the house on the Heerengracht. Not that Allaert would be living there any more; Allaert was married and had a house of his own, and here was his bride behind him—a mild, doe-faced, long-limbed young creature in a dress the color of sand, neither a beauty like Saskia nor plain like Lysbeth and Margheretha. "How well you look, Rembrandt, how exceedingly *well* you look," said Allaert; and they stepped back, still holding each other by the upper arms, as if by sinking their fingers into each other's muscles they could undo the strangeness that had come with those gone years.

Their efforts to talk to each other were continually interrupted—by one introduction after another, by an argument between Tulp and Hendrik as to what herbs should be sprinkled over the dried peas and beans, by a sudden blaze on the hearth: the fat on the joint had caught fire. No, Allaert hadn't been doing much painting lately; their rooms were so crowded with wedding gifts that there wasn't any place to set up an easel, but he did try his hand at it now and again at his parents' house. What he said of his mother—that she had been ailing, that she had gone to see *The Anatomy Lesson*, that she often wondered why Rembrandt had never dropped in—was partly lost because Dr. Kolkoen had finally inveigled Saskia into sitting beside him on the couch and was trying to fasten the little blue bow to her crown.

Everything—the flirting, the cooking, and the conversation—came to a stop on the arrival of Frans van Pellicorne, the last of the expected guests. He had fulfilled in his manhood what Allaert had promised in his youth; while Allaert had faded like a fine spring sun that begins to draw water before noon, van Pellicorne's stripling brilliance had only intensified. He kept his face clean-shaven, possibly because he was said to resemble Alexander the Great. His luxuriant hair, brushed back in deep waves from his smooth forehead, was a peculiar tawny sort of red. His manly body under his clothes could scarcely have asserted itself more if he had chosen to come in sandals and a lion-skin; his pale grey breeches were of a stuff thin enough to show the line of his thighs, and his bottle-green jacket, laced with silver, spanned tight over his massive chest. Allaert asked him how he had managed to get so brown at this time of year—his skin was only a shade lighter than his hair. "In Spain, in the orange groves of Granada and the gardens of Seville," he said, and thereby fell afoul of Margheretha, who made a sour face.

"What's the matter? Don't you care for Spain, Margheretha van Meer?" he asked, walking over to the couch and sitting down on Saskia's left—Kolkoen, on her right, was still trying to get the ribbon fastened to her crown.

"Not in the least," said Margheretha shortly.

"But how can you know? Have you ever been there?"

"No, Heer van Pellicorne, and I can't imagine myself going."

"You're making a mistake, let me tell you. There are some marvelous things to see."

"Yes, I'm sure," she said. "Like the plaza in front of the palace where they burned the Protestant martyrs by the hundreds. Like the prison where they poisoned our envoys or starved them to death."

It took the eminence and authority of Dr. Tulp to extricate them from that; he made a convenient crisis of getting the leek and potato soup out of the pan and into the tureen—Delft ware, borrowed from the shop for the night. And Rembrandt wondered whether Margheretha had lashed out at this glittering Alexander because she had found him sinfully attractive, or because his own attentions to Saskia van Uylenburgh had tried her bitterly. She seemed, poor thing, ashamed of herself; and he was glad to see her placed at the table between Allaert and Dr. Tulp, both of whom were kind enough to be considerate of her sensibilities.

His own place was not entirely to his liking. As the guest of honor, he sat at his host's right hand and was given Allaert's doe-eyed Lotje for his other neighbor. Saskia was within speaking distance on Hendrik's left, but she was flanked on the other side by Frans van Pellicorne, who looked thoroughly pleased with himself. And really he had no reason for complacency; even if Margheretha had been the one to make the scene, he had shown up far from well in the argument. An Amsterdam Regent's son should have considered twice before squandering good Dutch money in that Babylon, that madhouse, that cesspool . . . "Good God," said Hendrik, jumping up and hitting himself on the forehead with the back of his hand, "the wine's still in the bucket; I simply forgot it. You're on the end, there, Matthys, you can get it without too much trouble. Suppose you be our Ganymede—you'll find the goblets on the shelf over the bed."

The ample goblets were filled, but nobody was to taste the wine before the toast; and since Hendrik not only got up but also stepped behind his chair, it was plain that the toast was going to be something of an oration. "We all know why we are gathered here and what genius we are about to honor at this unworthy little spread—"

"Unworthy little spread!" said Frans van Pellicorne into Saskia's ear. "How many courses does he serve when he's entertaining really important guests?"

She laughed. "You're not supposed to take it seriously—it's oratory," she said.

"—yet I cannot let the occasion pass, ladies and gentlemen—and you, too, Matthys, if only you'd be good enough to sit down—without putting into a few words what all of us have in our hearts."

"The fewer the better," said Dr. Tulp.

"Not Hals, not Elias, not de Keyser, not anybody in our beloved Fatherland has risen to the heights of *The Anatomy Lesson*. We did not have to be told after the picture was hung; we who know him and have clasped his hand have been convinced of his genius from the start. Therefore, not in happy amazement but in serene satisfaction at seeing our predictions justified and our certainties come to flower, I give you, ladies and gentlemen, our crowned Apelles, the glory of Amsterdam: Rembrandt van Rijn!"

She leaned forward a little and lifted her goblet and looked at him over the brim, and the fatuous speech was redeemed by the bright spots of color on her cheeks and the pleasure in her eyes. Frans van Pellicorne set her bowl of soup directly in front of her, but she was not aware of it. She pursed her lips after the first sip of wine and parted them again, and it was as if she had sent him a congratulatory kiss.

"By the way, Rembrandt, did we ever tell you what we did with The

Child?" said Kolkoen. He was finished with his soup, having eaten it fast but carefully enough to keep the point of his goatish beard out of it. "Tulp bought him a grave, and we wrapped him in a couple of old sheets and put him in a two-florin coffin. We thought you'd like to know he got a decent burial."

"God knows he deserved it—he certainly served his turn," said Tulp.

"It was very kind of you, Doctor," said Margheretha. "I don't suppose any service was allowed, though I could never understand—"

"Let's not get into religion again, Margheretha van Meer," said Matthys. "We had enough trouble with that before. Anyhow, he's buried, and all of us got considerable benefit out of him. Van Loenen took a couple of his ribs, and I kept a kneecap for myself."

Rembrandt tried to occupy himself with his soup, but he had little appetite. Even if Saskia had looked at him again—and she would not, Frans van Pellicorne kept leaning toward her, grazing her shoulder with his and whispering into her ear—he doubted that he could have recaptured his earlier high-heartedness. Nothing could have restored it but earnest and knowledgeable talk about the picture, and plainly nobody wanted to talk about that. Van Pellicorne was telling Saskia a questionable joke; Lysbeth and Margheretha were complimenting Allaert's Lotje on the way she arranged her hair; and Matthys and Dr. Tulp were recalling other corpses as if they had been old friends. They were finished with the picture, they had officially put the picture behind them when Hendrik sat down after his tawdry toast: so solitary and so fleeting are a painter's glories in this world.

During the fish course, which consisted of chopped herring with vinegar and capers, nothing came about to draw him out of his gloom. To talk to Hendrik was to be bored, and to talk to Allaert was to become involved with the three young women around him—Lysbeth and Lotje were exchanging recipes, and Margheretha seemed to be using her salad as a means of swallowing her tears. "And how is the master these days?" he said flatly, throwing it down into the middle of the nonsense.

"Not too well," said Allaert. "He complains of not being able to get his breath."

"I'm sorry to hear it. He wrote me a very pleasant little note."

"Did he? He said he intended to. It's the strangest thing—he's always so sure he's going to die of the plague or the sweating sickness, and all the time he's eating and drinking himself to death."

For some reason he fell to thinking of my lord Constantyn Huyghens. If he had been here, he would have talked about *The Anatomy Lesson* and in terms that nobody at this table, including the little witch who was allowing van Pellicorne to feed her capers, could have understood. Space and mass, light and shadow, motion and stillness, life and death—he would have discerned them all and given due praise, stopping now and again to make a sound in his throat like the sound of doves . . .

"I'm sorry, Matthys," said Hendrik, "but I'm afraid I'll have to trouble you again, this time to gather up the salad plates. I can't move here, I'm simply wedged in."

"Sit still, Dr. Kolkoen, I'll get them," said Margheretha. "Lysbeth can bring the joint to the table for you to carve, Hendrik, and I'll look after the peas and beans, and Dr. Tulp can pour the wine."

While all of that was in progress, Saskia van Uylenburgh behaved herself, probably because Frans van Pellicorne had gone a bit too far in his attentions. She sat back in her chair, her face lifted into the candlelight, her eyes half shut and her mouth closed in a wistful smile. She should not have done it—she should not have taken capers with her tongue and lips from Alexander's fingers; but nothing could detract from the beauty of the dreaming, smiling lips.

"Nobody," said Hendrik, slicing into the joint, "is to eat before we have another toast. We are about to begin the latter half of the supper, and the next two courses are in honor of my cousin here. Even the genius of Apollo"—he bowed to Rembrandt—"must sometimes give way to the charms of Aphrodite." He turned to her and lifted her hand and kissed it, and she crinkled her cheeks and nose in a delightful grimace. "This time I'll be brief; the object is before us and calls for no eulogy— the lady's person is her praise. Ladies and gentlemen"—he raised his glass in one hand, still holding her little fingers in the other—"I give you Saskia van Uylenburgh, Friesland's most enchanting rose."

"Now there's a gift that I'll take wrapped or unwrapped," Matthys Kolkoen said.

She blushed, and her face quivered a little before she could smile again. Rembrandt wished that she had not smiled, had only turned a disdainful glare upon the coarse-mouthed bachelor; but then he found it impossible to imagine her glaring at anybody at all.

"Pull yourself together, Matthys, we're not in a tavern," said Dr. Tulp. "The joint's excellent, Hendrik, and so are the beans and peas. I concede to you, you were right about the thyme."

But nothing was to be gained from Dr. Kolkoen's disgrace. If Pan and his goatish beard were put down, glittering Alexander was again in the ascendancy, seeing how much charm could be crowded into the circumscribed bounds of decency. Would Saskia van Uylenburgh care to see Hooft's *Granida*? It was a delightful play, with some haunting lyric songs, and it would give him great pleasure to take her. Could he change cuts of the joint with her? Hers seemed a little rare, and ladies were inclined to like theirs better done.

Their little duet went on over a swell of noise: the clatter of knives against plates, calls for the butter and the salt, and increasingly exhilarated talk over the refilled goblets of wine. Rembrandt tried to disre-

189

gard them, even entered into a discussion between Kolkoen and Margheretha about the intentions of the Swedes, which Matthys had begun to show that he had not been ruffled by his superior's reproof; but the talk was involved, and Margheretha, woman though she was, showed herself much better informed than the other two. He was not eating, he was merely pushing food around on his plate when he heard Saskia saying his name. He refrained from looking up; he was no Kolkoen, no van Pellicorne, to dance attendance on her whenever she chose: if she wanted him to look at her, she would have to call him again.

"Rembrandt van Rijn, are you deaf? I'm talking to you."

"No, I'm not deaf, but you'll admit there are a good many distractions."

"What I've been trying to ask you is, did you bring your crayons?"

"My what?"

"Your crayons, your crayons. Don't you remember you said you would? You promised in your very own parlor that you were going to draw me tonight."

Perhaps it was her purpose to indicate that she had been in his parlor, and never in van Pellicorne's. "Yes, I brought them, but I told you before we needn't do it unless you want to."

"But of course I want to! You know I want to—I told you so!" Her cherubic head, with its curls all disheveled and fiery in the candlelight, was thrust far forward so that she could continue to look at him across the busy hands of the carving host. "We don't have to clear the table because we're the guests of honor. Let's do it while the others work. Let's start just as soon as we finish the sweet."

Though it was only an indifferent pudding, flabby and mildly flavored with lemon rind, that sweet had more savor for him than anything else he had eaten tonight. Saskia did not finish hers; she abandoned a little mound of it—along with Frans van Pellicorne—in order to squeeze in back of her cousin's chair and stand behind "crowned Apelles," laying her little hands on his shoulders so that he could feel their warmth and pressure through the cloth. "I don't see your crayons —where are they?" she said.

"Here in my pocket." He turned and found that if he had moved his head another inch his cheek would have rested on her breast.

"And paper? Have you got paper?"

"Yes, here in my other pocket."

"All right, come then." Her hand reached down to his, which closed without intention over the softness and the warmth and the dimples, as if his fingers were moving with a life of their own. "You'll excuse us," she said to the company, "if we leave you to your chatter and go about more important business. I am about to be sketched by Rembrandt van Rijn."

And where could he draw her but on that couch where Matthys Kolkoen had lolled at the beginning of the evening?—though he saw to it, before he seated her on the bearskin, that no print of the other man's body remained. It was dark there while he settled her into her pose, while he tilted back her head and crossed her warm, moist hands in her lap and pushed back her living curls, hearing meanwhile the thudding of his own unruly heart. Then, in the princely pride that was his by reason of her smile and her submissiveness and his mint-new glory, he called imperiously for candles, and candles were set for him on the shelf above the couch and on the floor. Seven candles there were in all, and the radiance that darted out from all of them converged upon her, lighting up her hair, her jewels, her eyes, her parted lips. Blessed to be a painter and have a painter's liberty to stare. To draw was to caress, and he drew them with a touch at once sure and tremulous, masterful and tender—the full eyelids, the temples shadowed by the springy ringlets, the hollow at the base of the round throat.

"Is the model permitted to talk, Master?"

"Yes, certainly, provided she doesn't turn her head."

"Is this dress suitable?"

"Any dress would be suitable. Besides, it doesn't matter. I'm not drawing the dress, I'm drawing you."

"Which of these people do you know the best?—aside from Hendrik, I mean."

"Allaert van Hoorn and Dr. Tulp. Heer van Pellicorne I scarcely know at all. I have a commission to paint his uncle, the Burgomaster. *He's* a very quiet, unassuming sort of man, for all his honors—"

"Is he? It certainly doesn't seem to be a family trait."

Out of the exhilaration that came from *that,* he did three swift sketches from various angles. To do the last he knelt in front of her on the floor, so close that the scent of her, moist and innocent like the scent of a bathed baby, came into his nostrils and hastened his heart.

"How many times will you draw me?"

"Oh, three or four hundred, God willing."

"But I wasn't asking for flattery. All I meant was, how many times tonight?"

"No more tonight—there's no more paper."

"No more paper? That's a pity. But I suppose we ought to be getting back to the others."

Those others—he became aware of them only after he had gotten up from his knees—were talking about going downstairs to dance in the shop; Hendrik had a clavier for sale down there, and Dr. Tulp could play it, more or less.

"Well, aren't you going to show me what you've done with me?" she said.

"Not until I've worked over it a bit with red chalk and bister."

"And when will you be doing that?"

He knew that she meant to be thinking of him, wherever she was, while he was working over the lines of cheek and neck and breast, and the knowledge made the hair on his arms rise with an eerie and delicious creeping. "Tonight, I imagine," he said, folding the paper and putting it back into his pocket. "Tonight when I get home, while my memory can be depended upon, and then again tomorrow when I get up and my mind is clear enough to show me my mistakes." She looked at him through her half-lidded eyes, and the creeping sensation moved from his arms to his spine. Would she think of him tonight when she stepped out of her petticoat? Would she think of him tomorrow when she sat up, stretching and yawning and sweetly disheveled, in her warm bed? He took her hand and drew her up from the couch. The imprint of her haunches was on the bearskin—he wanted nobody else to see it, and he was glad, when they rejoined the others, to hear that they were ready to start the dancing downstairs.

It was strange to dance in the shop, among the statues and paintings and silverware and china, to the light of insufficient candles and the twang of the plucked strings and the bursting, thrushlike notes of Margheretha's flute. The place was not well kept: he saw a mouse scuttle under the counter; when Saskia collided in the shadow with a Chinese ceremonial robe, two clouds of dust arose from the vacant sleeves; vague images of his own and other bodies came up into the tarnished or misted mirrors, and now and again a cobweb trailed across his face. His skin was so charged and responsive that not only *her* hand but every hand he touched in the round and the promenade begot a tingling or a shock. His pulse was racing and his breath was shallow, but his arms and legs had never felt so light, so free. Why he should think of such a thing he did not know, but when a sudden turn in the serpentine line sent Lotje stumbling against him, he saw her in her nakedness, knew exactly how she would look against a sheet. Kolkoen, gyrating with a Moorish dagger in his hand against a length of French velvet, was Pan indeed, his bony body stored with the knowledge of innumerable bawdy nights; and Frans van Pellicorne, executing the most complicated steps with a fierce precision, seemed to be asserting through his clothing how superbly he could do something else. And *she*—she rippled like a line of fire through the pattern of the dance, her hair borne out by the wind of her motion, her face tilted upward as if she were listening to the whispers of some invisible and erotic god. Once, after taking his hands according to the requirements of the measure, she exceeded those requirements by drawing him close —so close that he felt as if two flames were licking out at him from the points of her breasts. Once again, coming unexpectedly upon him at the turn in the double line, she laughed aloud and reached up and pulled hard on a lock of his hair. Allaert lost his sash and shouted that it made no difference. Somebody crashed into the Venetian crystal, and Hendrik, out of breath, announced that he didn't care. Exhaustion came, but it was the wild, triumphal exhaustion of a swimmer—fire had turned into water now—and he panted toward her past eyes and masks and plumes and hands that were blurred as if by rolling waves. It was not until they had been at it for more than half an hour that he became dimly aware of one mirror which he should not look at: it flung up to him, out of the spray of delight, a drowned face—Margheretha's face distorted by blowing into the flute, the mouth grotesquely puckered, tears standing in the pale and bulging eyes . . .

They were thirsty at the end of it, and another round of wine was brought down, and he drank it though he knew he should not, knew that his body, charged as it was, would surely make poison out of it. He was ill-situated, too, while he drank it: the final eruption of the crazy dance had flung him into a corner between Allaert and Lysbeth, both of whom, without saying a word, made him feel that he had done something preposterous and ought to be ashamed of himself. *She*—undoubtedly as helpless as he in the terminal explosion—had landed against the counter and was not to be blamed if she had been lifted up and seated among the damasks and the laces by Frans van Pellicorne. Still, he couldn't exactly be pleased that she was looking down at Alexander's aristocratic face and taking her goblet from his sunburned hand.

"What are you working at now?" said Allaert.

"Portraits. An old philosopher reading. *A Rape of Proserpine.*" He hesitated and felt his face flush as he mentioned the *Proserpine*, remembering his earlier vision of what nobody but Allaert ought to think about.

"Whom did you get to sit for Proserpine?"

"Nobody. My imagination. My all-too-ready imagination."

Allaert laughed and clapped him on the shoulder, but he could not reciprocate. He could only stare gloomily at *her* perched over there on the counter, kicking her heels against the wood and showing her ankles in their pretty green stockings.

"Rembrandt's working on a beautiful *Minerva*, too—very profound and quiet, more like the sort of thing he used to do in Leyden. Margheretha van Meer's sitting for that," Lysbeth said.

"It's only a sketch. I haven't done anything worth mentioning since *The Anatomy Lesson.*"

Suddenly he saw it as it must look now in the lightlessness of the deserted Surgeons' Meeting Chamber—the shapes blurred and indistinct, the colors bled out in the dark. A senseless pity for it and for himself took hold of him, and he swallowed the rest of his wine and shuddered. *She* was blowing something out of van Pellicorne's hair, and *The Anatomy Lesson* was closed away and robbed of the eyes that gave it existence, and Matthys Kolkoen was calling for more music, and unless he was prepared to be brutally rude he would have to lead his sister onto the floor or say that he was too drunk to dance.

And indeed the last swallow had been potent enough with him to justify his sitting out the next and final measure, a formal and courtly one to be performed after the English fashion by twos. He let himself down onto a heap of collapsing and dusty cushions and watched the couples walking out: Allaert and Lysbeth, Hendrik and Margheretha— the flute was silenced, the clavier could carry the burden—Saskia and Frans van Pellicorne. It was so stately a dance that it was difficult to take exception to it: the movements were slow and rigid, and the only contact called for was the contact of fingertips. Yet, in the uneasy light of the burned-down candles that sputtered and waved in the currents of air drawn after the passing and bowing figures, he conjectured that looks were being exchanged between Saskia and the Burgomaster's nephew; and those guessed-at looks and the sure malaise begotten by the wine made his heart as heavy as a stone. Suppose she was calculating which was the more desirable, Alexander or himself. An Amsterdam burgher or the son of a Leyden miller . . . A classic profile or a coarse Dutch face . . . Old wealth, securely invested, or the promise of a new fortune, with wings attached to every florin . . . practiced courtship grown exquisite in the gardens of Granada or rough longing, inarticulate and amazed at itself . . .

Lotje, carrying her own cushion, crept round the fringes of the dance, seated herself beside him, and smiled shyly up into his face. "You look as if you had a headache," she said.

"I do." Only the ache was really under his ribs, in the vicinity of his heart.

"What time do you think it is?"

"One—half past one—I don't know."

"We should be going soon. Will you come to visit us one of these days?"

"Yes, certainly." He could not make it sound as cordial as he wished. He was thinking how Saskia was bound to go back to Friesland, and how in that far province—it seemed farther away to him than India or the New Continent—she would say provocatively some evening to a suitable husband, "I danced one night in a shop in Amsterdam, among dusty Oriental robes and tarnished mirrors, and I made two conquests there: a burgomaster's nephew and a famous painter named Rembrandt van Rijn."

"May I take your greetings to my mother-in-law?"

"Oh, yes, do, by all means."

"May I tell her you'll be calling on her too?"

"Yes, of course, as soon as I've worked off a couple of my commissions."

"She'd like to see you. She hasn't been well, you know."

He wasn't quite well either. The wine had gone to his head; he knew it when he tried to shift his position on the unsteady heap of cushions and saw the candles, the dancing couples, the staring statues, and the festoons of cloth come floating together before his eyes. "If you'll excuse me for a moment, Lotje, I think I'd better step out for a breath of air," he said, getting to his feet.

"But you're surely not thinking of leaving, are you?" Hendrik called to him; and it occurred to him as a novel and remarkable thought that he *could* take himself off, could seem to care the less about what he was willing to leave behind. "Yes," he said. "I've had too much to drink and I've got to paint tomorrow."

"What about me—do you intend to walk away and just leave me here?" asked Lysbeth over the twanging melody.

"Don't worry, Lysbeth van Rijn," said Allaert, turning her about. "Lotje and I will take you home. Come to see us, Rembrandt. Good night."

He opened the door into the street, making the shop bell jingle weirdly into the black emptiness outside, but before he could leave she was there on the threshold, breathing into his face. The childish scent of her was in his nostrils, and her eyes, wider than he had ever seen them, were shining earnestly at him through the dark. "When will I see you again?" she asked, and seized him hard by the wrist, as if he might escape forever.

"Whenever you please, Saskia van Uylenburgh."

"Tomorrow?"

"But tomorrow"—he was surprised that he should remember it in his drunkenness—"tomorrow I'll be busy all day painting the Burgomaster and his son."

"Day after tomorrow?"

"Yes, at one o'clock."

Her eyes grew narrow and witching, and he knew that she was scheming to pay him off for his busy tomorrow. "I'll be elsewhere that day until three. Would you want to see me at three?" she said.

"Whenever you choose to come I'll be wanting to see you."

Her hand reached up in the shadow—he did not know at first what she meant to do—and plucked off his crown. "Take mine off too. The party is over," she said, and stood meekly before him, with the wind stirring her skirt and hair, while he took the hard little garland out of her warm and living curls. "Good night and God be with you, to see that you don't tumble into the canal." She did not return his crown or ask him for hers; she bowed as one bows at the end of a dance, and shut the door. He stripped away the blue ribbon that Matthys Kolkoen had fastened among the boxwood leaves and carried the garland with him through the gusty, unpeopled streets, glad for the blind windows and the empty alleys, glad to be able to do whatever he liked with his prize —to look at it, to fondle it, to hold it against his chest, his cheek, his mouth.

*

April, May, June—it seemed to him afterwards that those months, unlike the others of his life, had passed not through his mind but through his body. They and the things that came to pass in them were

195

intensified by the pounding of his heart, the tingling of his skin, the hurrying current of his blood. It was only natural that they should be innocent of thought—he had so little time for thinking—never before had he crowded so much into every swollen day, so many planned pleasures to be tasted and so much work to do. Only while he was washing and dressing between a sitting and a party did he have any time for sober consideration, and even those hours, gilded with pale spring twilight or alive with the splash of rain on the new green leaves, saw thoughts give way to sensations and conjectures dissolve into dreams.

There was a dreamlike cast over his whole existence, possibly because he was doing for the first time so many things he would never have guessed he could enjoy. With that always-changing yet always-partly-the-same group of semi-intimates who constituted his circle, he rowed up the Amstel on a chilly moon-whitened night to an orchard behind a tavern, where he drank strange wine whose savor he never found again and stared through boughs of peach and cherry blossom at the slowly veering pattern of the stars. He went berry-picking on an afternoon canopied with lead-colored thunderclouds and so laden with moisture that the black fruit seemed encased in a film of water, and her cheek, when he brushed it with the back of his hand, was wet as if with tears. He visited villages along the river, crossed bridges from one unknown bank to another, walked through useless gateways into vacant ruins, came upon frogs croaking swollen-throated in deserted Catholic shrines. And over all these scenes—or so it seemed to him in recollection—some part of her or one of her belongings was superimposed: her lace handkerchief floated over the berry patch, her sun-saturated hair flamed up against an arch of smoke-grey stone, her muslin scarf blew out and undulated between him and the stars.

If there was something elegiac about that spring, it was probably because his hope of what they would say when she was posing for him never came to fruition. Twenty times at least in those three months she climbed to his rooms on the Bloemgracht; but every such occasion was a loss of ground, something to be expunged or compensated for when they met again in company. It was true—and perhaps not altogether regrettable—that she grew rigid and remote as soon as she took the pose, so that the face he painted above the exquisite points of her lace collar was only a feeble and phlegmatic likeness of what he knew her to be. He was convinced he could have dispelled the constraint if only they had really been left to themselves, but the whole world seemed to be in an elaborate conspiracy to see to it that they were never alone. Patrons kept bringing their wives or fiancées to have a look at unfinished likenesses. The apprentices Flinck and Bol, obviously and ridiculously besotted with her, used every pretext to haunt the place beyond their regular hours. Drape-makers, chimney sweeps, and grocers' delivery boys kept making appearances; and when everybody else was well out of the way Lysbeth asserted her propinquity by moving the furniture noisily in the living room.

But there was one hot, bright Sunday in June that gave promise of better things between them. With the sittings and the evening parties and the little jaunts with their friends, they had been meeting almost every day; and this particular Sunday had seemed blank to him because he was without hope of seeing her—she went invariably to hear her uncle's sermons, and there was to be a family trip to Haarlem in the afternoon. It was his habit to get up as early as usual on Sunday and use the apprentice-free hours to paint away in peace, and starved for a sight of her though he was, he stayed at his easel in a room almost blinding with sun and scented with the dying fragrance of some roses that Allaert and Lotje had brought back for him from their country place. And suddenly, while he was adding a few highlights to the cool olive-green and violet surface of his *Rape of Proserpine*, he heard light footsteps on the stairs—footsteps that could have belonged to nobody else. She was coming to him in the little noontide space between the service and the trip, and she must have come in haste because she wanted a sight of him: her face, flushed and moist in the sunlight, and the disorder of her dress of peach-colored muslin told him so.

"What a happy surprise!" he said, laying down his brushes and wiping his damp forehead with the sleeve of his shirt. "Have you eaten? Can I give you something?"

"Yes, if it won't be any trouble." She sat down, not on the chair where the rigidity always came upon her, but on the long stool where Flinck and Bol usually settled themselves to sketch and adore her. The diaphanous folds of the dress flowed over her knees and lay on the floor around her feet. "I hurried so, and I'm going to have to hurry back again, and I'm terribly thirsty. Get me a mug of milk."

He went to get it in the kitchen: Lysbeth, who was happy to play hostess to everybody else, plainly felt herself degraded to a servant's status if she had to wait on Saskia and never handed her a napkin without looking distinctly put upon. When he came back with the foamy milk in his finest Delft mug, he found her self-possessed enough to think of covering her tracks: "You know, to save my life I couldn't remember whether I was supposed to sit for you tomorrow or day after tomorrow. I asked Hendrik at church, and he couldn't remember, either," she said.

As he bent to hand her the mug, it occurred to him that he might stop all such devious nonsense by kissing her—her lips were parted; her milky teeth were gleaming; her tight little necklace of pearls was sunken into the soft and faintly flushed flesh of her throat, and his urgency was such that the mug trembled in his hand. But there was something in her eyes that told him she would deplore the act though she might not regret the desire, and he contented himself with lifting a loose, warm lock of hair from her brow. "Day after tomorrow at one," he said, "though we'll be seeing each other tomorrow evening at Kolkoen's, you know."

"I see you so much I don't know what to wear any more. You've seen all my dresses half a dozen times." Over the rim of the mug, she gave him a beautiful, tremulous smile.

"I never saw this one."

"No—I know—it was just finished. I stopped at the dressmaker's to get it yesterday afternoon."

He knew that Lysbeth would be listening and that the dress would be an affront to her—because of his dreamy preoccupation he had not remembered to ask her what clothes she needed for summer wear. Now that he thought of it, his sister owned no lawns, no muslins, no linens; it was probably her lack of such things that had made her look almost as dowdy at the last dance as Margheretha van Meer. "This is a beautiful color," he said, daring to pick up and finger a soft fold of the cloth so close to her neck that the back of his thumb surreptitiously brushed her damp skin. "Did you buy anything else?" The vapid question permitted him to prolong the touch.

"Oh, just some ribbons and a poke of cherries and a damask cushion for my Aunt Sylvius." She drew back a little to indicate that he should take his hand away, but as she did so she let her head drop to one side so that her cheek brushed his wrist in a secretive caress. "What I really wanted to buy and couldn't was something I saw in the furniture shop where I got the cushion. It was French, I think—something between a chair and a bed. You should have seen it—it was simply beautiful. The frame and the legs were all carved and gilded, and there was a griffin or a dragon or something at the foot, and up at the head there was a wonderful little crying Cupid with his hands tied. It was all covered with quilted satin, and there were marvelous velvet cushions with embroidery and tassels, and there was a damask coverlet and a velvet canopy—"

Her eyes narrowed and her cheeks flushed as her hands sketched out the lines of Cupid and griffin and canopy. Plainly—and he loved her the more for it—she was subject to the same passion for such finds as he carried in his own blood. "Since you want it so much, why didn't you buy it?" he said.

"Buy it? Oh, Lord, where do you think I would put it? It wouldn't do at all in my Uncle Sylvius's house—it's very ornate, very worldly; in among all those chaste sober pieces of theirs it would look like a *sin*. And I couldn't send it up to Friesland either; a trip like that would batter it to bits. To tell the truth, I was thinking *you* ought to buy it. It would be wonderful for your mythological things—Hendrik thinks so too."

In spite of the hard, quick steps that were crossing the floor in the parlor, he entertained the possibility. To hold such a thing in his possession until a time when he might have the right to give her gifts . . .

To look at it on nights when longing broke his sleep, to imagine her weighting down the cushions with her moist and rosy nakedness . . . The thought was intoxicating, like the smell of the withered roses shedding their petals in the heat. "Maybe I will buy it. Maybe you'll look at it with me some day this week," he said.

"Whenever you like."

"Whenever *I* like! You're so busy you never have a minute."

"I had a minute today," she said, giving him back the empty mug and looking with a strange mixture of archness and tenderness into his eyes. "But now I must be going. They've rented a carriage, and I don't want them counting how many pennies are being wasted while it's waiting in the street. Don't take me to the door—Lysbeth was getting your meal ready when I came in, and you shouldn't keep her waiting either. God be with you until tomorrow night."

He stayed where he was, partly because he had no desire to encounter his sister and partly because he wished to allow the sensations of that sweet visit to seep in; to remove himself from the spot where he could still inhale the heavy scent of the roses seemed to him a violence. He stared at the space above the stool, as if her ringleted head were still inhabiting it, until Lysbeth came in. "I hope you're about ready to sit down now. The soup's half cold already," she said.

"Well, that's no great loss on a day as hot as this." He meant no harm; he was too happy to harbor any resentment.

She only gave him a dour look and went into the parlor where the table was laid for two. The affronted servant's manner that she assumed in Saskia's presence had not yet left her. The unnecessary courtesies she performed—putting the salt and butter in front of him, shaking out his napkin and handing it to him—were intended as reproofs.

"Wouldn't you like to buy yourself some summer things?" he said, after he had swallowed several spoonfuls of the lukewarm soup.

"Summer things?"

"Dresses. I thought maybe you'd like to have a couple of those light bright-colored dresses like the one Saskia had on."

"Oh, I don't think so." She pushed away her soup and stared at the wall above his head. "Actually, there aren't more than ten or twelve really hot days in the year, and I've always been able to get through them by taking off my jacket. A person doesn't have much use for that kind of dress."

"Yes, but wouldn't you like to have one just because they're pretty?"

"It would be a waste of money. Besides, I'd feel uncomfortable— they're too conspicuous."

"Whatever you like. If there's anything you need, feel free to buy it." His annoyance sounded in his voice in spite of himself.

"I'm perfectly satisfied, I don't want a thing. I guess in some ways I'm like Margheretha; I don't like to clutter up my life with a lot of things I don't need."

It would have been easier for him to put up with the malice behind the speech if she had not uttered it with an air of wide-eyed candor. He was nettled enough to want to ask her why she didn't go and live with Margheretha in her bare and shabby house; but he knew that a quarrel would only pull him further away from the visit, and he stolidly consumed his soup, deliberately recalling meanwhile how the moist cheek had felt against his wrist.

But his sister was not ready to abandon the subject. She set her elbow on the table, rested her cheek on her hand, and looked at him with a false affability. "Of course, I might feel differently about it if we had a great deal of money," she said. "If we didn't have to care how much we spent, I might even take it into my head to want something like the little couch that Saskia van Uylenburgh was talking about—who knows?"

"I've told you we don't have to worry about money. I've got more portrait commissions than I can take care of, and if I wanted a thing like that couch, I fancy I could afford it."

"Have you any idea what a thing like that would cost?"

"No, but I can look at it and find out."

"But surely you're not thinking of buying it?" Her delight at catching him up warred with her horror at his intentions and pulled her face awry.

"Why shouldn't I? God knows I don't allow myself many indulgences—"

"Then I'd like to know where the money's going. No matter what you earn, we're still behind with the bills."

"I've told you not to bother your head about the bills. Hendrik says it's high time I raised my price. In a couple of months we'll have more than enough."

She removed his soup bowl and passed him a dish of cherries with elaborate politeness. "I don't know what you mean by that," she said, "but you certainly can't believe we're ever going to have more than enough in the sense that Saskia van Uylenburgh and Frans van Pellicorne do. They turn up at our parties, and that's all very nice, but it shouldn't blind a person to the fact that they're simply out of our class. Margheretha tells me their families have been piling up fortunes for generations, and you've got to remember you had nothing to start with, nothing at all. If you saved every penny you made—and so far we haven't saved anything—we'd never be able to match the kind of life they live. Their houses, their trips, their servants, the food they eat, what they put on their backs—it just isn't within a painter's reach."

"It's within Rubens' reach." It was a foolish and transparent boast: Rubens painted in Flanders for the Catholic Church, and bishops were more generous patrons than the wary burghers of Amsterdam. "I'm only just beginning—if you don't mind, let's wait and see how well I

200

do," he said, and left his cherries untouched and took himself off without another word into the studio.

And there, for the first time in three months, thought imposed itself on sensation: he could not give himself up to the image of her lifted face, to the recollection of her touch, or to the smell of the roses. Questions, all the more urgent because they had been so long suppressed, rose in his mind, so insistent that it was as if his own voice were addressing him peremptorily from various parts of the room. The sittings, the parties, the magical trips—had she come to them only as diversions from the life to which she must inevitably return? Had she touched his cheek, taken his hand, tugged at his hair only to learn how it is to make light love to an interesting specimen of a lesser breed? Were she and Frans van Pellicorne really of a world apart—and therefore close together—by virtue of the mellowed money in their coffers and the old blood in their veins?

Assailed by these questions, not knowing what he was doing, he took up a sheet of drawing paper and tore it into shreds. His hands trembled; his throat was suddenly dry; he wanted to say aloud—he would certainly have said it if Lysbeth had not been nearby—what he had never put into words in all these tender, brooding months: "I love her, I love her." He saw, too, letting the torn bits of paper fall behind him like scattered petals, that this intolerable agitation could be appeased only if he married her, though never until this instant had he pictured himself taking a wife. Only by asking her outright if she would have him could he exorcise those unknown suitors who waited for her in Friesland and the tawny Alexander who pursued her here in Amsterdam. Only by publishing the banns could he be relieved of the fierce jealousy, the tormenting uncertainty, the unnerving fright.

And quickly, knowing that he could not endure the suspense without going out of his mind, he made his plans: he had been a fool to go about his wooing in such a haphazard fashion, depending on chance encounters, reassuring himself with looks and touches and smiles. As soon as possible—not Monday because they would be at Matthys' rooms, not Tuesday because they were going to the country with Allaert and Lotje, but certainly on Wednesday—he would present himself at the house of Pastor Sylvius, with all the proper speeches learned by heart and with a nosegay in his hand. He could not see himself doing it, but it would have to be done. The possibility of acceptance was as unimaginable to him as that of rejection; it was enough that he could envision himself standing on that unknown threshold on Wednesday at eight o'clock.

Having reached that decision—prudent or insane as it might prove itself—he went back to Proserpine's abduction to the kingdom of Hades. The canvas was too cool, too earthy-green, too smoothly surfaced in spite of its violence, and he worked at it for an hour, striding at it and away from it, breathing the scent of the wilted roses and treading on the shreds of paper; and before he was finished, some of his own wild distress had gotten itself transferred into the glint on the nose of the hellish steed, the somber shining of the ghastly chariot, the flecks of foam churned up from the River of the Dead.

*

The nosegay, the memorized speeches, the collar of fine pleated linen that he had bought for the occasion—they had seemed unreal to him back in his room, and here on the path to the front door of Pastor Sylvius's house they seemed downright preposterous. That house, small as it was, had a dignity more unnerving than the splendor of Lastman's or the grey stone, many-windowed magnificence of the van Hoorn mansion on the Heerengracht. The lawns, beaded by a recent rain, were perfectly cropped, and the flowerbeds were exquisitely tended even though they were no longer in bloom. The leaded casements reflecting a sunset muted behind undispersed thunderclouds, the wrought-iron balustrade and the ancient bronze knocker—all of them reminded him that the young woman whose hand he was about to ask for had cousins in distinguished pulpits and great universities and was the daughter of a burgomaster of Leeuwarden, a man so intimate with the good, gone Prince of Orange that he had been with him on the day of his assassination.

If his nerves were unstrung by the exterior of that solemn and respectable residence, the inside of it was more unsettling still. In the little hallway was a middle-aged maid in an impressive cap, who asked his name in a whisper and announced it in a jarring shout. To his left was a study lined with books; and to his right, on the other side of a drawn portiere, was a room that was crowded with chattering guests. The presence of those guests was so unexpected that he must have stood a full minute before he handed the maid his gloves and his plumed hat and found the courage to walk in. It was no consolation that all the visitors were known to him—the plump, warm-hearted writing master Coppenol, and Allaert and Lotje, and Vrouw van Hoorn, whom he had not yet found time to call upon. Their presence would make an opportunity for the delivery of the speeches unlikely if not impossible; their faces, set against discreet drapery or the carved backs of old and precious chairs, were so unwelcome that he could not even bring himself to smile. And *she*—he had been foolish enough to imagine that she would run to the door to let him in—she was not even in the room. It was Allaert who took him over to the aged and delicate pastor and his wife, who sat as if enthroned in tall, matched chairs near the window, he in his long black gown and she in her sober grey, with the pink of her scalp showing through the severely parted white of her hair. Their eyes, keen but reserved, rested upon him—his heart sank to note it—with no particular curiosity or interest. "You're very welcome, Heer van Rijn," said

202

the pastor in a quiet, unsteady voice; and the lady, smiling a pinched and social smile, reached out her veined hand and took unto herself as a hostess's due the bouquet he had intended for his love.

In the exchange that followed among the three of them, ordinary talk about the convenience of the New Haarlem Road and the foibles of the weather, he knew he was conducting himself with neither wit nor grace. His mind kept flying back to the time when he had asked Saskia if he might pay his visit. Had he specifically mentioned Wednesday as the day he wanted to call, or was it she who had suggested it? Had she taken some impish delight in imagining him coming to what he thought would be a private interview and finding the parlor filled with guests? Or was it something worse than that—had she, suspecting and rejecting his intentions, deliberately chosen an evening when it would be impossible for him to make them known? The old pastor was certainly not behaving as if anything crucial were impending: his pale face with its scant silky beard neither sought nor avoided the newcomer's look; his beautiful spare hands, as white as paper, lay crossed on the lap of his robe with perfect serenity. His wife completed some remark about the recent thunderstorm with an explanation of Saskia's absence: the storm had broken so suddenly that Saskia had gotten wet closing the casements in the driving rain and had gone upstairs to change her dress. But it was put very casually, and before she finished she turned it into an excuse for the temporary absence of the fruit—Saskia had asked them to wait until she arranged it before they served.

Their little private conversation had run out and he was walking toward an empty chair with a disheartening conviction of having been dismissed, when she parted the rust-colored velvet portieres and came into the room, her hair wreathed with ribbons and curlier than usual, probably because of the rain. It was doubtless what Lysbeth had said about the clothes she and van Pellicorne put on their backs that made him more acutely aware of the precious things in which she moved—the amber satin of her dress, the pearl-studded buckle, the lace of her petticoat showing at every step, the glint of gold chains and garnets at her round throat and on her plump little wrists. "Ah, so here you are, visiting us at last," she said, and came up to him and gave him her hand. Her palm, softly padded like a cat's paw, lingered long enough to make him doubt she would do anything to frustrate or embarrass him. "Do sit down—I can't stay; I've got to fix the fruit dish. I'll be back in a minute," she said, and smiled at him, and was gone.

He reminded himself that he had not yet greeted Vrouw van Hoorn in the flurry of the introductions; in fact, he had not really seen her, but only ascertained that she was there. Now, with the image of Saskia's glowing cheeks and vital lips still in his mind, he turned and saw a face that startled him: the long cheeks hollowed out, the eyes smaller than he remembered, the mouth, vaguely smiling, of a peculiar purplish red. She was sitting very erect in one of the carved chairs, with a pillow behind the small of her back and a fan and a lace handkerchief spread out on the grey silk that draped her knees. She did not look at him, and after the first shocking instant he did not look directly at her. "You remember me, don't you?" she said, and something in the melancholy fall of her voice impelled him to a piece of French courtesy that he had never performed for anybody else: before he settled into his seat, he came and kissed her cold, dry hand.

"No backgammon this evening, Vrouw Sylvius?" said Allaert.

"Oh, yes, only I thought we'd wait a little. We're expecting one more visitor." She was indicating her gratefulness for her bouquet by sniffing at it, and something in her face as she looked coquettishly at Allaert over the flowers reminded Rembrandt of his mother looking at him in the almost-forgotten kitchen in Leyden. But the likeness was superficial; his mother in her bombazine and this one in her fine grey woolen were worlds apart.

"May I ask who else is coming?" said Lotje.

"A man—but you're not supposed to be interested any more. You're settled now for good or for ill," said the pastor, giving her a teasing look.

Who? thought Rembrandt. Frans van Pellicorne?

But the good writing master Coppenol, with his round head and his smooth hair and his little porcine eyes and mouth, relieved the anxiety by saying that Lotje was in no danger from Heer Maurits Huyghens; that gentleman—he turned the compliment with as much flourish as he copied out a line of poetry—was head over heels in love with Lotje's mother-in-law.

"Huyghens?" said Rembrandt, driven beyond awareness of where he was by the magic of the name. "Could he be related to my lord Constantyn Huyghens?"

"Why, yes," said the pastor, "they're brothers. Are you acquainted with my lord?"

Two things militated against his making much of it: the recollection was still too precious to use, and to explain his connection with the Prince's secretary would be to cast himself in the role of a painter who was patronized and paid by, not intimate with, the great. "Slightly, your honor. I met him once, more than two years ago, when he happened to be in Leyden. I doubt he'd remember me," he said.

"Maurits is in Amsterdam a good deal oftener than his brother," said the hostess, carefully wiping a streak of pollen from the end of her aristocratic nose. "The Prince won't let poor Constantyn out of his sight." Whereupon the talk turned to politics; to the clever but not altogether blameless way the Prince was playing off the old ally France against the old enemy Spain, to the difference between political and personal morality and the paradox of good kings who had been wretched specimens of humanity and very admirable people who had been sorry rulers indeed . . .

He was out of it, completely out of it. Though he had outstripped

Thomas de Keyser and Nicolaas Elias, he had no friends to tell him what was going on at The Hague; though he had patience to execute almost every thread in rendering a piece of Flemish lace, he could not force himself to read the weekly news review. Saskia came back carrying a large salver of fruit, but his pleasure in the sight of her was tainted by a realization that she was dispensing the fruit according to some mysterious protocol which she had doubtless been trained in from her childhood and which he knew nothing about. She crossed and recrossed the room, going first to Vrouw van Hoorn, then to the pastor and his wife, then to Master Coppenol, then to Lotje, and then to himself, leaving Allaert until the last. He stared somberly at the splendid platter, wondering if he would betray his ignorance by his selection of the fruit. "That peach there in the middle—take that one," she said, bringing her face almost lovingly close to his. "It's just soft enough; I felt it." And he picked it up with a mingled surge of joy and pain, thinking that however far from him she was he could still take to his lips something she had touched.

"If anybody here is tired of seeing the same thing Wednesday after Wednesday, blame my wife here," Pastor Sylvius said. "I made so bold as to suggest a salad or a little cold partridge tonight for a change, but she wouldn't hear of it. You might as well know what's to be expected: as long as it's in season, you'll be getting nothing but fruit."

During the mild and decorous protest raised by the others in praise of fruit in season, it broke upon Rembrandt that what he was attending was the Sylviuses' "at home"—Wednesday evening here was like Friday evening at Pieter Lastman's, the time when friends were expected to drop in. Now that he stopped to think of it, he remembered that Saskia had made three or four gratuitous remarks to indicate that the pastor and his lady kept open house on Wednesdays; if he had chosen the wrong evening to make his crucial visit, he had only himself to blame. Having made the rounds with the fruit three times, always in the same order, she set the salver on a beautiful old table chastely bare of everything but a Chinese vase and a couple of books, and taking a handful of cherries, stationed herself behind her aunt's chair. "What a lovely nosegay! Where did you get it?" she said.

"Heer van Rijn brought it. Wasn't that kind of him?" She held it up for her niece to smell, and Saskia lowered her head above it, but not quickly enough to hide the blush that spread over her neck and face. He felt in his bones that she knew it was for her that he had brought it, but why had she blushed—in pleasure or in pity or in shame? It was impossible to tell, and he was only the more confused when she lifted her head and he saw that large, brilliant tears were standing in her eyes.

The hostess said they might as well begin their backgammon—there was no telling how late Heer Huyghens was going to be—and all the accouterments, including a little table of exquisite workmanship, were brought in by the maid and set so close to Vrouw van Hoorn that she did not have to lean away from her pillow in order to play. While Saskia, Vrouw Sylvius, and Allaert gathered close to her around the table, it occurred to Rembrandt that it might not be amiss to have some sort of conversation with his host, even if none of the memorized speeches could possibly be delivered. But Master Coppenol balked him by laying a beautifully kept, plump little hand on his arm to keep him in his chair. "I suppose you're so sought after these days that you couldn't consider another commission, could you?" he said.

"I *do* have more than I can handle. I'd rather not take on anything new." Annoyed that the role of paid artisan was being thrust upon him, he said it without much grace.

"Especially if it was a portrait? I wouldn't blame you if every now and again you got tired of that sort of thing."

But he couldn't give way to a growing conviction that he *was* getting tired of that sort of thing. Some half-stifled voice inside him had been asking persistently of late why it was that burghers who wanted to be painted always had such vapid faces that a person was forced to get whatever painter's satisfaction he could out of a minute and showy treatment of their plumes, their gloves, their jewelry, their silks. Before his prickly conversation with Lysbeth, he had actually rejected a commission or two, hoping to gain time for some raw and passionate scene from the Old Testament—Jacob asleep on his pillow of stones or Hagar and Ishmael famished in the wilderness. But ever since last Sunday he realized he must keep grasping at everything within reach, at least until he knew whether he was accepted or refused. "Who wants a portrait?" he said.

"I do." Fortunately nobody was listening; those at the board were absorbed in the game, and Lotje had crossed the room to talk with Pastor Sylvius.

"What did you have in mind? Bust or full-length?" he asked, thinking that there were certain interesting paradoxes to be captured here—grace in spite of paunchiness, and a queer combination of shrewdness and kindness in the small bright eyes.

"Nothing so grand; I'd never be able to afford it. What I'd really like is an etching. Those beggars of yours, and the one you did of the pancake woman—they're little masterpieces, and I'd like to be the subject of a little masterpiece. You etch as well as you paint—a fact that hardly anybody knows."

If the little gentleman was getting satisfaction out of knowing more than most, if it pleased him to think he might get a jewel at a negligible price, his complacency had grounds: being a penman, he was an expert in line. The etchings *had* been neglected in favor of the paintings, and it was so good to hear them praised that for almost half an hour he forgot to look over his shoulder at the bright and curly head. Master Coppenol said things that he wanted to hear, even if he said them pompously: it was gratifying that somebody should realize how much vitality he managed to get into a few scratched lines, how aptly he used the burr thrown up by the needle, what a rare velvety quality he got into his blacks, how almost imperceptibly his surfaces moved from dark to light . . . And before the first round of backgammon was over he had let himself be caught, all the more willingly since the whole transaction was carried on so discreetly that only the compliments could have been heard and nobody could have guessed that anything was being bought and sold.

It was Lotje who interrupted their private talk. She came up behind Master Coppenol and laid her hand on his shoulder—a smooth, unobjectionable hand like so many it was his fate to paint, a hand memorable for nothing but its rings. "You two have been enjoying each other's company much too long," she said. "Go and talk to Pastor Sylvius, Master Coppenol. I have a thing or two I want to say to Rembrandt." And she sat down authoritatively, like a teacher in front of a class, in the writing master's abandoned chair.

"You know," she said, forcing her flat brown eyes to gaze at him gravely, "to me you and Allaert are just like brothers. He has no real brothers, and you're his closest friend, the one he talks about most— and that, if you don't mind my saying so, makes me feel as if I'm your sister, so I hope you won't object if I talk to you quite frankly, the way a sister would."

He was surprised and a little saddened by her claim to closeness. Though he and Allaert were always exchanging words and gestures that indicated intimacy, they were not intimate; their short embraces, their repeated and earnest utterances of each other's first names, their way of staring intently, if blankly, at each other were nothing but means of hiding their acute awareness of their separation. "Lecture me all you like, Lotje," he said. "I'm touched and flattered by your interest."

"I hope it won't sound like a lecture—I certainly don't mean it that way. I only wanted to ask you, why didn't you ever come to the Sylviuses' 'at homes' before?"

"I was never invited."

"People don't send out *cards* for 'at homes'—they simply let other people know they're going to have them, and the other people are supposed to drop in. Now, I know Saskia van Uylenburgh told you the Sylviuses were *having* them"—her voice, already a mere cultivated murmur, dropped to a whisper—"I know because I heard her mention it to you. And when you didn't take it up, it probably hurt her feelings—I know it would have hurt *mine* if I had been in her place."

He certainly didn't want to hurt Saskia's feelings, yet he was irritated by the whole elaborate and useless fabric of this kind of society: did it matter who asked whom or which of the guests was the first to be offered the fruit? "I suppose it was stupid of me not to realize—"

"Not stupid, Rembrandt. Only careless."

"But isn't it all rather silly? If she wanted me to come, couldn't she have told me so?"

She allowed her smooth pale brown head to droop to one side to indicate her bafflement. She gave him a look of coy reproach, and expelled an indulgent if exasperated sigh. "Really, now, you know better," she said. "She couldn't ask you—"

"Why not?"

"Because a woman just can't ask a man. It would be bold and indelicate; and Saskia van Uylenburgh, though she's very lively and free, wouldn't under any circumstances be bold. Allaert didn't want me to mention it to you—he thought you might be offended—but I didn't see how I could offend you by offering you a piece of well-intentioned advice. If I were you, I'd come to the Sylviuses' every Wednesday evening and stay at least an hour, though I wouldn't bring a present every time. That won't be necessary, the first time is enough."

He wished he could have believed in that sisterly relationship which she avowed. If he had not felt an impassable distance between them—and the present exchange had widened rather than diminished it—he could have put her knowledge to excellent use. There were urgent questions that he wanted to ask her. Would he do better to apologize to his love for his oversight or to forget it? Had Matthys Kolkoen and Frans van Pellicorne outstripped him in assiduous attendance at the Wednesday evenings? Would it be proper or calamitous for him to mention marriage to his host tonight? But she, with her straight back and her schoolteacher's air and her bland face—he could ask her nothing.

"To tell the truth, you don't visit nearly as much as you ought to," she said.

He knew, and the knowledge was galling to him, that she was thinking how he had failed, in spite of repeated hints and open invitations, to pay his respects to her ailing mother-in-law. Those hollowed cheeks, those sunken eyes and purplish lips put him so plainly in the wrong that his only response was anger. "It's easy for you to say that, Lotje. You've got nothing to do but visit," he said. "Every hour I take away from my easel means something lost. What I could paint today won't be there for me to paint tomorrow, like napkins to be hemmed and silver to be polished. If I don't get it down today, I may never get it down."

"Oh, I know that. Believe me, I know it, and Allaert knows it, and his mother, too. Only—"

"Only what?"

"Only there are some claims"—she twisted her beautiful linen handkerchief and tied a knot in it—"some claims that we have to answer if we want to live with anybody besides ourselves. Even the most gifted of us have to stop sometimes"—she meant to finish, she refused to be silenced even by the sharp voice of the maid announcing Heer Maurits Huyghens—"to show our respect—our consideration for—well, love and friendship and birth and—and death."

He supposed all that was so, but he was glad to be relieved of the necessity to agree. As the newcomer entered the parlor she got up and went over to the players on the other side of the room, and whatever guilt and affronted pride she had left him with he was able to dissipate in his disappointment in the guest. Heer Maurits Huyghens, standing against the rust-colored portieres, would have been unprepossessing even without the contrast of his subtle and urbane brother. His body was short and stocky in bottle-green woolen; his manner was anxious and rigid; and his face—pallid and of a yellowish cast—had a peculiarly squashed look, like a wax mask that has been pushed awry by a destructive hand. But he too was adept at the mysterious protocol; he shook hands with everybody in what was obviously a prescribed order, though it was not the order in which Saskia had passed the fruit. He did not hear Rembrandt's name, for he mumbled only a vague approximation of it, though for that there was some excuse: the maid had come in to light the candles, and there was a great to-do about a minor accident —some wax had dripped from her taper and spotted Lotje's dress.

The arrival, the newly lighted candles, the end of the backgammon, and the consequent shifting of everybody's position except Vrouw van Hoorn's promised more liveliness. There was more conversation, but it was not the sort that Rembrandt could take part in: everybody wanted to hear what was going on at The Hague. There was idle talk about Prince Frederik Hendrik's horses and his wife's appetite, minute talk about the tactics that had succeeded so brilliantly at the siege of Maestricht, obscure talk about the possibility of a negotiated peace with Spain. And his sense of isolation was deepened because Saskia did not come to take the empty chair at his side, but seated herself instead on the little stool at Pastor Sylvius's feet.

Was it true that he had hurt her feelings? Had she gone so far as to tell Lotje so? As it had seemed inconceivable to him in the old days at Lastman's that Allaert could be lonely, so he found it hard to believe she could have vulnerable sensibilities. Yet he had seen her hurt at the rudeness of a tapster in a village inn, pained at the loss of a handkerchief that was a gift from one of her sisters; and this very evening, as she had lowered her head over his bouquet, her eyes had filled with tears. Like all the others, she had her question to put to Heer Maurits Huyghens, a foolish little question about the masked dances that were in fashion at The Hague. She introduced it ineptly, when the talk was on heavier matters, so that he was embarrassed for her; and his love was made more poignant by his knowledge of her fallibility—dear, trivial, tender little fool that she was, he had never loved her so much!

With the questioning over, the party fell back into little groups; and since nobody joined him, he was left sitting solitary and conspicuous. He had begun to wonder whether he should take his leave, when the host, having patted the bright curly head, got up from his place near the window and came across the room to his stranded guest. "We haven't had more than a word together, have we?" he said. "I have no pictures to show you, more's the pity, but maybe you'd be interested in seeing what I have in the way of books."

If, as they crossed the little hall, his heart hastened at the thought that Pastor Sylvius might be making an opportunity for a private interview, he was enough in command of himself to realize as soon as the delicate old scholar faced him in the decorous quiet of the study that he had no aim except the avowed one of showing his books. Books in English, books in Latin, books in German and Greek—books giving off a smell of faded leather and dry, aged paper—the pastor took them down one after the other from the orderly shelves and turned the pages as if the print could nourish and bless his old hands. How anybody could care so much for words on paper he had never been able to understand, but it was impossible to doubt the man's sincerity. And when he pulled out of a closed cupboard what was obviously his prize—a great Hebrew Old Testament bound in wine-red leather and closed with ornate metal clasps—he succeeded in conveying some of his enthusiasm to his visitor: it was as if in looking at the large Hebrew characters, stern and virile, he were seeing the authentic Word of God. "Might I come some day and copy a page or two?" he asked. "I often have to do Hebrew texts when I'm painting the Sacred Books in Old Testament scenes, and I've never seen anything as clear and beautiful as this."

"Come any time you like and copy whatever you want."

"Do you read Hebrew, your honor?"

"I read it a little, very haltingly. There was a time when it was a serious offense to know Hebrew or Greek and read the Testaments in the originals. Thank God that time is past, and please God we never bring it back again by growing as bigoted as our predecessors."

It was possible that the exquisite old man was trying to let him know that to ally oneself with the Sylviuses and van Uylenburghs was not to sign oneself over to the strictures of militant Calvinism—it was possible but not probable. His keen eyes did not raise themselves to his visitor's face, and his frail hands kept turning the stiff and rustling pages as he identified familiar passages. Yet every now and again he allowed himself to brush shoulders with his guest, and that brief familiarity seemed to imply that the young man's person was acceptable.

But the quiet and gratifying interlude in the study was short-lived: not more than a quarter of an hour could have gone by before Heer Maurits Huyghens broke in. "Van Rijn—Rembrandt van Rijn—is that who you are?" he said in a clipped baritone utterly devoid of graciousness. "I didn't get the name the first time because of all the fuss about the lady's dress."

Though he himself had felt that too much was made over the spot of wax, he found himself ranged with the others now that this inferior member of the Huyghens family seemed to be censuring them. "Yes, van Rijn," he said, and he said it curtly, avoiding the eyes and the squashed nose and staring at the low and yellowish brow.

"Good. I wanted to see you about a commission. If I hadn't run into you here, I would have had to call on you tomorrow. You remember my brother Constantyn—he bought some things from you in Leyden— anyhow, he says you're the person to order a portrait from, and he knows about such things. But I have business to attend to—I can't be staying here very long—so it'll have to be done at once."

If he had been making a conscious effort, Heer Maurits Huyghens could not have put him more definitely into the category of the paid artisan. "I have more portrait commissions than I can take care of," he said coldly, and would have added that he preferred to set his own time, if the old pastor had not broken in.

"Yes, Maurits," he said in a pacifying voice. "I'm sure Heer van Rijn would like to oblige you, but Saskia tells me every minute of his time is taken for weeks ahead."

"But couldn't you edge me in somehow? I'm going to be in Amsterdam for eight days."

"I'm afraid not. I have sittings on Thursday, Friday, and Saturday—"

"What about Sunday? You wouldn't have any scruples, would you, about working on the Lord's Day—"

"No, it isn't that," he said.

"Then what is it? I wouldn't be demanding or critical. My brother assures me that your work is the best to be had in the Netherlands."

If he gave way at last before the ungracious persistence, it was neither because he could not stand firm nor because he wished to ingratiate himself with Pastor Sylvius; it was only because he had a sudden vivid recollection of that bitter cold evening in the outbuilding behind his father's mill when the dapper little figure had bent close to his *Judas*, taking it in with his luminous eyes and murmuring over it with a sound like a dove.

It was the pastor who forestalled any unseemly discussion about the price: the instant the appointment was made, he stepped between his guests, took each of them by the elbow, and marched them across the hall into the sitting room. "There, now, you have a chance to talk to your old friend—she's alone at last," he said, and gave Rembrandt an almost imperceptible push in the direction of Vrouw van Hoorn's chair.

The game had been removed, but not the little table. She was alone at it now, sitting forward with her elbows on top of it and her face between her two veined hands. Because she was pulling the loose skin of her cheeks and forehead upward and backward with her fingertips, much of the change in her was obliterated: he saw her for the first time this evening as the same woman who had stood in front of the fan of laurel leaves, and he was disturbed to find himself face to face with the embodiment of that memory. It had been easier for him to deal with Allaert, whom the years had transformed almost into a stranger; it had been easier for him to deal with her earlier tonight when the ravages of her illness had dissociated her from what she had been in the past. "I'm glad you came over, even if you were so long about it," she said with utter simplicity. "You disappeared for a while, and I thought you were gone."

"Oh, no." He could not bring himself to fabricate a gallant speech about its being unthinkable that he would leave without coming over to her. "I was in the study with the pastor. He was showing me his books."

"Did he show you his Hebrew Bible?"

"Yes. It's a beautiful thing."

"I'll tell you something—he must be quite taken with you if he showed you that. That's something he shows only to his favorite guests."

She sighed then and shifted her back against the pillow, and he could not tell whether she had been assailed by pain or was out of patience with the halting triviality of what was being said. He stared at the darkened window behind her—every now and again it was purpled by a flicker of distant lightning—and told himself that he must find some way to join the present to the past, must establish some connection between the two who were making empty conversation here in Pastor Sylvius's parlor and the two who had talked years ago in the little chamber in the house on the Heerengracht. But what could he say? To ask how things went with her would be out of the question—it was all too obvious from the loose rings on her fingers and the purple tinge in her lips and the almost fleshless collarbone shining through the thin stuff of her dress. Nor could he talk of Allaert without artificial protestations about a friendship that did not really exist. And how, after his inexcusable neglect, could he be so crude and presumptuous as to talk about himself?

"I wanted to tell you: I went to see your *Anatomy Lesson* twice—"

"That was very good of you."

"To tell God's truth, it *would* have been very good of me if it hadn't been the painting it is. I somehow find it very hard to get upstairs these days; I'm miserably short of breath. But it was certainly worth the effort; there's no other Regents' piece in the Netherlands like it. The rest of them, even the best, are official pronouncements, like funeral speeches and inaugural orations. Yours is the only one that isn't a comment. Yours is the thing itself."

Nobody else had spoken of his picture in such words. He crossed his arms on the table and bent a little closer to her, close enough to catch the remembered smell of her perfume—the vague and powdery smell of crushed dried flowers. "Do you mean that I managed to keep myself out of it?" he said.

"Oh, no, God forbid! You were in it, unquestionably. What you managed to keep out of it was—well, everybody else. I don't know why

212

it should be, but I keep thinking of your painting in terms of saying something, and what you didn't say was what everybody else has said—all the old words the audience is waiting for. Anyway I went to see it twice, and both times it addressed me directly, and I wanted you to know that I listened with all my mind and heart."

In return for that he could give her only a formula of gratefulness worn thin by frequent use: though none of the scores who had complimented him had said anything like what she had said, he could not find the words to tell her so. She smiled at him, still molding the weary flesh of her face into some semblance of vitality and youth; and the pale flicker showed again at the window behind her head, calling into being for an instant a black cluster of leaves outside.

"I've often thought of that time at Allaert's nameday party. I don't know what came over me—I must have thought I was a sibyl, I made so many prophecies—and very gloomy prophecies they were, as I remember them," she said. "I kept telling you what a long, hard time you were going to have before you made your way, and here you are in your middle twenties, and everybody says you're the first painter in Amsterdam."

Sharp and transitory as the light at the window, that instant came back to him: the long wait for the names that she never uttered—Dürer, Titian, Michelangelo—the carefully measured praise, the warning about the mistakes and disappointments that were bound to come. Well, the account was settled; she was unsaying those wounding things that had blighted his hopes, but he did not feel the hot exultation that would have flooded up in him if she had done it a year ago. All he could feel was an aching regret that he should have carried his grievance against her so long, a melting shame that some unyielding core of bitterness had kept him from her and forced her to use her weak and breathy voice to gainsay herself.

A gust of wind and a few large spattering drops came hard against the casement. "Oh, is it raining?" she said, turning her head without moving her supporting fingers. "I'd better hurry then—I haven't said what I wanted to, and Allaert and Lotje'll be here in a minute to rush me off—they act as if I might melt if I were out in a little rain. That same evening, I believe I told you I'd come some day and ask you to do my portrait. I must have sounded patronizing then—the way it's worked out, if you were to do my portrait now, you'd be doing a great favor for *me*—"

And without warning he was on the point of weeping; he had to tighten his throat against an upward rush of tears. As if in some pale, unearthly illumination he saw the line of his life shooting up while theirs was sinking—her pain, the ruin of her beauty, the glittering Allaert faded into mediocrity—and his heart was swollen with pity. "Let me paint your portrait," he said, barely able to keep himself from sobbing. "I've never painted anybody like you. I could make it something wonderful. You've no idea how much I could get into it—the wisdom and the beauty and the kindness—"

When he dared to look at her, he saw that her eyes also were wet, though her mouth was curved in a quiet smile. "Oh, no. Not that I wouldn't love to have you do it, but we couldn't—not now, anyway," she said. "It isn't because I'd mind seeing myself the way I am—I wouldn't mind that at all. Only, you've no idea how much of your time it would take; we'd never get finished. I'm ridiculously feeble—I spend more time in bed than out of it these days—and you'd scarcely get started before I'd have to take a rest. But it's good of you to offer, and you don't have to paint me for me to see how it would be—" She took her hands away from her cheeks, reached across the table, and moved her fingertips down the side of his face in a dry and ghostly caress. "I have a good imagination, and I can imagine how it would be, and that's enough."

Not caring who might see him, he caught that hand and covered it with kisses. It did not withdraw itself until he had recorded upon it his sorrow, his belated contrition, his stifled love. And when he relinquished it, her face—loose and ravaged though it was without the supporting fingers—was nevertheless so serene that he could draw serenity from it. "Just as I told you, they've noticed that it's raining, and they're coming to march me off," she said.

They came, Lotje and Allaert, to gather up her fan and her handkerchief and to drape a shawl around her shoulders, to talk about the storm that was coming and the fact that Father would be worrying—he had forgotten Father; it was as if Father did not exist.

"You'll come with us, won't you, Rembrandt?" said Allaert. "We'll take Mother home first, and then we'll take you."

Under the circumstances he could not have refused, even though there was nothing to be gained but a few minutes of silence or superficial talk in their carriage. For some incomprehensible reason he was glad that fortune had not dealt so fabulously with him that he had a carriage of his own, glad that he could accept at least this favor from them. Sustained by the conviction that he was doing the proper thing, he went to bid the Sylviuses good night. The pastor shook his hand cordially, and the pastor's wife thanked him again for the bouquet, but Saskia barely looked at him and gave him only her fingertips. "I'm sorry we're going so early. It's because of the storm," he said.

"I *thought* you might be staying a little longer," said Saskia, opening the door. "But naturally you wouldn't want to get caught in a storm. The important thing is not to get yourself wet." Whereupon, without so much as a smile, she closed the door behind him and went back into the room; he could see her through the window as the carriage started off—her head high and her cheeks flushed—making another round with her salver of fruit.

It was more than a week before he had any news of her. The portrait, which was his only fixed excuse for seeing her at regular intervals, was finished; there were no little suppers arranged, since everybody was enjoying the last of the summer weather in the country; and he waited with apprehension and yearning for the unnamed time when he would see her again. But when the occasion came, it was in a form that left him disturbed and nettled. A note was slipped under his door, a strangely formal note written in the old lady's pale and elegant script, asking him to come to the Sylviuses' on Friday evening. Friday was not an "at home," and something in the stiffness of the note convinced him he was being summoned rather than invited; he supposed his intentions had somehow gotten themselves conveyed to the elderly couple, and that they wanted a more private situation in which to look him over and decide whether he was an appropriate suitor for so richly dowered a bride.

He was uneasy over his lack of savings, and he had half a mind to let them know, if they inquired about his financial status, that he would be better off by a thousand florins if their nephew Hendrik ever saw fit to discharge his obligations. It gave him some satisfaction to reject at least part of their hospitality in his answer: Vrouw Sylvius had said it would be a pleasure to have him sit down to supper with them, but since he was already committed to take supper with the Tulps that night, he wrote that he could not come until eight and did not trouble to add the customary formula of regret. His nervousness made him unusually talkative over the Tulps' ample and relaxed table; he paid noisy court to the lively, sharp-tongued wife and the shy, blond little daughter, who was so taken with him that she sat on his knee while she was eating her sweet. It was the doctor who hurried him off, trying meanwhile to pacify the little girl, whose small, thin fingers clutched at his jacket—she began to whimper as soon as he opened the door and wanted to follow him into the dusky street.

The few flower stalls still open had little to offer, and the nosegay he took with him this time was a dreary and haphazard collection of drying boxwood sprigs and half a dozen autumnal roses. It made no difference, he told himself, walking up the orderly path with the failing chirp of a late cricket in his ears; whatever he brought, the old lady was bound to confiscate. Having rapped twice, he set his face into a cold and preoccupied frown suitable for the eye of the sharp parlormaid; and he felt both foolish and unnerved when it was Saskia—and a pale Saskia, strangely diffident and subdued—who opened the door.

She was wearing, probably for the last time in the dying summer season, the peach-colored muslin dress in which she had come to him that Sunday when for the first time he had known himself to be in love. But then she had been all animation, all breathless motion, and tonight she was almost alien to him in her stillness and her gravity: she had the strained air of somebody waiting, and her eyes were blurred as if she had lately wept. When he shook hands with her—she gave him only the cold tips of her dimpled fingers—he wondered whether she could be suffering from some womanish ailment or had just had a serious argument with her guardians. But once they had entered the living room, the easy cordiality of the pastor and his wife dispelled the second conjecture: the old lady did not reach for the bouquet but merely nodded toward the roses and said with a kind of doting tenderness, "Saskia, I take it these are for you." And this turn of events was so unexpected that he could make only a poor business of presenting the nosegay: his bow was too formal and his eyes refused to meet the strange, wan eyes of his beloved. The host and hostess settled into their matched chairs on either side of the table near the window; he took a seat to the right of Vrouw Sylvius, and Saskia sank down in a descending cloud of peach-colored muslin on the little stool at the pastor's feet.

She looked so sad and listless with her head bent and her shoulders drooping and the shoddy flowers lying on her knees that he did not find it easy to carry on conversation. The decorous atmosphere was the more chilling after Dr. Tulp's comfortable family supper; and the persistent suspicion that he was under careful scrutiny made him all the more inarticulate. He tried to talk of the afternoons he had spent doing the portrait of Heer Maurits Huyghens, but the subject was singularly unrewarding; that gentleman had proved even less amiable on closer observation, and the only piece of intelligence he had collected during the sittings was the fact that the Prince had a mania for Flemish painting—a bit of information it was quite impossible to work in.

"It was good of you to take that commission," said the pastor, laying his veined and delicate hand on Saskia's curls. "I could see you didn't want it."

"Oh, I'm glad enough to get commissions. It was only that I was pressed for time," he said.

"Your mother must be very proud of the wonderful reputation you've made yourself here," said the pastor's lady. "Next time you write her, please offer her my congratulations on your success."

The graciousness of that—the easy assumption that such social amenities could pass between a woman of Vrouw Sylvius's station and his mother had a strange impact upon him: he looked around him, and it was as if he were seeing the room and the people in it for the first time. These walls and floors and ceilings, like the humbler ones in Leyden, were also a human habitation, the scene of human closeness and estrangement, human passion and serenity. These two old people here, for all their ruffs and the fine cloth that covered their bodies, were also open to rheumatic twinges and the aching weariness of the waning years. And it was profoundly moving that the girl in the peach-colored muslin should have lost a little of her bloom tonight, should, like any

216

other daughter of Eve, be vulnerable to family stresses or the changes of the moon.

Whereupon he fell to talking almost as freely as he had talked to Saskia near the gold-streaked window at Hendrik's supper party. If they were drawing him out, they were doing it with the most considerate of questions; if he was leaving himself exposed to the scrutiny of their tired and knowing eyes, he did not care. Being the painter of *The Anatomy Lesson of Doctor Tulp,* he did not hesitate to recount his lack of success with Pieter Lastman. Though he suppressed the sordidness of the years in the cluttered outbuilding behind the mill, he did not attempt to cover up the poverty or the isolation. What he was now, he neither exaggerated nor diminished, and in the shadowy room where the talk had been so earnest that nobody had thought of calling for candles, he gave what he knew to be a just account of himself.

It had gone so well—the pastor had nodded with such grave comprehension and the pastor's wife had laid such a motherly hand on his sleeve—it had gone so well that he could see no reason for the sudden descent of an embarrassing silence. Vrouw Sylvius was looking anxiously out the window at the fading light; her husband was studying his own hands while a nervous smile played at the corners of his lips; and Saskia, her head suddenly high and two spots of red burning in the paleness of her cheeks, took the shabby nosegay out of her lap and, plainly wanting to indicate that she rejected it, laid it on the floor.

"It's getting dark," said the little old lady.

Her husband coughed, and Saskia flicked a boxwood leaf from her knee.

"Yes, it's getting dark," Vrouw Sylvius repeated in a quavering but determined voice, "and if you two children want to take a walk in the garden, you'd better do it soon."

"Aunt!" said Saskia.

"Oh," said Rembrandt, "yes, of course. I've never seen your garden." He got up, bewildered, and offered his arm to Saskia since Vrouw Sylvius did not rise. And it was not until the two of them had passed wordless through a doorway, had walked down a little aisle of clipped hedges and issued into a garden already chilly and dried with the advance of autumn—it was not until she turned, still wordless, and faced him under a yellowing sycamore, that he understood. They had fashioned for him the occasion which he had not had the wit and courage to fashion for himself; they had sent him into the garden to make his declaration of love.

"If you didn't want to come out here, you didn't have to," she said in a voice that was choked by tears. "I never told my aunt to send you out here with me. You can go right back in as soon as you please."

There was so little light left that he could see her only dimly. Her hair was a mist, her face was a tear-streaked oval, her eyes—they would not look at him—were wet and bright. "Why should I want to go back? I want to stay with you forever."

"Nobody would know it from the way you act—"

He came a step closer to her, over crumbling leaves; and the innocent fragrance of her came up to him with the smell of drying summer things. "I was afraid," he said. "I didn't dare."

"Afraid of what?"

"Afraid to ask, afraid you wouldn't have me."

She covered her face and sobbed aloud, and he felt her sobs like thrusts of pain in his own chest. "*I* wouldn't have *you*—after the shameless way you've made me run after you!" she said.

He reached for her, but she was not easy to encompass. Before she would let him hold her, she had to vent her ruined pride upon him—she beat his chest with her little soft fists. "You never came, you never said you loved me, I had to tell Lotje, you even had to be sent out here with me tonight," she said, and then subsided against him; and the first kiss he set upon her was salted with the salt of her weeping.

"Oh, but I love you, I love you," he said, crushing and cradling her against him, driven half out of his mind by the antitheses of passion and tenderness, pride and remorse, exultation and regret.

"Do you? Are you certain?"

"Certain, certain. I knew it the instant I saw you, that time when you and Hendrik walked into the room—"

"I'm not what you ought to have." She was sobbing again. "I'm not intelligent."

"You're so much beyond anything I ever dreamed that I can't believe I'm holding you."

"Well, you are, and you've got to stop it now because I ought to go back in there and tell them—they're worried about me."

But he held her there yet a little, kissing her round forehead and her living hair, tasting her lips, saying to himself: Here she is against me, these are her lips that I kiss . . . Her hand that had struck him moved tenderly and childishly, as if to wipe the blows away, over the cloth of his jacket; and he remembered to look to her pride. "Will you marry me, then?" he asked, and she laughed, half-mocking, half-gratified, and he felt the warm breath of her laughter against his shoulder.

"What else?" She stepped away from him and tidied her dress and hair and wiped her face with the back of her hand and started up the boxwood aisle toward the lighted open door.

Vrouw Sylvius stood in the hallway, ostentatiously busy picking dead leaves from a bunch of greens on a little table, but she raised her head as soon as she heard their steps; and in spite of the enforced serenity of her face, he could tell by the irrepressible question in her eyes how many times his beloved had cried against her breast. Saskia nodded and the two women embraced, the white hair with its neat part coming up against the fiery curls. "I wish you two as much happiness as I've had with my husband," she said, looking at him with wet eyes over her niece's shoulder. "I couldn't wish you anything better. Go into the study, Rembrandt, and talk a little with the pastor. Saskia and I are going upstairs, but she'll be down again before you leave. God bless you, dear nephew, and good night."

It was a solemn figure that confronted him in the study, enthroned behind a desk and between two tall brass candlesticks whose candles burned with steady flames. Though some of the solemnity was doubtless ritualistic, and probably emphasized by the fact that the pastor was not really the bestowing father but was actually speaking for the dead, the keen and sunken eyes admonished him into remembering much that he wished he could have forgotten—his neglected accounts, his empty purse, his exploits with the girls on Pieter-Jacob Street. "Sit down, my son," he said, and it was impossible to tell whether he was addressing a member of his family or one of the errant sheep God had given into his care.

He sat in the chair that had been placed for him, his knees against the back of the desk and his face in the candlelight.

"I wanted to talk to you a little . . ."

He felt the blood stinging in the thin skin of his cheeks, and sustained himself with the thought that he had three things in his favor: his God-given talent, his peasant good health, and his sturdy virility.

"I wanted to talk to you a little about your wife-to-be. I wish I knew her better than I do—she isn't mine, and whatever I say you must take with some reservation, realizing that there's a great deal I can't know—"

"I'm sure there's very little you don't know, your honor."

"No, that's not really so." He smiled a melancholy smile and curved his thin fingers around the base of the candlestick. "She's elusive—and besides, she's so young and we're so old. My wife, too—she doesn't feel she knows her well. For example, I've sometimes thought she was more fragile, more vulnerable than her high spirits would lead one to believe. That may be because she's been an orphan so long, and everybody's been sorry for her and treated her with maybe too much gentleness."

"I can understand how they would," he said, so sure of himself on that score that he had no trouble making his eyes meet the weary, sunken ones on the other side of the desk. "I couldn't be anything but gentle with her—she's so precious to me."

"I'm glad of that—I'm very glad of that. You can't see it now, of course, but there will probably be times when she'll fall short of what the usual husband demands of the usual wife. She has all the graces and none of the skills; she can dance and arrange fruit and flowers and charm the most crotchety old Calvinist pastor into forgetting Doomsday for a

219

while, but my wife tells me that she's totally incapable of sewing a straight seam or making a pot of stew. Not that you won't be able to afford enough servants between you. Her father left her forty thousand florins"—he said the incredible sum distinctly, as if to murmur it would be affected and vulgar—"and you yourself can hope for an excellent living, I understand. I mention it only because I wanted to let you know that you'll be kinder to her if you don't spend it—as you'd naturally want to—to spoil her and indulge her and deck her out. The kindest thing you can do for her is to have others do the sort of thing she's never learned to do herself."

He did not answer; he was far too dazed by the forty thousand. A fourth of that sum seemed inexhaustible, but he felt no impulse to point out that they could live in luxury on it for a lifetime. Its very magnitude made it awesome, made it something he would be almost afraid to touch.

The pastor's spare fingers kept rubbing the smooth base of the candlestick. "There's something else, and I don't quite know how to put it," he said. "If I told you she was heedless, you might think her a great deal worse than she is. And yet there's no other word for it—she *is* heedless, not so much for others as for herself. Life burns very bright in her, and it's a beautiful thing to witness. But it's as if everything were consumed in the present—she never thinks about the future, and she hardly ever mentions the past. The sorrows of this world simply have no place in her consideration. Not that I mean she isn't sympathetic—she has the tenderest heart on earth—but she doesn't seem to believe there'll ever be any difficulties for her; all she anticipates is one long carnival, so that it's hard for a person to imagine her nursing sick children or seeing them grow up and leave her—it's hard to imagine her getting old—"

Something in that frightened him; he found that his hands were clasped hard on the edge of the desk and that his knees were aching from pressing against the wood. "She's young, and she's probably always been so happy she scarcely knows what trouble is," he said. "And I suppose life will remedy that—all of us, even the happiest, come to that knowledge soon enough."

"Yes, I suppose so. Only"—the thin hand went up and molded the wax that was dripping down the side of the candle—"only, if misfortunes come, as they certainly must, don't expect fortitude of her or be hard with her for the lack of it. She's a child, my son, and I'm afraid she'll always be a child."

"I hope I'll have enough fortitude for both of us."

"I hope so. I truly hope so." He sighed like a man who was finished discharging a heavy duty, and leaned back in his carved chair and smiled. "My wife and I are very happy that you'll be living in Amsterdam—she'll not be leaving us that way," he said. "She wants me to tell you—that is, she told me to tell you *if* you asked for her—that she'd think it very good of you if you were willing to wait until June."

"June?" He who had never believed he would have her at all could not bear to think he would not have her in a week. "Why does she want to put it off until June?"

The pastor moved his thin shoulders in an almost imperceptible shrug. "I don't know, I really don't know," he said. "It's certainly not that she has any doubt about it. Her heart is set on it; she tells my wife that from the day after she got here she's thought of nothing but you. I think it may have something to do with her birthday—in June she'll be twenty-one and her own mistress. And there you have it again, I don't really know her—if she's waiting for the reason I suspect, then she's showing herself far from heedless, then she's delaying something she wants with all her soul out of consideration—well, out of consideration for me."

"I don't believe I understand, your honor."

"You see, she's an orphan; and if she marries before she comes of age, then I'm the one to give her, I take the responsibility. Not, you understand, that I'd hold back in the least; little as we've seen of you, my wife and I are satisfied, completely satisfied. But I imagine she has some crazy notion that she's the one that ought to take the—the legal steps—"

He had paused, even stammered a little, and it seemed to Rembrandt that he had been on the point of saying "the risk." He was surprised to find that he was not in the least affronted; staring at the pale old face between the still flames of the candles, he knew his own heedlessness, his way of wandering off into that world in which he painted, the imperious impulses of his unruly heart—and his exultation was made the more intense by the realization that he was afraid. "Any husband is a risk," he said after long silence. "And I suppose I'm more of a risk than most because I can't honestly say that I know myself."

"You're good, my son; that much I'd swear to. And now I'll not sit here and lecture you any longer—it's a role I don't fancy, and I'm not at home in it without my pulpit. God bless you and give you as much happiness as a son of Adam can expect outside of Paradise. I'll go and call your bride."

They were alone together then, he and Saskia, in the empty parlor. She had wept a good deal in the interim; he could tell it from the red circles around her eyes. She had taken his nosegay apart and wore one of the roses in her hair and another thrust into the brooch between her breasts, and that second rose gave him occasion for the only intimacy he dared to claim that night. With the curtains still open and so many candles burning and the footfalls of the old couple wandering back and forth in the room above their heads, he did not even venture to hold her as he had held her in the garden; but once, on the pretense that he wanted to smell the rose, he brought his face very close to her breast. And strangely—not passionately, but almost as if it were a piece

221

of ritual—she dragged down the peach-colored muslin to bare the beautiful, veined round of living flesh almost to the nipple; and there, once he had kissed it, she cradled his head. For him too, admonished and chastened as he was, that first closeness was almost without passion. Wonderment, gratefulness, tenderness, and the knowledge of their mutual mortality so wrought with him while he pressed his cheek against the yielding softness that when he raised his head the rumpled cloth of her dress was spotted with his tears.

BOOK V

1634
-
1637

Three deaths, as fleeting as the shadows of summer clouds, passed in that year across the rich green meadow of his happiness. In July while he was still in Friesland, lingering there after the wedding among her married sisters—all of them blond and lively but none half as beautiful as she—news came that his brother Gerrit had died. Nobody suggested that he hie himself out of his marriage bed and make the journey from Anna-Parochie to Leyden: Gerrit had so long been close to death that his going was merely the fulfillment of a melancholy expectation and called for no more than a letter and a promise that he would soon be home to visit the grave with his bride. The news came in the afternoon, and was troubling mostly because his little love did not seem to know what to do with it—they had been swinging on a rope swing and cutting the last of a prodigious yield of roses before the letter arrived; and she stood in the garden, her eyes questioning and her face puckered, knowing that neither the shears nor the swing would be proper any longer, and wondering whether she ought to weep. He let her know at once that tears were not required and that certainly nothing was to be done to fend off the company invited to dine with them at her sister's house that night. But the rest of the afternoon was marred by awkwardness: she and her sister and brother-in-law were rigid and subdued out of respect for a grief he did not feel, and the arrival of the guests—whom they insisted on considering an imposition on him—was so welcome and enlivening that he was obliged to keep warning himself not to indulge in immoderate gaiety. A couple of times during the evening he had to remind himself what he was being so circumspect about, and when the visitors went home and he and she were alone together in the fresh and airy room upstairs, it was she who made it plain by certain modest maneuvers in undressing that tonight was no night for making love. Lying on his back and sensing her warm, damp body under the thin lawn nightgown, breathing in the scent of her person with the other generative scents of the summer night, he expected hours of wakefulness and longing; but there was something deliciously benumbing in the suspended desire, and he soon fell asleep.

When he wakened next morning, he remembered Gerrit with a start. Dawn was in the room, grey but many-hued like mother-of-pearl; and he recalled another dawn long ago, on those same dunes where he had questioned his greatness, when he and his brother had dragged through the dank and rotting grasses a piece of booty from the sea—a mermaid from the prow of some wrecked ship, her face worn expressionless by the waves, and grey lichen and salt crusted over her breasts. He could still remember the strange foamy shapes of the salt clusters, and above them his brother's face looking seaward. This mermaid, Gerrit had told him in an awed whisper, could have dipped her scaly tail in the warm waters around Cyprus or Japan, could have bathed in the purple tides of the Adriatic or stood frozen to the elbows in some ice-locked port on the Baltic Sea. He was grieving that such a face should have greyed and dwindled and soured, that such wide-ranging dreams should have spiraled down to a house and a room and a bed and a grave, when she turned against him in her sleep. She was always at her loveliest when she turned so, half awake, in the mornings; sleep worked some magical renewal on her flesh, making it soft and smooth as an infant's; sleep moistened her mouth and warmed her neck and loosened her curls. And his sorrow was not so strong that he could reject what her propriety had withheld from him last night; he took her and took her again and yet again; and when they appeared among her kinfolk at the breakfast table, everybody, including themselves, was confused as to what to be embarrassed about—too little grief or too much love.

Afterwards, when friends back in Amsterdam said what a pity it was that his loss should have come upon him during his marriage holiday in Friesland, he nodded politely, but he confessed to himself that there had been no diminution of his long delight. It was almost as if his brother's going increased his own capacity for savoring the world; and months later, when he mentioned that peculiar fact to Dr. Tulp, he said in sudden shame that there must be something unforgivably selfish in his character. "I wouldn't say so. I think it's more or less natural, though most people wouldn't admit it," the good doctor said. "For my part, I'll tell you frankly: I never want my wife or my supper or my glass of wine as much as after I've signed a certificate of death."

It was on a raw and wintry afternoon, besmirched by soot and beaten by rain and sleet, that his apprentice Ferdinand Bol came back from an errand and interrupted him at his work to tell him that Pieter Lastman had died. He was hard put to it to school his face into the proper mask of regret; what he really felt was a surge of anger—anger and fierce bafflement that no honor ever forthcoming and nothing he would ever paint could wring from that stilled mouth the admission that he was something other than he had seemed back in the lean and bitter days. That finality, that stepping away from him into everlasting silence, was all the more galling because he had been intending to visit the master, frankly in order to boast. For my lord Constantyn Huyghens had finally reappeared with an order from the Prince of Orange for a large painting—with the probability of more to follow—on the Passion of Our Lord.

He was putting what he hoped would be the final touches on a *Descent from the Cross* when Bol came in, and perhaps the accession of anger was intensified by something he had been feeling in spite of himself about the work under his hand. It was magnificent, of course—

226

everybody said so—powerful, daring, rich in movement and pathos; but it left him strangely unsatisfied, so much so that he had little urge to work on it and took an inordinate pleasure in standing around and hearing it praised. Could it be that his discontent had its source in the marriage he was trying to bring about between what he felt impelled to paint and the grandiose sort of thing that happened to be the fashion at The Hague?

The fashion at The Hague . . . The flair for the ornate, the theatrical, the obviously noble—it did not upset him that the Prince of Orange was bitten with it; the wonder was that a prince should concern himself with painting at all. But the dazzling commission had been tarnished by the fact that the Prince's secretary had caught—or had always had— a touch of the same infection: having him there at last, murmuring over the paintings and gazing at them with his lustrous eyes, would have been more gratifying if he had not had a tendency to settle and gaze and murmur in the wrong place. Dissatisfaction gnawed at him every time he set to work on the picture and must have been there when Bol came in with the news. In the presence of his apprentice he was able to stifle the inner turmoil, but later in the day he vented it on van Vliet for putting too much acid on an etching plate.

Four sittings had been scheduled for the day of the master's funeral, and it seemed excessive to cancel them, especially since nobody had remembered to invite him to the services. Still, he arranged to step out to watch the funeral train go by, and had the moral satisfaction of standing bareheaded in the icy rain for half an hour before the solemn line approached, walking under the stripped sycamore boughs. Notables of the city—Hooft and Vondel and the Burgomaster van Pellicorne— preceded the coffin; young men, some of them doubtless former apprentices, staggered under the weight of the big black box; but few followed it, and none who did wore the crepes or veils reserved for members of the family.

The coffin passed so close to him that he had to stifle a reasonless impulse to put out his hand and touch the wet black velvet pall; he looked with fright and awe at the young shoulders bending under the weight of the big body that used to move around the studio with so much liveliness and grace; and pity closed his throat when the followers thinned out so soon, leaving the blank street empty under the dripping trees. No wife, no sister, no brother—no child to inherit and preserve the splendor he had accumulated in his great deserted house—nobody to go home and weep out of sheer bereavement—nobody to visit his grave . . . And the pity grew in spite of the ineradicable remembrance of how his own love had been offered and rejected; the pity nagged at him so constantly that he thought of buying up every Lastman canvas on the market, and did indeed buy two and hang them in his workroom, where there was usually light and talk and a fire. In the days after that he found himself for the first time covertly watching his wife and counting the days between her times of the moon. "Have I counted wrong, or are you late this time?" he asked one night when they were sitting alone by the hearth, with sleet driving against the windowpanes; and he was disappointed when she told him that he must have counted wrong: since Pieter Lastman's funeral, there was nothing he wanted so much as a child.

The skaters had disappeared from the canals—the ice had begun to break and the icicles were falling from the roofs and the trees—when word that Vrouw van Hoorn had departed this earth was brought to his door by a liveried servant in a mourning hat, after the manner of the fashionable world. He and Saskia were alone in the workroom when the messenger came; Lysbeth, in a fit of sulks, had gone early to bed, and the warm serenity he had come to value more than almost any other state had settled down upon the two of them—he scratching at his etching plate and she dreaming over her embroidery. Their own preference and the pressure of his work had led them to live more and more to themselves; and they enjoyed themselves with others chiefly when others came to them, when a visitor—Master Coppenol or Dr. Tulp or the Sylviuses or the learned Jewish doctor Ephraim Bonus—dropped in without an invitation. It was just such a casual guest that he expected to see when he opened the door, and the stiff and sober figure on the threshold was as startling as an apparition.

The announcement that was handed to him—together with a pair of printed tickets to admit him and his wife to the services, the funeral, and the cold midday meal thereafter—was not the usual impersonal one. It was written in Lotje's hand, and it told of a peaceful though protracted passing, and of the need that the writer and Allaert felt to have those they loved around them at the time of their loss. He stared long and blankly at the note before he thanked the servant and gave him the required piece of money. The fact that he had been informed as if he were a member of their family or their dearest friend—was it the closing act of an elaborate pretense or the ritualistic fulfillment of a stifled reality? How much had the dead woman loved him? How much might he have loved her and her son and her mild daughter-in-law if he had not deliberately built a wall against them around his vulnerable heart?

The messenger still lingered, stiff and deferential, in the open doorway, with snow-edged stoops and dark gleaming water behind him. Would Heer van Rijn, he asked at last, be good enough to carry a lantern in the funeral procession? The young Vrouw van Hoorn had asked him to make the request but not to press it, since she knew and respected the gentleman's distaste for public display. He was on the point of saying no: he had never attended a great funeral, to say nothing of carrying a lantern like one of the principal mourners, and he was afraid he would not know how to conduct himself. But all at once, breathing in the wintry evening some evanescent scent that was a promise of the spring she would never see, he gave the servant his consent; and afterwards, when he had closed the door and was back at his worktable, he could not explain the strange impulse to Saskia, who kept looking at him every time she reached for her scissors and snipped a thread. If there had ever been a time when he was justified in putting a barrier between himself and this woman whose world had seemed inimical to him, that time was past. And now that he could no longer wait upon her in that great world or any other, could he do any less than walk behind her to her grave?

*

If he looked at it one way, his sister Lysbeth was a touchy and ungrateful creature who meddled in affairs that were none of her business, and she and nobody else was responsible for the present difficulty. If he looked at it another, he himself was not completely innocent: his quarrel with Lysbeth had sprung out of his trouble with van Vliet, and his trouble with van Vliet could be traced to his discontent with the Passion pictures for the Prince; and whatever was the matter with those he could blame only on himself.

The big *Descent from the Cross* had been finished and out of the studio now for months, and the fact that it was actually hanging in one of the magnificent rooms in the Prince's house at The Hague had given it unquestionable authenticity. Everything he had hoped to accomplish in it, his recollection assured him that he had accomplished; and he was laboring away at two of its fellows, an *Ascension* and a *Resurrection,* with the speed and daring that rises out of a precariously established self-confidence. It was unfortunate, then, that van Vliet, as slavishly devoted and as inept as ever, should have been so besotted over the *Descent* that he could not bear to see it hauled out of the house without making a sketch of it for his own folio. And it was still more unfortunate that for weeks he had been working in secret—by way of giving his master a happy surprise—over an etching which would put at least a faint reflection of the glories of that painting into fifteen or twenty eager hands.

Luckily, he came upon that etching in its executor's absence, late at night, when he wandered with a candle into the studio to see how the paint was drying on a double portrait of him and Saskia: the sight of it was more maddening than anything that had happened to him since the death of Pieter Lastman. The light of his candle caught it by accident where it was drying on a worktable, with a casual assortment of small vases to hide it and to weight it down, and the effect upon him was like a thrust in the stomach. Everything in his painting that he had managed to forget—the ostentatious flourishes, the vulgar writhing of the lines, the excessiveness of the gestures and the facial expressions—was not only preserved in van Vliet's etching but came blasting out

229

of it. He kept looking at it as a man prods at an ulcer in his mouth with his tongue; he went from the etching to all of van Vliet's work he could lay his hands on and back to the etching again; sweat drenched his nightshirt in spite of the chill of the April night. And slowly, while he went alternately to cool himself at a window and to warm himself in the ghostly breath of a heap of ashes on the hearth, the problem was transformed: he ceased to think about the Passion paintings and began to ask himself what he ought to do with van Vliet. Wasn't it time to put a stop to his blundering efforts and his multiplication of ugly and useless things? Desire and backbreaking labor were not enough to make a man an artist, no matter what he had told himself back in the Leyden days. Not only the *Descent from the Cross*—no, everything the fellow touched was falsified and vulgarized. And before he went back to the bedroom and fell asleep at last, eased by the healing currents that seemed to flow through the thin stuff of her nightgown from her warm hip and thigh, he had made the decision: there was no help for it—he and the poor ape would have to part.

There was only one hour during the following day when he could take on the wretched encounter—the time he had reserved for working on the *Ascension,* which under the circumstances he had no desire to touch. But that hour was unluckily late in the afternoon; and for most of the day he was forced into hypocritical friendliness with his apprentice—had to watch him pick up his print, sure that it had not been discovered, and hide it in his folio; had to accept a clean palette and brushes from his thick hand; had to joke with him as usual at the midday meal; had to listen in silence when Lysbeth told him what household chores she wanted him to do next week, when he would not be there. It was four o'clock, and the spring sun was shining with incongruous cheerfulness through the studio windows when he found himself alone with van Vliet at last and set about the miserable interview.

His speech was long, but van Vliet did not interrupt him; he merely stood staring down at his own chest and turning the buttons on his dirty jacket with his big hairy hand. The just and carefully chosen phrases were tainted by the realization that much was to be gained from van Vliet's departure—so much that he would feel nothing but relief when the scene was over and the poor devil was on the other side of the door. Flinck and Bol were young gentlemen, and other apprentices of the same kind would be coming to him soon, and this lumbering provincial would be more and more out of place. Certain patrons had raised their eyebrows at his blundering ways and his ignorant language; and Saskia, fire-quick and volatile, was constantly exasperated by his slow motion and his slow-wittedness. If there had been genius or even talent in him, it would have been the teacher's manifest duty to endure and excuse the rest. But the four years here and the five in Leyden had changed him not at all; and to advise him to go and make a decent living at something more suitable was an act of charity . . . So at least

Rembrandt told himself, gazing at the bright window as he finished up his speech, unable to look any longer at the thick-thumbed, fumbling hands.

"Am I to go soon, Master?"

It was a wounding question. He remembered that he himself had not put it to Pieter Lastman; stricken as he was on that bitter afternoon, he had packed up his belongings and left the house on the same night. "Oh, no, there's no particular hurry. Take as long as you like. But I always think it's a good thing to make a fresh start as soon as possible," he said.

"Would you have any idea what I could make a fresh start at?"

There was no irony in that, and no accusation. Poor van Vliet would be incapable of making a scathing reference to any of the matters his master had not thought of until this moment: his unmoored condition, his limited skills, his poverty. He needed advice, and in his need he turned blindly toward the only source of help he had known these nine long years. "Why don't you go back to Leyden and see if you can't get work at the Elzhevirs' press? You're good with plates; you ought to make a fine printer," he said.

"There are presses in Amsterdam, too, aren't there?" It came after a long pause, like a turtle heaving itself up out of the mud.

"Yes, certainly. Bleau's, for one. I only thought you might be happier back home."

"I won't be happy in any case"—it was not a reproach, it was simply an observation—"but I think I wouldn't feel as bad if I stayed in Amsterdam. That way, I wouldn't have to tell my people what's happened until I'd got myself something else. And besides, I'd be able to see you —not often, of course, because I know how busy you are—"

He turned aside from the stupid, guileless face—hating himself, hating his new splendor, hating the Passion pictures—and opened the top drawer of a chest under the window. There was money in it, and several precious stones, and his best brushes—brushes which van Vliet had kept soft and clean for him for years. "Here, take this to help you over the first few weeks," he said, bringing a handful of florins and thrusting them into the thick, yellowish palm.

"Thank you. You've been very good to me, Master."

"No, I haven't." He almost shouted it in his pain. "If I'd been good to you, I'd have told you what I'm telling you now after the first year."

"It's not your fault. You never said I could paint. And I enjoyed it even if I didn't learn too much. Don't think that I'm sorry."

Though he plainly had nothing more to say, he stood for a little longer, bewildered, not knowing what to do, looking down at the crumpled pieces of paper on the floor. Then he sighed and bestirred himself and went to get his folio. For one sick instant Rembrandt thought he was on the point of taking out the appalling print and offering it as a parting gift; but if that intention had kindled in the primal confusion of his brain, it went out almost at once. "I'll get a few things together here, if you don't mind," he said, tying up the leather thongs and looking in perplexity at two of his oils that stood, still wet, against the wall. "Your sister has your supper ready, so don't wait for me. Thank you again, and God bless you, and good night."

After such an encounter, he could scarcely cope with food, and that was a pity: it was a Saturday evening, and on Saturdays Lysbeth always outdid herself to prepare a fine spread. Her object was not so much to crown the working week as to honor an old custom brought out of their life in Leyden; the memory of home was embodied on their Saturday table in the form of a dish he had ceased to care for long ago—the famous "cold dish" made of sugared bread sops floating in a bowl of beer. He found the "cold dish" and the roast goose and the salad arranged festively on the board that Saskia had set with china plates and glass goblets—laying the table was her one household responsibility. But even this her sister-in-law seldom let pass without covertly suggesting that she had not completely mastered it; and tonight, just as his darling —her shoulders draped in a beautiful collar of point lace and her face eager and rosy between her new pearl earrings—sat down in her chair, Lysbeth took away his napkin, which was slightly crumpled at one corner, and handed him an irreproachable one from the sideboard; and Saskia wet her underlip with the tip of her tongue and sighed.

He and she were in the habit of exchanging quick glances over these quirks of Lysbeth's, but tonight she did not raise her bright lashes. When she looked at him, as she did while he was forcing himself to get down a couple of sops and a long draught of the oversweet beer, her eyes did not flicker with malicious amusement; they shone with deep, still solicitude. She might not know anything about housekeeping or the obscure authors who occupied Margheretha van Meer, but she knew *him* in and out and could be depended upon to catch the slightest shadow that passed across his face. There was no way for him to hide his distress; he showed it so plainly that his little wife could do no more than nibble a lettuce leaf and pick at the browned skin on the goose. She added what she could to their uneasy suppertime talk, carefully selecting topics to give nobody any offense: the new building for the Municipal Orphanage on the Kalverstraat, the stillness of the city since the Council had passed its ordinance against the use of carriages inside the gates. But after about a quarter of an hour her anxiety got the better of her caution. "What's the matter, Rembrandt? You aren't sick or anything, are you?" she said.

He assured her that he was perfectly all right and added that he would like to see her as concerned about her own health as she was about his. With Lysbeth there, ready to catch any sign of doting on his part, he did not tell her that he wished she would eat more of her meat and remember to change her shoes after she had been out in the rain. They had learned to suppress much of what they felt and thought when they met at the table in the presence of his sister after the day's absence, and Saskia usually hoarded a dozen things to talk about while they were undressing for bed. But this evening she could not wait; she pushed her scarcely touched plate aside and asked him whether anything had gone wrong at the studio.

"No, nothing's gone wrong," he said, wishing he could postpone the account until Lysbeth was in a better humor. "But I had a very upsetting talk with van Vliet this afternoon. I told him I couldn't keep him any more. I guess I should have done it long ago."

It would have been better if Saskia had stifled the quick smile that dimpled her face; there was too much of sheer relief in it, and it did not completely harmonize with the high-minded pronouncement she delivered after it, tilting her head and securing the pearl in her left ear. "Well, certainly nobody can blame you for letting him go," she said, careful to avoid her sister-in-law's pale, amazed eyes. "He'll be much better off in some other trade. He never belonged in a studio."

"Excuse me," said Lysbeth, "but just what is it you object to—his manners or the way he paints?"

It should have been he who did the answering, but his wife came in before he could think of a mollifying reply. "Both," she said, looking straight at Lysbeth. "He can't paint—he never could—even I can tell that much. And besides, he doesn't wash himself often enough."

"I'm no expert myself," said Lysbeth, throwing down her napkin, "so I wouldn't presume to pass judgment on the way he paints. But if he isn't dainty enough to suit everybody's taste, maybe it's because he works like a horse around here. God knows how I'm going to get the windows cleaned and the fires laid and the heavy shopping done. There'll be nobody around to bother with that sort of thing once *he's* gone."

He could not blame his love if she lost her temper. The taunt about her failure to attend to the housekeeping was undeserved inasmuch as his sister had refused to divide the labors, had jealously kept hold on everything but the most trivial responsibilities. How well Saskia could look to a house was still to be seen: Lysbeth had allowed her to look to nothing but setting the table and arranging the roses. He hoped she would tell his sister so, but anger had robbed her of the ability to offer a just argument. "Whatever needs to be done will get done, whether van Vliet's here or not," she said.

"Yes—but how well?" said Lysbeth.

"Well enough. Well enough, at any rate, to suit me. Some people are much too fussy about those little things."

"Well, maybe I *am* too fussy," said Lysbeth. She got up and carried the "cold dish" from the table to the serving board, and there was something exasperatingly symbolic about the gesture: it was as if she were moving the homely and unwanted virtues of the Leyden life out of the sphere of their sophistication and heedlessness. "Maybe it doesn't make any difference if nobody washes the windows or if the chimney stops up so the room gets filled with smoke. Maybe it's foolish to concern yourself if a bolt of good cloth gets eaten up by moths."

Saskia's eyes grew moist, and her upper lip trembled. Among the fine things she had ordered sent down from Friesland—many of which she had given to Lysbeth in a carnival of generosity—was a shawl from Cashmere with telltale holes in the corner of it; and some two weeks after his wife's possessions had arrived, redolent of her past and her person and her perfume, a moth had gotten into a bolt of woolen that Lysbeth had bought at a bargain. He could still see the riddled spot; it had given him something of a shock when Lysbeth had shown it to him, though she had said she didn't care and had seemed completely satisfied when he told her to buy another bolt without worrying about the price.

"What do you mean—moths? There was only one moth, so far as I remember," he said loudly, fortified by the recollection of his wife's open-handedness. "I must say, I think it's a little petty to brood over it all these months."

"Oh, I know—I know how petty both of you think I am," said Lysbeth with a sob in her voice. She did not look at him; she looked—as she had frequently looked at the *Descent from the Cross,* rolling up her eyes in false appreciation of its false pathos—at the empty wall above his head. "You're busy with important matters, your lives are filled with important people, and I know how I annoy you with my old-fashioned ways—"

"But nobody ever said you annoyed them," said Saskia, appalled by the first sight of her sister-in-law in tears.

"Maybe you don't say it, but I'm not such a fool I don't know what you're thinking. Everything's settled between the two of you. Nobody bothers to ask me about van Vliet; nobody gives a thought to how I'm supposed to get along here after he's gone."

"I didn't ask anybody about van Vliet. What I do about my apprentices is my own business," he said, feeling the goose meat turn into a greasy lump in his stomach. "It's my studio, and I have a right to dismiss any apprentice who isn't up to the mark."

"Now, really, aren't you hiding the real reason from yourself?" she said, abandoning the sobs for an infuriating drawl that had a mad and incongruous note of flirtation in it. "You knew what kind of painter he was before you brought him to Amsterdam. *I* thought you brought him to help around the house, and he never gave you any cause for complaint on that score, God knows. Isn't it more because we've all gotten so elegant that he doesn't fit in, not even as a drudge? Isn't it more because you're ashamed of him in front of Flinck and Bol"—she said the names in a shrill falsetto, intended, he supposed, to imitate patrician speech—"them and your wealthy patrons and your distinguished guests?"

"Suppose that was part of the reason," he said, glaring at her across the dishes. "Suppose he does embarrass me—does that make me a dog?"

"Nobody said you were a dog. All I said was: you're ashamed of him and you got rid of him as soon as you didn't need him any more."

"I gave him his chance, and he made small use of it. He's lived with cultivated people day in, day out and never learned to wash his neck. He's eaten with human beings, and he still eats like an animal. He's heard decent language, and the sort of stuff that comes out of his mouth is what you'd expect out of a drayman. If he hasn't learned anything in all these years, I'm not the only one to blame—it's his fault, too."

The frozen silence that followed his shouting, ominous as it was, sickened him less than the cruel things she had driven him to say about the poor ape who had gone away so peaceably. Remembering the thick hands fumbling with the leather thongs on the folio, he was so distressed that he did not dare to look at Saskia—he knew that the comprehension in her eyes would melt him to tears. He sat on the edge of his chair, twisting and wringing his napkin under the table, but seeing to it that all of him that appeared above the board was immovable and stern. If his sister should scream or hurl a goblet at him—her face, red and puffy with rage, told him that she was capable of anything—he would not flinch, he would remain the embodiment of justice and affronted authority.

But when her voice came out of her, it was low and controlled. "I know what you're implying—you put me in the same class with van Vliet," she said. "You can't say I don't take a bath often enough, and you can't say I eat like an animal, but I wouldn't swear for my language, and I haven't turned into a fine lady in spite of all the wonderful opportunities you've given me."

"Don't be ridiculous. Nobody's talking about you, and you know it."

"The plain, ordinary life we lived back in Leyden"—she gestured toward it where it stood behind her on the sideboard in the form of the "cold dish"—"you're finished with it, you're ashamed of it, you don't want van Vliet or anybody else sticking it into the faces of your fine new friends. And since you're throwing it overboard piece by piece—van Vliet's gone now, he's been discarded like an old shoe—I'll not sit around and wait till my turn comes. I'll leave before I'm asked to—I'll pack right away and take the first canal boat out of here."

If he did not answer her outburst at once, it was only because he was stricken silent by surprise: it had simply never occurred to him that she could go. For the first time, staring at her mottled forehead, he imagined what these rooms could be like without her: no need to stifle amorous cries or amorous laughter, the right to eat one's breakfast any time and naked if one pleased, the right to break the inexorable regularity of the supper hour, to take small journeys without the constraining third in the coach, to arrange a social evening without inviting somebody who would pay his sister court and soothe her touchy sensibilities . . .

"Oh, don't be silly, Lysbeth. We wouldn't think of any such thing," said Saskia without conviction.

"It's nonsense," he said with a brusque heartiness that struck him as inept and spurious. "Of course she doesn't mean a word of it."

"I'll show you whether it's nonsense," she said, getting up so violently that the table shook. "All I need is a room, and they have one for me now in Leyden. I don't stay where I'm not wanted. I'm moving out tonight."

She actually walked out of the room—an act that he witnessed as if it were some detached and distant thing happening in a play. He stared after her, still wordless, even when he heard her slam the door; he could not bring himself to look at Saskia, though he was acutely aware of her quick breathing.

"It's certainly a pity she should take it that way," said his wife in a voice that somehow turned the statement into a question.

"It certainly is." He laid his napkin on the table. "I suppose I'd better go and put a stop to all this foolishness right away."

"Yes, I suppose you'd better." A faint breath came to him across the board, and he could not determine whether she had merely exhaled in relaxation after the excitement or was sighing with regret.

He got up slowly, walked around behind her, and bent down to kiss the curls at the back of her head.

"Oh, don't start *that* sort of thing," she said, laughing strangely. "The longer you stay here, the angrier she's going to be."

He knew that what she said was true, but he blew at the spot behind her ear, pinched her elbow, and kissed the nape of her neck before he went into the hall.

The door was closed. Lysbeth had not locked it, but the spring dampness had swelled the wood, and he had to shove against it with his shoulder, so that he came bursting into her room without poise, even a little foolishly. The chaos he had expected to find there did not exist. She was packing, yes, but not the clothes and furs he had bought to indulge her in her unhappiness—those hung, bruising reminders of cheerful attempts and their futility, in her open closet; poor isolated heaps of necessities—petticoats, nightgowns, plain skirts and jackets—were all that she had laid out on the bed. Her aspect, too, had changed; as she went back and forth from chest and closet to the bed and the open packing case, her bearing was almost dignified. And he knew with a start that the possibility of her departure, which he had entertained for the first time only a few minutes ago, had been with her constantly from the day he had set his heart on Saskia.

"Honestly, Lysbeth, I wish you wouldn't do that," he said, standing helplessly between the door and the bed. "Nothing I said about van Vliet had anything to do with you."

"I liked van Vliet," she said in a flat, drained voice, taking the worst two pairs of shoes out of the bottom of the closet.

"I know you did. I liked him too."

"How could you like him if you said he ate like an animal?"

"You plagued me into saying whatever I said."

"Still, whether I plagued you or not, it happened to be what you really thought."

"It wasn't what I really thought—it was exaggerated. Anyway, it had nothing to do with you, and I wish you'd put those things back in the closet and come and eat your sweet."

"I've eaten my last meal under this roof," she said; and, though the wording of it was pretentious and shopworn, her quiet, measured manner of uttering it gave it an authentic finality.

"But why?"

"Don't ask me why," she said, putting some folded nightgowns into the packing case. "You know."

He did know now, though he had given it no thought beforehand. He knew what it was to lie solitary in this room while two lay embracing in another, knew the bitterness of cleaning up the remains of a feast prepared for the conviviality of others, knew what it was to be gaily welcomed but never eagerly waited for, praised by the mouth but never yearned for by the heart. "Please," he said in a voice roughened by his distress. "If you go like this, I'll never forgive myself."

"Oh, I wouldn't worry about that if I were you. You'll forget it soon enough."

What she said was true, in spite of its pointless flippancy; they would not miss her at their lovers' breakfasts and suppers, and few of their friends would wish her back to witness and pass judgment on a merriment she had never really shared. "Surely you know that's not the case," he said.

"Why lie about it? If a person learns anything in a life as miserable as mine, he learns to tell himself the truth."

She lied to herself, of course, as often as most unhappy mortals. Yet now, because there was nothing of the theatrical in her manner or her voice, he knew that, for once, she was facing reality. She was going back to her mother's lovelessness and Adriaen's censure; she was trading light work for backbreaking labor, loose-handed luxury for mean penuriousness. "The fact that I'm married and love my wife doesn't mean that I don't want you in my house," he said.

"Even if you wanted me—which you don't—I wouldn't stay. Two women don't belong under the same roof-tiles, as the old saying goes. It's *her* house, not mine, and things won't get any more peaceable as time goes on. Besides, I'm tired of trying to be something I'm not. I'd rather be home scrubbing the kitchen floor."

He looked again at the desolate collection of finery hanging in the closet. "Take those with you—they're yours—I want you to have them," he said, his heart made heavy as a stone by the realization that with these words he had accepted her offer to go.

"I won't need them—where would I wear them?"

"I don't know, but take them anyway."

"Because they'd be a reproach to you, hanging there? All right, I'll get them out, but you're making too much of it. There's only one thing, as far as I can see, that you've got to reproach yourself with: you should have sent me away sooner, when I still had something to go back to. There's nothing now—nothing—Hendrik Isaakszoon's married, and Gerrit's dead."

*

It was eleven o'clock according to the chimes that echoed in the dark emptiness of the Surgeons' Guild Hall, and Nicolaas Pieterszoon, otherwise known as Dr. Tulp, knew that the window behind him, a solitary, candle-lighted square in a great block of blackness, might soon attract the attention of the city watch, who would be making their rounds in the wintry street. He seldom worked so late in the little office dignified by the name of the Master's Chamber; and the night guardsmen, bored with their duties, would probably use it as an excuse to force their way in, hoping to find some ghastly business—a charity patient under the influence of weird Oriental drugs or an illegally-come-by corpse being prepared for midnight dissection—going on inside.

Actually, he was only looking at a dried specimen of foxglove, which was glued to a piece of parchment crowded with minute notes in his own hand. The notes yielded him nothing, though he had read them over and over. He knew without reading that the hard dark leaves, dried and ground down to powder, had been administered blindly by generations of physicians before him, and that the result had sometimes been a cure, sometimes a derangement of the pulse, and sometimes a vomiting fit. There was some secret here, impenetrable and provocative: he could not solve it and he could not leave it; he began and ended every session with his specimens by staring at the flower until the crimson pattern on the inside of the bell had burned itself into his brain. "Ah, well," he said aloud, and pushed the parchment away and rubbed his aching eyes: that downy blossom and rough leaf would plainly yield him nothing again tonight.

The sensible thing to do at such an hour would have been to go home to bed; yet, now that he remembered it, he still had a call to make. At about nine o'clock his punctilious little Portuguese colleague, Dr. Bonus, had seen the light in the window and come up to tell him that the wife of their mutual friend Rembrandt had just been delivered of a boy. The midwife, after the manner of her kind, had refused to admit as early as she should have that the matter was more than she could handle, and things were at a desperate pass when the doctor had finally been called in. But the poor young woman had suffered no lasting damage and was resting comfortably under a sedative that he trusted his colleague would approve of, and the child seemed healthy enough.

Still, the husband had been upset; and though the melancholy little Jew would not have gone so far as to make any suggestions to his eminent Dutch associate, he had managed to intimate that a visit from an old and trusted friend would be welcome, no matter how late he dropped in.

If that obligation had not come into his mind while he was putting the parchment specimen sheets back into the compartments in the cabinet, he would have remembered it on his way out: he seldom passed through the meeting hall without having a look at *The Anatomy Lesson*. He walked up close to it tonight, shielding the flame of the candle he carried with him against the erratic December gusts; and when he drew away his curving fingers, life and death, as startling as ever, sprang into being on the shadowy wall. Much had changed since the time of the painting: Kolkoen's head had gone bald, and his own eyes had sunken and reddened a little, and The Child had gone through secret and terrible transformations under the earth; but the captured, everlasting moment gainsaid the fluid actuality. Strange, he thought, walking down the winding stairs with the fluttering light in his hand, strange that nothing the young man had painted since had moved him like this. To tell God's truth—he admitted it to himself as he stepped out into the sleet-spattered street—nothing the young man had painted since had moved him at all. Doubtless part of his fascination with *The Anatomy Lesson* could be chalked up to sheer vanity; it was natural that he should prefer his own hands and face to Belshazzar's. But that was by no means the whole story. Something else was missing—something else . . .

He walked through a night that was wild and filled with sound—shrill, taunting whistle of wind coming out of the alleyways, and the far-off bellow of the churned-up sea. There was plague in Amsterdam; it was, in fact, a night very like another twelve years ago when he had walked from the Pest House to Pieter Lastman's—God rest his soul—to pick up some drawings left for him in the painter's vestibule: crude, groping things, but of such a nature that they had meaning for a man who had looked all day at death. It was years since he had taken them out of their folio, and he had not remembered or regretted them in the days of *The Anatomy Lesson,* but he regretted them now. As he walked almost blindly, with his hat pulled down against the sleet, over stone bridges and along black canals, he asked himself if it hadn't been a mistake to get such a splendid commission for the lad, if there hadn't been something demoralizing about the very brilliance of that first success. Few besides himself would care for the coarse and crumpled drawings, and all Amsterdam was fluttering over those "speaking portraits" of its eminent citizens, that Belshazzar frozen with fear, that twisted, theatrical Christ being put up on or taken down from the Cross. But he remained convinced that something had been lost, and he could not think himself more obtuse than the rest . . .

Somebody was still awake in the rooms on the Bloemgracht. Firelight and candlelight made wan squares of the row of second-floor windows above the blackness of the warehouse; and he did not have to knock—nobody had remembered to bar the downstairs door. The parlor at the top of the long flight was dim and disorderly: the fire had died down, and the solitary candle on the table revealed some unwashed dishes, a soiled napkin, a sheet of sketching paper, and a little heap of herring bones. The rest of the place was so dark that he took it to be empty until Rembrandt heaved himself up off the couch and out of what must have been a heavy dream.

"It's me—Tulp." He took off his drenched hat and cloak and came to stand close to the fire. "Bonus stopped in at the Surgeons' Guild to tell me—he says the lady's doing beautifully now."

"If she is, it's a God's wonder." Still numb and lumbering with sleep, he went to the table and lighted two more candles. The sight of him was something of a shock—he was in his stocking feet, his crumpled shirt was open far enough to show the reddish mat on his chest, his eyes were swollen, and his hair stood wildly out from his leonine head. Also, possibly because the doctor had been remembering him as he had looked in earlier days, he seemed surprisingly thick-set and burly. His massive neck, red and creased, rose like a pillar out of his wrinkled collar; his shoulders were as broad as a wrestler's, and his muscles bulged against the stuff of his sleeves. "I can't say how glad I am to see you," he said. "Excuse me—I know I'm incoherent—I fell asleep, and I'm not altogether awake."

"I'm sorry if I got you up."

"Oh, it wouldn't have lasted. I can't get myself quiet. I keep starting up. I keep imagining it's still going on—"

"Well, it isn't. Bonus says everything's in good order."

"I suppose it is—no thanks to that midwife." He lowered his voice to a whisper. "I hope she fries in Hell. Do you know, she let things go until it was almost—"

"Well, it wasn't, so you might as well stop worrying about it. They're all like that; there's not one of them wants to admit she isn't capable of handling the business. Is she gone?"

"No, not yet, more's the pity. She had to wash, and then she had to dress, and then she was totally exhausted and had to lie down, and then she needed a cut of beef and a mug of beer—"

"She'll be about her business as soon as she lays eyes on me. Shall we go in and have a look at the mother and the baby?"

"Yes, I suppose so." He ran his hand over the crazily disordered locks at the back of his head and brought up a fierce, impatient sigh. "That is, provided the silly wet nurse decides that it's permissible. I haven't seen either Saskia or the baby for more than ten minutes. The nurse's chief function—for which a person pays her enough, God knows—seems to be to throw the father out of the room."

The sleeping quarters too were dimly lighted by a hearth fire and a

240

single candle. The doctor stopped on the threshold to accustom his eyes to the shadow: the huge wicker basket-bed in which the wet nurse sat to suckle the baby would be somewhere on the floor, hooded over by its arch of dried and braided reeds and heaped with pillows and blankets and swaddling bands. He scented it before he saw it in the semi-dark; its reedy smell dominated the other familiar scents of a confinement room for a lady of fashion—dried lavender and warmed linens and perfumed oil for the infant's skin. The wet nurse, fat and falsely jolly, peeped round the arch of the basket-bed and nodded her permission for them to enter, her lips pursed on a row of pins, her big lap filled with swaddling bands. Saskia was almost invisible in the deeper shadow of the partly curtained corner bed. The midwife rose—gaunt, weary, and resentful—from the splendor of the carved and gilded couch near the window, and stepped into the candlelight. "It's a late hour for visitors," she said.

"It's the doctor, Vrouw Scheepen," said the wet nurse, without removing the pins.

"What—another one?" She picked up her cloak and started toward the door. "Good night to you, Doctor. And good night to you, too, Heer van Rijn. You can depend on one thing: your wife will never die for lack of medical attention," she said, and before anyone could answer, she was gone.

"Is my wife asleep?" said Rembrandt, his voice still rough with anger.

"I think she is, the darling!" The wet nurse spat the pins into her fat red hand. "Are you asleep, lambkin?" She leaned far out of her wicker boat in the direction of the bed. "Wake up, dearest. Your husband's here, and another doctor to see how beautifully you've done. Open your pretty eyes."

"I'm awake, Nurse," said Saskia out of the darkness. "But don't take the baby yet—let me keep him awhile."

"I think we could use another candle," said Rembrandt. "It's so damnably dark in here a person could fall on his face."

The wet nurse heaved herself out of the creaking wicker, and, eager to appease and please, lighted three candles. The doctor claimed one and carried it over to the corner bed, where its light caught the fiery brightness of the mother's spread hair. Her face—witching, triumphant, and utterly satisfied—smiled up at him. The child, still loosely wrapped in woolen, not yet swaddled, lay in the curve of her arm with its round head against the band of linen that had been laid across her swollen breasts. It was well with her; he knew it by the clearness of her eyes and the muted glow of her skin. He held the candle closer to look at the infant, a fine male and big enough, though he wished it had been a little quicker to move when he touched it.

"What do you think of him, Doctor? Is he all right?" said Saskia.

"Yes, sweetheart, he has everything he ought to have—ears and eyes and nose and all four of his members, and a fifth one, too." She giggled, and he kissed her lightly on her moist brow. "You've nothing to do now but lie there and enjoy him."

"Hadn't he ought to be swaddled, though, Doctor?" said the nurse.

"Yes, in a minute. Only, suppose we let his father hold him a little first." He picked up the warm bundle and turned and held it out to Rembrandt, who took it from him with more apprehension than eagerness. Yet it required only a few breaths and a little languid stirring in the woolen wrappings to drain the hardness from the tired face. Tenderness took the sharp lines away, tenderness loosened the corners of the bitter mouth. The rough, unshaven cheek brushed lightly, carefully against the round, downy crown, and the cold, light eyes were blurred by tears.

"What are you going to name him?" the doctor asked to break the silence.

"Rombartus, after Saskia's father. He's so little and feeble I'm afraid I'll hurt him."

"There's more strength in him than you'd think. Here, Nurse, you're right, he really ought to be swaddled. And you—you kiss your wife good night and come out and give me a goblet of wine. It's the least I deserve for walking over here on a night like this."

On his way out he heard her calling her husband "my poor bear" and asking him whether anybody had given him something hot for supper. Not wanting to provide them with still another unwelcome listener, he wandered, candle in hand, into the studio. Through its uncurtained window he could see a few scattered lights where other human beings still waited up to hold the mirror to the mouth of the newborn or lay the coins on the eyelids of the dead. He did not look at the canvases that shimmered around him; he set his candle on the worktable and stood with his forehead pressed against the chill pane until his host came in, tidied up now, with his hair combed and his collar fastened and his feet in soft shoes. "You look better now," said the doctor.

"Do I?" He filled two goblets and drew two painter's stools close to the table. "I can't say I feel much better. The sounds that came out of her toward the end of it— I tell you, they weren't human. What I don't understand is how anybody ever wants a second one. I'll never forget it, not as long as I live."

"Well, I can tell you, *she's* forgotten it already. None of them remember it after it's over; all of them tell you it's as if they went through it in a dream. The best thing for you to do is to put it out of your mind, and you'll be doing that as soon as you get back to those."

The pictures he gestured at stood at the very edge of the circle of illumination. Here and there a ghostly radiance emanated from them— glitter of a knife, sheen of a satin turban, exquisite intricacy of a bit of lace. Their creator looked at them and shrugged his heavy shoulders. "Tonight I just can't imagine myself getting back to them," he said.

"Why not?"

"Oh, I don't know. They seem like something *I* went through in a dream."

The doctor got down from his stool with his goblet in his hand. "Show me what you've got here," he said, certainly not because he had any inclination to look at the pictures, only because it occurred to him that they might leap to life again for their maker if he saw them through another man's eyes. His host's apathy was evident in the way he took up the light and carried it forward until it shone on the canvases.

Christ—ineffectually dramatic, a little like a bad actor—ascending into heaven on a cloud pushed up by seraphim . . . Samson, furious, shaking his fist into his father-in-law's face . . . Portraits—fine ladies and elegant gentlemen—and one of Rembrandt himself befurred and beplumed and bejeweled. A strong vertical shadow down the middle of his face reduced the breadth of his peasant's nose and minimized the fullness of his peasant's lips; and the eyes, one in the light and one in the shadow, were cold and worldly wise and startlingly cruel . . .

Unnerved by those eyes, the doctor made up his mind to disregard what was painted and concern himself only with the painting. That, he supposed, was something to marvel at; he wished he were conversant enough with the art to find words to describe the thick, majestic brush strokes, the tender blendings that led almost imperceptibly from brilliant lights into deep shadows, the thick incrustations of layer upon layer of paint that gave a solid immediacy to the precious things—the pearls, the gleaming satins, and the bits of gold. He said what he could in praise of one thing and another, and was able to warm more quickly to his subject because the baby had begun to cry lustily in the other room. But Rembrandt remained indifferent. "They weren't painted to be seen by candlelight," he said, turning away and setting the candlestick down on the table. "Anyway, as I told you, none of them really stirs me tonight."

"That's probably because you've just gone through a violent incident. It always takes a while to recover."

"It shouldn't. It didn't in the past." They returned to their places on the stools, and his host sat with his elbows on his knees and his chin on his clenched hands, his eyes mere slits beneath his heavy eyelids. "After my father died, I remember I ached to get back to it, and when I did I painted better than before."

And suddenly the doctor was assailed by a recollection so sharp that his fingers moved involuntarily on the worktable between them. He saw Hendrik Uylenburgh's shop on a warm spring day, and the lad from Leyden standing in his mourning clothes among the tawdry treasures— earnest, ardent, tremulous with wonder and gratefulness. Where was he now, that raw and eager dreamer? Scarcely a vestige of him could be found in the grim and sullen figure hunched on the other side of the candle; yet there was a massive and leonine strength in that figure, a strength that suggested it could sustain a blow even after a violent incident. Perhaps it needed, even wanted, the bitter truth . . . He waited until the infant, lulled by the syrupy cooing of the wet nurse, fell silent, and his own voice was steady enough to mask his gravity in a kind of casualness. "Isn't it possible," he said, "that you aren't doing exactly what you want to? That would account for your unwillingness to get down to it again."

There was an instant when the stocky shape, by its very motionlessness, seemed to be entertaining the possibility; but it was only an instant. He shook the thought off—actually shook himself as a dog will shake off sleep or water—let out a short, curious laugh, and sat erect with his hands clasped around one knee. "No, nothing like that. I'm doing exactly what I want to," he said.

"Are you sure?"

"Oh, yes, perfectly sure. Though I wouldn't expect you to see what I'm after—it isn't your sort of thing."

The doctor flushed and looked down at the graining of the wood. "I never set myself up as an authority. I admit I know next to nothing about painting," he said.

"Oh, *painting*—you know more about painting than most. I don't mean that. If you don't see what I'm after it's not because you don't understand painting—it's because you and I have a completely different way of looking at things. You see things as they actually are and you're willing to stop at that, but what I aim at in those"—he turned toward the righteously infuriated Samson, the transported Christ, the terrified Belshazzar—"is life raised to its highest significance. If I don't convince you it's no more than I expected; you'd be the hardest person in the world to convince."

"And how do I happen to come by that dubious distinction?"

"Probably it's the profession that you're in. By the time people get to your office or the hospital or the Pest House, they'd scarcely serve as models for paintings like those. Seeing them in that state day in, day out, how could you possibly believe in magnificence?"

To hear that he was an expert only in the sordid dregs of life, to be told that his labors made him blind to splendor—it hurt his feelings, and few could hurt them any more: only his little daughter and one or two of the more brilliant students under his direction. "I suppose I have my blind spots," he said, refusing to encounter the pale eyes, though he sensed that they were only unconcerned, not intentionally cruel. "Rubens, for instance—I never saw a canvas of his that I'd care to look at twice, though people pay little fortunes for his things, even the ones he lets his apprentices finish—" He broke off, knowing that his hurt had goaded him into a wounding remark: the young painter had recently bought a Rubens himself.

"You don't like him? Well, I wouldn't expect you to. He's no Dürer, I'll admit—and yet he does have other things. If he gives you short measure on whatever it is you're looking for—depth? understanding?

compassion?—there's nobody else that can match his movement and his richness and his color. And if anybody could take what he lacks and add it to what he has"—he looked over his shoulder avidly at a painting they had not seen tonight, something unfinished, with bits of moist paint shimmering in the semi-dark—"then he'd really get everything in a painter's power: the strongest sweep of motion and the ultimate expressiveness."

"Would that be possible? Wouldn't the one exclude the other? I mean, if you see the world as splendor, could you see it as—"

He was not permitted to finish. His host slid down from the stool, snatched up the candle, and waved the flickering light of it in an extravagant sweep down the length of the unfinished canvas, a large *Sacrifice of Abraham*. "Look—I almost got them both into that," he said, "the splendor and whatever else you're looking for. The old man—he's a patriarch, yes, with all the dignity and power his action calls for. But you can't say he isn't a father in deep trouble. I almost did it there, especially in the face."

The doctor was able to say truthfully, though for him it was small praise, that he much preferred this painting to any Rubens he had ever seen; he refrained from adding that anybody who imagined a father could look like that with his son under the knife should pay a few visits to the hospital. His host put down the candle, came up behind him, and laid an affectionate hand on his shoulder; and when he looked up he saw a self-confident face smiling at him, the eyes warmed by a sudden surge of guileless friendliness. "Yes, I almost did it there, and one of these days I'll do it to your satisfaction," he said. "You're hard to convince, but I'll convince you yet—wait and see. You did me so much good tonight; I feel entirely different now. I don't know what came over me—really, I've got nothing to complain about. I have my wife and my baby—thank God for that! I've got my work and my reputation, and the reputation's your doing; I could still be slaving away unknown in Leyden if it weren't for you. Everything's better with me than I ever dared to dream."

"Then go to sleep while you're still in a good humor. Myself, I got up at five this morning, and I'd better be on my way."

"It was good of you to walk over, especially in such filthy weather. I'll see you again on Sunday—on Sunday we're having the christening feast, you know. Your wife'll come with you, of course, and maybe you'll bring your little Gretha. Do bring her, by all means; little girls are always taken with babies, and there'll be all sorts of things she'll like to eat—raisin tarts and cookies and gingerbread."

*

He had probably begun worrying before he was aware of it. Looking back, he remembered certain hours, certain seemingly pleasant occasions that had been tarnished for him by he knew not what, certain foods that he had put from him because they were tainted by a nameless fear. But the first time he knew—really knew—that something was the matter was on that bleak February evening when he stood in the studio alone, leafing through his drawings because Flinck had wanted to borrow a figure from one of them, a little sketch of Joseph expounding his dreams.

The recent drawings had not yet been filed away in the big neat folios. Though he had managed to paint and sketch and work at his etchings with reasonable regularity of late, some things had to be neglected to give him time for coping with the nurse and diverting Saskia and playing with the baby; and such minor matters as filing and framing had gotten out of hand. The sketches of the last three months lay where he had tossed them when he finished them—face down in a wooden box, the earliest on the bottom and the others on top; and not being able to remember when he had done the little Joseph, he carried the whole batch over to the worktable, laid it down between two candles, and began with the first, a gloomy sketch of Saskia lying in bed after her confinement, her chin supported on her fist and a mournful—no, almost a tormented—look in her wide, sleepless eyes.

There were merrier pictures after that one—it seemed to him that in the first weeks he had done almost nothing but draw the baby. He doubted there was one of the little creature's gestures or expressions that he had not committed to paper; evening after evening he had sat in the bedroom drawing his first-born, releasing through chalk and crayon and ink what he could not release in words and dared not release in caresses upon so frail a being—the wondering intensity of his love. While he drew, he had a pretext for staring in a way that would otherwise have seemed like doting. By drawing them, he could in a manner fondle the round, downy crown with its mortal soft-spot where the skull had not yet quite closed over, the tender creases in the neck, the soft belly with its umbilical protuberance, and the small, proud insignia of manhood below. There were sketches of Christ carrying the Cross and Mary surprised by the angel; there were sketches of actors and musicians and beggars, but always he returned to the little one. Rombartus stiffly confined in his fresh swaddlings, Rombartus looking in amazement at his own curled hand, Rombartus hanging from the nipple of the nurse's breast, drowsy, like a bee replete with honey yet too happy to detach itself from the flower—the nurse bathing Rombartus, Saskia, erect and wary, carrying Rombartus downstairs . . . And suddenly there were no more pictures of the baby. The sequence had come to a dead stop: in the dozen loose sheets that followed, the little form did not turn up again. It was then that he asked himself why he had abandoned such a dear and fruitful subject, why for the last three weeks he had made not one drawing of the child.

Quite forgetting the Joseph sketch he had come looking for, he put the drawings back in the box, blew out one of the candles, and went with the other into the bedroom, still questioning himself but feeling the question now as a suffocating fullness in his chest. There, in the uneasy mingling of candlelight and firelight, with the smell of oil and lavender in his nostrils, he took his usual place on the carved chair close to the bottom of the corner bed. Saskia, in a new red dressing gown of French velvet, was sitting before a long mirror while the nurse stood behind her and brushed her hair. The baby lay in its cradle near the fire, none of him visible over the ornate and painted sides except the crown of his head. And while he stared at the downy roundness, his heart seemed to shrink in him as it had seemed to swell a moment ago. If weeks had passed without his having drawn the child, something even more alarming had been going on in the last few days: in the last few days he had not even looked at the child.

Not out of lack of love, certainly—if he had stayed away from the cradle, if he had not asked to have the little creature laid on his knees, if he had not gotten up at night to ease his yearning by staring down at the sleeping, guileless, expressionless face, it had not been because there had been any diminution in the great, aching surges of his love; it had been because some change had taken place in the baby, some change that he could not bear to see, some change that had first begun to manifest itself weeks ago, not long after the last of those drawings had been tossed into the box. And finally, after sitting for a good ten minutes, grasping the carved claws on the arms of his chair as if he could rouse his courage by hurting his hands on the wood, he went over to the cradle, catching, as he passed the long mirror, a fixed and worried look, not unlike the one he had gotten down on the first of the sketches, in his wife's strangely still and secretive eyes.

No, he could not deceive himself: it was not, as he had hoped to discover, that the intensity of his involvement had given rise to groundless anxiety. The baby in the cradle was not the baby in the drawings; it lay listless on its pillow, it would have been flaccid without the support of the swaddling bands, and there were webby, bluish circles around its closed eyes. He bent over and touched it under the chin with his forefinger. It did not stir, and its motionlessness was so tormenting to him that he could not contain himself, had to prod it hard—in the chest, in the belly—until it wakened and began to cry.

The cry was more dreadful than the stillness before it. It was no lusty protest, no angry claim to the right to sleep; it was a helpless whimper, a vague complaint that annoyance should be added to a heavier misery. The eyes—deep grey-blue—came open slowly, tearless and lusterless, fixed on nothing. He went down on his knees beside the cradle, jarring it into a crazy rocking, and the whimper turned into a thin and powerless cry. Saskia, appalled, was staring at his reflection in the mirror, but her voice when she spoke was merely exasperated. "Now why on earth did you have to go and wake him?" she said.

247

"Can I pick him up?"

"Whatever for, at this hour of night? He ought to be asleep."

"I'd just like to pick him up."

"If you do," said the nurse, "his swaddlings will come loose, and we'll have to wrap him all over again."

He abandoned the idea, took one more long and ungratifying look, waited until the feeble whimper had given way to dull sleep, and went back to his station in the carved chair. He took a knife out of his pocket and began to clean his fingernails, keeping his eyes fixed on what he was doing; but every now and again he could sense that the eyes in the mirror were darting covert looks in his direction.

"A little of the baby's oil wouldn't be amiss for the ends of your hair, lambkin," said the nurse to Saskia, curling a lock of it around her fat red finger. "The ends are splitting the tiniest little bit, and that will stunt the growth if we let it go."

He had hoped the nurse would be taking herself off by now: at this hour of the evening she usually retreated into the kitchen, allowing the two of them a little privacy while she consumed incredible quantities of bread and butter, cheese and beer. But she meant to apply herself to the splitting ends at once, and he could not face the prospect of stifling his anxiety until he and his wife were alone. Turning round in the chair so that he was looking full at the lovely, rosy face in the mirror, where it seemed to be floating in a cloud of loose and fiery hair, he asked in what he hoped was a casual voice, "Does the baby seem quite well to you, darling?"

"Well? What do you mean? Why shouldn't he be well?"

"I don't know—I poked him because he looked—well, a little listless—"

"Listless? I should think he would be listless! You'd be, too, if you were wakened up like that. The poor little thing was fast asleep."

"That's a father for you!" said the nurse, nudging her lambkin with a familiarity he hated. "Always looking for something to fuss about. Let me assure your honor, the child's the living image of health. He coos, he stretches, he gurgles, he belches—he does everything he ought to. As for appetite, he sucks me almost dry."

"And these last few days, Nurse, it hasn't seemed to you that he's maybe a little weaker?"

"Weaker, your honor? He's strong as a little horse."

"Weaker!" said Saskia. "He got hold of me by the ear this morning, and I thought he'd pull it off my head."

She turned round then, taking off her jingling rings and tossing them from hand to hand, and gave him a warm and beautiful smile. Now that he remembered it, he *had* heard her protesting the strength of the little one's grasp on her ear this morning while he was in the studio correcting a drawing of Bol's; and the pleasure he had felt in the noisy incident came back, and his relief was such that he did not withdraw to the studio

248

where he might be tempted into looking at the drawings again, but sat on the couch in the parlor where he could hear the nurse telling her mistress that his honor was getting moody for lack of diversion and would be less inclined to look for troubles that weren't there if he went to a tavern and had a mug or two with some of his men friends every now and again . . .

He did not take her advice and go to the Crown or the Barrel, but he found other pretexts for leaving the house, and would often go shopping instead of sending one of the servants. Some superstitious conviction that the eye of God was on him, that he had better chasten his rebellious, grasping heart, kept him out of the fine shops and away from the auctions; but he spent an unconscionable time selecting turnips and cabbages and cuts of meat. Sometimes the mere act of stocking household plenty would give him the sense that all was well under his roof, and then he would chatter easily with the market people about his wife and his baby and the prodigious amount of butter the wet nurse devoured. But then again there was no comfort in it: he wanted to be back home gazing at the child before he had reached the first of the stalls that he meant to visit, and the rest of it would be a grim struggle to buy every item on the shopping list before he hurried back to blot out the preposterous notion that he would find the baby dead. It was on one of those grimmer expeditions—he was standing, burdened down by parcels, in a stall in the fish market, with the grey and yellow scaliness of dead sea-creatures under his nose—that he met Dr. Ephraim Bonus one Friday afternoon. Assailed as they were by the reek of the fish, the shouts of the quarreling fishwives, and the icy wind that swept in from the churning yellowish water beyond the wharf, it was inconsiderate of him to hold the sad little Portuguese there in desultory conversation; but even when the doctor turned up the collar of his cloak against the February blast, he could not let him go.

"I've always wanted to ask you, Doctor," he said, stepping out of the way of an annoyed customer, "was there something unusually difficult about my wife's confinement—more so than the ordinary first birth, I mean?"

"Well, I'd say it was difficult, even for a first baby, but I've seen worse ones. Why do you ask? Isn't she quite herself?"

"Oh, yes, she's fine, she's glowing. Only, when there's a hard delivery, doesn't it sometimes—isn't it possible that there might be some harm—some aftereffect on the baby?" It came out more ominously than he had intended, partly because he was shuddering in the dank cold and partly because, laden down with packages as he was, he could not make the proper minimizing gestures with his hands.

The sad, small face peered at him between the black turned-up collar and the damp hat-brim. "There was no *injury* to the baby," he said with careful emphasis. "No bruises, no marks—I made sure of that."

"Good! Good! I'm terribly glad to hear you say so." If it had not been for the bundles, he would have seized the chance to shake hands and go his way, cherishing the warmth that was returning around his heart.

"Still," said the doctor, "things could happen and not show themselves until later. Is there anything you've noticed—"

"No, nothing—no marks, no discolorations—nothing like that at all!"

"Is his appetite normal? Is he gaining weight? Is he active enough?" The melancholy eyes under the drooping black brim entreated him, like the eyes of a father, not to obscure the business with evasions, to come out with the truth.

"Well, the fact is—and it may very well be my imagination, the nurse and Saskia both tell me it's nothing *but* my imagination—but the truth is, I thought I did notice a little listlessness. He doesn't cry the way he did at first; he—he whimpers—" He had brought out the last word unwillingly, and it seemed to him that he had somehow betrayed the little creature, had marked it, in order to relieve his own unmanly fright, with some dark and baseless calumny.

"What about the eyes—did you happen to notice the eyes?"

"No," he said, God knows why, "I can't say I noticed anything about the eyes."

"Suppose I drop in, tomorrow or the next day, just to have a look. It's probably nothing, and there's no need to upset your wife. I'll just stop by, as if I were paying the lady a social call. It's probably only a simple cold—everybody's catching a cold these days—and if you stand here bareheaded like that much longer, you'll be catching one and carrying it home to the baby yourself."

The fact that the doctor did not make his appearance at the rooms on the Bloemgracht either that evening or the next was reassuring—he could not have been too disturbed by the symptoms described; otherwise he would have come at once. The child was whimpering less, and when the nurse went out to visit a friend for a couple of hours he and Saskia were very merry together, so raucously and skittishly merry that they somehow could not settle down to making love. On the third day, after the noon meal, Bol and Flinck talked him into going with them to an auction—not to buy, only to look. He was exposed to a beautiful Domenichino, a stark Seghers etching of the quay, and a time-softened Roman urn with twisted dolphins for handles, but still he did not fall into temptation; and on his return he was certain that the threat had been withdrawn. Even when the slovenly Katje told him that the doctor was in the bedroom with the mistress and the nurse and the baby, he was not disturbed: the sounds that issued from that room were so gay, so filled with life that he was certain the good doctor's auguries could only be the best. "Rembrandt," called his wife, "there's a friend of ours in here. Come in."

"Never mind," called the visitor, "I'm just leaving; I'll see you out there."

As he stepped from the hallway into the parlor, the little doctor paused on the threshold and closed the door between, carefully and without making a sound. Rembrandt was right about his wife, he said— the lady was glowing, and that was something to be grateful for: many a young mother had not survived such a delivery, or had survived it only as a pitiful ghost of herself. As for the baby—it was too early for any-body to be alarmed, though it didn't do to be too sanguine, either. The baby *was* a little slow to respond to sound and touch, and its eyes were somewhat duller than he could have wished. No, it wasn't a cold; a cold or any other childhood disease would have made itself known by now— that was why he had stayed away for the three days. The symptoms could be manifestations of some inward injury at birth, and that injury could be light or serious, a person simply couldn't know: there was nothing to do but wait and see, hard as he knew it was to wait . . .

And the only thing that made him less hateful than Dr. Claas Duarts-zoon back in Leyden was the fact that he *did* know how hard it was to wait, that he himself had waited in infection-ridden ships to see whether he would be admitted at the harbors, had waited in Amster-dam to see whether the Surgeons' Guild would permit him, Jew that he was, to practice, had gone home with the proper papers and waited to see whether anybody would need him enough to claim the keenness of his eye and the sureness of his hand. That old sorrow, lived with for so long that he took it for granted, shone out of his still brown eyes and steadied his hearer, who made no futile protests and asked no futile questions—only winced once when a burst of Saskia's laughter went like a needle through his heart.

"She doesn't seem to realize that anything's the matter, does she?" he asked, putting his hand to his jaw because it had begun to shake.

"That's natural. We have a peculiar capacity for closing our eyes to anything we don't want to see."

"Hadn't we better tell her?" He did not know whether he asked it out of fear that shock might do her irreparable harm or out of the gnaw-ing yearning to be utterly with her in this—to kneel with her beside the doomed cradle, to weep with his head on her breast.

"What would be the use? It may turn out to be nothing—it could still be nothing, though I rather doubt it. But whatever it is, why should she be told beforehand? The longer she knows, the more she'll suffer. She'll know, God help her, soon enough."

To endure it alone, to hold his peace in the terrible conviction that she would know soon enough would have been easier if he had not been sure that in a sense she knew already. She had not really exiled the fear-ful thing from her mind; it was more as if she had relegated it to some dim outer reaches of her consciousness and drawn a curtain across it behind which, muffled and inexorable and ominous, it continued to unfold. But to deal with her as she was trying to deal with herself—with *that* excluded—was to taint every look they tried to exchange with hypocrisy. Unable to be with her completely, he found it better to be with her as little as possible. He put on a brash show of re-establishing the life they had led before the coming of the little creature: he laid in loaves and fowl and joints of meat and kegs of wine, he prodded the slovenly Katje into making elaborate soups and puddings, he filled the rooms and the evenings with guests. Bonus, Tulp, Hendrik Uylenburgh, the Sylviuses, Allaert and Lotje, Bol and Flinck, Frans van Pellicorne and the cool young personage to whom he had just been affianced —they came and went and came again. Something was arranged—a dance, a few rounds of backgammon, a little concert—for almost every night. In those days it occurred to him for the first time that he was growing too heavy; his body, stuffed with company food, dulled with unaccustomed drinking, and made as unresponsive as a stone by the weight of his sorrow, wanted to sink against his will into every empty chair. And she—doubtless unusually light because the weight of the doomed unborn no longer dragged down her body—she could not sit still under the titillations of the flute and the viol, must kiss Tulp on the back of his neck, must perch like a five-year-old on her uncle's knee. She had never been more beautiful, nor more gratified with her beauty, than she was now that her fine gowns could be brought out of the closet and made to close at the waist with only the slightest alteration. She took on for him again—though he could have possessed her any time he had the heart for it—the elusiveness of the first weeks of their courtship: he found himself picking up the warm pearls just taken from the white round of her neck, he found himself burying his face in the folds of her empty red dressing gown and pressing the soles of her house slippers against his chest.

Yet the dark business continued to unfold, and the drawn curtain was not completely effective: her extravagant motions were often intended, he knew, to distract attention from something that made itself known even behind the heavy folds. She talked too persistently to the mildly puzzled Lotje about how loudly the baby had cried and how much the baby had eaten; she demanded too many reassurances from Tulp and Bonus about things she knew could not have mattered—a little rash, a distaste for barley broth; she too assiduously avoided conversation with her aunt, who spent more time in the bedroom than the others and whose clear old eyes had begun to be clouded by doubt. Any evening without diversion had become intolerable to her; and the one night when he had not been able to arrange anything she insisted that he take her to the theater, though a wild February squall was trying to rip the hanging signs from the shops, was blowing the lanterns out and filling the air with flecks of foam. Once there, she sat like a figure carved out of stone, staring fixedly at the stage; and he knew that like himself she was frozen with fear—had dragged him out only to flout her own terror, had remained there watching the foolish comedy only to prove to herself that she was a happy young mother like any other, out in public for the first time to receive congratulations on a propitious confinement and not in the least apprehensive about what she would find when she opened the bedroom door.

She found nothing that night: the nurse, who was finishing her beer, cheese, and bread and butter beside the cradle, got up—shaking rind and greasy crumbs onto the carpet—to assure her lambkin that the little darling had slept like an angel; and the gay undressing thereafter was quite according to custom, except that Saskia took a double dose of the mild sedative that Dr. Bonus had recently refilled and put on her dressing table without a word. She fell asleep almost at once, and he did not lie awake long either. Perhaps because he was exhausted by strain, perhaps because he was benumbed by the heaviness of his diet, sleep came at him like a brutal enemy these days: sleep smote him as the butcher smites the ox with a hammer, beating him down into a blackness too thick for dreams. It was a wonder, then, that so slight a noise as she made a few hours later should have wakened him. She whimpered, no more loudly than the baby; and when he had said her name twice without answer he saw in the dim light of the dying fire that tears were running over her cheeks, and he knew that she was weeping in her sleep.

"What's the matter, darling?" he said in a whisper.

"Far down—under the water—"

"What, dear—what's the matter?"

"I can't reach it—"

"Saskia—"

"Let's go home. There's no use, and I'm terribly cold. Hold me, make me warm, I'm freezing to death."

He held her, but there was little warmth in him to give to her. He waited until the sleeping potion had reasserted itself, stilling the whimper, sealing up the tears, blotting out the image of the drowning shape borne farther and farther away in its trailing swaddlings. Then, when she was warmed through and had turned onto her side, her breath even and evenly stirring the bright lock that lay across her lips, he crept out of the bed and went over to the cradle. The carved and painted sides still shone in the light of the embers, but the inside was dark—dark as the voiceless, imageless well of death. A sound, barely detectable, rose out of that blackness—feeble breath laboring with phlegm—not rattling yet, only striving, and he snatched the little one up, covered its shrunken, puckered face with kisses, beat it gently on the back until it made a coughing sound and spewed a little onto his nightshirt and began to take in air again. Why had he done it? To prolong the suffering? To postpone the ordained passage for an hour, a day, a week? It would not live, it could not live, and yet a pale gleam of exultation illumined the

253

depth of that shadow: he loved it, he loved it, and he had snatched it up out of death.

For something close to an hour he walked back and forth with the baby in his arms. He did not actually pray, for he addressed nobody and asked for nothing, but detached phrases—"O Lord, I am heartily sorry," "Shall these bones live?" "If it were not so, I would have told you"— went through his brain and issued in audible whispers from his lips. The child slept, drawing its precarious breath at least with no discomfort, and he feared the sudden assault of sleep himself, feared that he might stumble and fall. By the last quivering light of the embers he laid it back in its cradle, making a deep hollow in the pillow so that the poor head would not roll, as it was wont to do these days, grotesquely to one side. All this he did very aptly and quietly, but on his way back to the bed he tripped over the nurse's bundle of sewing, and Saskia woke and started up from the bolster, her eyes shining wildly through the dark.

"What's the matter?"

"Nothing—nothing."

"What are you doing out of bed?"

"Nothing—I couldn't sleep and I went to look at the baby. He's all right now. He wasn't breathing quite evenly; I think he had a little phlegm on his chest."

"Oh, for God's sake, you'll drive me out of my mind with it. Always fussing, always getting up and looking, never letting a person get a decent night's sleep—"

"I'm sorry. I'm terribly sorry."

"If you keep it up, I swear I'll put him in the nurse's room."

"Don't do that."

"He's old enough—"

"We'll talk about it tomorrow. You're only making yourself more wide-awake. Lie down. Here, let me cover you. Go to sleep."

He got into bed beside her, and she turned her face from him; but then, as sleep surged back upon her, she let herself curl against him. "Hold me, make me warm," she said, exactly as she had said it in her dream. "I'm freezing to death."

After that, by wordless agreement, they put an end both to going out and arranging social evenings at home. Actually, there was no longer any necessity for inviting visitors; they came without invitation. The Sylviuses found half a dozen pretexts for dragging their fragile and rheumatic bodies through the wretched weather, and both of the doctors dropped in almost every day, explaining at first that a sick call or a visit to the apothecary had happily brought them into the neighborhood, and toward the end not bothering to explain at all. And on the rare occasions when none of these appeared, Bol and Flinck—the one dark and grave and the other blond and gentle—were always to be counted upon. Their love for their master's wife, which had waned a little in the days of her mundane connubial fulfillment, waxed again: the solemn, brooding Bol took to referring to her reverently as "madame" or "my lady," and Flinck could not see her pick up the baby without retiring into the studio and shedding tears.

But there was the half-hour of wakefulness left over after everybody had gone home. There was the cradle and the terrible stillness in the cradle; there was the nurse with her futile and wounding reassurances: Had they heard the little fellow gurgle while the pastor was reading his sermon? If only the two young men had taken themselves off a little earlier, she would have given them a fine show tonight—she had scarcely been able to get the swaddlings right, she had never seen such lively hands and feet . . .

Yet an evening came when even she was silenced. While she got her mistress into the red velvet dressing gown and began to fuss over the fiery hair, her big, loose face was emptied for once of all pretense; she sighed a wheezing sigh and kept glancing toward the cradle with apprehensive eyes.

"That's enough, Nurse," said Saskia, pushing away the brush.

"Don't you want any oil, lambkin?"

"No, no oil tonight." She got up more quickly and deliberately than usual and walked straight to the cradle. He watched her from his usual station in the carved chair, watched the swaddled body as she took it up from the pillows, was so certain that the life had already departed from it that he almost cried aloud when it moved its withered hands. As she seated herself with it on the stool in front of the fire and began to sing to it, he reached down to the floor beside him and picked up the needle and the etching plate that he had left there last night. To etch would be impossible, of course, yet he could simulate the motions of etching. She sang, and he dragged the needle along the edge of the copper plate, and thought—God forgive him!—that the line of her back was something he might use some day in a picture of Hagar crouched over the thirsting Ishmael in the wilderness.

She paused in her lullaby, only for an instant. She took a deep, shaken breath and began again, but tonelessly and in another key. That change of key was strange and disintegrating, like the tremor of an earthquake. He got up, letting the plate fall clanging to the floor, and came to her, and saw by the loosened jaw and the rolled-up eyes that the child was dead.

"Here, darling, let me take him."

"No, not yet." She said it angrily, fiercely. "Let me alone. Can't you see he hasn't gone to sleep?"

"Please, Saskia, let me have him. He isn't well—he's worse—"

"He is not, he is not!"

"Oh, now, lamb, *do* let your husband have him," said the nurse, coming up and giving him a wild, conspiratorial look. "I think he's very sick —I think—I'm afraid he's gone."

"He is not!" she said, leaping up with the little corpse at her breast, its head lolling backward over the curve of her arm. "He is not gone, and you're a liar, Nurse, you've always been a hateful, piggish, filthy liar! Get out, get out of this house. Leave us alone! Leave us alone!"

He had sense enough to shout after the retreating nurse that she should stop at the doctor's house and tell him to come at once. Bonus came as fast as he could—hatless and cloakless through the rain, his nightshirt stuffed into his breeches; but half an hour must have passed between the time when the nurse went out and the doctor came in. And all through that half-hour she had fought him off with one arm and sung the toneless lullaby by turns; she had walked with the baby through every room in the house, cradling it, talking to it, calling it by all the tender names they had called it together in the happy days. It was only by speaking to her as an affronted father would speak to an offending child that the little doctor was able to get the infant out of her arms, and it was close to morning before she could be convinced that the pastor and the undertaker must be called, that the baby was dead.

*

The other two, Dr. Matthys Kolkoen and Dr. Joris Valckaert, had paid their bills, left something for the barmaid, and slipped into the misty April dusk to pace the streets as springtime cats and restless bachelors will. But Dr. Tulp stayed behind at the liquor-anointed table and ordered another glass of the sour white wine; there was nothing he wanted to look for, and nobody expected him home before seven o'clock.

He was sorry to see them go: Dr. Valckaert had been holding forth on wounds, and he knew wounds, having been with the army at the siege of Breda. Among the three of them they had covered every known treatment for every sort of damage that weapons could inflict on the fragile hide of man, and at the end of a conversation bloody enough to drive a party of young burgher exquisites to a more distant table, they had come to the usual inconclusive conclusion. "My very honorable colleagues," Matthys had said, finishing off his measure, "allow me to sum up the results of this learned discussion: some wounds heal and some wounds don't."

He was not quite willing to leave it at that. The energy his companions would expend in another sort of search would stay curdling within him, good husband and disillusioned dreamer of women that he was, unless he could spend it on the question in hand. The answer probably lay less in the nature of the wound than in the nature of the wounded. Some carried in their blood the mysterious capacity to close great gashes, and some died of next to nothing, and nobody could tell why.

And here in the purpling dusk, with the customers almost all gone home to their suppers and the barmaids murmuring girlish matters behind the half-open door of the kitchen, he let his mind travel up whatever questionable alley it would and fell to wondering whether what could be said of bodies could be applied to spirits, too. Take poor old Seghers, for instance: the man had gotten a mortal thrust when his cousins had cheated him out of a paltry inheritance in his youth, and nothing he did after that could be called the gesture of a sound being. All of it —marrying a sordid slut to spite himself, begetting a crowd of children to increase his poverty, making etching after etching obsessively to fill up his meaningless days—was the thrashing about of a man who feels himself in the grip of his own slow death. Another man might have survived the starvation, the filthy living quarters, the raw cheap liquor, the sleepless nights spent over the copper plates and the etching press; but he had not really died an accidental death when he had tumbled, old and sodden with brandy, over the railing of a balcony and cracked his skull on the cobblestones below. The fall had been intentional, whether the old man knew it or not; the fall had been his blundering way of giving himself the coup de grâce.

Some of those frantic and wonderful prints of his were to be seen on New Doelen Street in the collection of a painter with a stronger capacity for healing and renewal. Rembrandt van Rijn was no Seghers, though he had certainly looked it on the day of his baby's funeral. Only a little more than two years had gone by, and nobody could have guessed, seeing the artist and his wife strolling on the Dam as he had seen them last Sunday afternoon, that either of them had lived down a calamity. Hale, high-hearted—sleek in silks and glittering with jewels and bursting with witty stories and bits of happy news to tell—such were Rembrandt and his Saskia this spring.

And it wasn't one of those superficial closings-over either, with festering going on underneath. One look at the *Danaë Welcoming the Golden Shower*, or whatever he meant to call the glowing nude of Saskia lying on the gilded couch with the griffin and the Cupid, would prove that the recovery had been complete. He shook his head at the barmaid who was coming with a taper to light the lamp on his table: it was easier for him to conjure up that picture in the accumulating dusk. It was a work utterly innocent of the taint of theatricality that had disturbed him in the canvases shown him on the night of the birth; splendid as it was with its shimmering white and its flickerings of gold, it remained in the world and of the world. All that was in the painting lay within the grasp of man—joy, and the remembrance of joy, and the promise of its renewal; and these needed no exaggeration. The lips parted and the breasts swelled and the warm belly held the honey-colored shadows in its tender hollows. The thighs lay softly against each other, and the moist, luxuriant triangle widened between them and above them, and love itself was enough and more than enough.

The four apprentices who were working in the young master's studio these days had taught themselves to talk about the picture in the safe terminology of the painter's trade. One of them would invite you to walk up to it under the pretext of seeing how delicately the half-tones carried the most brilliant light into the deepest shade. Another would ask you whether you had noticed the marvelous difference between the inanimate softness of the pillows and the living resilience of the flesh, and a third would join in with feverish enthusiasm about how the amber darkness of the hair—which hair you were left to decide for yourself— drew in the vibrant reds, the deep, rich browns, the flickering or gleaming golds. But the coyness was theirs; there was no trace of it in the canvas. The canvas spoke directly, unashamedly, and with gratefulness of the inexhaustible delights of love.

Such a recovery could not have been made in a month or even a year, of course: at first the hurt had been crusted over by something like protective scabs not altogether wholesome in themselves. The young couple had moved to a shockingly expensive set of rooms near the Military Club on New Doelen Street; they had put in their place her Friesland relatives who took it on themselves to suggest a little more caution; and they had drawn on her fortune for whatever caught their fancies—a statue of Augustus and a Ruysdael landscape and furs and lace and pearls. But all the while the healing process was going on apace, as anybody who visited them could see. She was doing what she could to keep the house in order and the servants in line; their dealings with each other were deepened by tenderness; and he was using some of the money to buy himself a little time: he accepted fewer commissions now and reserved certain days for painting whatever he pleased.

They saw more people over there on New Doelen Street than in the early days of their marriage; their rooms—airy, spacious, but still somewhat disorderly with the clutter of life and an overabundance of precious things—were crowded twice a week by lively company. Bonus, bound to them because he had shared their bitter herbs, haunted the place and brought with him others of his kind: a couple who had made a small fortune by importing brandy, and another couple sufficiently well off to keep a foreign bookshop for the pure love of it. Pastor Sylvius was seldom there any more; an indefinable disorder of the stomach had so enfeebled him that he spent most of his leisure propped up in bed. Still, there was no shortage of theological discussion: before retiring, he had introduced the young people to another preacher—the Jovian, bearded Swalmius, a lion among the discredited sect of the Mennonites; and Swalmius had brought his colleague Anslo, who also preached the radical doctrines of a sect that refused in Christ's name to be enrolled in the City Guard, to sign a lease, or to uncover their heads to anybody but God. For a while the evenings had been in need of the leavening of youth, but lately the young officers from the nearby Military Club had begun to stop by in a neighborly way. Arriving just as the graver, middle-aged element was beginning to thin out, they were willing to sit

258

around and talk town gossip and politics until the middle of the night.

A vital place—he felt the pull of it. Sipping his wine and watching the last of the drinkers let himself out into the springtime street, he played with the thought of wandering over there himself this evening when his wife had gotten over the notion that she had something important to say to him and his daughter had been put to bed. But he knew that his need for such company was as illusory as his wife's demand for significant conversation. Bonus, with his professional deference, would bore him; he found Anslo's religious ardor embarrassing; and he would not have the patience to follow the arguments of the learned and subtle Swalmius. And by the time the military contingent came whistling up the stairs, he would probably wish them all in hell with their flamboyant manners and their vivacity and their young appetites. April or not, he was not in his twenties any more. He had lectured for three hours, sat for three more through a meeting of the Board of Regents for the Old Men's Home, gone to a consultation, and spent what was left of him with Kolkoen and Valckaert; and by half past ten he would be ready for bed.

Yet there were many Amsterdam notables who would have envied him his right to come and go there as he pleased. To know an artist who was being mentioned in the same breath with Rubens was something to boast about, especially since Rembrandt consented to know so few: he rejected in a month more invitations to dances and concerts and little suppers than Ruysdael or Moyaert received in a year. Even to have him accept a protrait commission had become something of a distinction, since those whom he decided to oblige—at a fee of four or five hundred florins and with the understanding that they would sit for him as many times as he considered necessary—took on a certain luster. After all, if he chose to paint them, they must be more fascinating than the others whose florins he refused. But if any of them hoped to win him to purposes of their own in his leisure hours, they found him evasive or downright rude. He took no trouble to hide the fact that the business of painting them was as tedious as it was lucrative; he told the well-to-do young officers, who were only too glad to spread it in the more elegant salons, that it was enough to have to listen to these stilted burghers during the day—his evenings he meant to spend as he chose.

Those patrons of his did have a good deal to put up with. Even a physician who had learned to discount the complaints of cranky patients had to admit as much. What they paid, in addition to their florins, had been brought home to him the other day by a story that the dyspeptic German von Sandrart had told with malicious enjoyment. The lady in question—she had let von Sandrart know that the next time she sat for a portrait it would be in *his* studio—had waited three months after Heer van Rijn had done her the inestimable favor of putting her on his list.

Thereafter, the master, taciturn to the point of incivility, had subjected her to ten long sittings, and when she said "long" she meant somewhere between two and three hours, broken only by brief and grudgingly permitted rests. Her hands went numb, her foot fell asleep, her neck got a crick in it. She scarcely dared to wipe her nose or swallow, and nobody had even thought to offer her a cup of tea. And when she had summoned up the courage to point out that her likeness was suffering from the strain, that the lines of her exhaustion were appearing on the canvas, he had said, "My dear Vrouw Schnellius, the only time your face has any character is toward the end of the sitting, when you're so worn out that you allow it to be what God intended."

Amusing, of course, and with a tonic sting to it like the white wine that he finished off in his darkening corner, shaking his head at the barmaid who approached to offer him a third. Amusing, but a little cruel and more than a little indiscreet: anybody who indulged his arrogance and his passion for the truth to that extent would have to reckon with powerful enemies. Von Sandrart was an enemy by situation and nature; nobody was clamoring to be on *his* list these days, and he could marshal with him a clique that for years had held a monopoly on "the higher thought" in Amsterdam. Over at Muiden they would not be happy to learn that their pre-eminence in intellectual conversation was being challenged on New Doelen Street by a group of artists, officers, Mennonites, and Jews.

Hooft, von Sandrart, Vondel, Tesselschade Visscher—he himself had seen little enough of them. He had visited their haunt, Hooft's seignorial castle on the Amstel River, only two or three times, and had always been hard put to it to keep himself awake. It was wearisome to sit around while they handed each other laurels, and whatever sense they made was buried under the coy indirection of their manner of address. Still, that draughty castle was known here and abroad as "the nursery of genius"; and Hooft had written a celebrated history of the Spanish invasion, and the plays and verses of Vondel were certainly the best ever written—small compliment though that was—in the recalcitrant medium of the mother tongue. The Muiden Circle, as they called themselves in compliment to the pile of ancient stones on the river where most of their eggs had been hatched, enjoyed a reputation that could not be ignored; and yet the invitation they had extended to Heer van Rijn had never even been answered—it seemed he had been moving at the time, and along with several other unwelcome effusions, it had gotten lost.

Not that it would have been necessary for him to pay them the sort of court they had come to take for granted. There was no call for him to write a congratulatory note to Tesselschade Visscher on her tedious poem about the Amstel, nor could he be expected to compliment von Sandrart on his muddy, mannered canvases when he met him at an auction, or to stand in line at a reception in order to be presented to the almost sainted Hooft. Still, it wouldn't have hurt him to say a good word to Vondel on the opening performance of his latest play—an embarrassing encounter of more than ten years ago at Vrouw van Hoorn's was scarcely an excuse. To come up to a group that was waiting for the author in the wings, to shake hands with the two or three whom he knew and to turn his back on the others, to walk away, well known as he was, before the poet made his appearance, to give everybody the impression that he was above offering felicitations—no, it was just a little too much.

And it would really be hard for anybody to work up an active antipathy toward Vondel. Even at those opening performances, his inability to find appropriate answers to compliments kept him from seeming vainglorious, and he could not part from a new acquaintance without making it plain that he earned his living not by his art but by keeping a hosiery shop. It seemed unnecessarily severe, too, to pass cold judgment on the productions of a man who was always glad to present an elaborate poem, free of charge, as his contribution to any worthy charity.

Down at the Surgeons' Guild, on the doctor's worktable, one of those poems lay buried under lecture notes and the mounted specimens of pharmaceutical plants: as one of the Regents, it was he who had arranged for the poet to read it aloud at a supper to be given for the benefit of the Old Men's Home in the gardens of that institution early in May. And why—it broke upon him just as the barmaid went to the fireplace to rekindle her taper—why couldn't that occasion be used to bring Vondel and the somewhat difficult young lion of the hour together? They might well have more to say to each other than to any of the stiff and self-righteous burghers who would be milling around them, and the next time von Sandrart had a damaging story to tell about Heer van Rijn over at Muiden, the poet might be depended upon to say that the painter wasn't as objectionable as he was made out to be . . .

The barmaid, restless in her suppertime idleness, was lighting the lamps on all the other little tables. The wicks flared up slowly in the misty darkness, lighting the young round of her chin and showing the scars that a case of the pox had left on her tired and dreaming face. He reached into his leather pouch, careful not to make an ostentatious jingle with his coins, and began to figure out what he ought to leave her. Kolkoen had left three pennies, and he had stayed twice as long as Kolkoen and could do no less than make it six, and six seemed small, six should certainly be doubled to twelve, if only because it was April, the sorriest time of the year to have the sort of cheeks nobody would care to kiss . . .

Scars . . . As he laid the pennies in the shadow of his crumpled napkin, he glanced at the jagged one a broken vial had left on his wrist. It had healed quickly: quick healing was in his nature; and yet, now that he remembered it, a far less spectacular laceration—a cut on his upper arm made by a nail while he was reaching into a packing crate—had been months closing over. The question was not answered; he was back where he had been an hour ago—some wounds would heal and some would not. A man could mend cleanly after the loss of a first-born son and could fester under the surface for God knows how many years because a little group of notables at one of Vrouw van Hoorn's "big evenings" had looked at him with less than compassionate eyes.

*

It was a warm evening, the first balmy evening of the year, with the pear and apple and cherry trees in bloom. It was an evening for sketching, making love, or talking with old and easy friends: the last thing in the world he would have chosen to do was waste it among strangers in the gardens of the Old Men's Home at a function whose only purpose was to collect florins that could have been gathered just as easily by a few young women going from door to door in the service of sweet charity.

They were there, he and Saskia, walking up and down the tidy little paths between the neat squares of lawn, examining the scrupulously clean interiors of the tiny and monotonous houses, maintaining the artificial smiles necessary for greeting strangers and admiring dreary little trees and barren bleaching courts—they were there because Dr. Tulp had been so persistent about it. The doctor was to make a speech, yes, but it seemed a little silly that a man of his years and position should want his friends to hear anything he might have to say to some hundred burghers who needed no oratory to convince them that they ought to give to an institution they had been supporting for years. It was a pity, too, that the accursed banquet had fallen on a Friday, since Friday was one of the two evenings when he and Saskia set out beer and salad and herring for their friends, and he had been forced to spread the word that nobody was to drop in tonight.

"Oh, this *is* tiresome," said Saskia, waving prettily over the heads of the thickening crowd at old Burgomaster van Pellicorne. "Maybe we can leave as soon as the speeches are over. If we got back, say, before eleven, we could put a light in the parlor window, and some of the officers might see it and come up."

"We can't leave right after the speeches. We'll have to stay to congratulate him. Otherwise, in a crowd like this, he'd never know we were here."

His brusque tone rose entirely from annoyance with that crowd: burghers and their ladies, most of them past forty, making a tour that they had made a dozen times before and smiling benignly over their ruffs at the wizened beneficiaries—well scrubbed, well warned, and on their best behavior—who piped or croaked their obviously rehearsed remarks about points of interest. He was sure he was having a worse time of it than she was. She seemed entirely at ease, smiling and bowing and finding something pleasant to say to everybody who stopped them —he supposed she had acquired a talent for that sort of thing in Friesland. Not that he questioned his right to be here: he was a distinguished citizen of Amsterdam even if he did not have the right to wear the burgher ruff, and he would give his ten or twenty florins to the Old Men's Home like everybody else. But he did not look like everybody else, and that was disquieting. He and Saskia, worried only that they would not make a brilliant enough showing, had decked themselves out —he in olive-green velvet and she in saffron satin—and had adorned themselves with jewels for an occasion that apparently called for a black and brown sobriety. And von Sandrart, the only other painter present, was plainly more conversant with the requirements than he was: the rigid German, standing in a circle of admiring ladies, was dressed irreproachably in black woolen with a very modest quantity of lace at his yellowish neck and scrawny wrists.

They were looking at the herb garden when a low and tentative female voice said his name. He turned and realized in a moment that it was Margheretha van Meer, her figure more curved and womanly now in her dove-grey woolen dress, and her hair bound in a severe but ample and queenly knot. Her blue overprominent eyes were lighted up with pleasure as she put her hand into his for an instant; then she withdrew it and slipped it over the arm of a tall, blond young man who had come up behind her and stopped at her side. "This is my husband, Pastor Elias Simonszoon," she said. "Elias, this is the famous painter Rembrandt van Rijn and his wife Saskia van Uylenburgh." Their constraint was lightened a little by a round of handshakes and bows and smiles.

The husband—and it was strangely upsetting to note it—was very comely in a fine-grained way; the husband, discounting the somber clothes and the austere black beaver of his calling, undoubtedly made a more pleasing first impression than himself. He explained that he and Margheretha, whose name he said with a proud, shy possessiveness, were here at the banquet only because he happened to assist Pastor Portius in his duties at the Old Men's Home, not because anybody had any illusions—oh, heavens, no—about what an assistant minister could give, especially with a wife and two children to keep.

"Two!" said Saskia, and her clear eyes clouded.

"Yes," said Margheretha. "The boy just had his second birthday, and the little girl is two months old." Whereupon a flush spread up from her neck and suffused her whole face, and she fixed her eyes on the rows of thyme and basil at her feet.

"We're very lucky in our children," said the friendly pastor. "Both of them are fine and healthy, thank God. And you, Heer van Rijn, have you started a family yet?"

"No, not yet," said Saskia; and he knew by the blithe, hard tone of it that he need not squeeze her arm to let her know there was no necessity to tell the others that they had had a child and the child was dead.

263

There was nothing to be embarrassed about, yet through all the trivial talk which followed he felt embarrassed nevertheless. He also took an inexplicable pleasure in learning that assistant pastors made less in a year than his income from his apprentices alone. Not that the pastor was complaining; he thanked God at the end of every speech for one thing or another, and his hand, closing over his wife's, seemed to indicate that nothing could distress a man who had found himself such a companion. She said nothing, only kept moving the toe of her plain black slipper back and forth along the edge of the herb bed until a long halt in the conversation made it plain that it was time for them to go their separate ways.

"I wanted to ask you, how is your sister Lysbeth?" she said.

"Lysbeth? She's pretty well."

"I think of her often. Give her my love."

"I'll remember to do that the next time we're in Leyden."

"Oh, is she in Leyden?"

"Why, yes. Didn't you know? She hasn't been with Saskia and me these last three years."

"Is that so? I'm glad to hear it. That is, I don't mean I'm glad to hear she isn't with you and Saskia. I only mean, I felt a little hurt because she never called on me, and now, of course, if she's in Leyden, that explains it, and I won't be wondering any more. You know, Elias, we're keeping these good people much too long—there must be dozens of others here who will be wanting to talk to them. It was very good to see you—to see both of you." The bright, protruding eyes permitted themselves to focus for one more instant on his face and then turned full upon Saskia, to take in and punish themselves with that beauty, those fiery curls caught up in the emerald-green veil, that breast still high and firm and flawless, that round neck with its double strand of pearls.

Unnerved as he was by the incident, it took him a while to notice that the genial master of the banquet was urging the guests to sit down to their suppers. He settled with his wife at the table that happened to be closest and applied himself without appetite to the large bowl of barley broth flavored with carrots and parsley; and what little savor the food might have had for him was spoiled by thoughts of Lysbeth and troubling recollections of his recent visits back home. She could make herself pleasant enough with strangers, his Saskia, but she had never been able to delight, bedazzle, or even appease the members of his family. Whether they were impervious out of innate dullness or because Lysbeth had sown an ineradicable prejudice among them, he could not tell, but none of them liked her. His mother regarded her with the same indulgent forbearance she used to show the kittens and puppies that the children brought into the kitchen, pitying their innocence and helplessness, putting up with them patiently while they were underfoot, and not in the least sorry when they took themselves off to wherever they belonged. Her presence in the house gave his sister an opportunity to practice her Christianity with a vengeance: she arranged that the place closest to the fire should be reserved for Saskia, that the best cut of meat appeared on Saskia's plate, that the tablecloth, whether it was dirty or not, should be changed every night for Saskia's sake. Poor Antje, forced by her loyalty to Lysbeth to maintain a coolness that her good nature would not permit her really to feel, spoke so seldom and so haltingly that anybody would have thought her hopelessly stupid. And Adriaen could not let a day go by without pressing the stranger in their midst into some damaging confession: yes, she *did* keep two servants; no, they hadn't been to church since her Uncle Sylvius had taken to his bed; it was true that they entertained frequently, but they did it only in the smallest way, with herring and beer.

No, nothing was to be gained by dragging her along with him when he went to Leyden—so he told himself while he conducted a not altogether coherent conversation with the well-endowed spinster on his left about the spiritual needs of those who had reached "the sunset of their days." Henceforth he would arrange his own visits home to coincide with the little trips she made to Friesland to assist at the confinements, namedays and anniversaries of Hiskia and Titia and the rest. Looking back on it now, he could not see why he had begrudged her those journeys in the beginning: short separations made for ardent reunions; and the nights when she had lain against him, drowsy after the jogging of the coach and eager to enjoy again the warmth of his body, were among the nights that he remembered best. Whether or not she got on with his people, whether or not she showed up like a hummingbird among wrens in this drab assembly, he was content. "I certainly agree with you there," he said in reply to something his neighbor had asserted with vehemence. And he suppressed a foolish impulse to tell his wife to take off her earrings: it was true that they were too elaborate and that they kept catching in the veiling, but to remove them in public would be a kind of capitulation.

"Look at them, the dears!" said a plump old lady in a ruff, seated close to the head of the board. She was nodding toward the table where the old men were seated, their bald or white or iron-grey pates bent over the soup bowls, their napkins tucked like bibs under their chins. Some of their faces were tragic and austere; some were sly or bitter or evil; some seemed already to be half-obliterated, melting away in decrepitude—"dears" they were not, and he was damned if he would say so. And while the empty bowls were being taken away and the plates of roast beef and cabbage were being handed round, he kept an eye on that table and was half-disappointed because the dishes set under the dribbled chins were no different from those being served to the retired or incumbent burgomasters, the Regents' ladies, and the scions of the old aristocracy. But this even-handed portioning was no reason for him to stifle his chill and knowing smile; it cost the rich and the fortunate little enough to dispense a fine dinner to their dependents once a year, and they were more than repaid by their complacent conviction of their own civic virtue.

No, he did not like them, he was not at ease with them, even though they tried to be cordial after his little wife had skillfully identified him for their benefit. Why shouldn't they be cordial? Doubtless they or their friends or their relatives were trying to get onto his list. And he listened with nothing more than cool patience while a burgomaster's widow delivered the old, shopworn compliments on his *Anatomy Lesson*, while the silly old lady said that the lace in his portraits was so real that a person wanted to finger it, while the aged judge with the rheumy eyes told him that he went to look at his Passion pictures every time he visited The Hague.

As they ate their way through the second course, the noise and the conviviality increased, possibly because there was an endless supply of excellent beer donated for the occasion by one of the larger local breweries. A burst of laughter went up at one table, a volley of coy protests at another. Grave ladies, beyond the time of beauty but conscious of the little that was left to them, came erectly across the darkening gardens, carrying lighted lamps which they set down on the boards among the fat loaves and the steaming gravy bowls and the tall pitchers of beer. Two or three daring souls left their tables and wandered over to others, and soon a third of the company had gotten up, going with mugs of beer and slices of buttered bread in their hands to do a little visiting with friends and acquaintances.

He felt conspicuous and a little pained that nobody was coming up to chat with him—Tulp wouldn't, that was certain, placed as he was with Vondel at the head of the main table; and Vrouw Schnellius had intercepted the impressive advance of Burgomaster van Pellicorne. "The gravy's nice, but I can't say I care for the cabbage," said Saskia. "I do wish we had been able to eat our supper at home tonight, just you and I by ourselves." Like him, she was feeling forlorn, in spite of her smile and her splendid dress. So it was with real pleasure that he saw Allaert and Lotje coming toward them, weaving their way among the ladies who were carrying out the empty plates and their charitable sisters who were bringing in the sweet. The new arrivals were well known, distinguished in their rich brown clothes, and as friendly as anybody could wish—Lotje came up behind Saskia and kissed her long and affectionately on the top of her head.

"I should scold you, I really should scold you both," she said, smiling down at the two of them. "We haven't laid eyes on you since little Cornelis's christening supper, and he's walking and talking now—he's saying almost everything."

"You haven't come to us either," said Saskia, flushing.

"That's true enough," said Allaert, clapping his old friend on the shoulder, "but then it's a good deal easier for you to come to us than for us to come to you. Lotje always has a bad conscience when she leaves the little fellow alone with the nurse, and so do I, to tell the truth. But you two are as free as the air—you can come and go as you please."

Lotje's mild eyes made plain that she remembered the cost of that freedom. Stroking Saskia's shoulders in a way that reminded him of the tender and tentative gestures of her dead mother-in-law, she began to praise Saskia's veil, Saskia's earrings, Saskia's dress—all of which did not make them feel any more comfortable under the eyes of their neighbors at the table.

"And what have you got to report of yourself?" said Allaert.

It was a stupid and unwelcome question. It forced a person to stare at his own life as if it were another man's, to ask himself—with the ruin and emptiness of old age under his very nose—what he had accomplished or experienced that was of any significance. "The usual thing," he said in a dejected voice. "A lot of portrait commissions, a few Biblical things on my own, and I've taken on a couple of new apprentices."

"Good heavens, I should think that would be plenty."

But somehow it wasn't, or at least tonight he felt that it wasn't. Still watching the old men's faces, he asked himself whether this was to be the sum and all of it: painting with increasing mastery and decreasing involvement, learning that such-and-such a canvas had been hung in the palace of some German Landgraef, moving from one suite of rooms to another, discarding chairs and drapes and bedcovers for better ones, making new friends and being estranged from old ones. "And what about you, Allaert—what do you have to report of yourself?" he said.

"Nothing, really." The long, pale face with its nondescript beard looked quizzical, seemed more amused than appalled at the vacuity. "We'll be living in the country most of the summer; the country air's supposed to be good for children. We're putting up a barn and buying some goats—I might even invest in a few cows. I wish you'd come out to see us; there'd be plenty of time for talking."

Yes, he thought, nodding politely, but what would there be for us to talk about?

While the others were moving back to their places Saskia whispered into Lotje's ear that she was almost certain that she was pregnant; and he was embarrassed to see that Lotje believed her, that tears actually came into the still, brown eyes. Hardly a month had passed since the death of Rombartus without Saskia's imagining that she was with child again. Those who saw her regularly—the officers, the Portuguese Jews, and the Mennonites—either teased her when she made her announcements or showed a guarded enthusiasm; and he did not know for whom he was most embarrassed—his wife or Lotje or himself.

The young couple said their farewells and got themselves out of the way of the women who were serving the thick, rich slices of gingerbread. As he watched them going arm in arm across the darkened lawn, his eye lighted again on Dr. Tulp, who sat side by side with the poet Vondel at a table where almost everybody flaunted the burgher ruff and showed some sign of self-assurance: erect shoulders, hands quietly folded on the edge of the board, a gracious if somewhat artificial smile. "The Muiden Circle seems to be very well represented here tonight," he said to the spinster on his left.

"Oh, yes, they would be. Joost van den Vondel's going to read a poem in honor of the occasion. Not that they wouldn't have come anyway—they can always be depended upon in any good cause."

He glanced at Saskia, whose pretty mouth was drooping with chagrin. A speech, a poem, standing in a long line to offer congratulations—it would be late; the officers would pass, and there would be no light in the window. And he did not want to listen to the poem any more than she did: it was bound to be one of those high-flown odes stuffed with noble sentiments and tricked out with far-fetched classical allusions; and those poor devils over there—sodden with an unlimited issue of beer, finished with the one elaborate meal they got in twelve months, with the looked-for event behind them now and nothing to do but go back to their barren little coops and wait it out, if they could, for another three hundred and sixty-five days—they were scarcely anything to be classical about.

The ringing of the bell drew his attention back to the speakers' table, where the master of the banquet had risen to make an announcement. "Friends and distinguished fellow-citizens of Amsterdam," he said, "we are about to hear a short address by a gentleman who requires no introduction. Permit me to present our beloved and respected Master of the Surgeons' Guild, Dr. Nicolaas Pieterszoon, better known as Dr. Tulp."

The dry dark hair, the bony and thoughtful face, the penetrating eyes that came up into the light of the lamp had changed little from what had been set down in *The Anatomy Lesson*. The doctor waited until the well-bred clapping was over, and then bowed briefly from the waist; and in the briskness of his bow and the tightness of his face there was a suggestion that he took the applause, his honored place in the community, and the short address he was about to make as matters of minor consequence. Yet all that he said was earnest and direct, in spite of the wry smile that tensed the corners of his mouth whenever he paused for emphasis or breath. They were here to celebrate a year of work well done, he said, but he trusted they knew the difference between celebrating an occasion and congratulating themselves. It was good that the year had seen certain improvements: enough trees planted to constitute a little orchard, an increase in the allotments of bread and herring, more peat for the hearths, more books for the little library. This was all to the good, but he felt called upon to remind them that actually it was very little—how little, they might realize if every generous donor would limit himself just for tomorrow to what he had provided for others here. Was he about to enjoy a cup of warm sack? Sack wasn't heard of in the little houses. An easy chair with cushions and a padded back? Here they sat on wood. An extra coverlet? But a sheet and a single blanket here were considered quite enough. A lamp to read by late into the sleepless night? But here, though the aged slept lightly, the supply of oil was short, and every light had to be extinguished at nine. Amsterdam was a charitable city, the most charitable city in Europe, no doubt. Yet, while the gap between what a man had and what he was willing to give was still so wide, nobody here, including the speaker—he stepped back into the shadow, as if to disclaim another round of the discreet applause—nobody here had reason to congratulate himself.

Saskia, her eyes brilliant with easy tears, put up her dimpled hand and pulled off her big pearl earrings: it was fortunate, he thought, that there were no receptacles for such donations in the gardens—otherwise she would certainly have given them then and there. He patted her on the knee and showed her, by spreading his ten fingers three times, that he meant to give thirty florins. She nodded and smiled at him and tapped her beer mug lightly with her spoon, like those around her, when the master of the banquet announced severely that the next and final item for the evening would be a poem written expressly for this occasion by Heer Joost van den Vondel, whose works were the glory of the mother tongue and the pride of Amsterdam.

He got up, a thick and aging shopkeeper in a brown jacket and a rather limp linen collar, and moved into the lamplight holding some of the pride of Amsterdam and the glory of the mother tongue on an excessive length of parchment between his pudgy hands. It was strange that his presence should seem so much less commanding than on that evening a decade ago in the little room that opened onto Vrouw van Hoorn's reception hall. Had his collar been crumpled then? Had the same creases—deep but unimpressive, like the cracks in a well-browned pancake—shown in his face? Had the same wisps of hair wandered over his innocuous round brow? The eyes looked sad: he had buried his wife a few months ago, and it was rumored that at The Hague their patience with his harmless and quirkish radicalism had begun to rub thin. His mouth was robbed of some of its determination by the dejected droop of the little goatee and the not-too-carefully trimmed moustache, and his chin was soft, uncertain, even a little tremulous.

But any expectation of modesty on the grounds of such unassuming looks was unjustified. The voice that came out of the well-fleshed chest was bombastic, stentorian. The first stanza—and who would care to listen to more than the first?—was a pastiche of theology and philosophy, preceded by the invocation of the usual classic gods. And it was all the more sickening because of those around him: Tesselschade Visscher looked as if she were being ravished, Hooft wore the expression of a man beholding a beatific vision, and von Sandrart kept nodding his head at every rhyme, as if the business of getting two ill-assorted words to jingle were an astonishing accomplishment.

"But what's it all about?" asked Saskia in a whisper.

He shrugged and spread his hands and did not care who might see him. He supposed it was about "the sunset of one's days"; it advanced the fatuous proposition that because certain of the gods had taken on old age—to wit, Saturn, Jupiter, and Neptune—it was godlike to grow old. He entertained himself through the rest of it by looking at the old men's table and posing such gratifying questions as: How would Jupiter have looked if he had lost his teeth? Did Saturn suffer from a weak bladder? Did the sea nymphs ever get together and complain of Neptune's senile obscenities? And since these questions provoked a nervous, tickling kind of laugh in his chest, he was relieved that his neighbors at the board, doubtless put off by his tightly compressed lips, did not solicit any admiring comments from *him* during the thunderous applause.

That applause and the celebratory ringing of the bell by the master of the banquet signalized the end of the whole tiresome business. People got up, draining off what was left at the bottom of their beer mugs—he could imagine how many of them would be following Dr. Tulp's suggestions tomorrow. A queue of congratulators was already forming, and he took his little wife by the hand and actually ran with her in and out among the knots of people to the spot where the speakers of the evening stood under the sparse trees. They might yet be home in time to catch a few of the gentlemen coming from the Military Club. He'd have to remember to tell Captain Banning Coq what he'd thought about the sea nymphs and Neptune—the lads of the City Guard enjoyed that sort of thing. Saskia stood in front of him in the line, and he improved the time by spanning her waist and letting his thumbs wander down as far as her hips. If the officers dropped in, that would be all to the good, and if they didn't—well, he could think of other ways to spend a merry hour.

But the business was not to be disposed of as quickly as he had hoped. The good doctor told him, with an annoying assumption of fatherly authority, that he'd better not go skipping off like that, he'd better stay at least long enough to congratulate the other speaker of the evening.

"But I don't know him, and we were planning to—"

"You ought to know him."

"We're expecting some of the officers to drop by and—"

"And he's expecting you to come up and talk to him."

"But why on earth—"

"Because I told him you would. Now, just wait a few minutes and I'll take you over and present you. Your company will wait, and God knows it's seldom enough that I ask a favor of *you*."

Except for the bevy of charitable ladies responsible for clearing away the debris of the banquet, the garden was almost deserted by the time

Tulp dragged the two of them up to utter the required asininities. Vondel had just rolled up the long piece of parchment from which he had read his masterpiece and was handing it to von Sandrart, but in spite of the fact that the German took the thing as if it were a scroll of Holy Writ, it was difficult to converse with the mild-mannered poet and retain any real truculence. They had scarcely been talking for two minutes when Vondel mentioned the hosiery trade by which he made his living and added that while poetry could be written in snatches between one customer and another, such a large and splendid work as *The Anatomy Lesson* would naturally call for total immersion and complete dedication. The pancake creases in his broad face, seen at close range, seemed homely and comfortable; his brown eyes, heavily lidded above and emphasized by deep pouches below, were shyly benevolent, and if the exasperating German had not been standing by to hear, it would have been possible to say what everybody else had doubtless said: It was a pleasure and a privilege to hear the magnificent poem you read for us tonight.

But he could not say it—at any rate he did not say it. When Tulp, standing paternally behind him and his wife, gave him a pat on the shoulder that was more like a prod, all he could get out was, "That was a very learned piece we had from you, Heer van den Vondel. It was so packed I'm afraid I missed some of it, just hearing it read off like that. I hope we'll be seeing it in print."

"It can be read before it is put in print," said the German. "This beautiful copy of it, in Heer van den Vondel's own handwriting, is to be hung on the wall in the Regents' room of this institution."

"Was there any certain stanza you found especially hard to follow, Heer van Rijn?" asked the poet.

"Oh, no, no certain stanza." If they began to explore particulars, he would certainly be lost. "I only meant that in general it was a little hard to grasp at first reading."

"I wonder if many of the audience had that feeling." He looked genuinely worried: his mouth drooped under the limp moustache, and two long furrows broke up the placidity of his round brow.

"Of course not," said Tulp, giving his protégé another prod and putting his free arm around Saskia's waist. "Everybody enjoyed it—that was perfectly plain. All my friend here is trying to say is that it'll yield even more on repeated reading. Poetry's a very concentrated thing— myself, I never really get hold of a poem until I've read it at least twice."

"Nobody whatsoever," said von Sandrart, "should have the smallest trouble with the comprehension of this work. This work was written to be understood upon hearing. It is clear enough to be comprehended by a little child."

"Really?" said Rembrandt, sensing a return of the nervous tickling that had stirred in his chest. "Those old men, for instance—do you think they didn't have any trouble with the classical allusions?"

"Well, now, that's a good point," said Vondel, putting up a plump hand and brushing back a disorderly wisp of hair. "No, Joachim, I'm afraid he's right. The old men couldn't possibly have grasped it; it was written for the donors. The fact is, I've often wondered whether it's possible to write anything that appeals to both the simple, uneducated man and the man of taste and cultivation."

"I do not know," said von Sandrart, "why a man with your distinction should give himself this bother. He who is mounted on Pegasus and is going to the stars—how can he perturb his mind with thinking about the common grooms he has left in the stable below? These people who cannot understand what is your meaning—you must banish them out from your mind or you will make a sickening wreck of what you are writing. It is enough for them that they are allowed to listen and pick up any little piece which falls in their hands."

Common grooms in the stable? In spite of Tulp's marked pressure on his shoulder and Saskia's lighter pressure on his forearm, he could not contain himself. It seemed to him that it was not only on the pitiful old men that the German had pinned his execrable label; Harmen Gerritszoon, the unlettered miller of Leyden—he had been degraded and insulted too. "Excuse me," he said in a voice charged enough to startle a charitable lady who was gathering soiled napkins at a nearby table, "but am I to understand, Heer von Sandrart, that these old men, these common grooms as you choose to call them, are to be put in a lower order because they never heard of Diana and Proserpine? I know next to nothing about poetry, but I can tell you this much as a painter: look at their faces and you'll find more there than you'll see in any number of your gentlemen of taste and cultivation. I know, I've painted them both, and when I find myself running dry it's to these common grooms that I go to renew myself."

There was an instant of silence in which his colleague's eyes, small and yellowed, looked him over from head to foot. "Yes, Heer van Rijn, that is obvious. I would say that is very obvious to look at your painting."

"Yes, and a lot of other things are obvious too," he said, pulling his arm free of Saskia's restraining hand. "It's obvious for instance that people have had their bellies full of Diana and Proserpine. It was bad enough when the Romans imitated the Greeks, and even worse when the Italians started imitating the Romans. But when *we* imitate the imitators of the imitators—that's going too far, that's trying to wring blood out of dry bones. Your Pegasus died a long time ago, Herr von Sandrart, and all that's left in that stable now is a tired old gelding standing so deep in his own dung he'll never be able to move, to say nothing about flying to the stars."

He was too exhilarated to consider the consequences; and the stillness that followed proved him irrefutable, even if Saskia was blushing and Tulp looked appalled. He was not sorry, however, that the doctor

272

should take it upon himself to point out that Heer van Rijn was speaking, of course, not of poets but of a certain group of painters, most of whom were Flemish: there was nothing to be gained by hurting the feelings of the shopkeeper-author, though his own origins should have prompted him to reprimand his toady for making such objectionable distinctions. He did not seem angry; he only rubbed his innocent forehead with his knuckles and said that an argument was always refreshing and that an honest clash of opinions furnished a person with food for thought.

But later, when he and Saskia were hurrying arm in arm along the dark canal, she would not let herself be drawn into his excited talk about the incident. Why she should be silent—whether she was sorry for Vondel or would have liked her husband to argue in the coolly courteous manner of her family in Friesland—he could not tell; but he was exasperated by her detachment and her moodiness. What reason had he to restrain himself in front of these fools who scratched each other's backs at Muiden? He had no cause to be wary—he was not hoping to be a burgomaster, like Tulp; he had more patrons than he could use. If any regrets rose in him during that walk, he downed them by gloating over the aptness of his thrusts and the sharpness of his wit—he had certainly been in fine fettle tonight. And his exhilaration mounted when the deep strokes of the clock in the City Hall came to a stop at the count of eleven. He would have an appreciative audience after all: it was still early enough for some of the lads from the Military Club to drop in, and in the telling he would be able to savor the evening's doings all over again.

*

It was a good six months after the charity supper before his wife was with child again, and even after Dr. Bonus had assured her that this time she was making no mistake, there was something strangely unconvincing about that second pregnancy. There had been so many other occasions when the Portuguese Jewish ladies had told her to be careful on the stairs and the Mennonites had promised to pray for her safe delivery and the officers had proposed toasts to "the one who will be with us soon" that there was bound to be something artificial about all the fluttering. And later, when she *did* have to go into those shapeless clothes that she had worn before the birth of Rombartus, and the protuberance was really keeping her back from the table at which the toasts were given—later she herself seemed dubious about her state.

As her body grew thicker, her face grew incongruously childish and thin. Her eyes seemed larger because of the bluish circles around them; her lips, drooping and often parted, looked like the lips of a little girl; and the flesh of her cheeks, tightening or falling away, showed beneath the delicate stretched skin the shape of the bones. It was just such a face as he needed for the angel he intended to paint in the Apocryphal story

273

of Tobit, and he drew it over and over. The Mennonite preacher Anslo, comparing those sketches with some earlier ones for a Flora and a Delilah, found a theological reason for the transformation. "She wouldn't serve for a pagan goddess or a Canaanite woman now, would she, my friend? She has an other-world look, a look that comes like a special grace from God to certain women about to give birth," he said. "More than anything else, that look convinces me that the spirit enters the child while the child is still in the womb. What I mean is: your wife knows, without exactly knowing in so many words, that what she's about to bring into the world is a living soul."

It was a soul, if it could be called anything, that she brought forth after long and terrible labor in the steaming heat of midsummer. This time the delivery was properly supervised: Bonus was there before the midwife and left the room only once, to relieve his bladder, in all the seven ghastly hours. But the infant, a girl child who would have been called Cornelia after his mother, uttered no cry when it was turned upside down and slapped on the buttocks; and they had scarcely gotten it cleansed of its envelope of blood and slime before it gasped a little and was dead.

The death of the child, he supposed, was enough to account for the dragging slowness of the mother's recovery. She lay abed for three weeks instead of the accepted two, listless between drowse and drowse, alive only three times a day, after she had swallowed the prescribed goblet of elderberry wine. In her sleep and her listlessness she seemed always to be remembering: she was back in Friesland with her sisters, or in the gardens and taverns where he had courted her, or in their old rooms on the Bloemgracht, or in her cousin Hendrik's shop, dancing among the dusty ceremonial robes—though everybody was bored by this time with Hendrik's affectations and chronic unsuccess, he was urged to come more often now for Saskia's sake. It was hard to keep at work, distracted as he was by the thought of her lying alone in their bedroom; half a dozen times a day he would excuse himself to his apprentices, lay down his brushes, and go to her. He would draw up a stool close to the bed and take the cool inert fingers between his hands or let his head come down where the coverlet was raised by the twin mounds of her knees; and peace would come upon him then, a dazed and dreaming peace. At first he was constantly waiting for the times when she would be revived by the strengthening drink, but afterwards he realized that she yielded him more comfort in her drowsy state. Once the wine had begun to course through her body, she said whatever came into her head, and her talk was the talk of one avid for the world. On such occasions she would tell him that she needed a new beaver cloak, or she might call in a servant and order an elaborate supper, which later she would push away untouched; or she might ask to have her jewel case set open on the coverlet so that she could look at her garnets and pearls. The only time she spoke of the baby was when she recounted her difficult delivery, and she disconcerted poor Anslo by refusing to dignify the living soul even to the extent of assigning sex to it: she referred to the little thing with conscious malice as "it," though everybody else said "your daughter" or "Cornelia" or "she."

It was impossible to tell when her confinement came to an end. Three or four times she got up and announced herself completely well, only to retreat again after an interval of feverish activity to the inert isolation of the corner bed. Dr. Bonus could find no reason for these relapses: when they asked her to describe her symptoms, all she could say was that she felt wretched, wretched, worse than she had ever felt in her life; and she said it with a kind of angry vehemence, her eyes clouding over with tears. It was Tulp who conjectured that she was feigning illness because some streak of pride in her would not allow her to admit her grief over the death of the child. And if that was so she certainly should not be permitted to hide in the bedroom and mourn there alone, he said; she should be indulged and distracted by the members of her household and by sympathetic and warm-hearted company. If she fancied she was ill and had to lie down, provision should be made for her to lie down in the parlor. That little couch, the one with the gilded Cupid on it—couldn't that be carried in?

It was, and she lay evening after evening on those quilted pillows on which she had been Danaë—and would, in due time, be Danaë again, by the grace of God. Even if they had not been told that she needed attention and indulgence, everybody who came to the rooms on New Doelen Street would have been drawn to her as the bee is drawn to nectar. Anslo and Swalmius in their somber ministerial black, Captain Banning Coq and young Lieutenant Ruytenberg tricked out in the insignia of the City Guard, the apprentices with the day's pigment on their shirts and under their fingernails—all of them waited their turns to offer her a nosegay, a bottle of French wine, a bar of fine soap, or a precious packet of Chinese tea.

It was the Portuguese bookseller's wife, Vrouw Pinero, a spry little creature with a face as wrinkled as a piece of dried fruit, who brought her the kitten. Why she had chosen this particular one of the litter of six born in her husband's bookshop was obvious. Its colors were Saskia's colors, tiger-orange and creamy white; it played with a tassel on one of the cushions with Saskia's impulsiveness; it settled down and washed its small, curled paw with Saskia's daintiness. And for something more than a week it seemed that Vrouw Pinero had found her precisely what she needed, a magnetic point to fix the erratic needle of her days. She put it to bed in a lined basket in the kitchen near the hearth, she let it crawl up on her chest and lick her chin, she spoiled it dreadfully by giving it goose liver and adding cream and sugar to its milk. And then Rembrandt was suddenly aware that she was putting it down when it jumped on her knee, was closing it up in the kitchen, had forgotten to replenish its food. It was one of the apprentices who told him that the little creature had running eyes, an affliction that he soon cured with the help of an eyewash concocted by Tulp. "Your cat's almost better; why don't you let him out of the kitchen?" he asked her one evening before any of the guests had arrived. She shrugged, and her face took on the stubborn look that always came upon it when she was asked to describe her symptoms. "No, not tonight. Some other time, maybe in a day or two. It isn't that I don't like him, it's only that it makes me sad to look at him," she said.

And when something finally did absorb her, it was a matter so trivial and so alien to his own tastes that he could take little pleasure in her revival. Maria de Medici was to pay an official visit to Amsterdam, and the town decided to outdo itself by way of a welcome, with floats on the river and pageants in the New Theater, with trumpet players in all the towers and triumphal arches over all the main streets; and he could not understand how his little wife could be sent into such a flutter over a woman whose family was distinguished in Italy chiefly for tyranny and in France for the slaughter of the Protestants in the Saint Bartholomew Massacre.

But interested she was, so interested that the skirts and jackets whose buttons and lacings had been too much for her to bother with came out of the closet again; and although it would be months before the Medici woman would arrive, she began to care for her hair and skin and nails as if she were going to a grand ball the following night. Captain Banning Coq and Lieutenant Ruytenberg were constantly bringing in fuel for her giddy fire: there was to be a dress parade down the length of the Breestraat; all the past and present burgomasters had gone to their tailors to be fitted for new gowns and hoods; Vondel had been appointed by the City Council to head a committee of poets and artists, the former to compose the pageant and the odes of welcome, the latter to design the arches and costumes and paint the scenes and banners for the New Theater and the City Hall. The Mennonites had never seemed to Rembrandt more genuinely endowed with Christian charity than when they listened unprotesting to all this worldly nonsense; they even agreed with Saskia when she argued that her husband's reputation as a painter might suffer if he did not bear his part in the general hubbub, if he refused to show his face at Hooft's castle at Muiden where the Committee for Poetry and Art was to meet.

Service on talkative public boards, the designing of gimcrack costumes and banners, and the making of gilded foliage and paper flowers were certainly not his meat. Yet when he found time to think of the Maria de Medici business—which was seldom, since the Prince had just ordered two more Passion pictures—he found himself willing to be drawn in, partly for Saskia's sake and partly because he might be given a chance to make up for the unfortunate scene that had taken place in the gardens of the Old Men's Home. Now that the exhilaration had drained away, the recollection of that scene kept coming back like a bad taste in his mouth. He especially wished he had never painted the two mad pictures that had sprung directly out of it: a bawling, fat, pissing *Ganymede Carried Away by the Eagle* and a hilarious *Diana Surprised by Actaeon,* in which the beefy huntsman seemed ready to jump out of his skin with delight over the twenty-one flabby nude females splashing and squealing in a typical Arcadian glade. Both canvases had found purchasers, and both purchasers had invited their intimates to enjoy the joke; for three or four months he could scarcely cross town without running into somebody who wanted to laugh with him over "those marvelous caricatures of the classical pretensions at Muiden." And though there was no indication that any members of the sainted Circle had ever seen those pictures, it was still a discomfiting possibility . . .

He was occupied with other matters that evening early in September when Coq and Ruytenberg failed to make their expected appearance at nine o'clock. He had been working all day, with the bafflement that usually set in when he returned to a style that time had discredited, on a series of sketches for the Prince's *Resurrection.* Nothing, not the angel nor the Roman soldiers nor the wan Presence rising from the opened tomb, would come out right: as soon as one thing seemed acceptable it destroyed his confidence in everything else. He could neither solve his problem nor relinquish it, so he carried his board and sketching paper and chalk into the parlor and set to work there, though he soon realized that he would be plagued by minor annoyances and distractions. Saskia, probably to gain attention, was coughing an exasperating little cough—she was forever coughing these days. Her little beast, which had grown by this time into a persistent and unlovely cat, kept jumping onto his knee and thrusting its moist nose against his chin. And the only three visitors who had as yet turned up—Swalmius, Anslo, and Dr. Bonus—had moved away from Saskia's gilded couch, since the military was not there to compete with them, and were sitting around a table, airing their differences as to the nature and attributes of God.

At one time or another he had drawn or painted each of them, and looking at the abandoned sketches strewn around his feet he wished he were at work on one of them now. The burly Anslo grasped the handle of his beer mug in one thick hand, but was too preoccupied to drink; his vital body seemed to strain the seams of his sober jacket; his cheeks shone ruddy above the black beard that covered the lower part of his face. Swalmius, seen in profile, seemed by comparison self-possessed and mellow; the light of the single candle shone directly upon him, making his Jovian beard and his greying yellow curls serenely aureate. And between them sat the little Portuguese Jew, his moustache drooping, his shoulders hunched, assent and protest passing by turns, like sunlight and shadows of clouds on a windy day, across his melancholy face.

"No, if there's one thing I'm convinced of, it's this," said Swalmius in his oratorical bass, "we must see Him as a Father."

"I beg your pardon, I have to take exception," said Anslo in an appealing tenor that issued incongruously from the sturdy instrument of his chest. "Say *feel* Him as a Father, if you like, and I'll agree to that. But *see* Him, no. He's not to be seen, not as a Father or anything else."

"Yet He plainly wished to come within the scope of our vision. He entered into the flesh precisely so that we might perceive Him," said Swalmius, addressing Anslo in the indulgent tone that a teacher might use with a well-meaning but stubborn boy.

"No, not perceive Him in the wholeness of His divine nature, if I may be permitted to say so. Only those of His attributes that He considered suitable for the limitations of the human mind and the human senses—"

"Are you actually going so far as to make Him divisible? As I understand it, He—not a segment of Him—made Himself incarnate by an act of His will for our salvation in the body of Jesus Christ our Lord."

"And you will pardon me," said the doctor, "if I disagree with both of you. My objection to this incarnation is precisely that it confines Him in any degree to what is perceptible. He is not to be molded into the shape of any body or limited in time so that He or any shadowing forth of Him begins with a birth and ends with a death."

There was no use in listening to Swalmius's reply; he had heard the old arguments before, and it was no wonder that they should be delivered somewhat offhandedly, though with the customary eloquence. Saskia, sadly neglected, was coughing and staring into the darkness beyond the window; the cat was walking on the sketches—which was no great loss; the city clocks had just marked the half-hour with a booming note made heavy by the misty autumn air, and Coq and Ruytenberg had not yet come. He laid down his piece of chalk and looked at the drawing on his knee, found it as facile in its nobility as Swalmius's discourse, and fetched up a sigh.

"I'm sure our hostess must be bored with us," said Bonus, "but our host ought to have something to contribute to the discussion. A God confined in time and space could be painted on canvas; such a God would make an absurdity of the law against graven images. What do you say, Rembrandt—can you paint God?"

"I don't know. I've never tried it."

"But you've painted God incarnate. You've painted our Lord and Saviour over and over," said Swalmius.

'Yes, I know that," said the little Jew, put out at last by the tutorial manner of the senior pastor. "But when you paint Jesus do you conceive of yourself as painting God the Creator of the Universe?"

Before he answered he removed the unbeautiful cat, which had seated itself on the sketch of a Roman soldier starting back in unconvincing awe before a slant of supernatural light, and set it as far away as he could without getting up from the stool. "I'm not sure I know what you mean by that," he said. "I haven't really followed the argument."

"He means," said Anslo, "can you put the attributes of God the Father into the person of God the Son?"

"What attributes are you talking about?"

"Why, those attributes," said Bonus, smiling his melancholy smile, "which are indescribable because they are inconceivable. The Torah counsels me against naming Him, to say nothing of describing Him, which I would certainly be doing if I tried to catalogue His attributes. If further clarification is necessary, I'll have to leave it to one of my learned friends."

But neither of them was called upon. Captain Banning Coq, more formal than usual in black velvet and a ruff and a fine new beaver with a rippling brim, walked into the room.

"You're very elegant this evening, Captain," Anslo called after him as he made for the couch to pay his respects to the mistress of the house.

"More so than I care to be," he said.

"And where's the lieutenant?" asked Saskia, sitting up with her back propped against the pillows and offering him first her hand and then her cheek to kiss.

"The lieutenant? Oh, he's been detained—he asked me to bring all of you his apologies."

He had been detained before, but never in such elusive terms, and Rembrandt found himself unexplainably annoyed. "You'll be giving him a bad reputation by putting it like that. It sounds as if he's looking for a playmate on Pieter-Jacob Street."

Saskia laughed and Anslo blushed and Swalmius knitted his Olympian brow. Banning Coq sat down on a chair close to the couch and cleared his throat as if he wanted to break the silence but could find no subject for conversation.

"You're late yourself," said Rembrandt in a tone that was churlish and possessive—after all, the man had not forfeited his right to go where he pleased by dropping in here two or three times a week.

"Yes, I know," he said, taking off his fine hat and shoving it under the chair as if he were ashamed of it. "As a matter of fact, both Ruytenberg and I were over at Muiden. They're still holding conferences over there, but I'd had enough of it, so I left him behind to see the rest of it through."

"Muiden?" said Rembrandt. "And what in God's name would you be doing over there?"

"Nothing, to tell the truth—absolutely nothing—it was a great waste of time," the captain said. "We were called over there in connection with this stupid affair for Maria de Medici. If it weren't that the two of us have to be responsible for the parade of the City Guard, neither of us would have had a thing to do with the whole idiotic business. You never saw anything as inane as what's been going on all day over at Hooft's—grown men and women playing with gilded nutshells and paper flowers."

His little wife, suddenly gone so pale that there was scarcely any difference between the color of her skin and the color of her lips, swung her feet to the floor and sat on the edge of the gilded couch, her elbows on her knees, her chin supported between her tightened fists. "Then— then they've already appointed the committee of artists? I didn't think they'd done that yet," she said.

"Oh, yes, they're all appointed, the poor devils. They're appointed and about their business, and a fine business it is—painting scenes for the stupid pageants and designing costumes for fat middle-aged ladies who are supposed to represent Amsterdam and Virtue and Navigation and Fortitude—"

"Who's on the committee?" she asked in a scarcely audible voice.

"Nobody of the slightest importance, my dear lady. Most of them are people like your husband's former apprentice Flinck—people with plenty of time to waste because they have no commissions to speak of. Poor Flinck, I really felt sorry for him; he looked as if he was bored to death. He told me confidentially that he would never have let himself in for it if Vondel hadn't insisted. It's hard for a person to refuse Vondel: he's always offering his own services for this sort of thing."

"So Rembrandt isn't invited?"

Pathetic as she was with her mouth shaking and the tears standing in her eyes, she begot less pity in him than anger. Wasn't it bad enough that he had been passed over and slighted, that over at Muiden they should be laughing up their sleeves at him? Wasn't it bad enough that Flinck, whom he had trained and been fond of, should have deserted and superseded him? Was it necessary also that she should make a public spectacle of his shame and expose her own weakness and embarrass his guests?

"No, my dear," said the captain, "your husband won't be in charge of such weighty matters as making crowns out of paper; he'll have to occupy his time painting Passion canvases for His Highness at The Hague. It's a pity, I'm sorry for him, but I imagine he'll get on. And inasmuch as I've had nothing but weak tea and miserable little cakes since noon, I wonder if I could impose on your hospitality to the extent of a plate of herring and a mug of beer?"

"Let me get it for you, Captain," said Saskia, getting up and smoothing down her skirt and forcing her wan, uncertain mouth into a smile. "I'm well enough to be a hostess, so don't anybody protest."

Nobody did: it must have been as obvious to the rest of them as to her husband that she wished to go to the kitchen where she could dry her eyes and wipe her nose. He felt an almost irrepressible urge to follow her; his anger had given way to the realization of how bruisingly dear she was to him in her vulnerability and her childishness. The cat, instantly alert to accompany anybody into the kitchen, went out with her; but she was too intent upon maintaining her precarious poise to notice it. He discarded the drawing on which he had been working and began another of an angel lifting the slab over the grave; but his hand was unsteady, and he was off to a bad start.

"And what have I missed this evening?" said Banning Coq in the pained silence.

He wanted no more oil and honey from that quarter. "Nothing worth mentioning," he said.

"Now, that's a gracious thing to say," said Anslo. "The fact is, we were having what I would consider a very significant discussion. Pastor Swalmius holds that we must envision God—"

"Ah," said Saskia, coming back with the plate and the mug, "are we to do that all over again?" And having placed the mug in the captain's hand and balanced the plate on his knee with an unconvincing show of vivacity and flirtatiousness, she went back to the couch and subsided against the cushion, staring at her lap as ruefully as a child might stare at a tumbled tower of blocks. He could not bear to look at her; he gripped the chalk, and hunching himself over his drawing, corrected the angelic arm that effortlessly lifted the great slab of stone. It was a good arm, now, but simply because it was as it ought to be it discredited the heavenly messenger's ordinary face.

"But we can't leave the discussion where we did," said the little doctor. "You never gave me an answer."

"I've forgotten the question."

"I asked you, when you paint Jesus, does it seem to you that you're painting God?"

He thought unwillingly of all the versions of Christ that he had ever painted, from the One who summoned Lazarus out of his grave with the masterful flourish of an actor to the fine nude on the Cross that suffered only in its thorn-pressed forehead and pierced feet. Even the One who transformed Himself into a burst of light before His apostles at Emmaus —of Him he had been inordinately proud—was a miracle-maker, not a divinity. "What do you want of me? I never said I was pious, did I? If you're looking for somebody to consider in your argument, consider Dürer or Grünewald. They painted Him out of the need of their souls —or I suppose they did. I'm painting Him for the Prince to hang up at The Hague."

The two pastors at the far table exchanged a look which probably meant that he should be forgiven for his irreverence, unsettled as he was by the Medici business. "Really," said Swalmius, "you're abusing yourself unnecessarily. Every time you've painted Him, you've painted at least one of His attributes. Take your *Raising of Lazarus* for instance —that certainly conveys His majesty and power."

"Yes," said Anslo. "Every time I look at it, I think how it is written that He spoke 'as one having authority.' "

The cat, its mouth still trailing a shred of the herring that she had fed it in the kitchen, came up to him and rubbed against his legs, wanting the stroking that he could not give it in his pain and self-disgust.

281

No, he thought, not "as one having authority"; more as one knowing his lines and certain that his audience will applaud. "That's the worst of them all," he said.

"You're very hard on yourself this evening. Maybe we *ought* to change the subject," said the captain miserably.

He did not answer. He was thinking of another passage, a foreshadowing of Him from the prophet: "He was despised and rejected of men, a man of sorrows and acquainted with grief." And at the same moment he saw the washerwoman Rinske Dobbels as he had drawn her against Pieter Lastman's antiquities—ugly in her nakedness, yet worthy of the pity that he had been able to bestow upon her in his own obscurity and loneliness. Oh, I was better then, I was closer to it then, whatever it is, he thought. What has gone out of me? What have I lost . . . ? And just at that moment the cat jumped onto his knee and thrust its fishy mouth into his face, startling him so that he struck it harder than he had intended, struck it so hard that it landed a foot away from him and uttered a shrill, amazed cry.

"Poor kitty, what did he do to you?" said Saskia.

The captain cleared his throat again, and Anslo lifted his beer mug and took a long draught.

"No," said Bonus, "I stand where I stood before. To try to know Him, even to imagine that we can know Him is the sin of pride you people are always talking about. Limited as we are in our perceptions, what more can we know of Him than the wood louse knows of the tree it feeds upon?"

The cat came back, its tail down, and stood on the drawings, looking up into his face. As the tree is to the wood louse, as God is to my feeble and distorted senses, so I am to that cat, he thought—a being unbounded in time, with neither birth nor death, a source of nourishment and healing and punishment, the possessor of vast, inconceivable power. With my left hand I stroke him, and with my right I chastise him; and if I were angry enough I could strike him dead. And there he stands on my sketches, knowing no more of my sketches than I know of the force that draws the sea or the power that propels the comets and sets an orderly orbit for the stars . . .

"Let the drawing alone now, darling," said Saskia. "Whatever you're doing, you'll spoil it. Come and sit by me."

He did not get up and go to her at once. He could not, for a terrible possibility held him there staring into the cat's unblinking eyes. How do I know, he thought, letting the drawing slide from his knee—how do I know that if the Unknowable were ultimately revealed, He would not prove as arbitrary, as selfish, as mean and meaningless as I myself?

*

The great reception given by the city of Amsterdam for Maria de Medici, Queen Mother of the Most Christian—and very Catholic—

King of France, was coming to its conclusion at last. They were finishing it off with a flourish: every bell in the city banging away, every trumpeter on the municipal payroll bursting his lungs, every town pigeon startled out of the evening quiet of his roost. And Dr. Tulp, standing by on the wharf with the other members of the Official Committee to Attend Her Majesty, looked up at the sudden soaring of the flocks and wondered what the poor birds could be making of all that noise.

It was over now, and the thousands who had stood at the windows and on the roofs and balconies of the houses in the Rokin to watch the splendid water festival could collect their scarves and children and make their way down unfamiliar stairs into the torchlit twilight streets. None of them could have found fault with anything; the royal visitor had clapped her hands and said that she had never been greeted by such a crowd, no, not even in Paris, and the reception could be stamped, like a well-salted barrel of herring, as a product of Amsterdam that had come up to the mark. The water was still strewn with gilded leaves and paper crowns, but the trappings of the carnival would soon be cleared away: the boats disguised as Charon's bark and Neptune's shell would be stripped and sent about their usual business of hauling or fishing; the triumphal arches would be taken down out of the way of traffic; the banners and costumes and false beards would be laid by in musty chests and closets; and the artificial island built out there in the watery waste to impress a queen and provide a stage for a foolish pageant would be reclaimed—as better things had been reclaimed in a harsher and more heroic past—by the sure encroachment of the sea.

Everything was proceeding according to schedule. Before the fanfare began to slacken, the gilded carriage rolled up with the cavalry guard before and behind it; and the royal guest herself—a horse-faced personage whose smile had been rigid to begin with and was as hard as iron by this time of the day—got into the cushioned interior, blew a few unconvincing kisses through the glass, and was off with a clatter to a welcome night's rest.

Once the carriage was out of the way, the doctor watched the swarming houses until he caught sight of his own wife and daughter coming out. He had meant to walk home with them, but one glimpse of his daughter's transported face was enough to steer him in the opposite direction. For the last twelve hours he had been producing enthusiasm by the yard, and he simply did not have the heart for any more of it, not even for the gratification of his family. Anyway, his wife's brother was with them and would take them home: *he* would have enough energy left for enjoyment in retrospect—after all, *he* had not been exposed from nine till nine to the Queen Mother's iron grin and the strictures of royal etiquette.

He crossed the wharf and managed to get through the press without interruption by avoiding the eyes of Tesselschade Visscher and nodding abstractedly, like a man in a desperate hurry, to Frans van Pellicorne; but out toward the edge of the crowd he found himself face to face with an aged past-burgomaster, whose name he had unfortunately forgotten, and was forced to nod in agreement while the greybeard, in a tremulous voice, told him that the pageant had been unforgettable, simply unforgettable, and that two of the odes had moved him to tears. And the best thing about the whole affair, he said, laying his withered hand urgently on the doctor's sleeve, was that it was a communal creation, an activity in which all of Amsterdam, rich and poor, high and low, had borne a worthy and memorable part.

All of Amsterdam? Scarcely, he thought as he pushed his way through groups of his fellow-citizens—immovable and imperturbable, exasperating with their shrill voices and their cranky children—toward the deserted center of town. Inclusive as public life was in this city, there were many that had no portion in it, and some of the best of them would be sitting out the evening in Rembrandt's rooms on New Doelen Street.

And inasmuch as he had given the last twelve hours to the Scribes and the Pharisees, he felt impelled to make a gesture in the direction of the Samaritans. Not that the young painter was suffering exclusion undeservedly: if he smarted in his rooms tonight and drew his curtains against the torchlit revelry, he had nobody to blame but himself. Still, it was one thing to refuse to condone a fault and quite another to withhold such balm as was available to soothe the sore. To make a casual visit, to say that a mug of beer with friends was a pleasure after a day of vacant formalities, to recount a few of the inanities that would discredit what the host and his visitors had not been asked to share—he liked the notion. He stopped at a corner under a sputtering torch, removed the scarlet armband that had identified him as a member of the Official Committee, and started for New Doelen Street.

Once there, he saw from the pavement below that the drapes were not drawn and the windows were standing wide open. Loud talk and a burst of laughter came to him on his way up the stairs; and he was surprised that there should be so much merriment up there, especially since none of the military could be in the company, required as they were to stand futile ceremonial guard in front of the state chambers where the Queen Mother slept, until the night watch came to relieve them at eleven o'clock. And when he entered the spacious front parlor he saw that the gathering was small, so small that they might be suspected of affecting boisterousness to hide their sense of isolation. The Mennonite Anslo, the Portuguese-Jewish bookseller Pinero and his sprightly wrinkled wife, and the melancholy Bonus were the only visitors who had turned up; and the new arrival looked with a pang at the great mound of herring salad that the little hostess was beginning to serve: if the present company was expected to consume it, they would have to stay and eat all night.

She dropped the serving spoon and came to the threshold to greet him—plump, rosy, gratifyingly light on her feet again, wearing a plum-colored dress and a double row of pearls that would have been worthy of an evening in the Prince's chambers at The Hague. It was hard to remember that she was well into her twenties now, a wife of five years and the mother of two dead infants; in scent and color and softness and guilelessness she was so much like an infant herself. "Oh, look who's come! They must have finished putting the Queen Mother to bed," she said, and lifted her dimpled hand and snatched the respectable new black beaver from his head. He bent and kissed her cheek—there was a freshness in it like the smell of crab-apple blossoms—and looked at her to see what he could find in her face. If she was regretting the lost carnival, she was showing no sign of it: the delicate flesh around her eyes crinkled as she gave him a smile. For her husband's sake she had put on an act of caring nothing about the whole stupid business months ago, and had probably ended by believing it herself. Or perhaps not quite completely—at any rate, she did not want him to see her as deserted. In her eager, breathy voice she told him that tonight's party would be a late one because the captain and the lieutenant were detained at the State House by their duties—they and five or six of the others were expected, but not until half past eleven.

It seemed at first that the host was taking the situation as lightly as the hostess. He was telling Bonus about a strange cramp in the arm that was troubling one of the apprentices, and he stopped only long enough to smile and nod from the other end of the room, as casually as if his first patron had dropped in on any ordinary evening. But the branch of candles on the long table at which he sat lighted up a jacket of unusual splendor; the Flemish lace collar that lay negligently on his massive shoulders was enough to make the finest burgher ruff look dull and staid, and the garnet earring that dangled from his left ear spotted his cheek with a wine-red glow. He, too, was showing that he could dress better for an evening at home than von Sandrart or Frans van Pellicorne or Allaert van Hoorn could have dressed for the Queen Mother's ball.

Dr. Tulp came over and joined the medical conversation. Dr. Bonus suggested hot applications, and he suggested daily exercises, and the host asked detailed questions as if his apprentice's cramp were the only concern he had in the world. But his hand, which looked all the more raw and hairy coming out of the gold-embroidered cuff of the jacket, began to beat an uneven rhythm on the table, and just when poor Bonus was learnedly explaining the difference between muscular tension and muscular strain, he turned unceremoniously away and looked up into the newcomer's face. "Well, what about it? How did it come off? I mean the water festival and all the rest of the goings-on," he said.

"Yes," said Saskia, carrying two plates of herring to Pinero and his wife, "how did it come off? Did Vrouw Bicker sink Neptune's shell? I was sure she would; she weighs as much as a cow, even without that shield and that helmet and all those yards of gold and purple stuff."

285

He gave them what they wanted then—an account of the proceedings that was harsher than he had intended. Vrouw Bicker's bulk, the ugly quarrel over precedence that had delayed the Procession of the Burgomasters, the definite similarity between the Queen Mother's profile and that of the cavalry captain's horse, the utter vacuity of the royal conversation—he described them all with a zest he would have regretted even if his host had not interrupted to ask whether public life in general wasn't made up of just such meaningless trivialities. What was intended, of course, was a thrust at the eminent Dr. Tulp, who was hoping to be a burgomaster one of these days himself.

The grave and passionate Anslo had also been disturbed by the description, though for a different reason. He shook his head at the salad that Saskia was holding out to him, and threw up his well-fleshed hands in one of those ardent, careless, heartfelt gestures that stirred the souls of female Mennonites. "It's all very well for you to joke about it, Doctor," he said in his resonant tenor. "You can afford to; religion's no particular concern of yours. But to me it's no laughing matter. To me, the day when a Queen of France, Catholic and reactionary, is entertained by a liberal, Protestant city is a sorry day, a tragic day, a very black day indeed."

Rembrandt hunched over the table and fetched up a short impatient sigh that bent the flames of the candles. "What would you expect?" he said, staring gloomily at the gold embroidery on his cuff. "Amsterdam's no Leyden; your Amsterdammers didn't have anything to forgive. *Their* dykes were safe; nobody burned *their* relatives. With them, it was only a matter of digging up the florins to buy themselves peace."

The doctor looked at him in some surprise. If the Leydener had been cherishing a fierce affection for his native city, he had certainly managed to keep it well hidden; besides, it was a little ironical that he should be speaking so scornfully of florins while the light of his garnet earring quivered on his cheek and the lace of his Flemish collar foamed over his chest. "I never realized that you judged the town so harshly. I always thought you rather liked it. You've prospered in it, anyway," he said.

"Oh, yes, I've prospered in it. But that doesn't make it any the less corrupt."

"Corrupt?" said Bonus. "That's a little strong, I'd say. If you call Amsterdam corrupt, then how would you describe a city like Seville?"

"Give me Seville, rotten as it is," said the host. "There a person at least knows where he stands. I'd find Inquisitors and Jesuits easier to deal with than these mealy-mouthed hypocrites who play both sides at once."

The little Jewish doctor shrugged and exchanged a look with his eminent colleague. No account, according to his melancholy eyes, was to be taken of such pronouncements; they issued out of a galled and captious heart. Anslo, too, held his peace, kneading a bit of melted wax on the candle with his plump, adept fingers; and the subject would probably have been dropped if the lean Pinero, hard to make out where he sat in the shadow by the window, had not cleared his throat and bent forward in his chair. "I agree with Dr. Bonus—'corrupt' is scarcely the word for Amsterdam," he said in a cultivated if somewhat twangy baritone. "Corruption presupposes evil, and your good burghers here couldn't possibly muster up the subtlety for evil. The worst you can accuse them of is an inveterate tendency to do the sensible thing. No matter how much they argue about theology and politics, primarily they're navigating merchants whose lives depend on the comings and goings of ships. For all their talk about grace and freedom, what they really want is a chain of open waterways and tax-free markets all around the world. Protestantism's a minor concern in Amsterdam—though I hope you understand I don't mean that as an insult to the city or the religion under consideration."

The doctor had succeeded in making him out in the shadow: a man so thin as to be almost emaciated, with a frog-wide mouth and bulging grey-green eyes that dominated an otherwise insignificant face, a man in whose very ugliness there was a kind of distinction.

"Who's going to be insulted at anything *you* say?" said his withered little wife, twisting up her dried-prune face. "Everybody knows you by this time—when you say one thing, you're as likely as not to mean the opposite."

"What did I mean?"

"Well, for one thing, I'm sure you couldn't have meant that the Amsterdammers aren't really enlightened and devoted to freedom. As *you* know and *I* know, my good man, they were enlightened and generous enough to take in the Jews."

"Yes, my girl," he said, tilting back in his chair and speaking in a singsong voice that half expressed and half caricatured connubial affection. "They certainly took in the poor Jews. And I might add that the poor Jews, poverty-stricken and plague-ridden as many of them were, happened to be expert traders with established connections in crucial Eastern ports—an asset not altogether unrelated to navigation and marketing. Kind to the Jews they were, I'll grant, in spite of the New Testaments they passed out to us as we stepped on shore. But I wonder if they would have worked up quite as warm a welcome if it had been English tinsmiths or Swedish ironmongers or German bakers —good Protestants and true—who wanted to come in."

"You can wonder all you like," said the lady sharply, "but so far there's nothing to be said against them. Even if they put on a show for the Medici woman, they've supported their fellow-Protestants in France, and I don't imagine that exactly improves their standing with the French crown."

Her husband did not answer at once because the orange and white cat had wandered in from the kitchen and used his bony knee as a stopping place between the rug and the window sill. "So far, yes," he said at last. "But I'd stake everything I have that a day will come—and in our lifetime, too—when Dutch ships will take Dutch musketmen to drive your French Protestants out of their last citadel."

Anslo squeezed a piece of candle wax into a ball and flung it from him. "God forbid I live to see it," he said, pounding the top of the polished table as he would have pounded the crude pulpit in his Mennonite chapel. "And if I do, I'll agree with our host that we're rotten, rotten to the core."

"No, I still wouldn't call it rotten," said Pinero, "only intelligently self-interested."

The little hostess, plainly eager to put a stop to such a heavy-hearted discourse, uncovered a bread platter and was about to pass it when her husband's eyes, pale and icy, froze her where she stood. "And what's the difference between that sort of self-interest and corruption? It's all the same, whatever you call it. What *I'd* call it is selling your birthright for a mess of pottage," he said.

And Dr. Tulp, watching the freezing glance dart from Saskia to the bookseller, was startled when it settled accusingly on his own face. Ah, he thought, that's intended for me, too. He's seeing me in a line of burgomasters, ready to shake hands with emissaries from Catholic France and Catholic Spain. And what about him with his expensive wife and his neglected family and his ample rooms and his art collection and his garnet earring—what's come over *him* in the last ten years? What do those falsely noble pictures back there in his studio have to do with the compassionate drawings I picked up out of Lastman's vestibule? The terrible truth he had in those raw hands of his—*that* was the birthright he traded for a mess of pottage. For the sake of a lordly life and a dream of glory, he wasted himself and was lost.

"Enough of this," said Vrouw Pinero. "With your permission I'll enjoy my herring salad."

"Yes, Saskia," said Anslo, sighing deeply, "weren't you about to pass the bread?"

The host's accusation had been too indirect for the doctor to take it upon himself; he could not say that no amount of consorting with the great ones of the city had made him squander what he owed to the pharmacopoeia and the clinic and the operating room. This was a social evening, and all he could do was try to salvage it with some amusing story that would put everybody back into an amiable state; but before he had a chance to introduce it footsteps and laughter sounded on the stairs, and the glow flowed back into Saskia's cheeks and the ice broke up in Rembrandt's eyes.

"Here they come—the brave soldiers back from the bloody battle," said Heer Pinero.

The doctor rose, bowed to everybody including the cat, crossed the room, and took his respectable beaver from a peg near the door. There were protests and repeated invitations to stay at least for a mug of beer, but he disregarded them and made his farewells with less cordiality than he could have wished. The room, filled with loud voices and the rattle of swords and young men's easy laughter, was suddenly utterly alien to him: all he wanted was to take himself and his aching questions back into the night.

BOOK VI

1640
-
1642

"There, now, I'm awfully sorry—I've gone and done it again," said old Jacob, the tapster at the Military Club, staring down at the puddle of beer he had just sloshed over Banning Coq's aristocratic hand.

"Never mind," the captain said, drying his knuckles on his napkin and taking up his mug, the third he had ordered in the last half-hour. "Just get a rag and wipe it up." It was almost impossible to get into a temper with the poor old clown, bald as an egg and crippled with gout and cursed with a nose that almost met his jutting chin: there was something disarming about the very enormity of his ineptitude and ugliness.

He tasted his beer and wished he hadn't ordered any more. With the reputation of his highly respectable burgher family and his own position as captain to maintain, he was not in the habit of drinking a great deal, not in the public and smoky confines of the clubroom at any rate. Besides—with the air as thick as it was from the exhalations of clay pipes and the black murk that kept pouring from the damp peat in the chimney places at both ends of the long, low chamber—his second mug had been enough to slow up his thinking, and the third was bound to give him a headache. Still, if Ruytenberg kept him waiting, what was there to do but drink? He had just come from a harassing evening at his parents' house, and he was in no mood to talk to any of the twenty-odd men playing dice and drinking at the little tables set here and there in the flickering light of the oil lamps and the muted red of the fires. And he certainly did not mean to walk around in the court while he waited for the lieutenant; it had gotten much colder since nightfall, and the panes of the six big crossbow windows were white with stars and fronds of frost.

He wouldn't have come over at all if Ruytenberg hadn't owed him twenty florins that he had promised to drop off here tonight: unless the creditor was here to accept it, the debtor, careless popinjay that he was, would think an attempt to pay was the same thing as payment and put the whole business out of his head. Perhaps he had already forgotten; it was half past ten, and some of the groups were beginning to break up, saying good night and reaching under the table for their hats and swords. He nodded to those that passed him without actually seeing them; the faces he was really looking at were the ones above their heads, the dozen or so painted faces in the great military canvas by Cornelis Ketel that hung in front of him on the paneled wall.

Out of fashion and smoke-befouled as that canvas was after fifty years, the captain liked it—there was more life and color in it than in any of the later and reputedly better ones that decorated the room.

293

The citizen-soldiers in the Ketel piece had an authenticity he could not account for: perhaps it came from the outdated splendor of their regalia, perhaps it was because most of them had already been dead when he was a child. He looked at the strangely naked faces, at the tooled leather and the antiquated weapons, at the feet set in their soft, ornate shoes on the square tiles of the floor; and dead though they were, they had more life in them than the eight burgher officers Aert Pieterszoon had arranged at a military banquet in the canvas to the captain's left. Those fellows, some of whom could still be seen idling on the musket range and giving the younger men unwanted advice, had no vitality at all.

"That Ketel picture could do with a good scrubbing, your honor," said old Jacob, sopping up the spilled beer.

"You can't scrub a picture—it would ruin it."

"Yes, I suppose it would. Well, no matter. I hear we'll be getting some new ones one of these days."

Two had been ordered. The troop of Corporal Bicker, spurred by the visit of Maria de Medici, had hired the eminent German von Sandrart to do them standing around that horse-faced lady's sculptured bust; and the retired officers, the Guildmasters of the Military Club, had put in an order with Govaert Flinck. He looked about him at the still unadorned sections of the walls and saw that the only good spots for large paintings were the two which had already been spoken for. Once those were occupied, all that would remain would be a shadowy expanse, big enough but almost black, between a window and the projecting chimney place. If there was ever to be a painting of him and *his* men—and he certainly didn't mean to let his captaincy go by uncommemorated—they would be lost over there in the dark.

"Well, Jacob, whoever orders the next one won't have much of a spot to hang it in, will he?"

"No, it's pretty dark over there. It's safe, though—whatever gets put in that corner won't be banged by a musket butt or ripped up by a lance."

The captain continued to contemplate the spot after the old fellow had gone back to his bottles and kegs. It was too bad, really—the spot was as black as Hell and so placed that any troop marching there would seem to march either out of the window or into the chimney place. Nothing but the brightest sort of painting could make itself visible there in the evenings; even Ketel's colors, rich as they were, would be obliterated. He found himself envisioning the blue-green of waves on a day in summer, a clear scarlet touched with orange, bright yellows, mellow bits of gold . . . Now, how the devil could he have summoned up such colors? He closed his eyes, and they came back to him in an Oriental turban, a stretch of blue-green sky behind a fleeing Delilah, a saffron robe on one of Belshazzar's guests. Why, they came from just up the street, from Rembrandt's studio, of course. Only one man could paint radiantly enough to undo the blackness of that murky corner: Rembrandt van Rijn.

The idea was so gratifying that he could not understand why it had never occurred to him before. He took a big draught of his beer and turned his chair so that he could stare directly into the shadowy expanse. Oh, it could be made splendid: he peopled it with a martial confusion of beings unfurling their standards and loading their muskets and beating their drums, but chiefly with himself. And if his heart raced at the thought of his own image stepping plumed and lordly out of that darkness, he could truthfully say he had other aims besides satisfying his own vanity. If such a canvas could exalt him, it could do as much for its painter. Rembrandt had the Prince's benediction, yes—his Passion series hung in The Hague; but somehow his reputation in Amsterdam had never come up to expectations. Seven years had passed since he had made such a stir with his *Anatomy Lesson of Doctor Tulp*, and though his fortunes could not be said to have declined in the interim, his name no longer provoked the same excitement: others—Pieterszoon, von Sandrart, even his former apprentice Govaert Flinck—were more eagerly sought after than he. What he needed was another chance to give his talents a vast, dramatic public display; what he needed was a commission to paint the troop of Captain Banning Coq. Give him that, and he was bound to turn out a masterpiece which would put every other painting in Amsterdam in the shade.

When Lieutenant Ruytenberg finally arrived, his nose red from the cold, and snow caught in his trim little beard and luxuriant chestnut curls, he apologized for his lateness and pulled the twenty florins out of his purse at the same instant, proffering the money as if it constituted an excuse for the delay. His superior found it almost as difficult as his inferiors did to be seriously annoyed with him—he stayed so young, he was always so merry; even when he was at a disadvantage he carried himself with so much grace. "Excuse me if I shiver," he said, hunching himself over the table in a way that would have seemed unmanly in anybody else. "It's devilishly cold outside."

"Were you playing dice?" asked the captain.

"Dice? No—backgammon. I took that twenty and fifteen more from a very jolly Englishman at the Crown."

"I suggest you hold onto the fifteen for a couple of days."

"Oh, I mean to." He always had the most virtuous intentions. "But why?"

"Because"—he could not refrain from broaching the subject immediately—"you'll be asked to subscribe for it. It's just occurred to me that there's only one spot left for a picture of the troop, and if we don't claim it in a hurry, somebody else will."

The lieutenant wrinkled up his nose. Plainly it had not been good strategy to connect the painting with the coins that jingled in his purse:

he had probably settled his mind on something he wanted and now he would see his contribution as a deprivation. "I thought all the places were spoken for already," he said.

"No, there's that big one over in the corner."

"That? God, that's a rotten spot—black as the bottom of a privy. Whoever gets himself stuck in there will be paying for the privilege of consigning himself to obscurity."

The captain smiled a little; the lieutenant had a way with language and liked his gift to be appreciated. "It's bad, but it's not as bad as you're making out," he said. "Whatever gets hung there will last, at any rate. Nobody will bang it with weapons or anoint it with beer."

"But who'll ever *see* it?"

"That would depend on the painter."

"Christ, Banning, what's he going to paint with? Hot coals? Molten iron? *You'd* have to wear black velvet—do you know how much of you anybody would be able to see from the middle of the room? Damned little—your sash and your sword and your hands and your face."

He should have been discouraged at such a prospect, but it only whetted his interest. He liked the thought of the parts just named, together with the gloss of his velvet which only Rembrandt could bring out, starting mysteriously from the dark. "Well, *you* wouldn't suffer," he said. "You're allowed to wear anything you like. That yellow jerkin of yours, the one with the gold braid on it—that would show up bright enough."

The merry eyes on the other side of the table kindled; he loved that braid-trimmed jerkin and he hadn't had an occasion to wear it since Maria de Medici's visit. But old Jacob came and set his beer in front of him, and in paying for it he began to feel tenderly disposed again toward what he had in his purse. "Nobody could paint anything—not even my jerkin—so that it would show up in that black hole," he said.

"Pieterszoon couldn't, von Sandrart couldn't, Flinck couldn't, I'll grant you. But there's one person that could, and magnificently, too—our friend up the street."

"Rembrandt? I hadn't thought of him."

"Well, think of him for a minute. Think of the colors in that *Marriage Feast of Samson* and the one where Belshazzar sees the writing on the wall—with colors like that a dark spot would be a downright advantage. The way he'd do it the braid on your jerkin would show up even from the other chimney place."

The lieutenant was tempted but not snared. He stared past the head of his superior, and it was obvious from the stillness of his amber-colored pupils that he was seeing himself—the perfect citizen-soldier, the darling of the troop—on that blank wall.

"I'll tell you what," said Banning Coq. "I'll hold the twenty you just gave me and use it as a down payment on your part of the subscription."

"I wouldn't think of it—"

296

"Why not? After all, it's only gambling money. This is our last chance, and I don't like to think of my captaincy going by without some memento. Besides, it would be such an easy way to do a really splendid favor for a friend."

The effect of that was better than he had expected; the lieutenant needed nothing so much as to think well of himself. That bright image of his character which he saw in the mirror of his consciousness had been tarnished this evening by three smoky blasts of accusation: he was the sort of man who would take a present of money, he did not feel the required loyalty toward his captain and his troop, and he did not leap eagerly at an opportunity to do a good turn for somebody who had repeatedly been his host. "I couldn't accept such an offer, and I didn't say I wouldn't come in if I were asked," he said. "I was only trying to look at it from all possible viewpoints. It isn't a thing to be undertaken lightly, you know."

"I don't undertake things lightly," said the captain. "If I say we ought to move quickly, it's only because in another day or so we could lose the chance to move at all. I'm sure none of the men in the troop will hold back, even though most of them aren't personally acquainted with Rembrandt. They'll want to claim the spot, and they'll trust my judgment enough to leave the choice of the painter to me."

"Oh, for God's sake, Banning, you needn't make it sound as if I wouldn't want a painting and didn't trust your judgment. If anybody's to do it, I'd want it to be Rembrandt as much as you would. Little as I know about painting, I'd say he was Amsterdam's best, even if he isn't the fashion at the moment. And anyway, I'd want to make him some return, considering the amount of hospitality I've consumed at his place."

"Of course you would." The time had come to wipe the smoky film from the bright mirror. He looked steadily, with a paternal warmth that was not justified by the minor difference in their ages, into the amber-colored eyes. "Actually, with me it's more than just a return for hospitality." There was no better way to make a man think well of his own nature than to speak ill of oneself in his presence. "I've never quite forgiven myself for not being able to get him appointed to the Committee of Artists for the Medici business. That hurt him—I could see it hurt him, couldn't you?—and what's more, it hurt her, the poor little witch, and just when she was at her weakest, too, after she lost her second child."

He had stumbled quite by chance into mentioning Saskia, but it was a felicitous chance: the lieutenant's eyes turned actually tender. "Let's not tell them anything about it, Banning, until it's been officially agreed upon. I wouldn't want either of them to be hurt again, and there *could* be difficulties," he said. But the captain knew that whatever difficulties the darling of the troop was envisioning now had been transformed from possible means of keeping his florins into annoying obstacles to be overcome, and that the transformation had been wrought by the recollection of the pretty little face, childishly tearful over the collapse of a dream.

"What obstacles do you foresee?" he asked, confident that he was now consulting a fellow-conspirator.

"My mother's friends say his commissions have been falling off."

"Well, if any of the troop should bring that up, it's easily answered: he's been too busy with the Prince's Passion series to accept more portrait commissions."

"He isn't liked over at Muiden, either. That *Diana* he painted and that *Ganymede*—"

"Oh, those! I consider those an advantage. If the opportunity arises, I wish you'd see that some of the junior officers got a look at them. They couldn't be anything but amused."

"There'll be some who'll object on the grounds that he'll take his own good time about it. Everybody knows how long it takes him to turn things out."

"What difference does that make? The longer he's about it, the better it'll be. Anyway, there's no hurry about getting the painting, only about reserving the place."

"Well, go ahead then; put in your reservation tomorrow."

The captain pushed back his mug, smoothed his moustache, and saw to it that his face took on a look of weighty deliberation. "I didn't mean we should rush into it—not until everything's been carefully considered," he said, staring out into the almost empty room: the last two groups of guardsmen were wrapping their mufflers around their necks and starting for the door. "It'll involve a great deal of money, and you and I will have to assume at least a third of it between us, partly because we're the major officers and partly because we'll naturally be up in front, painted at full length and in detail."

"How much do you think we'll have to assume?"

It was better to come straight out with it. "Oh, five hundred florins or thereabouts," he said.

"Five hundred florins?" The lieutenant shivered again and made it plain, by rubbing his hands, that the shiver rose not from the preposterousness of the sum but from the draft that the departing guardsmen had let in through the door.

"Yes, I imagine it would be something like that, though I'd think it only reasonable if three hundred or three hundred and fifty came out of my purse. Your share wouldn't be more than a hundred and fifty then, though I'd want as much attention to go to you as to me. The troop wouldn't be what it is if it hadn't been commanded by both of us —I've always said as much."

It was a noble speech, spoken impressively into the almost abandoned clubroom. The waning peat fires on the hearths, the lamps burning up the last of their day's supply of oil, the faint sheen on the paneled walls, the solemn faces looking out of the ancient pictures, even old Jacob whistling tunelessly while he corked up his bottles and wiped off his counter—all these made for an atmosphere worthy of earnest purposes and high sentiments.

"He and Saskia could do with another spectacular success," said the captain. "If the money started to pour in again from commissions, they'd know how to use it magnificently. She's the sort of woman that ought to wear pearls—God made her for it. And he—well, he only needs a chance to show the other idiots what he's made of."

Slowly, the lieutenant wiped the beer from his moustache and opened his purse to take out a tip for Jacob. He shivered again and turned toward the frosted windows. "Just look at those panes," he said, "it must be terribly cold." And the captain waited—merely waited— until his junior officer drew out of the sweet dark privacy of the purse the other fifteen florins and laid them on the beer-stained wood beside his captain's mug. "You keep them—otherwise I'll spend them, and I suppose I ought to hold onto them for the subscription," he said.

*

For almost an hour he had been standing on the little stone bridge sketching the people skating down there below him in the grey-green light of the frigid dusk. The hour was against him now: he remembered rather than saw the red on their cheeks and noses and the bright colors of their knitted jackets and stockings; and his gloveless hands would no longer obey him, and his vision was misted with tears from the bitter cold.

There was no reason for exposing himself any longer to the cut of the wind that came in, wet and cruel, from the stormy reaches of the sea. He had more than enough to fill up the little panel on which he had wanted to catch the effect of the slanting northern light on the snow. Last night in the studio—with the windows whitened by frost and the drafts moving across his feet—he had covered the whole blank surface first with glue and then with a pale underwash of chalk, which would shine through the paint and give whatever was laid upon it a kind of eerie gleam; and today, between four and five, he had learned all he had to know about what light did to ice and what congealed winter moisture did to distant chimneys and roofs and hills. If he stayed where he was—about a quarter of an hour's walk from home—it was because he meant to be deliberately late to supper in order to worry her. There were those who seemed to think he doted on her and spoiled her, and they might be right: she had certainly turned upon him this afternoon like a spiteful, pampered child and given him more of her saucy tongue than any self-respecting husband should bear.

It had all begun about the moths that had eaten into his Russian bear-skin in the storage closet. Moths were a sore subject with her since the first days of their marriage when Lysbeth had accused her of infesting the rooms with them. The moths had chewed into the bearskin in several places and had riddled God knows what else among his precious possessions: the purple velvet coverlet was probably a ruin, to say nothing of a Persian shawl he had never even painted—he hadn't looked, he hadn't wanted to see. But even more exasperating than the loss was the way she took the matter: moths, according to her, were to be expected and borne with; a certain percentage of a person's belongings was to be written off to them every so often—like storms and floods and earthquakes, they were an act of God. He had told her in so many words that moths could be found only in dirty houses; and she, red in the face and hoarse—partly from the cold she had and partly from fury—had challenged him to *show* her, just show her any dirt in their rooms. And he had obliged her, expecting to find only a dusty window sill or an unswept hearth, and had found so much more that he had been driven into a shouting rage. The closets in every room were shambles. The brass and copper was sorely in need of polishing. Cobwebs hung from every ceiling except the one in the parlor, and a heap of soiled clothes that had somehow not gotten into the wash made a sordid display when she opened her dressing-room door. The house was downright slovenly, and he had taken a fierce delight in telling her so.

Had she been shocked, repentant, humbled? Not she; she had told him brazenly that it was his fault, all of it. When she had promised at the altar to love and obey him she had not bargained to clean up after seven apprentices, to see that his supper was on the table whenever he chose to come and get it—be it five or eleven—or to keep moths out of closets crammed with crazy old stuff. There weren't enough rooms, and they weren't big enough to accommodate the kind of lives they lived. She needed at least three servants, and she was permitted only two. If he insisted on hoarding money—hers as well as his—then he could expect to put up with a few moths, and if he didn't like it, he could always go somewhere else.

He had taken her at her word, stopping only long enough to pick up what he would need for sketching. He had eaten a chop and a dish of cabbage in a tavern, had walked the full circle of the Prinzen Canal, had warmed himself for an hour in the Regents' room of the orphanage and looked at pictures he had not seen since he and Jan Lievens had studied them on holiday afternoons back in the Lastman days. The sketching he had put off as long as possible, knowing that the late hour would be the dreary one; and now, with the chalk worn down and the paper used up, he stood on the bridge and stared into the last silvery aura of the waning sun and began to be sorry for Saskia, since he had quite exhausted the business of being sorry for himself.

He told himself without conviction that *he* hadn't bargained for what he'd gotten either, hadn't promised at the altar to endure without protest all the ruin she was working on him and herself and their household by her heedlessness. Yet something like a promise, something equivalent to a promise, really, nagged at him while the sea wind whined in his ears: old Sylvius, the only blood relative of hers he had ever learned to love, had explained to him what a child she was, poised in the present without a sense of the future or a knowledge of the past; and he had nodded as if he understood and accepted her for what she was; and what had passed between him and old Sylvius was all the more binding because the pastor, locked now in the bitter cold of his grave, was beyond saying "I told you so." These last few weeks the old man had been continually in his thoughts; he was etching a posthumous portrait of him for Vrouw Sylvius, and even in the heat of this afternoon's quarrel he had seen the austere face—solemn, forbearing, looking at him with reserved tenderness. To point out her failings to her was one thing; to shout abuses at her was another. And when he remembered what he had said—that lady though she was supposed to be, she kept their house like a slattern and let priceless treasures go to waste while she sat at the mirror curling her hair around her finger—he was sick at heart and wretchedly cold.

He turned back to the icy prospect, trying to forget. A gull soared up, beaten inland by the blast; he caught its poise and desolation on the corner of the crowded paper with a line or two. She had looked piteous when he left, in spite of the defiant face she had tried to put on. Her cheeks, swollen from her heavy cold, had reminded him of how she had looked straining to bring forth her two doomed children; and remembering that, he wondered how *he,* who had only sown the blighted seed, not carried and given birth, could ever have addressed her with anything but compassion and love. To quarrel with her was cruel, like setting a potted rose out into an ice-green evening like this—cruel and useless too, since she was what she was and would not change, and he had chosen her as she was and could not find it in his bruised heart to wish her to be anything else . . .

He sighed, dropped the end of his chalk over the side of the bridge, and watched a curly dog come up and sniff at it as if it might be something to eat. He folded the sheet of sketches and put it into his pocket, and found the lining badly ripped—she was always saying she was going to mend it, but she never did. He turned and walked down the slope of the bridge and stopped short because he saw her coming up to him in her little beaver hat and her scarlet tippet lined with squirrel, and he could not quite believe it was she. She ran, careless of who might see her; and the tears started out of her eyes, and she said his name in her poor hoarse voice and laid her head against his chest.

"What are you doing out in this terrible weather with your cold?" It was not a reproach; tears stung in his own eyes as he kissed her cold, chapped chin. He turned her around and began to walk with her—

after all, they could not stand kissing on a public bridge—but he held her close as they walked, letting warmth and reconciliation flow from the hand that clasped her waist through the bulk of fur and cloth.

"I couldn't stay alone—I thought you were never coming back."

"Why would you think that?" he asked, though that had been precisely what he had wanted her to think.

"I couldn't stay by myself, so I walked over to Vrouw Pinero's—"

Another good ten minutes' walk, and yesterday she had been feverish, and this morning he had advised her to stay in bed.

"And I felt so dreadful that I cried, and Vrouw Pinero asked what was the matter, and I told her how the moths had gotten into the bearskin rug—"

It was not a rug, and when she had wanted to use it as one, he had told her distinctly that it was too precious to be walked on—but he let that pass.

"And Vrouw Pinero said I should have used camphor and she'd give me some, and I told her I was afraid even to look in the closet again, and she said that was nonsense and she'd come back with me and look. She did—she's the kindest woman!—and it wasn't as bad as I'd thought. The purple velvet coverlet is perfectly all right, and there were only a few holes in that old shawl."

The shawl was *not* old; he had bought it less than four months ago. But he managed to hold his peace.

"So now that closet is very orderly; we cleaned it and dusted it and put camphor in all the woolens and velvets. And then Vrouw Pinero went home, and I cleaned out the other closets, too. I did it all by myself because Maartje was out shopping for supper and Liesje was washing. I was all right while I was doing it—I kept thinking how pleased you'd be—but after I finished I was in such a sweat, and I felt terribly sad because it was four o'clock and I began to think you'd never come."

He took her hand, warm and pliant in its little olive-green glove, and kneaded it gently, and held it first against his lips and then against his chest. "I was just coming when I saw you on the bridge," he said. "How did you know to look for me there?"

"That was where you said you were yesterday. If I hadn't found you, I don't know what I would have done. I never was sadder, not in all my life. After I finished the cleaning, I sat on the floor and cried—" She coughed a little, and looked up at him apologetically, as if coughing were a fault. "Please make it up with me, please say you forgive me," she said.

That annoyed him: he was not a priest, it was not his province to forgive; and besides, he could not really say she was forgiven. The ruin of the bearskin and the shawl was no light loss, and all her cleaning and Vrouw Pinero's camphor could not bring them back.

"Well, then, don't forgive me if you don't want to," she said mournfully, letting her hand drop out of his slackened grasp. "I don't forgive you either for saying I'm a slattern and for staying away so long that I didn't know whether you were alive or dead."

"That's ridiculous. Nothing could have happened to me."

"Everything I say is ridiculous. You think I'm a fool."

"I never said you were a fool."

"No, but that's what you think. Anyway, it doesn't matter—you think worse things than that: you think I'm wasteful and slovenly and careless. You think I don't care what becomes of your things."

"I think you should see to it that the closets are cleaned. That's what we pay the servants for, and God knows we pay them enough."

"We don't pay them so very much. My sister Titia pays her maid half again as much as you do—"

"Titia will run her household in her way, and I'll run mine in mine."

"Oh, I'm sure of that. You're as stubborn as a donkey, and so tight-fisted it makes a person sick."

"*Somebody* in our house had better be tight-fisted—"

"Oh, yes, at home, but not at the auctions—it's different when you lay out thirty or forty florins in one afternoon at an auction. *That's* not wasteful, *that's* not careless, *that's* not anything to ask forgiveness for!"

She had stopped a few doors from their own house, by a brick stoop where two children were making snowballs and staring at the quarreling grownups with half-frightened, half-delighted eyes. He took her by the elbow and jerked her along, more roughly in his embarrassment than he had intended. "There's no necessity for you to ask my forgiveness. I don't forgive people, it's not in my nature, and I wish you'd be good enough to lower your voice," he said.

"You raised yours first!" She had meant to shout it, but because of her hoarseness it came out in a pitiable squeak.

"Go ahead, then, shout as much as you like. Tomorrow you'll have no voice," he said.

"I don't need one—not to talk to *you,* anyway."

"I have no objection to that. I could do with a little peace and quiet."

"You'll get it."

"The sooner the better." He walked before her up the path, disregarding the fact that she might slip on the ice. He took out his key, thrust it into the lock, opened the door, and stepped back for her to walk in.

"Go on in. What are you waiting for?" she said behind him.

He took off his hat and held it against his chest while he made her a bow, extending his hand toward the doorway in a mockingly courteous gesture.

"Don't bow to me!" She walked in, shoving him aside, actually striking him with her little gloved fist as she passed. "You look ridiculous when you bow—you're nobody to bow at a person. You're a boor, that's what you are—a selfish, grasping, cruel boor."

The blow, light as it was, was infuriating, but not as infuriating as the name she had shouted into his face. A boor, he told himself, going into the bedroom and banging the door—that was what Pieter Lastman had doubtless called the miller's son from Leyden; a boor was what the distinguished group of them had thought, seeing him on the threshold of Vrouw van Hoorn's little room; a boor was what her relatives probably named him behind his back; and how else would the mutual back-scratchers over at Muiden refer to him except as "the boor"? He tore off his jacket and hurled it onto a chair; he let his muffler fall in the middle of the floor to show her that *he* could be careless too. The fire was burning decently enough, but he went at it with the poker, jamming the logs against the bricks and sending up a red eruption of sparks. She did well to stay out there in the parlor: let her call him a boor again, and he'd take her by the shoulders and shake her within an inch of her life.

When he had finished making his clatter with the poker he heard, even through the closed door, that she was coughing. She's doing that to make herself pathetic and to accuse me, he thought, stepping out of his cold, damp shoes and into the warmth of his slippers, which she had put in front of the fire—there were some things that she always remembered. But the coughing went on with such persistence that he could not believe she was affecting it; and his chill unbelief turned into a hot anger: now she had gone and made herself sick—refusing to stay in bed and running out to Vrouw Pinero's and getting herself into a sweat with that silly cleaning and going to look for him as if he were a lost child and she had to bring him home.

She stopped coughing, and in the silence broken only by the snap and whisper of the flames on the hearth he tried to reason out what could be done about the untenable situation. He could not stay forever in the bedroom while she sat in the parlor—both of them would have to eat supper; he could not go out again—he was chilled through and too sick at heart to face a noisy crowd in a tavern; and furthermore, he knew her—she would follow him even into a drinking house where no respectable woman would show her face. She had struck him, and perhaps now she was sorry and would ask for a forgiveness which this time he would not withhold. He ran a brush over his hair—the wind had made it stick out like the hair of a boor—and went into the parlor to see what she was about.

What he saw was almost enough to gall him back into his unthinking fury. She was sitting on the floor in an exasperatingly theatrical manner, to indicate, he supposed, her contrition and submission. She was sitting on the floor beside the couch on which she had been Danaë, her arm resting on one of the brocaded pillows, her head on her arm, her hair all loose and fiery and disheveled, and her eyes fixed on a wrinkled handkerchief spread over her bent knee.

"Get up," he said, sick with pity and rage. "There's no reason for you to sit on the floor like that."

She did not answer. Her eyes went on staring at the handkerchief; and he stared with her and saw in the middle of the creased linen a spot of blood.

"Where did that come from?"

"That blood? From my mouth, I think, when I was coughing." She made a ball of the handkerchief and covered it with her hand.

Out in the bitter weather, in a sweat, out to find him . . . Many died of inflammation of the lungs, and she was frail as a winter rose. A gasping sob came up in his throat, which he turned into a kind of bellow for Maartje, who came in from the kitchen with a saucepan in her hand.

"Go and get Dr. Bonus—"

"Where should I go and get him, your honor?"

He did not know, he could not think; all he could do was snatch the handkerchief out of her grasp and see—as if he could read it and augur by it—the size and color of the spot of blood. "At his house, at the hospital—"

"Don't send the poor girl on a fool's errand," said Saskia in a startlingly natural voice. "We're having an evening, don't you remember? Either he or Tulp is bound to drop in."

"Then what does your honor want me to do?"

"Nothing," she said, smiling wanly and getting up. "Take the meat off the spit before it burns and set the table for supper. As for me, I think I'll wash my face."

He held out his hand to her then, and she gave him her moist, warm fingers, looking at him with such contrition, such pleading love that he could scarcely hold back his tears. "I'm not sick, nothing hurts me, I'm perfectly all right," she said.

*

The good Dr. Tulp—he had never looked better, in spite of his burgher ruff and his carefully brushed hair—lifted his ear from Saskia's chest, which had been divided from him only by her filmy chemise, and smiled. "Nothing there, my friend—certainly nothing that I can hear, anyway. And that means nothing serious, no inflammation of the lungs," he said.

The sigh that Rembrandt sighed then seemed to change everything within the range of his vision. The parlor, washed before in a sickly, yellowish cast, seemed of a sudden ethereally bright. She had insisted on lighting five or six candles, probably to show him that there was no question of calling off the party; they shed a pure radiance over the prepared order and beauty of the room, and how he could ever have thought it dirty and slovenly, he did not know.

She was not coy, she did not hurry to get the buttons fastened over the rich creaminess of the upper part of her breast. She sat on the edge of her couch, dealing gravely with one button after another and smiling at him uncertainly as if—poor love!—the blessed news might put her back into his ill grace. "But where did the blood come from?" she said, for the blood had gotten her those bruising kisses, that unstinted and passionate forgiveness. "There really was some—he knows, he saw it—a spot about as big as that." She showed the doctor the garnet in her ring.

"Oh, blood can come from a number of things, sweetheart. Blood isn't necessarily a sign of either inflammation or weakness of the lungs. It could come from your throat, for instance. Were you coughing very hard?"

"Yes, and shouting, too, because we had an argument, and I was screaming at *him*," she said, and laughed and hung her head.

"Well, that'll teach you to be a more obedient wife," said the doctor, passing his hand over the soft, candlelit confusion of her hair. "These colds of yours are bad enough as it is; you shouldn't go running about outdoors, and you shouldn't strain your voice when your throat is sore. In fact, it wouldn't do you a bit of harm if you stayed in a nice warm bed for a couple of days."

"Please, not this evening—tomorrow!" she said. "I'll keep myself warm. You can put me in the chair by the hearth and wrap me up, and I'll never move. We've been sad all day, and now there's no reason to be sad any more, and I do so want to enjoy myself."

"Very well, you have my permission, provided you stay where we put you."

"And you, my poor bear, do *you* think it's all right for me to stay up?"

The word "bear," close as it was to the word "boor," had a strange effect upon him. It tightened his throat, and he had to swallow and blink his eyes. "If the doctor says it won't hurt you, I don't suppose it will," he told her in so rough a tone that he had to mitigate it by bending over and kissing her forehead. It was sweetly damp, beneficently cool—thank God, there was no fever in her now.

She did up the last of the buttons, and the doctor pulled the chosen chair close to the cheerful blaze at the other end of the room and suggested a heavy blanket because of the draft across the floor.

"Get one out of the closet in the bedroom; I want you to see how beautiful that closet is," she said. "I've been a wretched housekeeper, but I'm going to be better now, I promise. When you come next week, Doctor, you'll scarcely recognize this place—all the brass and copper will be polished, and there won't be a cobweb anywhere."

He was glad to be alone in the bedroom, even though he could no longer get down on his knees and thank God. He opened the door of her orderly closet, and there, where the spare bedclothes were stored and the air was pungent with camphor, he let his forehead rest against some soft folded thing and allowed the smarting tears to come as they would. She was not dying—there was no limit save the inevitable common one set upon their nights and days. God strike me dumb, he thought, if I ever raise my voice to her again. But he could not think: God strike me blind, or, God drain the power from my right hand.

He noted matters to compliment her on, like the polished floor and the neat pile of pillowcases, then stopped in the middle of the room with the blanket over his arm and decided he had better remove his own disorder: his jacket sagged on a chair and his muffler lay on the floor. As he picked up the jacket, something crackled in the pocket—he had forgotten the sketches, the marvelous sketches; the thought of them came back like an added benediction, and he could scarcely wait to see whether they were as good as he recalled. But to linger brooding over them seemed a solitary self-indulgence that might tarnish their reconciliation, so he laid the folded paper on top of the blanket and went back into the other room. It was a pleasure to wrap her up, gay and fragrant as she was, in a series of complicated folds. "The closet is beautiful," he said, stuffing a loose end of the blanket into the space between her yielding haunches and the hard back of the chair. "The pillowcases look fine, and a person could see his face in the floor the way you've polished it."

"If I'm not allowed to move around, what are we going to do about the salad? I didn't tell Maartje to make it—I always make it myself, the way Hiskia taught me—and now Maartje's gone to bed."

"It makes no difference. They'll eat plain fish for once."

"That's right. After all, they don't come here to eat; they come to see you."

"Not me—*you*," he said, and kissed her on the cheek and carried his folded paper to the table where he could spread it out in the candle-light.

Tulp wandered over and made such a fuss about the sketches that one would have thought he was my lord Constantyn Huyghens. The naked tree, the seated boy putting on his skates, even the desolate gull in the corner of the page—there was nothing that did not draw his enthusiastic comment. At first his praise was something to luxuriate in, but the very excessiveness of it became painful when one remembered that they were only little sketches for a casual piece and that there had been no such ardent words for *Belshazzar* or *Samson's Wedding Feast* or *The Sacrifice of Abraham*. If an admonition was implied, the artist wanted no part of it—he avoided the intelligent eyes and looked at the chair in which his darling sat swathed in the blanket, probably congratulating herself less on escaping a sentence of death than on the rejuvenescence of their fervor and their trust.

But before there was any necessity for him to acknowledge the disturbing compliments, the downstairs door banged and the steps shook under hurrying booted feet. "That must be Coq and Ruytenberg!" said Saskia with a delight that caused him not the faintest surge of jealousy —let her live to be coddled and adored and flirted with so long as her lungs took in the air and her eyes saw the light of the sun! He excused himself to Tulp to let the newcomers in, and they were as merry as he could wish them, their faces glowing healthy from the cold and each of them holding what was obviously an expensive bottle of wine.

"These," said Coq, gesturing at Ruytenberg's bottle with his own, "are for a celebration."

"What are we supposed to celebrate? Has one of you been promoted?" It was a foolish question: the captain, being at the top of the pyramid, could not be promoted, and Ruytenberg could not better his present rank unless he took the captain's place.

"No, of course not," said the lieutenant. "We'll tell you in a minute. Only, what's come over our hostess? Are you jealous, that you've got her all wrapped up so that nobody can see her?"

There were explanations and expressions of sympathy, offers of kisses and warnings of infection, boasts of indifference to every risk including the plague, and a couple of kisses that found their mark on her swollen cheek and her chapped chin. Wine, they said, was a specific, and wine they would administer as soon as they divulged what was supposed to be celebrated. Tulp, possibly envious because the arrival of the younger men had made her so gay, was still studying the sketches; and it was not until Ruytenberg commanded everybody's attention by rapping on a brass candlestick with his ring that he came over to their end of the room.

"How would you like sixteen hundred florins?" said the lieutenant to Rembrandt.

"Anybody would like sixteen hundred florins," said Saskia.

"He naturally doesn't know what you're talking about," said the captain. "That's a silly way to begin."

"Very well," said Ruytenberg, "I'll take it from another direction. How would you like a commission to do a Regents' piece, a commission much larger than the one this learned gentleman"—he made a deep bow to the doctor—"secured for you some years ago?"

Rembrandt did not answer—he was struck wordless by a surmise of what was coming: saw it as a flamboyant waving of banners, a thrusting of serried lances, a crossing of the diagonal lines of drawn swords.

"In a word," said the captain, "how would you like to paint the troop of Captain Banning Coq marching out to parade? Sixteen hundred florins was subscribed this evening, and we've reserved a tremendous place for it in the clubroom at the Doelen. Every member of the troop is on the list, and all of them are agreed that you're the master and can make of it what you please."

"Except," said Ruytenberg, "that it will have to be very bright—the corner it's to hang in is damnably dark."

"It'll be bright if he does it; that goes without saying," the captain said.

He could see it in its brightness so vividly that for an instant the vision drove out even the thought of the gain and the glory. He could see how to make the noonday sun drench the canvas, dispelling any shadows that could gather in any corner. There would be banners and sashes and drums and maybe an urchin's fantastic jacket for color. There would be lines of light on lances, curves of light along the barrels of the muskets, slants of light on the beveled edges of sword blades, pools of light on the polished boots and shoes. Light and color would come first; around those he would arrange the portraits—no monotonous rows of heads presented as if on platters to the viewer, but living beings caught in the excitement of their simultaneous action as the others had been caught in the stillness of their common absorption with the dissection of The Child . . .

"Well, what do you say?" asked the lieutenant. "We can't pull the corks until you've accepted."

His fame would be on the rise again; life would yield him the impossibilities he had asked of it when he had dreamed of Amsterdam in Leyden—it was as if a great flotilla of galleons heavy with treasure were bearing toward him at full sail over a blindingly brilliant sea. "Of course I accept," he said. "I believe I can give you a wonderful picture—" He broke off, thinking that military noise must somehow be gotten onto the canvas, the shouts of a crowd of men over the tramp of feet and the roll of drums. To paint clamor in bursts of color and a confusion of crossing lines and changing lights—that was a worthy challenge to his skill. "I can't think of anything I'd rather do," he said. "Thank you—thanks to both of you—thanks very much."

The corks were pulled, and Saskia sent the captain to get the goblets. As he crossed the room he was transformed into the central figure in the painting: he would march in the forefront, of course, and a fine figure he would be to pivot all the movement on, with his strong square shoulders and his light flowing hair and his pointed beard and his large, full eyes. And Ruytenberg was no mean model either; slight though he was, he would provide whatever his superior lacked—a certain elegance and grace.

They drank the first toast to their hostess's health and the second to the painting, and as she drank with them, looking at her husband over the rim of the goblet, her infantine skin was suffused with a fresh pink tide of hope and her lips were parted in wonder at the fame and splendor bearing in her direction. "It's been a long, long time since you've had anything like this," she said.

"I never had anything like this except *The Anatomy Lesson*."

"No," said Dr. Tulp, "this is not to be compared with *The Anatomy Lesson.* That was good enough to start with, but this is simply in a different class. There were only eight of us in that, and not one of the lot was what you would call a really lucrative patron—the sort that comes back to be done at full length, or the sort that sends in his wife or his cousin or his aunt. Once the word of *this* gets around, you'll have more than you can handle even if you double your price."

It was true, and he could not help rejoicing in it. In the years that had passed between the two commissions, he had grown weary of hearing *The Anatomy Lesson* mentioned as his most notable canvas; he had learned to hate the stolid burgher taste that put its austere sobriety above the richness and the splendor of *Samson's Wedding Feast* or *The Sacrifice of Abraham.*

"The doctor's right," said Ruytenberg. "There are over twenty of us, and every last man of us could bring you others, and those others could bring you still others, ad infinitum. The sixteen hundred florins, though it's a tidy little sum in itself, is only the beginning. Wait until you see what happens once the canvas is on the wall."

The captain filled a glass for his host, and he drained it off, letting the heat of the wine flood up and the dreams flood in. A house of his own, more princely than Lastman's, in a quarter of the city as opulent as the Heerengracht . . . A salon crowded with antiquities and precious canvases . . . Such plumes and furs and cloaks as had never decked the person of a miller's son or a boor . . . Three servants, four servants if necessary, to keep the whole vast expanse as impeccable as his mother's little kitchen . . . And Saskia draped in damask and roped in pearls, going shod in gilded leather and careless as a queen through the regal rooms . . .

"It *should* make a difference," she said, tilting her head luxuriously against the back of her chair and half closing her eyes.

"It'll make an enormous difference," said the doctor. "Your one problem will be to keep from hurting people's feelings. You'll have to find a gracious way of saying no to everybody you refuse."

Saying no to importunate burghers in a marble vestibule—he liked the idea. He contemplated it while his wife was going on about how crowded they were here, how there were scarcely any closets to store things in, how the apprentices overflowed the studio. He barely listened until she asked the captain whether he didn't think that sooner or later they ought to move to a larger place.

"Let's not spend our florins before we've got them," he said, pleasantly but firmly. "Let's wait and see how it works out."

"Oh," said Ruytenberg, giving him a merry poke with his elbow, "why are you always spoiling her pleasure? There's no harm in her having something to dream about."

And there was this to be said for the lieutenant's way of looking at it: unlike himself, she had no visionary lights and colors and lines to distract her. His own high-heartedness could be transmuted into yellow and scarlet and sea-green images; but there was nothing that she could put between herself and the swift advance of those full-sailed dreams.

*

No matter how much he strove to obliterate it, the façade of the great house on the Breestraat kept coming up before him. He wondered, then and afterwards, whether it would have wrought so potently with him if he had first seen it at any other time than a mildly sunny January afternoon. Light—his angel and his daemon—kept him staring there in spite of his better judgment. As if gold could be diluted in water and floated over a surface, a pale wash of light had gathered on the rough rosy oblongs of the bricks and the smooth facings of ornamental stone. Every pane of the three lordly tiers of double windows had served as a mirror to catch the watery blue essence of a day that bore promise of spring; and the tiles of the roof, wet with the residue of melted snow, gleamed gold and turquoise and green like the scales of a dolphin leaping up out of a legendary sea.

"Go and look at it," she had said to him. "What harm can it do to look at it?" And he had gone and looked at it and advised her to put it out of her head, though she, to tell the truth, turned out to be less obsessed with it than he. Her mind, swift and volatile these days with a general resurgence of health and love and hope, had darted off to more easily gotten things, but he could not keep it out of his thoughts even when he was painting. It was out of the question, that house on the Breestraat—it was finer than Lastman's, too fine even for the rich and noted painter everybody assured him he was about to be—yet he wanted it more than anything, more even than a living child.

And because the image and the yearning were always there, he taught himself to escape them by plunging into his teaching. The exigencies of the studio—the necessity of answering the questions raised by half a dozen young men—made it impossible for his mind to wander off to something else. His mornings went briskly because he made plans at breakfast instead of brooding; the noonday meal, never more for him than bread and cheese and beer, he took at some apprentice's easel, eating with one hand and pointing out errors with the other; and by late afternoon, if things went well, he was so exhausted that the remaining hour before supper could be consumed in sleep.

If things went well—but there were always accidents. And there was one Thursday toward the end of February—the weather had turned cold, ice would have formed on that not-to-be-remembered roof again —when everything flew out at once, like the cogs and screws and springs of a ruined clock. Flew out without warning, since the lesson in drawing from life that he had been conducting had yielded some excellent results, and the departing apprentices had left the room in the best possible order, and the model—a reasonably presentable woman—before going off to the bedroom to dress, had promised to come back next week. Nobody was left with him but the dark, somber Bol, who had stayed on in the capacity of senior apprentice for love of him and Saskia, and the lively Hoogstraten, who was lovable even though he drove a person mad with the number and nervous exactitude of his questions; and these two had taken it upon themselves to brush and fold the precious cloaks and coverlets against which the obliging model had been displaying herself as Bathsheba after her bath. "Well, now, that's very kind of you," he said, walking over to them and encouraging the yawn that would assure him he was ready for his nap. "Lay them by, all in the same chest. And remind me, Bol, to tell the others tomorrow to hold onto their sketches. We'll have a chance to work on this again; she says she'll come back next Thursday."

"I'll make a note of it, Master." He went to the other end of the room to make a note of it, with his soft dark hair flying long and loose below his velvet beret. He made a note of everything, not out of any obsession with orderliness, only because he knew what chaos his remote and passionate nature could make of everyday affairs if he did not rein it in with calendars and lists.

"And if you don't mind, Master," said little Hoogstraten in his shrill, insistent voice, "can I ask you just one question? When a person is doing a sketch that he intends eventually to turn into an etching—now, you understand, I'm speaking *only* of a sketch done specifically for an etching—should he indicate, or *try* to indicate, in the sketch the various thicknesses and thinnesses of the line that he means to produce on the etching plate by means of the burr?"

The small pale face with its wan blue eyes and its wispy and colorless wreath of hair was so earnest that he reproached himself for lack of patience. Yet the question was, as usual, unanswerable and futile. "I don't know, Hoogstraten," he said, suppressing the matured yawn. "To tell the truth, I never thought about it. I make a sketch, and afterwards I look at it and think: This is a good sketch and would probably make a good etching. I never think of the burr until I'm working on the plate, and even then I can't say I really *think* of it—the burr takes care of itself."

"You mean, Master, that you're not conscious of what effect you're going to get with the burr? You mean the results of the burr are purely accidental?"

"No, I couldn't mean that. I know what I'm doing. It's just that I don't think about it. It's more like—"

He was not called upon to provide the simile. Something intense was going on between the model and the maid on the other side of the door, and the next thing he heard was the model's voice, shrill with a sense of injury, saying, "What do you take me for?"

"What could be the matter with Vrouw Poorter?" he asked. Some-

312

thing in the remembrance of Pieter Lastman, saying, "Now, Rinske," had impelled him to call every one of his models—beggar, drunkard, or whore—by the last name.

"I don't know, Master," said Bol. "Would you like me to go and find out?"

Maartje's voice, objectionably curt and superior, was going on to the effect that Madame had said the bedroom was to be cleaned today, absolutely. "No," he said. "You stay here and close the shutters. I'd better go myself."

They were standing face to face in the little hallway—the poor woman in her nakedness and Maartje in her starched workdress with a bucket of soapy water in her hand. The bedroom floor, stretching behind the maid, was sopping wet and gave off the smell of soap and drenched wood.

"She went and put my clothes in the parlor."

"And where else was I supposed to put them? I'm not having her track up my clean bedroom floor when she goes to get dressed."

"And I'm not walking into your parlor born-naked either, with the door standing open for everybody to come in. I don't make a show of myself any more than I've got to—"

The maid, endowed with all the bigotry of the ignorant and convinced that what went on in his studio was only one shade better than what went on in a whorehouse, could not suppress her ugly, knowing smile.

"I'm not coming back here any more. There are some things a person doesn't have to put up with."

"Please listen to me a minute, Vrouw Poorter. Maartje will get your clothes out of the parlor and put them in the bedroom, where they belong. As for your coming back next Thursday, I certainly hope you will. It ought to be plain to everybody in this house that you're very valuable to me, and we'll see to it that the bedroom is yours to use whenever you please."

"Your honor can very well stand there and say so," said the servant. "But when am I supposed to clean it, I'd like to know? Madame never got up until after nine, and then she was in there dressing until ten, and after that she takes a notion to go out and shop with Vrouw Lazzara and gets dressed all over again, and she isn't finished with *that* until two o'clock in the afternoon."

"What Madame does," he said icily, "is her own business. Go get Vrouw Poorter's clothes and keep a civil tongue in your head or you'll have something to regret."

She set the bucket down so violently that the water sloshed over and stopped spreading barely an inch from the toe of his shoe. He was too disheartened to do more than wait in silence until she reappeared, holding the cheap clothing between her thumb and forefinger as if it carried some infection. "Lay those back on the bed where you got them," he said; and now that the maid was properly humiliated he could see some reason for her exasperation: she had engaged herself to work for a couple and had found herself waiting on eight, with no one to help her but an ill-trained girl from the orphanage. The studio flowed over into the house, and the house flowed over into the studio, and their mingling made something as squalid as the grey-blue water in the bucket with its splinters and its spots of grease and its dead suds.

Going back into the studio, he found that Hoogstraten was gone; but Bol, only vaguely distinguishable in the faint light that was left with the shutters closed, sat idle on the edge of the worktable—he was always unwilling to take himself off, always hopeful that he might be asked to supper. "I've been thinking, Master," he said in a melancholy voice, "that a resolution ought to be offered before the Saint Lucas Guild. Kiel and Hoogstraten think so too, and I'm sure all your former apprentices —with the possible exception of Govaert Flinck—would be more than happy to give us their support."

He had no idea what the apprentice was talking about. Though he was naturally a member of the Saint Lucas Guild, he never went to the monthly suppers and attended only the most crucial of the meetings. Bol usually brought him such news as might concern him; but if the young man had mentioned a resolution to him before—he took it to be a resolution of grievance from the mournful tone and the slightly bent head—he must not have been paying attention. "Why would Flinck hold back?" he asked, trusting Bol's candor to yield him a clue.

There was an instant of charged silence in which he got the impression that the undefined resolution had some direct application to himself. The young man shifted his haunches on the worktable and began to crack the knuckles of his fine, long fingers. "Oh, well, nothing's to be expected of *him*. He's much too close with the lot of them—Vondel and von Sandrart and Hooft and Tesselschade Visscher and the rest of the Muiden crew," he said.

Now he was certain he was involved, and deeply so. He buttressed himself against the wall and remembered the splashing *Diana* and the pissing *Ganymede* and the things he had said to von Sandrart at the charity supper. His heart, hastened by the argument in the hallway, began to beat still harder, and he could not bring himself to request enlightenment, could only ask Bol what he thought von Sandrart could have to do with it.

"Well, now, if Vondel makes a statement that isn't exactly flattering to you," said his assistant, "you can be sure that it was prompted by von Sandrart. He was jealous to begin with, and now he has this business of the military Regents' piece sticking in his throat—everybody knows you're getting more space and a bigger fee than he is. Excuse me, Master, it's a bad habit, and I know it annoys you—" He stopped cracking his knuckles and laid his loosely folded hands on his paint-stained knee. "But this much I will say: I can't imagine Vondel, without any prompting from anybody else, just sitting down and writing in a preface to his play that Rubens is the glory of the art of painting in the Netherlands. It's von Sandrart who's responsible, and he ought to be put in his place. Kiel's been working on the wording of the resolution; he thinks it ought to go something like this: 'Inasmuch as Amsterdam is the unrivaled center of Dutch painting and harbors such famous masters as Heer Rembrandt van Rijn, it seems strange to us, the Brothers of the Guild of Saint Lucas, that Heer van den Vondel should have to reach so far afield as Flanders to find a painter worthy of mention in the preface of his play . . .'"

He had seen a copy of that play on the counter of a bookshop a week ago. The name of it, as he remembered, was *The Brothers*, and he had leafed idly through it, never thinking to look at the preface. The style, as indirect and ornate as the style of the poem that had irked him in the gardens of the Old Men's Home, had made him wince, and he had pushed the book away and never thought of it again.

"'. . . Therefore be it resolved that the Brothers of Saint Lucas . . .'"

He straightened his shoulders, resisting an impulse to sag against the wall. "To tell the truth, Ferdinand, I didn't know anything about it. I couldn't make out what you were talking about," he said.

"Oh, Master, I'm sorry!" The slender young body slid down from the worktable; the large dark eyes, too close and too compassionate, gazed into his face. He was hard put to it to keep from thrusting out his hand to ward the young man off, and was the more undone by a sudden remembrance of his mother extending her arm to forestall his sister's embrace.

"We thought you knew all about it, Master."

There was gall for him in the "we": they had whispered about it here; they had commiserated with him and made plans to defend him behind his back. "I should have known, that's certain. The trouble is, I never read anything but the Bible and history."

"Why should you waste your time reading such stuff as *The Brothers*? My sister saw it, and she tells me it's deadly dull—nothing but noble speeches from beginning to end. He'll probably be turning Catholic one of these days, which is enough to explain why he should have a preference for Rubens—all those Mary Magdalens and Mary Mothers with their rolled-up eyes."

Rubens, Rubens—he turned his back on his assistant and walked to one of the shuttered windows to secure a loose latch and hide his sudden burning hatred for Rubens. Rubens with his Helene Fourment and his house with a park for a garden and his commissions from the Count of This-and-That and the Bishop of Such-and-Such! Vondel and von Sandrart dared to aim their barbs at him, his apprentices dared to pity him, his wife dared to call him a boor because he did not live like Rubens, which is to say like a manorial lord. And there—for sale and ready

315

to be inhabited next summer—was that peerless house, that magnificent edifice of aureate brick and gleaming stone. Sixteen hundred florins for the Regents' piece, and God knows how much more to come from the commissions that were bound to pour in, and Saskia's whole fortune scarcely touched—they were living out their golden years in a colorless and dreary situation between wealth and poverty, splendor and squalor, not knowing whether they were princes or poor artisans: it was ridiculous!

The young man, frightened or wounded or both, had gone to the other side of the studio and was taking his cloak from a peg. "You know, Master, we'd never think of submitting such a resolution until you'd seen it in writing and approved it."

"Actually, Ferdinand, I don't see much good in offering a resolution. Nothing's to be gained from that sort of thing, though it was kind of you to think of it. Maybe it's better to bide our time until they see for themselves—"

"Which they will, Master, as soon as the Regents' piece is hung."

"Yes, God willing. Good night, sleep well, I'll see you tomorrow at nine."

Yet he could not bear to think of tomorrow, with its mean, small life conducted in its mean, small way and circumscribed by these wretched rooms. He had already made the leap in time and space and stood now in his thoughts where he soon would stand in actuality—his whole existence released and transformed by the amplitude of a new and worthy shell. What patron would dare to complain of the number of sittings he required if he met the artist in such an entrance hall? What Amsterdam stocking-vendor would dare throw Rubens in his face if he lived like Rubens, displaying to the chance visitor such a collection of canvases and antiquities as the Flemish master had not troubled himself to acquire—a collection that remained obscure, unguessed simply because it had never been assembled in a suitable salon? The days were over when the life of the house and the life of the studio would taint each other with sordid antagonisms and distractions. That third story—his mind soared to it with fierce, joyous strength—was high above the petty noises of the street, crossed by sea-borne winds, and drenched with light. There, in separate cubicles, his apprentices could work in solitude and peace, there his models could undress and dress in little rooms of their own, there in deep closets he could lay aside the precious things he had used today and would use again tomorrow, there in a remote chamber he could set up his own easel, let his face do what it would in his solitary transports, paint as he needed to paint and deserved to paint —beyond mean annoyance, beyond sound, beyond question and reproach, princely and accountable to nobody, vulnerable to nothing and confined by nothing—free—

He heard Saskia's voice addressing Maartje in the parlor; she had come back from her shopping trip. Too exultant, too out of control to

316

dare to show his face even to her, he called to her from the studio not to take off her cloak. "Why not? Where are we going?" she asked. And he had to wait a moment to master his voice before he could tell her that they must go and look at that house at once—before the sun had withdrawn from the windows, while the bricks were still rosy and the ornamental stone was still shining and the icy tiles of the roof were still washed in gold.

*

It was hard for others to understand why he was not disheartened by the long wait. Almost a year, they said, before the present owners would bestir themselves and move out! And another six months before the remodeling necessary to accommodate his household and his apprentices could be done and he could move in! But what seemed preposterous to outsiders seemed only natural to him: so vast a transformation was to take place in his whole life that the wonder was that it could be accomplished in so short a time as a year and a half. He did not resent it, either, when half the price of the house had to be withdrawn from the bank and put into the hands of the owner. True, Saskia's fortune was diminished by something like a third and he got nothing immediate out of the investment except the right to dream. But her money had really been wisely placed—what could serve her better than a regal house?—and the amount they would lose in interest from the bank was probably no more than the rent they paid on New Doelen Street. Besides, he had neither the leisure nor the inclination to compute in detail what they had gained or lost. With so many men to sketch for the Regents' piece, with the portrait commissions and the apprentices, with his cramped household in such confusion and his wife in her third pregnancy—and just as erratic and willful as she had been during the last fruitless one—he found it hard enough to keep his first glorious concept of the great canvas fresh without toiling over columns of figures that would have baffled a municipal accountant.

Yet he was sensible enough to refuse to buy any furnishings until he could buy them out of the first installment paid him by the Military Guild. In his last encounter with the young man at the bank, that knowing personage, his eyes flashing cold-green behind the lenses of his spectacles, had tried to convince him that he might do better by withdrawing two-thirds of Saskia's money and paying for the house in full, since the delay involved paying more than he would be drawing in interest; but the yards of figures and percentages that had been reeled off had so confused and frightened him that he wanted no transactions except those characterized by simplicity. It was a pleasure, then, to work from a given sum in a given place—eight hundred florins received from Captain Banning Coq and deposited in a gilded box in the top drawer of his chest. That way, a man knew what he had and what he could afford to spend, even if the arrangement sent the lieutenant into spasms of laughter and made the wry Pinero shake his head. It proved a delight to Saskia, at any rate. After one of their shopping trips she would run to the gilded box and arrange the coins in two heaps, one to represent what they had spent and one to represent what they still could spend—though it was unfortunately true that the shopkeepers from whom they bought the tall leather chairs, the great oak tables, the gold frames, and the ornate mirrors could never give them a bill to the penny then and there: some item always had to be refinished or mended at an additional cost which they were assured would be nothing for them to worry their heads about.

And he was so happy in the thought of those stored new possessions that he was not distressed when the final accounting turned out to have little enough to do with their conjectures over the heaped contents of the gilded box. If they had bought more things than they remembered, they had bought nothing useless, nothing unbeautiful. If many negligible sums added up to something that a person couldn't shrug off, what was to be done about it? Warped wood must be sanded and refinished, tarnished mirrors must be resilvered, cracked leather must be replaced. And Anslo's suggestion that the imperfections could be taken care of little by little was characteristic of a Mennonite mind, alien or even inimical to magnificence. Anslo was the sort that could sit on a cushion for three years without noticing that the frieze had split and the stuffing was coming through.

Besides, a sudden accession of skill and power when he made his first assays at the great canvas had left him almost staggered by his own capacities; and the conviction that he could do whatever he pleased with the brush flowed over into the rest of his life and assured him that there was no exigency he could not master, no demand that could prove too much. He was still only thirty-three, and if more money should be needed for the opulent life the two of them would live henceforth, it would be forthcoming, part of it out of the higher prices bound to come with his foreordained success and part of it with the doubling of his production. These days he could paint endlessly. With all the shopping and all the catering to her erratic moods, he was painting more than he had ever painted: his mind was never sodden, his body never weary any more. When he lay in bed beside her forbidden person these nights, it was no longer baffled desire that kept him awake. Visions of great, radiant canvases came and went before his staring eyes, visions so nourishing and renewing in themselves that he had no need for the healing properties of sleep.

It did not occur to him until December, after the Saint Nicolaas Feast, that his relationship with her had become a little less close than he could wish. The visits to the house—emptied at last of those intruders, the former owners—the trips to the shops, the endless discussions about remodeling and their newly acquired possessions had made for a stream of high-hearted talk between them; but the house and the furnishings were all they ever talked about. He never told her anything about the Regents' piece—which he was doing in a rented warehouse because the canvas was too big to be accommodated in their present quarters—and she scarcely ever mentioned the child. He realized that their reasons for silence about what concerned them most were opposite: he did not need to talk to her because his hopes were so high, and she could not bring herself to talk to him because her hopes were so low. That realization disturbed him and disrupted the easy ripple of their shallow conversations; whereupon she, too, grew disturbed and restless and skittish, complaining that she was sick of sitting in the parlor with nothing to do while he closed himself away from her in his studio or kept himself out of reach in the warehouse—no matter what Dr. Tulp and Dr. Bonus said, she was going to Friesland, where there were people for her to talk to and things for her to do. He forbade the journey, not so much because he feared it would harm the child—he took it for granted that the child was doomed—but out of apprehension that she might miscarry on some lonely stretch of the highway. That fear and his awareness of her hopelessness about the baby made him too tender to reject her next request: if she couldn't go to Friesland, then might she ask her sister Titia to come and stay with her in Amsterdam? He had no particular antipathy to Titia, who was the most reserved and sensible of the bubbling lot, but he could not face the idea of wasting a week away from his painting to attend the round of little suppers that would doubtless be given to enliven her stay. If a week was to be wasted, he would waste it on his own; and he told her, without raising more than a tepid objection, that while Titia was visiting with her he would take himself to Leyden for a belated stay with his family.

Wishing to carry some part of his new grandeur back into a world from which he had no desire to separate himself, he went to the gilded box and took from it a good number of the coins that yet remained, in order to buy gifts for each of them—gifts splendid enough to convince them of the golden change in his fortune and to let them know that long silences and desultory visiting did not indicate a weakening of family ties. He bought their presents as carefully as he had bought his damasks and marble basins and Japanese vases, giving much thought to their suitability and none at all to the cost. For his mother he bought a regal gown of soft velvet, lined with fur at the collar and the flowing sleeves, as well as an ancient brooch in which massive goldwork supported a flawless amethyst. For Lysbeth he chose a costly muff and tippet of the finest grey squirrel; for the good Antje a gathered skirt and matching jacket, dark blue satin with embroidery of a lighter blue. For days he could not make up his mind which had the better chance of succeeding in the unlikely business of pleasing Adriaen—a Bible or a clock; and when he decided on the Bible he kept visiting bookshops until he found one so beautiful—so clearly printed on such fine, soft paper, so impressively bound in time-muted calfskin, so richly secured with gold clasps

—that he would have spent twice the price to have found another for himself.

Yet the giving of those gifts—he presented them in the first half-hour he spent under his mother's roof in an effort to overcome the family's almost withering lassitude and disinclination to ask him about his affairs—yielded him little satisfaction. His mother, her face as immobile and furrowed as a walnut shell, did not pull herself out of her chair to try on her robe, only stroked it a little when he laid it across her knees, and seemed awed, even distressed by the evident costliness of the brooch, as though such an expenditure required her to live more years than she could hope to in order to make the investment worth while. The squirrel muff and tippet had been a bad choice for Lysbeth: she made a point of letting him know that she had small use for that sort of thing now, since her feet were usually so swollen that she couldn't get them into decent shoes and she seldom went into the city any more. And nothing Antje said in praise of the beautiful blue skirt and jacket could gainsay the obvious fact that she shrank into sad insignificance under the richness of its color and the fullness of its folds. Only Adriaen seemed genuinely if grudgingly gratified: though he could not bring himself to praise the beauty of the binding and the clasps, he could be seen fondling them with his cracked and leathery hands. And he did manage to say that he and Antje had never owned a fine Bible and that this one, with its big clear print, put scarcely any strain on his weakening eyes.

While the mournful business of gift-giving was dragging to its conclusion, the donor became more and more acutely aware of the surroundings. The parlor was almost unchanged, yet the room and all its accouterments seemed to have faded and shrunken. Could those candlesticks possibly be the ones that had been proudly taken out and lighted for Master van Swanenburgh? That small, paled-out map—could it be the glorious and dream-begetting piece of cartography against which Harmen Gerritszoon had been in the habit of resting his bald head? And his own young face a little to the left of the disheartening map—an old study in oils that he had not bothered to take with him because the manner was so broad and the subject was so common, with its thick neck and tousled hair and coarse peasant mouth—was I ever that one? he asked himself. Which is real—the gallant decked out in gold chains and brown velvet handing out his bounty like a manorial lord, or that one up there, raw as the malt-mash from which he got his shelter and nourishment and the rough clothes on his back?

During much of that first night, lying in the corner bed which had once been shared by the two who had begotten him—his mother had left it to him, saying that she would be perfectly comfortable with Lysbeth—he kept telling himself in his wakefulness that his depression was of no significance. It was only that in coming back to the house where he had spent his childhood he had, in some inexplicable way, grown childish—they had hurt his feelings by their listless acceptance of his gifts, they had affronted him with their lack of interest in his coming wealth and happiness. And what else could he have expected, if he had not been indulging in boyish self-deception? Adriaen had always borne him resentment and had felt little respect for his craft; Lysbeth was doubly inimical because she had tried to live his better life and failed, and poor little Antje could not have shown him more cordiality without overstepping her role as keeper of the peace. As for his mother, she would certainly be different tomorrow when the others were out of the way; after all, she had to live with them and could not offend them with what they would consider doting—in fact, her leaving his glories unmentioned might very well have been prompted by her wish to spare him their disparaging insinuations and knowing looks. By the time sleep began to break the order of his thoughts and loosen his aching arms and legs, he had decided that the best way to be alone with her would be to paint her; while painting her in the brooch and the fur-lined robe he could convince her of the abundance of his blessings and heal the unnerving break between his present and his past.

But things began unpropitiously the following morning. The journey, the tepid welcome, and the sense of being unmoored from the gone years had so drained him that he did not wake up until after ten. Doubtless they had remarked in his absence that this was the way he lived, going to bed past midnight after bouts of eating and drinking—Adriaen had made some mention last night of the increase in his girth—and lying around in shameful ease until some equally ungodly hour. His mind was clear and active, but a fit of queasiness made him incapable of looking as cheerful as so fortunate a man should look or of eating enough to show that he appreciated the food. There was trouble, too, about setting up his easel: he did not dare to suggest putting it into the immaculate parlor or into any of their bedrooms; he did not want it in the kitchen where his mother and he would constantly be intruded upon, and he felt a reasonless distaste for spending most of the day in the room where he had slept his uneasy sleep. In the end he settled on the last of these, but when everything was ready there—the easel set up, the palette prepared, the armless chair pulled up into the meager square of pale sunlight—he still could not begin: even with Antje to help her, it took his mother such a long time to deck herself out in her unfamiliar finery. Lysbeth had told them—heaping coals of fire, no doubt—that the noonday meal would be postponed until one so that he would have more hours for painting, but by the time the dressing was over and his mother came in, bearing down heavily upon her cane, the clocks in the belfries were already striking twelve.

The hour was whittled down further because there was another problem: the little withered body was so regal in its gold and fur and velvet that it made an almost insignificant thing of the small head, balding now and wrapped by Antje in fold on fold of white cloth. "We must get you some kind of hood, Mother. The robe and the brooch are too much unless you have some kind of hood," he said; and another fifteen minutes was frittered away before Antje could lay her hand on one that he had given to Lysbeth while she lived with him on the Bloemgracht, a brown woolen hood lined in brocade and trimmed with fringes that ended in steel beads—a thing long unused and redolent of camphor and high intentions and defeat.

He had not been working for more than ten minutes when he knew that this would be the best of the many likenesses of his mother that he had done: he was, as he knew when he stood before the great Regents' canvas in the Amsterdam warehouse, a consummate master now. The marvelous network of wrinkles in the darkened flesh of her face, the deep pile of the velvet and the sun-warmed sworls of the fur—he flew from one to the other and back again, intoxicated by his capability. And he did not realize that little was coming of his determination to talk with her until he became aware that he somehow kept bypassing her sad and questioning eyes.

"That Regents' piece I was telling you about, Mother—it's going to be the biggest thing I've ever done."

She did not answer at once, and something in the forward thrust and slight tilt of her head suggested that her hearing was less acute than in the past. That fact might explain the smallness of the part she had played in last night's talk, and also the quizzical look.

"Yes, it's going to be enormous, bigger than that whole wall over there," he said, gesturing out its vastness with his brush.

"And how much money will you get for it?" she asked in a tone so muted and lifeless that it seemed to be reproving the volume and excitement of his.

"Sixteen hundred florins."

"Sixteen hundred florins?" The incredulity that turned it into a question arose out of disappointment, not out of astonishment. "How many people did you say were going to be in it?"

"About twenty." He covered the curtness of his answer by frowning at a stubborn lump of paint on his palette knife.

"Well, I suppose you know what these things are worth," she said, all the more remote and judicial because she remained motionless in her pose, with her hands clasped on the head of her cane. "But for painting twenty people, I thought a person would get more than that." Her gaze, which he had asked her to keep fixed on the copper basin on the chest of drawers, showed no inclination to move toward his face.

No wonder she was disappointed! In her ignorance she had taken her notion of the cost of a single portrait and multiplied it by twenty, and it was hard for him to keep from saying, "Don't be a fool!" The level stretch beyond the leaded panes, a mudflat broken only by a few mean houses, reminded him how limited her life had been. "That isn't the way it goes, Mother. Each of the sitters doesn't pay what he'd pay if he were sitting singly—say four or five hundred florins; nobody ever heard of such a thing. For this sort of canvas, sixteen hundred florins is a very good price. In fact, it's the largest price the Military Guild has ever paid anybody. Ketel and Elias"—he chose the names that even she would be likely to recognize—"got considerably less."

"I suppose it *is* a great deal of money." It was her mouth alone that admitted it, pale and turned in over her shrunken gums; there was no retreat, no recognition of anything complimentary to him in her averted, wary eyes. "But I don't imagine it would go very far toward paying for the new house you bought."

He stifled his annoyance at her implication that they had no other funds, no assurance for the future and nothing laid by. "We're not paying for the house out of *that*," he said. "We drew on Saskia's fortune to pay for the house—it was a tremendous amount of money, you know, and we'd scarcely taken anything out of it."

"Oh, Saskia's fortune . . ." Her voice, cold and uninvolved, let him know—and by intention—that Saskia's money was beyond the province of her concern. *His* doings, *his* money—these she might regard with interest, but Saskia and what was Saskia's were unreal, not to be taken into account at all.

It was natural then that when he found the words to answer they should come out with a certain stridency. "Not that we'll have to draw on Saskia's fortune again. Saskia's fortune"—he repeated it deliberately—"will stay in the bank. The rest of the payments for the house will be coming out of my painting. Everybody says I'll have more patrons than I can accept, once the Regents' piece is hung."

"Really? Does one picture make all that difference?"

"Yes, when it's the sort of picture this one happens to be. Many of the men in it will be wanting single portraits, or their friends and relatives will. Most of them come from wealthy families and can afford that sort of thing. Anyway, I don't think you realize what an honor it is to be asked to do a canvas like that. A man's reputation is built up by such a commission. It widens his circle of buyers, it permits him to raise his price."

The sharpness of his speech had transformed her pose in a subtle way. The tilt of her head—it had been somewhat reserved and querulous before—reminded him now of the half-timorous look of a listening bird. "But who am I to talk?" she said, closing her thin old hands harder on the cane and breathing out a sigh. "You know perfectly well that I never saw sixteen hundred florins at one time in my life. I can't imagine how you live or what it would cost you, and anyhow, I keep forgetting that you won't be having as many people to depend on you as Harmen did."

He could not help wincing at that. If he had consigned the little creature under Saskia's belt to death, it was to stifle hope, to forestall futile suffering, but *she* had no right to take their childlessness for granted, to be so casual about the pointless birthpangs and the wasted blood. "I wouldn't depend on that, Mother, if I were you. Saskia's pregnant again—I meant to tell you—and neither one of us is exactly old. I may yet have a large family to support."

"Ah, well"—she was still unruffled, her bright and beady eyes were still fixed on the copper basin—"a baby in your case wouldn't necessarily be an extra expense. When a woman has a child"—he felt her glance flit briefly across his vulnerable face—"she doesn't usually want so many other things."

And now he was so wounded that he did not dare to lay his unsteady brush to the painting. Guileless as she seemed, sitting there with her frail head trembling under the weight of the heavy hood and her frail hands opening and closing on her cane, she had given him—and not unknowingly—two bitter thrusts. That she should refuse to say "your wife" or "Saskia," that she should push his beloved into a great and nameless category by calling her "a woman" was bad enough. And it was far worse that she should let him know in so offhand a way that she and the rest of the world were well aware of what he had regarded as a secret between himself and the kind, dead Sylvius: Saskia's lightness, Saskia's heedlessness. He would not have her judged in her elusive, incalculable beauty by those whose lives were measured out in malt sacks and bounded by dismal houses and little barren fields. He would not have her judged at all—to hold his peace was to betray her and their shared dreams of splendor. "I don't believe you understand Saskia, Mother," he said, "and I don't suppose you ever will. Saskia doesn't have to watch herself like any ordinary housewife; she wasn't brought up in that kind of family. The Uylenburghs have always been able to do pretty much as they pleased."

And now that he had said it and gotten nothing for it but silence and a stricken look, he felt a wrenching inside, as though something had been uprooted from his chest. He had thought only to place the beloved and himself where they had every right to be—in a shining circle, among the lords of the earth, beyond the force of the petty laws that applied under this roof; he had not seen how it would be to stand on the outer side of the bright circumference, consigned forever to the inferior place. Oh, he had deceived himself to think that change of fortune and absence and the years were powerless to dissolve the ties of blood! To climb above the station of one's family was to leave them irretrievably behind, and what could the abandoned be expected to feel except jealousy and resentment and pain? With every visit, he had been more an alien, more the questionable stranger within their gates. Every present he had ever brought—tokens from a world they would never inhabit—had been a mockery and a further irritation. To try to speak to them of their own affairs was to reveal how little he knew of their lives, how little he really cared; and *his* dearest concerns—wife, painting, glory, children, house—were so remote from them that they heard with indifference or listened with enmity. "Therefore a man shall forsake his mother and his father and cleave unto his wife" . . . the Bible was right, but there was no need to exhort a man to the act of separation: let him live his life a step beyond the circumscribed horizon, and the separation happened of itself.

The silence was so heavy with remorse that he found it difficult to go on painting; but paint he did, laying the brush to the wrinkled cheek and the withered hands in hard resignation, as if every stroke were a bitter kiss of everlasting farewell. She did not speak or look at him again, and it was a relief when Lysbeth called from the foot of the stairs that the food was on the table. Small kindnesses were still possible: he could at least help her out of the armless chair, support her by sinking his fingers into her slack side until she got her balance on her cane, remove the weight of the hood from her poor trembling head.

During the meal he did what he could, being an alien sojourner, to indicate all that was left in him: his good intentions. He ate with a show of appetite some of the "cold dish" and the herring and the gingerbread; he was alert to pass everything, and he filled up the uneasy silences with remarks that could offend nobody, remarks for the most part about his mother—how lively she was, how well she looked, how steadily she had kept the pose, never so much as turning her head. But it was all unreal —his voice was strange to his own ears, and his eyes grew strained and blurred with looking at the flat, rejecting surfaces of other eyes. And when he was permitted his solitude at last—she could not sit for him again until tomorrow, she would go and nap in Lysbeth's room, she always slept away the afternoon these days—he counted with the frustration of confinement and the torment of loneliness the days he still must spend in this house, separated from and in some strange way betraying the beloved.

For what did they know or care of the life that she and he had together—of their watch over Rombartus's doomed cradle, of their quarrels and reconciliations, of the hours they had spent wandering hand in hand like awed children through the splendid rooms emptied and cleaned to receive their happiness? To these sorrows they were indifferent; these joys could raise no warmth around their hearts, and to be where she was not was to ask, "What am I?" and "Why do I live?" No, he would not deceive himself—aside from the life he knew in front of the easel, there was no life except in her presence. Only with her was he more than a painting shadow; love, the source of life, dwelt for him only in her person—Saskia, Saskia, nobody else.

*

The canal boat deposited him and the eleven other passengers at the Leyden Gate in a wintry sunset; a thin film of ice cracked like a shattered windowpane under its advancing prow, and the wharf and the roofs beyond it were sprinkled with a fine powdering of snow. But he could not delight in the look of the city which he knew now to be his heart's home, he could not give himself joyously to his reunion with the one being he loved until he had rid himself of a foolish anxiety. All through the journey, above the shrill whip-crack of the wind and the grating boisterousness of the other travelers, he had been nagged by the thought that in his absence something could have happened to the Regents' piece. One heavily painted corner of the great canvas, fastened with nails to the wall of the warehouse room, might have pulled loose and folded over, cracking and sticking; or one of the workmen on the first floor of the building might have left a burning candle behind in the shavings and sawdust that always cluttered the place. Perhaps, too—he thought of it for the first time during his brisk walk through streets he was not yet prepared to take pleasure in—the painting was something less than what he had comforted himself with in his isolation. Did the pattern of the slanting lances really overmaster the military confusion? Was the yellow on Ruytenberg's jerkin as saturated with sunlight as he had seen it behind his closed eyelids on those sleepless nights? Were the lesser portraits—the ones in the background—truly beginning to emerge as living beings, identifiable personalities, out of the dark?

The warehouse on the Bloemgracht was, of course, intact. The lantern he borrowed from a shopkeeper in the neighborhood revealed the enormous oblong fixed solidly to the wall. As for the painting—it was more rather than less than he had envisioned. The metal of the weapons so clearly carried the design, the colors were so pure and vibrant, the half-born faces in the shadow so surely promised to be living if summary likenesses that he could not leave it without working on it then and there—he worked on it, in fact, until the bells in the steeples boomed out eight o'clock.

He was hungry then, so hungry that he had to stop at a tavern to take away the gnawing emptiness. He ordered only cheese and beer, since she might be keeping supper until he arrived; but he ate rind and all, tasting in anticipation the food they would eat together in their blessedly empty rooms. She, too, would probably be glad enough to be rid of a guest, to be freed of the necessity of considering another person's needs, to be able to say whatever came into her head. On the walk home he felt light-headed, like a man out of doors for the first time after a long illness: every bright window, every snow-paled roof and ledge and steeple, every lantern borne past him in the thickening dark seemed a thing wonderful and precious, a cause for breathing deeply and blowing out clouds of mist and lifting up a thankful heart.

The downstairs door was locked for once—he was glad to see that she was being more circumspect about such matters—and he let himself in with his key. Six candles were burning in the parlor, three on the table and three on the mantelpiece, and the stillness and emptiness of the room was accentuated by the whispering of a small well-laid fire.

He was about to call her when he saw a cloak that he had never seen before, a dark blue cloak with a collar of some kind of curly grey fur, tossed over one of the chairs. Had she rifled the gilded box and bought it in his absence? Its very modesty made that seem unlikely, and just as he came up close enough to notice that it was worn where the hand would hold it shut, the other door, the one to the hall, came open, and Titia—why Titia? Titia was to have gone home yesterday—came walking in.

"Oh," she said, plainly embarrassed, "I startled you—I'm sorry. You expected me to be gone."

"On the contrary. I'm very glad to see you," he said, congratulating himself that he could produce the required words even if they came out without conviction.

"I meant to go yesterday, but Saskia's been ailing—"

"Saskia? What's the matter?" She ailing, and he apart from her, among her enemies . . . "Did she lose the baby?"

"Oh, no, nothing as bad as that—I'm sorry if I made you think so. It's nothing but another one of her colds, but she was coughing, and Dr. Bonus thought she just *might* lose the baby if she didn't stay off her feet. She's to keep to her bed for another day or two, and I thought you wouldn't mind under the circumstances if I stayed on to see to the house and keep her company. That's my cloak—I ran out a while ago to get her some fresh rusks. I shouldn't have tossed it down like that, I know."

For the first time he looked at her and looked with kindness. Titia, who had always been the least striking among her sisters, had almost completely lost her looks. Her face was white rather than creamy, her eyes and hair both seemed to have faded, and her lips, wan and childishly parted, gave him a timid smile. Only a boor would have forced so inoffensive and well-meaning a creature into making an apology, and late and strange as it was for him to do it, he crossed the room and gave her a kiss. "Thanks very much, dear; I'm really very grateful," he said. "No, let the cloak alone, don't be foolish. It's all right where it is—I only wondered whose it was. It was very good of you to run out after rusks."

"Oh, it was no trouble at all. You'd better go to Saskia—she was getting restless, she thought you might have decided to stay another couple of days. She says you're sure to be hungry—I've made you a kettle of pea soup with a nice piece of bacon. I'll put it on a tray so you can eat it in the bedroom. You go ahead—you can't imagine how she's missed you, she's talked of nothing else."

Her voice, breathy and hurrying like Saskia's, trailed behind her as she went into the kitchen. Her back, thin and forcibly erect, was somehow appealing with the loose pale ringlets spilling over her unpretentious white collar, and he dropped his cloak and hat and gloves over hers—it would seem like a reproach to her to hang them in the closet.

But his charitable mood did not outlast his first fifteen minutes in the bedroom. Not that he found his wife sicker than her sister had led him to believe; in fact, lying rosy and beribboned in the corner bed, with the protuberance thrusting up the new velvet coverlet, she looked as if she were in glowing health. But the evening was not *their* evening and the room was not *their* room: how was a man to kiss his wife without reserve under the eyes of her sister, and where was he to sit since Titia, with the carelessness of a woman used to having a lady's maid pick up after her, had left something—a robe, a pair of gloves, a petticoat—on every chair? He took himself with his tray to a stool near the foot of the bed and ate in silence while the two of them chattered on. He was annoyed to learn that the visitor had been sleeping here instead of in the spare room prepared for her, and he was childishly disappointed in his soup—it was far too thick and peppery. From the stuff of their talk it grew plain that Saskia had been courting a cold: they had been to two little suppers, to a play and a concert, and they had been out on innumerable shopping trips. Whenever his glance settled on her where she lay with her hands clasped behind the nape of her neck and the ribbons bobbing in her curls, she sniffled; and it was obvious that she was making as much as she could of her little affliction in order to forestall his irritation. "Isn't the soup lovely? Titia made it for you," she said; and the remark was like a nudge in the ribs: he wasn't being as cordial to Titia as she could wish. She was much less concerned over their marred reunion than over seeing to it that he was a proper host; there was nothing in her manner to heal the bruise that he had gotten in Leyden or to fill up the emptiness.

Titia, uneasy again, went over to the chest of drawers and began to gather up her belongings.

"What are you doing, darling?" said Saskia.

"Gathering up my things to take them over to the other room—"

"But there's no great hurry about that, is there, Rembrandt?"

She was nudging him again, insisting that he be nice to Titia. Well, if she wanted him to be nice, he would show her how nice he could be. "No hurry at all," he said, smiling an artificial smile at the wan little person who kept darting back and forth with her arms loaded with underclothing. "In fact, why do anything tonight? I'm not in a hurry to move in; I can sleep perfectly well in the other room."

It was the guest—not *she*—who was appalled at that. The guest protested, but she insisted, pointing out that moving Titia's dresses from one closet to another would only keep him up longer when he plainly wanted to get to sleep as soon as he could.

Poor Titia stood immobilized, wrong if she stayed and kept him out of his bed and wrong if she moved and robbed him of his sleep. Her last frail claim to beauty had collapsed a moment ago when, unable to locate her nightcap, she had taken a pair of spectacles out of her pocket and set them far down on the bridge of her peaked nose—in spectacles, she looked depressingly like an unmarried aunt. "It would only be for to-night—I'm on my way tomorrow," she said.

"Tomorrow? Why tomorrow? Stay a while longer. Now that we're all together, it'll be pleasanter for you," said the husky voice from the bed.

"Certainly. We're hoping you'll stay three or four more days at least." He drank off the last lukewarm swallow of the unwanted soup and looked at Titia with false, overplayed cordiality. "Actually, you'd be doing me a kindness by staying. Saskia needs somebody to keep her company, and *I* certainly won't be available—I mean to spend every spare moment I've got at the warehouse working on the Regents' piece."

Titia did not go the next day, nor the following one, nor the one after that; and since she stayed on in a kind of captivity, only because he and Saskia kept pressing her with invitations to outspite each other, the days of her visit were tarnished, like his days in Leyden, with the yellowish cast of unreality. He woke in anger, alone and unrefreshed in the unfamiliar bed; he ate his breakfast in grim solitude because they had chattered through half the night and were sleeping until an indecent hour; he went into the studio in anger, banging the door behind him and hoping the noise would jar their dreams. He felt the more justified in his rage because he had renounced his people for the sake of his bond with her, and she—it meant more to her to make her sister at home than to hear of his bitter alienation from his family, or to help him turn his troubled mind toward the serene splendor of their future, or to lie in his arms with her head against his chest. Since the ultimate intimacy was forbidden them because of her pregnancy, she had no use for him: Titia was plainly a better companion than he. He could see how anger gnawed at her when she saw him get up from the table and start for the warehouse immediately after supper, so he made a point of rising at the end of the main course, leaving his beer unfinished and rejecting the sweet. And because he suspected that she waited in anxiety for him to come home, he stopped at a tavern on the way back and climbed the stairs and closed the door so quietly that she could not be sure when he came in.

On the third evening after his return and the last of Titia's stay—her belongings were packed, and Bol had arranged to take her to the wharf at seven tomorrow morning—his anger turned into something more sickly and disintegrating. He himself had caught a cold—certainly not from any contact with her, more likely because he had worked himself into a sweat at the warehouse; and the phantasmagoric cast that had colored his life since his homecoming was deepened by his feverishness. She was up and about for the first time that evening, and set the table herself as if for some high occasion with the best goblets and the finest cloth; and though he made it clear to her that only his clogged nose and aching throat kept him from going back to his canvas, he was glad his cold had saved him from spoiling her celebration.

He bore himself courteously at supper—at no time during the visit had he been really boorish to his sister-in-law—and ate of the goose and drank of the wine with the dry, insatiable appetite of a person with a cold. They had probably made some sort of agreement between them to appease him and draw him out, and he found himself talking more than he had meant to about the Regents' piece and the portrait of Pastor Anslo ordered by the little Mennonite congregation. He even caught himself addressing his wife directly two or three times—a thing that he had deliberately avoided doing since his return—and the ease of their exchange made their hostility seem unreal, though no more unreal than everything else.

At Titia's invitation—it was her last night with them and she had seen so little of him, she said—he came and sat with them in the bedroom, bringing his drawing board and paper and chalk and settling down on the stool at the foot of the bed. Saskia, either exhausted by her first exertions or apprehensive about what he was going to say to her once her sister was gone, climbed to safety again under the coverlet and sat against the heaped goose-feather pillows, and the chatter went on, though somewhat half-heartedly, perhaps because they had talked themselves out and perhaps because he was there. He took some pleasure in sketching in spite of having to stop every now and again to blow his nose or wipe his eyes. He made one delightful little drawing of Titia, busy like an aging lady over her lace-making, her thin ringlets loose in the lamplight and her spectacles far down on her nose; and the sketch was charitable, even loving—a fact that also confused him, considering that he had felt nothing for her but irritation since the night of his return.

"I must look dreadful in this condition," said Saskia plaintively.

"I don't know what makes you say so. You look well enough to me," he said.

"That's not so. I must look dreadful to you. I know because you haven't sketched me, not for days."

"I'll sketch you now," he told her, neither coldly nor with cordiality, but in a noncommittal voice. And he spent the remainder of the evening making a series of small drawings from which he pitilessly barred all fantasy, all appreciation of her beauty, all show of doting tenderness—five little drawings in each of which her face came out at once harried and slack, swollen with the strain of her pregnancy, strangely full in the lips and somber in the eyes.

"Show them to me," she said, holding out her hand for them.

"No, they're not particularly pretty."

"I'm not particularly pretty myself."

Whereby she forced him to make her a more affectionate and gallant speech than the situation called for or his heart could freely provide; and his eyes, clouded by his persistence at drawing, again saw everything in the room in the sickly yellowish light.

Luckily, both the women wanted to go to bed early, Titia because she would have to get up at six and Saskia because her exertions—or her worries—had made her tired. He kissed each of them on the forehead with equal detachment before he gathered up his sketches and went into the studio; his nose was so stuffed by now that he knew he would have to blow until his head was clear before he himself could go to sleep. He placed the candle on the worktable and laid out the evening's productions in the small circle of wavering light—the flame kept bending and swaying because a gale was blowing in from the sea. The one of Titia pleased him, but those of Saskia were somehow disturbing: they were honest enough in themselves, but there was some taint of pretense in them—probably her pretense of illness.

He took up the last of the drawings and studied it closely. Her pose —the head sunken deep into the pillow and the arms trailing over the coverlet—would have been effective if it had not been spoiled for him by the thought that nobody with a minor affliction had a right to look so pathetically limp and sad; but give the pose to somebody gravely ill, somebody on the point of dying, and the taint of affectation would be gone. The lines of the drawing were sparse and light and deft; he could imagine them on a copper plate, and he thought how pleasant it would be to have some large, elaborate etching to work on here at home in the evenings once her sister was out of the house and the two of them had made their peace. He held the sketch a little closer to the candle—it seemed to change and breathe in the uncertain light of the blown flame —and tried to think of a subject that would allow him to put it to use. What women in Scripture had been seriously sick? Sarah? Rebecca? Judith? Magdalen? Mary or Martha? Mary Mother? There were many legends about the last illness and death of the Virgin: Saint John had been with her, and others of the apostles, and angels had waited in the room, ready to transport her soul to Paradise. And highly Catholic though the subject was, and likely even to lead him into an unhealthy kind of pathos, he made up his mind to etch Mary Mother at the instant of her death.

Now that his choice was made, he knew he would do better to go to bed at once. He was in no condition for drawing: his head was aching and his eyes were undependable and his nose was so stuffed that it kept making a wheezing sound. But he could not abandon the figures that were crowding so swiftly in upon him; he had to reach for a big piece of paper and get the lines and masses and shadows down in at least a summary fashion in a larger sketch: he could not trust his feverish brain to hold so much intact through a troubled night. His hand, not as adept as usual but adept enough for his purpose, drew a canopied couch and a dying female form upon it, three angels moving vaguely above the canopy in a cloud of light, and a group of mourners merely suggested by slashing lines—apostles and saintly women, servants and children, weeping or standing by in silent awe. When the first fierce effort was over, he noticed with surprise that he had left the whole lower part of the sheet of paper blank: he had separated himself from the death scene by a big vacant stretch of foreground, as though what went on behind that emptiness was too pitiful to approach. Such an expanse could not, of course, remain in the final rendering; and he did what he could to remedy the error—he drew three steps leading up to the couch, which he decided to put on a kind of dais, and he added an ornamental foot-piece to the couch itself, pulling it out with curved and fanciful lines into the empty space. It was not until he straightened up, his head throbbing and his eyes half blind, that he realized there was something familiar about that ornamental foot-piece. It was impossible for him to deceive himself—it was very like the one at the bottom of *her* little couch, the one on which she had been Danaë and would be Danaë again and yet again, with the grace of God.

A draft from the leaded window made the flame of the candle waver. The flickering light was somehow ominous—awkwardly he put out his hand to steady it and was thrown into consternation when he almost knocked it over: to be in the dark at that moment seemed as terrible to him as to lie, still living, in the shut blackness of the grave. His chalk rolled off the edge of the worktable, and he could not reach after it with his nerveless fingers. But what has come over me, why am I terrified? he asked himself. Surely not because I have given my Protestant soul to a Catholic subject. And surely not because I have put a dying woman on Saskia's couch—what other couch should I put her on? I see that couch a dozen times a day, and it is only natural that the griffin at the foot of it should be engraved on my brain . . . But much as he despised himself for doing it, he sat down again and rubbed at the chalky lines with his thumb—rubbed and rubbed until no trace of the gilded beast remained.

As he started for the door he realized that he was shaking, but it was only to be expected that his fever should be followed by this chill which made it difficult for him to undo his clothing and turn back the covers with his trembling hands. The warmth under the heaped quilts and blankets pervaded his body; he could feel his sickness and the murky illusions of his sickness subsiding in him and around him: it was not terrible, only restful and comforting to his tired eyes, to lie in the dark. And before he fell asleep he was thinking in a sane and craftsmanly manner of certain changes he meant to make in the sketch tomorrow: there should be a chair and a seated figure to fill up the vacant space at the foot of the dais, and the cloud of light around the angels should be only a little more intense than the light around the dying woman's face.

*

The monthly meeting of the Board of Regents of the Old Men's Home adjourned much earlier than usual. Two of the more garrulous members were absent; the June heat, accumulated in the wood and

332

leather and rich carpets of the little chamber, robbed everybody of the inclination to gossip; and Dr. Tulp found himself at four o'clock with nothing in the world to do.

These unexpected periods of respite, these blessed spots of blankness on the crowded pages of his days, were, he supposed, his reward for filling his life almost to bursting. Another man's wife and daughter, accustomed to seeing him come home early now and again, would have minor pleasures or duties ready for him on such occasions; but his, having learned to get on without him, would show something close to consternation if he turned up before five. Another Board member could not hope to get across the length of the Old Men's gardens without an invitation to have a tankard in a tavern, but his colleagues, remembering how many boards he served on, how many hours he spent in the hospital and the Pest House, and how little time he had left for his pharmacopoeia, would never venture to make such a suggestion. There were certain losses entailed, of course: lads at the Surgeons' Guild whom he would have enjoyed talking to asked him their pre-worded questions as briefly as if a battle were going on; patients felt that they were imposing on him if they described their symptoms; and his wife took it for granted—and seemed a little put out if it proved otherwise— that Saturday was the only day that could be spared for love. In return for all of which he got such hours as this—hours as empty as the hours of a homeless vagabond or a drunkard sitting in sweet, dull vacuity on the stoop of an inn, hours when nobody wanted anything of him and the jangling insistence of his obligations stopped all at once, and he could feel his body seeping up the sun. When he was handed such an hour, he never marred it with conscience, never asked himself what he ought to be doing, only what it was that he most wanted to do. So, if he made his way toward the van Rijns' new place on Saint Anthonies Breestraat, it was not because he ought to see how the poor thing was doing now that her third one was buried beside the other two nor because custom required one to visit a man in his new home and wish him luck. It was because the big house was bound to be cool and Saskia would be wearing a thin summer dress, and the proud possessor of so many rooms and so much new furniture would be too busy talking to object to a weary silence on the part of his guest.

She *was* wearing thin clothes, a blue-grey dress that made her look unusually slight in the solid splendor of the new entrance hall. The place *was* cool and reposeful—coolness seemed to come up from the big black and white tiles in the pattern of a Saint George Cross, and serenity emanated from the great carved chest, the antique statues, the pictures in their heavy gilded frames, the tall leather chairs. But there were others there, Vrouw Pinero and the queenly Vrouw Lazzara; they came up behind her like crows trailing after a bluebird; and in their matronliness and their black bonnets they made him wonder how it was that nothing—not the terrible deliveries, not the stresses of a stormy if ardent marriage, not even the little bodies lowered in their coffins—had taught her to grow old. "Oh," she said, bright-eyed and breathless, "I wish you had come an hour ago. I've just finished taking these ladies all through the house, and I swear—as proud of it as I am and as much as I love you—I simply haven't the strength to run up another flight of stairs."

"Do sit down, Saskia," said Vrouw Lazzara.

She subsided onto a chair and fanned herself with her hand. Nobody could sweat as becomingly as she: little beads stood like dew on the bridge of her nose, and her curls were plastered to the lovely round of her brow.

"I didn't come to see the house; there'll be plenty of occasions for that. I came to see you and your husband," he said.

"As for seeing my husband, I'm sorry to disappoint you, but you'll have to do as well as you can with only me. He isn't in, he's over near the Bourse, up to his ears in the law. No, don't look so alarmed, it's only a bankruptcy business—my poor cousin Hendrik's gone into bankruptcy."

"I'm sorry to hear it."

"So am I, I can tell you. Especially since he owes my husband a thousand florins—he's owed it to him for years. Rembrandt's over at the lawyer's now, seeing if there's a chance of getting any of it back. I don't suppose you know anything about that sort of thing?"

"No, not really." It was difficult for him to keep his face in order, shocked as he was by the enormity of the sum and surprised at the lack of circumspection that allowed her to discuss a private financial matter in the presence of visitors. "Those businesses are usually complicated, and even a lawyer would have to know the particulars before he could judge—"

"Well, I'm no lawyer," she said, smiling up at them and crossing and uncrossing her plump little feet, "but I'd wager Rembrandt won't get a penny of it back. Which is very regrettable, because he'll come home in one of his bearish states, and I did so want him to take me to a play tonight."

"Madame," said a not-altogether-respectful voice somewhere above their heads.

He looked up and realized for the first time that a handsome balcony with a balustrade of polished spindles opened out from the second floor over the reception hall. Leaning over the railing was a maid whose elegant cap framed a sullen and resentful face.

"Really, Saskia," said Vrouw Lazzara, pulling herself up to all of her regal height, "you should teach that girl that she isn't supposed to shout at you. If she wants to ask you something she can always walk downstairs."

"I know, I told her that yesterday, but she doesn't remember. What do you want, Maartje?"

"That big statue in the studio—the one the apprentices are drawing —am I supposed to scrub that too?"

"Yes, certainly. I told you to scrub everything in there, didn't I? But wait a minute, now that I come to think of it, maybe you'd better not— it's plaster, it might melt or something. I guess you'd better let it alone."

Vrouw Pinero stepped into the middle of the big expanse of black and white tiles and addressed the sulky personage on the balcony. "Stone and tile you scrub. Plaster you wipe off with a cloth that is barely damp. And don't shout at your mistress over the balcony, especially when she's entertaining guests. It's never done, never," she said.

Whereupon the servant disappeared into the darkness behind the balustrade, and the two ladies made their farewells, and he was left with her in an entrance hall whose magnificence seemed authentic only after the others were gone. Its grandeur called for one of two things—either a great assembly such as used to gather in the old days at the house of the van Hoorns, or for emptiness. Anything between made its spaciousness and its splendor either chilling or ridiculous.

"It's terribly big, isn't it?" she said ruefully.

"Impressive—very impressive."

"Oh, if you think this is impressive, wait until you see the salon."

"Sit still. I'll see it another time."

"No, I want to show it to you." She got up with a child's sprightliness and laid her hand in his, moist and warm and so innocently self-surrendering that a man reproached himself for taking too much pleasure in the touch. "Rembrandt would never forgive me if I neglected to take you in there," she said, leading him through a hallway whose shadows yielded him the opaque curve of a marble wine-cooler and the flash of a big mirror. "It's for guests, and we'll never have a more important guest than you: he always says you were the first, if it hadn't been for you he might never have made a start."

He stopped behind her on the threshold, prepared for splendor, but not such splendor. The room—an enormous oblong carpeted with Oriental rugs and ceilinged with great dark beams—could have accommodated a court reception. The three tall casement windows were draped in saffron-colored damask; the wainscoting, three rows of squares made of some rare and highly polished wood, went two-thirds of the way up the wall. The space was so large that for an instant he had the impression that it was only partially furnished: the precious things—the carved table, the ten Spanish chairs covered with green velvet, the statues of gods or emperors, the unbelievable collection of Brouwers and Ruysdaels and Lastmans and Seghers—seemed like little islands on the surface of a broad, blank sea. "How many beautiful things you two have accumulated!" he said.

"Oh, do you think so?" she asked, drawing him in beside her and looking up at him in gratification. "I'm so glad. To me—and to Rembrandt too—once we got them in here they seemed a little lost. Won't you sit down? The chairs *are* to sit on, though nobody's done it—"

"Haven't you had an evening since you moved in?"

"An evening? Here? Oh, no." She lifted his hand and brushed it lightly against her cheek. "You know we wouldn't have an evening without inviting *you*," she said, drawing him with her toward a pair of princely chairs set close to the great oak table. She sat down, her cloudy skirt spread over the velvet and her hair on fire in the light from the window, and propping her elbow on the table top and resting her moist chin against her hand, looked up ruefully into his face. "We haven't had any evenings, not yet. We're not doing anything—we're waiting, simply waiting," she said.

"And what are you waiting for?" he asked, letting himself down circumspectly onto the new green velvet. He hoped that they wouldn't be waiting for another doomed child.

"Why, for the picture to be finished—the Regents' piece. The first of our evenings here is going to be a celebration for it, like a christening feast, with all his friends and patrons in and all the hard work over and nothing to do but eat and drink and dance. You couldn't even *talk* to him about an evening now: every spare minute he's got he's off at the warehouse painting away, and even when he's around he's so preoccupied he doesn't hear half of what a person says."

"And in the meantime I suppose you keep yourself busy with the house."

"It *ought* to keep me busy; there's enough of it, God knows." She fetched up a sigh that lifted her breasts, still strangely virginal under the intricate pleatings and tuckings of the blue-grey cloth. "But to tell you the truth, I don't do very much—whatever I try turns out to do more harm than good. I'll ruin something precious yet; if I haven't done it up to now it's only because Vrouw Pinero always stops me before I make a fatal mistake."

"Maybe you ought to get yourself more capable servants."

"That's true, we certainly should, but good servants cost money, and Rembrandt's gotten himself into such a worry over the amount we're spending these days. Actually, I suppose he's got good reason: every time you turn around there's another expense."

"Like this business of your cousin Hendrik—"

"Oh, that's the least of it. I sometimes think the Regents' piece will cost him more than he'll ever get out of it. He has to keep on renting the warehouse because the canvas is too big to be worked on anywhere else, even here, and while he's busy with that he can't do much of anything else. As for the apprentices—we thought he'd make considerably more from them now that they're living with us and he's raised their fees, but actually the gain's ridiculously small. It's extra work to clean up after them upstairs, and he sees to it that they get better food than he expects for himself, and there just isn't enough to take care of the bills. Last month and the month before and this month too we had to take out a little more of mine—he still insists on calling it mine—"

He put up his hand, less to fend off a fly that had come zooming through the window than to have something between himself and her candid eyes: he did not want her to see the worry that must certainly be showing in his face, and he was glad when the silence was broken by the grating of a key in a distant lock and the loud reverberations of a banged faraway door. "That's Rembrandt," she said, shaking out her curls. "Don't say anything about my telling Maartje to scrub the plaster, will you? He doesn't have to know."

The host came in so grim that it was hard to imagine him concerning himself about a plaster cast. Something, either the heat or his exasperation over the business at the lawyer's chambers, had prompted him to turn his elegance into a caricature of itself: his bottle-green jacket hung over his arm, his shirt was crumpled and pasted with sweat to the barrel-like curves of his chest, his little beard was matted, and his hair stood out like the mane of a lion around his head. "I knew it was you—I saw the hat in the reception hall and knew it was you," he said, coming up to shake hands.

"I'm afraid I chose a bad moment."

"Nonsense. You know I'm always glad to see you, though I can't say I'm in a state for anybody else."

"Was it as bad as all that?" asked Saskia.

"Bad? It was ruinous. It's gone, all of it." He flung the damp jacket with its sharp silver buttons onto the top of the polished table and turned to the doctor. "A thousand florins—to say nothing of the interest that would have accumulated on it—gone, just gone."

"I know, Saskia was telling me. Couldn't you salvage anything at all?"

"Two hundred, if I wanted to be a dog about it. I took it and handed it over to Hendrik on the way out—the poor devil, it's all he's got. You couldn't leave a friend without a cent to his name, could you? After all, he's got to eat and pay his rent."

It occurred to the doctor that a man without an amethyst earring might with more decency have claimed some part of the two hundred; but he did not say so, he only pursed his lips and shook his head.

"Damn it," said his host, slapping vainly after the veering fly, "I'm in no position to take such a big loss. I've no idea where the money goes, but it certainly goes." He walked to the back of his wife's chair and stood looking mournfully down on the sunlit round of her little head. "It's not the house—I'm sure we can afford that—but I've got to stop buying pictures and antiquities. You may not believe it, but I've made a new beginning. That little Palma Vecchio I asked to have put by for me—I stopped on my way back from the Bourse and told them to sell it elsewhere. No more of that sort of thing for me—not until the Regents' piece is done, anyway—and no more pearls and furs for you, my love." He bent and pressed his mouth down onto her clustering curls.

"Oh, I don't need anything, I have plenty," said Saskia, laughing.

He straightened and let his hands, raw and hairy, pass over the cool curves of her arms. "From now on we'll be living like monks—we'll subsist on fish and cheese and beer."

"That'll be no great hardship for you—that's all you eat anyway. Feed the apprentices a diet like that, and maybe we'll really save something."

"They're growing lads, they need their meat and greens. Master van Swanenburgh and Master Lastman always fed *us* well enough, God rest their souls. We'll save in other ways—but this sort of talk can scarcely interest the doctor." His pale eyes, suddenly bright with a surge of penitence and affection, sought the eyes of his guest.

"Your house is beautiful."

"Oh, I forgot—this is the first time you've been in it. You mustn't judge it from the way it looks now. It takes more things to fill it up than I thought it would. Has Saskia taken you around to see it?"

"No, darling, I haven't. We got to talking, and besides, I was a little tired."

"That's right. Don't go rushing up and down stairs in this heat." He bent and kissed her again on the top of her head. "But isn't she blooming, when you consider everything she's been through? Have you ever seen her looking better?"

Once, the doctor thought, once only: at a little supper in the bachelor's quarters of that same bankrupt Hendrik, before you were living like a famous painter or I was somebody for burgomasters to reckon with or she had eaten the fruits of love. She danced into an empty Oriental ceremonial robe, and dust was shaken out of the vacant sleeves; she danced that night as if there were no limit to the air that mortal lungs can draw through parted mortal lips. The measure has grown statelier now: you do not blush so much, and I think twice before I speak, and she—proud as she is of her new house and much as she loves me for old time's sake—can't be forever running up and down the stairs. "No indeed, never—she doesn't look a day over twenty," he said, hoping that his voice was casual enough to distract attention from the tears standing in his eyes.

"Why should I? I have nothing to age me."

In the warm stillness the doctor thought how all that might have aged her had been taken early away—the little seeking mouths, the clamoring voices, the importunate hands. Snip off the buds . . . so his mother had said at work in her garden God knows how many years ago: snip off the buds if you want to get a perfect Guelder rose . . .

"Maartje will age you—Maartje would age anybody," said Rembrandt.

"Oh, she's not as bad as that. Tell me, how was poor Hendrik?"

"Reasonably cheerful, considering the circumstances. I imagine he'll feel the shock of it later. He asked me to give you his love. Oh, and there was something else he wanted me to tell you—I almost forgot: he said you'd want to know that his sister wrote him to say your old Aunt Saskia died."

"Aunt Saskia?" She tilted back her head, and her cheeks crinkled like clotted cream, and all the doctor's mournful musings broke up with the giddy transformation that was coming about in her face. "Do you know what that means? I'm her godchild, and there's two thousand for me in her will—that's twice as much as we lost by poor Hendrik. Isn't it wonderful? I'm sorry she died, of course, but then she was close to ninety, and all I can think is: Isn't it wonderful?"

It was plainly so wonderful to both of them that they needed privacy to enjoy it: the doctor's presence kept them trimming the wings of their exultation down to the proportions of common decency. Yet they managed, in spite of the hampering circumstances, to establish the fact that it really was two thousand florins, that they should have it in autumn since the courts of Friesland were usually quick about such matters, that no more of her dowry need be touched—the legacy would certainly last until he had finished the Regents' piece . . .

It was a subject they could not completely abandon during the short remainder of his visit. They forced it into the background while they asked the required questions about his wife and his pharmacopoeia and his daughter and the chances of his serving on a mission to the Prince at The Hague; they held it in abeyance while they begged him to stay to supper but it asserted itself once more while they were walking him across the tiled floor of the reception hall.

"You'll buy the Palma Vecchio now, won't you, darling?" she said, stopping to look up at an empty place on the wall evidently reserved for that treasure. "How much was it—a hundred and fifty florins? We'd never notice, not with two thousand coming in."

And it was gratifying—so gratifying that he felt almost exhilarated on his walk home—to hear that Aunt Saskia's demise had not shattered the husband's good intentions: nothing was going to be bought— not the Palma Vecchio nor the Japanese teacups nor the silver forks nor the bonnet with the ostrich plumes—absolutely nothing until he had finished the Regents' piece.

*

In the court outside the Military Club, Captain Banning Coq had sensed an unmistakable softness in the January air: the icicles hanging from the iron grillework had visibly dwindled, the caps of snow had fallen from the stacked lances, and there were faint purple edges to the sunset clouds. But inside, the penetrating damp of a hard winter had stored itself and was scarcely mitigated by the two sluggish fires, and wet cloaks and mufflers still cluttered the chairs. Well, it couldn't be too much longer before Ruytenberg would get there, even allowing for his usual lateness—so the captain thought as he let himself down into his usual seat and stared at a wan patch of radiance on the darkening wall.

Doubtless the emptiness of that wall was what the lieutenant wanted to see him about. He had a note in his pocket, delivered that afternoon by one of Ruytenberg's servingmen: "See me this evening at the club-house if you can. It seems that some of the lads were raising a fuss about the Regents' piece last night." He supposed they had good reason: a year had gone by since the first installment had been paid, and he had never been able to wrest from the painter even an approximate date on which the painting would be done. The idea of angling further for some sort of commitment was one that he didn't relish; the last time he had tried it his usually amiable host over in the new quarters on Saint Anthonies Breestraat had almost taken offense. It seemed that the completion of a masterpiece, like the growth of a barley grain in the husk or a child in the womb, followed its own unhurried, inexorable course. It seemed that those who kept asking questions were guilty of indecent prying that was likely to blast the sensitive, inchoate thing. As for the down payment—he had been given to understand that it bought nothing but the finished piece and that anybody who imagined it entitled him to come spying around the warehouse was crass, presumptuous, and totally ignorant of the mysterious workings of art.

That the painting *was* coming on, the captain never doubted. Their conversations in the splendid new salon were about the Regents' piece and nothing else. But listening to talk about it and making inquiries about its progress were two different matters; the mere words "And when do you think you might . . . ?" were enough to bring a stubborn hardness into the heavy jaw and an icy warning into the pale eyes. Last Friday evening—possibly because he had *not* made any efforts to elicit information—the artist had rewarded him with a little present, the sketch from which he had been working. "Here, you can have this; I won't be needing it any more," he had said somewhat haughtily, tossing it across a plate of buttered bread. "All the figures are on the canvas now, and the big divisions of space are set, and so are the major areas of light and shade." But grateful as the captain was for such reassuring news, he knew it would be bad strategy to repeat it to Ruytenberg or any of the others who were objecting to the long delay. They would conclude that the work was almost finished, and he, watching the ghostly patch of light fade out on the polished wood before him, was afraid that spring would come and go and maybe summer too before anything would cover that empty wall.

"What's the captain's pleasure?" said old Jacob, coming up to the table with a spotted napkin over his shoulder. "We have a delicious cabbage soup this evening—"

"It doesn't smell delicious—but I'll take it anyway. Why don't you stir up the fires? It's downright dank in here tonight."

Now that he had vented some of his irritation on old Jacob, he could contemplate the little discussion that lay before him with more equanimity. He would make them understand that they had no course but patience, that the painter could not be hurried without prejudice to the painting, that insistence might plague him into throwing up his hands and refusing to finish the thing. Were they willing to wait for the picture until June or July, or would they prefer to do without it? Heer van Rijn —it ought to be obvious from the kind of house he lived in—was a man of means and wouldn't think twice about returning their down payment. Heer van Rijn—he had no scruples about exaggerating—had more people clamoring at his door for portraits than he could hope to take care of in two or three years . . . And, with his plans well laid, he allowed himself his usual indulgence: he stared at the wall and evoked the painting that in any event would be hanging on it one of these days.

The soup and the lieutenant arrived almost simultaneously and were equally unsatisfactory. The soup tasted more or less as it had smelled; and the lieutenant, instead of stating his business and having done with it, sighed and fell into a hunched and weary pose on the other side of the table, staring ruefully at the spotted board and distorting his cheek against the palm of his hand.

"I suppose," said the captain, annoyed that he should be forced to indicate anxiety by broaching the subject, "the lads have begun to complain about the delay."

"The delay? No, *that* they're more or less resigned to, though I'm sure they'd still want me to ask you when he expects to be finished."

"How the devil should I know? He's at it enough; he's at it day and night. Why don't you drop over there and ask him yourself?"

There was a thrust in that: the lieutenant, discouraged by a shortage of gaiety and the presence of what he considered an inordinate number of Jews, had been slack in his visiting of late. "Much good that would do me," he said, without changing his disconsolate position. "The last time I asked him, he glared at me as if I'd committed a crime."

"Well, if he's touchy these days, it's no great wonder. The third child gone, and his mother dead, and a thousand florins gone over the mill-wheel in that bankruptcy of Uylenburgh's—"

"Still, he could tell a person how he's coming along."

"He did tell me, and you could have heard too if you'd troubled yourself to drop in there with me last Friday evening. He says that all the men are on the canvas—"

"I'm glad to hear it," he said without the slightest show of gladness. "I'm very glad to hear it, and I only hope it's true. Nobody bothers *you* about it—they wouldn't dare. But not a week goes by when somebody isn't at *me,* and this week it's been worse than ever because of that epigram of Vondel's. I wish he would have waited to circulate the damned thing until the picture was on the wall."

Two things were disturbing: he could not imagine what, other than the artist's slowness, could be upsetting the lads, nor could he understand how, man about town that he was, a circulating epigram could have bypassed him. "Oh, well, Vondel . . . ," he said, playing for time and sending a covert glance around the sparsely populated clubroom. None of the members of his own company were there, which meant that they could at least talk freely, whatever it was that they were going to talk about.

"You didn't hear it, did you, Banning?" said the lieutenant, not without satisfaction. "I'm surprised you didn't; it certainly made the rounds. It's on Rembrandt's painting of Anslo, the one he did for the Mennonite congregation. I suppose it's clever the way Vondel put it: he cut the painter down by making a great to-do over the sitter—rather a neat trick, you'll admit. Wait a minute, I think I can say it:

> *"O Rembrandt, give us Anslo's voice in art.*
> *Not for his visible aspect do we seek*
> *But that which the ear discerns, his nobler part.*
> *Truly to see Cornelis, hear him speak."*

"If that's supposed to be amusing, I have a feeble sense of humor."

"I didn't say it was amusing. I said it was unfortunate. The lads got hold of it just when they were all worked up over the delay. If it hadn't been for that epigram, it would never have come into their heads to go to the warehouse—"

"To the warehouse?"

"Yes, that's what I wanted to talk to you about. A couple of the lads —Schellingwou and Cruysbergen, to be exact—went over there last evening. I told them not to, I told them he'd be furious and so would you, but they'd had more than their measure of beer and they wouldn't pay attention."

How many times, strolling past that warehouse, he had put down his own desire to go in and feed his hungry eyes—he who had been the originator of the whole plan, he who was the artist's intimate friend, he who had laid out a larger percentage of the down payment than anybody else! And to think that two of his inferiors, in their cups and as arrogant as if they had had every right in the world, had simply presented themselves at that forbidden door! Cruysbergen and Schellingwou, of all people—the one a shallow gallant who knew more about dice than about art, and the other the son of an upstart family, a fellow who ought to thank God that his vulgar face was about to be immortalized in a masterpiece. "Surely they didn't get in," he said.

"Oh, yes, they got in." The lieutenant hunched even more despondently over the table. His eye, scarcely visible between his knuckles and the damp brim of his beaver, did what it could to avoid the captain's look. "Nobody was there but Bol, and he told them he had orders that nobody was to see the picture, but they were drunk and insistent, and I guess there wasn't much he could do."

"And I suppose, connoisseurs that they are, they're ready now to give us their expert opinions," he said in a voice whose icy sarcasm somehow failed to come off.

"Well, they had a few objections . . ."

"And what were their objections?"

"Oh, what's the good of going over it, Banning? Even if the figures *are* all put on, the painting's far from finished, and they were drunk, and the light was poor, and, besides, you can hear what they've got to say yourself. They told me this morning they'd like to have a word with you, and I thought the best way to arrange it was to say they could probably find us here tonight."

The soup, unappetizing before, became intolerable. He pushed it away and did not know where to look—not at the blobs of grease floating on the surface, not at the lieutenant's evasive eye, not at the doorway where the two of them would soon be coming in. No new arrivals had swelled the little company in the clubroom, but even the ten or twelve guardsmen sitting in pairs at the distant tables made up too large an audience for the scene that might take place. "I can't see that there was any call to arrange a conference with those two," he said after an uneasy silence. "Cruysbergen thinks he knows everything and wouldn't be able to tell a Dürer from a Titian, and Schellingwou's a stupid ass who ought to keep his mouth shut and thank the Lord that he's in the Company at all."

"That's true enough, but they put their money down like everybody else. You know, Banning, now that I look back on it I wish we had shouldered the whole expense ourselves. That way, nobody would have had the right to complain."

That way, thought the captain, I'd have been out of pocket eleven or twelve hundred florins. Your word's as good as your bond, and your bond's worth nothing . . .

"That way, even if the picture *was* a bit fantastical and out of the ordinary, nobody would have the insolence to protest."

"Fantastical—is that their objection, that it's fantastical?" The captain's voice was loud enough to draw the attention of some who sat at other tables.

"I don't remember what word they used. I gathered that it wasn't what they'd expected—"

"And just what *had* they expected—something like those?" He gestured at the other canvases, its predecessors—the dull, serried ranks, the somber and unleavened faces scarcely visible in the uneven light of the fire.

"Who knows? Anyway, we'll soon find out—here they come."

The fact that the two of them were together was in itself disquieting: only a strong cause could bring such divergent natures into even a temporary unity. Cruysbergen, tall and slender, bore his comely body with cynical offhand ease, and Schellingwou had plainly just risen from a family supper and washed his face and put on a fresh white collar for the important interview. He crossed the big room diffidently behind his striding companion, his bull neck bent, his bullet head inclined, and his pudgy workaday hands hanging respectfully and a little helplessly at his sides. Perhaps it was his uncertain bearing that made him more acceptable to the captain than the self-assured dandy who came up to the table before him. If Schellingwou was thick and dull—more Germanic than Dutch—that was no fault of his; if he had overdone the martial treatment of his moustache by twisting the oiled ends up to emphasize a pair of porcine eyes, it was excusable in a man who took his military rank with grim seriousness. "A good evening to you, my captain and my lieutenant," he said. His companion, whose handsome face seemed the harder because it was framed in a cloud of loose and silky chestnut-colored hair, merely nodded, as if one salutation were enough in a situation as strained as this.

"Sit down, gentlemen," said the captain in what he hoped was a firm, if amiable, voice.

Cruysbergen eased himself into one of the proffered chairs, but Schellingwou remained standing, looking sadly down at the others. "We came because we had a little complaint to make, you know," he said.

"So the lieutenant told me. Sit down, I'm sure we can settle it. Jacob, over here again, if you please—we'll be needing a couple more tankards of beer."

"We were over at the warehouse last night," said Cruysbergen, not without belligerence.

He was hard put to it not to blast out at the insolent dandy. "If anybody had asked me, I would have advised strongly against it, since it went contrary to Heer van Rijn's wishes," he said. "But what's done is done, and I suppose you wanted to see how the work was coming along —I gather there's been some complaint about the delay."

"Well, yes," said Schellingwou, "a lot of the men *have* been saying he seems to be taking his own good time about it, but—"

"But there isn't much we can do about that, is there? Hurry him and you run the risk of spoiling the thing. I'm impatient too, but I keep telling myself he isn't delaying for his own pleasure. After all, the fee's the same regardless of time, and if he didn't have the picture so much at heart, it would be easy enough for him to turn out something shoddy and pocket his florins and go on to something else. Actually, we're lucky that he's willing to put so much effort into it—"

"I'm not so sure about that," said Cruysbergen. "Maybe the more he does to it, the more there'll be to object to."

Schellingwou blushed, the redness spreading slowly up from his fresh white collar to the puffy flesh around his little piggish eyes. "What he means, my captain," he said, looking miserably down at the tankard of beer which Jacob set before him, "is that some of the men are worried he'll only be making it more and more fantastical."

"Fantastical? How do you mean—fantastical?" It was impossible for him to control either his voice or his body, and he jarred the table so that the beer sloshed over onto the wood. "Everybody says there's nobody like him in Holland for color and movement and light; the best people in Amsterdam wait for months to sit for him; he suits the Prince and Constantyn Huyghens and Burgomaster van Pellicorne. And you two have the audacity to walk in there drunk and set yourselves up as judges of a man of his reputation!"

Schellingwou withered, but Cruysbergen sat precisely as he had been sitting from the start, his long body lolling back, his head tilted on one side, his eyes fixed steadily upon the captain's face. "I never said I was a judge of painting," he said in a voice that had only grown more arrogant, "but it doesn't take much taste to see that my face is half covered up by somebody else's arm. What I get for my money is what can be seen over the other fellow's sleeve: my eyes, my forehead, and my hat—which, I'll admit, is very nicely painted in."

But that was impossible. Something must come to mind in a moment to explain that out of existence: the bad light, the unfinished condition of the canvas, the unstable state of the drunkard's eyes. He looked at Ruytenberg, but Ruytenberg only played with his gloves and looked at the wall.

"He's telling you God's truth, my captain," said the unhappy Schellingwou. "And in my case it's even worse—nobody would know me, not even my wife. I'm in the back row, and I had a hard time convincing myself it was me. There's nothing but a small chunk of cheek and one eye and a bit of chin."

"Five or six of us are like that: there's not enough showing so that we're even recognizable," said Cruysbergen. "When we laid down our money we understood that the least we'd get would be likenesses. Nobody wants to pay to have his hat preserved for posterity."

"There must be some misunderstanding; it was taken for granted from the start that everybody would have a likeness," the captain said. A faint hope began to glow in his consciousness. "It isn't finished, you know; he keeps changing it. That's it: he must have made some changes, and some of you lads are painted out—temporarily of course—while the changes are going on. You, for instance, Cruysbergen: no doubt he had you fully painted in, and then, for some reason—to improve the design or something like that—he raised that fellow's arm so that it came across your face. But now that he's finished with that, he'll paint you in again; he'd never do just the top of your face, that much I know."

"Yes," said the lieutenant, "many's the time I've seen him scrape off a whole figure and repaint it." He pushed the untouched tankard closer to Schellingwou, who obediently took a few swallows, getting the foam on his chin.

"The painting will be satisfactory to everybody; I'll take the responsibility for that," said the captain, sick at his own placating tone. "The whole incident was very unfortunate. It's a pity you people walked in there and got yourselves upset over nothing. But I assure you on my word of honor that everything will be worked out to everybody's satisfaction—each member of the Company will be given proper attention."

"I hope so," said Cruysbergen, getting up without touching his beer. "We don't expect too much, you know—nothing like the attention that was given to the lieutenant's jerkin and the rosette on your shoe."

Once they were gone Ruytenberg pulled on one of his gloves and heaved up a sigh. "We barely came out of that with our skins," he said. "It was clever of you to improvise the repainting business."

"I didn't improvise it." He rejected the praise and the implication coldly. "It so happens I'm confident that the case is more or less as I described it."

"Really? How can you be sure when you haven't seen the picture?"

"I've seen the sketch of the picture. In fact, he gave it to me when I was over there last Friday night." He tried to summon up an image of that sketch, but it would not come: he saw nothing but crossing lines and bursts of light and a sharp little rendering of his own face. Had he or had he not noticed that certain of the faces toward the back were almost out of sight? He vaguely remembered an instant of uneasiness— probably he had had his doubts and had put them down by assuring himself that everything amiss would be set right in the final piece . . .

"Where have you got it?" asked Ruytenberg.

"At home in my album."

"That's splendid. Why didn't you say so? Suppose we walk over and have a look at it. Then we'll be able to tell what all the fuss is about."

But the lieutenant's suggestion was somehow more unnerving than the encounter with Schellingwou and Cruysbergen. Impatient as the captain was to look at the sketch, he meant to do his looking by himself; if some of the members of the Company had been crowded out behind the others, he wanted that shattering fact to break upon him in solitude. "That wouldn't be convenient," he said, getting up and staring straight into the small pert face. "There are guests at my house; once I'm in, I'll have to join the company. Anyway, I'm the one that did the ordering, and I'm the one who'll have to take the full responsibility."

*

For months now the painting had waxed and the world had dwindled away. The light of the painting had grown and encompassed him and left the world and all the comings and goings thereof in the shadow.

Vibrantly awake and acutely aware of himself, he painted the lieutenant's boots and the faces bobbing up at the back of the crowd and the streaming banner in the middle plane. His mother's dead face, the voices of his apprentices, the breathless talk of his little wife, the splendor and spaciousness of his new house—these were scarcely discernible where they lay on the dark side of the planet; these he knew only dully and remotely as in a muted dream.

In that world of incandescent light, time melted to nothing. These soldiers, for instance: they were the parading burghers of Amsterdam who had never fired at anything but a target; yet they were also their own forerunners, the ones who had driven the broken ranks of the Spanish blackbeards over the dunes into the muddy tides. The ghosts of those fallen sons of Leyden, evoked for him in his childhood by his father, sprang up full-armed in him now and issued onto the canvas through his daemonic hand. Harmen Gerritszoon himself was not a moldered corpse nor an old man remembering, wordless and loose-handed, in the sun; he was a boy dodging through the martial noise and magnificence. Then by some magical elision the boy was not his father, the boy was himself. And if time was canceled out, how could reason stand? The logic of theory and the common sense of burghers were both consumed in that waxing effulgence, and why should he try to preserve them? Who, being made a member of that ageless and glorious Company of Heroes, would be mean enough to object to the obliteration of some part of his earthy person? The flames went up higher every day, and rank was forgotten together with the immutable law of light and shadow. With the conflagration burning up his own brain, his own heart, the sparks must fall wherever they would.

In those months he realized for the first time that it was only in the act of painting—not in meditation, not in converse with his fellows, not even in the act of love—that he could break open the fruit of life and know its ultimate sweetness. From all the carnival nights and days of his years he had come away still hungry: here and here only was he really fed. Insights and visions utterly unavailable to him through contemplation yielded themselves graciously as the softness of the brush bent to the cloth; all the eloquence locked up in his halting tongue was spent in the suave strokes down the fall of the banner; he painted a bit of braid, a button, a waving plume more tenderly than he had ever touched her lips. His quarrels with the world were fought and settled in the converging lines of muskets and lances; old sorrows melted away in the peaceful spots of grey-green shade, and sometimes his happiness was such that he could not keep himself from singing aloud.

Always when he had finished the day's work he pulled his stool as far away from the painting as possible—nothing but that stool and a rickety worktable shared the enormous upper room with the canvas—and sat down to gaze at his masterpiece from a vantage point not nearly distant enough, his hands hanging between his knees, his head resting

347

against the cold wall. Bol, coming upon him on one such occasion, remarked that he looked exhausted, but he had rejected the word. "Exhausted" meant depleted, collapsed; and he preferred to think of himself as "spent"—and well spent, too: everything poured out, everything
freely given to that blazing image which had become his only reality.
Loving it so much, loving it beyond even himself, he delighted in being
prodigal for its sake. He squandered paint on it; he laid on the most
precious colors in fat, sleek layers, building the surface up until bits of
it actually stuck out: the drummer's sleeve was thick enough to slice,
and the gold braid on the lieutenant's jerkin was solid enough to grate
a nutmeg on. His strength, too, he paid out gladly; sometimes, when
he sat down, his knees were as unstable as water, and his hands were
seized with a trembling, and jagged silver lines—small lightning flashes
begotten by avid staring—flickered before his eyes. Nor was he miserly
with his hours: on days when he was free he scarcely bothered to wash
his face in his haste to leave the regal rooms of the new house. He was
as unconcerned about the food put before him on the great oak table
as a dog intent on finishing what it had left undone last night with a
mate or a deadly enemy; he did not know what it was that he chewed
and washed down with beer. He did not hear her words, either, only
her voice talking at him constantly of things that could not concern
him: it was as an incorporeal thing, seen through the remembered realities of muskets and lances that he perceived her face. Yet sometimes
when he sat dreaming in the warehouse with the sweat drenching his
shirt and the cold of the wall invading his aching shoulders, a vision of
her would intrude itself, a vision in which she was dressed in clothes
she had discarded long ago. He would see her in peach-colored muslin,
sinking down breathless onto the low stool in the old studio and asking
for a mug of milk; he would see her in the big straw hat that had
adorned her rosy cheek with flecks of light and shadow on the day of
their betrothal; he would see her in her crimson dressing gown, bending
over the cradle where the doomed Rombartus—or was it one of the
others, also buried?—slept a drugged and whimpering sleep. And always he would exorcise her as a troublesome spirit, though never without feeling a bruise on his heart. Well, troublesome she was, like everything that intruded upon his obsession—troublesome like food and drink
and sleep and the cloud that passed between the painting and the sun.
Later he would take her into his life again; later, later . . . only not
now while the wonderful canvas erupted before him, the golds and the
scarlets blaring like trumpets, the blacks and the blue-greens vibrant
like the roll of drums.

She never suggested that she come to the warehouse, and he never
invited her. Even Bol and Hoogstraten, who were as unobtrusive as
shadows and had been welcome enough in the beginning, knew now
that he could no longer bear to have them in the room; they satisfied

their aching curiosity by coming after supper, when the sun and he were gone, to stare at the marvel by candlelight. When they spoke of it in her presence, she made it obvious, a little childishly and pettishly, that she had other matters to occupy her mind: she did not care if he hurried in and out like a man possessed, if she had never been asked to see the picture, if weeks went by without a visitor—only it *did* seem to her that he could find a minute to draw the tulip she wanted to embroider on her tablecloth. He drew that tulip for her one February evening when they had been broken in upon by Coq and Ruytenberg, who had wanted a premature showing of the picture, a request which he had firmly, even harshly refused. And at the end of the next afternoon's short reign of winter sunlight, when his triumphal gazing at the day's accomplishments was interrupted by the sound of footfalls on the stair, he started up from his stool in anger, thinking that his importunate patrons were flouting his express prohibition—and was strangely unnerved to find that it was she. She stopped on the threshold, stopped short as if before a curtain of flame. The picture was there in front of her—vast, tumultuous, incandescent in the oblique rays of the sun—and no light he had ever seen was lovelier than the light that came flooding into her eyes. "Oh, God!" she said after long silence, putting her gloved hand up to her trembling lips; and he thought that the two things he would wish to remember on his deathbed were Constantyn Huyghens' sound of mating doves and her "Oh, God!"

After that, unfortunately, she felt called upon to be more specific. Her comments, plainly patched together out of remarks heard from the apprentices, would have annoyed him if her bright glance had not kept sweeping over the whole tremendous area of the canvas, if every now and again some snowy ruff or shining lance or effulgent plume had not shattered the order of her sentences and driven the borrowed compliments out of her head. Satisfied as he was already, he did not listen. He looked at her as he had not looked for weeks; his eyes, appeased with his earlier staring at the picture, were capable for the moment of taking her in. Her face was as fresh as a pink rose between the wintry beaver skins of her hat and tippet; and when he came and kissed her into silence, what he gave her was not the ghostly, half-awakened sort of kiss he had been giving her these many nights, but a hard, an almost bruising kiss.

"I suppose I get that as a reward for praising your picture," she said, pushing him off a little.

"Not at all—I kissed you because I wanted to."

"Really? Maybe there's something about this time of day, then—if so, I'll come again. No, don't worry, I'm only teasing. I came to tell you something important—otherwise, I never would have dared to break in on you."

From her sprightliness he could conclude only that she brought pleasant news: it was as if her old Aunt Saskia had died over again and the florins collected months ago were just about to come in. "And what did you want to tell me?"

"First I want to tell you your shirt is soaking wet. Don't go out like that—you'll get a cold if you do."

"Don't worry about *my* getting colds. You're the one—"

"Second, there's paint on your forehead."

"Yes, I know."

"And third, I'm pregnant—"

"Pregnant?"

"Yes." Her tremulous affirmation rode over the protest in his voice and the appalled look he could not keep out of his eyes. "I've just been to Dr. Bonus and he tells me there couldn't be the slightest doubt."

But, Jesus, was she mad that she should be pleased about it? Had she really no recollection of the past, no sight into the future that she should smile at him because she was destined to wrench her body for the fourth time to bear fruit for the grave? His own face congealed into a witless mask, and he damned her childishness and their evil luck and most of all himself. He was the one who had sown the blighted seed in her, and what was worse, had sown it heedlessly, scarcely even wanting, turning to her between sleep and sleep to cleanse himself of *that,* so that tomorrow he could see with clearer eyes and paint with a steadier hand. And even now, aware as he was that the old, monotonous agony might shatter her completely, he could not keep himself from looking over his shoulder at that painted blaze of light and power, could not help thinking how her suffering would encroach upon his hours, take his mind out of this brightness and thrust it back onto the turbid and darkling side of the world . . .

"You don't seem particularly pleased about it," she said.

"Oh, but I am—I certainly am." Out of the early years when he had still hoped, he drew the proper gestures, the proper facial expression. He put his arm around her shoulders in an imitation of the former tenderness; he smiled according to the dim remembrance of a former smile.

"If you're worried, I suppose I can't blame you." She drew herself out of his embrace and looked down at her small feet, booted in black velvet and set among puddles of oil and blotches of paint. "But you needn't be so sure it's going to die, either—"

"I never thought any such thing."

"Didn't you? You'd be a fool if you didn't. Still, it might not die— Bonus said it could be perfectly healthy. But if you think I shouldn't go talking to people about it, I won't. There's no need for anybody to suspect until it begins to show."

He did not answer because the late sunlight had moved to a new area of the canvas and was lighting up the silvery blue-green of the standard bearer's jerkin with a glow that was almost phosphorescent; but she took his silence for an assent to her promise of circumspection, and such an assent implied a reproof.

"Not that there would be anybody for me to talk to," she said. "I won't be going out much—Dr. Bonus wants me to keep off my feet—and nobody ever comes to our place any more. For all the company we have these days, it's ridiculous for us to live in a mansion; we might as well have stayed on New Doelen Street."

He could not pull his gaze away from the greenish radiance. "It won't be like this forever, it's bound to be finished some time," he said. But the finishing of the painting meant bereavement, and his voice carried a hint of his regret.

"Oh, you don't care if you never finish. If you had your way, you'd go on with it for another year."

A nagging memory buzzed through his thoughts like an aggravating fly: the men were put out by his slowness—two of them, drunken and insolent, had heckled poor Bol into letting them into the warehouse to see how much he had done. The incident had been so coarse and shameful that he had courteously refrained from embarrassing Coq and Ruytenberg by mentioning it, but he never thought of it without a strange confusion of panic and rage. "I'm scarcely dawdling. I work like a dray-horse, as you ought to be able to see," he said.

She straightened her hat and fastened her tippet. "Go ahead and work. I'll be on my way. I've held you back for fifteen minutes at the most, and I wouldn't keep you any longer for the world."

"I didn't mean you were holding me back. In fact, I was finished for the day. Don't be angry—wait until I've changed my shirt and I'll walk home with you."

He wanted desperately to have her agree to that. He wanted to stroll arm in arm with her through the busy streets, saying whatever might soothe and sustain her, guiding her around the puddles left by the melting ice, perhaps stopping with her at a pancake shop—for some reason he had never been able to fathom, she was always delighted to drink a cup of tea with him in a noisy public place. But when she had put her anger aside and had turned to him again with utter guilelessness, he felt no relief, no happiness. It was almost more than he could bear to walk away and close the door on that patch of blue-green satin gleaming as it might never gleam again for him or anybody else in the strange light of the withdrawing sun.

*

As spring came and passed into summer—damp, brooding, heavy with the sound of great warm drops falling on the furry surfaces of leaves—he found it necessary more and more often to abandon the light of the picture for the dark side of the world. She changed as she always did when the mass and weight increased within her, and her face laid stronger claims upon him because it was less beautiful with the lips and eyelids swollen and a determination to hope rather than hope itself steadying her long looks. That wounding thing she had said about its being ridiculous for them, solitary as they were, to live in a mansion kept nagging at him until he made up his mind to give an "evening." But when he sat with her, writing down the names of those to be invited, there was no pleasure in it; there was something almost elegiac about that list. Lotje and Allaert, Frans and Vrouw van Pellicorne, Hendrik Uylenburgh, the Tulps, Dr. Bonus, the good writing-master Coppenol, Margheretha van Meer and her churchly husband, Anslo, Swalmius, the Pineros, the Lazzaras, and Coq and Ruytenberg—though many of them were currently his friends and two at least were connected with the miracle at the warehouse, all seemed as far away as Jan Lievens and little Hessels. Everything, save only her and the picture, seemed to belong to the past.

Their "evening" was not a success in his estimation, though she seemed to enjoy it. It was difficult to take care of company in a new house. At the last minute there was a wild scramble for goblets and napkins that had been stored nobody knew where, and the extra spit in the kitchen, never tested to date, had a broken chain and would not turn—though that particular dilemma was a blessing in a way: it gave the constrained and ill-assorted assembly something to talk about. Then, too, though he had invited everybody he could think of, the little groups of hesitantly conversing humanity seemed too small for the palatial rooms. From their pedestals Caligula and Augustus and Faustina stared with cold marble eyes over the scattered guests in wordless disparagement of a gathering not to be compared with the gorgeous receptions they had known in their day. The world had declined from what it had been at the high tide of history or else—the thought sustained him through the mishaps and insufficiencies of the evening—the world had never been and never would be as glorious as what stood behind the locked door of the warehouse.

That "evening" did not quiet his nagging conscience as he had hoped it would. She seemed lonelier than ever after it was over, so lonely that he decided on a further indulgence: his free Saturdays, which he had been spending on the picture, he would devote to her from this time on. The mornings would be given to leisurely talk, the afternoons to shopping trips, the evenings to a play or a visit if somebody invited them out, though that was unlikely because they had been so withdrawn of late that nobody thought to ask them any more. On the first Saturday he conducted himself admirably, even holding his tongue when the pleasure of his company led her into high-hearted spending; but the second Saturday was marred by a letter from home, a dour letter in Adriaen's crabbed hand. Lysbeth was sick, gravely so according to Dr. Duartszoon. Whether she would want to see Rembrandt or Rembrandt would want to see her, the writer would not presume to judge;

yet he felt it his duty to make the facts of the matter plain: her feet and legs were swollen to half again their normal size, her pulse was fluttering and scarcely perceptible, and for hours on end she labored for breath.

The news distressed his little wife profoundly, though he did not show her the letter and did what he could to minimize the distressing physical details. She refused to go shopping and rejected a suggestion that they take their noonday meal in an eating place; and after lunch she went into the bedroom, where he found her weeping on the bed. More because she insisted than through any will of his own—he was strangely without any impulse, as though his mind and heart, incapable of the proper grieving, had dulled themselves to everything else—he went slowly about the business of packing to go to Leyden; he would set out late on Monday, after he had assigned a problem to his apprentices. But on Monday there was no longer any need for his going: another letter in the same stiff handwriting delivered and arraigned and rejected him. It was a letter that Antje must certainly not have seen. Antje, the only one left of those who had shown him kindness in that emptied house, would never have assented to such scourging bitterness:

My dear Brother:

It will not be a surprise to you to learn that our sister Lysbeth was summoned to the bosom of our Lord and Saviour last night.

Though it would be possible to delay the funeral until you and your wife could stand at the grave with us, I have decided not to do so. Both Antje and myself are worn out with long watching, and until the body is laid away neither of us will be able to rest.

Do not reproach yourself unduly that you are not here to assist at the obsequies. I did not expect you to come. I have borne the burden of Lysbeth's sickness as I bore all the others. After the years I spent—and Antje with me—seeing to our crippled brother, our aged mother, and a mill which has always lain like a stone on my shoulders, it seems to me a small duty, in which I need no assistance, to lay our sister in her grave.

Your brother,
Adriaen Harmenszoon

Grief struck him then for all three buried without his having truly mourned them: Gerrit, his far-searching eyes sealed up in everlasting darkness; his mother, her rustling skirts pressed down forever around her motionless feet; Lysbeth, her puffy, futilely seeking hands folded at last. He would have taken the boat to Leyden that same night if it had not been for the scalding letter: it would have been a privilege, it might even have opened the floodgates of his churning heart to see, to touch, to lie across those graves. "Go home," Saskia said, standing apart from him, in awe of his person because it held such sorrow. "Go home and make your peace with your brother—tell him I kept you here, lay the blame on me." But he could not go: he lacked the courage to withstand the moist, accusing glance; he did not have the humility for saying, "I am heartily sorry," or the good will for saying, "God knows I am grateful that you carried such burdens for me."

He did not go, and he might as well have gone, for all the good the staying did him. For the first time in years he could not depend on his fingers to do what he wished; something—had God's judgment indeed been visited upon him?—something had simply gone out of his hand. He did not go to the warehouse because he knew that once there he could never resist the impulse to work at the painting, and he was afraid he might mar any part of the canvas he touched. For half the night he walked the vast, reproachful, unfamiliar rooms, too fearful of dreams to be able to close his eyes. He could not eat, especially not meat; all flesh, even the flesh of the first summer fruits, seemed to carry the taint of corruption. "If you don't feel like painting, why don't you do some drawings?" she said, coming up to him, beautiful in her shy self-mistrust and her need to help him. "I'll sit for you, or you can draw Liesje or Maartje or the cat or whatever you please." But though he sketched with some diligence on Tuesday, Wednesday, Thursday, and Friday, his trouble did not lesson: the lines on the paper were so loose and characterless that he burned the sketches in the kitchen fire before any of the lads could see what a state he was in. On Saturday, baffled by the chalk and still afraid of the brush, he made a desperate attempt at etching. Three orders had come in for copies of *The Death of the Virgin,* and the big copper plate was in need of retouching, and he discovered with infinite relief that the needle was congenial to his grasp. All Saturday morning he worked near the open window, and the warmth of the sun penetrated his nerveless hand, and he knew while he worked that though he was sinful and mortal, yet for the time being he did no ill and lived.

It was close to noon and the business of cleaning the etching plate was almost finished when he remembered that he had meant to give the day to his wife. She deserved it the more for the tenderness she had shown him in his grief, for her own subdued mourning for his sister, and for her eagerness to take something more than her due portion of the blame. He washed his hands and face and came into the big dining room where she and Liesje were laying the table. "Wouldn't you rather go out?" he said. "I thought we might go to one of those orchard taverns on the Amstel. It's warm enough to sit outside."

"Oh, but why should you stop when you've just gotten started?" She went on laying the folded napkins on the plates, her swollen lips curved in a grateful smile. "Anyway, everything's ready here; Liesje's sliced the cold chicken and Maartje's made us a beautiful dish of new peas."

"But I'd like to go, provided you would."

"It isn't that I wouldn't like to, darling—you know I always enjoy it so much. Only, maybe we ought to wait until next Saturday—"

354

"I've finished what I was doing."

He had not said it with complete conviction, and he knew by the vagueness of her eyes that she did not entirely believe him. "Well, if you're finished," she said, arranging the silverware, "why don't you rest? To tell the truth, I'm tired myself. I was just saying to Liesje that as soon as we eat I think I'll have a little sleep."

By the end of the meal he was convinced she had refused as much for her own sake as for his. The heat which had healed and consoled him was plainly less salutary to her in her heavy condition; she was too rosy and too pale by turns, beads of sweat stood under her eyes and on her forehead, and she scarcely touched the food, explaining that it made her breathless to stuff herself in weather like this. Her hand, eager to assure him that she was still grateful for his offer, kept moving across the big oak table to touch his. They did not speak of Lysbeth, only of the gratifying fact that he was back at work again; and she kept patting his wrist and uttering the same congratulatory sentence over and over. Seeing that she did not want the sweet, he rejected it too and went with her into the bedroom, where he pulled the curtains, heaped the pillows, and loosened the fastenings of her dress. "You're much too indulgent with me these days—you're spoiling me—and what will I do when the baby's born and you forget all about me again?" she said, lying back against the pillows, with the protuberance at which he did not dare to look, doomed as it was, rising under the folds of her thin blue-grey skirt.

"I'll never forget about you," he said, and sat down on the edge of the bed to prove it. But he did not have to sit for long; within ten minutes she was—or was pretending to be—asleep.

*

Back in the studio, he laid the touched-up copper plate on the press. He would entrust the printing to Bol, since he wanted impeccable copies —they were to go to the bookshop of Clement de Jonghe, the pale, silky-haired, deep-eyed collector and seller who had come shyly to his house to offer his expert services in place of the mediocre ones of the ruined Hendrik Uylenburgh. It was a pleasure to think of those expressive hands picking up the finished prints, of those comprehending eyes taking in every delicate variation in light and shade. The *Death of the Virgin* was a master print, the best he had done; yet some haunting disquiet hung over the shining copper surface until he identified the taint: in the beginning, he remembered, he had been disturbed because he had made use of the foot of Saskia's little couch and the weary droop of Saskia's head. And how shallow and fantastic those imaginary terrors seemed to him now, side by side with actual self-arraignment, actual death . . .

She was asleep in the curtained bedroom, and the servants were barely audible in the downstairs reaches of the kitchen. The heat of the summer afternoon scarcely encroached upon this spacious, lordly studio where order increased the sense of coolness and openness: everything—or almost everything—was in its proper place. Here in his eagle's home, under the tiled roof, with the street far below him, he nurtured the precarious sense of life: years to paint and draw and etch, evenings alive with the earnest talk of friends, her body disburdened of the child—they were young, the tides of desire would come washing in again, there would be nights of love-making and the nourishing peace of sleep after love. Almost without knowing it, he had his chalk and drawing board and was drawing with a good, obedient hand. The great mirror of Venetian glass tilted against the west wall had caught his image and given him a subject, and sketching himself, he forgot where he was, watched the sunlight withdrawing as though he saw it from another planet, heard the bell on the front door downstairs make a muted jingle as one who sleeps in a summer field hears the belled flock go by through the drawn and fragrant curtain of his dream.

It was a good sketch, it could serve as a subject for an etching . . . The front door was closed again, and footfalls sounded on the stair between the first and second floor. Somebody spoke—Liesje, and somebody else—Saskia—answered . . . It was a very good sketch, especially effective around the wrinkled forehead and the tired eyes . . . A wagon went by, jolting over the cobblestones, and the voices of playing children came up to him from the street . . . The lines would be better, softer, once he had brushed a little wash along them. He would do that now—no, later—this new house had a way of suddenly oppressing the heart with the weight of its silences. Silent it was now, utterly silent, but before the stillness had come down upon it, hadn't he heard somebody—Saskia—wildly saying, "Oh, my God"?

He laid the sketch on the worktable, weighting it down with a Chinese seal, and stepped into the hall to listen. Silence—total silence—lay before him on the landing and drew him down the stairs. He crossed the long hall and went into the bedroom. Curtained as it was—the drapes and the walls dim gold with the brightness that sifted through the silken warp and woof—he could not see at once whether she was there; but in a moment he made her out sitting on the edge of the bed, her hair loose, her dress still unfastened and gaping, a letter—Jesus, not *another* letter—trailing from her hand.

"What happened, Saskia? What's the matter?"

"Nothing in Leyden. This is from Friesland." Her eyes shone up at him through the strange, molten light, begging him to forgive her for whatever she was about to add to his pain. "It's about Titia—it came just now. Poor Titia's dead."

He opened his mouth, but no sound would come. It was not only that death could keep striking over and over. It was not even that death could strike the young—three infants in their cradles, and Gerrit and Lysbeth and Titia. It was something more terrible still. She sat on the bed with the letter held out in her hand, and what he saw was not the letter but the remembered handkerchief spotted with blood.

"She died last Tuesday. She's buried by now. They didn't think I ought to come, in my condition—"

"What did she die of?" His jaw was so loose, his tongue so thick, that his voice came out like the voice of an idiot.

"An inflammation of the lungs—a hemorrhage from the lungs. She had a peaceful end, they say. She bled a good deal, and then she fell asleep and died in her sleep."

"How old was Titia?" How many years are left, dear God?

"Thirty-three. No, thirty-four, now that I come to think of it. She was three years older than I am. She seemed to be ailing when she was here, didn't she? One night she coughed so much that I made her a mug of hot wine." The recollection of that old gesture of concern and tenderness loosed the tears in the wide, still eyes that gazed steadily before her through the amber light. The tears rolled down over the pale cheeks and past the corners of her swollen lips. Then suddenly she sighed and her whole face grew intent and earnest. "Poor bear, I know what you're thinking. But honestly, you mustn't think it—it isn't so," she said.

"I'm too stunned to take it in—I'm not thinking anything."

"Yes, you are—you're thinking it's the same with me as it was with Titia, because I had a cold and coughed up a little spot of blood that time. You're afraid the baby'll die and I'll die with it. But that's not so —I swear to God it isn't so." She dropped the letter onto the embroidered coverlet and stood up in the soft confusion of her rumpled and unfastened dress: her blouse had fallen down, and one childish shoulder and half of one firm white breast were bare. "I'm better now than I ever was—this time the baby's not draining me at all. I know it sounds strange, but I'm telling you the truth: the baby's actually putting strength back into me. None of the others I carried were like this one. With the others, when they moved, it was like a fish just barely making his fins go in the water. But this one kicks and turns over whenever I'm excited—happy or sad, it doesn't matter. Here—feel it." She came and took his hand and pressed it down triumphantly upon the warm protuberance. "Feel it—it's doing it now."

The vitality of the creature kicking and stretching the pliant membrane of her flesh was not to be doubted. The movement was actually visible; her loosened skirt had fallen down around her ankles, and the fine lawn of her petticoat was stirred by the thrusting of hands and feet. "Do you see him?" she said, looking down at a raised mound near the arch of her ribs. "I know he's a boy, too, somehow—I don't know how I know it, but I do."

"He certainly feels healthy, and God knows I'm glad of it, though you mustn't think I've worried about either you or him," he said. He was able to utter it with conviction because the rippling movements under his palm were almost as reassuring to him as to her.

"Poor Titia—she was always the frail one. They worried over her from the time she was a baby; they never thought she'd see her first communion, much less get married. I was always different—I never had anything worse than a cold. And with this baby I won't even have a hard delivery; he's got so much life in him I'm sure he'll leap straight out."

Standing with her in his arms now—her wet, cool cheek pressed to his chin, her life-bearing belly swollen against him, her full breast with its hard nipple thrusting at his chest—he could only believe her, could only reproach himself for staining her bright confidence with his own sick sense of mortality. It was true; no other child had ever moved like that within her. It was true; her face, strained as it was, bore no resemblance to the drained, dry face of Titia. Many months had passed since she had showed him the red spot on the handkerchief, and he had heard his mother say many a time that certain sicknesses could be miraculously withdrawn from a woman when she gave birth to a healthy child. For the first time he yearned for that birth, remembered how it was to hear the thin wail of the newborn above the chatter of the midwife. It was time to clean and repair the wicker basket, time to count the blankets and diapers and lay them in lavender, time to polish the cradle and put the little goose-feather pillows out to air in the sun. But not *that* cradle, not *those* pillows. He could not repress it—he found himself saying, "Let's buy another cradle."

She nodded, rubbing her cheek against his neck. "Whatever you like. A new cradle would be very nice. But it isn't necessary, not to ward off bad luck. I know nothing's going to happen to this one," she said.

*

In those days, for a reason he could not grasp at first, images of stained-glass windows—a few that he had seen and many he had heard described by visitors from France—kept forming in the shadow behind his closed eyes. In thoughts and in dreams he kept seeing those windows—the nameless white saints with blood-red wounds, the amber-colored crowns and scarlet cloaks and bits of azure sky set in their heavy dark network of leadings, their translucent hues the more radiant because they were bounded in black. It was not until months afterwards that he knew the source of these images. Time had been shattered like that for him into intense and separate particles: mornings and afternoons and evenings bloomed one at a time in light-drenched brilliance, and at the edges of each—separating them and connecting them and forming the overall pattern in which each had its place—were the somber, leaden lines of dark.

In the dulled green and moted yellow of late summer he locked up the warehouse with the unfinished Regents' piece inside. It did not matter what Coq and Ruytenberg might think about his taking a holiday; they and their subordinates would suffer from the loss of time much less than he. He painted what could be painted in the spacious studio at home, within reach of her voice, no more than a flight of stairs away from her—a couple of lucrative portraits, a serene *Sacrifice of Manoah* in which wife and husband, no longer young, prayed earnestly to be given a son, a *David Embracing Absalom* in which grief stood side by side with tenderness. The hour in which he painted became a separate shining area of peace; but when he went downstairs to see how it was with her, it was in lead-grey fear until he found her well; and after that the next hour also cast its isolated glow. The Everlasting Designer —if this was indeed His conception—was like the creator of those effulgent wheels and burning arches of glass at least in this: His bits of brightness almost obliterated His underlying pattern of dark.

If the life they led while they waited was confined—she spent most of her days lying idle on their bed, she would risk nothing that could endanger the baby—it was a more carefully regulated life than they had ever known. Weeks before her time was due, she found a reliable midwife, the widow of a city trumpeter, and gave her a room in the house; and the conscientious woman set herself to righting whatever was amiss. Accounts were put in order, bills were paid when they arrived, meals appeared on the table at the proper hour, and even the maids improved. Vrouw Dircx, the midwife, seldom intruded upon them; she would consent to sit down to their Sunday supper with them only after they had invited her repeatedly. It was almost impossible to learn anything about her past life—the whole purpose of her conversation seemed to be to disparage herself. If she mentioned that she mourned her husband as the only friend she had ever had, she let them know too that he had been a man of small education from a poverty-stricken family. If she expressed fondness for her native village, she added at once that hardly anybody had ever heard of it. Might she thank them again, she said, for the room they had given her—how could she ever accustom herself again to the little chicken coop in which she had always lived? And now she would take herself upstairs, if they would excuse her, which she was sure they would: she knew well enough what poor company she must be . . . Her sad, colorless face with its deep-set eyes and its pale, loose mouth was animated only when she was dealing with the maids or the butcher boy or the chimney sweep. Rembrandt was surprised to learn that she was only forty-one: her tired gait, her constant reference to her advanced age, and the frequent sighs that shook her double chin and heavy breasts had led him to believe she was fifty at least.

She showed her mettle on the night of the delivery. Saskia was merry and at ease that evening at supper—Pinero had dropped by, and he and she and Rembrandt had stayed on at the table eating nuts and drinking wine. Hearing the town clock strike half past seven, she excused herself: she should be back in bed, the baby was letting her know he had had enough of this good cheer, she said, and started for the front stairs. The host and the guest went on cracking walnuts and shaking their heads over the troubles likely to rise out of the new alliance with the unstable Royal House of England; Pinero was accusing Frederik Hendrik of licking the boots of the Royalists when he was stopped short by a low, amazed cry. The two men ran to the front stairway, but Vrouw Dircx was there before them, was raising the white-faced Saskia from the step onto which she had let herself down in a spasm of pain. "I'll never be able to get up there—I can't walk," she said, in a voice she might have used if she had caught her skirt on a nail—a voice frighteningly incongruous with her big, tormented eyes.

They called to her that she should sit still, that they were coming to carry her.

"There's no need of that," said the midwife. "I'll see to it myself."

Her manner of seeing to it was to pick up her mistress as if she had been no heavier than a bolster. Sick, aged, weary-hearted as she dubbed herself, she carried Saskia up the rest of the stairs like an Amazon, even finding breath to say over her shoulder that everything was progressing nicely and nobody should distress himself. Pinero left to summon Bonus, and Rembrandt remained alone at the foot of the stairway, incapable of anything but stupidly repeating to himself: This is the time, this is the terrible waited-for thing. A few shrill animal cries, some of them like the howls of a beaten dog, some of them like the squeals of a pig under the butcher's knife, tore through the vast reaches of the house and gave way to stillness. He clung to the banister, unable to go up, too weak and too terrified to raise his voice and ask whether she was dead. But before Pinero came back with Bonus, Vrouw Dircx appeared on the balcony above him, smiling and wiping her bloody hands on the big white servant's apron that she never took off in his presence, not even to sit at supper on Sunday night. "Your honor has a fine male child up here," she said. "A fine male child, fat and lusty."

"And Saskia?"

"Splendid, splendid."

"Splendid?" He sank onto the lowest step, trying not to sob, grinding his cheeks against his wrists.

"I'll have her in proper condition to receive your honor if you'll give me just ten minutes."

So it had happened just as she had told him it would, and everything she had foreseen took authenticity from this first instance of her prescience. If the child had leaped into life as she had foretold, then all his terrors were emanations of his own sick mind, and she would surely live.

If a space of shadow intervened between that luminous evening and the more public joy of the christening feast, that was only to be ex-

pected. She was frail enough to be weakened even by an easy birth—
Vrouw Dircx and Tulp and Bonus kept telling him so. And sometimes
her aspect was as reassuring as their expert opinion: if every now and
then she fell back against her pillows as though she had been swimming a great distance, if she had no strength for eating her porridge and
wished they would keep it warm for her until later, all that they had to
do to renew her was to bring her the baby, to lay the baby where he
could lift his blind blue eyes to her and press his small, fine fingers into
her breast. Lay Titus in her arms—Titus he was to be in memory of
the dead Titia—and she was herself again; it was as if a cloud had
passed from the face of the sun and the whole varicolored stuff of life
was flooded with direct light. It was the custom for the mother to sit
bolstered up in bed with the baby beside her while the christening feast
was going on below and for the guests to leave the table by twos and
threes and pay their respects upstairs. And every visitor came down
from her smiling: nobody had ever seen a more blooming mother, nobody could imagine a healthier or more beautiful child.

Beautiful he was—even from the first it was plain that he was a van
Uylenburgh: small nose, exquisitely demarcated lips, hair that was
silky and fiery blond and soon began to curl. He was so neatly fashioned that there was small temptation to touch him—it was enough to
look, and the father schooled himself to look without drawing: the
chalk and the inkpot had once been unlucky, and he did not bring them
into the happy room. Anyway, there were such fair and subtle har-
monies of color in the baby that it would be better to wait until he could
be painted with the sort of palette that had been laid out long ago for the
Danaë—yellow and amber, cream-white and milk-white, and that
other hue, too delicate to be degraded by the word "pink," which flushes
the inner petals of the guelder-rose. One night two or three weeks after
the christening, when he was imagining such colors thick and soft under
his brush, it occurred to him that whatever was crude or earthy in his
seed had been purged away while it lay within the flawless temple of
her body: Titus would never be cursed with his flat nose, his little eyes,
his massive head, his raw and hairy hands. But the exultation begotten
by that thought was stricken dead in its flight: those in their graves in
Leyden had no continuation of life in the perfect little body—a realization so shattering that he had to leave the room and withdraw to the
balcony. "Forgive me, Mother and Father. Forgive me, Lysbeth and
Gerrit," he said in a whisper; and the broad splendor of the reception
hall blurred below him, and the tiles of the floor wavered, and he bowed
his head on the polished balustrade and wept.

It was October before she was up and about again, sprightly but so
thin that her rings were loose on her fingers and her little shoes kept
slipping off and all the splendid dresses brought out of the storage closet
had to be taken in. There was no need to hire a seamstress because
Vrouw Dircx was also expert with the needle. In fact, Vrouw Dircx was

so expert with everything—from the bleaching of linen to the preparation of a little feast out of nothing for an unexpected guest—that nobody thought of letting her go. In a strange conversation held with him one evening in his studio, she renounced the salary at which they had hired her as preposterous. Her duties as midwife had been ridiculously light, she said; her duties as nurse were lighter still, since Titus's disposition was as angelic as his person; and her present occupations were only a little supervising and busy-work to keep her mind off her griefs. If there was any chance of her staying for another month or so—she presumed to mention it only because the mistress seemed to be taking it for granted—then she could not in good conscience accept more than half of what they had hired her at. Something about the big stolid presence standing humbly before him was unnerving: the fact that she expected so little of him somehow discredited him, and he could restore his own sense of decency only by offering her considerably more. "A month, Geertje?" he said, embarrassed because he was using her given name for the first time. "Don't talk about a month, for God's sake. I've no idea what we'd do if you were gone." And since she did not answer, only sighed profoundly, he somehow talked himself into raising the half-salary she asked for to three-fourths, and offering her a housekeeper's position in his family for as long as she cared to stay.

With such a trustworthy nurse on hand, Saskia could be persuaded to make a few sallies into the world while the fine autumn weather lasted. They went once to the Sylviuses' house, where he had come ten years ago to ask for her, and that was a mournful evening: the little old lady, too frail and uncertain on her feet to live alone any longer, was going to her son, a pastor in Friesland; and the books and candlesticks and cushions were packed, and the hostess, a relict in a barren place, was so slow and remote that she could give them only confused and ghostly congratulations. The next week they went to Anslo's, and that was better: Lazzara, Pinero, Bonus, Swalmius, and Menasseh ben Israel—the rabbi of the great Sephardic Synagogue and the owner of a Hebrew printing press in the Breestraat—had a rousing argument about the relative values of reason and revelation; and the women seemed glad to retreat into a corner and go on among themselves about infants and midwives and deliveries. On that occasion Saskia was, if anything, too lively. He watched her from the other side of the room, caring less about the theological discussion than about her evident pleasure at coming into her own at last, a mother among mothers, who could boast about the flawlessness of Titus's skin and the amiability of his disposition and the strength in his fingers—boasts that would have been unseemly if the others had not known how many years she had had nothing to boast about. Her face, flushed and wonderfully mobile, looked in its thinness like a child's; her tortoise-shell comb seemed out of place in the disheveled looseness of her candlelighted hair. She glanced at him once as if she expected him to shake his head at her, but he only smiled. Still, he should have tried to check her, not for her vaunting but for wearing herself out: the next morning she complained of dizziness, and Tulp came by at his request and suggested that she spend a couple of days in bed. She was wan and dreamy thereafter, almost too wan and dreamy to go to a little supper arranged in their honor by Coppenol; but she could not find it in her heart to disappoint the good writing master; and once they were there among old friends—Lotje and Allaert, the Tulps, her cousin Hendrik, and Frans van Pellicorne and his handsome but unfruitful wife—she was in excellent spirits, perhaps because she had profited by her spell of rest.

Actually, when winter came and it was unthinkable that she should go out in the sea-cold squalls, they were happier. Their life, drawn by Titus out of the great stretches of the house into the bedroom, was merry and cozy. The chimney had a marvelous draft, and there was always a good fire; whatever they needed for their comfort or entertainment—a big chair, a few smaller ones to accommodate occasional guests, an embroidery frame for her, a little drawing desk for him—could be carried in, and there was still room to spare. Vrouw Dircx withdrew to her melancholy meditations as soon as she had seen them comfortably settled, and did not return, unless they rang the bell to summon her, until it was time to turn down the bed and warm the sheets with a heated stone. Bol was often with them and would spend whole hours lying on the floor while the baby reached for his face and pulled his hair; Coq and Ruytenberg turned up only twice, perhaps because they were annoyed that he had not yet returned to the Regents' piece and perhaps because they were not at home with simple domesticity; but what with the Mennonite theologians and their Jewish neighbors and an occasional visit from Allaert and Lotje, there was no lack of company. In fact, he and she and Titus were by themselves so seldom that an evening on which nobody arrived was a holiday evening, filled with a tremulous contentment, warmed by firelight and candlelight and an amber glow of peace . . .

There was one such evening, in February toward the end of the worst winter in a decade, that he never forgot. Long afterwards, when the room was orderly again and all the things brought into it had been dispersed to their proper places, he could recall the dear disorder: the extra chairs hiding the pattern of the carpet, the table blocking off the damask drape, the cradle and the heap of drying diapers on the hearth, her embroidery scissors and his jerkin and Titus's rattle on the bed. He had been working on a large drawing of *Isaac Blessing Jacob*, and he loved it for more than the spare eloquence of the lines and the way the three figures emerged out of the shadows: he had gotten into it—he knew not how or why—a sense of righted wrong, of peace after contention, of reconciliation at the last. He was putting the final strokes of

363

ink-wash on the pillow behind the dying patriarch when he realized that she had been sitting longer than usual wordless and motionless behind her embroidery frame. "What are you thinking?" he said.

"Only that it's all worked out so well—much better than I thought it would—"

"What has, darling?"

"Everything. Everything, I mean, between you and me." She took up the scissors and snipped off a length of scarlet thread—she had been stitching at the tulip he had drawn for her months ago; and her hand was so thin that the candle burning behind it shadowed forth the bones.

"Everything between you and me is completely the way it ought to be," he said.

"*Now* it is—right now—this evening." She laid the scissors down in her lap, where it jingled among her discarded bracelets and rings; and he too, seeing her earnestness, put by the drawing and the brush and sought her eyes, which would not look at him but fixed themselves on something far off and invisible. "Let me tell you what I mean, and don't stop me, because I'll feel much better if I get it said. And don't think for a minute I'm saying it because I'm sad or sick or anything like that. I've never been happier, and every day I feel a little better—I'm so much better, in fact, that I want you to go back to the warehouse tomorrow and start to work again on your Regents' piece. It's so beautiful, and I keep thinking how the paint might get too hard or you might stop feeling the way you did about it in the beginning—and I wouldn't want that to happen, not for anything in the world."

"It can wait. Nothing can happen."

"It *can't* wait, and things *can* happen, and I want you to go down there tomorrow for certain, though that isn't exactly what I wanted to talk to you about." She pushed the embroidery frame aside so that there was nothing between them but the fire on the hearth and the sleeping Titus in his cradle and the unfinished drawing he had just put down at his feet. Her body, bent forward with her elbows on her knees and her chin on her curled hands, seemed small for the great carved chair in which she sat, small for the voluminous folds of her emerald dressing gown—a thing of stiff satin that stood away from her shoulders and breasts. "My Uncle Sylvius was right, God rest his soul," she said. "He told me I was too young and light-headed to get married to anybody that wasn't old enough to be a father to me. He said I'd give you more grief than happiness, and he was right. Only, I couldn't help it, I loved you so—even when we quarreled, no matter what terrible things I said, I always, always loved you so—"

"Oh, but he was wrong about that—"

"No, really, he wasn't. I know how silly and stupid I was, my darling. I never knew what to do with a house or money. I couldn't even learn to scold a servant or keep a closet clean. I spoiled too much, and I bought too much."

"I was the one that bought too much—I spent more than you did." Since she was smiling, he did what he could to steady his trembling lips and answer her smile. "Anyway, I didn't marry you because I expected you to keep clean closets and save money—that wasn't important. I married you to love you, and I've had more than my share of joy in that, God knows!"

"Did you? I'm glad to hear you say so. But honestly, sometimes I think I was a bad bargain even there—I was sick so much and pregnant so much, and that would have been all right if it hadn't been that I felt you were cheated because all the other babies died."

A fan of sparks went up from the logs and disappeared against the soot at the back of the chimney; and he knew with a sudden expansion of the heart that she—yes, and he with her—had been talking as if all of it were over, as if it were being looked back upon from a distance, like the kitchen in Leyden and the attic in Pieter Lastman's house. "I'm not cheated. I have more than I deserve. You give me everything I want," he said; and his heart was the fuller because only with a conscious effort was he able to put it in the present.

"Don't feel unhappy about it, poor boy. There's no reason now for either of us to feel unhappy." She lifted her chin and shook out her fiery curls with the old vivacity. "Now that *he's* here"—she made a gesture in the direction of the cradle—"now that I've had him for you and he's so beautiful and perfect, I hardly ever think of how hard it must have been to put up with me. Because now that I've done one thing the way it ought to be done—and maybe even better than most women could— I know you don't blame me for anything else."

"Blame you?" It was all he could do to speak without releasing the sob in his chest.

"Well, you know what I mean—I'm sure you know what I mean, my darling. And what I *didn't* mean was to make you sad. I'm not sad, not in the least, believe me. I have everything I wanted—you and the baby and all that any woman could ever ask of the best and kindest of husbands—and I wanted you to know I feel contented and happy now because I've made some return by giving him to you." She got up then, almost as swift and light on her feet as she had been in the old days, crossed to the hearth, and swept the sleeping Titus, coverlet and all, out of his cradle. He stood up quickly, afraid that the weight of the baby would be too much for her or that she might be overtaken by one of her spells of dizziness, but she came to him proud and unfaltering, smiling over the round and drowsy head. "Take him—he won't wake up— just take him and hold him. You've taken him from Geertje but never from me. Hold out your arms—I want to give him to you," she said.

He did as he was bidden. This was a ritual for her, and he had never been able to perform a ritual without embarrassment: as he took the yawning, half-awakened bundle from her he recalled how he had blushed when he had put the wedding ring on her finger, how self-consciously he had walked down the aisle to kneel for the last time beside his mother's coffin, how hard it had been for him in his youth to swallow the communion bread. But this time—he remembered it afterwards with profound gratefulness—he bore himself freely, returned her look, and even managed to say, "You know—don't you?—how much I thank you for him, dear love."

What came thereafter he could not clearly call to mind, though that evening must have been the same as all their other evenings: Titus laid back on the goose-feather pillows, a bite of something eaten in mild good cheer at the table near the window, the bell rung for Geertje, Geertje come and gone, and the two of them lying close against each other between the warmed and scented sheets. She must have slept more peacefully than usual that night; otherwise his quiet weeping would surely have wakened her. This much he knew—he did not think of the drawing of Isaac and Jacob again until the following morning. It was a blessed thing to remember that he had wondered what it was when he opened his eyes and saw it lying on the floor in the thin light of the rising winter sun.

*

After that, whenever he had any free hours he betook himself to the Regents' piece. He could not doubt that she wanted him there; considering what each of them knew—and knew that the other knew—it was too charged and tremulous for them to be alone together now. Even after she grew too weak to walk the little distance from their bed to the table under the window, even after she coughed blood—and a great deal of it—even now that her arms were too feeble to hold and support the child and could only lie around it as the green spurs, no longer needed, lie around the opened under-petals of a rose, he went his way as if nothing had happened. The intensity of their oneness could not have been sustained if they had been together long; and besides, she was never alone: Geertje was always there, and Ferdinand Bol was always there.

It was strange how much store she had come to set in these weeks on his senior apprentice. She would raise her voice—so husky and feeble sometimes that it was necessary to come close to the bed to hear her —to ask whether Ferdinand was in the house; she would rouse herself out of some long, incommunicable dream to order a favorite dish of his for the noonday table; it was at his urging and on his arm that she walked to the window to see the first green of a belated spring on the poplars and the sycamores. With him in the room, she no longer seemed to notice the absence of Coq and Ruytenberg; and when others came— Anslo and Swalmius, Tulp, the Lazzaras and the Pineros, Allaert and Lotje, the van Pellicornes, Dr. Bonus and the learned Rabbi Menasseh ben Israel—she would summon up her strength to break into their conversation with an almost imperious reference to some affair of *his:*

366

"Has your sister decided yet which of those two young men she likes the most?" or, "Don't think of painting Vrouw Noordhoek for less than a hundred florins—she's nowhere as poor as she's making herself out to be."

Remembering that old, grave talk with Pastor Sylvius, her husband attributed her involvement with his apprentice to the attraction that youth holds for youth. She seemed to be growing always younger in her sickness; the river of time had somehow changed its course and was flowing backward for her. Her face looking up at him from the hollow in the plump pillow had changed, but not into the face of an aging woman: a newcomer might at first glance have taken her for a half-grown girl. One newcomer he did bring to her in the hope of giving her some part of that glittering world of dances and state receptions and high names at whose boundaries she had beaten and fluttered like a moth against a closed window. Of all the lucrative portraits he had done lately to stop the fearful shrinking of the sum in the bank, the only one he cared about was a likeness—expressly ordered *as* a likeness, severe and without flattery—of the recently widowed Vrouw Anna Weijmar Six, who had succeeded Vrouw van Hoorn as the keeper of Amsterdam's most cultivated salon. She made it plain that she wished to know him better; there was something almost insensitive in the regularity with which she sent him invitations to supper or a Sunday in the country, invitations which he just as regularly refused. Since her notes were usually accompanied by something like a jar of jam "to tempt the appetite of the invalid" he would read them to Saskia; and once early in April she begged him to go to the little supper currently in question: she was curious about the Six house and wanted him to describe it for her, she said. He went at her urging and found himself surprisingly at home, not with the company but with the winsome son Jan, who knew Latin, Greek, and Hebrew, collected paintings, etchings, and books, and was at work on a poetic tragedy. Jan Six was what Allaert would have been if Allaert had not faded, what Frans van Pellicorne would have been if there had been anything under his glitter and gallantry. He was, in fact, at once so attractive and so unassuming that it was impossible to refuse his request to visit the house on the Breestraat and see the canvases and the collection; and when he appeared in the reception hall with a bunch of violets for Vrouw van Rijn, her husband asked if he wouldn't present them in person: she was less weak than usual that day, and it occurred to him that she would be pleased with the attention.

Pleased she was, but only briefly. This scholar-gallant, this rising sun of the aristocracy, for all his gracious consideration, was a being too bright for her long-sheltered eyes. She gave him her hand to kiss and showed her appreciation by thrusting her nose into the violets; she spoke of his mother's kindness and her hopes of calling on her soon; but her eyes—very large and immediately expressive now of any distraction or distress—kept looking at the ceiling, and Rembrandt knew she was thinking of Ferdinand Bol at work in the room above. And when the distinguished visitor had left and she asked to have his violets put on the table under the window, it was plain that she did not want their purple richness detracting from the charm of the faded anemone that the senior apprentice had left on the little table near her bed.

No, there was no use trying to extend the reaches of her life. Her life had been gathered in—for how many months now he dared not ask himself—like the nets of the fishermen off the Leyden dunes at even-tide. What she had, she had, and she wanted no more. He and Titus and Ferdinand Bol made up the whole of her tally and were enough—so she let him know by the faint, fretful line that deepened between her eyebrows when he spoke of others. And to tell God's truth, he had been doing his own gathering in. The apprentices in the orderly upper work-rooms, the discreet and devoted visitors who came late and went home early, the patrons and the young man at the bank and the people in the shops were alien to him, though they served in one way or another to deaden the inner pain and to make the hours go by. Even the baby was on the other side of the meshes, though he held him and talked to him and spoke of every happy change in him for her sake. Later . . . he would love him later, though he could not conceive of that "later." What except utter darkness could be lying for him beyond the last brush stroke and the last breath?

That spring transmuted the Regents' piece. Subtly, little by little and almost without his realizing what was going on, the painting underwent an all-encompassing change. The change had nothing to do with other changes he had earlier told himself that he might make: the faces that were blotted out by casques or lifted arms or waving plumes would have to be sacrificed—who would expect him to concern himself with such things at a time like this? The transformation with which he *could* concern himself was indescribable, could not even have been communicated to the attentive Jan Six. All that he could say of it, even to himself, was that what had originally been a bright and fluid dream, and then had been fastened down into an actuality, was drawing loose, floating away, taking unto itself a profound but aerial radiance which had not been there even when it had first been a dream. The difference was the difference between the blast of trumpets and the shuddering golden tones of the organ. It was the difference between the metallic gold in rings and the liquid gold of sunset in the greying troughs between the waves. It had less to do with the central figures than with the rank and file, and less to do with *them* than with the auxiliary presences —little girls and a dog and a couple of half-grown lads running about, figures that he had added to distribute the patches of intense color and to provide a touch of fantasy. The river of time flowed backward here also, drawing these figures on its swift surface. They were his father and his brother Gerrit and himself caught up in the prelude of a long-since-finished battle. The dog was all the frightened beasts ever provoked by the meaningless blusterings of men. And the noonday sun that poured its glory and its living heat upon the heads of these marchers was no sun that could be changed with the rotation of the earth. He himself was timeless inasmuch as he had re-created light unwavering and eternal: a hundred years might come and go, but this sun of his would neither rise nor set.

Certain small areas of the painting—the sunlit edge of the drummer's hat, the face of the girl in the saffron-colored dress with the sea-blue collar, the sunken warmth of the noonday light on the marble pillar at the rear—he left unfinished, not out of fear that he might spoil them but because he needed them as a joy deferred, as something to think of when he wakened in the morning with his eyes blurred by troubled sleep and his mouth as dry as ashes. If there had been any prodding from Coq and Ruytenberg, he would probably have forced himself to press on to the conclusion, but lately he never encountered either of the gentlemen. They and the rest of the citizen-soldiers of Amsterdam —he had heard of it in a vague way, as if it were some rumor carried to the wharf by a ship out of India or Japan—were occupied with the Grand Public Reception being prepared for Queen Henrietta Maria of England and her daughter, the Princess Royal, who had lately been affianced to Frederik Hendrik's eldest son. An unfortunate alliance, an almost Catholic alliance, surely an anti-Protestant alliance and one that would indicate that the Republic of Holland was fulfilling Pinero's gloomy prophecies. Not that *he* cared greatly which way that wind might blow: a God who could stare mercilessly at what was young and beautiful wasting away could scarcely concern Himself whether people took bread and wine in remembrance of Him or imagined that they ate His flesh and drank His blood. If the sight of paper garlands and silken banners hanging from balconies went through him like a knife, it was for a reason that had nothing to do with the Republic of Holland or the Kingdom of Heaven. Those parades that *she* had never seen, those splendid state balls that she had never danced at, those regal banquets at which she had never sat bejeweled in the flowering of her loveliness —it was the thought of them that made him weep in the street.

There was one May morning when he could not shut out the wounding public merriment even after he had gotten himself into the safety of the warehouse and bolted the door behind him. A chorus of girls from the orphanage had chosen an open field across the canal as a practice ground for their celebratory antics; and from nine to eleven they kept singing an inane ditty—composed no doubt by Vondel or some other ass from Muiden—about the fair young bride who had ventured over the stormy sea. At the end of every verse each of the girls was to whip out a streamer of colored ribbon, a maneuver at which they proved themselves singularly inept—the flat-chested mistress who was conducting the rehearsal chided over and over through her nose, "No, Klaartje, no, Lotje; we will begin again, we will take it from the start." Every time the vacuous words were repeated to the vacuous tune, the fury in him mounted; he could barely restrain himself from leaning, shirtless and hairy-chested as he was, out of the second-story window and shouting curses at them across the canal. Hate curdled in him, and when he heard the unaccustomed sound of footfalls on the stairway he immediately attached them to a hateful image: they must be coming again, the drunken soldiers, to see what they were getting for their filthy florins, and this time he would give them more than they were looking for.

But it was only Dr. Tulp on the threshold, gazing in awe at the flaming canvas; mastering, like the man of reason that he was, whatever cry of admiration came up into his throat; waiting until he could formulate his response to that glory in sane human speech—and the wait was long. "That is like nothing I ever laid eyes on before," he said at last, without taking his grave and kindled look from the Regents' piece. "Nobody I know of has surpassed it." And the silence sounded late and bitterly with the names implied: Dürer, Titian, Michelangelo.

Quickly, to blot out the remembrance of another scene in Hendrik Uylenburgh's shop in the morning of his years, when the good doctor, still young and reckless, had grasped him by the arm and said, "The world's in the palm of your hand"—quickly, to stifle the thought that cheese was sold over the counter where he had seen the Oriental sword, and that the doctor had grown grey and dry and that he himself had grown middle-aged and heavy—quickly he began to say something which would plant both of them firmly in the present: he must bring his daughter Gretha to see their new house; it must be months since he and Saskia had seen her . . .

As his voice trailed off, the doctor pushed him back a little and stepped in and closed the door. Still shrill and vapid through the open windows came the song of the fair young bride from across the sea. The doctor took off his hat, loosened his ruff, wet his lips, and seated himself on a high painter's stool, with his bared and grizzled head close to the lieutenant's marvelously painted sword. "It was about Saskia—the state of Saskia's health—that I dropped in to talk to you," he said.

His heart began to race and he felt a vertiginous sickness, so strong that he almost forgot what was behind him, almost rested his shoulder for support against Banning Coq's wet glove.

"I thought I ought to tell you that it's no minor illness she's got," said the doctor.

Must it be thrust in his face, turned this way and that? "Surely you didn't think I couldn't see that?"

"Well, yes—no— I don't know. I couldn't be sure, and I didn't want it to come as a shock. That's why I stopped in—because I didn't want you to have to face it without preparing yourself."

"I've prepared myself." He said it arrogantly, as though there was

370

cause to take pride in it. "I've been preparing myself ever since last winter. Anyway, how in God's name can a person prepare himself?"

"I don't know," said the doctor, staring down at his own fine hands with a kind of contempt, as if all they had done in his life was to be discounted in the face of their ultimate impotence.

"If you mean praying and running to some preacher—"

"I don't mean that, as you ought to know. I mean accepting it, getting yourself used to it, taking it into your mind a little more from one day to another. I didn't realize you'd been doing that. If I'd known, I wouldn't have come—" His careful, practiced voice could not fall at the end of the sentence, could only waver. He got up from the stool and reached for his hat and thought better of it—opened his arms and held them out instead, as a father holds out his arms to a hurt and passionate child. And as they had once embraced in Hendrik Uylenburgh's shop, so they embraced here under the painted radiance; their cheeks, pressed together for an instant, were wet; and whether it was the doctor or he or both of them that wept he did not know.

"God forgive me—you've been good to me, and I never deserved it," said Rembrandt, wrenching himself free.

"It was easy to be good to you; I was somehow taken with you from the beginning. As for her—you know I was always immensely taken with her," the doctor said.

He took up his position again then on the high stool, interlocking his long white fingers between his knees, and did what he had plainly come to do—took, insofar as he could, the black mystery out of death by explaining its workings in the terms of one who is its familiar. She would die easily—he did not shun the word and use in its place such pastors' words as "depart" or "pass away"—she would die easily, probably soon after her next hemorrhage, and not of strangulation, not of failure of the lungs, but of a gradual enfeebling of her heart. There would be no great pain and very likely no apprehension either. Death in such cases always came suddenly, unexpectedly, and often came in sleep. When it did come, she would look no different than before its visitation. Her eyes might be open or they might be closed, and her lips might part as if in surprise, but that was all. And not to show consternation, not to call her back from peace to a few last minutes of needless fright—that was the one important thing.

Medicines he had—he got up again and took them out of his pocket: two drops of this in a glass of water in case of restlessness, a spoonful of this if she should complain of any pain in the chest, and this powder—something of his own compounding and very effective even if he said so himself—to induce sleep. It was a good thing to come down here and work at the warehouse; her little store of vitality could be doled out more pleasurably for her if conversations were not protracted, and she seemed happy and placid with the good Vrouw Dircx

371

and Ferdinand and the child. As for eating and drinking, give her whatever she asked for: some blessed dispensation saw to it that nothing could do much harm when nothing could any longer do much good. And so good-bye, and let God keep them both and let them never think themselves forgotten even for an hour—if thoughts or prayers from an old friend could serve, she would be what she had been when she had danced in Hendrik Uylenburgh's shop ten years ago.

He was gone then, and for something like half an hour it was possible to live with resignation, walking the paint-spattered planks of the floor to the beat of the stupid song and silently, freely weeping. It was possible to see oneself as a child of time, mortal and coming to the end of a mortal love. But something shattered that—the vision that the doctor had conjured up of her face moist and flushed and lifted to him in the swiftness of the dance. She approached, she withdrew, she changed with the fluidity of living fire; she was Danaë, known and waiting to be known again on her carved couch; she was the beloved, virginal but ardent, running breathless into his studio on a summer Sunday morning; she was a little child in Friesland at dawn on a nameday feast—he could have sworn that he had seen her so!—her face shining rosy and white and expectant from the aureate cloud of her hair. And to negate time, to gainsay death, to grasp at immortality, he took up his brushes and his palette and went and stood before the little girl in the saffron dress, the one to whom he had not yet given a face. There, in the midst of the splendid martial confusion, he painted her as she had been revealed to him, in the guise that her volatile spirit must have worn in those days when he had walked on the Leyden dunes and thought of greatness as the only shield between himself and death. Had she been denied the carnival in honor of Maria de Medici? Would she be lying in her grave when the trumpets sounded again for the Queen of England and the fair young bride? No matter; he was placing her in a burst of glory beyond anything that petty man could sustain for a few paltry hours. Tenderness, sorrow, strange exultation in his own greatness moved his hand until she stood before him in her invulnerable, changeless youth —Saskia satisfied, Saskia happy, Saskia at a high celebration that would last forever and forever, Amen.

BOOK VII

1642
-
1645

Now that the things whereby he had lived were accomplished—she laid away in her grave and the house emptied of the pomp of her funeral, the last touch of paint put on the Regents' piece and the great canvas locked up to dry in the warehouse—now that whatever cords had bound him to the world were cut, he wondered how he himself continued to live.

It was not he who ordered that the leftover funeral meats be sent to the Old Men's Home, not he who dispensed the appropriate sum to the pallbearers and paid the tailor for the mourning clothes, not he who ordered a grave to be reserved beside hers under the floor of the Old Church. It was a spiritless image of himself, a body lifeless and mechanical and yet sickeningly aware that it was made of corruptible matter, which went daily about the meaningless business of rising, dressing, washing, eating. And all the while it asked itself why it persisted in this travesty, why it was not lying in that waiting grave.

People came and went; for days after the funeral the house was seldom free of people. Old patrons, neighbors, art dealers, former apprentices, members of the Saint Lucas Guild and the Surgeons' Guild and the Company of Captain Banning Coq presented themselves in the stark orderliness of the grand reception hall to assure him that they grasped the enormity of his loss. Geertje Dircx and the new little servant girl—he believed her name was Klaartje—came to the back parlor and announced the callers: the writing master Coppenol, Heer and Vrouw Pinero, Dr. Matthys Kolkoen, Heer and Vrouw Lazzara—it was as if, joined as they were with the past, they had come to give him a message from his dead. To those she had known and loved he gave himself up with initial fervor, bestowing and taking such embraces as would have been unthinkable before, heedless of his shaken voice and the tears that stood in his eyes. But the illusion was fleeting, and once it was dispelled he stared in vague wonder at those he had so wildly taken to himself. What were they doing here? Was she not dead and buried? What could they say of her? And his tongue was tied, and his eyes were fixed, and he wished the intruders gone.

He was scarcely out of bed before he began to yearn for the coming on of evening: only the evening was tolerable, undisturbed by guests, relieved of the burden of the many hours to be lived through, dulled by the supper lying heavy in his stomach and the sure approach of early sleep. The time between seven and ten he spent in the back parlor with Geertje and Titus. Even the new little girl—her name *was* Klaartje, that much he had gotten into his bewildered brain—intruded only for a minute upon his isolation to bring in Geertje's mending and prepare a place before the fire for the child. Geertje had found her to take the place of the sullen Maartje, who had broken her contract and run away, having no intention, as she said, of letting herself in for a funeral after all that sickness and everything else. Liesje, too, was gone; a tailor had asked for her in marriage. The new one was thirteen, a country orphan with a shy, tearful smile; and whether she was continually in that tremulous state out of respect for his afflictions or because of her own sorrows and apprehensions, he did not know. An evening would come when he would find heart to reassure her with a kindly word, but now he felt only relief when she went back to the kitchen and he was free to sag into something that could almost be taken for peace.

For Geertje's presence made no difference. Sharing the light from his candlestick, she sat across from him at the big round table, mending or totaling up the household accounts or writing on smoothed pieces of wrapping paper reminders of what she must do tomorrow: send Klaartje out for oil, tell Dr. Bonus that Titus would not eat his barley broth, get another broom. There was something calming about those notes of hers; they sketched out the modest boundaries of a life so muted and circumscribed that he could contemplate it without pain or agitation. The big devitalized body in its grey frieze garments was as undemanding as a massive and unbeautiful civic statue; the slow movements of the thick hands going about their minor duties impinged on him no more than the moving hands of a clock. Her large dark eyes, with whites that were yellow and clouded, were so mild and vacant that he sensed nothing when they passed from the pen or the needle to his face; and when she found it necessary to ask him something she never startled him but always pushed the silence out a little with a sigh before she rent it with a word. Subdued as she was by nature, and doubly so now in her mourning for her mistress, she could not offer any assault to his jangling nerves; and though she doted on Titus, some animal instinct—missing in Lotje and Vrouw Lazzara and the bustling, ruddy, tearful Vrouw Anna Weijmar Six—kept her from calling his attention to the child.

"What a comfort he must be to you in your sorrow!" "How fortunate it is that she left something of herself behind her!" "God in His mercy has given you good reason to go on living"—no day went by without some variation on that old, false tune; and it seemed to him that they sang it to spare themselves, to avoid facing the utter desolation of his state. Titus was not Saskia. That Titus lived—God forgive him, but it was the truth—was a minor matter now that Saskia was dead. Only a mind eager to escape the confrontation of sorrow could think to ease him by pointing out on the small rosy face a likeness of that flickering smile, quenched now, buried in the dark. Let them speak no more of what lived again only to mock him: the silky curls and the round forehead with its beads of summer sweat, the willful little ways and the creases in the neck and the guileless radiance in the eyes. Only fools who had never known love or remorse could dream that such shadows of shadows might soothe the open wounds of regret and love. Titus? What had he to do with Titus? On the worst days he could not even look at him; and on the better ones, when the balm of some recollection had softened him to tears, the most he could say for him was that he was better than nothing: living flesh was a less tormenting thing to weep against than a vacant dressing gown or an empty shoe.

In his raw weakness he was not above resenting the amount of fuss that went on over the baby. One evening close to the end of August, a grey and oppressive evening when the haze of suspended moisture in the air made sheer breathing an effort, he found himself out of sorts because the good Geertje, instead of coming over to him at the table at once, sat down beside Titus on the spread comforter, tried long and vainly to interest the little one in his rattle, and continued to squat there, foolish and graceless, sighing heavily at her unsuccess. The boy, having knocked the rattle out of her hand, turned over on his belly and was chewing at the quilt. Secretively, still unconscious of her master's look, she felt the back of the round head and the creased place behind the knee with apprehension, as if she expected to detect a fever. "What's the trouble now, Geertje? Is something the matter with him?" he said.

"Oh, no, your honor, nothing at all. He's as cool as a roll of butter in spite of this dreadful heat." She got up with a creaking of knee joints and made her slow, stolid way to her chair. "But Dr. Bonus was here this afternoon and thought he looked a little washed out."

"Anybody would look washed out in this weather."

"That's what I thought."

She opened her workbasket and laid out a threaded needle and a scissors. Some strange mixture of feelings—stifled fright, jealousy, utter incapacity for dealing with any new burden—made him refrain from his usual courteous gesture: he did not push the candlestick toward her to give her the best of the light. She made no move to get what was her due, merely took up one of his black stockings and pulled it over her fist and began to darn it in the shadow. "Did Bonus have anything else to say?" he said.

"Well, certainly nothing that needs to alarm your honor. Only that it might be a good idea to guard against the mother's sickness cropping up in the boy—"

"And just what does he suggest? How's a person to guard against it?" His voice was rough against malignant destiny—whatever it could do to him, it probably would.

"Just a few simple things, your honor. Good rich food, which he already has. Mostly, he ought to have long airings, and it's my fault if he hasn't had those. The doctor wants him out of the house every fine day for at least an hour. He's got to have plenty of fresh air."

"Well, take him out, that's easy." His relief at her cheerful, casual tone was like every other relief he had experienced since the day of the funeral—only a cause for asking himself what he could take heart in now that *she* was dead.

"I ought to find it easy," said Geertje, fixing her discolored eyes on the tip of her finger poking through a hole in the stocking. "But I don't get around the way I used to, as I told your honor from the start."

His memory provided him with reproving images of Geertje scrubbing the vast marble floor in the reception hall, sponging the statues in the salon, stirring a caldron of soup for the apprentices, bathing the baby, laying the sopping linens out to dry. His sister Lysbeth, younger than this one, had sunk under the burden of a smaller house. Women's labors, and women's mute, animal patience under their daily obligations, moved him enough to make him push the candlestick in her direction. "God knows you've got enough to do as it is," he said. "Why don't you let Klaartje take him out? She looks as if she could do with a little fresh air herself."

"Klaartje? Oh, no, your honor, I couldn't think of such a thing. Last week she lost her prayer book, and now she doesn't know where she left her shawl, and likely as not she might turn up some day and say she can't remember where she left the baby. If I let him out of here with Klaartje, I wouldn't have a minute's peace—I'd feel my mistress's beautiful eyes reproaching me from heaven."

He tried to keep his face unchanged. If what she said was downright mawkish, if he looked ridiculous holding up her stockinged hand and lifting her eyes to the ceiling, it was no fault of hers: she was, as she had told him a dozen times, common and ignorant, and it was her very humbleness that made her acceptable to him in these intolerable days. He blotted out the tawdry vision of a winged Saskia suspended in a cheap aura of glory and applied himself to practical considerations. "I imagine Klaartje has enough to do anyway, cleaning up after the apprentices. We'll have to get somebody else, somebody older and stronger, somebody who can take some of the heavy things off your hands," he said.

"Another one instead of Klaartje?" she asked in melancholy resignation; and he saw other images—Geertje patiently teaching the country orphan how to polish silver and set the table, Geertje brushing and braiding the girl's thick blond hair.

"No, of course not, I wouldn't think of letting Klaartje go. We'll get another one, a third one. With a house of this size and the apprentices and the baby, the two of you aren't enough."

"But it seems to me your honor's spending too much already, what with—"

She stopped, stripped the stocking off her hand, and stared at it in dumb confusion; and he knew that what she had kept herself from saying was "what with no commissions coming in." But there was no reason to be concerned over the lack of commissions; while he had been

378

absorbed in the Regents' piece, he had discouraged prospective patrons, and those close enough to him to know that he was no longer occupied with the big canvas would never impose themselves upon him in his grief. "Really, Geertje," he said, "there's no reason to worry about expenses. There'll be plenty of money, plenty of commissions, once the Regents' piece is hung."

"Well, don't trouble yourself with it, your honor. For a short time like that, I'm sure Klaartje and I can hold out."

He did not answer immediately, thinking while she stitched at a frayed napkin that she had a poor widow's notion of money matters: actually there was no cause for "holding out," and if he did not tell her so it was only because he did want to hurt her feelings by belittling the crisis or her usefulness. Saskia had left her only partly consumed fortune to Titus, and *he* was the executor, without check or supervision. If he drew at once on that as yet undetermined sum—he must go to the bank and try to make order out of that confusion of figures one of these days—if he spent something to hire another servant, he would be exercising only the most scrupulously conceived of his rights: more help in the house was needed not for his benefit but for the child's. He glanced at the baby sleeping on the comforter, and another image of *her*—a blessed antidote for Geertje's wooden angel—manifested itself. He saw her sitting up in her bed to sign her will, strangely hopeful, feverishly radiant, as though in making arrangements in the face of death, she had magically exorcised or made a laughing matter of it. "But you must add another clause, you poor man," she had said to the lawyer. "You must write that all this is invalid and my property is to be divided equally in case I bear another child."

"Very well, Geertje, let's leave it as it is for the time being," he said tardily. "In fact, I see no reason why I shouldn't be the one to take the baby out. I'm simply wasting my mornings. The demands made on me are few enough."

Few enough, troublingly, few, almost nonexistent . . . But wasn't that the way he wanted it? Lying late abed, stunned into static grief by that empty pillow. Sitting long over the sickening business of consuming an unwanted breakfast. Wandering through the house and tormenting himself with its useless, vacant splendor, or stumbling upon some chair, some cushion they had bought together and going up to his eagle's nest to beat his fists against the wall and weep. Waiting for the afternoon when he would start to teach and then finding the teaching an insupportable burden. Taking comfort in the lengthening shadows because they pointed him toward evening and the best of his hours—and now that he had it, what was so good about this hour?

She sighed into the wordless stillness. "It might do your honor good," she said. "It might hearten your honor to get around a little outside."

About that, he thought, there was no need for hurry or effort. Inevitably, once the Regents' piece was hung in the Military Club, he would be drawn back into the tide of things whether he liked or not. It would be as it had been after *The Anatomy Lesson* was displayed at the Surgeons' Guild and he was dragged by the sheer pull of fame out of his solitary preoccupation and into the life of Amsterdam. The burghers of the city would not permit the painter of that hidden splendor in the warehouse to rot away in brooding apathy. He would be forced to lock his sorrow up within him; he would be forced to carry his spiritless body into the great salons; he would be forced to talk and drink and smile. Meanwhile, it was just as well for him to begin by going out with Titus . . .

Geertje yawned, and he knew that he too must have yawned—she never yawned before him. "Why don't you put away your mending?" he said. "You need your rest."

She gave him in a long look the only human contact he could endure these days—mute understanding, unspoken pity. "As soon as I've finished this napkin, your honor, but don't wait up for me. God keep you. Go to bed."

*

But it turned out to be a depressing business, dragging the child through the streets of the city. When the needed sun was there, the heartless and complacent crowds had to be taken with it; and Titus, eager to glory in his new walking, squirmed and fretted against being carried and, given his way, was like as not to start for a canal or a chestnut-roaster's fire. So, by the end of September, after Dr. Bonus had agreed that two days in the open country were better than seven short walks in the city, Rembrandt went every Tuesday and Saturday through the Haarlem Gate toward one of the villages that lay that way; and anybody would have thought he was setting out for the Indies, weighted down as he was with a hamper of food and a drawing board and half a dozen diapers and a rolled quilt for Titus to sit on and a flask of boiled milk—to say nothing of the child.

Geertje had been right when she told him he was not going to find these expeditions easy. So many unaccustomed duties were involved— changing diapers and washing the fouled ones in streams, offering food on the end of a spoon to a small mouth that stubbornly shut itself, learning to know that "wa" meant "water" and "mook" meant "milk"—and his mind was so slow and his fingers so awkward that he might have abandoned the plan after one attempt if there had not been so much stuff for drawings to tempt him on. The exasperating obligations toward the child only whetted his appetite for work: once he had grabbed the wormy apple out of the little fist, he could draw the grained and twisted trunk of the ancient tree; once he had tied the elusive darter to the stile at the end of a rope, like a recalcitrant puppy, he could sketch the scarcely visible towers beyond the flat and rusty meadowland; once the moist eyelids with their flame-colored lashes were closed, he could try to capture a mass of clouds borne in from the water on a mild wind and lying almost motionless now, like some legendary mountainous continent in the heavens. But whatever he brought back with him from those expeditions was slight and incomplete: conscience kept him from forgetting what lay on the quilt beside him or sat close to him and hammered with a spoon on his knee—a conscience the more acute, he knew, because he felt so little love.

His inability to kindle to this masterpiece of hers, this only living seed of his, was something he did not fully understand. He pondered it on the outskirts of Hillegom and Omval and Amersfoort, by the placid water of the Amstel, or in the grottoes around Koestverloren—miniature forests made up of damp caves and a few wild fruit-bearing trees. What had become of whatever poor capacity for love he had once possessed? Had it died with her and been buried in her grave? Or did he reject the boy for the very reason that others believed he would cherish him, because he was so like the dead and was forever mocking sorrow with her sidelong look and her elusive smile?

Allaert's Lotje had said once that nobody can ever deceive a baby, that a baby knows perfectly well who loves it and who doesn't; but either Lotje did not know what she was talking about or he did not know his own heart, for Titus was content, even elated, in his company. With no backward look at Klaartje or Geertje he would set out on those Tuesday and Saturday jaunts, perched on his father's shoulder and shouting strings of incomprehensible words into the dawn. With utter confidence he would sit down on a knee already occupied by an etching plate or lay his head, warm and damp from much stamping about, on his father's thigh. "Da-da"—his name for his father—he attached to other things large and solid and beloved: a sun-warmed rock that he could slide on, a friendly hound that bounded out to meet them when they passed the gates of Rhenen, a big mossy stump from which he could see, beyond the rolling hayfields, the place where the Amstel veered toward the sea.

One cool afternoon late in September, when they were wandering over the mowed fields near Amersfoort with a breeze in their faces and the distant creak of windmills in their ears, they came upon a scene he would have given much to stay and witness; but he had to forgo it for Titus's sake. In a clearing in front of one of the farmhouses a huge hog, mute and stolid and almost the color of the earth it had spent its life wallowing and rejoicing in, lay on its side, fattened and bound for the kill, its neck stretched out in unconscious readiness for the knife, its cloven, dirt-caked feet no longer kicking against the ropes that fettered them. Not far off, in the moted light at the entrance of a barn, a peasant was grimly sharpening his knife; and three small children ran about on the patch of grass between the barn door and the sacrifice. The children were plainly delighted, either at the prospect of violence or the promise of a feast; and their cruel excitement somehow got into Titus's blood

—his chin went up, his back straightened, and he curled his hands into quivering fists. No promise of fish or windmills was enough to lure him away; and at the last minute—the peasant was trying the blade on his thumb and nodding over it approvingly—it was necessary to pick up a kicking, screaming bundle and carry it off in the direction of a clump of willows. He managed to keep his irritation in check only until the branches of those willows closed him and his protesting burden away from the butchery. Then, knowing how much he had wanted to draw that prostrate pig, how much he had denied himself in order to save the stubborn child from a scene he would probably have enjoyed like the rest of his heartless kind, he put him down hard on his bottom among the twisted roots and let him howl until he was red in the face.

In angry determination not to be cheated, he took his paper and his chalk out of his pocket and, turning his back on his shrieking, flailing son, set himself to capture the pig, dumb and hopeless in the face of its final agony. His hand trembled, possibly because it was shaken by some nameless tide of emotion, probably only because it was strained from grasping the child; and with the sun shimmering through the quaking willow leaves, he did not hope for much. He would do the thing in detail later, in an etching, with the bristling hairs and the exposed underparts and the hanging cloven feet incisively drawn in. Now, with this small devil incarnate howling to burst his lungs, it would be a wonder if he caught more than the basic shape: the pitiful thrust of the neck, the heavy swell of the fattened side.

Yet when he was finished and had gotten the thing into a steady patch of shadow where he could look at it without squinting, he saw that it was good in spite of the trembling, good in spite of the boy's hatefulness, good without effort, in a stark, unstriving kind of simplicity. While the child's cries gave way to long quavering sobs, he crouched over the paper and felt his heart hasten and a smile part his panting mouth: this readied hog, sketched in a few minutes and almost without thought, could call up more real pity than his Isaac under Abraham's knife, his weeping Hagar, his Christ at the whipping post, his beaten Samaritan. A prickling crept up his back as he realized that the hog had in it, cleansed and perfected, much of what had stirred his father in the little sketches scattered on the floor of the outbuilding behind the mill, much of what had drawn Vrouw van Hoorn and Dr. Tulp to the crude sketch of Rinske Dobbels, much of what he had lacked these many years when his pride and stubbornness had not let him admit it even to himself.

Who knows? he thought in the bitter self-mockery that was constantly with him these days—a person who can draw a pig ready for slaughter may yet learn to draw Jesus on the Cross. The thought unstrung him: he began by laughing in a spasmodic, crazy way; but the tickling in his chest turned almost at once into a fit of weeping as unrestrained as the child's, and he had to cover the drawing with his hand lest it be ruined by his tears.

He did not know how long he sat hunched there, weeping—long enough, he supposed, for the poor beast to have been flayed and disemboweled, long enough for Titus to have quieted down at last. He smeared away the tears from his burning face with his sleeve and looked for Titus where he had set him down, but he stood close at hand—a baby, a blubbered baby that had made his uncertain way over the gnarled humps of the roots and now stood at his father's knee, staring in fearful wonderment at his father's face.

A baby, a blubbered baby in a little rust-colored dress and soiled white stockings . . . Through the mist in his eyes he saw the child as someone strange and isolated, someone he had never seen in and of himself before. What had Geertje dressed him in for their earlier expeditions? Had his red-blond hair always been brushed like that into a roll that nodded over his round, puckered forehead? Either he did not remember or he had never really looked. The delicate face, still a little blunted with infantine fat—had he closed his eyes every time he had begun to take it in? And if that was so—the boy continued to stare at him in amazement that a great rock should crack—what had he seen in place of this guileless and potentially beautiful creature standing so still in the flicker of shadow and sun?

The beloved, of course, the dead beloved. But it was not out of love triumphant and bereaved that he had turned away from this shadow of her shadow. If her eyes had looked at him joyous and loving out of these eyes, he would have shut them up with tender fingers and covered the moist lids and bright lashes with kisses. If her happiness had curved these lips, he would have gathered from them a medicine to heal his lacerated heart. But it was Saskia weeping on the bridge above the frozen canal, it was Saskia begging for reassurance before the Regents' piece in the warehouse, it was Saskia pushed aside and left to her fear and her loneliness so that the great canvas might prosper—it was a wronged Saskia that he saw in the forlorn being she had left behind, saw and could not bear to see.

"God forgive me—forgive me, Saskia," he said aloud. His hand, groping about in his pain in the loose earth beside him, brought up a pebble which for some reason he held out to the child. Titus was pacified and took the pebble and stared at it and said, "Da-da," and this strange reconciliation brought on another fit of sobbing so fierce that he was afraid it might be heard above the rustling of the wind in the drying foliage.

When he was finished with weeping he lay back exhausted on the ground and sat Titus on his chest, as he remembered sitting on his own father when he was a baby. It seemed to him as he lay with his shoulders pressing into the cool sod that the earth beneath him was honeycombed with the last abiding places of multitudes—what spot in this little land had not been used as a grave?—and in the tired peace that comes after long weeping, he tried to call up an image of all those dead.

But he could find no form in which to embody them: not Geertje's painted angels, nor the more austere heavenly hosts of his mother's pious dreamings, nor the Hebraic children of God resting in Abraham's bosom, nor the Catholic saints bearing the implements of their martyrdom, nor the Protestant elect, orderly and seemly in their modest crowns. Either the dead slept everlastingly and knew nothing, or they wakened utterly and were delivered from the limitations of this corruptible body and these groping senses; and in either case it was vain to call upon them and ask them to forgive. If they slept below in dreamless quiet, no begging voice could reach them; and if they moved disembodied and aerial beyond the fogs that becloud the firmament, they would scarcely have withheld their pity until they heard the cries sent up out of a guilty and remorseful heart.

He saw her then, not as a bodiless spirit—for, as Margheretha van Meer had admitted once, the miserable children of the earth can never be delivered from eyes and hands and lips—but as a remote and peaceful watcher, older now, older than she had lived to be, standing in the shaken light and shadow with one hand stretched out in a kind of benediction and the other laid against her breast. Her eyes knew him but did not see him; her eyes shed light upon him but would not let his look come in. So he would paint her some day when his peace was secure and his bowels had ceased to yearn within him. Meanwhile he must teach himself to foster what she had given to him with so much pain and pride . . .

Titus slid off his chest and walked unsteadily away to investigate a patch of ferns. He sat up, aching in every muscle, and began to collect what was strewn about him: the drawing of the doomed pig, the chalk, the little drawing board, the pebble—why should he want it?—that he had put into the boy's hand. He knew that his face must be red and raw, seared by the violence of his repeated weeping, but he did not wait for it to right itself: in these latter days of September, the sea mists rolled landward as early as five o'clock, and he did not want Titus exposed to any unwholesomeness that lurked in those mists.

*

He had told himself beforehand that it would be a mistake to make too much of the evening when the Regents' piece was to be put on display at the Military Club. The occasion would not be a public one: out of courtesy to the subscribers who, as he had too often been reminded, had laid out their florins, the clubhouse dining room would serve nobody that evening but members of Captain Banning Coq's Company. No knowledgeable collectors, no particularly promising patrons, no fellow-members of the Saint Lucas Guild would be there—only the skittle-playing, horse-obsessed haunters of the musket range, whose opinions meant nothing to him. If he put in a request that young Six and Ferdi-

384

nand Bol be allowed to attend, it was not that he needed anybody's support; it was only that he did not want to share a table with Coq and Ruytenberg or sit with strangers and be bored to death.

It was unfortunate that the canvas was to be presented on that particular Saturday evening. The afternoon, spent in the fields with Titus, had had for him a deep, disarming, incommunicable sweetness which he would have liked to brood upon until he slept. This first week of October had been unusually dry, and the grass and dead leaves they had walked on had rustled and crackled and given off a desiccated fragrance as of incense; and he had known a strange happiness at the thought that all things dead eventually came to this—a blameless dryness so innocent as to take upon itself a kind of holiness. With winter coming on, the tainted sickness might go out of his mourning: the dead are harried by decay all summer long, but in winter they lie almost secure in their graves. Such thoughts had made him incapable of bothering about what he wore and how he looked—he put on his unironed and spotted mourning jacket and neglected to go to the barber's even though his hair, unwashed and unmanageable and fast growing grizzled, stood out like an ailing lion's mane. There would be nobody there he would care to impress: Bol saw him all day long slopping about in his painter's blouse, with his bare feet thrust into ancient slippers; and Six, born as he was to the gold braid and spotless linen of the Regents' class, measured his greatness by his eccentricity. Also, to come to an affair of Coq's and Ruytenberg's in a slightly slovenly state was to pay them off for the evenings when she had lain feverish in the great new house and they could not find the time to come.

He got to the clubhouse early, senselessly prolonging the occasion by his desire to hurry to it and get it over with, and the dining room was almost empty when he stepped in. Old Jacob, setting out the mugs and bottles, said something about "bad luck with the fires"; and indeed they were miserable fires—new peat, not properly dried, poured out black smoke and begot the disheartening thought that within a year or two the whole bright surface of his canvas would be coated with grime. For the moment no harm was being done: the painting, hung this afternoon by Bol and four of the other apprentices, was under a great tarpaulin. He ordered beer and cheese, sat down at a table for four in the middle of the room, and stared at the covered picture and was depressed by the size of it. It seemed much bigger here than in the empty warehouse, where it had stood like a god in his temple with nothing to detract from it; and he had to admit that it was certainly too big jammed in there between the crossbow window and the chimney piece: the men were bound to look as if they were marching straight into the fireplace.

Cheese, bread, a large tankard of beer, and a salad of cucumbers and radishes were put in front of him by the old servant. Whatever his honor might care to order during the evening came to him with the compliments of the Company, said Jacob, tremulous with pride over the manly generosity of the hosts. He begged, too, to call the attention of the guest of honor to the little bunches of boxwood and bayberries put on all the tables to mark this important occasion; and it was good he had mentioned them—doubtless somebody ought to be thanked for the gesture, and the hero of the evening knew he would never have noticed them himself. The beer was excellent, the salad creditable, the cheese not as good as what he would have been nibbling at home in the good Geertje's society. As others, arriving by twos and threes, began to seat themselves toward the edges of the room, he wished he had not chosen a central table where every stray glance would light on him; but to move now, carrying his food with him, would seem like a retreat.

Bol and Six were not late, but he took it ill that they were not early. So much time had gone by since he had first sketched the guardsmen—so many violent things had happened to *him,* and *they* had passed through so many subtle transformations on the canvas—that he was afraid some of them might come and sit with him and force him into admitting that he had forgotten even their names. Grief robbed a man of the useful, middle part of his nature: either it made him responsive and intense, as he had been this afternoon, or it left him slack and witless, as he was tonight. In such a mood of self-mistrust it was easy to notice and magnify disturbing things, to imagine that the general failure to stare at the draped picture indicated disinterest, to feel that Coq and Ruytenberg ought to have been on hand to greet him, to observe that the soldier who had arrived earliest was greeted by Jacob as Heer Cruysbergen, a name he vaguely connected with one of the men who had forced Bol to let them into the warehouse to have a look at the mystery.

Bol and Six came together, the former in decent grey wool with pewter buttons, the latter in buff-colored velvet and a magnificent peacock-blue cloak. The two young heads, one dark and brooding and the other fair and insouciant, were so comely that a king could not have asked for more impressive companions. "There's no use pretending otherwise, Master," said Bol, sitting down and staring ruefully at the muffled canvas. "Seeing it down here is disheartening, somehow, after the way it looked in the warehouse. But you soon get used to it, and—as I was saying to Jan—we've got to remember that nobody else saw it the way we did, off by itself." And the silence was filled with the mournful thought: "Nobody else but Tulp and the dead."

Since he was preoccupied, the two young men chatted with each other; and he felt himself growing more raw and stupid by the minute. Was the man who was entering now the drummer of the Company or one of the rank and file who happened also to have a squarish beard? Should he be put out with the captain and the lieutenant for merely waving heartily to him from the door without coming over to his table, or had they more cause to take offense at him because he had crowded them out by bringing his own companions? Once the tarpaulin was off the picture, would his heart and the occasion quicken? Or would he know that the best time was already past, that never again would the painting be what it had been to him and to her when it had stood in an isolation worthy of its greatness and its uniqueness, making her stop with her little hand at her lips and gasp and say, "Oh, my God"?

"Is there to be a speech?" said Jan Six, lifting his bright face to old Jacob, who was serving the two young men also with "the compliments of the Company."

"A short one, as I understand it, your honor." The rheumy old eyes took in the loose yellow curls, the cleft square chin resting against the collar of buff velvet, the masculine but well-cared-for hand. He knew this youth at sight; everybody in Amsterdam knew him and took it for granted that he would be a burgomaster, and treated him accordingly.

"And who's to make the speech?"

"The captain, your honor. He'll start as soon as all of them are here —there's only two of them missing now, if I'm counting right. May I suggest that you gentlemen don't fill up too much on cheese and salad? There's a partridge on the spit for your table."

When the missing two arrived, they proved sufficiently important for the short postponement. One of them was the ensign and the other the senior member of the troop, a silvery-grey musketeer as conscious of his dignity as if he had regularly stood in the path of a cannonade. The noise, which had had a certain halting and forced quality until now, surged to a heartening volume. At the crest of it Captain Banning Coq got up, silhouetted against the smoking fireplace at the upper end of the room, and banged on the table with his tankard; and everybody fell silent at once, perhaps because the talk lacked real conviction and perhaps because military discipline had taught them to hold their tongues at the first command.

The captain was dressed in the clothes in which he had been painted, but if his intention was to prove that his portrait was a "speaking likeness," that plan did not entirely come off, at least not for the painter. Had he changed, aged, somehow at once both softened and dwindled? The chest that supported the scarlet sash was not really monumental; the eyes were shrewd rather than knowing; the voice that would have issued out of the picture would have been more compelling than this voice—too smooth, too ingratiating, pitched too high, as if to cover up some insecurity, some doubt.

"Comrades," he said, "we are about to set eyes on what we have long been waiting to see—"

Nobody said, "Too long," but he paused almost imperceptibly, as if he were expecting something of the sort; and it was necessary to tell oneself that nobody here could build or demolish a reputation, that a painter would be in a sorry way if he had to depend on the enthusiasm of these foppish toy soldiers.

"As soon as the tarpaulin is removed from what waits for us over there, I am sure that every one of you will say that he never waited to a better purpose, never laid down his florins in a nobler or more gratifying cause. When you see what Heer van Rijn has given you"—he made a gesture toward Heer van Rijn's table and waited for applause, and there *was* applause and some clanking of knives and banging of tankards— "when you see what I glimpsed only briefly this afternoon and cannot wait to feast my eyes on, you will know what I mean. But why talk about it? Lieutenant, Ensign, take off the tarpaulin." He went on only long enough to cover the thud of their boots across the length of the room. "Show us this wonder, this glory that will keep the Company marching forever, its banner unfurled, its lances raised, its drum beating down the corridors of time."

With military precision, the ensign and the lieutenant loosened their corners. The great cloth slid down and a great "Oh!" went up—how else?—no dolt could fail to exclaim over the brilliance of the color, no clod could see without wonder a sudden burst of noonday light irradiate a twilight room. Amazement at gold and sea-blue and scarlet, at pulsing brightness and overwhelming size—these alone were enough to make it easy for them to do the expected thing, and that first "Oh!" of theirs was vibrant and long. But before it had subsided the painter was deaf to it, overwhelmed as he was with his own discontents: it was horrible, horrible that the great canvas should be crowded in like that. They were not marching down the corridors of time, they were marching into the fireplace; his figures, contrasted with the figures in the other paintings along the walls, looked so large as to seem overdone, so vigorous as to seem aggressive, so exuberant as to be—dear God, he blushed as he had blushed in the van Hoorn sitting room—in questionable taste. Nor was it as much comfort to him as it should have been that Jan Six, aristocrat of aristocrats and the only connoisseur in the lot of them, had sprung out of his chair to stare at it avidly and was now looking down at its creator with tears of admiration standing in his eyes. "A great moment, a moment in history," he said. And Ferdinand Bol, stroking his tankard, probably because he did not dare to lay a comforting hand on his master's arm, said, "Nobody else will notice the crowding, Master, remember that. It's only we who saw it in the warehouse." *She* had seen it in the warehouse, and what did it matter what anybody thought of it? He cared about nothing, nothing, now that she was dead.

So he could not care much if they were a little put off, once they had gotten over their first amazement, by its uniqueness. The silence now was the uneasy silence of the uninitiate who must engage in a worried search for safe little words to cover their ignorance. Somebody in a corner lighted on "really unbelievable colors." Somebody else, a touch more clever, mentioned the "coming-outness and going-inness of it"— not bad for a young dandy who knew nothing about perspective. A third venturesome soul said loudly that there was so much in it that a person didn't know where to start. The captain, up there by the fireplace,

388

lifted his tankard again, perhaps to call them to silence and a round of standing applause; but if that had been his intention, he abandoned it and sat down. They were disquieted, they were disconcerted, they had begun to go in groups to get a closer look at the thing. The applause could wait—it was better to let them alone to gape and reassure each other and themselves.

Yet the dozen of them who wandered up to the picture were not doing the sort of thing the painter would have expected. They did not feel the thick braid on the lieutenant's jacket; they did not point out the barking dog or the running boys or the radiant face of the child-Saskia or anything else that should have caught their fancies. They looked—how could he have been so stupid as not to have known it beforehand? —only for their own images. "Where am I?" "Is that me over where you're standing, Dirk?" "You're here, Isak—at least I think this is you" —that was all they said.

And they said these things so tentatively, they sought themselves out with so much embarrassment, and some of them looked so crestfallen when they finally discovered themselves in the back row half-muffled by a banner or almost crossed out by a lance, that an unnerving transformation took place in his own feelings: he was sorry for them in their constraint and their disappointment and their ignorance. Their desires —and he could not wish it otherwise—had been cut to pieces by the fierce wings of his desire. While he smiled back at Jan Six and shook hands with the captain, who had finally come up, while he nodded to Ruytenberg and bowed to others who offered him at a distance various gestures of congratulation and applause, he was stricken by the thought of how many had been robbed of what was rightfully their own so that he might soar at will: Mother and Father, Adriaen and Lysbeth, poor van Vliet and Vrouw van Hoorn and Master van Swanenburgh, yes, and *she,* too, the one beloved, lying beside him quick with new life and heavy with the fear of death, and he forgetful, unresponsive, even cruel, borne upward and away from her on the reckless pinions of his dreams.

"Oh, yes, there I am—at least, I guess that's me," said one of the older men. "It's just that it took me a while to recognize myself, what with Hendrik's gorget covering up my chin."

"Don't tell us you mind a little thing like that," said a drawling voice from the shadow at the edge of the room. "You apparently don't understand how this is done, you're complaining about the very thing that makes this painting great. Anybody can paint faces you can see and recognize—like these up here and here and here—" The speaker had risen tall out of the shadow and was flinging his lean arm toward the Ketel and the Elias and the new von Sandrart canvas on the wall. "The remarkable thing about this painting is that it's not a group portrait at all: it's a great design. You're only showing your ignorance if you complain because somebody's gorget is more important than your chin."

Everybody in the room turned his head toward the center table, where the captain stood with one hand on the back of the master's chair and the master sat stupefied. Was this the voice that had forced Bol to open the warehouse door on the grounds that anybody who had paid his florins had a right to come in? Was this an enemy speaking in crude sarcasm or a befuddled fool quoting with decent intent some dictum he did not understand? And if he was quoting, whom was he quoting? The demanding face not quite visible in the twilight, the sudden babbling everywhere—what should be done, how could it be dealt with? One thing was certain: he could not deal with it, slow and thick-witted and utterly at a loss as he was tonight . . .

"Heer Cruysbergen," said the captain, "this is not the occasion for that sort of remark. We're here to—"

"You're right, my captain. This is not the occasion, I'll admit. The painting is finished. No changes are possible. All we can do now is get together and celebrate the completion of the masterpiece. And before it was completed, that wasn't the occasion either, as I remember. Before it was completed, the genius mustn't be upset: he was working it out according to his own lights, and it would be sacrilege to mention that your face happened to be chopped up by a musket butt."

It was unfortunate—it somehow made the occasion more ghastly still —that old Jacob should have chosen that moment to come up with the roast partridge and preserved quinces and fresh rusks. An appalled silence gripped the crowd of them, kept them watching with a kind of fascination while the dishes were set down one after the other before the honor guest; and it was his apprentice—not he—who found the heart to break the ugly hush.

"This much should be explained—this much should be explained in all justice," said Ferdinand Bol, with his eyes cast down and his hands lying open on either side of the partridge. "You do yourselves a disservice and you do the painter an injury, an unforgivable injury, if you look at those figures up there as separate portraits. My master painted the Company all together, as one great totality." His voice trembled, and he closed his outstretched hands and bit his lower lip. "My master painted a military fellowship, a fellowship larger and more significant than any single one of you as he stands alone. And it was all the more honor that he paid you by painting you like that—the honor of being part of something greater than yourself."

His gentle voice begot a gentle surge of deprecation and reassurance: the soldier, they said, was speaking for himself; if some agreed with him, there were also some who didn't; and no matter what he thought about the picture, he ought to control himself like a guardsman and a gentleman. But when their voices had subsided, the mocking voice again asserted itself. "Heer Bol," said Cruysbergen, somehow turning the very name into an insult, "maybe we differ about what's an honor, you and I. To stare over somebody else's sleeve like an idiot is an honor I can do without."

The captain stiffened, but that was all. He had his sketch at home in his album to show to his children and grandchildren. He had his Company where he wanted it, taking up the largest area of the wall. He had his image of himself—magnified, glorified—marching down the corridors of time. Having used the painter, he was finished with the painter; he had no intention of defending him if it meant alienating any of the companions he would be meeting on the musket range day after day and clinking a merry tankard with night after night. As for Lieutenant Ruytenberg, *he* was gazing out the crossbow window as if he had to supervise the coming down of the dark. And what else was to be expected of a man who had flirted with blooming health only to run away at the first rumor of ill luck, the first omen of death?

It was Jan Six who started up to take on the sickening business—his hair shaken loose, his hands up and clenched near his chest, his whole young body taut and belligerent. "God in heaven," he said, "is a man supposed to sit and listen to this? I've never heard anything so coarse, so disgusting, so arrogant and ignorant—never in all my days. You over there—how dare you raise your voice against your betters? This man, great beyond your conception, has been good enough to put your stupid face into a masterpiece, and you criticize, you complain, *you* protest! That he should have turned a crowd like you into a thing like that and then have to listen to you whine about your florins and what's in front of your faces—no, I can't understand it, it's too much for me. If the name of a single one of you survives"—the sweep of his arm indicated that he meant to include the captain, too—"it will be only because you had the great good fortune to get yourself painted by Rembrandt van Rijn."

The strong young hand came down on the master's shoulder, and somehow the ardent voice and the reckless generosity of the defense shook him at last out of his dull incapacity. He got to his feet and glared across the room at the still unabashed and sneering face, and icy fury contracted his heart. "What do you want?" he shouted, and his voice was like the bellow of a steer, and old Jacob, who had begun to light the lamps, stood still with the taper and its flame shaking in his hands. "What do you want? Your miserable florins back? Here, you can have them." He reached for the heavy purse at his hip and turned to Banning Coq. "What did he pay? What was his share?"

"Please—please—let's not—" said the captain.

"Oh, no, let's have an end of it. He protests, he isn't satisfied, and neither am I—I wouldn't take his filthy money for anything. There, he couldn't have paid more for it than that," he said, and flung down a fistful of jangling gold and silver coins among the dishes on the table.

"Don't think you can make it right by throwing around your money," said the bitter voice. "You can't pay a man off for making a fool of him. What do I want? I want you to paint me out of the damned thing. But I'm not likely to get it, of course: you're the genius, your holy handiwork can't be tampered with, and I'm only a soldier—not a captain, not a lieutenant—only a soldier who'll have to put up with the jokes I'll be hearing about that picture to the end of my days."

And inasmuch as it was true, how could it be answered? This one too, arrogant and loathsome though he was, had been slashed by the reckless wings. His face had been blotted out for a high purpose, yes, but he had no portion in that purpose; and he would have to explain over and over—to his comrades, his wife, his children—why this violence had been done to his particular face. While the babble surged up again, Bol collected the coins that had fallen under the rim of the meat platter and in among the rusks, and the master noticed that his apprentice's face was white, and knew that his own was red, that his thin skin showed the stain of an uneradicable shame.

"Cruysbergen's drunk, as usual," said the captain softly.

But it was not enough, and he could not bring himself to answer graciously or even to turn his head; and Banning Coq, having done what he considered his duty, wandered back to his table near the smoking fire.

If the rest of them had abandoned the subject and set about their eating and drinking, it might have been possible for the guest of honor also to eat and drink. As it was, with muted discussions going on all around him, he found it unthinkable to touch the partridge and equally unthinkable to sit staring at it there untouched. Whether it was wise or not, it was certainly a relief when Jan Six got up, flung his splendid peacock-blue cloak around his shoulders, and tossed his head in the direction of the door. "Come, let's take ourselves off," he said, "we don't have to sit and listen to this. We'll stop at my place—my mother will be delighted. The sooner we get out of here the better."

But they could not leave without passing close to Cruysbergen's table. The rebels had gathered there and were for the most part on their feet, talking loudly and pointing over the more seemly heads at the great canvas, which was growing brighter every minute as old Jacob kindled one after another of the lamps. "And look at all that empty room in the back—why couldn't he have put some of us there?" said a pale plump fellow with a drooping moustache and tired eyes. "That dog barking at Isak and those boys running around in the crowd—why did he have to stick them in if he was short of space?"

"That's right," said Cruysbergen. "And what about that silly little girl with the fuzzy hair—whose daughter is she that she should have a full-length portrait for nothing?"

It was too much. That many would be dissatisfied—this he supposed he had feared and expected in the secret places of his mind. That he had come off badly with Cruysbergen and been abandoned by Coq and Ruytenberg—this he deserved. That the celebratory occasion had turned into one of his worst humiliations—this he would teach himself to bear. But that a coarse, jeering voice should desecrate his vision of *her,* that everything left of her gone childhood and her innocent earthly happiness should be slandered and abused—this went like a bruising fist into the softness of his heart. He walked as briskly as his two young companions down the darkened street, answering them now and then and answering to the point; but his eyes were blind and he was thankful for the stretches of windowless dark where he could chew his trembling lips and allow himself to weep.

*

"Go on, I'm listening," said Vrouw Anna Weijmar Six, looking over the rim of her hand mirror at her son Jan, who stood some five feet away from her in the sunny, curtained alcove of her dressing room, his stance outwardly respectful but not without a hint of impatience, his head turned politely in her direction but his elbows planted carelessly behind him on the window sill.

He could imagine how hard she was listening. She was engaged, with a practical shamelessness that he had never learned either to admire or to deprecate, in the business of pulling a few stiff white hairs out of her plump, pink little chin. He supposed he ought to be sorry for her: the necessity to remove such hairs was a sign that all the vestiges of youth were past. But she went after them with so much vigor, she plucked them out with such evident relish that sympathy seemed out of place.

"I really *am* listening," she said, fingering the plucked, unblemished surface. "And anyway, if I weren't, it wouldn't really matter—I've heard it all before. Once from Banning Coq's mother, and once from Ruytenberg's sister, and at least twice from you."

Once from me, he thought—as usual, you exaggerate. If he had gone on too much about it, it had been to others, not to her; and considering the fuss she made over a stained drape or a spoiled pudding, he wondered that she should object to hearing about that miserable spectacle at the Military Club. "I'm sorry. If it bores you, I'll see that I keep it to myself," he said, hating the middle-aged and the circumspect, with their stiff white hairs and their lukewarm blood.

"I never said it bored me. Talk about it as much as you like, if it relieves your feelings. Only"—she laid the tweezers on her dressing table and the looking glass in her lap—"I keep feeling there's something you want from me, something you think I ought to do."

Something she ought to do—well, he should hope so! What was their ancient and honorable name good for if it couldn't be brought to the aid of a great man wronged, a prophet badgered by Pharisees? If such a one, sunken as he was in the morass of his personal sorrows, could be forced to struggle too with the creatures of the slime, Amsterdam was a wilderness of stolid ignorance.

"I can't have him paint me, Jan; I've already had him paint me. And

393

if I asked him so soon again, it might seem patronizing and obvious."

He saw that it might, and gave her a grudging nod. "Still, you could always send others his way—members of your Regents' Board, relatives, friends—"

"Believe it or not, dear, I've tried it." She got up, so simply and severely dressed in her neat grey woolen that he could not even condemn her ostentation, and laid the mirror beside the tweezers and came to him in the alcove. "Three times last week I tried it, and it just didn't work at all."

"Whom did you try it with, and how did you try it?"

"Why should I tell you? Anybody I'd name you'd only take exception to," she said with infuriating equanimity. "Besides, I haven't stopped trying. I'll certainly keep asking wherever I think it's wise, and maybe eventually I'll have some success, though I want you to know it isn't going to be as easy as you seem to think."

"It's disgraceful that anybody should have to go around asking for commissions for him. People should be clamoring at his door."

"Scores of them *were,* that's just the trouble. And it wasn't so long ago either—not long enough for them to have forgotten how he behaved himself."

Behaved himself—little girls should keep their dresses down, little boys should lower their voices, servants should pause and cough slightly before crossing a threshold—that was her idea of morality! "And just how, according to his inferiors," he said icily, "did the master behave himself?"

"A little arrogantly, to say the least. There were some he told to come back in a couple of years. Others he gave to understand he'd rather not see them again at all."

"Is that just gossip, or do you know of specific cases?"

"Well, there's the case of Amalia van Wylick—that's one I got first-. hand. She can be something of a plague, and I know he was busy with the *Sacrifice of Abraham* when she came, but he needn't have said she had an uninteresting face. Once a woman's been told that, she's scarcely likely to come back for more."

His cheeks went hot out of anger and shame for the master. "If *I* had the choice of painting Amalia van Wylick or Abraham and Isaac, I know what *my* choice would be," he said.

"Of course, but that isn't the question. The question is, where is he going to get commissions? I tried to talk Amalia out of her hurt feelings, but I did no good, and it's a pity, because she would have paid him an excellent price."

Money again—the whole sickening business at the Military Club had had the taint of money on it. Money was so hateful that there was something unnerving about even the rejection of it: he saw again, with a vague sense of nausea, the coins scattered among the festive food. "The master isn't in need of money. His wife left him a fortune," he said. "What he needs—and it's shameful that he should have to go begging for it when it's showered on people like Flinck and von Sandrart—is the patronage of old, solid names."

"Well, he has mine for whatever it's worth, and he's welcome to use it as he likes. But he's offended some of the others enough to make them glad for an opportunity to pay him off. He's made himself enemies—more than I would have thought—and I'm afraid he'll be needing more support than yours and Tulp's and mine."

He chewed his lower lip and thought of the Regents among whom she would charitably, graciously continue to look for possible patrons—the pompous men and busy little women running around in well-intentioned civic activity, getting under each other's feet in their zeal to do good. "What's the matter with his peers? Why don't *they* bestir themselves to defend him?" he said.

"His peers?" She let herself down onto a stool close to the sun-drenched curtains and scratched her head in perplexity. "If you mean people of learning, people of accomplishment—*you're* the writer, *you're* the scholar, I should think *you'd* be the one to know the answer to that. I'd be glad to give a supper party and invite any number of them if you think it would do him any good."

The learned, the accomplished—he tallied them off one after the other and dismissed them. This one was a toady of von Sandrart's; that one was forever running over to Muiden to spend the weekend in Hooft's drafty castle; another couldn't open his mouth until Joost van den Vondel told him what to say. Their antagonism to the master was old and rooted deep; and his little fool of an apprentice Houbraken hadn't helped matters any by saying that the painting of Banning Coq's Company made every other piece in the club, including von Sandrart's, look like a playing card. The power of the Muiden Circle was as arbitrarily theirs as the wealth and influence of the house of Six; and he was ashamed to think of himself as one of the inheritors.

"You know, I've been a little worried about you, dear. You seem so nervous."

Her choice of words would madden anybody. A prophet showing his scorn for the Pharisees—that was "misbehaving." A protest against utter injustice—that was "nervousness." "I'm not in the least nervous. It wasn't I that spilled the chocolate," he said.

She had been the chocolate-spiller, a couple of hours ago at the noon-day table. She said, "Touché," not managing the French too well, and looked up at him from her place on the stool with a rueful little smile. "But there's no reason for us to be quarreling with each other, is there?" she asked, putting up her hand and feeling her chin again with obvious satisfaction. "I'm concerned about him, too; it was I that introduced him to you in the first place, wasn't it? I'll do whatever I can, I promise. I'll keep asking people about commissions, and I'll arrange a supper party whenever you—"

"A supper party is a ridiculous idea!"

"Is it? I thought you were the one who made the suggestion."

She confused him—he couldn't for the life of him remember which of them had suggested it. "Do whatever you think," he said, and started for the door.

"Are you going to work on your play, darling?" she asked as he put his hand to the doorknob.

He *had* been intending to work on his play, but now that she had mentioned it he would do no such thing. "No. I'm going to walk over to Dr. Tulp's."

"To see the doctor about Heer van Rijn? I'd wait until evening if I were you. I doubt he'll be there at this time of day."

"Whether he's there or nor, it'll decrease my nervousness to walk," he said with bitterness.

And when he was out in the hall, with the closed door between them, he could scarcely master an impulse to kick at the beautiful paneled wood. He knew that she was laughing at him—lovingly, tenderly, with an indulgent shake of her greying head—but laughing at him nevertheless on the other side of that door.

*

Houses were bound to look dreary toward the end of winter—so his mother and Lysbeth and Saskia had always said. Nothing but a thorough spring cleaning could get rid of the mud and melted snow tracked over the tiles and carpets, the soot that contrary drafts drove down the chimney, the smoke that kept pouring out of the fireplace. Everybody's house was dreary in February, but how dreary? he asked himself that bleak Sunday afternoon, walking up and down a salon used now only by the apprentices when he set them to sketching the Caligula or making drawings from the Ruysdaels or the Brouwers. Was there another great house on the Breestraat or in all Amsterdam that was really as dreary as this?

Of course, there was no discounting the fact that the place was depressing for reasons other than the seasonal grime. It was not Geertje's nor Klaartje's fault if he remembered that *she* had hoped to have crowds of guests with music and dancing, celebratory occasions that had never materialized. Nor could any amount of soap and polish make up for the absence of certain pieces of furniture that were to have been bought in a future that never arrived: the empty spaces needed sideboards and cabinets and suits of armor and lengths of Flemish tapestry. Nevertheless, striding back and forth in the seldom occupied chamber, past a bleak hearth where only an occasional fire was kindled to keep the apprentices' hands from stiffening, he saw things that could not be accounted for by February disenchantment or the bruise of old regret. Must there be cobwebs dangling from the ceiling? Must the ashes of a fire burned out two weeks ago still be strewn over the hearthstones?

Couldn't somebody have gotten that blotch of yellow ocher out of the carpet? How long had it been since the picture frames had been dusted? He ran his forefinger along the frame of the Rubens and gathered up a damp grey film on the tip. "Good God!" he said, and shuddered, as if he had reached into the apple bin and touched a dead mouse. As for the weather's making the house look dreary, here it was working the other way: the panes of the beautiful leaded casements were so grimed over that they made the rain-swept prospect outside more disheartening still.

Wiping his hand on the side of his wrinkled breeches, he started back to the small sitting room in the rear where such life as the house contained centered itself on Sunday afternoons. All these lordly chambers to accommodate four who might as well be living in a cottage in Zuytbroek for all they got out of their surroundings: the heavy, aging woman forever at her accounts or her mending, the raw little adolescent servant dreaming and chewing the end of her blond braid, the boy in common frieze—no reason to deck him out since nobody here went to church and no after-service visitors came by—and he himself in his wilted shirt and his shoddiest jacket, filling up the empty hours between a spare noonday meal and an indifferent supper by examining possessions that he never used . . . He caught an image of himself, unkempt and grizzled, in the ornamented mirror he and Saskia had bought for the little hall. "Good God!" he said again, thinking with how much more seemliness and dignity Harmen Gerritszoon had spent the Sunday afternoons of his life. His eyes settled on the beautiful ancient wine-cooler, carved out of marble, which stood on a gilded table under the big glass. Had they ever heaped it with snow and put a precious bottle in it, he and Saskia? He could not remember . . . At the moment it was filled—the blood rushed into his face and the veins in his neck showed swollen at the sight—with a collection of worn stockings, a pincushion bristling with needles, a couple of balls of yarn, and a spool of thread.

He snatched the tawdry assortment out of the wine-cooler, jagging his fingers, and strode with it, dropping things behind him, into the back parlor where the three of them sat just as he had expected to find them, like peasants, without candles, making the most of the dull rose glow of the fire. "God in Heaven," he said, and knew how often he must have cried out against all that was amiss, knew it by the fact that they scarcely bothered to turn their heads. Even the boy, making a tower of blocks on the hearthstones, looked at him indifferently, reaching out meanwhile to find another block for the tower.

"What's the matter, your honor?" said Geertje.

"What's this? What do you call this?" he asked, holding out what he had left of his findings.

She peered at it; she could not make it out. Her eyes were failing, and the expanse of the big round table, dark without candles, stretched between. "What's what, your honor?"

The little Klaartje got up from the hearth and stood behind her. "It's your mending, Vrouw Dircx. His honor picked up your mending some place where you left it," she said.

"Where did I leave it? Oh, yes, out in the wine-cooler. I brought it down when I went up to change my apron after I washed the dishes. I meant to work at it later and I thought I'd save myself another trip upstairs."

"But, Geertje, it was lying in the wine-cooler, in the *wine-cooler*—"

"I'm sorry, your honor. I know that's no place to put it, but I didn't think it would do any harm. After all, nobody's likely to come in and find it there."

There was no insolence in her, only a drab imperturbability. That she should have lived all this time in the deserted house and never guessed that he was wounded by its emptiness—no, it was more than his patience could bear. "A wine-cooler is not a repository for old stockings. Nobody buys hand-carved Italian marble to put old stockings in," he said, knowing that his eyes were bulging and that a big vein was pulsing in the middle of his brow.

She got to her feet then and did what she had not done since the day of the funeral: she made him the servile curtsy, with a bending of her wrinkled neck and a creaking of her knees. By the gesture she divested herself, dumbly and resignedly, of the confidence that had been between them on the evenings when they had sat in mutual sorrow and silence, sharing the light of the same candle; and, so divested, she was exposed enough to put him to shame. "Forget about it—it's nothing," he said.

"Oh, no, your honor, it's not nothing. It was a bad mistake, and if your honor will be good enough to overlook it I'll see that nothing like it ever happens again."

If only she could have kept silent! The words, craven and meaningless, spoken by rote to countless masters by countless servants, stirred up his subsiding bile. "The fact that the house isn't crowded with visitors is no reason why it should be kept like a pigsty," he said.

"I didn't know your honor thought I kept it like a pigsty."

"I didn't say you did, though there's plenty the matter here, God knows."

"If your honor would mention what's to be done, I'd do my best to do it."

"Dust the picture frames. Scrub up the tile in the reception hall. Take the paint spots out of the carpet. Polish the brass and copper and silver. Wash the windows—you can't see the outside for the grime on the panes." He knew when he was halfway through it that it was a preposterous list. Two strong men could scarcely have coped with it, and he was shouting at an aging woman and a frail young girl. Yet he went on, naming things he had not even known he was aware of: sooty hearthstones, dusty bins, smeared lamps, grimy window sills. Somewhere in the midst of it the tower of blocks came down and the boy began to wail and the little Klaartje covered her face with her apron and burst into tears. Only the thick and weary woman on the other side of the table did not collapse, stood motionless like a dumb beast under the lashing of his words, her eyes dull and fixed, her face as grey as a stone. When his voice and his fury had both given out, she still stood unmoved: it was the weeping Klaartje who picked Titus up and carried him screaming out of the room. There was a long silence in which he heard the blood beat like a hammer in his ears. Then she curtsied again, gathered up the things he had strewn over the table and put them into her apron, and said in the same craven voice, "Your honor is right. I have made a pigsty of your honor's house. With what strength I have, I'll try to mend it. I'll do what I can."

"Geertje," he said, putting out his hand.

But she did not see him. She also left the small back chamber, and he could hear her sighing as she labored through the hall.

Time went by, dark pounding minutes when the surge and fall of his blood seemed to keep pace with the glow and fall of the dying fire. He sat down in the empty room, aimless and ravaged, and could think of nothing he wished to do. He simply stared before him, and by and by the little Klaartje came back, leading a pacified Titus. Having settled the boy on the hearth and given him his big felt ball to play with, she came with a burning length of twisted paper to light the candles; and her face was so pale that the chapped spots on her cheeks and chin showed purplish in the growing light. She said nothing—what could she say, poor thing?—and he said nothing. Once she had lighted the candles and folded up Geertje's shawl, she sat down on the hearth with the boy and they rolled the ball back and forth between them; and when the child's laughter broke the silence it was a kind of indecency. Not caring that the girl would hear him, he sighed heavily and moved uneasily in his chair, conscious of a coldness at his back and around his feet. A chill, he thought, a chill of the spirit, setting in after the soul's fever . . . But the flames of the newly lighted candles were waving and bending crazily, and a strange smell was in the room—smell of a wind-swept rainy street—and Klaartje half rose from the hearth and looked at him over the rim of the table with large, scared eyes. "There's a big draft in here, your honor. Something must have blown open. I'll go and see to it," she said.

She went, but there was no change. The cold smell kept filling his nostrils, and the current of air along the floor was strong enough to bestir him into getting up and lifting Titus out of the range of it onto one of the chairs. When Klaartje came back, she was paler still, really blue around the lips. "Please, your honor, if you don't mind, maybe you'd come into the salon with me and see if you can do anything with Vrouw Dircx," she said. "She's—she's started cleaning the windows in there, and the wind's driving in, and everything's getting soaked in the rain."

He went without believing her, but when they crossed the threshold of the salon he saw that one of the great casements was really standing open, and Geertje Dircx—up on a stool, with the wind slapping her apron and her black housedress around her heavy, uncertainly balanced body, with rain and tears running down her face and her greying hair wildly disordered by the blast—was rubbing fiercely at the leaded panes.

"Geertje," he said, "for God's sake, Geertje—" By the fixed eyes and the stony cheeks he knew she had not heard him, was not aware that he was there. Cold and afraid and sick with the nausea of his spent fury, he walked across the room into the rainy gust and took her by the skirt, but even that did no good. "Geertje," he shouted above the noise of the wind and the rain, "get down this minute. I mean it. I command it." And still she did not hear or see.

Klaartje came up and stepped between them then, bearing herself with an unaccustomed self-assurance that made him wonder whether she could have witnessed such scenes before. "Dear Vrouw Dircx," she said in a piercing, reedy little voice, "here's his honor asking you to step down, don't you see? It's no day to be cleaning casements—his honor never meant any such thing. Come down, come down like a good soul, and let me close the window. The lovely carpet is getting spoiled, and there are terrible drafts all over the house, and your little angel will catch his death of cold."

The hand that held the scrub-rag stopped its wild, repetitive motion. She shook herself, and looked down and reeled a little, and let them take her hands while she got to the floor. When Klaartje banged the window shut, she started at the sound and shuddered like somebody frightened out of a deep sleep. "What? What? What window was that?" she said.

"Everything's all right now, Vrouw Dircx," said the little servant, and the false reassurance in her voice made him certain that for her this was nothing new. "His honor isn't angry, and there's a fire in the parlor, and we'll get you warm, we'll go and sit with Titus, and I'll make us all a nice cup of tea—"

"No, thank you, Klaartje, not just now," she said, passing her hand over her forehead. "I seem to be a little dizzy. If his honor will excuse me, I think I'll go up and lie down in my room and try to get some sleep."

"Certainly his honor will excuse you," said Klaartje. "Maybe he'd help me get you upstairs since you're a little dizzy."

She walked well enough, both on the level and on the staircase; and if he supported her by laying his arm around her waist it was not that she really stood in need of steadying, only to indicate his contrition, though he had an uncanny notion that she had forgotten much of what had been said. Breathing somewhat heavily, she gave Klaartje instructions on the way up: the black bean soup needed only to be heated over a low fire; there was a dish of fish heads for the cat outside on the window sill; Heer Bol was not expected to supper, and there was no need to set her own place at the table—she felt so qualmish she doubted she'd want anything to eat tonight . . . He left the two of them at the door of her room—he disliked entering because there was always a woman-smell that offended him in there—and going into his own princely chamber, dank and bleak in the dying light of the winter afternoon, he began to break up some kindling, thinking he would wrest from the misery of the day at least the cheer of a good fire.

Klaartje was talking in the same false, cajoling way; he heard her call back from the stairway that she would see to everything; he heard the ringing of pots in the kitchen, and he wondered whether he himself would be able to eat. Then, after another silence—the kindling was broken and laid, and he stood staring vacantly at the cold, oppressive majesty of the mantelpiece—he heard a sob: she was weeping alone in her room, poor Geertje, weeping as he had wept in the weeks after the funeral; and sometimes she had come then and stood at his door, her big face washed over with tears, and a steaming cup of broth—her idea of comfort—held out in her hands.

His eyes lighted on a little box lying on top of the mantel. It was months since he had seen it or thought of it; it contained a gift he had bought for Saskia on the day of her death, a small gold chain set with pearls. Why not? he thought, taking the dusty box down from the mantel. He would never have the heart or the face to take it back to the jeweler's after all these months, and a present—such a rich present as masters did not give to servants—might somehow atone for the moment when he had robbed her of their shared grief and confidence.

He went down the dark hall and into her room, breathing shallowly to avoid the smell. Here, too, there were no candles: her big body, flat on its back and draped in the thick folds of her housedress, showed charcoal-black against the universal grey. He could not see her face—it was covered by one thick arm, flung up and bent across it—but the creased neck was shiny with tears. He took the chain out of the box and approached the bed. "Geertje," he said in a voice that actually conveyed some of his regret, "I brought you a little present."

She heaved up a sigh that shook the stolid length of her body. "Your honor didn't need to bring me anything. It was my fault. All I want is your honor's forgiveness," she said.

"You have that already. I'm the one that ought to apologize. I don't know what got into me. But things haven't been going very well for me these days."

The thing that had not been going very well came down on him like a ruined wall, utterly crushing his spirit. The great canvas at the Military Club—who looked at it, who spoke of it now? The crowds it was to have drawn to this splendid house of his—where were they? How many kisses, what last dear confidences had he sacrificed for it, certain —dear God, how certain!—that it would prove itself worth any sacrifice? And now Banning Coq apologized for it, and Hooft and Vondel ignored it, and von Sandrart sneered at it, and Bol and the youngsters got into shameful public quarrels over it at Guild meetings and in taverns, and he was worse off than he had been before he laid the brush to it—and she was dead.

"I know how it is, your honor," said Geertje, turning her head in his direction without withdrawing her arm. "Believe me, I understand."

But he could console himself no more with such understanding than with the loyalty of his apprentices. "It's a chain I brought you, Geertje," he said in a voice not unlike Klaartje's. "I bought it the day Saskia died, and I never had a chance to give it to her, and now I want to give it to you."

She sat up, disheveled and breathless, looking less at the chain than at the hairy hand that offered it; and before he could guess her intention and step away, she had seized that hand and was kissing it and weeping upon it.

"Don't do that!" he said, so sharply that he had to make amends with a softening explanation. "That isn't how things are between you and me. Take your chain and wear it, Geertje; and if I ever lose my temper again, remember that it's because of other things, not you."

He left her lying on her side with the chain gleaming between the pillow and her wet cheek, and went downstairs. Titus was playing cheerfully on the hearth, so he followed Klaartje into the kitchen, where she was pouring the black bean soup from a caldron into the tureen— he took the caldron from her, pitying her childish back, and hung it on the hook over the embers. "Tell me, Klaartje, has Vrouw Dircx ever behaved like this before?" he said.

"Like what, your honor?" She was chopping pickled beets for a salad, and her eyes fixed themselves on the work and rejected his searching glance.

"Like she did in the salon—opening the window and starting to clean it on a day like this."

"Vrouw Dircx was dreadfully upset, your honor. She worships your honor, and—if you'll excuse my saying so—your honor did scare her half out of her wits shouting at her like that—"

He waited, and the small chapped hands continued to chop, but less expertly—the cubes of beet flew off the cutting board and onto the floor.

"If your honor means does she sometimes get dizzy and seem a little mixed up, why then I'd have to say yes, she does—not very often, only now and again. But then it's a big house for her to have on her hands, and I'm not much help, though I do whatever I can."

"How old are you, Klaartje?"

"Fourteen, your honor." She dropped the knife and turned her blue, scared look upon him. "Your honor's not thinking of letting me go?"

"Oh, no, no. Nothing of the sort, Klaartje. Only—" He saw there was no use pursuing Vrouw Dircx's eccentricities with her beneficiary and staunchest defender. "Only I thought maybe we ought to have still another girl, somebody younger than Vrouw Dircx but older than you."

"Oh, yes, that would be wonderful. Three of us certainly ought to be able to keep the place in hand. And unless your honor has somebody in mind, I know exactly the girl for the situation."

"Who would that be, Klaartje?"

"Well, her name's Hendrikje Stoffels, and she lives in my village, in Ransdorp, and she's twenty or over, and a fine housekeeper, and handsome, too—the sort of girl your honor would be proud to have open the door to his patrons."

Retreating from the thought of his shrunken patrons' list, he diverted himself by conjuring up a picture of this Hendrikje Stoffels of Ransdorp. He made her blond like Klaartje, tall enough to reach the tops of mantels and picture frames, as serene in her bearing as Margheretha van Meer, but full and round of arm and breast and shoulder —a country Juno, slow-moving and statuesque.

"She'd love it here," the little Klaartje was saying. "And if she stays where she is, you know what'll happen to her: she'll marry some dolt, some farmer or shoemaker—"

"Worse things could happen to her." He had said it inadvertently, thinking of Lysbeth—poor Lysbeth and poor Hendrik Isaakszoon.

"Do you really think so, Master? I don't. I'm terribly glad to be out of Ransdorp."

"Can you write, Klaartje?"

"Oh, yes, your honor. We all learned to write in Ransdorp."

"I wish you would write to this Stoffels girl then and ask her if she'd like to come. Do it right away."

"Gladly, your honor."

For an instant he was warmed by an old vision: he saw the house— irreproachable, shining, and splendid—as it had never been and he had always hoped it would be. But that was a short-lived comfort: when he turned and went into the other room to be with the boy, he knew that whatever came to pass—if all the brass were polished, if all the dust were wiped away, if every candle in the house were lighted—the shriveled heart in him would be the same. What would I do with it, how would I live in it? he thought; and he was grateful that the boy left his play and came to sit on his knee. "Dada is tired," said Titus; and spent as a man who has swum a long way through icy water, he laid his cheek against the warm, round head and breathed the fragrance of the silky curls.

*

The Stoffels girl had come from Ransdorp, and spring had come, softening the lanterns in the streets and the lights in the windows, and now that the house was at its best—better even than it had been when *she* had lived and been mistress in it—it seemed strange to him that some indefinable restlessness should make him forever eager to get out. Five nights out of seven he rose from his well-cooked supper and wandered off, leaving the swept hearths and the shining casements and the lighted candles behind him, taking long walks and inhaling the mingled scents of April—warm rain on cobblestones, the smell of crab apples in bloom in some faraway orchard, the strangely generative smell of the calmed sea. Where he settled after those walks—at the Lazzaras' or the Pineros', at the house of the learned and neighborly Rabbi Menasseh ben Israel, in the salon of Anna Weijmar Six or the Tulps' small parlor —made little difference; all that he wanted was to be elsewhere and to stay elsewhere until eleven, when everybody but the faithful Geertje would have gone to bed.

In the six weeks of her stay he had scarcely looked at the Stoffels girl, or had looked at her only enough to smile wryly at the portrait he had painted in his thoughts when Klaartje had recommended her. She was dark, and her hair was thick and a little coarse, as luxuriant hair is likely to be, with coppery lights in it when she sat close to a candle. She was small: she had to stand on a stool to reach the tops of mantels and picture frames, and he knew without ever having come close to her that the top of her head would reach no higher than his nose. He could see why Klaartje, who was childish and very flat, was forever going on to Geertje about the Stoffels girl's figure; it was womanly and full, swelling out at the breasts and going in at the waist and coming out again at the hips. It was true, he supposed, that she was just the sort of girl he would be proud to have open the door to his patrons—if he had had anything to speak of in the way of patrons. There was a trimness about her in her grey housedress and her big starched apron; her eyes were large and dark and still, and the pure duskiness of her cheek and neck were set off by the severity of her clothes. Geertje was wrong in remarking that she didn't get around as fast as she should: her movements were even and continuous rather than slow—the graceful, lithe movements of a young cat. He guessed that she was clever enough to make herself seem not too clever before a predecessor who might turn out to be an enemy. He felt rather than saw her laughing in the kitchen when Geertje said that to go to bed with new-washed hair was the best way in the world to get lice; and though Titus was obviously taken with her and tried to win her embraces, as he won everybody else's, with smiles and slantwise looks, she did not melt to him, but treated him with a measured coolness and set him on Geertje's lap much oftener than she held him on her own.

There was no sense of stress in the house to drive him out. On the contrary, since the coming of the Stoffels girl there had been no more outbursts from him, no more tears from Klaartje, no dizzy spells or hand-kissings on Geertje's part: it was as if that trim, self-contained, soft-stepping presence exuded peace. Perhaps, he told himself in his

April wanderings, it was just because peace had been established under his roof that he felt free to go about his business; though where he went and what he did when he got there had little enough purpose in it—the arrival of a possible new patron at the Six salon was enough to make him leave it for the cozy little parlor at Rabbi Menasseh ben Israel's. Much as he needed patrons, he shrank from taking them on; he was absorbed that year in the most profitless and enlightening of tasks—he was busy painting himself. As a man who gets up from a long illness will stare at his image in a mirror, wanting to know what is left of him after the fever and the delirium, so he set himself to contemplate the thickening, aging man who had somehow survived Saskia's death. Mercilessly he set down the fixed, empty eyes, the double chin, the deepened furrow between the eyebrows, the heavy cheeks, the dry hair with its first streaks of grey and all its reddish luster gone. And having known himself so nakedly during the day, he saw no reason to put on a mask for the evening. He wandered in where he pleased, sprawled in what attitude he liked, listened or did not listen as he chose, answered in halting, passionate sentences when a question moved him, shrugged or snorted if it did not seem worth answering. Freedom was what he wanted, not old French wine or elevated conversation, freedom to be the wretched but singular thing he was; and he found that freedom chiefly among those other survivors, the Jews, stamped like himself with indifference to trivialities and the brusque capacity to dispense with amenities that comes only to those whose spirits have been stretched on the rack of isolation and loss.

One night toward the end of April he stayed later than usual at the Pineros'. Either he or the assembly in general had been extraordinarily excited. Though the talk had been political and he himself for the last two years had been so remote from such matters that he scarcely knew whether France or England or Denmark was the current enemy, he plunged into the argument loudly and truculently, not caring at all that he twice made a fool of himself; and it was past midnight when he got up to go. A sea-borne wind was moving in the street, sending shreds of clouds across the mild, close face of the yellow moon. There was motion all about him—new leaves turning in the breeze, moonlight coming and going on the black water of the canal, curtains flapping at open windows—and the fever in him did not abate on the short way home. Though he was perfectly sober, he felt as little in possession of himself as if he had downed five or six mugs of beer; and he hoped he would not have to show his flushed and animated face, he hoped that Geertje would have given him up and gone to bed.

Evidently she had. The house was locked up, the fires were banked, and no light was left for him except the new candle on the big round table in the back sitting room. His empty beer mug, his neatly folded napkin, his plate provided with a peeled hard-boiled egg and a strip of smoked herring and a piece of buttered bread—they looked like an arrangement for a still life in the limited, steady light. He shrugged and sighed, thinking how the poor soul must have worried before going upstairs and leaving the lighted candle behind her, weighing the danger of fire against the danger of his annoyance at finding himself in the dark. He decided to eat, not because he wanted the food but to spare her a pang at discovering tomorrow morning what he had left uneaten.

Going to get the beer needed to wash down the food, he started for the kitchen with his mug, but stopped in momentary alarm because the Stoffels girl came out of a black corner into the candlelight. She had plainly been dozing in her chair: her apron was a little rumpled and her rich hair was lying looser than usual against her cheek. But her eyes, wide awake at once and fixed intently upon him, had rid themselves completely of whatever dream she had been dreaming, as the eyes of the young and healthy will. He was disconcerted, as if it were he who had been caught exposed and vulnerable after sleep; and she made him a deep curtsy, her warm mouth grave and controlled. "Let me get the beer for your honor. I waited up in Vrouw Dircx's place. She was afraid to leave the candle, and I wasn't particularly sleepy," she said.

"And where is Vrouw Dircx?" His voice carried a note of displeasure, and he did not know why, since he had been wishing the woman in bed.

"Upstairs with Titus, your honor." She came and stopped in front of him only long enough to take the mug out of his fingers. "Titus had a nightmare and wanted to get in bed with somebody, and Klaartje was asleep, so I thought Vrouw Dircx had better take him in with her, seeing as he's used to her."

She said most of it on the way out to the kitchen, and he smiled behind her. Clever, he thought, you certainly are clever. Used to her or not, you know damned well whom he'd like to curl up against after a nightmare, and how much ground you'd lose with the housekeeper if he got into the habit of crawling in with you. Then it occurred to him that he had not thanked her or even given her a decent greeting. "Bring in another mug for yourself," he said, but that too seemed curt and cold, since he had not called her by name.

She came back from the dark kitchen—like a cat, she was apparently familiar enough to find whatever she wanted in the blackness—carrying his mug and another for herself. He sat and ate and drank, staring at his plate so steadily that it was some minutes before he realized that she was standing on the other side of the table. "I'm sorry, sit down, Hendrikje. If I ask you to have a mug of beer with me, I naturally mean that you should have it sitting down."

"Thank you, your honor." She subsided with a rustle of her starched apron into the chair where Geertje usually sat, but without any of Geertje's spiritless lassitude. She sat on the edge of the chair gazing at the pool of candlelight reflected in the polished wood, and he could look at her because her eyes were almost hidden by her full, moist eyelids:

406

she sat with her back erect, her head slightly bent, and her elbows close to her sides so that the upper rounds of her arms pressed against and thrust forward the firm, confined mounds of her breasts.

"Did your honor have a pleasant evening?"

"Pleasant enough. Noisy, at any rate. And you?"

"It was quiet as the tomb around here, your honor. Vrouw Dircx did the accounts, and Klaartje knitted, and I polished the silver. There wasn't a sound out of Titus until after eleven. Poor little fellow"—she smiled for the first time, and he saw the gleam of her teeth between her red-brown lips—"he dreamed he was being chased by a bear."

Bear . . . boor . . . dear bear . . . my poor bear . . . Tears smarted in his eyes, and his throat closed spasmodically to smother a sob. She did not see; her look was still fixed on the reflection in the wood. He swallowed and pushed his plate aside and thought he had probably been offensive again by failing to offer her anything to eat. "Aren't you hungry? Wouldn't you like something?" he said.

"No, thank you, your honor. It's a habit I never got into. We were poor at home, and if we had three meals a day, it was something to thank God for. And now I suppose it's all to the good—that I never got into the way of munching at bedtime, I mean. I never was what you'd call slender, and the good food in your honor's house puts flesh on me, so I have to watch myself."

"I eat too much, I know—I'm getting heavy—"

"Not as heavy as your honor makes himself look in those pictures, if you'll excuse my saying so." She glanced up at him shyly; her dark eyes were warmed for an instant with an offer of merriment to be shared, and her half-suppressed smile begot a dimple in her cheek and a soft crinkling at the corners of her lips.

"No? Don't you think so?"

"No, really, your honor. It's very strange the way your honor goes at it—I was thinking so the other day when I was cleaning up the studio. Most people get all trimmed up to have their portraits painted, but your honor messes himself up and glares in the mirror as if you were trying to make a fright of yourself."

He was certainly out of control tonight. A moment ago he had been on the point of sobbing; and now laughter, equally uncalled-for or at least disproportionate, was tickling in his chest: there was something wildly comical about the fact that she took his uncompromising insight into his shattered state as an attempt to "make a fright" of himself. Yet he could not laugh; some nameless reticence kept him from laughing with the warm, full being on the other side of the board at this hour of the night. He knitted his brows and controlled his mouth, and ended by being more remote and austere with her than there was any occasion to be. "I trimmed myself up when I was young. I'm past that now, Hendrikje," he said.

"Oh, Lord, it'll be a sorry business if your honor begins that sort of thing. What I mean is: Vrouw Dircx is always making herself twice her age, and if your honor makes himself out to be sixty when he can't be even forty, it'll certainly be gloomy here."

"I'm thirty-nine," he said, on an inexplicable impulse to lay out all the facts. "How old are you?"

"I, your honor? Nineteen or twenty—I'm not sure. There were eight of us at home, and nobody bothered to count the birthdays."

"Eight?" he said, thinking of the three little graves. "Eight out of how many?"

"Eight out of eight, your honor."

"All of them lived?"

"Yes." She sighed, drawing her straight brown eyebrows together. Why? Was she feeling a resurgence of longing for the other seven or remembering how their grubby hands had snatched her portion from her dish or broken in importunately upon her sleep? "Oh, yes, in spite of the pox and the poor rations and all the moving from one place to another, every one of us lived. My father was a sergeant in the army, and we followed him because we would have starved if we hadn't. It's hard for children to have to move so much; everything you come to care for you lose. Even a tree or a fence or a corner in a yard—it's yours only for so long, and then you're gone. But it's late, and I'm going on too much, and it couldn't possibly interest your honor. Would you care for another mug of beer?"

It was only when she was on her feet again, the detached and irreproachable servant smoothing the last trace of a wrinkle out of her apron, that he realized how much she had been transformed while she was sitting at the table; and he saw the change with regret. Now it was finished, and she had been the one to put an end to it—a realization that troubled his pride. "No, thank you, one mug is enough," he said. "I'll blow out the candle. You can go upstairs."

If she was wounded by the curt dismissal, she did not show it. There was a pertness in her exit, probably unintentional, because of the flapping of the great bow at the back of her apron and the sway of her hips. He waited deliberately until her footfalls had stopped sounding above him before he snuffed out the flame and made his way into the shadowy hall. On the climb up he thought of his cool bed and the recollections that came to him these nights before he slept: now and again, between dreaming and waking, he would still mistake a current of air for the stirring of her hair across his face, the fall of the quilt against his shoulder for the touch of her hand; and sometimes it was shattering and bitter, and sometimes it was inexpressibly sweet . . . He started at the sound of padding footsteps and felt a strange combination of exasperation and relief when he saw in the moonlight from the high window that it was Geertje who was waiting for him at the head of the stairs. She was grotesque in her nightclothes, with her hair in two thin braids; the chain he had given her shone on her lusterless neck, and with the plaits and the necklace she looked like one of the aborigines from the New Continent. "I thought I'd just go down and see that everything's safe," she said.

"Everything's all right. The doors are locked, the fires are banked, and I blew the candle out myself."

"Your honor must have had an enjoyable evening."

It was an oblique reference to the lateness of his return, and he resented it. "Yes, very enjoyable. It's good to stop watching the clock once in a while," he said.

"There's no earthly reason why your honor shouldn't stay out as late as he likes." But she followed that immediately with another veiled reproof. "Poor Titus was terribly upset—did Hendrikje tell you?" She peered at him earnestly and breathed her heavy breath too close to his face.

"Hendrikje told me he had a bad dream."

"Yes. He asked for you, but I took him in with me and he went to sleep right away. If your honor doesn't mind, I won't disturb him. I'll keep him in with me the rest of the night."

"Of course I don't mind. It would be ridiculous to disturb him. And very likely we're disturbing him now, standing out here and whispering like this."

She curtsied, preposterous in her aboriginal garb, complete except for the feathers. "That's true," she said in a voice that reminded him chillingly of the voice that had answered his tirade last winter. "There's nothing to talk about, now that I know everything downstairs is all right. You were the last one up—I could tell by the footsteps. Well, God bless your honor, and good night."

In his room, with the door closed behind him and his forehead resting against the cool pane of the moonlit window, he let the excitement of the evening ebb away and was surprised to find so much that was ugly and disturbing left behind by the withdrawing tide. He was irritated by the bouncing streamers at the small of Hendrikje Stoffels' back, irritated that Geertje Dircx should lie awake identifying people's footsteps, irritated that she should know or care what hour he returned or how much time he spent thereafter in the back parlor, irritated that the boy—flesh of his flesh—should be sleeping in the woman-heavy air of her room, curled for protection against her voluminous side. The light beyond the window kept changing with the racing clouds: the roofs now black, now faintly gilded; the water in the canal now invisible, now sleek and gleaming like a serpent's skin. Though it was by no means cold, prickles rose on his arms and he shivered; and the great bell in the Old Church had struck two before he felt calm enough to stretch himself out between the chill, unrumpled sheets.

*

It might never have occurred to him to resume his country outings with Titus if it had not been for Dr. Tulp. The doctor visited the house on the Breestraat frequently these days, stopping to chat and take wine and walnuts in the back parlor, stepping into the salon to look at his favorite Seghers, climbing to the third floor to see what was going on in the studio. He plainly admired the new self-portraits and stood long and thoughtfully before an unfinished posthumous painting of Saskia: she bent forward from the canvas, more serene than life had ever permitted her to be, with more wrinkles than the years had ever given her, her eyes fixed and solemn and her hand laid quiet over her quieted breast. But though he had much to say for the way the work was coming on and for the impeccable and comfortable condition of the house, it was plain that he thought of that splendid edifice chiefly as a place to escape from and of the artist's preoccupation with the naked self and its elusive recollections as a not altogether wholesome business that ought to be broken off now and then. The advancing years had made him only more tenaciously perceptive. He stood with his fine, sallow face thrust up, and it seemed to his host that he was sniffing out matters that he himself would prefer to ignore. The tightening strain between Geertje and Hendrikje Stoffels, the way Titus had of playing the one off against the other, the adolescent brooding of the little Klaartje, a certain huffiness on the part of the formerly devoted Ferdinand Bol— the doctor seemed to sense them all. "And you yourself—just look at you," he said at the end of his discourse on Titus's need for air and exercise. "You've gotten yourself a belly. Your cheeks are flabby and you have a double chin. You never even get yourself dressed up any more."

"What should I dress up for?"

"Nothing. Just for the pleasure of it."

"I can't see much pleasure in squeezing yourself into a tight jerkin and breeches."

"Take off eight or ten pounds and you won't have to squeeze. Get out in the country with the boy, and while you're at it, take the women. The old one looks like a peeled potato, the young one looks like a limp stalk of celery, and the one in between—even she's losing her looks."

She wasn't losing her looks—that was the wrong way to put it; her looks were ripening, but she was playing them down. If her face seemed less lovely to the visitor, it was because she had taught it to be less open, less vital, more circumspect; and for that the master himself, more than the stresses and labors of his household, was to blame. The truth of the matter was that he did not know how to treat her: he kept veering in his behavior toward her like a dry twig in an eddying stream; and she, at first markedly responsive to every change in his manner, had fallen into perplexity, and from that into an unbecoming rigidity. The ebullience he had felt for the first time in the parlor of the Pineros kept cropping up again through his grief, like weeds through the stony soil of a devastated land; and when that mood was on him he laughed with her, invited her droll comments on whatever he was painting, offered to walk with her to market to carry the milk. Then sorrow would settle in again, and in his vulnerability he would ask himself how he could have enjoyed her high spirits and her dry wit, and how he could have slighted poor Geertje, his fellow-in-ruin, the mute companion of his weeks of mourning, for a chit who would be running out of his house and getting married one of these days. At such times, in the quarrels that broke out between her and Geertje—she quarreled now, getting her back up like a cat at criticisms uttered or implied—he felt bound to take the older woman's part; and twice he had told the younger one that her pertness was unsuitable to her age and her place. "Yes, your honor. Whatever you say, your honor," she had said, thrusting out that full, dark red lip of hers, making a mockery of her submission with that lip and the glint in her eyes. And thereafter, sorry that he had been stern with her, he would be kind again, too eagerly kind . . . But by now she had had her fill of this veering: let him be what he liked—*she* was the same to him, morning, noon, and night. She held herself stiff, she walked as if she had been too stringently corseted or had been trained in court etiquette from her cradle. Her mobile face was as blank as the painted face of a manikin—but she had by no means lost her looks.

"Couldn't you take the whole family out to the country for a week or so?" said the doctor. "Allaert and Lotje won't be going out to their place until the first of July, and I'm sure they'd be glad to lend it to you."

"That's out of the question. In the first place, I wouldn't ask them for such a favor. In the second, what do you think I'd do about the apprentices? In the third—" He broke off, unable to say aloud that he could not drag himself away from the canvases up in the eagle's nest, from his own grieving face and hers looking down at him with steady, empty eyes.

"Well, if you won't, you won't. But the boy needs sun, and from the looks of the rest of you here, the least you could do is get yourselves a thorough airing. It's easy enough to decide on a Sunday and take a little trip."

But it was not as easy as the doctor seemed to think. The practical plans were simple enough to work out: he decided on the Sunday and the place—a little grove up the Amstel; he learned what canal boats would take them and bring them home; but the people involved were distinctly recalcitrant. It had occurred to him that Ferdinand Bol should make one of the party, and his first disappointment was the young man's incomprehensible response to the invitation. "No, thank you, I don't believe I can. No, I'm certain I can't," he said, wiping off the top of the grinding slab—they were alone in the studio that evening. "I'd better stay home next Sunday, I think."

"Why? You're not going to services, are you?" Bol was something of a freethinker and often complained of his father's piety.

"No, I'm not going to services. It's just that I'm tired."

"An outing isn't supposed to tire you. It's supposed to be a way to get a rest."

"Is everybody going?" His dark eyes turned to the posthumous portrait of Saskia as he asked the question. The unfinished figure was painted on thinly and looked wan and lifeless in the oblique light of the declining sun.

"That's the way I'd planned it."

"Is Vrouw Dircx going?"

"Of course—why not?"

"And Hendrikje Stoffels—is she going too?"

"Naturally." He flushed and added, "And so is Klaartje."

"Well, I hope you have a pleasant time of it, Master. I'm sure you will."

The form of address startled him a little. He was no longer young Bol's master; besides, the old title had been dropped in the last days of Saskia's illness, when Bol, watching with him over the sickbed, had learned to call him, hesitantly and shyly, by his first name. He did not like it that "Master" should be injecting itself again, and he did what he could to force the young man to look him in the eye. "There'll be blankets and bottles and baskets to carry. I could use your help," he said.

"Oh, I think you'll be able to manage without me." He folded up the rag with which he had been cleaning the grinding slab, took his hat from the peg, and jammed it down over his dark crown with an air of finality. "You'll have Hendrikje Stoffels—she can do as much as I can." And with that he looked again at the posthumous portrait, said a cool good night, and left without fixing his eyes on the master's face.

Then everything went wrong with the women. Klaartje was depressed when she learned the date—Vrouw Dircx explained to him in Biblical parlance that it was a bad day for the poor little thing because "the manner of women would be upon her"; Hendrikje wanted to know if they couldn't put off starting until noon—she had taken of late to attending the Reformed services, probably to look around for a likely young fellow; and Geertje grew maudlin over similar holidays she had taken with her husband in "the springtime of her days." They wearied him, all of them; he was sick of women with their mysterious afflictions and their secretive doings and their sentimental recollections; and for the first time in his life he wished he were in the army, camping out among rude males, indulging in horseplay and filthy talk, waiting for the general engagement in which all bad blood, all bile, all nameless angers could be released.

In the quarrel that broke out the Saturday afternoon before the too-much-talked-of outing, he would probably have taken Hendrikje's part against Geertje if the young woman had not already offended him by suggesting that they wait to start until after church. It so happened that on this occasion Hendrikje was right: the goose that Geertje was roasting for the outdoor supper would *not* be as suitable as ham; roast fowl *would* get greasy and unappetizing lying about in the sun. But when he heard the two of them in the kitchen, at each other like a young cat and a weary old mastiff, he strode out there and intervened, throwing the weight of his authority against the ham. "Vrouw Dircx is the housekeeper here. She plans what's to be eaten," he said. "If she's decided on roast goose, roast goose it'll be."

"Yes, your honor. Whatever your honor likes. I only thought—"

"Don't think and don't argue. There's too much thinking and arguing going on around this place."

The dark, still eyes met his and briefly kindled to life in the beautiful, forcibly rigid face. "I suppose I can promise your honor that I won't argue, though it's hard," she said. "But as for thinking—I don't see how I can put a stop to *that,* even to make sure I have a roof over my head."

He saw what a stupid and wounding thing he had said and was on the point of making her an apology, but he was not given the opportunity. Vrouw Dircx, given license by his earlier sharpness, told her how her rebellious and unfortunate nature would ruin any gifts she had as a serving maid: her face and her figure might make her suitable for the parlor, but her impertinence was bound to land her in the scullery. And when the lecture was over—she listened to the bitter end of it with narrowed eyes and a flaming face—she turned and ran out of the room.

When she was gone, Geertje gave him a cheerful conspiratorial look, expecting him to share in her triumph; but he only thrust his hands into his pockets and stared grimly at the accursed goose sputtering on the spit. "I want her to obey you—you're the housekeeper," he said at last in a flat and tired voice. "But I think it would be better if you didn't lecture her. In the future, I'd rather you'd leave the lecturing to me."

"Certainly, your honor."

Not knowing what to expect, he had not dared to glance up at her, and he was sufficiently reassured by her reasonable tone to minimize his implied reproof. "You see," he said, "I'm a little concerned about her—she came from a big family, and she lives a lonely life with us here. She has nothing but her work, and I imagine that she'd like to take some pride in that—"

"God forbid"—the voice was less controlled and queerly vibrant—"God forbid that *I* should rob her of her satisfactions."

"I'm sure you don't mean to, Geertje, but you do give her less credit than you give Klaartje."

"Oh, as for that, she doesn't need it as much as Klaartje—"

"Klaartje *is* a scared little thing—"

"Not only that, your honor. I'm the only one that ever has a good

413

word to say for Klaartje. Hendrikje Stoffels gets her praise from other people; she doesn't need anything extra from me."

There was something in the breathy, shaken voice that warned him not to pursue the meaning of that cryptic statement. He had intended to stay in the kitchen long enough to help her take the goose off the spit; but now it seemed wise to get out, to leave her alone to release on the pots and pans whatever trembled in her. In the back parlor, where Klaartje was laying the table, he tried to distract himself by making a few sketches for a canvas on the Holy Family. Titus came and stood by him, watching intently while the shapes of cradle and infant and ministering cherubim came into being on the paper; and the closeness of the boy and the dream of what he meant to paint—the quiet browns and reds, the harmony and restfulness of the Mother and Child and Joseph and the cloud of winged innocents from heaven—almost gave him an illusion of peace until he heard Hendrikje's light step in the room. Though she had washed her face, she had not been able to do away with all the signs of her weeping: her cheeks were chafed, the end of her nose was raw, and her eyelids were red and swollen. He looked at her earnestly, hoping that he might give her some comfort and reassurance, but she did not turn once in his direction. She busied herself with the silver and the napkins which she had taken from the chest, and her smooth, strong, shapely hand straightening out a napkin made him amend the hand of the Virgin lifting the corner of the coverlet from the sleeping Child.

Looking up from that finished hand, he saw that Titus had left him and was standing beside Hendrikje, his face lifted, his beseeching amber look fixed on her marred cheeks and eyes, his own face puckered with the reflection of her grief and shame. It seemed for a moment that he might break into a wail and bring down the whole precarious fabric of their mutual pretense, but caution—and what a sorry business that it should already be working in so small a being—caution taught him to control himself: he only encircled her leg with his arms and pressed his melancholy little face into the softness of her thigh. She dropped the linen that she had been holding and looked down at him in surprise and gratefulness, but gratefulness was too strong an emotion for her to cope with—she also was on the point of giving way to painfully mastered tears. "Go out to the kitchen and tell Vrouw Dircx to wash your hands for you," she said. "Just look at your little hands—they're all dirty, and it's almost time to eat."

The conversation at the evening meal was no better than he had expected. Klaartje, the only one who had no idea that anything was amiss, was so benumbed by her condition that she could add nothing to the halting talk: her mouth hung open, her cheek lay listlessly against her hand, her hair was limp, and there were bluish circles under her eyes. Talk about any household matter was likely to prove dangerous, and what was there to talk to Vrouw Dircx about except household matters?

Hendrikje Stoffels took very small portions and had trouble swallowing even those; Geertje made a few uncalled-for disparaging remarks about her own cooking which forced the master into saying that everything was delicious; and the child, glancing sidewise through his fair hair at Hendrikje, scarcely touched what was on his plate. Still, they managed somehow to get through the dreary business until Geertje rose, somber and massive, to clear the table. She was reaching for a dish of hard-boiled eggs that nobody had touched when Klaartje bestirred herself out of her sickly dream. "If it won't be too much trouble, Vrouw Dircx, I'd be grateful if you'd put a couple of those eggs into the hamper for me tomorrow. The way my stomach's been lately, I think I'd better not risk eating the goose," she said.

The housekeeper muttered something and went out with her trayful of melancholy leavings. Neither of the girls rose to help her—Klaartje because she was torpid and ailing, Hendrikje no doubt because she did not dare. It crossed his mind that Geertje was out there in the kitchen longer than usual—she always came back promptly with some sweet or wine and nuts—but he told himself that the time only seemed long, stretched out as it was by the silence and the stress. Klaartje sat hunched over the table, her flat chest rising and falling laboriously as if the mere act of breathing were all that could be expected of her; Titus sat perfectly still, and his resemblance to Saskia—a scared Saskia holding out a blood-spotted handkerchief—was uncanny; Hendrikje sat in the erect, defensive position which had become her habitual one, her haunches resting only on the edge of the chair, her head up, her elbows pressed against her sides, her breasts thrust forward, round and firm and strangely obvious in the candlelight.

"Excuse me, your honor."

It was Geertje's voice, addressing him from the threshold. He looked up from what he should not have been looking at and saw that the housekeeper was empty-handed, swaying a little, and grey in the face.

"What's the matter, Geertje?" She undid him utterly when her yellowish eyes stared at him in that vacant way, and his voice carried his fright.

"Nothing—it's just that I feel a little dizzy. I—with your permission, I'll go upstairs—I have a bad pain in my head."

"Oh, isn't that a pity?" said Klaartje, suddenly alert and taking on that false, cajoling voice he had never forgotten. "But never mind, Vrouw Dircx, we'll get you upstairs and you can lie down and it'll pass."

It was Klaartje who went to support her where she stood swaying— he could not go to her. It was not only that she looked ill, ugly, stricken; it was that her sagging cheeks, her hanging lower lip, her hair disordered at the temples as if she had been in some physical struggle made her look guilty and brutalized. "Yes, take her up and make her comfortable, Klaartje," he said; and the two women—the old heavy one lurching against and almost upsetting the slight young one—made their grotesque progress across the room. How will they ever get up the steps? he wondered, but still he could not make himself rise from his chair.

The last halting footfalls had grown silent above their heads before Hendrikje Stoffels asked him if he wanted anything to finish the meal. "God, no." Repulsive as the thought of food was to him, the words came out with a brusqueness he had not intended, and he added, with over-compensatory kindness, "Don't you?"

"No, your honor, nothing." She would not look at him: she lifted her head a little as if she were sniffing the air. A strange smell, at once savory and disgusting, was coming in from the kitchen. "Something's burning out there," she said, getting up so violently that her chair fell over behind her.

He went after her, thinking that Geertje, in her dazed state, had forgotten to take the goose off the spit. The spit was empty, but the goose was burning nevertheless. It lay sputtering and charring in the red embers on the hearth, black in the pinkish glow, giving off smoke and that clinging, choking smell.

"My God, look what she's done!" said Hendrikje, reaching for the tongs. "She's burned the goose—she came out here and threw it into the fire."

Back in the other room, alone at the table, Titus was letting out the long-suppressed wail at last.

"But why would she do such a thing?" he asked, staring at the blackened goose with as much horror as if it had been a living thing consigned to the flames.

The big, still eyes looked at him in amazement. "Why? Surely your honor must have seen it a long time ago—it's plain the woman's mad."

*

In spite of its propitious beginning, it was not what Dr. Tulp would call a satisfactory evening. Usually when Jan Six dropped in the time went quickly, and here it was not quite nine and the host was thinking it must be ten and wondering when he could go to bed.

His wife was doing better with it than he was. She sat sharp-featured and erect near the three-branched candlestick, filling up the silences with minor observations and the click of her knitting needles; it meant more to her than to him that the young man should prefer their little parlor to the great salons, that the son of the most brilliant family in the Regents' class should appear casually on their threshold, like a cousin, his hat held diffidently in his hand. And ordinarily the doctor found his own satisfaction in those visits: the young man's mind, rebellious and restless, churned up just the sort of questions that had tormented the doctor in his own youth. But tonight there were none of the usual eruptions, and now that the conversation had been going on for more than an hour he was suddenly aware that neither he nor his wife were bearing any part in it. Jan Six was talking to their daughter Gretha, and Gretha was talking to Jan Six, and they would probably have gotten on better if the master and mistress of the establishment had taken a walk and left them to themselves.

He leaned forward in his chair by the fireless chimney place—it was June, and, though the evening was cool, there was too much moist softness in it for a fire—he leaned forward and looked at the girl where she sat on a bench near the darkening window, addressing slow, earnest questions to the visitor at her side. For the first time he realized that she was decked out, had been decking herself out almost every evening in the last few weeks, spending time in front of the mirror that she used to spend with him in his office, trying vainly—he knew how vainly, because for years he had tried it himself—to brush the dry fuzziness out of her hair. Tonight she was wearing a dress that he had never seen before, a white lawn stitched with a blue pattern at neck and waist, not so thin as to seem immodest on a girl of fifteen, but not so heavy as to conceal the fine, spare sweep of her shin and thigh. Her hair was brushed up in a cloud and held in place by a blue silk net. Had he or had he not seen her start up from her seat at the sound of the knocker? Now that he remembered it, it was then that she had gone to the vase and taken a rose and thrust it, in the Spanish fashion, behind her ear— an ear adorned with one of her mother's pearls.

He glanced at his wife and wondered whether she was busy with like conjectures. If so, her keen practicality would impel her to point out that if the girl had gotten any such ideas into her head, it would be their duty to drive them straight out: Gretha was a child, and Jan was twenty; Gretha was a Tulp, and Jan was a Six; Gretha's dowry was decent, but Jan was heir to a fortune and could reach as high as the House of Orange itself. Snap off the flower in the bud, save her the heartbreak, bring in half a dozen suitable young men if she was ready for that sort of thing . . . But was she? In spite of the long, lithe body and the grave, waiting look and the earrings and the rose, he found it painful to think of her as a woman: the child was still there in the easy movements and the throaty voice and the slightly parted mouth, and the child was what he loved. Besides, even if she *were* looking higher than she should, would that be as devastating as women always seemed to think? Were the months of melting heartbreak more destructive, really, than the cold strictures of circumspection? Far too much was made of the business—nobody died of it except in English ballads. He had seen them die of boredom, of hidden guilt, of isolation or spleen or driving restlessness; but nobody—at least nobody who had landed in *his* office —had ever died of unrequited love.

The present exchange between the two young ones dealt with *Macbeth*, recently given in Amsterdam by the English players; and it had gone on long enough for his wife's gratification to turn into uneasiness: she rolled up her knitting and asked if somebody wouldn't like some raisin cake and wine. Gretha rose with her, too well brought up to be tardy about it, and went into the kitchen; and he was left alone with Jan Six, who seemed to have forgotten his existence and did not show himself too happy to be reminded of it.

It was fortunate, then, that the bang of the knocker broke in upon their halting conversation; Rembrandt was at the door, decently shaved and brushed and buttoned into a spanned jacket—the doctor remembered that he had pointed out to the poor devil some weeks ago how he never even took the trouble to dress up any more. "Come in," he said, "and make yourself comfortable. Here's Jan; he'll be delighted to see you. How's—" He broke off, appalled, because in one of those strange lapses of memory he had almost said, "How's Saskia?" He substituted, "How's the painting?" and got no answer, since the women were just coming back and there was that flurry of excitement which passes over a moribund social occasion on the arrival of a new guest.

It did not last: the newcomer seemed too preoccupied to draw the separate parts of the little gathering together. In fact, once the food had been served and the young ones had returned to their bench by the black window, Rembrandt seated himself on a low stool with his back to them, facing his host and hostess; and nothing but an outright request, which the doctor was too proud or too pained to make, would have drawn Jan and Gretha in. Well, he thought, looking down on Rembrandt's reddish mane with the streaks of grey in it, he's here again with his troubles, but at least he'll be addressing them to *me*—which will make me feel less like an intruder in my own parlor.

"Don't you care for the raisin cake?" asked his wife. He realized he had not been eating it, only crumbling it on his plate.

"There's nothing wrong with the cake," he said. "It's just that I can't stuff myself any more before I go to bed. I suppose I'm getting old."

"Vrouw Dollaerd doesn't seem to think so," she said, looking at him archly, raising her fine black brows and giving him a mocking smile.

Whereupon poor Rembrandt was obliged to ask, "Who's Vrouw Dollaerd?" and then was obliged to listen to a colored-up version of a story that should never have been passed along to her in the first place. Vrouw Dollaerd was mad for the doctor—wrote him love letters, hemmed him handkerchiefs, made him nosegays, was so beside herself that yesterday she had flung her arms around his neck in a public place.

"Look," he said to Rembrandt, "maybe you ought to know that the public place she's referring to is the Old Women's Home, and Vrouw Dollaerd is eighty-one. The poor old creature's out of her head."

And strangely, for he would have thought it the last subject that would engage his visitor's attention, Rembrandt seized upon the wretched business and would not let it go. This Vrouw Dollaerd—how had her madness first shown itself? Aside from this love-making, did she do other peculiar things? Was there actually any sharp dividing line between the sane and the insane? When Hercules Seghers tore up his last shirt and tried out different processes of colored etching on it, was that madness? And Sweelinck—when he suddenly forgot he was playing the organ for a full church and terrified the assembly with an ear-splitting imitation of a great storm, was he mad?

The doctor stared at the furrowed forehead and wondered what tricks the brain behind it had been playing of late. Did the poor fellow ever catch himself wondering, as he himself had been on the point of asking a while ago, how Saskia was, and consider the possibility that he was going out of his mind?

"No," he said, setting his cluttered plate and his empty goblet on the hearth, "I wouldn't say that either Seghers or Sweelinck was mad. But then it's hard to be positive about these things. Vrouw Dollaerd, for instance—they won't take her out of the Old Women's Home and put her in the madhouse for writing me love letters—only if she stopped eating or made some really shocking scene or did physical violence to herself or somebody else." The whole matter was dreary: it made the back of his neck creep, breathing upon him from behind the breath of old age and senile ardors and final dissolution. "And how are things going at your place? Titus looked well enough the last time I saw him. Is Klaartje any better—has the port I recommended given her any more color?" he said.

Titus was lively, and Klaartje was improving. In a week, she'd be leaving—a hat-maker, a friend of Vrouw Pinero's, had offered her a place in his shop, and it would be a crime to hold her to her contract: the wages were better, and the shop would be a good place for her to meet young men. But to get back to that other business: What did the doctor consider a really shocking scene, one that would definitely indicate madness?

"Who's to say?" asked the host with some exasperation. "Unprovoked shrieking and raving, taking off your clothes in public, something of that sort. Certainly not getting irritable in a bad situation or forgetting now and again that the dead are dead—that's to be taken for granted, that's in the course of things."

The broad peasant face flushed. "Oh," he said, "I do well enough. I wasn't thinking about myself."

"Then whom were you thinking about?"

"Geertje. She's made a couple of scenes lately—nothing like what you were saying, but they *were* scenes, and Hendrikje Stoffels is convinced she's out of her senses."

The doctor cracked his knuckles; had he suppressed from the beginning the feeling that there was something uncanny, something distinctly off-key about the big, silent woman? His wife also might have scented some trouble; her brows drew together, her lips parted, and the tip of her tongue came out. "Why, has Vrouw Dircx been writing you love letters and hemming you handkerchiefs?" she said.

"Oh, no, God forbid. She just got upset and made a couple of scenes. I doubt I would ever have thought of it if Hendrikje Stoffels hadn't brought it up."

The doctor did not answer. He was thinking how this new maid, unlike the other two, had never become a familiar household accessory. She was no "Geertje," no "Klaartje"—she was invariably "Hendrikje Stoffels"—alien, not to be taken for granted, kept at arm's length, and referred to with strained formality. Why? Because she was proud and reserved and ungiving? He doubted it; her person emanated too much warmth. And beautiful as she was, she was like some fine animal whose intelligence had not spoiled her body but had stayed where it belonged, in her large, still, knowing eyes.

"What kind of scenes?" said his wife, carefully wiping the corners of her mouth with her napkin.

Well, nothing, really—nothing to be alarmed at. Cleaning a window on a very rainy day—but he had been shouting at her about the slovenly condition of the house, he had brought that on himself. And then somebody had hurt her feelings about a goose she had been roasting, and she had taken it off the spit and thrown it into the fire. She had felt terrible about that, had gone out the next day and changed her will so that her wretched little savings would go to Titus. She doted on Titus, she was a second mother to Titus—

Remembering the story of a madwoman who had strangled her own infant with a coil of her hair, the doctor felt an icy prickling down his spine. "Look here, don't take it so lightly. It isn't sane behavior to clean windows in the rain, and it's worse to cremate a goose," he said. "If you have the slightest doubt, give her the rest of her year's salary and get her out of the place."

"Why?"

"Why? I don't want to upset you, you've got troubles enough as it is, but it isn't sensible to leave a woman in charge of a helpless child if you suspect her of being mad."

"But you don't realize how much I owe her. She sat with me through the whole period of mourning. She looked after me when I wasn't fit to—"

"Well, that's a pity, and I can imagine how you feel about it. But whatever she did for you, you can't afford to keep her if she has fits of insanity. Give her a good settlement, or, better still, arrange a little pension for her. And do it soon, before she burns something else than a goose."

"Do you really think—"

"I don't think anything. Nobody can be sure. She might go on for years no worse than she is, and then again you might wake up some morning and find God knows what on your hands. Get her out before that happens. You're out of your head yourself if you take that sort of risk."

His wife nodded agreement, and he glanced up to see whether the pair at the window might come in with their advice, but they had evidently heard nothing. Gretha, either thoughtful or sleepy, was resting her head against the windowpane, and Jan Six was staring at her quiet, childish face.

"But I can't do that," said Rembrandt. "It's not only that I can't treat her so shabbily after all she's done for me, and for Saskia, too, and the boy. You see, if she were to go, there I'd be, alone in the house with Hendrikje Stoffels—" He set his plate and goblet on the hearth and took to gazing at the floor, his hands hanging raw and hairy between his spread knees.

"Since when," asked the doctor's wife, "have *you* been troubling yourself about the proprieties? Suppose you *were* alone with her until you found another girl to take Klaartje's place—nobody would know it and anybody who did wouldn't give it a second thought."

How stupid can a clever woman be? thought the doctor, looking at the big, sad, thickened body hunched over on the stool. It's not the neighbors he's afraid of, you fool—it's Hendrikje Stoffels and himself. Look at his fingernails chewed ragged. Look at his belly, swollen with the food he's stuffed into it to smother another need. Look at the way he's given up embracing women—even you and Gretha. It's plain enough he hasn't been to Pieter-Jacob Street; since he buried her, he hasn't touched a woman, and he was never made for abstinence—he with his bull's body and his sensuous brain . . .

"Hendrikje Stoffels," said the visitor with the same strained formality, "is a young unmarried woman, not much past twenty. It would be unthinkable for us to be alone together in that house."

"Oh, nonsense," said the lady. "It's a big enough house for the two of you to lose each other in. Go live up in the attic with the apprentices for the time being if you're—" She did not finish, but the unspoken word hung in the air, vibrant with the throb of long-stifled and illicit desire—the word "afraid."

In the silence that followed—his wife did what she could to shrink it to parlor proportions by going grimly at her knitting—the doctor looked at his guest as he might look at one of his patients, asking himself the pertinent questions. Was the poor devil to live celibate for the rest of his life? Preposterous. Was he to resort to whores? Unthinkable, whores being what they were: this was neither Paris nor Seville nor Rome, this was Amsterdam. Was his best solution then to marry an heiress? So Jan Six had intimated, but Jan was not concerned at the moment. The heiress proposition was worth considering—he himself had thought of it seriously enough to line up candidates in his mind. But the day when a family like the Uylenburghs would raise no cry if he asked for a daughter of theirs was over: his reputation had declined, his capacity to earn money had dwindled, and his person was not what it had been. He was aged beyond his years, slovenly and seedy, so careless in his dress that he seemed to be putting himself deliberately beyond consideration. And maybe that was precisely his aim; maybe he would have as little use for an heiress as an heiress would have for him. Who was he, with his heart in a grave and his mind forever fixed on some canvas, to fetch and carry for a woman? Who was he, who had never brought himself to speak out his devotion to the first beloved, to mouth the required flatteries? But Hendrikje Stoffels was another matter: the doctor had not the slightest trouble imagining his friend rushing at the healthy serving girl from Ransdorp, and the healthy serving girl from Ransdorp, pliant as a tame cat, opening herself without forethought or legal requirement to the strong and desperate embrace . . .

"Well, I'll have to think about it," said Rembrandt.

"Don't think too long. Don't think until the woman sets your house on fire or does something to Titus."

"She'd never do anything to Titus. She loves Titus—"

"That makes me all the more uneasy. The mad ones have a way of moving from love to hate without giving notice. There was a young woman here in town who strangled her own baby—"

"Good heavens, Nicolaas, what's the matter with you? Why would you tell him such a thing?"

"To let him know there are worse things than flouting the proprieties. Anyway, as you said a while ago, my dear, why *he* should be worried about the proprieties, I don't know."

In the uncomfortable stillness the great bells in all the towers of the city rang out eleven, dropping the separate tones through the moist summer air like so many ripe fruits released from the bough. Jan Six rose and said it was time for him to be going; failing to get the hoped-for protest from his host, he kissed Gretha's hand in the French fashion, bowed to his elders, and went to get his hat; and Rembrandt, buttoning his jerkin, followed him into the hall. When the doctor returned from seeing them out, he found that his wife had already gone upstairs. Only Gretha, with the rose wilted enough to dangle against her neck, was still there, sitting on the bench by the window, looking down in grave and gratified wonderment at the back of her hand. "What's the matter?" he said gruffly. "Stung by a wasp?"

"No, Father," she said, not lifting her eyes from the spot that had been kissed. "Are you going up now, too?"

"Yes, I'm tired."

"You seem tired. I wish you a pleasant night."

A pleasant night . . . he turned his back on her and started up the staircase, actually stamping. A pleasant night, to him, meant sleep. He was sick of love—his own and everybody else's. All he wanted was to forget about the very existence of love.

*

422

All through the summer, in spite of the doctor's warnings—and they were repeated—Rembrandt did nothing. Or rather, he confined himself to watching, an activity that was stressful in itself and the more so because Hendrikje Stoffels was watching too, and all observations ended with a meeting of their eyes. Hendrikje Stoffels, having expressed herself once over the charred remains of the goose, made no further comment; but almost as if she had heard the exchange in the Tulp parlor, she saw to it—and he was grateful—that even after Klaartje had left and her duties increased, Titus and the housekeeper were seldom together alone.

And what was the fruit of all his watching? In September he was as uncertain as he had been in June, though instances kept multiplying. Geertje talked to herself, moving her lips without making a sound; but for all he knew, that was neither new nor sinister: probably she had been doing it since her coming and he had not noticed it. Geertje glared; her eyes became downright malevolent when Hendrikje Stoffels so far forgot herself as to embrace Titus or to chatter on at supper about some comical household incident, but that, too, was only to be expected: how could she take pleasure in cheerful talk or a nimble wit when she herself was so sad and slow? There were no more crises like the window-washing and the goose-burning, yet he could not hide from himself that she was impelled toward such crises. She avoided them by going out of the house whenever there was a threat in the air; and though she had not walked on the Breestraat for months, she was often to be seen now from the upper windows, a basket on her arm and her shawl over her shoulders, making her way to market to buy something that was suddenly needed and looking strangely more grotesque as she plodded heavy-footed through the sunlight than she had ever looked in the shadowy back room. Sometimes she went out in the evenings too, stung to it because he and Hendrikje Stoffels had fallen into conversation; and then it was as if she had said aloud to them, "There! The house is yours! Rejoice in it!"—the invariable result of which was that the two of them fell silent, and Hendrikje, once Titus had been washed and put into his long white nightgown, went early to bed.

Titus, though he stayed rosy and plump, still gave his father some concern that summer. Geertje no longer made any move to take him out with her; and the master of the house, performing the duties of his teaching with a kind of fierce meticulousness as if such dependability could somehow make up for his other failures, seldom had time to spare. But Ferdinand Bol took the lad into the fields at least twice a week, and Vrouw Lazzara and Rabbi Menasseh ben Israel stopped for him whenever they were going for a stroll, and anyway he would soon be old enough to play unsupervised with the other little ones on the street. But having so many new people to indulge him had a questionable effect on his disposition. He became confused, capricious, demanding; and sometimes, coming back from a walk with one of the others and finding that Geertje was not in the house, he would set up a wail.

One morning toward the middle of September, the atmosphere at the breakfast table seemed more charged than usual, so charged that the master did not gulp down his food and take himself upstairs to his apprentices, but lingered over his cheese and beer, watching the two women covertly as they cleared the table and went back and forth, a few paces apart like animals that do not trust each other, between the back room and the kitchen. Hendrikje Stoffels was wearing a new skirt and bodice, brought to her as a nameday present from her family in Ransdorp by a turnip farmer who had carted his crop into town; and Rembrandt took the clothes to be the source of the tension: the skirt and bodice were a brilliant scarlet, and Geertje had said last night that she didn't know when Hendrikje would find an occasion to wear them—certainly not to church, nobody would appear in church in such a color; and not around the house either, since maids didn't wear red, not in respectable families. It was probably the young woman's insolence in putting on her present in spite of the warning that had stirred up Geertje's animosity. At any rate, she was bent on getting out of the house, and soon; she was so eager to be gone that she snatched his plate away before he had finished the last few bites. With her hair disorderly and her shawl flung carelessly over her shoulders, she left like a Fury rushing out of Hell, without remembering to say good-bye to Titus. He fell to whimpering, and his father stayed to soothe him until Vrouw Lazzara came and took him out; but even when that was settled he was in no state to go up to the apprentices: he continued to sit staring down at his crumpled napkin until Hendrikje came in from the kitchen and said, "Does your honor want anything else?"

"No. Only . . ." He had been on the point of suggesting to her, as considerately as possible, that it might be better if she did not wear the scarlet skirt and bodice; but suddenly the idea struck him as unjust, even tyrannical. Why shouldn't she wear the nameday present given to her, probably at great sacrifice, by her people in Ransdorp? And where could she make use of it, if not in his house? In order to watch over Titus, to keep an eye on Geertje, to do what would otherwise have remained undone now that Klaartje was gone, she never went out to sit with a young man in a pancake shop or to take a stroll on the Bourse or along the walls. She had every right to wear it, to bloom like a late red poppy in the rusty autumnal drabness of their world, to take pleasure in her own image reflected in the mirrors and casements. Scarlet was her color, scarlet set her off, darkening her luxuriant hair and warming the dusky pillar of her throat and deepening her eyes. "Only, I've been wondering what could have gotten into Vrouw Dircx this morning," he said.

"What I've got on my back, your honor—that's what got into her." She stood on the other side of the table, high-headed, almost bold, hold-

424

ing herself erect and full-breasted, inviting him to see what she had on her back and to speak ill of it if he could.

He did not speak ill of it. All he said was, "Oh, that?" shrugging his shoulders.

"I thought I wouldn't wear it. I thought I'd lay it by, but then I said to myself it wouldn't make any difference. The way she is, if it hadn't been my skirt and bodice, it would have been something else."

The way she is . . . The phrase, said almost casually, was somehow more frightening than the more explicit terminology used in the Tulp parlor. "Why, is she worse? Does she seem worse to you?" he said.

"If you're asking me, your honor, she's much worse. When I first came, she was sane most of the time and a little peculiar now and again. These days it's the other way around. She's mad—that's the only thing a person can call it. She goes around glaring and muttering, she walks the floor half the night, you should hear the way the wall shakes when she throws herself down on her bed. I only wonder she hasn't been picked up on the street, the way she looks and keeps talking to herself. Vrouw Pinero got me out in the kitchen the other evening when they were here for supper and asked me what could have come over you that you didn't see how it was. She made me swear I'd never leave Titus and her by themselves."

"Good God—is it as bad as that?"

"I'm only telling you what Vrouw Pinero said—"

"But what am I going to do about it? I can't shove her out of the house and lock the door on her, I can't throw her out into the street."

"Of course you can't, your honor." Her eyes warmed, her carefully mastered mouth loosened. She sat down, for the first time without waiting for his permission, and looked at him companionably across the board, her elbows on the table, her dusky cheeks between her strong and beautiful hands. "Of course you can't, nobody would expect you to, and it wouldn't be called for. Did you know she's got a brother in Gouda? All your honor would have to do is write him a letter and tell him to come and get her, because she's failing in her brain and nobody but a relative can take the responsibility for her any more. Who'd expect you to turn your house upside down because one of your servants happened to go mad? Anybody would think you were more than generous if you paid her way to Gouda and gave her her salary for the rest of the year."

"Has she told you anything about this brother in Gouda?"

"No, your honor, but I know he writes her at least once a month— long letters, too, very good and kind. In a couple of them he asked her if she didn't want to come there so he could look after her. He's a decent man, the sort of man that would answer your honor right away, I'm sure."

"But maybe there aren't any such letters. People like her have a way of imagining things—"

"Oh, no, I'm sure about the letters. I've seen them."

"She showed them to you?"

"Now is that likely, your honor, considering the way she feels about me? But after she burned the goose, I got to wondering who we could go to if all of a sudden she went stark raving mad. So I waited until she was out, and then I went up to her room and took the letters out of her drawer and read them. She has a whole bundle of them from her brother Willem in Gouda, and he's certainly the person that you should—"

Oh, but he could not let it pass—the image of this girl, the poor wretch's enemy, rifling her drawer, reading her letters. He saw her as she had been in the old days after the funeral, the dull, unasking sharer of his grief, sitting where this one sat on the other side of the table, mending his stockings, writing herself reminders on scraps of paper, fetching up a sigh before she could bring herself to break in upon his sorrow. "It wasn't right for you to read her letters," he said so sharply that she started out of her chair and stood at attention. "You had no right to do such a thing."

"No?" Though her cheeks flushed to a bright pink, there was no contrition in her, no servile show of submission; on the contrary, she actually tossed her head. "Your honor sounds like one of those preachers he's always talking against. I'm sorry I did it, then, but the day may come when your honor won't be sorry. If it does, I have her brother's street and number written down. And if it doesn't, there's no harm done —she doesn't ever have to know."

She hurried off to the kitchen with her loosened hair bobbing against her neck and the folds of her scarlet skirt agitated behind her, and he went up to his apprentices and started to teach, raising his voice and striding back and forth, trying to shout down the thoughts that had sprung up while she was standing there. She should be tamed, this Hendrikje Stoffels, and he had been terrifyingly close to taming her, to coming round the great table that had always been between them, to laying his hands on her upper arms, to closing his fingers round that dusky flesh, warm and living under the sliding cloth . . .

He was angry enough to pretend not to hear her when she called to him some time later from the second-floor hall, to let him know, he supposed, that the noonday meal was on the table. After a short silence, during which he could see Ferdinand Bol's dark, sad eyes fixed upon him, she called again, this time with a note of urgency. "What's the excitement about?" he said to Bol, and felt that in saying it he seemed false and awkward. "You'd think the world would fall in if the soup got cold."

"She can't be calling us down to eat," said his assistant. "The bells sounded eleven only a few minutes ago."

"Then it's some other nonsense." He flung off his painter's apron with an unconvincing show of exasperation and stamped downstairs.

426

But it was no household matter that had made her call up to him. An official messenger of the City Council, wearing the tall black hat and scarlet sash and carrying the wand of his office, was standing, stiff and embarrassed, in the reception hall. He put his wand to his hat brim, plainly awed by the splendor of the place. "I take it that you're Heer van Rijn, master painter," he said.

"Yes." He could not keep himself from glancing apprehensively at the great roll of official papers crushed between the fellow's ribs and elbow.

"I'm sorry to say, sir, that in the course of my duty I must serve certain legal papers on you."

What had he done? What bill had he forgotten to pay in the confusion of this miserable household? What law had he transgressed, not even knowing of its existence? And why must he stand there under her candid, curious eyes, getting redder and redder in the face? "Why? What's the matter? If it's an unpaid bill—"

"Not that, sir. It's a suit for breach of promise."

"A suit for breach of promise? With a woman, you mean?"

"Yes, sir. Here it is. Please take it. It's my obligation to see that it gets directly into your hands."

"But who in the world would be charging me with breach of promise?"

"It's all there in the document, Heer van Rijn. If you have a protest, you can state it, of course, to the City Council. A good morning to you, sir," he added without irony, and left, careful not to bang the splendid door.

"Geertje!" said Hendrikje Stoffels. "She did it—it's Geertje."

And Geertje it was, her name looking weirdly incongruous in the ornate and impressive black script with the city seal affixed beneath it. One Vrouw Geertje Dircx, widow and midwife and long-time servant of the master painter Rembrandt van Rijn, did on this day depose before the proper representatives of the City Council that the said Heer van Rijn, after giving her every assurance of his intention to take her to wife; after living alone with her, subsequent to his wife's death, for several weeks in his house on the Breestraat; after pledging his troth to her with a chain set with pearls which had been the property of the said deceased wife, had indicated that he did not intend to fulfill his obligations . . . There was much more, but he did not read it. The great parchment document fell out of his hands. Hendrikje picked it up and read it without asking permission, read it avidly, catching her breath now and again and saying, "This is impossible!" "This is madness!" "Oh, good God!" and he was so undone that she had almost completed it when he came and snatched it away from her. "Who told you you could read that?" he said.

She did not answer—she took to the stairs.

"Where are you going?" he shouted after her.

"Up to my room, for that paper—the one I wrote her brother Willem's address on," she said.

*

When he walked out of the house that harsh November afternoon, not saying where he was going or when he intended to come back, he wished he would never again have to set eyes on the shining casements and the lordly façade. He had managed to love it still as the place where Saskia had crept closer to him and died; he had even been able to sustain the contrast between its splendor and the sickening failure of the Regents' piece; he had forced himself now and again to make a show of conviviality in it with the Tulps and Jan Six and his Jewish neighbors, though all those little entertainments had been ringed round by lonely and often reproachful ghosts. But it seemed to him that afternoon as he walked through mud and sleet in whatever direction his feet carried him that the house on the Breestraat had been tainted for good by the business of Geertje: what had gone on there in the weeks between the serving of the legal parchment and this morning's violent removal to Gouda had shamed every room. It was as if a noble mausoleum had been desecrated by mad mummers' rites from which nothing could ever purify it, ever make of it again what it had been in the tragic but rational past.

She had gone mad, utterly mad, the poor devil. The accusations she had made against him in that long sheet of official writing were not aimed at him in spite or in a desperate attempt to make him yield to her wishes: in her twisted brain they were facts, obvious and incontrovertible. He had loved her and meant to take her as his wife, and she had been worthy of that love; where else—she had sobbed and shrieked it at him, kneeling on the floor and clasping his knees and rubbing her wet face against them—where else would he find one like her to mend his clothes and keep his accounts and be a second mother to his child? She had been so convinced, had invented or exaggerated so many incidents that proved his deep affection and honorable intentions, that he could not look forward without apprehension to the arrival of her brother Willem. He, too, might be convinced; he, too, might insist on dragging the affair into the courts; and those who were gloating over the fate of the Regents' piece might be given something more succulent to exult over. But Willem, a sad and shaggy man who looked a little like a tamed and emasculated goat, had seen the matter through sane if not exactly intelligent eyes. Poor girl—he had insisted on calling her a girl, though she had turned with shocking speed into an old, old woman, with her loose flesh hanging in heavy folds on her big bones, and the hair at her temples gone white—poor girl, she had always been a little on the queer side, and particularly so since her husband's death. His honor had been patient with her beyond anybody's expectations. To take the six months' pay that his honor offered was to accept, under the stress of poverty, much more than was called for by the situation. The necklace that his honor had so graciously given her and even more graciously refused to take back would be sold to buy her what little luxuries she might be allowed in the madhouse at Gouda. For to the madhouse at Gouda she would have to go if she continued as wild as she was—raving, hurling a mug at Hendrikje Stoffels, snatching up Titus and trying to run away with him, drinking mustard-water because she took it to be poison and vomiting all over the place—in this state neither he nor his wife could be responsible for looking after her.

It was the summons for breach of promise that had attenuated the whole ghastly business. Willem had to go twice to the City Hall to declare and depose; the poor woman, weak after her dose of mustard-water, had to be brought in and shown to the proper authorities; Hendrikje Stoffels and the master had to compose and copy and swear to their accounts of the affair; and five days—days of nightmare, ripped by the shrieks of the disturbed Titus, hounded by the presence of a stranger in the house, darkened by threats of some new violence—went over their heads before the proper documents of dismissal could be produced and the seal of the city affixed thereto. The Saturday settled for their departure to Gouda was a dreadful day for traveling, with sleet coming in on a northeasterly gale and the temperature steadily falling; and in the aimless sickness of his spirit he could have found it in his heart to ask them to stay until the weather improved—after so much misery, what would be lost by one day more? But by one o'clock Hendrikje Stoffels had gotten their baggage into the reception hall and found them a wagon ride half the way to Gouda and packed them a basket of cold fowl and rusks and cookies to be eaten on the trip. She had helped poor Willem to half drag and half entice the wild-haired, grotesquely bundled woman down the stairs; in an attempt to forestall a violent farewell, she had gotten herself between Geertje and the master and had received for her trouble a bloody scratch that ran from the corner of her eye to the corner of her lip. And when they were gone she had not sagged in womanly weakness or looked to him for thanks or pity or said one word to indicate her weariness; instead, erect and energetic, she had gone about the business of cleaning up the confusion they had left behind.

"You'd better walk over to Bonus's and see if something shouldn't be done about that scratch," he said, taking his hat and cloak from the closet and starting for the door.

She had not asked him where he was going or when he would be back; she had merely said that there was no reason to bother Dr. Bonus about it—she had treated such scratches before with black soap and vinegar. And he had gone his way, wanting only to put the house behind him, to benumb himself with the cold, to walk until exhaustion and exposure made him incapable of contemplating what his life had once

429

been and what it had become, what shards and ashes God or fate had left in his hands. For three hours now he had been walking down desolate alleys from which even the chestnut sellers and beggars had retreated, behind the dank walls of churches, out onto the wharves where the fishwives sat huddled under the roofs of their stalls and the spray dashed in and struck him in the face. He was drenched to his skin and assailed by recurrent chills before it occurred to him that if he could not bring himself to go back to the Breestraat, he could stop to warm himself at a tavern; but when he looked into his purse he found that all he had was three pennies—never, not even in the poverty of his adolescence, had he found himself without enough money to satisfy his bodily needs. It was this realization that sobered him into turning away from the wharves toward that vacant magnificence which he, in the heedlessness of his young manhood and the arrogance of early success and the heady fantasies of triumphant love, had been fool enough to believe he could turn into a home.

The front of the house, sighted from the stone bridge, affected him like a returning sickness; but the cold and faltering lump in his chest began to thaw and grow steadier the moment he had unlocked the door and stepped inside. It was not only that all the candles had been lighted as if for a festal evening, that the tiles of the floor had been scrubbed, that waves of warmth and the fragrance of baking gingerbread broke upon him from the farther rooms. It was something else, something indefinable, as if lustral waters had been scattered; as if the very soundlessness—no shouting, no weeping, no footfalls hurrying to avert or control a crisis—were, like Noah's rainbow, a sign and a covenant of divine good will, a promise of continuing peace. He stood close to the door for a little, savoring the quiet, until Hendrikje Stoffels came in, dressed in the scarlet skirt and bodice that had not appeared since the morning the city messenger had come. "Ah, look at your honor—you're drenched to the bone," she said, coming and taking his dripping hat and cloak.

"Yes. I was walking." Since she showed no tendency to question such behavior, he did not offer an explanation. He stepped out of his sodden shoes onto the tiles, which were still warm from their recent scrubbing. "And how did it go here while I was gone?"

"Very well, your honor. Titus quieted down very nicely. He napped for a while, and now he's in the kitchen with me pretending he's helping me with the cooking. If your honor would like to wash up before supper, there's a good fire and a kettle of hot water up in the bedroom."

"Thanks. I'd like that very much."

"And don't be in any hurry—supper will wait until you're ready, and so will Titus. He didn't eat anything at noon with all that excitement, so I gave him a bowl of soup about three o'clock."

The melting process that was working within him kept him from giving her more than an appreciative nod. Clinging to the balustrade from

sheer weariness—he wondered whether she would think him drunk—
he made his way upstairs. There, too, were the brightness, the orderliness, the blessed quiet in which the ringing of his wind-buffeted ears
was almost good to listen to. She had set Geertje's room to rights and
half closed the door upon it, as if decency had told her it would be unseemly to exhibit it in its emptiness, and pity had kept her from sealing it away from the warmth of the rest of the house. A candle burned,
prodigal but gracious, beside Titus's little bed; and to herself she had
given the celebratory luxury of a serene yellow lamp.

His own bedroom was softly radiant with candlelight and firelight. A
stool had been drawn up to the hearth; beside it were his slippers, and
draped over it was a robe of brown woolen lined in the front with
beaver—he had not seen it for years and wondered how she had found
it in the chaos of his storage chest. Standing on the hearth, he stripped
off his dank and clinging clothes and added hot water from the kettle to
the cold water that she had made ready for him in the big copper basin;
he immersed a towel and wrung it out and drew the steaming linen over
his aching body, shuddering in pain and pleasure at the penetrating
heat. Four times he washed himself from his crown to the soles of his
feet, knowing that supper would wait, stopping often to stare in benumbed blessedness at the changing shapes cast onto the wall by the
fire. Then, since she had set a brandy cruet and a little silver goblet
on the hearth for him, he drank before he took up the warmed and
furry weight of the robe and breathed the healing smell of camphor that
rose from its shaken folds. But this won't do, he told himself: I can't go
down to her with nothing but this robe on; and he looked about and
saw that she had laid out the other needful things on the bed. Thereafter, he followed the vaguely remembered rules for the gentleman
who is to sup comfortably in his own house: underclothing, shirt unbuttoned at the neck, breeches and stockings and slippers, and the robe
on top. He ran a comb through his snarled mop, not going to the mirror,
preferring to see himself for this one evening as he had been when he
had bought the forgotten piece of furry finery: well-fleshed rather
than heavy, high-colored rather than florid, resilient still, with a lion's
mane undulled by grey, and a pair of keen, unclouded eyes.

Downstairs again in the back parlor, he saw that the kindness which
had prompted her to leave the door of Geertje's room ajar had also kept
her from laying a place for herself tonight and that she had brought in a
copper bowl of boxwood sprigs to fill the empty place formerly sacred
to poor Geertje. While he was contemplating these arrangements, she
came in from the kitchen with Titus holding onto her apron strings from
behind and pretending to drive her like a pony. She was carrying a
tureen of savory soup made of clams and dumplings and flavored with
pepper and parsley; and her face, heated by the cooking, showed
rosy through the cloud of steam. "Won't you sit down with us?" he said,
unable still to call her by her name.

431

"No, thank you very much, your honor. I have a cut of mutton that will need watching on the spit. Anyway, I've gotten used to eating on the wing. Sit down and try the soup—I hope it's to your taste. I'll be back in a minute with the rusks."

It was all to his taste, from the excellent soup to the shelled walnuts and sliced apple arranged in a pattern on a fine old blue glass dish. Actually he was surprised to find that he had a sense of taste: for months he had been stolidly stuffing himself with more food than he wanted without troubling to savor it, and tonight he ate slowly and prudently, like a man concluding a long fast, but with an appreciation so keen that a crisp sliver of mutton seemed an infinitely precious thing. The fire crackled behind him, and the heat came through the heavy robe and relaxed the tightened muscles in his back and shoulders. Titus sat at his right, conveniently if callously resigned to the loss of his old companion. And every now and again—on the wing, as she had said—Hendrikje Stoffels appeared to clear away one course and place another, her beautiful dark hands looking more pliant and vital than ever against the whiteness of the clean tablecloth, her hair loosened a little by the haste of her comings and goings, her person giving off a scent so muted that it was less a scent than a freshness, like the smell of new-washed clothes carried in out of the sun.

The larger of the two squares of gingerbread that she brought in steaming from the oven was for Titus, she said, rumpling his fiery curls with her dusky fingers; in Ransdorp they would consider him a skinny gosling, and she would love him better and be able to squeeze him harder without being afraid of breaking him if there were more flesh on his silly little bones. The boy laughed as a child will to invite hugging and tickling, but she gave in to him only after all his gingerbread and milk had disappeared; and she made it plain that she would be doing him a great favor to leave the table uncleared while she took him upstairs and told him his story and popped him into bed.

"Will you come into bed with me, Hendrikje?" he said, getting obediently down from his chair and taking her outstretched hand.

Did she flush, or was it only the scarlet of her bodice reflected on her cheeks and her round and lineless forehead? "Not tonight. I have too much to do tonight. Tomorrow night, if you're good all day," she said. Then, to take away the sting of her refusal, she picked him up and carried him upstairs; and the sound of their laughter floated down to him where he sat over the last of his walnuts and wine.

While she was gone, he tried to dispel his dreaming ease enough to rehearse the things he wanted to say to her: thanks for the orderliness of the house and the excellence of the supper, praise for the skill and warm-heartedness with which she had managed the boy, questions about the scratch—was it at all swollen, did it hurt? His goblet was empty, and he reached for the decanter and then paused, his hairy hand on the crystal stopper. He had taken brandy upstairs and two goblets

432

of wine during the meal, and a third one would certainly put him somewhat beyond self-possession. But why in his own house—after such a day, such a year, such a life—did he have to set a watch on himself? He remembered irrelevantly then how Vrouw Tulp had suggested that when Geertje Dircx was gone he could go up to the attic and sleep with the apprentices; and he thought what a foolish idea it was, how ridiculous he would look to Hendrikje Stoffels dragging his things up there tonight; and while he was laughing over that he poured his third goblet of wine. It did nothing beyond spreading a delicious warmth through every part of him, a warmth that made him sigh and close his eyes and fall into a kind of waking sleep from which he roused himself easily enough when he heard her light feet hurrying back downstairs.

She paused close to him only long enough to pick up the wine goblet and the blue glass dish and then went off to the kitchen. When she came again, he saw that her dealings with Titus had rumpled and changed her: her large dark eyes were warm from gazing with love at something exquisite and loving; her mouth was parted and smiling, and a lock of thick waving hair had fallen over her brow. "I'll put myself in order in a minute, your honor," she said, returning and holding his look.

"Don't," he said, and it was as if another man had found the courage to speak, not he. "I like you very well as you are."

"Titus pulled the comb out of my hair. Titus—" She fell silent and put her hand to her breast, fastening an undone button on the scarlet bodice. He could hear the blood pounding in his ears, he could feel the hair rising on his arms and chest. "What about that scratch—how is it?" he said in a queer voice, getting up and taking her by the chin and turning her cheek to the candlelight.

She did not answer. She let her head come down so that her lips brushed against his palm and her warm breath filled the cup of his hand.

"Hendrikje," he said, pulling her against him, pressing his mouth against her forehead and letting the hard and fiery pillar of his need delight and torment itself against the yielding softness under the skirt. "I wouldn't want to force you—"

"Does it seem to your honor that I'm being forced?" Almost solemnly she broke the embrace and drew back from him, but only to undo the buttons of bodice and blouse and uncover for him the round, dark, richly nippled breasts. "Here?" she asked, the word driven out of her in a cry by the violence of his kissing. Then, since he said nothing, she sank down on the hearth and drew him with her; nor did they get up again before every candle in the room had burned out and only a few flickering embers were left of the fire.

*

If his happiness was so overwhelming that he could scarcely believe

433

in it—if passion had renewed his body and affection had salved his spirit and order and purpose had made a home of the ruin that had been his world—how could he be expected to behave with circumspection? He could no more remove the brooding smile from his face than he could warn her to stop singing over her work or to drain her bearing of some of the new and touching dignity. What they were to each other it was impossible to hide; and before the Saint Nicolaas Feast everybody who came into the house knew how it was with them and took it as much for granted as if there had been a wedding supper with toasts to the bridegroom and a veil and wreath for the bride.

Titus knew it: three nights after Geertje's going he had wakened out of a bad dream and come to look for Hendrikje straight to his father's bed. There, showing nothing but gratification, he got under the coverlet and lay down between the two of them, with the warmth of the hairy chest on one side of him and the yielding firmness of the ripe breasts on the other; and there they let him sleep out the night. The apprentices knew it and stopped saying, "Hendrikje, will you hand me this or that?" The baker's boy and the butcher's boy and the greengrocer learned to take off their hats before conducting business with her in the kitchen, and maids from neighboring houses knocked discreetly before opening the back door. As for his friends, old ones like Tulp and Bonus and Pinero as well as recent ones like Rabbi Menasseh ben Israel and Jan Six—though they seemed to think it too pointed as yet to bring her sweets or tea or ribbons, they never missed an occasion to open a casement for her or offer her a comfortable chair.

His delight in drawing and painting her was almost as intense as his delight in having her. Sometimes in the middle of the night, between one surge of desire and another, he would get up and put on his robe and ask her to take again some attitude that had enchanted him: he drew her sitting on a heap of Oriental cushions, her curved nakedness ruddy in the light of the fire; he drew her stretching her leg and looking thoughtfully at her toes; he drew her bracing herself on her elbow and peeping out to see what he could be doing, her bosom shining in the candle glow that fell between the parted curtains of the bed. These drawings, at least, he was discreet enough to hide; he laid them, to her unexpressed but obvious distress, between the pages of the great Bible.

Nobody spoke of the matter—he never even caught the apprentices whispering—but he supposed all of them must be wondering whether he intended to marry her at once, or not at all, or only if their nights bore fruit. He did mean to marry her, of course, and the question of possible children had nothing to do with it. There was only the matter of some vaguely remembered clause in Saskia's will that would have to be cleared up first, and since they were both immersed in the happiness of the present, he saw no reason to believe that the future would not take care of itself. He could think no further ahead than the oncoming Saint Nicolaas Feast, and he was considering gifts that the most elementary discretion would forbid—a crimson velvet dress, a gold chain for her dusky throat, jeweled rings for her smooth, dark, pliant hands—that afternoon when Ferdinand Bol gave the first pause to his high and racing heart.

Snow had been falling in great white starry flakes since morning, and he had been watching it through the upper windows while he taught, hoping that it would continue to come down, that he and she could walk together, bemused and warmed by love, in the new white radiance tonight. Now, with the lessons over and all the lads except Ferdinand gone out to stroll or sketch or carry on snow fights, he stepped up to the dark casement and took his comb out of his pocket and ran it through his hair, meaning to make himself as comely as possible before he went down to her and their fine supper and their happiness. Perhaps it was this absorption in his own person that made him start when his assistant coughed behind him. "Oh, so you're finished," he said, turning and thrusting the comb back into his pocket. "I'll see you tomorrow, then. Good night."

But the young man, standing beside an empty easel with the pale light of one lamp behind him, did not move. "I don't want to keep you, I know you want to get downstairs to—to your supper, but I wonder if you could give me time for just a word," he said.

"Certainly, Ferdinand," he said with an attempt at cordiality. But he did not draw up one of the stools and settle down on it: his assistant had made it plain that the exchange was to be brief not only by saying so but by extinguishing every lamp in the room except the one burning wanly between the empty easel and the posthumous portrait of Saskia. He stood halfway between his master and that light, his cloak over his arm and his hat in his hands; and the master did no more than ease his haunches down onto the cold and insufficient support of the window sill.

"I wanted to tell you I've made up my mind to leave."

Was there a note of arraignment in that? It was impossible to see the young man's face—only the dark hair was lighted up like an aura around it. The shoulders were erect, almost challenging, and over one of them he could see the thinly painted face of the dead, still unfinished, no depth or answering look as yet in the eyes. But if there were implications, he refused to take them up; he would not allow them to taint his high-heartedness. "Well," he said, "you're certainly ready to set up a studio of your own. I imagine our friends wonder why you didn't do it years ago."

"It was my happiness to stay with you, Master." The earnest voice, quiet and tremulous, was an unconscious reproof to the easy and superficial warmth of his own. "And when there was unhappiness here —when things went ill with you and yours—I was even more tied to *that*. This"—he made a vague, helpless gesture with his cumbered hands—"this was my home."

435

"Don't think I haven't appreciated it." It was the sort of remark a person might make to somebody who had served him well in a shop, and he did what he could to amend it. "They were bad years, God knows, what with the way things went with the Regents' piece and this business of Geertje—" He broke off, seeing two unrelated images, either one of which would have been enough to unman him a couple of months ago: the great canvas as it had been the last time he had laid eyes on it, already dimmed by smoke, with a lance and a musket rested heedlessly against it; and a wilted anemone—Ferdinand Bol's flower—on the table beside the dying woman's bed.

"I'd stay longer if I thought I was needed. But I believe I'm right in thinking you won't be needing me any more."

He was not speaking of the duties of the studio—in those he was obviously needed as much as ever. He was speaking of whatever support he had provided, or imagined he had provided, as a fellow-mourner: lighting lamps beside her picture, preserving, with youth's wild negation of change and forgetfulness and death, those little arrangements of vase and bowl and silver platter that *she* had invented and liked, those dusty twigs of boxwood or marjoram that her hands had thrust under the foot of a statue or into the frame of a looking-glass . . . The silence had hung between them too long. "I'll miss you, Ferdinand—but I suppose you know that," he said.

"I'll miss you, too, Master. But it will be better this way. Things change—they have to—it's only right that they should—"

But you're only saying that, you don't believe it, not yet, he thought. Ten years from now you may be able to forgive me—it will take you that long to see how I could want to live, why I didn't go down with her into her grave.

"God bless you, Master, and give you something in the way of happiness—"

So long as *you* don't have to see it, he thought; so long as *you* don't have to witness the living betraying the dead. As if getting through life weren't an endless chain of betrayals; as if I hadn't betrayed Lysbeth and van Vliet to make way for her, as now, to make way for Hendrikje, I betray her and you and Geertje; as if the lighting of a lamp, the saving of a twig of herbs could undo the inexorable law of change which sees to it that nobody but the buried are ever released from the pain of giving pain . . . "God bless you, too," he said, getting up and taking his back away from the chilly casement. "The best of luck in your new place. And give yourself a little pleasure now and again; a person's time is shorter than you young people think."

He wished that the young man would come then and embrace him, that the arm which had supported her dying head would clasp his shoulders, that the forgiveness which passes understanding would be meted out to him in his human unworthiness. But there was no embrace; there was a brief, reserved handclasp, which he returned in kind;

and then, without another word, Ferdinand Bol and all the relics of the past that clung about his person were necessarily and properly gone.

Yet haste to remove himself from the bleakness of the empty room seemed unfitting. He went back to the window and stood there for a long while, looking at the snow on the black branches and the curved bridge and the sills of the lighted casements, thinking of the countless graves it was piling up on tonight. Either they slept down there in their cold darkness and knew nothing, or they knew all things and forgave them all: kings forgave their crowned sons, and withered mothers forgave their blooming daughters, and dead painters forgave the apprentices who had taken the skills and the tools from their rigid hands—so he had said to himself before, and he said it again, more urgently now, because there was more in him now to be forgiven . . . Rest in peace, Mother and Father. Rest in peace, Gerrit and Lysbeth. Rest in peace, Vrouw van Hoorn, with the fortuitous concatenations of this life resolved into an unimaginable harmony. And you, too, beloved, rest in peace—he went and took the lamp from beside the unfinished picture —and give me the absolution I must have before I can make your eyes look otherwise than dead . . .

On the way down, carrying the lamp in one hand and drying his cheeks with the other, he remembered again the musket and the lance set carelessly against the beautifully painted gold braid and silver-blue satin, and the bright image of her childish person darkened already, destined like everything else to be filmed over by the smoke and grime of the years. Well, Saskia, he thought, at any rate your boy is content; *your* masterpiece is being dealt with more tenderly than mine. And it was a comfort, a kind of dispensation that it was not Hendrikje but Titus, rosy and eager for his supper, who stood waiting for him at the foot of the stairs.

BOOK VIII

1648

-

1654

When Jan Lievens presented himself at the house on the Breestraat—forty-three now and balding and so long away from his Motherland that now and again he lapsed unconsciously into English—through at least the first part of the evening the sharer of his unhappy stay at Lastman's felt that he deserved every possible consideration. He had had an excellent place at the Court of King Charles I and had lost it when the Court had other things, including the safety of their heads, to think about. He had had a generous patron and had lost him, too—fallen as he now was into the hands of the indignant Scots, discredited abroad by his poverty and at home by the net of lies in which he had entangled himself. And Jan Lievens, who had eaten at that royal table, painted those royal princes and princesses, collected that royal pension month in, month out, seemed to Rembrandt such an appalling example of chaos and change that he regretted that his old companion should have come to him on an evening when his back parlor was occupied by his Jewish friends and Jan Six and Gretha Tulp and Pastor Swalmius, all of whom were delighted to hear that the Romanizing popinjay English King had been put in his proper place.

The table with its abundance of good wine and sliced goose and nuts and apples seemed too festive; the salon with its splendid collection seemed so blatant an assertion of prosperity that he did not offer to show it; even Hendrikje seemed too fine in her scarlet velvet dress and her saffron silk shawl. Through the whole evening—a very noisy one, because his guests were in such high spirits over the English news—he kept signaling the exile to stay on until the rest were gone. And Jan Lievens was willing to accommodate, was less eager to nurse his misfortunes in solitude than his host would have imagined. Handsome still, if somewhat thickened and softened, he sat at the table and consumed a gratifying quantity of roast goose and wine. Jan Six and Gretha seemed to be drawn to him, and it was to these young ones that he held forth in a manner so little changed that to see it was to be plunged back into forgotten pancake shops: his hands still made wide gestures; his rich baritone still gave weight to the old broad assertions; the national cataclysm notwithstanding, he had not lost the trick of running his white well-fleshed hand through the black waves of his thinning hair.

It was after eleven when the others went out into a street submerged in the first thick mist of an early autumn. Coming back from seeing them on their way—Lievens had remained at the table, peeling an apple—he met Hendrikje in the reception hall with a four-branched brass candlestick in her hand. "Where are you going, darling?" he said, thinking it would be pleasant to have her there to look at while he listened to Lievens' melancholy tale.

"To take this up to the studio. I thought you'd want to show Heer Lievens your paintings."

"Yes, I suppose I will, but later. You can take that up if you like, though, and then come down again. I imagine we'll be sitting in the back room for quite a while."

"No . . ." She did not look at him across the flames of the candles, and from the way she wet her lips with the tip of her tongue he was sure that something in Jan Lievens had reminded her that she was a sergeant's daughter from Ransdorp and that her hand, loaded though it was with gold and garnets and pearls, did not wear a wedding ring. "No, I'd rather go straight to bed."

He did not protest as she went up the splendid staircase. She would have come back if he had insisted; since the first time he had laid hands on her, he was the master and she was all compliance, all yielding and giving tenderness. But if she had sensed, or imagined she had sensed, some sign of disapproval in the poor devil in the back parlor, he did not want her exposed to it. In an hour he would find her still awake in their firelit bedroom, and with that expectation running in his blood he hurried back to his guest.

The first thing he meant to do was ask his old friend if he stood in need of ready money. Through most of the boisterous evening, he had been trying to figure out how much he could spare, a calculation made more difficult by the unnerving realization that he did not know how much he had. Such money as was lying around in drawers and gilt boxes and Chinese jars, along with uncashed bank drafts from the buyers of two portraits and a couple of serene versions of *The Holy Family*—the amount of that he knew generally. But Saskia's money, what was still left in the bank after the payments on the house and its furnishings—of *that* he had not yet been able to form a clear estimate. He guessed it must be close to twenty thousand florins; at least it had been close to that before he began to make minor withdrawals six or seven months ago. Hendrikje, excellent manager that she was, created plenty out of next to nothing; and current expenses could almost be covered by the apprentices' fees and the payments from such patrons as turned up from time to time. If he had not, under the expansive influence of his recent happiness, indulged himself occasionally at the auctions, he would have been three, four, maybe five hundred florins to the good; but that was done, and everything he had bought had been a bargain —the English crisis had slowed up trade and brought the prices down. And even if he had been more straitened than he was, he would still have been impelled to do what he did the instant he seated himself opposite his visitor. "You left in a hurry, I know, and I don't imagine you had time to collect all that was due you on your commissions," he

442

said, trying to make the matter more casual by picking at a bit of cold goose. "If there's anything I can do for you, just say so. It so happens I have a fair amount of cash in the house—if you wanted, you could take it with you tonight."

The reaction to that was a suppressed smile and a lifting of the eyebrows. "Well, now, my dear fellow," said Jan Lievens—he had picked up the "my dear fellow" in England and had tried it on all the males this evening, including the Olympian Swalmius—"that's very generous of you, but actually I've never been better off in my life. It's true I left in a hurry, but not without collecting. They have a kind of honor there that makes them the more eager to pay off simply *because* they're in a desperate case. With what I've saved—most of the time I was invited out to dine—with what I've saved and what I collected just before I left, I came out of it with something over eleven thousand florins—no fortune, of course, but enough for the time being. Thank you very much just the same."

"I'm delighted to hear it," he said with a heartiness made false by his embarrassment. Eleven thousand earned in the craft and laid by to be used freely seemed like a fortune to him: whatever was left of Saskia's was by law and by right not his but Titus's, and when he withdrew any of it he felt ashamed for days. "Then I suppose you won't be in a hurry about setting up a studio."

"No, I don't imagine I'll be getting around to that before midwinter. You see, I'll be going to Utrecht next month to be married; you'll admit it's about time. I thought of it once in England—she was a perfectly charming girl—but now I'm very glad I didn't. I couldn't have done better anywhere than I'll be doing now: she's twenty-seven, but she's from a good family, and her dowry's thirty thousand, and she's the only child of rather elderly parents, and I don't imagine we'll have anything to worry about for the rest of our days."

Rembrandt pushed away his plate and wondered why his old companion should be stirring up such dislike in him. Jealousy at the thought of all those florins? A sudden recollection of poor Lysbeth sitting in the bitter-cold outbuilding and saying stupid things that she hoped would be considered clever? Sheer exasperation with himself for mistaking somebody far better off than he himself was for a stranded beggar? The old, buried pain that the tawdry and the mediocre were bound to be the darlings of princes because princes—with the exception of William of Orange, who had not been born to the purple—were tawdry and mediocre themselves? He rose and filled his guest's goblet with wine—decent wine, but Jan Lievens was probably accustomed to better. "Well, I wish you happiness," he said without conviction.

"Thanks. I imagine it'll work out nicely. You wouldn't know of a house for us, would you? I'll want a fine one, naturally, but nothing as —as overwhelming as this." He had managed to give the word an implication of ostentation; his eyes took in the polished floor, the Oriental carpet, the beautiful wainscoting, and were not impressed. "Something with fewer rooms, a little more simple—"

He shook his head, though he knew exactly what sort of house was wanted and would have been able to recommend two or three. They were what people referred to as "the new houses": all the floors were done in large tiles laid in a diamond pattern, and the walls were not divided into plaster and wainscoting—they were either all plaster, painted in some pale and characterless color, or all wood. It was not for the old, dear profusion of priceless things that these rooms were made, but for the display of a single precious object: a globe, a lonely canvas, a solitary piece of ancient statuary, a fine old lute hung in isolation on one of the blank walls. "You'll have no trouble finding what you want," he said. "That's the only kind of house they've been building for a number of years."

"Five or six rooms would be plenty."

"And where are you going to put your apprentices?"

"Apprentices? To tell the truth, my dear fellow, I'm finished with apprentices. Teaching is just too wearisome: if I can't live off my painting, I'd rather starve. Somebody this evening was saying you have eleven of those fellows on your hands. I don't know how you do it; it would bore me to death."

He could not say that Saskia's money, Titus's money, could dwindle away in a few years if it were not for the apprentices' fees. Besides, no matter how bitterly he sometimes resented the time it took from his painting, he considered it his moral duty and fatherly pleasure to hand down what he knew to the young and eager ones. "They don't bore me at all. On the contrary, I like them. And one of the ways I get to know what I'm doing myself is to think it out so that I can explain it to them," he said.

"By the way, what *are* you doing?" said Jan Lievens; and it was plain from the burst of vitality in his voice that he had forced himself to ask the question, that he cared no more about his old friend's paintings than he cared about what had become of the English girl he had considered marrying.

"Oh, a couple of portraits. Some Biblical subjects I've always wanted to work on—" And he could not keep himself from adding: "The last big thing I did was a Regents' piece for Captain Banning Coq's Company."

"Oh, yes, I heard about that." He said it quickly, nervously, as if he had heard enough to make him want to bury the subject as fast as he could. "They tell me you were painting it just when your wife was in her last illness." "They," whoever they were, must have used that last illness to explain what they considered a regrettable anomaly. "You know"—the guest produced a sprightly smile, recovering with admirable speed from another man's misfortunes—"it wasn't until tonight that I knew you had married again."

"I'm not married." It came out of him more belligerently than he intended.

"Oh, really? I got the idea—the young woman makes such a fine appearance—you mean, she's only your housekeeper?"

It was a question he had never been asked before, and in his anger and embarrassment he answered it as bluntly as he could. "She lives with me. She's my mistress."

"Oh, I'm sorry, I didn't realize—" His visitor flushed and tried to cover his confusion by tossing off the last of his wine.

"That's how it stands. We've been living together for close to a year."

"Well, your friends certainly seem to accept her completely. Amsterdam must have changed since I was here. The young Tulp girl—she's the daughter of the famous physician, isn't she?—she was saying how wonderfully she gets on with your Tobias—"

"His name is Titus."

"Yes, of course, Titus. I'm sure it works out beautifully with your friends, but don't you have to worry about your patrons? After all, this isn't Rome or Paris, and there must be numbers of people—especially women—who are very narrow-minded about these things. Won't they hesitate to come to a house where—?"

Of which number, Rembrandt thought, the heiress from Utrecht is no doubt a conspicuous example. "Those who want to come can come. Those who don't can stay home and go to the devil," he said.

"But why make yourself unnecessary trouble? Unless, of course, you're not willing to commit yourself—"

"I am committed. Would you care for another glass of wine?"

"No, thank you—it's excellent, but I've had plenty. I know it's none of my business, but I can't imagine why you would—"

"Because," he said furiously, "my wife left her money to Titus, and it's at my disposal only so long as I don't remarry. The minute I get married, I can't touch the money—it stays in the bank until Titus reaches his majority."

The long silence that followed was made terrible for him not by his guest's embarrassment but by the realization that he had brutally raised his voice against the dispensation of the dead. If he had thought that dispensation inequitable before, he had exorcised the thought with work which memorialized the past—her posthumous portrait, a new etching of the dead Sylvius, a panel made from the drawing he had done on the wintry bridge that day when she had come to him after their quarrel for reconciliation and tenderness. Now, only now did he feel that the demands of her love had made her on her deathbed unwise and unjust. It was as if her dead hand lay heavy on the florins in the bank, and he in his rage and his frustration—yes, and in his assertion of

445

his right to live warmly and merrily on the earth under which she lay—had struck away that dead hand.

"That *is* a pity," said Jan Lievens, "especially at a time when you could probably use the money—"

"I'm not short of money."

"Oh, I didn't mean you actually needed any. You're living like a king here, as anybody can see. But hadn't we better go up to your studio before it gets too late?" He rose and wiped his fingers on his napkin; and it was plain that anything, even an unwelcome hour of looking at canvases, would be preferable to the marsh into which he had stumbled. "I've been wanting all evening to see what you're doing."

He wished he could say, "Some other time," and see the visitor to the door. But that would be foolish: it would indicate that he was undone—and he was *not* undone—by the questionable state of his means and the irregularity of his household. He handed a candlestick to Jan Lievens, took another for himself, and started for the reception hall and the stairway, thinking how even a devotee of "the new houses" could scarcely fail to be impressed by what the moving lights called out of the midnight darkness: the ancient wine-cooler, the great mirror with its heavy frame, the Ruysdaels and the Perennises hung in unimportant spots where most people would have hung an etching, the marble tiles, the polished balustrade. And if there was not too much up there to be shown, even so self-centered and unperceptive a man as Lievens would realize he was seeing the fruit of lean and bitter days.

The four-branched candelabra Hendrikje had set on the worktable in the studio was still burning brightly. "We'd better talk softly," he said almost defiantly, jerking his head toward the closed door at the opposite end of the room. "Five of the lads are in there sleeping."

"You mean they stay with you?"

"Five out of the eleven stay with me."

"But don't you find it burdensome having them under your feet?"

"They're not under my feet. A house the size of this could accommodate twice as many. Anyway, as I told you, I like them, and so does Hendrikje. These things over here"—he put down his candle and picked up a pile of unframed paintings that stood against the wall under the black casement—"these are studies." There were only two finished canvases to show, and it seemed wise to save them for the last.

He laid the studies out flat on the worktable, and turned sick at what the candlelight did to the irregular surfaces, falling straight down upon them. Two were of young rabbinical students reverend in their rags; one was of a handsome Sephardic merchant melancholy in silk and velvet; the last was a likeness of the little country girl Hendrikje had found to help with the housework. But varied as the subjects were, the concentrated yellow light reduced them all to the same rawness and violence; the brush strokes showed like gashes; the rich impasto cast ugly ridges of shadow; the subtle transitions from color to color, dark to light, seemed coarse and obvious. Jan Lievens looked at them in some surprise; and the host was about to hold them up parallel with the candle-stick so that the distortion would be less, when the visitor said, "Your subjects certainly are unusual. Am I wrong, or aren't three of them Jews?"

It had come out as a kind of complaint, and he was glad to have a righteous cause on which to vent his stored fury. "Yes," he said. "I didn't realize you had any objection to Jews."

"Oh, I don't, not in the least. It's only that there aren't any of them in England, you know."

"Well, there are plenty of them here, as you saw by the company downstairs tonight."

"And very interesting, colorful people they are. I haven't a thing against them—"

"That's very generous of you," he said; but his old friend was touching the ridged impasto with the tip of his finger, and the irony was lost.

"You're painting more thickly—aren't you?—than you used to back in Leyden."

That, too, was a complaint, and he had an almost uncontrollable impulse to strike the white finger with its well-cared-for nail from those rich and living mounds and ridges. "Paint's one thing I never try to save money on," he said.

"No, but I'm serious. Isn't it the fashion here—it is in England—to paint thinner? Anthony van Dyck, God rest his soul—I saw a great deal of him at Court, and he always said a painting ought to be as sleek as a piece of silk."

He could not answer. It was not only that it was impossible to tell this shallow fool who had loved nothing, lost nothing, suffered nothing, that a painting was life, and that life with its bloody births and consuming passions and annihilating bereavements was no piece of silk. It was also the embittering knowledge that with Rubens dead matters had not worked out as he had always expected: it was not Rembrandt van Rijn upon whom the mantle of Rubens' greatness had descended; it was Anthony van Dyck, whom nobody in the Netherlands had cared much about, who had snatched the glory in his last years and pulled it down with him into his grave. His own lads had mentioned now and again with derision calculated to please their master the toying with glazes, the transparent vacancy of the smooth surface, the tendency to turn every female sitter into a Venus which some Amsterdam studios were affecting of late. *That* influence, courtly and superficial, was what the Dutch were taking unto themselves. However strongly they had made their political stand with the rebellious Roundheads, their tastes were exactly where a person would expect the tastes of a self-indulgent race of merchants to be . . .

"This one," said Lievens, "is very interesting."

He did not bother to ascertain what his visitor was referring to. "Interesting" meant either so poor as to be beneath the most negligible compliment or so puzzling as to be beyond comprehension. "Those are studies," he said, "and you can't see them anyway, not in this light. I should have put them on easels. The paintings ought to show up better; there are two of them over there against the wall."

Unfortunately it was Jan Lievens, not he, who took up the four-branched candlestick and directed its light not on *Abraham Visited by the Angel,* which his host had wished to show him first, but on *Susanna and the Elders,* which was to have been saved for the last, since it seemed the likelier of the two to please, being at once less venturesome in texture and more splendid in color and detail. The canvas bloomed gratifyingly in the candlelight: a cast of gold which took well to such illumination lay over the magical landscape with its timeless battlements, over the purple-blue robes of the Elders, the scarlet cloak and slippers that the bather had left behind her, the stepping-stones leading down into the water, and the loosened hair and almost naked body of the young woman herself. In that yellow radiance, it seemed foreign to its painter, and he wondered why he had done it. Because he had lately come upon a number of honey-colored Venetian things at the auctions? Because the house, refurbished by Hendrikje, had revived the old foolish dream of splendor? Because now that his spirit had turned toward the sober and terrible truth, he had looked back and allowed himself one last piece of shimmering fantasy?

"That's lovely," said Lievens. "That's the sort of thing I'd imagined you'd be doing. I'm sure anybody, including the English, would be taken with it on first sight—they'd even overlook the impasto. If you could only do it the way van Dyck did—keep the same brilliance and still get a little more smoothness, a little more gloss—"

"Gloss is a thing that doesn't concern me. I wouldn't bother to wipe my ass on gloss."

He was as much amazed as Lievens at what he had said, but even in the appalled silence that followed he could not be sorry. He took the candlestick out of his visitor's hand and waved it across the other canvas —drab, harsh—the Angel of the Lord, a fierce piece of radiance, descended incongruously, as if by accident, among unbeautiful mortals in a dark, crude, and somber world. "That's the way I paint now, and that's the way I mean to keep on painting," he said, walking away and taking the light with him.

"Well, really, Rembrandt, you might at least let me see it—"

"What's the use? You wouldn't care for it. Come back downstairs and have another glass of wine."

The parlor looked ravaged now, with the candles burned down and the empty walnut shells strewn about; and he knew that his guest was as eager to take himself off as he was to see him depart. Yet tact required that whatever ugly wounds had been exhibited upstairs should now be covered, and Jan Lievens let himself down onto the chair he had been warming earlier in the evening and blithely held out his goblet. It was he who talked of old times, dwelling on the Leyden days with a sentimentality that would have been sickening even if a person had not kept remembering what had gone on between him and Lysbeth. He had been home to visit his parents—thank God, both of them were well; he had dropped in on Dou and found him a real provincial celebrity with more commissions than he could handle; he had taken a walk around the Old Wall—good heavens, how small that wall did seem to him now! —he had visited a few graves—scarcely, thought Rembrandt, Lysbeth's grave . . .

The host drank also, though wine was the last thing he wanted; and while the facile melancholy talk went on he wondered why this old friend of his, whom he had welcomed heartily with the best intentions, should have made such a determined effort to reduce him to a state of depression and doubt. He saw then that his generosity had been an insult, that his good fortune had been a goad and a reproach, that his ill luck had been a source of satisfaction—and how could it be otherwise, how could a mediocrity do anything but chafe in the presence of a master before whom he had crawled in his last evil days at Lastman's and for six hard years in the outbuilding behind the mill? Back home from his profitable and not inglorious stay in England, he would naturally wish to believe that their positions had been reversed; there were those who were happy to encourage him in that belief with tales of dwindling commissions and the neglected Regents' piece; he, with his glazes and his silky smoothness, had something he could teach his teacher, and it was only human that he should exult in that change. It was easy to imagine him saying tomorrow, "I spent the evening with my old friend Rembrandt van Rijn—you remember him, don't you? He lives in one of those big old gloomy places on the Breestraat, and saddles himself with apprentices. In his younger days he had a great deal of talent, and I suppose he's very capable still, but he's so stubborn and wrong-headed that a person can't talk to him for his own good. He lays the paint on a quarter of an inch thick, and—would you believe it in this day and age? —he *likes* a raw surface, he has no use for gloss."

And once the visitor had gone his way after the strongest assurances of lasting friendship and the most affectionate of good nights, it was impossible for the host to see his situation as he had seen it before. Was he or was he not in a precarious financial condition? he asked himself, going from room to room to snuff out the candles. Would the number of his patrons really shrink because he was living with a mistress? Was there something childish in him that he should enjoy teaching a crowd of fumbling youths? Could the Dutch, who had taken to his work because they had been nurtured on the honesty of Brouwer and Seghers and Hals and the splendor of Rubens, suddenly pass him by because they had been seduced by a silken and vapid simplicity? Was this really a dreary old house, crowded beyond reason with canvases and antiquities? But it was no hour for a weary and harassed man to answer such questions. The clock in a nearby steeple sounded one, and Hendrikje would be waiting up for him, and knowing well enough what could be depended upon to bring on forgetfulness and sleep, he banked the feeble fire and went upstairs to bed.

*

By now the letter was dog-eared and wrinkled and spotted with paint; he parted with it only when he got into bed; he had been carrying it around in his pocket for ten days. It had arrived with the first snow, and the snow and the letter had exorcised the miasmal autumn and the empty-heartedness that had been with him like a sickness ever since the coming of Jan Lievens; and whenever things went wrong—when an expected patron did not keep his appointment, when he had to make still another withdrawal from the bank, when he quarreled with Hendrikje about her running out to services every Sunday morning and exposing herself to possible rebukes from the elect—whenever things went wrong, he took the limp paper out and read the letter over again.

It was, though he had not dared to believe it until he saw the signature at the bottom of the long official paper, from my lord Constantyn Huyghens, still the Prince's secretary at The Hague. It said, quite incredibly, that Prince Frederik Hendrik had a mind to add two more canvases to the five by Rembrandt that had given him so much pleasure, and that he—my lord—would be in Amsterdam on the eighteenth of November and would be grateful if the master could reserve the evening to discuss the subjects and come to an agreement about the price. The warmth of the tone was enough to obliterate any discouraging afterthoughts: he had wondered only briefly why the Prince should have let ten years elapse between commissions and whether his mind would have turned toward Rembrandt van Rijn if Rubens had not been dead.

Old remembrances, as perceptible as smoke or a scent, had risen from that paper: the days of glory and high spirits when the *Anatomy Lesson of Doctor Tulp* had drawn crowds to the Surgeons' Guildhall; the evening when the little secretary with his lustrous eyes and his glossy beard had stayed in the outbuilding behind the mill, unmindful of the cold, murmuring over the *Judas* with the throaty sound of a dove. A man carries two lives within him, he thought, the life he dreams and the life he lives; and only rarely—the young would hang themselves if anybody ever told them how rarely—do the two converge. But not caring whether afterwards he would be forced to call himself a fool, he had been permitting himself to hope, to trust that another such convergence was about to come to pass.

The only thing about the letter that troubled him was the postscript: "I learned from a friend of mine after writing this that your fellow-painter Jan Lievens—do you remember that he was with us the night

I bought your *Judas*?—has recently settled in Amsterdam. It would be a pleasure to see him, provided, of course, it would be agreeable to him and to you." It was *not* agreeable, but he did not see on what grounds he could refuse; and once he had given the invitation, he got in return the malicious gratification of having Jan Lievens pulled up short at the mention of commissions from the House of Orange. Then, too, there was the business of his lady wife from Utrecht: though they had been settled in one of "the new houses" for over a month, she had not paid a call, afflicted as she was on various occasions by difficulties with a maid, the arrival of out-of-town cousins, preoccupation with draperies, and a cold in the head. But now, miraculously, her health had been restored, her affairs had subsided into order, and she could think of nothing more delightful than a visit to the friend of her husband's youth—especially if her coming could coincide with that of the distinguished gentleman from The Hague. Hendrikje, who seldom lost her temper, said that if Vrouw Lievens appeared *she* would spend the evening in the bedroom—not that it made any difference: Hannie, the new little maid, the latest import from Ransdorp, was perfectly capable of serving a tray of cold meats and fruit. He had made it plain to her and to Jan Lievens that the evening of the eighteenth of November would not be a convenient occasion for receiving the heiress from Utrecht; but even after that she had said, though with a rueful and tender gaiety, that she was still determined to stay upstairs. Nothing from a loving request to a surly command had been able to change her mind: she had said firmly that the evening was to be *his* evening, and that if she injected the faintest note of embarrassment into it she would never forgive herself; and sorry as he was to have her exiled from his triumph, he was forced to admit to himself, once the matter was settled, that his dominant feeling was relief.

To show that she had no wounded sensibilities, she spent the whole day preparing the company dishes and cleaning the salon. With a kerchief over her hair and her skirt tucked up around her knees—she had beautiful legs, perhaps a little too full at the calf but tapering to the trimmest of ankles and provocative even in thick black work-stockings—she moved the stepladder methodically from place to place around the enormous room and climbed up to give a thorough cleaning to the profusion on the walls: the Turkish powder horn, the trophies made of ancient weapons and plumes and bittern feathers, the Chinese scrolls and the Japanese figurines, the frames of the Brouwers, the Seghers, the Ruysdaels, the Carraccis, the Percellus, the Lastmans and the Rubens. Carel Fabritius—as young as Bol had been when he had first come to the studio and as taken with Hendrikje as Bol had been with Saskia—Carel Fabritius, very comely with his candid face and his guileless blue-grey eyes and his disorderly chestnut-colored hair, abandoned his easel and helped with the cleaning, holding the ladder for her and stepping onto the pedestals to dust Faustina, Caligula, Tiberius, Augustus, Otho,

Galba, and Vespasian. Titus and the lissome little Hannie joined them when the dishes from the noonday meal were washed and put away; sitting on the rich Persian carpet, they polished the metal pieces, Hannie busy with tongs and candlesticks and Titus rubbing away at old medallions. To see so many at work over his possessions was to know how much he owned: in what other Amsterdam house could my lord Constantyn Huyghens find such exquisitely chosen opulence? And for once he abandoned the business of the studio and spent the day in the salon. Cheer and gratefulness welled up in him; he who could seldom bring himself to say a word of thanks praised each of the workers over and over, clapped Carel Fabritius on the shoulder, kissed Hendrikje loudly on the cheek, and carried Titus pig-a-back around the room so that he could move his delicate little fingers over the ancient muskets and through the silky feathers and plumes.

Supper and the hour after it were made a little uneasy because it was impossible to tell from the letter just when my lord would come. He might arrive at eight, intending to spend the evening, or he might come as late as ten, meaning to discharge the business with dispatch at the end of more important calls. Hendrikje was certain he would appear early; and by half past seven she had the supper dishes back on the shelves, Titus bathed and put to bed, and Hannie, her hair piled in a silky coil on top of her head, dressed in impeccable black bombazine with a richly embroidered apron tied pitilessly tight around her slender waist. Hannie was to answer the knocker, light the candles, carry in the wine and food, keep the marble wine-cooler filled with snow, and sit, whenever she was not otherwise occupied, as still as a statue in the reception hall. Having set the girl's comb at a more becoming angle, topped the pyramid of oranges and figs with a strip of sugared ginger, and opened and tasted the wine, the mistress of the house finally snatched the kerchief from her head and ran upstairs to brush what she had laid out for Rembrandt to wear.

Once dressed—it was almost eight o'clock by then—he could not settle down to anything. He wandered restlessly from one room to another; he went into the small back hall to see in the big mirror how he looked in his bottle-green jacket—well enough, he supposed, since he had diminished a little and Hendrikje had done some clever letting-out in crucial places; he ate a fig and went into the kitchen to dabble his fingers in the water basin; and by the time the quarter-hour sounded from the nearby steeples he was almost ready to resort to a book. But there was no need for that: somebody was scraping his feet at the top of the snowy front steps; and even though it was probably only Lievens, he could not stand on formality, must thwart poor Hannie, who gave him an exasperated look, must open his own door. And my lord Constantyn Huyghens, there on the threshold, was enough to summon back the exhilaration of the afternoon. His eyes still shone in spite of the pouches beneath them, his mouth still parted in a shy smile in spite of the wrinkles on either side of it; he took his host by both hands, and the wringing pressure of his fingers was as giving as an embrace. "How glad I am to see you! How well you look! How very good to see you after all this time! I'm afraid to think how long it is," he said, stepping into the bright hall, still holding onto one of Rembrandt's hands.

"Ten years, my lord, though it's hard to believe it, looking at you."

"Me? I've aged deplorably." He raised his head—the glossy little beard was gone—and looked around, no doubt expecting to see Jan Lievens. Hannie came up and took his beaver and his black cloak starred all over with snow, and helped him brush the dampness from his ruff—in a day when the ruff was falling out of fashion and giving place to the French lace collar, it was strangely heartening to find him faithful to it still. "And your charming wife—how is she?" he said.

"She died, my lord."

"Died?"

"Yes, you wouldn't have known it. She died of an inflammation of the lungs three years ago."

"Died—that lovely Saskia!" The velvety eyes looked straight at him, made no attempt to evade the spectacle of his sorrow. "Good God, I had no idea. I would have written you—I hope you know. Dead at her age, and here you are in this big house all by yourself—"

"No, it isn't quite like that." He wondered what the little secretary would have thought of him if he had blurted out exactly how it was. "I have a son, Titus—we had others, but they died when they were little things. Anyway, I have Titus here with me; he's four years old. And I have a housekeeper"—he thought of her sitting over her knitting upstairs and knew she would have wanted him to say exactly that—"a housekeeper, and a maid, and eleven apprentices, five of them living here in the attic. No, you couldn't say that I was alone."

"And you've gone on teaching and painting through all that trouble—"

The earnest and unwavering gaze, the tremor in the voice, the small hand falling on his bottle-green sleeve—surely they deserved some portion of the truth. "Actually," he said, "I've found it easier to teach than to paint—the teaching takes a person out of himself. In these last three years I *have* been painting, it's true, but not nearly as much as I did before she died."

"But that's only to be expected. The wonder is you've painted at all, what with the child and your house and your apprentices, to say nothing of the shock of such a loss. I only hope you haven't forced it, I only hope you've given yourself time to work back into it." He withdrew his fingers, but not before he had passed them gently over the hairy wrist of his host.

"Too much time, I'm afraid. In three years a man could get himself forgotten. There are so many changes, so many new names—"

"Nonsense! Anybody with your achievements can afford to lie fallow for a while—"

"I'll be doing better. My household's more orderly now—"

"You're obviously doing well enough as it is. This house, this beautiful house—I knew you had moved, I got your address from the Saint Lucas Guild—but when I found the place I was certain there had been some mistake. Nobody but Rubens, God rest his soul—and he lived off the Church—nobody else in the Netherlands ever painted himself into such a splendid house as this."

And what would you say, he thought, if I told you that this splendid house is only half paid for, and that the money which bought that half was Saskia's, not mine? What price would you offer me for the two canvases if you knew that my old apprentice Flinck has twice as many commissions as I do, that no buyers have come for the *Susanna* and the *Abraham,* that my Regents' piece went out like a bonfire on a rainy night . . . ? "I love the house. Foolish as it is to keep it, I get a great deal of pleasure out of it now that my housekeeper has gotten it in hand," he said.

"Why shouldn't you keep it? With five apprentices living in, you'd have to have a roomy house—and why shouldn't you have a beautiful one if you can?"

"So I tell myself . . ." The little Hannie had come back and settled on the seat by the entrance to wait for the next thud of the knocker; a cold draft from under the door was stirring the hem of her skirt and blowing across the visitor's wet feet. "But why am I keeping you standing here?" he said, taking the secretary by the elbow. "Come into the salon where we can sit by the fire."

He paused on the threshold because my lord had stopped there, plainly wonder-struck by the prospect before him—gold and marble, copper and silver and rich painted surfaces gleaming in a prodigality of candlelight. It came into his mind as his visitor made the long-remembered murmuring sound that everything here, at least, could be honestly called the fruit of his work and evidence of his past success; conscience had kept him from laying out a single florin of Saskia's for any of this. "That's Rubens' *Hero and Leander,* isn't it?" said the little secretary. "I didn't know you owned it; it's one of the best. And two Carraccis, and all those Brouwers—good Lord, man, you must have almost everything he painted in this one room!"

"I believe I do," he said, trying to control the twitching of his lips, trying to keep down the surge of pride.

"What a collection! I'll tell you outright, though I beg you not to repeat it—Frederik Hendrik's collection doesn't come up to it. That marvelous Ruysdael—that Percellus—those Seghers—" He was off, drawn by this and that, and his host, suddenly unstrung, could only let himself down onto the nearest chair and follow him with his eyes.

"Imagine," said the visitor, turning back to Rembrandt with his hand on Vespasian's marble foot, "just imagine what it must mean to your boy, your Titus, to be growing up in such a beautiful place among all these wonderful things. If your wife—God rest her soul—didn't have many years to take pleasure in it, at least the child will profit by it. And you—I find it so with my boys, and I'm sure you will with yours—through him, you'll enjoy it all over again."

He could not answer, he could only nod and tighten his lips against what he knew would be a weak and foolish smile. For the first time he was seeing the house and the collection as something less transitory than his mortal self, as a legacy, a rich and solid accretion deposited by his labors through the years. On another winter evening, perhaps when he himself was no longer above the earth, another young wife would light other candles in these silver candlesticks and draw the curtains close against the night. Couples as young as he and Saskia had been when they danced in Hendrik Uylenburgh's dusty shop would turn away from the ancient marble emperors at the sound of the clavier to dance in the middle of this never-danced-on floor. Titus—as self-possessed as Frans van Pellicorne and as radiant as everybody had expected Allaert van Hoorn to be—Titus would lead his lady out, and the lines of dancers would whirl around, and the hair of the girls would ripple like living fire. And after the dance there would be the yearning and the begetting, and one generation would follow another, and all of them would know at least once or twice in the allotted number of their years a day when the reality converged with the dream . . . But we have no clavier, I must buy a clavier, he told himself, rubbing his knuckles across his stinging eyes. We must have music here, so that Hendrikje can teach the boy to dance while she is young and nimble. I'll sit and watch—how long is it since I've danced? Not since I danced with you, dear heart.

He started at the sound of the knocker. He had quite forgotten Jan Lievens; and my lord turned away from Vespasian as if he had forgotten him too. "Oh, yes," he said, "that'll be your old friend from Leyden. When I think of that first night and the two of you there in the coldest, barest studio I've ever seen—when I see you here in this house with all these priceless things, God knows I don't discount your misfortunes, but I can't help being gratified at what a splendid life you've made for yourself."

Jan Lievens, crossing the threshold and clapping his host on the shoulder on his way to shake hands with the secretary, had gone to some trouble to manifest that he, too, had made a splendid life for himself. Lace spilled around his wrists and shoulders; his jacket and breeches were of copper-colored velvet; an emerald ring, the gift of Queen Henrietta Maria, flashed on his finger, and a silver chain with a medallion bearing the likeness of King Charles ornamented his chest. Presented with such a display of trophies, what could my lord do but ask about England; and what would he get but a lengthy and circumstantial answer from one who fancied himself in the role of the insider who had seen every act of the royal tragedy at first hand? The three of them crossed to the fire at last and settled themselves in tall carved chairs near a table, which Hannie was quick to furnish with fruit and meat and wine. Expansive, self-confident, so delighted with the occasion that he was even capable of bestowing a compliment on the vintage, Jan Lievens sat back and gave them the benefit of his experience for the better part of an hour.

But he could not spoil the evening: my lord Constantyn Huyghens listened politely to tales of the gallantry of Prince Rupert and the sufferings of the Queen, but his velvety glance wandered now and then to a Seghers or a Brouwer or the Rubens, and often settled, warm and affectionate, on the face of his host. Twice he interrupted to praise the efficiency of Hannie and the beauty of the pyramid of fruit; once he permitted himself to say that all those remarkable qualities of the Queen's which Heer Lievens admired so much—her ardor, her articulateness, her eagerness to take an active part in governmental affairs—had unfortunately done her poor husband no good; and it was he who held up his forefinger for silence during the count of ten strokes from the nearby steeple and said that, much as he hated to stop such an enlightening conversation, he'd better get down to the Prince's business.

Subjects, prices—it was sad that the golden gratification of the evening should be tarnished by such things. The host got up and refilled the goblets and passed the fruit to hold off the moment when he would be told precisely which incidents in the life of Christ the princely patron had set his heart on, and how much—suppose it was a really disgraceful sum, smaller by far than what he had been offered in his better days?—would be forthcoming from the treasury.

"Perhaps," said the little secretary, "in your present state of mind, with so much trouble behind you, you'd rather not work on one of the large dramatic scenes. Maybe you'd like to do something more intimate—"

"Have I any choice?"

"Oh, all the choice in the world. Though Prince Frederik Hendrik would like to know what he can expect—you can write me when you've made up your mind—he said expressly that the subjects should be left to you."

"That was very gracious of him."

"Gracious, but wise, too. He knows he'll get a better pair of Rembrandts"—he said the name exactly as he would have said "Raphaels" or "Titians"—"if you're doing what pleases you best. As to the price, I hope it will be acceptable. Things have changed, of course, since you did the Passion pieces—"

"Yes, my lord, I know that." The grave and steady gaze gave him to understand that he was not to be shamed before his fellow-painter: solid excuses would be provided for the falling off—the Prince was old, the House of Orange was poor in comparison with other reigning houses, prices had come down disturbingly of late . . .

"The Prince is perfectly aware that he isn't dealing with a relative newcomer now, and he hopes that double the price you received for the other Passion pictures will seem right to you."

"Twelve hundred florins each?"

"Yes, if that's satisfactory."

He had closed his hand on the stem of his goblet so hard that the carved crystal was biting into his skin. He loosened it now and hoped that no one would notice the look of witless happiness on his face. "It's more than satisfactory," he said in a calmer voice than he had imagined himself capable of. "It's very generous indeed."

"He'll be delighted to hear that you think so. And when can we hope to have the pictures? By the end of summer, do you think?"

"Earlier than that, my lord. By April at the latest. I'm in a position to start work on them at once."

It was an indirect confession that he had no other business of significance on hand, but if my lord caught the implication, it did not upset him in the least; he smiled and nodded and turned, courtier that he was, to the member of the party who had for the last ten minutes been out of things. "And you, Heer Lievens, I suppose you're as glad to be back as we are to have you here," he said. "I can imagine how hard it must be to pull up roots after eighteen years, but there'll be some compensations, too—you'll be free to paint whatever you like. And after doing Court portraits year in, year out, I'd think that would be something of a relief."

"On the contrary, my lord"—he straightened and laid his hand over the medallion as if to protect it from some impiety—"all I feel is a deep sense of loss."

"Eighteen years *is* a long time. I can understand how you'd grow attached to the royal family—"

"It wasn't only the personal loss. I lost even more as a painter. Over there I was at the center of the most exciting development my craft has seen in half a century. I had the inestimable privilege, you know, of working side by side with Anthony van Dyck—"

"Yes, of course. Somehow it hadn't occurred to me that the two of you were at the Court together."

"He'd mastered a new kind of technique, and he was generous enough to share his discoveries with me—something wonderfully fresh that painters are only groping toward here in the Netherlands."

"Really?"

"Yes. He understood the exquisiteness of the glazed surface, the wonderful possibilities of"—he tossed back his hair and aimed a look at once pained and challenging at his host—"of gloss. He set the trend, my lord. What he laid down is something we'll be elaborating on for the rest of our lifetime. Titian, Rubens, Carracci—he's outdated them all, whether we on this side of the water are too stubborn to see it or not."

"Do you really think so, Heer Lievens? Skill and suavity—those he certainly had. But the canvases of his that I've seen struck me as rather remote and lifeless—"

"Dignified and idealized, if I may say so, my lord. He showed us once and for all that there's no necessity to lay on paint a quarter of an inch thick, that nothing's to be gained by painting every freckle and wrinkle in. But I won't go on about it—Rembrandt and I were over the same ground not too long ago, and there's no use arguing with him: if he's determined to misdirect his marvelous talent, there's nothing I can do. All I can say is: it's a little foolhardy for a man to set himself against the trend."

Constantyn Huyghens got up, came round to the back of Rembrandt's chair, and laid his hands like an affectionate boy on his host's shoulders. "The devil with the trend," he said, laughing. "This one here doesn't have to bother about the trend; he'll make the trend himself."

"So it may seem from The Hague and Amsterdam, my lord, but over in England—"

"England's a little world off to itself, Heer Lievens, and from the look of things at the moment, what they'll be making there is gunpowder, not trends. The Continent's the place to see which way the wind is blowing, and there, as you know, I've been around a little."

"Oh, without a doubt what's going on in France and Italy remains important. I mean to make the tour myself next summer—"

"And when you do, every collector you visit will show you as one of his most precious finds an etching by Rembrandt van Rijn. And where the etchings go, I've always found the canvases follow. Give our friend here another three, four years, and what he's painting now will be hanging in the Ruffo collection or the Medici palace or the Farnese gallery. He's got his admirers everywhere from Stockholm to Palermo. He's making a trend of his own, and God forbid he should trim himself down to anybody else's specifications."

The small white hands clasped and kneaded his shoulders before they left them, and he felt his heart dilate. What if it were so? What if, without having stirred from this city, he had begun to direct the eyes and hands of other artists, making them see and paint the world as no man before him had ever seen or painted it? What if the Farnese or the Medici were to teach the Regents of Amsterdam what fools they had been to turn their backs on his masterpiece? What if it were really so?

My lord spent the last half-hour of his visit making himself pleasant to Jan Lievens; perhaps it was his eagerness to mitigate his forthrightness that kept him from asking whether they mightn't walk up to see what was in the studio. But in the reception hall, where poor Hannie was finding it difficult, sleepy as she was, to sit like a statue on the seat by the door, the little secretary made up for even that omission. "I wanted to ask a favor—in fact, I don't dare show my face back in my rooms without asking it," he said, fastening his cloak under his chin. "I brought my two older boys down here with me this time, and I was wondering—you can always say no if it isn't convenient—if I could drop in with them just for a few minutes tomorrow afternoon."

"Surely, my lord—you know that the three of you would be more than welcome."

"I understand you'll be working, and I don't want to interrupt you, but they're really very well behaved: they'd just slip into your studio and stand there and watch you for a little while. I want them to be able to say they've seen Rembrandt at work. It would mean a great deal to them and to me. It would be something for them to remember for the rest of their days."

*

So far, the day had not gone at all as Hendrikje had planned it. It was a mild March day, pale blue after a night of rain—the first day that seemed like spring; and she had wanted to give the house a general airing the way her mother used to in Ransdorp, opening all the doors and windows so that the light gusts could carry off the accumulated smells of winter. But her eagerness had dwindled away at the breakfast table: how could she concern herself about an airing when *he* was so disturbed by the letter that had just come from Friesland? Not since the days of Geertje's crazy doings had she seen him drumming his fingers on the table like that, his mouth so tight, the line between his eyebrows so deep.

It had been upsetting that he should leave the table with his herring untouched, and even more upsetting that he should have taken himself out of the house without saying where he was going or when he was coming back, with the apprentices waiting for him upstairs. It was only after the door had banged shut behind him that she had begun to ache a little because he had said not one word to her about whatever was bothering him. Certainly he had not gone to any pains to hide the letter from her—he had left the three closely scrawled sheets in the bedroom, scattered over the spread, and that sign of his trust in her after the liberties she had taken with brother Willem's letters made her all the more reluctant to go and find out for herself.

But now it was half past nine, almost an hour since he had gone out, and she was so worried about how he might deal with whatever trouble he was in that every other consideration flew out of her head. Nobody was there to see her: Hannie had gone to dust the master's studio while he was out of it; the boarding apprentices had finished their morning meal and gone to their easels, and Titus was standing at the window in the salon, fascinated by the nesting birds that kept coming into the poplar boughs with bits of straw in their bills. Leaving the dishes half-stacked on the big round table, she wiped her fingers—it would not do to spot the letter with butter and herring oil—and went upstairs.

Yet once she was in their own room, with the pure sky on the other side of the clean panes and the innocent birds chirping and darting through the pale March sunlight, she did not pick up the scattered sheets at once. To spy on him even for his own good would somehow spoil the blessed hour they had had here last night when the year's first thunder had wakened them to each other and the big warm rain. But certain phrases—"the prices you are rumored to have paid for canvases," "your earlier carelessness about everything concerning money," "the princely manner in which you choose to live"—emerged out of the scrawl and drew her down; and before she knew what she was doing she was kneeling beside the bed with the letter in her hands.

It came from Titus's uncle—he kept saying he had a right to know one thing and another on the grounds that he *was* Titus's uncle. The Uylenburghs up there in Friesland were worried about Titus—and how dared they stick their noses in at this late date, when they had been content to leave the helpless child in the hands of that madwoman, when they had never turned up once to comfort the widower or help him set his house in order or lay a wreath on the poor dead mother's grave? It seemed, so far as she could make out from the roundabout language, that they wanted to know just how much money was in the bank for Titus and whether it would still be there when he was old enough to claim it. It seemed they were afraid that it might be "used in unsound speculation in paintings," or "drained off in the purchase of antiquities and other useless luxuries." By that mention of "luxuries" were they trying to insinuate that he was loading *her* down with clothes and jewels? She would rather go in rags than deck herself out at Titus's expense, and she hoped he would tell them so. But here she was, letting a letter of theirs poison her mind against him, and why should she suspect for a minute that he would rob his own child? The whole business was nothing but spite, something they had thought up to plague him with because it had come to their ears at last that he had taken a common serving girl and made her his wife in everything but the name. They couldn't really believe he was in any serious trouble about money, not with his reputation and a collection like the one in the salon and such a house as this . . .

And now poor Titus—what had come over her that she should have left him alone downstairs?—was calling her from the reception hall. "In a minute, I'll be down in a minute, darling," she said, arranging the hateful sheets of paper on the bed in what she hoped was a reasonable likeness of their earlier disorder and smoothing out the dents that her elbows had made in the spread. Downstairs, she found the child at once exasperated and disconsolate, with the kite that Heer Fabritius had made for him in one hand and the unfinished tail of it in the other. There would be no general airing of the house this morning, that was plain—she would have to help him tie the bits of cloth to the string, as she had promised him last night.

"Where were you, Hendrikje?" he said, not coming to meet her, standing small and affronted in the middle of the big tiled floor.

"Just up in the bedroom."

"But what were you doing up there so long?"

"Nothing—mending a hole in my stocking. Did you want me to tie the ribbons on the tail of your kite? Come along, we'll do it right this minute. Get the ribbons and put them on the table in the back parlor—"

"I can't. The table's all full of dirty dishes."

Dear God, so it is, she thought. I never finished, and what will *he* think if he comes home and finds the room untidied? "That's easily mended," she said, putting her hand on his shoulder and edging him toward the incriminating confusion. At least Titus was as presentable as usual—she could not help it, even on this stay-at-home morning she had dressed him in scarlet velvet for the sheer pleasure of it; and once a week, no matter how bad the weather was, she washed his silky, fiery hair. Whatever they might think up there in Friesland, no prince with royal aunts and uncles could look so fresh and fine as he . . .

While she carried out the plates and mugs and silver for Hannie to wash, while she folded the napkins and put a clean cloth on the table, she could not keep from making up answers to those high-handed ones up there. Wasn't it enough that he had resigned himself to living out of wedlock instead of trying to change the poor dead woman's will? Wasn't it enough that she herself couldn't look forward like any peasant's wife to having children, but had to wait in shame and fright every month in the hope that there wouldn't be anything under her belt to bring down the wrath of Pastor Broekhuyzen and the congregation? And if they were worried about money, wasn't she doing Geertje's work and her own and a lot of other little things nobody had ever done here before? Vrouw Pinero and Vrouw Lazzara seemed to think so, and so did Dr. Tulp and Heer Six. "Are you angry, Hendrikje?" said Titus, sitting at the table and watching her over the heap of orange and green and purple bits of cloth and ribbon that Heer Fabritius—who also had a high respect for her and her doings—had collected for him in the studio.

"No, I'm just in a hurry. Now, if you hand me the ribbons one at a time, I'll tie them on," she said.

Every now and then she halted their enterprise in order to embrace him. She needed that closeness—his neck as smooth and cool as the petal of a tulip, his breath smelling sweetly of butter and milk—because exasperating phrases from the accursed letter continued to come into her head. Was there a grain of truth in all of that? Could it be said of *him,* as the neighbors had said of her own poor father between campaigns, that he was "living beyond his means"? For himself he wanted nothing but bread and fish and Amsterdam beer, but he was always bringing something home for her or Titus, and when guests were expected he went merrily to market and carried home the makings of a

461

feast—a suckling pig, a pudding stuffed with raisins, the best French wine. That he should spend money that really belonged to this little one here on such luxuries or on gloves and necklaces for her, or even on pictures—no, she refused to believe it. Titus's uncle simply did not know his man if he could imagine such a thing.

Yet, with the steeple clocks striking ten and the apprentices wrestling and yelling up in the attic, with a patron stopping by to pick up an etching that had been promised and that nobody had any idea where to look for, she could not rid herself of anger and a nagging uneasiness. And when he finally made his appearance—he walked in half an hour later, behaving as if it were the usual thing for him to step out with everything at loose ends—she could not reach her hand to him or hold up her face to be kissed. "You might have told me Heer Smid was coming for his etching. Nobody knew where it was, and he had to go away without it," she said.

"Don't worry about it," he said, sitting down on the other side of Titus and unfastening the top button of his jacket. "It's not as if I'd lost a sale, you know—I'll send one of the lads over to his house with it this afternoon."

"The lads, by the way, have been running around and making a terrible fuss up there."

"Have they? Well, it's their time they're wasting, not mine."

"But where *were* you, anyway?" she said before she could stop herself.

"Yes," said Titus, "where *were* you, anyway?" And though his parroting of her complaining tone was winsome and comical, she could not smile.

"At the bank."

"At the bank? Taking out money, you mean?" That, too, she had not meant to say. She had been so utterly at ease with him, voicing whatever came into her thoughts, that she had lost the servant's prudent art of holding her tongue.

"No, I had to go to the bank to see about something. That letter you handed me at breakfast—that was from Saskia's people. They want to know how much I have on hand—according to the will a certain fixed sum's to be kept intact for Titus—and I can scarcely tell them without finding out."

"You mean you didn't know?" she said. Even her father, considered by the family the most feckless of men where money was concerned, had known what there was in the wooden box under the bed.

It was strange and disarming to see a boyish flush spread up over his wrinkled brow. "Well, not exactly," he said, playing with the tail of the kite. "It's not quite as much as I thought it was—it somehow never is—but I suppose it'll be enough."

"Enough for what?"

462

"Oh, Lord, don't ask me." He reached behind Titus and patted her on the hip. "To explain it would be too much for me—I'm amazed that I got it straight myself. If you mean is it enough to cover what Titus's mother left him, no, it's not, but the man at the bank says they'd be out of their minds up there if they thought of it like that. What's in the bank is nothing beside the value of the house and the collection, and whatever's lacking in cash could easily be made up from those, with plenty to spare."

It seemed simple and reassuring, though that was probably only because her Ransdorp limitations kept her from grasping its real complexity. "The house itself must be worth a fortune," she said.

"Oh, it is, though these fine old places are going out of fashion and there isn't the market for them there used to be. Not that I have any notion of selling it or, for that matter, of *his* ever wanting to sell it." He laid his hand on the princely little head. "I've always taken it for granted he'll want to live in it, and I trust when that time comes there won't be any mortgage on it any more."

"Mortgage?"

"Oh, yes, naturally there's a mortgage. The house is only half paid for, you know."

She knew nothing of the sort, and her dismay must have been plain. In Ransdorp when people didn't pay for their houses, the sellers put them out. In Ransdorp to live in a house that was only half paid for was like living close to a dyke with a crack in it: men walked the floor and women wrung their hands until the last florin was laid down and the fearful papers were consumed in the fireplace.

"It's nothing to worry about—three or four more commissions like the one from the Prince would take care of the whole business," he said.

"But what about the man who sold it to you? Doesn't he mind?"

"Thyss? Why should he mind? The longer I put off paying the principal, the more interest he collects. Besides, he couldn't really lose his money. No matter how much fashions change, the house would always be worth at least *that* much."

She should have nodded and held her peace, but she could not help herself; fear was oozing into her like dank water. "But suppose all of a sudden he did turn up and ask for it—then what would you do?"

He frowned at the pile of bright ribbons, and she knew that he was really frowning at her insistence. What had come over her that she should read his letters and ask him questions as if she were his wedded wife? "It's very unlikely that any such thing would happen," he said, more coldly than he had spoken to her since Geertje's going. "And if it did, I could always raise the money."

"By borrowing?"

"No, of course not, why should I borrow? What's in the salon would bring in twice the amount of the mortgage. It's a security, that collection, though I don't exactly relish the thought of selling any of it. I can imagine better ways of spending a morning than asking myself which I'd hand over first—the Rubens or the Brouwers."

"If we're not in trouble, you don't have to think of it."

"We *aren't* in trouble. Thyss is perfectly content to leave things as they are, and I can give Saskia's people a satisfactory answer, so let's let it rest. There's plenty to take the joy out of life without inventing extra things to worry about."

To her amazement she found that she was weeping. "I'm sorry, love, I'm terribly sorry, I certainly didn't want to put unhappy thoughts into your head," she said. "I'm bound to be stupid about these things; the only way I can see them is the way we saw them at home in Ransdorp, which is wrong, of course—"

Titus rested his cheek and shoulder against her; Titus touched her, but *he* did not. "You're right about the lads, at any rate," he said in a voice that only tried to be friendly. "I can hear them all the way down here. I'd better go up and see what's going on." And he would have left her without another word if her guilt and desolation had not driven a sob out of her throat—a short little sob like a hiccough that stopped him on the threshold and brought the kindness back into his face.

"Now, don't be foolish, Hendrikje. This is ridiculous. I don't even know how we got into it," he said. "The way things look, I'll be doing better than I've ever done in my life. More commissions will be coming from The Hague, and I told you what my lord Huyghens said about the way my reputation's growing on the Continent. We've got nothing to worry about, darling, absolutely nothing. Life's short enough—let's enjoy it while we can."

"I'm sorry. I'm terribly sorry—"

"Well, forget about it. Finish the boy's kite and go and fly it with him for a while—you ought to get out more than you do, you're closed up in the house too much."

And when he was gone she sighed a shaking sigh at her own morbidity and hurried to tie the last gaudy ribbons onto the string. What he had said about her was true: no doubt she needed an airing as much as the house did. All that was called for to get rid of these foolish worries was an hour in the March wind and the mild spring sun.

*

He stopped on the threshold of the kitchen with his cloak over his arm and watched the two of them at their peaceful occupations: Hendrikje at the worktable, sorting the good dried peas from those that had gone dark and bad, and Titus at his little desk near the fireplace, learning the alphabet. "H, I, J, K," he chanted, looking like a singing angel: he was six now and in his first year at the Dame school, and the three

464

inches he had grown had taken away the last of his baby fat and given him an ethereal look. "L, M, N," murmured Hendrikje, digging into the yellow-green heap of dried peas with her beautiful dark hands. "Are you going out this evening, dearest?"

"Yes, just down to the rabbi's. I thought"—he had asked her so often that the suggestion was more ritual than anything else—"I thought you might like to come with me tonight."

"Oh, I'd *like* to come, you know that." It was the usual beginning, accompanied by the usual smile. "I always like to be where you are, but really I shouldn't—"

"Why not? The peas can wait—"

"It isn't the peas. It's just that I'm tired and I'd have to get all dressed up—"

"Nonsense. You could go exactly as you are. All you need is a necklace and a couple of bracelets."

"Besides, I wouldn't enjoy myself—I'd be worrying about Titus. I just don't feel comfortable leaving him in this big house by himself."

There was no use telling her that he wouldn't be by himself, that Hannie or any of the five apprentices could sit with him. Her reluctance was based on the feeling, directly traceable to Pastor Broekhuyzen and his accursed congregation, that no matter what *his* friends might think, only a Jezebel would go paying social calls with her paramour. She was willing to sin, but she could not bring herself to flaunt it; and her dark, still eyes begged him to spare her the bitter and impious little jokes he had often favored her with in the past.

Well, he did not want to quarrel with her, this evening or any evening. He always had the better of her—she had no tongue for quarreling —and she looked so young and mild and defenseless with her begging eyes and her slightly parted mouth and her round, unwrinkled brow. "Whatever you like, Hendrikje," he said, and came over to the worktable and kissed her, breathing the smell of freshly dried linen that never left her warm flesh and her thick hair.

"When you come home tonight, Father, I'll say the alphabet all through for you," said Titus.

"Indeed you won't. When your father comes home you'll have been fast asleep for hours."

She said it partly to assert her authority and partly to make plain that she did not expect him to come running home early for her sake. And the generous way she took his freedom for granted, the lively interest with which she asked him what he had done and who had been there, the genuine delight she showed over a pear or a pastry brought for her from somebody else's table—these made him all the more eager to come home to her, so eager that in the three years of their oneness he doubted he had kept her waiting after eleven more than twice.

"Take your hat, dear; it's raining," she said, turning back to the peas. And even though it was only a few doors down to Menasseh ben Israel's, he got his hat, not because he wanted it but because she had thought of his grizzled head with concern and love.

It was probably better anyway that he was going by himself, he thought, hearing on the brim of his beaver the light tapping of the unseasonable February rain. Jan Six would be there, just back from The Hague; Jan Six would be able to tell him whether the new Prince meant to match up to his father as a collector of canvases; and if the report turned out to be discouraging, he did not want her looking as if she expected the roof to be snatched from over her head, the way she had last spring when she had heard that Prince Frederik Hendrik was dead. The fact that he was selling more etchings, and many of them abroad, steadied her not in the slightest: she would withhold her rejoicing until she could be shown a signed order for a painting from one of the Farnese or the Medici. The probability that young Prince Willem would want to celebrate his succession by commissioning a whole series of canvases was no reassurance to her; she could only mourn that the old Prince, who *had* ordered and paid a week before the appointed date, would be doing no ordering any more. And something of her Ransdorp grimness was infecting him, too: he was glad to get out of the rain and the dark and into the rabbi's little front parlor, luxurious with tan leather and green velvet and crowded with exotic and precious things.

The rabbi had taken as much trouble to prepare himself for the casual evening as his venerable calling allowed: his stout body was buttoned into a good black jacket and breeches, he had combed his beard and his flowing moustaches, and he had brushed his hair until the reverend streaks of grey showed silver in the candlelight. But though he took the visitor by both hands with his usual cordiality and asked after the lad and wanted to know what was on the easel at the moment, some preoccupation showed in his pale eyes: he seemed eager to turn his guest over to Heer Pinero and Jan Six, who had settled themselves in armchairs on either side of the chimney place. And once he and the newcomer had drawn their chairs up to the blaze, he beside the bookseller and Rembrandt beside Jan, he showed no inclination to enter into the talk, but fixed his sleepy eyes on the carpet and clasped and unclasped his small, plump hands. They were speaking of the English crisis, but he was plainly thinking of something else—was so distracted that he had forgotten for once to draw the curtains over the blank, dark panes.

"If they've gone so far as to imprison him," said Pinero, "they'll certainly chop his head off. It's his life or theirs now. They can't afford to retreat."

"No, I don't suppose they can," said Jan, staring solemnly at the bookseller's long legs in their loose dun-colored hose. "And I suppose it wouldn't be any more than he deserved. For all his high-minded pronouncements and his gallantry, nobody can deny that he's been deceitful—"

"Deceitful?" Pinero said, squirming in his tall chair and distorting his sallow face against the palm of his hand. "If we sent people to the block for being deceitful, we'd have more headless bodies lying around than we could bury in a year. He's got to be beheaded, I'll grant you, but not because he's deceitful, whatever that is. He's got to be done away with because he'll have power if he lives, and he's a fool, and a fool with power makes trouble for everybody."

Jan Six, so chided, left the floor to his elders, but none of them saw fit to claim it. Pinero yawned, the rabbi turned the great seal ring on his stubby finger, and for some minutes all of them sat staring into the fire. In that devitalized silence Rembrandt wondered when it would be seemly to ask whether painting was in or out at The Hague these days. Certainly this was not the moment for such a question; it would be better to wait until they had been warmed by a goblet of the rabbi's good wine.

The rabbi's good wine was carried in by a young woman, a daughter of Israel, who made the whole room momentarily alien because a white coif covered her hair and half of her forehead; and that stark, naked-looking face of hers brought everything Hebraic in the room into the foreground: the seven-branched candlestick on the mantel, the great Torah lying open on the table, the blank walls innocent of graven images, the silver tray on which a single word was etched in Hebrew lettering.

"She's new, isn't she?" Pinero asked as soon as she was gone. "Where did you get her?"

"She's one of the ones that just came in from Poland," said the rabbi sadly. "She was eager enough to work for me at first, but she's already changed her mind. If she stays another month, it will be a great surprise to me. I *thought* I kept the dietary laws, but she thinks otherwise. I *imagined* I was reasonably pious, but in her eyes I'm only a little better than an infidel. Ah, well, there's no call to worry about her. Give her a month or two and she'll find herself a Polish rabbinical student and shave her head and marry him. They'll live in some rat-infested attic, but their geese—if they can afford any—will be killed in exactly the proper manner, and she won't be called upon to expose herself to the eyes of the gentiles or put a pot on a hook on Friday nights. It's a dreary subject, drearier than you gentlemen know. Let's have done with it. Heer Six, suppose you tell us what goes on at The Hague."

The young man shifted uneasily and laid his fine, strong hand on Rembrandt's sleeve. "The first thing I wanted to tell you was that I saw all your pictures, the old ones and the new ones," he said. "They're in the Prince's private chambers, and whoever hung them certainly knew what he was doing. The light is marvelous—not strong enough to make reflections, but bright enough to bring out all the reds and golds."

"And what about Prince Willem—do you think he likes them?"

Jan pressed his fingers down harder on the master's arm before he replied. "I'm afraid he's not interested in anybody's pictures; in fact, I doubt if he'd know a Raphael from a Michelangelo. Cannons, siege engines, fortifications—that's the sort of thing he's interested in: if his father hadn't so arranged the peace with Spain that there'd be no getting out of it, he'd be marching south this minute. He's positively hot for marching—he'd march on anything, including Amsterdam."

"You're saying that as a joke, of course," said Pinero, stretching and rubbing his sides. "But maybe it's quite within the range of possibility."

It was wounding that all of them, close friends as they were and avowedly interested in his painting, could have passed so lightly over the annihilation of his hopes for new orders from The Hague. Did they notice the stiffness of his face? Were they as painfully aware as he that he was too borne down by nagging private troubles to give much thought to the larger concerns of the land? He leaned forward in his chair, disengaged his arm from Jan's fingers, and made himself look as absorbed as he could. "How would you describe him? What sort of person is he?" he said.

"Actually, a singularly colorless creature." The speaker himself, clasping his hands around his knees and bringing his bright hair into the firelight, looked colorful enough. "So colorless and limp that a person wonders where he gets the vitality for his military ambition. It's impossible to say just yet which of half a dozen likely enemies will serve his turn: if it can't be Spain—and it looks as if it can't—there's always Denmark or England or Sweden or France. No, it's a sad, confusing place up there; I came back without regrets. There's only one piece of really good news I can deliver, and that's for you," he said, turning toward the rabbi.

"I could do with a little good news at the moment."

"Prince Willem says—and he said it emphatically and in my presence —that he has every intention of continuing his family's policy of hospitality toward the Jews."

The rabbi sighed, got up and refilled his visitors' goblets, and let himself heavily down onto his tall chair again. "I wonder if the Prince has any idea what he's bringing down on himself by making such a promise," he said. "I'm profoundly grateful for his generosity, of course, but does he know—do any of them up there know—what kind of Jews this Polish pogrom is likely to bring in?"

"The House of Orange never had reason to regret the ones that came from Spain and Portugal—"

"Yes," said the rabbi, "that's true enough, but being hospitable to the Poles isn't exactly the same thing. We Sephardim came with good manners—different, perhaps, but good. Three months, four months after we arrived, there was nothing peculiar about us but our religion and our accents. If you met us in the street, we looked like anybody else."

"And that's only half of it," said Pinero. "We had something to offer —we had valuable trading connections in the Eastern ports, connections that you good people could use."

"And what's to prevent the Polish Jews from doing something useful?" said Jan.

"Everything, Heer Six, just everything. They're peasants, ignorant peasants—fanatical and dirty and destitute. And what with the English troubles and the new Prince at The Hague, it's a good deal harder to find work than it used to be. A healthy Dutch villager can walk the streets for weeks before he finds himself a place, to say nothing of an alien who'd rather die of starvation than work on the Sabbath and hasn't the brains or the inclination to learn a word of Dutch."

"Thousands are coming, only the good God knows how many thousands," said the rabbi. "Every week another Jewish village in Poland is burned to the ground, and all they bring with them is the clothes on their backs. You've seen them, Heer van Rijn—this street is full of them. There's hardly a property owner in the Jewish section that hasn't taken one of them in."

Certainly he had seen them. He had even sketched a few of them in their tall hats and greasy cloaks and tunics made of old sacks tied in at the waist with pieces of rope. Their faces were covered with moth-eaten mufflers up to their fearful staring eyes; their feet and legs were wrapped in filthy rags; their walk—he had scolded Titus for imitating it—was a strange, unsteady amble, like the movement of a bear taught to walk on its hind legs. Their women, in their tattered shawls and ugly wigs, looked like witches, and their children were nothing but big, terrible eyes and protruding bones—Hendrikje had offered food to them, but they shook their heads and clapped their hands over their mouths and ran away.

The daughter of Israel came in again, her eyes half-lidded against the eyes of the uncircumcised, her look fixed on the tray of food she carried, beautifully arranged and ornamented with slices of apple preserved in cloves and cinnamon. There was a plump yellow cheese encircled with flakes of whitefish; there were pickled olives, green and black; there were pots of quince and cherry jam; there were strips of sugared ginger and a heap of steaming buttered rusks. The rabbi was famous for his exquisite little spreads, and the company welcomed this one with more than the customary enthusiasm: here, if everything else had ended in disheartened silence—the English crisis, the tastes and ambitions of Prince Willem, the troubles that plagued the Jewish community—here at last was something to talk about.

They deplored the current custom of spoiling the most delicate fish by dousing it with vinegar and smothering it in capers. They agreed that the worst loaf baked at home was better than any brought in from

469

the bakery. They compared Portuguese wines with French, Italian olives with Spanish. Their host told them how a little orange rind grated into the batter did wonders for pancakes—he had learned the trick in his youth in France, when he and his family had taken temporary refuge in the Protestant citadel of La Rochelle. And they would probably have gone on delighting their palates and teasing their satiety for another hour if a soft, rhythmical knock had not sounded on the door. It was a strange knock, three quick taps and another one after a pause, and the rabbi plainly recognized it as a signal. "Oh, my soul, that's Nahum again," he said, throwing down his napkin in annoyance and starting for the entrance hall. "What can he want at this hour of the night?"

The drenched figure that stepped onto the spotless tiles looked, in his ragged cloak and filthy leg-wrappings, like a fragment of the outer darkness thrown into the warmth and the light. His face was indistinguishable because the upper half was shadowed by his tall fur hat and the lower half was buried in his muffler; but his voice, though nothing could be made of the alien words that he addressed to the rabbi, came out of him with urgency and authority.

"That's Hebrew they're speaking, if you're curious, Rembrandt," said Pinero. "He's one of the Ashkenazim from Poland we were telling you about. It's only a couple of months since he got here, but whatever goes on he's in the middle of it—if it's any kind of trouble, I mean. This time, it's an old man he's got on his hands at the synagogue. Nahum's afraid he's got inflammation of the lungs; he doesn't think it would be safe to leave him there in the cold all night."

With a courtly gesture that seemed a little ridiculous under the circumstances, the rabbi waved the newcomer toward the sitting room. Before coming in he divested himself of the tall fur hat that might not have passed under the lintel, the muffler that might have swung out and shattered some precious thing, the greasy cloak unfit to be seen in candlelight; and it was possible to see that he was slight and young, probably in his early thirties. Jan Six broke the silence by indicating a gentile's interest and concern. "Where does *he* live?" he said.

"Nahum? Nowhere, really," said Pinero. "Places have been found for him, but he always turns them over to others. He sleeps in the synagogue—that is, if he sleeps at all."

Was it this houselessness and the text it summoned up—"Foxes have holes, and the birds of the air have nests, but the Son of Man has nowhere to lay His head"—was it this houselessness or something in the man himself that made him not merely another to add to the many wretched figures he had drawn, but one that summed up and transcended them all? Standing abashed in the comfortable little parlor as if he were indecent in his threadbare smock and drenched and dirty leggings, he put the room and all the others in the room to shame. His hair, parted in the middle and wet and of a dark reddish color, fell in limp waves on either side of his bearded face—a face so sallow, so exhausted, so vul-

470

nerably soft from hunger and weariness that it seemed already to have been encroached upon by death. The mouth, parted between the scant beard and the red moustache, was full and Slavic; the cheekbones, too, were Slavic, high and straining against the pale moist skin under the eyes. But the eyes themselves belonged to no race or nation: they were dark and very large in spite of the sleep-heavy lids that yearned to close over their wet and stricken brightness. They moved slowly around the little circle near the fire in mute greeting, and it seemed to Rembrandt that they paused on him for a moment—probably it was only because he was the rawest and rudest of those assembled here.

"Nahum has a difficult situation on his hands," said the rabbi. "There's an old man down at the synagogue—"

"Yes, so I heard. Well, he can take him to my house. I've got two there already, but my wife will see to it one way or another," Pinero said.

And that vast salon, peopled only with statues, and that empty reception hall, and that little chamber where poor Geertje used to sleep . . . He opened his mouth to make his offer, but the bookseller smiled at him wryly and shook his head. "Never mind, it won't do. God bless you for it, but it won't do, not with these Ashkenazim," he said. "Better give yourself a killing chill sleeping in the synagogue than go to bed under the roof of the uncircumcised."

Yet the visitor out of the night, though he knew no Dutch, had plainly caught the burden of the exchange. He turned and looked at Rembrandt across Jan Six's bright curls, and a wan light came welling into his tired eyes; and before he turned back to the rabbi for his final directions he made a timeless Eastern gesture in the direction of the painter: he put his listless hand first to his forehead and then to his heart.

After that and another exchange in Hebrew, he stepped backward, plainly eager to be on his way; but the rabbi stopped him long enough to offer him the tray. Of all the exquisite plenty on the etched silver surface he would take nothing but a rusk, and Rembrandt observed how the spare fingers broke the crust: three times he had done *The Supper at Emmaus,* and he had never been satisfied with the way the hands dealt with the bread . . .

Whether the others had been as shaken as he by that abashed and compelling presence, he did not know; but during the time it took for the rabbi to give him back his fur hat and his cloak and his muffler and see him out into the dark from which he had come, none of the three who waited in the parlor said a word. It was the rabbi, coming in and standing close to the fire as if he had been chilled out there in the hall, who broke the uneasy silence. "You see, it's just as I told you," he said with a sigh. "They're different, they're completely different."

"Is it their doctrines—I mean, is their ritual quite different from yours?" asked Jan Six. "As different, say, as the Lutheran is from the Reformed?"

"Oh, it's a little different, but that's not really it. They're different themselves; a person can't understand them, can't make out what they think or what they want. If we came to an agreement on every item of the dietary law, the difficulty would still be there. This Nahum, now—I see him every day but it never gets any better between us. I might as well be talking to an African or a Chinese. They're a different breed, they come from a different world."

And suddenly, with an immediacy that made him grip the arms of his chair, Rembrandt knew that this alien and unwanted thing, this stark insistence on the bitter actuality that embarrassed and admonished them all, was the substance of Christ Himself. As this foreign and unsettling Nahum had stood in the rabbi's parlor, so He must have stood in the courts of the Temple among the Scribes and Pharisees, incapable of their rational compromise, urgent with the afflictions of the multitude, Himself remembering and forcing others to remember the black chambers of the heart, and the hungry mouths and the begging hands and the goods ill-gotten and ill-kept so long as others had no bread, and the flesh that holds together only for a little while, forever exposed to the inescapable assault of death.

They were talking of the differences between Sephardic and Ashkenazi ritual, but he did not listen; he could only stare in front of him while a canvas sprang into being in his brain: Nahum as Christ—for was not Christ an outcast Jew? It was not as he had done it in the past: the Lord did not sit like a disguised king, making Himself known to His amazed and terrified apostles, blinding them with His light; the Lord sat a little hunched over, chastened and weary with the yoke that had only lately slipped from His slight shoulders, marked by the death that He had suffered and mild with pity for those who still must suffer it, a plea for recognition, rather than the demand for it, in His great wet eyes that had seen too much. As for the radiance that streamed from Him, it did not stream and it was not a radiance: it was the faintest of halos, no more obvious than the shattered light that Menasseh ben Israel's candles had shed around Nahum's head. "It's late, I must be going," he said, getting up from his chair.

"But it's barely ten—"

"I know, but I must be going. I mean to sketch awhile before I go to bed."

"You may as well let him go," said the bookseller. "His daemon's upon him, isn't it, Rembrandt? Well, when you shake him off, ask my wife and me to supper at your place—it's weeks since we've been there."

The purpose of that, he knew, was to remind him that there were some among the sons of Abraham who had no foolish scruples about eating food out of a gentile kitchen. But why should Jan Six follow him to the door and look at him so gravely and cling so long to his hand? Yes, of course, because the young man was sorry to have brought such depressing news from The Hague: he could not know how little weight that news bore now, how nothing was of any importance but the driving necessity to fix on paper—at once, before mortal forgetfulness set in—those sallow, death-touched cheeks, those hands, those eyes.

*

Considering how much Amsterdam was gaining from the signing of the Peace of Münster—the right to trade openly now with her former Spanish enemies and the relief of witnessing the formal cessation of hostilities that had harried three generations—it was strange that the city should have put on such a shabby celebration. It was as if the civic imagination had collapsed after the splendid entertainment for Maria de Medici and the scarcely less impressive one for the English Queen and the Princess Royal. Nobody was willing to take on the expense of a water pageant or the detail and tedium of a great public banquet; and in their listlessness they had retrogressed. Speeches in front of the City Hall and tar barrels burning outside the doors of loyal citizens—these had been sufficient before the Spanish war and ought to be sufficient after it. Like their ancestors, they would do their thanksgiving in their homes over roast goose, singing the old songs of Dutch freedom with their friends and telling the old tales of Spanish tyranny to their children, waiting up until the tar barrels were safely burned out, and then going sanely to bed.

Dr. Nicolaas Tulp, or Burgomaster Nicolaas Pieterszoon as he was listed now in the municipal annals, had been excused from speech-making because he was suffering from a laryngeal affliction. He had been thankful for that minor ailment: though he bowed to the Peace and accepted it as the last fruit of Frederik Hendrik's solid if limited wisdom, he could not speak in its praise, and wandering through the streets in the June twilight, he could not regret, either, that even the minimum requirement of a tar barrel had not been complied with by many a family. Every here and there somebody had failed to set out one of those crackling casks of smoke and smell and flame; and he was gratified at the thought that some of the omissions were probably due to disapproval rather than lethargy.

Mennonites, Quakers, and the pastors and deacons of the Reformed congregations had not fulfilled the request of the City Fathers. Their fireless stoops and curtained windows made plain that they could not rejoice over a compact with the murderers of their spiritual ancestors, a compact all the more shameful because it had been made behind the backs of their old and faithful allies, the Protestants of France. The Protestant cause, though it was rising toward the flood in London, was at a sorry ebb in Paris; and those who still supported it in Marseilles and L'Isle and La Rochelle would lose what little strength they had, now that their only powerful friends had come to terms with priest-ridden Spain. The Swedish envoys had been disturbed, and the Danish

473

envoys had been affronted; and all along the wharves where those who fished the northern waters lived, there was no smoke, no singing, no fire. The Jewish section—the doctor wandered through it on his way to Rembrandt's house, for where else should he go on a night of municipal merrymaking?—the Jewish section had unanimously rejected the tar barrel, and understandably so. Nobody would expect them to rejoice over a treaty with the country that had packed their forebears into leaky ships and pushed them off to sail from port to port, dying of plague and starvation and exposure to the pitiless Mediterranean sun.

If there was no tar barrel in front of the splendid entrance to the house on the Breestraat, if the curtains were drawn as though the master would not lend one ray of his candlelight to the equivocal brightness of the celebratory evening, the doctor, for all his official status as burgomaster, could only smile. A son of Leyden, the city that had smashed her dykes to drown the enemy, a friend of Jews and Mennonites—it was sound and worthy in him that he had disregarded the request. The heat of the thousands of fires was oppressive, the fumes of the burning tar were painful to the doctor's aching throat; and it would be good to be away from them both, to cease to brood on the listlessness of the speeches and the thinness of the applause and the silent reproach of the empty stoops, perhaps even to forget that he had been forced, as a burgomaster, to set one of the accursed things outside his own front door.

The recollection of those other nights of civic celebration when he had visited the master were so strong that he expected to find there what he had found in the past—a houseful of guests. Did he expect also to see the dead come running to greet him, her living arms held out to encircle him, her breathing mouth offering him his kiss. Maybe so, maybe so; for when the comely seven-year-old boy opened the door, what he said in his heart was, "This is all that's left of her."

"A good evening to you, Doctor," said the lad, looking at him with her eyes, at once candid and enigmatic, smiling at him with her faintly rosy lips. "We haven't got any tar barrel because Hendrikje says it would be disrespectful to Pastor Broekhuyzen and my papa says it would be disrespectful to my Grandfather van Uylenburgh and my Grandfather van Rijn, so we haven't got any, have you?"

By the age of seven, boy children objected to being kissed; so he mastered his longing and laid his hand on the summer-moist and fiery hair. "Yes, I've got one," he said, "but that's only because I'm a burgomaster, and burgomasters absolutely must have them. Do you like tar barrels?"

"Not particularly. They smell." The small nose wrinkled. It had grown somewhat flatter, a little more like Rembrandt's, with the years. "And it hurts when the smoke gets in your eyes."

"It certainly does, and makes you cough, too. Isn't anybody here tonight?"

"Nobody but Hendrikje and my papa. Hendrikje is playing dice with me in the back parlor, and Papa's up in the studio. Won't you come in?" The grace of the slight, childish arm extended in a gesture of invitation —she could not have taught him that, the good young woman from Ransdorp: that could only have been carried in the blood.

Yet the good young woman from Ransdorp—she got up to greet him, dusky, high-headed, and full-breasted, in a blouse of white linen and a skirt of saffron silk—could have stood up with the best of them at the City Hall tonight as she motioned him, with a restrained but authentic cordiality, to a chair at the big round table. "Rembrandt will be delighted to see you. Titus, run up and tell your father that Dr. Tulp's here; and don't slip on the stairs—remember they've just been polished," she said.

While they talked about tar barrels and speeches and the handicaps of a rasping throat, he wondered whether she was happily childless by design or unhappily so by accident; whether her imprisonment in this house—she went only to church and to market—was maddening or reassuring to her; whether she feared and hated or accepted and pitied the dead. One thing was certain: she loved the boy as much as she could have loved the fruit of her own body; her quiet eyes, now that he had returned from summoning his father, were seldom turned away from his. "Titus beat me at dice seven times this evening, didn't you, Titus?" she said. And the lad was constantly drawn to her too, would stand against her side, let his head rest on her shoulder, and did not seem to mind her supple fingers rearranging his disorderly curls.

The master of the house came into this serenity bemused and disheveled, his hair standing out like a mane and his shirt collar undone. Plainly he had been summoned out of deep absorption, but he resolutely set himself to dispel it: he rubbed his hands and asked Hendrikje what sort of hospitality was this—where was the rest of the cake they had had at supper, where were the nuts and raisins and wine? She went into the kitchen, and the boy went with her, and for a moment the guest and the host looked silently at each other over the flames of the candles, paler than usual in the smoky twilight atmosphere. "It's good to see you. You always came—didn't you?—after the big city festivals. Don't think I don't remember," Rembrandt said at last.

"But I'm afraid I dragged you away from something you wanted to finish."

"No, no, not in the least." He clapped the doctor on the shoulder and sat down at the big table beside him. "Anyway, I'd be in a sorry way if I waited to see a good friend until I've finished what I'm working on now. It's likely to take me three or four years."

He knew without the risk of asking that it would not be another Regents' piece. After the unhappy reception of the last one, another such commission could come only after a decade of forgetting. "Another big Biblical canvas?" he said.

"No, a Biblical etching. My etchings get abroad though my paintings don't, and I agree with my lord Constantyn Huyghens—my buyers will be coming mostly from abroad. I'll show it to you later if you're in a frame of mind to do any looking. How's the great conflagration? I suppose I ought to go out and see it—I doubt we'll be making peace again in my lifetime—but somehow I can't bestir myself."

She came back with a big tray of sweets, and Titus walked behind her, proudly carrying the decanter. Once she had put out the napkins and the silver—as she bent near him, Rembrandt reached up and grazed the curve of her smooth cheek with the back of his hand—she excused herself and took the boy off to bed. And in all of that she had been so quiet, so unobtrusive that they could take up the conversation exactly where it had been left when she entered. "You're wiser to stay where you are," said the doctor. "The tar barrels were a bad idea—too much smell and too little to see. I put one of the accursed things out on my own front stoop, but that was only because I had to—"

"Naturally, Heer Burgomaster." He laughed as he said it, but it was not said entirely in jest: the old reproach, the old mockery was there in the tired, red-rimmed eyes.

To let it lie, to refuse to squabble with an old friend over tar barrels would have been the better course; but he could not forget that he had come a long way through smoke and stifling heat not to be jibed at but to fill up his empty heart. "It's easy for you—you can simply wash your hands of it," he said. "All you need is your canvas and your paint, and that's a very enviable position to be in."

"No, really, there's more to it than that." The rough fingers, which had been picking off bits of nutshell, rested on his sleeve. "You know how many times I've tried to paint Christ—fifteen, twenty times at least—and do you know something? After I finished each of them, it always made me sick."

"Oh, come now, you're exaggerating."

"No, I mean it—I hated to look at them. And now I want to show you something. Come on"—he got up abruptly and took the candlestick from the table—"let's go upstairs."

There was something sorrowful and eerie about the great house when it was emptied of everybody but the little family. Their footfalls on the stairs called up resounding echoes. The strange light that brooded over the city, an orange-tinged gloom of smoke and flame more suitable to invasion and destruction than to celebration, was reflected in the polished surfaces of the balustrade and the little tables in the halls. Hannie and the lads—so the host said, puffing a little—had gone out to see the tar barrels; nobody was up here, they could have the place to themselves. Over this way, to his own haunt, his eagle's eyrie. Through the window they could see the darkening city: the canals red bands of light, the foliage turned metallic in the glare, the distant streets marked out by leaping tongues of fire.

And then that strange, transmuted world fell out of consciousness. There was no room for anything except the canvas onto which the raw hand trained the candlelight. Time was undone, and the doctor stood on the threshold of a bare room in an inn at Emmaus, bleak in itself, but washed in a pale, brownish gold. The quietness in that room was so profound, the miracle that came to pass there manifested itself so unobtrusively, that the doctor could hear the slow beating of his own mortal heart. As for Him, with His shattered halo and His drained face and His great begging eyes—he was truly the risen Christ, with the torments of the Cross and the chill of the tomb upon Him still. And the doctor knew that his own face had assumed the puzzled look on the face of the young servant who stood by while the bread was being broken, asking himself, "What has come over them? What is this?"

"Who was the model for this one?" he said, and his voice sounded peculiar to him in the echoing emptiness of the attic. "Where did you get him?"

"At Menasseh ben Israel's. He came there one night last winter. He's one of the Ashkenazim. Or I should say he *was* one of them—he died, he worked himself to death. I used to go back there thinking I'd find others, but I've learned now that the rabbi's house isn't really the place."

"The place for what?"

"The place to see the Ashkenazim. The synagogue's where they come first; some of them are nothing but skin and bones when they get there. I have to be careful they don't see what I'm doing—they're not like the Sephardim, they're really mad on the subject of graven images—I have to stand behind a pillar and get what I can in the dark."

"And how do you intend to use them?"

"Come over here—I'll show you."

He went from the picture, carrying the candlestick with him; and whether the subtle radiance that remained where the light had fallen actually emanated from the canvas or was made of the stuff of remembrance, the doctor did not know. Tardily, for he was loath to leave what had so stirred him, he followed his host to the worktable, where the glow of the candles picked out a large copper etching plate and a confusion of sketches: the halt, the blind, the starved, the utterly destitute. "It's going to be an etching of Jesus healing the sick," he said. "It's what I was telling you about downstairs—I don't suppose I'll finish it for years. Over here will be the sufferers, most of them in the shadow. Here, a little to one side, I'll have Him standing, and He'll be like the Christ in the *Emmaus,* partly light, partly dark. And over here in the full light —I don't know why, but that's the way it's got to be—over here are the ones that question: the rich young man that wanted to follow Him and couldn't, and the priests of the Temple and the Scribes and Pharisees."

It was a drawing of some of the latter that the doctor's eye happened to light upon. The faces were marvelously eloquent—some reserved and melancholy, some languidly unconcerned, some jesting. "And where did you come by these?" he said.

"You mean those Pharisees? They were a committee of Sephardim that came down to look into something or other. I'll be filling in a lot more of them later—" He broke off because footfalls were sounding through the empty house. "That's Hendrikje going back downstairs, Titus must be asleep. We'd better go too."

"I don't understand you," said the doctor, following him out into the eerie hallway and down the long staircase. "All these years you've been carping at the preachers: you couldn't ever bring yourself to join a congregation; you had to pick quarrels even with the harmless Mennonites. You can't bear fanatics, yet here you are, drawing fanatics, getting the best things you've ever done out of the Ashkenazim, who, as you say, are mad on the subject of graven images and almost everything else."

He did not pause to answer, he flung his answer back over his shoulder. "It's not their fanaticism that I'm concerned with. You ought to understand that. It's their misery, their utter misery," he said.

*

There was more than one reason for Rembrandt's desire to go back to Leyden that autumn. In the first place, an immersion in that humble, frugal atmosphere from which he had come might cure Hendrikje of something that had been troubling him—her ineradicable habit of bearing herself respectfully, if with dignity; her obvious intention, especially when guests were in their house, of keeping her place. There was nothing in him or in their life together to encourage such self-effacement: he had grown careless of his clothes, dressing only in what he could paint or etch in; their table was plain unless visitors sat down to supper with them; and those visitors—save only Jan Six and his Gretha and the Tulps—came neither from the Regents' nor the wealthy burgher class. Nothing but the great house and the exquisite child were left of the splendid life he and Saskia had lived, or dreamed that they might live; and it distressed him that Hendrikje should so often sit silent, afraid that a slip of the tongue on the part of the servant girl from Ransdorp might shatter a splendor that did not exist.

He had gone with her twice to her family, where nobody asked any questions: everybody in the crowded house had taken it for granted that she was married or as good as married, and had made no end of fuss over the little fairy-tale prince they had brought with them. But if they went to Leyden, they would not take Titus. Titus was nine now, and should not miss a week at Latin school, and would be perfectly safe with Hannie and Carel Fabritius if Vrouw Pinero or Vrouw Lazzara stopped by every day to see that things were going as they should. Besides, much as it troubled his fatherly affection and his loyalty to the dead to admit it, he knew that whatever was to come about in Adriaen's house would only be confused by the boy's resemblance to his mother.

There was another reason for going now in September before the autumn rains set in and winter came to freeze up good intentions until next spring. Adriaen's last letter—he wrote once a year as if he were constrained to send an annual report to some distant and disinterested official—had been disquieting. Not that the content was otherwise than usual: Antje's rheumatic hands and feet, the falling away of still another customer, the floor that needed mending, old Dr. Duartszoon's comment that there was nothing much to be done about a man's bad liver—these, from one year to another, were much the same. But the handwriting, tight and angular in the past, had undergone a change: the tops of the tall letters wavered like things seen through water; and this unsteadiness was enough to make him show a page to the good writing master Coppenol, who said, "Your brother's getting old, isn't he?" and then, on learning that he was only in his fifties, asked whether he had been very sick or had a palsied hand.

Finally, those things that he was painting and etching—a *Golgotha,* an *Ecce Homo,* the *Christ Healing the Sick*—somehow refused to move along now that the thought of home had gotten into his head. By September he had arrived at an impasse with everything: he never sketched one of the Ashkenazim any more without asking himself, "How is it with Adriaen? Does he crawl out on that slanted roof to mend the sails? Does he still labor up those steps with sacks on his back? Is he in pain?"

Yet once they got there, in a red autumnal sunset, with the rosy light in the little parlor picking out every cherished and well-tended object, he saw that the primary purpose of the visit was not to be accomplished: the daughter of the poor Ransdorp sergeant, who had owned next to nothing and moved constantly from place to place, was awed by the order and propriety, the sense of decent living and ancestral permanence. Here was such a house as her own people had dreamed of: a sound house, lived in for generations and completely paid for. The tin Sunday plates, set out for their supper, were just such plates as she had coveted in her childhood, and they carried more authenticity than all the Delft china and Venetian glass she handled daily on the Breestraat; she bore herself as humbly before Adriaen and Antje as she bore herself in the presence of Allaert and Lotje van Hoorn; the faded map in the parlor pleased her more, probably because it did not intimidate her, than his Rubens. And when she had taken off her cloak and hood and was invited to seat herself, she would have settled down on that old trunk where he had sat, listening to the bees and wanting the fullness of his own life, on the day of his father's funeral, if her brother-in-law— she had not been in the house ten minutes before Adriaen addressed her as "Sister"—had not insisted that she take one of the good leather chairs.

They sat in the roseate dusk, moted with malt dust, while they waited for the soup to come to a boil and the lamb to get a little crisper. During the halting talk, made the more halting because Rembrandt could not speak of his accomplishments without seeming to boast or of his afflictions without inviting censure, he looked first at Antje and then at Adriaen and was somberly glad that he had come. The change in them was so marked that he wondered if he would have known them if they had turned up unexpectedly at his door in Amsterdam. Dear God, he thought in fear and pity, have *I* changed as much, have *I* grown as old? Antje's flat and undistinguished features seemed more recessive still, now that there was so much fat on her. Her hair, pulled back from her round forehead and knotted severely at the nape of her neck, was iron-grey; her eyes seemed to have sunk into her head, and her lids were red and swollen, and nobody could have known where her waist was if it had not been for her apron band. As for Adriaen, he was so thin that he obviously should not try to carry sacks; his shoulders were stooped, his face was broken up by hollows and wrinkles, and his lips, between his decently trimmed moustache and his scant white beard, seemed to have closed in upon themselves. The bright, wet, eagle's look—the visitor would have been glad to see it even if it had been turned upon him in judgment—if it was there at all, was shadowed out of sight by the heavy pouches under his eyes and by his beetling, whitened brows. An old man who could not heave himself out of a chair without a suppressed sigh, a sick man whose skin shone dry and yellow even in the reddish twilight, a man who had given up all hope of joy or even solace and took pride only in the fact that he had somehow endured—such a one his brother Adriaen was now.

"Rembrandt tells me you're troubled with rheumy aches in your hands, Sister," said Hendrikje, fixing her respectful look on Antje.

"A little, as you see." She held out her red and knotted hands as if they were a curiosity that might interest the visitor.

"Isn't it hard for you to do the washing and the scrubbing with your poor hands in such a condition?"

"It was at first, Sister, but a person gets used to it. I'm well enough. It's him"—she nodded in the direction of her husband, who looked at her almost malevolently—"it's him I worry about."

There would be one way to help them, thought Rembrandt: I could sell the Augustus or a Carracci and give them money. But the moist look—old eagle roused from his sleep—fastened upon him for an instant, and he knew that Adriaen would find his florins as unacceptable as Nahum had found the proffered shelter in those vast, unpeopled rooms of his. It was too late; whatever he offered would be categorically refused. And why not, why not?—especially since the time to bear the heavy load was short, the seal of death was on those shrunken, purplish lips. Pride in his endurance, pride in his silence under the intolerable burden—this was all he had salvaged out of his bitter life, and no number of florins could ever make up for the relinquishing of that hard, just pride.

"Is there anything I can do for you at the mill while I'm here?" he asked, hoping that his voice would carry something of his contrition. "Are there any loose roof tiles I could reset for you—any repairs on the sails?"

"No. No, thank you. Hendrik Isaakszoon's eldest comes over every now and again to do that sort of thing. He'll take no pay for it, God bless him, but Antje always makes him a pudding at the Saint Nicolaas Feast." And then, as if some unexpected upheaval of stifled feeling had cracked the dry surface of his self-respect, he added, quite incongruously, that he had never had a gift which gave him so much pleasure as that beautiful Bible.

Antje said that the soup was surely heated by now and started for the kitchen, with Hendrikje behind her offering to help; and Adriaen, plainly fearful of a solitary minute with his brother, pulled himself sighing out of his chair and said, "Come, Rembrandt; we'll go out and keep them company."

It was a great wonder that the conversation at the table went as well as it did. Hendrikje, now that she was a little less shy, was doubtless responsible for that: she talked with Antje about household matters and repeated to Adriaen some of the more memorable pronouncements of Pastor Broekhuyzen; and as if she had been warned off by some sixth sense, she refrained from mentioning Titus. He himself was little help. If amends could not be made by the sacrifice of an ancient statue or a prized canvas, did that mean that no amends could be made ever at all? "O Lord, I am heartily sorry—" the words sprang into his mind as he took the piece of gingerbread that Antje was offering him, and he did not know whether it was the beginning of some prayer that they had all reeled off together in church, or a portion of Holy Writ, or the cry of his own shamed and smitten heart. But a person could not say, "Adriaen, I am heartily sorry," as easily as, "This is excellent gingerbread." A person had to wait for the proper moment, and the moment might not come.

"And the little boy, Saskia's son—how is it with him?" said the good Antje.

"He's getting on, he's healthy," said Hendrikje, and a flush suffused the duskiness of her face. "I can't be a mother to him—a mother is a mother, that I know—but I do the best I can. Do you grow your own vegetables here, Sister? Yes, of course you do. There are no good carrots like these in Amsterdam. A person forgets how good a carrot can be."

"Yes," said Adriaen, rejecting the cake and looking at it sadly, "we keep the garden going. Not only the vegetables, but the flowers too. We had fine hyacinths just where Father put them along the path in the back. And the tulips, too—they did very well this year."

O Lord, O Adriaen, I am heartily sorry . . . How fortunate the Catholics were that they could lie on the cathedral floor with their arms stretched out as if they were on the cross in penance for their grievous sins and their even more grievous blind mistakes, and rise again purified. For such a one as he—what penance, what purification? Only with the brush, saying on canvas what his stumbling tongue could never bring out. And even though it was not the time to broach it—Antje was giving Hendrikje a recipe for pickled beets—he could not restrain himself. "Unless it would be a bother to you, Adriaen, I'd like to do your portrait," he said.

"My portrait?" He said it without a trace of the coy self-disparagement with which everybody else, except only their father, had responded to such a request. "Well, if it will help you to keep your hand in, I'm willing. It's slow over at the mill—the mash is laid and it's too early yet to pick the sprouts—and I could use a spell of sitting still."

And still he sat, as still as a statue, in the chair where their mother had sat before him. Every afternoon, as soon as the dishes from the noonday meal were washed and put away, the two of them left the women and went up to the little room, where their silence became—or so at least it could be hoped—a kind of communication. Some irrational connection between the act of painting and the Catholic act of penance on the cold cathedral floor kept him laboring as he had never labored even in the ecstatic hours he had spent in front of the Regents' piece. Though the weather had turned frosty, sweat ran down his back and made his shirt cling to his skin. He painted until there was a fluttering in his ears and spots obscured the stern, unstirring shape before his eyes. And it was as if God stood with him at least where the brush was concerned—the paint, pliable and obedient on the canvas, lent itself to every sort of stroke from the boldest and most violent to the most delicate and tender: he gouged out a fold in the cloth with his thumbnail, drew a loose white hair with the butt end of the brush, molded a lumpy bit of flesh with his fingertips. Once and once only he thought with snorting scorn of Jan Lievens and his gloss and his silky smoothness; but he exorcised the consideration as a piece of unworthy vanity: he could not be proud, not now, not here—in humbleness and contrition he was painting a truly worthy pride. And when the end of the painting came, close to the end of the visit, he was gratified that the shrunken and taciturn mouth could give him any praise at all. "That's good," said Adriaen. "Father would have liked it"; and the withered and spotted hand, falling only for an instant on his sweat-dampened sleeve, was something to cherish, though in his aching weariness he wanted an embrace.

On the day before their going, he and Hendrikje went to Old Saint Peter's, carrying four sprigs of boxwood to lay on the graves. It was a grey day, and the church was chilly and deserted, and he was remorseful and shamed before her because he could not remember the family place and go to it at once: *she* had known exactly where to find her grandparents and an old aunt in the rambling and disorderly churchyard at Ransdorp, and her eyes—though they did not reproach him—seemed to be asking him quietly how he could forget. Father, Gerrit, Mother, Lysbeth—they lay in the order of their going with the whitewashed span of the arches above them. No painted or carven saints looked down on them; nothing was there with them except the pipes of the organ and the great, bleak cross. And to give them the sprigs of boxwood—she passed them to him one by one in her summer-browned hand—afforded him no comfort. Tears, the only acceptable gift, he could not summon up at will; and getting up from his knees and standing beside her in a constrained and falsely pious attitude, he did not know whether to curse the foolishness of all such rituals or the emptiness of his own heart.

It was then that, looking at her out of the corner of his eye, he saw that she was staring not at the bronze plaques over their lost faces, but at the scant space of floor left between them and the next group of graves. Two more, only two more of his kin could lie there; and which two and how soon he knew too well. Young as she was—and she had never looked younger or more beautiful to him than now, standing in the austerity of this stripped place with her dark eyes fixed on the floor and her hood flung back from the warm curve of her cheek and the disordered luxuriance of her hair—young as she was, he did not want to drag her forward with him into the ranks of the generation that is the next to die: her mother and father still stood between her and the bleak wind from that uncharted land. "Shall we go now, dear?" he said.

"Yes, in a minute. May they rest in peace . . . we always say that in Ransdorp. I was thinking how sick your poor brother looks. And Antje—she'll follow him soon enough. What would she do in the world without him?"

What was there in that to release the frozen grieving? Her serene acceptance of what he would have kept from her? Her piety for those whom she had never known? Her pity for those whom she had seen for the first time only a week ago? Her implication that love can be more faithful than he had known it to be, that love can draw the living out of the world to the dear dead? Whatever it was, it was enough to make him weep long and hard, first on the cold, unanswering stones and then against her living breast.

*

Ever since the middle of the morning he had been trying to get her to share the high-heartedness that had come upon him with the letter from Italy. "Do you realize who this Ruffo is? He's the chief collector in Sicily," he said. "And he's not just angling, either. It's an outright commission: eight hundred florins for an *Aristotle Contemplating a Bust of Homer*. Think of it—I'm coming into my own in Italy; it's working out just the way my lord Constantyn Huyghens said."

She had been glad to hear it, of course, but not as glad as he had wanted her to be. She had not been able to understand why an Italian order was better than a Dutch one, or how eight hundred florins, staggering sum though it was, would do more to ease his worries than the two thousand four hundred he had gotten from Prince Frederik Hendrik four years ago. She had, in fact, fallen so woefully short of his celebratory mood that he had gone to the attic, where the lads at least had been properly impressed. There had been whistling and stamping and clapping up there; and afterwards, when they had all come down to the noonday meal, there had been so much talk about the fame of this Ruffo that she could only accuse herself of faint-heartedness and ignorance.

She had tried to mend the ignorance a little by asking Vrouw Lazzara who Aristotle was and why he would have contemplated Homer's bust. But Vrouw Lazzara had given her too much help, and by suppertime she had Aristotle confused with Plato and Plato confused with Alexander. She would not have dared to expose her scattered bits of learning even if she had had the heart; and she did not: she had fallen again into useless, sinful grieving over her dead child.

The child, she had been telling herself since they had laid it in its grave six months ago, had never been theirs to keep. The child was the fruit of sin, and the fruit of sin is death. Titus had wept with an abandon that amazed her in a boy of eleven—he had wanted this little sister with the dusky skin and the dark fuzz on her round head; Rembrandt had wept a little too, and a little was much for him; but *she* had not wept. Fear of God's hand that could do this and worse had held her erect and frozen at the grave; and in these last six months the tears she had not spent there had come unexpected and unrelieving out of her eyes, and sorrow always began to gather again as soon as they were released, like the Biblical clouds that return after the rain. Nor was there any comfort in the good Vrouw Pinero's repeating, "Come, you're young, you'll have another." She did not want another—her joy in the little unseeing eyes and the groping, sucking mouth and the curled hands had been great, but not as great as the fright she had carried about with her when it had been almost impossible for her to hide what was within. For a while she had come to church in a loose black cloak and taken the Lord's Communion with a liar's lips; then, when the loosest of cloaks would no longer serve, she had told Pastor Broekhuyzen that she would be away for three months, nursing a sick sister in Ransdorp. And in those last three months, all through a sweltering summer, she had not stepped out of the house, had even been afraid to stand at a window for a breath of air . . .

These thoughts and the nagging worries that no eight hundred florins could dispel and the remorse over her incapacity to rejoice with him when he had a rare occasion for rejoicing had hounded her all day.

Usually the somber mood was lifted by Titus's return, but this evening he was not coming: he and six of his school-fellows were cooking supper over a bonfire and going skating on the frozen canal. During the meal she revived a little, probably because she had eaten almost nothing during the day; and she ventured at least to tell him that she had asked Vrouw Lazzara about Aristotle and Homer, and he seemed pleased by that. Homer himself, he said, was another subject that Ruffo had suggested for a later canvas, if the Aristotle turned out as well as he had been led to expect.

There was to be an organ recital at the Old Church—he had mentioned it earlier in the week—and she had been hoping that they would go. To be among people without having to deal with them, to sit wrapped cozily in wool and fur against the bitter February night, to have all thought overridden by the shuddering low notes and the shrilling high ones, to hold onto his hand secretively, as if they were as innocent as the young lovers who came to such public affairs to exchange tentative touches and quick looks—this was as much as she felt she could sustain tonight. But in his excitement over the Ruffo letter he had completely forgotten the organ recital; he built up the fire on the hearth in the back parlor, brought a bottle of wine from the kitchen, and pulled up his chair to the blaze face to face with hers so that they might talk. His talk was desultory: he had been talking about the letter all day long and everything that could be said about it had been said, and he could not settle himself enough to become interested in anything else. Watching his intense, exhilarated face in the changing firelight—he had wanted no candles—she felt rigid and apprehensive. When he was stirred up like that, it usually ended in love-making; and tonight the last thing on earth she wanted was to make love.

Love demanded a free mind, and hers was swarming with worries. Love demanded a high heart, and hers was weighted down with grieving for the dead child. Love demanded a warm and pliant body, and hers was cold and loath to move, and the good fire did not ease it. Love demanded friendliness at least, and she would have been a hypocrite if she had said she felt friendly toward him tonight. He seemed a flighty boy to her, getting himself so stirred up over this Ruffo business; he seemed callously glad to have Titus out of the house for once and even expressed the hope that he would be spending more and more evenings with his school-fellows; he seemed selfish and careless of her wants, not even noticing that she had put on her peacock-blue woolen and a fresh linen collar in expectation of going out with him tonight.

"Aren't you feeling well?" he said after a listless silence had hung a long time between them.

"I'm all right. It's just that I'm a little tired."

"Maybe you aren't leaving enough for Hannie to do. Where is she, anyway?"

"She's gone to bed." The Hannie business was annoying too. The girl was quick and apt and never sat down without permission. He had no idea how much the girl did, how much there was always left to do. Whatever went wrong, whenever the mistress of the house was tired, he had only one solution: heap more work on the shoulders of the girl.

"Are you angry about anything, darling?" he said.

"No, of course not. What would I have to be angry about?"

"Nothing that I know of. Then suppose you come over and sit on my lap."

That was the way with men: they whistled, and you were cold-hearted if you didn't come running. For days, weeks—completely taken up with *Ecce Homo* or *Nole Me Tangere* or heaven knows what —they put you and your yearnings out of their mind, they noticed you no more than they noticed the warped board on the stair. And then, all of a sudden, you somehow got into their sight again, and you were expected to be warm and eager and grateful—no, it was too much, it was a kind of tyranny.

She came nevertheless and disposed herself awkwardly, her haunches on his lap, her arm around his neck, her legs hanging uncomfortably over the arm of his chair. When she turned her head to kiss him, her neck ached; when she gave him her mouth, her lips felt abused under the purposeful intensity of his kiss.

"What's the matter, Hendrikje—don't you love me?"

That, too, was a tyrant's question. There was no answer except a long string of accusations: If I didn't love you, would I live with you unmarried, would I walk around in a loose black cloak in mortal fear of Pastor Broekhuyzen, would I have closed myself up in the house for months, would I work like a horse to keep your rooms clean and your apprentices fed, would I accept without complaint the fact that we didn't go to the organ recital tonight? "Of course I love you. You ought to know that," she said.

"I mean, don't you want me?"

And that was the most unjust and unanswerable of all: his practiced hand, seeking under her skirt, had called up something, surely, but not the melting thing that she had always taken for desire. She wanted him and she did not want him. Having him, she would feel anger and outrage; and not having him, she would feel self-accusation and just enough nagging need to make it impossible to sleep. "Don't *ask* me such questions. If you want to make love, make love. Just don't *ask* me things like that," she said.

His hand fell slack and still upon her thigh. He drew back his head, and in the changing light of the fire she saw his dear, rejected, bewildered face. What had come over her that her heart should fail to open at his touch? How was it that she could find fault with him and hurt him? Oh, it had nothing to do with him and her—they were the best of lovers. It was all the other things: the way the florins ran through his hands, her pain that Titus should be leaving them for friends of his own, her futile brooding over the dead child. And the tears, the unexpected and unrelieving tears, came small and stinging out of the corners of her eyes.

"Don't cry," he said, looking less depressed than perplexed. "If not tonight, some other night."

"No, tonight. I love you, I want you."

"Let's wait until later, we'll see." He put her off his lap gently, and, much less shaken than she was, went to the big round table. "Come, we'll have a glass of wine."

But though the clouds were returning after the rain, though the nagging need, first roused and then neglected, had left her even more rigid and uncertain than before, she was determined that it would be tonight. This room which he had made ready for rejoicing and the love that comes after rejoicing was so woundingly lovely to her that she begged him not to light the candles, and she was saying she wanted to sit on his lap again in the firelight when the knocking sounded on the front door.

She went to answer it; she would not have it that *he* should shoulder any of Hannie's duties; and it was an impressive figure and one she had never seen before who invaded their sore privacy. The newcomer, in the light of the candle she carried, was massive and imposing, with a round head, a swarthy, soft, creased skin, a pair of stubby but well-tended hands, and an expansive chest. When he took off his hat, his hair showed cropped and grey. He was in his middle fifties, and was, by the ruff around his neck and the crimson jewel that dangled at his ear, a wealthy member of the burgher class. "Is the master at home this evening?" he asked, courteously enough, but with a certain twang of annoyance in his voice, a certain uneasiness in his pale blue eyes.

"Yes, your honor." She flushed because Rembrandt had forbidden her to use that servile form of address to anybody. "He's in the back parlor. Please step in."

She felt the blue, uncomfortable glance behind her as she preceded him, lighting his way. She could not tell why she should feel apprehensive; many that were strange to her came here, and some arrived late in the evening: patrons, fathers wanting to place their sons in the studio, old friends of Rembrandt's whom she did not know. But she was disturbed and made the more so by Rembrandt's response: he actually started out of his chair as if she were ushering in an apparition.

"Oh, good evening. It's good to see you," he said, taking one of the chairs away from the festal fire and setting it close to the table for the guest, who waited with stiff courtesy for her to put down the candlestick and seat herself. "Won't you join us in a glass of this?" The hairy hand was awkward and unsteady as it poured out the wine.

"It's an odd hour to be stopping in, I know," said the stranger, nodding a constrained thanks at the goblet, the faceted stem of which he took in his stubby fingers. "I came on an impulse—it happened I was visiting in the neighborhood—"

"Oh, it's no inconvenience to us—we were spending a quiet evening at home."

This was no patron, no father of a prospective apprentice, that much was certain. Rembrandt was strangely eager to appease, and with patrons and fathers he always bore himself with brusque and casual pride, exchanging a minimum of amenities and getting down to business at once. But tonight—and it was unsettling to witness it—he began to ask nervously after the visitor's health, the visitor's shipping ventures, the visitor's family. And the visitor also grew more uneasy by the minute and answered those questions either with nods or monosyllables, shifting his powerful shoulders as if he had a pain in them.

"As I was saying, Heer van Rijn, I came on an impulse. I never thought I'd *have* to come at all. I've been expecting for some months now that you'd stop at my office, at least with some sort of explanation—"

"I had every intention of doing that, Heer Thyss. In fact, if you hadn't come tonight, I would have come to you in the course of the week—"

Heer Thyss? she thought, clasping her cold, rigid hands on her knees under the shelter of the table. Heer Thyss, the owner of this half-paid-for house . . .

"But since you know what I'm here about, I may as well come out with the whole business. You owe me a large sum of money, Heer van Rijn, and you've been behaving as if the debt just didn't exist. You've never made any payments on the principal, and in the last eight months, you've even stopped paying the interest."

Stopped paying the interest! Her heart labored and faltered, as it had labored and faltered last summer when the child had dragged her down.

"At the very least I must ask you to let me have the interest for the past eight months. Trade is bad, as you know, and I'm feeling the pinch like anybody else. Furthermore"—a flush spread over his swarthy cheeks—"it's fourteen years since you bought this house, and it seems to me it's about time you started paying off the principal."

For an instant the face that she so loved and had so cruelly rejected was terrible to see—white and spotted with red blotches, exposed and undone. Then the redness spread over the whole of it, and it hardened. A proud and steely glint came into the eyes. "As for the interest, Heer Thyss, I'll give you a draft for that tomorrow," he said. "It was an oversight on my part—I've had a number of things to press and distract me—"

"Yes, naturally." The powerful and stately body shifted on the chair, protesting against the indignity of the scene, protesting that he should be driven like a usurer to demand what he had waited for far beyond the bounds required by decency. "We're all distracted. We're all pressed."

"As for the payments on the principal, I'm afraid I'll have to put those off a little longer, perhaps another five or six months. I have expectations—"

"Do you?" He raised his pale eyes—really, they were humane and reasonable—to the eyes of the debtor. "I'm very glad to hear it. Another Regents' piece?"

"No, Heer Thyss. Actually, it's something better. Just this morning I received a large order from the Italian collector Ruffo."

The cropped grey head went down again, and the blue eyes gazed at a few drops of wine on the table. It was plain that the great name meant as little to Heer Thyss as it meant to her—he let out a short sigh. "Another five or six months would be possible, I suppose. If you can really give me the assurance—"

"Oh, if you have any doubts about that," said Rembrandt, with something of the old arrogance, "I can set them at rest by showing you Ruffo's order. Hendrikje, if you please, step into the salon and get—"

"No," said Heer Thyss, shaking his head. "Sit still, madame. I assure you, Heer van Rijn, I don't want to see it. Your word was good enough for me when I sold you this place. I know you've had your difficulties in the meantime, and I've waited, depending on your word, and I'll continue to wait another six months, if I can expect the interest."

It was a generous speech, considering the circumstances, and she wondered why he should take offense at it, why his raw hands should close into fists at his sides. She supposed it was because he hated mercy more than reproof; to be granted unearned grace—that was to him the unbearable thing. "The interest, as I told you, will be ready tomorrow morning," he said.

"Good, then." He lifted his goblet to his host, without lifting his glance. "I'll be on my way. That's all I wanted to know." And he would have stood up—she was already reaching for the candlestick to light him out—if more knocking, loud and lively, had not sounded on the door.

She was senselessly afraid to unfasten the latch again: it seemed to her that some threat, dark and nameless, was out there waiting to rush in. But it was only Heer Lievens, wearing a plumed hat and breathing fumes of brandy. "Still up and merrymaking, eh, Hendrikje?" he said.

"Still up, at any rate, Heer Lievens."

"Where's your husband? In the back, as usual?" He had recently taken to calling Rembrandt her husband, and she could not tell whether he did it out of good nature or to cast a semblance of propriety over their situation.

"Yes, but he's got a visitor—"

"I should think he'd have a dozen tonight. Come—" He took the can-

489

dlestick from her and held her by the elbow and steered her in the direction from which she had come. "I ran into Fabritius and Maes at the tavern, and they told me the marvelous news, and I couldn't go home without looking in to offer my congratulations."

He swept ahead of her into the parlor. Unhindered by the presence of Heer Thyss, offering him no more than a nod in spite of his ruff and his dignified bearing and the crimson jewel in his ear, he walked up to his old friend and kissed him loudly, in the French fashion, first on one flushed and spotted cheek and then on the other. "But what are you doing here, so solemn and private, keeping your good fortune to yourself?" he said. "We were all drinking to you and the Ruffo order at the tavern—your lads are as pleased as if it had happened to them. Imagine it—Ruffo! With a start like this, in a month or two you'll be selling at staggering prices to the Farnese and the Medici."

Rembrandt accepted the embrace but did not return it. His hand rose feebly and fell again, and the gesture stirred in her an almost uncontrollable pity: she wanted to take that hand and made a warm place for it between her breasts. "Heer Thyss," he said, "permit me to present Heer Lievens. Heer Lievens"—he went scarlet again as he said it, for no reason that she could make out—"was Court Painter to King Charles of England."

"Ah, yes, I've heard of you, Heer Lievens. In fact, you married the daughter of a business associate of mine in Utrecht," he said, offering his swarthy hand.

"So you've been drinking a toast to my old friend's good fortune," said Lievens, taking up the bottle of Rhenish. "Shall we have another?"

"No, thank you very much. I was just going." He was not cowed, would probably not have been cowed even by an order from the Medici; but she could see that he was impressed. "Good night, madame. Good night, Heer Lievens. Good night, Heer van Rijn—I wish you joy and continued good fortune."

Once she had seen him out, she stood, breathing heavily and trying to compose herself, with her back against the closed door. Were they discredited and disgraced or had they suddenly been swept up to some unimaginable peak of security and well-being? Should she be happy and bear herself in the streets with pride, or should she be wretched and creep around corners in the dark, the way a debtor would in Ransdorp? She did not know what to feel, and knew at last that she could feel nothing, nothing but the return of the cold and unrelieving tears.

She did not come back into the parlor, where the two of them were sitting at the table poring over the Ruffo letter; she only paused in the doorway to say good night.

"I'll be coming up soon, dear," he said, without lifting his eyes from the page.

But she did not believe him; his mind was grinding away again, and she knew herself forgotten. The bed was empty and cold, and her neck kept aching. She said the Lord's Prayer and the long Act of Contrition, but none of it could soothe her, none of it could put her erratic thoughts to rest. It was not until she heard Titus coming through the hall to his room—whistling softly, with his skates clicking behind him—that she was able to stop listening for the bells to toll off the quarter-hours in the steeples and give herself over to a benumbing but unkindly sleep.

*

Now that the *Aristotle* had been completed and sent off to Sicily, he was surprised to find that he was not waiting eagerly, as he would have waited in the old days, for his patron's response. When the expected letter came—a warm letter in which the great collector announced himself so pleased that he was placing an order for a *Homer Reciting the Iliad* and an *Alexander* doing whatever the painter saw fit—it could not bring on the heady exhilaration that lesser orders from more insignificant sources had brought on in the past. It was as if the world beyond the great casement windows had faded; as if the grass, the trees, the placid water in the canal, the distant steeples, the very sky itself had lost the intensity of color and the sharpness of line they had worn in his youth.

But there were compensations for this bleeding away. He found himself in his new state less open to distress as well as to exultation: the crises, the disappointments, the small shocks were also muted and confined. He thought little about Thyss's visit; the blush that had spread over his face every time he remembered it ceased to rise; he paid the interest because that was the limited thing called for and possible, and he laid by in the gilded box to which Saskia's household arithmetic had been confined five hundred florins of the *Aristotle* money toward an eventual payment on the principal. But the time of that payment receded in his mind because there were no further reminders from his creditor; in fact, he began to think that the worthy burgher, convinced of his good intentions now, might well remain satisfied for quite some period with interest and nothing but interest. And if it should turn out that such was not the case he could always sell something to add to what was laid by: one of the Carraccis or the Percellus or perhaps even one of the Brouwers.

He did make certain other minor moves, more to set Hendrikje's mind at rest than because he felt there was any need. She was pregnant again; and pregnancy, instead of making her more languid and silent as it had made Saskia, had stirred her into driving restlessness. He sold a double necklace of Saskia's pearls; he took a small sum from Jan Six at the young man's urging and gave him paintings worth twice the amount as security; he tried to collect something on the ancient debt owed him by Hendrik Uylenburgh and got nothing and was ashamed of himself even for asking—the poor devil was so pitiful in his cheap little

491

shop among his gimcracks that nobody wanted to buy. Whatever was brought in by such measures was laid by in the gilded box, and there was no longer the temptation to remove it since there was nothing in the washed-out world around him that he felt the desire to possess. Quiet, colorless day moved into drab night and out of it again, and nothing delighted or disturbed him. It was *she,* not he, who went into a white and shaking state that morning in July when a messenger from the City Hall, the same bony fellow who had come about Geertje, turned up at their front door.

What he brought was a formal statement that Heer Thyss wanted his principal and had registered his demand for it with the City Fathers. He supposed he had been waiting for it in his dull way; he merely glanced at the parchment and did not bother to read it through. She wept in the presence of the messenger and wept when the messenger was gone; she wrung her hands over the assertive mound of her belly; she entreated him to go at once to Heer Six or Heer Pinero or Heer van Hoorn and ask for a loan. "Nonsense," he said, annoyed that she should force him to envision himself asking for charity among his friends, showing his insolvency as freely as poor Antje had shown her crippled hands. "There's no need to borrow—the only thing that's called for is selling."

"And who in God's name are you going to sell to?"

"That's Clement de Jonghe's business, not mine. You sell things through your agent. That's what you have an agent for."

"Well, go and see him," she said, starting for the closet to get his hat.

"If it's all the same to you," he said coldly, "I'll finish my breakfast first." And stolidly, not addressing another word to her, he consumed without wanting any of it a rusk, a slice of cheese, a large portion of herring, and two mugs of beer.

Yet in spite of the fact that he thought himself impervious and was certain that he looked it, there must have been some outward sign of urgency that he did not admit. Though he walked into Clement de Jonghe's fine airy shop as casually as he might have walked into it any morning to look at the great folios and the etchings laid out on the carved tables, though he saw to it that the bell on the door made only the most discreet tinkle, and waved at the proprietor in a way meant to indicate that there was no hurry, the young man glanced at him anxiously and hastened to wind up the conversation he was having with a talkative female customer. Once she was gone, taking her perfume with her and leaving the whole bright place to smell of new etchings and old books, de Jonghe came over to him where he sat at one of the tables, and did not perch as usual on the edge of it, ready for flight at the sound of the bell, but sank, grave and attentive, into an adjoining chair.

If he was unwilling to come straight out with his difficulties, it was for his agent's sake rather than his own. The young man, who continued to look like a worried and somewhat sickly youth even in his middle thirties, seemed so vulnerable with his childishly fair hair and his earnest eyes and the little puckers of concern in his innocent forehead, that it seemed a pity to burden him with such stuff. His affection for beautiful things extended to those who made them, and Rembrandt knew that a flaw in his own fortunes would make his agent wince as he would have winced at a rip in a brilliant canvas or a crack in a precious vase. "Are you well, Clement?" he asked, partly to show a friend's interest and partly to gain time for wording his business.

"Oh, yes, I'm well. But how are things with you?—that's the question," the agent said.

And suddenly he knew by the mingled confusion and compassion in the gentle profile that the trouble he brought would not be news. Clement de Jonghe must have gotten wind of it—he and how many others it was hard to tell; he tried not to think how Jan Lievens and the Muiden Circle would take it. "The fact is, I'm in a minor financial dilemma. Thyss—he's the man I bought my house from—"

"Yes, I know." And it was he who told Rembrandt what Rembrandt had come to tell him. "I wish to God I could be of help to you," he said, opening and closing a book of Flemish etchings with a carelessness that betrayed his distress. "I know how generous you've been to my predecessor, and I'd like to lend you whatever you need—in fact, I really ought to: what I've taken in from your etchings is no small amount, to say nothing of the honor that your reputation has brought to my shop. But honestly"—he fixed his earnest brown eyes on the uneasy eyes of his visitor—"things have never been so bad here, I haven't a loose florin to my name. Last year I bought too much, and this year—what with the English war, and the difficulty between Amsterdam and the House of Orange and the general uncertainty—I've sold less than I ever have since I opened the place. I'm desperate enough to let things go for less than I paid for them just to see them move."

Rembrandt nodded knowingly in answer. It somehow eased him that this dilemma of his should be diluted in a general dilemma: if he was doing ill, Clement de Jonghe was also doing ill, and so was all Amsterdam; and the upper Atlantic was strewn with the wreckage of the navies of England and Holland, and the new Prince was already the old Prince—dead and buried before he had had a chance to reign, cut off by a fever after he had marched in a peevish fit, just as Pinero had said he would, against the burghers of Amsterdam. No shots had been exchanged during that mad confrontation; the Prince's silent cannons had merely been brought up to face the silent cannons of the city on the walls. But in those three days of charged stillness, confidence had been destroyed: a creeping paralysis had fallen over the swarming beehive of business, prices had gone down until nothing seemed worth selling, and the buyers, afraid of whatever preposterous event might be coming next, were tepid and few. "Believe me, there was no such idea in my head," he said, giving the sad young man a pat on the shoulder. "What I thought of was handing over something from the collection for you to sell. I don't imagine Thyss will be wanting his whole principal at once. I imagine he'd be satisfied with three thousand florins, and I've got close to two thousand laid by."

"But I'm afraid you're wrong about that." The pale forehead was positively covered with puckers. "Thyss is caught in a cleft stick himself, I've been told; he'll be needing everything he can get. The English fleet sank two of his ships, the poor devil. And what makes it worse is that his daughter's been betrothed—he'll have to produce her dowry, and I understand it's a large one, by the end of the year."

"Well, then," he said, with a recurrence of the strange detachment, "I suppose I'll have to give you several things."

"Your Percellus, your Carraccis, those antique statues—to sell on *this* market? Excuse me, it isn't any of my business—you know what you want to do and my place is to carry out your wishes—but that strikes me as a very unwise move. Your things would be bought, of course, even at a time like this—you have the best collection in the city —but they'd go for a pittance."

He could not summon up courage to ask what a pittance might amount to, and for some moments, uninterrupted by the bell on the door, they looked through the leaded windows onto a street where others in a less desperate state came and went under the blinding summer sun. "But I must sell, market or no market," he said at last.

"Must you? Isn't there—excuse me, I only ask because I'd like to help you figure it out—isn't there a considerable sum at the bank? I mean the money left by Vrouw van Rijn."

"Left to Titus, not to me."

"But you have the right to draw on it, don't you?"

"Oh, yes. I was appointed the executor."

The young man sighed and straightened, as if somebody had lifted a sack from his frail shoulders. "In that case, draw on it. Draw on it right away, and pay your mortgage," he said.

"If I did that, I'd be robbing Titus."

"But what about the collection—doesn't that belong to Titus, too? He's *your* heir as well as his mother's—God rest her soul—and you do him no favor by throwing away his patrimony. Ten years from now he won't thank you for selling an eight-hundred-florin Rubens for three or four hundred, which is the most I could hope to get for it now."

Three or four hundred . . . The shrinkage *was* appalling. "Maybe," he said, willing in this new exigency to throw overboard what was dearest to him to appease the cruel sharks of fate, "maybe it would be a better idea to sell some of the Seghers or the Brouwers."

"The Seghers or the Brouwers? Not those, for heaven's sake! Even if money were loose at the moment—and it's never been tighter—they'd stand around in the shop for months, and in the end they'd go for noth-

494

ing at all. They're out of fashion; their wonderful strength and rugged-
ness is exactly what would tell against them. Everybody wants smoothness now, everybody wants gloss."

He did not answer. He sat with his head in his hands and swallowed
the latest bitter potion: Seghers and Brouwer despised and rejected,
and the world fallen into the hands of van Dyke and all the other
courtly, emasculated fools . . .

"No," said the young man, with so much muted and hesitant compassion that it was plain he knew what deeper trouble than mere money
lay under this, "no, I wouldn't sell a thing if I were you—not a sketch,
not a print. Fashions come and go: this smooth, vapid school happens
to be in at the moment, but a day will come when—"

"If I live to see it!" It was a harsh and indecent cry, forced out of him
by the recollection of all those miraculously molded surfaces: the wrinkled hands of his mother lying on the Bible, the golden opulence of
Danaë's hair, the thick embroidery on Ruytenberg's jerkin, the kneaded
and death-ridden hollows on the cheeks of Adriaen. And he had no
right to let such a cry escape him, no right to force the young man to
look at his wounds.

"We'll live to see it, Master." The "we" and the "Master" were all
he could offer in the way of comfort, and Rembrandt lifted his head and
smiled weakly to show that it was enough. "We'll live to see it, all right
—but that can wait. What's urgent now is that you get Thyss his money,
and in my opinion it's only the maddest kind of scruple that keeps you
from going to the bank."

"Oh, I'll go to the bank if you think that's the sensible way to do it."

"I'm sure it's the sensible way to do it. When will you go?"

"Now—I might as well."

"Good. Would you like me to go with you?"

That, too, was gracious, but he shook his head. "Oh, no; thanks just
the same, Clement. I'm perfectly in command of myself, I can manage
it alone."

Now that he had settled his mind on the bank, it was reassuring, it
was almost pleasant to walk into the place and initiate the business. The
procedure was so normal, so simple: you went up the sparsely peopled
aisle through a sun-drenched and lazy quiet; you presented yourself to
a clerk who was almost like an old friend—you had joked so often
with him about the hazy concept you had of your own affairs. But there
was something different about the familiar face behind the heaped ledgers: the tired grey eyes, blurred by the thick lenses, first widened and
then blinked as if they had been awaiting his appearance in dread. "Ah,
Heer van Rijn," said the clerk in an unhappy voice, "I'm afraid I can't
serve you this morning. You'll have to see Heer Schippers"—he motioned toward somebody in the grander and more shadowy reaches behind him—"he asked me to send you back to him as soon as you came
in."

But who was Heer Schippers, and why was he being shunted off to him? To be cut away from the only spot in the great chamber where he had ever carried on any dealings was disturbing. He sighted Heer Schippers rising and beckoning to him from behind an impressive desk—a smooth-faced man whose inexpressive visage reminded him of a peeled almond, the remote and official mask above his impeccable ruff topped by sleek black hair growing in a widow's peak into the linelessness of his sallow brow. "Good morning, Heer van Rijn," he said in a voice which somehow conveyed that he did not like whatever business was afoot; and the uneasiness was not lessened by the quick, noncommittal pressure of his hand.

"Good morning. My friend out there at the counter said there was something you wanted to see me about—"

Heer Schippers nodded and let himself down again into his tall leather chair. His eyes, dark and uncommunicative, passed over the neat pile of papers, the piece of polished quartz, the plumed pen and green glass inkstand on the gleaming top of his desk, and it was humiliating to stand staring while he made up his mind to speak. "Is there any irregularity in my last draft—I mean the one from Ruffo?" he said.

"Oh, no, no irregularity—"

"I ask because it's the first direct payment I've ever received from abroad, and I thought there might have been some mistake—"

"No, nothing like *that*." The emphasis on the last word implied that Heer Schippers only wished the difficulty had been a matter so trivial. "Your draft from Italy was cleared some time ago. It's only that I take it you came in this morning to make a withdrawal—"

"Yes. I want to withdraw ten thousand florins."

"And I'm in the unfortunate position of having to tell you that you can't." The dark eyes moved quickly across his face and away again, fixing themselves on the plumed pen.

"I can't? What do you mean? There's considerably more than that in the account—there must be close to sixteen—"

"It isn't that, Heer van Rijn. There's fifteen thousand four hundred and seventy-two florins in the account, to be precise—Jahggers totaled it up for me. The trouble is"—he swallowed on it, his ruff moved if the mask of his face did not—"the trouble is, you can't withdraw anything at all."

"Can't withdraw anything? What are you talking about? Why can't I?"

"Because of an order that came to us last week from the Orphans Court. Wait a minute—here it is." He took it out of a drawer and held it, long and crackling and heavy with cords and seals, across the desk.

"But what is this?" He could not make anything out of the minute black script because his sight was jarred by the fierce and sudden hammering of his heart.

"You mean you didn't know anything about it?"

"How would I know about it?"

"Well, they usually inform the person before they issue the papers—in my opinion, that's the more courteous way to go about it. At any rate, to put it briefly, it's an order from the Orphans Court to stop all payment"—he resorted to the parchment in order to put the words into the mouths of the members of the Orphans Court and get them safely out of his own—" 'to stop all payment on the monies bequeathed by Saskia van Uylenburgh, deceased, to her son Titus, excepting only such as may be required for his proper upbringing and education—' "

"But why would they issue an order like that? Who would have—?"

"The van Uylenburgh family filed a request with the Court of Friesland. Any further withdrawal must be approved by them—"

"But this is crazy—this was done out of sheer malice. Where would they get the right?"

"Oh, they can do it—they have done it, as you can see." He lowered his voice, probably to indicate to Rembrandt that there was no point in drawing attention to the isolated place mercifully provided for such shameful revelations. "They got the court here to approve the request"—he read from the parchment again—" 'on the grounds that the present executor is neither sound nor dependable in his dealings with the said monies and may have dissipated them entirely before the rightful heir comes into his majority.' "

"But that's a lie—"

"That may well be, Heer van Rijn—I'm not in a position to judge. But the Orphans Court here took it seriously enough to order a stoppage of payment: this appendix was attached to it in our City Hall. There's the Amsterdam seal, and these names are the members of the local Orphans Court—you can see that their signatures are all duly filled in."

That seal, those names—stolid, impervious, and mighty—overwhelmed him with the conviction that he walked in a world which ceased to be indifferent to him only when it reached out to crush him. "And what am I supposed to do—just sit back and let them do it?" he said.

"No, there are countermeasures you can take. You can go to the City Hall and enter a request to have the order rescinded."

"And how long would that take?"

"Three months, five months—I don't know—in their dealings with us they've always been terribly slow."

"But I need my money—I need it at once—"

He should not have said it—it deprived him of his last vestige of status and authority. The sallow face before him became again as uncommunicative as a peeled almond between the ruff and the widow's peak. "And we're naturally sorry we can't release it to you," said Heer Schippers, rolling up the parchment and putting it back into the drawer. "But you see how it is—there's nothing that the bank can do, the whole

497

matter is simply out of our hands. If we were to give you two florins after that document arrived, we'd be flying in the face of the law."

"A fine law it is if it can be used in a family quarrel!"

"These things aren't always fair, Heer van Rijn; I realize that. But you can see it's completely out of our jurisdiction. The thing for you to do is go to the City Hall and get a copy of the order and prepare your answer with the help of your legal counselor. All I can say"—he rose to indicate that it was all he *would* say—"is that I hope you can settle it to your satisfaction, and I trust we'll be having the pleasure of serving you soon again."

To walk back down the main aisle and out of the bank seemed utterly beyond his capacity. Shame—shame in the guise of a wet, thick heat—broke upon him in successive and increasing waves, driving the sweat out of his heavy flesh, making him acutely aware not only of his public disgrace but of his ugliness. Their eyes were upon him—the eyes of all the clerks and officials; they saw the wetness staining the back of his collar, the sag of his shoulders, the uncouth disorder of his hair; they were thinking in scorn or in pity—and either was equally annihilating—how his dead wife's family had seen to it at last that he could not lay his raw and hairy hands on what had never really been his own. Others too—those who were in the bank to deposit or withdraw rightfully, legally, like good citizens of Amsterdam—were staring at him because he had raised his voice back there at the desk; some of them he probably knew—he could not tell since he could not lift his eyes from the floor, where the checkerboard tiles seemed to melt at the edges because of the mounting waves of heat and the terrible pounding of his heart. The door was there, open and blinding, like the mouth of a cave; and once he had stepped out of it beyond the reach of their stares he waited for some sort of relief, but he felt nothing except stifling heat and choking ignominy. What am I to do, where am I to go? he asked himself, standing against the wall of the building and wiping the sweat from his cheeks lest the passers-by should take the shameful stuff for still more shameful tears. To the City Hall? But how could he go to the City Hall with a hideous red drenched face, and no voice left in him to ask for what he wanted, and no power in his benumbed and throbbing brain to find the words in which to make his request?

He could not stand where he was forever—people had begun to look at him. There was no way of hiding his face, but his hands at least he could get out of sight, into the pockets of his breeches. There he found a stick of chalk and a little sketch of a dog that he had crumpled unknowingly during his interview with Heer Schippers, and these he held onto like the hands of friends; these supported him through the burning streets and the maze of curious or indifferent faces until he came again, with the sketch a damp, squeezed ball and the chalk broken in two, to what had once been his own door.

He did not go to the City Hall that day or any other. After pondering his case through two steaming weeks of summer, he saw that he did not have a case, not such a one, at any rate, as would be acceptable in the sight of the Law. His case rested on what he had etched or painted while the money dribbled away and his untended affairs piled up behind him: the death-touched face of Nahum transformed into the compassionate face of the Christ, the halt and the blind gathered around the Saviour, the portrait of Adriaen. And what would the gentlemen of the Orphans Court care for such items in his defense—what, indeed, would anybody care?

Such moves as were made in those oppressive days to fend off what he felt to be the inevitable calamity were made not by him but by his friends, who had learned not from his mouth but from the mouth of rampant rumor how matters stood with him now. If Thyss was appeased for the time being with three thousand florins, backed up by Ruffo's order for a *Homer* and an *Alexander* at eight hundred florins each, it was because Jan Six or Clement de Jonghe or Dr. Tulp found buyers for one thing or another that had been gathering dust in his eagle's eyrie, or scraped a little out of their own tills, or got a small loan from one of their friends. These odds and ends, added to what was in the gilded box, relieved him of the imminent bailiff's sale and put upon him instead the burden of being grateful for mercy—a burden so unbearable that, like poor Hendrikje, he could not bring himself to show his face in the streets.

Hendrikje, as he realized whenever she passed, pear-shaped and panting, across the blank stare that was his vision, got neither assurance nor consolation from her alliance with him. She bore herself like any poor servant who had been fool enough to get pregnant and had nowhere to hide. And this bearing of hers and the blow that it gave his already bruised heart would have made him furious if he had not recognized that she, too, was right in her way—as right as the Law. She *was* a poor servant girl in trouble; the splendor through which she crept, the massive possessions behind which she tried to hide were spurious and briefly held. And she was deserted, too: he had withdrawn from her as he had withdrawn from everything else. The one thing he could not bear, and she knew it, was to have her come weeping to him for comfort and love: he was thrown into panic by the thought of what might come to pass in him if tenderness were to stir the brooding and miasmal silence that had settled upon his days.

Titus sustained her: Titus lifted whatever was too heavy for her, and opened the windows for her at the first sign of a breeze, and followed her into the kitchen when anybody came to the door. Titus, almost twelve and conversant with the mysteries of childbearing, as students in Latin school in a great city were bound to be, would ask in his changing voice whether she was sick at the stomach in the mornings and when she expected her pains to begin. He had caught, with the exquisite apparatus of his sympathy, the fact that she was ashamed to be seen; and he invented all sorts of excuses for getting in front of her and shielding her from the eyes of others. And even in her vulnerability and her sorrow she was considerate of him, too, considerate enough to sense that he was afraid that this little sister—he insisted it would be a little sister—might go the way of the other one. So, when she talked at all, it was mostly to boast of her own good health and the liveliness of the being in her womb. "Dear Lord," she would say, "if you could feel how it's kicking!" or, "No matter what I'm thinking about when I go to bed, I drop off as soon as my head touches the pillow. In all my life, God never gave me such good, sound sleep."

They *did* sleep, both she and the lad: in his sleepless nights of wandering he often stood, with the candle shaded by his curved hand, and looked down upon one or the other of them—whatever stifled love still lived in him was released by the sight. The young woman's face, resigned and humble even in her dreams, had a doomed and earthy beauty —so Eve must have looked, he thought, sleeping with damp hair and faintly puckered brow and lips half parted as if to breathe were to sigh, outside the shut gates of Paradise. For a little while at least the boy still slept within those gates, his forehead lineless and dewy, his mouth sometimes curled by an enigmatic smile, his beautiful hand—already manlier than the rosy face or the slender body—lying open in the tangle of his fiery curls. It was a good thing for the lad's sake that the calamity should be put off for another year or so. Slowly he would absorb it and grow accustomed to it, would make his farewells to one object after another, would anchor his young hopes on a new life in another place. Yet a day came when there was no comfort for his father in the thought of such a slow and merciful detachment. A day came toward the end of that ghastly and smothering July when there was reason to wish that everything would crash down at once, consigning the three of them to a disgrace so great that it could not be increased, burying the three of them, alone with each other and their misery, from everybody's eyes.

It was a Saturday afternoon, and he was up in his studio—he was teaching himself to stop calling it his eagle's eyrie—he was by himself up there, thinking about his apprentices: how when they left him they usually broke with him completely, as Flinck and Bol and Juriaen Ovens had done; and how while they were with him they were utterly with him, waiting for his every halting word as if it were Scripture, fighting his battles for him in taverns that he never entered, competing with each other to do him kindnesses. That paradox had held him motionless on his high stool for almost half an hour when it occurred to him that he had heard no noises from downstairs, neither talking nor walking about. Titus was out: he went every Saturday to the Tulps', where Gretha was teaching him to play the lute, but what about Hendrikje and Hannie? Hendrikje, now that he thought of it, had made a disquieting impression on him at the noonday table. He remembered how she had looked standing at the end of the board and ladling out the soup; and he wondered now what he had not stopped to ask himself then: why, on a day as hot as this, she should have confined her hair in a heavy black net and put on a dress with sleeves that reached down to her wrists.

He slid from his stool and came down into rooms that looked peculiar to him because for days the curtains had been drawn against a pitiless glare, and now there was no sun and the clean panes of the windows revealed a sky that was pale grey but did not promise the relief of rain. There was nobody in the reception hall or in the salon where she had taken to sitting of late because it was cooler there than anywhere else. There was nobody in the back parlor, either, and only the little Hannie was in the kitchen, sitting at the worktable and scouring the big black caldron. "Where's your mistress?" he said.

"She's gone out, your honor."

"Gone out?"

"Yes, about half an hour ago."

"But why would she—she hasn't been going out—where would she—?"

"I don't know, your honor. She just went out, she didn't say where. All she said was, she didn't think she'd be gone more than a couple of hours."

He downed an impulse to show his disturbance—this sudden departure was strange after weeks of total confinement, and the little servant must have felt the strangeness, too: her thin hands, slick with soap, moved nervously over the black belly of the pot.

He turned then and went into the salon, where he could do his wondering in private; and walking back and forth past statues and painted surfaces that were remote from his disquiet and almost ugly in the grey glare, he slowly puzzled it out. She would not have gone to Dr. Bonus because of any worry about the child; she would have sent Hannie out to bring the doctor here. She would not have gone to consult with any of his friends about his current troubles: except for Vrouw Pinero, who stopped by to visit with her almost every day, she was in awe of all his friends and would never have presented herself at their doors. And suddenly it broke upon him as a certainty that she must have gone to the pawnbroker's, poor devil, to sell something he had given her—the fur jacket or the pearl earrings or the Chinese shawl. Some household bill must have been presented to her, and she had not wanted to distress him with it and had dragged herself, misshapen and short of breath as she was, to dicker with a pawnbroker instead. And the thought of her going about such business in her condition and parting with one of the few gifts he had been able to give her was so piteous to him that he could not distract himself, but must sit close to the window, watching for her to come up the street.

He sat there for a long time, jarred every fifteen minutes by the chimes in the steeples, first cheered and then depressed by half a dozen passers-by who seemed to be and were not she. By the fourth time the chimes assaulted his ears, concern had turned into anxiety, and anxiety was turning into fright. Had she stumbled on some lightless stairway to a pawnbroker's cellar? Had the strain of going about in daylight, fearful that some member of the congregation might see her swollen body, brought on her pains prematurely? Was she sitting now on some stranger's stoop, unable to get back home? The alarming possibilities multiplied until he was on the point of going out to look for her, when he saw her—and this time it was nobody else—coming slowly up the street. Her face, under the pale grey light, was bled of color; the lips had a purplish cast, and there were purplish circles around her eyes. The net that held back her hair had been pulled to one side—she had probably disarranged it unknowingly by wiping the sweat from her forehead— and the slant of it and the uncertainty of her gait made her look drunken: at one point not ten steps from the house she reeled and almost walked into a tree. He went quickly to the door to open it for her then, telling himself not to vent his anxiety on her in any unkind word, meaning to take her in his arms and pull the disfiguring net away and stroke her head.

But though the hall was shadowy, he saw something in her that fended him off: she looked like a thing so beaten and sore, so broken that the lightest touch would give her pain. "Oh, you were worried. I'm sorry you were worried," she said, and even her voice was not her own.

"You needn't have done it. There was no reason for you to do it."

"I had to do it. I had to go, once they sent for me—"

"Once who sent for you?" he said, alienated enough by the strangeness to see her as if she had been a stranger, a village woman made ugly by the drawing on of her time, grotesque in the tight decency of her dress, her face as forbidding as a nun's because of its drained whiteness and the hard marble look where the hair was pulled back tight from the cheeks and brow.

"The Elders. At least I didn't have to see the pastor—"

She broke off then, realizing by his shock that she had revealed what he had not guessed, and walked past him into the salon, where she let herself sink down onto the same chair on which he had sat waiting for her, imagining everything but the preposterous truth. He came only as far as the doorway; he could not bring himself to cross the threshold. "Surely you didn't go to church?" he said.

"Yes. They sent for me, and I went—I had to." She bent her arm and drew it across her sweating face and let her head loll against the back

502

of the chair, staring not at him but at the ceiling. "It was bad, but now that it's over it doesn't seem as bad as I thought it would be."

"What could have made you do a thing like that?"

"When they send for you to reprimand you, you have to go—otherwise you can never get back into the flock again. And now I'm reprimanded and it's over—for the time being it's over, anyway—"

"You mean you went to the Elders and confessed?"

"What else was I to do? They knew—then sent for me."

"God Almighty!" he said, beating the door frame with his fist as if it were the crawling, ignorant core of piety inside her. "Haven't we got enough without that? Isn't it enough that we have to go to our friends for money like beggars? Do you have to hold us up for your goddamned church to spit on too?"

She bore with the blasphemy, but it was plain, too, that she expected him to bear with the piety. "It won't go any further than the Elders," she said. "They won't talk about it, not even to their wives. They're men of God, and they'll show me God's charity."

"Men of God!" It was not only her impervious trust in the sanctimonious crew that had haled her up for the pleasure of hearing her confess her shame which made him so furious he could have split his knuckles on the door frame. It was also that something alien and utterly at odds with his spirit should intrude upon the only thing they had in common now: their oneness in the black hour of their disgrace. "Men of God—there's not one of them that Jesus would have touched." He knew, he had seen Him in the dying Nahum and painted Him at Emmaus and etched Him among the halt and the blind. "Jesus wouldn't have had any more use for those hypocrites than He had for the Pharisees."

"Maybe so, maybe He wouldn't." She said it with a short sigh, impatiently, as if, really, it made no difference. "But it's the rule of the congregation that a woman's to be reprimanded if she has a child out of wedlock. They didn't call me in the first time, though I'm sure they knew from the way they talked today; but this time they *had* to call me in, that's the rule."

"The rule, the rule—to hell with the rule!" he shouted, and stopped only because there was somebody behind him. Titus had come home and was walking, elegant and incongruous, into this pain and sordidness. Hendrikje saw him too, and it was wounding that at such a moment she should care enough how she looked in the eyes of the lad to snatch the horrid net from her head and shake out her hair. "What I don't understand—what I'll never understand is why you went along with it," he said, going on exactly as if a third had not joined them, had not set the lute, with a hollow jangle of tone, against Augustus's pedestal.

"If they send for you," she repeated flatly, "you go, that's all there is to it."

503

"You go, that's all there is to it," he said in a hateful caricature of her voice. "Do you know why you go? Because you're gullible and superstitious. You may be clever about other things, but you're stupid about this—stupid—"

She did not answer, only spread her hands on her knees in a gesture of acceptance. As she had accepted the summons and the bigotted judgment that she was sinful, so she accepted his accusation of stupidity. It was the boy who protested, darting between the two of them, standing between them with his head thrown back and his arms crossed over his chest and anger whitening his hardened lips. "Don't you call her stupid!" he said.

"Titus," she said, and her voice was her own again, "don't talk like that to your father. This is none of your business—it's between him and me. Anyway, you're too young to know what we're talking about."

The manly belligerence collapsed; the lad was shamed, turned back into a child. His arms came helplessly down to his sides, and a deep blush suffused the pallor of his face. "I'm sorry," he said, and hung his head, and went like a chidden puppy to stand beside her, waiting for her reassuring and forgiving touch.

She did not withhold it—with her face turned aside, she reached out her arm and drew him a little roughly against her poor misshapen side, making a sound that was both a sob and a laugh. It was enough to set the two of them weeping—she with her head still turned away and the boy with his flushed cheek laid against her loosened hair; and the sound of their weeping in the great empty room, the smallness of them clinging together in the forfeited splendor cracked the bands of rage that constricted his own heart. He came and stood above them, and drew the two heads, the fair one and the dark one, against his chest.

"It's over—let's forget it," he said, his own voice thick with weeping. "I'm sorry, too—none of it would have happened except for me. I'm sorry about this"—he laid his hand tenderly on her belly—"and I'm sorry"—he gestured at the mocking magnificence around him—"I'm terribly sorry about this."

"No matter, no matter." Sobbing, she patted them as though they both were children, him on the hip, Titus on the head.

"The only thing I'm not sorry about is *this*," he said, embracing them both, making a oneness of the three of them; and they wept together then, all three, hard at first over what they had lost and more quietly afterward over what was left to them; and it was she who knew when the time to stop had come, she who gently loosened their grasp upon her and said that she was weak and wanted a cup of tea.

*

It was not that he had allowed himself to grow particularly attached to Carel Fabritius. When the young man had taken over the senior apprenticeship from Ferdinand Bol, there was little room for thought of anybody but Hendrikje; and once those pleasures had been assimilated into everyday experience, there were worries coming on the heels of worries, and Carel Fabritius had been nothing more than a part of the periphery that lay beyond the accumulation of crises and confusion. If he had been removed from the studio by the usual course of events —a sudden urge to go wandering across the Continent or a decision to open a place of his own—his going would have prompted only a reasonable regret; and if he had died in bed of the sweating sickness or an inflammation of the lungs, his master would not have mourned him otherwise than formally, following his bier with due solemnity but without tears. It was the manner of his going—the senselessness and the suddenness and the bloody ugliness of the thing—that made his image unforgettable after his person had been obliterated. Now that all that was left of him was what nobody, not even his parents, could look at, shut into the nailed-up coffin and sent home from Delft, a person saw him everywhere: bending over the cradle where the new Cornelia kicked and cried, offering Hendrikje a peeled apple, stepping back from his easel in the compartment where his unfinished landscape still stood, returning with Titus from skating on the canal, with the wind spots red on his milky cheeks and the snowflakes lying in his chestnut hair.

He had asked permission to make that trip to Delft with even more than his usual diffidence: it was no time to beg for leave, he knew, with Hendrikje still weak after a difficult childbirth and the master just returned from Adriaen's funeral in Leyden. Yet the portrait commission had been the first ever offered him, and the sacristan who wanted it had been unwilling to wait, and he would paint as fast as possible and be back in Amsterdam in no time at all . . . Whether the permission had been granted freely or sourly, Rembrandt could not remember, though he knew that there had been no hard feelings at parting. Carel Fabritius, leaving forever on that grey December morning, had not only thanked him profusely but had turned back at the threshold to hold him in a strong embrace. Not that there had been any presentiments—the young man had been high-hearted over the journey and his hope of painting a great portrait. He shouted over his shoulder that he would do his master credit in Delft; and Rembrandt, going back to his breakfast, had heard him whistling all the way up the empty street.

Things had gone well enough without him, as well as the dreary round could be expected to go in the doomed house in those savorless days. Kiel had taken over Carel's duties, and Hendrikje, after having lost by mourning for Adriaen what small gains she had made, had begun to eat and occupy herself with light duties; and the return of her serenity had a pacifying effect on the two-month-old Cornelia, who stopped yowling for half the night. As for the master of the house, his brother's death had left him merely stunned and idle. He had been teaching as usual, but he had not been painting, and he snatched at every pretext for staying out of the studio. The most recent of such pretexts was an ancient gold-plated helmet he meant to use for Ruffo's *Alexander:* it needed polishing and could not be trusted to anybody else because the precious plating was worn so thin that it could easily be rubbed away. With this, then, he had been occupying himself, sitting on the floor close to the cradle, rubbing for a while and then looking at the baby, trying to find in the baby some living trace of one of the many that lay in Leyden graves.

It was not until the next day that he realized he was spending so much time on the golden helmet because he had nothing to put under it: he could not for the life of him conjure up an Alexander of Macedon. Those glittering figures performing their high acts on the crests of history, those more-than-human creatures whom he had desired to paint so much that he had been willing to stay out the bitter months with Lastman—where had they gone? Now that he had the skill to paint them, not one remained; they had been obliterated beyond his purpose by the onslaughts of age and bereavement and apprehension and loss. A comely young man, radiant and self-confident, should have been easy enough to find in Amsterdam. But he had so little hope of success that he could not bring himself to walk the frozen, iron-grey streets in search of such a one—since he had been back from Leyden, he had not stepped out of the house.

Allaert van Hoorn—had *he* been Alexander in the days when Lastman had stared besotted at him? Maybe so, but knowledge threw its shadow back over recollection, stubbling the flawless cheeks with a scraggly little beard, making the eyes small and the neck thin. Frans van Pellicorne? On the night of the dance at Hendrik Uylenburgh's, if he remembered right, he had actually attached the name of Alexander to that mercurial and manly presence; but whatever the Burgomaster's nephew had seemed to him then was unavailable to him now, obscured under layers of fat and ribaldry and laziness. No, he would not do, and neither would anybody else, not even Jan Six, whose rich hair had lost its first luster and whose mouth was too sternly set against what he took to be a stupid and wrong-headed world. The fact was that the human species was incapable of harboring for more than a short time that grandeur with which it foolishly dreamed it could invest itself. And even if he had chanced to see some handsome and unblemished face at the zenith of youth and power and fulfillment, he could not have kept it unclouded in his thoughts long enough to set it down in paint; it would have been blotted out by the other image that he had brought back with him from Leyden: the face—austere, ungiving, dour even in death—of his brother Adriaen.

He was thinking such thoughts that afternoon when Hannie returned from the fish market without the fish and came clattering through the kitchen and into the parlor without even taking off her wooden clogs. The clatter and her white face were startling enough to make Hendrikje, who had been nursing the baby in front of the fire, get up and pluck her nipple from the sucking lips.

"Oh, madame, oh, your honor, the most terrible thing—"

"Not Titus?" said Hendrikje. "Not—"

"No, madame, not Titus. It's poor Heer Fabritius—"

"Why, what happened?" he asked, dropping the polishing rag.

"He's dead, your honor."

"Dead? Carel?"

"Yes, I heard it at the fish market—everybody's talking about it—"

Cornelia began to shriek, groping after the withdrawn nipple; and Hendrikje took the brownish puckered thing and thrust it back into the seeking mouth. "My God, what happened to him? Did he get the plague?" she said.

"No, it was an accident, madame. The big powder mill at Delft blew up—it exploded—nobody knows how. They say it was a terrible explosion, the worst ever in Holland. Poor Heer Fabritius was blown to bits."

Oh, but it couldn't be—the girl and all the people in the fish market must be wrong about it—the thing was too preposterous. He wanted to reverse time, to go back as if he had been God Himself to the instant before the explosion and gather the explosion back into the folds of that which had not been because it should not be. But it *had* been, and time was irreversible, and what came with that knowledge was a white fury —rage against the cruelty, the brutal ugliness, rage above all against the senselessness. "Stop it!" he said, trying to vent some particle of that boundless protest upon something other than the eyeless, featureless Being that stood at the center of the endless and meaningless suffering— this death and all the rest. "Stop it!" He could not bear the sound of the futile grieving: Hendrikje's moan and Hannie's whimper and the infant's shrill, unrelenting cry.

"God rest his poor soul," said Hendrikje, sobbing. "God forgive him his sins and take him to His bosom—"

He turned upon her, letting the helmet fall to the floor with a clang. "Stop that nonsense. This isn't one of your sniveling church funerals. There's nobody to hear you, and if He did, He wouldn't care."

"Don't say it, Rembrandt, don't say it," said Hendrikje.

He did not answer. He turned his back on her and went upstairs.

The first thing he saw in the grey light of that forfeited haunt was the quiet luminousness of the *Christ at Emmaus*. The upturned eyes were there behind the white web of his anger, but he would not look at them; with a violence that endangered the canvas—what did it matter, who cared for it, who wanted it?—he turned it to the wall. Nobody had lighted a fire here, and he stood in the draft between the open door and the bleak window, giving himself up to the cold and staring at the portrait of his brother—*that* face he could bear. In the big room next to this one, young Kiel was instructing the others; Hannie would come up in a minute and terminate the lesson with her news. He held off a half-formed thought, waiting for the footfalls, which ascended, and the babble, which broke out, and the piercing cry of the youngest of them, who had loved Carel Fabritius as little Hessels had once loved him in Lastman's studio. He waited until what was necessary—and useless—had taken place, and then walked up and stared into the painted face of the dying Adriaen.

Alexander of Macedon? Allaert van Hoorn? Frans van Pellicorne? Jan Six—oh, they were gaudy tinsel; here was the hero, the unprotesting bearer of sacks who knew this life for what it was: a weight laid on the back to break it. Here was wisdom: the foregone, lived-out conclusion that everything comes to nothing. Here was courage: to keep silent and endure . . . The babble died down, and there was an end to the weeping. Kiel came and stood on the threshold—God, how like children these lads in their twenties came to look when a man was fifty!—young, blubbered, half-shamed and half-proud in the new dignity that had come upon him now that the powder mill at Delft had blown his predecessor from the face of the indifferent earth. "Is there anything I can do for you, Master?" he said.

"No, nothing."

"If you're going to stay up here, can't I make you a fire?"

"No, I'm warm enough." Warmer than the dead, he thought, turning away from the young man and back to the portrait.

"But isn't there something else I could—?"

"Yes, wait a minute." The thought that he had held suspended until the futile outcry was over formed itself now, became articulate: the nameless and uncomplaining hero must be commemorated; he who had endured in silence must be preserved in time, had a better right to such a commemoration than any Alexander of Macedon. "Run downstairs and get me that helmet," he said.

"The one you were polishing? Yes, Master, right away."

But even without the helmet, he had begun. He had snatched up a sheet of paper and a bit of chalk and was making the sketch, drawing the sunken cheeks and the stern eyes and the dour lips partly from the portrait before him and partly from his knowledge of how they must look now in the closed grave. The apprentice returned with the helmet and laid it on the table beside him, but he scarcely glanced at it as he set the darkly glittering, crested thing on the cold forehead, far down, like a crown.

BOOK IX

1655
-
1659

It was seldom enough that Dr. Tulp awakened in a room and a bed other than his own. Merchants, bankers, judges, even pastors could arrange for little jaunts into the country; but physicians could not—or at least should not—put themselves out of reach for more than three or four hours. It was not until the first week in June that his daughter, married to Jan Six last Christmas, had finally pried him loose from Amsterdam and carried him off to Ijemond, their country estate; and awakening to the smell of frying sausage, he felt as amazed as if he had been dropped into the bright, raftered chamber from the beak of a great bird, like the hero in some Oriental tale.

So much trouble had been taken to prepare the room for him, with half a dozen drawers emptied for his handful of belongings, that he reproached himself for having to leave after a single night. Stay until Monday, he thought, echoing what Gretha had said last night as she bent over the footboard of the bed she had wanted him in so long. "Stay until Monday, Father, do. After all, what could go wrong?" But a dozen things could go wrong; there were always legs and arms and ribs to be broken, fevers to shoot up without warning, mild little headaches to turn into intolerable pains—there was plague again this year in Amsterdam. He had come on Saturday morning and had said he would leave on Sunday afternoon, and nothing, not the savor of an elaborate breakfast nor the freshness of the green countryside in the sweet and hazy air of early summer, was going to change his intentions. He sat up and reached for a robe—Jan's Indian silk one, because he had not bothered to bring along one of his own—and stepped into his slippers. Some day when he was old—he had to depend on longevity, he could bear the unbroken drive only by promising himself a terminal rest—some day when these hands were no longer supple enough for their only purpose and when his presence as burgomaster was required only on state occasions, he would come to Ijemond and sleep in their company bed as long as they wanted him to.

He washed himself in the big brass basin, lathering the virginal soap and crumpling the fresh towels and strewing a few drops of water about. He combed his hair—it was quite white at the temples now—using their silver comb instead of his own. Then he smelled the fresh bouquet of roses and crossed the polished floor to survey himself in the pier-glass, half-pleased, half-scornful at the sight of himself wrapped in Jan's Eastern splendor. They really don't harmonize, the robe and I, he thought, and went downstairs.

It was a pleasant place they had, with the green of orchards and meadows filling up the many windows and reflected in the gleaming wood; it was a pleasant life they lived here, unconcerned about formality, their days not marked off too strictly from their nights. He caught them kissing as he turned out of the hallway into the long, bright room where the table was laid for breakfast: not all women liked to be reminded in daylight of what had passed in the dark, and he hoped that Jan realized his luck. Considering that it was Sunday morning, with churchgoers coming past their undraped windows, there was something amusingly defiant in the way these two had gotten themselves up to miss the service for his sake: Jan in a second Indian robe of almost violent green—good Lord, how many of them did he own?—and she in a fantastic, beribboned, cherry-colored thing. "What will you have, Father, beer or tea?" she said, blowing him a kiss. "Whatever you refuse today, you can have tomorrow, because it would be ridiculous, just ridiculous, for you to think of going back this afternoon."

"It certainly would," said Jan. "You haven't even seen the new barn."

He shook his head, hoping that his regret was showing in his eyes, and started for a chair.

"No, Father. Not that one—this one." She patted the tall, carved, velvet-seated chair at the head of the board.

"Isn't that Jan's?"

"Yes, but it's yours as long as you're here. It's the best place to see the portrait from. Would you prefer ham or sausage?"

"Sausage, tea, and rusks," he said. "And nothing—not you, nor your elegant wrappers, nor your French menus, nor your portrait—can make me change my mind. Much as I hate to, I'll have to take the three o'clock boat."

The portrait dominated the affectionate banter and the serving of food; the portrait, seen yesterday in candlelight and now for the first time in daylight, was more vital, more immediately present even than its subject, the young man who chatted at his side. Gretha had not been exaggerating when she wrote home from Ijemond that the master had outdone himself—the Jan Six at the table, splendid as he was, dwindled in the presence of the Jan Six on the wall. He was older up there than he was in life: wisdom and determination and some grief not yet experienced had hardened and sharpened the aristocratic face without robbing it of its gallantry; the clothes, merely rich and tasteful in the actual world, were exalted in the painting to a high significance—the cloak, the gloves, the formal beaver were the vestments of the Regent as the surplice or cassock were the vestments of the priest; the gesture was purposeful and sure—the young man drew on his glove not because the hour for a casual leave-taking had come but to set out on some pressing business. And the execution matched the magnificence of the intent: threatened and shamed and harried though the creator was, he had only taken a surer grasp on his brush—the surface was one shimmering, intricate network of bold, firm strokes and daring, brilliant swirls.

"You do like it, don't you, Father?" Gretha said.

"Naturally I like it. Anybody but a fool would like it." But Holland these days was crammed with fools—fools that wanted the surface of a canvas to look and feel like a piece of window glass.

"It looks exactly like me, don't you think?"

"No, not quite—but it will later. It'll look like you—or you'll look like it—when you've come out on the other side of the fire."

What fire he did not know, though there was bound to be at least one in every life—a consideration with which he did not want to taint the freshness of the morning and the newness of their love. If as a man he knew the transitory nature of all happiness, if as a physician he knew the fearful vulnerability of all flesh, if as a burgomaster he knew that the best years of the Republic had passed and that these two might live to see Catholic armies marching again across the long-untrampled dunes, he saw no reason for telling them so. "It was good for him to have this portrait to work on," he said. "You can tell that from what he's made out of it."

It was to their credit that they did not want to drop the unhappy subject. "It's seven weeks since we've been home, Father. How is it with him now?" she asked, and the concern in her face was all the more touching by contrast with the fashionable collar of her dressing gown.

"He's well enough. A little thinner, maybe, than when you saw him last, but that's only to be expected in his situation."

"There's no way to avoid it then?"

"No, none that I can see. The best I could do with the City Council was to get the bankruptcy suit postponed. He'll have another month to finish the canvases he's working on and collect whatever little sums are outstanding, but after that they'll sell him out."

The young man looked as solemn, if not as effective, as he looked in his portrait. "Surely there *must* be other steps to take," he said, waving away the serving man in impressive grey livery who was advancing on him with a platter of ham. "If you can think of anything for me to do, Father, I could come back to the city any time at all."

"What's there to do, Jan?" He ate ostentatiously food that he did not want in order to be innocent of spoiling the festive breakfast. "I've been to Thyss, and there's nothing to be gained in that quarter—Thyss needs his money, he's in trouble himself. I've been to the Orphans Court, and they won't rescind their order to stop payment, and they're perfectly right from their standpoint: he *would* use up Titus's inheritance in a few more years. To borrow enough money to get him out looks hopeless —he needs too much, fifteen thousand florins would scarcely do. I thought of going to Huyghens, but *that* he wouldn't hear of. There's only one Regents' piece coming up, a big one for the Old Men's Home,

513

and I spoke for him in connection with that, but it did no good—it's to go to his former pupil Ferdinand Bol, ironically enough. All his friends have ordered portraits—you and Clement de Jonghe and young Breuning at the Court and even poor Coppenol, who isn't, as you know, exactly wealthy—and all of you have paid in advance. But it's nothing, it's a mere fraction of what he would need."

"Fifteen thousand florins," said Jan, looking mournfully at the bouquet of pink roses in the silver vase on the table. "That would be a very large sum to risk . . ."

"Oh, there's no question of *risk*." A taint of bitterness had come into his voice, begotten by the prodigal display of heavy plate and priceless crystal, by the servant coming and going in his livery, by the green reflections that ornamental orchard and unused meadowland cast on the white ceiling and the gleaming floor. "To *lend* him anything would be useless: he'd never be able to pay it back—he doesn't paint fast, and he's out of fashion. It would have to be handed to him outright, it would have to be a gift." He saw his daughter's cheeks flush almost to the color of her wrapper. She did not look at her husband; she only stirred and stirred her tea. And what, he asked himself, had he been saying? What right had he to thrust the possibility of such a solution in their faces? "Huyghens is the one person I know who could think of handing out an amount like that, and he won't hear of my asking Huyghens, so there's an end of it," he said.

But that there *was* an end of it, that his son-in-law should only shake his head and sigh, was galling—more so than Thyss's desperate and dogged refusal, more so than the cool and official negative from the gentlemen of the Orphans Court in response to his eloquent plea. Perhaps Rembrandt had been right in forbidding him to make any such advance to my lord Constantyn Huyghens; perhaps my lord also would have shaken his head and sighed. The rich—the very rich, like Six and Huyghens—might all produce the same Olympian melancholy on such occasions: that Jan Six meant to produce nothing else was obvious, at any rate. Money to the monied was plainly a sacred possession, and their inalienable right to keep it to themselves was as taken for granted as their exclusive claims on the persons of their women. To give fifteen thousand florins to another man was as out of the question as leading your wife to his bed . . .

"Will you have some more sausage, Father?"

"Yes. It's excellent." He took and ate it, though he certainly did not want it. From the nearby church from which they had so gaily absented themselves for him came the choral singing of the opening psalm, and he sought for something to say that would indicate to these two that he would not be knocking at their inviolable citadel any more. "Your congregation over there seems to be short of men," he said at last. "Or maybe it only sounds that way because of the distance—"

"Are you talking about the psalm, Father?" Her eyes passed over the sad and uncommunicative eyes of her husband, who was resting his cheek against his fist, and fixed themselves on him. "I wasn't listening; I was thinking about *them*—what on earth are they going to do? It's not only a question of him—there's poor Hendrikje and Titus and the little girl—"

He reached under the table and patted her on the knee in gratefulness for what he knew was a valiant and futile effort. "Oh, they'll get along somehow. People have survived worse things, you know."

Her husband bestirred himself, taking his cheek from his curled fist. He had kept his silence not without strain: the mark of his knuckles was there, a double dent in the firm, clean-shaven flesh of his face, and his eyes were not without uneasiness. "It will be terribly difficult for them." He shoved his plate aside—it was to his credit that he had eaten little. "In fact, it will be downright sordid to stand around and watch their possessions being carried out of the house—"

"Oh, he needn't stand and watch," said the doctor, almost lightly. "He doesn't have to be on hand until later."

The brooding eyes of the young aristocrat, so much less confident than the eyes in the portrait, brought themselves to encounter the eyes of his father-in-law at last. "I hate to mention it, I know it's almost nothing, yet it might be of some help to them," he said. "I'd like to invite them to come and stay here while the business is going on. Two weeks —a month—as long as they please—"

It *was* almost nothing, compared with fifteen thousand florins—in a way, it was worse than nothing: to live for a while in such rural elegance would only emphasize the squalor and the dinginess of the life that was to come.

"It wouldn't change their situation, of course," said Gretha. "It's only that the others—especially Titus and the baby—might get some good out of a little holiday."

"It's very kind of you to think of it, Jan." He got it out with a creditable show of warmth. "It *would* be good for Hendrikje and the children, and, whether he came or not, he'd appreciate your generosity." This time he touched his daughter in full sight, patting her hand where it lay cool and inert on the crumpled linen of her napkin, and feeling as he did so that he had dragged the conversation out of troubled waters and moored it safely to the flat bank of banality.

"What should we do, Father? Write him a little note?"

"Yes, that would be a nice way to do it. Write it this afternoon, and I'll take it back with me. I've been thinking I'd stop in to see him tonight."

"Don't go. Stay until Monday."

He shook his head. The distress in her voice was simulated now; it was hard to remember how earnestly she had said the same words last night. Her husband's entreaties were longer but just as empty of real conviction. They would be sorry to see him onto the boat, of course,

515

and in a week or two they would begin to beg him for another visit; but he knew they would not find themselves unhappy to sit down at the table in the mild summer dusk without him, alone except for the servants carrying in the candles and the pudding and the cold sliced meats. They would have their world to themselves then, a world in which Jan Six was as open-handed as any patron of the arts could be expected to be—but a world in which a gift of fifteen thousand florins was simply preposterous. If they referred tonight to this morning's talk, it would only be to assure each other that no suggestion of the sort had ever been made: a sane man—and Father, God bless him, was eminently sane—could never have thought of any such thing.

*

All the way home on the canal boat, and later, too, over Sunday supper at his own table, the doctor had been irritated by the thought of the letter he had promised to deliver tonight. He answered his wife's natural questions in a summary fashion, his attention fixed all the while on the crackling paper in his pocket. He had kept it there to make sure he would not forget it; that he wanted to forget it, he knew well enough.

Walking slowly now through the mild June darkness, he wondered why he had been foolish enough to volunteer to carry it. If an invitation was all Jan Six could bring himself to offer the man he regularly called a true prophet among Pharisees, let him send the paltry thing by the post. There had been no call for *him* to implicate himself in the business; and realizing that he would have to say something or other on presenting the accursed document, he had an almost irrepressible impulse to throw it into the black water of the canal when he turned onto the Breestraat and write to them at Ijemond that it had somehow gotten lost.

But then his annoyance went soft in him and turned into something close to pity. He was sorry for the importance they had put upon their trivial gesture, sorry when he remembered how Jan had unsealed the letter in order to add that the cherries in their orchard would be ripe, how Gretha had planned to buy toys for the little girl. Their intentions were decent, according to their lights, and the very splendor of the house he was approaching was an argument in their defense: was any man required, even out of his superfluity, to hand out fifteen thousand florins so that another man, even the greatest of living painters, could live in a palatial house and indulge an avid appetite for canvases and antiquities?

It was Titus who answered the knocker, standing with a single light in front of eerie stretches of darkness. Hannie had been dismissed two months ago, and the prodigal consumption of candles had ceased: reception hall and salon were as black as caves. Perhaps because the solitary yellow flame emphasized the hollows in the boy's cheeks and temples, he seemed a little peaked and wan for a lad of fourteen. "I'm not too late, I hope? You people weren't on your way to bed, were you?" he said.

"To bed? At ten o'clock? Oh, Lord, no—the worse things get, the later we sit up." His eyes shone, and he gave the visitor a quick smile; obviously he was doing his best to transform the squalid breakdown into a kind of carnival. "I'd ask you to come back and see Hendrikje, but she's bathing Cornelia in the kitchen, and you'd get nothing for your pains but a good splashing. It's dreadful, the way she splashes. There's more water on the floor than in the basin before we're through."

"I see you were helping," said the doctor, noticing that the front of the lad's shirt was drenched, noticing too that it was a very fine and delicate shirt which was threadbare at the seams.

"I always help. Hendrikje's so tired, and Cornelia's so squirmy—I can hold onto her better than anybody else." Then suddenly he sighed, as if the effort of sustaining the lively chatter was too much for him. "Why don't you go up and see Father? Just go on up—here, you can have this candle. He's up there all the time these days." The wistfulness broke through, could not be gainsaid by the queer shrug of the young shoulders. "He almost never sits in the back parlor any more."

"But won't you need your light to get back to the kitchen?"

"Oh, no. I could find my way blindfolded by this time. The great candle famine"—he delivered his phrase with relish, pressing the light into the doctor's hand and reviving his smile—"the great candle famine set in during April, and I've had plenty of time to learn my way about. Do go up and see Father—he'll be delighted. I'm off to the kitchen to wipe up the floor after that little porpoise."

On the way up the staircase the doctor wondered whether that strained liveliness, that precocious charm could outlast the calamitous summer, whether it would still be there next winter, jesting about cramped quarters and mended linens and meager suppers, turning the raw stuff of poverty and failure into witticisms. For the first time he had felt a surge of fondness for Titus Rembrandtszoon van Rijn, not as an offshoot of Saskia and not as an object of solicitude or a source of satisfaction for Rembrandt, but as a separate being—exquisite, gallant, and vulnerable—picking his way through the ruins as well as he could.

The studio, too, was ill-lighted: the master was making two candles suffice for whatever he was doing. He was not painting; he was sitting in the far corner, tailor-fashion on the floor. In the meager light his hunched body—still thick and heavy though the clothes had begun to hang loosely on it—and the aura of his unkempt mane and the glint of his small eyes were troll-like and grotesque. What he was doing, the doctor finally made out, was sanding down an empty picture frame. "Oh, so it's you," he said, without getting up. "I thought it was Hendrikje." Then, giving vent to some mad and mocking impulse, he lifted the frame and stuck his head through it and made a grimace. "Beautiful, isn't it?" he said.

517

"At this point in our lives none of us looks exactly like Adonis."

"Oh"—he put down the frame and stretched out his legs in their loose hose and paint-spattered breeches—"the Heer Burgomaster looks elegant enough."

"Next time I come," he said in bitterness, "I'll see to it that I mess myself up on the way. If I look objectionably respectable, it's because I was at Ijemond this afternoon."

For a moment he was afraid that a futile hope might leaven the creased and sagging face; but out of Ijemond the master plainly expected nothing. "Don't move, if you don't mind," he said. "I've been measuring the canvases for frames, and I've got everything laid out on the floor."

For the first time, then, the doctor looked at what was spread out at his feet. On the planks between him and his host stretched piece after piece of somber splendor. A young man—Titus, perhaps—riding on a ponderous charger away from sullen hills, with his eyes fixed grimly on an unseen but terrible destination. Two coldly shimmering renderings of Joseph accused by Potiphar's wife, the face of the wife in one of them cynical and vulgar and hideously hard. The carcass of a slaughtered ox —corpse and nourishment, sacrifice and commodity—suspended in the shadow of a butcher's cellar. Faces—Clement de Jonghe's, Breuning's, Titus's—brooding in sorrow or incomprehensible mirth or dazed resignation upon some secret inner revelation. A Flora, fearfully unsettling because she could have been either Saskia or Hendrikje, holding out a meager handful of wan flowers. A Christ at the whipping post, emaciated, done for, scarcely able to stand on His feet, looking like the starved beggars that were carried into the hospital or the Pest House.

He put his hand under the dripping candle and thought of the few crude and powerful drawings he had picked up out of Lastman's vestibule on a plague-ridden night some thirty years ago. That first bitter knowledge, buried long under ambition and love and the distractions of the world, had heaved itself up out of its grave: what lay here at his feet was the old declaration, lifted by skill to a black and shimmering splendor, that to be human is to suffer bereavement and agony and death. "Jesus Christ!" he said, not in blasphemy, only calling upon the Sufferer to witness the suffering.

For an instant the small glittering eyes on the other side of the shadowy room signaled thanks. Then they turned mocking again, looked at him as they had looked through the empty picture frame. "Lovely, aren't they?" the master said in a voice utterly unworthy of what he was talking across. "Just the sort of thing everybody will want to hang in his parlor. Sweet, soothing—and I hope you notice what pains I've taken to get a beautiful gloss."

"Look," he said, "if you have enough understanding to paint like that, you ought to accept the fact that we live in a world of fools."

He did not answer. He got up at last and pointed to the picture of the

518

slaughtered ox, the beauty of its varied surfaces wildly incongruous with the ugliness of its subject, the reds and creams and scarlets clothing raw flesh and tendon and bone and dead fat in a shocking richness. "Doesn't it look like a Crucifixion?—the way it's hanging there, I mean. It is—on a lower order, of course. The Body and the Blood . . . and that's what we eat."

Take a few more steps in that direction and you'll end up with Geertje Dircx, the doctor thought. Sure of his vision in the dimness now, he walked between the paintings and set his candle on the long worktable where one copper etching plate after another sprang into burnished existence out of the dark. "I don't see the point of limiting yourself to a couple of candles. You won't save money with that sort of thing, and it can't be healthy, not for your eyes and not for your mind either," he said.

"Oh, it was Hendrikje's idea to save the candles. She started doing it in the kitchen and the back parlor." He rubbed an even wilder disorder into his hair. "She thought she'd save them for me to use up here, but now I find I don't want them, not many of them at any rate. If I'm not painting, I'd rather be in the dark."

"That's crazy."

"Oh, no doubt. A lot of things about me are crazy. I work as if I were crazy, that I'll admit. Look at that—" He nodded grimly and without pride at the exhibition that stretched out before them. "And that's not all, either; there are others standing against the wall. I never covered so many canvases so fast before."

"Then isn't it time you stopped and rested?"

"Rested? How would I rest?"

"Jan and Gretha want you people to come and stay awhile with them at Ijemond." He pulled the letter out of his pocket, no longer sorry for it, seeing nothing in it now but its insufficiency; and his host did not trouble to unfold it, only stuffed it into the pocket of his breeches. "Maybe you ought to go. Maybe it would do you good."

"Do me good! God almighty—a stay in the country—picnics and little walks and little suppers and all the rest of that—" He stifled the obscenity. "No, I don't think it would do me any good," he said in a quieter voice. "I'll stay where I am until they cart me out, if it's all the same to you."

"That might be all right for you. But I should think it would be upsetting for Hendrikje and Titus. They'd be better off elsewhere—"

"Then let them go elsewhere," he said in scorn and fury. "Who's stopping them? Let them go to Ijemond or any place else, and good riddance—"

"They wouldn't think of going without you—you know that."

"The more fools they! The only thing I want is to be left alone."

It was so: the paintings on the floor and the being out of whom they had issued—dirty, hateful, deliberately repellent, as unapproachable as a beast with a javelin sticking in its belly—proved as much. It would be better for him, too, to withdraw his galling presence; but he must manage to make his withdrawal without reproach, remembering that his bruised sensibilities were nothing beside this agony of solitude and rejection and shame. "I can understand how you would feel that way," he said. "It was the children's idea—Jan's and Gretha's—and I couldn't refuse to pass it along. If there's anything I can do for you, and I know that's a foolish thing to say because there really isn't"—he took up the candle and started to pick his way between the terrible and splendid canvases—"but if there is, please send for me."

"Wait a minute. I want to thank you—"

"For what?"

"Oh, I don't know. For being the one in a thousand that doesn't get sick at the stomach looking at stuff like this."

"That's no reason for thanks."

"It's reason enough. Good night, Nicolaas—"

He had seldom used the first name before, had seldom said anything but "Doctor" and "Heer Burgomaster" and had been saying them in recent years with growing irony. But to come back and embrace him was obviously impossible; and the doctor only paused on the threshold, briefly and without turning, and said, "Good night."

The light of the candle, falling before him to the foot of the stairs, revealed Titus sitting on the lowest step, lighted up the boy's white, lifted face and kindled his fiery curls. "Is Father still working, Doctor?" he asked, without getting up.

"Yes, I believe he is." The sound of the sanding had begun again while he was still on the upper staircase. "Why? You aren't going to wait up for him, are you?" He sat down beside the lonely watcher, putting the candle on the floor and laying his arm companionably around the slight shoulders.

"I don't know. Sometimes I stay up and have a mug of beer with him when he's finished, but he didn't seem in that sort of humor at supper. What do *you* think?"

"I think you ought to go to bed and get a good night's rest."

"I'm not really sleepy."

The swollen eyelids and the fine mouth, drooping and almost drained of color, belied the statement. "Sleepy or not, you should go to bed. And I'll tell you something else you should do; you should go to Ijemond to visit Gretha and Jan—they want you and Hendrikje and Cornelia to come and stay for a month while the moving's going on."

For an instant the comely face lit up with visions of country gardens and prize cattle and fruit trees; then it put off such childish things and grew inappropriately manly. "What about Father—isn't *he* invited?"

"Of course he's invited. But he wanted no part of it when I mentioned it this evening. He'll stay here, but he has no objections to your going, and you know yourself that Hendrikje needs a rest."

"Oh, but she'd never go without him, even if he didn't want her."

"What about you? Couldn't you go, even if the others didn't? You look as if you could do with a holiday."

"It wouldn't be a holiday. Hendrikje wouldn't leave him, and I couldn't leave Hendrikje or him either, and I'd miss Cornelia, and they'd miss me. Whether they know it or not, I'm a help to them. I've learned to be practically everything—a good bargainer at the market, and a washerwoman, and even a chimney sweep. I help them a lot."

"I'm sure you do."

"So you see, I couldn't possibly go, much as I'd like to. None of us could, as long as *he* stays. And he'll stay until the last minute if things up in the studio keep going the way they're going now. I can imagine them taking the stool out from under him and he'd still go on painting until they came back and moved the easel too."

He ended with a husky ripple of laughter, like Saskia's, a sound that was particularly eerie in the black, still house. The doctor laughed too, though he found the picture the lad had evoked anything but amusing.

"But don't let me keep you, Doctor. Other people go to bed at a decent hour, even if we don't. You don't think, then, that he'd want me to wait up for him?"

"I think you ought to go to bed."

"All right. I will." He rose and took the candle and escorted the visitor across the shining tiles. "And thank you again," he said, "for your very kind invitation. I'll write Gretha and Jan a note—I'm an excellent secretary too. Oh, and Hendrikje asked me to give you her best regards." He opened the massive door and stood looking out for a minute at the dark and balmy street as if he were amazed to find it there, as if he only half believed that any world could exist other than the ruined one within the walls. "My respects to your wife, Doctor. It's always delightful to see you. Thank you for the visit, and everything. Good night."

*

Now that the bankruptcy proceedings were grinding inexorably on, now that the doors of what had once been his house were bolted against him, now that he and whatever he could call his own—his paints, his easel, his manikin, a few rolls of canvas, and enough clothes for a man to be decent in—had been transported to the Crown Inn, his first feeling was relief. To be dispossessed was also to be disburdened—there were so many things he did not have to trouble his sore and weary mind with any more. When he went out in the company of others—Tulp or Clement de Jonghe or Pinero—he noticed that on their way through the bare reception hall of the inn they always turned their heads aside from the two rooms where his treasures, draped in tarpaulins, were stored until they could be put on public sale; but he himself felt no need to spare his eyes the ghostly sight. He made a point of looking into those rooms, glaring at the familiar shapes that showed through the cloth with scorn and loathing, feeling a kind of exultation of contempt as he said to himself, "Oh, yes, there's the Rubens, and that would be the Percellus, and that round knob must be Vespasian's bald head." And he wondered whether any of the ships' captains engaged in the recent naval battles with the English, after their battered vessels had held together hour after hour only by the grace of God, had felt the same surge of demoniac glee at the impact of the cannon ball that splintered them to bits.

But this ecstasy of destruction was brief and intermittent. Most of the time he was utterly quiet, closed in by a white and empty peace. The simplicity of his existence never ceased to strike him with wonder: he was amazed that a man could live solitary in an inn, with no obligations except the legal one to wait there with his possessions until the sale took place, and have all his wants attended to at the small sum of three florins a day. Three florins a day and the hospitality of the Pineros, who were housing his family as casually as they had housed several series of Ashkenazim, bought for him this changeless isolation, this voiceless quiet, this rest that was a foretaste of the rest he would know in his grave. And except on the infrequent occasions when somebody took him out to buy him a mug of beer, he had infinite leisure—leisure from seven in the morning when he woke out of a heavy and vacant sleep until seven in the evening when either Titus or Hendrikje visited him at the inn—leisure to ponder, to remember, to let the dark water of his thought flow wherever it would, leisure to contemplate and to paint himself.

Who else was there to paint? He could not afford to hire a model. Besides, as the destructive frenzy seized him when he glared at the objects in their swathings of tarpaulin, so a solemn preoccupation held him when he saw, in the very decent mirror that the innkeeper Heer Schumann had found and set up for him, his own ravaged face. For hours he would stare at that self which he had come to consider his one indubitable possession: at the flesh that had collapsed and loosened under the strain and the loss of weight, at the eyes—almost expressionless, uncommitted, merely waiting—gazing out from between the thick eyebrows and the heavy pouches, at the lips folded upon each other in a way that suggested more tenderness than he would have thought he possessed, at the peasant nose that had not been chiseled a whit more elegantly by the hand of pain. He would stare for half an hour and then wander slowly over to the easel—there was no need for hurry, nobody wanted him for anything—and put down a few strokes and stroll back to the mirror to give himself up to that deep staring again. And he neither liked nor disliked that self which he was setting down—only knew that, like the earth, it *was*. Was, in spite of inner convulsions. Was, in spite of the inevitable erosion wrought upon it by the tides of the years.

It could scarcely be said that he was working to complete that self-portrait. Sometimes whole days were given up to the dark cavern of a nostril or the highlight on a dry and grizzled patch of hair; and Hendrikje, coming in after a two-day absence, would take it for granted that he had not been working on it at all. But he never bothered to set her right; though he could not say he waited for her coming—in his present state he waited for nothing—it was as if the painting were no longer in the room once she was there; in fact, the very room itself seemed to have changed.

In the daytime, without her, his quarters, though they were large and light, were as austere as the cell of a monk. A long time ago the Crown Inn had been a municipal orphanage for girls; and some of the bleakness of the massed but solitary lives which had once been lived there seemed to cling to the big blank windows, the worn floor planks, and the white and peeling walls. But when *she* came, Heer Schumann, who was much taken with her, brought in an extra lamp "so that husband and wife could be cheerful together"; and the ghosts of the orphans were exorcised, and he became aware of the cheap, bright cover on the bed, and the glow of the ancient wooden stools and chairs, and the soft summer shadows of the trees on the Kalverstraat lessening the starkness of the windowpanes. At such times she came closer to him than she had been in many months; and her beauty and her desire were incomprehensible to him, almost as surprising as the three-florin charge that covered everything.

What had come over her or him? Had she really changed, or was it only that he saw her anew now that there were days when he did not see her at all? She *could* have changed: it could have been the birth of a healthy child that had made her hair as thick and lustrous as in the days when she had shaken it loose in defiance of Geertje; the opulence that had swelled her breasts with milk could, he supposed, have suffused the rest of her body—her dusky throat, her softly downy thighs that smelled like drying grain, her pliant, seeking hands. Whatever it was, Heer Schumann learned very quickly that, once he had gone his way after bringing them the second lamp, it would not be discreet to return and rap on the door and suggest that they come down and join him in a goblet of wine. Wine, milk, and honey flowed in them and between them: they were in each other's arms for one thing or another—passion or sheer outworn excesses of powerless tenderness—as soon as the good innkeeper had left them to themselves. After the cold austerity of the day, like a change in season, came the melting, debilitating richness of the night; and their celebration of the rites of love would have been worthy of a bridal bed. The only difference between this late blooming and the early one was the completeness with which it was over once it *was* over. They rose from the rumpled coverlet with a workaday alacrity when it was time for her to return to the Pineros'; and he felt no need to brush her thigh with his as they walked through the nighttime desertion of water-lapped, leaf-whispering streets. Back in his room, he

523

did not think of her while he undressed; back in his bed, he did not grope after her in his dreams—he had no dreams, he had nothing but the deep, dividing sleep.

Coming out of that sleep into the mild quiet of the summer morning, lying on his back and having to tell himself where he was and why this particular ceiling, flaked and sadly in need of repainting, should meet his opening eyes, he was closer to the old world, the one he used to live in, than at any other time of the day or night. How did it look on the inside, the great house on the Breestraat, with all its curtains drawn and the walls stripped of their treasures? Why hadn't it occurred to him to carry off his etching plates before the place was locked against him? How was it with Titus—did his friends abuse him with his father's disgrace? And the little Cornelia—would she know him when she saw him again or shrink away as from a burly stranger?

Then, as the light strengthened on the self-portrait, those thoughts would dissolve as fog dissolves in the sun. He would get up and go, slipperless and half-naked, to the easel to see whether the night's drying had drained yesterday's work of any of its intensity. If there had been some falling off, he would begin to correct it without even stopping to wash his pasty eyes or rinse his mouth of the taste of sleep. One touch of the brush to the canvas, and he was transformed again into the three-directional starer: he staring at his reflection in Heer Schumann's mirror, and the reflection staring at him, and the image on the easel—more monumental, more allied to eternity than what appeared in the polished glass—staring at nothing with its vague and uncommitted eyes. What am I? he would think. A pig, a frowzy pig, go put on your dressing gown before the chambermaid looks in on your hairy chest and your drooping belly . . . And he would obey himself, and make himself decent, and add a few more strokes before breakfast; and then it would seem to him that what looked out through the mask of collapsing flesh and sagging wrinkles, piggish though its human vestments were, was an imprisoned and degraded god.

Though he never knew at the beginning of the day who would be with him to help him bring it to a close, Titus or Hendrikje—which of them came depended on whether Cornelia was too fretful to be left with Titus—he fancied he could tell by some sixth sense whether the evening would be dragged out for him by responsibility or made brief by love. When Titus was there, recollections of the departed orphans repossessed the place, though he could not understand why Titus should be connected with them, overmothered as he was and as gay as ever in the midst of the family crisis. There was an evening in the middle of July when the sixth sense failed him: his waiting had attuned itself to one of those great, soft, sea-scented winds that rushed through the trees and cooled the feverish rooms and gave the city the benefit of a storm that had broken somewhere else; and he was certain that she would come to him that evening cool of cheek and loose of hair, that they would lie side by side uncovered, letting the steady and ample wind move soothingly across their nakedness. But it was Titus who came, and later than usual too, when expectation had risen to a shrill pitch and the chimes were jangling nine o'clock.

The boy walked in wearing a cloak—strange in such weather. From the rigid way he held himself it was obvious that he was carrying something heavy in his right hand, and that he had worn the cloak to hide it. "I'm sorry I'm late, Father," he said in a breathy voice, "but I brought you a sort of present, and I had to wait until it was dark before I could pick it up. Cornelia was a bit cross, but Hendrikje says to tell you she'll be sure to come tomorrow. Also, she said to give you her love."

His first thought was to curse Cornelia's crossness, his second to wonder what good Hendrikje imagined her love could do him at that distance, and his third to remind himself that the boy was standing there, eager to show his present and dragged down on one side by the weight of it. "Well, now, what have you brought me?" he asked, gruffly because he was unsettled and unexpectedly tender.

"Wait, I'll show you. Close your eyes a minute. I want to make a proper display—I'm going to lay them out on the bed."

He closed his eyes—in fact to go along with the lad's high-hearted mysteriousness, he went and stood in the corner like a child playing a game until he heard the young voice behind him say, "There now. All ready."

He turned and looked at the bed. In the faint light of the single lamp, beautifully arranged over the cheap coverlet, lay ten copper squares. Not new ones—his heart began to race at the sight. Used ones—his, unquestionably his—eaten into by acid and stained with ink. *Christ Preaching to the Halt and the Blind, David Praying, The Agony in the Garden, The Good Samaritan, The Blind Tobit,* two of the better landscapes, a portrait of Saskia, *The Flight into Egypt,* and a large and elaborate *Descent from the Cross*—all of them were here, most unbelievably, since the law had compelled him to leave them along with the seventy-odd paintings in the dark tomb of that forbidden house. It was like witnessing a resurrection from the dead. "Dear God, how did you come by these?" he said, and his voice was tremulous. "Was it Tulp— was it Breuning—who got them out of there for me?"

"I did."

"You did?" The lad, cloakless now and looking exposed and vulnerable in his worn shirt and skimpy breeches, stood to the side of the door, his face triumphant but tired, his head tilted back against the flaked wall. "Did you go to the City Hall and get permission?"

"Oh, no, that wouldn't have done any good. I just got into the house and took them. Yes, I broke in tonight and stole them—that's the only way to put it," he said.

"Broke in, you say? Stole them?"

"Yes. I forced the lock on the kitchen window and climbed in. I didn't dare light a candle, but it wasn't so dark that I couldn't feel my way up to the studio; and once I was up there it was easy enough to find the worktable, and I took whatever I could lay my hands on and came out the way I went in. I hope they're good ones—ones that you would have wanted to save—"

For a minute he stood wordless, staring at the plates and thinking what marvelously good ones they were, how God—if God was ever with anybody—must have been with him in this, putting almost all that he had sorrowed over under the groping hand. Then he thought of that groping, of this slight and protected being exposing himself to seizure by the city guardsmen by forcing a lock and slipping through a casement, of this scarcely-more-than-a-child going blind through the stripped and eerie house, with memories of lost felicities ready at every turn to assail his not yet calloused heart. "It was good of you—it was very good of you, Titus," he said in a choked voice. "When I think of your taking such a risk—one of the guardsmen might easily have caught you, you know—when I think of that and the way you must have felt walking around in there all alone—" But he did not finish it. The words he should have said and had meant to say—"I would rather have done without the etchings"—would not come out of him. His eyes, avid, turned back to the squares of copper glinting on the bed, and he could not lie now any more than he had been able to lie that night when he had stood in the lavender-scented, newly ordered closet and offered God anything as a price for Saskia's life, anything but the skill of his own right hand . . .

"Really," said Titus, "I wasn't a bit frightened."

Oh, but he must have been, and terribly. The fright was suspended now, held off by the headiness of success; but tonight in his borrowed bed at Pinero's he would probably lie sleepless, with a pounding heart and dry, unclosing eyes. And that realization brought on another—that it was not Titus but he himself who should have thought of the exploit and carried it out. While he had been painting that image which was scarcely visible now without Heer Schumann's second lamp, it was the lad who had been thinking the thoughts and executing the obligations of the man of the household: Titus had been tending Cornelia and helping Hendrikje and filching the etching plates from which the four of them might get their daily bread. And there was pain and reproach in that—so much pain and reproach that he could not take the thin body into an embrace.

"They *are* good ones, aren't they?" said Titus, as if the collapse of high-heartedness had cast some doubt upon the value of the booty.

"They couldn't have been better if Clement de Jonghe himself had picked them out by daylight," he said, and hoped that the speech would compensate for the touch and the kiss he could not find the heart to give.

"But now that I come to think of it, maybe they won't be any good to you without a press to run them off on—"

"Oh, there's no difficulty there. Clement has a press, and so does Rabbi Menasseh ben Israel. We can always find a press. Sit down—you must be tired."

"No, not a bit." He straightened so that his bright hair rested against the peeling plaster. "I feel as if I could stay up all nght."

"Sit down anyway." He motioned him to the only comfortable chair. "Sit down and tell me what you've been doing with yourself—aside from breaking into houses and stealing things."

The lad was the owner of a nimble Uylenburgh tongue; and what came out of him, breathless and hasty, once he had flung himself into the chair and dangled his legs over the arm of it, had the offhand tone and amusing hyperboles of a budding gentleman. To begin with, he had become an expert baby-feeder. The secret of it was dodging: a baby spouted like a whale for the sheer joy of it, and you had to know by the look in the eyes when the spoonful you had just put in was going to come out. Oh, yes, and he was putting his lessons on the lute to excellent use: he and two of his fellows had picked up a florin amongst them by playing at a dance last Saturday evening, in addition to which they had gotten a free supper—cold duck and pastries and French wine. And Vrouw Pinero's window frames had needed repainting, and he had gone over them for her—considering everything, he didn't see how he could do less.

Every now and again as he rambled on, too charmed with his own spirited delivery to notice that his father was appalled by these scraps and patches of his vacant gypsy life, his eyes wandered to the burnished display on the bed, and the corners of his mouth were indented by a smile. There lay the justification for his shabby and chaotic existence, and for this redeeming accomplishment he wanted and deserved a little more praise. "That etching of Christ—the one healing the halt and the blind," said Rembrandt somewhat self-consciously, "is probably the best thing I've ever done. Years went into it—years. You can't imagine what it does for me to see it lying there."

"I'm glad. I'm awfully glad, Father. It was sheer luck; I could just as well have picked up some perfectly useless old thing, you know."

"And if you had"—he said it slowly and emphatically—"I would have been just as grateful. It was a very kind thing for you to do for me."

"*De rien,*" he said in the good French that he had picked up from Jan and Gretha. "And you, Father—what have *you* been doing with yourself?"

"Nothing. Sitting—thinking. Looking out of the window. Painting that—" He raised the lamp and held it so that the hard uncompromising image appeared like an actual being summoned out of the dark.

"Oh, that's marvelous. It's so impressive it almost puts a person off."

But he did not like it, that was plain. His face lost its mobility as he stared at it, and he drew up his knees until they almost touched his chin.

He was afraid of, perhaps even repelled by, the ravaged and ungiving face; and his father, taking the light away, thought how it was no great wonder: if somebody had shown him such a thing thirty-odd years ago, he too would have rejected the harsh judgment it passed on a world that looked dewy and green and limitless. "It's a kind of companion piece to the one of your Uncle Adriaen in the golden helmet," he said.

"Yes, I can see that. They're both very stern and strong."

"Look at it later, Titus."

"When it's finished, you mean?"

"No." He laughed tonelessly and carried the lamp over to the bed and trained its light on the display of etching plates. "I mean much later. I mean when you're fifty."

They talked then like conspirators about the disposition of the loot. It would not do, he said, to keep the plates in the inn, much as he wanted them there: somebody connected with the bankruptcy proceedings might ferret them out, and they would be confiscated, taken away from him for good. Titus was for burying them in a churchyard, but much as he hated to deprive the boy of another exciting adventure, he explained that they would be safest in the hands of a friend. Titus was to take them home tonight to Pinero, who would then pass them on to Bonus for safekeeping: the rabbi was omitted from the circuit out of consideration for the sanctity of his profession.

It was hard to have them carried off so quickly. He had wanted to repossess them by feeling the infinitely complicated and varied grooves with the tips of his fingers, but this he could not bring himself to do with anybody else standing by. It was hard, too, to see the evening coming to an end so early: it was only half past ten, and he never began to undress until midnight; but the boy was incapable of either sustaining or abandoning the strained jocularity that was the only sort of communication he thought proper to the occasion, and would plainly be better off, whether he slept or not, in the quiet of his bed. Once he had gone his way, wrapped again in the unseasonable cloak and pulled down on the right side by the weight of the etching plates, something melancholy and haunting, something almost as perceptible as the smell of a burnt-out clay pipe, remained in the air and could not be dispelled, not even by the warm and steady wind that kept blowing in from the sea. For a long time he walked back and forth between the open casement and the bed on which the imprints of the plates could still be made out. Once, passing the chair where the slight body had flung itself down after its exertions and its draining triumph, he put out his hand as if to touch the place where the fiery curls had spread themselves. But before the gesture was complete, he thought of the painting, carried the lamp over to the easel, found a brush and added a few touches—a heavier line along the furrow between the brows, a darker patch of shadow at the corner of the lips.

When the canvases and antiquities that were the one remaining manifestation of his glory were taken from their swathings and cleaned and offered in public auction at the Crown Inn on a fine summer day, he seriously wondered if he could be going mad. The gentlemen in their beavers and the ladies in their plumes and pearls who made their tepid and unsatisfactory bids were puzzled, even shocked, by the way he bore himself; they had plainly expected him to closet himself decently away from this culminating act of his ruin or walk shamed and meek through the spectacle with a bowed head. They with their offers of fifty florins for what would have been a bargain at three hundred, they with their flaccid faces expressionless even in avidity, with their circumspect fingers in their shrunken purses—for even the most fortunate were finding it an inauspicious year—they could not be expected to understand the exultation of destruction that drove him downstairs to see the worst of it, to walk brazenly back and forth between them and his forgone belongings, even to let out a contemptuous laugh at the fool who offered twenty miserable florins for a Brouwer.

No, he was not behaving, either at the auction or in his daily doings, like a man in his proper senses. He took no interest in crucial matters and got himself worked up over the most trivial details: so Hendrikje let him know with a spirit worthy of the days when she had tossed her head at Geertje Dircx, and so Dr. Tulp pointed out when he stopped at the inn to take him out for a mug of beer. How was it, they wanted to know, that he fell into a cursing rage when the chambermaid gave him an ill-ironed sheet, and merely shrugged his shoulders when he was told that the auction bids were so low that the Orphans Court had stopped the sale before a third of the goods was disposed of, postponing it until fall for Titus's sake in hope that the unrest in Europe might subside and prices rise. How could he get himself into a froth because Titus had played the lute in a dance hall when he couldn't bestir himself even to talk about finding a place for himself and his family to live in? And what sort of man was it who could barely bring himself to thank the Pineros for their inexhaustible hospitality and yet was moved to the point of tears because none of his students had come to the auction and taken advantage of his fallen state by buying at a minor cost objects they had lived with in his house and had learned to love?

He was not really troubled by Hendrikje's resentment; he supposed it was justified, and it added a certain tang to their connection. That her diffidence should have dropped from her, that she should walk pertly, clicking her heels, that her large eyes should sometimes sharpen with impatience—these things along with her figure, lithe and trim again now that she was neither pregnant nor nursing, turned her back into the Ransdorp girl whose comings and goings he had covertly watched with stifled desire. Their union these days was as likely as not to come at the end of a spat, and he knew with a questionable pleasure what her complete acquiescence had robbed him of in his first possession of her: the pleasure of compelling, of insisting, of mastering—a pleasure not without its sting of cruelty. As the summer waned, they talked less as they walked through the deserted streets; but they kissed more fiercely, more clingingly in the shadow of Pinero's stoop. He made her stay beside him in that generative darkness longer than she should, with Cornelia likely to waken the household by her cries and Titus too uneasy to fall asleep until he heard her come in. And when she outstayed the chimes to submit to some unflagging embrace, he felt his face take on the foolish self-congratulatory smile of one who has won again at cards or dice; he walked back at a lively pace, kicking whatever twig or bit of gravel lay in his path, knowing—and indulging—the vulgarity of that smile.

Sometimes she talked of the house they would have after the second auction, but he did not listen: the thought of that crowded existence in cheap and unfamiliar rooms, the thought of the noise and the confusion and the attempts at cheer gave him nothing but a conviction of his utter incapacity to live again like other men. These vacant walls, this battered furniture that belonged to anybody and nobody, this floor scuffed by the soles of others who had come and gone ingloriously—he no more wished to leave them than a patient who is gravely ill wishes to leave his hospital bed. He was not even troubled because there were more evenings to be spent in solitude: Titus was back at Latin school and had his lessons to prepare; Vrouw Pinero was in bed with an unshakable rheum and Hendrikje could do no less than tenderly nurse her; Tulp, when he was not occupied with municipal business, was reading the proofs of his *Pharmacopoeia,* which was coming off the press at last. To paint after supper had become impossible, partly because the sun was gone now by the time he came back upstairs and partly because even the lightest supper brought on a sodden weariness—he could not stand at the easel while his body labored to digest the beer and cheese and bread. So he had borrowed enough from Coppenol to buy half a dozen copper plates, an etching needle, and a vial of acid; and he spent the empty evenings hunched over the shaky little table that Heer Schumann had ordered brought up for him from the kitchen. In the weak glare of the single lamp, he etched stolidly and interminably, disregarding the pain that tightened like a cord around his forehead, avoiding the mirror when he stood up to undress, afraid to see his own inflamed and sunken eyes.

And since the world had dwindled to the confines of the inn, his models were those that he saw constantly around him. Heer Schumann's wife, listening to the tales of a sea captain just back from the Indies, became the Samaritan woman listening to Jesus at the well; the old porter, sleeping with his head against the wall in the dusky common room, became Saint Francis in ecstasy under a great tree; the butcher, stepping backward in protest before the innkeeper's accusation that the sausage was not fresh, became Saint Jerome astounded by a heavenly revelation. The remaining three of the six precious copper plates were given over to the chambermaid, the woman he had berated so mercilessly because of the wrinkles in his sheet; and one of them, in which he placed her cold and naked to the waist beside a stove, was done with such care that it constituted in his own mind—though she would never see it—the apology he could not bring himself to give.

He was scratching away one evening in September at the crosshatchings on her swollen foot when somebody knocked at the door. He was puzzled—it was half past ten, too late for Hendrikje or Titus— puzzled and embarrassed too, since he was in no condition to receive a visitor: the top button of his shirt was gone, his breeches were wrinkled and spotted, and he smelled of sweat because he had not bathed for several days. The knock sounded again, and he pushed the etching plate away and went to the door, wiping his palms on his sides. His vision was shimmery from long staring, and it was a moment before he realized that the person on the other side of the threshold was Jan Lievens, standing with his hands outstretched and a look of solemn compassion on his big, smooth face—just such a look as one might fix on the chief mourner at a funeral.

If he had thought at all about Jan Lievens in the wreckage of the last year, it had been only to be thankful that he had chosen this particular year to spend in Italy. It had never occurred to him that the traveler was bound to come back; and to have him here now, seeing his host in a sordid and slovenly state and so red in the eyes that he might well have been weeping, was unnerving. There were only two choices: the unthinkable one of slamming the door in his irreproachably sorrowful face or submitting to his pity by taking his offered hands. "Well, now, Jan, when did you get back?" he said in a voice that sounded false, shaking the hands with a vigor that rejected their proffered sympathy.

"Only this afternoon. I'm still walking on deck; we had a rough sea all the way back." He followed his host into the room, making it seem for the first time crowded as well as mean—where was he to put his fine black beaver with its nodding plumes, and which of the rickety chairs could accommodate his ample body? "I would have come earlier if I'd had any idea, but I didn't find out until tonight. I had supper at the house and saw my poor girl to bed—she was horribly seasick all the way home—and then I went down to the Barrel to pick up what I could in the way of news. I ran into young Flinck down there, and that's how I heard about this—"

"Here, sit down, Jan." He snatched up his old dressing gown, a disgraceful piece of worn and spotted splendor, from the one good chair and tossed it on the bed.

"How shocked I was, you can imagine—I couldn't believe it." He let himself down, shaking his head from side to side and fetching up a sigh. "Such a terrible thing—I felt I had to come over and see you—"

"Thanks. That's very good of you." He would have regretted the dryness of his own response if he had not felt that every word addressed to him had been practiced on the way, if he had not kept wondering how the large and earnest face had looked when the "news" had first come out.

"And is it really as bad as they've been telling me?"

Perhaps the best way to end it—and God knows he wanted it ended—was to make a statement so extreme that no further discussion would be possible. "Oh, yes," he said cordially, almost hilariously, sitting down on the stool and resting his wet back against the edge of the table, "everything's as bad as it can possibly be."

"Really?"

"Yes, really. Everything's gone. The house, the collection, my own canvases, the furniture, Hendrikje's jewels—everything." He flung his arms back in reckless self-abandon along the table and let the buttonless top of his shirt gape to show his shaggy, sweat-drenched chest.

The visitor was put out by the incongruous gesture; he started like a frightened horse and ran his fingers through his hair. "But this is only a temporary situation," he said primly, as if he were delivering a reprimand. "The thing to think about is what comes next—"

"What comes next is the second auction sale—which will probably be as much of a fiasco as the first one."

"Still, *some* money is bound to come out of it—money that you can use to make a fresh start."

"No, that's where you're wrong. If it's anything like the first auction, there won't even be enough to pay off the creditors—" He felt no shame, only an out-of-hand pleasure in shattering the easy optimism. "All I have to live on is what comes out of my etchings—Clement de Jonghe's paid me in advance for a set of twenty."

"And your good lady and the children?"

"They're living with friends—Jewish friends."

"Oh"—the soft white hand went up again and traveled through the loose locks—"I've always said the Jews were the most hospitable people in the world. But as soon as the sale's over, you'll be together again, and that should be a great comfort to all of you. Have you started to look around for a place?"

"No—not yet." It came out stupidly, haltingly, as if it were a confession—at the thought of looking around and being together, the brief hilarity had collapsed. He simply could not imagine himself inspecting a succession of sordid houses, conjecturing which rooms would serve for what and whom, and haggling over the rent.

"Well," said the visitor, "hadn't you better begin to look? You'll want room for teaching, and it isn't easy to find a place with enough space and the right light for a studio."

He thought of the apprentices he would still have with him—the loyalty of four or five of them at the most would survive this shameful and aimless interim. And how could he raise his weary voice to teach principles that his present condition had discredited? The wonder was that he could paint, that he should be painting better than he had ever painted before. He looked over his shoulder at the easel, where the somber self-portrait stared through the shadow beyond the wan light of the solitary lamp. See it, speak of it, tell me what it is worth, he thought. But he knew that not more than ten men in Amsterdam would know what it was worth, and that Jan Lievens would be the last imaginable candidate for that company.

"Yes, what you ought to do is find yourself a place where you can take a few commissions," said Jan, straightening in his chair as if it were he who had to bestir himself for the fresh start. "Come to think of it, there's no earthly reason why you shouldn't be working on portraits here. I've got some people on my waiting list who'd be glad to come if they knew you were taking commissions. This may not be as comfortable as a studio, but you could bring the price down a little to make up for that—charge them, say, two hundred florins apiece."

Two hundred florins . . . Hard as it was to take a favor from somebody who would never have seen the English Court if it had not been for the strict supervision imposed upon him in the cold outbuilding behind the mill, he took his arms from the table and said, "Thanks. A few commissions would be a great help."

"Good! I'll look into it right away. You should hear from me before the end of the week. I see you've been painting." The visitor's big body, still lithe in spite of its accumulated weight, came up out of the chair and wandered over to the easel. "Well, I'm glad to see you haven't lost any ground over all this," he said.

"No, I don't believe I have. Whoever comes to me will get his two hundred florins' worth." If there was no sting in it, that was only because his contempt could not stir the unleavened mass of his despair. He sat on his stool as a schoolboy in disgrace sits in his corner, his head bent and his hands hanging loose between his knees.

"There's only one thing," said Jan, "and that's the question of surface. In paintings that you do for yourself, naturally, it makes no difference. But in commissioned portraits—"

He did not break the painful silence. He could not utter the offhand "Of course" that would spare his visitor the necessity of speaking charged words and bring him perhaps a thousand desperately needed florins. He sat stubbornly silent, staring at his hanging hands.

"If you could—and that's a silly way to put it, there's no question that you could if you only wanted to—if you could give them what they're all asking for, not only in Amsterdam but all over Europe—"

"What?" he said flatly. "A silky finish? I can't. I paint the way I paint. God help me, I can't do otherwise." He was glad he had said it:

lifelessly though it had come out of him, it proved that there was still some redness glowing at the core of his charred heart.

"But then, you see, I can't do as much for you as I would like to—"

"Don't let it disturb you. There's no call for you to do anything for me."

"Oh, yes, there is. We studied together, we learned together—"

Liar! he thought. You ate the fruit of my labor and grew fat and sleek and fashionable on it. You took of me and corrupted what you took, corrupted it enough to make it fit fare for the world. He did not answer because his chin had begun to shake as if he had palsy.

"Still, I should be able to do something. There are one or two on my list, older people who might prefer your way of going at it. Anyway, I'll see."

Four hundred florins . . . He remembered the day when he would have spent as much for a pear-shaped pearl that had caught Saskia's fancy. The shaking was subsiding; he got up from the stool to prove to himself that he could stand. For Hendrikje's sake, for the sake of the children, for the sake of the Pineros, he stifled the burning impulse to shout at Jan Lievens that he could take his commissions and—but that was foolish, that was a child's way, there was nothing to be gained by obscenity.

Without another word of praise the visitor turned his back on what Michelangelo would have been glad to have painted, crossed the little room, and put his arm around his host—an arm that could not be shaken off because, if it was presumptuous and patronizing, it was also well-meaning and affectionate. "I'll do my best for you, believe me. And don't take it too much to heart. You'll see, your day will come again."

Yes, he thought while the smooth hand reached for the elegant beaver, my day will come again when we're both of us dead, and I don't imagine there will be any opportunity for *me* to patronize *you* in the Kingdom of Heaven.

"Get a good sleep. Your eyes look tired."

"That's nothing. They're red because I've been doing too much etching."

"Well, don't overstrain them. My compliments to your good lady. You'll be hearing from me in a week at the latest. Take care of yourself, my dear fellow. Good night."

And now that the visitor had taken himself off, the rage broke out through the blackened crust. He imagined himself sinking his fingers into the soft white throat and knocking the impervious head against the wall, making wild and obscene speeches of rejection to the patrons charitably sent his way, overturning the rickety table with a crash of wood and a clang of copper that would startle the dull sleepers beneath him to a knowledge of what a caged beast it was that paced above their heads. Beast? Beast and demigod, seething with a fury that the rest of their puny lot would never know. They would take him for a drunkard, they would take him for a madman if he roared and struck out; even what stood on the easel could not bear witness to his right to their respect. The somber face that stared uncommitted out of the shadow could not vouch for him; it was too honest, too stricken, too naked in its pain. Striding past the mirror he caught another image—ponderous, unassailable, overwhelming. Oh, he would paint himself for what he was in spite of what they were trying to make of him—as a pasha raised above the groveling wretches of his court, with a great stick held like a scepter in his mighty hand, his massive person upright on a chair that might have been a throne, his chest and thighs wrapped in drapings of scarlet and gold.

Scarlet and gold—he had the stuff of them in the spotted and threadbare dressing gown. He put it on and snatched a worn biretta of black velvet from a peg and set it crownwise on his head; for the moment his maulstick would serve as the great staff he meant to hold—he would borrow the old porter's walking-stick tomorrow. He dragged the armchair across the bare planks to the mirror and laughed contemptuously when he got an unintelligible curse from below. The light was not right; as he pulled the lamp to the very edge of his worktable, he thought with savage satisfaction that it could easily tip over, that the flames could fan out with the spreading oil, consuming the floor, the bedspread, the flimsy stuff that swathed his body, himself. It did not tip over, of course; but the fierce rage in him burned itself out in that imaginary conflagration, and he was able to give himself over to the image in the glass, to fix that image so firmly in his mind that its weight and its splendor and its arrogance would be there tomorrow when his chin and hand no longer shook with the just anger of an affronted demigod.

Oh, he was tired. His eyes burned almost intolerably—mortal eyes staring at an immortal image. He saw it completed and hung in some public edifice where thousands as yet unborn would come and go. Most of them would stare at it from far away: the very mass and majesty of it would hold the ordinary looker off, would keep him at such a distance as was kept in Eastern courts between the petitioner and the pasha's throne. But some few would draw closer, their eyes fixed in wonder, their lips fallen apart. And for those few—he bent forward, close to the mirror, to see himself as they would see him—he would record the cabalistic truth unavailable to the rest: the doomed fleshiness of cheeks past their prime, the unspent, soured tenderness at the corners of the mouth, the grief beyond comfort in the small moist eyes.

✱

If she blamed him for anything these days, she blamed him for bringing the two children—yes, and herself, too—into these miserable furnished rooms. He had had plenty of time between the disastrous summer sale and the scarcely less disastrous autumn one to look for a decent place, and what had he done in those months except sit in the inn, brooding and scratching out a few etchings and painting two pictures of himself that nobody would ever buy? Like a barge stuck in the mud, he had stayed where he was, stolid and impervious, answering her nagging always in the same toneless voice: "Let it alone. Something will come up."

And this was what had come up—these three cramped rooms under a sloping roof, this hole of an attic that simmered even in October, this clutter of another man's mean life—lumpy beds, a table that had never been scoured and smelled of stale beer and soured cabbage soup, a cupboard filled with cracked and greasy dishes, closets she hated to open because they gave off an odor of old sweat and damp rags. She could not even clean the place properly because it was theirs only for a few months—it belonged to the brother of the old porter at the Crown, who had gone to Dordt to dispose of some little property left by his mother—and she was sure the owner liked his filth and would be appalled to smell fresh soap when he came back.

The temporary nature of the arrangement was almost as upsetting as the squalor. She had had her fill of waiting: waiting in the great doomed house, waiting at the Pineros' while he sat at the inn, and now waiting again until he roused himself out of his torpor—or was stung out of it by vermin or the return of the porter's brother—to find a place where they could really live, where he could have a room to paint in and she could take out what linens she had salvaged from the wreckage and set such a decent table as her mother had set in Ransdorp and make up fresh and spotless beds. It was not the lack of money that kept him in this sordid place: Jan Lievens had sent two very good patrons his way, the old merchant Tripp and his faded and distinguished wife, whose portraits he had done—thank God!—in their own fine house; she would have dropped dead of shame if he had dragged either of them up to *this*. It was sheer soddenness, a maddening unwillingness to move, to try to make anything better, that kept him from going out to look. And she could not rouse him, she could not shame him, she could get nowhere by telling him what he was doing to the children—her own misery she did not even dare to talk about. All that he did whenever she brought up the subject was look at her with small, dull eyes and say, "Let it alone, will you? Just let it alone."

It was only in the early evenings, when the small, bleak windows became beautiful in the autumn twilights, that she softened a little. She put off the lighting of the lamp as long as she could, not, as he thought, to save oil, but to allow the hateful furniture to be blotted out by the dark. She sat as far away from him as the confines of the room would permit, close to the window in spite of the chill currents of air, Cornelia fed and washed and fallen into an uncertain sleep on her knee. Usually their silence was unbroken for hours: Titus studied in his own wretched cubbyhole or went out to earn a supper and a few silver coins with his lute; she could not talk to Rembrandt without upbraiding him; and he had seen to it that no visitors stopped in. Yet the silence was often mitigated by groping and uncertain music: a man whom she had never seen but whom she took to be very old because of the deep, quavering notes he produced, kept practicing the cello downstairs. Those throbbing tones, guttural as a sob deep down in the chest, those phrases repeated over and over like some desperate question—they lacerated the raw nerves of her man so much that she did not dare to show what pleasure they gave her, how bereaved she felt when they did not stir the stagnant quiet. In the lampless shadow, her tears, dried up in the hot exasperation of the day, came slow and soothing out of her eyes and fell on the burrowing head of the little girl and on her own chapped hands. She wept for her dreams in the days when she had thought of him as inaccessible and yearned to have him touch her; for the duties and dignities of which she had been robbed; for this little one of theirs closed into a world of dirt and gloom and ugliness; for the princely boy going about like a beggar and covering his hopelessness with a mask of feverish gaiety; for the great master who was sinking further and further into the slough of his defeat and turning into an old and shattered man under her eyes. Hanging onto the fragmentary music she would try, too, to grasp the fragmentary stuff of memory: How had his hair felt under her fingers before it had dried and grizzled? How had he borne himself among his friends on a company evening, with his ox-strong body encased in bottle-green velvet? Why could she not summon up that earlier voice of his, the vibrant voice with which he had bade his guests good night or called her to a midnight feast of nuts and wine, the prelude to love? Her tears would fall faster then and the little Cornelia would whimper in her lap, aware in some strange way of her distress. Finally that whimpering or something else—a musical phrase repeated too often, a book flung down by Titus in the next room, a burst of drunken laughter in the street—would pull him out of his long dream. "Jesus Christ!" he would say to shock and wound her. "Why don't you light the lamp? Aren't things dreary enough without sitting around in the dark?"

Apparently the porter's brother liked Dordt well enough to want to stay there as long as his Amsterdam rent was taken care of. The autumn sunsets turned to wintry ones, the portraits of the venerable Tripps were finished and paid for, the Saint Nicolaas Feast—not to be mentioned, for who could buy gifts even for the little girl?—was drawing on, and they were still there. They were no longer a family clinging together as they had clung in the days of the calamity. Like a raft that has come whole through rough waters and then fallen apart under repeated batterings in some shallow bay, they had split up and gone in separate directions. The head of the house had taken to frequenting taverns for the first time in his life, and often he would stay away until twelve or one and come back as sullen and wordless as he had gone out, sober, but with the smell of brandy on his breath. Titus appeared and disappeared as he saw fit, and she could not add to his distress by asking him over and over where he had been; his only comfort was his belief in his own independence, and he turned cold at her solicitude and stared her down with alien eyes. Even the little Cornelia she could not have with her constantly: the child was forever wanting to visit the Pineros, and would clench her fists and turn red in the face to hear that it was time to go home, and how was it possible to reject the good woman's offer to keep her there awhile in the bright and cheerful house? All this *he* saw —dull-eyed and stricken though he was, he could not keep himself from seeing it—but he made no move to look for that other place which she thought of now with no more real belief than she could summon up these days when she thought of Paradise.

The day before the Saint Nicolaas Feast seemed to her the dreariest day she had ever lived through. Titus, though he was on holiday from the Latin school, had gotten up early and gone off on some unnamed business; Cornelia was with the Pineros; and *he,* after drawing listlessly all day and then tearing up everything he had done, had let himself down at the table, heavy and unapproachable, his elbows on the board, his hand shading his eyes. The evening meal was ready, but he plainly took it ill that she should presume to break in on whatever desolate thoughts were passing through his mind with such paltry doings as setting out dishes and putting on lentil soup. He did not move to make way for her: she worked over him and around him; and if she held her tongue, it was not out of consideration for him—she could have beaten her fists against his stolid back—but only because she did not wish to weep in his presence; and all day long recollections of the Saint Nicolaas Feasts of her childhood—the polished apple, the sweets wrapped in twisted paper, the precious bit of colored ribbon left overnight in the sabot on the hearth—had been calling up tears. She had just set his filled bowl and his wooden spoon before him without a word when the door creaked open and Titus walked in.

The lad looked cold, thin, and incongruously merry. His comely face, pinched and blue at the end of the nose and around his lips, seemed nevertheless so self-satisfied that she wondered whether he had been with a girl. But his eyes belied any such conjecture: they looked at her innocently; they looked at her in the almost-forgotten way, with warmth and love. "Oh, lentil soup!" he said, as appreciatively as in the old days he used to say, "Oh, roast duckling!" And, having nodded to his father and blown her a kiss, he went away to wash his hands.

"What's *he* been up to?" said Rembrandt, taking his hand away from his forehead and straightening his maddeningly unresponsive back at last.

"I don't know, I'm sure. I never ask him what he's up to. It makes him feel like a child."

"Well, he *is* a child, isn't he?"

"It would be a God's pity if he was, considering—"

"Considering what?"

"The things he's got to put up with."

The moist eyes blinked and stared as if they were taking in for the first time the dirty walls, the tawdry furniture, the cracked dishes, the peasants' fare. "Where's Cornelia?" he said in the voice of one who has not quite detached himself from sleep.

"Cornelia's been gone for three days, in case you haven't noticed. She's at the Pineros'." She set down the platter of bread with such violence that it was a wonder she did not crack the dish.

"Well, that's good, isn't it?" he said.

"Good for her, maybe, but not so good for me."

"What's the matter? Do you miss her?"

"Miss her? Why shouldn't I miss her? What else have I got in this God-forsaken—" She broke off, feeling the upward surge of the stifled weeping; and Titus came back, jaunty in his shirt sleeves, still mysteriously merry, and sat down and patted her hand.

"I thought you weren't going to school today," said his father.

"I didn't."

"Then what in the name of Jesus have you been doing all day?"

"Oh"—the bright head, bent over the soup bowl, lifted itself, the lips smiling, the eyes brilliant—"the most scandalous things—stealing and gambling and seducing women and all that."

There was an ache in her chest to hear him even mouth such matters; she wished him a little boy again, leaning against her thigh while she beat the batter for a cake. Backward, always backward, back to his childhood, back further still to her own—there was no happiness save in the past.

"Actually, I was engaged in the most innocent business," he said, licking the dark broth from the corners of his pale and delicate lips. " 'Innocent' is too mild a word for it. My activities were praiseworthy, filial, downright Christian and benevolent. Since eight o'clock this morning I've been walking from one end of Amsterdam to the other, looking for a house. And, believe it or not, I think I've found one."

His voice had quavered a little on the last sentence, and his lashes, long and fiery bright, came down over his eyes. In this, too, his gaiety was a gaudy but fragile banner to fly over his none-too-dependable courage: he was afraid that the massive paternal presence would heave itself out of its stupor and reduce him to a guilty schoolboy who had taken too much upon himself.

"Who told you to go looking for a house?" said his father, but he said it without wrath. Indeed, a smile, the first that she had seen for days, stirred the creases in his flaccid cheeks.

"Nobody. Certainly not Hendrikje." His knee nudged lightly against hers under the table. "I only thought we'd have to get out of here *some day,* and since I had a holiday, it seemed a good idea to go out and get the lay of the land. All in all, I saw seventeen places"—he hurried on, hoping to carry the skirmish through before his father's smile died away —"nine of which were dreadful—dark and damp and cold. Five of the remaining eight were fit to live in, but either there wasn't any room for a studio or the light wasn't right. I kept trying to find good light for you, Father—" He gave him a beautiful look in which fear and love and pity and respect were all commingled. "I wanted to find a place with light as good as any you've ever had before."

There was no answer, only a loud clearing of the throat; but there was no anger either, and she sighed audibly and released a bit of bread she had kneaded into a hard lump in her nervous hand. If he was thinking that the boy had done what it was his place to do, he was not going to assert his usurped rights: the time for an outburst had passed.

"Nine and five makes fourteen places I eliminated for one reason or another, and that narrowed the choice down to three," said Titus. "Two out of those three seemed too expensive, and really, they weren't nice enough to be worth it. But the third—the third, Father, if I say so myself, is a jewel of a find. It's clean, big, airy, positively drenched in light, and there's a park across the way, with statues and a fountain and a labyrinth of hedges—a perfect place for Cornelia to run about."

"Surely," said Rembrandt, "you didn't have the gall to rent it." But his face gainsaid the words: the smile had deepened, and he looked across the table at the lad with something akin to pride.

"Rent it? Dear God, you know I wouldn't do such a thing. Commit you to a place you haven't even laid eyes on? The idea never came into my head. I just thought I'd do the first rough looking for you. Only, I guess you'd better go and look at it soon. It's such a bargain that somebody else is likely to snatch it up—"

"And when," he asked, "would you like me to go and sign the papers?" Though the words were ironic, the voice carried no bitterness. "Tomorrow's the Saint Nicolaas Feast—the landlord would scarcely want to do business then—"

"Why not? I would think the prospect of rent coming in would be an extra reason to make merry over the goose."

"You're in a dreadful hurry, aren't you?"

Suspended and quizzical, the lad weighed the situation, saw that a laugh might be worth the risk, shook back his radiant curls, and laughed convincingly. "Yes, I suppose I am, Father. This place has served its turn, but I don't suppose any of us is head over heels in love with it. And when I think of that house on the Rozengracht—the windows are so big, and so much light comes streaming in, and the labyrinth will be so beautiful next spring—"

"Very well, then. We'll go and see about it tomorrow, the three of us."

He had yielded the field so graciously that she stared at him in surprise. What had undone him? The lad's charm, the lad's daring—a stirring of satisfaction at the thought that he had fathered such a one, buoyant in defeat, handsome in threadbare clothes, capable of finding his way about in an indifferent city, adept so early in diplomacy? Or was it relief at having the burdensome duty done, even if another had done it for him?

Tears came into her eyes, and she got up and turned away to hide them. "Will anybody have any more lentil soup? There's enough in the pot for a couple more bowls," she said.

Titus said nothing, only licked the thick brownness from both sides of his wooden spoon.

"Give it to the lad. He deserves it, after all the walking he's done."

"There's more than a bowlful."

"Is there? Well, I've had plenty. Why don't you take the rest of it yourself?"

*

There was nothing he could say against the house on the Rozengracht. Now that they had been living in it for months, it seemed even more suitable than at first sight. It was just such a place as his mother and father and Adriaen and Antje would have been gratified to see him settled in: though the old house in Leyden could have gone into it twice, it was only a larger specimen of the same variety; and they, if they had visited him there—why should that comfort him, since they were beyond all visiting?—would have sat unconstrained in the clean and sparsely furnished parlor, would have slept as comfortably as at home in the corner beds, would have lingered at their ease in the big kitchen, sopping up the gravy with their rusks from the somewhat battered plates that Hendrikje had carried back triumphantly from some second-hand shop. It was the sort of place he should always have lived in, a place in keeping with his Ransdorp woman and his childhood recollections and his broad, flat nose and his peasant's blood. His neighbors—distant enough to give him no trouble yet close enough to relieve Hendrikje's loneliness—his neighbors, with their noisy offspring and their careless way of wandering into their gardens in their shirt sleeves, with their overdressed processions to the little neighborhood church for Sunday services and Wednesday evening prayers, were so like the ones of his early years that it was a long time before he realized he had reason to blush for them when Allaert and Lotje or Jan and Gretha stopped in.

No, he had no complaints against the scrubbed and modest house, or the uncrowded street that led up to it, or the rolling meadows that lay behind it, or Heer Lingelbach's labyrinth with its tasteless statues. The only trouble was that he could not make these things his own, that he had to keep saying to himself with a kind of wonderment, "Oh, yes, this is the back garden, and this is the canal, and that house three doors below belongs to the Wingerts." Consciously, deliberately, he studied the front entrance, the decent brick doorway, the door painted a faded bluish grey, the clumps of tulips at the end of the path. But though he memorized what he saw as he had memorized the opening lines of the *Aeneid* at Latin school, it refused to become part of his life in the same way as the malt-dusted doorway of the mill or the dark landing of the hallway in that first place of his and Saskia's.

The four apprentices who had come back and the two new ones for whom he had Clement de Jonghe to thank had settled into the studio more easily than he; they behaved, in fact, as if they enjoyed a sacrifice that bore testimony to their loyalty. The thing he was most afraid of— that he would be unable to teach what his ill success seemed to discredit —never interfered with the instruction. What troubled him in the studio was what troubled him in the rest of the house, the fact that every now and again he had to make a conscious effort of the will to take the long, bright, alien chamber in. "Now, where was I?" he would ask the lads, realizing that he had stopped in the middle of a sentence, and the "Where was I?" might just as well have been the dazed "Where am I?" of somebody coming out of unconsciousness.

But what really distressed him, what made him think he must do something to pull himself out of this numbness and distraction, was the realization that Cornelia had been separated from him by a kind of veil for the whole five years of her existence. All that time she had been there and probably trying desperately to get at him; but nothing—not her yelling nor her stamping nor her lunges at his legs—had gotten her through; he even had difficulty summoning up a clear image of her. But I certainly know what she looks like, he told himself: her hair is black and straight, and somebody, either Hendrikje or Titus, cuts it in an even bang across her forehead to keep it out of her eyes. Her eyes are a strange color—dark, light, I don't know—an indefinite, smoky color. And there's a crinkling all over her face when she smiles, like the crinkling on top of clotted cream . . .

That night he watched her over the bread and fish covertly, taking a shamed and secret inventory of what he should have known as well as the palm of his hand. If she had been slight, she could have been called witching; but what some day might be witching could only be called trollish now. A little troll, he thought, noticing that her nose was flat at the bridge and flared out in a round and wriggling bulb at the tip —a little troll with fierce black hair and devilish eyes and small white milk-teeth behind the small pale lips. He realized, too, that what had been giving their meals such an air of stress was the fact that she assailed them with unremitting talk that was as difficult to disregard as the shrill passage of a flock of birds. Everything she had encountered in the course of the day, from the black cow's hair in the milk pail to the green bug on the lettuce leaf that looked like lettuce walking, came bursting out and beat wildly around their heads. It was Titus who saw that her father's eye was on her. "Oh, do be quiet long enough to let us swallow our food, will you?" he said. "If only you were a boy, a person could put up with you in hopes your voice would change. You're enough to split anybody's ears, you penny tin whistle, you crazy little hazelnut."

Her father held her on his lap that evening while Hendrikje mended and Titus studied. Worn out with chattering or secure within the curve of his arm, she soon fell asleep, one knee poking into his belly, the other leg stretched out in its darned scarlet stocking, with the foot dangling in its small scuffed shoe. She smelled of butter and clean sweat and the grass she had been playing in; and when the others were not looking, he kissed her lightly freckled cheek, consciously and dutifully, but not without some stirring of love. What have I come to, he thought, that I need to remind myself to love my own little one, that I am hard put to it to remember the names of my apprentices, that I try to hang my cloak on a peg that was in the Breestraat house, that I do not know whether the tulips are coming into bud or have already bloomed and dropped their petals? For an instant he saw himself as others must see him—sodden, impervious, seldom replying, often not even hearing, habitually twisting his knuckles against his benumbed forehead or rubbing his burning eyes. And what he envisioned brought so much consternation that all through the evening he kept asking himself how it might be changed. Less food? No more than a single mug of beer at supper? Cold baths? Long walks with Cornelia, the sort he had taken with Titus after that other cataclysm? Oh, he must bestir himself, he must take Hendrikje out for a stroll this very night, and tomorrow and each day thereafter he would do at least one of the things he used to do: go to the market on the wharf and buy the fish, talk with the lads while they were tidying up the studio, get a portfolio to put his scattered drawings in . . .

It was the hope that he might become what he had once been by doing what he had done in the past—it was that hope rather than any remaining pull toward the old forsworn splendor that brought him to the auction the following Saturday afternoon. He went alone—the apprentices were off before the midday meal to a picnic—and he would have gone with an empty purse if Hendrikje had not given him twenty-five florins with which to make the final payment on some recently bought second-hand furniture.

It was a fine afternoon, sun-warmed and breezy, and he walked through it with the poignant but timorous pleasure of an invalid going out for the first time after a long illness, aware of the small pink sycamore blossoms that floated along in the canals, consciously straightening his shoulders, reminding himself to swing his arms and hold up his head. Several people, two of whom he did not know, bowed to him and said, "A good day to you, Master"; and by the time he reached the empty warehouse where the sale was to be held he felt a muted well-being, a perceptible lifting of his heart.

He counted himself fortunate that there was nobody with whom he would have to converse in the group of twenty-odd people gathered under the bare rafters. Flinck was there, with the sour-faced von Sandrart on one side of him and the aging Tesselschade Visscher on the other; but his one-time apprentice had the grace and sensitivity to blush, even after all these years, over the betrayal that had done him so much good: he talked with forced intentness to his fellow-members of the Muiden Circle and avoided meeting his former master's eyes. There were no other luminaries in the negligible gathering; even if he had not heard it stated mournfully all around him he would have known that nothing of much value would be put up today. The room was warm in spite of the smallness of the crowd; and he had to remind himself not to loosen his belt or undo the top button of his collar or run his hand through his carefully brushed hair.

He sat on the last of the four benches, not to isolate himself from the proceedings but to get a better view of the moted slant of afternoon sun that poured through a skylight onto the spot where the auctioneer would stand. The broad band of brightness was interesting in itself—it illustrated an old theory of his that the air in which we move is not nothing, but a delicate and evanescent medium, with a being of its own, like water; and he was so absorbed in studying it that he did not notice the two young men who were suddenly there, murmuring, "Excuse us, Master," while they tried to pass him and share his bench.

The first one was dark, with black ringlets cut short and clustering low over his forehead and temples. By the rich hair and the swarthiness of the soft young face and the note of fantasy in his clothes it was plain that the fellow was an Italian. His companion was straw-blond, Dutch and grave, with dark blue eyes in his narrow and bony face; and once he had squeezed past the bulk of the master, he left a respectful gap on the bench before settling his lean haunches on the wood. Then, in a sudden access of courage, he turned and said in a hurrying voice that he would like to give his friend and fellow-painter here the honor of an introduction to the only Dutch master who could match swords—or was it brushes?—with Titian and Michelangelo. This was Signor Baldinucci, in Amsterdam on a visit from Rome, and this was the master of masters, Heer Rembrandt van Rijn . . .

The stiff little speech was immediately buried under a heap of incomprehensible Southern verbiage; and the words, falling like olives shaken from an opulent tree, were more or less summarized by the young Dutchman: "Signor Baldinucci asks me to express his overwhelming admiration," he said. "He has seen your etchings by the dozen in his native land and can only fall back in speechless wonder at them." A faint smile, a Northern judgment on the Southern excess, pulled up one corner of his thin, pale lips. "He wishes me to add that we spent the entire morning at the Military Club, studying your great Regents' piece—the superb color, the startling movement, the bold chiaroscuro, and several other things I can't quite make out. As for me, what can I say, now that he's finished? What's there to say about such a canvas but 'Oh, my God!'?"

"You haven't told me your name," said Rembrandt, more brusquely than he had intended because it had been so long since he had heard himself praised.

"Koninck, Master. Philips Koninck. I studied with other masters, but I never learned anything to speak of until I saw your canvases. Though I didn't have the means to be an apprentice in your studio, what little I know came from the walls of the Military Club and the Surgeons' Guild."

He had his usual difficulty expressing thanks, and he could not offer a look instead because his eyes were shameful with unreleased tears. Touch was easier, and he reached across the empty space and laid his hand briefly on the young man's knee. After that, with the tremulous mood of the convalescent upon him again, he could not pay much attention to the auction. He was surprised and a little frightened to find himself where he was; he was short of breath and uncomfortably aware of his own heartbeat; he saw everything—the smoothly painted landscapes and still lifes, the tentatively raised hands of the tepid bidders, the auctioneer making up for his shabby clothes and undistinguished person with much gesturing and the mouthing of inappropriate old saws —he saw everything but the beam of sunlight as if it were a scene in some dull play. Tesselschade Visscher, egged on by Flinck and von Sandrart, offered a hundred florins for the most fashionable of the canvases, a sickening collection of animal carnage—dead fawn, dead swan, dead cock, dead pigeon—hung against an antique altar surmounted by an emperor's bust and adorned with fat cupids whose sentimental faces made the slaughter below them doubly appalling. A man in a plumed beaver put down sixty for an almost empty autumn landscape after he had satisfied himself that the surface was sufficiently glossy; a young married couple bought at fifty a vapid girl staring calf-eyed at a man who strummed on an ill-drawn lute; and somebody else spent eighty on a picture of a goldfinch in a tasseled cage. He would have pulled himself up and gone to make the payment at the furniture market—he was already trying to think of something more than a curt good-bye to say to his young neighbors—if the auctioneer had not mentioned that there were five or six drawings to be put up, too; and he permitted himself to open the top button of his collar and resigned himself to another half-hour of the heat.

"They say," said Philips Koninck, "that one of those drawings is a Seghers."

"A Seghers?" And suddenly it was as if he were about to see not the work of the dead and discredited painter but the man himself—he who had let his wife and children starve, he who had used up their clothes and bed linens in futile and maddening attempts to make colored etchings, he whose frustration and self-disgust had driven him to drink and whose drunkenness had toppled his body over the balcony into dark peace, the confining skull cracked open and the brains that had boiled in vain spilled out at last on the paving stones . . .

The Seghers drawing came up late and as a kind of anticlimax, after a Juriaen Ovens had gone to Govaert Flinck at twenty florins, and three others equally modish and vacuous—an Asselyn, a Victors, and a Trek—had been knocked down at prices ranging between eleven and eighteen. "Ah, yes," said the auctioneer, "and there's this one, too, beautifully preserved, a Hercules Seghers; and the scandals of his life alone, ladies and gentlemen, will provide your guests with plenty to talk about on a dull evening." Whereupon he stepped forward and held it up, and small as it was—an oblong of white paper not much larger than a letter—it was visible from the last bench and drew from the thick, inert body of the master who sat there something that he hoped was no louder than a sigh.

It was nothing, really, but fierce verticals and horizontals set down with rigid firmness—masts and hulls and furled sails of ships at anchor near a wharf, and yet it was more than that: the desperate daring of ships and the desperate daring of Hercules Seghers were fused in those few hard lines. He felt as he gazed at it that another gaze was turned upon him—the jaundiced, knowing gaze of von Sandrart was on his avid, sweating face. And it was the guttural German voice that began the bidding. "Four florins," it said.

"Four florins for a Seghers," said Koninck in a mournful whisper. He opened his purse, emptied it into his hand, and counted the coins quickly. "Eleven," he said aloud, venturing all he had. "I bid eleven."

"Twelve," said von Sandrart, and added to Tesselschade Visscher that anybody who upped the bidding beyond that was an idiot: it was nothing but lines—up and down, back and forth; it was Seghers at his worst, and Seghers at his best was none too good.

Oh, it was an insult not to be borne, it presumed upon his shame, his bankruptcy, his helplessness; it took for granted that there was nothing in the purse at his side. Heavily, knowing what he looked like —an aging lump of a man whose face was crimsoned with anger and oily with sweat—heavily he heaved himself up off the bench, using the shoulder of young Koninck as a prop. "Twenty-five florins. If the drawing weren't worth it—which it certainly is—I would offer that much to preserve the honor of the painter," he said.

"Twenty-five florins?" said the auctioneer.

"Yes. On the spot." He planted his purse beside him on the bench, so that the coins in it jingled.

The Italian looked at him as if he had gone crazy. Von Sandrart snorted and then shrugged, Govaert Flinck blushed, and Tesselschade Visscher threw up her plump hands. But all of them mattered less than the bony face that young Koninck lifted to him, the big eyes saying what the spare mouth could never utter: I will remember this—and you—to the end of my days.

"Is there anybody," asked the auctioneer, "who wishes to top that bid? Would *you* wish to top it, Herr von Sandrart?"

"I?" said the German. "I am not such a fool."

"Very good, then, ladies and gentlemen. This authentic Hercules Seghers goes at twenty-five florins—a very generous offer which honors both the painter and the bidder—to the most eminent master Rembrandt van Rijn."

In a daze, with his heart stammering in his chest, he got himself somehow to the slant of moted sunlight, where he emptied his purse and paid the price. The glory was dispersed before the last florin was handed over: other images came between him and the marvelous hard lines— images of Hendrikje's shocked eyes and Titus's mouth fallen open, images of uncurtained windows and meager suppers and battered chairs. A sickness seized him, the more disintegrating because he could not tell whether it was of the flesh or the spirit; he had to sit down on the front bench, had to pretend he was gloating over his purchase when what he was really engaged in was a struggle to get his breath down deep into his chest, which seemed to have somehow changed, been barricaded against air, as if his ribs had suddenly fallen in. Whatever it was, it passed in a few minutes. But there was left in him now only so much strength as would carry him home; and when the two young men who had shared his folly and his glory asked him at the door if he would do them the honor of drinking a mug of beer with them, he could not find words to answer or sense to explain, could only smile weakly, foolishly, and shake his head.

*

It was no easy matter for the Heer Burgomaster Tulp to visit his old friend after the move to the Rozengracht. Municipal business usually held him late at the City Council—trivial ceremonial business about which his colleagues were willing to bicker for hours, or weighty and complicated business which they would often have settled with their eyes closed if he had not pointed out the consequences. More often than not, it was seven before he could seat himself at his own table or at one of those official meals where the stresses of circumspection were added to the labors of digestion; and though he had kept an abstemious stomach and was convinced that he had lived less on the bulk of food than on the evanescent spirits of good wine, digestion had become a labor for him: he was growing old.

Any man of sixty would have found it somewhat trying to walk to the outskirts of the city at the end of a day of work and with a full stomach; and the honors that had lighted upon his dry white head and his consciously erect shoulders made it harder for him than it would have been for most. It was only through thinly populated and out-of-the-way streets that he could walk without being bowed to, or offered a piece of advice from one of the townsmen whose rights he had been appointed to guard and whose private interests he was expected to advance. And though he no longer saw patients in his office and made the rounds of hospital and Pest House only seldom, he was not relieved of the obligations of the role he bitterly missed; scarcely a day went by when somebody did not stop him and make him responsible for one or another of the inevitable flaws or breakdowns in the human anatomy.

No, it was never an idle, pleasant stroll, and often it was a dizzying and disintegrating experience because it made him realize that only change is permanent. Landmarks he had known for almost half a century were gone and strange buildings to whose very beauties his spirit was hostile had taken their places; babies that he had drawn from their mothers' wombs were young men and women, stopping him to show him *their* babies; orchards had turned into factories and meadows into streets. Even his own hands were strange to him now that the small white knobs, as hard as bone, had marred his fingers—fingers so inept and stiff that they had their troubles with buckles and buttons and really should not be trusted with the lancet any more.

Yet there was one evening in August when he made the painful journey more quickly than usual and with a lighter heart, in spite of his after-supper weariness and the stiffness in his right knee. He had good news to deliver at his destination: the Surgeons' Guild, now under the presidency of the learned and amiable Dr. Deijman, wanted another Regents' piece for their Guild Hall and had finally bowed to the unflagging arguments of their most eminent member and former president, who had urged at every opportunity that the commission should go to Rembrandt van Rijn.

He tried during that walk to forget the other occasion when he had told the same sort of news: the awkward young man arrived from Leyden with a mourning band around his hat; the little shop with its stock not yet discredited; the ardent, blind assertion that wealth and glory had come, without the sour afterthought that wealth and glory, like meadows and old houses, also pass. Had they embraced that morning? he asked himself as he walked along the margin of Heer Lingelbach's labyrinth—an atrocity, really, with its boxwood cut into fantastic shapes and its bad statues smiling inanely in the misty orange-tinted twilight. As he remembered it, they *had* embraced. That too was gone—the business of embracing. His old body, scrubbed and austere as a monk's, kept to itself these days. Sleep, untouching sleep, was all that he and his wife shared now on the cool, unrumpled sheets. Gretha gave him a peck on the cheek, and Jan gave him a clap on the shoulder, and their little girl curtsied and was taken off to the nursery: and once in a tavern not so long ago he had been so drunk that if he had been anybody but the Heer Doctor and the Heer Burgomaster he would have caught the serving girl by the wrist and kissed her out of sheer loneliness . . . This place, too, with its tawdry imitation of the rustic and the antique, had once been open meadow, where innocent cows had chewed their cuds and bumped their moist muzzles against each other . . . "We step, and we do not step into the same river"—who had said it?—one of the Greeks. But which of the Greeks he could not remember; there were times when his mind seemed as inept as his knobby hands.

As he walked up the path to the decent, ugly house, the face of the little girl suddenly appeared above the clipped hedges: straight black bangs pushed fiercely to one side, button nose, small and beautifully shaped mouth with gleaming teeth, eyes that were turned into slate-grey crescents by a grimace. "Do you want my papa?" she asked, dodging out of the range of his hand as it reached across the hedge to touch her head. "Because if you do, you won't see him. He isn't here!" She made the last statement as if she had scored a great point in a secret game. "He went away. He was mad at everybody. He was mad at Titus *and* Mama. The only one he wasn't mad at was *me*."

"Then I suppose I'll go in and talk to Titus and your mama." His disappointment and the sturdy way she stood behind the hedge—her stocky legs apart, her square chin thrust out, her hands clasped behind her back to discourage a person from trying to touch *them* either—impelled him to add sardonically, "That is, if *you* have no objections."

It was Titus who answered his knock; and in the orange light he looked wan and depressed. "Oh, it's you, Heer Doctor," he said. "What a pleasure!" And though the old remembered pitch was gone—his voice had settled long ago to a pleasing baritone—the cordiality was still there, together with the courtliness.

"Cornelia tells me your father's out." He said it ruefully: though he was scarcely counting on the sort of response he had gotten in Hendrik Uylenburgh's shop, he was pained at the realization that there was to be no response at all.

"Yes, unfortunately. He ought to be back soon though. Won't you step in? I'll go out to the kitchen and tell Hendrikje you're here."

The lights had not yet been kindled in the front room. He let himself down onto one of the hard and serviceable chairs and used the solitary moment to rub his accursed knee. It was pleasant, at any rate, to think of what the nine hundred florins forthcoming from the Surgeons' Guild could do to a room like this: drape the stark windows, build a mantelpiece around the bleak fireplace, pad the chairs with leather, break the cold expanse of the barest of the walls with a chest. The barest of the walls—he noticed that there was something on it, something small in a fine frame of teak or ebony. Horizontals and verticals—ships—a Hercules Seghers. But Titus returned just then, carrying a lighted lamp; and he suppressed an impulse to get up and look because the young man passed the drawing with what seemed a conscious disregard and placed the lamp on the farthest window sill, so that none of

549

the light, still weak in the orange dusk, settled on that wall. He sat down then in one of a pair of chairs opposite the doctor, and began to chatter with forced blitheness about insignificant things.

Nodding and making the appropriate answers, the visitor watched him covertly. Was he well? That flush on his cheekbones—was it fever or only rawness after weeping? Did the chest under his respectable linen shirt seem a little concave? His right hand, narrow and veined, hung down listlessly over the arm of the chair until he sensed the doctor's look upon it; then it grew animated with the old elegant gestures. The visitor was on the point of saying, "Tell me, Titus, is anything the matter?" when Hendrikje came in carrying a tray with wine and goblets and thin slices of gingerbread. She was duskier than ever, tanned with summer gardening; her body strained richly at the seams of her old blue dress; and her hair was braided and coiled in a heavy, glossy coronet around her head. It was strange to see the exquisite young man waiting on her as if she were the fragile mistress of some French salon: he took the tray from her and placed it on the sill beside the lamp; he served for her, offering her a plate and a goblet first; he would not sit down until she had settled herself in her chair. "You want to see Rembrandt, and God knows when he'll be back," she said as soon as the amenities had been taken care of and Titus was seated beside her. "I hope he won't be staying out half the night again. He'd be terribly sorry, I know, to miss a visit with *you*."

It struck him that he had never seen her so handsome, so self-possessed, exuding so much confidence and well-being and serenity. The calamity had been for her a blessed relief: she had told him on other occasions how much she loved this house, how utterly at home she felt in this neighborhood, how not a soul hereabouts—including the Reverend Kemperer—ever took her to be anything but Vrouw van Rijn. Evidently Rembrandt's walking out in a rage this evening had troubled her only as a breeze momentarily ruffles the surface of a deep pond: whatever had gone wrong she was plainly certain she could set right. The doctor shrugged and smiled at her over his goblet. "Oh, he'll probably be back before I'm on my way," he said.

"Maybe yes and maybe no," said Titus in a melancholy voice.

"Don't worry. Just don't worry. We've had enough of that." She reached across the little space between the chairs and patted the young man's hanging hand, and he curled his pale fingers around her brown ones and managed to produce a smile. "I'd worry if we were wrong, Titus, but this time we're right."

"Maybe—"

"No, dear, there's no 'maybe' about it. Doctor, I ask you, could anybody in his right mind pay twenty-five florins for *that*? And another three today for African wood to make a frame for it. Twenty-eight florins hung on the wall, and the little girl—go get her, Titus—the little girl runs around in skirts up to her knees, and I watch everything, even how many carrots I put in a stew."

But the doctor was worn with a day of weighing counterclaims and dispensing considered advice; he had come to deliver good tidings and share in the rejoicing, and he wanted to dodge the question as deliberately as Cornelia—whom Titus had gone to bring in out of the garden—had dodged his hand. "Ah, well, Hendrikje, I wouldn't be too hard with him. He's had the collecting habit for years, and nobody breaks a habit just like that." He tried to snap his fingers, but the hateful knobby things only slid noiselessly against each other. "Anyway, that twenty-eight florins won't make much difference. He's got a good commission coming his way—that's what I dropped in to tell him about."

She looked at him quizzically, raising her straight dark eyebrows as if she had heard that tune too often and was surprised that he should be singing it too. Then she immediately assumed a serene and cheerful expression, doubtless because the young man was there, holding the sullen little one by the plump upper round of her arm. "Thanks, Titus. All right, now, Cornelia, it's after eight. Wash your hands and face and go upstairs," she said.

"It's *not* after eight."

"Just wash your hands and face and—"

"It is *not*. I didn't hear the bells."

"Bells or no bells, do what I tell you—go to bed."

"And *you* go to the devil. You and Titus can both go to the devil."

Not one of the three of them started or ventured a smile. The child, frightened by her own audacity and awed by the silent and expressionless court around her, stared malevolently at the floor and then turned and stamped loudly up the stairs.

"She learned that from *him*," said Hendrikje. "That's what he said before he went out because I complained about the money he spent on the frame."

"Forget about it," said the doctor. "She will, too. As I was saying, there'll be good money coming in—nine hundred florins."

"Nine hundred florins? Dear God, for what?"

"The Surgeons' Guild is ordering another Regents' piece."

"Really? Is it settled?" Her tone was guarded; she had rejoiced over nothing too many times before.

"Oh, yes, it's all settled. They signed the papers this afternoon. I wouldn't have come to tell him otherwise."

"Of course you wouldn't." But there was no easing in her manner. Her eyes, large and thoughtful, looked at him and yet were plainly considering something else.

"It's the kind of thing I'm sure he'll want to do," he said.

"Oh, yes, it'll be very good for him. It's just what he needs, especially right now. Only, the nine hundred florins—I wonder if we'll

551

ever see them. The creditors weren't all paid off by those sales, you know, and the minute they hear he has a commission like that you can be sure they'll be after him again. Especially if he keeps running to the auctions and giving people the notion that he's got money to throw away—"

"I don't think he'll be doing that, Hendrikje," he said; but he avoided her dark look, troubled as he was by the thought of the unsatisfied creditors and the suspicion that what he offered in his friend's defense was a peacemaker's easy lie.

"It isn't that I want anything for myself, Doctor," she said, laying her hand on Titus's wrist. "It's only for the children. You know how young ones are: they *will* grow out of their clothes and they have to be properly fed. *He* never wants anything himself but cheese and herring, so he thinks that ought to be good enough for everybody else—and it's good enough for me, God knows. But young bones need meat to grow on, and I never knew a child that didn't hanker after a treat once in a while —it's no sin to want an orange or a fig or a piece of gingerbread."

Oranges, figs, counsel and kisses, a light left in a dark bedroom, endless patience to answer questions—these were motherly means of binding a child; and it was all the more to her credit that she had so bound the lad, especially since he was not her own, especially since she might have felt his charm and his aristocratic comeliness as a reproach. If the thin fingers that stroked the back of her hand indicated unwavering solidarity and devotion, it was no more than she had come by honestly, giving and getting love day in, day out, when the father remembered to look for it only when his spirit was too broken to brood over visions or his hand too tired to control the brush. And yet, and yet . . . He could not justify it, but he felt a twinge of distress at the sight of their oneness, a distress so keen that he wanted it reduced to a matter of florins and pennies, taken out of the area of love and laid safely in some neat category marked out by the law. "I really ought to ask Abraham Franzen about this. He's my attorney at law—Rembrandt knows him. Let me ask him if there wouldn't be some way to put the money out of reach of the creditors," he said.

"Maybe it could be fixed some way so that the money wouldn't legally be in his hands at all." Her eyes were veiled now, focused on her lap. "Maybe Titus could be his agent . . ."

The young man did not move an eyelash or a fingertip. His look was unavailable too, fastened on the toe of his shoe; and the very fact that no glance passed between him and his foster mother suggested somehow that they had talked this matter over before. "But there's one thing we're losing sight of," he said. "After all, Titus is only eighteen. Until he comes of age, he can't really act in an official capacity."

"But isn't he doing that already, law or no law?" she said.

"Yes, Doctor." The young man crossed his legs with studied ease, leaned forward, and clasped his hands around his knee. "When I sell

Father's etchings to the dealers—and I *have* sold a great many of them, I haven't been doing anything else since I'm out of Latin school—when I bargain for the prices and keep the accounts and do the collecting, wouldn't you call that acting in an official capacity?"

The sky beyond the stark window had paled out now to an even, watery blue, and the strengthened lamplight made the young face vulnerable and appealing in its eagerness and its pride. "Of course, Titus, it certainly is," he said quickly. "All I meant was, a few years will have to go by before you can put your signature on a legal document."

"Oh, as to signing papers—Hendrikje here could always sign the papers."

They *had* talked about it—he knew it as surely as if he had heard them. They had made a plan, a plot, a benevolent plot of course, to save themselves and the little one from the old man, and the old man from himself; and they were convinced that he—just and circumspect citizen that he was—would make a willing third in their conspiracy. But she was in her thirties, and the boy was in his teens, and neither of them could know how painful it would be for another old man with knobby fingers and a stiff knee and a mind still loyal to razed buildings and gone stretches of meadowland to take their part against the beaten, the almost-forgotten, the prematurely old.

Her voice moved serenely, reasonably into the charged stillness. "If there was some way of doing it—if Titus and I could form a kind of partnership to sell his work, he wouldn't have to deal with the creditors any more. He'd be free to teach and paint, and that's what he keeps saying he wants more than anything in the world."

A partnership? Then it had gone as far as that between them. While the master stood bemused at his easel or drank as he must be drinking tonight in some neighborhood tavern, they had already thought out the terms without the help of any legal adviser: what they wanted was not only the right to dispose of his works but control of the purse strings too. And now he could not bring himself to look at either of them; instead he stared blankly at the cool, remote blueness on the other side of the windowpane.

"Besides, it would give Titus a start in life, something he could keep on doing later. And Titus needs something like that, the good Lord knows."

He had to nod—about that she was right enough; so far the boy had gotten nothing but the poorest of pickings at the feast: his tastes and manners shaped to fit a life beyond his means and most of his inheritance frittered away. Nobody had troubled to provide him with any skills but the unremunerative ones of the aristocrat; he possessed nothing, really, but his wit and his charm, and the least he could ask for was an opportunity to put them to use. Managing his father's business—if he didn't do that, what *was* he supposed to do? And yet, and yet . . . How would it feel to have a stripling ask, no matter how wittily or graciously, what had become of twenty-five florins spent on a Hercules Seghers, or ten laid out for a nameday gift, or two squandered in a tavern on an evening when all things present seemed meaningless and all things past were dimmed and nothing had any reality but the waiting grave?

She had seized upon his nod; now her eyes were wide and intent. "Really, Doctor," she said, "it's the only way, as far as I can see. If we don't do it, and do it soon, we'll be out of this house and back in some filthy attic—and what that's like, only a person who's been through it can understand."

"But to ask a man to give up control of his own money—"

"Believe me, Doctor, we don't like the idea any better than you do," said Titus. "There's no telling how he's going to take it—"

No, he thought, there certainly isn't—he might rear up like a tormented lion and roar the two of you out of your wits. And the thought gave him a secret and malicious pleasure, so that he had to stifle a smile.

"Titus is more worried about that than I am," she said. "As I figure it, either it'll suit him and he'll take it the way he took it when we rented this house, or he'll act pretty much the same way he acted about the bankruptcy."

The way he acted about the bankruptcy . . . She had a remarkable head on her shoulders, this sergeant's daughter from Ransdorp. She had seen what it would never have occurred to him to count on—the black streak of self-destructiveness that had made the master stop to stare at the shapes under the tarpaulin, that had impelled him to parade in front of the little crowd of bidders, that had been the source of the terrible and tragic self-portrait painted at the inn, in which his suffering, his nervelessness, his utter disgrace had been set down on canvas for himself and everybody else to see. His need to plunge still further into misery and shame as a gesture of defiance—she could depend upon it, she knew it all too well.

"Still," said Titus, picking nervously at a loose thread on his cuff, "I wish it were settled."

"So do I," said Hendrikje. "We can't afford not to settle it, with all that money coming in. Last week one of those old creditors of his got wind of what he'd spent for the drawing and turned up here to ask for something on account, and you can imagine how hard it was to convince him there just wasn't anything to be handed out. And there'll be other ones like him, you can be sure, as soon as news of this Regents' piece gets around."

"Maybe we could avoid the fireworks altogether," said the young man, resorting to the old feverish gaiety, "if we brought the business up while you were here—especially after you'd set the stage by telling him about the commission—I don't imagine he'd say the sort of thing he would if the three of us were by ourselves."

The doctor looked straight into the amber eyes—they were anxious

and supplicating and seemed doubly so in the artificially merry face—
and shook his head. Just, sane, and necessary as this plan of theirs might
be, he would have no part in it, not even as a spectator. "No, I don't
think so," he said with a coolness he knew he might some day regret, for
the boy would need friends and he did not want to shut him out. "No, I
believe I'd better be going. It's a long walk back, and I have a stiff knee
joint, and tomorrow's another day, and a very crowded one for me. You
two can tell him about the commission. Oh, yes, and ask him if he'll
stop by at the Guild Hall tomorrow. I'll be there around four, and I'd
like to present him to Dr. Deijman. As to the nine hundred florins—
it'll be several weeks before anything will be forthcoming, so there's no
great hurry to settle with him about—about the partnership. I'd let him
enjoy himself a little if I were you. After all, it's a long time since he's
had a big commission—a long time, for that matter, since he's had anything to congratulate himself about."

The lad, obviously abashed, and just as obviously undeterred from
his purpose, shook hands with him constrainedly and retreated to another room. It was she who went with the visitor to the door and walked
with him along the hedge to the end of the path. In the still, cool evening, with the dim wall of the house behind her and the pale grass
around her feet, the dark, rich figure under the colorless sky was less
Hendrikje Stoffels than woman—the bearer of children and the giver
of nourishment.

"I'm afraid you think ill of me, Doctor, and I'm sorry for it," she said.

"I don't think ill of you. You'll do what you have to do—"

"What I have to do for the children, Doctor. Not for myself." She
said it without pride, but with a stern dignity; and he could do no less
than nod again before he bade her good night.

His knee gave him less trouble than on his way over, but that was
probably because his mind was giving him more. From behind one of
the fantastically cut hedges of Heer Lingelbach's labyrinth, over the
splashing of the fountain, rose a cascade of girl's laughter, such laughter
as a person takes for granted in his youth and almost never hears in his
latter days. So *she* had laughed, the dead one, dancing among the Turkish swords and Chinese ceremonial robes in her cousin's dusty shop,
stopping to catch her breath and pressing her perfumed handkerchief
against her round, moist brow. She had been no mere breeder and giver
of nourishment: she had been volatile, swift, like running water, or
fire, and to remember her even now quickened the tide of his turgid
blood. She was a man's woman, a maker of children only to fulfill the
claims of love—to conspire with the son against the sire would have
been for her unthinkable, to have bound and weakened the sharer of
her bed would have been merely a way of depleting her singular treasure and robbing herself thereby . . . But now that he had remembered her and taken his late delight in her, almost as if those looks, those
kisses had fallen not on his friend's face but on his own, the sound

reason by which a man must govern his life reasserted itself. Had she lived, how would it be with her now? What would she be—he did not want to envision it—but an aging, withering child? Could she have remained unshaken while their hopes went out like candles at a banquet, one by one? Could she have stood unmoved while the great house in the Breestraat was stripped of its glories, or lain beside him uncomplaining at the inn to ease the slow agony of his disgrace? Could she have been a fortress for his children, and a maid and mistress in his house, and an advocate for those who *would* grow and *would* eat and *would* live on when their begetters were at rest in their graves?

He turned and looked back at the house, less ugly now because there were yellow lights at the windows. What would come about in those rooms would come about—he could do nothing to stop it, any more than he could stop the burghers of Amsterdam from loosening their old Protestant ties with the North and turning to Spain and France, any more than he could put an end to the plague or cure a sated and self-indulgent generation of a passion for vapid family scenes and flattering portraits whose surfaces were slick as silk. Things change . . . we step, and we do not step into the same river. That was from Heraclitus, and he went his way smiling with satisfaction that his rusty brain should have ground the answer out at last.

BOOK X

1660 - 1662

Actually, though she and Titus had been so hesitant and devious about sending him to the City Hall on their business, Rembrandt was not put out with what they wanted him to do. If they were managing his affairs for him—and they *had* been managing them, and very shrewdly, too, for a number of months now—it was natural for them to want the City Council to grant the boy an early majority so that he could bring whatever bargaining he was doing to a close without running home to have his foster mother put her name on the necessary documents. After the first weeks of silent, self-devouring resentment he had come round to accepting their arrangement almost cheerfully. Having seen nothing since the Seghers that had stirred up the old avidity, he wanted no extra money in his purse; if his unsatisfied creditors walked past him with averted eyes in the street, at least they no longer intruded upon the peace of his house; and a single month's accounts had been enough to prove that Hendrikje and the lad were doing much better for him than he could do for himself. He had no obligations any more except the teaching and painting; and so much time was left for those—such long, intent mornings and such serene, unbroken afternoons—that he wondered how many of the hours of his life he had frittered away picking through the immense rubbish heap of his business. It was an unusual thing, then, and a not altogether welcome break in the calm rhythm of his days, for him to leave the studio that afternoon in November and go to see the new Burgomaster Jan Six at the new City Hall.

Like Dr. Tulp, and unlike almost everybody else in Amsterdam, he had no enthusiasm for the fine, proud public building. It belonged in the same category as "the new houses"—clean of line, spare of ornament, pretentious in its very claim to unpretentiousness. He had been one of the few who had regretted that the old Town Hall, whose place it had so completely usurped, had burned down by what the Amsterdammers called "a lucky accident." He had made a careful, tender drawing of the ruin, recording what was left of the reverend tower while others around him had muttered against it for standing so rugged in the midst of the wreckage—it would cost thousands of florins, they said, to pull it down. And though nine years had passed between the night of the fire and this windy afternoon, he could not see the altered horizon without a sense of loss.

The new Town Hall, with its modish stone facing and its regular bands of monotonous windows and its little domed tower set in the middle of its gabled roof, looked like an upstart under the bleak grey sky. Its unbroken oblong mass dwarfed the few who walked the unworn and colorless area of paving stones around it; its isolation gave it a kind of raw haughtiness. Looking up at all those windows, it was impossible not to think that too many municipal officials and clerks and clerks' assistants sat at too many desks inside, trying to record and remember too much.

Nor was the interior any more hospitable with its splendid decoration in gold and silver, its arched ceilings carved and painted in the classical manner, its marble arcades letting in the wintry light in chilling profusion, its vast, pale marble floor. From the center of the great hall he glanced, but only for a moment and without emotion, at the four tremendous spaces still awaiting canvases: two great oblongs above ornate fireplaces with pillared marble mantelpieces, and two huge lunettes, very high up, stretching between the arc of the ceiling and the top of the second-story arcade. The work of Govaert Flinck, his former apprentice and earliest renegade, was to fill them all; but he had known that for months, and the bitterness had passed. He was working at what he wanted to work at—that was the phoenix which had risen for him out of the ashes of his poverty and his shame, and he was satisfied. He thought of the *Saint Peter Denying Christ* on his easel at home, all scarlet and red-brown and firelight and shadow, with the divine face turning out of the darkness to mark the fulfillment of the prophecy and deliver the reproach; and he was troubled less by the stretches of waiting wall than by the smell of damp plaster and the penetrating cold of a building that had not stood long enough to be dried out by the sun.

The young Burgomaster, in his second-story office, was also feeling the cold. He sat with a cloak over his shoulders behind a desk covered with an accumulation of papers ornamented with wax seals and streamers of ribbon. More and more, as he moved into his late thirties, he had grown to resemble his portrait, possibly because the restoration of the Stuarts threatened to cause almost as much international difficulty as their fall, and possibly because poor Gretha had miscarried twice. His mouth was firm almost to hardness; there was a single horizontal furrow across his brow and a steely keenness in his eyes. But he rose with no diminution of the old respect and hurried out from behind his parchment barricade and embraced the master. What the ordinary run of citizens had rejected and forgotten *he* made a point of valuing still, as he valued the fine old chairs that had come down to him through four generations and the heavy gold medallion, definitely out of fashion now but the pride of his maternal grandfather, which hung around his neck on a long gold chain. The Weijmars, the Sixes, the Tulps—Rembrandt van Rijn was *their* painter, a sort of living family heirloom, to be treated on all occasions, public or private, with every mark of honor; and it occurred to the aging master as the smooth cheek touched his that a broader fame might have earned him less warmth in this particular quarter: he provided the young Burgomaster with something to be at odds with the commonality about.

Sitting on the corner of his desk, Jan Six asked how things were going over at the Rozengracht: Was the little agency flourishing? Did Cornelia like the Dame school now that she had grown used to it? What pictures were in the making besides that splendid *Peter Denying Christ*? Two portraits of Titus, a series of single figures of the Apostles?—he could hardly wait to see them; and since Gretha was getting her strength back, they would be coming over soon. There was no need to hurry the conversation or to twist it in the direction of the business to be broached. The talk ended, as the master knew it would, with Jan's asking cordially, "And what can I do for you?"

There was no need either to plead the convenience of an early majority for Titus; Jan offered at once to take the request to the City Council. "It'll probably be a few months before it's granted—things *do* get behind here," he said, looking ruefully at the clutter on his desk. "But I'm sure the Council will grant it. I only wish everything I wanted to do in your behalf could be as easy. But the older people get, the more stubborn they are, and we seem to have more octogenarians around the City Hall than they have at the Old Men's Home."

He knew that he ought to ask what foredoomed good offices the new Burgomaster had been engaging in of late, but he could not bring himself to put the question. Though it would be churlish to say that he wanted no kind attempts to restore his ruined reputation, that any such attempts were bound to bring nothing but new embarrassments, such was precisely his case: he wanted to submerge himself in the peace of his obscurity, he wanted all of them to let him alone. "Heaven knows," he said after a long silence, "I hate to ask you or your mother or your father-in-law for any more favors. You've all done enough and more than enough." And he put up his hand to fasten the cloak under his chin.

"But you're not going, are you, Master? I was about to ask my secretary to bring us some brandy. Won't you sit down and stay awhile?"

"No, Jan, you're busy, your desk's covered with papers. And, anyway, I must be going—I told the lads I'd look in on them before they closed up the studio."

"In that case, I suppose all I can do is walk you downstairs."

And that, he knew, was another attempt to confer an honor: it could do a man no harm to be seen with the Burgomaster's arm over his shoulder. Stopping a third of the way down the staircase, above the heads of those who walked the marble floor, Jan Six looked out over the dizzying prospect of arches and arcades and carved capitals, and fetched up a sigh. "Those spaces—I never look at them without thinking what *you* could have done with them," he said.

How was a person to answer? He could not even shrug, because the hand was still on his shoulder.

"I tried, you know," said his companion. "I really tried."

But don't tell me about it, he thought, feeling the blood mounting to

561

his cheeks. "I'm sure you did, Jan, and it was very good of you. You know I'm grateful," he said.

"Unfortunately, there's nothing for you to be grateful for. And I'm convinced that there could have been, if only the City Council hadn't seen fit to hand the whole business over to old Vondel."

He turned his back on the broad, cold view, planted his elbow on the balustrade, and resigned himself to listening to what he might have heard more comfortably in Jan Six's office over brandy—the story of the most recent useless effort made by the Weijmars and the Sixes in his behalf and to his shame. It was not as he had convinced himself it had been: he had not been merely forgotten in the choosing of the artist for this remunerative and dignifying commission. His overzealous friend had gone to Vondel in spite of his father-in-law's warnings that there had always been bad blood between the master and the Muiden Circle; Jan Six had not been able to believe that Rembrandt would not be called in, especially after he had been told what subjects the poet had assigned for the canvases. Scenes of rebellion, scenes of martial prowess, scenes to commemorate the victorious issue of the long struggle with Spain—who could do them better than the painter of the Regents' piece at the Military Club? Surely anybody, even a doddering old poet gone soft and Catholic, could see what such a master could do for the City Hall. But the doddering poet had not seen it, had explained in his pompously benign manner that the scenes were to refer to the war with Spain only symbolically, by presenting other fights for freedom, preferably classical ones that would fall in nicely with the marble arcades. The lunette over there, for instance—the master was forced to look toward it over his shoulder—was to hold a canvas that could be a marvelous thing: a painting of the Batavian Julius Civilis, the first Dutch rebel, taking a sword-oath with his chieftains that he would drive the Romans from the Fatherland. And who was to do it—it and the other lunette and the two pieces over the mantels? Flinck—the name lent itself perfectly to derision. By toadying to the proper people at Muiden, Flinck had put himself in the way of five or six thousand florins, to say nothing of what the commission would do for his reputation. Arguments were useless—the assignment was already given out. Nobody else could achieve the proper classical atmosphere, nobody else could be trusted to render in color and line the poem in which Vondel had described the art that ought ideally to adorn the City Hall and uplift the minds of the citizenry—nobody but Flinck.

The master could understand the young man's infatuation with his own eloquence. Inarticulate as he himself was, he had been carried away in the same fashion that evening in the garden of the Old Men's Home, when he and Saskia had come up in their excessive finery to offer unwilling congratulations to the benign poet and he had said certain things to von Sandrart that would have been better left unsaid—things that he might not have to be reckoning with now when there was no high-heartedness left and it was only dreary to have enemies in high places. "Oh, well, it was bound to be Flinck, and I suppose he'll do the sort of thing that's wanted and do it solidly," he said.

"He's certainly not killing himself to get it done in a hurry."

"It's a big commission, Jan." One of the lunettes alone was much larger than the Regents' piece at the Military Club.

"It's a month since he reported to the City Council that the cartoons were finished. What the devil are cartoons? Sketches?"

"No, a stage beyond the sketches. Full-size drawings of what's to go onto the canvas. The Italians use them a lot; they prick little holes into the outlines and then blow red chalk-dust through the pricked cartoons. It's an accepted way of working—for some people, I suppose, it's the best. I don't do it because anything more than a sketch ties me down—I keep changing things, inventing things as I go along—" He broke off, obsessed for an instant by the thought of inventing things on so vast and regal a surface.

"Naturally you would change as you went along," said Jan Six. "I should think anybody with a grain of imagination would want to."

"Not necessarily. Michelangelo used cartoons."

"Don't tell that to poor old Vondel. It's all he needs to convince him that Flinck is a second Michelangelo."

"Has anyone seen the cartoons?" He regretted the pointless curiosity that had driven the question out of him. He did not want to be involved even to the extent of being curious; he wanted to be let alone.

"No. He was supposed to bring them in for the applause of the City Council last Monday, but he didn't turn up. It seems he hasn't been feeling too well."

He did not ask, "What's the trouble?" His spirit had not leaped at a black conjecture, though his conscience behaved precisely as if it had; his conscience, knowing too much of mortality—how many had he seen into their graves?—made some ritualistic motion of warding off: it was as if his conscience were crossing itself. "He'll be turning up with them one of these days," he said after a protracted silence. "And when he does, I'm sure everybody will be satisfied."

"They're bound to be. Vondel will see to that."

Something—perhaps the strange way his own heart would halt and stammer of late—something made him say, "Flinck's by no means a poor artist. Even without Vondel to convince them, the members of the City Council would like what he did. He turns out a very respectable canvas—"

The young Burgomaster linked arms with him and started on down the staircase. "He ought to," he said. "After all, he got his training from you."

That was true enough, but again it would have been better left unmentioned. Bitterness was futile, and, worse still, it was distracting; it marred his pleasure over the accomplishment of his little mission and his escape from the ornate and alien coldness of the new City Hall. It was not until he had walked half a mile that he could forget how much he *had* taught Govaert Flinck, how large and beautifully placed the empty lunettes were, how tepid a talent it was that must settle every line and shadow beforehand by means of cartoons.

*

The sudden death of Govaert Flinck, coming in his early maturity and at the apex of his fame, was a shock to everybody including the scion of the house of Six. Possibly because his lively tongue had run away with him a few days earlier on the staircase of the City Hall, he was so upset by the news and so scrupulous not to take advantage of it in unseemly haste that he did not mention the vacant commission even to his mother for two weeks. His delay was based on an amiable conviction that the members of the Muiden Circle were so deep in grief that they could not give much thought to the empty spaces: in the society in which he moved, it was considered gross vulgarity in an heir to ask the amount of an estate before the bronze plaque had been set into the church floor above the dead benefactor. And he was appalled, he felt that his own decency had been shamefully taken advantage of when his secretary told him that Vondel had decided within a week that Jan Lievens and Juriaen Ovens were each to have one of the oblongs and one of the lunettes.

"But, good God, why the hurry?" he asked, looking over the piled-up papers at the greyish old face. "The poor fellow is scarcely cold in his grave."

"I wouldn't know, your honor," said the secretary. "Perhaps it isn't so; I'm only telling you what I heard next door in Heer Cornelis's office. You could probably find out more about it from the Heer Burgomaster Tulp."

Some of his outrage veered off from Vondel and ran in the direction of his father-in-law, who very likely had gotten the ill news some time earlier and had kept it to himself. The doctor had not been with him in this affair from the beginning. He had shown so much concern over a possible failure that he would not even envision how much their friend stood to gain from a possible success; he had answered every argument with the same rigid and circumspect counsel: "Let him alone, Jan. He's been through too much. He's content, or relatively so, with things the way they are. All he wants is to be let alone." The hopelessness was probably due in part to the fact that *The Anatomy Lesson of Doctor Deijman* had made such a small ripple in the community; but the doctor was forgetting that to be displayed at the Surgeons' Guild was one thing and to be on view at the new City Hall was quite another. Lievens and Ovens—it was unthinkable, and he could not imagine himself sitting through the remainder of the afternoon with it gnawing at his mind.

"All right," he told the secretary, "that's just what I'll do. If anybody wants me, he can find me upstairs."

But that office where he had meant to relieve himself by shouting what he thought of Vondel and his friends was unavailable to him. Something about the massive oak door told him, before he turned the handle, that it was locked: the doctor had finished his day's business early and was gone. Gone to the Pest House again, he thought, with no less exasperation than he would have thought, Gone partridge hunting. He rattled the handle, knocked on the beautifully beveled panel all in vain, and started back down the marble steps, mouthing to himself the tasteful oaths of a gentleman.

At the turn of the stairway he stopped and looked over. No matter what frame of mind he was in—even on the days when he had been heartsick about Gretha's weakness and his daughter's disappointment over the little brother that God had decided not to send after all—he could take pleasure in the serene nobility of the prospect below. At this time of day, close to half past four—the crowds of the curious had moved to neighboring taverns; and those who remained, set widely apart on the great floor, were present on legitimate business. From his dizzying vantage point he could identify the few whose smallness provided a scale for the magnificence of the place: Vrouw van Spiegel and Vrouw van Huydencooper were waiting under the Shield of the City for their husbands to take them to the dinner at Burgomaster de Graef's; Heer Keister was expecting Heer Cornelis to join him in their usual preprandial brandy; and the little messenger running across the polished marble was hurrying to get the municipal mail to the boat before it left the Utrecht Gate. And there—he drew in his breath and grasped the cold balustrade—there, in front of the great mantelpiece to the left was the arch-enemy, the arch-dodderer, the venerable Joost van den Vondel, standing in conversation with Tesselschade Visscher. With their dear, dead friend scarcely buried, they were disgracefully, unbelievably engaged in talking about his successors. At least they were looking up at the vast expanse above the marble mantel with bland satisfaction, as though they were already seeing there the work of some new protégé.

His indignation propelled him further down the stairs to a place from which he could see them more clearly: the round head of the poet, with its grey locks flowing down from the bald spot in the middle, as if he had been tonsured, and the faded, sand-colored hair of the great lady of Dutch letters, piled up intricately and topped with an ostrich plume. Both were impressively dressed, she with the remains of a large, pale beauty encased in black satin and he in grey woolen whose austerity suggested the cloisters he had been frequenting of late. They were old, more than old enough to have been his parents; they had been notables when he had still been in his cradle; they had borne their dignity so long that his own seemed by contrast a crass novelty; and he had to remind himself that he was a burgomaster, son of an illustrious house and heir to a prodigious fortune, in order to keep himself from retreating to his office. But who and what, after all, was Joost van den Vondel? The author of dramas that were puerile put side by side with Corneille's and Shakespeare's, the producer of facile lyrics that were jingles compared to Crashaw's and Donne's. He had kept a stocking shop, he had gone Catholic, his son had run away to the Indies with stolen money—matters which the Amsterdammers had seen fit to overlook, though they had never forgotten that Rembrandt's father had kept a malt mill in Leyden, that Rembrandt's wife had worn too many jewels, that Rembrandt's house had been the haunt of Mennonites and Jews. And, close to the bottom of the stairs, he saw in a flash the reason for the difference and gathered therefrom the courage to stride across the resounding marble floor. Joost van den Vondel, being vacuous in himself, had been able to assume a pose and a mask—a pose of venerable calm, a mask of unassailable dignity that lesser folk could admire and depend upon. And Rembrandt van Rijn, great in his art and great in his spirit, could not be contained in any preconceived mold. The mighty self had smashed whatever acceptable form the world had tried to confine it in. The passion, the rage, the grief, the fierce and uncontrollable need to search and to know had always broken through.

It was this insight that gave him the confidence to accost the two. "A good day to you, madame," he said, looking straight into the eyes of Tesselschade Visscher—large greenish eyes that had learned to be fervent over nothing. "And to you, too, Heer van den Vondel." It was gratifying to encounter exactly what he had envisioned: a benign imperturbability. "I happened to see you from the staircase, and I thought that now might be as good a time as any to bring up a matter that's been on my mind for several days."

He saw by a slight narrowing of the deep-set eyes of the poet and a faint flutter of the plump, smooth hands of his votary that the two of them knew perfectly well what matter. Vondel's puzzled question, "And what would that be, Heer Burgomaster?" was only a bid for more time.

"Now that Govaert Flinck is dead—God rest his soul—"

"It was a terrible loss," said Tesselschade Visscher, shaking her head and agitating her ostrich plume and lifting her moist eyes to the vaulting. "An irreparable loss."

"In the flower of his prime," said the poet, stressing the words as if he were testing their right to be included in a forthcoming elegy.

"Stricken as all of you must be," said the young Burgomaster, keeping down the devilish smile that twitched the corners of his mouth, "I don't suppose you've given much thought to who will be doing the canvases now that he's gone."

To tell a lie was not in the estimable role that the poet and the community had established for Joost van den Vondel. Luckily he had his Tesselschade there to provide the necessary diverting action: she raised her eyes again to the vast arches and talked as fast as a female author who had written hundreds of lines saying absolutely nothing about the River Amstel could be expected to talk in an emergency. Poor Govaert, he had thought of nothing but those paintings, even on his deathbed. He had bequeathed to Joost—a sacred legacy—the finished cartoons. Whatever went up there could only be a bloodless shadow of what would have come into being if he had lived.

"Yes," said Jan Six, "but something will have to go up there."

The poet laid his stubby fingers on the tight sleeve of his handmaid. Plainly, the brash young man was more than a woman could be expected to cope with. "After what little thought I've been able to give the matter, I've more or less come to the conclusion that the commission should be evenly divided between Jan Lievens and Juriaen Ovens," he said.

"And what about Rembrandt?"

"If I remember rightly Heer Burgomaster, you came to me once before in Heer van Rijn's behalf." He said it coldly, with the affronted dignity of a schoolmaster who is forced to correct the same error twice. "So I can only repeat now what I told you then: his work is unsuited to the spirit of the City Hall. He has no feeling for the classical. His figures, though some of them have strength, are utterly devoid of grace. On the other hand, Heer Lievens and Heer Ovens—"

"Are nonentities, ciphers." He said it loudly enough to draw the stares of the few who were loitering about. "Ciphers, Heer van den Vondel, who wouldn't even know how to hold a brush if *he* hadn't taught them. It was a poor imitation of what *he* was doing that got Lievens his post at the English Court. As for Ovens, I remember when he was Rembrandt's apprentice, and one of the weakest of the lot. He's fit to design tapestry, maybe, but he's no painter, no painter at all."

Vrouw van Spiegel and Vrouw van Huydencooper were listening, and Tesselschade Visscher's large, pale eyes turned deprecatingly in their direction. To be shouted at in public was also uncongenial to Joost van den Vondel's exalted role: a less rigid man might have laughed or shouted back, but he could only draw up his dumpy body to its insufficient height and begin to shake.

"You see, Heer Burgomaster," said Tesselschade Visscher, laying a plump and appeasing hand on his cuff, "it's no time to talk about poor Govaert's successors. The wound is too fresh, we're all too upset, and particularly Joost—which is only to be expected considering how closely they worked together on this. Lievens and Ovens were the first ones who came to mind, and they do seem the painters most amenable to classical concepts, you'll admit. I myself was saying to Joost that it's a pity von Sandrart happens to be in Germany. Von Sandrart is beyond argument a more masterful artist than either of the other two."

"And so is Rembrandt."

"But not amenable, not classical—"

"He hasn't been asked to be either classical or amenable. I tell you,

Heer van den Vondel, it will be a calculated affront to my family and a lasting disgrace to Amsterdam if this man is passed over for somebody whose reputation he made and one of the worst of the youngsters trained in his studio."

The bells were sounding five, and the arcades were suddenly alive with those who had been waiting in their offices for the signal to go home, and the growing audience plainly put the poet even more out of countenance. "Actually, I haven't spoken formally to either Lievens or Ovens yet," he said in an aggrieved voice, "but apparently what goes on in my little office is general gossip in no time, so I suppose they know."

"Which means you couldn't possibly drop either of them," said the serviceable Visscher.

"No, I certainly couldn't, that's out of the question. But Lievens doesn't seem eager to take on anything that will hold him in town too long, and he may be willing to confine himself to one of the lunettes. In that case, Juriaen could take both the spaces over the mantel, which would leave the other lunette for Heer van Rijn."

In the chatter and scuffle of the five-o'clock exodus, Jan Six considered the offer. He could bargain for more: the poet's cracked mask and the curiosity of minor civil servants staring at the constellation of notables were in his favor; but perhaps if he refused to be grasping his cause would be served more effectively. He could imagine what the public response would be if three of the spaces were filled with the muddy inanities of Lievens and Ovens and the fourth blazed with the warm golds and fiery scarlets, the rich crimsons and shimmering blues and greens that broke the gloom in the Military Club. The contrast would be glaring—let the Amsterdammers see it for themselves.

"I'm sure," he said, looking up significantly at the lunette where Julius Civilis was to perform the sword-oath with his Batavian chieftains, "that Heer van Rijn wouldn't want more than *that*. He's busy at the moment with a series of *Apostles* and a marvelous *Peter Denying Christ,* and large public commissions are the last thing he's thinking about. If he accepts—and I believe I can convince him to—the gain will be less his than Amsterdam's."

The Burgomasters van Spiegel and van Huydencooper, walking together out of the shadow of the lower arcade, sighted the little group and came over to exchange greetings before they joined their ladies; and Jan welcomed them with more than his usual cordiality. God could not have sent him a better pair of witnesses—whatever they heard here would spread like fire at Burgomaster de Graef's supper, and would spread so fast and far that it would be utterly beyond recall. "We've just been talking about what's to be done with the commission that poor Govaert Flinck left behind him, God rest his soul," he said, while the newcomers shook hands all around. "It's all been decided—the work will be split three ways."

"Lievens and Ovens and who else?" asked van Huydencooper. "Von Sandrart?"

"No," said Tesselschade Visscher ruefully. "Rembrandt van Rijn."

*

That in the eyes of the Amsterdammers his day was over, that he was forgotten in favor of the new school that had risen in England and was flourishing in Delft—these things he had taught himself to accept, and to these he was resigned. But never, not from the evening when he had walked discredited out of the Military Club, had it occurred to him to doubt his own greatness. What he painted during the long series of calamities, in the gloom of the desolated house on the Breestraat and the isolation of the Crown Inn and the small and barren studio of his present house was to him manifestly excellent, such work as he would have submitted with confidence to a jury of his dead peers—Dürer and Titian and Michelangelo. Nor was he utterly alone in his assurance; in fact, now that he lived on the outskirts of the city and those who came the long road to visit him were his staunchest supporters, he heard nothing but unmitigated praise. Dr. Tulp, Jan Six and Gretha, the young Philips Koninck who had sought him out in his retreat, the mild and aging little poet Jeremias de Dekker whom he had met one night in a tavern and who kept repeating that the world would remember him not for his own poor verses but because he had known the master—all these sustained him, all these held out to him the hope of a final justification, even if it were to come after he had lain a century in his grave.

It had never occurred to him to ask himself what his family thought: he had always taken it for granted that Hendrikje and Titus were his ardent partisans, that when they saw the worn old man, carelessly dressed and exhausted with his day's labors, staring into the peat fire on the hearth or resting his burning eyes by holding a wet towel against them, they saw in him the greatest of living painters and felt an unwavering respect and compassion for the shattered presence because it had done so much and would yet do more before the coming on of the ultimate night. And it was a faint doubt about Titus's fidelity, raised in that first year when the young man and Hendrikje were conducting the little agency, which taught him that he was still capable of receiving a bruise on his heart.

The lad was out in the world these days—much more than he himself had ever been—meeting dealers, talking to collectors, attending auctions, drinking with men of consequence, men who lived in "the new houses" and informed themselves about "the new art." Talkative as he was, at the supper table he seldom had anything to say concerning those encounters. His gaiety, rubbed a little thin by his exertions, went all to being gallant to his foster mother, to tenderly teasing Cornelia, to asking dutiful questions about whatever painting happened to

569

be on the easel. He had, of course, a sound reason for keeping the stresses of the market place out of the house on the Rozengracht: hadn't they set up the partnership in order to let his father work in peace? Yet it was impossible not to wonder what hanger-on of the Muiden Circle, what devotee of van Dyke, what friend of an old enemy he had run into; it was impossible not to conjecture what remembered barbs or snide shrugs or cold disparagements were hidden behind his quick but tired smile.

In the days when Clement de Jonghe was handling his work, the master had never entertained an instant's doubt as to his agent's enthusiasm. The gentle and cultivated young dealer had always made it obvious that his shop was honored by a Rembrandt canvas, even an unsalable one: if the Amsterdammers did not buy, the fault lay not with the painting but with public triviality or thick-headedness. Clement had never asked what had been and still was an obvious and legitimate question: Why continue to paint scenes from the Bible when there were no ecclesiastics to buy them and no church walls to hang them on, when the House of Orange—the sole great patron of religious painting in the Dutch Republic—had ceased to be interested in collecting anything but the good will of the House of Stuart? Clement had spoken scornfully of the quick turnover in still life and genre as a mark of the decline in taste, and he had seen the infatuation with the glossy surface as a passing fashion, to be taken no more seriously than the passion for Japanese teacups and French lace. But if his fine way of brushing off such matters was not adopted by Titus, the master could not in justice disregard the fact that to his former dealer he had been one valued client among others, whereas the little business conducted from the Rozengracht depended upon him alone.

Certainly his son never took exception to anything he wanted to work at. He followed the progress of the portrait of Jeremias de Dekker —a portrait that would be given as a token of friendship to the sad and undistinguished sitter—as eagerly as he followed the progress of any of the lucrative portrait commissions he had brought in; he showed no impatience when yet another *Apostle* was begun; he ran upstairs before he had even washed his hands when he was told that the Christ figure on the Peter canvas had finally been sketched in; he spent his Sundays sitting for his own likeness in a monk's cowl, and his melancholy and guileless sweetness needed little changing to transform it into religious meditation. Yet now and again something disturbing would pass his lips. He said of his own portrait, "It's wonderful—I only wish I could afford to buy it." He asked whether, now that the de Dekker was finished, his father was intending to do the same honor for Koninck. He said that the face of Saint Peter was so impressive that it might well convince an aging prospective patron to order a portrait; and he added that one corner of the canvas—the corner with the Roman sword and helmet—would have made a splendid still life in itself. Mild hints at the

570

worst, showing like scarcely visible weeds in the rich greensward of the young man's filial devotion. But enough to set up nagging questions: Does he see me still as I was represented to him from his childhood by Tulp and Pinero and Six and the rest—a peerless master whom time will justify? Or does he measure me now by what he hears in the market place: "Your father's portraits are laid on so thick that a person could pick them up by the nose." "Your father paints in a style that has been dead for a generation." "When will your father stop painting our Lord and His Apostles and Abraham and Joseph and confine himself to ordinary things?"

Such doubts gnawed at him most keenly when he had just finished a canvas, partly because he still longed for unstinted praise and partly because he was always too absorbed in what he had completed to turn at once to painting something else. It was so with him that afternoon late in November when he laid the last touch of white on the eyebrow of the lying Saint Peter, and took the canvas from the easel, and set it against the wall to dry. Nobody would buy it, no crowds would come to the Rozengracht to marvel at it, but—so he told himself with an urgency that would make it impossible to sit out the evening before the fire in peace—it was great indubitably. It had come great out of him without any conscious effort to make it so: it was as natural as a stone, as common as clay, and nevertheless sublime. He had done in it effortlessly what he had desperately strained to do when he had painted the *Sacrifice of Abraham*—he had evoked and made manifest a high moment in human history. Every skill that the years had taught him he had lavished on that scene, yet no skill asserted itself: everything was brought into the service of the awesome simplicity. And the moment of betrayal, so honestly and completely rendered in itself, drew in the past and the future—held the remembrance of the bread broken in the upper room and the thin light of Good Friday morning showing above the eastern hills, waking the cock that would crow twice in fulfillment of the prophecy.

And what now? he asked himself as he fenced the canvas in with pieces of a broken easel. Should I call the lad to come up and see it? If I do, will he say it's a pity we don't live in Brussels where there would be room for it in the bishop's palace? Shall I go downstairs and have a mug of beer and get a wet towel and bathe my eyes? But before he had time to make a decision there was a stamping on the stairs—nobody could teach Cornelia to stop stamping; she was forever needing a new pair of shoes. "Papa, Mama says you're to come down right away because Gretha and Jan are here," she said.

While he bent over the basin to freshen himself for his visitors, the little girl stood staring at the big canvas, placing herself not only outside the makeshift fence but a good two feet away from it, as if the life-size figures and the somber burning of the colors in the darkening room had put awe into her heart. He watched her covertly over his shoulder while he dabbled in the water. By the time her generation would begin to attend the auctions, the glossy finish, the endless groupings of fruit and game and flowers, the coy scenes of fashionable domestic life would have become outworn and tiresome affectations. Perhaps her contemporaries would turn back to him, would come in little troops to see the undervalued *Anatomy Lesson of Doctor Deijman*, would ask how it was that such a master had been overlooked by the fools who commissioned the paintings in the City Hall . . . "Come," he said, "we'll go down now."

"Is the man angry, Papa?" She pointed at Saint Peter drawing himself up in a false pretense of righteous fury.

"Yes, I suppose he's angry."

"Who is he mad at?"

"That maid, those soldiers. But mostly, I suppose, he's mad at himself."

Hendrikje had worked such wonders with the front room that even the elegant guests did not seem out of place in it. She had made some dark green drapes to mitigate the starkness of the windows; with Titus's help she had mended and polished an old Portuguese chest bought for next to nothing because the back of it was worm-eaten; she had plaited a hemp rug for the hearth and made some bright pillows for the chairs and set potted plants on the window sills. A peat fire burned slowly on the hearth, and a lamp shone yellow on the renovated chest. How she had come by the wine and oranges he did not know, but when he walked into the room with the little one dragging on his hand, she was offering decent hospitality to the visitors. Titus went before her, spreading respectable napkins on the knees of the comely young Burgomaster and his pale wife, who gave the host a wan smile, as if to indicate that no mention need be made of *her* dreary affairs.

"My papa is finished painting the man who is very mad," Cornelia shouted—it was as impossible to teach her that she could make herself heard in an ordinary voice as to make her understand that she could get from one place to another without charging like an elephant.

"She means the *Saint Peter*," said Rembrandt. "I just took it off the easel."

"Oh, did you finish it, Father?" It was Titus who asked, with as much gratification as the most mistrustful parent could wish. "Why didn't you call me? As soon as we've finished the sweet let's all go upstairs."

But for various legitimate reasons they didn't. The autumnal darkness came down with unexpected suddenness, and he did not want them to see the wet canvas in the glare of a lamp; Gretha was still too weak to venture the steep staircase; and her husband seemed at once strangely alert and unaccountably preoccupied. Hendrikje was plainly sorry to see the project forgotten; as she came to take his empty plate and goblet, her large, quiet eyes sought his, and her beauty, put out of mind as usual while the canvas was being completed, struck him anew.

572

"Oh, well, you'll come back sometime when it's lighter," she said to the visitors; but her dusky fingers brushed his in taking his plate—she soothed him with love in his disappointment as she would have soothed a child.

Actually he was scarcely aware of any disappointment. What they thought of the picture could make little difference, and the fact that the otherwise empty and tormenting interval was being filled up with their amiable chatter was enough to compensate for the postponement of praise. He watched Titus sitting tailor-fashion on the hearth, with his back to the chimney and his fiery curls caught now and again in the light of the slow flames; he watched Cornelia playing the little troll to Gretha's faery queen; he watched Hendrikje, no longer afraid of anybody, carry on an easy exchange with the scion of the house of Six; and he was satisfied. He was passive in his weariness—he only half listened; and it was through a warm and cloudy doze that Jan's voice came to him, saying, "But don't fall asleep, Master. I have something important to talk to you about."

"Was I dozing? I'm sorry," he said, and did not add that he had been laboring at the easel until they arrived, since that might be taken as a reproof for their neglect of the painting upstairs.

"I came to offer you a commission—"

"A commission?" asked Titus, bending forward with an alertness that was brash perhaps, but certainly guileless. "What is it, Jan? A portrait?"

"Something better than that—"

Hendrikje stopped beside the Portuguese chest and set down the tray she was taking back into the kitchen. "Not another Regents' piece?" she said.

"Better than that, too. You know those tremendous spaces they've reserved for canvases in the City Hall? Well, the Council wants your good man here to do one of the lunettes."

"They want *me* to do one?" said Rembrandt, coming raw out of his somnolence. "I thought Vondel handed those commissions over to Lievens and Ovens."

"That was the original plan," said the young Burgomaster with a smile in which malice, triumph, and complacency were combined. "But Heer van den Vondel has changed his mind—with a little pressure. The way it stands now, Ovens is to have the spaces over the chimney pieces, Lievens gets one of the lunettes, and the other one goes to you."

What little he had eaten went hard in his stomach. He could not raise his eyes to the eager couple sitting in the visitors' chairs; he could not look at Hendrikje or Titus or even the little one; he could only stare, embarrassed and baffled, at his own paint-stained fingertips. How many people of consequence had Jan Six pursued into corners and beaten down? What objections had he been forced to counter: "Your family is entitled to its peculiar tastes, but must you foist them on the city?"

"What has he done that's any good since the *Anatomy Lesson* for your father-in-law?" "Do you want another fiasco like that monstrous thing at the Military Club?" Jan Six meant it all kindly, of course; but it was time to put a stop to well-intentioned intercession—a man could get too much of it, a man had a right to live out his latter years in peace. "Look, Jan," he said at last in a flat and steady voice, "I know they didn't want me for that commission. If they had, they would have come and asked me, especially the second time around, after poor Flinck died. If they're offering me a lunette at the last minute, it's only because of what you've done for me. I'm grateful for that, God knows; but to undertake a thing like this when you're not really wanted, to force yourself on people who've always been dead set against you—it's more than I want to take on at my age and after all the rest."

"We know the way you feel about it, and we don't blame you," said Gretha with something of her father's calm reasonableness. "It's only that we thought this particular commission was too good to be missed—it opens up so many possibilities."

"Everybody in Amsterdam will see it," said her husband. "And twelve hundred florins isn't a bad fee either, not in times like these."

He continued to sit in what must have seemed a stubborn silence, unable to raise his eyes, not weighing the matter, only trying to find some blessed formula that would put an end once and for all to these humiliating kindnesses without doing hurt to his loyal partisans. It was Titus's voice, not his, that broke the uneasy silence; and he was surprised that it should be so restrained and dubious.

"Twelve hundred florins *is* a good fee," the young man said. "But then again, we've got to consider what this sort of commission would do to everything else we have on hand. That lunette is enormous—whatever Father did for it, he'd probably want to do very broadly, very boldly. Somebody who's looking for a painstaking likeness might even be put off by that, and we sell more portraits than anything else. It sounds good at first, but three or four portraits would bring in as much as the fee, and maybe in the long run it wouldn't be wise."

"Cornelia, go and wash your face," said Hendrikje harshly. It was obvious that, for her at least, the twelve hundred florins had been whisked out of sight by the circumspect little pronouncement of her foster son. "The way you look, a person would think you were an Indian instead of a Christian child."

The master was thankful for the diversion. They watched the little one's furious retreat, they listened to her angry stamping out to the kitchen, they did not see his flushed and agitated face. So he does not want me in the public eye, he thought; he is afraid to have anything of mine put up in the City Hall. He's heard enough from my enemies to convince him that I'm safe and dependable only if I'm tied down to minor things—"painstaking likenesses" and such. But give the stubborn old bull a wider range—give him another big canvas like the one at the Military Club—and nothing will come of it but wild experiments and sickening failure and loss of money for food and rent and occasion to blush before those who say, "There, now, he's done it again. Didn't I tell you so?"

"We ought to look at it from all angles, of course," said Jan, addressing the young man who sat on the hearth with his elbow on his knee and his chin on his closed hand, plainly not a little proud of his own prescience. "But one thing you mustn't do is confuse it with the commission your father had from Captain Banning Coq, God rest his soul. The trouble over that came up because certain people wanted detailed likenesses which weren't possible without spoiling the overall design—a problem that doesn't present itself here at all. The canvas for the City Hall is to be historical; it's to represent the sword-oath that Julius Civilis took with his chieftains when they swore to get the Romans out of Friesland. It's to be a work of the imagination, pure and simple. The only text for it is a few lines from Tacitus."

"But such a text!" said Gretha, her wan cheeks taking on color for the first time. "A person can't read it without thinking: that's for the master, that's for Rembrandt. It's your kind of scene and your kind of illumination—torches or bonfires at night, and the warriors gathering at an old castle seat somewhere in the Teuteberger Forest—"

He saw—how could he help seeing?—the legendary figures emerging out of the primordial darkness of the forest to people the vast arc of the lunette, their shields and corselets rich with barbaric ornament, the lines of their crossing swords like the clash of rude metal, their lighted faces speaking revolt, their shadowy backs and shoulders speaking indomitable power.

"Civilis himself—he's also for you," said Jan. "He was old, you know —old and strong and bitter like your brother the way you painted him in the golden helmet. A man with a price on his head, half blind; it says in Tacitus that he lost an eye. When I think of what you could do with that one-eyed face—"

He also thought of what he could do with it. It sprang into being— hard as stone, inaccessible as the head of an eagle—in the black desolation of the Teuteberger Forest and his own days. Like Adriaen in the golden helmet, like himself at the Crown Inn, it endured and showed its implacable scorn for the lightsome world that made it suffer. Its harsh and hard-won majesty did honor to the crown that pressed upon its wrinkled brow, and the reprisal it threatened—as it had not been in vain against the ranks of the invading Romans—might not be in vain against the burghers and Regents of Amsterdam, against all the unseeing and uncaring lords of the earth.

"I still believe," said Titus, "we ought to give some consideration to—"

But he never finished. One contemptuous glance from his father was enough to make him stammer into silence. And for months now, he thought, I have been telling myself that I wanted only obscurity and peace. For months I have been deceiving myself, convincing myself that there was nothing left of the ancient conflagration in my heart . . .

"Actually," Jan Six was saying, "I suppose I might have done better for you; I might have gotten all four of the spaces if I had known how to play my cards and bide my time. But then, on the other hand, though the money's less, maybe it's better as it is—better, I mean, to have the contrast there for everybody to see: *your* masterpiece and *their* flabby stuff all together in the same place."

He nodded at Jan, but he looked at the bright bent head of Titus. To have *him* see the difference, to tear from *his* mind whatever had been put there in the market place, to have *him* come and say, "Father, I never knew how great you were until today"—that would be sweeter than to overturn the market place itself. To make them all eat their words, and to make this one eat his suspicions—no, not since he had suffered in Lastman's studio had he wanted anything so much.

"You'll take it then, won't you?" asked Gretha.

"Yes, I'll take it." But where was he to work on a canvas the size of that lunette? His studio would never hold the vast, barbaric thing. Besides, he wanted nobody to see it until it was done, and how much haggling would he have to do with Hendrikje and the lad before he could afford a warehouse to work in? But he would get that money, no fear of that, even if approval had to be gotten from Titus's relatives for another withdrawal from the dwindling sum in the bank. "I'll take it, but where am I to do it? This place will never hold a thing that big."

"Jan thought of that on the way over," said Gretha. "His mother has a warehouse near the Dam, and the first floor is empty. She'd be honored to have you use it, I know."

"Jan thinks of everything," said Hendrikje, smiling and picking up the tray. The twelve hundred florins that Titus had tossed out the window had been conjured back; and it gave the master a sour pleasure to know that for the first time she could not help rejoicing over what, for her foster son, was a defeat.

The visitors stood up and embraced him. As he helped her into her beaver cloak in the dark hallway, Gretha remembered to mention what a pity it was that they hadn't gotten upstairs to see the *Saint Peter*, but the picture and the pain he had felt detaching himself from it this afternoon seemed far away from him now.

"We really *are* sorry," said Jan, puzzled by his silence.

"Oh, it makes no difference. There'll be plenty of time for that later," he said.

*

It was months since Dr. Tulp had paid a visit to Rembrandt. He had pretexts enough for not presenting himself at the house on the Rozengracht: scarcely a day that winter went by without its sleet or rain or snow or blinding fog, and walking to the distant suburb was a different matter from strolling over to the Breestraat. But actually, as he knew, if an unseasonable spell of balmy weather had broken the cheerless succession of days, he would not have taken himself to that street where the crows sat disconsolate in the stripped trees of Heer Lingelbach's labyrinth. Ever since he had heard that the master had been engaged to paint the sword-oath of Julius Civilis, he could not think of him without exasperation and apprehension; and he did not want to carry his misgivings into that house where, according to Jan and Gretha, everybody was high-hearted over the long-delayed vindication that was certain to come.

Such news as he had of what went on there he got in spite of himself. Whenever his son-in-law brought the subject up—which he did repeatedly—the doctor maintained a dour silence. He was annoyed and disquieted, and why should he try to hide it? Annoyed at Jan's inexhaustible complacency over his *coup,* annoyed at Gretha's obvious conviction that this wise and honorable man of hers could do no wrong, annoyed above all that what they chattered about so happily and persistently might be the beginning of still another in the master's series of embittering encounters with a hostile world.

It was not until the first warm days of March set in and his ostensible excuse for keeping to himself dwindled away with the icicles that he began to ask himself, in the melting mood of spring, whether his exasperation was justified. In the solitude of his office at the new City Hall, he found himself pushing his memory back to the Lastman days, trying to see his long connection with Rembrandt as a landowner might try to see his estate from the window of a high castle, in its entirety. He had always believed—not rationally, only with the darker certainty of the heart—that the destiny of Rembrandt, the intention of Rembrandt's soul, had been there from the beginning, like an amphibious creature awkwardly pulling itself up out of the mud, striving to establish itself in those drawings of drunken old men and wretched washerwomen which had so unnerved the proprietor of that fashionable studio. And when he dug out those crude drawings, brittle and discolored, from among other remains of a gone life that he found it difficult to believe he had once lived, he was only confirmed in his conviction. Left to himself, would the artist have gone on like that? he wondered. Would he have headed straight for his bitter destination if it hadn't been for the success that I myself set in motion for him? What would he have come to if that success had not diverted him from tragedy to splendor: splendid clothes, a splendid wife, a splendid collection, a splendid house, and splendid canvases by the scores, growing always grander and more opulent until the black year of Saskia's death? And much as the doctor had suffered with him over the termination of all that, there had been some compensation. In the terrible and pitiless self-portraits, in the likenesses of Christ changed from a meretricious miracle worker to a man

577

of sorrows acquainted with grief, in the exiled Jews and hard-pressed workers of Amsterdam transformed into Apostles, in the great Biblical canvases that no longer glittered with Oriental majesty but endowed patriarchs and disciples with a common, timeless humanity, the doctor had seen the original intent of his friend's spirit breaking through. Once it had become plain that financial ruin and the eclipse of reputation would not crush the painter, he had told himself that some good, perhaps the greatest good, might heave itself up out of the wreckage. Over there on the Rozengracht, rejected by the world which had touched him with its corruption, Rembrandt van Rijn could give himself over entirely to the only preoccupation that could hold a man of his greatness in his latter years: the rediscovery of the buried soul's intent, the pursuit in art of what might mean nothing to a vitiated generation, but everything to himself.

Yet sometimes in that memory-laden spring the doctor would smile at himself with the old irony. Whose inward peace am I trying to establish here—my friend's or my own? he would ask himself. Which concerns me most: that he should dedicate the end of his life to an inward search, or that *I* should be spared the painful business of watching another futile effort, another shameful defeat, another protracted agony? As for the joys of detachment and inwardness, they are sweet enough when I manage to snatch them out of the harrying demands of my busy life; but would they be sweet if they *were* my life, if I had nothing else? Do I call the hour blessed when I can close my eyes and search my mind in solitude only because I live in the world and can take its esteem for granted? . . . Whereupon a frightening thought would take hold of him, a thought that neither reason nor experience nor insight could exorcise: When the external world which presses upon us loses its meaning and its savor, is it possible that meaning and savor pass also out of the inward world, leaving us nothing but a succession of brackish days to be waded through until the obliteration of all consciousness comes as a welcome release?

He could not answer that question any more than he could explain why some wounds heal and some do not; and the fact that it stood unsolved in his mind made him a little more cordial with his son-in-law. Though he continued to maintain a marked silence when the *Julius Civilis* was injected into the conversation, he showed himself interested in other reports from the master's house: two more *Apostles* were finished; Rembrandt was doing a peculiar portrait of Titus that scarcely did the young man justice—he slouched in his chair in a thoroughly uncharacteristic way, and his face looked ironic, even snide; Hendrikje had that place of theirs looking almost as good on the inside as one of the new houses—Titus had hung his lute on a peg over the Portuguese chest, and the two of them had laid tiles in the front hall . . . Yet, though his exasperation was subsiding and the first warm winds were blowing the smell of new-turned gardens over the city, the doctor could not bring himself to walk to the Rozengracht.

He was leaving the City Hall a little earlier than usual on one of those mild days—bound for the Dam, where a precious packet of German medical books was being held in a shop for him—when Jan came up behind him and laid an arm around his shoulder. It turned out that he, too, was going to the Dam to do an errand for Gretha, so they walked together, the doctor leaving the choice of the way to his son-in-law. It was an unfamiliar way, through a crowded section where their halting conversation was interrupted by the shouts of porters and the rattle of carts jolting over cobblestones. As they turned into an unknown street, taken up partly by warehouses and partly by a rope factory, Jan stopped and pointed to a solid old brick building, dull red in the late-afternoon sun. "That's Mother's warehouse, the one where Rembrandt works," he said.

The doctor did not answer, and they walked down the street in silence until the younger man stopped in front of the big brick structure. "He's probably up there now—what do you say to going in for a minute?" he asked in a casual tone that was not quite convincing. "He'd be terribly pleased—especially at a visit from *you*."

At first thought it seemed a good way to end a period of separation which had been going on too long: Jan's easy talk would fill up any silences that might rise out of the master's resentment over what he probably took for sheer neglect; they would not have to stay too long, since they could plead their errands; and any amenities which passed now would take the constraint out of the overdue visit to the Rozengracht. But then it occurred to him that he would find something in addition to his old friend behind the blank windows: the *Julius Civilis* would be there, to be examined and commented upon, and it had never entered his mind that he would be forced to have any dealings with that painting before it was hung, for good or ill, in the City Hall. "Not today," he said testily, convinced now that he had been led by the nose down unfamiliar streets to this particular door. "It's getting late—the shop will be closing soon, and I want my books."

"The shop won't close. It's not much after five, and we'll only be here a minute." And with a high-handedness that would have been objectionable in anybody less charming—he looked so fine in his buff-colored jacket and his blue-green breeches, he smiled so disarmingly over his shoulder through such luxuriant and well-brushed curls—he walked up to the stoop and knocked loudly on the door.

The doctor felt relief and a certain malicious pleasure at the utter silence that followed. No voice, no steps, nobody at any of the three tall windows—obviously nobody was there. "We'll do it another time," he said, turning back to the street.

But his son-in-law only thrust his hand into his pocket and pulled out

579

a chain strung with numerous keys. "Oh, I can get in, whether he's here or not," he said. "Come on, let's at least have a look at the canvas. I'm sure he wouldn't mind at all." And there was no time to weigh the moral considerations involved, no time to argue that an unfinished painting was nothing to be looked at, before the right key was found and the smell of oil and paint came through the opened door.

Jan went in ahead of him, stopped dead before he was well out of the doorway, and made a sound that might have indicated either awe or consternation. Most of the huge oblong canvas nailed to the opposite wall was already covered; the areas of white in the upper corners, which asserted themselves first, were the parts of the cloth that lay beyond the arc of the lunette. What glowed within that arc was so vast that it dwarfed even the remembrance of the military Regents' piece, so strange that the doctor suspended thought until he could grow accustomed to it, as a diver grows accustomed to the eerie light—less light than a weird mutation of darkness—that passes through the restless upper waters to the heavy downward reaches of the sea. What, and by what illumination, was he looking at? A castle encroached upon by the inexorable darkness of the forest that presses always against every citadel of man, waiting to reclaim and obliterate? A porch, a portico of the half-built or half-ruined seat of a barbaric king, revealed by torchlight or firelight or some unearthly and indefinable radiance that seemed to issue from the garments, the ancient weapons, the ghostly and timeless bodies of the conspirators themselves, emitting a faint glow in the midst of the owl-haunted, leaf-whispering night . . .

"What *is* it?" said Jan.

"Exactly what the City Council ordered, my lad." His voice quavered with bitter laughter. "Julius Civilis taking the sword-oath with the Batavian chieftains." And why should the Amsterdammers complain if they were getting more than their money's worth—if the crude and overwhelming presence that dominated the expanse with his stern, ravaged face, his clenched hand, his fantastic crown made superfluous by the invincible, staring single eye was more than Julius Civilis outfacing the Romans, was man outfacing life and death?

"I never imagined it would be anything like this—"

"How could you? How could anybody? It's something new in the world."

He wrenched his glance from the king's face to the faces of the other conspirators. Masklike, almost translucent, beyond the petty emotions of time-bound mortals, they emerged out of the immemorial shadow with that strange glow upon them or within them—their swords, their corselets, their lifted goblets shining, their eye sockets holding blank, impenetrable pools of dark. Each was less himself than a part of the awesome company; and the touching of their swords was as intimate as if they had cut their wrists in the ancient Hebraic manner and each was taking into his veins a little of the others' blood.

"Of course," said Jan, "it will look altogether different once it's finished."

"The devil it will!" His voice, echoing in the bare room, was as strange to him as that room itself—the first floor of a warehouse unaccountably flooded with the delusive light of day, when the only reality was the one he could not stop staring at, the reality of the impenetrable night. "It's almost finished now—can't you see that? Those arabesques he makes with the butt end of his brush or the tip of his finger"—he pointed to some of them in the muted areas of blue and yellowed white and paled russet—"he never makes those until he's almost through."

"But it *looks* unfinished—"

"It won't when you see it up where it belongs. It's painted to be looked at from below, from the main hall and the arcades. From there —the more's the pity!—what you consider the crudeness of it will be lost. Let the fools stay down where they belong, and they'll imagine they have what they want."

"But some of them will be bound to see it before he gets it up there. After all, he'll have to bring it in and take it up the scaffold; and the members of the City Council will naturally be curious to have a look—"

"Well, see to it that they don't, just see to it that they don't," he said, wheeling away from the fearful wonder and turning what he knew to be a disordered face on his son-in-law. "Get him to hang it on a Sunday, when the place is empty."

"They won't like that. They'll naturally want to be present at the hanging. What shall I do?"

"Why ask me? *I* had no hand in it. Maneuver them out of a formal hanging the way you maneuvered them into giving him the commission."

The young Burgomaster, belittled by the giants on the canvas, sighed and sagged against the wall. "Look, are you sure he painted it intentionally in that—that peculiar way? Are you sure he wasn't in a hurry—just careless?" he said.

"Careless, do you call a thing like that? Don't be a fool."

"Well, maybe it's not carelessness, maybe it's something else. His eyes look bad to me, he keeps rubbing them—maybe his sight is failing—"

"If only everybody could see the way he does with his bad eyes."

"You think it'll be all right then—with the City Council, I mean."

"All right with the City Council?" He said it harshly, he said it with a sneer; he did not know out of what subterranean waters such hate could well up in him against this comely, well-intentioned, cultivated man whom his daughter and all the notables of Amsterdam loved. "No, of course it won't be all right with the City Council. They'll hate it— you know that. Look at their hero, their Julius Civilis—a barbarian with a peasant's face—a big, raw peasant with the crudeness and power of a brute. It isn't a picture of civic solidarity, it's a picture of revolt. And there's something else, too: nobody likes to think of himself as mortal—especially not the members of the City Council—and in some way, I don't know how, that canvas is drenched in death."

The handsome face before him lost all color. "Then what am I to do?"

"What are *you* to do?" He stopped himself before he had uttered the devastating "What is *he* to do?" It was bad enough with his son-in-law as it stood—the dignitaries of the City Hall displeased, his judgment discredited, Vondel triumphant; it would be too much to remind him now of what he would see soon enough: that his good offices had done irreparable harm to the master for whom he had such deep affection—not fifteen thousand florins' worth, to be sure, but a deep affection nevertheless.

"Do you think I could ask him—very tactfully, of course—to make it more definite, to smooth it out a little just in case they should see it at close range—"

"No. In the first place, he wouldn't do it. And in the second, he shouldn't. It's the way his"—he broke off, to say "his soul" would sound affected and overdramatic—"it's the way he intended it to be."

"Yes," said his son-in-law, despondent and contrite. "You're right about that. He's convinced it's the best thing he's ever done—he keeps saying so."

"And it is, it certainly is." The doctor was back in the world again, seeing the world beyond the dusty windows where porters would run about and wagons would rattle over the cobblestones and children would roll their hoops season after season no matter what became of Rembrandt van Rijn. "No doubt it is, but don't comfort yourself with that. Don't expect the City Council to see what you don't see yourself."

His son-in-law was also back in the world: he straightened, shook out his chestnut locks, and smiled a gentle, self-disparaging smile. The vast and dreadful affair had somehow been reduced in his mind to proportions that could be dealt with. What he had done could be categorized under the heading of natural human error—and he had a right to make a few errors like anybody else. "I did wade in over my depth that time, didn't I?" he said.

"Never mind. It'll work itself out somehow."

"Would you like to stop off and have a brandy, Father? You look tired."

"No, no, I want to get to the bookshop." He too would try to put the matter behind him; he too would walk out without turning to look again at that somber vision which surpassed and therefore shut off the desires of ordinary men; he too would spend the evening as remote from the glorious calamity as he could keep himself, reading and warming his aching legs before the fire. "I want my books. I've got to have my books."

Two months and more had gone by since the painting had been taken out of the warehouse and fastened into the big curved empty space in the City Hall; and so far as Hendrikje could make out, Rembrandt was satisfied. How he could be satisfied, she did not understand: she herself had expected God knows what—some public ceremony, some banquet of burgomasters to which she could have sent him off in his old suit of chestnut-colored velvet, well brushed and with a freshly ironed shirt, something which would have shown that his work was gloriously finished and gratefully received, some occasion from which he could have come back to her triumphant and justified. But if she was disturbed by the absence of any such celebration, she had to admit she knew nothing about these things—perhaps it was no longer the custom to celebrate. *He* showed no disappointment: he went back to work on the *Apostles* and the *Homer* he was doing for Ruffo and another new painting of himself; and who was she to raise questions when he seemed content?

The fact that the painting had been hung on a Sunday, without ceremony and with nobody but her and Titus and the apprentices standing by, had not seemed to trouble him: Jan Six had said it would be hazardous to get the huge canvas up with clerks and visitors milling about, and he had accepted the explanation. It was she, not he, who found something strangely rehearsed in Jan's and Gretha's praise; it was she, not he, whose spirits were dashed by the grim brevity with which Dr. Tulp announced that this was certainly his masterpiece. And when she had gone into a panic this morning because a messenger had come to request that he present himself that afternoon at Burgomaster van Spiegel's office, he had laughed at her apprehension and told her that the summons was probably for nothing more important than to give him some silly scroll to express the Council's gratitude. *He* had no worries, that much was plain. If he had had the slightest misgiving, he would never have asked Titus to come with him. Matters between him and Titus had been distant and strained ever since their difference over this commission, and his only reason for taking the young man with him, so far as she could see, would be to have him witness some ceremony, casual and belated though it might be, to mark his success.

But now it was four hours since they had walked out together, and every conjecture she had seized on to ease her anxiety was worn out. More time had passed than could possibly have been used up in the longest of ceremonies and the most dawdling of walks from the City Hall, more time than it would take to drink even three or four mugs of beer if they had stopped in a tavern to make their peace. Cornelia had been home from Dame school for hours; the most diligent of the apprentices had closed up shop and gone his way; the meat put into the pot for five o'clock supper was simmering to shreds. And the great pile of mending that she had laid out to keep from showing her distress to the little girl was reduced to a torn kerchief and a pair of stockings so riddled with holes that they could not be salvaged, and the grey November dusk had faded, and yet she could not bring herself to light the lamps: it seemed so preposterous that the hour of lamp-lighting should have come with them still gone.

"Mama, it's dark in here," said Cornelia. She was sitting on the Portuguese chest with her doll in her lap, a handsome and expensive doll that Jan and Gretha had given her last Saint Nicolaas Feast; but the poor thing had been so assailed with beatings and kisses that it looked like a bundle of rags.

"I'm sorry, dear, I forgot. I'd better take the stew off the fire too."

"That's better," said Cornelia, when the wicks had been kindled and the front room had been given a yellow, deceptive air of evening cheerfulness. "Now I can see my doll's face."

She did not give voice to the angry thing she thought: that the doll *had* no face, that by last Easter most of the paint had been kissed away or scrubbed off with a vengeful scrubbing brush. *He* had promised to repaint it, but the *Julius Civilis* business had crowded the intention out of his head; and the recollection of that promise, unfulfilled though it was, closed her throat and stung her eyes as if he were gone for good and all, as if she were remembering some melting kindness bestowed by one long dead.

"*Where* do you think they are, Mama?"

"For the tenth time, Cornelia, I don't know. They went to the City Hall. I think they'll be coming back very soon now."

"But I'm hungry."

"All right, then, come into the kitchen and I'll get you a glass of milk."

But they did not go to the kitchen; before the little one had gotten down from the chest, Hendrikje heard the sound of the opening of the front door. "There they are!" she said, springing up and overturning the heap of mending, only to see that Titus had walked in alone.

Her first impulse was to ask, "Good God, what happened?" Not because there was anything ominous in Titus's face—the worst that she could read there was a mild annoyance; only because the very absence of the big warm bulk of the man she wanted to scold and embrace was somehow frightening. "Where's your father? Is your father all right?" she said.

"He's down at the warehouse. I suppose he's all right—he seemed all right to me."

"But what's he doing at the—"

"I'm hungry!" said Cornelia, dragging at her hand. "I want my milk. You promised me my milk."

"Oh, very well, I'll get you your whole supper. Let me get her settled down and I'll be back in a minute," she said over her shoulder. But the incapacity of her hands as she served out the overcooked food reminded her that the one who stood in need of settling down was herself.

When she came back, Titus was on his knees gathering up the scattered mending, and for once she was exasperated with his courtesy. "What's your father doing at the warehouse?" she said.

"Cleaning it up, airing it out, I guess." His voice was level, but it had a weary fall. "You see, the picture will be back there some time this evening—"

"What picture? What are you talking about?"

"The *Julius Civilis*. That's what they wanted to discuss with him. It seems"—now that he had the mending collected, he remained on his knees, sorting it into orderly heaps, with his face turned away from her—"it seems they had some changes to suggest."

"Changes to suggest?" No scrolls, no formal speech of gratitude—changes to suggest: the vision of his bewildered face, his heavy body sagging under the blow unnerved her so that she must let herself down into a chair. "*Who* had changes to suggest? What's going on?"

Patiently, and a little wearily too, as if by this time he had had his fill of the business, he recounted what had gone on in the office of the Burgomaster van Spiegel. Heer van den Vondel and certain members of the City Council hadn't been completely satisfied, and now that the three other canvases were up, they had voiced what he himself had been hearing rumored for weeks: their feeling that no one of the four canvases ought to be strikingly different from the rest. The painting wasn't *rejected,* he hoped she understood. It was only returned temporarily for certain alterations.

For the first time in her life she felt otherwise than loving toward the gracious young man who laid the heaps of mending on the window sill and seated himself across from her—disturbed, naturally, but not outraged; regretful, of course, but not crushed; deploring an unfortunate situation instead of being appalled in the face of a calamity. "Alterations?" she said, choking on the pity that welled up in her when she thought of that huge thing he had labored over for months and considered his masterpiece sagging down like the flag of a defeated company from the place where he had been so proud to see it hung. "What alterations? It's finished—isn't it? What sort of changes could they want him to make?"

He looked at her wide-eyed, plainly amazed that she was not aware of what he had seen from the beginning: that the unfortunate business could have had no other end. And maybe it couldn't, and maybe she *had* known it in some secret place in her heart; but oh, the pitiable body in its old rubbed chestnut-colored velvet, the small reddened eyes blinking in amazement, the mind stupefied, unwilling to believe what the ears were forced to hear, the hand coming down for support on the edge of the Burgomaster's desk—the poor wrinkled hand!

The young man's amber eyes, half hidden by the moist eyelids and the fiery lashes, stared ruefully down at his own hands. "They were very considerate of him—very considerate," he said in an appeasing voice. "They didn't dictate any particular changes; they just want him to bring it more into line with the others. They said they were sure he'd know best how to proceed himself. They said they would pay him an extra stipend, and a generous one, for any additional time he spends on it. They said—"

"Who are *they?*"

"Burgomaster van Spiegel and Heer van den Vondel—"

"He hates Heer van den Vondel—"

"Does he?"

"Does he? Good God, you ought to know that, with all the things *you* seem to know."

She had reproached him before, but never mocked him. She saw the quick, pained, unbelieving glance, the sudden collapse of the slight shoulders, but she had no compassion for them. Standing halfway as she did between the son and the father, the young and the old, she could look in only one direction now. "Something else I don't understand— why in the name of Jesus did you leave him by himself after a thing like that?"

"He didn't want me. He told me to come home. Besides, I knew you might be wondering, and I was worried about you."

"Worried about me? *He's* the one to worry about. I'll be surprised if he doesn't—"

"Honestly, Hendrikje, I think you're making too much of it. He didn't seem as upset as all that; there wasn't any quarrel or anything of that sort. He bought a sausage and a loaf of bread and went down there to stay the evening so that he'd be on hand when they came with the picture, and I went with him and helped him sweep up. I offered to stay, but he said I'd better go home and tell you not to wait. He expects to be back here about nine tonight."

She did not ask him what time it was now—she did not dare. The period of waiting had not come to a stop; it had only been lengthened and intensified, and she did not know what she was to do with her unbearable self between now and nine o'clock. Carry the mending back upstairs. Knit away at the red stockings she was making for Cornelia. Where was Cornelia?—oh, yes, in the kitchen, eating her supper; and the poor young man who sat staring at her and searching for other comforting words to say to her—he probably needed his supper too. "Did you eat on the way home?" she said.

"No. The fact is, I haven't had anything since noon." It was a bid for a concern which she could not feel, a loving service she could give him only automatically.

"Well, come, then," she said. "The meat's gone to shreds, but it'll be better than nothing." And she went before him into the kitchen and ladled out the stew and set his dish on the table opposite Cornelia's, which—together with the small blunt face above it—was ugly with cold gravy and bits of meat.

He followed her at a distance into the ember-lighted kitchen. She had hurt him, and that was amazing to her; she could not care that she had hurt him, and that was more amazing still. He went to the fire as she moved away from it, lighted the taper, and kindled the lamp in the middle of the board; and there was something almost insolent in that: it was as if he had said, "*I* refuse to make a wake of it. *I* see no reason to sit mourning in the dark."

"Where's my papa?" said Cornelia.

"Working," he told her offhandedly. "Why don't you wipe your face, you grubby little bug? What do you think you've got a napkin for?" But Cornelia was sullen, and his little sally did not break the charged, unhappy stillness. "What about you?" he said, turning courteously to his foster mother where she stood by the kettle. "Aren't you going to have something to eat?"

"Me? How could I put food in my stomach?"

She had not meant it as a judgment on him, but plainly he took it as such: he sat back from the board and fetched up a sharp sigh in which there was both regret and exasperation. "Whatever you like," he said, in as icy a voice as his guileless nature could muster up, and fell to with a ravenous haste utterly at odds with his usual pickiness, putting great loads of meat into his mouth and tearing at the rusks.

And cruel as it was—he was young, he was tired, he had been sent away by his father and had found no love in his foster mother—cruel as it was, she could not allow him to eat in peace. While he ate, while he helped her to clear the table and wash the dishes, while he sat in the front room and tried to lose himself in the history of Josephus, she plagued him with questions that only tightened the knot of her anxiety. Had Jan Six been at the meeting?—she shot it at him over the tense, irregular click of her knitting needles. No, nobody had been there but the Burgomaster van Spiegel and Heer van den Vondel—he answered flatly, without raising his eyes from the page. And the Heer Burgomaster Tulp—wasn't *he* around either? No, he couldn't very well have been there whether he wanted to or not; he was away with some committee at The Hague. How long had the discussion lasted? Half an hour, three-quarters of an hour—he wasn't sure. What time was it now? A little after nine. Did he think his father would actually work on the canvas tonight? He didn't know, but he doubted it; it would be a foolish thing to do—there was only one lamp at the warehouse now. And goaded by the bells that were sounding half past nine, infuriated by the matter-of-fact tone and frustrated in her fierce efforts to know how it was with *him* in his misery, she struck out again. "I'll let you alone. Go on, read your book. I'll not bother you any more," she said.

Whereupon the little one, who had been dozing on some cushions on

587

the floor, came out of her sleep, completely alert, with a look of triumphant malice on her trollish face. "Mama and Titus are fighting—Mama's mad at Titus," she said, and lay down again with a look of utter gratification on her face.

It was Titus who lifted her from the heaped cushions an hour later and carried her up to bed, Titus who went into the kitchen and banked the fire and barred the back door. Her own hands, so cold and nerveless now that they could not even make a pretense of knitting, were incapable of any of the nightly duties. She sat staring straight before her, wondering wildly what there might be in the warehouse that she had never seen: a knife with which a man could cut his wrists, a rope with which a man could hang himself? Titus came back and stood in the middle of the room, uncertain and dejected; and it suddenly occurred to her that he had too much pride in his manly self-possession to show her what he feared or how he ached for his father's sake.

"Look, Titus, it's close to eleven," she said in a shaken voice.

"Yes, I know."

"I'm terribly worried for him—"

"It *is* late, but really, I'm sure he's only—"

"How can you be sure of anything, after such a terrible business? Get me my cloak and tell me the way—"

"You'd never find it. You can't go over there by yourself."

"Then come with me."

"And leave Cornelia?"

It seemed obvious to her that it was better to leave Cornelia to the possibility of waking in nightmare solitude than to leave *him* with a rope or a knife in the black company of his shame. "I'm not worried about her. I can't think about anybody but *him*," she said. And the young man did not answer, only helped her into her cloak and opened the door and followed her into the dank cold of the November night.

She realized with a strong poignancy that she had never walked the nighttime streets of the city without *him* beside her. Other walks—exultant walks through new-fallen snow after she had become his woman and the mistress of his house on the Breestraat, languorous walks from the Crown Inn to the Pineros' house through the fragrant heat of the summer nights, recent walks along the Rozen Canal and through the deserted mazes of Heer Lingelbach's labyrinth—she remembered them all, and his arm around her waist, his thigh brushing against her thigh. To be in the city, to be in the world without him was an unbearable thought: she clasped her hands under her cloak and prayed to be spared such loneliness—better to be the first to die than to walk these terrible streets alone. For every section that they walked through, from the most sordid to the most splendid, seemed to her filled with a deadly malevolence. In Ransdorp it had been different: a person could walk Ransdorp from one end to the other in fifteen minutes, and say to himself all the way, "There sleeps Granny Schaarp, and there the Schilders are eating bread and herring, and under the slant of that gable are little Klaus and Dirk and Isaak, three in one big bed, tired out after their day at the Fair . . ." But if she had never come away from the Ransdorp comfort she would never have known the richer comfort of lying locked in the round of his powerful arms, of feeling the rise and fall of his hairy chest . . . Lord Jesus, she prayed, keep the knife and the rope out of his reach. Take me first, let me be the first to fall into Thine everlasting sleep.

Titus pointed out three tall, dimly lighted windows in a black hulk of a building and said, "This is the place"; and there was no time for her fears to forgather before she saw *him* through the dusty glass, saw him sitting on a stool with his shoulders hunched, his head down, his hands hanging between his spread knees. She caught Titus's hand before it could touch the latch and begged with her eyes for a little more time, time to tell herself: I must not run into his arms, I must not add to his weakness by showing him how much I have been afraid of it, I must not double his afflictions by asking him to comfort me.

And once she was inside, she saw certain signs that steadied her: there *was* a knife on the rickety table at the far end of the room, but he had used it only for slicing sausage; he had not been so undone that he had not thought to hang the velvet jacket on a peg near the door; and the huge canvas was not tacked limp to the wall before him, it had been nailed taut and flat to the peeled plaster—and that, for some reason, was the most comforting sight of all. "What are you two doing here?" he said in a voice thickened by the phlegm of long silence. His eyes, small and bloodshot but dry and bright, looked at her keenly, sternly, as if he expected an accounting. Then they returned to the canvas without resting on Titus at all.

"It's very late—it must be past midnight—"

"Is it?" He stirred and sighed as if the intrusion of any fact from the outer world, even the time of day, was painful to him. "I had no idea—I was sitting here thinking," he said.

She looked at what he had been thinking about: the old, old forest, the ancient warriors, the frightening darkness and the even more frightening unearthly light. Now that she was seeing them straight on and only ten or twelve feet away, the bodies and faces looked wild and crude, not like human beings, more like maskers in the firelight of some carnival of her childhood—tremendous maskers on stilts, or almost transparent ghosts. For an instant she wondered whether this was how the City Fathers had seen them, looking at them from the upper arcade, but that question went down at once under the hot surge of her loyalty and love. To stand against him for the children's sake was one thing; to side with the City Fathers was another. Who were they to judge him? If he said the picture was great, then it *was* great! "I was worried for you. I asked Titus to bring me," she said. "I got so upset I couldn't stay in the house any more."

She expected him to chide her for having left Cornelia, but he said nothing, and she knew that he had forgotten Cornelia. At the same moment she knew that it was quite otherwise with Titus; he remembered Titus all too well. If he had not turned to him once since they had opened the door, if he had let the young man step back and seat himself on the window sill without so much as turning his head, it was because he was deliberately rejecting him and wanted to make that rejection known, even in his confusion and his pain.

"I waited and waited—"

"I'm sorry. I just forgot about the time, and I suppose I had good reason."

"Of course you did, I know you did. But it'll be better at home—I'll give you some tea and brandy, and maybe you'll sleep."

"You heard?—they want me to change it." Without lifting his hands from between his knees, he made a gesture that reminded her of the fall of shot birds.

"They're fools—idiots!" she said, fighting back the tears and looking toward Titus, hoping that Titus would come into it now, would provide him the comfort of more eloquent abuse. "You don't have to do what they tell you—once Ruffo pays you, we'll return their money. If they dont want it in the City Hall, you can always hang it somewhere else—"

He shook his head. "There's no place else to put it," he said. "It's too big. There's not another wall to hold it—certainly not here in Amsterdam and maybe not in all Holland."

That undid her, that begot such fierce pity in her that she could have bent double. It seemed to her that it was not the picture but he himself who had grown to such huge and grotesque proportions that there was no longer any place for him in the city or the world. She could not speak, and it was appalling that Titus, still sitting remote on his perch in the tall window, could fling such a self-contained and reasonable voice into that desolation. "That's right, Hendrikje, there's no place else to put it. Either it goes back to the City Hall or it's rolled up and put away to be cracked and ruined," he said. "That's why I say their suggestions are worth thinking about. Better to make a few alterations than—"

"*What* alterations?"

It was the same drained voice that had uttered the rest of the weary words, and Titus could not see from where he sat that the veins had started out in the thick neck and the balding forehead, that the big hands were clenched now between the spread knees. He slid down from the sill and came forward, standing with grace and self-assurance between his father and the canvas; and she knew that the persuasive arts he meant to practice here were the ones that he had learned to use with pride and success in the market place.

"You wouldn't have to do too much, Father, not really. I don't believe they'd even notice if you didn't touch the background," he said. "Vondel kept harping on the central group"—he gestured toward the

590

central group, the crossed swords, the terrible one-eyed face of the hero, the shimmering forms gathered around him—"and I'm sure if you'd work up those figures a little more, make them a little more definite and detailed, everybody would be satisfied. There's really no choice in the matter: either you change it or—"

He broke off with his mouth hanging open because his father had heaved himself up like a bear after long baiting and was thudding across the bare planks of the floor. Where? To the rickety table, to snatch up the knife, to come hurrying back—wild, red in the face—with the knife in his hand. For a moment she stood stupefied, paralyzed by the fear that he was provoked enough to aim it at Titus's chest. "Change it?" he shouted into the echoing emptiness. "I'll show you how I'll change it." And he lunged at it with the blade, plunging it in and sawing a big raw gash through tree and warrior and column; then he turned the knife at an angle and made a kind of flap, and letting go of the knife, caught at the edge of the flap with both hands and tore with all his might, so that the canvas ripped and shrieked like a living thing.

"My God, Father, what are you doing?"

"Changing it the way *I* want it changed," he said, and wrenched his jacket from the peg and flung back the door and started out into the dark.

She stayed only long enough to see the young man put up his hand to touch the cruel gash, the hideous rip as if he could not believe in them, as if only his shaking fingers could prove to him that they were there. He was deathly white, he was clutching his stomach now as if he was going to vomit, he was certainly in no condition to be left by himself. But she had stood with the children too long against him while he had been bowing and breaking under the blows of poverty and disgrace and the years. "There's no good in staying here. Come home as soon as you get hold of yourself," she said, and went after the beloved into the black, unpeopled night.

*

For a week thereafter he was kept in the house by the first confining sickness he had had since his childhood—a feverish rheum that filled his head with mucus and reduced his voice to a croak or a whisper and set his heart galloping like a runaway horse. The symptoms of his illness seemed to have been malevolently contrived to goad his unabating anger: it was infuriating to have to blow and wipe until there was no skin left on the end of his nose, infuriating to strain his throat in order to make ridiculous sounds, infuriating to feel even in his dreams the crazy thumping in his chest. And when the rheum thickened and the fever subsided, his fury did not decrease as he had foolishly told himself it would. The lessening of his bodily misery only allowed him to brood more constantly on his shame and his rage; he could not begin to teach

591

as yet because a few sentences were enough to bring on a coughing fit, and he could find nothing whatever to do with himself.

There was no solace for him, only exasperation or a deeper pain, in the company of his family. Cornelia harassed him with her ceaseless talking; Titus came home only to eat and sleep, seldom speaking and never meeting his father's glance; and Hendrikje's efforts to show her concern and compassion put an obligation on him that he could not discharge: his rage and humiliation shut him off so completely that nothing she could say, no look she could give him, no tender service she could perform for him was able to break through. All the canvases he had begun before he had accepted the accursed commission had been finished, and no new subject could stir anything in him but a cold contempt. He felt an actual physical nausea at the thought of stretching canvas or mixing paints or holding a brush, and the worst of it was that his etching—a thing which had always absorbed and renewed him when he could not paint, a pursuit he had been able to follow even in the aimless desolation after Saskia's death—was simply not available to him any more. His eyes could no longer endure the cruel shining of the copper plate; to stare at it for longer than a few minutes was to bring on a blurring of his vision and an unmanning fear that he would outlast his sight—a thought that made him realize what people meant when they spoke of "a living death."

When he was well enough to come downstairs and sit in the little parlor, it was not the parlor that he saw, with its fire and its decent furniture and the candles that Hendrikje had squandered the cost of a supper on in order to soothe his spirit and ease his eyes; it was the bleak warehouse and the awful image of the ravaged canvas—an image that stopped his heart in its wild careening and made him shiver and cover his face. Sometimes that image begot an overwhelming pity in him: he mourned over it as he had mourned over the body of his first child. And then again it was not pity that he felt, but guilt—he could not have been more appalled if he had shed human blood. Closed in that darkness and isolation was his offspring and his victim, gashed and ripped by his own hand; and the realization was so terrible to him that he would deliberately ward it off by thinking of the warehouse itself. The warehouse was dirty, paint-spotted, sordid with things he had left there —a pair of shamefully worn slippers, a sweaty painter's smock, ends of old loaves and sausages, bones of smoked herring, a jug of soured milk —and Jan Six, who had not shown his face in the Burgomaster van Spiegel's office or on any occasion since, had a key and might walk in and see the condition of his mother's property. Besides, he could not bear that anybody, least of all Jan Six, should see the mutilated painting. As soon as his voice was reasonably dependable, he sent for his senior apprentice and gave directions which he would have given his son if he had not been filled with white-hot enmity: Take the nails out of the painting, lay it face down on the floor, and cut it up into manageable pieces—after all, it could be used again and there was no sense in wasting good canvas. The lad had come back from that assignment obviously shaken. He had done as the master had ordered, or *almost* as the master had ordered, he said. But somehow he had not been able to cut up the central group around the hero—*that* he had found intact, and he could never have forgiven himself if he had not kept it so. He had brought it back to the studio, and he wondered whether his master would want him to mount it on a stretcher: there would be just enough room to stand it upright against the wall . . . But he could not look into the pleading, diffident young eyes; he could only turn aside and shake his head. "No, roll it up and put it away somewhere. What's the sense of stretching it? I don't want to see it," he said.

Certainly he did not want it to haunt him in the studio when he found the voice and the strength to teach again. The whole affair was so dreadful that he could only hope to obliterate it, to act as if it had never taken place. And now the desire to expunge became the obsession of his waking hours: he would have no peace until the borrowed warehouse was cleansed of its clutter, until every nail hole was plastered over and every spattering of paint was scrubbed from the floor and the key to the hateful place was back in the pocket of the scion of the house of Six. "If it's preying on your mind," said Hendrikje, "why don't you send some of the apprentices over there to clean it up?" But he mumbled a sullen refusal, for he knew that he would believe in that cleansing, that expunging, that obliteration only if he scrubbed and plastered and carried out the accumulated rubbish with his own hands.

He went there one afternoon when the sky was lead-colored with unfallen snow. He went alone, carrying the soap and scrubbing brush and rags in a bucket, together with the cold supper which Hendrikje had wrapped up for him: white meat of chicken, a couple of apples, rusks, and a slice of gingerbread. He felt as he took the long and exhausting walk from the Rozengracht to the Dam such desolate isolation as he had not known since the Lastman days; he encountered nobody he knew, and those unknowns that he did encounter filled him with loathing—the children looked fat and smug and spoiled, the women either coarse or silly, the men hard and cold in their leanness or bloated and self-satisfied in their obesity. By the time he had come to the bleak warehouse, he felt himself an exile, and a willing one, not only from the citizens of Amsterdam but from all mankind.

Chilly as the big room was, he flung one of the windows open: the smell of the painting remained though the painting was gone, and the smell was as sickening to him as if it were rising from decay. He worked in intensifying darkness, emptying old, caked receptacles, collecting refuse, sweeping the strewn litter into a heap, filling his bucket with ice-cold water out of the storage barrel; and while he worked he was hounded by a persistent memory.

He saw himself clearing out the studio in the outbuilding behind the mill to make it respectable for my lord Constantyn Huyghens. He saw the velvet draped over van Vliet's empty easel, the ostrich plume stuck into the mug that held his pens and brushes, the paintings lined up against the wall: Jan Lievens' and Gerard Dou's and his own—paintings that had not come into his mind for thirty years. He fell, then, to thinking of the others who had worked with him in his youth: how Lievens had fitted the soft and malleable stuff of his nature into the mold of the times and had risen to such fame and wealth as to be invited to paint a lunette which still hung in the City Hall; how little Dou, content to be a provincial notable, had prospered in Leyden by painting the faces of its unpretentious citizens and the humdrum scenes in their dull rooms and quiet streets; how van Vliet had mercifully fallen out of the ken of everybody who had known him before—the last time anybody had heard of him he had been working for a maker of sails. He saw their several lives unfolding predictably within the boundaries they had set for themselves; only he of the lot of them had walked vulnerable toward the ultimate greatness that lies beyond all orderly boundaries—and fallen, as Vrouw van Hoorn had told him he would, again and again, publicly, shamefully into the mud . . .

He felt the mucus accumulating in his head and went over and closed the window. Out there the streets had changed: the leaden clouds had burst like worn feather beds, and the air was softly agitated with large, slowly falling flakes of snow. It was growing dark—some of the whiteness showed sharp between the bricks of walls and chimneys—but he decided to defer his supper, to keep it as a reward and a rest when the floor was scrubbed clean. He kindled the wan lamp, sighed and rubbed his aching shoulders and remembered his father making just such a motion. Something, perhaps the recollection and perhaps the sight of the new snowfall, soothed him; and he got down and began to scrub slowly, rhythmically, his mind drained of everything but the motion, so that it was almost as if he were scrubbing in his sleep. He had been in this state of dreamlike suspension for some time—the window had turned quite black and the flame of the lamp intensely yellow—when he heard a tentative knocking on the door. One of the apprentices, he thought. Hendrikje must have sent one of the apprentices to help him, and he was exasperated by this solicitous intrusion and waited for a second knock before he shouted in a hoarse and surly voice, "It's not latched. Walk in."

The door moved slowly backward, and the presence on the threshold was such that he wondered whether it was really there, whether he had not called it up out of some forgotten corridor of his past. The intruder was a small man, dressed as impeccably as Master van Swanenburgh used to dress to pay a formal visit: black beaver, black velvet jacket and breeches, black shoes with silver buckles, black gloves, and a large white linen collar so stiffly starched and impressive that it looked for an instant like the outmoded ruff. And—pink, fresh, almost infantine against all this blackness and whiteness—the broad Dutch face showed between the dip of the beaver and the rise of the collar, a singularly guileless and puzzled face made softer by reddish curls threaded with white and flecked with melting snow. "Excuse me," said the stranger in a gentle tenor voice, "but is this the warehouse of Vrouw Anna Weijmar Six?"

"Yes, it is." Since the small and inoffensive apparition apparently wanted no dealings with him, had obviously only come from Jan's mother on some errand in connection with the property, he did not bother to put down the scrubbing brush or get up off his knees.

"Good. They told me over on the Rozengracht that this is the place where I can find Master Rembrandt van Rijn." Whereupon he began to look for Master Rembrandt van Rijn as if he were in some cupboard or in the antechamber with the water barrel, and would come out now, washed and brushed and in the clothing of a gentleman.

"*I'm* van Rijn," he said, letting the brush slide into the bucket and shaking the grey and soapy drippings from his fingers.

For an instant the pink face puckered in childlike surprise: little dents appeared where another man would have had wrinkles, in the fresh cheeks and between the sandy eyebrows. Then he subsided into immediate self-possession, as if he had seen stranger things in his fifty-odd years. The corners of his mouth moved in a cordial smile, and he stripped off his glove and held out his small well-fleshed hand to shake hands formally and—most informally—to help the man who was squatting before him to his feet. "I don't mind the wetness, it's only a little soapy water after all," he said, insisting on the contact with a kind of warm authority. "It's a great honor to make your acquaintance, Master. I'm Duart Simonszoon van Hudde, the treasurer of the Syndics of the Drapers' Guild. I hope you'll excuse me for coming over here at this hour—your good wife seemed disturbed about it and did everything she could to put me off—but there's a meeting of the Syndics tomorrow, and I *did* want to settle my business with you tonight."

But what business could the man have with him—this impeccable little burgher who held the purse strings of the oldest and most respected merchants' guild in Holland? He stared at him and said nothing, and the eyes of the newcomer—of an indefinite color, neither blue nor brown nor grey—gazed back at him shyly but without embarrassment. "Don't you want to dry your hands, Heer van Rijn?" he said after a long but unstressful silence. "They'll chap and crack, and that's unpleasant for anybody, and especially so for a painter, I would think."

He bowed and went into the antechamber and plunged his arms into the icy water in the storage barrel and dried himself carefully. Peculiar as the whole incident was, he would have been scarcely more surprised to find the caller vanished when he came back than he was to see him sitting at his ease on one of the high paint-spattered stools, with his heels on the topmost rung and his hands curled around his knees. "It's a long way from the Rozengracht, and I sat down without begging your leave," he said. "Won't you sit down too? I'm here on behalf of the other four Syndics of the Cloth Hall, to talk over the possibility of your doing something for us—a commission, you know, a Regents' piece."

He stopped in the act of pulling up another stool—stopped and straightened to his full height, his cheeks turning hot and the old wild pulse of rage and shame hammering in his chest. Then the fellow *had* come from the house of Six: they had been up to their old scheming in his favor, and this Duart Simonszoon van Hudde had stepped out of the snowy night to bring him the sop that was to soothe him in his disgrace. He wheeled around and glared at the visitor. "Who sent you?" he said.

"Who sent me? Why, I suppose you could say the Syndics of the Cloth Hall sent me, though, to tell you the truth, I made the choice by myself—"

"Not Jan Six? Not Anna Weijmar Six?"

"The young Burgomaster? His mother?" The whole rosy face was broken up with little depressions of confusion. "Unfortunately, I can't claim the honor of counting either of them among my acquaintances. That's the trouble with being a member of the Board of Syndics. We work so hard at it, Heer van Rijn, that there's not much time left for meeting the people we'd like to meet."

"Am I to understand you came to offer me a commission?"

"Yes, with certain reservations. But then, by the time a man comes to our age, he takes it for granted that everything comes with certain reservations—isn't that so?"

He looked up so eagerly, he smiled with such a strange mingling of resignation and cheerfulness that it was impossible not to nod back at him. "So the Six family didn't send you? You don't know them?" he said.

"Why, no, nobody sent me—nobody but the Syndics of the Cloth Hall, and as I said a moment ago, they left the matter pretty much to me. I suppose it's because I own a few things—a Hals, a Seghers, a Brouwer—that they do me the honor of considering me an expert. And though it's nothing to boast of, I do know a little more about it than the other four. Look, my friend"—his tenor voice took on a sudden reedy tone of concern—"won't you please sit down? You've been doing manual labor here, your wife says you've been ill, and I'm sure you must be very tired."

Tired he was, so tired that his heart, once he was settled face to face with his visitor, left off pounding and moved as weakly as a dying fish. Over its irregular movements he heard the visitor talking; through the mist that the paroxysm and its aftermath had put before his eyes he saw the candid face. Nobody had sent the treasurer of the Syndics of the Cloth Hall. The said treasurer, charged by his fellow Board members to find the proper painter for their Regents' piece, had gone about the business with the same uncompromising thoroughness and invio-

lable honesty that had made the woolens of Amsterdam the most faultless item on the European market for the last hundred years. He had
made a list of all the notable painters in the city and had gone from one
Guild Hall and charitable institution and private house to another, examining and evaluating their productions. It had been an education,
Heer van Rijn, a real education. Some whom he had thought of as minor
painters had risen markedly in his esteem, and some whom he had approached with the highest hopes had turned out to be downright trivial.
And now that *that* part of the business was over—to tell the truth, he
had come to his decision some time ago and had gone on only to satisfy
his conscience—he knew that the one painter who could handle the
commission properly was Rembrandt van Rijn. If it had been possible
for the Syndics to call back the great Dürer from the dead, they could
not hope to get a better product than they would get right here—he
bent forward, too earnest to smile, and laid his hand briefly on the
stained and icy hand.

"Thank you, Heer van Hudde," he said; and realizing that his unbelief had made the thanks sound cold, he added, "Those are kind
words, and I stand in need of a few kind words these days."

"We hope, then, Master, that you'll consider the commission—"

"*You're* the one to do the considering, Heer van Hudde. I couldn't
say I've given much satisfaction with such commissions in the past.
Plenty of bad blood came out of what I did for Banning Coq, God rest
his soul, and the *Anatomy Lesson of Doctor Deijman* pleased nobody
very much, and this last one they'll not be hanging up again—that lunette I did for the City Hall."

"No?" said the visitor, shaking his head and pursing his mild pink
mouth and making a clucking sound. "But aren't they *dreadful?*—the
pictures that are up there for good, I mean. So blown-up, so false, if
you'll excuse my saying so. My, my, if poor Seghers could see what
they've got up there he'd turn over in his grave."

That speech, delivered without malice in the quiet tenor, had an unmanning effect upon him. It was as if some hidden spring of life within
him, long sealed over with ice, had suddenly been released to well up
and infuse his weary body with some freshening essence, to fill his aching eyes with tears. "I don't paint like that. I paint what I see, not something that people believe they ought to see," he said.

"I know it, my dear friend, I know it." The small and rosy hand, as
undeliberate as a child's, reached out again and patted him on the wrist.
"That's why the other four agreed with me that you're the one we should
get. And now"—he took a piece of paper out of his pocket, unfolded
it, and spread it on his knee—"now shall we go through this list of what
I referred to earlier as the reservations?"

There was a change in him then: it was as if he had assumed the
tasseled mortarboard of the professor. He took a stub of crayon out of
his pocket and held it poised between thumb and finger; and it was plain

that he was a man about to speak in his official capacity, but his authority was so old and well worn and sat so comfortably upon him that it could not give offense. "First of all, let's consider the kind of painting that our members want," he said. "We're an ancient guild, Heer van Rijn, and all five of us feel that any painting for the Guild Hall should be—well, why mince words?—a little old-fashioned. Innovations such as you introduced, and perfectly properly I'm sure, in the lunette for the City Hall are very interesting, but in our particular case they simply won't do. Close up or far away—wherever the viewer stands—a table must look like a table, an account book like an account book, a money-bag like a moneybag. I've not the slightest doubt that you can do what's required; any number of your paintings prove it. But the question is: Would you *want* to do it that way? That's something we'd better settle from the start."

He should have bridled, he should have said that the painter's concept of his subject was inalienably his own affair; and why he continued to sit courteously listening he did not know. Was it because he was too weary, body and soul, to assert his rights? Was it because the little treasurer saw nothing preposterous in his request and would have been amazed to learn that he had overstepped himself? Or was it that the fresh and blameless face before him, precluding visionary fantasy, could be painted only with directness and truth? "I would give you recognizable objects and good likenesses, worked up to the smallest detail," he said at last.

"Good!" He uttered it with real satisfaction, checked off the first item on his list with his stub of crayon, and smiled an open and gratified smile. "Now, as to what we would like to have brought out—if such things ever *can* be brought out—it's not so much our dignity as our honesty. The one thing you can say of the five of us is that our honesty has never been called into question. We examine and classify and stamp every bolt of cloth that comes off the looms in this city, and we have never—it may seem a small matter to you, but it's everything to us—let one flawed yard of goods go through our hands. We don't expect you to make us handsome or intelligent or aristocratic. Honest and conscientious—that's what we've been in our duties, and that's what we mean to be until we die, and that's what we want to look like when we're hung up in the Cloth Hall."

He did not speak, he only nodded, trying to envision the group—five men who could say of themselves that the creeping corruption of the times had not tainted them, that in their calling they had never lied to themselves or among themselves or to the buyers on the market—it was an assembly he wanted to see.

The visitor nodded too and made another check mark on his list. Then he lifted his face, which had grown even more schoolmasterly, and fixed the painter with his steady, earnest eyes. "And now, third and last—except, of course, for the monetary terms—there's this business of giving every one of the sitters his just due. That's very important. I wouldn't want to make a final commitment until we had come to an understanding about that," he said. "Far be it from me to criticize the very important canvas you did for the late lamented Captain Banning Coq—as a pure piece of painting, it's as fine as any in Holland, I have no doubt. But if certain members of that Company had their complaints, I must say I can't really blame them. A few of the faces are cut up by intervening objects and others are lost in shadows. They'd naturally feel cheated and a little ridiculous, though I'm certain that wasn't your intention. No doubt you were carried away by the enthusiasm of youth— a tendency we won't have to reckon with here, the more's the pity: you and I are both beyond such transports now. There are to be six sitters in our Regents' piece: five Syndics and our loyal servant who has been with us over twenty years and deserves to be memorialized as much as we do. And every one of the six must be a finished portrait, each man getting what he deserves and no man profiting by the suppression of any of the rest."

It must have been taxing for him to deliver himself of all that: he had wrinkled his paper by pressing his elbow nervously down on it. It was hard, too, to answer him, to ask without implications of scorn or anger—for which there was really no cause—"What do you want, then, Heer van Hudde? Five Syndics and a servant all sitting in one long row?"

"Oh, no, certainly not, Heer van Rijn. You only say that because you're worn out with your sickness and aren't drawing on your remarkable imagination. Arrange us any way you like—some sitting, some standing—anything you want. One could be speaking and one could be thinking and another could be listening—but why should I say such things to *you*? Come down to the Cloth Hall—we'd like you to paint us in the room we meet in—come down and have a look at us and move us around as you please. I'm sure you'll find an arrangement that will be completely satisfactory to all parties concerned; there must be dozens of possibilities."

He had never been inside the Cloth Hall, though the fame of its integrity had brought many to visit it from England and Denmark and Poland and Germany and France. He would go tomorrow or the day after—with trimmed hair and a shaven face and in decent clothes, so that Heer Duart Simonszoon van Hudde would not think he was always as slovenly as he was tonight. "I won't do it like the one for the Military Guild," he said. "You're quite right—some of the men *did* have reason to complain about what I did to them." And though he had uttered it with difficulty, it was as if some long illness passed miraculously from him as he spoke.

"You'll consider it, then, in spite of the reservations?" He checked the last item off, folded up the paper, and returned it to his pocket.

"Yes, definitely." He sighed and straightened on his stool and became aware of the room again: the half-scrubbed floor, the steady flame of the lamp, the snow piled up outside so that a thin, uneven band of it showed at the bottom of the black windowpane.

"It's an honorable commission, Heer van Rijn, even if I say so myself, and I'm happy to be able to offer you a solid and equitable price. Each of the Syndics is prepared to put down two hundred florins, and an additional two hundred for the portrait of our good servingman will be provided by the president and the secretary and myself. That's twelve hundred in all—will that be satisfactory?"

"Entirely satisfactory, Heer van Hudde."

"Well, good, then; very good!" said the little visitor, sliding down from his stool, his broad face dimpled all over with the dents of his gratification. "We'll be expecting you to call on us at the Cloth Hall one of these days. Not that there's any hurry. Eager as we are, I'd rather see you stay at home until you're quite yourself again. And, if I may say so, I wouldn't stay here much longer without a fire if I were you. You've got a long walk ahead of you, and the sooner you're in bed the better. There's no use trying to tell you how delighted I am that we've come to an agreement—I only hope you know."

The small figure was over the threshold, moving off in a swirl of big flakes, before Rembrandt realized that there was a way to exchange kindness for kindness, to make some return for the faith that had survived the twists and turns of fashion, to let some of the clean waters that had welled up in him at the touch of this stranger flow out of his closed spirit into the world. "Heer van Hudde, Heer van Hudde," he shouted, running out after him into the soft, agitated whiteness. "Wait a moment —there was something I wanted to say—" The treasurer of the Syndics of the Cloth Hall stopped short while the flakes gathered on his beaver and the fine velvet in which he had dressed himself to pay a formal call on the Master Rembrandt van Rijn. "You said it would be twelve hundred florins—let it be a thousand," the master said.

"A thousand? Why a thousand?"

"Because the portrait of your servingman—*I* would like to make a gift of that to him and to the Drapers' Guild and to you."

For an instant he was afraid that the purity of their exchange would be shattered by some protest, but no protest came. The small mouth opened, closed, and shaped itself into a smile. "Well, now, that's very generous of you, very generous indeed," he said; and the light touch that he laid upon the bare chapped arm before he went his way was as giving and as satisfying as an embrace.

✳

The board had been spread in the meeting chamber of the Syndics of the Cloth Hall, and the candles had been lighted, even though the golden midsummer sunlight still lay in squares on the good china plates and the crystal goblets, on the beautiful wainscoting and the pale wall above it, and on the finished picture which hung on that wall, itself a source of light. Summer—ripe, peaceful summer—would bloom in it forever: so he thought as he saw it from the threshold, saw the white and black and cream and scarlet of it across the festal table. He stood there, decent in the grey jacket and breeches that Hendrikje had insisted he buy for the occasion, unnoticed by the loyal servant of twenty years' service who was laying pears and peaches on the boxwood garland in the middle of the board; he stood there and thanked God—listening or unlistening—that such a blasted tree, beaten by so many storms and rooted in such inhospitable soil, should have borne such fruit. Nothing as radiant and whole and true had ever before issued from him. He hoped that they also would know it, the five who were to sit with him at this little supper which, in their courteous fashion, they had arranged to celebrate the consummation of his eight months of labor. But whether they knew it or not was a secondary consideration: God and the great dead against whom he had measured himself all his days would know if He or they knew anything; and, furthermore, he knew it himself.

The frame of the picture—they had ordered it without thought of cost from the best frame-maker in the city—put a gilded but simple boundary around the best of his works and the best that a man could hope to find on earth. The light of the liberal sun fell on the six faces and merged there with the inner light of the human spirit unclouded by compromise, glowing in ripe serenity. The black velvet, the black beaver hats, the fine scarlet and gold of the Oriental carpet that covered the table at which they sat, the ancient wood of the wainscoting behind them, the account book and the moneybag they touched with their seasoned and eloquent hands—all these, carefully as he had wrought them, were mere accessories to the faces; and the faces, varied as they were and perfect likenesses, were subordinate to the ultimate intention: the light of Man shining in the light of the world. He looked his fill and then cleared his throat to make his presence known to the servant, who had laid the last yellow pear in the waxy green of the boxwood. "Oh, your honor, I hadn't seen you," he said, straightening and smiling and glancing up at the picture. "It does look fine, doesn't it? It's almost upsetting—I'm here and I'm there—it's almost as if there were two of me. And now, before the others come, may I thank your honor for the portrait? Wonderful as it is in itself—and I've never seen anything like it—it's still more wonderful because of your honor's generosity."

The best he could do in return for that was to bring himself to look cordially at the well-known face: the merry mouth, the lineless cheeks, the gentle eyes, the balding brow. "The table looks very festive—very elegant," he said.

"Thank you. I'm glad your honor thinks so. The extra place is for a friend of your honor's, the Burgomaster Tulp. Heer van Hudde thought you might find it pleasant to have him here, since he was the subject of your first Regents' piece and has known your honor for so many years."

"That was very kind of Heer van Hudde," he said, feeling the easy tears filming his eyes and doing his best to keep them out of his voice. The celebratory supper, the elaborate garland on the table, the beautiful frame, even the fact that the other pictures had been removed for this one evening so that nothing would draw attention from his masterpiece—all these, gracious as they were, were formal courtesies. But that the treasurer of the Syndics should have thought of inviting his old friend to share the occasion—this surpassed graciousness, this came from the heart.

"Your honor will sit here at the head," said the servant. "Heer van Hudde, because it was he who arranged this happy business, will sit at your left; and Burgomaster Tulp, as the guest of the Syndics, will sit at your right. Wait—I think I hear them coming. I believe the gentlemen would like your honor to stand over there, a little to one side of the picture. They'll want to shake your hand and thank you separately before you all sit down to supper, you know."

He had not known it, nor was he prepared for the grave procedure that followed. Each one of the Syndics, dressed in the formal clothes in which he had been painted, stepped in by himself, paused just this side of the threshold, and looked up at the painting solemnly and with complete attention, as if he had never laid eyes on it before. The second waited outside the room until the first had come at an unhurried pace across the broad carpet, to take the master's hand and express his gratification and move on to his appointed place at the board in the mingled sun and candlelight. It was a ritual so perfectly planned that his own awkwardness could not mar it: it overrode whatever rigid and insufficient things he said in response to their varied compliments; and it reached its consummation with the last of the line, when the good doctor came in and kissed his cheek and held him in his arms as he had done in Hendrik Uylenburgh's shop thirty years ago.

Once they were seated and grace had been said, the atmosphere was lightened by a fine flurry of unfolding napkins; and while the servant poured out the excellent white wine, everybody began to jest about what they should toast. Their beavers, said the secretary; plainly their beavers were the most significant part of the picture for the master, since he had repainted them nine or ten times. The president proposed his own eyebrows because they, too, had given no end of trouble, but then withdrew his suggestion in favor of Heer van Hudde's hand, which had grown stiff with holding the moneybag a dozen unsatisfactory ways. There was a warmth in all that jesting which told him they looked back on the long sessions of sitting—the puttings on and the scrapings off, the tag-ends of time when they had hurried away from a completed piece of Guild business to slip into the chairs he had set for them, the days when the sun had stubbornly refused to shine for him—as the stuff of happy memory. And lest he should be taking their harmless levity

ill—he had not been able to call up one feeble sally to add to theirs—
the president rapped his plate with his knife, rose and lifted his goblet,
and said in a voice quavering partly with age and partly with feeling:
"To the brush of Rembrandt van Rijn, which he does not dip into paint
like other masters, but into the light of God's pure sun."

As the brightness at the windows faded and the quiet shining of the
candles intensified, the servant brought in the great tureen of soup and
ladled it out and set it still steaming before them—a rich and creamy
whiteness dappled with bits of melted butter and broken here and there
by the tender green of summer leeks. They ate with seemly slowness,
talking of this and that: of the boy Prince Willem and his mother and
the great Pensionary de Witte, who was gathering more power into his
hands than any citizen since Oldenbarneveldt, of French belligerence
and Flemish complacency, of the fate of the settlers who might be left
to their own devices if the great land was lost in the West, and of the
hazards of the merchant vessels moving across the northern and the
eastern seas. But whatever they talked of, they returned unfailingly
to the business of the evening, to the canvas that shone scarcely less
now that the light of day was withdrawn and it was left to shine with its
own light. "The pages of the account book are so real that you can hear
them crack and rustle," said the vice-president. "The scarlet in that
carpet burns like a fire," said the secretary. "I pity poor Heer van
Hudde," said the president. "Here we are, saying it all beforehand, and
poor Heer van Hudde is the one who has to make a speech."

Little was expected of the guest of honor. They were so at ease with
him and each other that he had to furnish nothing but a "Thank you"
and a nod and a smile. Now that the windows had darkened, he was
more aware of the city than he had been when he was only able to see the
roofs and canals and sycamores and poplars which had become so familiar to him over the eight months he had sketched and painted: out
there lay Amsterdam, where the names of Lievens and von Sandrart
and Juriaen Ovens meant more than his—it was only in this one small
chamber that he was the painter of painters, the peer of Dürer and
Titian and Michelangelo. But it was a serenely melancholy thought
rather than a bitter one; the worst it could do to him was to make way
for the remembrance of another celebratory evening, when Hendrik
Uylenburgh had made a foolish speech and the dead beloved had come
to stand beside him and watch the sun go down, her face and hair on
fire with the molten gold. What had he hoped for then? More than he
had gotten? No, it was only that what he had gotten was more exalted
and more terrible, different only as that which was wrought by destiny
or the hand of God was different from what men, poor artificers that
they were, fashioned vainly and shallowly in their waking dreams. For
one generation gave way to another, and the nations coalesced and
drifted apart like bits of light on a wind-troubled pool, and only one
who was blind in his vanity would presume to say what tomorrow would

bring. But tonight was tonight, and the picture hung on the wall gloriously completed, and Heer van Hudde was tapping on his goblet and getting up to make a speech, partly from carefully written notes, but mostly from the heart.

"Great and beloved Master, dear and respected Burgomaster and Physician, good friends who have had an equal share with me in this happy enterprise, I promise to speak briefly, but I pray God I may speak sufficiently," he said. "They say that the time of miracles is past, and yet it seems to me that what we celebrate here tonight is a kind of secular miracle, a blessing given to us in spite of so many possibilities to the contrary that we ought to bow our heads and offer thanks with all our hearts. We have our Regents' piece, our incomparable Regents' piece, but we must not take such a rare thing for granted. Think for a minute how much might have stood in the way of it, and it may seem to some of you as it seems to me: that there is a Providence that concerns itself with such things. Heer van Rijn might not have lived to be called to our service—I know that he was one of a numerous family and that all the other issue of his mother and father are now with God. Any one of us might have gone his way before the painting was finished—life is a precarious possession even for the young, and we are already growing old. I might have been misled by bad taste or bad advice into engaging some other master, and Heer van Rijn might have had his reasons for turning me away when I came to offer him the commission. Good friends, when you come to think of it, what might *not* have happened? The full brightness of the sun might never have shone on that gold and scarlet carpet on our table; we might, like many other guilds, have ripped out our fine old wainscoting and replaced it with plaster ten years ago; our good and loyal servant might have been so burdened with private cares that he would have been unable to smile; those troublesome beavers of ours might never have been arranged to the master's satisfaction—and any one of these possibilities would have been enough to diminish the unique treasure which hangs, to our honor and for the preservation of our memory, finished and safe on that wall. Vision itself is vulnerable, and Heer van Rijn has eyes to paint and we have eyes to see. For all these reasons, and many more, I offer thanks to that Providence which works its miracles quietly in spite of a thousand possibilities that stand against them, but in thanking Providence I do not in the least stint my thanks to our honored master here. I say to him now what I said to him on our first meeting: we could not have been better served if the great Dürer himself had risen from the dead to paint us. And to our thanks will be added those of our children who will see us living here when we live no more, and the gratefulness of generations who will look at us when we are long since forgotten, and think that man is good and life is worthy, even if there is much of it that lies in the dark. Dr. Tulp, old friends and fellow Syndics—yes, and you, too, Mathias, put down the tureen and join us in this: I give you, by the grace of Providence, Heer Rembrandt van Rijn."

They had the kindness not to look at him during the long and decorous applause. They looked at the painting or at each other, and it made no difference that his throat was tight, that his eyes, seeing the faces of his dead—Gerrit, Father, Mother, Lysbeth, Saskia, Adriaen—had to blink against the stinging tears. Them, too, he had memorialized, setting them beyond time in such guises as his groping and limited spirit had perceived them in—and however he had misunderstood them or whatever ill he had done them, it was either forgotten or forgiven now . . . The president and Heer van Hudde were urging the Burgomaster to his feet: surely he would give them a word or two; it was the least he could do in payment for his supper, they said. And the guest of honor wrung his napkin under the table and hoped that the doctor would be casual or dry or jocular: it would not do to weep, he simply must not weep . . .

"Syndics of the Cloth Hall, gracious hosts and honorable gentlemen, I have known this one here since he was a lad from Leyden grinding pigments in Lastman's studio," the doctor said, clapping him on the shoulder hard enough to make him take hold of himself. "When *I* thought he was remarkable, the world thought he was nothing to be particularly excited about. When *I* had the feeling that he had declined, the world was ready to clamor at his door. When *I* was sure he was a giant among painters, the world consigned him to a minor place. And the work of his that seemed to me his best before this one that I love so much"—he gestured toward it with his stiffened fingers, he smiled his fine cool smile at it—"that work they rejected outright. In fact, now that the pattern has changed, now that I find myself in accord with five burghers of Amsterdam, all men of culture and substance, about a canvas of his, I wonder whether I have lost my good judgment. But since you insist on agreeing with me in spite of my questionable record, since you see in this one here"—he touched him again—"a peer of Dürer, let's drink to that. I give you this dear and difficult friend, this sturdy and indomitable spirit who walked his own way and was followed only by the choicest of followers—you and me, dear gentlemen, and a few equally admirable others—the glory of Holland, if not now, then in due time: Rembrandt van Rijn."

There was laughter after that, laughter and more talk and the clink of china while the servant carried off the soup bowls and brought in the first course: an exquisite piece of boned whitefish, covered with the grated yolks of eggs and lying on a nest of parsley. He himself could not yet take part in the easy and cultivated conversation. A profound stillness was upon him, a peace that he could not bring himself to break with blundering words. He stared at the steady flames of the candles and took the first bite of the food, and the savor that he found in it was not merely the savor of the yield of the pure summer brook. It was a nourishment not only for his flesh but for his spirit; and if he could have found the words, he would have told them that he was taking a secular communion, not unlike the good Heer van Hudde's secular miracle—that he had returned after anger and loathing and long loneliness, chastened and absolved, to take his portion at the love-feast of the human race.

BOOK XI

1666
-
1669

And now, as he advanced toward that place in which time is no more, the chronology of the world, the orderly reckoning of years and months and days, was mercifully weakened in him. He could no more remember what had happened first than a man standing in his autumnal garden could see which of the leaves heaped up against his wall—the gold, the ashen brown, the red, the yellow-green—had gone past him earliest on the always hastening flow of the wind. Often during the day and for hours in the night—for his sleep was brief and broken—he would try to put the accumulating events into their proper succession, but the effort only confused him and deepened his conviction of general dissolution and futility. What had come first, Titus's withdrawal or Hendrikje's mortal sickness? He could see the separate scenes clearly enough to tell what season they had taken place in: in one there were fronds of frost on the window, in another there was a bowl of violets on the table, and a third was crossed by the thin rays of a late September sun. But when he tried to place them in a regular order, dull sleep pressed down upon him, or the miseries of his failing body distracted him—his aching teeth, the painful stiffness of his joints, his burning eyes. What came after what, what led into what? It was useless; he did not know and he would never know.

When was it—in the sultry air of what month in what summer had he become aware that for days, maybe even weeks, Hendrikje had scarcely touched her food? When had he glanced up from the meat and beets and rusks on her plate and seen that the flesh of her face had a greyish cast and was stretched tight and dry over the bones?

"How is it that you aren't eating?"

"Who can eat on a day like this?"

"But you haven't *been* eating."

"I'm eating less, but what's the difference? All the women in my family get fat in their forties, and I'd rather be thin."

"Don't get thin—I like you very well the way you are."

"Do you really, now?"

She had asked it half in jest and half in earnest: his decreasing ardor, which might have caught fire at a stronger yearning, had found less and less in her of late at which to kindle itself. She had been going up to bed early, sometimes an hour or two before him, and his urgency had seldom been such as to impel him to break her heavy sleep. Had he or had he not put his hand across the sun-reddened tablecloth and laid it over hers and told her that her body was as dear to him as ever, even if he did not claim it as often as in the old days? That would have depended on whether Titus had sat at supper with them that evening, and he could not for the life of him remember when it was that Titus had begun to absent himself three or four nights a week to take his meal on the other side of town in the society of Magdalena and Vrouw van Loo.

Had the young man been shouldered out, or had he simply deserted a melancholy household for a more cheerful one? That, too, could be answered only if the chronology could be properly arranged; and, God help him, his mind went blank, he felt a vertiginous pressure in his head whenever he made the attempt. The first short, bitter conversation between father and son had taken place in the autumn—but which autumn? The autumn after the calamity of the lunette for the City Hall and the hanging of the Syndics' Regents' piece—an autumn when she had resolutely turned away from the boy in order to show that her loyalties were all for him? Or another autumn, the next one perhaps, after the fright had gripped his vitals like a black inexorable hand? The autumn when he had heard her making the strange noise in the back yard and had run out to her and found her retching and seen the grass around her stained with the stuff from her poor, pale, gasping mouth? "My God, Hendrikje, what are you doing? Are you coughing blood?"

"Oh, no, not coughing it, just vomiting it," she had said, as if there could be comfort in that; for she knew, poor devil, how her predecessor had died, that predecessor against whom she had never uttered one jealous word, for whose soul she had regularly prayed, and whose child she could not have brought up more tenderly if he had been her own. "It's nothing, I tell you, nothing. It's the grapes. I should never eat grapes, especially with the skins."

Which autumn? He could not remember, but he could recall the chill room and the fire gone down to embers on the hearth, and her upstairs in her exhausted sleep, and himself waiting for the boy to come back because he had a word or two to say to him: in the last four days he had come home only to change his clothes and go to bed. "This is a home, not a boarding house"—that was what he had meant to say; but instead a stream of bitter things he had not even known he thought came spurting out of him because the young man had walked so blithe and merry into his hopelessness and his solitude, whistling shrilly enough to wake the woman and the girl upstairs.

"Where have you been? To the van Loos' again?" He said the name in a spiteful, affected voice meant to mock the mincing pretensions of Vrouw and Magdalena van Loo. They were minor offshoots of the Uylenburgh stock who had come after the death of Heer van Loo to settle in Amsterdam; and they had used a little money much more circumspectly than he had used a great deal, so that their house on the Singel was filled with small precious things and could lay claim to a kind of faded elegance. The mother looked like an old wooden Virgin in a cap with pink ribbons; the daughter was a washed-out copy of Saskia, a girl of seventeen whose limp hair and inexpressive face and languid manners struck him as an insult to the dead beloved. But whatever the two women were, the lad had taken to them and they to him; and his eyes had grown narrow and his mouth had turned hard at what his father had done to their name. "Yes. Where else should I be? Would you rather have me drinking in a tavern? Or would you prefer that I went to visit the whores on Pieter-Jacob Street?"

"For four days you've used this house as nothing but a place to wash and sleep in—"

"What else am I to do here? Sit like a stone for you to glare at? You've been furious with me ever since I said you'd better let the *Julius Civilis* thing alone—and all the more furious since it turned out that I was right. I should think you'd be glad to be rid of me. I should think everybody here, except maybe Cornelia, would prefer me out of sight."

What things he had said in answer to that he could not remember, but they could certainly not have been forgotten, could only have burned deeper and been the more galling when the liking for the colorless girl had turned into affection and the affection had turned, unbelievably, into what the young man had deceived himself into thinking was love. Love that limp little Magdalena? Wait eagerly all day to hear that childish, lisping voice? Walk the streets at night with that wispy nonentity? It had seemed to him that Titus, for some inexplicable reason, had deliberately chosen the exact reverse of everything that his life at home should have taught him to love.

How soon after that had the dear helpmeet, the unfaltering worker, pulled herself out of bed on a chill grey morning and gotten half her clothes onto her dried and shrunken body, and then fallen back against the bolster, white in the face but smiling as if she had caught herself at some foolish thing, and said, "You know, I'm afraid I just can't do it any more"? This time Dr. Tulp had seen no reason to tell him what he already knew, had only dragged himself stiff-kneed night after night to the Rozengracht, to bring always stronger and stronger drops that put longer and longer intervals of sleep between the assaults of the pain. When she was awake, she moaned and held the covers away from her stomach as if the weight of a comforter or a blanket was unendurable. Sometimes she cried out, and then looked stern and shook her head as if somebody else, not she, had been guilty of the impropriety. She had asked for the pastor, and he had sent Cornelia to bring him, watching her from an upper window as she hurried off toward the church: sturdy and purposeful, a little woman in her exigency, her hair lifted behind her in the wind of her haste—her mother's dark, luxuriant hair. And the pastor had come, a kind and unobtrusive old man with a mild and almost toothless pink mouth, and had prayed alone with her up there. Himself, he had sat downstairs with her daughter at his feet, stroking the child's head as it rested against his knee; and he had recognized what prayers were being said, not by the words, since they were too quietly uttered to be made out, but by the rise and fall of the old voice: "The Lord is my Shepherd, I shall not want," "In my Father's house are many mansions," "Our Father who art in Heaven."

"God has given your good wife a little respite, Heer van Rijn. We prayed together, and then we talked awhile, and now she has fallen into a quiet sleep."

He had not said what had leaped into his mind: that Dr. Tulp's drops, not God's mercy, were responsible for that respite. He had stood near the door, wordless and awkward, with his arm around the girl's shoulders, wondering when the pastor would leave him to suffer in solitude.

"You're not of our persuasion—I understand that. You've seen the face of Our Lord through some other window, with the Quakers or perhaps with the Mennonites—"

He could not tell whether *she* had said so, or whether the pastor had come to that conclusion himself. It had seemed to him a convenient and charitable conclusion, and he had not gainsaid it, had only mumbled that he supposed he was more of a Mennonite than anything else.

"It doesn't matter, Heer van Rijn. All that matters is that a man should know the grace of God in his heart, should partake of the Saviour's abounding love. And I'm sure that such has been the case with you—otherwise you wouldn't have had so much love to give. Your wife has often spoken to me of your strong and abiding love for her and the children. Never once in her life, she said, did she have to ask herself whether your thoughts had turned elsewhere. I thought that might be a comfort to you, I thought that was something you might like to hear. Good day, Heer van Rijn. Good day, dear child. May the Lord be with you and keep you and make His countenance to shine upon you and give you peace."

It had been one afternoon not too long thereafter, when Titus was sitting at her bedside—for in the last days Titus *did* sit at her bedside, shocked and thin and almost as pale as she—it had been only a few days later that he had gone to ask the old poet Jeremias de Dekker to sell for him that grave which he had bought in the Old Church so that he might lie beside Saskia and to buy with such money as could be gotten for it a grave in the West Church, where the organ music that Hendrikje had loved would send its vibrations down through the marble blocks beneath which she would lie, where the feet of the pious would move above her, coming to the altar to receive the bread and the wine, the Body and the Blood. And even though he could not tell her of this thing that he had done, it had given him strength: strength to hold her in his arms during the last assault and the last futile struggle, strength to straighten her limbs and close her eyes and spread her hair on the bolster before he let the children or any stranger who had not seen her in her life and her beauty come into the room and see her in her death . . .

Winter, and the leaves piled up, and the snow laid over them, as earth is laid over the lost face, and confusion is laid over memory. Winter, and the evil days come when a man says, "I have no pleasure in them." Was it that winter or the one which came after it that the good Vrouw Lingelbach—who had been doing their wash along with her own and teaching Cornelia to mend and make a simple pottage—had come to the door one morning with a little old woman named Rebecca Willems, a creature so bent and wrinkled that he had been shocked to find that the difference between her age and his own was only seven or eight years? This Rebecca, Vrouw Lingelbach had said, had neither kith nor kin nor bed nor hearthstone; and if they would give her a place to sleep and what little food she needed, would serve them to the limits of her strength and her devotion. He had accepted her, and Cornelia had welcomed her; and between the old woman's experience and the girl's vitality, much that was squalid, much that jangled the raw nerves had disappeared, and he had at least had a decent place in which to sit empty-handed and stare out the iron and frozen days.

Quiet—old Rebecca fallen asleep and emitting little rhythmic puffs of breath, and Cornelia sitting on the hearth beside his chair and knitting steadily in the changing light of the peat fire, knitting and knitting and saying scarcely a word. What was it—Titus's desertion to the van Loos, her mother's death, his reaching out to touch her now that there was no one else for him to touch—that had put a stop to her chatter and lightened her step and quieted her darting eyes? That was another thing he would never know.

"Where's your brother?—it's almost midnight."

"He and Magdalena went skating on the Singel."

"You'd think they would have tired themselves out by now."

"I guess they did. I guess they must have gone to Vrouw van Loo's to drink tea." And then, after long stillness, and with a little uneasy laugh, "I guess they'd come *here* to drink tea if you ever asked them to."

"Why should I ask them? I've got company enough."

"Do you really, Father? So do I, so do I."

And into another evening much like that one—for to those whose lives are over, all evenings are more or less the same—had come the lad from Dordt, seventeen or thereabouts, his thin and handsome face peaked by the frost, snow powdering his fashionable velvets, snow in his silky pale brown locks, in the thick lashes that made his large eyes seem even larger, in the folds of the big cowhide bag he dragged in with him out of the bitter night. His name was Aert de Gelder, and he had come from Dordt to enroll as an apprentice. Every objection that had been offered to him he had parried with such courteous persistence that the master was convinced it would be useless to turn him away that evening, that he would only appear next morning at the door.

"But I'm sick, young man. I'm tired out, I've lost my wife, I scarcely have strength to teach the two that are still with me."

"You don't have to teach me, Master. I can learn by watching. If only you'll let me stay and watch you paint—"

"I scarcely ever paint any more."

"Holland will lose a good painter if you turn me away. I have a gift, but I need to learn, and the only painter I have any respect for is yourself. I'll pay whatever fee you name, if you'll only let me stay in your studio and study what you *have* painted and ask a few questions. I'll not disturb you, I'll not intrude—look, couldn't we try it for a week and see how it goes?"

A week, a month, a year, two years—he did not know, he could not remember. But during whatever stretch of time it had gone on, this Aert de Gelder had given him not one instant of regret. The young aristocrat who had kept his own manservant in Dordt became on the Rozengracht the servant of his master, ready to grind the pigments and lay the wet towels across the burning eyes and run to the fish market and take the heavy pail out of Cornelia's hands. His questions had been so penetrating that it was diverting to answer them; his fingers had proved so apt that they had learned at once how to imitate the light strokes and lay on the heavy impasto; he resurrected and revivified the old unfashionable convictions by stating them with the wonder and vigor of youth. Again and again he went to see the *Anatomy Lesson of Doctor Tulp,* the *Company of Captain Banning Coq,* the *Anatomy Lesson of Doctor Deijman,* and the *Syndics of the Cloth Hall;* and nothing could convince him that the painter of those would never stand at his easel again.

"Why should I? I get on with what comes out of the teaching and the etchings. And anyway you can see how my arm shakes."

"You could always steady it with the maulstick, Master. The only trouble is that you haven't used it for so long."

Some weeks after that—it was spring by then, he could remember the bunch of violets on the breakfast table—he said over the rusks and herring that he was going upstairs to paint and wanted nobody to disturb him: if he was to get anything done, and he doubted very much that he would, it would have to be done in solitude. His voice, like his temper, wavered between kindness and vengefulness; he wanted to please the boy, but he also wanted to show him that making a beginning after such a calamity was not the simple matter his callow optimism had led him to think. Alone in the little studio, he opened the casements to the cool April air and went and faced himself in the looking glass. The image that he saw in the clear bluish light appalled him—the flesh of the face shrunken and pulled awry by deep wrinkles, the eyes small and bloodshot and blurred by weeping, the hair unkempt and completely grizzled, the mouth flattened over the gaps left by lost teeth and drawn down at the corners in mortal disgust as though the taste of existence was bile on his tongue. He hated the wreck that stared back at him, and he was seized with a frenzy to set it down at its worst: he turned back his collar so that the loose flesh of the jowls and neck would be visible; he found an old beret and set it on his head at a crazy slant. What he painted then—or rather laid on in great lumps with his palette knife—what he molded with his fingers and scratched with his thumbnail and scored with the butt end of his brush absorbed him utterly; in his feverish obsession with it he forgot his shaking arm, his rusty finger joints, the blearing and burning of his eyes. The evil days were in it, the days when the keepers of the house trembled and those that looked out of the windows were darkened and the grinders ceased because they were few. The colors of death were in it: ashen brown and wild streaks of scarlet, dull grey and sickly yellowed green. But when he paused to take breath and look at it from a distance, he saw that the old skills were in it too—coarsened by violence, stiffened by long disuse, but surviving nevertheless in this ruined flesh, this dulled brain, this cooling blood. And when he showed it to Rebecca and Cornelia and Aert de Gelder, he was not given occasion to say, "There, now, I hope you're satisfied—you see how it is with me when I try to paint." The old woman said, "Lord save us, your honor, it's like you when you're in a bad humor sure as one pea is like another." Cornelia said, "I can't keep looking at it, Father—I'll cry if I do." And the apprentice from Dordt said, "Who ever painted the terrible truth as honestly as that?"

Yet it was not entirely honest, and he knew as much and was nagged by the fear that this wild and bitter image might be the last record of himself he would leave on earth. In a week or so he was trying to catch himself by surprise, glancing suddenly at his image when he happened to pass a mirror; and what he saw was always desolate but sometimes less distorted by the madness of despair. The skill to render the subtleties and contradictions inextricably bound up with mortal existence—had he lost it completely after Hendrikje's death? Fearfully, with Aert de Gelder looking over his shoulder, he rummaged through the canvases that stood unwanted in his studio, trying to see what half-forgotten means he had used to embody those contradictions and bring them into a dark harmony. It occurred to him then, perhaps because he had turned up a couple of the *Apostles,* that he might deal with himself with more detachment if he painted himself as Saint Paul—an old man pondering in prison some Hebraic text, weary of the world and the struggle, waiting for the final release; and he began to work up that concept slowly, circumspectly, sketching himself as exhaustively as he had sketched Heer van Hudde and the rest. Once he had prepared the canvas and laid on the first brush strokes, he did not allow himself to stand at the easel for longer than a couple of hours; and he invited Aert de Gelder to come in and sit behind him because he knew the presence of the lad would rein him in and forestall any furious and reasonless flights. And it was as if Heer van Hudde's secular Providence had stooped once more to sustain him, to take him from one peak and set him on another as though he had never fallen into the black gorge be-tween: his brush was what it had been in the old days, obedient in his hand. But he knew no exultation to find it so; it was Aert de Gelder, not he, who stood and stared for another half-hour at the day's accom-plishment and came to the table too exhilarated to eat.

After supper, the four of them would usually sit in the parlor, crossed now by the fragrant winds of summer. Rebecca would doze and Cor-nelia would knit and Aert would ask the questions he had been hoard-ing up all day: "How much yellow did you add to the white in the tur-ban, Master?" "Where could I find some Hebrew lettering?—I'd like to learn to copy it too." "Is it best, do you tihnk, to stop painting a little before you want to or to go on until you have to stop because you're tired?"

On one such evening, with the smell of mown grass blowing in from the meadows and the canvas almost finished, so many old mem-ories came pressing in upon him that he wished even this devoted pres-ence to withdraw and leave him to himself, so that he could say over and over, as a monk tells his beads, the long roll call of his dead. Silence had descended after the meal because Rebecca had gone to vespers and had asked Cornelia to come with her; Titus, as usual, was at the van Loos', and Aert de Gelder, perceptive enough to sense the melancholy in the air, had been making a pretense of reading the Bible in the wan-ing light. But the young will be served, and he could not contain him-self forever. "Master, I've been wanting to ask you: when you conceived of your self-portrait, which came into your mind first—the colors or the forms?" he said.

It was an unanswerable question, and he brushed it away fretfully. "It isn't a self-portrait. It's the Apostle Paul," he told him in a voice more querulous than was justified.

"Yes, of course, excuse me; I'm always forgetting. But which came first—?"

"I can't tell you. I don't know."

"Then maybe you can tell me what text you were thinking of—I've been trying to find a suitable one here in the Bible. Is it this: 'I have run a good race, I have finished the course'?"

"No, it's something altogether different. I don't know where to tell you to look for it—I couldn't find it myself—but it's somewhere in the Acts or the Epistles. 'Lord, when shall I be delivered from the body of this death?' "

*

They kept urging him to paint—Tulp and Aert de Gelder and Cor-nelia and Jeremias de Dekker—so he painted. Some old men, when their affairs in the world were finished, played backgammon all day long; some occupied themselves with the cultivation of hyacinths and tulips; some sat on the stoops and watched the children playing in the

street. With the same listlessness, the same detachment, he painted—
it was his way of filling up the empty days. Only, there were very few
subjects now that he could bring himself to work on. To tell the impious
truth, there were only two faces that could draw and hold him: his own,
stunned before what he had known and drained by what he had suffered,
and the imagined face of Him whom *she* had taken to be God incarnate.

God the Father he had never been able to visualize; the Holy Spirit
he had never imagined as anything but a rayed iridescence; and even
those winged messengers whose movement he had tried to capture with
the aid of the swinging manikin were lost to him now. But the Son still
took shape for him, if only as seen in a glass darkly; and his chief quarrel with the world these days was that the Rozengracht was so far from
the synagogue of the Ashkenazim and the Jewish section of the Breestraat, where he might hope to see Him suddenly materialize in one of
His kind.

Nevertheless, he went to look for Him whenever he could elude Aert
and Cornelia. Much as they irritated him with their solicitude, they had
sound reasons for wanting him close to home. There had been plague
in Amsterdam—one-tenth of the population had died of it, and it was
not yet completely past: on those unauthorized wanderings of his he
often came upon a door painted with the scarlet cross. Besides, there had
been times when even a short walk in his own neighborhood had set his
heart fluttering, caused the veins to stand out like ropes on his hands,
and made his head feel at once enormously expanded and eerily light.

Heat was his most insidious enemy, and that summer the heat lingered, thick and humid, far into September. The leaves fell as if from
sheer exhaustion, scarcely yellowed at the edges; the brief rains did
nothing more than raise steam from the cobblestones. And yet he
argued with the young ones that morning that there was nothing the
matter with the weather—it was a fine autumn day, a little warm perhaps, but comfortable because of the freshening mist.

But apparently the citizens of Amsterdam were not in agreement
with him; they had taken to their houses and closed their shutters against
the sun. On his weaving, enervating stroll from the Rozengracht to
the Breestraat, he met only those who exposed themselves out of necessity: the porters, the city messengers, the wagoners taking loads of
wilted vegetables back from an almost empty market, the pastor or doctor called out on urgent business and plainly unhappy with his obligation.

It was two in the afternoon when he reached the Jewish section of
the Breestraat and found himself a wall to lean against in a patch of
shadow. It had been a futile journey; even here the life that usually
churned around him—the young rabbinical students at their endless
arguments, the noisy children, the women thrusting their heads out of
the windows and calling to each other in their mysterious language—
had all withdrawn into the blessed dark of the curtained rooms. One

subject only was available to him: an old beggar who was making the rounds of the neighborhood with a thoroughness that belied the pious resignation of his face, exhibiting his torn clothes and his reverend beard and collecting his coin at every door. He set himself to sketching the beggar only in order to distract himself from a mounting panic: either he was sick, or his fear of sickness was a sickness in itself—a crawling nausea, a sudden and drenching flow of sweat, a pain at the back of his head.

But if I'm really sick I ought to go inside somewhere, he thought. A drink of water, a chair to sit in, a few minutes of the cooling darkness, and I will be myself again. But that thought only begot another which intensified his fright: there was nobody here any more whom he could find to call upon in his exigency—the Lazzaras had moved to Rotterdam years ago; the good Pineros had gone to their graves within a few months of each other; the melancholy Dr. Bonus and the urbane Rabbi Menasseh ben Israel were also to be counted among the dead; and of all the rabbis and merchants who had sat for him in his studio, there was not one whose house he would have been able to identify. Mortality and change—this one gone and that one and the other, and new lives going on in the rooms they had once inhabited, yes, and in his own rooms, too, in the great house whose chimneys he could see from where he stood—mortality and change unstrung his knees, so that he had to move to prove to himself that he was not dying, had to walk ten or twelve paces in the merciless heat of the bleared sun.

Ten or twelve paces was as much as he could manage. He stopped before a great house of yellowish stone and let himself down at the bottom of a flight of steps that led up to its impressive door. I can feel the cool stone through the cloth of my breeches, I can see, I am alive, he told himself; tonight when I am back home with Aert and Cornelia and Rebecca I will laugh at this. And though he went on sweating even more profusely, though the pain in his head had not decreased and his fluttering heart had not righted itself, the fear subsided. He took the chalk out of his pocket and was working again on his drawing of the beggar when a man came out of the house next door and approached and stopped in front of him at the bottom of the stairs.

It was an impressive stranger who looked with large and penetrating eyes first at him and then at his drawing—a man in his early forties, lean and swarthy, with a hawk nose and a mass of wavy auburn hair. He was dressed in elegant things that had crumpled in the weather; his bronze-colored breeches were fine but wrinkled, and his rich silk shirt was darkened with sweat and left unbuttoned over the matted hair on his lean chest. His person had suffered less in the heat than his clothing: his bearing was erect; and the upturned ends of his carefully trimmed moustache, unwilted, gave his whole face, netted over by premature furrows and wrinkles, an air of keen attentiveness. "So you've been sketching our friend the perennial beggar," he said in Dutch that was surprisingly easy, since he was obviously one of the Portuguese Jews. "Yes, and you've caught him, too"—he took the sketch and held it a little away from him as far-sighted people will—"all his sanctimoniousness, and in such a few lines. Really, this is a marvelous drawing—I've seldom seen the like of it. May I ask your name?"

"Rembrandt van Rijn."

"Rembrandt van Rijn? Of course, of course—who else? But what are you doing, Master, sitting here on my doorstep? Will you do us the honor of coming in?"

To reject the invitation would have been both churlish and foolish. The stranger evidently knew and esteemed him—he held the sketch with extreme care in one hand while he extended the other to help him up off the step; besides, wasn't he offering what had seemed an urgent necessity a few minutes ago: a shadowy retreat from the oppressive glare of the sun? "I'm Miguel de Barrios," he said, suiting his pace to his visitor's as they started up the stairs. "I'm a poet, but you wouldn't know of me. I write for the Sephardim, in their tongue." He swung the great door open and led his guest by the elbow through a reception hall that smelled of sandalwood and dried reeds and gave off the coolness of marble and old wood. "Here, to your right, Master," he said, and drew back a rustling crimson curtain to reveal a room that was blessedly dark.

It was a big room, almost as big as the lost salon where he had once displayed his canvases and statues and antiquities. He was able to make out the boundaries of it by the faint glimmer of gilt along the foliated molding and by the edges of the muted red Oriental carpet that bloomed with a vague pattern of flowers. The drapes, drawn so carefully over the two tall front windows that no dart of painful light came in unsifted by their warp and woof, were of a strange and splendid color, or seemed so in the light which they seeped up and contained—something between a coppery pink and gold. Here and there, as his eyes accustomed themselves to the deep shadow, objects of Eastern opulence emerged from it: cushions of scarlet and crimson, a beautiful old chair whose seat was padded in olive-green, a great vessel of chased brass set on the hearth and filled with tall dried reeds, a screen of polished wood so intricately carved that it looked like lace. And though there was much here that he wanted to see, he was so taken with the penumbral aspect of the objects that half-revealed and half-concealed themselves that he shook his head when his host asked him if he would like to have the curtains pulled aside. "Not unless *you* wish it, Heer de Barrios," he said. "It'll only heat up your room, and I'm perfectly comfortable in the dark."

Two chairs with a small inlaid table between them manifested themselves in the area of light near the windows, and, at the younger man's courteous gesture of invitation, he subsided into one of them and took the damp handkerchief from his pocket and wiped his sweaty face while his host went back to the doorway and called in a voice that fetched up echoes in the other rooms, "Abigail! Come down for a minute, will you, Abigail? We have a guest." Then, having pulled up a third chair out of the darkness, he too sat down, his swarthy face and loose auburn locks burnished in the roseate light. "My wife," he explained. "She's upstairs with the children. She'll be delighted; she knows your work, too. Two of our friends have portraits by you—Judith de Lana and Rabbi Eleazer ben Salamon. In fact, several years ago, not long after we were married, we wanted to have you paint a pair of portraits for us, but we couldn't find you. You weren't at the place down the street, and somebody said you were in Hull, and somebody else said you were at the Court in Sweden, and for all I knew, you—had gone into retirement and weren't painting any more."

Though the intelligent face had not permitted itself to change, he knew by the slight pause that this Miguel de Barrios had been on the point of saying, "For all I knew, you were dead." And perhaps I might as well be, he thought. Perhaps I came within an inch of it on your front steps. Perhaps your curtained chamber here is so congenial to my spirit because it is so like what I am drawn to now—the darkness of the grave . . .

The crimson curtain rustled, and he looked toward the doorway and saw a woman, as obscure as the other splendors that had vaguely emerged before his eyes. It was only when she moved into the coppery radiance around their little table that she became corporeal enough for him to see that her hair was pale red, her forehead high and prominent, her eyes grey and heavy-lidded, her mouth rather wide and moist and curved in an uncertain smile. What color she was dressed in he could not tell because the silken stuff was drenched with the color of the curtains; but her whole person was made precious, like some Eastern idol, by the flash of jewels and the shimmer of gold—garnets at her round throat and in her ears, pearls at her wrists, and a brooch of carved amber between her small, high breasts.

"Heer van Rijn—Heer *Rembrandt* van Rijn, Abigail," said her husband.

"No, not really?" Her face—not aged or wrinkled, merely molded by her thirty-odd years out of the young girl's smooth mask into something more subtle and expressive—told him all her wonder and her pleasure. "You'll never believe me, Master," she said in a quiet voice pitched somewhat lower than most women's voices, "but not long after we were married we went to look for you at the house down the street—such a big house, all closed up, and nobody there—"

"Yes, I was telling the master about that," said her husband. And the guest was sorry that he would not hear it again from her, perhaps because it could not be told too often to a man isolated and half forgotten, perhaps because she had somehow managed, by the rise and fall of her voice and a slight movement of her beautiful bejeweled hands, to evoke the great house with its covered windows and its smokeless chimneys and the two of them knocking in vain on the barred door.

"He was sketching our perennial beggar out on the front steps," the husband said. "A wonderful sketch—you'll have to see it. But first we ought to have some chilled wine."

"Oh, yes—especially in this heat. You'll do us the honor, won't you, Master? You'll have a goblet with us, and a slice of cake, and a bit of fruit?"

"Yes, thanks, if it won't be any trouble to you." He could not understand why he was willing to stay; now that the sweat had ceased to flow and the pain at the back of his head was gone, he should have wanted only to escape. The cultivated graciousness of these two and the elegance of their house should have made him uneasy about the benumbed state of his brain and the wretched state of his clothing, yet he felt at his ease and talked without constraint to her husband while she was gone. If there was any tension in him, it was only the hushed expectation with which he waited until she returned bearing a tray that was as exquisite as herself—damask napkins and Venetian goblets and small knives with carved ivory handles, a bottle of wine still damp with the cool water in which it had lain, thin slices of loaf cake dark with nuts and honey, and a pyramid of grapes and pears. As she set his goblet before him and bent to fill it from the bottle, she did not lower her full eyelids as he had thought she would; she gave him a long, grey, serious look. And as she turned away from him to serve her husband, he could have sworn—where or under what circumstances he did not know—that he had seen her before.

"Excuse me, Vrouw de Barrios," he said, "but your face is very familiar to me. Could I have seen you at Dr. Bonus's, or the Pineros' or the Lazzaras', or perhaps at the house of Rabbi Menasseh ben Israel?"

She had seated herself between the two of them and was spreading her napkin in her lap. "No," she said, shaking her head slowly and smiling. "I'm sure I never met you before, Master. If I had been presented to you, I would have remembered it. I'm afraid it's just that many of us look alike—I mean the women of my race with red hair."

It was the husband who carried the conversation for the most part thereafter, asking whether his guest had read the writings of Descartes or Cominius, moving agilely when he saw that this was not a bookish man to a variety of other subjects: the raising of children—they had three and stood in hope of having another; the lacy screen—it was Moorish handiwork; their country house—they had come back from it at the end of August, thinking, idiots that they were, that the worst of the summer was over; the game of chess at which he had just been roundly beaten by his cousin Emmanuel next door. She did not talk, but he could watch the fluid grace of her hands, pale and soft but wonderfully skillful, snipping small sprigs of grapes from the enormous bunch with a jeweled scissors, taking up one of the ivory-handled knives—pink like her almond-shaped nails in the glow of the curtain—and peeling a pear, round and round, so that the skin came off all in one piece. And when the pear was ready she put it on his plate and gave him another of her suppressed and somewhat melancholy smiles.

"Far be it from me," said her husband, "to take advantage of the happy chance that brought you to my doorstep. We're fortunate enough to have made your acquaintance, and if what I have in mind isn't congenial to you, you only need to refuse. Abigail and I have never had those portraits done—she wanted no other master, and I agreed with her. Do you think you might care to paint us now?"

"Yes, would you care to paint us now, Master?" Her hand, cool and a little moist from the pear, rested for an instant on his wrist, and he had again the strange conviction that he had known her before.

"I see no reason why not, so long as I have my health." He had it now—the moment of panic outside on the steps when he had thought he was dying seemed far away. "But I'm slow—I warn you—"

"That makes no difference to either of us, does it, Miguel?" she said, touching her husband's arm. "I have servants, and sometimes whole days go by when I scarcely raise a finger. As for my husband, he can make up his poetry just as well while he's sitting for you. God has been good to both of us; we can do pretty much as we please." She stood up then, and gathered up the goblets and plates and set them on the tray; and the guest, too, heaved himself out of his chair, thinking that he might well have overstayed the time allotted to him by the rules of courtesy.

"But you're not thinking of going?" said the poet.

"No, please, you're not thinking of going? I only thought I'd clear away the leavings—I'm sure an artist wouldn't want to look at old parings and seeds and crumbs. Stay a little longer—stay until it's cooler outside." And now more than ever he was convinced that he had seen her somewhere, perhaps years ago, perhaps when she had been a child.

"But I can't, I really can't, much as I'd like to. They'll be worrying about me at home. You've no idea how they keep track of me and pester me to tell them where I'm going and get themselves into a state if I'm half an hour late for supper," he said.

"Your wife, Master? Your children?"

"No, Vrouw de Barrios. My wife's dead."

"Peace be with her!"

"My daughter, my apprentice, the old woman who keeps my house for me, they fuss and they worry—"

"But that," she said, holding her bright head a little to one side and lowering her full eyelids, "must be because they love you."

There was a little more talk then in which she bore no part. The husband offered four hundred florins for each of the portraits—a generous but not an ostentatious fee—and asked for a pen and wrote down in a strong angular hand the place where he could find the master; he had no

622

intention of losing him a second time, he said. Pulling the rustling curtain aside on the lighter reception hall and ushering his guest toward the door—the wife remained in the shadowy room behind them—he asked, "And when shall we come to you, Heer van Rijn?"

The thought that they would come to him was somehow painful, like the light that came in under the big door. "Couldn't I come to *you,* Heer de Barrios? I'd rather do it that way," he said.

"But why, Master? It's a long way from the Rozengracht to the Breestraat. We can take the walk more easily than you, for the next several weeks at any rate. Abigail's only in her second month, and we're always walking. We take a walk almost every night before we go to bed."

As I used to do with Saskia, as I did with Hendrikje, he thought—arm in arm, thigh brushing against thigh . . . "Still, I'd rather come here, if it's all the same to you. Your salon, the things that are in it—I don't mean to paint *them,* of course, but somehow I can't imagine painting the two of you anywhere else."

"As you like, as you like," said the poet. "Name your day. Next Tuesday? Next Wednesday?"

And now that he stood on the steps again, now that the harsh street and the bleared sun were pressing in upon him, he rejected both Tuesday and Wednesday and said that he could come on Thursday. Why? Certainly not to protect his dignity—they had credited him with far more of that than he believed he possessed. Only because he would not have a dream in a shadowy room deceive him into believing that there was anything he wanted any more, anything he could wish to hasten toward in the empty world.

*

Nothing, not even the *Syndics of the Cloth Hall,* had ever gone as well for him as the portrait of Miguel de Barrios. By mid-October the canvas was finished, and the sitter, laying down the magnifying glass which he had wanted in the picture because his far-sighted eyes could read nothing without it, said, "Perfect, perfect. I beg you, not one stroke more."

He needed the reassurance and was grateful for it: his whole procedure had been a departure; and who in his sixties can have confidence when he goes blindly, led by an inner voice which he does not fully understand, into a land where he has never been before?

The five good Syndics and their amiable servant existed solidly in reason and sunlight and harmonious company. Miguel de Barrios emerged out of darkness, not quite corporeal and in solitude, and no reasonable language could transmit what showed in the furrowed face, the secretive and compressed lips, the large all-seeing and yet not-quite-seeing eyes. As the brass vessel and the Moorish screen had manifested themselves in the shadow of the salon that first afternoon, so Mi-

623

guel de Barrios manifested himself in the black vacancy of the universe; he was there on the canvas forever, yet his image said only, "Look at this passing miracle: for a moment I am here—and who knows why? And then in a moment—who knows why?—I am gone." Still, it was precisely out of that somber declaration that the painting drew its dark splendor; it left a trail of wordless wonder behind it, like a falling star.

And the skill with which it had been painted was as amazing to its creator as whatever it was that he had gotten into it. He was old, he was sick—it was preposterous that he should paint with such skill. Light passed into shadow and shadow into light by more subtle gradations than he had ever attained in his most vigorous years; paint seemed to mold itself under the warmth of his fingers before he had actually touched it; his brush was like a living thing, an extension of himself, every sable hair of it bending to his only half-known will.

And if this is the way it has gone with the husband, what marvels can I expect when I paint the wife? he asked himself in the days when he knew with regret and exultation that the first half of his task was almost done. Every time he had come to their house, he had seen her at least once, though always very briefly: it was as if she guessed that her presence might disturb or even blight the unfolding of this first miracle. "Good day, Master," she would say, bringing in wine and cold sliced meat and putting them on the inlaid table. "I only thought I'd leave this here in case you stopped for a little rest." And then she would go out so quickly that he could not even match her face with his memory of it or know for certain whether the dress she had been wearing was russet or scarlet, greenish blue or bluish green. But she could not obliterate herself completely: her step sounded on the stair, she would call to a servant or to one of the children, he would hear her singing quietly to herself. He would notice, looking up to rest his eyes, that there was a cashmere shawl lying over the arm of a chair and would know that she had left it there; he would become suddenly aware that there were scarlet leaves instead of the dried reeds in the vessel on the hearth, and would think how she must have arranged them with her supple, bejeweled hands.

Yet the first afternoon she sat for him, an afternoon when the sky was grey and the leaves kept blowing past the uncurtained windows, began in such frustration that he wondered whether his skill had burned itself out in one final conflagration. It was not only that she was shy, so shy and rigid that every pose she took froze into artificiality, with a look of self-depreciation and apology driving everything else out of her face; it was also the disturbing realization that, like some apprentice who has not yet mastered the rudiments of his craft, he could not get a creditable likeness. Miguel de Barrios he had sketched once, in ten or fifteen minutes, using a single sheet of paper. But Abigail de Barrios was another matter; in the first half-hour of the sitting, he made seven sketches and dropped them all despondently on the Oriental rug. He could not understand it—all his life he had been so adept at catching likenesses that he had deliberately tried to depart from them, altering the features subtly or extensively in order to bring out some significance or heighten some mood or capture some fleeting impression. And now, with his model there before him in the carved chair with the olive-green cushions, sitting motionless in the light shed upon her by an ancient five-branched candlestick, he could not draw what he saw; and in his bafflement he felt like walking out of the house and testing whether he could draw anything—a stoop, a tree trunk, a blank wall.

"Do you have a headache, Master?" she asked because he was thrusting his knuckles into his forehead in his desperation. "Shall I tell one of the servants to bring you a wet towel?"

"No, no. I don't have a headache. A wet towel wouldn't help. It's peculiar, but I simply can't get a decent likeness of you. It's never happened to me before."

"It's dark in here, even with the candles. Maybe I ought to send for another candlestick."

"No, thanks, it's not the light either. I don't know what it is—I just can't make you look like yourself."

Seeing that he was no longer sketching, she abandoned the set position and looked at him almost flirtatiously, her head on one side, her eyes half hidden by her full eyelids, her hand playing with the soft folds of semi-transparent cloth over her breast. "Maybe you don't want to draw me," she said, half laughing, half in earnest. "Maybe you want to draw somebody else."

"Why wouldn't I want to draw you? I've been looking forward to it from the beginning—"

"Yes, but do you remember the first time you came—you told me you were sure you'd seen me before. Maybe it's the other person, the one I remind you of, that you really want to paint—"

"Yes, I remember that; but if such a person exists, only God knows who it would be."

"Maybe somebody back in your childhood, somebody you've completely forgotten?"

"No . . ." Her look had left him, was fixed on the discarded sketches now, and he also stared at them where they lay scattered among the exotic Eastern flowers. No, not in childhood, he thought. Later, when the blood had already been infused with the wine of love, when monstrous childish imaginings had been put away, when the flesh knew what it willed, and every fair face, every female body moving in a crowd was made aureate with the pulsing light of desire . . . He pushed back his grizzled hair and looked at the lines which old, spent passion and stifled remembrance had impelled him to draw in red chalk on the rejected sheets of paper at his feet. In one of them she had the shy, sorrowful smile of Margheretha van Meer; in another her hand was the hand of Vrouw van Hoorn reaching out to touch his raw and hairy wrist. In another, Saskia's fiery curls lay moist against her brow; and three times, though her bosom was small even in her pregnancy, he had given her Hendrikje's full and nourishing breasts. "No, it's all of them," he said, and wondered that he should have said it aloud—what would he say to her if she asked him to explain?

But she did not pursue the matter. Possibly she thought he was muttering in his dotage, and possibly he was: dotage might well be the superimposing of a life's fleeting images one upon another so that there was no way of knowing in what year a man lived, what room he stood in, what face he saw with his blurred and remembering eyes. Sometimes at home he would catch himself saying, "Saskia—Hendrikje—Cornelia, you forgot to give me a napkin," or, "Ferdinand—Carel—Aert, you're getting too much red in it," or, "Maartje—Geertje—Rebecca, where have you put my shoes?" Yes, he was sure that he was muttering in his dotage, and that her silent withdrawal and resumption of the pose—her neck slightly bent, her eyes looking out and away, her hand holding a withered carnation into a pale area of candlelight—was another instance of her exquisite courtesy. Yet the freezing shyness was gone from her mobile face; and if it was pity that had thawed it, he did not care: time that had taken his loves away had also pulled out of his heart the galling sting of pride. Tell yourself that I am old and a little mad, he thought; tell yourself that my reason comes and goes like the glow of embers in a burnt-out fire—what else should you tell yourself? What would I have told myself, in the years of my health and my glory, if I had met such a one as I am now? And he took up the chalk and began to draw again, not trying to exorcise the others from her image, only using her image more consciously to contain them, to bring them into harmony, to set them at peace with each other and her, to wash them all in the same latter-day light of a disembodied and unasking love.

Yet if pity kept her from trying to follow him into the impenetrable maze of his shifting memory, it did not prevent her from trying to draw a little closer to whatever he was now. When he laid down his chalk—decisively, to let her know he had produced a satisfactory sketch at last—she did not ask to see it; she used the brief rest to say, "If I remember right, you told us that same afternoon that you live with an apprentice and an old woman who keeps your house, and that you have one child."

"One child?" Was he really so embittered against the lad, so remote from him and finished with him, that he could give a stranger the impression that he didn't exist? "No, Vrouw de Barrios, I have two children—a girl in her early teens by my second wife and a young man in his twenties by my first one. Both of them are at home with me—the girl helps to keep house and the boy sells my etchings and canvases. Titus works very hard, I don't see too much of him, and I don't imagine he'll be living with me long—he'll be getting married one of these days."

"Yes, so it goes," she said, sighing as if she were envisioning the day when a child of her own would be going from her. "Children *will* grow up and marry, and everybody goes home from the wedding in high spirits—everybody but the parents. It's easier, I suppose, if both the mother and father are left—then they have each other. But it must be very hard when one of them is gone. Still, if it's a good marriage—"

"A good marriage—I'd scarcely call it that," he said, setting the stretched canvas down hard on the easel.

"No?" She looked surprised and frightened; a pucker showed between her two pale eyebrows, and the flower jerked slightly in her hand. "The young lady—she's not acceptable then?" she asked, and added at once, as if to soften the harshness of it, "I mean, your boy's beyond her—might have done better for himself?"

He could not answer, not even to relieve her evident contrition for bringing up the painful subject. He picked up his palette and began to load it with the paint he meant to use in making the outline—a recessive grey compounded of black and a touch of ocher and white. Titus *had* been beyond Magdalena van Loo, but—he asked it of himself with a sharp constriction of the heart—was he beyond her now? A change had taken place, a transformation so gradual that its stages had been imperceptible; and to realize how great the change had been was appalling enough without the guilty questions that came in its train. Am I to blame for the sunken cheeks and the listlessness and the silence? he thought. Did the blight first come upon him when I went at my canvas with a carving knife? Did I rob him of the love he should have had from his foster mother in her last years? And is it any wonder that a son of mine, after living in my welter of spurious splendor and aimless squalor, should find the dull house on the Singel a place of order and plenty and peace? "Oh, there's nothing really wrong with the young woman except that she's dull and colorless," he said. "I suppose I've got no grounds to blame him—any way you look at it, he hasn't had an easy life of it with me. I raised him like a prince, and now he goes around peddling my things like any art dealer's poor assistant. His mother left him a fortune, and by the time he's old enough to get it most of it will be gone."

"I can see how he'd be bitter about that now, but don't you think he'll get over it later?" she said, looking at him with earnest, timid eyes.

"But it isn't the fortune that's the trouble. Strange as it must seem, I'd swear he doesn't give much thought to the money. I'm the one that's bitter, to tell the truth. I can't forgive him for caring less than my apprentice does for the things I paint. He's pleasant enough about my canvases, you understand, but I can imagine him being just as pleasant to half a dozen other painters. He simply doesn't see anything in my work to be particularly excited about."

"But isn't that just because he's young and has always had your things around him? Give him a little time, Master, and I'm sure the day will come when he'll give you your due."

"I doubt it." He fell silent and brushed on the outline—the head held sideward in gentle attentiveness, the frail round of the shoulders, the delicate hand holding the withered carnation. "Besides, how long can I wait? I'm an old man, Vrouw de Barrios—sick, forgotten by almost everybody. I paint because there's no other way for me to fill up my time. When I'm not painting, I'm waiting to die. That's all I ever think about—my death."

"Do you think of it so much then, Master?" For the first time she forgot the pose and let the dried flower drop into her lap. Her hands made a slight but infinitely expressive gesture: it was as if she took his ruined face between the warm palms of her hands. "That's dreadful, I know —there was a year when I was always thinking of it, and I was young then, I couldn't have been more than twenty-two. I was perfectly healthy, but I couldn't go to sleep. I was afraid to close my eyes, afraid I was going to die in the night. I couldn't understand then what was going on inside of me, but now I know what it was: something had happened that made me turn away from everybody—there wasn't anybody I could imagine loving any more. And ever since then I've thought it's the unspent love locked up inside that goes sick in us and brings on that kind of obsession with death."

"That may be true, but I'm beyond loving anybody."

"You?" she said, womanly and bantering and tender, looking without false shame at the outline, the magical reflection of her body that he had evoked while he stood there before her asserting his emptiness and his lovelessness. "Nobody could look at that—or those"—she flushed and glanced down at the discarded sketches—"and believe any such thing!"

He did not gainsay her—he could not gainsay her. If he had seen in her husband's somber face some mystery of existence itself, if his dead had come back to him sweet and incorruptible to show their lost faces in the sketches scattered on the rug, if his son had been revealed to him stripped of an old, false guise and pitiable in actuality, it was because whatever had been sickening unspent within him had flowed out toward her in love. She settled her fair and gracious body back into the pose, and he took up his brush and finished the outline, working longest on the hands and the dried flower—though the face would be the largest area of brightness, he wanted a kind of halo to float above the hands as if they themselves were emanating light. She said nothing more during the remainder of the sitting; and though he was grateful that what had passed between them was not to be diluted with banalities, the silence made him nervous, so nervous that he realized he had left his hat behind him only when the wind assailed his head on the other side of the closed door.

The door was unlocked, and he stepped back into a room that was dark and emptied of her presence. But she was nearby, and so was her husband; the voice of Miguel de Barrios came to him through the olive-green curtain that divided the salon from a smaller sitting room. "Only the outline? He's certainly dragging it out this time," said the poet. "He didn't take anything like that amount of trouble with me. You have a cavalier, that much is plain." And then her voice came in, rich and a little heated—he would remember it to the end of his days—saying: "I don't, of course, but if I did, it wouldn't be anything to tease me with. Any woman who pleased him would have reason to be proud and grateful. It's the last thing on earth I'd want to joke about."

*

After that afternoon, it was impossible for him to see Titus any longer as the aloof and coolly censorious representative of the market place. He saw him as he was, or at least as he had envisioned him in Abigail de Barrios's parlor—confused, exhausted, dispossessed; but the new image did not make it easier for him to deal with his son in pity and with love. The young man's curt or constrained "We're going to be married a week from Saturday—would you care to be present?" was so galling that he felt his rage spotting his face; it was only with effort that he could say, in a grotesque caricature of cordiality, "Why, certainly. How could you think anything else?"

The last twenty years had not shaped him in a mold suitable for weddings: his clothes were ill-fitting and threadbare; to enter a church after he had refused to attend service with Hendrikje stirred up old self-recriminations; and he knew as little how to conduct himself at the ceremony as he knew what to say to Titus's mother-in-law and Titus's bride. Cornelia was no help; some of her stifled belligerence had broken out as soon as she knew that the date was set; she had even rejected his offer of money to buy a new dress for the occasion: "No, indeed," she had said, "I'll go in my old blue—it's quite good enough. The van Loos can take me or leave me as I am, it's all the same to me." Standing beside him while the "I, Magdalena, take thee, Titus" was being murmured, she glared at the pastor and the greens and the little bride, who certainly did not look strong enough, under the weight of all that satin and velvet and all those pious admonitions, to bear the additional burden of her animosity. He himself managed to maintain an air of cheerful attentiveness during the ceremony and at the long, insipid supper that came after it; only once, in the vestibule of the church, when the wedded couple greeted their guests, did he lose control of his face, and that was when Titus went up to the wooden old lady in the beribboned cap and embraced her and said, "Well, Mother, now I can really call you Mother." He thought then of the one who had brought him forth in labor and held him out, with the certainty of her death upon her, as her gift and her masterpiece; he thought also of the one who had raised him with more pride and love than she had given to her own, and it seemed to him that his heart was about to burst.

So light, so faithless, so careless of old loyalties—it gnawed at him for weeks. "Now I can really call you Mother"—oh, well, the boy would tire of the old woman in due time, would sigh impatiently when he found her a too-frequent guest at his table, would resent it when the little Magdalena dragged him out on a winter night to go and sit awhile with poor Mother, who asks so little of us, who only wants us to stop by and have a cup of tea . . . *He* never dragged *her* along to the house on the Rozengracht. When he came, it was during the day—to deliver money for etchings, to introduce somebody who wanted a portrait, to tell his father, quite without malicious intent, that what he was getting from his mother's bequest would make it possible for him and Magdalena to buy the furniture they needed for their parlor. His mother's bequest—it made the old man heartsick to hear it mentioned: even with the limited withdrawals permitted by the Friesland relatives for Titus's needs, it had shrunk to a wretched fraction of the magnificent round sum she had named in her will; it was just about enough to close the gap in the meager requirements of two who lived in a modest set of rooms near the Apple Market and had to ask themselves which they could indulge in this week—a roast goose, a bottle of wine, or a pair of tickets to a new comedy.

And yet, for all the awkwardness of his attempts at reconciliation, apparently they had not been entirely futile. One Sunday morning, when all of them were eating breakfast, old Rebecca produced a letter that had been thrust under the door last night after they had gone to bed. The letter was from Titus, and it was long and cordial enough to make him wonder whether the young man simply fell into an amiable form of address when he took up a pen, or whether he felt more than he could make plain when he and his father were face to face. The purpose of the letter—important enough to bring him all the way across town at an hour when he knew that the doors of his father's house would be barred—was to state that Cosimo de Medici was in Amsterdam buying canvases; that he, Titus, had persuaded the map-maker Bleau, who was shepherding the Duke around, to send him to Rembrandt's studio, and that the great Italian collector could be expected to arrive Monday at two o'clock. Also—and this part of the letter the recipient read three times—the writer would like very much to come early enough to sit down to the noonday meal with his father and sister and help set up whatever pictures his father might want to show the distinguished visitor.

Yet the recalcitrant stuff of his life would yield no more gracefully to the simple business of sitting down to a meal with his son than it had yielded to the wedding. Cornelia took it ill that the menu should diverge from the usual simple fare, and he himself saw that it would be impossible for Titus to sit down with only his father and sister: what was to be done with Aert and Rebecca, who always sat at table now—were they to be told to eat in the kitchen, like servants in some grand establishment? Obviously not, but the alternative was almost as painful: old Rebecca had a way of breaking in with irrelevant observations; and the relationship between his son and his apprentice had always been remote and cold. So, if a meat pie and an elaborate salad were finally wrested from Cornelia, if the table was laid with the good tin plates and the best linen, there was nothing festive about the proceedings: he himself was apprehensive, Rebecca was flustered, Cornelia had gone to some lengths to make herself as unattractive as she could, and Aert, for much the same reason, had gotten himself up splendidly in a royal-blue jacket and breeches, an outfit he had never appeared in since he had changed the gentleman's role in Dordt for the disciple's role in Amsterdam.

If it had been Aert's intention to outshine Titus, he need not have put himself to so much trouble. Titus, though he had dressed himself in the claret-colored finery he had been married in, looked not ten but twenty years older than the apprentice—hollow in the cheeks, pinched in the nose, white around the lips. His excitement over the likelihood of making a sale to the greatest of Italian collectors was the one thing that intermittently revived him from a listlessness which had become even more marked since his wedding. Only when he said that the Medici seldom offered less than five hundred florins, and that the prospective buyer was pious and might carry off one of the Biblical scenes, did color and vitality come into his tired face. Is he ill? his father wondered, seating him at the head of the table between himself and Cornelia. Probably not—probably it's only that he and Magdalena have been at it too much. But the question remained, adding to the other stresses a solicitude that could not be expressed. The meal at least gave them something to make vacuous conversation about; but he found himself remembering other meals, more meager ones in more wretched places, when Hendrikje had ladled out the pottage and the lad had invented tender and whimsical names for the little troll; and his heart was heavy, and he longed for a thick broth of lentils and bacon as though he could have taken in with it all that was irretrievably gone.

"And what are you working on at the moment, Father?"

It was a dutiful question, put with at least a show of honest interest; and it was unjust of Cornelia—though he had nobody but himself to blame after his talk about unconcern and disloyalty—to give her brother a look that said: "As if you cared!"

"The portrait of Vrouw de Barrios—it's almost finished."

"I wish I could have seen it—"

"What? Haven't you seen it yet?" asked Aert de Gelder.

"Why, it's never been here, has it? I thought all the work was done at their house on the Breestraat—"

"It was, but they didn't mind letting me in," said the apprentice. "I've been over there twice."

The implication of neglect and the invidious comparison were so blatantly there that the master was hard put to it not to reach under the table and pat his son's knee. "The portrait of Vrouw de Barrios, and a *Lucrece*, and a *Christ at the Pillar*," he said, trying to override the interruption.

"No matter what Vrouw Lingelbach says, kidney is the best part of a meat pie," said old Rebecca. "A meat pie that has no kidney in it isn't fit to eat."

"You're quite right, I agree with you completely, Vrouw Willems," said Aert. "The *Christ at the Pillar* is a marvel. And the *Lucrece* looks as if every color in it had been painted over a base of gold."

"Is it finished?" asked Titus. "It sounds like the sort of thing that might catch the Duke's eye—"

"No, it's not quite finished, is it, Master? You said last night that there were still a few things to be done to the curtain and the dress."

He nodded at his apprentice, probably too curtly, and regretted that also—the young cannot be expected to stifle their jealousy or hide their devotion. Besides, it was touching that the aristocrat from Dordt could never show a merry face at the little feasts Cornelia set out to celebrate a sale; at such times he ate as a mourner eats at a funeral banquet, sparingly, to make it plain that he would have preferred to have the picture back and live on salt herring and bread.

"Do you know what, your honor? The Hinkels have bought another cow," said Rebecca.

"Have they really? That'll be very convenient for us," said Cornelia. "They'll never use up all that milk themselves, and I don't doubt they'll let us have what's left at a good price."

She had spoken with so much premature womanliness that she amused and delighted her brother. He laughed his old courtly, half-teasing laughter, and reached behind her head with his thin hand to tug affectionately on her luxuriant hair. "A housekeeper and a penny-squeezer already," he said. "She's learning her trade early. She'll be running off and getting married one of these days."

"Me?" she said, turning on him with frigid dignity. "Not likely. So long as Father needs me here, *I'll* not be going anywhere else."

But in the old days the lad had loved her so much, had bathed her and carried her on his shoulders and made her toy houses out of painted paper and answered her endless questions with sweetness and patience, stroking this same hair that she no longer wanted him to touch . . . "Fill up your brother's beer mug, Cornelia. Don't you see that it's empty?" he said.

No, whatever he had hoped for from that meal was not forthcoming. Titus was silent during the remainder of it: Aert had barely grazed him —he cared nothing for Aert; but he loved Cornelia, and Cornelia had struck home. Nothing could rouse him out of his wan passiveness: when his father asked courteously after Magdalena, he said only that she was well; pressed for a description of the visiting dignitary, he delivered himself of a few terse phrases—young, nineteen or thereabouts, scrupulously Catholic, not at ease with people . . . All that could be hoped was that matters would go better in the studio. If it was unavoidable that Aert would accompany them, at least Cornelia and Rebecca would remain downstairs.

But by the time the three of them had put the little room in order for Cosimo de Medici, his sympathy for his son was on the wane. Each of the pictures displayed on the easels had received some dutiful comment from Titus: the self-portraits were "among the best"; the *Saint Peter Denying Christ* was "still one of his favorites"; the *Lucrece* was "just as brilliant as Aert had said it was"; the *Christ at the Pillar* contained a "remarkable juxtaposition of gentleness and brutality"—but whatever the young man said was made unacceptable, even distasteful, by the ultimate praise he could not find it in his heart to give. And there was less cause to stifle exasperation because Titus, more at ease in his role of agent, did not look so peaked and pathetic as he had downstairs. He ordered Aert around, properly confident that the apprentice knew less than he about the arts of display and the whims of buyers; and with his obligation to make appropriate comments discharged, he talked a little about his own affairs. Though the market was still tight—how could it be otherwise with so much unrest, domestic and foreign?—he was selling more etchings and canvases than he had sold a year ago. His father's work was, of course, the mainstay of his little business, but other painters were coming to him too—young ones who might be worth watching, who might in time make a name for themselves. Take Maarten Booms, for instance—he was doing landscapes, little pastorals in soft browns and greens, with considerable originality and taste. And his comments on this Maarten Booms were so similar in tone to those he had applied to the masterpieces around him that it was hard to tell whether he had any notion of how vast a difference there was between a Maarten Booms and a Rembrandt van Rijn.

"Yes, I saw one of his paintings at an auction," said Aert de Gelder, who was deliberately soiling his fine suit by rigorously dusting everything in the room, though all that Titus had suggested was that he run a rag over the chair in which the Duke would sit. "That is, I *think* it was his—so many painters do those flat green things with cows and sheep that it's hard to tell one from the other."

"There's a good deal of interest in pastoral painting these days—"

"Is there? I wouldn't know. It's a genre I never felt tempted to try myself."

It was an unhappy business, and he had to admit it would not have been much better if he and Titus had been there alone. He felt himself face to face again with the lack of faith and the betrayal that had driven him to go at the *Julius Civilis* with the carving knife: the rage was gone, but the bruise continued to ache. And the only antidote against it was the hope that the young Cosimo would do something to set things right, would stop on the threshold bedazzled by the profusion of riches gathered in this little room and utter in his first transport what Titus had never said.

But the instrument provided for the working of that longed-for miracle could not have been worse. Cornelia, who had conducted him upstairs, stood behind him long enough to indicate over his slack shoulder her amazement and disgust that this should be one of the illustrious Medici, a duke of Florence and a lord of Tuscany. He was lean, loose-jointed, saddle-nosed, with a sallow complexion and lank black hair; his clothes were grey and baggy and monkish; he wore the pettish expression of a gentleman forced to wait in line for a ticket—he obviously wished to be anywhere but where he found himself. The burnished golds, the vibrant scarlets, the cold greens and rich browns that assailed him here were bound to affront him; he was so colorless that he should have restricted himself to naked rooms with blank stone walls. He had plainly learned not to offer his hand to be kissed—the Dutch had had their fill of that sort of thing in the days when the Spaniards had swarmed over the land; he merely nodded his longish head when the three of them bowed, and nervously fingered a heavy gold medallion bearing the image of Saint Catherine of Sienna, his only ornament. "I will tell you from the beginning that I know nothing of pictures, nothing in the smallest," he said in Dutch. "I buy them, yes. I care for them, no. That I am buying pictures—it is an act of filial piety, to the pleasure of my father and my uncles, who had it in their heads before they were delivered out of the flesh by God to fill up two very big galleries. Five hundred florins for a little one. Six hundred florins for a big one. What shall I take?"

The master and the apprentice were so appalled that they remained on the opposite side of the room, but Titus, accustomed to the eccentricities of prospective patrons and probably warned by the map-maker Bleau of what he might expect, stepped up to the Duke with practiced grace. "That would depend on what pleases your Highness," he said. "We're proud to be able to offer your Highness a considerable variety. Something from the New Testament, perhaps? Would your Highness step over and look at this superb *Christ at the Pillar*?"

He stepped over, but he kept his distance as though the very smell of paint were enough to hold him off. He looked, he sighed, he jiggled the medallion of Saint Catherine, he shook his head. "No, no New Testament. That might not be good."

"Good, your Highness? It's an excellent canvas, painted with the skill of a master who has been working in the craft for more than forty years—"

"This is not what I mean. I mean this is a Protestant country. I mean

634

it might be heretical or even have a blasphemy hiding in it. I do not know—I would have to ask my confessor, and he is not here. Something else."

"Something in the antique manner, your Highness? It isn't finished yet, but I'm sure my father could have this beautiful *Lucrece* ready for you in a day or so."

The Duke stood before the slight and tragic figure holding the naked dagger; he stared at the shimmering golds and browns, and he made a grimace. Perhaps he had been reminded of his young wife, a French princess who had run away from him and locked herself in a castle and threatened to throw a prayer book at his head if he came after her; perhaps the very richness of the textures and colors disturbed his piety.

"No?" said Titus, with the inexhaustible affability of the market place. "A head of Jesus, perhaps? There are several over here—just simple heads, so that there wouldn't be any doctrinal difficulties."

He walked past them twice, looking at them over his shoulder. "Why is it," he said, as if Rembrandt were not in the room, "that he makes our Lord and Saviour look always like some Jew?"

"Because that's what He was," said Aert de Gelder, unable any longer to control himself.

"It is so—he was," said the Duke, without turning to the speaker. "But of this I see no reason that I should be always reminding myself. In our country, by our painters, He looks like the Son of God, not like a Jew."

"Perhaps one of these remarkable self-portraits would be more to your Highness's liking," said Titus. "There are ten on display here, and there are several others that we could bring out."

"No, don't bring any more out. It is sufficient." Evidently the very thought of having to look at more of them made him tired. "Maybe I will take that one," he said, stopping before a painting done soon after the meeting with Saskia. "Or no, maybe that one—" He cast the briefest of glances at one that glittered with the sumptuousness and the arrogance of the good years. "Then again, maybe that one." He flung his limp hand in the direction of a more somber likeness; and the gesture, at once careless and erratic, was like that of a housewife in a greengrocer's shop unable to decide which is the best of three available cabbage heads.

"Your Highness is having some difficulty making a choice because these three are so outstanding," said Titus. It was a lie and a perfectly conscious one: there were others that were better, and Titus knew as much. "Perhaps, then, you would care to take two or even the three."

"No. One." The voice was brusque and cold enough to make the master blush for his son. "It will become monotonous. Who wants to see three copies of the same face?"

"As your Highness wishes."

"I wish this one," he said, tapping the corner of the somber portrait with his bony knuckles. "Now, in regard to the payment: is it big, is it little, is it in between?"

"I should say it's somewhere in between, your Highness. But it's very meticulously painted."

"Is it? I take your word for it. As I said, I do not know and I do not care about these things. Five hundred and fifty florins—Bleau will give you tomorrow a draft for it. It is to show respect to my father and my uncles, God rest their souls."

"God rest their souls," said Titus and Aert and the master. Whereupon the Duke nodded again, addressed a "Good day" to Rembrandt, to whom he had not directed a single word before, and asked to be shown back downstairs. It was Titus who conducted him; Aert remained behind, muttering, "God help me to control myself!" and striking the wall with his fist. The display was gratifying, but the master's first concern was to get his apprentice out of the studio so that he could give his full attention to whatever wounds his son had received in the sickening affair. "Go take off that fine suit and try to brush the dust out of it," he said.

"But such ignorance, Master, such insolence, such bigotry—"

"You can thank God you're a painter—it's not the painter, it's the agent that has to put up with this sort of thing. Now go and change your clothes and ask Cornelia what we're to have for supper. Five hundred and fifty florins is worth celebrating, no matter where it comes from. And tell her I said she should give you enough money to buy a bottle of good French wine."

But when Aert was gone and there was no longer any need to put a creditable face on the matter, he collapsed before the thought of his son smiling and wheedling and gesticulating before this wretched Italian. It was his own doing that the young man's liberal and noble grace had been debased into something just this side of obsequiousness. It was his doing that five hundred florins more or less should be significant enough to justify a lie. The son of any workman in Amsterdam, trained by a prudent father to the carpenter's or the glazier's or the weaver's trade, could sneer and spit on the ground like a free Dutchman at the bigoted Italian tyrant passing in the street. His and his only had to say, "Yes, your Highness," and, "No, your Highness," and, "Whatever your Highness wishes," even though he had come of a great Friesland house, hot partisans of the rebel Prince Willem of Orange, and had been left a sum that should have kept him in comfort for the rest of his days.

It was not enough to say, "O Lord, I am heartily sorry," in solitude: the confession would have to be made to the victim, who was coming back upstairs. And perhaps, after such a confession, all that had kept them divided would be taken away, perhaps they would weep a little together and embrace . . .

The young man walked into the room, smiling faintly and directing his glance—it was a habit he had acquired in the last few years—not at his father's eyes but, with a false show of candor and attentiveness, at the middle of his father's brow. "Well, that's over. And now I'll help you put these canvases where they belong before I go," he said.

"Titus—"

"Yes, Father?" He was removing the *Christ at the Pillar* from one of the easels, holding it expertly from the back by the stretcher, for there were still patches of paint on it that had not quite dried. To admit that the Duke's visit had been a fiasco and a disgrace was the first and essential step toward any possible reconciliation; but his son showed no sign of being affronted or disgraced. His face, bled of excitement now, was a mask—a fragile mask and a pitiable one, but a mask nevertheless.

"I wanted to tell you that I'm sorry—"

"*You're* sorry, Father? *I'm* the one to say I'm sorry. Not that the Duke's rudeness and lack of taste are any fault of mine. He is what he is—a person puts up with him because he pays good prices and whatever he buys goes into the Pitti or the Uffizi. It's something to be hung in a collection that's probably the finest in the world."

His tone was blithe, shallow, and easy. He wanted no confession, no act of contrition; he wanted only to go back to his business and his supper and his Magdalena with the soothing conviction that he had done a good day's work and had comported himself under trying circumstances with grace and aptitude. Once he had stacked the self-portraits and returned them to the closet, he stopped a good five paces away from his father and gave him another unconvincing smile.

"No, Titus, what I wanted to tell you was: I'm sorry that it worked out the way it did. I mean, I'm sorry that the way I lived, the way I dealt with what was yours, should have forced you into this position, this trade—"

The mask did not so much as waver. It was amazing that, ravaged and pale as it was, it should still be so uncommunicative and expressionless. "Oh, it's a good enough trade, Father, I've no complaints against it. Besides, I never showed any talent for anything else," he said. "I make enough to keep the two of us, and in time I'll be doing better. Is there anything else you want me to do up here? If not, I'll take myself off; I have an appointment at a shop near the Dam at half past three."

"Will you work very late today?"

"Five—six—I'm usually home by seven."

"I should think it would be a terrible strain to do this sort of thing hour after hour. Are you sure you're well enough?"

"Well? Oh, yes, perfectly well. Why do you ask, Father?" For one instant the amber eyes, so like the eyes of the dead beloved, fixed themselves on his, and what he saw in them was fright.

"No reason, really. Only, you look a little wan. Maybe you should ask Tulp to have a look at you."

"I did go to see about myself—it must have been some six weeks ago.

Magdalena worries over nothing, so I went to her doctor to please her. He says there's nothing the matter—nothing but a little exhaustion. Anyway, *you're* the one to think about. You look worn out—after a session like the one this afternoon anybody would be. I'll be going now, and you lie down and take a rest."

He did lie down in his bedroom, barring the door against Aert and the others; but the recollection of the airy voice, the ungiving eyes, the impenetrable face, the spirit so alienated as to be quite unreachable made it impossible for him to rest. No position he could take on the pillow would ease the nagging pain at the back of his head, and whenever he began to sink into sleep, his heart knocked him back into bleak wakefulness. It was spoiled, spoiled—all that had ever been between him and Titus was ruined past mending; and the young man and the young man's life—God forgive him, they were ruined past mending too. And when images of the pictures flashed across this desolation, when he told himself defiantly that the self-portraits and the *Christ at the Pillar* and the *Lucrece* were great, he answered himself sardonically that they had better be, considering how many lives he had blighted for their sake.

*

He was sick again after the visit of Cosimo de Medici—scarcely able to open his eyes when Titus came to show him the draft from Bleau, somehow getting it into his head that he had come back from walking on the dunes and found the house in Leyden barred against him, taking Cornelia to be Lysbeth and asking her questions that frightened her and made her cry: "Was Hendrik Isaakszoon here this evening? Did Gerrit get upstairs all right? Mother and Father—are they both asleep?" He was sick for he did not know how long, and then well again, though with two differences: it was sometimes an effort for him to stand up straight—it was as if the earth itself, like a great magnet, drew him from one side or another; and as he had been delivered earlier from the tyranny of time, so he was delivered from the tyranny of place—he no longer needed to see whomever or whatever he wanted; it was all there, like grain brought in from the harvest fields and laid up in the storehouse of his brain.

He did not, for instance, feel impelled to go to the Breestraat to look at the finished portrait of Abigail de Barrios; he had it, every stroke of it—the reddish curls lying over the whiteness of the forehead, the eyes moist and understanding and sorrowful and tender, the almost transparent cloth gathered over the delicate swell of the bosom, the aura of light that floated around the hands. They were kind, she and her husband: they did not mean to have done with him now that they had their portraits. They sent him an invitation to come whenever he liked to their regular Wednesday "evenings"; and when they learned he was ailing, they sent him things redolent of that first afternoon when he had

638

walked out of the glare into their blessed curtained darkness: a loaf of honey cake, a piece of sandalwood to make his pillow fragrant, a pyramid of fruit. When he was well enough and the weather was right—the days only briefly warm and the dusks cooled by the mild mists of August—he went to one of those evenings to let her know that he was still among the living and that he had begun to paint again. He found little occasion to speak to her: she seemed more shy than ever and in a state of constant worry over the company of ten or twelve that she had brought under her roof to enjoy themselves. But she did peel a pear for him, taking the gold and russet skin off in one piece; she did keep furnishing him with the names that would not stay in his head and kept changing into other names—Dr. Bonus, Vrouw Lazzara, Heer Pinero, Rabbi Menasseh ben Israel; she did take him up to the nursery to see her children—three little girls dressed in pink and salmon and crimson, and blooming in the light of the candles like so many autumn roses. And when an hour of noise and movement proved as much as he could bear, she went to the door with him and kissed him good night.

He did not go again, for many reasons. The distance was too great, and he was assailed from without by the strange pull of the earth and from within by the fierce knocking of his heart. Aert and Cornelia and Rebecca had plainly spent the evening in a state of acute worry about him. And nothing was to be gained from seeing her again face to face; in fact—he knew it without sorrow—another meeting might bring about a diminution, even a loss. Abigail de Barrios moving about among her friends, giving flustered orders to her servants, kissing the foreheads of her daughters, might detract from or even blot out the Abigail that he had painted, the one that was locked in the storehouse with all the other rich garnerings of his years. She had kissed him once, and on some other evening she might forget to kiss him, or the business of kissing might become an obligation or a ritual.

Besides, he might miss a visit from Titus if he went out after supper. Something—perhaps the sight of his father lying almost unreachable in his sickness, perhaps the recollection of what had been said after the fiasco with the Duke—something impelled Titus to come now and again all the way from the Apple Market to the Rozengracht, even when there was no business to be settled, to sit with the old man for an hour or two. Those little visits were fortunately uneventful: Aert, who was with his master from breakfast to supper, either tending him in his sickness or serving him in the studio, seemed content with his bounty, perhaps because it was given more liberally these days; and Cornelia, too, had undergone a change. "I bought a little extra cheese, just in case Titus might stop by," she would say, coming in from market. Or, "Look, Rebecca, would you please remember to put more beer into the water pail every time you take some out?—a person can never tell when there will be a guest." And once, coming into his studio on a night when he could not sleep, he found her there in her nightgown before an old, fair portrait of her brother, kneeling on the floor and weeping with the wild intensity of her childhood, chewing on a lock of her hair to keep herself from waking the household with her sobs. "Oh, my God," she said, "how is it that he has changed so much?" And he could give her no answer, could only stand behind her supporting her shaking shoulders with his unsteady knees and stroking her head.

Changed he had, appallingly, so that even the most unwilling eyes must see it. The question was no longer, "Are you sick?" but, "How sick are you? Sick past mending? Sick unto death?" Sometimes when they sat making their desultory talk in the front room, the young man would say he wanted a breath of air and would go into the little back yard where Hendrikje had first made the retching sound, and his father knew that he had gone there to cough blood. But no notice was taken of these matters; it was as if there were a pact between the two of them to disregard the manifestations of each other's mortality. When the one-sided dragging brought the old man into collision with a chair, the son said, "Light the lamp, Cornelia, we can't see where we're going." When the young man was seized with a spasm of coughing, the father said, "Have some wine—it'll ease the tickle in your throat."

As the summer waned and the nights grew more salubrious and congenial to sleep, he found his old body—out of step with the sun and running on its own eccentric rhythm—wanting to sleep less and less. Some thought would strike him, sharp and twanging like an arrow, and force him out of bed. It could be a grave and weighty thought, like the realization that Magdalena carried his grandchild and Titus's offspring in her poor little body; or it could be something utterly trivial, like the thought that old Rebecca must be losing her taste if she put so much salt and vinegar into the food. Whatever it was, it drove him to the window, where he would stand until his legs grew stiff, thrusting his head out the open casement and staring into the darkness that he knew to be Heer Lingelbach's labyrinth. Sometimes the sleep that would not remain with him in his bed came upon him as he stood, and he would dream half-awake. The blackness out there, alive with the stir of foliage, would be washed for him in a muted golden light, and great glossy leaves and tendrils would unfold in it—he would see an Oriental garden, but a very ancient one, perhaps the garden of Eden or the gardens that King David had laid out between the palaces he built in Jerusalem. There, in that dim gold, among growing things that half emerged from and were half lost in the blackness, she, the final beloved, appeared dressed in scarlet and greenish yellow, with pearls around her neck and pearls hanging from her ears and beaded bangles shimmering at her wrists. There was a night when a great fragrance, like the commingled smells of dried reeds and sandalwood, rose from leaves already fallen and trodden upon; and that scent was like a magic potion to him—it was by benefit of that scent that he saw her as she must have been in her youth, perhaps at the end of that year when there had been nobody she

640

loved. And while he dreamed—for surely this was dreaming—another figure stepped out of the shadow and laid one arm around her shoulder and extended the other to cup the virginal breast. Himself, yes, but in a guise more grave and gentle than any his spirit had worn in the course of its sojourn on the earth. The pale golden light shone on them both, and the leaves kept uncurling slowly around them; and she turned her head his way and looked at him with giving and accepting eyes, and laid her fingers over his seeking hand so that spirit and body, dream and reality, dissolved under her touch.

It did not leave him, that vision. Instead it congealed, or at least partly congealed, in his thoughts. The figures that had stood against the darkness of the labyrinth or the dusty gold of the Oriental garden never quite detached themselves from the misty air in which he saw them in his mind: there was no boundary line between them and it; they hovered there, edgeless and evanescent, glimmering coagulations of that from which they had issued and into which they would pass. His yearning to paint them was overwhelming and irrepressible; he desired to paint them as in his vigorous and imperious youth he had desired to perform the act of love. Yet he held back: he stretched his canvas and stopped, he prepared his palette and stopped again, knowing well that to paint them was to leave the real world behind and enter into the dream, and that on the other side of the dream was death.

"So you're going to start another big one, Master?" said Aert, taking the surrender for a renewal, a resurrection. "What is it going to be?"

And promptly, as though the dark angel of deliverance who stood waiting behind him had put it into his old, faltering mouth, he said, "Ruth and Boaz," and then wondered how long it would take the lad to catch him in his lie.

But Aert never caught him, and neither did Cornelia. What he evoked on the canvas, in the most beautiful strokes and moldings he had ever executed, plainly had nothing to do, so far as they were concerned, with Vrouw de Barrios or himself. Their total unawareness of what he was about showed him how great a distance lay between the darkly luminous dream world in which he painted and the light-drenched earthly world in which they lived. They said they had never seen such colors, such textures; they said it was less like a painting than like music; they marveled at the gravity and tenderness in the lover's face and the exquisite expressiveness of the young woman's hands. They walked on tiptoe past the door of his studio as if their profane footfalls might disturb some holy mystery; but they never guessed that what he was doing in there was equivalent to the act of love, that his spirit had passed from his outworn body into his brush, that he was taking unto himself and possessing utterly the woman whom he did not even visit any more, that when he came down to the table too tired to eat or talk he was spent with satisfied desire.

Titus came by one evening when the picture was close to completion and went by himself to look at it and stayed so long that the old man was afraid he had fallen into a faint up there alone. But when he went after him, he found him sitting on a stool drawn up close to the easel, with the lamp on the floor beside him, and his eyes—very large now in a face from which most of the flesh had fallen away—gazing as fixedly at the canvas as he himself had gazed into the night when the vision had first taken shape under the whispering leaves of the deserted labyrinth. The young man said nothing, only sighed and rose and picked up the lamp; but there was that in the look he turned upon his father which told the old man he was not walking unaccompanied out of the earthly light into the dark.

While he worked on the picture, he thought of it as the last one he would ever paint. It might well have been: he would certainly not have plunged immediately into its successor if another offering of pears and grapes and an affectionate little letter had not come to him from Vrouw de Barrios. It was as if her living self—still there in the shadowy house on the Breestraat, still calling to children and servants across the big room, still setting a table for her friends and looking toward her husband for the nod that would tell her she was doing well—it was as if her actual self had raised a sad and gentle protest against her transformation into a dream for the dying; and he was ashamed, he blushed when he read the letter as he used to blush for the passionate conjectures of his youth. It occurred to him then, since he had nothing else to do, that he could put himself on decent terms with her real being and fill up his empty days and gratify Aert's insatiable desire to see him working miracles at the easel by painting a portrait of her and the three little girls and Heer de Barrios. He would send it to them as a present if he was given time to finish it, and he took a blameless if somewhat feverish pleasure in the thought of Aert coming back from the Breestraat and telling him about their surprise and delight. The colors would be those he had seen in the curtained room that first hot afternoon, along with the pink and salmon and crimson the little girls had worn the evening when she had kissed him, and to these he would add the colors of sweet and transitory flesh and blood.

To set a guard on himself—he did not trust his wayward spirit—he told Aert he was about to paint a portrait of the de Barrios family. He would have been glad to leave it at that; but his apprentice, still bemused with admiration over what he called the *Ruth and Boaz*, was importunate for a foretaste of what he was sure would be even more glorious. "Tell me how you envision it, Master," he said. And the eager face before him, handsome and beardless still, looking at him with clear eyes under a soft fall of brown hair, stirred him to a rare burst of eloquence: he told Ferdinand—Carel—Aert not only about the palette that he had decided upon but also how the figures were to be arranged so that each of the five would be bound to all the others by a kind of chain of touch, and how the background was to be nothing—a throbbing, infinitely variegated expanse of dark. One little girl, the eldest, was to hold a basket of fruit—and where was that basket Vrouw de Barrios had sent him? Another was to smile up at her elder sister, and a third was to sit on her mother's knee with one hand touching her mother's breast. Changes might come about in the execution, of course, but they would be minor. He had the overall pattern perfectly clear; he could see it as plainly as if it were hanging on the wall of the de Barrios salon.

It occurred to him as he began work on it that the process of conception for the family portrait was the reverse of that which had brought the other canvas into being. In the *Ruth and Boaz*—he had taught himself to call it that when he was forced to call it anything—a vision had materialized into a picture; but now, as he labored with always shallower breath, always dimmer sight, a picture was dissolving into a vision. The children were not the de Barrios children—to tell God's truth, he could not remember what the de Barrios children looked like. The children were vague embodiments of a blitheness too frail to be called pure joy: their very freshness was such as says, "I am here only to depart." The reds, the crimsons, the coppery pinks, the pale golds and cold bluish greens with which he conjured them up were the colors of autumn and dying fires; the background shadow, pressing in on them, encroached upon the edges of their figures; even the eyes of the youngest were deepened by that shadow, as though she carried in her being the knowledge of the dark land from which she had come and into which she would go again when the years had swept through her and emptied her of her desires and her enmities and her loves.

In the sorrowful ecstasy of his labors with these unearthly children —his, his, the fruit of his spirit as surely as Titus and Cornelia were the fruit of his loins!—he almost forgot that he had a body. He ate to please old Rebecca and Cornelia; he lay down to rest because Aert would not go to bed before his master did; he seldom bathed and got quite out of the habit of taking off his working clothes at night. And the divine carelessness that showed itself in his dealings with his person extended to his dealings with his brush. Cloth, pearls, a fur-lined sleeve, a bit of green satin over a little chest, the salmon-colored toe of a tiny shoe—he did not trouble to plan and work them out: he laid the paint on in thick masses, or washed it on thin, or twisted it this way and that in wild and beautiful arabesques, and whatever he had wanted to set down emerged complete.

"I'll be eager to see the de Barrios children when I take the picture over there," said Aert. "Are they really like that?"

"More or less, I suppose. Of course, it's very freely painted. I imagine I'll be able to do better likenesses of Heer and Vrouw de Barrios."

And he did—at least in the beginning, before the face of the Portuguese poet began to change weirdly and inexorably under the brushes that seemed now to need no guidance, to be painting of themselves. The nose of Miguel de Barrios remained, but everything else kept changing: the brow, the cheek, the neck, the lips. As he had stepped out of the blackness of the labyrinth, loving and still youthful, to lay his hand upon the last beloved, so he came, as he might have been if false hopes had not deluded and enmeshed him, into the pulsing darkness above the shining little heads. Serene and wise, dressed in sober black without ornament, he took his seat behind the children and claimed the shimmering progeny of his soul. And she, even she, was transmuted. Those remembered ones who had vaguely asserted themselves in the sketches scattered over her red rug arose from the dead and passed into her person: Vrouw van Hoorn, Saskia, Hendrikje touched with her hands, smiled witchingly with her lips, gazed through her large, still eyes; and in painting this final vision of her he painted, embraced, possessed, and paid late homage to them all.

After that there was no more talk of likenesses. Likenesses fell into the category of unmentionables, like Titus's cough and his own collisions with furniture; nor did Aert de Gelder ask him when he wanted the picture taken over to the poet's house. His daughter and his apprentice spoke of it still as *The Family Portrait*. Whether they saw the equivocal resemblances in it, he did not know; he knew only that their way of uttering the title had changed, as if he had brought into existence on that canvas, for man's everlasting hope, such a family as should have been and had never been in the world.

In their innocence they were unaware of much that was in it. Aert saw the dark background merely as a foil for the richness and muted radiance of the figures, and Cornelia took the death-tinged gazes of the mother and father as nothing more than the sobriety that comes upon older folk with increasing worries and obligations. But they were young, and he was glad there was a great deal in it that they did not understand, glad that he could go to his grave without touching these two good and faithful servants with the taint of his death.

Titus alone knew it for what it was—Titus, who could scarcely believe he would live to see the fruit of Magdalena's womb. He came often now, probably as often as his strength would allow; and as soon as he had greeted the members of the household—barely touching them with the tips of his fingers, for he knew what contagion he carried in him—he would go slowly, pausing for breath on the way, upstairs to the studio. He took it for granted that *Ruth and Boaz* and *The Family Portrait* were not for sale. "Even if you could spare them, Father, I'm afraid I couldn't," he said. And that was all he said until that unseasonably warm and misty evening when he excused himself and went into the back yard and stayed longer than usual and came in again, white in the face.

"Sit down," said his father, who had been scratching his unshaven cheeks and cracking his knuckles during the long agony. "Would you like Rebecca to bring you something—hot tea, maybe, or a goblet of wine?"

"No, not yet. Later, Father, if I may." The voice was a hoarse whisper, but it still carried some of the old courtliness. "I'll tell you what I *would* like, though: I'd like to go up to the studio."

They went, the old man carrying the lamp and leading the way and pretending to be more unsteady than he was so that he could pause and give the doomed one who followed him time to catch his breath. Halfway up the stairs he noticed that something was impeding him: one of his garters had come undone and his stocking was hanging loose around his ankle; and he knew how slovenly he was, how crumpled and spotted and grimy with old sweat. "God forgive me, I don't know when I last had a bath," he said, coming into the dark studio. The two pictures stood side by side on separate easels, and Titus took the lamp from him and set it between them so that they kindled in the sudden burst of light. But the young man's eyes, tremendous and watery with strain and suffering, did not turn at once to that unearthly radiance: he gazed at his father, and then, very close to his father, he went down on his knees.

"Excuse me," he said, "may I pull up your stocking and fasten your garter? If you walk around like that, I'm afraid you might trip on the stairs." And then, unbelievably, the serviceable gesture was transformed into an embrace—the death-marked face was pressed urgently against his chest, the poor thin arms had clasped him around the knees so hard that he was afraid he could not keep standing on his feet. Through his shirt he felt the pressure of a desperate kiss, and laying his hands upon the almost fleshless shoulder blades, he set his mouth to the sweat-drenched brow.

"Titus, Titus—"

"I love you, Father."

"I love you, too."

"Those pictures—those two pictures—if I had the strength I'd come and look at them every night. Everything else I see, everything I sell makes me sick with disgust. It's only those"—still clasping, he turned his great desolate eyes upon them—"that can give me any comfort. When I'm looking at them, I don't suffer. When I'm looking at them, I can bear it, I'm almost at peace."

*

All of it was over now—the services for the dead, and the burial, and the long walk back to the Rozengracht. The box containing the earthly remains of Titus Rembrandtszoon van Rijn had been lowered into a grave in the West Church not too far from the place where Hendrikje lay; and the old man, leaning heavily on Cornelia's arm because of the downward pull of the earth, had come home to the comforts that Aert and Rebecca had prepared for his comfortlessness—the hot tea with brandy in it, the bed turned back at midday, the curtains drawn against the light, the cool towel laid wet over his smarting eyes.

He had given himself up to their ministrations, had even pretended to sleep so that they might be released from their futile service to him. They had left him—and not quite left him: they had stayed, all three of them, on the second floor, and Cornelia had left his door standing a little ajar. Why? Because she thought that being closed up in a room might remind him of being closed up in a coffin? She had not come to know as yet, poor child, that the living are more straitly confined than the dead, fettered to their bodies, imprisoned in the world . . .

He could hear the two women talking softly in the studio, the old one eager for the details of a ritual in which she could see herself as the central figure, the young one trying to transform something unbearably immediate into the finished stuff of memory.

"Was it a fine funeral, dear?"

"Oh, yes, beautiful. Sixteen pallbearers and three dozen candles and a beautiful pall for the coffin—"

"Sixteen pallbearers! My, my! Then he was buried like a proper gentleman!"

And strangely, he too took some satisfaction in it. That enough of Saskia's fortune had been left to see this son of hers to his last rest with dignity—this brought the warm tears back into his aching eyes.

"And what about the services? Was there much reading?"

"Not too much, Rebecca. But that was out of consideration for poor Magdalena, I think. Poor Magdalena's so big, you know, I wonder she can drag herself around. She and Vrouw van Loo asked us to come and sit down with them at the funeral table. They were very kind and gracious, I hated to refuse; but I was afraid for Father, and I'm sure they understood."

"Sh, you two," said Aert in a loud whisper. "Close his door or close this one or stop talking. He ought to get some sleep."

Sleep should have come to him easily: for the last three nights, ever since the foreknown tidings had been brought to him, he had scarcely closed his eyes; and a kind of blessed vagueness began to inundate his thoughts in the stillness, blurring the recollection of the raw oblong in the church floor, making it possible for him to see it as it would be by and by, closed over with marble paving slabs, marked with a bronze plaque that said: "Titus Rembrandtszoon van Rijn, 1641-1668, At Rest in the Lord," ornamented on Easter mornings with white and purple tulips or hyacinths . . . Tulips in the yard of the house in Leyden, and bees about their business among them, and the cousins from Zuytbroek sitting down at the funeral table after the burial of Harmen Gerritszoon . . . What had they brought, those cousins? Yes, a chopped herring salad, all the way from Zuytbroek, and Heer and Vrouw Lingelbach had told the old woman not to trouble to make supper, they would bring the supper, and that was good of them, very good, and he was tired, very tired . . .

But then, before the sun had withdrawn from the pulled curtains, he was wide awake again—sleep and the thin crust of resignation were shattered by the wild pounding of his heart. Why, why, had the young one gone and he remained with this misshapen thing in his chest, so swollen that it almost smothered him when he turned on his left side in his sleep? It was beyond reason and mercy that it should keep up its crazy, useless beating in spite of every ecstasy that should have burst it, every loss that should have strangled it. He hated it with a sick loathing: it was more than he could bear to keep dragging it back and forth, back and forth in the bleak prison of the world; the carving knife that he had taken to the *Julius Civilis*—he could turn it just as easily against himself. Reject the senseless or malevolent scheme in which the father survived the son—have done with it, he thought, curse God and die. And the obsession was so powerful with him that he tried forcibly to turn his mind to something else, lest he give the two young ones and the old woman another corpse to deal with when the first was scarcely out of sight. But there was nothing to think of, nothing to hope for, nothing to want: whatever came into his mind—people, painting, food, the cycle of the seasons, the alternation of day and night—came tainted with the taste of death. He got out of bed then and walked, on feet that were white and puffed up and netted over with broken veins, into the studio —blessedly empty, for the other three had taken themselves downstairs to the front room or the kitchen as soon as they had satisfied themselves that he slept. Not to look at the canvases, no—the canvases too were steeped in mortality. Only to delude himself with a madman's hope that if he stood where he had stood that evening with his stocking hanging around his ankle he could gainsay finality, could experience again that desperate embrace.

"Come," he said imperiously to him who was beyond all summoning. "Hold me, kiss me, this is where I stood, this is the spot where you went down on your knees; and I bent over you, so, and steadied myself, and your shoulder blades were under my hands, and you said, 'I love you, Father,' and I said, 'I love you, too.' " And how this mockery of the actual, this affront to the immutable laws of the finite and the perishable could have been any help to him, he did not know; but when he was finished with it, he was less aware of his hateful heart.

There was only one thing that stood between him and the black disgust which would make every knife, every high window, every vial of sleeping drops a temptation to him—the possibility of wresting that high remembered moment out of the universal ruin. While he sat at the table and forced himself to eat a little of Vrouw Lingelbach's supper so that the lad and the girl and the old woman would not go fasting by his example, he felt a passionate longing to be painting it just as it had been: his son and himself, with the marks of their doom upon them, clinging to each other on the verge of dissolution. He could envision every detail; the person of the buried dead was as immediate to him with its emaciated arms and its big feverish eyes as his own ravaged image seen in a mirror. But how could he paint it?—to paint it would be as shameful in the eyes of the world as walking naked in the street. Whoever would see it—Aert or Cornelia or Tulp or Rebecca—would conclude with good reason that grief had unhinged his mind. If he was to paint it in peace, without letting consternation loose upon the lot of them, without exposing himself to their apprehension or their aching solicitude, he would have to transform it as he had transformed the vision of Abigail de Barrios that had come to him out of the blackness of the labyrinth. And the dark angel who had prompted him to say, "Ruth and Boaz," served him again, offered him as thick a cloak for his last inordinate sorrow as for his last preposterous love. The Prodigal Son—yes, that was it—he would tell them all that what he was painting was the return of the Prodigal Son . . .

Rebecca found the place in Luke for him that same evening, and he sat before the peat fire on the hearth, reading the text over and over because the solemn cadences, more than the words themselves or their meanings, called up rich colors in his dulled, half-dreaming brain: a vibrant red, a clay-darkened white, a streak of pure yellow, an ocher tawny as a lion's skin and touched here and there with patches of gold. He did not speak of his vision; it would have jarred the quiet exchange among the others. Their talk was the simple, almost ritualistic talk that had served generation after generation at such times—as suitable here as it had been forty years ago in the house in Leyden: the pastor had read the service beautifully, especially the Twenty-Third Psalm; a surprising number of people had come to the services, many from the art shops and the Saint Lucas Guild; it had been good of Vrouw Lingelbach to cook their supper—enough was left for another meal tomorrow night . . . He nodded now and then and even made a remark or two: Bleau and Maarten Booms had been there, and young Philips Koninck too, just back from Germany. And none of them could have guessed that the only thing that kept him from rending the decent web which custom had taught them to weave over the terrible day was the business of bending the parable to his purpose—a task so arduous that as soon as he pulled up the blanket that night, he slept from sheer exhaustion.

The next day he sketched a little, but to no purpose: his hand shook, the images wavered in his mind and blurred on the paper before his aching eyes, and he had to put the drawing aside, telling himself that he had begun too soon. The sight of Cornelia going desperately about her usual business made him recall the threadbare saying that the day after the funeral was always worse than the day of the funeral itself—her eyes were red, her cheeks were wan and splotched, she kept running her hands through her hair and gnawing at her lower lip. He followed her upstairs, where she had gone to distract herself by giving his room a thorough cleaning; but she was not at work when he came in—she was kneeling by his bed with the bucket and scrubbing brush untouched on the floor beside her. Her head was bowed, her face was hidden by the rich fall of her disheveled hair, and her arms, dusky and round and beautiful like her mother's, were flung wide across the coverlet.

"Come, child," he said, "there's no good in crying."

"I'm not crying, Father." She raised her head and turned her face to prove it; and he saw the dry glitter of her dark brown eyes. "It's just that I keep wondering if Titus knew I loved him."

He remembered—and knew that she was remembering—the miserable noonday meal when the dead had come to sit down at table and make peace, and she had pulled away from his loving touch. He came and sat on the edge of the bed and stroked her damp and tangled hair. "Of course he knew it. He couldn't have helped knowing it. You mustn't worry about that," he said.

"But how could he know it when I was so hateful to him?"

"You weren't hateful to him—"

"I was, you know I was—the day he was here with the Duke."

"If he thought you were hateful to him—and I doubt he did—then he must have known why. He must have known you were angry with him because of me or jealous that he'd gone away from us to have a life of his own. And he would have known you loved him or else you wouldn't have been jealous and angry like that."

"Do you believe that, Father? Isn't it only that you're trying to make it easier for me?"

"Certainly I believe it. Look, Cornelia, when I was young I said terrible things to my father—I thought they would turn him against me forever. But they didn't—he knew I loved him, and I knew he knew it. That's something we can't hide, no matter what we do to cover it up."

That talk with Cornelia wrought a profound transformation in his vision of the picture, relieved it of its fearful urgency, washed it of its consuming bitterness. Now he was no longer able to see the moment of reconciliation between himself and his son as an isolated thing, existing solitary in the universal emptiness. He could never think of it without thinking also of the night when he had come back from his wanderings on the dunes and, seeing in the light of the single lamp the seal of mortality on the face of Harmen Gerritszoon, had fallen on his father's neck and asked forgiveness and been forgiven. As he had known from the first evening that the picture must carry the solemn cadences of the parable and must have in it certain colors—the burnished ocher, the inexplicable yellow, the living red, the clay-tinged white of dying flesh— so he knew now that it must somehow encompass the everlasting cycle of revolt and return, estrangement and reconciliation. "Forgive us our trespasses as we forgive those who trespass against us"—that, too, is part of the text, he told himself. As I sinned against my father and he forgave me, so I have been sinned against by my son and have forgiven; and he who pressed his dying mouth against me will also be sinned against even in his grave, for the fruit of Magdalena's womb will reproach him with his death as if it had been a desertion, and will in time pass on the sickness which is life to others, who will likewise sin in the monstrous blindness and heedlessness of their youth, and come to ask forgiveness, and be forgiven . . .

"Another big one, Master?" said Aert when he was told to cut and stretch the canvas. It was hard for him to keep the wonder out of his face. Only a kind of adoptive filial piety kept him still laboring like a servant in this stricken and lonely house: he had obviously been sure that *The Family Portrait* was the last.

"Yes, *The Prodigal Son.* I've already made a few sketches—the father and the young man—"

"Will there be just those two figures in it?"

"No, there will be others—four others as I see it now—bystanders, simply there and looking on, not having any idea what's taking place."

"Why are you adding them? To fill up the background?"

"Partly that, but partly to show how when a mystery happens nobody understands."

"Will they be coarse figures then, Master? Grotesques?—I've never seen you do a grotesque."

"Scarcely. They'll be just the opposite—the way I picture them, they'll be very dignified. You don't have to turn a man into a grotesque because he doesn't understand a mystery—otherwise, it wouldn't be much of a mystery." Grotesques indeed—it was preposterous—had there not been Tulps and Huyghens and van Huddes among them? He turned his back on the lad and looked at his supply of pigments. "You'll have to go and get me some ocher and some vermilion tomorrow," he said.

"Certainly, Master. Before you're up. The first thing in the morning. And will you include anything to suggest the Divine Presence? An angel, or perhaps God looking on out of a concentration of light?"

"Of course not." He said it in utter impatience and contempt. "You've been with me six years—you've seen what's happened here—you know what I am. How could you believe there'd be place for anything like that in a painting of mine?"

His work on that painting was serene and unhurried. It was always changing; as it had changed in his mind during the first months of mourning, so it changed now, even more radically, under his brush. If none of his three faithful servants recognized the dead in the figure that kneeled in contrition before the father, it was no great wonder: some of his own coarse earthiness had imposed itself upon the body of the penitent, and then that too had been painted out, and what was left was suffering itself, kneeling in the shape of man—the head shorn, the body muffled up in rags made splendid for some unaccountable reason by the ocher and the gold, one foot bare, the other in an almost soleless sandal, the face emerging only vaguely out of the shadow, pressed against the sustaining body of the father and wearing a look of weary, bemused, almost blissful peace.

And if the son had undergone more transformations than he could remember in his own weariness, what was to be said of the father, who had never, not since the first strokes had been laid on the canvas, been either himself or Harmen Gerritszoon? The father was old, older than himself, older than the miller of Leyden, older than the Patriarchs, older perhaps than time itself. The eyes of the father—and this he understood no more than he understood why the rags should be golden—the eyes of the father were blind. Yet the groping figure stooping over the prodigal in an accession of love and wonderment had a grave splendor, a muted magnificence. Light gathered on his wrinkled brow and drooping eyelids, light shone in the beard around his murmuring, pitying mouth; and all that could flow from one being to another on the current of love—compassion, forgiveness, the assurance of unfailing solicitude—passed from his hands into the young flesh that he touched through the radiance of the rags.

The watchers, too—those who looked out of the dark behind the two who had met and embraced and been reconciled—offered in their quiet surprise and almost querulous questioning a profounder tribute to the miracle than the agitated bodies and terror-stricken faces he had painted in his youth. And the darkness itself—it was Cornelia who noticed it—was not the vacant shadow in which the figures of *The Family Portrait* glimmered: it was infused here and there with such faint light as appears in the upper reaches of the sky before the coming of the dawn. It was as if something moved in the void, some nameless current going its inexplicable way, drawing an incomprehensible pattern between perishing star and perishing star.

"Don't be angry, Master," said Aert when it was almost finished. "I know you don't like me to say so, but I still think you've gotten the Divine Presence into it. If you hadn't, why would I feel like going down on my knees every time I look at it? Besides, that red cloak over the father's shoulders—that's the sort of cloak the early Flemish painters used to put on the Heavenly King."

"Think what you want about it," he said, for he had no real answer. If the son was more than Titus and more than himself and had become sheer man, broken and penitent, then the canvas bore testimony to his glimpse of a father who was such a One as could receive all humanity in an absolving embrace.

*

All through the warmly wan October afternoon he had sat in the parlor, idle and empty-handed, and listened to the noises in the street, noises so strangely muffled and far away that they seemed to be coming from another world. But there was no rest for him in the dozing and the aimless sitting; whenever the chimes in the steeples sounded an hour which he meant to count and always forgot to, he was troubled by the thought that there was something he ought to do.

Work on the picture? He drummed on the arm of his chair in exasperation at the foolish question that kept coming back after repeated dismissals. He couldn't work on the picture, hadn't been able to work on it yesterday or several days before. He hadn't even been able to see the picture, though he was sure none of the other three had guessed it—not since the dream or whatever it was had come upon him in the night. A kind of knock on the head, or *in* the head . . . A noise such as his father must have heard when they broke the dykes in Leyden and let the sea crash in on the Spaniards . . . A sheet of light first white, then crimson-purple, then gold . . . And afterwards such deep sleep that when he had awakened he believed he had dreamed it, and would have sworn he had dreamed it even now if some residue of the light had not been with him still—filaments of it, downy feathers of it, flakes of it settling around the edges of everything he tried to see.

Work on the picture? That was ridiculous. There had been times when he could not even remember what picture, though for the moment he could see it plainly in his mind's eye: the blind old Simeon in the Temple, holding the Child. He had gotten the text from old Rebecca an endless while ago. But maybe only a couple of weeks had really passed since she had read it to him after supper in the kitchen; it all seemed so distant—the time that was divided from the present by the dream of thundering waters and exploding light. She had read, if he remembered right, how the blind old Simeon had been in the Temple and sensed the presence of the infant Jesus, how he had taken Him from His mother and held Him in his arms because God had promised him he would live to see the Light of Israel, and how afterwards he had gone away content because the prophecy had been fulfilled, content and ready for death. "Ready for death"—no, those were not the real words, those were dull and flat like all the words of his making. Somebody—Cornelia, all aureate at the edges—came in and asked in a far-off voice if he wanted a bit of boiled beef or a bowl of lentil soup for supper, and he said, "A little of both," to please her. The brightness that had gathered around her remained, like a deserted halo, long after she was gone. And secretly, with a kindly craftiness, he figured out the safest way to walk to the table without stumbling over anything. The girl, the apprentice, the old women—he did not want them knowing and worrying. He had not told them about the blow on the head and the noise and the light; he had managed to find his way about in the bright confusion and to answer whatever they asked him as if he were not addled, only very tired, very old.

He was successful with his eating, could swallow the shreds of meat without choking on them, could bring the trembling spoon up the long distance without spilling any of the lentil soup. Though it was autumn, there were still broad, melting rays of sunlight falling slantwise across the table and the three faces. The rays were real, not like the drifting bits of radiance; the rays were there because they ate their supper very early so that his food could settle before he went to bed; and it occurred to him vaguely that they would rather eat later and would do so, by lamplight, when he was gone. Perhaps this evening he would give them a surprise, would sit up far beyond his usual hour, watching for the moon to come up, cloudy and shapeless beyond the pane. Yes, he would surprise them; the food had not pacified him, the usual sodden quiet was not settling in: there was something gnawing at him, some deep restlessness, something he wanted to do.

The women and the apprentice carried out the rusks and meat and soup and replaced them with a bunch of grapes from Vrouw de Barrios: she had cut them with her supple fingers and a little jeweled scissors from a vine otherwise quite barren and bereft of leaves in Heer Lingelbach's labyrinth—but that was nonsense and he had better watch himself, he had almost toppled his goblet of wine. There was a knocking at the door, and for an instant he thought it was Titus and did not judge himself too severely for the mistake: when the living were dissolving into light there wasn't too much difference between them and the dead. It was not Titus, nor Hendrikje coming back from seeing Geertje and brother Willem into the wagon bound for Gouda, nor Saskia returned from Vrouw Pinero's where she had been instructed in the care and preservation of precious things. It was Dr. Tulp, so misty that a person could be excused for thinking he wore the burgher ruff. "And how is it going with everybody here?" he said in the faraway sound to which all voices had shrunken after the crash of the inwashing sea.

"Well enough, well enough." It was himself that said it. And he supposed it was no lie: he who had pursued light all his days could do worse than find himself immersed in an endless drift of it, and he felt himself smile.

There was talk among the others that he did not attend to. He kept eating grapes because to pull them off their stems and break them against his toothless gums and ferret out the seeds with his numb tongue released a little of the restlessness.

"You shouldn't eat so many of those, Father. They'll give you a stomach ache," said Cornelia.

"Let him alone," said the doctor. "They can't really hurt him." And he heard the same voice saying some sad and consoling thing about nothing doing much harm when it comes to the point that nothing does much good. But it was not speaking in the warehouse where the golds and scarlets of the military Regents' piece blazed in the summer sun. It was speaking here at the table, asking him, "How's the baby?"

The baby? What baby? Rombartus caught up out of the black cradle and held for an instant in love beyond the grasp of death? No, that was long ago . . . The Baby in the picture? But as he had left it, how could anybody tell it was a baby? It was a mere lump at the core of the brightness it emanated. Aert would be able to give it shape, Aert could mold it so expertly after his master's fashion that hardly anybody would be able to tell who had finished it . . .

"I say, Rembrandt, how's the baby?"

"What baby are you talking about, Nicolaas?"

"Why, your grandchild—Titus's baby, Magdalena's baby."

"Oh, yes, of course." But he had put that baby so thoroughly out of his mind that he was always thinking sorrowfully how it had gone out in black nothingness—Titus's line, Saskia's line. "What did they call that baby?"

"Titia, Father. Titia, after Titus."

He swallowed the last grape whole and knew what it was that had been hounding him, taking the peace out of his enforced rest. "I tell you what, Cornelia," he said, looking at her blurred and shining shape on the other side of the table. "Let's go and see the baby. I never saw it. Let's go over there and see it tonight."

"Oh, no, Father, you're tired—"

"Go tomorrow, Master—"

"Yes, your honor, go tomorrow—"

"Let him go tonight if he wants to. I'll be going in the same direction, and by the time you're ready to start back, the carts will be coming in and you can get one of the wagoners to give you a lift. But we'd better take a couple of lanterns, Cornelia. There's a mist now, and by the time you come home you'll scarcely be able to see your hand in front of your face."

It had been kind of his old friend to mention the fog; otherwise he might have believed he was in Simeon's state, almost totally blind. The streets were dark when the three of them set out, so dark and misty that he could really perceive nothing but the lanterns, the ones that Cornelia and the doctor carried and those that went before them, their bearers blotted out, their swollen and roseate shapes seeming to move of themselves. As a candle will draw swarms of moths on a midsummer evening, so the lanterns drew the flakes and feathers and filaments. They were like planets going through the void, like souls incandescent in the blackness of unbeing, and they so held and awed him that he forgot to be wary in his walking and sometimes lurched against Tulp on his left and Cornelia on his right. They were going to finish the Baby in the painting. They were doing no such thing—that was more of his nonsense; they were going to the Singel in a procession of worlds or spirits to see Titus's child. And the way was long and passed through peculiar layers of air, sometimes so hot that he clawed at his muffler and sometimes so cold that he could not keep himself from shivering. The other two did not seem to notice these variations; they spoke quietly of he did not know what because the moving lanterns somehow slid between him and their voices, eclipsing whole sentences. And suddenly he said, "I should have carried a lantern too. I did carry one at Vrouw van Hoorn's funeral. I thought I couldn't do it, but I suppose I did it as well as anybody else."

"Naturally," said the doctor. "Here, take this one. This is where I leave you. Good night."

His mind grew clearer as they crossed the great vacant Apple Market and the curved stone bridge that spanned the Singel. He knew that the house whose lighted windows Cornelia pointed out to him belonged to the van Loos and that the old woman who let them in was Titus's mother-in-law, the same whom the lad had been happy to call "Mother" —and why not, since both of the others were dead? Whatever trouble he had in the hall and the unfamiliar room to which Vrouw van Loo conducted them was trouble with his sight: it was as if the lantern handed to him by the doctor had burned a great hole into the scene and sparks still clung to the margins of the hole as they would cling to kindled paper and whatever he wanted to see had to be glimpsed beyond the edges of that hole and those sparks.

What a pity it was, the old woman said, that she should be receiving them in a bedroom on their first visit! But poor Magdalena was ailing, had not been herself since the christening, had been forbidden by the doctor to get out of bed, could scarcely make herself heard because of the terrible cold she had on her chest . . . He strained to see above the blank spot and was able to make out the young woman sitting in a corner bed with a folded bolster behind her. She smiled such a wan, slow smile as he had seen on Saskia's dying lips; her face was bluish white against the garish scarlet of the shawl around her emaciated shoulders; and her hand, listless beyond prudishness, was tardy in covering the breast at which she had been suckling the child. "Look, Titia," she said in a cracked whisper, "here's your grandfather come to see you, and your Aunt Cornelia too." Whereupon he managed to say something —God knows what—but at least he called her "Daughter," and Cornelia led him to a chair close to the bed, and he sank into it, too weary to control the movement of his body, coming down with a thud that made the wood creak.

"Put back the blanket, dear, so that Heer van Rijn can see the little thing," said the old woman; and the languid, death-touched fingers pushed the white woolen aside to reveal what Simeon had held up under his old, blind eyes. Only this one is a girl, he thought, and was surprised to learn from Cornelia's soft "Oh, now, Father, you knew it was a girl" that he had spoken aloud, had probably uttered something not altogether kind.

And certainly he intended nothing but kindness. The girl-child was so small and frail in her nakedness that he could have wept for pity even if his mind had not undergone another of those peculiar mutations, even if he had not seen the vulnerable little being floating among the swollen lanterns, the drifting worlds, the going souls across vast expanses of dark. Great tears gathered in his eyes, warm and burning; and Cornelia got down on her knees beside him and said the words that would not come out of his tightened throat: "Oh, but it's a lovely baby, Magdalena! Such perfect little hands! Such beautiful little feet!"

They forgave him for his doddering nonsense, and he was glad that he had grown old enough to dodder and be forgiven. Cornelia took his hand and laid it on the baby's belly, fresh and smooth under his dry, numb touch; and Magdalena patted his wrist. "I'm sorry it wasn't a boy," she said in her poor hoarse voice. "I was hoping to have a little boy to show you, one you'd think was just like Titus. But she can't help it, poor thing."

They wept a little then, all of them, for the dead and the dying and the newly-born; and the weeping cleared his eyes and his thoughts, and he found wit enough to say that he was happy it was a girl: women were very serviceable and beautiful and good—he stroked Cornelia's warm hair while he said it—and he was glad that another one had come into the world . . .

They stayed a little longer, waiting for the carts to begin to come by; but how they spent the time or what they talked of he did not know. He was trying to remember what Simeon had said when he handed the Baby back to His mother, and he was so afraid of making trouble by another unfortunate reference to it that he felt nothing but relief when they were safely on the other side of the front door. The first wagoner that Cornelia hailed agreed to take them all the way to the Rozengracht and refused the coin she offered. Was this the bread cast upon the waters returning after many days? The light whirled around him now as the snow had whirled that night when he had run out to tell Heer van Hudde that he meant to paint the portrait of the good and faithful servant free. "Good and faithful servant . . ." "And God go with you . . ." No, that was what the Mennonites said when they bade you good night—that had nothing whatever to do with Simeon. The cart was filled with grain sacks; and as he rested his back against them and tried to answer Cornelia, who was going on as women will about the beauty of the child, he saw his father and Adriaen beating the malt dust from their breeches, and the flat fields stretching endlessly away, and the turning sails of the mill . . .

And now they were all home—Gerrit and Lysbeth and Adriaen and himself—and their father was washing his hands because he never said grace without washing them, and their mother was putting out the good tin plates because this was the anniversary of the Spanish retreat. No, he was wandering again: the lamp that he took to be on the kitchen table in Leyden was really in Cornelia's hand—she was walking before him up the stairs, and Aert and old Rebecca were coming up behind

656

him, saying that he must be very tired and ought to sleep well . . . such a long walk, such a good night's sleep . . .

But now that they were in the upper hall, he refused to turn into his bedroom; he insisted on spending the night where he had often spent it these many months, on the couch in the studio. No matter what they said, he would never settle down until he remembered the text, and lying close to the painting and breathing the smell of the wet paint might summon those longed-for words back into his faltering brain. By the lamps that Aert and Cornelia carried he saw vague spots of other pictures ranged against the wall—*Ruth and Boaz, The Family Portrait, The Prodigal Son*. They were not welcome tonight: when he lay down on the couch, too tired to take his clothes off, he turned his back against them to keep them from distracting him from the *Simeon in the Temple*, but he remembered rather than saw the blind old man thrusting his dying face into the radiance that streamed from the unfinished body of the Child he held in his withered hands. And when the last of the lights had been carried out of the room, he stared into the darkness and watched the flakes and filaments and downy feathers pausing, hanging suspended, withdrawing from their whirling dance. There was peace in the pausing and in the faraway good nights and in the departing footsteps going quietly down the hall. Peace . . . he had it, held it for an instant while the velvety shadow, also beautiful and worthy, obliterated the last of the filaments of brightness. "Lord, I have seen the light"—that was what old Simeon had said. "Now let Thy servant depart in peace."

ABOUT THE AUTHOR

GLADYS SCHMITT, the eldest child of Leonore and Henry Schmitt, was born in 1909 in Pittsburgh and has spent most of her life there. She was educated in Pittsburgh public schools and at the University of Pittsburgh, where she majored in literature and the history of art. She worked on *Scholastic Magazine* for ten years, three of them in New York; and for the last nineteen years she has taught at Carnegie Tech's College of Fine Arts in Pittsburgh, where she is Professor of English.

In all seven of her novels she has depended upon the counsel of her husband, Simon Goldfield, who works closely with her in every phase of her writing, from planning chapters to reshaping sentences. Dorothy Schmitt, her sister, types her manuscripts. Their adopted daughter, Mrs. Robert Culley, is a painter.

Miss Schmitt teaches mornings, writes in the afternoons, and gives evenings to friends, theater and music. She lives in a large Tudor house ideal for the casual hospitality she and her husband most enjoy. She characterizes her life as regular and confined, but nourishing and exciting.

During her research for REMBRANDT, Miss Schmitt consulted all important sources relating to the artist and his times, many of them available only in Dutch.

"Helen Hollick has it all. She tells a great story, gets her history right, and writes consistently readable books."—*Bernard Cornwell*

"If only all historical fiction could be this good."—*Historical Novels Review*

"Hollick joggles a cast of characters and a bloody, tangled plot with great skill."—*Publishers Weekly*

"A wonderful book… breathes new life into an ancient legend. Compelling, convincing, and unforgettable."—*Sharon Penman*

"An epic tale… Helen Hollick has done her homework meticulously and her story, for all its high drama, gleams with convincing Dark Age detail." —*The Lady Magazine*

"Uniquely compelling… bound to have a lasting and resounding impact on Arthurian literature."—*Books Magazine*

"Helen Hollick joins the ranks of Rosemary Sutcliff, Mary Stewart, and Marion Bradley with this splendid novel."—*Pendragon Magazine*

"Weaves together fact, legend and inspired imagination to create a world so real we can breathe the smoke of its fires and revel in the Romano-British lust for life, love and honour."—*Historical Novels Review*

"Stripped of its medieval trappings, the story of Arthur's rise loses none of its legendary power… this [is a] well-researched, skillfully constructed trilogy opener."—*Library Journal*

ALSO BY HELEN HOLLICK

Pendragon's Banner: *Book Two of the Pendragon's Banner Trilogy*
Shadow of the King: *Book Three of the Pendragon's Banner Trilogy*
Harold the King: *The Story of the Battle of Hastings*
Sea Witch: *The First Voyage of Pirate Cpt. Jesamiah Acorne*
Pirate Code: *The Second Voyage of Cpt. Jesamiah Acorne*
A Hollow Crown: *The Story of Emma, Queen of Saxon England*

FOR CHILDREN:

Come and Tell Me: *A keep yourself safe story*

The
KINGMAKING

HELEN HOLLICK

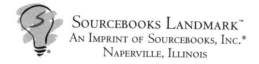

SOURCEBOOKS LANDMARK™
AN IMPRINT OF SOURCEBOOKS, INC.®
NAPERVILLE, ILLINOIS

Published by Sourcebooks Landmark, an imprint of Sourcebooks, Inc.
P.O. Box 4410, Naperville, Illinois 60567-4410
(630) 961-3900
Fax: (630) 961-2168
www.sourcebooks.com

Originally published in Great Britain by William Heinemann.

Library of Congress Cataloging-in-Publication Data

Hollick, Helen.
  The kingmaking / Helen Hollick.
      p. cm. -- (Pendragon's banner trilogy ; bk. 1) 1. Arthur, King--Fiction.
2.   Great Britain--History--To 1066--Fiction. 3.   Arthurian romances--
Adaptations. 4. Kings and rulers--Fiction. 5. Britons--Fiction. I. Title.
  PR6058.O4464K56 2009
  823'.914--dc22
                              2008051869

            Printed and bound in the United States of America
                 VP 10 9 8 7 6 5 4 3 2 1

For Sharon Penman

with my love and gratitude

ACKNOWLEDGMENTS

WITH ANY BOOK OF HISTORICAL FICTION THERE MUST BE, TO MAKE IT become believable, a great amount of research into the background facts. I am indebted to so many for their patience and generous help. *The Kingmaking* was first published in 1994; several successful adult novels later I find I have many of the same people to thank:

My friends and family did not mind the many years of hearing about "when I write my book," and have all shared in the excitement and pleasure of the reality. A large thank you to Mal for his expertise on the practical side; he understands computers so much better than I do. My grateful thanks to Charles Evans-Gunther who answered so many obscure questions, and to various members of the now sadly demised Dragon Society for their articles and inspiration. Staff of various libraries and museums answered my letters and questions with enthusiasm, which I gratefully appreciated, given that before actual publication I could not claim to be a proven author.

Thank you to Lynne Drew, my previous editor at Heinemann, who guided me through my first days as a professional author and most especially to the editorial and production teams, past and present, at Discovered Authors (UK) and the staff at Sourcebooks, Inc. I am so fortunate to have the opportunity to work with so many genuinely nice people.

My grateful appreciation to Jerry for his help with arranging questions for the Reading Group Guide.

My ex-agent, Mic, took me under her wing on the basis of a few chapters, and encouraged me to get the rest of it right; I remain grateful to her for that.

My love goes to my husband Ron for willingly driving me miles to see things like deserted, wind-swept hill forts, and to my daughter Katharine for never complaining about having to come with us. Thank you to both of them for their support and encouragement—and for ignoring the undusted rooms, unvacuumed carpets, and frequently forgotten dinners. These years later, the domestic side hasn't changed one bit… except Kathy has now learnt to cook. Survival instincts perhaps?

Finally, a special thank you to historical fiction author Sharon Penman, who has given me so much support and belief in myself. She is a wonderful, highly valued and treasured friend and to her *The Kingmaking* is dedicated.

Helen Hollick
2009

Britain circa AD455

Place Names

Agealesthrep	Aylesford, Kent
Caer Arfon	Caernarfon
Caer Dydd	Cardiff
Caer Gloui	Gloucester
Caer Leon	Caerleon
Camulodunum	Colchester
Cantii	Kent
Ceredigion	Area around Cardigan Bay
Crae Ford	Crayford, Kent
Dubris	Dover
Dumnonia	Devon and Cornwall
Dun Pelidr	Traprain Law
Durobrivae	Rochester
Durovernum	Canterbury
Eboracum	York
Eryri	Snowdonia
Gaul	France
Hafren	River Severn
Hibernia	Ireland
Iceni Way	Ickneild Way
Less Britain	Brittany
Ligre	River Loire
Londinium	London
Mon	Anglesey
Portus Adurni	Portchester Castle, Porsmouth
Rutupiae	Richborough
Summer Land	Somerset
Tamesis	River Thames
Tanatus	Thanet
Vectis	Isle fo Wight
Venta Bulgarium	Winchester
Yns Witrin	Glastonbury Tor
Yr Wyddfa	Mount Snowdon

People

Scotti:	Migrated from Ireland to modern Western Scotland
Angles/Saxons/Jutes:	Anglo-Saxons, English, or Saex
Picti:	Tribespeople from Caledonia, Eastern Scotland
British:	Celts/Welsh
Hibernian:	Irish

Pronunciation

A basic guide to the rough pronunciation to some of the Welsh names.

Abloyc	*ab-loy-c*
Bedwyr	*bed-oo-ear*
Cei	*kay*
Cunedda	*kin-eth-a*
Cymraes	*cum-rice*
Dogmail	*dog-my-l*
Dunaut	*din-eye-t*
Enniaun	*en-nee-eyen*
Gorlois	*gor-loys*
Gwenhwyfar	*gwen-hwee-var*
Gwynllyw	*gwin-(h)lee-oo*
Iawn	*yown*
Llacheu	*(h)lak-eye*
Melwas	*mel-oo-as*
Meriaun	*merry-eyen*
Morgause	*mor-gice*
Rumaun	*rim-eyen*
Typiaunan	*typ-ee-eye-nan*
Uthr	*oo-tha*
Ygrainne	*ig-rine-ya*

Circa 450 AD

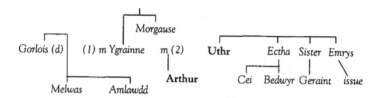

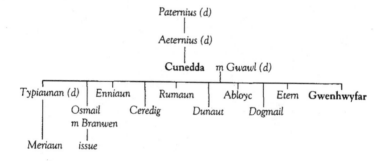

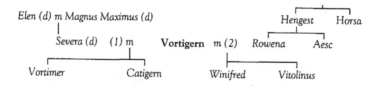

PART ONE

THE SPINNING

MAY 450

ONE

H<small>E WAS TEN AND FIVE YEARS OF AGE AND, FOR THE FIRST TIME IN HIS LIFE,</small> experiencing the exhilaration of the open sea and, for this short while, the novelty of leisure. The boy, with a grin fixed as wide as a new moon, folded his arms on the rail and leaned forward to watch the churn of foam boiling about the ship's bows. Salt spray spattered his face, tingling against skin that bore the faintest trace of manhood about the upper lip and chin. The sharp, sea-tang smell burst up his nostrils like a cast spear to his brain and hammered behind his eye sockets. He tossed his head high, back, bracing his body with his hands against the leap and plunge of the deck, and laughed with the pure energy of unequalled pleasure.

His eye sought the furl of the Dragon Banner flying proud from the mast-head. He twisted his body to see it better—a snake-like tubular shape, curling and writhing with a life of its own. Streamers shrieked with the passing of the wind, and the head flashed gold in a display of fire sparked by the caught rays of the sun. Ah, but it was good to be out in the open! Out on the sea, heading for Britain with Uthr Pendragon's war host!

A sister ship, the same as this great war-beast, save that she flew no dragon, plunged into the cleft of a tossing wave, thrust herself forward, gallantly keeping pace. The boy waved to men on board, grinning the wider to receive a brief flung acknowledgement.

Then he saw Morgause watching him, standing as straight and stiff as the single mast.

A fine-bred lady, Morgause, with the figure of a goddess and the vanity of an empress. She held her cloak tight around her shoulders, her slender fingers clasping a rose-coloured silk veil that held her sun-gold hair in place against the ripping wind.

If the ship was the perfection of sail, then she, to look upon, was surely the perfection of woman. Venus, Uthr called her in the intimacy of their lovers' bed. Perfection to the naked eye, often marred when examined close by a flaw within—hers the arrogance and cruelty that came with high ambition.

The boy's pleasure faded as fast as a tossed stone sinks below the surface of a calm pond. Why did the Lord Uthr need bring her? Why her and not his wife—although she could be as bad, with her constant praying to God and perpetual muttered litanies. An invading army was no place for a woman, not even for the mistress of the man who considered himself to be Britain's rightful king.

Her eyes—cold, calculating, ice-blue eyes—bore into him; evil eyes that never smiled except at the indulgence of her own twisted pleasures. His right hand was behind his back; he made the protective sign against evil, knew she was aware he made that sign. Strange, from tales he had always assumed witches to be ugly, dark creatures, not having the beautiful fair skin of Morgause.

He tried again to feel the joy of the ship but the excitement had faded, lost under this shadow of her foreboding. Instead, the lad ducked below deck and made his way to where Uthr's soldiers squatted playing dice or board and counter games. He was safe from her down here—she would not come where the men lodged—although it was so much better to be out there, in the air and sunlight…

Lord Uthr, called the Pendragon, approached Morgause from behind and wrapped his great oak-branch arms around her slender waist. She stiffened and pulled away from him, not caring at this moment for intimacy.

"You ought not let the boy do as he pleases, Uthr," she said. "Give him leave to take holiday and he will be fit for nought when it comes to returning to duties."

Uthr laughed, a deep bear-growl rumble. "He's just a lad. Leave him."

Morgause made no answer. She had no intention of letting the boy run wild, unchecked and undisciplined. Why Uthr had brought him she had no idea. He was nurtured as foster son by Uthr's brother—but a war host was no place for a boy who, in truth, was no more than the bastard brat of a long-dead servant girl. Uthr found the boy to his liking, but to her mind he was a lazy, rough-edged, insolent whelp who needed regular beating to remind him of his place. Common gossip favoured the foster father, Ectha, as the brat's unknown sire—although there had been some who had whispered of it being Uthr himself. He had the more likely reputation, would once have rutted with any whore available. A smile slithered across Morgause's lips, so carefully painted with vegetable dye. Not now. Now, he lay only with Morgause, youngest sister to his God-possessed wife.

"They say, below decks," Uthr said, nibbling at her ear—she attempted to brush him aside—"I have brought you with the intention of finding you a suitable husband." He ignored her flailing hand. "Shall I do that, my pretty one? When I have lopped the tyrant Vortigern's head from his noble shoulders and placed myself as King of all Britain, shall I wed you to some noble lord?" He swivelled her around, aimed a large wet kiss at her lips, smudging the red colouring. "Or shall I set aside my wife Ygrainne and wed you myself? Queen Morgause. It has a nice ring!"

She would have felt pleased had she known him to be serious. But Uthr was always jesting, always making fun of her aspirations. Curtly she answered, "My lord will do with me as he may please."

"Ha!" Uthr laughed again. "At this moment it pleases me to stand here on this swaying deck and kiss you." He glanced around. "It would please me even more had I a tankard of wine in my free hand! Where's the boy got to?"

Morgause said nothing, glanced instead at the wake foaming behind the speeding ship. Happen Providence would supply a discreet chance to tip the brat overboard before they reached Britain?

Instead, Fortuna followed the boy. Showing herself in the guise of squalling rain and a blustering westerly wind, she came stamping over the horizon with the dawn. Uthr's soldiers, landmen not seafarers, huddled below deck groaning as their stomachs heaved up to their throats. The Less Britain sailors scurried regardless, taking a reef into the square sail and jibing close to the wind. Thunder was brewing, would be upon them before mid-morning. For the boy, the storm was thrilling. To his delight, he found himself and Uthr the only passengers braving the deck.

Weather-seasoned sailors grinned at him as they scuttled about, great waves of spray soaking their clothes to the skin, the wind beating in their faces and snarling through the Dragon Banner overhead. Uthr ruffled the lad's hair, sharing his wild exhilaration.

"Is a battle like this?" the boy asked, eyes wide as a silver salver, salt-encrusted hands gripping the ropes along the rails. "Is it as exciting?"

Uthr laughed, making a hasty grab at his cloak that swirled in a gust of mauling wind. "Aye, lad. Danger breeds a sharpness that courses through your blood as hot as a man's lust for a beautiful woman." He watched fascinated as lightning lit the blue-black sky from horizon to horizon. "Always," he shouted through the following roar of thunder, "be aware. Keep your head, your sense. When you throw a spear, throw your soul with it. Let your sword be one with your arm." He made accompanying gestures, casting an imaginary spear, cleaving the air with a sword. "Keep tight control, boy. You will feel fear; fear pumps your blood the faster, but let not the fright touch your face. Keep it close, tucked well behind the shield of calm expression." He put his arm around the lad's shoulders and declared with a gusted laugh, "The same applies to handling women." He grinned. "The secret there, lad, is to let them *think* they hold control!"

Involuntarily, the boy glanced astern at the timbered cabin that was, for this voyage, Uthr and Morgause's. Uthr must have seen, for he too looked.

"You are right to fear that one, for she's a woman who seeks what dangles beyond her reach. I have her tamed, but Morgause can scratch as dangerous as a cornered wild cat."

The boy ducked his head, chewed his lip. Aye, did he not know it!

Thunder bellowed overhead. Uthr made to stride away but paused, waving his hand in the direction of the shuttered cabin. "She's no sea-maiden, my prized whore. You'll see no more of her these next days, not until we make harbour." He winked and strode for'ard to speak with the captain.

And he was right. Not even when the first haze of the Gwynedd coastline came into view, nor as the shore grew larger, with detail coming clear, did Morgause show herself.

The boy stood on deck, spellbound as the great ship, with her following sister, swung landward. Gwynedd—where the Lion Lord Cunedda ruled. Where valleys nestled green and lush, and mountains heaved upwards to caress the sky. He had heard much of Gwynedd, and found this first view of peaks plunging like an eagle's swoop towards a plain that, by contrast, lay as flat as the sea, not disappointing.

The two ships swept into the straits between the mainland and the Isle of Mon. A lively wind, the tail end of the storm, danced across the sea chasing a galloping herd of white-crested waves that pranced to meet the nearing shore.

A movement there! Two dark specks against the spring vegetation of green, yellow, white, and pink. The boy squinted his eyes, attempting to make out clearer shapes. Two riders—not adult, for they lacked height and build—were urging their horses to a fast pace. A chestnut and a smaller, black-coated hill pony.

The oars lifted then dipped to kiss the white foam. The sail dropped and the ship, tossing her prow like a mare held over-long curbed and kicking high her heels, leapt for the harbour sheltering beneath the imposing fortress that was Caer Arfon.

TWO

H EELS DRUMMING, THE TWO CHILDREN URGED THEIR PONIES INTO A GALLOP, the flat land along this seaward stretch allowing the pace faster. The boy, better mounted, was forging ahead on his chestnut gelding, enjoying the reckless speed.

"Etern, wait!" Gwenhwyfar shouted, pleading. She saw her brother disappear into a gully but her words were snatched by the teasing wind; she doubted he had heard. Relief brought a smile when she found him waiting impatiently, his excited horse tossing flecks of foam, hooves fidgeting. The boy's eyes were darting from her approach to the haze of sea, and the sprawl of buildings beside the estuary. He wanted to get back.

At ten and four, Etern was the elder by two summers. He had his sister's copper-gold hair and expressive green eyes, but was taller by a full head and shoulders. He frowned at her, shouted, "Kick him on, make him earn his keep!"

"He's going as fast as he can!" Gwenhwyfar hurled a retort sharp with ruffled anger. Reaching her brother, she hauled at the iron-tough mouth of her sweating pony, noticed, with a twinge of envy, how the handsome Aquila was barely damp. One dark stain on his neck, a slight quiver to his deep chest, nothing more.

"That pony's too fat for his own good," Etern observed with critical disapproval. "About time Da gave you something decent to ride." Instantly, he regretted the barbed sarcasm. He smiled an apology, smoothing his sister's puckering temper with "Still, I suppose he does well for his age, but you are growing out of him. Look, your feet are almost to the ground!" He laughed suddenly, impatience swinging to humour.

Gwenhwyfar laughed with him, her mouth wide, head tossing, seeing with her brother the absurdity of her lengthening body astride this short-legged, barrel-bellied pony. Fondly, she patted his neck, her palm slapping on the wetness that was beginning to steam. "He has served me well enough."

"He cannot carry you forever though—would he not make a pony for brother Osmail's son now? The lad will soon see his third summer—time he was riding."

Gwenhwyfar snorted disdain; brother Osmail was not a favourite of hers, and even less so his fastidiously intolerant wife. "If Branwen has her way he will be fit for nought save women's work or the priesthood." Pulling on the reins and giving a thumping kick with her heel, she brought her stubborn pony away from the grass he was eagerly snatching at and persuaded him to walk on.

Etern grimaced, echoing his sister's distaste for the boy's prospects, and nudged Aquila to follow.

For some yards they rode in silence, the horses picking their way through the dull tangle of last season's heather and the fresh colours of mayflowers. The wind brought a sharp tang of the sea to mingle with the smell of warm earth and sweet-scented, sun-speckled plants. Overhead, a flight of gulls, one with a fish flapping from his beak, wheeled shrieking and squabbling. Etern brought Aquila up to the pony's side, rode companionably with his sister.

"What possessed our brother to wed a woman such as Branwen?" A question Gwenhwyfar was often heard to ask, particularly after some fresh outburst of disagreement with her sister-by-law. "Were there not milder-tempered maids to choose from?"

Aquila was beginning to dance, becoming bored with the sedate pace. He blew through his nostrils and tossed his head, his mane brushing Etern's face. The boy shortened the reins, intending to curb the impatience, managing only to increase the bend to the horse's neck and the jog in his step. "Osmail seems happy to have a son born, another on the way, and a plump woman to keep him warm at night."

The wind lifted the loose hair always escaping from Gwenhwyfar's braids. She gave Etern a look that could have scorched the mayblossom brown. "There are enough plump women around Caer Arfon to keep an entire legion warm! No need to wed such a dragon!"

Aquila leapt sideways at some imagined fright. When Etern had enticed him back on to the sheep-track they were following Gwenhwyfar added, with a wicked grin, "And Branwen is not plump, she's as fat as Da's best breeding sow." She pushed her pony into an ambling trot. "Come, brother, Splinter has his wind; those two ships will have docked by now."

Traders' ships were becoming a rarity along this coast. The chequered sails of the Saex sea wolves, aye, or the earth red of the pirates from Hibernia; both a menace to trader or traveller. But sleek, powerful craft like those two fighting

the heavy swell of the straits and a bruising westerly wind were uncommon
enough to set brother and sister hastening home. Coming down from the hills,
the eager canter had increased to a furious gallop, Etern pointing ahead, shouting excitedly, "It's the Pendragon, Gwen! I can see the Dragon Banner!"

"*Uthr Pendragon*," he whooped, his voice crying back into the mountains and
hurling towards the afternoon sky.

Gwenhwyfar held her counsel, but as they approached the incline leading up
to the stronghold's outer defences she faltered an opinion. It may be his banner,
but need he be aboard?"

Her brother blew a crude noise through his lips. "Of course he's aboard! The
Dragon flies only above its lord!" He swivelled to face her, his expression animated. "Think on it! Uthr Pendragon at Caer Arfon!"

A tale told often around the hearth fires, of the time when, soon, Uthr the
Pendragon, the exiled High Lord of all Britain, would raise his war host and
come to claim his rightful place as supreme king. A tale of hope fashioned by
old harpers and young soldiers. Tales were tales, along with the legends of past
gods and heroes; Gwenhwyfar had long since learnt such tales were not always
to be believed.

They trotted through the open gateway between ditch and palisade fencing
and entered the bustle of the settlement that crowded against the towering turf
walls of the stronghold, Cunedda's fortress of Caer Arfon. Within a few strides,
Gwenhwyfar believed her brother right.

A festive mood bubbled, tripping over dwelling-place threshold and market-
seller's stalls, spilling like heady wine into alley and street. People were jostling,
laughing, and dancing, making merry as they will when spirits are lifted to the
stars with the promise of hope against the oppression of a tyrant's rule. For even
here, under the protection of their beloved Lion Lord, the despised King Vortigern
cast his greedy shadow.

The ponies clattered through the cobbled archway into the sanctuary of the
stronghold proper, their ears pricking as they neared the stables and the promise
of corn. Here, within the imposing walls, turreted and top-fenced, swelled the
normal bustle of a powerful lord's domain. Kennels for hunting dogs, barns for
gathered grain, roundhouse dwelling places for servants and slaves, a latrine, and
bathhouse. Smoking cooking pits near the kitchen place, the well, and the impressive structure that was Cunedda's Hall, with, beyond, the family apartments,
stone built, lime-washed and roofed with slate.

With the horses settled, brother and sister ran, slowing only to slip past the open kitchen door from where a shrill voice could be heard scolding some unfortunate.

"Branwen!" Gwenhwyfar mouthed, exchanging a wary glance with her brother. Safe, they hared for the Hall, heart of the Caer and of Gwynedd.

A crowd pushed to enter at the wide-open oak doors. Men mostly, warriors already gathering for Cunedda's spring hosting, but with a few women of the settlement elbowing their way through. A tumult of noise poured from within.

Etern cocked his head to listen at a side door. He pushed it open and crept through, his sister close as a shadow behind him. The vast building was bursting with excited people. Merchants, Eldermen, a handful of headmen who had ridden hard when the two ships were first sighted.

A bear-pawed hand thumped down on Gwenhwyfar's shoulder and spun her around. She looked up, startled, met with an elder brother's heavy frown. With a none too gentle shake Enniaun growled, "I wondered how long before you two bobbed up." He eyed Gwenhwyfar's appearance. "You been fighting a battle?" He poked a finger at a particularly large stain on her tunic. "Would it not be polite for our father's two youngest to have washed and changed before entering his Hall?" He twirled Gwenhwyfar round, studying an even larger grass stain on the seat of her bracae. "God's truth! The pair of you are dirtier than midden slaves!"

Brushing ineffectually at the offending mark on her chest, Gwenhwyfar smiled innocently. "We were in a hurry. No one will notice us if we stay at the back."

"I will notice—and have no doubt Da will."

Gwenhwyfar exchanged a wry glance with Etern. Enniaun was right, of course. Dismally they slouched out again and stood dejected for a moment, heads and shoulders slumped. "We could creep in through the servants' door from the kitchens," Gwenhwyfar suggested.

Etern shrugged. "Da would still see us—or worse, Branwen. Best do as Enniaun says. Just wash the bits that show, put on a clean tunic and comb your hair. Meet you back here!" He said the last quickly, off and running towards the boys' place before he had finished.

Gwenhwyfar envied him those quarters. No twittering chatter from an array of cousins for him! Nor, she reflected as she trotted into the girls' chamber, a mess of discarded garments strewn over floor and cot.

Grumbling to herself she flung someone's crumpled tunic from her bed and kicked her own dusty boots beneath. Stuffing her tunic into the chest of soiled garments destined for the laundry slaves, she washed from a pitcher of cold water and tugged a comb through her tangled hair, cursing her misfortune at being born a girl.

After nine brothers she was the only daughter. In a sheltered recess of her heart, Gwenhwyfar sometimes wondered whether her mother might have survived the birth of the last delivered had she borne a tenth son. Making a face in the hand-held bronze mirror, she studied herself. A squarish chin, nose a little too long, mouth rather too wide, lips too thin. She did not consider herself pretty, did not particularly care whether she was or not. Gwenhwyfar thought, behaved, more like a boy than a girl; learning to run, fight, and ride as was the old way for British-born women. The old way, before the Romans came with their tidy ideas. She could handle a weapon, sword or spear, as competently as Etern; could plan an ambush with unrivalled cunning—much to the annoyance of family and servants who often fell foul of her mischief.

She stuck her tongue out at her slightly distorted image in the polished metal, put the mirror down and again attacked her hair with the comb. Her personal bane, this! Cunedda refused to allow her to wear her hair short. He suffered her in boys' clothing—discreetly admired her courage and determination, but wailed, "*Leave something to remind us occasionally that you will be woman-grown one day!*"

Hastily she rebraided its thick mass, her fingers flying in and out, then struggled into a fresh tunic. Glancing at her bed, which she shared with Ceridwen, Cunedda's youngest niece, she grinned. All was tidy. The others would be in for a scolding from Branwen when she saw the state of the place! Gwenhwyfar laughed wickedly and skittered back to Etern, leaping up a short flight of wooden steps to where he waited.

"What took you so long?"

"This damn mane of mine, it takes ages to braid—one day I'm going to defy Da and hack it off!"

Eyes widening, Etern stared in horror. "You would not dare!"

Restraining a smile, Gwenhwyfar retorted, "Would I not?" For a wild heart-beat Etern believed her!

A second time Enniaun appraised them, nodded his satisfaction. "You will pass." Then, "Do you not have female garments, Gwenhwyfar—more suitable than boys' bracae for an occasion such as this, hm?"

Her eyes grew round with indignation. Those were words more suited to the dragon Branwen, not a beloved elder brother! "I wear a gown on the Lord's day! Is that not enough?" she answered.

Etern giggled. "Only because our Holy Father told Da one Sabbath you looked more like a street slave! Da was livid, I recall."

Gwenhwyfar grinned back at him. She had reluctantly agreed to wear more suitable clothing in the chapel, not to pacify Branwen who grumbled the girl ought always dress as befitted her sex, nor for the priest, but because her Da had been embarrassed in public by a man he regarded as a pompous ass.

"You will find space over there. Go quietly, mind." Enniaun smiled to himself as the children wormed their way through to where he had indicated. Etern on the threshold of manhood, a fine boy, and Gwenhwyfar, so like her mother. The same vivacious face, sparkling eyes and trilling laugh. The same iron will.

Enniaun was close past Etern's age when Gwenhwyfar was given life and their mother's taken. To the end of his days he would never forget seeing his Da crumpled with tear-stained face, rocking a pitifully crying baby, nor his choking words. "*Aye, little one, I miss your Mam too.*" He turned his attention away from his sister, squatting hunkered on her heels, chin cupped in hand, eyes intent upon Uthr—a man so often heard of yet barely remembered by the elder brothers; never seen by the younger ones.

None in this Hall failed to share her excitement. Cunedda's people loved Uthr, and what he stood for—freedom, revenge. They were a proud people, with long, long memories. Under Uthr and Cunedda they had once fought Vortigern and lost. Defeated and shamed, Cunedda had surrendered to the King, who claimed the North in forfeit. Giving instead, in gracious compassion, a shabby, forgotten corner of Britain, racked by poverty and plague, and violated by sea pirates. Vortigern intended the giving as an insult. Cunedda had no choice but to accept, and had come with his loyal people to this struggling, dismal corner of valleys and mountains with a heavy heart and bitter pain. Finding a dejected settlement loosely propped beside the remains of a Roman fortress, he turned that heaviness to determination, pain into optimism. He created pride and wealth in place of squalor and shame, hope in place of resignation. The passing years saw the raiders set to flight, the ruins rebuilt and hearts raised as high as the mountains of Eryri. Demand, encourage, bully, and praise; the Lion gave might and wisdom, received back from his new land of Gwynedd loyalty and profound respect. Cunedda won enough of both to choose his own friends—and to blow dust in the face of those who objected. But none forgot Uthr, the rightful king; and none forgot Vortigern, sitting safe within his guarded estates and comfortable strongholds in the wealthy south and west.

Cunedda's people—once the proud Votadini, now the even prouder people of Gwynedd—cherished their memories. Of a war begun and lost; of Vortigern hiring the Saxons to fight against them, and the resulting blood and death and sorrow. Memories that whistled on a summer dawn, of sons slaughtered and women taken; or on a frosted winter's night, of hearth fires grown cold and dwelling places lying derelict. Dun Pelidr, the ancient fortress rising like a whale hump from a sea of flat land, fallen empty and dark, Cunedda's fortress where he had governed, as had his father, and his father before him. Dun Pelidr where rotted the butchered bones of Cunedda's eldest son.

Ah, in Gwynedd Vortigern's cruelties were well remembered! It had taken time to reforge strength, to rebuild all that had been lost, but they had it all now, all and more. By moving Cunedda to Gwynedd, Vortigern had intended him to sink into oblivion, but the King had judged wrong, and now Uthr was back from exile!

Accompanied by his three sons, an Elderman came before Uthr, bowed, and exchanged a brief word before finding seating. The Hall was filling. Soon there would be standing room only; then the porch would crowd with men, and latecomers would need wait outside, the speeches relayed by those who could hear. Glancing round, Gwenhwyfar recognised many of those already seated or waiting to greet the Pendragon and Cunedda; many, she did not know. That one, from the emblem on his shoulder, must be from north Dyfed, and the one seated beside him. Several to the left had come from across the Straits, from the sea wolf plagued Isle of Mon. Word must have flown fast and well guarded ahead of Uthr's coming, for so many notables to be so quickly gathered in this chieftain's hall!

Her attention wandering, Gwenhwyfar gazed fondly about her: at the smoke-blackened beams arching under the reed-thatch roof, carrying the carved heads and faces of protective and watchful spirits; at the fresh-painted white daub walls, hung with bright tapestries and splendid skins, lined with ranks of spears, swords, and shields. Her brothers sat clustered in a group, chattering among themselves, their faces eager and animated. Ceredig, kind natured and easy to talk to, the next born after Enniaun. He was stockier than the others and not so tall, though like many of them he carried the same bush of red hair as their Da. With a wife and three young daughters, he was awaiting an opportunity to claim his own land. Seated at the fore of the group were the twins Rumaun and Dunaut, as like as two spears made from the same shaft, both tall and exceptionally handsome, both with wives and young children. Rumaun was bending forward, telling a no doubt lewd tale to Meriaun, only born child of dead

Typiaunan. Next to him, Abloyc, legs spread, hands behind his head, thrust himself back laughing. By the turn of summer Abloyc was to wed a chieftain's lass from Dyfed, a blue-eyed, vivacious girl. Gwenhwyfar had met her several times and liked her. And then sleek Dogmail, smiling at a passing serving lass. His bed companion? You never knew with Dogmail exactly who his latest love would be. He loved them all, he said, all women. Osmail was not there. Gwenhwyfar scanned the crowded Hall. Ah, there he was, seated beside an Elderman from the small coastal stronghold of Conwy. Engrossed in serious conversation, judging by the concentrated frown on his face. She turned her attention back to Uthr. A bull-muscled man, richly dressed in a combination of Roman and Brythonic fighting gear, as were most of the fighting men. But Uthr eclipsed all others, as the sun would outshine an evening star.

Gwenhwyfar shivered, excitement tingling along her spine. Sa, tales are not true? As she glanced across the Hall indignation flushed across her cheeks, glowered in her eyes. What insolence! Among the Pendragon's personal guard sat a boy hunkered on his heels, openly staring at her with a lopsided grin. Gwenhwyfar turned to Etern, intending to exclaim at the impertinence, but her mouth dropped open as she saw her brother nod and grin back at the boy. Of all the…! She decided to ignore the both of them.

Uthr's purple cloak, spun of the finest wool, was fastened at his left shoulder with a brooch the size of a man's clenched fist. Around his throat he wore a torque of twisted gold shaped like a dragon—a great serpent beast with ruby eyes and gaping jaws, its gold scales winking in the dancing light of the torches. A royal torque, a king's insignia—and Uthr wore it like a king determined on absolute power.

All the while, though she directed her mind to the Pendragon, Gwenhwyfar could feel eyes on her. Eyes belonging to a boy with hair cut ridiculously short in the Roman style, and a nose too long and straight for a face with an etched laugh that could only be described as shameless. Gwenhwyfar tossed a braid behind her shoulder and lifted her chin higher.

Cunedda was coming to his feet, striding forward a step, and holding his arms high to silence the rumble of talk.

Gwenhwyfar shuffled her body around so as to turn her back on the boy.

"Lord Uthr!" Cunedda's voice boomed up to the roof, shuddering the dust from settled corners to swirl a while among the hearth fire smoke curling around the cobwebbed rafters. "First I speak words of welcome, as custom and honour demands. I say to you, for myself and my people," he gestured with spread hands at the intent assembly, "welcome to Gwynedd and to my Hall. Welcome, as my foster brother, unseen for over many years and truly missed." He grinned at Uthr, then said in a lower tone, "Despite your tendency to get us both into serious trouble!"

Laughter rippled, and a few handclaps joined enthusiastically by Uthr himself. Stories of these two men's youthful exploits were popular hearth tales, told for the most part with good humour and much laughter. For some, though, they were useful to be spread as malicious gossip. Cunedda might be well respected, but Uthr had left many enemies along his trail.

The lord of Gwynedd let quiet settle before stepping up to the man he had waited so long to receive. He clasped Uthr's arm in recognition of friendship; Uthr stood, returning the gesture. Before the cheering crowd, the two embraced, holding each other close, not heeding their ready tears.

Stepping back, reluctant to relinquish the embrace of friendship Cunedda spoke directly to Uthr, but pitched his trembling voice so all might hear. "And welcome, double welcome, as rightful King of all Britain!"

As one the assembly leapt to its feet, roaring agreement, hands waving or striking the air, heads back, mouths wide, feet stamping. Gwenhwyfar stamped and yelled with them. Through each season of her twelve years of life her brothers and father had spoken with admiration for this man, Uthr Pendragon. Barely a moon waned without someone bringing up the question of when he would raise an army and come against the tyrant Vortigern. And now it was happening! Uthr was actually here in her Da's Hall! Here he stood, as large as a bear, as imposing as a dragon, ready to renew his war on Vortigern!

The Pendragon held his arms high, humbly acknowledging the acclaim. Deep, dark eyes, set in the earth brown face of an outdoor man, gazed solemnly over those standing before him cheering and shouting.

Gwenhwyfar wondered if Uthr had noticed herself and Etern, knew them to be Cunedda's youngest born. As the thought came the Pendragon's piercing gaze fell upon her. She flushed pink, but summoned enough courage to return his scrutiny.

Unexpectedly, she met something other than stern power. Kindness shone there, and laughter. She smiled a half-shy girl's greeting. Uthr's mouth twitched in response and Gwenhwyfar found it impossible to control the laugh that burst from her as he winked.

The boy must have seen it too, for when Gwenhwyfar turned her head she caught him grinning straight at her. With immense difficulty, she repressed the childish urge to stick her tongue out at the mongrel whelp.

THREE

POURING WINE FOR GUESTS AND GWYNEDD'S WARRIORS WAS ONE OF THE FEW women's tasks Gwenhwyfar quite enjoyed. To make her way round benches that groaned under the weight of so many, to slide nimbly between the jostling arms of animated revellers without spilling a drop of her Da's most precious wine, carried a pleasing benefit. You could take a while to fill a tankard or goblet, and listen to interesting talk. Men with the drink in them seemed to forget the wine-bearer had ears! Gwenhwyfar learnt much of the comings and goings beyond Caer Arfon by that innocent pouring of wine!

Four suns had set since Uthr's arrival, followed by three heat-hazed days busy from dawn's first light to the fall of dusk—aye, and beyond, into damp-scented, sound-heightened darkness, that carried the clang, clang of the swordsmith's hammer as far as the sleeping hills. By day, horses were brought up from the pasture for the fitting and checking of harness and hooves. Men were drilled, the echoing tramp, tramp of their feet mingling with their shouted war cries. Other men busy with leather and metalwork; a constant bustle of making and mending, and among it all the cheery leave-taking of messengers, swift-bound for allied lords of Dyfed and Gwent. And all the time there came the steady arrival of Cunedda's warriors called by the great boom and boom of the war horns sounding along the wind from ridge to ridge that first sunset, summoning shepherds, mountain or valley dwellers. Fathers and sons, headmen with their shield-bearers—the fighting men of Gwynedd coming eager to fulfill their service of the war spear.

The hill from the Caer, rising in an incline beyond the Stone Ground to where the tumbled stones and timber of the old Roman fortress of Segontium had once stood, was clustered with tents and campfires. Uthr's men alongside Gwynedd's, and those from beyond the Dovey river. Men who welcomed Cunedda's strong hand against the sea wolves, proud to offer their spears alongside his own. Aiee! This would be a hosting to stir a tale-teller's harp for many a winter's night to come!

The noise of excited talk and merry laughter swirled and buffeted against the high rafters, mingling with the dark waft of hearth smoke. Carrying a new-filled jug on her hip, Gwenhwyfar made her way along the row of benches to where her brothers sat with her father, and Lord Uthr. She poured for the Pendragon, listening to the conversation of the moment—talk of Vortigern's two grown sons by his first wife, a woman long since cold in her grave.

She moved with casual slowness to her father, shifting the weight of the heavy jug and pouring carefully. So-o, Vortigern and Catigern were becoming more outspoken against the second-taken wife? Gwenhwyfar knew much of her. Rowena, daughter to the Saxon warlord Hengest. The marriage had caused outrage some ten and eight years past, culminating in that brief flurried war of Cunedda's unsuccessful rebellion, and Uthr's simultaneous attempt to take the throne. Cunedda had lost his eldest son and his northern stronghold, and Uthr too, had lost his vast holding of land and had fled into exile. Many good men had died through Vortigern's wanting of that Saex bitch! How he had paraded his victory, rubbing the sting of salt into the raw wound and neatly sidestepping remaining criticism by declaring his marriage a treaty of alliance.

"He says," said Cunedda, talking of Vortigern to Uthr, "he still regards Rowena as a hostage for peace."

Uthr barked a shout of laughter. "And treats her as such? My arse he does! That lecherous toad married her because he was hard for her. Mind, Hengest is a crafty bastard. *You want to bed my daughter? Certainly, Vortigern, but not without a bride price of a claim to British land!*"

Uthr emptied his goblet in one long draught. Wiping his mouth with the back of his hand he crooked a finger at Gwenhwyfar, who was serving her eldest brother, and held out the empty vessel for her to refill. To Cunedda, he added, "That Saex pirate knew what he was about when he paraded a ten and six year old beauty before a man known for his whoring. I hear she's pregnant again?"

Gwenhwyfar filled one brother's goblet, moved to another. That also was common knowledge. The Queen's birthing would be within the month, the sixth born, and all who despised the King and his bitch hoped for it to be the fifth to die. One child only had survived, a daughter who had the fair skin and sharp temper of her mother.

From a nearby corner someone called her, holding his goblet high. There was still wine in her jug but she walked deliberately past and made her way towards the women's side, where she filled a goblet for herself and sat. She flicked a glance at the one who had hailed her, Etern, her youngest brother, seated cross-legged on the floor among the boys of the Caer. Let someone else serve him, him and that boy! For these three days she had seen nought of Etern so taken with the insolent whelp was he! Well, she, Gwenhwyfar, would have no tangle with him!

Spirits soared and voices grew loud with the laughter of full bellies and good wine. Again it was Gwenhwyfar's turn to take round the wine, and again she found herself pouring for the Pendragon.

He nodded his thanks, grinned broadly at her and said to Cunedda, "Your daughter will one day make a fine match for some aspiring princeling. Have you plans for betrothal?"

Feeling her face grow pink Gwenhwyfar held her jug steady as she poured. Her Da, though, had been distracted by some shout of laughter along the table and so no answer came. It was not her place, a woman and a child at that, to pass comment, but Gwenhwyfar was never one for bowing to convention.

"My lord, I have no intention of being married off to some unlanded, un-blooded upstart who wishes to use me for his own ambition!"

Attention caught, Cunedda flashed his daughter a frown of disapproval, but Uthr sat back in his chair and roared amusement.

He thumped the Lion on the shoulder and declared, "Your lass, my friend, and no mistake! She has your wit—temper too no doubt." He chuckled again, reached out to hold Gwenhwyfar's chin in his cupped hand and scanned her face. "Aye, but I can see her mother's beauty shadowed beneath this childhood awkwardness." He released her, said with a decisive nod, "You'd do well for a king's wife, girl. I full agree—aim high!" He reached his arm behind her, play-fully patted her backside with his palm.

"I will wed none but the highest, my lord!"

"Queen, eh?" Uthr chuckled. "Even you, at your age, could do a better job than the present one!" More laughter, echoed by others at table and those with-in hearing.

Cunedda nodded quick agreement and made attempt to turn the conver-sation, but Uthr, his humorous eyes lingering on Gwenhwyfar, pursued the thing. "I give you a promise, lass." He raised his wine and said in a louder voice, "When I have parted Vortigern's head from his shoulders, I shall bear you in mind should I need a new wife as queen!"

To Gwenhwyfar's extreme annoyance, Etern and the boy joined with the answering shout of hilarity.

Passing their corner, the boys called for her to leave the wine. Saying nothing, she thumped the jug on the table, stepping deliberately on what she thought was her brother's toe. No matter that it was the boy who yelped.

He looked up at her, brown eyes meeting her green. Taking hold of her arm with his fingers he said, with no hiding of the laughter in his voice, "I am grown quite tall and have yet more growing before I finish. Would I be high enough for you?" His laughter broke with a splutter as he collapsed against Etern, whose arms came about the boy's shoulders, their amusement exploding into joint hilarity.

Gwenhwyfar glared distastefully at the both of them.

"You behave like half-witted mooncalves!" earned herself more laughter.

She turned away abruptly. Arthur had entered Gwenhwyfar's life, and she hated him.

FOUR

LADY MORGAUSE WAS IN A BOILING TEMPER. THE MEAT, SHE CONSIDERED, HAD been raw on one side, blackened on the other, and the wine sour. The Hall was draughty and full of choking hearth and torch smoke; loud with men's drunken laughter and the cloying stench of male sweat. She had a headache as thick as beeswax. And that girl had dared flaunt herself before the Pendragon! His eyes had roamed to her all evening, followed her as she left to seek her bed-chamber with the rest of that gaggle of girls. Ah, and Morgause knew only too well Uthr's gleam of interest, that curving smile of his!

The iron-rimmed heels of her boots click-clicked on the path in step with her anger, her lips pressed tight, body rigid, as she stormed along the rough-laid path. She hissed an embellished oath as her cloak snagged on a nail protruding from a leaning fence, jerked the material free with impatient fingers, cursing again at the sound of ripping. There was little light out here. A flaring torch set here and there, a shaft of pale, flickering yellow from the open doorway of some hovel of a dwelling place, There was no moon, the faint silver of midnight star-light not quite enough to illuminate the way to the latrines. Not that light was needed; the stink provided guidance enough.

She entered the dim-lit, square-built chamber, her nose wrinkling as the smell of human waste assailed her nostrils. Seating herself at the nearest accommoda-tion, she emptied her bladder quickly with held breath, and would have run for the fresh air had dignity ever permitted Morgause to run.

She was used to the luxury of a Roman villa; light, airy rooms, tiled flooring, and paved courtyards. Hot water in the bathhouse—not the tepid, brownish slush that filled Cunedda's excuse for a bathing pool—and latrines cleaned twice daily. She snorted derisively. Small comfort that there *was* a bath-house and latrines in this squalid apology for a nobleman's residence! By the name of the Goddess, it was hard to believe civilisation had ever touched this backward place!

As she stepped outside, her sight was momentarily lost in the darkness. She walked forward impatiently and collided with someone running for the door. A flurry of arms, a swirl of hair and a gasped apology. Then the dim rush lighting from within the latrines flared briefly as the door opened and closed. Silence. Morgause stood, her breath not yet recovered from the foul stench. That wretched girl again! For a moment she almost made to follow the child with the intention of delivering a severe reprimand. Her hand went to push the door but she had no wish to re-enter the place without desperate need, and even less of a wish to stand hovering here, outside.

Turning back along the path, she swung right to skirt the Hall and strode towards the chamber allotted Uthr, her thoughts dwelling on Cunedda's daughter. Gwenhwyfar. A child on the edge of womanhood, a maiden. A pretty enough thing, though her legs and arms were too long, her body not yet full rounded but with enough promise to excite a man who took an interest in young girls. Morgause caught the swirl of her cloak as a freshening sea wind flapped at its length, and cast the folds across her shoulder. Uthr had made that remark in jest about marriage with the girl, but with Uthr who knew which was jest and which seed to take root? Morgause had long since learnt not to trust Uthr's seemingly idle remarks.

There was a light in his chamber, spreading in a narrow, spilt pool through the open door. Morgause hesitated. Was her lord already come from the Hall? Not yet, surely? A moment since he was still drinking deep with Cunedda, though many were seeking their sleeping furs or already lay snoring where the drink left them. With her mind half diverted by the irritating reflection of Gwenhwyfar, and that disturbing look of lust in Uthr's eye, Morgause entered the chamber.

There was a clatter, a gasp of indrawn breath. The boy Arthur was crouched beside a clothing chest set at the foot of the bed, his hand hovering inside, fingers clasped around a small scroll of parchment. Immediately Morgause was across the room, reaching out, roughly grabbing at him.

"What do you do here? How dare you pry into my lord Uthr's things!" She twisted Arthur's arm behind his back, brought him to his feet and shook him as a dog would shake a caught rat.

Fear and panic had ripped across Arthur's face at her unexpected entrance, his heartbeat leaping, breath catching. All was masked now, controlled, sealed tight behind a shield wall of defiance. He would not let this witch see his fear of her! She would like it if he showed how scared he was of her slapping hand and evil temper.

"I am not prying!" he defended, attempting to squirm away, to free his arm. "Lord Uthr bade me fetch something."

"You lie!" Morgause snatched at the parchment. He jerked aside, but not quickly enough. She had it, a sneer of triumph in her pinched nostrils and slit eyes. She moved from him a pace, but did not let go his arm, her grip tightening, claw like nails biting into the flesh beneath his woollen tunic. Arthur would have cried out but he knew to hide that also. Bite hard on your lip, or dig your own nails into the palm to divert the pain she inflicted, keep it hidden.

She was attempting to unroll the thing one handed, not succeeding. Impatient, she hissed, "What is in here?"

Truthfully, "I know not. Lord Uthr bade me fetch it." To add conviction, "It is for Lord Cunedda to see."

Morgause waved the scroll before his nose, her face coming close to his, both hands now on his arms, shaking, shaking. "You lie. You were stealing it! For some purpose of your own, you were thieving from Uthr!"

The defiance came easier now. He was not lying—no need to pretend, to think fast or fabricate untruths. "Why would I do that? Why should I steal from the man I love?" A mistake! Arthur saw it as he spoke, realised her anger had turned ugly.

Morgause's eyes narrowed. Her hand drew back, the gemstones in her many rings flashing in the subdued light, the gold and amber and jet bracelets tinkling and jangling at her wrist. Then the palm swept forward. Two stinging blows fell sharply across Arthur's cheek, leaving streaks of white that began to redden, would show the blue-black of bruising by morning. There would have come a third.

"Why indeed?" a man's voice drawled. "What use, woman, would a letter from my saintly youngest brother, Emrys, have for this boy?" Uthr stood in the doorway, leaning casually against the frame, his great bulk blotting out the darkness beyond, his hand resting lightly on the pommel of his sword.

She had not heard him come up behind her. Morgause spun to face him, not letting the boy go. "I caught him going through your things. It is not the first time he has stolen or lied."

Uthr pushed himself from his leaning position, strolled a little unsteadily into the chamber and towards a wine flagon, where he poured for himself. "You too have stolen, my lovely, aye, and lied on occasion." He raised his goblet in mock salute, said with a light chuckle and an amused smile, "Did you not steal me from my wife? And do you not, even after all these years, still lie to her about it?" Then, with the severity of command, "Let the boy go. He tells the truth."

Reluctant, lips pouting, Morgause released her hold. Uthr jerked his head at Arthur. "Take the parchment to Cunedda—you will find him in his own chamber—then return here." He winked, almost as a conspirator would. "I may have further need of your legs, lad."

There was triumph in Arthur's bold, eye-to-eye look as with a flourish, he took the scroll from Morgause's hand. He bowed his head at Uthr and left, his step jaunty. Beyond the door, he leapt into the air, striking his fist above his head, into the darkness. Sweet pleasure to have won over her! Sweet, rare-tasted pleasure! He cared little whether she heard his accompanying war yell of triumph.

Uthr said nothing more. He set his baldric and sword aside, unclasped his cloak, peeled off his leather tunic, belched, and took a further draught of wine.

Morgause, too, said nothing. She stood, fists clenched, willing Uthr to say something more, something she could answer. There was much she would say! Of that girl, Gwenhwyfar—what was she to Uthr, had he intentions there? Of the brat Arthur—whose son was he? Why had he been brought here? When was Uthr to set his wife aside and take Morgause in her stead! She waited, willing an argument. Still Uthr said nothing.

He sat on the bed, busied himself with plumping the pillows, fiddling with the furs, inspecting the clean linen. He raised one eyebrow in her direction. The glow from the few bee's wax candles fell soft, flattering on her skin, ringing her sun yellow hair like a golden coronet. Her breasts beneath the expensive silk of her robe rose and fell with the quick panting of her angered breath. Holding his goblet, he moved slowly, almost casually, and encircled her body with his arm. He kissed her, not gently, but with a roughness that came from the certain knowledge of possession.

"You ought not frown, my beauty, you will get wrinkles around your eyes." He ran his thumb under her chin, down her neck, his fingers slipped briefly beneath her bodice. Then he placed a swift kiss on her lips and swung away, back to stretch out on the bed, his goblet still in his hand.

"I'm tired, Morgause. Go to your own bed this night." He waved his free hand in the vague direction of the door and closed his eyes.

Morgause took three deep breaths. Very calm, but with ice hatred, she said, "So, I am to be dismissed like a common whore who is no longer needed?"

Uthr laughed. "Common, my lovely? Na, you were never common." Morgause did not miss the fact that he had not denied the word "whore," and had used the past tense.

She stalked to the door, sweeping her cloak around her high and wide, knocking the flagon of wine from the table, sending it spinning and clattering to the floor. "I hope your new maiden gives you a dose of the cock-pox!" she flung at him, and banged out through the door.

Uthr yawned. It had been a long day of greeting old friends and new, of good food and wine. He closed his eyes, sighed with tiredness—opened them again with a start. What new maid? He lifted himself on his elbow, peering curiously at the closed door in half a mind to call Morgause back. Na, leave it. He settled himself more comfortable, lying atop the furs, booted feet stretched the length of the bed. Ah, Morgause was so easy to bait into a flurry. Always had been jealous, that one, not like her eldest sister, his wife. Ygrainne was the placid one. He yawned again, felt the warm glow of approaching, welcomed sleep. How different sisters could be! The one meek, shut away for hours praying to her God, world weary with the shouldered burden of others' problems and troubles—and Morgause, a blaze of temper that crashed through all reasonable sense, with no thought beyond herself. The one a wife who would not be a wife; the other who could never fill her place. Happen he ought to seek a third party, another female who would be somewhere atween the two minds. His drowsing thoughts drifted to think of Cunedda's daughter. Her pretty face, her tilted, defiant chin. Now there was a maid who could be moulded into obedience without losing her spirit.

When Arthur returned he found Uthr sleeping, the empty goblet still in his hand. Gently he took it and covered the man he loved above life itself against the night cold. Then he found a sleeping fur for himself and, protective of his lord, curled on the floor before the door.

FIVE

GWENHWYFAR WOKE IN AS IRRITABLE A MOOD AS THE ONE SHE HAD FOSTERED on seeking her bed, only now she had the added discomfort of a headache. Probably a residue from the wine she had drunk last night—the children were only to have watered ale, but sampling what the adults drank often proved too tempting an opportunity to miss. She lay a moment, snuggled in the comfortable warmth of her bed, her cousin Ceridwen's back jammed close, the gentle rhythm of her sleeping breath rising and falling. Gwenhwyfar listened to the babble of birds greeting the day and watched, in a dreamy half sleep, as the shaft of light trooping through the single small window crept down the opposite wall and lengthened its march across the floor. She ought to get up. Branwen would come bustling in soon, banging the door, thumping the beds, tutting and squawking at the girls' laziness. She glanced across at the other beds. No one else was up, then.

Damn that boy, it was his fault she had this headache! His fault her mood was as sour as the taste in her mouth. Under her breath she swore a particularly obscene word that she had heard one of her elder brothers use. Did she have to wake with him on her mind! She repeated the word. And she had dreamt of him—curse him. Did he not even respect the privacy of sleep? Was it not enough to have sat laughing at her last night; to have taken Etern?

Forgetting Ceridwen still slept she plunged from the bed, grabbed her clothing, and dressed. She would find them both, give them a piece of her mind. She chuckled then—aye, and see how their heads throbbed this fine morning! Order her about, eh? Well, they had asked for wine and they had got it—Da's best fermentation, strong enough to blow the scalp off a seasoned warrior's head! She laughed again. The headache was lifting, her mood swinging into something more pleasurable.

Whistling, she ambled to the door, and ran slap into Branwen.

"Look where you go, child, and stop that noise; it is not a sound to befit a woman." She stamped into the room, pulling bed covers off the sleeping girls—daughters of Gwynedd's Elders, of Cunedda's elite warrior guard and a variety of kindred, some older than Gwenhwyfar, some, like Ceridwen, younger.

"Gwenhwyfar!" Her back to the door, Branwen lumbered around, the bulk of pregnancy making movement slow and cumbersome.

Gwenhwyfar was almost out of the door; she paused in midstride, looked back with a sweet, innocent smile on her face, murderous words in her head. "Aye, Branwen?"

"Where are you off to? There is much to be done this morning—you will help me."

"But I…" Gwenhwyfar ceased her protests; it was never profitable to argue with her brother's wife. Etern and Arthur would have to wait—happen their pounding heads would last long enough to be showing discomfort later.

Those two spoken words were enough to draw a frown from Branwen, accompanied by, "One day, young maid, you will become headwoman to a household." Her raised finger wagged with her scolding. "Come that day, you will need to know your duties." Branwen waddled through the door, motioning for Gwenhwyfar to follow. "The dear Lord knows how I try to impress this fact upon you!"

The morning dragged. A bright, sun-splendid morning with the birds busy about their nests and young, and the sky a perfect cloudless blue.

The storerooms were deliciously cool. An arrayed army of pots and jars: preserves ranked along rows of shelves and upon the floor; dried fruits, spices, and herbs; honey for sweetening and for adding to the ink used for the writing of ledgers and communications. Amphorae of oil for cooking and lighting. Salt, barrels of it. Further in, steps down to cooler, darker, slate-lined cellars where meat, smoked or salted, hung from low beams, and beyond, in a smaller chamber, cheeses made from cow's, goat's, and sheep's milk. Produce from the herds that grew fat from Gwynedd's ample grazing.

Branwen poked and peered, tutting often. A heady, potent scent clung to where the barrels of wine and ale were stored, a smell of last summer's end, when the fruit had been gathered and pressed in the great vats behind the granaries. The jugs of apple and pear and wild flower wines were in plentiful supply, so too the barrels of ale, but the fine imported wine drew a burst of exclaimed dismay, the vaulted ceiling echoing her clicking tongue. Branwen wagged her head. "We will need to keep close watch on these—I pray Lord Uthr will not stay long." She clicked her tongue again.

Behind the safe shadows of the smoking torch she held Gwenhwyfar grinned. There was enough wine in here to quench the thirst of two full Roman legions! Branwen did fuss so.

Then out from the stores and across the hard-packed earth of the courtyard heading for the little dark room where gathered herbs were dried and ground for cooking and healing and, beyond, to the linen chests, a particular pride of Branwen's. Few households could boast such fine-woven bedlinen!

Gwenhwyfar trotted at the woman's heels, her eyes drifting to the rise of hills beyond the Caer's turf and timber walling, only half listening to Branwen's list of chiding, so often had she heard the same round of complaints.

"Your father should send you for fostering where this disagreeable side to your nature would be whipped from you."

Dutifully Gwenhwyfar agreed. Do the tasks, nod your head. Quicker to see the thing through than start a battle of words.

There were steps up to the linen stores. Branwen tripped on the last, falling forward heavily with a startled cry. No matter how irritating she was, Gwenhwyfar would wish the woman no harm, for the sake of the child she carried if for little else. She put out her hand, concerned, offering help. "You ought to rest more with the babe so close to birthing."

Branwen heaved her bulk upright. Shaken, she replied, "Rest? Where would I find time to rest?" Fumbling with her girdle keys, she unlocked the door and a waft of lavender-scented, sun-bleached linen leapt out at them. "I expect to birth this child while sorting out some incompetent's mistake." Branwen moved inside, her fingers lovingly touching the laundered items, selected what was needed, and motioned for Gwenhwyfar to carry them. Rest? With the men preparing for war and such a large household to be responsible for—she peered narrow-eyed at Gwenhwyfar—and with this child who preferred the run of the hills and a sweating pony to educate into taking women's work seriously? Branwen sighed. It was the Lord's will that a woman should work to atone the sins of Eve. Rest? Rest!

Uthr's assigned chamber was close to Cunedda's own rooms built at an angle to the rear of the Hall. His room was empty, found to be muddled with armour, maps, and discarded clothing. A man's chamber. Bed furs lay in a heap, a wine flagon lay on its side on the floor, its contents long since soaked into the hard-stamped earth. More tutting from Branwen. She called for servants and muttering disapproval at the thoughtlessness of men, moved on to inspect the women's quarters, and to the chamber assigned to Lady Morgause.

Apprehension fluttered within Gwenhwyfar as she followed like a puppy in her sister-by-law's squat shadow. She was well aware who she had collided with last night at the latrines. Aware this lady was not someone to treat lightly. Her temper had been heard throughout the stronghold and was etched in the cold beauty of her face for all to see. Gwenhwyfar was no timid girl, but, oh, did she need to accompany Branwen beyond this particular threshold?

Morgause lay languishing on her bed. She barely bothered a glance at Branwen as she entered, but her brows rose fractionally as Gwenhwyfar came forward to place fresh linen for a servant to remake the bed. The girl risked a quick discreet look at the woman, her eyes darting away as they met with a dark expression of disapproval. She knew Morgause would say something, some disparaging remark.

And it came, silky smooth, laced with the sharpened edge of a dagger blade. "Gwenhwyfar. The maid who holds no respect for elders, who does not watch where she is going, and who thinks she can hold a man's attention by prattling silly nonsense!"

Frowning, Gwenhwyfar returned Morgause's stare. Whatever was she on about? "I apologised for my clumsiness, my lady. I was in desperate need to hurry." She lifted her shoulders in a slight shrug. "For the rest, I know not what you mean."

Morgause smiled. Gwenhwyfar noticed how that smile went no further than the lips, no trace of it touching her smooth cheek or blue eyes. A chiselled smile that could have belonged to a marble statue. If becoming a woman meant bustling tetchily from storeroom to storeroom, or lying a-bed while the sun rose high, making ambiguous, sarcastic comments, then na, Gwenhwyfar did not look forward to womanhood!

Branwen had cast a hard, disapproving glance at the girl, but to Gwenhwyfar's relief, said nothing. Branwen chided her many faults for her own good, but loyalty to your own came before courtesy to this immoral, painted woman. Politely, Branwen asked if the lady had all she required.

Morgause stretched, arching her slender body, and lazily rose from the bed, unconcerned at her nakedness. She was beautiful, and she knew it. Walking like a sleek cat across the room, she slid smoothly into a robe, seated herself on a stool, and motioned for the slave to begin on her hair.

"I would prefer quarters closer to my lord Uthr's." Morgause swept her lashes low and blinked several times, staring meaningfully at Branwen. "We are an inconvenient distance apart."

"Our unmarried women's chambers are all away from the men's." Branwen's reply was stiff.

Morgause waved her hand. "No matter. Distance increases desire." She glanced at Branwen's rigid stance and sober dress, her eyes lingering on the woman's advanced pregnancy. "I see you keep close to your man!"

Branwen tightened her lips, affronted. "The servants are instructed to bring all you need." She turned on her heels to leave.

Morgause waited until Branwen was almost through the door. "There is something…"

Branwen paused.

"The boy Arthur has orders to attend me. He has not made an appearance this day."

"I will instruct the servants to find him."

Seizing her chance Gwenhwyfar said eagerly, "Shall I go look for him?"

Morgause spread one of her dazzling smiles that sparked nothing of friendliness. "Do so."

Tossing an impish grin at Branwen, Gwenhwyfar skipped off before her brother's wife could countermand the order. She searched the Caer and made cursory enquiries through the bustling settlement, to discover the boy Arthur was nowhere to be found.

Nor, for that matter, was her brother Etern. Damn them both! No, damn Arthur; it was he who had captivated Etern!

By early afternoon she gave up the search and, instead, headed for her special private place, a sanctuary of quiet where she could think or dream. She fleetingly wondered whether she ought to report back to Morgause, but decided against the idea. It was Arthur, after all, who was in trouble with the woman, not herself. Sitting with her long legs twined around the sturdy bough of a large old tree at the far side of the orchard, she thought over the morning, wondering where Etern had got to and who Arthur was, beyond the scant information she had already gleaned. And then there was Morgause to consider.

Morgause, how different from Branwen! Gwenhwyfar giggled to herself, stretched her arms above her head and settled her back more comfortably against the sturdy old trunk. Uthr's mistress epitomised all Branwen detested. What fun! She would tell Etern of this morning's encounter. How he would laugh! Morgause with no shame, Branwen bristling with disgust! The Christian priest lay behind Branwen's fastidiousness, of course. Gwenhwyfar thought him a sanctimonious fool. Once, she had asked her Da why he tolerated the man. Cunedda had replied that it was politic to accept the Christian faith.

"*Jesu Christ poses no threat to Gwynedd or to me. He's as welcome to my hospitality and acknowledgement as any who bring peace and prosperity.*"

"*All very well,*" Gwenhwyfar thought now, closing her eyes against the dance of dappled sunlight. "*The Christ might be welcome, but need we suffer Branwen's morals?*"

Voices. Two people talking beyond the wall in the confined space of the herb garden. Morgause's shrill of laughter and an answering deep-throated chortle. Uthr. Gwenhwyfar's eyes snapped open: she sat hastily forward, grabbing at a branch to steady herself; the bough swayed, settled.

They had stopped not far from the overhang of her tree. Looking down through the glossy spring foliage, she could see them, standing close together against the sun warmed wall.

"Is it not pleasant here, Morgause? I said you would enjoy Gwynedd."

"No, it is not." A whine crept into her correct Latin—not for her the soldiers' clipped accent or the common British tongue. "I have barely seen you, Uthr." Then impatience. "And the boy has disappeared."

Gwenhwyfar chewed her fingernails. Should she make herself known? It was wrong to listen to private conversation, but...

Morgause was talking. "Arthur is becoming more disobedient as each day passes! He is at an age, Uthr, when he thinks he can rule the roost, but I tell you..."

The man sighed, interrupted, and peeping through the leaves Gwenhwyfar could see him stroking Morgause's slender arm.

"He's high spirited."

"He is a self-willed, spoilt brat."

From her hidden place Gwenhwyfar nodded her head in vigorous agreement with Morgause's sharp response. *Aye to that!*

Uthr was standing very close to his mistress; his hand had slid around her waist. "Leave the lad be, it is his first time away from the estate."

"I do not know what possessed you to bring him."

"I like him."

"Huh!"

They fell silent. Gwenhwyfar peeped again. Uthr's head was very close to Morgause. He kissed her, his hand sliding up to caress her breast. Irritably, Morgause pushed him away but did not step aside. "Not here, not where Cunedda's people may see."

"What? Becoming modest of a sudden?"

She ignored the sarcasm. "You ordered the boy to ensure I had all I needed."

Uthr tried again to kiss her but she jerked her head away. "The boy is a lazy good-for-nothing. I will thrash his backside when I catch up with him."

Uthr chuckled. "For punishment or pleasure?"

Morgause laughed, a false, forced sound. "My lord, what thoughts you have!"

Uthr laughed with her, but there was a rumbling growl beneath the flat humour. "I know your ways, Morgause, and have a distaste for them. I am fond of the lad. Leave him alone."

The laughter quite gone, and jealousy rising, Morgause sneered, "Fond of him? Do I not know it!" She swirled some few paces away. "Why did you bring him? Because you could not bear to be parted from him? Because you could choose which one of us warmed your bed at night—choosing him last night!"

Gwenhwyfar's grip almost slipped, so far out was she leaning. Uthr had stormed forward, his hand slapping a resonant blow across Morgause's cheek.

"You have a twisted mind, woman!"

"An open one! Why else are you so taken with a servant's by-blow? Why else did you persuade your brother to foster him?"

"The fostering was Ectha's decision, and I'm fond of the lad because he has the making of a good soldier."

Changing tack, Morgause began fiddling with the lacings of Uthr's tunic. "As I have the making of a good wife?"

"For someone, possibly."

"For you?" She was cuddling close.

"I already have a wife."

Morgause flounced away. "A wife? You call that God-kneeling, virgin-breed a wife?"

"She is a good woman." Uthr re-laced the ties. "As for the boy, I brought him because he needs the experience. Ectha's eldest own-born son, Cei, would also have come had he not been stupid enough to break his leg. Satisfied? Or do you need further explanation?"

He put his hands on Morgause's shoulders. She twitched, indicating she did not want his touch. "I say again: the boy came because I like him. Ygrainne is my wife; I happen still to like her. What do you want?" The last, to a servant hovering uncertain on the far side of the garden.

"Forgive me, Lord Cunedda sends for you. Urgent word comes from the South."

Uthr nodded curtly and waved the man away. He turned back to Morgause. "You, I love." He kissed her forehead and, without a backward glance, swung away across the garden.

After a while Morgause also left, walking away with quick, angry steps.

SIX

GWENHWYFAR RELEASED HER BREATH IN A LONG, SLOW EXHALATION. SHE WAS an honest girl, with a dislike of lies and deceits; it was wrong to listen to others' conversation, but if Uthr and Morgause had intended secrecy why talk in the public space of a garden? They had spoken of nothing of great importance, no confidences or intrigue. She chewed her lip, considering, her fingers toying with a braid of hair. Best to keep quiet. No one knew she had been in this tree, after all. Squinting through the green canopy at the floating blue sky, Gwenhwyfar checked the orchard. Two goats solemnly chewed the cud away to the left, geese were preening beneath the shade of a favourite tree, but no people. No one to ask awkward questions needing evasive answers. This heat was becoming oppressive, too close and stifling. She slithered from her bough and, swinging to the ground, strolled across the orchard for the Caer's western gate. She would go to the paddock, catch Splinter, and ride to the hills. It would be cooler there, more of a breeze. She might even paddle her feet in a stream, or swim in the pool beneath the waterfall.

Coming round the granary building she stopped short, her jaunty, whistled tune catching in mid note. Leaping back, Gwenhwyfar flattened herself against the roughness of the lime-washed wall, drew breath before tilting her head to peep round the corner.

Morgause was standing in the path of Arthur and Etern, whose horses were slithering to a startled halt. A flourish of spite panted through Gwenhwyfar. She watched, a satisfied smile creeping across her lips, as Morgause marched up to the two boys. Good, Arthur was to have a telling off!

His horse shied at the woman's sudden movement and shouting voice, colliding with Aquila, who bounded forward tossing his head and snorting.

"Take care, my lady! The horses are edgy for want of exercise!" Etern's rebuke was taut but polite. Morgause ignored him.

She took hold of Arthur's bridle. "Where have you been all morning?"

Suppressing anger and acute embarrassment, Arthur replied with curt civility, "Etern and I were first with Lord Uthr. We went then, at his suggestion, to speak with Lord Cunedda. He has commanded Etern to show me the horse runs." The boy looked at her scornfully. "Would you rather I ignore either of my lords for your benefit, lady?"

Uthr had lied! Morgause caught her breath, her fingers clamping tighter around the bridle straps. He had known of Arthur's whereabouts! He had known! The bastard had lied to her, shielding the boy. In a voice filled with hatred she spat out, "Do not think, boy, you will be permitted to run wild here in Gwynedd. I shall see to it that you do not."

She swished her skirts as she strode away, making the horses snort again, dancing in agitation. Etern stared after her, mouth slightly open.

Soothing his mount, Arthur said low to the woman's departing back, "I bet you will, you bitch." He brought his hand up in an obscene gesture.

Etern looked across at him, said mildly, "I take it you do not much like Lady Morgause."

Arthur laughed, breaking the tension. He squeezed his horse forward. "Na, not much. The only person to like her is Uthr!"

For Gwenhwyfar, that small moment of pleasure for Arthur's discomfort had passed. She did not like him, but disliked Morgause even more. The woman had a cloak of evil clinging to her, a darkness that made your flesh crawl and the hairs on the back of your neck prickle. A pulse of sympathy for Arthur flickered briefly. It must be unpleasant to be constantly under that woman's command. Gwenhwyfar slid from her hiding place and ran forward, waving her arm to attract attention. It would take only a moment to catch Splinter—she would ride with the boys.

"Etern! Hie, brother!"

The horses were trotting, eager to be away. Etern glanced over his shoulder, saw his sister and called, "Later! I am too busy for you now!" And he was gone, riding through the entrance tunnel running beneath the twin watchtowers.

Gwenhwyfar felt numb, stunned. She stood staring in disbelief, her arms hanging at her sides, her head empty of thought, incapable of movement. She and her brother had always done everything together. Always. "*Too busy for you*" hammered and hammered at her. Etern, her beloved brother. Too busy.

Fighting back tears, she walked into the stables, not certain where she was going, what she was doing, just doing it by habit. She lifted her pony's bridle from its peg and went from the Caer down to the paddock. Splinter was a friendly pony, easy to catch; he allowed her to slip reins over his head, put the bit in his mouth, and fasten straps in place. Not until she was mounted on his warm, bare back and cantering up the valley towards the gentler slopes of the higher hills did she let the tears come. In her misery, Gwenhwyfar urged the pony faster, let him have his head, his sturdy legs stretching forward, mane and tail streaming, her own hair coming loose from its braiding. The wind whistled in her ears; whipped away falling tears.

A ground-nesting bird shrilled alarm and scrambled into hasty flight, its whirring wings beating up from the grass almost beneath the pony's unshod feet. Splinter leapt to one side; squealing with surprise, Gwenhwyfar was thrown. Instinctively, she tucked in her head and rolled with the landing. Winded but unhurt, she lay still, her head burrowed into the crook of her arm. Then the ache took hold of her; sobs shook her body as she cried, her tears soaking into the grass that was already browning from the days of baking sun. The heartbreak of loneliness and betrayal stabbed and stabbed as her body heaved and choked out there on the wind-kissed hills, where the birds fluttered and chirped as if no wrong could ever be done to the world.

It was a long while before the grief was all spilled, before her body stopped its shuddering and the tears were cried dry. She lay broken and damaged, fragile among the warm heather and coarse grass, with the heat of the afternoon beating down on her back.

Soft whiskers from an inquisitive muzzle snuffed at her ear, rousing her. Stiffly, she sat up, head and eyes aching, throat dry and swollen. She fondled the pony, rubbing his broad forehead, pulling at his shaggy forelock. At least he was a friend. Wearily, Gwenhwyfar stood, found her legs were shaking. Stretching her hand to the reins, she leant against the pony's broad belly, patted and fussed over him a while longer.

There was a chill to the coming of evening, a whisper of rain heralding the clouds massing distant on the sea's horizon. A storm would grow with nightfall and the turn of the tide.

The girl made her way to a stream and drank, letting the cold, sweet taste trickle down her hot throat. She washed her face, patting handfuls of soothing water on red, sore eyes, then sat a while, hunched on the bank, watching the tumble of water as it rushed by, chattering and busy, down the hillside to join the slower flowing river and beyond that, the sparkle of the sea. A thought of Etern came to her. They had shared everything from the day she felt old enough to leave the security of her nurse's holding hand—probably afore that also, though she could remember nothing before her third summer. She knew he must leave her soon, for he was close to becoming a man, and men could not take time to ride and play with girls. But not yet, not this summer!

Unsure what to do next, aware that anger was replacing hurt, she rebraided her hair and dabbed vaguely at grass-stained knees. Vaulting on to the pony's back, she turned his head and jogged slowly home.

Evening had taken full hold by the time she made her way into the stable yard. The place was busy; many of the men had passed the day hunting, returning in high spirits with some fine buck and a variety of small game. Bustling slaves took charge of their weary horses, walking them around to dry the lathered sweat, or brushing matted coats. There was the noise and laughter of shared excitement, tossed jests, and mock insults from the men of Cunedda's Hall, men eager to share their day, to relive the pleasure of the chase.

Gwenhwyfar led Splinter into a quiet stall at the far end of the stable block and began rubbing down his coat with a twist of hay. It was still thick and shaggy from the winter, great tufts coming out in dusty handfuls as she groomed. His chest, neck, and belly were quite damp with sweat.

Her father insisted a rider be taught to tend a horse in addition to ride it. "*You cannot learn much of a horse by putting your backside on it. Know your mount. Know every hair on its body, then he will know you, and serve you well.*" Gwenhwyfar enjoyed the work. The regular strokes, the steady, relaxing chewing as Splinter tore at hay in the rack before him. Turbulent emotions subsided, jangled thoughts ebbing into a dream-like trance with the rhythm of her grooming and the drowsing warmth and smell of horse and stable.

Lost in her work, she disregarded two mounts being led into nearby stalls. Standing on the off side, bending to scrub at an obstinate stain, Gwenhwyfar was unaware of who led them. A laugh that was becoming unwelcomingly familiar attracted her attention.

"That scruff at the end there is surely not your Da's?" Gwenhwyfar's jaw set, her muscles freezing rigid. She remained taut, waiting for her brother's reply.

"Na, that's my sister's pony."

Again a laugh. "I would have thought even a sister could have done better!"

Somehow, Gwenhwyfar held her rising temper in check. Surely Etern would answer in her defence? She waited, but he only chuckled.

Arthur then asked, "Would this be the same sister who served at table last night?"

"Gwenhwyfar's my only sister. Aye, it was she who made a fool of herself in front of Uthr."

Gwenhwyfar bit her lip. Why say that?

"She had spirit," Arthur countered.

Who needs your approval! Gwenhwyfar mentally thrust a retort.

Arthur giggled, a stupid, childish sound, Gwenhwyfar thought. "The one sister, eh? Just as well it was nine boys and one girl, not vice versa! Nine girls… whooof!"

Etern responded with another laugh. "Aye, one can be trouble enough at times." He meant it; it was no amused jest.

Arthur was moving to the other side of his horse, attending to sweat patches left beneath the saddle. He had no experience of girls. His foster father had two born sons who, with himself, were the only children of the household. There were the servants' daughters, of course, and a few slave girls working in the kitchens, but beyond superficial contact Arthur had little to do with any of them. Gwenhwyfar had brought round the wine at table; he assumed all girls and women were set to serve, had no personal experience to suppose otherwise of Cunedda's daughter. He observed quite innocently, "I doubt her trailing skirts bother you over much."

Gwenhwyfar's temper erupted in a howl of rage. She sprang from behind her pony, causing him to start backward in alarm, all the hurt and anguish exploding behind her as she shouted, "I may be an unworthy girl to your insolent eyes, but I'll have you know I am high born of Gwynedd. I will not listen further to such insult! Splinter has served me with more loyalty than some I can name." Here she flicked a hand contemptuously in Etern's direction. "I am proud of my pony!"

Arthur stared, greatly amused at the furious whirl of hair and arms before him. He pointed at Splinter. "You are proud of that moth-chewed tuft of dune grass?" He rested a hand lightly on his own horse's sleek rump. "I know Gwynedd's famous for horseflesh—I assumed for riding not eating!" He grinned, expecting laughter from Etern. The other boy remained silent, recognising his sister's dangerous mood.

Arthur mistook the silence and teased further. "Tell me then, daughter of Gwynedd, do you ride this apology for a mount, or is he intended as a hearthrug?"

"Happen," Gwenhwyfar retorted with dignity, "it is fortunate I am a girl. It seems the bastard-born boys of Less Britain do not have manners bred into them!"

Moving with quick steps, Etern came from behind his horse. "That's no way to speak to a guest!"

Her answer was almost a snarl. First he had not wanted her, now he sided with this dung-heap of a boy! "He speaks disrespectfully to the daughter of his host!" To Arthur she snapped, "You will observe, bastard boy, I do not trail at my brother's heels, nor"—indicating her bracae—"do I wear skirts!"

"Gwenhwyfar! Enough!" Etern glared at her, his own anger rising at this show of rudeness to his new friend. He lifted his hands in expressive despair. "Forgive her, Arthur, she is upset."

Arthur gave a single nod of his head. What was there to forgive? Being snarled at, called a bastard? He was used to it. Everyone back home spoke to him so, save his foster father, Lord Uthr, and his young foster brother Bedwyr, who was too little to know anything anyway. He liked this girl; she was not like the servants, grubby drudges who poked fun, or whined or giggled and chattered. She reminded him of a wild cat he had once found caught in a snare. How it had spat and clawed and fought for freedom, even though a paw was almost severed! He turned, intending to fetch hay for his horse, waved his hand in a dismissive gesture. "There is nought to forgive, my friend. She's only a girl."

Furious, Gwenhwyfar reached for the nearest item to hand, which happened to be a bucket of water. She swung the thing up, hurling the contents at Arthur.

Etern stood speechless—as did Branwen.

Guessing Gwenhwyfar would not be far from the stables, Branwen had come in search of the irritating child, entering the building just as the water dowsed its victim.

"Master Arthur!" she screeched, rushing forward to dab ineffectually at the dripping boy. To Gwenhwyfar, "You wicked child! You heathen demon!" Branwen glared at her, furious. "I will see you whipped raw for this!" She flapped her hand at Etern. "Run for a cloak, a blanket, anything to turn a chill from the boy."

"Thank you for your concern." Arthur smiled politely, dropping the British tongue to speak in precise, correct Latin. "I have come to no harm, it was an accident. Gwenhwyfar was emptying the bucket and I walked in the way." He removed Branwen's hand that was patting rather personally at his wet bracae.

At that moment, Gwenhwyfar hated him more than ever. How dare he make excuses for her?

"It was no accident, as well you know!" she yelled. "I threw it deliberate and aimed well. Could as easily do it again." She whirled and seized a second bucket from the next stall, hurled the water. Prepared, Arthur ducked aside, and the full force sluiced over Branwen.

She stood speechless. Water dripped from her hair, soaked through her gown, spread in a puddle at her feet. Her mouth opened and closed once or twice, then her face puckered and turned a deep shade of puce. Without a word, she strode forward and clamped a hand around Gwenhwyfar's wrist. The girl made no sound as she was dragged forward and borne away, too proud to cry out at the twisting pain of that vicious grip.

Besides, there seemed little point in saying anything. What was there to say?

SEVEN

"WHERE ARE YOU TAKING ME?" PICKING AT THE FINGERS AROUND HER WRIST, Gwenhwyfar attempted to pull Branwen to a halt. This path from the stable yard was rough shale and gravel, a narrow way, pocked by foot worn hollows. Gwenhwyfar stumbled and fell forward, a stab of pain shooting up her left arm as she tried to save herself. Branwen hauled her upright and ploughed forward, a trireme under full oar.

"To your father," she replied curtly.

Few things frightened Gwenhwyfar. In weapon practice she could stand firm against a thrusting spear or sword blade; she was capable of mastering a wilful horse or outfacing a snarling dog. Not for her, the shriek of panic when a spider scuttled across the floor or a mouse ventured bold into a room. Punishment she could endure, but to face Cunedda's displeasure, witness his disappointment? Fool girl, what had she done!

"My wrist hurts. Please stop." She was close to tears, her hand throbbing, the fingers already swelling.

There was no turning Branwen when her mind was set. "It is time your father saw the wickedness that lies within you, child."

Sweeping up to Cunedda's private chambers, Branwen barely paused to seek admittance.

The Lion Lord of Gwynedd stood at a table studying a spread of maps and papers, his head bent to see clearer, fingers moving across the yellowish parchment. Grouped around the table were his sons and eldest grandson—and, pointing at some particular note of interest, Uthr. Cunedda glanced up at the unexpected entrance and frowned. Uthr withdrew his finger from the map, dark eyebrows raised in enquiry. Heads turning. Surprise, puzzlement and a flutter of amusement. A slight pause from both sides, men and woman.

Cunedda: "What means this interruption?"

Osmail: "Branwen? What do you here?"

At the front of the cluttered table, Abloyc, Rumaun, and Dunaut drew aside to allow the woman access, their grins widening as they noticed her wet and spoiled clothing.

"Gods!" Cunedda barked. "My maps!" He snatched the precious articles from threatening drips of water, tutting and barely listening as Branwen launched into the telling of her grievance.

Uthr tactfully busied himself with the view from the unshuttered window, choking back laughter at the account of Arthur's dowsing.

Abloyc, however, always one for merriment, gave a great bellow of delight, echoed by his brothers and nephew. Even Osmail permitted himself a smile, which faded rapidly under a sour look from his wife.

"Why bother me with this childish prank?" Cunedda snapped, with no sign of amusement. "Is it not your duty to settle household matters?" Then, annoyed, "By the Goddess, woman, we plan a war campaign here!"

Folding her arms, Branwen stood in a posture of defiant determination. "And I plan to put end to the devilment within your daughter. She is deceitful and rude, becoming quite unmanageable."

"I have not found her so." Cunedda stood behind his table, matching the defiance.

Ceredig, leaning against the wall, interrupted. "Mischievous I would agree to, even impudent, but not the words you use, sister-by-law." He winked surreptitiously at Gwenhwyfar.

Smiling back at him, Gwenhwyfar felt more at ease. Catching that slight gleam, Osmail frowned reproof.

Spreading her skirt, Branwen shook the sopping material, and picked disconsolately at her bodice and bedraggled hair. "Look at me! I am soaked through, my gown is ruined and the servants are laughing behind my back. How can I maintain discipline within the Caer while this girl runs wild?" A thin wail entered her voice. "I may take a chill from this. I tell you, Lord Cunedda, I will have her hide if harm comes to the child I carry!"

Straightening from where he had been leaning over the maps, Cunedda folded his arms, said drily, "Happen you ought to have changed your garments before coming here."

"I judged it best to bring this wicked deed direct to you."

Cunedda sighed, exchanged a brief glance of mutual resignation with Enniaun and crooked his finger at Gwenhwyfar. "Come here, child. Why?"

Gwenhwyfar answered without fear, to the point. "Because the boy was rude to me."

A smile threatened Cunedda's composure. His sons were snorting, holding laughter in check. They had gathered in a semicircle behind him, interested in this digression from serious discussion. Only Osmail stood apart, and Uthr, who remained beside the window.

Pointing towards Branwen, Cunedda asked, "And was your sister-by-law rude also?"

Again a direct reply. "She stepped in the way as I aimed a second bucket."

Uthr's laughter mingled with the rise of chuckles and Cunedda found he dared not look at any one of them for fear he would lose his hard held restraint. Curse the lass, the little vixen! With forced severity he queried, "You are, I assume, sorry for what happened?"

Standing spear-straight before him, Gwenhwyfar debated a truthful answer. She would not lie to her father. "For wetting Branwen I am." She paused. "Not for Arthur, save I'm sorry I missed him that second time."

Again Uthr spluttered, smothering the sound with a strangled cough. Enniaun, Abloyc, and the twins were laughing outright. Ceredig's shoulders were shaking, a hand covering his face, spluttering noises coming from between the fingers.

Branwen raised her arms in despair, ignoring these fool men. "Gwenhwyfar has disgraced our laws of hospitality, disgraced Gwynedd!"

"Oh, come, that is exaggeration!"

"A prank cannot be construed as anything more than high spirits." The laughter was abating, indignation creeping in as Branwen made more out of this than necessary.

Ill at ease, Cunedda shuffled a few papers. He agreed with his sons, but then Gwenhwyfar was running leeward to the acceptable of late.

Osmail came forward. It rankled that his brothers always sided against Branwen and himself, made their jests and snide little comments at their expense. Branwen ran this Caer. She was an efficient head woman, a good mother. They forgot that. Forgot where they would be without her.

"My wife has suffered gross humiliation, Father." He indicated her appearance. "Insolence cannot be tolerated."

"In my experience, the occasional dose of humility causes no harm," Cunedda observed. "Be that as it may, such behaviour will not do, my daughter. You are confined to the Caer for one week." He hooked a stool from beneath the table and sat down, turning his full attention back to his maps. The matter was settled.

"You are not serious!" Branwen's shrilled protest jarred through the room. The flat of her hand banged on the table, her other hand shooting out to jerk the girl nearer. "She deserves a public thrashing for this outrage, not mere confinement!"

The last shreds of laughter vanished, hostility snaking to the fore instead. Instinctively, the brothers gathered behind their father, Osmail in turn taking a step nearer to Branwen on their side of the table. Each side drew themselves up, frowns creasing deeper. Battle positions, second nature to a fighting man.

Thrusting the stool aside, Cunedda came sharp to his feet. "No child of mine receives public reprimand!" One had, once. Typiaunan. Butchered before the gloating eyes of Vortigern's hired Saex.

"She needs a thrashing, and a thrashing she will get!" That was Osmail. Osmail defying his father, his brothers.

Shocked gasps. Osmail turning against their lord? Even Branwen took a small, hesitant step away from her husband, then recovered to move even closer, standing shoulder to shoulder with him.

"Too long have your eyes been turned against discipline," she said.

Cunedda had no time for Branwen. A woman in your bed to while away a summer night, or to snuggle against when the winter winds and snows raged was one thing. But Branwen's incessant bad tempers—why his son kept her, he could not understand.

He regarded Osmail through slit eyes, looked at him for perhaps the first time in many years. Always a disappointment, Osmail. A clumsy child, dropping things, tripping over something, a molehill, his own sword. Spewing or swooning at the merest hint of blood, unable to handle a sword efficiently. Grizzling when a younger brother bested him on the practice ground. Cunedda had despaired of the lad as a child, rejected him as a man grown. He ought have gone into the Christian priesthood.

He turned his attention back to Branwen. "I have more important matters to attend than household squabbles." He raised a hand against the flood of answer and frowned at Gwenhwyfar. "You put me in an awkward position, daughter!"

Chewing her lip, Gwenhwyfar hung her head. For, that, she was sorry.

Striding to the front of the table, swearing beneath his breath, Cunedda unbuckled his belt. "Off with your tunic, girl, let's see this thing ended."

"Da, this is not warranted..." Abloyc had come round the table on the other side, his hand extended.

Ceredig with Dogmail, appalled, joined him. "A whipping is no punishment for a child's prank!"

Osmail stepped in their path. "One such prank, happen not, but how many more need we endure from this devilish girl?" He glowered at Cunedda. "You whipped us often enough as boys."

"Never for something so trivial!" countered Rumaun.

"Trivial! You call deliberately soaking my wife trivial!" Osmail bunched his fists, rage reddening his face, his anger all the more potent for knowing that his brothers were right. Branwen was overreacting in this silly nonsense, yet he had to declare for her, back her. He had not the chance of escaping her sour temper during the next few weeks as they had! "How dare you belittle her status!"

"Belittle her? God's teeth, she has welded her supremacy so tight, it would be easier to shift Yr Wyddfa a mile nearer the sea!"

Cunedda raised his hand for silence. "There is no time for argument, we have more pressing matters to discuss. Gwenhwyfar!"

She stood quite silent, staring steadily into Uthr Pendragon's eyes as the strap whistled through the air five times to strike across her back. It was Uthr who kept the cry from reaching beyond her throat, not her silent, watching brothers. Their mixture of sympathy and indignation would have unstoppered that tight control, but not with Uthr there. She would not disgrace her father before such a man by crying out, so she looked at Uthr and kept the pain from showing in her face and voice. When it was finished, her shoulders burnt like fire and her wrist throbbed sporadic drumbeats of pain, but the cry was jammed firm in her chest.

"Satisfied, Branwen? Now be gone." Cunedda swept his hand meaningfully towards the door. He felt anger and revulsion at himself for being pushed into administering a punishment he knew to be unjust, cursed the circumstances that left him no time to argue this dispute.

Bobbing a brief obeisance, clumsy in sodden skirts and advanced pregnancy, Branwen began to chivvy Gwenhwyfar out of the room, waited for someone to show the courtesy of opening the door. Abloyc was the nearest. Casually he leant against the wall and folded his arms, his expressive eyes daring her to make comment.

Branwen regarded her husband, a disdainful glance that ordered him to intervene. Resentment flashed across Osmail's soul. Before all his brothers she put him down, trod him into the dirt. He came forward and opened the door, saying with pent-up malice, "One day, woman, you will push me over this hurdle of restraint!"

Branwen snapped, "You have not the wit or the courage to even approach it, Osmail."

"A bitch wife and a coward husband." It was Dogmail who sneered, who said the words that they all thought.

Osmail turned, bunched his fist and hit him.

Dogmail fell backwards, sprawling across the table, sending maps and papers flying, his nose spouting blood.

"Jesu Christ!" Several brothers murmured the same incredulous expletive, standing gaping, mouths open, eyes wide. "Jesu!"

Osmail flexed his knuckles, felt the soreness and bruising swelling already. He said nothing, but stumped out the door, flinging it wider open as Gwenhwyfar darted back in and skidded to a halt, her own expression registering disbelief.

With no word, he pushed past, shouldering Branwen aside also. She called after him for an explanation, but he stumped on, shoulders hunched, rage boiling. He had never hit another man in temper before. Never hit a brother. A brother, by God, a dear brother! And that woman, that nagging, managing, arrogant… He slammed the outer door, crossed the courtyard, and disappeared into the smithy. There would be work to do. Best stay out of her way a while, she'd not be over pleased at all this.

Inside Cunedda's chamber all stayed still and quiet, exchanging glances, unspoken thoughts. Gwenhwyfar's eyes were enquiring, darting from one face to the other.

Dogmail dabbed at his nose, his head tipped back. "Well, well," he chuckled, "Osmail! Who'd have thought it!"

"What now, child?" rasped Cunedda, seeing Gwenhwyfar.

"Am I still confined within the Caer?"

The question eased any remaining aggression; back came the familiar laughter. Enniaun and Ceredig bent to retrieve papers, Abloyc was fetching a stool from across the room, Uthr approached the table. "Fearless your daughter, my friend!" he said with a grin.

Cunedda laughed, tension easing from hunched, tired shoulders. "She has the audacity of a vixen!" He ruffled Gwenhwyfar's unruly hair. "Na, lass, you have taken your punishment"—wagging a solemn finger—"but no more scrapes this day, eh?" He waved her away out of the door, and turned to his maps.

EIGHT

EYOND THE CLOSED DOOR, BRANWEN SHOOK GWENHWYFAR, SCOLDING HER impudence. Despite the punishment, she had achieved little. It was not enough, nowhere near enough. Taking firm hold, Branwen pulled the girl out of Cunedda's apartments and across a rear courtyard. Well, a lesson would be taught, a lesson to be remembered! To the Caer's chapel she took her, entering its dim interior by a side door.

Does she intend me to beg God's forgiveness then? Gwenhwyfar thought, defiance coursing at the idea. Never!

A square-cut stone altar dominated the little building, a single lamp upon it remaining always alight. Gwenhwyfar bobbed a reverence before it, deciding it best to comply with whatever crazed idea Branwen carried in her head—for now. Sometimes it was easier to swim with the current rather than fight against it. There was always a shallow pool somewhere ahead.

Branwen passed by the altar, however, crossing instead to the far side of the chapel, and only then, as she tugged open the door to a rarely used storeroom, did Gwenhwyfar begin to feel the first stirring of alarm.

The priest, she remembered, was not at Caer Arfon. He had ridden out the day of Uthr's arrival to attend some arranged meeting of holy men. The chapel was likely to be barely used for some weeks, save by a devout few.

Briefly Gwenhwyfar wondered if his absence was more than coincidental, the thought instantly forgotten as Branwen pushed her into the darkness beyond the door.

"You will stay here until I decide to release you. In God's sight you can dwell upon your wickedness." With satisfaction, Branwen slammed the door shut and pushed its bolt home.

Gwenhwyfar listened to the disappearing tap, tap of footsteps on the stone floor. The place was cold and rather damp. High to one side, a small ventilation brick through which the last rays of remaining daylight cast shafts of eerie half light. She sank to the floor and sat there dismally for a while, then bitter tears burst from her. She sobbed; it had been an awful day! A beating, her swollen wrist throbbing and throbbing, both pains of little consequence beside the loss of her brother's loyalty, that was unbearable! Her heart broke. Etern needed the companionship of a boy near his own age. This boy Arthur was foster kin to an acknowledged hero; naturally her brother would feel drawn to him. He needed no younger sister trotting at heel when the call of nearing manhood came.

For the first time in her life, Gwenhwyfar understood the sorrow of loneliness and rejection. It came hard to a child who had been close companion to one brother and under constant nurture from the others. Creeping miserably to a corner she felt a cloak hanging from a hook on the wall. Pulling it about her, seeking comfort from its small warmth, she sobbed more tears.

The sound of a man urinating against the stonework of the chapel wall woke her. She sat up with a start, unaware she had slept, disorientated at first by the dark and the chill. Did he not realise his blasphemy? Happen he cared as little for the Christ God as she did. No doubt he had mistaken his way to the latrine, or had not bothered seeking it.

She wondered whether to call out. As she hesitated the man belched and stumbled back towards voices that rose and fell from the direction of the Hall. The chance had passed—would she have taken it? To shout for help would be an admission of defeat, a blow to her pride. Hunched beneath the thin cloak, she sat listening to the distant rumble of thunder and the muted roar of a wild surf. How long had she slept? She felt uncomfortable, the growing urge to urinate becoming unbearable.

Had she seen a bowl of some sort on that shelf? Body and fingers stiff from cold Gwenhwyfar fumbled in the dark, knocked something over sending it crashing to the floor. The bowl. She choked back a sob, scrunched over the debris to an opposite corner and relieved herself, disconcerted as her urine splashed on the slate floor.

Even with her lack of conviction for the Christian faith, she felt ashamed at defiling holy territory. She thought of the man earlier, outside. He had probably been too deep in his wine to have noticed where and what he did.

Returning to the corner where the cloak lay, Gwenhwyfar huddled into its scant warmth, doubting sleep would return. The sound of scraping bolts; she had dozed then. Heavy headed and swollen eyed, she felt suddenly aware of shivering cold and gnawing hunger.

Branwen stood in the doorway, a flickering torch in her hand. Saying nothing she set down a pitcher of water and a platter of food. The door closed, and Branwen went away.

Numbed fingers felt for the food, tears pricking Gwenhwyfar's eyes once again as she almost knocked the pitcher over. She drank great gulps of the cool, sweet water, easing her tight throat then poured some over the hot swelling of her wrist. The pain eased slightly but came back almost at once. Frugally, she chewed the barley bread and goat's cheese; she had no idea how long Branwen intended to keep her locked away, or when the next meal would come. At the thought, she regretted drinking the water so thirstily.

For a while the darkness held no fear, nor the discomfort, though the hard floor did little to ease her hurts. But the isolation quickly became intolerable. Never before had Gwenhwyfar been entirely alone during the night hours. There had always been her nurse, or Ceridwen and the other girls, or a brother, or her Da. Always someone else's back to snuggle against, to feel safe beside.

Glaring flashes of light penetrated the blackness, followed by long, rolling booms of thunder. It must be late; sounds from the Hall had ceased. The Caer slept beneath the growling storm.

Never had Gwenhwyfar faced darkness totally alone.

Another great roar of thunder. The girls would be cowering in their beds, blankets over heads, giving little screams and moans. Gwenhwyfar would normally scoff at their silliness—but it was different alone, vulnerable, exposed. A muffled rustling stirred close by. Mice or rats? In the dark, the pattering movements sounded menacing, unfriendly. Gwenhwyfar's heart pounded; she pulled the cloak tighter around her, sitting wide eyed, shivering, as rain drummed outside and the storm swept over the bay and echoed around the mountains. She covered her ears with her hands, and found herself praying to whatever God was listening for the dawn to come, soon.

As it did, eventually. Daylight brought welcome sounds: fowl scratching nearby, birdsong and distant movement, some activity. Muffled calls of male voices, the snorting and stamping of horses.

The sun strode high overhead when Branwen returned. Gwenhwyfar stood firm in the centre of her cell to face her. "My father will have something to say when he hears of this outrage!"

As she set down fresh water, food and a chamber pot Branwen's laugh was low but victorious. "That will not be for some while. They rode out this morning, off to war. Laughing and joking as if they were riding to some holiday! Fool men, glorying in death and destruction!"

Gwenhwyfar swayed, unbelieving. Her father and brothers off to war at Uthr's side? Gone? Without a word of parting?

"You lie!" she shrieked, running forward. "My Da and brothers would never leave without bidding farewell."

Branwen barred the door with her own body, holding the girl at arm's distance. "You think not? A search was made for you, my dear, but you could not be found. It was assumed you were in hiding, ashamed at your conduct. The search was not over thorough."

"You lie!" Distraught, Gwenhwyfar threw herself at Branwen, fists beating and feet kicking. "I heard no call to march!"

Branwen gave Gwenhwyfar a push that sent her hurtling to the floor. "Did you not? How would you know? The hearing of such is a man's affair, not for a woman or child. There was a messenger last afternoon, I believe, some while before your disgraceful escapade, something about King Vortigern heading into Powys." She shut the door, wearing a thin, straight smile of satisfaction.

Stunned, cradling fresh pain from her injured wrist, Gwenhwyfar listened as Branwen walked away. She remembered the messenger who had arrived while Uthr talked with Morgause in the garden, who spoke of urgent news which had sent Uthr hurrying to her Da. And the bustle that morning. Horses, men laughing and shouting. The army marching!

NINE

ETERN SIGHED AND KICKED THE WOODEN PALISADE WITH THE TOE OF HIS BOOT; to emphasise his angry frustration, he kicked again. He turned to gaze at the hills, watched as colour flicked from dark to brilliant to dark again, cloud shadows chasing each other as if playing some frenzied children's game.

"I tell you, Arthur, Gwenhwyfar would not take herself off after a punishment."

Arthur was leaning over the wooden parapet, peering down at the clustered settlement with its huddle of round and rectangular houses, its market stalls, taverns, and other buildings that made up a thriving place where people lived and earned an honest, or not so honest, living. A busy place, even with the men gone off to war. Directly below, a blacksmith hammered at a bent wheel rim outside his forge. Arthur watched, fascinated, as the man's muscles rippled across naked shoulders, strength pushing a piston arm up and down.

"Aye," he said at length, "your sister's different from other girls." As an afterthought said, "Wears bracae, has excellent aim—a fine temper too, eh?"

Etern grinned at his friend's attempt to cheer him. He liked Arthur. He had some quality about him, a daring attitude that promised excitement, danger, and adventure. Why his sister had taken such a dislike to the lad, he could not understand. He missed Gwenhwyfar, her bright chatter, her mischief, but he enjoyed Arthur's company. Somehow, the two had not come together.

Arthur had a way of telling tales as good as any harper. He had told Etern of foreign lands, of Rome and Greece and India. Tales of strange beasts, long and striped or tall and spotted, elephants, lions, hairy apes. Of war and heroes, battles lost and battles won. Etern had learnt more these past days from Arthur, than from all those lectures droned by a succession of tutors. Arthur brought the past alive; his enthusiasm inspired Etern, who listened, thirsting for more. Gwenhwyfar would love to hear those tales—if only she would set aside her ridiculous animosity!

"My sister would not hide." Etern frowned into the glare of the afternoon sun. The storm of last night was quite gone, leaving the world washed and fresh, the air cooler and lighter. "No reasonable explanation would account for her missing the departure this morning. Gwenhwyfar finds it hard to accept she will never ride to battle—but that doesn't stop her wishing for it!" Etern chuckled. "She glories in my father's campaigns—and is as excited at Uthr's war host as you and I. To miss our standard flying high beside the Dragon as our men march to war?" He shook his head, then swung round to grip the fencing. "Never!" He strode a few paces along the walkway, his fingers skittering along the top of the palisade. From up here on the high turf wall there was a commanding view across the plain that slid on one side into a wave-tossed sea and, on the other, raised up to meet the mountains that clustered, like a king's guard, around the Snow Mountain, Yr Wyddfa.

Etern stopped his walking and frowned across at the purple haze that was the island of Mon. The Romans had stormed across those wind-whipped straits once long, long ago, to put an end to the Druids who had made their sacred place there. Aiee! There had been blood shed that night! When the wind blew just right, you could hear the screams of the spirits that haunted the groves and the shadows. Women priests had fought and died there—women among the men, fighting for what they believed in, useless against the strength and power of the Roman Eagles. They were gone now, the Druid priests, save for one or two crazy men who clung like limpets to the way things had been then, way, way back. The worship of the old gods and goddesses was remembered, of course, but as habit, something that was always done. Who thought twice about touching sacred wood, or offering the gods a pinch of spilt salt? The Christ had altered all that. The Old Ways were changing; the new, striding forward to acceptance.

Women went with the war host in those days, the days before Rome came to sweep the Old Ways into the midden heap and introduce the new, masculine way of things. Gwenhwyfar maintained that Rome was frightened of a woman's potential capability. She was probably right.

The memory of the past was strong today. The past, swirling and mingling with the present, spreading like a flare of torchlight, bright pathed into the future. Caer Arfon, built from the ruins of Segontium, and Cunedda, both already legend. Cunedda's wisdom and strength, the Caer's four-timbered corner towers, turf wall, and wooden palisade. Beyond the settlement, another defensive wall set atop a soaring rampart and plunging ditch.

"*Not built to keep the enemy out*," Cunedda had laughed once, with his youngest born, "*but to keep you two horrors in!*"

Cunedda might never return. His sons might never again stand and look to the beauty of the hills or across a tossing sea to Mon. War was bravery and excitement, but war was also death.

"Gwenhwyfar knows the reality behind the glory," Etern said quietly. "Some of those who passed under that arch over there will never return through it." His eyes pierced Arthur's. "We are a close family. We do not ride to battle without bidding farewell. Never would my sister have failed our father. Never against her will."

Arthur believed him. It was not a jest when he had said Gwenhwyfar was different from other girls. Oh, not different in the obvious sense. The serving girls back home, those drabs who toiled to fetch and carry, to clean and cook, were menials, workers, nothings. Gwenhwyfar was noble born, but there was something about her aside from class and family connection. Pride? Character? Whatever, he wanted to know her, befriend her. There was a lot, he thought, to the real knowing of a girl like Gwenhwyfar. That was it, though—she was still a girl, a child, but one day soon she would be a woman grown. Arthur felt a quick sense of pleasure at the thought. He shrugged, unsure how to answer Etern without sounding condescending.

"The few girls I know seem a mewling lot to me. Quick to seek their mothers' skirts."

Etern's sharp glare of reprimand told Arthur he had not then spoken tactfully.

"You forget—we have no mother's skirt. Gwenhwyfar may seem a tiresome girl-child to you, but I assure you, she is not." Etern's voice was shaking—with anger or emotion, Arthur was uncertain. "We have had it rough, living along this coast. Da and my brothers have fought long and hard to make Gwynedd the land it now is. Vortigern knew what he was doing when he took Da's northern lands and forced him to come here! Uthr had the soft side—exile to a wealthy, comfortable villa in the sun!" He rushed on, barely pausing for breath, arms waving, animated, pacing up and down. "Da's founding more than a place where we live and rule. He is founding a dynasty. Gwynedd is destined to become powerful, a land that nurtures princes and fathers of kings." Then he paused, with an earnest, pleading look at his companion. "Gwenhwyfar has grown with me, Arthur, learning from the first days we toddled together. She's a girl thrust into the violence of a man's world. She carries double the burden, for she needs to prove herself as strong and capable as her brothers." The frown slid from Etern's face and was replaced by a broad smile. "Although I grant her pranks can be pretty childish at times!"

"Like throwing water over people?" Arthur laughed with Etern. The two fell silent, brooding their own thoughts.

Below, the smith had finished the wheel, had returned inside his forge. A billow of steam and smoke hissed and curled from the open doorway, showing he was busy about some other matter.

"So," Arthur said, pushing himself away from the palisade and straightening his tunic. "If your sister's not moping or hiding in shame then she must be detained somewhere. Against her will."

Leaping forward, his face suddenly pale, Etern grasped Arthur by the shoulders. "Could she be lying hurt somewhere?" He swung his head left and right as if he might suddenly see her. "Happen she's fallen, or become trapped or…"

"Hold hard! Would she not have been found, either in the search this morning or since? Use your brain! Who was most affected by yesterday's piffling incident?"

Etern calmed down and dropped his hands. "Yourself and Branwen."

"Aye, and who has been parading around with the smug look of a cat who has found the cream?"

"Branwen."

Arthur nodded, then leant back against the palisade once more, his arm draping along the top. "I would surmise that Branwen has some knowledge of your sister's disappearance."

"What are you suggesting?" Etern's frown deepened. This hinted at a malice he felt reluctant to meet head on.

Looking away, Arthur studied the mist-swathed heights of Yr Wyddfa, beautiful against the cloud-patched blue sky. He had never seen mountains such as these. Quietly, to the hills he asked, "Have you ever been locked away as punishment?"

Etern shook his head and came to stand beside Arthur. "We are whipped, confined to quarters, or something. Why?"

A little laugh, forced in its humour. "Oh, suffice it to say I am familiar with such things." Arthur chewed his lip, his nails digging into the wood. "I clash often with Uthr's mistress." He jerked his shoulders in a shrug of indifference. "Branwen reminds me over much of Morgause, that's all."

The other boy guffawed, his head tossing back, delighted. "Hardly! They are as different as queen and peasant!"

Arthur snorted. "Which one the queen?" Then, serious again, Na, I did not mean like that."

Etern's frown returned as he thought on Arthur's insinuation. Was he suggesting Branwen would go against Cunedda's authority? That she would... The suggestion was ridiculous! He flicked a hand dismissively. "You talk nonsense."

For some moments Arthur continued gazing towards the hills, not seeing the shadows that now clung to the slopes, damping down the vivid colours, making the heights seem brooding and oppressive. Dark thoughts of black places and slamming doors chased through his mind, of her laughter and his heart thudding, thudding. "Do I? You lead a good life here, Etern of Gwynedd. Your father is an honourable lord. You say you know the realities. Do you? What do you truly know of hatred and malice? Out there," Arthur gestured towards the horizon, "out there, men die bloody deaths. There is no law, only an instinct to survive. Men take that instinct home to their womenfolk who become dulled by sickening reality. For that, the children suffer, because we are the poor sods who cannot fight back." He stopped abruptly. Morgause knew Uthr would never set aside his wife and take her instead. She knew the reality and took that knowing out on the one who could say or do nothing against her. Cei and Bedwyr were Ectha's own born, privileged, special, protected. But he, Arthur, was only a bastard foster child, at the witch's whim and mercy. He finished with one word, spoken so softly that Etern barely heard: "Yet."

Arthur was adept at rapid swings of mood. The cloud lifted from his face as the real cloud shadow lifted from the mountains. He strode purposefully for the descending steps, waving Etern to follow, calling cheerily, "Come on then. If Branwen has your sister shut in somewhere, we have to find her and let her out."

Etern trotted to catch up with him. "Swords and spears! Have you any idea of the size of this Caer? Then there's the settlement, beyond that the old fortress. It could take days!"

Arthur was running down the wooden steps; he jumped the last three. "I doubt Branwen would go where the men were billeted. The settlement, happen, but I'll wager your sister is within these walls. Aside, what else is there to do this afternoon?"

As dusk approached, they were on the verge of calling a halt. Squatting on the sheltered top floor of the north-east watchtower, Etern shared the barley bread begged from the kitchens, while Arthur recounted some lurid ghost tale. His gleeful cackles and eerie moans adding some impressive embellishments.

A sudden flap of wings. Etern leapt to his feet, heart bumping. A creature summoned by the story! Na, only a bird taking startled flight. Hand on thumping chest, he glowered reproach at Arthur's crowed amusement, then peered negligently through the narrow slit in the wall that gave little light but served well for ventilation. Suddenly he waved Arthur's laughter to silence. "Look! Over there, entering the chapel—Branwen!"

Arthur was on his feet, pushing Etern aside and squinnying through the opening. "Where?"

Losing interest, Etern returned to his bread. Branwen was always praying in the chapel.

"Now why," Arthur said thoughtfully, "would she be going to the chapel this time of the evening? Surely she ought to be supervising the Hall—it will be time for gathering soon."

"Why, indeed?" Etern's reply was grim. Crowding behind the small aperture, they waited, watching. Branwen reappeared, glanced around, and made her way back to the kitchens, unaware of her two observers.

Releasing his breath slowly, Etern slid his back down the wall and hunkered down on his heels. "In all truth, I thought we were on a fool's errand, though to follow it at least passed the day." He flicked a glance up at Arthur, who stood watching him reflectively. "It seems I owe you an apology."

Rather gloomily, Arthur squatted beside him, replied, "Branwen's close to dropping her child; happen it's a whim of hers to be alone—or something." He shrugged. Plenty of the young women at home disappeared to secluded sites for a short while; admitted, they usually reappeared dishevelled, pink faced, and hugging a secret pleasure. But surely a woman heavy with child would hardly be slipping away to meet her secret lover?

They waited a moment, each nurturing his own thoughts. "You had best fetch Osmail, Etern. I will go on ahead, over there." Arthur jerked his thumb in the direction of the chapel.

"She will be mortified if you find her in such a situation. You fetch my brother," Etern protested.

Equally emphatically Arthur countered with, "Where do I look? Where do I find one busy man among buildings I do not know? Go, Etern, don't argue."

Arthur gave the boy a firm push towards the south stairway, then ran to the north steps leading down beside the low orchard wall that met with the chapel and the door that, moments before, Branwen had pulled shut.

His enthusiasm waned as he approached the door, disappeared altogether as he reached tentatively out to push it open.

Inside, one lamp burnt upon the altar, throwing grotesque shadows leaping and flickering against the walls. There was a smell of stale incense, beeswax, and a mustiness Arthur found peculiar to all places of worship, Christian or otherwise.

Standing two paces beyond the threshold he allowed his eyes to grow used to the dim light, then began picking out the familiar cross shape of a Christian building. An unobtrusive door caught his attention. He walked to a recess, his steps sounding loud and unwelcome in this silent place, took a candle, and lit it from the burning lamp. Hesitant, he went up to that door.

His hand hovering over the bolt, he did not know what to expect, though he was certain he had the right place. He convinced himself the trembling of his hands was due to the fear of finding a girl's dead body, but the truth taunted him. The close confines of dark crowding walls made his palms sticky and his throat taste sour. Shut in; silence. Cannot get out, cannot get out. He took a breath and drew the bolt.

The candle cast a long, wavering shadow over a rumpled blanket to one side. The room smelt strongly of must and human waste. Apprehensive, Arthur took a pace forward. A movement from the shadows on his left made him whirl round and drop the candle. It fizzed out as a pitcher crashed over him, spewing water.

"Blood of Mithras!" he gasped, water and surprise taking away his breath. "Are you so damned determined to drown me?"

Gwenhwyfar stood speechless. The faint light from the single lamp barely illuminated her hands, covering her open mouth. Slowly, she raised them in a gesture of apologetic helplessness. "I thought you were Branwen come back." As if that explained everything!

"Aye, well." Arthur brushed at his wet shoulders. "As you can see, I am not." He shook his head, scraping water from dripping hair. "Your brother is fetching Osmail." Then, "Are you all right? You're shivering."

Without waiting for an answer, he fetched the blanket and draped it around her shoulders.

Gwenhwyfar felt flustered. Mixed feelings coursed through her: embarrassment, guilt, relief. She cradled her wrist, it hurt abominably. Without protest, she let Arthur lead her to the light and seat himself close beside her, but not touching, on the altar steps.

"I suppose we had best wait in here for the others," he said. They sat and waited. The silence within the chapel grew, the shadows darkening, advancing nearer.

Arthur was trembling, his teeth chattering slightly.

Gwenhwyfar had to say something, some words to explain, to ease the shame. "I am sorry. It smelt in there." Gwenhwyfar hung her head. "There was no utensil to use. I had to use the corner."

"The stink clings, doesn't it?" He spoke simply, as if he really did know, really did understand. "It's getting darker in here." He launched himself to his feet, went with rapid steps to the side door, and thrust it open as far back as it would go. Daylight was fading fast into a purple and red sky that promised another day of sun on the morrow.

He crossed to the main doors, intending to let in more light, and worried the handles. They were unyielding, locked.

"It's dreadful when you are alone in the dark," Gwenhwyfar said quietly, pulling the blanket closer against the numbing cold.

Again, Arthur answered, "I know." He returned to squat at her side, uneasily, watching the encroaching darkness.

She was unsure what more to say to him. Finally, "Are you all right?"

He was fiddling with a battered gold ring on his left hand and staring into the looming shadows. "When I was younger, not so long past, Morgause used to lock me up." He faltered, licked dry lips. "She would shut me in a place no more than a hole where there was no slit of light, nothing. It was like being inside a sealed tomb." He twirled the ring on his finger, round and around. "I never knew when she might decide to let me out. Each time I believed she might never come back, might leave me there to die, huddled alone in the dark."

"Why would she do such a thing?" Gwenhwyfar was appalled, could not, even after her own experience, comprehend such cruelty.

Arthur had no answer. He had asked himself the question many times, but had never found an explanation. Jealousy, hatred, just the pleasure of creating pain and fear—who knew with Morgause?

"Did your foster father, or Lady Ygrainne, never stop her?" In a family that knew each other's secrets, each other's fears and delights, Gwenhwyfar found it incomprehensible that such a wickedness could take place uncensored.

For Arthur, it was very different. "Ectha is frightened of her, Uthr besotted by her, and Ygrainne has no time for her, or me—hates me more than Morgause does. Lady Ygrainne spends her life with God. Morgause runs the household." He was sweating profusely now, beads of perspiration standing out on his forehead, trickling from his armpits and down his back. His breathing was becoming rapid. The walls were closing in, falling in, the roof pushing, pressing; the blackness engulfing, chewing him up, gorging itself on his fear.

Urgently he said, "Would you mind if we went outside?" Not waiting for an answer, he bolted for the open door.

Gwenhwyfar followed more sedately, her blanket trailing. Arthur stood with his back against the wall, eyes shut tight, taking great gulps of the cool, sweet air. She put a tentative hand on his arm.

"I was terrified last night," she admitted. "I was so alone; I wanted someone, anyone to come, but…" Her voice had changed, defiance mustering. She looked directly at him. His eyes were open now, looking back at her. "I'm not sorry for what I did, Arthur!"

Managing a weak laugh he said, "I am—I was wrong. Etern was frantic with worry about you." He put his hand over hers, held it. Her fingers were cold; he closed his own around them to bring more warmth. "So was I."

"I'm surprised my brother has even remembered I exist," Gwenhwyfar said bitterly.

"What?" Arthur pushed himself from the wall. "Bull's Blood, he talks of no one but you! *Gwenhwyfar this, Gwenhwyfar that*, or, *My sister found this trail, this bathing place, this whatever.* He says your father thinks of you as a true Cymraes, not someone watered by Roman wine!"

Gwenhwyfar shrugged, flattered, but not ready to show her pleasure. "I am of Gwynedd, not Rome."

"Bravely spoken, my Cymraes fach, my little British woman!" Arthur was feeling better.

His confidence was returning now the threat of those squeezing walls was gone. He still had hold of her hand. It pleased him to feel her closeness, her fingers in his own. "Etern is like a lost sheep without you, Gwenhwyfar. That's not healthy for a boy of his age!" He added the last with muffled laughter.

Gwenhwyfar smiled at him, her eyes crinkling. She remembered her hand, and shyly withdrew it. She liked him! He made her laugh. With mock sincerity Arthur said, "I grant you are an exceptional girl, Gwenhwyfar, but a man needs other men."

"A man needs a woman to comfort him through the night and to give him sons." Gwenhwyfar's retort came with a knowing grin.

"Aye, well." Arthur grinned back, unable to counter her argument. He still trembled slightly, but the violent fear had dwindled. Darkness seemed less terrible when shared with someone else.

"Am I forgiven my bad conduct?" he asked. He knelt before her, desperately wanting her friendship, needing her approval.

"Forgive me, lady. I offer my humble body as your friend and my sword as your servant." Earnestly he looked up into the dim outline of her pale face, seeking her eyes, red-rimmed but with the sparkle fast returning.

Gwenhwyfar giggled. She could see now why Etern had been so captivated. Arthur had a vitality that swept you along with his enthusiasm and wild ideas. And suddenly, she realised his long nose and short-cropped hair were not ugly at all; in fact, he was rather handsome, in a rough, rugged sort of way.

She took his proffered hand and laughed. "I forgive you and I accept your sword. Will you defend me to your death, from dragons and demons?"

"Dragons and demons certainly. Branwen and Morgause na!"

Gwenhwyfar roared with laughter, then caught her breath as movement jarred the swollen wrist.

"What's wrong? Are you hurt?" Arthur was on his feet, showing immediate concern.

"My wrist. I fell—it's nothing."

"Nothing be damned! I can see the swelling even in this poor light. Hie!" He waved attracting the attention of the two people approaching. "Here come your brothers!" Arthur ran forward, gesturing wildly as he explained the situation, urging Etern, who was anxiously herding Osmail, to hurry.

The big man looked displeased at what he was sure would turn out to be a boy's prank. Etern had babbled something about Branwen locking Gwenhwyfar in? What nonsense!

But as he came upon his sister, saw her pain and distress, his irritation became profound anger.

Branwen had done this? His wife, the mother of his children had deliberately and callously done this?

He squatted before Gwenhwyfar and examined her wrist, asked a few direct questions. After brushing aside her tears with one finger, he lifted her and strode back across the orchard tight-lipped, his expression grim.

Branwen had committed this disgrace. Aye, well, it would be her last! Push him to the limit, to that hurdle of endurance? He was over it, by God, over and spurring fast for manumission!

Etern exchanged a wry look with Arthur as Osmail walked away. "I have never seen my brother look so angry. By God!" He laughed suddenly. "Am I glad not to be in Branwen's boots this evening!"

Together the boys ambled across the orchard heading for the glow of torch-light streaming from the open doors of the Hall. The sound of tables being set up and women chattering drifted into the darkening stillness beneath the trees. A heavy dew had fallen, leaving a trail of silvered marks where the boys walked.

"Your sister," Arthur said, placing an arm around Etern's shoulders, "I like her."

Removing his arm, he pushed his hands through his bracae belt and, whistling, walked on ahead into the comforting welcome of Cunedda's Hall.

TEN

E ARLY AFTERNOON. ETERN POKED HIS HEAD ROUND THE DOOR AND GRINNED broadly. Gwenhwyfar, sitting cross-legged on the floor, tossed two wooden dice in the air and neatly caught them in her right hand. She grinned back at her brother.

"You are supposed to be in bed," Etern chided. "Alone?" he added, searching the chamber with his eyes.

"They," and Gwenhwyfar gave a little toss of her head indicating the beds that belonged to the other girls who shared this chamber, "have grown bored with gossip of Branwen's disgrace, and as my injury is not fatal they have decided to leave me and follow more interesting pursuits."

For most of the morning the girls had fussed around Gwenhwyfar, excited and curious, making a nuisance of themselves with their wittering and twitter-ing—plumping pillows, tut-tutting, and overemphasising sympathy, which was as shallow as a dried-up river ford. All this Gwenhwyfar suffered for the few scraps of information among the nonsense. Branwen had been ordered to her apartments by her outraged husband—and with the army's departure Morgause had apparently raged and stormed at not being allowed to accompany Uthr. Gwenhwyfar had attempted to pursue this line of conversation, but those silly lily-brained creatures had gone off at a tangent about hairstyles and face paint.

Few women went with the menfolk to war these days—not decent women anyway. The patched whore wagons trundled after any hosting, making their way as best they could along the rutted, disintegrating roads, but women no longer joined in the fighting—as Cunedda had been at pains to point out to his daughter many times. Some British women still learnt to handle weapons to defend themselves and their children according to the old ways, yet Morgause was no traditionalist; she was Roman bred and born.

Gwenhwyfar rolled the dice to the floor and smiled triumphantly. "Venus!" She glanced up. "Are you coming in, or are you a doorstop?"

Etern ambled over and sat cross-legged next to her. "Four counts of six in a row?" he queried, claiming the dice and beginning to shake them vigorously in his closed fist. "You cheated."

"I did not! I scored Venus fair. What would be the point of cheating myself?"

Throwing a total of five, Etern handed the dice to his sister. "Best of three throws?"

She nodded agreement and played her turn, then gave him the dice. Casually she asked, "Not with your friend today?"

"Who, Arthur? Na, he has been claimed by Morgause." Etern wrinkled his nose in disgust at his low score. "You know, Gwen, I don't much like the woman." He shivered, as if a chill had crept down his spine.

As Gwenhwyfar tossed her last throw she said, "Neither does Arthur."

Spreading his hands, Etern admitted defeat. "Canis to me, lowest score. Another go?"

"Na, I have had enough of dice." Gwenhwyfar stretched lazily and, climbing to her feet wandered to the window. The chamber was on the first floor, built above storage rooms, its single square window overlooking a courtyard and, to the far right, a vegetable garden. It was all very well to be ordered to spend a day in bed, but it was so boring! She felt fine, beyond a dull throb in her wrist, would rather be out doing things.

"Osmail was with me earlier," she said, watching three slaves tending the young spring growth. "Do you suppose he minds being left behind?" Then, as if on the same topic, "Cabbage for supper by the look of it."

Etern, coming to stand behind her, laughed. "Remember the time too much salt was put in for the cooking? Aye, I think he minds, but one of our brothers must stay to watch over Gwynedd."

"He has never professed to like the killing of men, our brother. All that Christian talk of love and turning the other cheek! Da despairs of Osmail, you know. He's the eldest and has no stomach for war." She had been leaning on the sill, looking out and down at the small empty courtyard below. "What does Morgause want with Arthur?"

Etern shook his head doubtfully. "She expects him to run errands for her, entertain her, I don't know. Why ask me?"

"Don't get cross."

Glowering at his sister's rebuke, Etern shuffled away from the window and plonked himself on the bed. "I'm bored," he admitted with a heavy sigh. "Da and the others away, you confined in here, Arthur with her." He nodded in the vague direction of Morgause's chamber.

Still at the window, Gwenhwyfar knelt on the floor and shuffled herself into a more comfortable position. Morgause's chamber was just visible, away across the vegetable plot and a little to the right. Gwenhwyfar fiddled with the bandage around her wrist, chewed her lips, watched a worm seeking blackbird hopping in the wake of the gardening slaves. "Why, I wonder, are her shutters closed?"

Lying back across the bed, Etern stretched his arms. "Whose shutters?"

"Surely the woman is not sleeping at this time of day?"

"What woman?" Etern sat up, irritated by the obtuse dialogue.

"Morgause."

Her brother lost interest. "Oh, her." He began lifting and bending his legs in some elaborate thigh exercise.

Folding her arms across the sill, Gwenhwyfar rested her chin on her hands, mindful of the injury. She whistled a few bars of a tune plaguing her mind. Suddenly she sat up straight and turned abruptly towards her brother. "I thought you said Arthur was with her?"

"What is this?" Etern demanded. "I am not his keeper."

Gwenhwyfar feigned indifference. She got up and moved vaguely around the room, touching this, tidying that. An uneasy feeling niggled, like an itch you could not reach.

Heading for the door, Etern stated, "I have a few things to see to. Call back later, shall I?"

Nodding at the other beds, Gwenhwyfar answered, "If the boneheads have not returned."

As his retreating laugh faded, she began dressing, awkward with the limited use of one hand. There was no logical reason for suspicion, no cause to doubt, yet her unease was becoming more insistent. All those things Arthur had said yesterday. Those confidences spoken, she was certain, through the need to ride the fear. It was the things he had not said that worried her. He was vulnerable to Morgause's spiteful whims when not protected by the Pendragon's presence—and Uthr had gone.

Gwenhwyfar slipped quietly from her chamber, down the back stairs, and across the courtyard, her leather sandals making barely a sound as she padded along the raised walkway running the length of the other wing. She stopped outside Morgause's room and listened at the door. Shutters, firmly closed, blocked any view inside. She could hear voices within: Morgause's penetrating lilt and Arthur's sullen responses.

This wing was a single storey construction of timber and stone. Living chambers were ranged along the ground floor, with the limited space beneath the low eaves of the slate roof seldom used, for access was difficult and headroom low.

Jogging to the rear, Gwenhwyfar clambered up the ladder and with difficulty lifted the trapdoor at its head. The thing was heavy, reluctant to move and hard to push with the use of only one hand. She found the need to climb higher, brace her shoulders against the unyielding door, and heave. It fell back with a startling thump, scattering a cloud of choking dust and musty straw. For a moment, Gwenhwyfar balanced on the top rung, coughing and blinking her eyes. She sneezed, took a breath, and carefully pulled herself up into the diffused light of the cavern beyond. Several slates were missing, and in places holes had worn through the plaster below the eaves, convenient for a number of nesting birds. Gwenhwyfar's ears caught the fluffing and flurry of feathers as brooding mothers squatted over their young, anxious at this unexpected intrusion. She could see their tiny heads and bright black eyes peeping nervously over nest rims at her, keeping so still. Feet pattered away from the broad shaft of light the open trapdoor let in, a squeaking of protest as mice scuttled to safety.

The place was empty save for a tumbled heap of wooden crates, several piles of discarded sacking, a few cracked amphorae and what looked like a battered saddle. Squirming through the layers of dust and sticky cobwebs, Gwenhwyfar crawled along to the far end that would be the ceiling of Morgause's chamber. She had to keep her weight on the timber rafters, for the plaster between crumbled most fearfully when she put hand or knee on it. In places, the fragile stuff had already worn, and she caught tantalising glimpses into the chambers below; for a moment, she was tempted to turn about and investigate the opposite far end, to spy down on where Branwen had apparently shut herself. She heard Arthur's voice, a sharp, "No!" With renewed determination she scurried forward.

The roof here sloped sharply down to the walls, and the narrow space was piled with collected dust and heaps of old leaves that had blown in through gaps in the tiling. Gwenhwyfar found she had to stretch out flat. Several small holes afforded a limited view of the chamber below. Spreading her weight along the rafters, she put her eye to the nearest and squinted down.

Morgause was talking in her low, singsong voice, husky and heavily slurred with over much wine. To her disgust, Gwenhwyfar could see nothing save the worn pattern of the rather crudely laid mosaic floor. She made to shift position, saw to her horror a puff of plaster collapse and scatter downwards in a fluttering shower. The rafter beneath her right knee creaked, sounding as loud as thunder to her ears. Heart thumping, she lay rigid, not daring to move.

"You do want to please me, do you not, boy?" Morgause was saying in her precise Latin. "Is that not why Uthr brought you, so you might please me?"

"You know damn well why he brought me. I am almost a man grown, I need the experience."

The woman laughed, a low, casual chuckle. Gwenhwyfar heard the sound of wine being poured, a jug clinking against a glass. Morgause's sickly sweet answer: "Experience, yes." The sound of movement, a rustling of silk garments and soft leather slippers. Morgause came into view briefly, carrying a second goblet, which she handed to Arthur somewhere beyond Gwenhwyfar's sight.

"It is time you became a man, boy." Morgause walked again beneath Gwenhwyfar's spyhole, carrying one goblet. Arthur must have taken the one offered.

The question was unexpected, floating upwards with the sun swirled flitterings of dust: "Do you find me beautiful?" There came no answer. "Or are you too much Uthr's boy?" Morgause's wine-smooth voice changed to a harsh rasp as she commanded, "Come here!"

Arthur did not move. He was standing pressed tight against the wall: it felt safer to have something solid at his back. He shook his head defiantly, wondering if he could make a run for the door. Three, four paces, draw back the bolt. He gulped the wine; it was strong but it steadied his quivering nerves—though he must not drink over much.

"You would do well to obey me, boy, to answer me." Morgause sprang forward. Arthur yelped, an involuntary sound as her hand caught viciously at his arm. He dropped the goblet, the fine blue glass shattering.

Pinning him against the wall, Morgause pressed her body close, the thin silk of her flame-coloured gown sharply outlining the curves of her body beneath. She smelt of strong perfume, a rich, spiced scent. Her breath bore a hint of chewed mint clouded by red wine. There was no denying Morgause was beautiful. Arthur swallowed, his eyes drifting towards the inviting swell of her breasts. He knew nothing of women, but his body was on the verge of wanting to know, that confusing time suspended halfway between boy and man.

She saw him looking, interested but indecisive. She adjusted her clothing and loosened the shoulder brooch, letting the folds of the bodice slip slightly. "These breasts should be suckling Uthr's son, but I have borne him only girl brats. Three—did you know that?" She moved a fraction away, the better to read his blank expression. "No, you could not. I was discreet with their bearing—remember my visits to kindred?"

He remembered well. Those glorious months of freedom from torment!

"I exposed them," she said with a small, careless gesture, drifting, to Arthur's small sigh of relief, further away. "I have no use for girls." She spun to face him, that soft seductive smile back again. "Do you wish to bed with me, Arthur?" She swayed her body, lithe and supple, so very sensuous. "Ygrainne bore Uthr two dead girls after the first boy died—did you know that also? Ah, I see you did not." Her smile was arrogant, all knowing. "There is no maleness in Uthr's seed."

Arthur felt hot, and a little sick. The sweat trickled down his back. His throat dry as he stammered in a high, cracked voice, "Uthr had that one son!"

Morgause spread her arms, her head lolling back with a scornful laugh. "His son? The thing died because it was not his!"

Both of them were out of sight now, and Gwenhwyfar squirmed forward, seeking another hole. That rafter creaked again, and another fragile cascade of dust spiralled down. She cursed under her breath.

Arthur's hissed response to Morgause's slander was shocked. "Lady Ygrainne would not do such a thing!" For all his dislike of her, he knew Ygrainne to be an honest woman. She would not kill a child or deceive her lord husband. Not now, not then. Morgause was standing so close, her breasts large beneath the loosely fitting bodice. He had never seen her naked. Arthur's heart was racing, his breathing coming shallow and fast. Curse the bitch! He hated her, wanted her dead, gone, anything. Wanted so much to reach out and touch.

Morgause knew, was goading him deliberately, her teasing subtle but intense. "Ygrainne has not always been such a blessed woman. She rutted with Uthr while still another man's wife." She ran her fingers lightly over his cheek, across his mouth, feeling the slight prickle of hair above his lip.

Arthur jerked his head aside, attempted to squirm away. She grabbed at him, pushing him harder against the wall.

To her fury, Gwenhwyfar, her teeth jammed into her bottom lip, could still not see anything, yet she dared not move.

"Everyone knows Ygrainne's first husband was a brute twice her age, and a heel-hound of Vortigern's at that." Arthur's voice was rising in pitch, panic beginning. "None gave her blame when she divorced the bastard and took Uthr as husband." He tried again to free himself, added with bravado, "Save you."

Morgause's lips were on his, her fingers searching beneath his tunic for the lacings of his bracae. Arthur kicked, hard. She screeched, her hand lashing out to strike him. Again and again her hand beat at his face; Arthur crumpled, covered his head with his arms. She used her fists and her feet, hitting and kicking at him.

Gwenhwyfar began to squirm backward. She must do something to stop this, fetch someone.

Then the fury ceased as abruptly as it began. Morgause squatted, held Arthur's bloodied face tight between her pinching fingers. "Why is Uthr so fond of you?" Her angered features were distorted and grotesque, like some foul spirit's mask. "You are his boy lover!"

The room was spinning, blood dribbled from a split lip, sparks and flashes shot before his eyes, but Arthur answered, furious at the insult to his lord. "Your mind is tangled in a weed garden of jealousy! You think because I love Uthr there must be something sordid, something obscene, because that is what you are, a foul-minded bitch! You cannot bear Uthr giving affection to anyone but yourself, can you?"

Her palm cracked sharply against his cheek. This time he did not flinch or try to hide away. He looked straight at her, let her hit him. "I'm not afraid of you," he said, though his voice shook. He was, desperately afraid, but anger had seized hold of him. "You are jealous of me," he taunted, "jealous because Uthr thinks more of me, a bastard son of a serving girl, than of you, his ageing whore!"

Morgause drew a sharp breath and flashed back, "Then you do bed with him!"

Arthur laughed. "You poor slut. You have so little idea of what love can really be—no idea of respect and admiration, pride and hope."

Her fist caught him a savage blow to the temple; he fell forward stunned, but the blows still came.

Gwenhwyfar did not know what to do. What could she do? She moved back quickly, not wanting to see more, or hear. That loose rafter creaked and groaned, then gave way. She screamed as the ceiling caved in.

Rafters, plaster, and dust cascaded down. Nesting birds took sudden flight, whirring wings and squawking alarm. Gwenhwyfar landed in a heap and sprawl among the cloud of debris, coughing and spluttering. The training of weapon handling and riding saved her from injury, for she rolled with the fall and was instantly on her feet, winded and covered in grime, but unharmed.

Arthur was crouched down, his hand cradling bruised ribs. He wiped at blood trickling from his nose, then reached forward tentatively to the sprawled form of Morgause. She lay on her back, one arm flung at a weird angle, dark blood oozing from a deep cut on her forehead.

"Oh, Mithras!" He spoke through a slow exhaled breath. "She's dead." He was uncertain whether to feel relief or what. There would be a deal of explaining to do over this.

"Nonsense!" Gwenhwyfar was recovering her wits. She pointed at the steady rise and fall of the woman's breathing. "We had best be from here. Now." She stepped to the door and opened it a little way. "Now, Arthur! Come on!"

He rose unsteadily to his feet; the room was spinning, his head ached, his face felt puffed and bruised. Gwenhwyfar grabbed at his hand, pulled him out of the door and quickly round the corner. The first comers were entering the court-yard seeking the cause of the noise.

Running, Gwenhwyfar took sanctuary within the nearest granary. A babble of voices and alarm filtered from outside with, once, the commanding voice of Osmail demanding explanation.

Beyond the stillness and quiet of the granary the noise passed by, gradu-ally dwindling. Gwenhwyfar brushed dirt and cobwebs from hair and clothing, wrinkled her nose at her grimed hands, guessed her face to be a similar colour. She fiddled with a tear to the shoulder of her tunic. She would need to wash herself and get this mended afore anyone asked questions.

Arthur had seated himself on a grain sack, his shoulders hunched, head resting between his hands. With thoughts shrivelling his insides, he suddenly felt sick. Morgause. Words and implications. Implying he was bedmate to his beloved lord, her hands on his body, mouth covering his. He tumbled forward spewing out the disgust.

Concerned, Gwenhwyfar hunkered beside him, one hand resting lightly on his back waiting for the violent shaking to cease, though her own body had not settled.

Embarrassed, Arthur stood, wiping at his mouth, disconcerted to find his legs were having difficulty supporting him.

Tactful, Gwenhwyfar retreated a few paces, squatting down on her heels. "Best get the thing out of you." A slight smile. "I have been long enough with Etern to know how a stomach reacts to distasteful things." The smile broadened. "My brother's guts are as unpredictable as a sea wind on a summer day!"

Arthur attempted to return the smile, said with an over lightness that did little to hide his discomfort, "Who need know of this?"

"Of what?" Gwenhwyfar had ambled to the door, was peeping out. Love of the Gods, but her wrist ached! People had drifted away about their business; all seemed quiet. "There's nothing for anyone to know. Some rafters gave way—it has been expected. We're not allowed up there, Da knows the timber's rotten." She turned suddenly to grin at him. "And I am unwilling to broadcast disobeyed orders!" She shrugged. "No one save Morgause knew you were in there." She threw the door wide, stepped out into the sunshine. "And she certainly did not see me!" She cocked her head on one side, looking back into the muted shadows within the great building. Colour was returning to Arthur's ashen face, blotched by the blood and bruising. "I would suggest you had a fall from a horse, or a fight with some low born in the settlement. None will query it."

She walked away, but returned a few seconds later with the need to say one thing more. Arthur had not moved.

In the doorway, she was silhouetted black against the brightness. "There are things that sometimes you wish others not to know, but between friends a secret can be as binding as the blood-tie of kinship. And the keeping can last as long."

JUNE 450

ELEVEN

THE BOYS, STRIPPED TO THE WAIST, WERE TURNING NEW SCYTHED HAY, making idle, breathless conversation as they tossed the sweet-smelling, drying grass. Arthur's bruising was a faint memory of shaded yellow against sun-tanned bronze skin; gone was that weary look of watchfulness and unease, replaced by relaxed laughter and happy contentment. His hair was longer, the close-cropped Roman style beginning to grow, with a slight curl, down his neck and flop across his forehead. Arthur enjoyed this work; it was hard but that was nothing to shy away from. Among friends and with the freedom to enjoy oneself, who noticed the soreness of sunburn or aching back and shoulders at the end of a long day? Lord and slave alike were out in the meadows for this haymaking. Animal feed must be gathered whether the menfolk were away or no, and the grain harvest would soon follow. Winter did not forget to call for the sake of a war hosting!

June had begun cool and cloudy with a wind that blew steadily from the sea, but as the month neared the longest day the wind veered and the sun blazed. If the rains held off these next weeks, it would be a good harvest. Wheat and barley were fast ripening, the green corn spreading wide smiles of rich gold.

Gwenhwyfar straightened, one hand easing her back, the other pushing the wide-brimmed, straw-plaited hat from her forehead. Etern tossed his pitch-fork, turning another few yards of hay to dry the underside. Arthur, working along the opposite side, looked up and regarded Gwenhwyfar, leaning now on her fork.

"If you're intending to stop work, lass, you could employ your rest by bring-ing us a skin of water!"

"I'll do better," she answered, happily compliant. Digging the prongs of the fork into the sun-baked soil, she unknotted the girdle that hitched her skirt to above her knees, letting the material fall full length. There were some advantages in being a girl after all! How much cooler to feel the swirl of thin-woven cloth around your legs, rather than the tight cling of bracae. "I'll fetch food and wine. It's time we rested—look, others are going off to the shade." She wiped at the sweat on her neck and face with the back of her hand.

Sitting beneath a chestnut tree, legs outstretched, spine secure against the broad trunk, Arthur remarked, "It's hot for the hosting. They'd not be able to get away from this noon heat if engaged in battle."

"Would you notice the sun, I wonder," Etern said through a mouthful of goat's cheese, "in the midst of fighting?"

"Happen not."

Passing along the skin of watered wine, Gwenhwyfar folded her arms behind her head and looked up into the bluest of blue skies. A few great puffs of cloud floated lazily, a shriek of swifts darted past. She closed her eyes, let the drone of bees and hum of grasshoppers float by as peaceful as a meandering river. The air was full of lazy summer scents, mingling with the salt tang of the sea. "We must hear soon," she pondered, "surely?"

Neither Etern nor Arthur made immediate answer. One or other of them proclaimed the same thing almost every day: "*We must hear soon.*" But nothing came, no word of the hosting. Good news, or bad.

"When I become War Lord," Arthur announced, "I'll set up efficient lines of communication."

Eyes snapping open, Gwenhwyfar chuckled, not unkindly. "Oh ho, so you are planning on the honour of War Lord? A high ambition for a fatherless servant's brat!"

Good-natured, Arthur lifted his shoulder then let it fall. "We've all got to harbour some plan. There'd be no point of expectation and hope otherwise."

Gwenhwyfar settled herself again, lying prone amid the swathe of uncut grass, chuckled drowsily. "Dream on, lad, for that's all that desire can lead to—more dreams!"

Arthur sat forward and absently picked up a stick, prodding a hole in the ground between his legs. "I'd have a fair chance if Uthr were my sire, but..." He sighed, rammed the stick too hard, snapping it in half.

"But Ectha is your foster father, and he has two sons of his own besides being as timid as a doe in fawn."

Arthur grinned at Gwenhwyfar's plain-spoken accuracy. "Aye, it'll be working the estate or serving as junior officer in some petty lord's hosting for me." He reclaimed the longer part of his broken stick, and twiddled it between his fingers. "I want to be part of a great army, want to lead—I've ideas to improve efficiency!" He tossed the stick aside. "Happen I'll have a chance when Uthr becomes king."

Kindly, laying her fingers lightly on his arm, Gwenhwyfar remarked, "That could be any day now."

Etern had stretched himself full length in the shade and closed his eyes to doze in this brief respite from work and sun. He opened one eye, squinted through the dappled brightness at his sister. Something had happened atween these two, some great event had twined them together as firm as stitching in leather harness. Neither had said what and, for all his questioning, he had gleaned no hint. He closed his eye again. It had something to do with that foul woman Morgause and the day the ceiling had collapsed into her chamber. He smiled at the recollection. It was not funny, of course, but there had been much secret pleasure throughout the Caer these past weeks. Bad-tempered Morgause confined to her bed with the pain of a fractured arm and dizzying headaches; Branwen similarly out the way from lingering disgrace and the birthing of her second-born son. Were it not for the worry of the hosting, life would be almost perfect!

"What for me?" Gwenhwyfar said idly. "I have no particular dreams," she beamed at Arthur, "beyond owning one of Da's best horses!"

Etern, without moving, added to her, "You, Gwen, will marry a lord in a strategic alliance. Your offspring will unite Gwynedd and whatever noble line this man comes from, making the strongest and most formidable family in the country!" He spoke carelessly, meaning no offence, stating fact. Alliances were for the female born to bring to the male line.

Gwenhwyfar, however, leapt to her feet, her fists bunching. "If that's all you hope for me, brother, then you had best think again!" She stamped her foot. "I will not be bargained out for breeding, not for all the 'strategic alliances' on offer!"

Etern sat up open mouthed, staggered at the unexpected explosion. Now what had he said!

"*If* I marry," his sister declared, "I will only wed with the strongest leader, a man who will unite Britain and drive out our enemies!" Her green eyes flashed with sparks of tawny gold; she tossed her head, the sunlight catching on those loose wisps of hair that would never be tamed, setting the colour glowing with vibrant reds and golds. "I mean it, this is no idle boast."

Etern exchanged a glance with his friend, who shrugged sympathy.

Arthur was thinking how pretty Gwenhwyfar was. A child still, with only the subtle hints of womanhood touching her face and figure, but it was there, the beauty, waiting to open like a flower from its budding. Morgause was beautiful, but she was like the ice and snow that set a dull winter's day bright with cold exhilaration. Gwenhwyfar's beauty would be softer, more like the gold and russets and warmth of a sunlit autumn day, with all its toss of wind swirled leaves and crackling orange flamed fires. Aye, and have the touch of frost that nipped your fingers of a morning and caught your breath sharp in your lungs!

"Vortigern's sons are already married," he said lightly, pushing an unexpected, alarmingly erotic thought aside. "Happen you are thinking of wedding one of their sons? Or the sons of Vortigern's sister are favoured, though the eldest, Gorlois, was unlucky in marriage." His caustic laugh was derisive. "He could not keep a wife—losing the first to God's kingdom, and the second to Uthr."

Etern chuckled, echoing Arthur's irony. The story of how the young Ygrainne met and fell in love with Uthr was well known, had almost become legend. The consequent fighting, heightened by Uthr's feud with Vortigern, was made all the more violent through Gorlois's desire for revenge against the man who had stolen his wife. Gorlois lost both wife and life, though Vortigern eventually won the victory of the warring.

Arthur buffeted his friend's shoulder with his fist. "There are always his two brothers to consider. Melwas or Amlawdd would serve."

Gwenhwyfar made a crude, insulting noise through her lips. "Both fat-bellied toads." She laughed, the sour temper evaporating as suddenly as it had come. "Vortigern is about to fall, his obnoxious kindred along with him."

"Aye, happen even now Uthr has removed his head and is marching in victory!" Etern scrambled to his feet, slicing through the air with an imaginary sword. "There will be a new line of sons for Britain."

Reluctant to quell this enthusiasm, Gwenhwyfar still felt impelled to interrupt. "What line, brother? Uthr has no sons. He would have to divorce Ygrainne and take a new wife." She chattered on with Etern, discussing possibilities. There was no shortage of noble-born ladies, and then Uthr's two surviving brothers had issue: Ectha's two boys, and Emrys, the youngest brother, an infant son.

Gwenhwyfar tossed a question at Arthur, unaware he had taken no part in this conversation. He sat quiet, shoulders hunched, systematically shredding a grass stalk. There was no place for him in the line of descendants. He was a bastard, unacknowledged. That Ectha had probably sired him was as nothing. He found it difficult to believe that Ectha, a quiet family man who still shed tears at the long ago death of his beloved wife could have, would have, so casually rutted with Ygrainne's serving maid.

"Would Uthr dare take Morgause as wife?" Gwenhwyfar repeated.

He glanced up, eyes flickering between Etern and Gwenhwyfar, not quite at them. "She would like that, has been hoping for such a thing for some while. A mistress is one thing, but marriage?" He spread his hands, indicating the difference. "The bitch likes to think—for us all to think—that Uthr loves her, but I believe he does not."

Leaning forward, hugging her knees, Gwenhwyfar asked with keen interest, "What makes you say so?"

Arthur threw aside a piece of the broken stalk. "Little things, like—oh, I don't know—he says things about her, lewd or coarse remarks, laughs with the men about her." He glanced again at Gwenhwyfar. "It seems to me, a man will say what he likes about his whore, but he keeps private the woman he loves."

Bats were flitting through the deepening blue of twilight as the outer defences of the settlement loomed ahead. The three had seized the chance to ride, heading for the glow of a brilliant red sunset. Racing their horses until they were blown, they turned and ambled home as the first stars brightened against the darkening night sky.

As they clattered under the inner archway into the stronghold old Marc, the gatekeeper, stepped forward and caught Aquila's bridle, causing the horse to skitter in alarm. Etern, almost unseated, shouted in quick anger, "Take care!"

Marc—his old, wrinkled face ashen grey—stroked the horse's damp neck, calming him. "My apologies, young master; I had no intention of alarming you." He spoke to Etern but his gaze drifted towards the lad Arthur, who rode on Aquila's off side.

"There be news. I have orders to tell you, and young Master Arthur here, to go direct to Lord Osmail."

Etern exchanged a swift glance with his friend and his sister. Good news? Bad?

Longing to go with them, disappointed that she had not been included, Gwenhwyfar slid from Splinter's back and ran to the boys' horses.

"I will see to these," she said, taking their bridles. "Go quickly."

Etern nodded his thanks and gave her shoulder a brief squeeze as he dismounted, aware of the effort the offer had taken. As their hurried footsteps echoed away, Gwenhwyfar turned to Marc. "What news?"

His hand still resting on Aquila's neck, the old soldier regarded Cunedda's only daughter with sad eyes. Her mother's gaze looked back at him. She touched his hand, felt a faint tremor beneath the twisted old knuckles. "What is it? Tell me."

"Bad," he said at length. "Terrible bad. The messenger's horse was on its last legs, ridden almost to death." He swallowed hard, seeing again the sight of the foundering horse, not an hour since, plunging through this same archway and staggering on the cobbles beyond, falling.

Tears slipped from Marc's short-sighted old eyes.

"They say," he said, "that Uthr be dead."

TWELVE

C UNEDDA RETURNED TO CAER ARFON IN GRIEF. BEHIND HIM CAME NO ELATED army marching proud beneath flying banners; no blaring of war horns or rousing marching songs. Instead, a weary, blood-grimed rabble, tottering to its knees, grateful for a place to rest and a chance to weep for the many dead. Tears fell from the eyes of a standard-bearer who defiantly carried the Dragon, tattered and stained with Uthr's own spilt blood.

Uthr's men and the men of Gwynedd, heads bowed, shoulders hunched, nursing disbelief and sorrow. The men of the Pendragon following wearily behind their lord's friend, hearts and spirits empty and lost. Defeated men, uncaring what happened to them, with no further cause to fight and no cherished lord for whom to lay down their lives.

Many a man marching that last, endless mile regretted missing death on the battlefield. The lucky ones had gone ahead with their beloved lord.

The people, mostly women, of the settlement stood watching as the host returned, lining the broad main thoroughfare or clustered at the gateways. A mother here, a wife there shouted their joy, welcoming a son or husband home; many, too many, threw their hands over their eyes and let loose their grief as they learnt their own would come home no more.

Others waited, silent, watching, remembering—as the straggle of wounded men limped or were carried past, bloodied, grey-faced men leaning on spears or friends, bundled into carts, draped over tired horses—remembering that other time of defeat, when Vortigern's hired Saex had come tramping in the wake of Cunedda's host. Remembering, too, what he had ordered done.

Beyond the cries of relief or sorrow, they stood fearful. Cunedda's stallion trailed his head; a front hoof stumbled on a sun baked rut. His rider automatically gathered the reins and collected the animal's balance. He heard the uneasy quiet, could see plain the nudging panic. His people remembered well the revenge of Vortigern. Cunedda entered his stronghold, dismounted, and stood for a moment with one hand on his stallion's weary neck, giving orders for seeing to the men's well-being. He stroked his hand along his horse's crest. Horses too had been lost, noble animals that gave courage without question. Few sights were more sickening than a horse with its belly slit open struggling to stand, not understanding why it could not. He saw Gwenhwyfar waiting before the open doors of the Hall.

Gone was the untidy urchin with dirt-smudged nose, ripped tunic, and scraped knees. Her hair, shining copper-gold in the sunlight, was neatly braided and looped. She wore a robe of palest green, the colour of spring and eternal life. In her hand, the chalice of welcome. A faint smile flickered to her father and brothers, thankful at least for their safe return. Cunedda stepped forward, sipped the red wine, handed the drinking vessel on to the son beside him.

Enniaun was the last to drink. He touched his lips to the red liquid and then spilt the rest on the threshold. "In honour and remembrance of those not with us," he murmured. "May the blood of their killers one day stain as this wine stains."

They stood, heads bowed, grouped around the spreading red puddle, watching as it soaked into the wooden boards of the steps, seeing again the blood of the battlefield.

"Welcome home, my father and brothers." Gwenhwyfar stammered over the words, her throat aching with sorrow. She wanted to cry, great gulping sobs, but held back her tears for the sake of her father and for the memory of Uthr, the Pendragon. She looked into Cunedda's grave eyes, saw the emptiness of grief there and spoke the words that pressed on the mind of every man and woman: "Da, will Vortigern come?"

Briefly Cunedda cradled his daughter's chin in his cupped hand. "Who knows, lass? Probably. I would, if I were he." He forced a crooked smile for her and suddenly pulled her close, holding her so tight she thought she would be crushed. Then his eye fell on Arthur, waiting with Etern a few steps within the Hall.

The two days of waiting for the hosting's return had been two days of bitter tears and lonely desperation for the lad. His eyes were red rimmed, puffy, and sore, his cheeks drawn hollows of wretched misery. Arthur had loved Uthr, loved him as he would never love Ectha, the man who fostered him, who might be his sire. It was Uthr who had given the boy his first sword, who had taught Arthur to fight, to use spear and shield, to ride, to hunt. Uthr who had taught him all he knew of battle and war, for Uthr had favoured Arthur, had never objected to the lad's constant questioning, his eagerness to learn. Arthur had never seen anything unusual in the attention, had assumed his lord was pleased to teach someone so enthusiastic—until Morgause had soured the dream, until she had planted seeds of doubt and disgust. Had Uthr tolerated a boy trotting constant at heel because he intended one day to use him in his bed? Now Arthur would never know.

The Lion Lord released Gwenhwyfar and walked up to the boy, placed a hand on his shoulder. "Come with me, lad, there is much to tell."

Arthur went with Cunedda. He would be sent home, back to Less Britain, back to dull Ectha and the banality of the estate. Gone were the hopes of an army life, shattered the dreams of becoming War Lord. Not now, not without Uthr. Cunedda led him through the silent Hall, past servants who stood uncertain of the future, through to his private chambers beyond.

Gwenhwyfar watched them go, stood staring blankly at that shut wooden door, feeling Arthur's sorrow as if it were her own pain. So many dreams left in ruins. So much blood spilt, and more yet to come. A tear dribbled down her cheek. Arthur had wanted so much, and one sword blade had taken it from him. Still she looked at that door. The death of one man—affecting, now, the lives of so many.

A hand settled softly on her shoulder. Surprised, she gasped, and turned around, her heart thundering. It was Osmail. Of all her brothers, Osmail offering comfort?

He stroked a finger around her face. "We'll be safe enough, lass," he said, a tenderness in his voice that she had never heard there before.

She smiled at him, at his own sad eyes, but he turned from her and walked away, that brief offer of love fading. All the same, she heard the thought he spoke aloud.

"I wish to God I had been there with the others."

Now that Cunedda had departed, a trill of conversation rippled, as if they were all released from a hag's binding spell. Slaves darted to pour wine and serve food for hungry men; wounded were ushered to medical aid, comfort, and rest. The war host, for better or worse, was home.

THIRTEEN

CEREDIG CLIMBED THE STEPS TO THE RAMPART WALK WITH A HEART AS HEAVY as his tired feet. The night seemed very still, almost at peace. The cloud-dabbed sky was pocked with stars, and a crisp mountain smell, mingling with the sharp tang of sea, threatened rain. Reaching the top, he turned sunwise along the walkway, nodding acknowledgement as the night watch snapped to attention. They had doubled the guard, though this night they would not be needed. Come tomorrow, and tomorrow…

The settlement, spreading below the rampart, gave the impression of normality; a light came and went in a doorway, a child cried. A man's voice called good night. The darkness cloaked an uneasy waiting.

Padding footsteps behind him, a light touch on his arm. A face, pale in the starlight, with eyes wide and anxious.

"You ought to be abed, little sister," Ceredig said, then shrugged noncommittally as she begged to walk his rounds with him. All the same, he shortened his long stride to match her slower pace.

They stopped to speak here and there with the sentries, exchanging a jest, sharing the grief of loss, enquiring after a bandaged wound.

Halfway along the eastern walkway Ceredig halted to stand before the palisade, looking out and beyond to the mountains, their familiar outline black against the dark sky. Companionably, Gwenhwyfar leant beside him, her elbows just about reaching the top of the wooden fencing. She folded her arms there, rested her chin, gazed with her brother into the night.

A hunting owl called, her mate answering. A dog-fox barked. All the normal sounds of night. Stars twinkled, clouds sailed by overhead. Normal. Save that Vortigern would be somewhere out there beyond Eryri.

A star trail fell across the sky, glimmered a while, faded.

"An omen sent for the Red Dragon of Uthr or the White of Vortigern's Saex?" Ceredig wondered aloud, shifting his weight to the left leg that seemed not to ache so much as the right.

Gwenhwyfar shrugged. "Without the Sight of a Myrddin, who can say?"

"Tck, those old Druids. What knew they, beyond mumbled charms and drug-induced prophecies?" Ceredig followed the Christian faith, though not as devoutly blinkered as his eldest brother.

They fell silent again, each sharing silent company with their own thoughts. The Druids, the ancient priesthood, were gone, their power destroyed by the might of Rome, replaced by the growing persuasion of Christ. Even those who clung to the old gods had abandoned the Druid influence.

"I wonder why stars fall as omens?" Gwenhwyfar mused.

"The problem with omens, sister, is that interpretation depends on which view you look from." Ceredig altered position to lean his shoulders against the fencing, looked down into the torch-lit courtyard below. Men were moving about, loading wagons, tending horses, seeing to armour and weapons. They would move out on the morrow to defend the passes, barricade the ways through the mountains. Vortigern would not find it easy to march into Gwynedd.

"We see a star's portent one way, sister; Vortigern's rabble another."

"Da said once that stars fall when a person dies or a child is born, marking a sorrow or greeting."

Ceredig made no reply. The whole sky would need to fall to mark this great sorrow.

Gwenhwyfar had not been able to sleep. This restless unease that swaddled the Caer pressed on her mind, setting her tossing and pitching in her bed. In the end, she had risen, dressed, and gone to find solace. The mountains always called when fear or sorrow battled against her heart. It was too dark to ride to their protective comfort, but the rampart walk gave a good view of their slumbering presence, so up she had come, softly up the steps to greet her friends. Had seen Ceredig walking his rounds.

Into the stillness she asked, as she had her father, "Will he come—Vortigern?"

Footfalls behind her, two men approaching. Gwenhwyfar whirled at the unexpected approach, her hand flying instinctively to the dagger in her tunic belt. She laughed in relief at the sight of another brother and her cousin.

"Who knows with Vortigern?" Enniaun said, coming up to lean his broad hands on the palisade.

Meriaun, shorter by a handspan and thinner, breathed in the night air, said as he exhaled, "He will have to come up the passes, or go the long way around the coast." Both their faces were shadowed with lines of apprehension, and a tiredness that went deeper than a lack of sleep. "Either way, he will lose many men."

The three men leaned together along the fencing, staring outwards. Ceredig gripped the wood between large, strong hands. Enniaun seemed more at ease, though it was the careworn relaxation of an experienced warrior. Worry about tomorrow when it comes, take today for what it offers. Difficult to set worry aside, but possible, with practice.

Meriaun stood next to Gwenhwyfar, his hand fiddle, fiddling with the rounded pommel of his sword. A babe newly born when Cunedda left the north, Meriaun had grown from boy to man beneath Gwynedd's sheltering mountains, had never known the desolation up beyond the Wall; nor his father. He knew the terror Vortigern aroused, though, and the hatred he had for him. His fingers tightened, the knuckles white against the iron. He thought, "*Let Vortigern come! Let him and I will kill him, here beneath the watching eye of Yr Wyddfa!*"

Enniaun spoke his thoughts aloud. "Vortigern goes as the impulse takes him. Our King is no brave-hearted seeker of blood. He prefers his comfort, the warmth and luxury of a palace, not the mud and slush of a tent and an army on the march. Is he satisfied with Uthr's death? Will he be content with the taking of a few hostages and the payment of a heavy fine? Or will he want a greater revenge—as he did at Dun Pelidr? Either way, Gwynedd will not escape lightly."

"Who is to secure the passes?" Ceredig asked. He had missed the orders, feeling the need to walk these ramparts.

"Dogmail the Beris pass; Dunaut and Rumaun head down to the Tremadog coast; myself, Aber Glaslyn ready to fall back towards the Black Ford if necessary; and Abloyc up to secure Llyn Ogwen. It ought to be enough, with men watching the northern coastal road."

"Safe. But for the sea."

"Even Vortigern's Saex cannot whistle up boats from nowhere!"

Silence drifted again. The mountains ringed Caer Arfon as securely as this palisade protected the Caer; but no defence was sure. Wood burnt. Passes could be breached.

"I am thinking there are two ways of approaching our passes," Ceredig said into the quiet, waving a hand out to the dark, waiting mountains. "With wisdom or foolishness." He patted his sister's shoulder and made ready to resume his rounds. "Go to bed, sweetheart, there is nothing to be done until morning." He walked some yards, stopped, and turned to face his kin, hand tight around the pommel of his sword. His voice was calm, but had a fierceness born of the certain knowledge that the deaths might not yet be ended. "I dislike Vortigern, but I freely admit he is not the fool."

FOURTEEN

I N THE ENCAMPMENT SET WITHIN THE CRUMBLING STONE WALLS OF THE OLD
Roman fort, Uthr's men sat weary and uncertain beside their night fires,
talking softly or dozing fitfully. Some nursed wounds that throbbed and ached;
most cradled their weapons, sword or spear, close at hand and ready. Waiting.
Bewildered, confused, and bereft, each man wrapped in his own thoughts of
loss and shattered hope. Leaderless men in a foreign territory, with the fear of
Vortigern at their backs.

Cunedda needed to put an end to this black mood before it got out of hand.
Men afraid could so easily follow a mistaken path. He needed calm, and new
heart. Come dawn's first light, word to rally before the Caer's Sacred Stone
had spread through the camp, and rumour surged with a force like that of the
Hafren's bore tide.

Uthr's men broke their fast with barley bread and porridge, sharing conclusions reached during the interminable night. What had Cunedda in mind? Each
held an idea as they assembled beside the men of Gwynedd before the hallowed
Stone, the symbol of a warrior's strength and the chieftain's right of leadership.
The whetstone, with its spiral carvings and score marks from many a warrior's
blade had come with Cunedda from the North. An ancient thing this Stone,
given, it was said, by the gods to the first of the Votadini. It was here, with a hand
upon this sacred, carved rock, that loyalty was vowed, promises exchanged, and
oaths sworn; here that Cunedda had proclaimed Gwynedd as his own. It was
before such stones, in the time before and before the coming of the Romans,
that kings were made.

Muttered theories passed back and forth from soldier to soldier, group to
group. Emotion was running high, with anger directed at Vortigern. Talk ceased
as Cunedda, Lion Lord of Gwynedd, and his family approached. Standard-bearers
carrying the two banners of the Lion and the Red Dragon took up positions
on either side of the Stone. A ragged cheer broke out as the first stirring of a

morning wind lifted the Dragon. Gwenhwyfar sensed the pride her father's men felt in her family. She had chosen to dress resplendently for Uthr—a gown the colour of a summer's green-blue sea, and a plaid cloak draped almost to her ankles and fastened by two huge gold and garnet brooches. Her hair hung loose, and at her throat, glinted a torque of twisted gold.

They stood beside the Stone, before the men, to honour the passing of a noble lord. How Gwenhwyfar wished it could have been to honour his victory! The waiting men looked on with mingled hope and doubt as Cunedda took a single step forward and raised his hands for silence.

"Friends! I grieve with you for the loss of our beloved Pendragon. As children he and I grew together at my father's stronghold; as men we fought our enemies—aye, and each other over a pretty girl!" Chuckles, a few cheers; the tension had eased. "It grieves me to realise never again will that valiant lord thunder his battle cry." Cunedda's voice cracked; for a moment he could not speak, so great was his sorrow. Somehow he managed to go on. "I say to you, Uthr is not gone! His spirit remains among us. With us, his hopes, ambitions, and dreams live on. He wished a Pendragon to sit on the throne of all Britain. Ha!" He barked the word, startling the few murmurs into stillness. "Do I hear some of you muttering that now this will not be?"

Cunedda paused, stared fiercely at the sea of faces. His stern gaze blazed out from beneath his bush of red hair, quelling dissent. The Lion would be heard!

"This banner"—he touched the Dragon reverently—"symbolises all we believe in, binds us together as one, and the Dragon is ours!"

An uncertain cheer drifted into the damp morning air, then a gruff voice rose clear above the others: "What good a banner if the name it leads be empty?"

The thin cheering died, fading to nods and mutterings of agreement.

Gwenhwyfar knew her father's ways, realised he was playing with these men, preparing them. But for what? She glanced from Etern's blank expression, along her brothers' frowns. Did they follow their father's thoughts? Arthur stood impassive to one side beyond Cunedda, pale-faced and oddly lost, a little uncomfortable. It would be hard for him with no one to stand between him and Morgause. Would the woman take herself away now her lord was dead? Gwenhwyfar caught a fluttered glimpse to the edge of the crowd, of Morgause's bright clothing, imagined she heard the loud jangle of bangles and necklace. Sa, she had come to listen then.

As they had snatched a hasty dawn meal, Etern had confided to his sister the opinion that the Pendragon's Banner was expected to pass into Gwynedd's keeping, with one of the sons taking it as his own. It seemed plausible. Had Uthr named Cunedda as heir, or was it to pass to Osmail, the eldest brother? Surely not to Osmail, who disliked war, who professed to putting love to God before the killing of men?

Enniaun then, a red-haired giant, taller by half a hand span than their father. Or Ceredig. Kind Ceredig, whose soft eyes could fill with sad tears at the telling of a harper's tale; Rumaun and Dunaut the twins, alike as two seeds. Abloyc, the humorous—always laughing, rarely serious save for occasions like this. Meriaun, the grandson; or Dogmail, at eight and ten a handsome man, loved by all the women, servant or high born. He doubted he would marry—"Over many beauties to choose from!" Etern? Impatient for manhood.

And Arthur. Gwenhwyfar wondered about Arthur. Traces of his tears were still visible. What future had he to face now?

Cunedda allowed the rumble of voices to circulate, to swell, then interrupted, his powerful voice carrying. "The name of Pendragon is not finished! Uthr's murder by a Saex-loving tyrant is not the end. Were we not all impatient to topple Vortigern from power? Uthr tried once and was forced into exile, to wait. This second time, we have rocked the foundations. Vortigern will fall, but we have to wait again, wait to put the final boot to his backside. We are not defeated. This is a new beginning, my friends, a new beginning!"

"How so?" The man who had questioned earlier spoke a second time. He had a loud, carrying voice that quickly attracted attention. Thrusting forward, he touched the mask of his wolfskin cloak in a gesture of respect, but for all that, stood defiant before Cunedda. "How can it be a beginning when the body of the lord we have served—some of us for many a year—lies mangled in Vortigern's hands? We cannot serve a memory, Cunedda!"

A ripple of assent.

"What is your name, soldier?" Cunedda asked in a kindly voice.

"*Waiting*," thought Gwenhwyfar. "*He's waiting like a cat watching its prey, judging the right moment to unleash his claws and pounce.*"

"Mabon. I served Lord Uthr for nigh on twenty year, from when I was still but a whelp green behind the ears; I fled with him from Dumnonia," he swept an arm behind him, indicating other men, "as did many of us here."

Cunedda pulled at his moustache, one hand cradling his bent elbow. "It was a Mabon, I recall, who raised the alarm that night when Vortigern's paid men came to murder Uthr in his bed."

"It was."

"You?"

"Aye, me." The veteran straightened his shoulders, his pride shining through a battle-grimed scowl.

Cunedda nodded at the man. "For your loyal service, I will recommend you for an honour, Mabon."

"With respect, Sir," Mabon replied, "I thank you, but to whom will you give such recommendation? We," again he swept his callused hand towards the men, "have no lord."

Direct into Cunedda's hands. "That," the Lion snapped, eyes blazing in triumph, "is where you are wrong!"

Dissent grumbled louder, each man talking rapidly to the man at his shoulder, heads shaking, a few fists being raised.

Cunedda boomed out, "Do you, Mabon, recollect Lady Ygrainne's condition when you found an urgent need to flee that night?"

"As if it were yesterday," Mabon answered forthright. "We were all concerned for my lady, heavy with child as she was."

Cunedda beckoned Mabon forward. "Come out here, man, so all may see and hear. Recount the tale to those who do not know."

Hesitant at first Mabon began to talk. He could not see the point of all this, but Cunedda must have his reasons.

"After the defeat, Uthr fled into his own secure lands of Dumnonia. He knew it would be only a matter of time afore Vortigern and the followers of the slain Gorlois made an attempt on his life. For some months we managed, our people were loyal, looking to Uthr and his new lady with affection. But there is always the risk of traitors. The attack came at a bad time—rough seas and foul weather."

The man was settling to his tale, confidence growing. "Lady Ygrainne had no choice but to take ship with us. It was she Gorlois's kin wanted dead, for her insult in leaving that lecherous bastard." He spat, nodded apology at Cunedda and, as the nearest female present, Gwenhwyfar. "The sea crossing was bad, bad enough for a fit man let alone a woman close to her time." Mabon shook his head. "She was delivered of a son soon after we disembarked in Less Britain. The child lived a day, no longer." He shook his head more vigorously at the enormity of the loss. "Uthr's only true born son. There have been no more."

Silence, save for the rustle of a spirited wind rising with the incoming tide. They all knew the tale but this time the recounting hit harder, rubbing salt into an open wound. No heir to carry the Dragon. No son to follow Uthr's dream and title.

Cunedda tugged at his moustache. "Were there not two women with child on that ship?"

Mabon frowned, startled, uncertain how the lord of Gwynedd came to know such small detail. "Aye, my lord." He spoke slowly, thinking what to say. "Caromy, my lady's maid, carried a child. She birthed a boy during the crossing." Mabon pursed his lips. "Poor lass had a bad time of it." He glanced sideways at Arthur, who stared back at him.

The story concluded lamely, a few beads of sweat standing out on Mabon's brow beneath the snarling head of the wolf cloak as Arthur's eyes continued to bore into the man.

"At first, tongues wagged that the child was Uthr's doing." He spread his hands. "He liked his women. Then Ectha took the boy in formal foster, so it was considered his had been the," he coughed, "indiscretion."

Pushing further Cunedda probed for more information. "And this son of Caromy's?" He smoothed his moustache with the tip of his index finger. "How did he fare?"

Mabon's resigned glance flickered between Arthur and Cunedda. "Ah, 'tis the shame of it, with all respect to the lad here." He nodded in apology to Arthur. "Caromy's child was a sickly thing, but 'twas the one that lived." He sighed, pointed to Arthur, "As you see, he thrived."

"The mother?"

"Took sick, died."

Throughout the telling, Arthur's expression remained impassive, almost bored. Gwenhwyfar, following the exchange of words and glances, felt herself teetering on the brink of excitement. She had not missed that familiar twitch about her father's lips; he was enjoying himself. For a heartbeat, she felt she knew what was to come, then it was gone like a seed lost to the wind. She waited, holding her breath.

Cunedda's voice suddenly roared like the creature he was named for. Many jumped; Gwenhwyfar almost squeaked. "I can add to the telling!"

His listeners shuffled in anticipation, eyes and ears riveted, locked on to Cunedda's muscular bulk. He placed a hand on Arthur's shoulder, brought the boy forward, then with apparent carelessness rested his other hand lightly on the Stone.

"Mahon has identified this lad to you as Arthur. I can tell you now of something I have held safe unto me these many years."

Gwenhwyfar took hold of Etern's arm, a thrill of anticipation streaking through her. She had known, deep down, where these things rested, unspoken and unheeded!

Excited talk, muttered questions. From the back, a few shouts. Raising the hand resting on Arthur's shoulder, Cunedda paused, waiting for complete silence to fall.

The incoming sea shuffled against the shore, and a gentle salt wind hissed from the hills. Two screeching gulls wheeled overhead.

To the misted blue of the new day, Cunedda boomed, "It was not the son of Uthr and Ygrainne who died, but Caromy's!"

The hand went back to Arthur; the other still touched the sacred Stone. He let the murmur rumble, heard the rise of hope begin to dawn as the men around him realised what was to come.

He went on, speaking fast. "The babes were exchanged, a deception to shield Uthr's firstborn from Vortigern's spite. Only four of us knew the truth of it: Uthr and Ygrainne, Caromy, and myself." Cunedda nodded grimly. "Now you know it. And by all the gods that ever were or ever shall be, Vortigern too shall know soon enough!"

The muttering had grown louder, men pushing closer, faces that a moment before were grey and lost coming alive, eager.

With ringing triumph Cunedda finished his speech. "There is another Pendragon—still young, I grant, we need wait for him to come of age. We, Uthr and I, had hoped we would not need to reveal him until he was ready, but that was not to be." Cunedda chivvied Arthur before him and shouted above the rising excitement, his voice ringing out almost to the watching mountains. "Here, before the hallowed sanctity of our Stone, I give you your next king! I give you the Pendragon—Arthur!"

He stepped back leaving Arthur to stand alone as a great clamour rose up into the sky. The lad smiled now, the pain and sorrow fading with that great roar of acclaim. Cunedda was wrong: five had known Uthr had his heir. Arthur had known, all these years in his dreams and thoughts, he had known Uthr to be his father. Why else had he loved the man so, and the man been so fond of a lad? He grinned, broadly, triumphantly, at the pride in Cunedda's face, the unexpected pleasure on those of his sons. Arthur winked boyishly at the exultant Gwenhwyfar.

Unexpected, Cunedda knelt before the lad, offering his sword as a token of his loyalty. Few heard the words he spoke, above that tumult of approval raised by those watching men. It did not matter, all knew the oath of allegiance.

"To you, Lord, I give my sword and shield, my heart and soul. To you, Lord, I give my life, to command as you will."

Arthur could not hide his consternation at so great a man kneeling at a boy's feet. With shaking fingers, he touched Cunedda's offered sword then, impulsively, he raised the man and embraced him as a friend.

It if were possible, the roar increased. Men of Gwynedd yelled their delight at seeing their lord accepted by the new Pendragon, and men of Uthr, heartsore and bruised, shouted and cheered, relieved to have their anxiety and uncertainty so splendidly lifted.

One by one the sons of Gwynedd stepped forward to follow their father's example. Etern too knelt.

"I am not yet come to manhood, I cannot swear oath to you. But this I can swear, Arthur, when the time comes you will not be wanting for a more loyal sword, for mine shall be yours, whenever you have need of it."

Arthur choked, almost unable to speak. He clasped his friend's arm and stammered, "Then I shall indeed be blessed with a greater fortune than I deserve!"

As Etern stepped aside, Gwenhwyfar, with head high, strode forward. The sun burst through a low covering of misty cloud, making her hair and jewels sparkle with dazzling brilliance. She knelt solemnly before Arthur, her grace and hint of woman's beauty showing clearly through the lankiness of her child's body, catching every watcher's attention.

The noise abated. No woman took the oath of loyalty. What was this girl-child about?

She held Arthur's eyes and her voice, young though it was, carried clear and bold.

"I too am of the blood of Gwynedd. Were I born male I would swear my oath, but I am woman-born. I have no shield or sword."

Arthur took her hands in his. Like a fool he felt a sudden urge to weep. Looking down at her earnest face, his dark eyes seeing deep into the hidden secrets of her tawny flecked green, he realised how much he wanted her for his own.

Tremulously Gwenhwyfar said, "I have something else to give, Lord." Her heart was hammering. "When I am woman-grown I shall have a greater gift to pledge. I offer you, my Lord, Arthur Pendragon, to use how you choose, my unborn sons!"

The family behind, ranged behind the Stone, roared delight and approval along with the excited host. Cunedda almost burst with pride as he shouted with the rest of them. Aye, his only daughter was as fine a woman as the one he had taken in marriage! Had he not always known it would be so?

Arthur gripped Gwenhwyfar's hands and raised her to her feet. He spoke quietly, words for her alone, not trusting the emotion to lie easy. "I accept your pledge, my Cymraes fach—only, before you take him, ensure your future husband agrees also!"

Gwenhwyfar tossed her head, a little annoyed. "I told you: I will not wed with any but the best."

Arthur grinned, suddenly confident, emboldened. "Would you consider a Pendragon the best?"

The men of the war host were jostling forward, eager to take the oath. Gwenhwyfar found herself swept aside, her answer lost to Arthur's ears.

"I will not bear my sons to anyone less."

FIFTEEN

M ORGAUSE WAS LEAVING. SHE HAD INFORMED CUNEDDA CURTLY LAST evening of her intention, demanding suitable escort and horses. He had not attempted to dissuade her.

She had stationed herself apart from the knot of women gathered on the far side of the Stone Ground, her expression as granite hard as the Stone itself. Watching the elated men swarm around Arthur, her fists clenched, the nails digging into the flesh of her palms. All the words and oaths and curses that were ever sworn swirled in her throat, ready to spew from between clenched teeth. It all made sense now! Uthr's excuses, the evasive replies. That was why he was so fond of the boy. That was why he had refused to divorce Ygrainne! Bastard. Lying, deceitful bastard! "*The Goddess rot your bones, Uthr Pendragon!*"

Her maid approached warily, sensing the mood. She whispered, indicating a group of waiting men and horses. Morgause walked to them with quick, angry steps, mounted the mare held for her, and prepared to ride out, then changed her mind. With rough hands and kicking heels she forced her mare through the tightly packed men, and halted before Arthur. For a long moment Morgause said nothing, just stared at the boy with malevolent hatred.

Arthur returned the look, unflinching, triumph sparking behind his dark eyes, this unexpected knowledge of identity provided a greater courage than he knew he possessed. "You are leaving us?" he said coolly in the neat, precise Latin she always used, added with a sarcastic smile, "You will not be missed."

The mare, uneasy at the press of men, swung away suddenly, eyes rolling, head lowered, and rear hooves lashing out. There came shouts of alarm, men darting backwards, jumping aside. Morgause yanked hard at the horse's bit, hauling her back. "You may have discovered you are no bastard, but I tell you this, your father certainly was!" She spat at Arthur and dug her heels into her mount, causing the mare to leap forward with a squeal of protest.

Several men fell beneath the plunging horse; one screamed as a thrashing hoof crashed on his leg, smashing the bone. Others crouched, arms protecting heads, or scrambled to safety. The instant reaction was rage. Hands reached out to stop her, grabbing at the bridle, countering her double insult. Morgause slashed faces, hands, heads with her riding whip, glaring and snarling like a savage cat.

Dabbing at the spittle, Arthur wiped it, repugnant, from his cheek. "Let the bitch go," he commanded in the men's British tongue. "We shall be well rid of her."

He strode quickly to the injured man, laid a sympathetic hand on his shoulder, ordered, "Send someone for a stretcher; see this man's well tended."

Morgause was galloping, driving the mare hard. Arthur stood and watched her leave. He ought to feel elated, joyful, at the very least relieved. Morgause was gone, gone from his life. No more of her slaps and tortures. No more of her venomous tongue and sharp sarcasm.

If only he could be certain. Certain that she really had gone from him. For good. But nothing was ever a certainty where that witch woman was concerned.

JULY 450

SIXTEEN

THE GRAIN HARVEST WAS RUINED. PERSISTENT RAIN WORKED THROUGH garments, soaking uncomfortable to the skin and aching into the joints of old bones and new-healing wounds. That glorious month of June had rumbled into a July, that brought a torrent of wind-driven hail from the west with all the fury of an angered boar. Had Vortigern used some dark power in the sending of that storm?

Within the one night, oats, wheat, and barley that had stood proud and golden, lay sodden and blackened. Fortunate that Gwynedd was not reliant on the growing of crops for survival; they had their sheep and cattle; the wild deer, fowl, and boar. The sea to fish. But the grain was needed for the horses, for the baking of bread, and for the staple poor man's diet of porridge.

When Arthur had taken up the title of Pendragon there came a flourish of exuberance and optimism which filled the next few days—even though Cunedda had ordered the lad home to safety in Less Britain.

Gwenhwyfar missed him. Missed his laughter and jaunty teasing. His friendship. Theirs had developed into a special liking, something that went beyond the sharing of seemingly endless summer days. Gwenhwyfar was a girl-child, but a girl on the brink of womanhood. With the coming of Arthur, she had felt as though she were walking in the wild foam of the surf—neither a girl on the firm, golden sand, nor a woman grown, in the open swell of the sea. She walked somewhere between, neither one nor yet the other, she could only look back to where the innocence of childhood romped, and ahead to the unknown future.

"Do not forget me!" he had called, as his ship slipped its moorings and the tide bore him away, that first night after his proclaiming.

"Never!" she had shouted back, standing on toe-tip to watch until the darkness took him. She would not forget Arthur. None would forget the vibrant boy who carried their dreams and their hopes of freedom. But nor could they forget Vortigern.

For a few days they shrugged off the threat of his coming, mocking his incompetence, carolling lewd songs, and passing even cruder jests at the King's expense. False bravado. With the coming of that storm, hope and gaiety fled Caer Arfon.

A depression settled, clinging like the grey swathing mist of low cloud that shrouded the brooding mountains. Even the sea rolled flat and grey.

Vortigern had come as far as Llyn Tegid and set up camp, entrenching himself and his stinking Saex mercenaries beside the river that fed the lake. Envoys began passing back and forth, riding dismally through the torrential rain. Cunedda's proud messengers, Vortigern's haughty emissary. A skirmish of words. The King demanding Cunedda surrender his sword and pay homage unconditionally; Cunedda playing for time with excuses and delays—seeking sanctuary from the inevitable.

How long, though, would Vortigern wait?

His patience would ebb, the relay of verbal procrastination eventually run its course. A few days; a week; ten days—twelve. It was to be the Lion Lord's homage to the king or battle. Cunedda wanted no further bloodshed, but Vortigern was not a man to trust, and his terms of surrender would not sit easy. One week turned slowly into two. Time had ended. So must the waiting.

Enniaun stirred more heat to the hearth, sending sparks and flames spitting high as he tossed wood to the reluctant blaze. The kindling was damp, more smoke than heat curling into the privacy of Cunedda's chamber. He shifted his brother Ceredig's boot aside and reseated himself within the circle around the hearth.

"To my mind," Osmail said, shuffling his cloak tighter about his shoulders, "it is naught but insanity for you to ride alone into Vortigern's encampment, Da."

With a snort of contempt, Cunedda hurled back, "Then I am insane." He raised a finger, pointed it at his eldest son.

"The moment I agree to ride out of my gates I hand my pride to Vortigern. Pride I can afford to lose, it's a thing easily restored. The life of a son is not."

Ceredig shifted his weight from a cramped ankle. "He would not dare harm any of us, Da. If we must humble Gwynedd before his army, then let us do so together. All of us."

"Aaghh!" Cunedda swarmed to his feet and stormed from the circle. "Must I tell you this again? Have you all lost your hearing and wits?" He stalked up to Ceredig and bent so as to speak directly to his face. "I have no choice but to submit without condition. I do have a choice as to who accompanies me. I take for escort thirty of my guard. No sons." His finger pointed at each face, looking back at him with mixed expression as he repeated, "No sons. Never again will I be forced to witness the cold-minded butchering of my own flesh and blood."

It was useless to argue further, but Enniaun made one last attempt. He spoke softly, edging away from the rash heat of the argument that had been tossed back and forth around the hearth this past hour or more. "It was different then, Da, as well you know."

"How? How was it different?" Cunedda stormed around the circle and jerked Enniaun roughly to his feet. "You know all about it, eh? You remember the taking and the killing at Dun Pelidr, do you boy?"

Enniaun hung his head, his fingers fiddling with the hilt of his dagger, teeth biting his lower lip. He remembered.

The fighting men had stumbled and dragged themselves up the steep sides of the Dun, weeping and bloodied. Knowing the bodies of their kinsmen had been left to the crows and the indecencies of Vortigern's hired Saex. For five nights and days they held out before the Saex managed to fire the wooden palisade. Even then, Cunedda's proud people clung to freedom for another half day, choking in the acrid smoke that blackened and invaded their crumbling fortress home. Held long enough for the wife of the eldest son to give safe birthing to their first child. Then Cunedda surrendered, opening the gates for the King to enter and take what he would, never dreaming the price of rebellion would be enforced evacuation—and the execution of that beloved eldest son.

Lifting his head, Enniaun gazed into his father's eyes. Remember? How could any forget the gathering of their belongings and being herded through those soot-blackened, body-strewn, mud- and blood-churned streets of Dun Pelidr? Forget the jeers and taunts of Saex barbarians and king's men. Forget the rise of vomit as the family and people of Cunedda walked proud beneath the still smouldering gateway and saw, hanging there by the entrails, the hacked body of Typiaunan, Cunedda's son.

He swallowed, made to reach a hand towards his father, hesitated. Said instead, "I remember, Da. We all, save Etern and Gwen who were not then born, remember."

Meriaun, that grandson born while the flames leapt high and the end was approaching, came to his feet, his hands spread. "I was a babe little more than a day born when the tribe left our old homeland. Smuggled from the Dun as a serving woman's child." His voice too, choked, and the tears trickled unashamed. "I knew only my grandsire's wife as Mother. The woman who birthed me chose to accompany her torn and mutilated lord into the next world. It was a brave love that gave her courage to drain her own blood from her veins."

Cunedda stood slumped, seeing again that terrible time. Slowly he shook his head. "And you ask me to take one or all of you into Vortigern's camp?"

He straightened, tilted his chin, defiant. "I go alone. If the King needs blood then he can have my old bones, not yours." He strode for the door, his decision final, halted as Osmail, still seated cross-legged before the hearth, said, "I am coming with you, Father. It matters not, my life. I am no warrior. Gwynedd needs me not." He looked up, an expression of pleading in his eyes. *Just this once, Da, acknowledge me. Think of me as the eldest, not dead Typiaunan.*

A stirring and shuffling as the brothers and Meriaun turned to stare at him. Osmail? Osmail offering this?

"Vortigern will demand a hostage to ensure future peace," he added. "Happen I can serve better thus than mouldering useless here." Still he held his father's eyes. "I ask only that you take care of my wife and sons."

For a fleeting moment Cunedda hovered on agreement. How much better to have at least the support of one son! He looked quickly away from Osmail's eye lest he see the truth, spoke as quickly. "No one comes with me save my chosen guard." He left the chamber shutting the door firmly behind him. *What use Osmail? What use his woman's stomach, his clumsy handling of weapons?*

Stiff, stretching cramped muscles, the family of Gwynedd rose from the hearth, followed their father through the door back into the Hall. Only Osmail remained seated before the sulky flames, tossing bits of broken twig into the fire. Hurting that no one—not brother, nephew, or father—had denied his acknowledgement of failure.

An hour after cockcrow Cunedda rode from his stronghold of Caer Arfon. A chill spray of mud splattered the horses' legs as they rode down from the Caer. Steadying his stallion from a jogging trot, Cunedda looked back at the gateway aware it might be his last look, willing to accept it so for the lives of his sons and the peace of Gwynedd.

No good, this remembering of the past! He urged his horse into a canter. Uthr had lost that war too, and Cunedda had lost everything including dignity. Vortigern had enjoyed humbling him, seeing him near destroyed; enjoyed the added insult of granting a dark, mountainous corner where starving peasants lived in rancid poverty, and raiding pirates plundered what little remained.

Gwynedd. Cunedda smiled grimly. Vortigern had played a wrong move! Gwynedd had rebuilt Cunedda's pride twofold, and what could be regained once, could be gained a second time. Na, Cunedda would not sacrifice Gwynedd or his sons to Vortigern. An easy price to pay, a bent knee and a few spoken words of homage. He set his face for Llyn Tegid, riding at a steady canter.

SEVENTEEN

THREE DAYS HE WAS GONE. THREE DAYS OF WAITING IN THE HUSHED CAER, where at any moment the war horns of the King's hired Saex were expected to boom and crash through the passes and heights of the mountains. Three days of discomfort for Cunedda's escort, squatting, huddled beneath sodden cloaks, beside hissing campfires and glaring across the river at Vortigern's encampment.

And then Cunedda brought his men home to Caer Arfon one mid-afternoon when a weak sun struggled to break through grey cloud pressing as chill as unsmelted iron. His expression was inscrutable; only his hands, clutching the reins, showed his great anger. Speaking not one word to those waiting to bid him welcome, he stormed into his Hall, issuing curt orders to stand all men down.

"Vortigern will not be making reprisal?" Etern asked, following, with his family and retainers.

Cunedda made no answer, went direct to his own chamber where he slammed the door behind him and bellowed for wine.

The evening gathering was a morose and dispirited meal with no singing, no laughter. One table called for the harper to tell a tale, but his heart was not in it, the chosen narrative a woeful story of lost love. Cunedda sat picking at his food, glancing often at his daughter. She caught his eye once and flashed him her most brilliant smile. He managed a smile back then busied himself with his pork. *How can I tell her? How do I tell what I have done to save Gwynedd?*

The talk across the tables came in hushed voices. Few of the hosting had yet disbanded. They would drift away on the morrow at first light, tramping back to their homesteads and families, back to salvage what they could from the ruins of the harvest. Eyes flitted again and again to the red-haired lord at his table. On every lip, the same question. At what cost, this surrender?

Uncertainty and disquiet swirled with the woodsmoke, as choking and blinding. Belatedly, Cunedda realised he had made a mistake; he must say some-thing, some few words to dispel this black mood. Those watching him were like whipped dogs, squirming low on their bellies, reluctant to approach the master for fear of further reprimand. Men and women, his people, were entitled to some explanation as part payment for unquestioning loyalty. But the great Cunedda was at a loss. What to say? How much to say? All of it, some?

Again he stole a glance at his beloved Gwenhwyfar, deep in earnest conversa-tion with Etern. The pair missed young Arthur; it had been good, that friend-ship, and for Gwenhwyfar something more than friendship? Cunedda had been pleased at that discovery. A short-lived pleasure that, now.

He pulled absently at his moustache. *Do I tell her? Do I share this misery or carry it alone, for as long as I need keep silence?* He exhaled slowly, coming to a decision. Na, let the lass hold the innocence and happiness of childhood while she might. It would be stolen from her soon enough. No need to sign for silence; Cunedda rising to his feet and clearing his throat settled the hushed conversation immediately.

"I have little to tell." He stood with the tips of his spread fingers resting lightly on the table. "I reached a personal agreement with the King. It is not to my lik-ing, but for the sake of Gwynedd I accepted the conditions."

He laid his hands flat, the wood smooth and cool beneath his sweating palms. "We took a gamble and lost. Vortigern has claimed a high payment of corn, cattle, horses, and such, for Gwynedd's surrender. He will take many of our young men also, to swell his British army. All that can be met," Winter would come hard this year, and the next. Happen the next too. Cunedda flicked his cloak, preparing to sit, then paused. "As to the other part of the settlement, that is for me to bear alone."

Low talk began again; wine was poured, food eaten. Cunedda plucked meat from a bone. His family knew not to question further.

Abruptly, Cunedda pushed back his chair, strode into the centre of the Hall, and cast the bone into the blazing hearth fire; burning fat spat from the flames. Anger brewed like fermenting fruit in his belly.

"There is one thing you need know!"

Faces turned expectantly towards him. Some sat with tankards half raised, others with meat or bread poised in their fingers. One man paused, bending to retrieve his dagger from the floor where it had fallen.

His voice like the great boom of the war horns Cunedda cried, "Uthr was betrayed—*we* were betrayed!" The words were as deadly as a viper's venom.

"Betrayed, by one who teaches love and peace. Vortigern knew where to find Uthr Pendragon!"

They had taken great care to hide this knowledge, to conceal their direction, changing course and changing it again. That Vortigern would know of Uthr's coming, and the war host was to be expected. Spies in Less Britain and the King's Saex pirates keeping close watch to the southern channel would ensure accurate intelligence. But Vortigern could never have been certain where the Pendragon was headed—Gwynedd, Dyfed, or home to Dumnonia? He gathered his army, made ready to march where and when needed, but would not have known so soon. Not so soon!

"One among us rode hard to tell Vortigern, to give him the edge in choosing the place to give battle." Cunedda paused, then roared his great anger, "It seems our holy priest did not approve our plans to overthrow tyranny!"

The response was immediate. A few protesting cries in defence of a holy man, hastily smothered as most let their anger go.

Cunedda raised his hands, shouted against the din. "I knew Vortigern's spies; knew them and fed them enough tit-bits to keep their bellies well fed, ensured they were safe detained when the time was ripe. But one, one I overlooked." His eyes narrowed as he looked around the incredulous faces. With a sudden hatred he said, "There was no meeting of holy men, only the meeting of one turd to another. It was a man of God who caused Uthr's death!"

This, Cunedda knew, was stretching the truth. Vortigern would have come soon enough anyway; Uthr could as easily have been slain in battle without a spy's tattling. Except the advantage had gone to Vortigern, allowing him to anticipate and outmanoeuvre the uprising before it was fully fledged.

Branwen came to her feet, outraged. She detested this backwater and its heathen people. Her only solace had become her faith in God and she had a sudden, alarming vision of that too being snatched from her.

"The father is a good man!" she cried, taking several quick steps to stand before Cunedda. "He is a man of God and answerable to Him only. You have no right to make such a vile accusation!"

Cunedda turned on her. "Enough of your tongue! If it were not for my son you would have been thrown beyond my walls afore now! I have ordered the stoning of better women than you!" He was standing before her now, one hand raised, finger pointing. "Your Christianity, lady, means betrayal and murder!"

Someone echoed agreement, cursing the priest and his God. Another spat upon the poxed Christian religion. Voices began to rise, the curses more volatile.

It needed little for frustrated, bewildered, and defeated men to reach for a revenge closer to home. Someone took up a torch, another cried for action. They rose as one and left the Hall, hands grasping more torches, the ululation of anger and defiance rising like the blood lust of the hunt.

The cheering swelled as the fire took hold of the squat chapel, the laughter rising with the flames licking up the walls, eating hungrily at the roof.

Branwen sat slumped in a heap by the hearth, weeping bitter tears at the roar and crackle of destruction. What was left to her now? Her church was gone!

Osmail stood helpless, torn between his faith and his father. His mouth worked but spilt no sound.

The three were the only occupants of the Hall; even the servants had run outside to witness the bright glare of burning. Cunedda was seated again, drinking deep draughts from his tankard. A small taste of revenge this, but as sweet as comb from the hive. He was aware his son followed the Christian religion with devoted passion. Aware, but suddenly, unreasonably, resentful.

His wife had loved Christ, and Christ had taken her from him. Damn Christ, all curses on the Christian God!

Brutally he said, "You may weep, woman. Shed your tears for a traitor whose action will bring more bitterness to this family than any pagan devil ever would."

Osmail knelt to comfort Branwen, then looked for a moment at his father who sat swilling wine, seeming to enjoy the frenzy outside. Osmail, who could never say the right words, do the right thing. Osmail, who believed in the love of God above all else. Osmail, who had at last discovered what it meant, how it felt, to be master.

He stood up and walked slowly over to his father. His throat felt dry, his heart pounded but this thing was for him to do, this last hurdle set for him to leap. "I shall leave on the morrow. My sons shall not be raised where God is not welcome."

"God is more than welcome. His traitorous servants are not."

"In my way, I am a servant of God," Osmail said. "Am I then a traitor?" He paused, willing his father to say something more, plead for him to stay. Nothing. No word.

"I will take Branwen to a holy house, somewhere that will appreciate generous funding." He did not add, "Where I and my wife will be welcome; where I will be useful." He had gone to Branwen's side. She looked up at him, her eyes full of wonderment. Was this her husband speaking? Was it Osmail saying these words she had prayed one day to hear? He helped her to her feet and she threaded her arm through his; went proud beside him as they walked from the Hall.

Only once did Osmail feel an urge to look back, to look one last time at his father. But he did not. To look back would be to admit weakness. And he could not risk losing this sudden-found, unexpected courage.

EIGHTEEN

THE FIRST PINK FINGERS OF DAWN WERE CREEPING ACROSS THE PALING NIGHT sky as Cunedda rode out alone, eyes hollow and red rimmed from lack of sleep, desperate to outrun the wallowing despair. He urged his stallion into a mad gallop along the sea-wet sand, and the wind clawed at his cloak, stinging his face like arrows. The horse stretched its body, the firm, taut muscles rippling, strong legs pounding, crested neck extended, his small pointed ears flat back and nostrils flaring. His tail arched, spreading like a banner. Distance was swallowed beneath his speed.

Cunedda let him run; let him go until he slowed of his own accord, head tossing, flecks of foam flying. The horse eased to a crab canter, slowed to a bouncing trot and finally down to a blowing walk. Cunedda brought him to a halt and slid, defeated, from the saddle to stand in the swirl of the incoming sea.

Not since his wife's death had grief torn so pitilessly at his heart.

The ugly submission to Vortigern weighed unbearable. Conscience wrestled with pride of leadership. Was he right to put Gwynedd before his children? Yet all of Gwynedd, all the people—rich, poor, Eldermen, farmer, peasant, servant, and slave—were they not all his children? Anger at the unjustness followed the outpouring of sorrow. The Dragon Banner flew for the new Pendragon. Like Uthr, this one would be back to fight openly or with more subtle means. Either way, the Red Dragon survived to claw its way to the throne. Vortigern knew this now, knew he had still to watch the shadows.

Cunedda laughed, a roar of desperate grief, remembering Vortigern's expression on learning of Arthur's existence—no further sense in hiding the truth. He had told the King outright, after kneeling in public homage and agreeing wholesale to Vortigern's terms. It had been most pleasant to see the King's sardonic smile of triumph wiped instant away.

The brief glow of pleasure faded. The tide swirled around Cunedda's boots, climbing up the beach. Because of Arthur's perilous position, ungrown and untried, he had no choice but to accept Vortigern's demands. No choice.

A single gull swept low with a harsh, mournful cry. Cunedda crumpled to his knees, slammed his fists into the surf and raged at the bird.

"By all the power I hold, and all the gods that ever were or will be, I shall see to it that the claws of the Dragon rake deep for this, Vortigern!"

APRIL 451

NINETEEN

T HEY WERE TRYING OUT SOME OF UTHR'S BEST WINE, STORED FOR SPECIAL occasions. What could be more special than an unexpected visit to the estate in Less Britain by Cunedda of Gwynedd! Besides, as Arthur pointed out, breaking the wax seal on an amphora of Vintage Greek, it would not keep forever.

They drank companionably, the young man and the elder, admiring the red glow of a sinking sun and exchanging talk of brave men and braver deeds. A cool, pleasant evening for early April. Spring had come early, bringing mild nights and sunny days, a promise of a fair summer. Cunedda had risked the sea voyage, for he had need to talk with Arthur, the kind of conversation that could not be well written on wax tablet or scrolled parchment, or conveyed by messenger. This was for him alone to say, but now that he was here the saying was not going to be so easy.

Arthur cut himself a chunk of soft goat cheese and said, almost flippantly, "So what brings the lord of Gwynedd to my mother's estate?" He lifted his goblet, a rare, fine glass of the palest green, and saluted his companion. "This wine is the best, but it does not warrant such a hazardous journey."

Cunedda loosed a brief smile. "Nor such a short stay. I remain but the one night; raiders are hovering off Gwynedd's shores. My sons are capable, but I do not like to leave her too long."

Arthur chuckled. "You make your land sound like a wayward mistress!"

Cunedda gave another small smile. Arthur would find out for himself one day, the gods willing. Held land was more than a mistress—was whore, wife, daughter, mother, all of those, with all their tempers and loves and smiles and sorrows.

Arthur's eyes had a question, one eye half closed, the other eyebrow raised. "Why have you come?"

Clearing his throat—this would not be well met—Cunedda placed the tips of his fingers together. "I will be open with you, lad, no shuffling around the arena exchanging feints."

Arthur nodded.

"I suggest, Arthur, you offer your sword to Vortigern."

A moment's silence—nothing moving, no sound, no breath—then the fine glass flew from the table shattering into tiny pieces as it hit the floor. Arthur's chair toppled backwards as he exploded to his feet in a torrent of abusive language, some words new even to Cunedda's ears.

Waiting for the violent diatribe to subside Cunedda sat patiently; the reaction had not been unexpected. Calmly he continued, "Come summer you will be seven and ten years of age, a man grown, the son of a war lord. Yet you sit here, idling away your time picking grapes and pressing wine!"

Arthur had been about to add further disparaging remarks, but Cunedda slammed the flat of his hand on the table, his expression fierce. "What do you intend, boy? To be a vine grower or a soldier?" Allowing him no time to reply, he went on, "You need experience of war, of leading men. How are you to gain it here?"

His pride stung, Arthur countered, "I serve with the local militia. A month back we sent scurrying a party of Saex who were attempting to set up a settlement to the south!"

Cunedda sipped his wine. "Sit down. Let us talk of men's business like men."

Glowering, Arthur sat.

"I have heard you train hard with the militia, that you do well."

Gruff. "You have sharp ears then."

"Would you rather I left you to rot?" The rebuke was sharp, to the point. Cunedda refilled his glass, handed it to Arthur, who took it and drank. With sympathy, the lord of Gwynedd took a breath and continued. "Where will you gain experience of war if not in Britain with Vortigern's British men?"

Arthur stared into the fading red glow in the western sky, his lips pouting. Where, indeed?

"Without experience, Arthur, men will laugh when you come to claim what is yours. Aside," Cunedda spread a hand, "if we do not soon drive out these Saex, there will be nothing left for you to claim."

Arthur answered, "I thought of approaching the King of Gaul, he and Uthr were friends. I have met with his son several times, we are of similar age," but he spoke with only half a heart. He did not, in all truth, really wish to fight to save some other king's land. Though he was reluctant to admit it, at least fighting for Vortigern would, indirectly, mean fighting for himself.

Reading Arthur accurately Cunedda offered, "Working for your own ends would give you more of an advantage."

The hot reply was defiant, anger and resentment rising again. "Not if I need bow before Vortigern!"

"You do not have to bow before him." Cunedda could be so damned persuasive, particularly when he spoke calmly, placidly, somehow making Arthur's raging seem like childish temper.

"Gather those men who once followed your father, and their sons, all who would follow the Dragon." Cunedda was leaning forward, eager, excited. "Offer their swords, under yours, to Vortigern. Gain time. Get to know the ways of war, and the hills and valleys of Britain; the marshes, the coast. The people. Let them get to know you." His smile for future planning crinkled to his eyes. "Befriend the tyrant, tell him the disagreement was between him and the father you did not know. Make him believe you are content with holding these estates, you want nothing more. Offer what you can, bribe where you can. Sit, listen, watch, and learn."

Petulant, reluctant to acknowledge Cunedda might be right, Arthur rasped, "And what if Vortigern will not accept me and takes a dagger to my back at the first opportunity?" He slammed his fist on the table. "Damn it, I am the Pendragon! He will not trust one of that title for a single handspan!"

"Of course he will not—no more than he trusts me—yet we get along reasonably well, if warily." Draining his goblet, Cunedda laid his hand on Arthur's arm. "Vortigern will take you and, providing you step carefully, he will tolerate you."

"Why? Tell me that. Why will he?" Arthur slumped back in his chair, arms folded, bottom lip thrust out. Stupid idea. Might as well fall on his own sword and make an end of it rather than offer himself to that murdering bastard.

"Why? Because Vortigern would prefer to keep you where he can see you. Where he can be certain you are not raising an army against him. Also, he's a desperate man. He has few British officers with a talent for soldiering. Even he has no wish to turn his entire army over to the Saxons!"

"Are you listening to yourself, Cunedda? You seriously expect me to fight under that—that toad who murdered my father!"

"Aye."

There was no point in saying anything further, for that was precisely what Cunedda was expecting. They argued some more, Arthur offering protests, Cunedda countering with adequate answers. Both knew Cunedda spoke sense, that Arthur had no choice. He needed experience, he needed to learn, and neither would come his way here in Less Britain.

"I would willingly have you with me, lad," Cunedda sighed, as a final thrust, "but were you to join with me I'd have more Saex in my mountains than there are blades of grass. Vortigern would never permit it."

Mid-afternoon the next day, a trading ship lifted her oars and glided down-river, making for the estuary. Aboard her, Cunedda, heading home, and by the turn of the month another ship carried Arthur, his cousin and foster brother Cei, and sixty seasoned swordsmen to Britain and mercenary service under the tyrant King Vortigern.

APRIL 453

TWENTY

COUNCILLORS DRIFTED FROM THE DILAPIDATED BASILICA OF LONDINIUM IN knots of twos and threes; huddled groups talking softly to one another, exchanging muted grievances, mostly against the King.

Arthur sighed exaggeratedly and tipped his stool back on its rear legs. "There's only one thing I dread more than a full meeting of Council."

Seated beside him, arms folded on the table, Cei looked with lazy enquiry at his foster brother and cousin, asked, "And what might that be?"

Arthur stood, scraping the stool over the cracked flooring. He stretched cramped muscles, reaching his arms up towards the equally cracked ceiling and yawned. "The next meeting!" He grinned and thumped his friend between the shoulder blades. "What a damned waste of time! There are days when I regret my decision to throw my soul in with Vortigern." He walked a few paces, flung his arm in the direction of the open door, declared with passion, "We ought to be out there, Cei, fighting these sea wolves who come to steal our cattle and land, not sitting here muttering about it!"

Cei nodded agreement, opened his mouth to reply, found another voice cut him short.

"Aye, but try telling our beloved King!"

Arthur spun round with a yelp of delight and clasped the newcomer's hand in greeting, jerking the arm up and down as if it were some rusted old water pump.

"Cunedda! You have come!" He motioned a thumb over his shoulder. "You have just missed the first pointless discussion."

Cunedda's hands were clasping Arthur's arms in firm greeting. "If only I had ridden faster!" They all three laughed at his open sarcasm.

"The Saex sit easy on their backsides and wait for us to talk ourselves into old age and beyond," said Cei sardonically, draining his ale tankard and setting it down on the table.

"All possibilities need exploring before action is committed." Cunedda so perfectly mimicked Vortigern's much-uttered phrase, even to the slight slurring of the Latin, a legacy of a sword wound to his left jaw.

"Meaning," Arthur translated through the ensuing laughter, "let us not rush into anything that's likely to cost over much from my treasury!" He gripped the older man's hand tighter. "Ah, Cunedda, it's good to see you!" His smile broadened. "I was not keen on persuading this Council into seeing sense on my own!"

"'Tis as good to see you again, boy." Placing his hand on Arthur's shoulder, Cunedda studied the young man before him. "You are taller than your father, though much like him." He approved of what he saw. A confident young man with an alert eagerness and self-assurance. Different colouring from Uthr, who had had quite black hair, Arthur's being more brown with a slight curl, but the same family trait of a long, prominent nose and that same piercing eye.

A leader of men, Uthr, superb in a fight but never one for patience or tact, too often a raging bull. At eighteen, it was too early to tell whether the same leadership qualities were strong in this lad. Cunedda frowned, his brows creasing into a deeper, more penetrating search of Arthur's animated face. Something simmered beneath the surface of those brown eyes beaming back at him, something ready to spill out when the heat was raised. This Pendragon possessed a more profound shrewdness than Uthr ever had, a sparkle that would rise to brilliance with the catch of sunlight.

Cunedda was reminded of an uncut diamond he had once seen. A thing of great value, he had been told, though for his life he could not understand why. A rough-hewn, rather dull, almost ugly object. And then the same stone after the jewelsmith had been at it; a gem so exquisite, so perfect, there were no words to describe the beauty that flashed and blazed within its cut and polished facets. Arthur reminded him of that diamond: rough-edged, unpolished, but beneath those disguising layers, ah, beneath!

Suddenly remembering his manners, Arthur indicated Cei, jolting Cunedda from his scrutiny. "You remember Cei, eldest son of Ectha my uncle and foster father? He is a second right arm to me."

"We met briefly when I visited Less Britain."

"Everything about it was brief, as I recall," Arthur growled. A pause, recollections of that unexpected visit. And the consequences.

"So," Cunedda said, "Vortigern has not put a dagger in your back? He accepted you, as I predicted he would."

Arthur's lip and nose wrinkled in distaste. "Na, no dagger. We have, shall we say, an uneasy understanding." He laughed suddenly. "You leave my back alone and I'll leave yours alone!"

As the slight moment of tension slipped past, Cunedda nodded and grasped Cei's hand, pleased to meet the young man again. "I have heard tell of your exploits with Arthur, they reach even as far as my distant mountains of Gwynedd!"

Cei's laugh was a deep-throated chuckle of wry amusement. "The blame for those lay firmly with Arthur; he's the planner, I merely follow orders! Though one or two of his schemes have turned out well."

Arthur interrupted with a snort of indignation. "Well? They are brilliant, man!"

Cei raised his eyebrows, unabashed. "All? What about last September— Glas Dhue?"

Rubbing his clean-shaven chin, Arthur grimaced then casually placed an arm around Cunedda's shoulders, steering the older man aside. "How's your brood? Are your sons with you?"

Cunedda roared his delight. "No need to turn the subject! I heard of Glas Dhue also! A brilliant—what—failure?"

Arthur scowled, then smiled good humouredly, appreciating the jest at his expense. "Had it not been for that sudden deluge turning firm ground into marsh, we would have sent fifty Saex into oblivion."

Understanding the frustrations of an unexpected change in the weather, Cunedda nodded. "You cannot win all the time, lad; learn by your mistakes, take defeat positively. Your father had his share of failure," he added sombrely, then smiled swiftly. It was well to turn the subject on occasion. "Three of my offspring are with me." He glanced at the few remaining men and said softly, "There's much to talk upon, in private." He glanced meaningfully at those last men who were noting with interest this friendly exchange between Lion and Dragon.

Few had forgotten where Gwynedd's loyalty lay.

Louder, for the benefit of curious ears, Cunedda remarked, "We attend Vortigern's welcoming entertainment this evening. Will you join me, Arthur? Cei also, of course."

Thanking him for the invitation, Cei made his apologies, pleading an alternative engagement.

Arthur leered. "With that well-endowed widow, no doubt?" he slapped Cei's shoulder. "Vortigern's feasting would be more rewarding!"

Countering swiftly, Cei retorted, "The King cannot offer such large," made a suggestive motion with his hands, "ripe fruit!"

Laughing together, the three men pushed their way through the crowded exit out into the open forum, where they took their leave, followed by more than a few speculative glances.

Vortigern's palace had seen better days when it had been the residence of the Roman Governor of Britain. Years of neglect had traded its opulence for cracked walls and peeling plaster. Rugs and spread furs hid fragmenting mosaic floors; the hypocaust heating was blocked and useless. Still, who noticed crumbling walls and the occasional hole in the ceiling when good wine flowed and excellent food was served?

They were all there, Vortigern and his kin: his sons by his first wife; the second wife, Rowena, with her father, Hengest the Saxon, and his son; the daughter born to Rowena and Vortigern, the Princess Winifred. The King's guests were the Elders and leaders of the governing territories of Britain who made up the Grand Council, some of whom had brought their wives and families, sons, brothers and uncles, as well as officers of the King's army and bodyguard, British and Saxon. A hotch-potch of nobility and rough chieftains, intent on clawing their way from tribal landholding to the prospect of eventual petty kingship.

Arthur ate with enthusiasm: army food was nothing special, the slop served in Londinium taverns as bad, and it was not often Vortigern opened his purse to pay for an extravagance such as this!

"How is your mother?" Enniaun asked politely, finishing the last of a fine roast fowl.

"I have no idea." Arthur selected more meat and bit into it hungrily.

"You do not keep contact with her then?"

With mouth full Arthur replied, "To what end? We never liked each other. My father's death and my coming to manhood did not alter that."

Etern, a man grown now with a moustache as red as his father's, said with a hint of reproach, "She is your mother."

His voice indifferent, Arthur answered, "Childbearing does not make a woman a mother."

"But surely, after all these years, now you are acknowledged as…"

Arthur cut off Etern's persistent questions quite philosophically. "In childhood I meant nothing to Lady Ygrainne, I mean nothing to her now." His plate empty, he chose a meat-filled pastry shaped in the form of a sucking pig. As a boy his life had been endorsed by periods of intense misery—the shame at being labelled bastard, the whisperings of speculation. And Morgause. Release came through Uthr's death. Arthur had understood his father's need to stay silent; Ygrainne's too, but not her coolness. It was not within him to forgive her for abandoning him to Morgause.

"You blame me for my father's death, don't you?" Arthur had asked Ygrainne before he left to serve in Vortigern's army. She had answered quite frankly: *"It was because of you I lost him."*

He had assumed she meant Uthr's death; only much later did he realise she meant Uthr's turning to Morgause.

Pulling at his moustache, Cunedda said thoughtfully, "She and your father were very much in love when Uthr took her from Gorlois."

Arthur gave a bark of scornful laughter, scattering golden pastry crumbs from his lips. "Nonsense! He wanted her wealth and her dead father's estate. Fighting Gorlois was an excuse to hit at Vortigern, fanning the flames of a war that was already brewing. Uthr would have done anything to further his bid for the kingdom. As would I." Another trait inherited from his father, cynicism.

Servants were bringing in the next course, the guests applauding the spectacular arrangements of boar and hare and swan, borne high on silver platters so huge they needed two men to carry them.

When eating had again commenced, Enniaun asked the Pendragon, his voice lowered, "And how is service with our King?"

The reply was succinct. "Oh, wonderful! He's a most uninspiring man."

Etern guffawed. "That must keep alive a desire to knock his head from his shoulders!" They laughed, then sobered on remembering their whereabouts.

"Vortigern treats you well, I hear, almost like one of his own brood?" Enniaun wiped boar meat juice from his dish with a hunk of wheat bread and nodded at Vortigern's two sullen sons seated at the high table. It was noticeable that they both ignored their father, their manner towards his Saxon wife verging on rudeness.

"Oh aye." Arthur stabbed at a portion of hare, busied himself with picking the meat from the bone, kept his expression guarded. "We fight and snarl at each other like whelps over a tossed bone."

Flicking a finger in Hengest's direction, Etern commented, "I'm not impressed by his choice of company."

Arthur scowled towards the high table, at the huge Saxon, a great bull-muscled man with arms like oak trees, thighs as sturdy as a ship's mast, and privy tackle, it was said, as penetrating as a well shot javelin. Unfortunately the Princess Winifred noticed his expression—and he looked hastily away. Like her mother, that one, a second arrogant and self-opinionated sow. Pretty, though, as her mother had once been, with flaxen hair and fair skin. But a temper like a rutting bear. He chewed at his meat, throwing a quick smile at the young woman sitting beside the princess. Her face came alive at that smile, eyes and mouth smiling back.

Arthur had come late to the banquet, hurrying and breathless, delayed by the need to tend an injury to his favourite horse. Entering as the guests were summoned to table, he had stood stunned at the sight of Gwenhwyfar waiting with her father and two brothers. He had not expected her to be with Cunedda, was unprepared to see her, a woman grown and so different from the girl he remembered. She had been as flustered as himself, her cheeks flushing pink as he kissed her hand; then their rather awkward embrace, as if greeting a stranger. A pity she was seated as Vortigern's guest, companion to the royal piglet, Winifred. He dare not glance often in her direction for fear of shifting this persistent throb beneath his bracae to something more noticeable on his face. Why? With other women he made much of his desire, had discovered they found the attention most flattering. With Gwenhwyfar, such crudity seemed obscene. She was beautiful and pure, a maiden to be respected, treated with honour. But by the Blood of the Bull, how he wanted to leap up from this table, cross the room in three strides, and kiss her! Not a polite kiss of greeting either, but a slow, lingering kiss that would last for days and take all breath from the world!

Enniaun was remarking, "Vortigern seems well at ease among those who wear a flaxen mane and carry a Saex sword."

"Jesu's love," Etern spat beneath his breath, "when will we be rid of him and these pox-ridden Saex! It is time you became king, Arthur!"

Taking a while to drain his goblet, Arthur wiped his mouth and shifted to a more comfortable position. The food might be good, but these benches were damned hard on the backside! "I am in the King's service, Etern, I command men of his cavalry. Such talk could soon see me kicking on the wrong end of a rope."

About to say more, Etern found Cunedda's stern gaze on him. *Not here, boy, not now.*

"Aside," Arthur said, setting his goblet down carefully. "Vortimer's the eldest son. When Vortigern dies, he takes up the royal torque, not I."

"Pig-swill!"

Laughing to himself, Arthur thought of his earlier analogies: Rowena the sow, Winifred the plump little piglet. Aye, pig-swill. Patiently, he waved aside Etern's derision. "I support Vortimer, he's as much against the King as are we. We cannot afford to fight among ourselves; if we do, we may as well stand back and invite Hengest in. He waits for a squabble in the front gate so he may creep in at the back." With a leisurely shrug, "Vortigern cannot live forever. Things will change when his eldest son comes to power."

"True enough," replied Enniaun, emphasising his point by flapping his eating dagger, "but Vortimer himself is no spring cockerel—he could journey to the next world before his father."

"Or," added Etern, "Vortigern's wife could yet bear a son."

They glanced furtively at Rowena, again heavy with child. A beautiful woman once but the years of constant pregnancies that ended in miscarriage or stillbirth had not been kind. None save her own people and the King much liked her.

A brooding silence descended on Cunedda's table, their individual thoughts broken by Etern. "Even if she did, who would want to follow a half Saex brat?"

His brother laughed, the humour cut short by Arthur's unexpectedly curt response. "Hengest and the Saex would."

Servants cleared away used dishes, removing uneaten food. Conversation turned to lighter matters. Several times Cunedda noticed Arthur looking at his daughter. Vortigern had expressed the wish to have Gwenhwyfar sit at table with his family—how could Cunedda refuse? He gulped a mouthful of strong wine, gestured to a slave to pour more. How did a lord refuse Vortigern the King without risking the loss of land and people?

Cunedda had known Uthr well, had run with him as a cub, fought with him, pursued women with him. Now he recognised that same look in his son's eyes, knew Arthur took after his father in more than a love of soldiering and a similarity of features. Women seemed drawn to a Pendragon as water was drawn downhill. How pleased he had been those summers past to discover his Gwenhwyfar had formed a friendship with Arthur—Gods, how pleased! He remembered how Uthr had first met with Ygrainne, then wed to another, and had wanted her. "*Nonsense*," Arthur had said when he had spoken of Uthr's love for her, but Uthr had started a war because of Ygrainne. The aim was to claim the kingship, but it started because of his desire for Ygrainne.

Ah, Uthr had loved Ygrainne, always, Ygrainne, and only Ygrainne. The others, all the others, had only fulfilled a passing need. Another thought, that again made Cunedda drain his wine. What if Vortigern were also to read Arthur's glances towards the girl? He should not have brought her to Londinium! He rolled his goblet between his hands, staring into the empty cup. A burst of laughter from the assembled company caused him to look up. How does a snared lord ignore a summons from the King?

Do not harbour dreams for my daughter, Arthur, Cunedda thought with anguish. *She cannot be yours.*

It was late when Vortigern at last withdrew. Rowena had retired earlier, taking the ladies with her. Reluctantly, Gwenhwyfar had left the banqueting hall with them, casting a pleading look at her father, who had responded with a gesture of helplessness. She had endured the princess's insults and snide remarks all evening, had swallowed her pride and her temper though her palm itched to slap the horrid girl's fat cheeks. They were almost the same age, no more than half a year between them, but that was their only similarity.

"*Do you ride?*" the princess had enquired.

"Aye," Gwenhwyfar had replied, to which Winifred had answered scornfully, "*Mother says horse riding bows your legs. I will only travel by litter.*" Such was the conversation for most of the evening.

To her relief, Gwenhwyfar discovered she was not obliged to accompany the ladies to the Queen's rooms, but was free to return to her own quarters, where poor Ceridwen lay abed with a feverish headache. She entered the semi-darkened room quietly, whirled a few joyful paces, and danced the rest of the way from door to bed.

Ceridwen sat up, her eyes bleary. The journey from Gwynedd had been exhausting—mentally, because of the excitement, as well as physically.

"You sound happy. The banquet was good then?"

Gwenhwyfar did a few more twirls before plonking herself on Ceridwen's bed. The goose feather mattress bounced up and down. "It was awful! The food was far too rich and I had to sit next to the Princess, a spoilt madam if ever I met one!"

Ceridwen frowned. Her head ached, her stomach still churned; had she missed something here? "May I ask then," she said timorously, "why you are so gay?" She twitched Gwenhwyfar's neat hair. "You have met someone! A lad." She sat up eagerly. "Who? What's he like?"

Gwenhwyfar was off the bed, hugging herself as she skipped away across the room, deliberately teasing. When the fluttering excitement became too much she ran back to Ceridwen and hugged her. "Arthur's here! Arthur the Pendragon. I assumed he would be on campaign or something, but no, he's here!" She lay back across the bed, arms flung wide, gazing up at the cracks on the ceiling. "Oh, Ceridwen, he has grown so tall, so…" she released her breath in a whoosh, "so wonderful!"

Ceridwen said nothing, snuggled into the warmth of her bed. It was only April, quite chilly at night, and this great echoing palace seemed rather musty and damp.

"Oh," she said, feigning indifference, "you're in love. I thought something exciting had happened."

Despite the girl's headache, Gwenhwyfar thumped her with a pillow.

Winifred lingered before seeking her bed. She detested her father's banquets— boring occasions for boring old men with boring conversations. She paused, her comb halfway down the tress of her unbound hair. She combed her own hair; the slaves were too clumsy, they pulled. One or two presentable young men this evening, but country clods, sons of over-ambitious petty lords. She would not waste time with such dismal prospects.

Winifred sighed, set the comb down, walked aimlessly towards the bed. Arthur, now, he was no dung-shoveller; he was the Pendragon, wealthy, in command of her father's cavalry. She twitched back the bed furs, slid beneath the smooth linen of the sheets. He was not exactly the most handsome young man, though, was he?

Snuffing out the lamp beside the bed, Winifred settled herself to sleep, lying with her arms crooked behind her head, thinking. Arthur Pendragon was the most presumptuous, impertinent, discourteous lout in all her father's army. She had paid him no heed before this night—but it interested her, this interaction between him and that rustic bred girl from wherever it was.

And there was nothing Winifred liked better than destroying a lovers' intrigue.

TWENTY-ONE

C UNEDDA SELECTED AN OLIVE AND STUDIED IT FOR A MOMENT, WONDERING for how much longer such succulent fruits would be obtainable. Leather, glass, metal, cloth, everything of quality was disappearing, becoming more difficult to get hold of. Cheap stuff—now that was readily available, shoddy goods, badly made, poorly crafted—ah, it was all going, gathering speed, rumbling away downhill.

This chamber, a fair sized room, overlooked the palace gardens, attractive in the moonlight but revealed by day to be a mess of cracked paths, weed-choked flower beds, and straggling, unkempt shrubs. Cunedda stood by a table, his two sons sprawling on couches, draped like discarded clothing.

"Your inspired use of cavalry, Arthur," he said, moving to the nearest couch and cuffing Etern's boots from the cushions before sitting down, "is earning you quite a reputation."

Arthur, perched on the edge of a stool, picked with the tip of his dagger at a morsel of meat caught between his teeth. "Most of my boyhood was spent with a good friend, an old soldier whose farm borders the estate. Gaius served in a Roman cavalry unit. I learned much from him." Warming to his subject, he expatiated. "I have tried to develop more than the basic tactics and skills within the limits of my own command." He frowned, busy with placing the dagger back in its sheath. "But in all skirmishes not under my sole command we are held back. My fine mounted men are used for reconnaissance or harrying the enemy when he's already in flight!" Contemptuously he sliced the air with his outstretched hand. "You, Sir," he said, looking straight at Cunedda, "use your horses with more intelligence, as the tribal British have always done."

"Indeed, some of Rome's best cavalrymen were British, and our ponies crossed with the better of Rome's imported mounts have proved more than their worth as war mounts." Cunedda sighed, nudged Etern further along the couch, stretched himself comfortably. He had drunk too much wine at that banquet; now it was swilling around in his belly with an over-indulgence of food, and the day's ride atop that. By the Gods, but he was tired. "Vortigern, like so many others, prefers infantry. Horses cost more to keep."

Arthur waved the Lion's words aside. "I know all that." His smile was a lop-sided grin, his right eye half shut and left eyebrow cocked, giving him a penetrating, self-assured expression that seemed to bore into Cunedda. "None the less, you have continued breeding good horses, Cunedda. You know there's more to using a horse than just placing your arse on its back to get from alpha to beta."

Cunedda swallowed down a belch and regarded the lad, undaunted by that off-putting gaze. Cautiously, "A cavalryman knows more than how to lullump along clutching at mane and saddle, aye."

"A good cavalryman is a *horseman*. Men under my command are all horse-men. They, Vortigern's mules," he jabbed a finger towards the window, "grunt and mumble, refusing to listen to any suggestions I attempt to put forward. The high ranking commanders of the army—I include Vortigern's sons here—argue that we have fought well enough with infantry for centuries so why change now?" He had his dagger out again, was twirling it between his fingers. "Fah! They see no further than day's end!"

Containing his amusement, Cunedda could almost see his old friend Uthr sitting before him, bellowing some tirade against whatever near-sighted stupidity had enraged him on this occasion.

Arthur was still talking. "Vortigern originally hired Hengest and his rabble because we do not have the men to furnish an effective army of infantry—Mithras, Rome could call on the entire Empire to swell ranks, but what have we? One stagnating little island, surrounded by water that every day brings yet another keel-load of Saex! How can we ever match the skill of Rome? Not with men on foot, for sure." Eagerly he swept on, Enniaun and Etern giving nods or murmurs of agreement. "Look at the success of Attila's Huns, who fight, eat, sleep—even copulate, so I've heard tell—on horseback."

Enniaun said sharply, "You sound as though you admire that Scourge of God!"

"As a commander and horseman, aye, I do."

Etern almost shared Arthur's view. "Attila was not infallible, though. Gaul defeated his dunghill mob."

"Not so," Arthur replied, leaning forward to rest his elbows on his knees. "Attila was *halted*." He stressed the word, "Halted, not defeated. He turned round and went for Rome itself instead." He cupped his chin thoughtfully in his hand.

"I wonder if our problems would have been less had he not died so prematurely—if he had continued into Gaul, and beyond."

Faces turned to look at him in astonishment. Arthur grinned, confident of his argument. "Would so many Saex have been eager to leave their kindred with Attila's sword coming daily closer to their throats?"

"On the dexter side," Enniaun said drily, "happen the Saex took to their keels because of Attila!"

"I heard," Etern said, a well padded cushion held close against his chest as if it were a companionable woman, "that Attila's remains were buried with three coffins containing all his wealth. One of gold, one of silver, one of iron."

"Aye," Arthur agreed, with a wistful sigh of slight envy, "I heard the same. His funeral songs were sung by squadrons of his men riding round and around his body, which lay beneath a silk-draped pavilion." He whistled between his teeth. "That must have been a sight worth the watching."

They fell silent for a while, lost in their own thoughts. Etern stood up and fetched more wine. He took the jug round, pouring for his brother and Arthur. "Think you this suggestion of Council to try another appeal for help to Gaul will be of use to us? Da says it will not."

"I am in agreement with him." Arthur wrinkled his upper lip. "Attila's gone, but his hordes remain, and despite my admiration for his horsemanship, Enniaun, I am afeared of what his rabble almost succeeded in doing! Na, Gaul has too many of her own problems. We are abandoned to our fate. 'Tis a pity that some of these fusty Councillors cannot see Rome has gone from Britain for ever and will not be returning, not now." He snorted, shaking his head. These older men were so blind—aye, and not only the older men! Uthr's own youngest brother, Emrys, claimed Rome would govern Britain again, and the Emperor would come swinging up the road from Dubris demanding to know what fool had let the country fall into such decay. "If we do not soon stop all this sitting around a council chamber endlessly talking instead of doing, there will be nothing worth coming back to anyway!"

Cunedda had been listening through the drowsy fug of wine to the exchange of talk. He said cautiously, "They are men, Arthur, who cannot perceive life outside the dominance of Rome. Others—influential, wealthy men—have tasted freedom from Imperial taxation and would not want a return of those binding restrictions.

Which is why Vortigern maintains such strong support. I do not want Rome, but then, I do not want Vortigern as an alternative. In my view we have exchanged one tyranny for another."

Enniaun sipped his wine. This was fine stuff, Vortigern's best. "Let them write their appeal. They may be right: when the unrest settles the Legions might be back. Although," he raised his goblet towards Arthur in salute, "I agree with you, lad."

"If we got ourselves organised there would be no need to seek help!" Arthur bounced to his feet, fists waving. "We can do it alone, drive out the Saex and make peace between neighbouring tribes!" Arthur slammed the arm of a couch with his fist. Damn it, he knew he was right, but how to make others see?

Cunedda sipped his wine reflectively. It was time for bed, but this talk was becoming interesting. He let a smile touch his mouth.

Seeing it, Arthur said, not without bitterness, "You too laugh at me then?"

"On the contrary. Continue."

For a moment Arthur was doubtful. His belly was full of men sniggering behind his back—and to his face. He would not have his father's friend also making mockery of his ideas. But then, those others were as useless as cracked pots; Cunedda was different, a man of wisdom and sense, a man who knew how it felt to be backed into a corner with only a broken sword for defence. He lifted a foot onto a stool and rested his arm across his thigh.

"I believe a strong, well-drilled cavalry force could tip the balance of survival in our favour." Now he had started, Arthur became eager to share his hopes, his plans. "Attila usually fought with three wings, left, right and centre, crashing forward at a gallop." He moved his hand ahead of him, but was interrupted by Enniaun.

"How many do you mean by strong?"

"Three alae comprising five hundred men each. Small enough to move fast and efficient. Large enough to be effective."

Enniaun half smiled. "Speaking kindly, lad, it is no surprise men laugh! That may not sound so many until you add on remounts and shield bearers and…"

Undeterred, Arthur would not allow him to finish. He had heard the arguments too many times before. "Disciplined cavalry, under able commanders, moving fast to where they are needed, when needed. Used not as a reserve or for scouting or carrying packs and men to battle, but as a *main, elite* force. Coming down on the enemy from the centre and the wings together."

"No infantry?"

"Aye, infantry and archers, where needed, local militia who know the land." As he talked, Arthur had straightened, setting his goblet down on a table to move freely about the room, gesturing with his arms. "Normally it is the cavalry

who back the foot. With my way of thinking I would reverse it. Cavalry swinging in here, militia with bows and javelins here." Carried away, his arm sent a
potted plant crashing to the floor.

Cunedda bit his lip, strangling a roar of laughter. He stood, retrieved the broken top half of the stem, looked at it with grave concern. "Aye, well, I imagine
the thing needed pruning." He managed to stammer the words before the effort
of restraint evaded him and he doubled up in laughter.

Enniaun, laughing also, bent to retrieve the bottom half. "Curb your enthusiasm, Arthur," he grinned, "else we will be answerable to Vortigern for wrecking
his apartment!"

Red-faced, stammering apologies, Arthur found his stool and sat down.

The laughter died, Cunedda dozed as lighter conversation gradually drifted
to more mundane matters. Wine was poured and drunk as the young men exchanged notes on the virtues of women.

Cunedda sat quiet, drifting from sleep to thought and back to sleep. They
needed time, a thing they never had! Time for Arthur to mature. Time for
the elders and the British army to realise the great potential of this young
Pendragon. Talk diminished momentarily, and Cunedda jerking awake asked, as
if an hour had not elapsed, "This use of cavalry, Arthur. Is it all formed of your
own ideas?"

"A compilation of my veteran friend, Attila's history, and what I have read—
the works of both Arrian and Xenophon on horsemanship are most informa-
tive." Arthur shrugged. How to put the vivid images of his dreams into words?
To face an enemy with a disciplined and united cavalry. An almighty, unstoppable force pounding down, forward... ah! "I have discussed the thing with
Cei; between us we have thrashed out the problems." He paused and said with
an impudent grin, "Or rather, I have put the ideas and Cei has pointed out
the pitfalls."

Pulling at his moustache, Cunedda asked, "And what conclusions, Pendragon,
have you reached regarding mounts for this wondrous cavalry? Until men like
my father's father began cross-breeding fine horses, Rome imported its stock
from Arabia. We do not have the ships or the funds to do that." He deliberately
cultivated a blank expression, talked in a flat tone. As if he could not guess
the answer!

Arthur beamed. "Your best horses are descended from those same desert bred
Roman imports. Strong, swift, surefooted, and stout-hearted warriors' mounts that
do well, even on poor pasturing and in a bad winter." Arthur's grin broadened,

showing straight, even teeth, white against his wind tanned skin. "I would come to Gwynedd." He lifted his hands. "Where else?"

Cunedda maintained his impassive expression; the muzziness of drink had cleared, that short sleep reviving his flagging energy. He barked, "You are talking thousands of horses, boy! Remounts, as my son said, and remounts and remounts. Horses die, horses fall sick. Mares need the seasons to breed, to drop and suckle their foals."

The Pendragon's buoyant confidence wavered. He chewed the corner of his bottom lip. Then, softly, "I know." He felt deflated, beaten. What nonsense was this? These men who would not listen were commanders, seasoned warriors, experienced with shield and sword, veterans of battle. They would not listen because he talked nonsense, a boy's prattling.

Cunedda took his time to drink a last cup of wine. When it was emptied he placed the goblet carefully beside him on the table and folded his arms across his belly, that still felt full.

"Are you so easily defeated then, boy?" he boomed, causing Arthur's dropping head to jolt upright, eyes wide, lips apart. "Your father stopped at nothing to gain what he wanted. Aye, he had to wait and wait again, but he never hung his head in defeat! Never. Even as that last sword slashed into his body he fought on, fought on his knees and kept fighting until the blood had all run from him!"

Angered at the unjustness of the taunt, Arthur thrust back with, "Na, he stopped at nothing to get his way! He wrecked my mother's life and my childhood. Because of his ambition you were forced to kneel before Vortigern in homage—twice. And for what, in the end? His death!"

Cunedda sucked in his breath, reeling at Arthur's attack—which struck all the harder, for he spoke the right of it. He pointed a finger, the golden lion's head of his ring seeming to leap at Arthur. "You do not ask the impossible. My great-grandsire ran four, happen five times the stock you need—the highlands were adequate then, of course. We were granted overlordship of the Votadini because of our horses." Cunedda shrugged, setting aside the pang of memory for those high hills and sweeping moors. He grinned, his face suddenly young. "I see no reason why Gwynedd could not do the same for you."

Arthur felt a sudden, soaring elation; he sprang to his feet and strode over to Cunedda, demanded, "My idea is not so stupid? This thing could succeed?"

Etern interrupted, coming also to his feet, caught up in the excitement. "We have good stallions and mares but it would take a while and a while to breed on such a scale again!"

Enniaun was behind him. "The initial outlay, then the supply for future years. It would only take one fight to go bad, and close on all the horses would need replacing."

"Na, my son, with careful management it can be done." Cunedda, pulling, as ever when thinking, at his moustache was making rapid calculations, taking into account the yearlings and foals to be dropped this year. Then there were the two- and three-year-old colts. Sales had been low for some while—the failing economy and unsettled times made men wary of paying out for extravagances. Who needed a fine-bred horse when oxen were more suited to pulling wagon or plough? "If I can be sure the Hibernian sea wolves have begun to understand my coastline is not for them, then I will be free to breed—and train—uninterrupted. Horses are not broken to carry a rider in battle overnight. It takes months, years."

He slapped his knee with the palm of his hand, and rose to embrace Arthur. "Aye, lad, I can breed you such a cavalry! Once you were up and leaping, you could raise additional stock elsewhere!" He offered his hand to Arthur, who took it warmly, returning the Lion's strong grip. Had it all been as easy as that?

Seating himself again, Cunedda leant back against the comfort of his couch and crossed his legs at the knee. "If, of course, you can come up with some equally brilliant method of payment. I do not breed horses for nought. I am wealthy, boy," Cunedda thrust his grim, determined face at Arthur, "and intend to stay so!"

There was always the sting in the tail. Uneasily, Arthur drew back a little, Etern and Enniaun on either side of him, waiting. He wiped a hand nervously over his mouth, found to his annoyance he was sweating. "I have thought of that also."

Cunedda waited.

The words were unexpectedly difficult to spit out. Why? It was a natural enough proposition, was it not? A common way of settling business. Words tumbled from Arthur's mouth like a stream at winter snow-melt.

"When I become king, I intend to raise taxes from my father's lands that shall then be returned to me, and from the fat merchants of the South. In the main it's they who demand the protection, so they must contribute towards the cost." That part was easy; this next made his tongue stick to the roof of his mouth. "Initially, I would accept the horses as a marriage portion with your daughter."

Cunedda's heart jolted, seemed to stop, then began pounding wildly. He felt sick, the surge of rich food and sweet wine rising almost into his mouth. Fool!

Damned blind, idiotic fool! Why had he not anticipated the obvious? What was he to say? How could he answer?

He studied the expectant faces of his two sons. They were nodding and smiling, agreeable to the idea, Etern even patting Arthur between the shoulders, especially pleased.

Cunedda stood. His bones ached; the tiredness had returned with a vengeance. He walked slowly across to the window, opened the casement, stood looking out at the river mist that lay over the dark gardens. Somewhere an owl screeched, its cry mournful in the darkness of early morning.

The pleased laughter behind him subsided. Why did he not answer?

He had known this day would come. These months, these years, he had known he must one day reveal the second part of that dirt-encrusted, enforced submission to Vortigern. He should have told of it then, but it had hurt too deeply. The buying of freedom by the binding of another. It hurt as much now, more, but it had to come out. He faced the room, turned to his sons and to Arthur.

"You cannot. Gwenhwyfar is already pledged."

TWENTY-TWO

STILLNESS. NO WORD, NO MURMUR. THEN, LIKE HOUNDS RELEASED FROM THE leash to the strong scent of a stag, the two brothers protested, shouting together, questioning, expressing outrage.

"Who to?"

"When?"

"Why?"

Nothing from Arthur. Oblivious to the surge of anger around him, he remained quiet, numbed, cheated.

The possibility had never occurred to him. She had never been far from his mind; always, since that night of childhood parting, he had assumed she would be his, one day. Gwenhwyfar had been special to him even then. She was his, damn it. *His!*

This evening, he had been so certain she still felt the same, that she had not changed. The long legs, awkward body, and freckled, usually grimed face were now just a memory. In their place, copper-gold hair, tamed though not altogether obedient, framing a perfect face, with gold-flecked emerald eyes that had flashed with pleasure whenever their gaze met across the banqueting hall. He wanted to hold her, take her for his own. To talk and laugh with her, share that special closeness they had found on the hills of Gwynedd. Arthur had always intended to come back for her. For her, not for the horses… that idea had come later.

His throat felt dry, choked. With a shaking hand, he reached for wine, hoped no one noticed the spillage as he lifted it to his lips. Mithras, he had been so sure of her! Had he been deceived then, by those innocent green eyes? She was devoted to another. Who? Whoever it was, he would kill him before he laid a finger to Gwenhwyfar!

"What means this, Father?" Etern demanded. His elder brother, with a calm that did not fool anyone, added in a low voice, "You said nought of this."

"Must I then discuss my plans with you?" snapped Cunedda. Enniaun was his favourite son, the eldest since Osmail had left Gwynedd. Cunedda had never raised his voice to him before.

"This must spoil your plans, Arthur," Etern remarked wryly. "I trust you were not considering marriage with our sister on the grounds of gaining Gwynedd's horses alone. Happen you would do better to wed one of our mares."

Cunedda remained by the window. Tears were brimming in his eyes as he held his hands, palm open in attempted apology, out to Arthur. "The horses are yours when you need them, lad. Payment can be negotiated later." He added, well intentioned, "There are plenty of wealthy young women ripe for the picking."

"But Da," Etern entreated, "Gwenhwyfar loves Arthur!" He looked pleadingly from his father to the Pendragon. "I know how much she loves you."

Arthur shrugged as if he did not much care. "Love?" he said off-handedly. "What has love to do with marriage? Happen you speak right, Cunedda." He grunted a single rasp of laughter. "I ought wed with Vortigern's daughter. Her dowry would buy ten times the number of horses I need." His jesting was flat and unconvincing. He walked to the table, refilled his goblet, and raised it to his lips to mask the stabbing hurt.

The one comfort, if it could be so described, this seemed not to be of Gwenhwyfar's doing.

Etern glared fiercely at his father. "Why have you not spoken of this? How could you betray my sister? Does she know of it?" He snorted. "I assume not, she would never have agreed!"

Cunedda rubbed his hands together; the palms were damp, sticky. "She does not know. I bargained hard for Vortigern's agreement that for the time being none save he and myself were to know. He was willing to have it so, a shared knowing between the two of us alone." Cunedda spat. "The King must leave his options open. For the sake of an alliance, there might have come a more urgent need to mate his nephew elsewhere."

An explosion of fury, like ill-set pottery within a kiln.

"What?"

"Vortigern's nephew? Melwas!"

"You agreed to wed my sister with that murdering braggart!"

"That slime-trailed, hag-spawned bastard!" Arthur hurled a couch over as he darted at Cunedda, taking hold of the older man by the loose folds of his tunic. "Melwas?" He hissed. "She's to marry Melwas? Are you serious? Are you the prime madman of all Britain?"

Etern was at his side, just as livid, made no movement to loose Arthur's clamped fingers. "Melwas is an evil, malignant snake!"

Enniaun, a pace behind, said, "He's hand in fist with Saex scum!"

Melwas, the second son of Vortigern's sister; brother to Gorlois, erstwhile husband of Uthr's wife Ygrainne. Melwas, captain of the King's personal guard. Melwas, who had lied and cheated and murdered his way to power, wealth, and a trusted position at the King's side. If the Pendragon had enemies, then Melwas was chief among them.

Softly, his words all the more menacing, Arthur said, "I shall never allow Gwenhwyfar to wed the likes of him."

When the time came for the telling, Cunedda had expected trouble from his sons, but he was unprepared for Arthur's passionate outburst.

Guilt at the enforced bargain heightening his reaction, he thrust Arthur's hand aside, then crossed to the table and upended it, scattering dishes and goblets and wine flagons on the floor. His shout of rage filled the room. "Do you think I want to see her wed to such a twisted creature?" His foot kicked at a wine jug, sending it spinning across the room, red wine spewing like spattered blood. "And you." He pointed at Arthur, his finger quivering. "Who are you to tell me what I can or cannot do with my daughter?"

He met the hostile gaze and held it, his breath coming fast, uneven, rasping in his throat. He groaned, passed a hand over his eyes, bent to right the table, replace the debris of tableware in order to occupy his hands, then said, "It is no easy thing to ride as lord to people who look to you for their safety and well being. Decisions must be made—decisions that are sometimes difficult but must, all the same, be taken."

His back to them, Cunedda the Lion Lord of Gwynedd buried his head in his hands, his shoulders hunched and shaking. His sons knew he was weeping. "What could I do when Vortigern demanded it?" he asked simply as he lifted his grey face. "What choice had I—Gwynedd or Gwenhwyfar?"

"You bargained our sister for land!" Etern cried. "What kind of greed is this!"

Cunedda aimed a stinging blow at his youngest son's cheek. He held the palm before his own eyes, staring at the redness, shocked that he could strike so easily. "See how Vortigern sets a son against his father." He let his hands drop useless to his side. "Defeat carries a price, son. For Uthr it was death. For us, it would have been the end of Gwynedd. Nor our death, not mine or yours, but Gwynedd's—her women, her children, her cattle, her crops. He gave me the choice, you see.

Gwenhwyfar for Melwas or Gwynedd for Hengest and his Saex, to do with as they will. Is it greed, Etern, to sacrifice one for the many?" Eyes pleading for understanding he added, "I could not lose my land. Not a second time."

Silence. What was there to say?

Etern tried one last protest. "We are strong. Stronger than when we were at Dun Pelidr. We have friends, many warriors on our side. How could he take our land and give it to the Saex? He could not, not now." He faltered. "Could he?"

Cunedda placed his two hands on Etern's shoulders and drew the lad to him in a tight embrace. "He did before, when he sent the Saex to destroy me. They did their job well. But most of them left after the burning and the butchering, left the north to its ghosts. With Gwynedd, it would be a death within life, for they would remain, make her their slave."

Arthur, shoulders slumped, offered his hand in submission and acceptance. Cunedda took it and patted the lad's arm.

Enniaun, subdued, with nothing more to say, retrieved goblets. Etern fetched fresh wine and passed the flagon round. They seated themselves, dwelt a while on the warm taste of rich red wine.

"I hoped, prayed, Vortigern would die—Gwenhwyfar even…" Cunedda broke off, appalled at his own thoughts. Na, not that! Anything to save his daughter from this monstrous betrothal, anything, but not that!

"Or Melwas." Etern spoke with calm menace. "Accidents can happen."

His father shook his head. "Think you that has not occurred to me? Na, I would not have murder on our hands; the revenge of the blood feud can soak through generations, can kill more innocents than a ravaging plague." He shook his head again. "For Melwas's death the King would take all my sons."

There was a longer silence, each thinking his own bitter thoughts.

At last Enniaun spoke. "My sister will not take kindly to this. Happen, when Melwas is let in on it, he may not want such a fire tempered woman." Empty laughter. It was a poor jest.

Enniaun added, "You ought have kept her safe in Gwynedd, Da, not brought her here."

Cunedda toyed with his goblet. "Do you think Vortigern needs my words at this Council? Does he truly need the few men we have brought, to fulfil our annual service within his army? I was ordered here for those things, and to bring Gwenhwyfar for Melwas."

Etern sneered, pointed an accusing finger. "So you jump to do as he bids!"

Dropping the goblet, Cunedda pressed his fingers to his temples. His head throbbed, hooves pounding his brain. Would they not understand? "Aye, I do as the King bids, boy. It took every trick and ounce of experience I had to retain Gwynedd after Uthr's wasted rebellion. I grovelled at Vortigern's feet, begged forgiveness, pleaded for Gwynedd to be spared. I have kept that humility and knelt cowed before his every word. To keep Gwynedd safe I will do anything, even give my daughter in marriage. As," he raised his head silently and looked eye to eye at Arthur, "as the Pendragon would do anything to gain his kingdom."

Arthur returned the challenge. He had swallowed his pride to come to Britain and serve under Vortigern, had bitten back anger, ignored whispered insults, followed idiotic orders, for the sake of waiting. Waiting for the time when he was old enough and experienced enough to raise his own host, to cut like sharpened iron through Vortigern's stinking skull! He nodded once, curtly. "Aye. I would do anything."

Enniaun emptied his goblet and refilled it. He drank another gulp, said, "Our mountains protect us, but we could not defend ourselves from Vortigern's unleashed Saxons if he decided to cede our territory to them. For how long could we withstand a siege, an assault from north, south, east and west?"

Reluctantly Etern nodded agreement. "Gwynedd is defensible, but not impregnable."

"I might add," heads spun round at the sound of Arthur's tired voice, "were Gwenhwyfar to wed another her life would be in danger. Vortigern and Melwas are both malevolent men."

He trailed wearily to the door. "Defy Vortigern and his nephew in this and she would spend the rest of her life watching shadows."

Etern extended a hand to Arthur. "Do not leave us, there is much to talk of."

Arthur shook his head. He steadied his breath, passed a hand over his cheeks, nose, and mouth, then forced a smile. "Happy endings are for lovers in harpers' tales." He left, calling for a slave to fetch his cloak.

"Happen the wind will change," Etern said.

His brother and father looked at him. He lifted his hands, let them fall. "Something may yet be awaiting to release us from this snare."

"After all these years? I doubt it."

TWENTY-THREE

WHISTLING A JAUNTY TUNE, CEI SAUNTERED THROUGH THE EMPTY STREETS, savouring the delights he had discovered during the evening. He chuckled to himself, recalling Arthur's teasing about his relationship with a rich widow. Aye, she was not young, but what did age matter compared to experience? He fingered the ruby ring on his finger, given impulsively when she had entreated him to stay the rest of the night. He had refused, having learnt from past mistakes not to linger too soon. Women had a habit of construing much from very little. He had left with promises to return another evening—happen he would at that. The streets were dark, and a dog barked somewhere. Cei yawned, ready for his own bed; it must be close on the third hour of the morning.

Someone hailed him, the voice loud in the nighttime silence, a guttural accent, Friesian. Curious, Cei strolled across the cobbled road, avoiding piles of dung. He nodded a greeting. "You're open late, taverner!"

The man was agitated, fingering the grubby apron covering his ample middle. "You are Lord Cei? I recognise you, you drink here with other officers."

Cei nodded again, amiably. "You serve good wine and hot food."

The man was pleased at that, but his smile of thanks faded with the return of unease. "I wish to close, it is so late, but I do not know what I should do with him." He pointed a stubby finger at a cavalry officer lying slumped across a table in the shadows beyond the open door.

Annoyed that one of the men should drink so heavily as to reach this state, Cei said harshly, "I'd toss him in the street if I were you. Let the sewer muck sober him." He made to move on. As the man said, it was late.

The taverner stepped hastily in his path and shook his head, embarrassed.

With a short, exasperated sigh, Cei strode over to the drunkard. As he was about to shake the man's shoulder, he broke into a chuckle. Ah no, the poor tavern keeper could not give this one to the street! Roused by Cei's persistent nudging, Arthur staggered unsteadily to his feet.

"He has drunk most of my best wine." The Friesian was hovering, put out by all this inconvenience.

Cei felt in his belt pouch and produced a small, battered coin. "For your trouble," he said, placing a supportive arm around Arthur's waist.

It was only a short journey to the palace but, hampered as he was by the almost dead weight of his companion, it took Cei a while to reach their assigned rooms, where, laughing, he waved Arthur's sleepy servant aside. "Go back to your bed, I shall tend your master." He seated Arthur on the bed and pulled off his boots. "An enjoyable evening, I assume. Trust you to spoil it by getting yourself over full of wine."

"I talked to them of the horses, Cei." Arthur's words were slurred. "Cunedda agrees with me. Think on it—he agrees!" He laughed with pleasure and fell backwards across the bed.

Cei frowned. "Is that why you are so drunk? Filled your belly to toast the hooves? Well, 'tis a good enough reason." Cei began to unbuckle the tunic, but Arthur, clumsily sitting up, stayed his hand.

"Why am I such a fool? My head has been so filled with dreams of cavalry that I never stopped to consider other details of life. My life. Hers."

"What are you rambling about, man? You have drunk more than I thought!"

"You would not believe a dowsing with a water bucket could create so much feeling, would you? She's a woman grown now and," Arthur paused, eyes as blurred as his speech, "and I love her." He grabbed at Cei's shoulders, pulling him close. Cei wrinkled his nose at the stink of wine.

"She makes me laugh, Cei, makes me feel I could take on Vortigern and his damned Saex friends single handed!" Arthur waved a hand expressively, then toppled sideways. He looked blankly up at Cei, not seeing him, filled only with a sense of emptiness, of great loss. "All that, and I can't have her."

"Who? Cannot have who? Ah, you are talking daft!"

Suddenly Arthur was asleep where he lay, lost in a swirling world of heavy wine, where hooves drummed and the dragon streamed before them. Swords clashed and glistened in sunlight. Sweat and blood, men fighting. Mingled, in the strange way of dreams, with a girl's shout of defiance drifting into laughter. Her face floating above the Pendragon's banner. An angry young girl, copper hair tumbling, face grubby, a bucket of swilling water in her hand; changing, shifting to a woman grown, serene and beautiful. Gwenhwyfar.

TWENTY-FOUR

GWENHWYFAR DID NOT PARTICULARLY LIKE SHOPPING; THE NOISE AND the bustle around the stalls and crowded, smelly streets held no appeal. She was not a frivolous young woman, and usually took minor interest in the acquisition of jewels or cloth and coloured ribbons. It therefore came as some surprise to her cousin Ceridwen when Gwenhwyfar enthusiastically agreed to go to the market with her—all the more so when she seemed to be enjoying herself.

The market of Londinium was, of course, far larger than their few street stalls at Caer Arfon. So many traders, so much to choose from! Pots and pans of glass or clay; fine gems; polished beads; materials for gown or cloak; silks and wools; every kind of weave in reds and blues and greens—a rainbow of colour. Spices and herbs, cooked food, raw food, shellfish, meat, gape-eyed sea fish, river fish, pasties and pies, sausages and cakes. Wine and ale. The girls ambled with the flow of the crowd, giggling together or prodding and poking, curious about some item, asking the price, wrinkling their noses at the telling. Too high!

Gwenhwyfar had bought ribbons—green, to match her eyes—Ceridwen, a fine bracelet crafted in jet and gold. They were making their way along the wider of the streets to a little tavern to take a tankard of wine and a pastry, when Gwenhwyfar squeaked, grabbed Ceridwen's arm, and pointed some distance ahead, through the milling of the Londinium crowd.

Arthur coming towards them, strolling beside the man Cei, his red cloak swinging, his dark head bobbing above the crush of shoppers and traders. He stopped, pointing to a stall; Gwenhwyfar lost sight of him, then spotted him again behind a trundled handcart. Impulsively, she called out, standing on toe-tip, waving to catch his attention. Twice only had she seen him these past five days since the banquet, both times at a distance, making it impossible to speak. He could not have heard or seen her this time either, for he turned without acknowledgement and disappeared down a narrow side street.

"Whatever are you doing?" said a contemptuous female voice, directly behind Gwenhwyfar. "Jumping up and down as if you have fleas in your undergarments!"

Gwenhwyfar whirled embarrassed, and found herself looking into the disdainful face of the Princess Winifred. She stammered, "I thought I saw someone I knew." Bear's breath! Why did she have to justify herself?

Winifred poked with a slender bejewelled finger at some saffron material on a stall near by, then peered haughtily along the crowded street. "Well, she has gone now, dear, whoever she was."

Condescending bitch. Gwenhwyfar would have enjoyed saying that aloud. Best not, keep smiling. To her dismay, Winifred linked arms and began walking with her; people melted aside with barely concealed scowls to allow them through. Winifred and her mother were tolerated but not liked, save by the merchants, who were falling over themselves to show their wares.

Gwenhwyfar twisted her neck to look down the side street into which Arthur had passed. He had gone; the street was empty except for a woman with three squawking children and a one-legged beggar. She did not notice Winifred also looking, for she too had seen Arthur, realised whose attention Gwenhwyfar had been attempting to catch. A smile slid across her mouth. Oh, he had gone— what a shame.

Until the night of the banquet she had not paid much mind to the Pendragon, had tried to avoid him. Her father detested "that boy" as he called him, and her cousin Melwas seized every opportunity to be as nasty as possible to Arthur. Some kin feud between them, to do with Arthur's father Uthr and Melwas's elder brother Gorlois. Silly, why dwell on the doings of men grown cold in their graves? However, days that would otherwise have been extremely boring, often proved most amusing whenever Melwas and the Pendragon were both at court, though such occasions were rare.

Melwas was not here at present, was away about the King's private business. He was expected back soon. Winifred hoped so: these tedious days of Council needed livening up.

The sneering attitude of father and cousin, both highly influential in Winifred's upbringing, had caused her own low opinion of Arthur. With that long nose and perpetual scowl he was not a handsome young man, but Gwenhwyfar's attraction to him had caused her to look again and see for the first time the character beneath his unprepossessing appearance. Discovering unexpectedly that Arthur had a possibility of being a most exciting man.

Resigned to her unwanted companion, Gwenhwyfar walked with Winifred, feigning polite interest in her purchases, answering yes or no to irritatingly personal questions. She would see him again, happen on the morrow, the Sabbath.

And she did.

Vortigern's Christian church was a splendid building, richly decorated and furnished to show his devotion to the faith. Everything about the King was deception. All attending the Council were expected at the bishop's special service. Chance put Gwenhwyfar opposite Arthur. Her heart raced as she took her place on the women's side and saw him standing there, tall and impressive, very bored.

Once, Gwenhwyfar raised her eyes to venture a glance across at him; she looked away again quickly, a blush heating her cheeks as she saw him watching her. She stood after that with head lowered, telling herself not to act like a moonstruck child. But how the thrill of his nearness made her tingle! Only a few feet away, she could practically hear his voice, smell him, touch him!

Winifred also enjoyed the service. For the same reasons as Gwenhwyfar.

There was an undignified rush from the church, Vortigern's Council, many of them non-Christians, retreating, eager for the pure air and sunshine. Eager, too, for the entertainment laid on for their benefit at Vortigern's expense. There were to be games of skill and challenge, displays by gymnasts and riders, then, later, feasting and dancing. The King was keen to keep his Council sweet. The congenial air of festival rarely failed.

Gwenhwyfar found herself swept forward with the crush, away from Arthur, and she was annoyed to see that Winifred had managed to waylay him. She did not see him again until the mounted displays.

His cavalry gave a daring exhibition of equestrian skills: throwing spears and fighting a mock battle; leaping on and off their horses at varying speeds and picking up articles from the ground at a gallop. One rider seemed to slip, went down under the horse's belly beneath the pounding feet, emerged on the other side, pulling himself back into the saddle, grinning. A horseman's trick! Arthur took the salute, resplendent in parade armour. Gwenhwyfar clapped and cheered, proud of him and his men.

And then the feasting, the banqueting hall filled with men and women, loud talk and much laughter. To her disgust, Gwenhwyfar found herself seated with the unwed women. Winifred, with her sickly sweet smile, beckoned her to sit beside her, welcomed her to the table. Why the princess was going out of her way to give this impression of friendship, Gwenhwyfar had not yet decided. It was so obviously false.

As usual for Winifred, she monopolised the conversation throughout the evening, whispering, not so quietly, various uncomplimentary remarks about her father's guests. Gwenhwyfar paid her scant attention beyond the demand of politeness, concentrating on her food and the entertainment—until Winifred said, "Ah, Lord Arthur has at last joined my father's captains, he can never arrive on time!" She giggled, coyly covering her mouth. "Did you see how he barely took his eye off me in church this morning?"

The others—silly creatures Gwenhwyfar thought them—giggled. One said, "Happen he has design on you, Princess. After all, you and he are a most eligible pair!"

Fury, most of it born of jealousy, swept over Gwenhwyfar like a surge tide. She announced without thinking, "It was hard to miss you. That gown you wore was bright enough to eclipse the sun!"

A hush fell over the girls.

Winifred looked at her with steel eyes. "Were you by chance speaking to me?"

Gwenhwyfar covered a stammer, said quickly with a glowing smile, "How could even a blind man have missed your beauty?" She cringed in self disgust at her enforced ingratiation. That was close! You did not cross Winifred, any more than you would taunt a basking adder!

The Princess extended her hand and patted Gwenhwyfar maternally, as if sharing some great secret. "Arthur has a liking for a pretty face. Mine, I have noticed, he likes in particular." To the others, "I would not object to him taking a liking to more than just my face!"

They tittered, simpering at Winifred's humour. Gwenhwyfar held a fixed smile and, with difficulty, her tongue still. Arthur, she hoped, would have preference for a better woman than Vortigern's Saex bitch.

It was herself he had watched, she was sure. But then, was she? The flicker of doubt, once planted, grew rapidly, refusing to be uprooted. Winifred had wealth and status. Na, Arthur would not be swayed by those. It was she, Gwenhwyfar, he wanted. They were pledged albeit a childhood promise, but made, all the same, with sincerity. He had not sought her out, though—had, now she thought of it, avoided her.

Winifred sipped wine, her expression smug. She had been right, then, the rustic girl Gwenhwyfar was indeed infatuated with Arthur. Were the feelings returned? She must find out. The Pendragon was suddenly more than a passing interest. Winifred wanted him for her own—and Winifred was used to getting what she wanted.

Soon the dancing began. Young men warmed to the women's sides and whisked chosen partners off to whirl the haze of food and drink from their heads. A knot of ambitious hopefuls clustered around the princess, who flashed her blue eyes at the flattery, making an elaborate game of choosing. She was ten and five years of age, ripe for betrothal, and this might be the only chance for many a chieftain's son to obtain a royal torque.

A shadow fell over the clustered group. Standing to one side, Gwenhwyfar looked up into Arthur's hawk eyes. He held her gaze briefly, then, coming to a decision, smiled warmly and walked towards her.

"You watched the display this afternoon?" he asked, making a surety of opening a conversation.

"Aye," Gwenhwyfar murmured as she bobbed a slight greeting, "your men are most impressive."

Motioning her admirers aside, Winifred bustled forward and laid her hand on Arthur's arm, her smile dazzling. "It was superb, my Lord! You rode so... manfully." Her blue eyes flicked up and down his body as she threaded her arm tight through his. "Let us dance," she said, leading him to join the whirl of laughing men and women. She glanced back at Gwenhwyfar with a victorious toss of her head.

Gwenhwyfar's body was shaking, her throat tight as if someone were steadily pressing two thumbs on her windpipe. The bitch. The fatherless tavern slut. The...

A voice, Ceridwen's, remote and distant. "Gwenhwyfar? Are you all right?"

Gwenhwyfar ignored her cousin's concern. For agonising minutes she stood rigid, fists clenched, watching as Arthur responded to Winifred's blatant flirting. His hands around her waist, he was laughing, his eyes never leaving the generous swell of her bosom under the thin silk garment that did little to conceal the delights beneath.

After much stamping and laughter, the dance came to a breathless end, the dancers breaking apart, dizzy from the pounding rhythm.

Gwenhwyfar seethed as Winifred demurely whispered something into Arthur's ear, watched helpless as he nodded and guided her out to the terrace, disappearing into the darkness of the gardens beyond.

Unable to hold back the tears of anger and hurt disappointment, Gwenhwyfar turned and fled.

TWENTY-FIVE

IT WAS QUITE LATE BEFORE THE SOUNDS OF REVELRY BEGAN TO FADE AWAY. Midnight had passed before the stragglers took their leave and those staying at the palace had staggered to their beds. Winifred sat stiff and silent, allowing her maidservant to undress her. If the girl noticed her mistress's disarranged hair or the bruising to her neck, she made no comment. She dismissed the girl, but did not go immediate to bed, sat naked before her mirror inspecting the marks on her white skin, lowering the polished bronze to examine the reflection of her breasts. Suddenly, she hurled the thing from her, smashing it against the far wall. Damn! Damn him and his insolence!

In a few months she would be ten and six, the age her mother had lured Vortigern to the marriage bed. If Rowena could do it, then so could her daughter. She would not be spurned by some—some *boy*! Going to her bed, Winifred drew the covers close around her skin. The feel of his hands on her breasts, his breath and lips on her neck, had been so very good. She pounded the pillow. Why then had he turned away from her and walked away? He had wanted her, that was plain—but he had walked away!

Whatever did that Gwynedd girl see in him? An arrogant, self-opinionated, ugly son of a rebel! Winifred drew up her knees, hugging them close. It had been so easy to lure Arthur into the seclusion of the palace gardens. She had backed away, of course, as he went to kiss her but then an unfortunate slip of the hand had caught her bodice on one of her rings. Naturally, he had helped her release it.

Why had he suddenly swung away, left her alone, her breasts exposed, and so very humiliated? She lay a long while, tossing, unable to get comfortable, unable to sleep. Her body felt hot, aching. She had enjoyed Arthur's touch, had wanted more. Still wanted more.

Her father disliked Arthur because he feared him—feared him because the Pendragon was a threat. Vortigern rarely made political mistakes, and never the same one twice over. He had let Uthr out of his sight; the son must be close watched. An idea germinated. What if Arthur were to be even more closely watched?

Winifred sat up, hugging her pillow to her chest. There had been talk again lately between her parents on the subject of her marriage. The arranged betrothal, some months past, she had put an end to. If they seriously thought she was going to some crusted old veteran's bed, then they had best think again! Winifred shivered with distaste, recalling the slimy feel of his dribbling mouth, and his rough, gnarled hands. A pity the poor old fool had suffered that seizure of the stomach! He ought never have eaten fruit before retiring. Winifred sniggered. Who would have thought that one small drip of poison on a single fruit could create such interesting, and rewarding, results!

Her idea was growing, becoming more appealing. This latest talk was something about a chieftain of her grandsire's. What—wed one of Hengest's Jutes and live in a midden-hut *Grubenhauser*? Ah, no, not when the Pendragon was on offer!

She slid from the bed, wrapped a light cloak around her, and padded from the chamber, her bare feet making no sound on the tiled floor. What better way for her father to keep Arthur under observation? As son-by-law he would be chained as firm as a tethered bull! And poor Gwenhwyfar! Winifred tossed back her head. Poor Gwenhwyfar, her lover lost to the Princess Winifred!

Arthur stirred, roused by the thin shaft of light as the door quietly opened and closed. He mumbled, moving restlessly in his sleep. Winifred held her breath. He must not wake! She clutched her cloak tighter around her throat, though it was not the chill of night that scuttled over her naked flesh. She stood a while, her breath coming fast between parted lips, her eyes fixed on the dark shape asleep in the bed.

In her own chamber, this had all seemed so easy! She slid the cloak from her shoulders, let it fall to the floor with a gentle swish. For a few heartbeats she almost retreated back to the soft, safe glow of the corridor beyond the door. The reality of doing, more daunting than she thought. Doubts came, followed rapidly by conviction. Rowena had ensnared Vortigern by the use of her body—and Winifred was every inch her mother's daughter.

Letting go the cloak, she padded across the floor. Arthur lay face down, his back uncovered, one arm flung carelessly above his head. His dark hair, curling slightly and long enough to touch his broad shoulders, spread in a tangle across the pillow.

Winifred resisted the temptation to run a finger down his spine. She had been kissed and fondled by young men, but had never allowed them to go over far. It amused her to encourage their manhood to rise and then push them from her, leaving them frustrated and rejected. As Arthur had rejected her. No one spurned Winifred. No one!

Deftly, she twitched back the covers and slid her body next to his. He stirred, stretched his arm to her, encircling her waist, pulling her closer, mumbling in dazed pleasure as her warmth touched him. Lazily he opened his eyes, lingering over the sensation, half unconscious, of soft flesh beneath his touch—then sat upright as realisation slammed him awake.

"Blood of Mithras!" he swore, recognising her. "What in the Bull's name are you playing at?"

Sweetly, "I am not playing, my Lord."

"If your father discovers you have been here he will flay me alive!"

I don't doubt it! she thought, said confidently, "He will not discover it; no one saw me come." She walked her fingers down the dark hairs of his chest and across his flat stomach. "You have a fine body; you ought use it, not deny its need. Do you not think the same of mine?"

Irritably, he brushed her hand aside and rolled off the bed. "Get out, Winifred, before…"

"Before what?" She stretched the length of the rumpled sheets, her thighs and breasts glistening in the dim lamplight, ran a fingernail seductively from her throat to the soft patch of pale hair that curled enticingly between her legs.

Arthur swallowed, at a loss, unsure what to do.

"You wanted me earlier," Winifred persisted, her voice silky. She beckoned, more sure of herself now, enjoying this new game. "You all but stripped me naked to touch me in the privacy of the gardens."

"I was drunk, but still knew when to call a halt." Arthur ran his hand through his hair. He could not bring himself to look away from her slender, so enticing body.

"Then are you no longer drunk?" she purred, raising herself on one elbow. "I am, with desire for you."

Arthur swung away, punching the air with a clenched fist. "You are a maiden—and more to the point, Vortigern's daughter."

"A maiden?" She had expected that, had used the same excuse herself on occasion when men became too insistent. "What makes you so sure?" She watched him from beneath lowered lashes, recognised the hesitation and pushed on. "I was betrothed not so long since. He was a dear man—older, but experienced, and very, very good to me." She flicked her eyes at him, pouted seductively. "How were we to know he would die before we could legalise our union in the marriage bed?"

She rose slowly in one fluid movement, crossed to Arthur and touched him intimately, a butterfly touch. She smiled. "It would seem you are interested after all." She took his hand, kissed the palm, and placed it on her breast. "There—round and smooth, awaiting your attention." Her arms encircled Arthur's waist, lips brushing his, and as her body pressed against him his response became undeniable.

With a low moan Arthur lifted her, his mouth covering hers, and carried her to the bed. Her body, young and new, responded delightfully to his lovemaking and at her urging he probed into her, her legs twining around him, drawing him in. She cried out, moaning with pleasure.

He froze. She had lied to him, the bitch! Astride her, he stared in disbelief, stunned that he had fallen so easily for her trickery.

Winifred moaned again impatiently, shifting beneath his body, the movement fuelling his need. Angrily he thrust harder, taking her maidenhood as savagely as he could.

Spent, panting, he rolled from her, horrified. "Mithras, get you from here, back to your bed. Say nought of this!"

"Must I go so soon?" She stretched her aching legs. "Can we not have more?" The afterglow of passion still lingered with a delicious throbbing. It had felt so good; why had she denied herself such pleasure for so long?

"That once should never have occurred. If your father…"

Winifred sat up slowly and leant back against the pillows. "Finds out? He would only hear of it from you, or me. You would not tell him—and I?" She slid down into the bed. "Will I ever have need to tell him?"

Cynically, "No doubt you could find some reason."

"My father wishes me to marry. I will wed, but one of my own choosing."

Arthur laughed. "There are many who would willingly take a girl's maidenhood, but not so many who would accept used goods as wife—save those eager for a fat dowry to compensate." He smiled at a private jest. He could use such a gift… but he was not yet that desperate.

Winifred's next words dispersed the private humour. "Or if a man and woman pledge themselves by the giving and taking of a first time." She was finding it difficult to steady her voice. She had been so certain she could win him—as her mother had won Vortigern; only, these things were not quite as easy as she had expected. "I will make you a good wife, Arthur." She stood up and moved towards him, resting her hands on his chest. "In time, an even better queen."

"I do not want a half Saex bitch as wife. Or queen."

She hit him then, the palm of her hand slapping hard against his cheek. "You bastard."

Arthur's expression remained impassive, inscrutable. He nodded once, with a thin, set smile, one eye half shut in that insolent way of his. "That's right."

Furious, she clawed his cheek with her nails, leaving bloody scratch marks. "No one," she breathed through flaring nostrils, "shall dare talk to me, Vortigern's daughter, the Princess Winifred, in that manner."

Arthur shrugged his shoulders, indifferent, ambled to where his clothes lay, pulled on his bracae.

"Princess? I assumed you were whoring this night."

"My father shall hear of this!" she cried furiously. "He shall know how you forced me here, took me against my will!"

Arthur turned slowly to face her. Was this a bluff? Would she be capable of crying rape convincingly enough? He studied her a moment. Winifred was indeed a beautiful creature; aye, but the beauty was all to the surface. Beneath that soft, enticing skin oozed putrid black poison. She was capable of lying, more than capable.

"You forget one thing, Princess." Arthur rested his backside on the edge of a table and folded his arms. "Your father has never trusted me. He has me watched at all hours, in all places."

The Pendragon twitched his eyebrow higher. "All places. We were followed into the garden"—he pursed his lips—"and a guard keeps constant watch over this chamber. Ah, Winifred." He spread his hands, palm uppermost. "Did you, then, forget the spies?"

"You lie!"

"If you say so!"

Winifred snatched up her cloak, flung it around herself. With a proud tilt of her head and the quirk of a triumphant smile, said, "Spies can be bribed to tell the story the way it might have been."

Arthur ambled to the bed, sat down, lounged back on his elbow. The self assured smile broadening, he nodded in agreement. "That they can."

Digesting his words, Winifred returned his direct gaze, her anger confronting his relaxed amusement. Striding towards the door, she threatened, "You

will take me as wife, Pendragon, or," she opened the door, "or I shall personally see to it you will not, shall we say, keep the equipment necessary for any
other marriage."

She stalked out, slamming the door shut behind her.

Arthur lay back on the bed, let his breath go slowly, stared up at the high ceiling. Two abandoned cobwebs were draped in the far corner, thick with dust. To
the left, a patch of brown damp stained the yellowing plaster. A crack zigzagged
from the centre almost to the wall. A crack, like the crooked scar running across
Vortigern's cheek.

After a while Arthur got up and sluiced cold water over his face and hair.
He felt dirty and disgusted with himself. How could he have been so easily
lured into this? What sickened his stomach was the knowledge that in the garden he had wanted her. He had been eager to leave that crowded room that
pressed in on him, making him feel hot and trapped, had willingly walked
her away to the cool shadows outside. Winifred was a beautiful young woman, her perfume pleasant, her skin soft, and her response to his first, exploring
kisses encouraging.

What had excited him about her? He detested her and her family. He had
lain with many women, barely remembered the first, taken with fumbling ineptitude. Ygrainne, his mother, had been furious to discover he had attended the
pagan ceremony of celebrating the successful harvest. Would have been more
furious had she discovered with whom he had come to manhood. A whore
Uthr had once favoured, a woman three times his age with three and thirty
times his experience.

Unexpectedly, that first time came back to him as he stood with his head
bowed over the basin of water in his chamber. She had caught his hand in hers,
whirled him around the blazing bonfire, her great, pendulous breasts bouncing
beneath her loose tunic. He had reached out tentatively to touch one, wondering what the pulpy flesh would feel like. She had laughed, scooped him up like
a toddler in her arms and whisked him away into the bushes where, in the dark,
other couples grunted. It had all happened so fast. He found himself lying naked
atop her gross bulk mouthing at her breast like a calf at some swollen udder. He
had not enjoyed the experience. Revulsion at her vast bulk and haggard age hit
him the next morning, the remembrance that his father had taken her when she
was young and pretty made the act somehow obscene. He had avoided women
for days afterwards.

The next had been a slave tending the goat herds some weeks later. Cei and he had been riding, had stopped to cool the horses, noticed the woman and two girls. Cei had grinned, swung off his horse and sauntered up to the woman. In a moment he was back with the girls while the woman returned to her goats, pleased with the more than adequate payment. Cei had taken his girl, there by the side of the track, with no more thought than a dog mounting a bitch. Arthur had followed his example, rather than look foolish in front of his elder cousin. The girl had been young, a maiden, her breasts new formed. He had been clumsy, hurting her; the blood that came frightened him, and her. More spots of blood stood out on her lip where she had bitten to stop herself from crying out. Some months later he caught sight of her again, labouring beneath a heavy basket of kindling, her belly swollen.

He wondered now, incongruously, what the child had been. Had he a daughter or son?

How many since?

He did not much like women. Women lied and cheated, set their little traps to lure you in, then, bang, bolted the door, leaving you shut in the dark to sweat and tremble, screaming to be let out. He reached to pour more water but his hands were shaking. He dropped the jug, bent to retrieve it and came face to nipple with one of the figures on the mosaic floor. He had not noticed the naked women before—seductive, suggestive, weaving a web of enchantment around their victim.

Arthur's stomach heaved. Wine and self-loathing spewed from him. "Shit," he muttered. "Holy, bloody shit!"

TWENTY-SIX

THE FIRST LIGHT OF DAWN TOUCHED THE EASTERN SKYLINE AS GWENHWYFAR opened her eyes. She had not slept well, had dozed fitfully and tossed about, dreams drifting and ebbing; strange dreams of unknown faces and far-off exotic places. Her head aching, she slid from the bed. One or two birds were starting to sing outside, their happy chirrups incongruous against her misery. It would probably be a bright sunny day too. Lashing rain and dramatic thunder would suit her mood better. Gwenhwyfar dressed and let herself out of the room. She would walk in the gardens.

She turned right outside the chamber, then left and left again. Na, that was wrong, she did not recognise this corridor. Damn the place! You could get lost in here, starve to death before anyone found you! Imagine stumbling for days through this maze of passages to be found, tongue hanging out, eyes bulging, gasping for water. She laughed, caught her breath suddenly, listening intently.

Footsteps walking fast—another corridor crossed this one a few yards ahead. Two men marched by, their boots rapping on the stone floor, swords and body armour jingling. One was Cei, Arthur's cousin, the other her brother Enniaun. Their steps halted as they banged on a door.

Curiosity getting the better of her, Gwenhwyfar ran forward to peep around the corner. If there had been an answer to their knocking, she could not have heard it. The men entered, then "Jesu Christ, Arthur! What's wrong? Are you ill?" After Cei's exclamation and the sound of steps running quickly into the room, the door was firm shut and she heard nothing more.

Hesitantly, she slipped forward and pressed her ear against the wood. Muffled voices interspersed with an occasional florid oath, then her brother's voice. She could not catch the conversation, but it was obvious the three inside were arguing Enniaun was hurling a string of curses—followed by an equally embellished retaliation from Arthur, then a crash.

Gwenhwyfar leapt back from the door in alarm, glancing quickly up and down the deserted corridor, expecting guards to come running or the door to be flung wide. Nothing happened. No one came.

Were they fighting? Cautiously, she wedged her ear tight against the door. Their voices were a low murmur, with the occasional word spoken louder. Words like "irresponsible," and "damn fool!" with, intriguingly, "What if her father discovers…" and "Worse, what if there comes a child?" Footsteps coming towards the door!

Heart pounding, Gwenhwyfar swung away, seeking a hiding place. Too late to run back up the corridor and round the corner—she would be heard if not seen! A door opposite stood open, with darkness beyond. Ducking round the doorpost, she ran in and set her back flat against the wall, breathing hard, heart thumping.

Outside, someone walked quickly away.

What was that other noise? A grunting, laboured sound. Gwenhwyfar's eyes were becoming used to the semi dark; the shutters at the small windows were not quite closed, dimly lighting the small room. It was bare of furniture and tapestries; nothing save a tankard on the floor and a tipped jug. A few feet away was a mound covered by a blanket which moved slightly. Warily, Gwenhwyfar stepped forward. She peered at the bewhiskered face of some unknown man who lay on his back, mouth open, snoring gently and stinking of strong ale.

Footsteps again. She tiptoed back to the door in time to see Enniaun re-enter Arthur's chamber carrying what looked like a water jug. No good to stay hidden here. That man, drunk though he was, could wake at any moment. Gwenhwyfar slipped out, along the corridor, noticed an entrance ahead leading into a secluded garden courtyard. Best to go out there. Arthur's door opened, she hesitated. Enniaun stepped out and instantly caught sight of her.

"What in the name of God are you doing here?" He strode towards his sister, wearing a frown of disapproval. "What are you about, girl?"

Smiling a greeting, Gwenhwyfar explained half truthfully, "I woke early, brother. As it seems to promise a fair day, I thought to watch the sun rise."

Enniaun's face softened, and he patted her shoulder absently as he used to do when she was a child. In British, he said, "I understand, lass. We are all feeling the need for Gwynedd."

Startled, Gwenhwyfar's eyes fluttered to his. Until that moment she had not realised that they had exchanged their native British tongue for formal Latin.

Suddenly, unbidden, she longed for the mountains and green valleys of Gwynedd. For the wild sea, hurrying streams, and lazy rivers. Enniaun was right:

she did feel that special longing, that inner something that went deeper than mere homesickness. "I want to go home," she said.

"We all do, but it cannot be, not yet. I leave immediate with Da and Etern and our men to go north. The Saex have pushed across the frontier and have run riot near Camulodunum." He did not add the rest, that farmsteads had been burnt to the ground, villas looted, the men slaughtered, and the women and children taken for pleasure or slaves. There were several wealthy estates in that area, and many of their owners were here at Council. Only one had brought his family.

To conceal the words unspoken, Enniaun confided, "Da is bound to serve his given days with Vortigern's army—he thought to take advantage of this opportunity to ride beneath the Pendragon's command. We," he indicated Cei, who had come from Arthur's chamber at the sound of voices, "came to rouse him."

As he spoke, Enniaun turned, Arthur was emerging from his room dressed in undertunic and bracae, his eyes tired-bruised, his face pinched, grey and unshaven. Four angry scratches stood out on his cheek. The blood was fresh, barely congealed. Only an animal's claws or a woman's nails could cause such a wound. Gwenhwyfar's quick mind considered it unlikely that he had suddenly developed a fondness for a pet cat.

A thrust of vindictive resentment stabbed at her—*serve him damned right! If he will have a woman with him for the night*—changing, within a heartbeat, to a plunge of pity. He looked so haggard and lonely.

Arthur spread his hands. "I heard you talking, Enniaun. Forgive my appearance, Lady Gwenhwyfar, I thought someone I have no wish to see had come." He shrugged, and added as if it would explain everything, "I have not slept well."

"Na?" said Gwenhwyfar in a tone that questioned the excuse. "I find the most effective method of dealing with mares that ride the night is to turn over and ignore them."

Arthur raised an eyebrow and nodded ruefully. "If I ever find myself in a similar situation again, I shall remember your advice."

Enniaun glanced shrewdly at his sister, more aware than Arthur of her way of thinking. Something did not quite ring true about her air of innocence. Bushy eyebrows drawing together, he wagged a warning finger at her. "We do not want unsavoury rumours spreading, Gwenhwyfar."

Was her brother referring to Arthur's woman or this Saex trouble? Both?

"Vortigern wishes us to delay, discuss tactics before we ride to teach these Saex a lesson." Unaware that Gwenhwyfar might be alerted to that other reason,

Arthur was talking about the uprising. "But Vortimer has decided to leave now. It's more prudent to head north before too many Saex learn of our coming."

"The Queen does not rise until well after the sun," Gwenhwyfar replied with straight innocence.

"That, young lady," Arthur replied, grinning, "could be considered a treasonable statement!" He winked. "But well said!" He began to walk back into his chamber. "I must dress, we are delaying over long."

"Arthur!" On impulse, Gwenhwyfar ran forward to pluck at his sleeve. He was a tall man, standing two fingers above six feet, his height as imposing as his direct gaze. The crown of Gwenhwyfar's head barely reached his chest. She looked up at him. "There's a man, drunk, in the room opposite yours." She pointed. "He looks as though he may be one of Vortigern's Saex." She felt suddenly foolish. Why would Arthur want to know where a drunken heathen lay? She dropped her eyes, looking at her neat Roman shoes, and said with a stammer, I thought you might need to know."

He laughed, a single snort, and putting a finger under her chin tilted her face up. Almost kissed her. "I know. He serves the King, but he also spies for the Queen." Arthur chuckled, happy to share a secret. "He was well pleased with a jug of strong ale to keep his solitary watch company." He grinned. "Given by one of my men." He glanced at Enniaun and Cei. "Keeping these spies occupied is costing me a fortune!"

Arthur took Gwenhwyfar's fingers in his hand and rubbed his sword-callused touch over her softness. Her skin was cold, but her answering grip, firm and steady. "My thanks for your concern."

Her answer was a radiant smile. She wanted to ask whether it was the princess he preferred; wanted to say that she loved him, said only, "Take care while you are gone."

The need to hold Gwenhwyfar in his arms and keep her close became almost too great for Arthur to bear. She was not like the others—no traps or deceit from Gwenhwyfar, no pretty smiles hiding malicious intent. Her earnest green eyes were gazing up at him, trusting and loving. He wanted to say so much to her, but how could he? What would be the point in saying that he loved her? It would only bring her more pain.

He forced a less potent, a more brotherly smile. "Aye, my Cymraes fach, I always do." He whirled away before he lost all sense and committed some other stupid deed. He had made one mistake that would send far-reaching ripples into the future months this ill-starred night already. There must not be another.

MAY 453

TWENTY-SEVEN

THE ATTACK WAS SWIFT, UNEXPECTED, ALL THE MORE STARTLING BECAUSE Arthur was lost in thought, pacing the new-cleared floor of a thirty-foot-deep defensive earthwork. The madness of the past two weeks had been fraught with chaos. The desperate ride north to Camulodunum, the assessing of damage… Men attacked, killed. Homesteads and farms burnt. A frenzy of bloody skirmishes.

Vortigern had not heeded warnings, left matters too late, and the Angli had swung together to unite their strength in a bid for independent supremacy. In a frenzy of bloodlust, they moved swiftly towards the gentle ridge that shouldered between the flat marshlands and dense woodlands of what had once been the territory of Queen Boudica's proud people, the Iceni. One satisfaction for Arthur, he—and others of his thinking—had been arguing for months that this would happen soon. It had needed only one man to rise into a position of power, one man to fire the young warriors and set the blood pulsing in the old. Icel was such a man—an English princeling seeking himself a kingdom.

English, Angli—how Vortigern stuck obstinately to the correct use of title! His wife and her kin were Jutes, this Icel an Anglian, and the settlers sprawling along the coast down towards Londinium were Saxons—"Saex" being the popular word used by the British for the lot of them. A loose, derisive play on the term for a foreigner and for the Saxon short-bladed sword.

Arthur bent to retrieve a lump of flint from the wall of the ditch, tugged at it, surprised at how firm the nodule was lodged. He pulled again, the thing coming free suddenly, showering him in a mist of chalk dust. He sneezed, wiped whitened fingers on his bracae that were already white-coated. The damned stuff was so dry, hard baked by the early heat and lack of spring rain. It got everywhere—in your boots, your hair, even inside your undergarments. The men had stripped off their tunics and were working bare skinned under the scorching sun.

He tossed the chunk of rock onto the pile of debris. This earthwork had lain abandoned for centuries, disused since the days when the Iceni lost the need for man-made boundaries to the supremacy of Rome. He sneezed again, cursed. It was a damn awful job clearing this scrub-choked, twenty-foot-wide ditch. And a waste of energy. The construction was wrongly sited for their purpose, with the rampart on the north side. It had been built as a gateway straddling the ancient Iceni Way. Built against an enemy coming from the south-west, not one firm entrenched to the north-east!

He turned to face the towering bank, shielding his eyes against the glare of new-cut chalk. All day had they been digging, all day in this insufferable heat, with no shade—and, with thirty men working, only a few handful of yards yet completed! Mithras's Blood, it would take months to reopen the entire seven mile length!

Winifred had not tattled to her father, nor her mother—he was certain of that. Could he trust Cei and Enniaun to remain silent? He had been indiscreet in telling them the truth of that night, but then, what use making excuses for the state they had found him in?

He had best go up to check the sentries in a moment, ensure they were not drowsing.

As for Vortigern's Saex spies, Arthur had handled them easily enough for months now, ensuring only harmless information filtered back to the King. Or Queen. That she had the upper hand at court was undeniable. It would be the queen who was the more likely to find out about him and Winifred. Na, it was safe kept. The girl could not betray him without betraying herself, and she had the more to lose. He laughed, walked along to the uncleared area ahead, where straggling bushes grew rampant and wild flowers clustered in brilliant profusion. Which was the greater? For her to have lost her virginity, or for him to lose his balls were her parents to find out? He pointed at a path of tufted grass along the lower slope, shouted a reprimand at the man who had missed its clearing, received a returned scowl of silent annoyance. The men thought as he did.

Ah, forget that night. It was a thing done—badly done, aye, but finished with.

Arthur plucked a yellow flower, idly wondering whether it had a name. Gwenhwyfar would know. She knew about plants and herbs. He tore the petals off one by one—Winifred, Gwenhwyfar, Winifred, Gwenhwyfar—threw the thing testily aside. Forget her, forget Gwenhwyfar. She was lost to him.

As the first flickering, swift-moving shadows topped the bank and began slithering fast down, with the startled cries of sweating, digging men and the whish and thud of spears brutally destroying or maiming, Arthur had a fleeting, incongruous thought, *Forget Gwenhwyfar? How?*

He had his sword out, was rushing to meet a Saex, full clad in war gear. They came together, Arthur's weapon parried by the Anglian's shorter blade. Arthur had no shield. He leapt aside from the returning thrust and yelled for help. Ducking low, Etern ran along the ditch, Enniaun hard at his heels, with the intention of giving aid to the men. But the Anglian Saex were swarming down the bank and coming up from the cover of uncleared undergrowth. Mithras, they were everywhere!

The three and twenty survivors of Arthur's work force tried to run for the weapons they had laid aside, found it useless, used instead the picks and shovels to hand.

A Saex sword hissed along Arthur's left arm, leaving a trail of oozing blood. Three more men fell, a fourth, a fifth. The virgin white chalk was turning a sickly, red tinged pink. Etern was down. No time to think, just fight. Use strength and muscle, cunning and wit. The Bull! From where did they come?

Enniaun saw Etern fall, sliced his sword through the nearest Saex abdomen, and turned to aid his brother; saw, as he lunged forward, Arthur fall to his knees. He was a big man, Enniaun, tall and powerfully built with broad shoulders, his bush of red hair this day tied back in a thong against the heat. His voice echoed along the sun-baked, bloodied ditch, an anguished, howled cry. Head down, shoulders hunched, he burst through the press of fighting men, uncertain where to help first. His much-loved brother or the more politically important Pendragon? A decision to be made as he ran, no time to think. Instinct.

Etern lay motionless. Arthur, still on his knees, was grappling a Saex with his hands, his sword lost. Another Saex was standing over Etern, axe raised to strike off the lad's head. One was coming at Arthur from behind... Enniaun shouted urgent warning to the Pendragon, caught hold of a spear as it whistled overhead, and flung the thing at the man about to mutilate Etern. Enniaun guessed his brother to be dead, so still was he lying. He took a step towards Arthur, saw him rise and swing his held opponent round, using him as a shield. A Saex short sword aimed at Arthur plunged into the wrong back. He was all right, up again, fighting. Relieved for that at least, Enniaun straddled his brother's body, swinging left and right with his sword, slicing through air and bone, whatever came within reach of the blade's vicious bite. Stories would be told later, around the Anglian hearth fires, of a red-haired giant among the British who killed with a magical, shining sword that spat blood.

For a moment Arthur held on to the dead Saex, manoeuvring behind him, gaining time to reach for a weapon. His fingers clenched, mercifully, round his own sword; he shoved the cumbersome body into his attacker and drove his blade deep into the entangled man, withdrew it and turned to face a new opponent. Something hit him from behind with a sharp thump to the back of the head, the butt of a spear knocking sense and awareness from him. He sprawled forward, the turmoil and shouting a haze of dizzy unreality.

Enniaun cried out, yelled for Arthur to get up, stepped forward intending to shield the Pendragon, felt a blow to his shoulder, saw a fountain of blood, and felt a curious numbness down his right arm. He stopped, looking in amazement at a spear tip that had passed clean through the flesh of his shoulder and was protruding obscenely from his tunic. Enniaun gaped at the slimy redness on the metal, not quite believing the oddity of having a spear sticking through his own body. The weirdest thing, it did not hurt, not much anyway.

There came more noise, shouting from the top of the bank, the bloodlust cries of battle, shadows and forms moving, darting. Enniaun saw nothing of it; he crumpled against the wall of red-spattered white chalk, felt and saw nothing more. Arthur, too, saw nothing of the frenzied activity, heard nought, save a wheezing breath in his own throat accompanied by a swirl of brightness fizzing behind his eyes. He was aware of someone standing over him, beginning to strip him of tunic and boots. His fingers moved, stiff, slow, closed around the smooth, hard surface of a rock, a lump of flint. He had it in his hand, brought his arm up, slowly, so slowly from the thump-thumping in his head, the burn of torn flesh along his arm. Up, lift up. The rock was so heavy, so damned heavy. He came up with it, hand pounding into the head of the thieving Saex squatting over him. A dull crunch, a muted gasp. Blood. Blood everywhere.

Curious, Arthur sat, staring at the flint in his hand, at the yellow and brown mixing of colour, at the exposed, cold, and dark interior of the stone. At the razor-sharp edge that had sliced, as sharp as any honed sword, through the face of the Saex. There was hardly anything left of the man's features, the eye and jaw gone. Spinning and whirling sensations brought vomit to Arthur's throat. He dropped the flint, lay down, and closed his eyes, vaguely aware the battle cries were no longer of the Saex, but British. That the Saex were fleeing along the ditch, scrabbling up the steep bank. Idly he wondered if Icel himself had taken part in the fighting.

A chill breeze woke him. His body was hot; the sweat and stink of blood and vomit assailed his nostrils. He opened his eyes, grimaced at the mess spewed down his chest and legs, grimaced, hoping it wasn't all his own contribution. Surely some of the blood came from a Saex?

"So you've decided to wake at last?"

Arthur looked up bleary-eyed, saw Etern squatting before him.

He said nothing, stared puzzled, one eye half shut, the other eyebrow raised. Looking sideways, he saw Enniaun lying there as grimed as himself, eyes closed but breathing steady. Back to Etern.

"I had hoped," he said, mouth dry, rasping as if it were full of chalk dust, "the next world would at least have a decent bathhouse. It seems not."

Etern laughed and playfully ruffled Arthur's chalk-matted hair. "We need wait and see. Not for us the knowing this time, my friend."

A gruffer voice, ahead and above. "You will wish you were in the other world, lad, when I finish with you." Etern drew his mouth down in a warning expression; Arthur forced his throbbing head up and saw Cunedda silhouetted against the evening sun. He stood, legs spread, fists bunched against his hips, stern and angry. Very angry.

"It came unexpected," Arthur said, without much conviction. A poor excuse and he knew it. Knew also he deserved the merciless tongue-lashing Cunedda launched into. There was, could be, no excuse for the danger he had placed his men in, for failing to supervise the sentries—paid for by their murder as they dozed in the shade of their own propped-up shields. For the carelessness of having no weapons to hand… the list went on and on.

Arthur sat listening, taking each verbal blow with a mounting sense of shame. He had been lax, careless. Men lay dead through his indifference to safety. He had not wanted this job of ditch clearing, had fussed and grumbled, and disregarded all the rules. You did not strip off your armour so close to enemy territory. You did not post a few idle sentries as sole guard along the ridge. You did not heap your weapons yards away. If Cunedda had not happened by on routine patrol… aye, well. A lesson in command learnt. A bitter, sharp lesson that had resulted in the death of over half his men, a jagged wound along his arm, Enniaun alive but wounded, and Etern with a lump to the back of his head the size of a hen's egg.

Oh, they would talk and laugh about the near disaster later. Arthur's first and last mistake. Etern's life saved by being struck unconscious, and Enniaun's shoulder that for the rest of his life ached whenever a cold easterly wind blew. But there was no laughter at this moment on Cunedda's outraged face, or in his harsh voice.

Nor was there laughter for Arthur, who when Cunedda walked angrily away hauled himself to his feet to supervise the burying of the dead; men under his command. Men he had not commanded well enough, who, through his negligence, had died.

It would not happen again.

Only one good thing came out of it all—the clearing of the earthwork was abandoned.

The Anglians later reused the fortification. Its construction attributed to their skills. Forgotten, as the years and the years passed, were the others who had come and gone, before the settling of the Anglo-Saxons.

TWENTY-EIGHT

GLANCING THROUGH THE OPEN WINDOW AT THE SUDDEN SHRILL OF A blackbird, Gwenhwyfar drove her sewing needle into her finger. "Damn the thing!" She flung the material to the floor and sucked at welling blood. She detested sewing. Her stitches never seemed to come out neat or even, the needle was always unthreading or the thread snagging and knotting.

"Is it so surprising the Pendragon grew tired of you and turned to me? You have the breeding of a sow, Gwenhwyfar of Gwynedd." Winifred sat working at an elegant tapestry, tossed her insult without bothering to glance up.

Gwenhwyfar hurled an ill-tempered response. "Better a well bred sow than a half breed runt!"

Four other young women in the room paused from their work, needles hovering in mid stitch, expressions appalled. No one spoke to the Princess like that and got away with it.

"You insolent bitch!" Winifred shrieked, her own sewing tumbling to the floor in her indignation.

"Bitch? It is not I who fill that description!"

"How dare you!" Springing to her feet, Winifred crossed the small chamber in three quick strides to slap Gwenhwyfar across the cheek.

With squeaks of alarm, the others drew back, holding their sewing to their breasts as if the flimsy material formed some sort of shield. Ceridwen alone came forward, her hand extended in appeal.

Gwenhwyfar too was standing, a dagger, which normally hung discreetly from her waist, in her hand, its tip pricking at Winifred's throat. With breathing controlled, her body loose, shoulders bent slightly forward, and arms flexed, Gwenhwyfar was ready for action; ready to fight, defend, or kill.

Frightened, Winifred had the sense to move a pace back, a little scream escaping her. "She threatens me! Threatens to kill me! Treason! This is treason—you are all witnesses to it!"

With a laugh, Gwenhwyfar lowered her weapon, sheathed it, and turned away in disgust. "You are pathetic, Winifred. A spoilt, conceited, half-breed baggage! Arthur loves me—we are pledged. If you think he feels anything more than a passing fancy to fondle your teats, then you are also a fool."

It was enough to tip the fear into fury. Rushing at her, arms whirling, Winifred took Gwenhwyfar by surprise. She staggered, trying to fend off the flailing fists, but Winifred caught hold of her hair, twisted a hank round her hand, and pulled while her feet kicked at shin and calf.

"Stop! Oh, stop!" Ceridwen fluttered around the locked pair, tugging vainly at Gwenhwyfar, trying to pull Winifred off, to stop the fight.

The Princess, unschooled in fighting, was pummelling anyhow with fist and toe, with no balance to her body or designed coordination. Gwenhwyfar, though, had always enjoyed the training for warfare, and had learnt well. Winifred had winded her; she let her blows come, caught her breath, then dropped suddenly to one knee. Winifred lost her balance and toppled forward with a shrill cry. Gwenhwyfar had no need to follow through, for Winifred lay gasping like a landed fish.

Guards and servants were running in.

"What is the meaning of this riot?" One commanding voice carried clear above the turmoil, which subsided abruptly as the queen swept into the chamber. Rowena stood a moment on the threshold surveying the whimpering heap that was her daughter, and Gwenhwyfar on one knee breathing hard. "Is this how women of Gwynedd behave? What is happening here?"

Nervously, Ceridwen bobbed a curtsy. "There was a difference of opinion, my lady."

Rowena addressed Winifred sharply. "Stop that noise, you cannot be so badly injured."

"Mother," Winifred made no attempt to rise, "she threatened me with her dagger, attacked me."

"You probably deserved it. Is this true, Gwenhwyfar? You hold a weapon?"

Undeterred by the queen's austere tone, Gwenhwyfar answered boldly, "I carry a dagger. Who does not?"

Rowena regarded her with a steady blue gaze. She was a small woman, standing shorter than Gwenhwyfar by a few inches. She was ageing also, no longer the sixteen-year-old beauty who had captured Vortigern. The beauty now was painted on, and the silky blonde hair had paled into streaked silver-grey. She had no figure, for the child she carried swelled her stomach to a great bulge, a thing Vortigern seemed to admire. In the hopes that this time, at last, his wife carried a boy that would live? All these years, and still Winifred the only living child!

Defiant against the hard scrutiny, Gwenhwyfar added, "It was my mother's weapon. I have carried it since childhood."

"Then you will carry it no more. Give it here." Rowena held out her hand, the fingers puffy and misshapen from pregnancy. "Quickly, girl. I am no common stall-holder to stand here arguing."

Reluctantly, Gwenhwyfar gave her the dagger.

"You will go to your own chamber. Remain there until I say otherwise."

Winifred scowled at her mother. "Is that all the punishment she..."

Rowena rounded on her. "Be silent!"

Petulant, the princess obeyed.

The Queen surveyed the chamber, with an expression as if they all carried some foul disease. Then, "Daughter, come with me," and she swept out, the heavy scent of her perfume lingering in her wake. Winifred, struggling unsteady to her feet, trotted obediently to heel.

Rowena said nothing more of the matter until later in the afternoon. She sat stitching an altar cloth by the light of a western window, patiently fashioning neat little stitches that steadily expanded this section of the Christ's crucifixion. It was incongruous, she reflected, that this Roman breed called her father's Jutes barbarian and savage, yet they thought nothing of this slow, tortured form of death. She sat back, easing a pain in her lower spine. How many weeks more to carry this wretched child? Please God, let it be a living son, and let this be the last! She pointed with her needle at her work and enquired of her daughter, "What think you of it, girl?"

"Is it difficult to work such small stitching?"

Rowena sighed in annoyance. "How like your father you are, always answering one question with another." She picked at a piece of fluff with her nail. "You were arguing with Cunedda's daughter. What about?"

Winifred found a sudden need to attend to her spindle. "No important matter, a misunderstanding."

"I see. Over what?"

Winifred struggled to sound indifferent. "A man."

"A man?" Rowena persisted, honey-sweet. "Which man?"

"Oh, no man in particular."

"It would not, by chance, be the Pendragon?"

Winifred dropped the spindle and stooped quickly to retrieve the spoilt wool. She forced a laugh. "The Pendragon? Why him?"

Did her mother know of that night? Those spies he had talked of… she was certain he had lied about them, for if her father had been told, he would not have remained silent on the matter. And yet he and the Pendragon went away, were north of here, fighting the Angli folk.

Rowena said scathingly, "The entire palace watched as you danced together at the feasting, my girl. And many tongues were set wagging when you both retired to the seclusion of the gardens."

Winifred blushed. "I needed air; the wine and heat…"

Rowena regarded her daughter with a stern eye. "I have no objection to your walking in the gardens with the Pendragon, child. As long as it is only *walking* that you do."

Feigning shock, Winifred exclaimed, "Mother! What more is there to do in a garden?"

Returning to her tapestry, Rowena sewed some half-dozen stitches. "If you are that naive, child, then it is time we talked of betrothal. There is a chieftain, loyal to my father, who would suit well."

Winifred felt suddenly afraid. God, no! She lowered her eyes. "You have the wisdom I do not yet possess."

Suddenly, like a striking snake, Rowena was on her feet and moving across the room as if she were a lithe girl, not a woman heavy with child. Her palm smacked across her daughter's face. "You stupid girl!"

Winifred squeaked, tried to draw back. "Why? What is it I have done?"

Rowena mimicked her. "What is it I have done?" Do you think you can entice the Pendragon by letting him mouth at you as though you were some tavern-slut? No, do not deny it—you were watched! Your father and I have men constantly following Arthur—he cannot be trusted. I am ashamed of you, do you hear? Ashamed!" She paced around the room, agitated. "At least, thank God, that is all you allowed him. Stupid, stupid girl, he could have taken matters further!" Rowena stood over her daughter like some goddess of darkness.

"And now this! Brawling like some street brat. You deserve a whipping for your behaviour!"

At that Winifred protested. "*I* deserve a whipping? What of that Gwynedd bitch who dared insult me! What of her?"

Rowena waved her hand dismissively. "She is of no consequence. It is you I am concerned with." She returned to her stool, but did not pick up her needle.

Winifred came to stand behind her mother. "Did you know the Pendragon is in love with her?"

"Is he?" Rowena kept her voice neutral. This she was not aware of. "And how do you know?"

Winifred folded her hands before her. "From the way he looks at her, and she at him." She laid her fingers briefly on her mother's shoulder, emphasising her point. "Gwenhwyfar said they were pledged." She moved away to the window so her mother should not see her scheming smile.

"Nonsense!" Rowena began stitching: the blue here needed particular care. But was it nonsense? Ja, she had noticed Arthur watching Gwenhwyfar, had taken it for a man's lusting. How strong would that make the Pendragon and Cunedda of Gwynedd? Too strong, dangerously so. Such a betrothal must never be allowed. She unpicked the last stitch, having formed it crooked. But wait—had not her husband said something recently about Gwenhwyfar being a possibility for Melwas? She began sewing, calm again. She must raise that idea again as soon as possible. And find a more suited wife for the Pendragon. She sighed. It would be so much easier to have the awful young man disposed of, but Vortigern had expressly said not. "*Too many would use the memory of his name. Na, my beloved, with his incredible talent for rubbing people the wrong way, it will only be a matter of time before he makes himself more enemies than friends. There will be few willing to follow him.*"

"Might not such a pledge cause a troublesome alliance against my father?" Winifred enquired innocently from her window seat. "What if it is not nonsense? What if Cunedda has agreed a match? My father could be placed in great danger should the Pendragon be allowed such a kin alliance."

Rowena peered at her stitching; the thread had knotted. Patiently she unravelled it. "She spoke idle fancy."

"Happen she did, but what if it was not?" Winifred hurried on. She must seize this opportunity to press her point, catch her mother's interest. Woden's breath! If she were to marry this chieftain of her grandsire's and be found on the wedding night not to be… She swallowed a hard lump. What did they do to women who went to the marriage bed no longer maiden? "It would be more prudent for Arthur to betroth a woman of my father's choosing; someone with whom he could be watched more easily."

"I would assume your father has already thought of that."

Winifred ducked her head, feigning modesty. "The Pendragon is an arrogant, toad-spawned dog-turd, but for my father I would wed with him."

Rowena continued sewing, a small smile touching the corners of her mouth. This sudden idea would have nothing to do with that episode in the palace gardens, by chance? Thank the God her husband's spies always reported to her first whenever her daughter was concerned! Vortigern would have had the girl flayed if he knew half the things she did! Foolish rosebud! That was no way to catch a man. You must dig a hole, hide the net, lure him forward and let him fall headlong in; not allow him to see the trap dangling!

At least the Pendragon had held the sense not to pluck this particular flower! There were one or two young men who had taken liberties with her daughter. She, the queen, had found it necessary to dispose of them without fuss. It was time the child was wed. But to the Pendragon?

Rowena never had discovered which girl Arthur had taken to his bed on that feasting night. There had been one—her servants had told of a virgin's blood on the sheets and the cling of perfume. Rowena liked to know all that went on— curse that drunken fool set to watch the Pendragon's chamber! She had not made him suffer enough for his neglect; slitting his throat had been over-quick, punishment ought have been longer drawn out. She smiled, amused. Mayhap the Romans had the right attitude to punishment after all! Then another thought, alarming. Could the girl have been Gwenhwyfar? No, unlikely.

The Pendragon for Winifred? The queen was warming to the idea. Vortigern was ageing, her father Hengest not yet in a safe position to make a bid for power, and he too was ageing. This child she bore, what if that too died or was a girl? Ja, there could be possibilities if Winifred were to wed Arthur. It was good to have a choice of roads to reach the same destination.

She said, "I will speak to your father about it."

Considering it prudent not to press the matter, Winifred asked permission to retire. She turned back at the door. "That dagger, Gwenhwyfar's. Can I have it?"

Rowena pointed vaguely to a table on the far side of the room. "It is over there. Take the thing—I have no use for it."

Well pleased with herself, Winifred found the dagger and, holding it clasped in both hands, left the room. "Spurn me, Pendragon? I told you, I always get my way. And as for you, Gwenhwyfar…"

She held the dagger to the light, admiring its fine craftsmanship, and walked along the corridor with a triumphant swagger. "You can be flower maiden at our wedding!"

JULY 453

TWENTY-NINE

VORTIMER WAS THE KING'S ELDEST SON BY HIS FIRST MARRIAGE, HIS BROTHER Catigern two years younger. Father and sons hated the sight of each other. Leaning across the wooden table, Vortimer offered his guest more wine, though he was already quite drunk.

Arthur accepted, holding his tankard out a little unsteadily. This endless patrolling, the pretence at keeping the Saex behind a hypothetical border sickened him. The fighting these last weeks had been sporadic—skirmishes only, nothing substantial. Icel had entrenched himself this far south, and here he would stay.

At least Icel was contained to the western edge of this great bulge of flat fenlands; but there would be no hope of salvation, of retrieving what was lost, unless Vortigern gave orders for a combined force to march against him—and that he would never do. The King had not the funds, nor the guts, to unite his own British. Too easily could such a hosting turn against him. The mood Arthur was in this night, it would not take much to encourage him to lead that force either! Good men had died in these pointless skirmishes, too many men to name. Their faces swam before Arthur's blurred vision; he raised his tankard in salute, drank in their memory.

"When are we going to drive this scum back to the sea where it washed in from?" he demanded venomously, crashing his drained tankard down.

Again, saying nothing, Vortimer filled the tankard. With the passing of the years, he was losing patience. Would his father never die, leave the way open for his son to salvage what he could without resorting to taking the throne by force? Vortimer's dark hair had long since turned grizzled and his eyes wore a permanent rim of red around sunken hollows. He was no longer a young man, fit and full of enthusiasm. "We cannot attack as you advocate, Arthur, we have not the men." How often had he made that self-same reply to Arthur, to his brother. To himself.

For answer Arthur made a crude noise through his lips. "And the King does not intend to muster enough British men."

"My brother, we are here for a matter of importance," said Catigern impatiently. "Is it not time we discussed that, not this same, endless quest?" Like Arthur, he took little pleasure in pointless action. Allowing the Pendragon to drink himself senseless this night seemed yet another waste of time. "We have talked around every other subject imaginable. Our matter must be raised now, brother." He looked meaningfully towards Arthur, who had the glazed look of one ready to sleep off excess liquor.

"What matter?" Arthur rose unsteadily to his feet, looking from one brother to the other. "Whatever, it must wait—I am for my bed." The room spun, and clumsily, with a surprised, distracted expression, Arthur sat down again.

"A thing of some delicacy," began Vortimer, uncertain how to broach the subject. He liked Arthur, admired him as a soldier and as a friend, though their ideas on warfare were very different. He had been amazed when the raw youth presented himself at court for duty with the army. Amazed but pleased, for Arthur was a useful man to have at your shoulder.

Vortimer took a breath and decided to tackle the problem head on. "From our spies we know much of our father's planning—and the bitch's scheming."

Belching, Arthur examined the flagons of wine, seeming surprised that all were nigh on empty.

"Will you listen, man!" Vortimer thumped the tabletop in frustration.

Catigern shook his head. "We should have talked of this earlier; he is too damned drunk now to listen!"

"I am not drunk, just bloody tired!" Arthur's words slurred together, he spoke part truth: it had been a long day in the saddle, with nothing to show for it come evening.

Standing behind the Pendragon, leaning over his shoulder, Catigern spoke urgently, with more force. "We have received word that Rowena is to arrange Winifred's marriage."

Arthur tapped a rhythmical beat on the table with his fingers, grinning inanely. "Well, good for her." He turned his head to face Catigern. "Do I know the unlucky bastard?"

Catigern put a hand to his head and groaned. "Will you be serious!"

His brother added, "Vortigern's daughter is to marry with a Jute chieftain—a thegn, I think the word is. One of Hengest's sworn men."

Arthur sat grinning happily. "Then we might be rid of her? Hooray for that!"

"God's truth! Na, we shall not be rid of her. There will be yet more Saex settling their feet over the door sill." Vortimer, across the table from Catigern, leaned closer to Arthur like a spider lurking hidden from a hovering fly. "Unless Rowena's babe is a boy, Winifred is the only child of the union. On Vortigern's death the Saex—her mother, her grandsire and, if this marriage goes ahead, her husband—will claim all on her behalf. Do you not see? That Saex rabble will claim the British throne!"

Arthur shrugged. "Then we had best hope for a boy to oust the princess. Mind, even then the brat will be half Saex."

"Or we can arrange some alternative marriage, Arthur, give Vortigern a better offer. One it would be impolitic for him to refuse. One that would cut Winifred off from her Saex kindred."

The craving for sleep taking hold, Arthur nodded slow agreement, wagged a ponderous finger. "Good idea. Who do you have in mind?"

Catigern let out the line, dangling the bait lower. "There is one man who could use Winifred's parentage to his own advantage and benefit from a hand-some dowry."

Vortimer added, "My brother and I are no longer young men. We may not live to see the day when our father falls. A sorry fact, but it must be faced head on."

Catigern again: "If any man aside from ourselves is to take the kingdom, we would like that man to be you."

"You have a claim through Uthr."

"You could add to that claim by wedding a wealthy heiress."

They stared solemnly at Arthur. He looked back at them, from one to the other, a sickening horror creeping over him.

"You are not serious! Oh na!" He was on his feet, backing away, hands up-raised. "Blood of the Bull, after all your ravings against Rowena you have the nerve to foist her bloody daughter on me? Are you out of your minds? Think again. No. Good night to you."

He strode to the door and flung it open. Vortimer said with quiet men-ace, "If you refuse this, Arthur, then you are no friend or," he paused for emphasis, "ally."

Arthur rounded on him, the blur of drink quite gone. "Do you think I fear you, Vortimer? You cannot threaten me. I have allied myself with you because it suits my purpose. My purpose, not yours. I could as easily stand with others."

"And end up like your father?" Catigern cut in. "Hacked to pieces on the battlefield?" This was going badly. Pausing for breath, he continued, treading softer, "This has been no light matter for us either. You—we—have no choice, you must see that!"

"And which one of you thought up the stinking idea?" Arthur glared at the two men.

Catigern hooked a stool forward with a foot. "It was suggested to us. We have thought upon it some days now."

Arthur sneered. "Suggested? By whom?"

Trying to evade the question, Vortimer said lightly, "No one of importance."

"By whom?"

"Damn it, Arthur! We had word that Rowena is to arrange a marriage for her daughter. She has suggested two possibilities to her husband. This Saex thegn or…"

"Or?"

"You."

Arthur laughed, punched the wall with his fist, bellowed, "And you, like the two fools you are, have neatly pushed me into her snare!"

"Nonsense!"

"It is a good arrangement!"

"Good?" Arthur stamped back to the table. "Who for? Me? Rowena and Vortigern? Winifred?" He kicked a stool aside. No one made a move to retrieve it.

Vortimer challenged, "Have you another in mind then? A woman who could bring as much as Winifred?"

Arthur opened his mouth to answer, closed it again. Defeated, he leant on the table, head bowed.

"Well, have you?" Catigern repeated his brother's question.

The Pendragon looked up and said quickly, stubbornly, "As it happens, aye, I have." Then he gave a long sigh. He righted the stool and sat down, toying with an empty tankard. His palms were sweating. "Na, there's no one. Not now."

Strange, he had not thought of Gwenhwyfar these past weeks. Death, often only a spear's length away, allowed no time for thinking. His mind slid back to the memory of her. Mithras, he still wanted her for his own, but he could not have her. What was it he had said to Cunedda about obtaining the wealth to buy his horses—that he might as well marry with Winifred? He groaned and put his head in his hands. It had been a jest, but the listening gods had obviously taken it seriously.

"Get it done quickly then. Before I change my mind. Only I tell you this," he stood up, the stool's legs scraping on the stone floor, "I will take her as wife in name. Nothing more."

Relieved that the matter had worked out easier than he had expected, Vortimer put a hand on Arthur's shoulder. "We ask nothing more."

Catigern rubbed his hands together. "At least," he said with forced jocularity, "you will have a virgin bride."

Arthur stared at him for some moments before bursting into laughter.

As he left the room Vortimer and his brother exchanged puzzled glances. To what reason the laughter, they had no idea.

AUGUST 453

THIRTY

CAMULODUNUM WINE WAS OF POOR QUALITY, BUT ARTHUR CARED LITTLE about the taste; it was the effect he chased, and the stuff packed enough punch to remain hammering in his head this sun-shining day. He was wallowing in a temperamental mood, ready to growl at anyone who crossed his path. Already by mid morning he had argued with Cei over some minor matter, had found his dog limping from a cut paw, and now faced an audience with Vortigern to receive orders that would probably conflict with common sense. The rest of the day did not bode well.

The town was untouched by the Anglian uprising, though its inhabitants remained badly shaken, demanding protection and assurances of future safety. Life in this damp, wind-swept corner, such as it was, was slowly returning to normal—or as normal as it could be with the King in residence and his daughter about to join him.

For Vortigern, each conflict was a greater headache. His British army awaited payment, and Hengest's Jute mercenaries also sought payment for their services, their demands growing daily louder. To pay them Vortigern needed to collect taxes, and those same men who demanded protection consistently avoided the paying of taxes—so the army grumbled, Hengest grumbled, and the civilians grumbled. God's eyes, the thing went round and round in a never-ending circle!

Every way he turned, he encountered problems. Problems with the economy, and with the threat of rebellion. The thing was spiralling out of control, like a dropped spindle twisting and jerking, knotting the thread, spoiling the wool. More and more men were coming to join Hengest, settling land that was not theirs for the taking. The British were openly quarrelling with each other and with himself, their King—and the Pendragon was gleefully stirring the dissent. Damn him to hell!

Melwas, now, he trusted implicitly, for his nephew was ambitious but not greedy. Vortigern had made it clear that he would do well out of loyal service to his King. The Summer Land, which had once been Uthr's, was now under Melwas's governorship, and he had the recent given promise of a prized bride. Another trouble: the Pendragon and Melwas fought like cat and dog, their bickering growing louder with each setting sun. Vortigern groaned. He wanted this interview as little as the Pendragon.

It was unfortunate that at the door of Vortigern's chamber Arthur encountered Melwas. The Pendragon stood his ground before the narrow doorway, in no mood for politeness.

Melwas had few good traits. A sour life had left its mark on his sallow, pockmarked skin and scowling features. He had few enjoyments, save women and fighting.

Disdainfully, he looked Arthur up and down, his nostrils wrinkling as if the man gave off some foul odour.

"So you're back," Arthur said cynically. "Some people are well content to be given the comfortable tasks while the rest of us are left with the men's work."

Melwas stood squarely before the door. "You ought to thank me, Pendragon—I have this very hour delivered your future wife to her father." He thrust his face closer. "There are none, save myself, the King would entrust with her safekeeping."

Arthur laughed. "Happen he can trust you for escort, but it seems he trusts me more in the longer term as her husband!"

Melwas jeered. "Trust you? This marriage tethers you." He raised his arm to push Arthur aside. "Out of my way, Pendragon; I have work to see to while you dally over the niceties of wedding plans."

"Dare to raise a hand to me, whore-son, and I will remove it from your arm." Arthur spoke soft, almost casually, his voice the more menacing for its total lack of venom. All he needed was an excuse, and this fat-bellied toad would be lying dead.

They loathed each other, these two men. The one corpulent, loose-jowled, and with the strength and stamina of a bull; the other tall and lean with dark hair curling almost to his shoulders, and dark hawk eyes that missed nothing. Each more than ready to kill the other.

It was Melwas's instinctive desire to draw his sword and butcher this arrogant whelp here and now, get the thing finished, but something made him hesitate, some warning that Arthur's words were no idle boast. He did not want a fight on Arthur's terms, so he said, "I doubt our King would appreciate blood spilt on his threshold. Let me pass." He pushed Arthur aside and walked away.

Their paths had crossed only a few times these recent months. As fate often wove the way of things, they were to meet as many times in as many days. Outside Vortigern's chamber, as Arthur was entering, then the following day, after yet another lecture from Vortigern on not harassing the more peaceful English settlers to the east of Icel's taken boundaries.

By early afternoon, Arthur's mood was far worse than the one of the morning. His head throbbed, his body felt strained and taut.

Cei was not sympathetic. "You never learn. Stay away from the drink, and its after effects will stay away from you." He had laughed at Arthur's coarse reply.

The horses were waiting, the men ready for afternoon patrol. Flies were irritating the animals, who were stamping hooves, kicking at their tender bellies, and tossing their heads. The heat, after the cold earlier in the month, had come back with a vengeance.

Eira, Arthur's grey stallion, matched his master's temper, laying his ears back and snapping at Cei's chestnut. "Another worthless patrol to while away what remains of a wasted day," Arthur complained as he gave the signal for his men to move off. He touched Eira's flank lightly with his heel and the stallion leapt forward, eager to be away from the hovering insects. Arthur restrained him with a firm hand on the rein, keeping him at a dancing walk, head tossing against the bit. The twin-towered, arched exit loomed ahead; a group of mounted officers burst from the right at a canter, intending to reach the narrow gate first.

Arthur swore as Eira shied, hurtling with a squeal to the left and colliding with Cei, whose stallion reared. Eira bounded forward, his head down, bucking. Somehow Arthur managed to get his hand up and bring him to a halt, head snaking, nostrils snorting.

Melwas sat his mount watching, amused. "That horse will kill someone before the year is out," adding in an aside to another officer, "with any luck, its rider."

Arthur glared, ready to reply with some colourful oath. Cei urged his chestnut forward, caught Arthur's arm. "Leave it. You know he goads on purpose. It would not be seemly to fight here." He nodded over his shoulder, back to where Vortigern had appeared, watching from a window.

Wheeling Eira to rejoin his turma, Arthur said, "Let the King's favourite ride through first—we need the air cleared of this stench."

Melwas caught the faint chuckle of amusement from Arthur's men, though he had not heard the words.

Sweeping a hand forward with elaborate politeness, Arthur indicated the other man should proceed. The instant Melwas had his back to him, made an obscene gesture. His men laughed.

Their paths crossed again within the span of another two days.

The patrols, as Arthur had predicted, were proving a waste of time. Ride in fast, bum the Saex in their hovels, that was the answer; not this senseless riding round and round chasing shadows. Then there were at least two British villas worth checking. Arthur and his men had found the owner of one a week since, footsore, bleeding and near death. He had stumbled through the darkness avoiding the rowdy groups of Saex, and made his way south to the British. He died an hour after reaching sanctuary, having told of how his family had been dragged from their hiding place and slaughtered; he had escaped because he was busy burying his massed wealth. "*Out in the field beyond the granary wall I put it!*" He coughed, spitting flecks of blood. Silver salvers, gold, jewels... Arthur had laid the man to rest. Happen he'd get the chance to go looking for it one day.

Hot and sweating, grimy and dry-throated returning from patrol, Arthur made his way to the bathhouse with Cei. The place was crowded with like-minded men thankful to cleanse their bodies of the day's work and heat. A storm was brewing, they agreed, though the black clouds were not yet visible. Come nightfall, rain and thunder would be upon them. What was drearier—riding patrol in dusty heat or lashing rain?

The bathhouse provided an opportunity to relax, to talk with friends and take life at an easier pace for a while. Arthur dozed in the steam of the hot room, let the dirt trickle from him with the opening of pores and sweating skin. Rousing himself, he plunged into the pool of the frigidarium, its coldness taking his breath away. He swam energetically, ignoring the scream of protest from his hot skin, the water sluicing away tiredness with the grime. He swam another width then heaved himself from the pool with a grunt of satisfaction. Taking a towel from a slave he rubbed himself vigorously until his body tingled refreshingly clean. Casting the towel down, he made for the changing rooms, waving a greeting to Cei, still reclining in the steam room and embarking on what promised to be an easy win at dice.

Whistling some soldier's tune, Arthur reached for his clothes. A sudden thump in the small of his back sent him reeling, gasping for air. His hands struggled for a hold, but he fell, his head striking sharply against the corner of the wooden bench. Men crowded round, lifting him from the floor. As their faces and the room spun before his eyes, Arthur focused on one in particular. Melwas.

The man feigned a concerned expression, asked if Arthur was all right, said something about the effect of strong wine.

Pushing the helpers aside, Arthur scrambled to his feet. "You punched me, you bastard whore son!"

Melwas raised his hands in innocent surprise. "I have just this moment entered the building!"

Another voice. "You lie, Melwas. I saw you."

The room fell silent, eyes turning to the speaker who stepped forward from the entrance. Etern pushed his way through the crowd to face Vortigern's nephew, the favoured one.

"So Gwynedd has pulled out already, eh?" Melwas sneered. "Had enough? Can't take hard work?"

Etern folded his arms and leant against a pillar, nodded a greeting to Arthur. "On the contrary, we have cleared our allotted area to the north; all is settled, quiet and under control. We have served our required time and now return to Londinium to collect my sister and cousin before going home."

A smirk. "Gwenhwyfar will not be leaving Londinium."

"Will she not? We shall see." Etern shifted his weight to the other leg, his gaze never leaving Melwas's face. "I followed you in," he said. "I watched as you passed behind Arthur. Saw your fist strike him."

Melwas turned a blotched, angry pink, his eyes narrowed, lips thin and colourless. "I would expect you to side with the Pendragon, Etern of Gwynedd," he snarled. "Traitors' dung clings."

Arthur lunged forward, but someone grabbed his arm and hauled him back. Melwas was facing Etern, who stood relaxed, casual, arms still folded, wearing an easy smile.

"You regard us from Gwynedd as traitors then, Melwas?"

"The whole warren is infested with them! It needs smoking, every last one cleansed from its lair, the Pendragon here along with the rest." Melwas flung a hand in Arthur's direction, but directed his accusation at Etern.

Shrugging off the arm that held him, Arthur stepped forward to stand beside Cunedda's son. "Even Gwenhwyfar?" he asked, his voice so low only those nearest caught the words.

Melwas leered. "The moment I have her in my bed she will be too busy satisfying my needs to draw breath for Gwynedd. With her belly full, she will have no time for thoughts."

Etern smiled lazily. "I should think my sister will have something to say on that score."

"Your sister will not be permitted her say. She is mine for bedding and breeding."

Arthur could listen to no more. "You bastard!" He flung the words as his fist came up, striking Melwas on the jaw.

Staggering, Melwas recovered his balance and brought a dagger to hand, bearing down on Arthur, who belatedly realised his lack of clothing and weapon. He leapt back, arching his unprotected body away from the swooping blade.

It all happened so swiftly. Etern lunged forward, grabbing at the sleeve of Melwas's tunic, dragging him to one side, away from Arthur. Melwas roared with anger and swung in the direction he was pulled, stabbing with the blade.

Etern clung to the woven cloth, stubbornly refusing to let go as he sank to his knees, aware of some dull ache in his chest. He coughed, spewing blood from his mouth, and fell slowly forward, ripping the tunic with his hand.

They stood stunned, frozen in disbelief as the life flowed from Etern, spreading in a grotesque dark puddle across the mosaic tiles.

Melwas clutched his cloak to him, away from the blood. He took in the hostile silence, dropped the dagger, sending it clattering to the floor. He fled, leaping over the sprawled body, running for the door. No one followed.

Arthur bent to Etern, turned him over, wiped the frothy blood from his blue-tinged lips, closed the eyes that stared in questioning surprise. He felt nothing, only a solid wedge of loss, a knot of desperate bereavement.

Tears spilt unchecked from his eyes, though whether he wept for Etern or Gwenhwyfar he would never know.

THIRTY-ONE

THE PURPLE MALEVOLENCE OF STORM DARKNESS WAS GATHERING IN THE northern sky, louring down into the western night-cluster of violent red, sunset-tinged cloud. Sitting alone in her chamber, Gwenhwyfar aimlessly combed out the tangles in her hair, watching fascinated as the storm loomed closer above the reds and greys of Londinium's jumbled rooftops. A streak of lightning ripped across the blackness, followed by the boom of thunder. She sighed: there would not be much sleep if that was going to be trumpeting all night. Turning at a sound in the doorway, she smiled a greeting as Ceridwen entered. "Any news?"

The girl dropped the packages she was clutching on a couch and ran her hand through wind tousled hair. Drops of water spattering the shoulders of her cloak scattered as she removed it and shook away the damp. "It's starting to rain, I got back just in time." She sat down and began to remove her boots, replacing them with softer house shoes. She leant forward, selected one of the packages and tossed it to Gwenhwyfar. "A present."

Catching it and eagerly unwrapping the folded cloth, Gwenhwyfar said, "You ought not go treating other people, my lass, but thank you all the same." She discovered a new comb, fine carved from elephant ivory, and held it beside her old one with its broken teeth. "This," she said, moving across to give Ceridwen a kiss of thanks, "I needed!"

A twelvemonth younger than Gwenhwyfar, Ceridwen was a slight girl, with fine features and a fragility of build that belied her strength. She had been a happy child, though timid, and was now a contented young woman eager to please, to serve her elder cousin as friend and companion. She displayed her other purchases: a roll of silk and a small wooden bird, carved so delicately that it seemed it might fly away if released from her hand.

Admiring the things, Gwenhwyfar asked again, "And is there any news?"

Ceridwen ignored the question; instead she fetched her own comb and stood to tend her damp, ruffled hair. Gwenhwyfar playfully pushed her towards the bed, tickling her ribs. "Tell me, you wretch!"

Laughing, Ceridwen fended her cousin off, calling pax. "You did not want to know of the Queen yesterday when I told you she was in labour."

"That was yesterday," Gwenhwyfar retorted.

Eager for the chance at her own teasing, Ceridwen adjusted her rumpled clothing and sat forward on the edge of the bed.

"You ought have come shopping with me, the market was full of the news."

Exasperated, Gwenhwyfar threatened more tickling. "If you don't tell me…"

Ceridwen laughed. "Apparently she's well after the birthing."

Gwenhwyfar buffeted her cousin with a pillow. "I don't give a Picti curse for the queen! The babe, Ceridwen, the babe?"

"Oh, the babe!" Ceridwen feigned deliberate misunderstanding. "You are interested in babies of a sudden!"

The pillow thwacked harder, amid a splutter of giggles from Ceridwen and a burst of feathers as the thing split. Giving in, she announced, "The Queen gave birth some hours past to a fine healthy boy!"

"What!" Gwenhwyfar leapt to her feet, a swirl of feathers drifting around her like a blizzard. "A boy! Good God!"

"I thought you would be pleased," Ceridwen said sarcastically, drawing her knees up to her chest.

Gwenhwyfar strolled to the window, hands joined, fingers on lips. After all these years the King's Saex wife had given him a living son! The window rattled with a gust of storm wind, the fragile glass quivering. Another flash of lightning, illuminating the lurid sky, and a crash of thunder. Outside, in the bedraggled gardens, the trees and bushes tossed under the assault of wind and rain. A slate from the roof tumbled past this first-floor window and crashed to the ground. Another gust caught the casement, the frail wood shuddering. Gwenhwyfar put her hand on the catch, intending to pull it more firmly shut. Lightning lit the British patrol guard struggling along the outer wall-walk that surrounded the palace, his hooded cloak pulled tight around his ears, the rain lashing his back. What did he think of this babe, then? The same thoughts that ran through Gwenhwyfar's mind, that must be in the minds of all who hated Vortigern? That a half breed Saex son might become king?

The wind gusted again, sending a swirl of leaves and twigs high into the sky, caught with a thud of anger at the window, ripping the catch from the rotten frame. The casement swung wide, two panes of glass shattering. Rain and the ice bite of the gale howled like a charging war host into the room.

Gwenhwyfar swore as the catch ripped her hand and the sharp edges of glass splintered.

Glancing up startled, Ceridwen saw Gwenhwyfar's hair blown in a great wild mass, the faded tapestries lifting from the walls; heard the wind rush through the room, the cry of the storm as it invaded the warmth and safety, breaching the defences. Gwenhwyfar gasped as blood dripped from her hand. Ceridwen jumped from the bed and, grabbing a cloth, made to wrap it round the jagged oozing gash running across her cousin's palm.

Gwenhwyfar stared at the blood drip, dripping on the tiles at her feet. The wind moaned in her ears; the room was spinning, her head swimming with the noise and whirl of confusion. She sank to the floor, her skin chalk white, lips tinged blue.

Running to the door Ceridwen shouted for help, ran back to Gwenhwyfar, frightened. Gwenhwyfar never fainted, never acted so strange. She patted her cousin's cold, clammy cheeks, calling her name.

Trembling, Gwenhwyfar responded, her senses floating in a misty profusion of semi reality. She clutched at the younger girl, mouthed something, the words refusing to come, spinning and spinning around in her head, catching in her dry throat. There was blood on the floor, running down her arm, staining tiles and gown, smeared across Ceridwen's cheek. Gwenhwyfar screamed, a long, unending howl of grief; she had seen Death revealed beneath his leering mask.

She was being lifted, carried. Voices, people clustering and flustering. Her head and hand throbbed. Her body ached. "Please go away." Did they? Or did she drift into the darkness of that other world, where reality becomes nothing and dreams leapt alive?

Thunder grumbled and the wind rattled at firmly closed shutters. Shadows from the two lamps leapt and danced, stirred by creeping draughts. Gwenhwyfar woke, felt a weight heavy at her feet that shifted as she moved. Ceridwen, sprawled asleep across the end of the bed. What had happened? For an anxious moment, Gwenhwyfar could not recall.

Ceridwen sat up, stiff from the awkward angle that she had slept in. Her hand tingled as it came to life. "Gwen? I have been so worried."

Fumbling for her cousin's hand, Gwenhwyfar drew her close with an urgent need to hold tight to something solid. Tears flowed, softly at first, then uncontrollably.

"Gwen, what's wrong?" Ceridwen felt more frightened than ever she remembered. This was not like Gwenhwyfar. Gwenhwyfar was strong, nothing frightened Gwenhwyfar. Gwenhwyfar never cried. Ceridwen shuffled up the bed, gathered her cousin close, rocking her as if she were an infant. "Please, tell me what's wrong."

Gwenhwyfar gulped, steadied her breath and gathered her confused thoughts. "I saw blood." Her teeth wouldn't stop chattering.

Ceridwen shook her head, not understanding. "But you are not afeared of blood, even your own."

Hugging herself, Gwenhwyfar tried to control the shaking, the great trembling that shuddered through her cold body. "Not my blood!" Her eyes were staring, frightened and shocked. "I saw a man's blood spreading on a tiled floor."

Ceridwen's eyes were puzzled. "Which man? Who? A brother, your father?"

Arthur? The thought roared like a charging boar into Gwenhwyfar's mind. *Not Arthur! Please, not Arthur!* Aloud, "I don't know! Oh, I don't know!"

THIRTY-TWO

Rainwater dripping from Cunedda's sodden cloak collected beneath his boots and drained into a missing square of the tessellated flooring. Gwenhwyfar watched the spreading puddle light-headed and distant, as if she were floating with the sensation of over much drink. What was it Da said? Etern dead? Etern was not dead, she had seen him alive and laughing; he had hugged her, kissed her before riding north with Da to fight the Saex.

There was no sense in all this! Etern could not be dead!

Morning spread dismal and gloomy beyond the shuttered windows. Rain beat against the patched glass, with squalls of wind squirming through cracks beneath doors and windows, rustling among the hanging tapestries, and flaring the flames of the braziers, everything damp and miserable. At any moment Etern would come swaggering through the door with a cheery wave of his hand, a laugh on his face and a careless tossed greeting as if he had never been away.

One little thought kept ticking and ticking in Gwenhwyfar's mind: *It was not Arthur. Thank the gods it was not Arthur!* The scream was there, hovering and wheedling closer to the surface. It was not Arthur! It was not Arthur, god damn it, it was her brother, her beloved brother! But she could only think of how it was not Arthur. What was wrong with her?

Cunedda was holding her firmly by the shoulders, saying again all he had just said, for he too could not believe it, needed to speak the words to hear the truth. "Melwas murdered your brother, my son. He was intending to strike at Arthur, but Etern deflected the thrust, took the blade through his chest."

Gwenhwyfar wanted to say, "I know, I saw it," but it had been her own blood she had seen, blood from her cut hand. The wind had broken the glass, and the glass had gashed her hand. Her blood, not Etern's. Hers. She stood mute, quite still, staring at that incongruous puddle of muddy rainwater beneath Cunedda's boots. Only the water was blood, spreading ghastly red.

Her father felt muddled and dizzy, exhausted. It had been a long, fast ride.

No time to stop for rest, for food or drink. Riding fast through the night, with the rain beating in your face, the horses feared of the thunder, the bursts of lightning. Etern, his youngest son! His son, dead! All his children had struggled through the infections and accidents of childhood. Now the sons were grown and at their father's side. To a soldier death followed constant at heel, like an unwelcome shadow; to die in battle could be accepted, expected. Typiaunan had died defending his territory and family—aye, though the killing had come at the hand of murderers. But to be stabbed by a dull blade in some bathhouse brawl? What sense was there in such a wicked death?

Cunedda said something else, had to say it twice over. Gwenhwyfar lifted her eyes, stared at him as though he were talking gibberish. Melwas? Coming for her—why should he do that? What had she to do with Melwas, the man who had killed her brother? She pressed her hands to her ears and turned away, shaking her head, almost losing hold of reality. Cunedda stopped her walking away, his hands on her arms, shaking her.

"Daughter, you must listen to me, must listen well! You are in danger. I want you to remain in this room while I arrange our leaving."

Gwenhwyfar broke free of his grasp, confused, uncertain. What was happening?

Her father limped to a chair, groaned as he sat. Just a few minutes' rest, just a moment to get his breath, to think. A cold numbness suffused his exhausted body. This day he felt his age, felt the ache of every battle scar. Enniaun was seeing to the horses; he could take a minute to rest. Wearily he pushed himself to his feet. Na, he could not, there were things that must be done.

Melwas had fled Camulodunum, could already be here in Londinium, could have dared come for Gwenhwyfar. Ah, but if he were to show his face Cunedda would run him through, strangle him with his bare hands, take a rope and... Talk sense, man! Revenge would come in its own time. For now, Gwenhwyfar must be made safe. If she fell into that murdering bastard's hands there would be little Cunedda could do to stop this abominable marriage—and over the smouldering ruins of Gwynedd's destruction, never would he allow that now! The agreement was finished, ended. The bloodprice of grieving kin demanded it so!

Over and over on that mad ride through swollen rivers, cloying mud and biting wind Cunedda had cursed himself. He should never have agreed to Vortigern's demands, never have come to Londinium!

"Da?" Gwenhwyfar said, standing forlorn and shattered, willing that some form of sense would return. Night had its own terrors, but the coming of day was bringing no comfort. She spread her hands, imploring. "I do not understand any of this." She ran her uninjured hand through her hair, clutching at its wild looseness, and stared hopelessly at the sagging man before her with a sudden feeling of standing on the edge of nothing, hovering between the solid and the void. Blackness beckoned, calling, pulling her forward. Gwenhwyfar wanted to scream, to pull back, but the emptiness lured her nearer; it would only need one step more.

Cunedda watched his daughter's spirit staring blind and scared through the dark, empty hollows of her anguished eyes. He should have told her years past, in the security of her own home; not here, not like this. "I have done you a great wrong, daughter. At the time I had no choice. Happen I ought to have sought harder for an alternative. Can you ever forgive me?"

He took her cold hands and began chafing away the numbness with his own stiffening fingers.

His voice seemed to come from a great distance. She answered flatly, "Forgive you for what, Da?" Her eyes appealed for help as her mind fought to accept this crazed, whirlpool reality.

Still holding her hand, Cunedda told her in a quick breath of the betrothal with Melwas. Gwenhwyfar listened, the words sounding as unreal as some weird harper's tale. She was shaking her head, backing away. Her safe, comfortable world was being torn apart, ripped to shreds by claws and teeth, fragmenting, dissolving. Etern was dead, and she was to marry with the man who had murdered him? This was surely some waking dream, a wizard's trickery!

She sank to the floor, her knees weak as that blackness brought her nearer the brink of madness. Her father knelt with her and cradled her to him. The cold and wet made his teeth chatter.

"I have done all I could, save murder." He choked back a sob, abandoned the effort to contain his grief, and let the anguish flood from him, his tears mingling with those of his daughter. "By all the pity of the Gods!" he cried, "was there no other way to stop this thing? Did I need to sacrifice my son for my daughter?"

They sat for a while together, holding each other for comfort. Then through the pain came the spear-lunge of sudden anger. Gwenhwyfar recoiled from her father. "Do you think I would have agreed to this obscenity?" Spirit and pride jerked her back from despair into awareness. "I would destroy myself rather than go to such a marriage bed!"

"And destroy Gwynedd in doing so?" Cunedda spoke more sharply than he intended.

"It is my right to refuse." She looked like a wild thing, hair unbound, eyes flashing, her teeth bared in a snarl of defiance. "It is my right to have a say in my marriage. By British law, my right!"

The reply was harsh, Cunedda's responding anger fuelled by her own. Anger breeds anger. "You forget—Vortigern rules by Roman law."

She wanted to hit him, hit something. To draw her dagger from her belt and plunge it into somebody. Vortigern, Melwas; Etern for being dead. Arthur for being alive. Only she had no dagger. The bitch queen had it. The anger vanished as suddenly as it had come, leaving a hollow loss of despair. She tried desperately not to cry.

Cunedda sighed, a drawn-out, helpless sound. "I had little choice, Gwen," He limped towards her and enfolded her with his lion paws. "I am sorry, lass."

"What can we do?" She buried her face in his chest, refusing to let the tears come. After a while she ventured a look at him.

Though his face usually had a sternness that made even the strongest quail, she knew the tenderness that underlay the necessary facade of a strong leader. But here was a strange expression, never seen before: anxiety and fear.

Cunedda forced a smile. "Ah, lass." He moved to a stool and seated himself slowly, his aches progressing into painful stiffness. He looked at his strong, brown hands, the palms callused from reins and weapons. "Our hands are tied by Vortigern's whims and fancies." He scowled. "It's time to return to Gwynedd. My place is in my own land, not dancing at Vortigern's heels. From this time forward, let him see to his own." He held out his arms, inviting her into his embrace. She responded, hugging him close. Over the years, his daughter had given cause for anger, laughter, or shed tears. The most tiresome of children, but held more dear than any fortune in gold or jewels. He stroked her hair back from her forehead, tucked a loose strand behind her ear. "You are more precious to me than Gwynedd, child."

She gave a tentative smile. "Nothing is more precious than Gwynedd, Da. We are mere bystanders in her history. Gwynedd is in her infancy; she will remain great long after our bodies have turned to dust. One day she will breed princes and great kings to be feared and loved throughout all Britain. Gwynedd shall make the laws, fight the battles, and keep the peace." Gwenhwyfar broadened her smile, gaining courage. "I would like to think we had some small part in the moulding of her proud future." She tightened her grasp around her father's waist, urgently needing his rock-steady firmness, and was startled to discover how his body shook.

"God's love! You are soaked, you will catch a fever like this!" She plunged into a rush of activity, running to the door, calling for servants to bring another brazier, food and wine, dry clothing. She kissed his cheek, suddenly calm about everything "You are wiser than that fool Vortigern. You will always outwit him."

Cunedda laughed, his own tension lifting. "Then let us pray your faith is strong. Outwitting Vortigern is no easy task!"

Warmed with hot broth and dressed in dry bracae and tunic, Cunedda sat for a while.

Rain still fell outside, the morning brightening to midday and beyond, through the shadow of heavy cloud. Gwenhwyfar, at her father's feet, poked at a glowing brazier. He toyed with her loose hair, so like her mother's. Suddenly, he missed Gwawl. Missed her strength and laughter, her warmth and unswerving love. He wondered if there was indeed an afterworld where life continued on. Was Etern with his mother? How pleased she would be to see him, how proud. He shook the fancy aside. The time would come to grieve, but not here, not now.

He lifted his head as a polite tap sounded at the door. Gwenhwyfar rose to answer it, but Cunedda waved her aside, going himself to the door, sword drawn. Outside stood a young man, his face hidden by the hood of a coarsely woven servant's cloak. A muttered exchange of words, then Cunedda closed the door and returned to the warmth of the brazier. A grim smile twitched beneath his moustache.

"Melwas is not here at the palace—he has taken shelter in a tavern some miles to the north." He nodded, satisfied. He was right to have made such haste, glad he was where he ought to be—na, not quite; he and his family ought to be in Gwynedd, but that would shortly be arranged. "Vortigern is expected to be returning to Londinium on the morrow. I intend to claim legal blood-right and ride from here in peace." He sighed. "I would that we could just go, but I want no Saex riding hard after us, demanding we follow the King's damned formalities. We will do this thing right. Melwas is in the wrong, not us. One cheering thought, Gwen!" Cunedda grinned. "The King is showing signs of his creeping age. He cannot ride as fast as I!" They laughed together, hiding their true feelings, sharing each other's sorrow as rain pattered steadily beyond the closed window shutters.

"Da?" Gwenhwyfar spoke softly, her voice rousing Cunedda from the pull of sleep. "Does Arthur know of this arranged betrothal?" It had been a thought hanging with her this past half hour.

"He does."

She fought back fresh tears. Cunedda slid an arm around her shoulder, pulling her to him as if he would never let her go. "By all the gods I wish I had ignored this agreement with Vortigern and accepted Arthur when he asked for you, but until this…" He faltered, searching for adequate words. "Until Melwas provided me with it, I had no escape. Arthur himself pointed out the greatest danger. Were I to let you marry with anyone else your life would be forever endangered."

One little spark of comfort began to grow in Gwenhwyfar, flaring warmer as she considered it. "Arthur asked for me?"

"Aye."

Gwenhwyfar, her head buried deep in her father's lap, let the tears fall. She had cried so much since that vision yesterday evening. Yesterday? Years past, it seemed. Could there be more tears left within her? At least now she understood why Arthur's attitude had changed so abruptly. Why he had danced with Winifred and not with her.

Cunedda's grip on her shoulder slackened and his breathing became low and even. Without disturbing him, Gwenhwyfar found a fur, placed it carefully over him and stood watching him sleep. There were grizzled streaks in his hair, she realised; the red was changing to grey. She had never thought of her father as old. She felt old herself—old and very weary. Her body ached, she was so tired.

Gwenhwyfar stumbled to the bed. She would lie down for a while, close her eyes, let the throbbing pain in her head ease.

She dreamt of muddled images. A glinting knife and red blood, Etern as boy and man, laughing—dying. Melwas with evil leering eyes.

And of Arthur.

THIRTY-THREE

LATE AFTERNOON. WITHOUT KNOCKING, CUNEDDA BURST INTO HIS DAUGHTER'S chamber, startling her and Ceridwen.

"Is your packing complete?" he asked curtly.

"Aye, Uncle." Ceridwen glanced at Gwenhwyfar for confirmation. "We are ready to leave as soon as you give the order."

"These here?" Cunedda pointed at two wooden chests standing to one side. Ceridwen nodded.

"Too much." He strode over to the nearest, heaved up the lid and, rummaging inside, began to throw clothing on the floor. He cursed and left it.

"Sort a few gowns, only what can be carried in saddlebags." He went over to the window. The shutters were open to let in a little light before night descended, and he frowned as the guard patrolling along the water-wall came within view. "Niece, you leave with Enniaun for Gwynedd within the hour."

"What of you?" Gwenhwyfar asked, stooping to retrieve the garments strewn about the floor.

"I shall stay to see through your marriage ceremony, arranged for the morrow."

Gwenhwyfar dropped the clothing. "But…"

Her father would not listen to protests. Pulling a cloak from the back of a chair, he tossed it at her. "Use this to bundle what you need for yourself."

His daughter, clutching the caught cloak, stamped her foot. "I will not wed that bastard!"

Cunedda's expression darkened. "Vortigern sends word that you must. He will be here to witness the handfasting, and has personally paid the blood-price for Etern's death. I am given the land along the coast down to the Ystwyth, and the right to the title of prince."

"You have bargained me away for that!"

"Enough, Gwenhwyfar!"

She bit back a retort, gripping the cloak tighter between her fingers. "I am to be hostage then?"

"So it seems."

She bent to pick up a gown, rolled it. Stopped. "Then why," she asked, "do I need to bundle clothing in this cloak?"

Cunedda's agitation changed to a grin. "Because I am secretly arranging for you to sail tonight to Ygrainne in Less Britain."

"What!" Gwenhwyfar flung the cloak aside. "Am I to be forced into exile?"

Drily, "Would you rather stay in Londinium to wed with Melwas?"

She cried then, caught between the one or the other, felt as she did when as a child she used to play at rolling down a slope. Tumbling down and down, over and over, faster and faster; head spinning, stomach churning. Never knowing when you were going to stop.

Cunedda took her shoulders and drew breath to steady his own racing pulse. "I have been this past hour with the King's envoy." His voice was hard. "Melwas also."

She gasped. "Melwas is in the palace?"

"Aye. Vortigern apparently backs his nephew." Cunedda's mouth drew tight as he held his anger in check. Time enough for that when he had his daughter safe. "Etern, it seems, drew blade first." He hushed his daughter's immediate protest. "I know, it is a lie. But witnesses have spoken for Melwas: money and sweet words can buy anything." He searched her face. Had she understood his meaning—how important it was to go, and go quickly? "Vortigern sends word that this marriage is the only way to ensure peace between us." Vortigern and his poxed kin could rot in their Christian hell for all Cunedda cared. He would bow and scrape to the envoy, agree all there was to agree, buy time—and get away. The King could not force Gwenhwyfar to marry if she was not here. And the extra land and title? Ah, well, Cunedda was considering the taking of them anyway. With or without Vortigern's gracious consent.

"I have a man securing a ship at this moment," he explained. "You sail at the first opportunity." He did not add the ifs. *If I can get you safely out of the palace; if you can make sail along the Tamesis before your leaving is discovered.*

"I see." Gwenhwyfar squared her chin against the churning panic. Given the King's present problems with the economy and the Saex, he would be hard pressed to follow her. She gathered up her belongings, flinging them on to the bed.

Ceridwen plucked up courage, from where she knew not, and stood before her uncle looking him straight in the eye. "I will not return to Gwynedd, my lord. I will go to Less Britain with my cousin."

Placing his hands on the girl's shoulders, Cunedda gave her an affectionate shake. "My dear, she may be gone for…" He paused. For how long?
"Some while."

"All the more reason to go with her."

Ceasing her bustle, Gwenhwyfar hugged her. "Are you sure?"

Ceridwen nodded. "I am sure."

"Then I'll be glad of your company."

Cunedda gave the younger girl a loving embrace. "I thank you, child, for your
loyalty. It will not go unrewarded."

Ceridwen blushed, stammering, "I seek no reward, Uncle."

"Come," said Gwenhwyfar, pushing Ceridwen forward. "Put on two of every
garment. It will be cold at sea by night and we know not what type of ship
to expect."

"In a while." Ceridwen was heading for the door, sensible, practical as ever.
"We may be hungry before sunrise. I will see what food I can beg. I have been
bringing meals up to you of late—no one will suspect."

"Go then. Be quick."

Gwenhwyfar stripped to her undergarments, rummaged among the rumpled clothes, and pulled on two layers. Cunedda had taken up her jewel casket
and emptied the items into a leather pouch. "There is extra in here. I shall
send more."

Taking it, Gwenhwyfar hid the pouch within the garments rolled in her
cloak. "Take care of Tan for me, Da."

Cunedda raised his eyebrows. "All this, and you take time to think of your
damned mare!"

Gwenhwyfar pulled a cord tight around the bundle, remarking lightly, "If I
were to think of more important things, my belly would freeze with fear and I
would be unable to set one foot before the other."

Her father nodded, knowing how she felt. "I will run her with my best stallion and will breed you a fine colt."

Gwenhwyfar smiled approval. "For the Pendragon, my gift to him."

Choking suddenly, her father held his arms wide, feeling the need to hold his
daughter. She ran to him, pressing close to his body.

For a while he held her, stroking her hair, breathing in her perfume. It would
be a while and a while afore they met again. Then he set her from him. There
was much to do. "I must wish your brother a safe journey home." He winked at
her. "He will take Tan with him."

Forcing a smile until he left the room, Gwenhwyfar slumped on to the bed. Left alone, the blackness edged nearer, bringing fresh fears and pain. She lay down and buried her head in a pillow, hugging its goose-down softness for comfort. The pit was before her again; only one step and she would be in, lost to despair. It was as if a long, silent scream were wailing and wailing inside her head.

Some fifteen minutes she lay there, only roused as Ceridwen ran terrified into the room. She threw a bundle of food on the floor and whirled to slam the door shut behind her, thudding the bolts home. She stood panting, her back pressed against the wood. "Melwas is coming!"

Gwenhwyfar's hands flew to her mouth, failed to stop the small scream escaping. Think quickly! Turn panic to action. "He must not suspect anything! Hide these bundles. Quickly!"

They tidied the room, cramming strewn clothing into chests, kicking things under the bed. Would Melwas notice her padded figure? They had never met, he might not.

They were prepared, but the stamp and thud of feet beyond the door made them jump all the same. Ceridwen stuffed her fingers in her mouth, trying to resist the impulse to hide behind her cousin. Melwas bellowed, demanding entry. Calmly Gwenhwyfar walked to the door and spoke through it. "What means this? I mourn my brother, will accept no visitors."

"I have urgent matters to discuss. Let me enter." From his tone, he was not about to go away.

Could she deny him entrance? Gwenhwyfar doubted it. She tried another feint. "I am alone, my lord, I cannot receive a man in my chamber." She motioned frantically to Ceridwen and whispered, "Hide yourself over there," pointing to the chests. Ceridwen crouched behind them and Gwenhwyfar flung bed furs over her. "And for the sake of the gods," she hissed, "remain still!" Ceridwen giggled nervously. "Do not let him stay long."

"That," Gwenhwyfar assured her, "I promise you."

Melwas was pounding on the door, but suddenly the noise ceased. Gwenhwyfar's heart beat as loud as his knocking. Had he gone? Na, he spoke again, level and explicit. "Draw the bolts or I shall have my men axe the door."

Gwenhwyfar waited a few moments, then straightened her shoulders and drew back the bolts. Melwas burst through, almost knocking her aside as he strode into the room, glaring around as if he expected to find some other man there. Gwenhwyfar remained at the door, holding it open. The men, Saex, were standing guard beyond.

Melwas moved to stand within an inch of her. "If you dare to deny me entrance again I shall order you whipped." He flung the door shut, challenging her to object.

She stood relaxed but alert. "To what do I owe this pleasure?"

"I have brought you a gift." He spoke triumphantly, gloating, knowing he had won out over Cunedda. He took her hand, led her away from the door and slipped a jewelled ring on her finger. "Tomorrow I shall add a marriage band." He raised her hand to his lips, his eyes never leaving hers. They were dark green with flashes of tawny gold. Attractive. But Melwas did not know her. Did not realise those sparks and flashes were signs of seething hatred. He turned her hand over to stroke the soft skin of her palm, and placed a kiss at the tip of each finger. Afterwards, Gwenhwyfar marvelled that she had mastered the overwhelming desire to snatch her hand away and spit in his face.

He was a short man, no more than five feet and a few inches, his lack of stature the more obvious because of his bulk. Clean-shaven, he wore his hair cut short in the Roman style, but was dressed like a Saex. His eyes were dark and set too close together, small eyes that darted suspiciously; Gwenhwyfar was reminded of a boar. A great ugly stinking boar.

Melwas grinned, a leer that passed beyond pleasantness. "You are indeed a fine woman. A good catch. Though I would have preferred you to be a trifle shorter." He let go of her hand.

She wiped his touch away on the back of her skirt, thought *Would you like me to cut my feet off at the ankles then?* She smiled placidly.

Melwas enjoyed talking, it seemed—best let him conduct the conversation. "Circumstances make it imperative that I take you as wife without further delay." As he spoke, his gaze had dropped to her bosom. She thanked the gods her choice of clothing for this cold weather concealed her body from the neck down!

"I had been told you were a skinny rake." He laughed lasciviously and moved closer, his body brushing against hers. "I like to have something to get hold of. Good firm teats and buttocks." Gwenhwyfar stood her ground. His mouth opened wider to reveal yellow-stained teeth, his breath foul. "Soon enough we shall have you broader, when I have my son breeding in you!" He bent to kiss her mouth, his lips flabby against hers, his flesh oily. God's truth, he stank!

Gwenhwyfar pulled away, fighting nausea and the desire to wipe his obscene taste from her mouth. "My lord, this is not seemly. I ought not to be alone with you."

His laughter shifted to a more malicious sound. "Why not? We are betrothed, the morrow sees our wedding day!" He smirked at her, drawing her to him, pressing his body tight against hers. "And after that," he added, "our wedding night."

Gwenhwyfar removed his hand from the lacings of her bodice. If he should discover the layers she wore! He tried again to unfasten her gown, but she wriggled and managed to break free.

"Come, Gwenhwyfar! Need we wait?" He grabbed suddenly at her hair, forestalling any further movement. She fumbled for her dagger, silently cursed.

"I suppose"—he nibbled at her ear, his breath hot on her neck—"I must express my regrets for your brother's death—though my action was purely in self-defence you understand. A regrettable incident." His lips sucked at her flesh. "He and the Pendragon were spoiling for a quarrel with me—in the name of God, I know not why." His hands moved to her buttocks.

Gwenhwyfar wanted to kill him, gouge his eyes out, rip his testicles from his body, slit his stomach. She managed to step away. "My brother has always been—" She stopped herself. "Always was imprudent." She choked over the words. "My lord," she had to have him gone! "I am flattered you desire me, and I too look forward to our wedding night, but would not haste spoil the excitement of anticipation?"

"I am not one for formality. I take what is mine, when and where I want it."

Gwenhwyfar walked quickly to the door and opened it. *I wager you do, you bastard.* She smiled, forcing all the pleasure she could into that sweet expression. "Our joyous union must be blessed by the priest, and waiting," she flicked a flirtatious look at him, "heightens reward."

Melwas grinned more broadly and hitched his sword belt arrogantly higher. Gwenhwyfar shuddered but kept her smile firm. "And your son must be legitimate born." She spoke with such conviction!

He kissed her again as he ambled past, eyes lingering on her deliciously rounded chest. "Until the morrow then."

"I await it eagerly." She flung the door closed behind him, slamming home the bolts. Leaning back against the door as Ceridwen had done, she swore all the most vile and obscene oaths she knew.

Ceridwen scrambled from her hiding place, face red from anger and holding her breath. "How dare he! What an arrogant spiteful beast!"

Going to the water pitcher, Gwenhwyfar scrubbed at her mouth with fresh, clean-tasting water and wiped her face and hands. His taste lingered; again she swilled water in her mouth and spat it from her.

"We must find my father, leave here now. We cannot wait until tonight."

Her cousin did not argue.

Opening the door, Gwenhwyfar found her way barred by crossed spears. "What is this outrage?" she demanded, taking hold of each spear, attempting to force them apart.

Saxons, large, fair-haired men—the palace swarmed with the creatures, Hengest's men. Melwas's too, it seemed. But then Melwas always had run with the King's mercenary pack.

Employing others to do the dirty work was no new thing. Rome had often done so, playing off one tribe's squabbles against another. Along the Tamesis and following the line of the Ancient Way, there were third, even fourth generation Saex settlers whose forefathers had fought alongside British auxiliary troops, with land given, according to custom, on retirement from service. Using the English was nothing new—except, unlike Rome, Vortigern had neither money nor land to give in exchange.

One of the guards spoke a few words of guttural British. "Orders, Lord Melwas. You remain chamber."

"Am I a prisoner then?"

The man shrugged, holding his spear firm across the doorway. "No speak British," he said. Gwenhwyfar had a deep suspicion that he did, and spoke it well.

"Must my cousin also stay?" She resisted the temptation to aim a foot at his shin. The guard shrugged again and threw a brief questioning glance at his companion. "Gwenhwyfar remain."

She snorted contempt and slammed the door shut. "Ceridwen, you must find my father. Hurry!"

Ceridwen bit her lip and reluctantly opened the door to slip unchallenged beneath the crossed spears, blushing slightly at the guards' appraising eyes. She peered along the corridor to make sure Melwas had gone, then hitched up her skirts and fled in the direction of Cunedda's chamber.

THIRTY-FOUR

A S SHE NEARED HER DESTINATION, CERIDWEN SLOWED HER ANXIOUS PACE, then stopped in dismay. Two Saxon guards stood resolutely before Cunedda's door. She twisted her skirt between her fingers. What to do? Had Enniaun gone? Where were the Gwynedd men? At the barracks or the guardhouse? Could she go there alone; would she have the courage? She must try!

A hand cupped her mouth, another curving round her waist, dragging her backwards kicking and struggling into a dimly lit room. The door banged shut, her assailant slackened his grip, and she bit his hand, teeth sinking into flesh. He yelped, but kept firm hold. "Jesu, girl, I am on your side!"

She kicked out, her foot thudding into his shin. He swore again. "I am here to help you, for the Christ's sake! Believe me. I am the Pendragon's man."

She stood still, breathing hard, body rigid, his hand clasped over her mouth.

"If I take my hand away will you be quiet?" He had a soft voice, kind.

Wide eyed, trembling with fear, Ceridwen nodded. Slowly he let go; she instantly whirled round and darted for the door. He caught her and swung her to face him, her small hands flying to his chest, hammering at his body.

"Listen to me, I said I was Arthur's man! Would you rather I let you walk into a viper's nest of Melwas's Saex?"

Her hand slapped his face.

"Fine. Have it your way." He let her go and flung the door wide, indicating with an extravagant gesture that she was free to leave. "Go. Melwas will be pleased to see you."

Doubtful, Ceridwen regarded the young man. Tall, fair haired, aged about twenty summers. His blue eyes glinted in the dim light, a tentative smile forming. Dressed in a simple tunic, weaponless, he appeared to be a servant, yet his stance, bright manner, and voice lacked servility.

"Who are you?" she demanded, her head held high and defiant, as she had seen Gwenhwyfar do.

"I am Iawn." He shut the door.

Ceridwen smiled shyly. "I apologise. You frightened me."

Iawn laughed, a pleasant sound, rich with humour. "Remind me not to frighten you too often, it could prove painful!" He inspected the deep teeth marks in his hand, winced, then laughed again as she darted forward to inspect the damage.

"I must get to my lord Cunedda," she said anxiously. "Gwenhwyfar is being held prisoner in her chamber."

"As is Cunedda."

"His son and the men?"

"Gone. Enniaun slipped the net, thank God."

"What shall I do? Gwenhwyfar must get away from here!"

Iawn sensed her distress and urgency, was suddenly reminded of his little sister. She would have been the age of this young woman had raiding Saex not butchered her two years past. He experienced an overpowering urge to protect this girl; wanted suddenly to gather her to him, take her to a place of safety.

If he had been at home that day, not out hunting, he might have saved his sister and mother. He bit his lip, forced down the rising nausea. God in Heaven, would the sight of their mutilated bodies never leave him be!

"Do not worry, little bird, we have things under control." He smiled, hunkered down to look directly into her anxious face, set his haunting nightmare aside. "There are many of us within the palace who secretly serve the Pendragon— and therefore Cunedda."

Ceridwen brightened, trusting him. "You are a spy, then I thought you were no servant!"

Iawn pouted. "Damn it, I have worked hard at this disguise. It has been no easy thing these past months fetching and carrying, bowing to the likes of them." He nodded towards the door indicating his contempt for Vortigern and his kindred.

His manner changed, his body becoming more stooped and huddled as he became a man whose only purpose was to serve "What be your orders, m'lady?" Even his voice changed into uncultured, poor man's speech.

Ceridwen clapped her hands. "Oh, that is good! You have a talent!"

He bowed modestly. "I take the character of a servant because they go unnoticed. You would be surprised at how many talk before us, assuming there is no intelligence atween a menial's ears."

He turned serious then and sat her on a stool, explaining carefully all that was planned, making her repeat her place in things twice over to ensure she had it aright. Satisfied at last, he saw her from the room, catching her hand as she passed through the doorway. He smiled.

"Ceridwen, take care of yourself."

THIRTY-FIVE

E XERCISING PATIENCE, IAWN WAITED FOR NIGHTFALL. IT WAS AN EASY MATTER to organise the escape of Cunedda's few remaining men from close confinement. Before Cunedda's door the silent blades of Iawn's and another of the Pendragon's men dealt with the Saex guard—and they were running unseen down narrow servants' stairs and out through the lengthening shadows of dusk heading for the water gate. Ignoring the soft scuttle of movement, the guard along the wall continued his patrol, obligingly looking the wrong way, turning his back as a shadow slid through the gate. He touched a finger to the pouch at his waist, hanging heavy with gold. So few British were loyal to Vortigern now; so many could no longer tolerate the increasing presence of Saex mercenaries and the dominance of the Queen.

Gwenhwyfar and Ceridwen were ready as gravel rattled against the small squares of unbroken window glass. Ceridwen slid the catch and peeped out, delighted to see Iawn's face staring up from below. He grinned and neatly caught the bundles they tossed down. Heart hammering a battle rhythm, Ceridwen gathered her skirts and climbed nervously out, her toes feeling for the wooden struts of the propped ladder. She felt Iawn's strong hands grasp her waist and swing her safely down. Briefly she clung to him, awkwardly murmuring her thanks. Gwenhwyfar followed quickly, unafraid.

"Your father's waiting beyond the water gate," Iawn whispered. "We freed him and the men first lest we should find the need for fighting." He looked about. No one. Nothing. "Make use of the shadows. Hurry."

The night was dark, with no moon, and low clouds covering the stars. It would rain again before dawn. The oars of a small fishing boat dipped steadily in and out of the water, pulling downriver towards the vague, distant shape of a moored ship.

"Iawn has found a fast craft." Cunedda spoke low, aware that sound carried easily over water. They had expected an alarm from the palace, the raising of the hunt, but nothing had come.

"The crew have been paid well, with the promise of more when I have word of your arrival. Here." Cunedda pulled a ring from his finger. "Send this so I may know you are safe."

Gwenhwyfar took it and slipped it on her own finger, where it hung loose and uncomfortable; nestled it in the pouch at her waist instead. When she looked up, the oarsmen were pulling alongside a timbered hull with a rope ladder snaking down and men leaning over to catch the bundles tossed up to them.

Ceridwen was ushered up the flimsy ladder, followed closely by Iawn, who steadied her feet, talking calmly to her as she nervously climbed. Anxiously she asked him, "Are you to come with us?"

He nodded.

She slipped her hand into his and held it tight. "Then the leaving is made that much more bearable."

In the fishing boat, Gwenhwyfar held her father close. "Where will you go?"

"Horses are waiting. I ride fast for home."

No time for more. Hands were pulling her forward, guiding her to the ladder. Before she knew it, she stood beside Ceridwen and Iawn on deck, and the little boat carrying her father was pulling away, out into the darkness. She realised suddenly she had not told him about her mother's dagger, that Rowena had given it to Winifred, and the bitch's brat had taken good care to let her know.

Cunedda called something as the ship slipped her moorings and eased into the strong tidal pull. Gwenhwyfar caught only the words "safe voyage." She leant over the bulwark, felt the leap of the ship as the wind took the unfurling sail, sending her racing forward, her bow wave creaming. No use calling out: what could he do about a dagger anyway? She waved, knowing he could not see her through the darkness, finally abandoned the struggle against tears. At least the dark hid those.

It was stupid, childish. Her thoughts were not that she might never see her family or home again, but that Winifred, a thieving, poxed Saex, possessed her mother's dagger!

THIRTY-SIX

THE DAY AFTER ETERN'S BLOODY KILLING, ARTHUR WENT DRUNK TO HIS marriage ceremony in Camulodunum. The thing had been agreed, arranged, there was no getting out of it. The handfasting had been set for three days hence, but the King, needing to ride urgently back to Londinium, brought the ceremony forward.

Arthur held himself well, despite vomiting profusely in the latrines before summoning the courage to enter Vortigern's quarters. The haze of best barley-brew helped, the only way he knew of getting through this god-damned day. It had helped him sleep too, though not enough to dim the memory of spilt blood and Etern's dead eyes.

The King noticed the way Arthur swayed slightly as he walked slowly into the private chapel. Hengest, standing beside his granddaughter, might have noticed too—happen they all had. Arthur did not particularly care.

It had occurred to him to run, but where was there to run to? Gwynedd? Ah now, Cunedda's mountains would be safe, but he did not want to be safe, he wanted Gwenhwyfar. And he could not have her.

Beside him, Vortigern's daughter spoke her vows in a clear voice, her self-satisfied smile wide with gloating. She was a tall, slender girl, and dressed in a fine silk gown, with flame-coloured veil and gold-trimmed leather sandals, her beauty was undeniable.

Her perfume, though, was strong, rather sickly. Standing so close, Arthur suddenly realised how much he hated her. And tonight he had to bed her! Or did he? He had taken her already. Vortimer, beside him, gave his elbow a squeeze of encouragement, but did not help matters by whispering, "Think on the pleasure of an untouched woman in your bed this night!"

A thought came. Arthur whispered back, loud enough for Winifred to hear, "A bride must be virgin pure, for if she comes to her husband's bed used, then he has the right to strip her naked and whip her through the streets." He looked at Winifred with loathing, his meaning plain. "Or accept her for the whore she is to do with as he pleases."

To her credit, Winifred's smile did not waver, but a small doubt began to niggle in her mind. She had the Pendragon. He was hers, but at what price? As the wedding entertainment and festivities gained momentum, the doubt grew. Happen the prize was not worth the winning after all.

Vortigern had left soon after the ceremony. For once, Arthur would have preferred to ride with him.

The Pendragon drank deeper and laughed louder, and eventually, as night fell, he allowed himself to be escorted to the bridal chamber where Winifred waited, the sheets drawn to her chin, her hair unbound. Sweet-scented flower petals were scattered around, the aroma of bees-wax candles.

They put him to bed beside her, scattered more petals and blessings, and left, laughing, tossing suggestive remarks and lewd advice over their shoulders.

Away to the south, a ship was steering into the flowing ebb current of the Tamesis river, her sails filling, carrying her swiftly for the open sea. Aboard her a passenger freed from an oath of betrothal; but Arthur did not know Cunedda had renounced all allegiance to the King, did not know that from now forward Gwynedd stood defiantly independent.

Tired, Arthur lay back, staring at the ceiling. Winifred had not moved; she sat with knees raised, the covers tucked beneath her chin. "I recall you were not so modest before." He took hold of the sheets and pulled them from her. Involuntarily, she made to cover her nakedness with her hands, but turned the reaction aside and let him look full at her rounded breasts and flat stomach.

"No child then?" he sneered. "No fault of mine. I know of several bastard born daughters." He threw the covers at her and turned his back saying, "Cover yourself. I have no need to look at you. I know already the slut I have."

There was nothing Winifred could say or do as his breathing deepened into sleep.

A face swam through Arthur's dreams, a face framed by wind-tossed copper hair. A woman with a laugh as welcome as a waterfall on a hot summer's day. Gwenhwyfar.

Sunlight flooded the room, the morning well underway when Arthur woke, sluiced himself with cold water, dressed, and made to leave. Almost as an afterthought he spoke to Winifred. "The thing is done, you are my wife. Enjoy the title; it's all you will ever have from me." He strode through the door and met with Vortimer waiting outside. Had the man been there all night?

Footsteps from along the corridor. Arthur peered through the dim light, saw Cei approaching, and stepped forward to speak with his cousin. They exchanged a few low words, then Arthur laughed, a high mocking sound that almost cracked into despair. He walked slowly back to Vortimer and stood before him, eyes narrowed, finger poking at his shoulder.

"Were you so scared I would wriggle free of this thing that you must stand guard at my door?" He poked again, harder, his face menacingly close. "Who had the idea to get me so quickly married to that whore in there? Which one, yourself or your poxed father, guessed Cunedda would call blood-right and disclaim all agreements past made?"

He kicked the bedchamber door open, glared at Winifred, sitting as she had last night, knees drawn up, sheets to her chin.

"I am the Pendragon. Remember that." He slammed the door behind him and stood with his back against it, eyes shut, breath rasping in his throat.

He need not have married her! Gwenhwyfar would by now be on her way to Less Britain, so Cunedda's urgent-sent messenger said, for temporary safekeeping. She was his, the Pendragon's, with Gwynedd's blessing, should he still want her.

Arthur wondered how a wedding night with Gwenhwyfar would have passed.

What to do? Two choices. Leave, declare Winifred a whore, and take ship for Less Britain to claim Gwenhwyfar as wife? He would need protect her against Melwas, for that bastard would sooner see her dead than with Arthur. Slowly he exhaled. He could live comfortably in Less Britain with Gwenhwyfar.

Or should he stay? Were he to leave Britain and abandon Winifred, Vortigern would never permit his return. Only as War Lord over some great invading army could Arthur then attempt to take the kingdom he so badly wanted. And Cunedda had been right: outside Britain, there was no army for him to command.

Gwenhwyfar or Winifred? Happiness or a kingdom? Choices. Na, there was no decision. The thing was done, the shuttle was moving through the loom, with the pattern well cast.

Suddenly, Arthur needed his men. The clash of weapons, the bark of orders, and the pounding of hooves. The smell of sweat and blood, a taste of fear and excitement.

Ignoring Vortimer, the Pendragon strode from the building. He wanted Gwenhwyfar but he was determined to be called king. When he had that, he could claim her.

He bellowed for someone to fetch Eira and rode to where, at this moment, the Pendragon belonged. With the army of Britain.

PART TWO

THE WEAVING

AUGUST 453

ONE

THE DAY HAD BEEN LONG AND HOT. UP HERE, THE EVER-PRESENT HILL WIND had helped cool the men down, but still they dripped sweat and were short tempered with the string of stubborn pack mules. Arthur called a halt early, although it was only mid-afternoon and they had plenty of light to cover a few more miles.

They made camp quickly and efficiently, securing the mule loads in a guarded tent beside the Pendragon's. Then relaxed a while, taking the opportunity to bathe in the cold waters of the lake, grateful to wash the itch and stink of stale sweat from their skins.

Arthur splashed with them, diving deep into the clear pool, the green depths quiet and mysterious beneath him, stretching down as if to reach the earth's heart. It seemed another dimension of being, amidst this weird light and diffused sound; another place; the other world of Faery, where time had no meaning. He pushed upwards, feet kicking against the pull of water, and for a panicked heartbeat it felt as if he were held there, trapped, being enticed down into that magic kingdom where no mortal dwelt. His head broke the surface, dazzling sunlight hitting him smart in the face. Men were laughing and jesting along the shore line, splashing each other, pushing companions into the cool water. Arthur gasped and sucked in sweet, clear air and struck out, relieved, towards them.

From the shore, where he rubbed himself vigorously with his tunic, the pool looked safe enough, but even so he shivered. Superstition! Even in a man of level thinking it was a powerful inheritance.

Cei noticed the shiver and grinned. "Too cold for you, huh?"

"Na," Arthur confessed, "too deep!"

Cei nodded understanding, his hand involuntarily making the sign of the Christian cross. "They say there is an island where the faery folk dwell, on one of these lakes, visible only at Beltaine. An evil place of pagan darkness where God's blessed face would not look."

"Aye, well, 'tis not Beltaine."

All the same, Arthur found it difficult to shrug aside that moment of fear when he had fought against the pull of water. How easy would it be to become lost within those silent depths? He shivered again, the memory lying heavy on his shoulder. As Cei had just now made the Christian sign of protection, Arthur's fingers formed the homed sign against the pagan lords of darkness.

Noticing, Cei gave him a sidelong glance of disapproval. He decided against comment, saying instead, "Should we not take a look at the morrow's ground?"

Arthur grinned back at him, grateful for the chance to turn his thoughts from the unreal to the practical. He strode briskly to the horse lines barking an order at an officer to take command. "And see to it no one goes near the mule loads while I am gone!"

"Do you not trust us then, sir?" called a soldier sitting outside a tent sorting his gear.

"Na, Lucius, I would rather trust a whore to stay virtuous in the men's bath-house!" Arthur answered brightly, a smile playing on his mouth. The men nearby laughed good-natured, knowing they would not have been picked for this duty were they not trusted. Escorting gold was not a task for the unreliable.

Vaulting into the saddle, Arthur heeled his stallion to canter away across the short, springy turf that in wetter months would be soft and bog bound. He reined in some distance up the hill, Cei bringing his mount round to stay close. They let the horses' heads drop to tear at the grass, which held little goodness in this bleak, wind-teased landscape.

Arthur shifted in the saddle and hooked his leg around one of the two for-ward pommel horns, rested his arm on his crooked knee. Eira grazed, his sensi-tive muzzle searching for choice eating.

"What are we doing here, Cei?" Arthur asked after watching the lazy swirl of smoke from campfires for a while.

"We are sitting up here thinking of the men down there preparing our sup-per," the big man beside him answered jovially. "And we are bringing a full load of gold from the mines to our bastard of a king. Your action was wrong, you know."

Arthur glanced sharply across at Cei and frowned. He had known Cei would eventually say something about what had happened.

"The mines must be kept working," he said.

"To fill Vortigern's treasury? Is that worth the killing and maiming of slaves?"

"Is it the death of a few slaves you object to then? Or that we are guarding and carrying gold for the King?" Arthur replied angrily, for Cei's words stung—the more so because he knew him to be right.

He had not wanted to accept these orders, given by the King's eldest son Vortimer, but then he had no desire to be pulled back from the marshlands and returned to Londinium either. The Anglian uprising was under control, the British somehow clinging to their supremacy—at least for a while, until the next thrust forward by encroaching settlers who were gaining in courage with every fresh outbreak of war fever. One day the dam would burst.

It had seemed a mundane task to ride westward to investigate rumours of unrest at the mines and to oversee the collection of a long overdue consignment of gold. But it was preferable to sitting idly kicking one's heels. Better than having to play husband to Winifred—mind, even shifting a midden heap was preferable to that.

The rumours had been amply borne out. The slaves were sullen and rebellious, their overseers drunken and slovenly, the mines unworked.

The Pendragon had handled the situation quickly and ruthlessly, hanging the commanding officer for gross negligence, publicly flogging two junior officers, and punishing those slaves who refused to work. There had been a brief flair of rebellion from slaves and guards, swiftly and decisively put down.

A handful of dead lay grotesquely bloodied as a result, women and children among the men. Even a handful were too many dead, but the mines were in business again, gold in production under the new, watchful eye of an honest and loyal man. Loyal to the Pendragon, anyway.

"I may not agree with Vortigern on most things, Cei," said Arthur, toying with the few incongruous black strands in the white mane hanging over Eira's withers.

His thoughts wandered, his sentence left unfinished. Strange how the horse's coat was white all over, save for black-tipped ears, black muzzle, knees, and hocks. The mane and tail, too, had strands of black, and a broad dark stripe ran from wither to dock. Arthur reflected on some young horses he had seen bred that were almost black at birth, turning to grey then white as they gained height and years. He wondered vaguely if even these few dark markings on Eira would gradually fade.

Cei shifted in his saddle. "You were saying?"

Arthur patted the horse and looked eye to eye at his friend, cousin, and second-in-command. "If I am to rule one day I shall need to control the economy." He snorted contemptuously. "Or lack of it." He swung his leg back into a riding position. "Even were I not to rule, I may soon need more than I have at present. Winifred's dowry will pay for the horses Cunedda is breeding for me. But it is not enough." He gave Eira one last pat, a firm slap on the neck. "The gold mine and a loyal overseer may come in useful."

Cei gathered his reins, pulling his chestnut's head away from the grass. He kicked him forward up the rising slope. "That I appreciate," he said, flinging the words over his shoulder, "but why gather the wealth for Vortigern? He is already in financial trouble. Another kick to the backside may just be enough to topple him." He pushed the horse into a canter.

Eira lifted his head and whinnied, his body shaking with the calling, impatient to catch up. His hooves danced, his head tossed. He needed no urging, bounded forward the moment Arthur relaxed pressure on the bit.

The two men cantered to the summit of the hill, the horses slowing as they reached the steeper incline, snorting and blowing.

Arthur could not answer Cei. The same question was in his own mind. He had no answer, save he had seized the opportunity to put as many miles as possible between himself and his Saex-bred wife.

They dismounted on the ridge. Below on one side the camp looked small and distant with ant size men scuttling between the tents. The late afternoon heat had left a haze on the horizon to the south, in the direction of the sea. A mist was rising, promising a cooler day on the morrow. On the far side of the hill, the ground sloped less steeply down to a valley where a river ran and the trackway twisted with the lie of the land, looping outcrops of rock, leaping from one side of the river to the other, avoiding boggy ground.

They hobbled the horses, let them find what nourishment they could, stood studying the route east.

"Do we follow the track?" Cei asked, chewing a blade of grass.

Arthur squatted, then absentmindedly took two ivory dice from his belt pouch and began idly tossing them in his hand, thinking. He rolled them, throwing a five and a one. He frowned. "It's a risk whether we take the track or keep to the hills. Either way, we may need to fight if we meet others: Hibernian, Saex, or British. Gold is of value to all." Then again, he could keep it himself; claim they had encountered raiders and lost the lot. But it was a matter of pride, really: would he allow raiders to take that which he was guarding?

He spoke quietly, regretfully, an apology in his voice. "The men need paying, Cei. Vortimer's British men; my men. Were I allowed to bring my full command with us, then happen I might have considered sharing it out among ourselves and heading off into the hills. But what then?" He retrieved the dice and threw again, double two. "What good would it do us? Could we pitch in with Cunedda in Gwynedd? Buy passage on a ship back to Less Britain? Is that what we want? There would be no goal in mind, no future, save for running like outlaw thieves."

Cei remained silent, brooding. Arthur was right no doubt, but still something irked him, like an unreachable itch between the shoulder blades. "I cannot help feeling we are nothing but slaves to Vortigern. We are under his son's direct command, we run at Vortimer's beck and call, but is not the one the same as the other?" Cei hunkered down next to Arthur, tossing his chewed stalk aside. "I am tired of it, Arthur. Tired of senseless skirmishes that gain us one step forward for every three we take backwards."

Arthur stared out over the hills, empty of life save for wind-bent trees, and birds. There were undoubtedly hares crouching in the grass, deer concealed in the clumps of alder, oak, elm and hazel woodland. Wolves too, lurking in the shadows.

"I had a dream once, Cei. As a boy, I talked of it to," he paused, remembering the warmth of Gwynedd, "to good friends. I was to be a great leader and command a king's army—that was before I knew Uthr Pendragon was my father. I thought then, as a boy, men would flock to my side. I expected to scythe through enemies like a farmer cutting wheat." He stopped. A falcon was hovering nearby, its wings folded, falling down into the grass. "A child expects the sun always to shine, Cei, thinks the sky is always blue."

The falcon had missed. It beat upward again in search of alternative supper. "I still have the dream, but it is so far removed from what it once was. I still want my banner flying higher than any other, but the glory has tarnished. Stupid, isn't it? I once lusted after war, all I want now is prosperity and peace; to see people, ordinary people, contended. To see children with full bellies." Arthur laughed, mocking himself. He stood up and kicked at a tussock of grass, put the dice away. "I suppose I have grown up."

Cei stood also, watching something, a disturbance of the air, a faint shimmer of movement. It grew as he watched, shielding his eyes, squinting to see more clearly. A dust cloud was visible some way to the north along the track.

Arthur saw it too. "Best alert the men," he said calmly. "One leisurely traveller does not make such an announcement."

Cei nodded his agreement. Releasing the hobbles from his horse, he mounted and cantered back, noting with pride the men had seen him coming and were waiting expectantly long before he reached the camp.

Arthur walked his horse to the cover of some bushes. It might have been wiser to return to camp, douse the fires, and seek safety in concealment, but curiosity had the better of him. He had a good view up the valley from here, and doubted he would be seen if he remained still.

No one coming from that direction could know of the load the mules carried, should not even know Arthur and his men were in the area. He rubbed at the stubble on his chin. Whoever was coming, was coming fast. He waited.

One horse, stumbling from tiredness, was ahead, neck outstretched, legs pounding. Behind, a group of thirty or so riders urging on almost spent mounts. They carried no standard. The animals were small, sturdy hill ponies; not as swift and well bred as Eira and others of his type. The stallion had seen the approaching horses; he neighed a high-pitched welcome.

Too late, Arthur grabbed for his muzzle, cursing. "Damn you! What has got into your thick skull this day? You are behaving like an unbroken colt."

Cei appeared, leading his horse quickly over the skylining ridge to join Arthur. "What do you make of it?"

"Someone is very keen to leave the pack behind."

"Hunter, or hunted?"

Arthur grinned. "We will not find out up here!" He ducked his head enquiringly towards the ridge behind them.

Cei replied with a nod. "I have left some men on the alert in camp; one is concealed up there," he pointed to the ridge, "as lookout. The others await your orders."

Arthur nodded, satisfied. "Have them form line of battle a little down this slope—near enough the ridge to show we have no hostile intent, but low enough should it be necessary to take action."

Cei acknowledged the order and turned to mount. Arthur vaulted into Eira's saddle and let the stallion walk forward, picking his own path down the uneven grass of the steep hillside. There was no doubt the riders had seen him. The one in front faltered, reining in his mount so hard the pony almost fell as it staggered to a halt.

Arthur's men came in a steady line over the ridge and took up positions, waiting, the Dragon Banner streaming proud above the bearer's head. The rider saw it and gave a shout and kicked it hard into a canter, heading for the Pendragon.

The animal carried two riders, a man with a smaller, cloaked figure clinging behind. Arthur nudged Eira into a trot, glanced over his shoulder to make sure Cei was following.

Shouting something, the man waved his hand frantically. The pony stumbled, regained its footing, but weariness and the double weight were too much; its head dropped, its forelegs buckled, and it went down, tipping the two riders to the grass. Instantly, the man was up, sword in hand, running to his companion.

The pursuers were gaining ground, closing in, anger glazing their expressions. Arthur recognised the leader; Brychan, a cross-breed Hibernian settler. Vortigern's man. A spawned cur-son of a fatherless mare! A toad-featured, pig's littered runt!

Arthur frowned darkly as Brychan thundered up to him shouting some abusive comment that, perhaps fortunately, was snatched away by the wind. The other man, coming up to him at a run, he did not know. He indicated Brychan. "Whoever you are, my friend, I see you have angered the King's sasnach dog."

Bringing his right hand to his left shoulder in formal salute, the man—a young man—eased his companion behind him a little. "I have something of his he does not wish me to have."

His mouth twitching into a smile, Arthur nodded. Aye, so he could see! She was small and slightly built, with dark hair and wide, frightened, brown eyes. Arthur judged her to be about ten and six years. He leant forward in the saddle, resting his arms on Eira's neck, and pointed casually with one finger. "Brychan's daughter?"

The said Brychan hauled at his frothing mount. He leapt from the saddle before the horse had come to a halt, rushed up the slope, drawing his sword as he ran. "You will die for this outrage, Gwynllyw!"

Arthur straightened, touched his heel lightly to Eira's flank. The big horse bounded forward, between the enraged Brychan and the young man, Gwynllyw, who shielded the terrified girl.

"There will be no killing without my consent." Arthur's tone was mellow, with no sense of threat or malice. Those who knew him well knew Arthur to be at his most dangerous when he seemed relaxed and easy. That good-humoured smile, that sidelong look with narrowed eye and cocked eyebrow.

Brychan's men approached, snarling like wolves. One man impulsively spurred his horse forward and Cei was suddenly before him; smiling, sitting his hose easily, hands light on the rein, a spear tip hovering at the man's throat.

"This is private business, Pendragon!" Brychan growled. "I order you aside!"

"No business is private before an envoy of the King." Lazily Arthur shifted his gaze from Brychan to the men. All carried weapons. "This looks like a war band to me. Does it not to you, Cei?"

"It does."

"Pah! I say again, this is a private matter!" Brychan stepped aside from Eira and waved his sword menacingly at the shrinking girl. "Come here this instant, girl! By the gods, I will have your hide flayed from your back for this insult to me!" The girl moved closer to Gwynllyw, clutching at his waist, her head shaking a silent no.

"She is mine, Brychan. I have claimed her—you have no right to deny us!"

"No right! By God she is my daughter and I say who she is to wed! Certainly not some upstart of a petty British chieftain! Gwladys! Come here, now! I order it!"

Arthur shifted his weight in the saddle. "It seems you are over free with orders, Brychan."

The two had crossed swords, figuratively, before, across Vortigern's Council Chamber. Brychan, son of a Hibernian wolf and a British noblewoman, had claimed his maternal grandsire's land, the barren hills between the rivers Usk and Taff, some few years before Uthr's death. Vortigern had welcomed him, a prospective ally, with open arms, granting him favours and friendship.

When Uthr had made his war call there had been few who rallied to him from these parts. Vortigern's gold and Brychan's influence bribed too well. Arthur detested Brychan.

"I say again, Pendragon—withdraw." Brychan swung round unexpectedly and struck Eira across the muzzle with the flat of his sword. The horse reared, squealing, front hooves raking the air in anger and pain. As the horse went up, Brychan darted forward and buffeted Gwynllyw with his shoulders, sending the man, winded, rolling down the hillside, and grabbed for the girl. Pushing his kicking and screaming daughter before him, he attempted to run the short distance back to the safe semi-circle of his men, surprised to find Arthur had moved no less swiftly.

Kicking himself free of the saddle, Arthur had dropped quickly, rolling away from Eira's plunging hooves to spring to his feet, sword raised, a yard in front of Brychan. He feinted to one side, dropped, and suddenly his sword was between Brychan and the girl. Arthur took hold of her, drawing her close to him with his left hand, the tip of his blade hovering over Brychan's heart.

He was winded as he spoke, exertion and the surge of blood heat taking his breath. "As I said, Brychan, this is my business."

At an angry movement from Brychan's men, Cei whistled low and threatened them with the spear he held. "I would not move a hair on your louse-riddled heads if I were you." He hoisted the spear aloft, waved it in a single circle. The Dragon dipped once in response, and the waiting line of ten riders along the slope above moved forward, coming at a steady walk, spears lowered, swords loose at their sides. "I have only to signal," Cei said, "and they will charge."

The hill men dropped back reluctantly, looking to their leader who signalled compliance with a curt nod of his head. They lowered their weapons and took a few paces back down the slope.

Arthur grinned. "Good. Happen now we can talk of this matter like civilised men." He paused, looked Brychan disdainfully up and down, and added with pointed rudeness. "At least, I can talk so with young Gwynllyw here."

Brychan growled and raised his fist, but with a laugh Arthur stepped back to a safer distance, taking the girl with him.

Following little used trackways and lonely hill routes, staying away from settlements where awkward questions could be asked had advantages when escorting a delivery of gold, but there were also disadvantages. The men foraged for food as they marched, at this time of year not a problem. This morning Arthur himself had brought down a fine buck—the butchered carcass would be roasting back at camp at this moment. The tents, good and strong, leather-made, were dry and windproof. There was water aplenty and few worries of raiding parties striking this far inland, which was why they were using this particular route. The one drawback was women; or the lack of them. A soldier welcomes the surfeit of willing girls to share his bed when stationed near town or settlement, grows used to long weeks of campaign or march without so much as a look at a female. But at odd times something occurs during these spells of enforced celibacy to remind the senses of what is being missed. Arthur held the girl close, his arm inside the folds of her cloak, encircling her slim body. As he had dragged her back, away from the proximity of her father, his hand had touched the firm, rounded swell of her breast and, suddenly, Arthur wanted her.

Beneath the cloak, Arthur shifted his hand. Her eyes flickered to his, her mouth closing in a bitten off gasp as he squeezed her waist. No woman could mistake his intent at that moment.

Gwynllyw saw it also. The Pendragon, personally, he did not know, but he had heard stories about his father and those now told of the son, heard enough to shout, "Gwladys is mine, Pendragon! Leave her be!"

Brychan countered swiftly with, "God rot you! She is not yours!"

Arthur laughed—he was enjoying this! He covered the few yards to where Eira stood, unconcerned and cropping grass. No trained warhorse moved far once the reins were dropped; such a small thing could save an unseated rider's life in battle. Arthur clicked his tongue and the horse lifted his head, ears pricking. The Pendragon lifted the girl to the horse's withers and vaulted up behind her into the saddle and, wheeling the animal round, cantered the distance between the angry group of Brychan's men and his own waiting line of cavalry. He stopped short just out of their hearing.

The girl sat rigid, back straight, arms still, her lips pressed tight together. She dared not open her mouth for if she did, the scream clamped between her teeth would start and never end.

Arthur bent his head, his mouth close to hers, his lips almost touching that exquisitely pretty mouth. When Eira shifted a hind leg, Arthur felt rather than saw movement to his left. He glanced up into the impassive face of Cei.

"If you kiss her, Arthur, I shall ride up this hill and return to camp with the men, leaving you as dog's meat for Gwynllyw and Brychan to chew between them."

Arthur forced a good-natured reply. "A bit of fun, Cei—harmless fun with a pretty girl."

"What was it someone said to me once? *I want to see contented people, children with full bellies?*" Cei looked Arthur straight in the eye. "I assumed you were talking of well-being and adequate food, but I must have got it wrong. You were obviously talking of lust and girls' bellies filled with childbearing!" Cei's cheeks were red-blotched with anger, his knuckles white as they clutched the reins. The two horses laid their ears back, sensing the fury. "Blood of Jesu! What are you doing, Pendragon? Are you determined to kill more men—our men—for the sake of a sea-wolf's daughter?"

Cei had never turned on Arthur before; had never commented on his more indelicate excesses.

"Is the Christian Jesu turning you soft-bellied then, Cei?" Arthur asked, surprised. "You were never averse to a pretty woman before."

"In the right place, at the right time, na. This is not the place nor the time."

Arthur regarded the girl cowering away from his holding arm, saw and felt her terror. He gestured defeated to Cei. "You are right, my friend."

He took a deep breath, assumed a calm, relaxed smile, and eased his hand on the girl's waist. "So, you do not wish to bed with me?" She said nothing. "Not with the Pendragon? I possess land and wealth—I could keep a mistress in comfort and jewels for many years." He sighed, "I see I am not tempting you." He brushed a strand of dark hair from her cheek, tucked it behind her ear. She was surprised at how gentle his touch was.

"I apologise, my dear, for all this." He gestured behind him to the hill men, and then forward to his own soldiers. "It was necessary, I needed you out of their hearing to talk alone with you. I had no other intention." He glanced at Cei. Happen the girl believed the lie. Cei certainly did not.

Arthur lifted her down, dismounted beside her, took her by the elbow, and walked a few paces.

"So you are not interested in me? Ah well, it was worth the asking!" He grinned suddenly, genuinely regretting his behaviour. He swept her a low bow, then took her hand in his and kissed it lightly.

A faint smile flickered on her pale face. This young man was absurd! For all the fear, she realised that she liked him! Things had happened so fast this day, so many reeling emotions coming tumbling one upon the other.

"It seems, as I cannot have you," Arthur glanced meaningfully at Cei, "who can? Your father or Gwynllyw? The choice is yours."

At the mention of Brychan her heart lurched. "He will kill me," she whispered, not daring to look at her father, who stood arms folded, foot tapping.

"I'd not allow him to. I would ensure no harm came to you."

Gwladys looked up at Arthur, wide-eyed, impressed. "You could do that for me?"

Arthur knew well he had no jurisdiction over Brychan at all, but still he answered with a swagger of importance. "Of course."

Cei snorted.

"I thank you, but I would rather go with Gwynllyw." She said it decisively, her eyes at last managing to meet his. Arthur was exciting and interesting, but Gwynllyw was steadfast and solid. And she needed a husband, not a lover whose attention could change with the wind.

"We had best sort this matter out then." With his broad smile, Arthur lifted her into Eira's saddle and set her comfortably wedged between the rear and fore saddle horns, walked at the horse's head, leading him by the bridle.

She had never been mounted on such a tall horse before. Her father's ponies stood below fourteen hands, and Gwynllyw's not much taller, but this beautiful creature with arched crest and proud-carried tail stood a full fifteen hands.

She stroked her fingers along the fine muscled neck, marvelling at the silkiness of coat and feeling of strength.

Bracing his shoulder against the animal's chest, Arthur eased the stallion to a halt before Brychan and motioned Gwynllyw forward. "It seems we have a difference of opinion here. On the one hand Brychan demands his daughter, on the other Gwynllyw demands a wife." Arthur paused, thrust his thumb through his sword belt, considering the matter. "Gwynllyw, have you a bride-price to offer?"

"Ten head of cattle and ten of swine. And I ask no dowry."

"That seems a fair exchange to me—does it not to you, Cei?"

Cei, still mounted, nodded agreement.

Brychan tried to speak, but Arthur motioned him to silence. "You could fight for her, of course."

Brychan snarled, "With pleasure!"

Gwynllyw growled, "Let me at the chance!"

Arthur just smiled with irritating amusement. "Brychan has, what, thirty men with him? But then, I have ten ranged behind me and another thirty t'other side of this ridge." He lifted Gwladys down from the saddle.

Brychan was glancing warily up the hill. He had been considering how many men the Pendragon had with him since the first sighting, and now a figure had been stated was it truth?

Arthur's grin faded. "Who owns this land we are on?"

"I do," said Gwynllyw. He gestured behind him. "We crossed the border stream some half-mile back."

Arthur slapped the young man's shoulder and grinned again. "That settles the matter then." He took hold of Gwladys's hand, placed it in Gwynllyw's, and turned to mount Eira.

With a roar, Brychan charged forward, but Arthur's sword came up, stopping him short. "Brychan, are you so slow to learn? I suggest, and suggest strongly, you get on that ragged hill pony of yours and take your men home." He thrust his face forward menacing. "You, Brychan, are on another's land, and to my mind are intent on unrest. By the power invested in me by the King, if you do not get your arse off this land this instant I will have my signaller call the remainder of my men and we will personally escort you off!"

Was it bluff? Brychan considered, considered hard, trying to read Arthur's face. Without success. Brychan despised the Pendragon. Finally, he acknowledged he had no choice, turned on his heel, and without a word returned to his men.

"I shall send bride-price for your daughter," Gwynllyw called.

Brychan mounted his pony and turned it, savagely pulling at the bit. "For brideprice there must be a daughter. I have but one daughter and she is within my stronghold with the women!"

Gwladys ran forward, distressed. "Father, please, I did not want it to be like this!"

He spat into the grass by her feet. "You have lost all right to call me father. You are no longer of my flesh nor of my blood." He trotted away without a backward glance, his men following silently.

Arthur had mounted, began to ride off, but Gwynllyw caught up with him, placed a hand on the rein.

"How can I thank you? You have done me a great service this day, although I admit to doubting your intentions for a while." He said it openly, honest, meant in friendship. Arthur took it as such, proffered his hand for the young man to grasp.

"You must never doubt my intentions, lad! Cei here has conscience enough to look after that side of things." Arthur winked at his friend. Gwynllyw did not understand, but shrugged aside the question forming in his mind, said instead, "My priest shall marry Gwladys and myself on the morrow. I would be honoured if you and your men would attend my wedding feast." He paused, reddened slightly. "But my stronghold is small. We are somewhat confined for room, a full turma would be difficult to accommodate."

Arthur roared his laughter, Cei joining in.

"God be praised! Have you not heard of Arthur, Gwynllyw? He is notorious for exaggeration! We have no more than ten and six men, including ourselves and officers!"

Gwynllyw saw the jest, saw Brychan had been made to look the fool, and gladly offered the welcome due all travellers.

TWO

For five days they took advantage of pleasant company, good wine, and relaxation. With the gold stored safely in Gwynllyw's own treasure house—a stone-built chamber below ground—Arthur too took advantage of the unexpected holiday. Let Vortigern wait and worry!

Gwladys settled well and quickly into her new household, welcomed by her husband's four sisters and widowed mother. The breeding of her grandmother adequately cleansed the stain of Hibernian blood and her devout Christian faith made her the more readily accepted.

At the wedding feast Arthur made promise of a wedding gift. He had not failed to notice Gwladys's shining eyes as she stroked Eira, had seen also Gwynllyw's appreciative appraisal. He mentioned Cunedda's breeding herds.

"I have heard of them—Gwynedd is well talked of. Is Eira one of Cunedda's then?" Gwynllyw asked, interested. He would be prepared to pay a handsome price, though he could ill afford it, for such an animal.

"Aye, Cei's too. We purchased them from Cunedda when we first came into Vortigern's service, but recently I have taken more. All my officers will soon be so mounted, and the men are to ride part-bred animals, hill ponies crossed with Cunedda's fine stallions."

It could have been the drink or the congenial company, but Arthur suddenly found himself telling Gwynllyw of his plans for a large cavalry force with all the men, not just the officers, mounted on horses like Eira—drilled, highly trained men and horses.

Gwynllyw was impressed, enthusiastic. "If I were not committed to my holding, I would gladly join such a company! At least I can give you my backing, for what it is worth."

"It may be worth a great deal, Gwynllyw. I thank you and…" Arthur stood up abruptly, banged the table with his empty tankard, and demanded silence. "I have not yet granted a gift to the bride and her husband! I shall send to Gwynedd to procure the foundation stock of Gwynllyw's own stables: one stallion and four mares—na," he winked at Gwynllyw's wife, "I shall make it five, one entirely for yourself. What say you, Gwladys?"

The girl leapt to her feet and flung her arms around Arthur's neck. "A mare of my own, like Eira!" She turned to her husband, smiling, delighted; thought, *Even my father does not possess such a fine beast!*

Seating himself, Arthur touched the place on his cheek where her lips had brushed, felt a twinge of regret that he had heeded Cei's conscience.

Cei, by his side, lightly tapped Arthur's arm, whispered, "I take it Vortigern's gold will be paying for such a lavish gift?"

"It is in our King's interest to encourage these smaller holdings. We need loyal men."

"We?" Cei sipped wine. "Or you?"

Arthur's face broke into a roguish grin, his interest swivelling to assess the serving slave pouring more wine into his tankard. He pinched her buttocks, said to Cei, "One day I will mean mine, but for now I am intent on more pressing needs." He fingered the girl's bodice, making a show of inspecting the lacing. She giggled as he whispered something in her ear, her eyes fluttering agreement to his suggestion. Arthur's grin broadened as he leant back in his chair.

"Well, this night is taken care of. As to the future, I think I have assured one man on my side."

Cei swallowed a mouthful of wine, said with a serious face, "How fortunate the Fates led Gwladys to be placed under your personal protection from any unwanted advances."

Arthur scowled and kicked Cei's leg beneath the table. He glanced at her, so obviously happy, the scowl deepening. Mithras, he needed a woman!

The fifth day. Clouds, puffballs of white cumulus billowing like ships in full sail against a blue sky. The heat had become oppressive, thick and clammy. The previous evening Gwynllyw had decided to hunt. The men had gathered at dawn calling the excited hunting dogs to order, had ridden out in joyful groups, singing and swapping tales of victorious battles and women won. The place seemed quiet and subdued without them.

Gwladys wandered through the small Caer, alone for the first time since her arrival. The scatter of buildings here were only one quarter the size of her father's huge complex of Hall, dwelling places, barns, and buildings. She preferred her husband's holding; it seemed more comfortable, more relaxed, than the constant buzz of activity at her father's.

She climbed to the top of the defence wall, hoping to find a cool breeze there, saw the ribbon of a river glistening among the trees. Whisking down the stairs, she snatched a light cloak from her chamber and, calling to a maidservant, announced, "I am going to the river!"

The water was inviting, cool, and deep. She walked for a while, watching ducks swim, a fish rise, a bird dive. No one was around. She was a strong swimmer—oh, why not! She stripped, waded into the water—how cold it was as it reached her thighs! She gasped as she plunged forward, swimming strongly. She felt clean and fresh.

She swam vigorously for a while, letting the coldness bite into her skin, then floated with her arms outstretched, enjoying the pleasurable sensation of water on her nakedness.

"You should not swim alone, it may not be safe."

She started and rolled over, taking in a mouthful of water as her head went down. Spluttering, she found firm ground beneath her feet, half stood, to hastily bob beneath the river's cover as she saw Arthur standing there on the bank. He was leading Eira, who stood fetlock deep in the current.

"I thought you were hunting!" she gasped, breathless from the ducking and from startled embarrassment.

Arthur patted his horse affectionately. "He must have picked up a stone, for the sole of his hoof is bruised. I dare not lame him—we ride out on the morrow." Arthur walked into the water beside the animal, lifted the leg to inspect the minor damage. "Cold water does wonders for leg injuries."

Gwladys felt a fool squatting down like this, but her clothes were on the bank, beyond him. How long had he been watching? She blushed, unsure what to do next.

"However beneficial to a horse's legs, river water is not over kind to a lady's skin," Arthur remarked.

"My clothes are behind you," she said, hoping he would move away, dismayed when he did not.

She had been swimming a good while, had not noticed the gather of clouds from the west. The soft fluffed whiteness of morning was dulling rapidly into rain grey. The sun disappeared, leaving the river in dark shade. Gwladys shivered, realised the Pendragon had no intention of moving.

It suddenly occurred to her she did not care. She was a married woman now, beyond his touch. She stood, waded past him and, scrambling up the bank, began rubbing herself dry with her light summer cloak. She squeaked as she felt his hands on her shoulders.

"You are shivering," he said, "let me help you get warm."

"Na! Na, thank you, my lord, I can manage!"

All the same, he took the thing from her, began to rub, gently, at her back, across her shoulders, down her throat.

She grabbed the cloak from him, reached for her clothes, dressed quickly, pulling on her tunic, her fingers fumbling with the lacings.

She trembled as his hands brushed hers, taking the irritating thongs from her to thread them easily, tying a neat bow.

"I am more used to untying these," he said in a soft, coaxing voice. He was so close. He smelt of horse and leather and male sweat. She stood still, eyes closed, as his lips brushed hers, parting them slowly for his tongue to flick over her white teeth.

She was about to put her arms around him, draw him nearer, when a female voice made her spring away alarmed, red-faced. She pulled her gown over her head, hiding her embarrassment beneath its concealment.

"My mistress sent me to fetch you, lady. She says the clouds are forming rain and you should never come to the river alone."

"Quite right, girl," replied Arthur briskly, taking the cloak and placing it around Gwladys's shoulders. "Exactly what I was saying." He ushered Gwladys forward, shooed her in the direction of the fortress, almost as if he were marshalling chickens. "Get yourself back, my lady."

He turned, smiling pleasantly to the servant girl. "You, girl, can walk back with me. Wait while I fetch Eira."

Gwladys, flustered, had trotted a few paces, then she stopped, horrified, and fled back to Arthur's side, grabbing urgently at his arm.

"What if she saw?" she whispered, frightened. "What if she tells my husband—he is bound not to think well of it! Oh, what shall I do?"

Arthur patted her hand. "What was there to see? A kiss from one friend to another—do not fret, my sweet, she saw nothing. Go on, get you home. Gwynllyw's mother spoke aright, it is to rain."

Reassured, Gwladys lifted up the hem of her skirts and ran. She found her mother-by-law waiting concerned and stern within the gates, a lecture on her lips. Chided, Gwladys listened and then burst into tears.

"There, child, I had no wish to upset you but think on it, we are not so far from your father's lands. What if he sent spies to steal you back?"

Gwladys's hand went to her throat. She had not thought of that. "He would not dare!"

"I doubt he would, but all the same it is worth remembering. Besides, the river can be dangerous. Never go out alone, especially near the water—who knows what devilments lurk beneath its surface?"

Gwladys bit her lip. She thanked the woman for her sound advice, walked with as much dignity as she could summon towards the chapel, and spent an hour prostrate before the altar praying to her God for forgiveness. What devilment, indeed!

Arthur squatted on the bank, holding Era's rein loosely as the horse nibbled at the lush grass.

"I have work to do, lord, may I not go?"

She was a pretty thing, if you could look below the matted hair and grime. "Why do servants not bother to wash?" Arthur asked.

"I do!" she replied hotly. "You'd be mucky if you'd spent a mornin' cleanin' out the bakehouse ovens!"

"You sound keen to get back to the task."

"I've finished. I were about to clean up when my lady sent me on this errand."

"So you need to bathe? Your errand is completed, the Lady Gwladys safely gone—now you can wash." He indicated the river. "Go ahead."

At first she hesitated, then, slowly, her fingers went to her bodice; she unlaced the thongs, pulled off her tunic and undergarments. She walked to the water, stepped in, ducked down, as relieved as Gwladys had been to wash away the clinging dirt.

Arthur watched her a while then pulled off his own boots, unbuckled his sword belt, and removed the light leather hunting tunic. "I think I will join you." He pulled some handfuls of bracken, offered one to her. "You scrub the sweat from my back, girl; I will scrub yours."

He unfastened the lacings of his bracae and slid naked into the water, concealing the gasp as its coldness hit his belly.

She stood uncertain, biting a black, chewed fingernail and glanced in the direction of the fortress. He was wading towards her, had reached her, caught her arm and tumbled her backwards. She screamed, from the cold more than surprise. He stifled the sound with his mouth, rolling her over in the shallows, holding her close. She responded, giggling.

The first rainfall for two weeks fell from a heavy grey sky. They did not even notice.

After, he paid her well and rode the next day from the stronghold with nothing but a casual memory and a temporary satisfaction.

FEBRUARY 454

THREE

Cei nudged Arthur's arm, indicated the two people entering Vortigern's audience chamber. Arthur frowned, screwing up his eyes to make out the faces through the crush of people and the smoke from the burning torches.

"Who is it?"

Cei gave a deep-throated chuckle. "A friend. Gwynllyw."

"Really!" Delighted, Arthur pushed his way through groups of men and women to greet the newcomers, making slow progress across the crowded room. "Gwynllyw! It is good to see you!" He clasped the man's offered hand. "Why come you here to Caer Leon through this day's foul weather? And with your wife too!" His look of pleasure turned to one of alarm. Usually the Hibernian sea-wolves did not raid during the winter months, but the weather, save for this day's miserable wetness, had been kind, the seas calm. "Not bad news, I trust?"

Gwynllyw returned the Pendragon's enthusiastic welcome. "I had no idea you would be at court—I had heard you were up at Eboracum! No, my friend, no bad tidings, save a summons by the King!" He was a shorter man than Arthur, square-built with broad shoulders and thickset legs, his face blunt-chinned and heavy-jawed. He needed to tilt his head back to look Arthur in the eyes. "The one disadvantage to building my new stronghold at Caer Dydd is the proximity to this place."

Laughing, Arthur moved behind Gwynllyw to kiss Gwladys. "You are even lovelier than I remember!" He stood back and, firmly clasping her hands, observed her state of advanced pregnancy. "Though somewhat larger!"

Gwladys blushed deep pink and flicked Arthur a glance from beneath lowered lashes. Her husband said with pride, "I thought it wise to establish full claim to my property so her father could not stir trouble," adding in an undertone, "Is Brychan here?"

Arthur tipped his head, indicating a group of men seated to the far right. "Aye, rats smell rotting vegetation from far off."

Grim, Gwynllyw answered, "I thought he might be." But Arthur had no chance to follow the remark, for Gwynllyw added, "I am receiving dark looks from Vortigern, we had best make our obedience—may we join you after?"

"Of course."

Arthur returned cheerfully to Cei. "Gwladys is pretty even in pregnancy," he remarked. "Some women run too fat with child."

"Any girl is pretty to you," retorted Cei affably.

"Save my wife."

"Many envy you."

"Then they must be hard pressed for pleasure." Arthur accepted dried fruits from a passing slave, chewed thoughtfully. Gwynllyw was presenting Gwladys to Rowena, the Queen making a gushing display of affectionate greeting. "Who are they anyway?"

Cei's reply was offhand. "No one in particular. Any man who seeks ambition and power would be glad to claw a way up through Winifred."

Arthur spat out a seed. "Be clawed *by* her, more like." He looked with distaste at his wife, seated beside her mother. They were both animatedly talking to Gwladys, about the child no doubt. Arthur snorted, finding it difficult to believe Winifred could be interested in anything so maternal. Rightly, he ought to have felt slighted by her adamant refusal to be with him, but he had no interest in where she placed her backside. The further away the better.

"Is there a rumour that she has taken a lover, then?" Casually Arthur glanced at Cei, knowing the man would not tattle idle gossip nor hold back truth if asked for a straight answer.

"Not that I have heard. All the same." Cei spread his hands, "were she mine, I would have her watched."

Arthur finished his fruit, wiped sticky hands on the seat of his bracae. Did he care what the bitch got up to? Not particularly. But then, a good excuse to be rid of her could prove useful.

Gwynllyw was approaching, hand outstretched to greet Cei.

Arthur whispered quickly, "Arrange it. As soon as possible."

"I'll do it now. Gwynllyw! How are you?" Cei stayed a few polite moments, then nodded to Arthur and took his leave.

Calling for wine and a stool, Arthur attended Gwladys, spoke fiercely to her husband. "By the Bull man, why drag her to this vipers' pit in her condition?"

Gwynllyw scowled. "Vortigern expressly asked to meet her. I think he is hatching some plot of reconciliation with Brychan."

"You have not softened towards each other yet then?"

Shaking his head, Gwynllyw puffed out his cheeks. "To Brychan, I am a low-born whore-son who ought to be dangling on a rope from the highest tree." He gave a great bellow of laughter. "And I suspect, Arthur, he would not object to having you dancing alongside me!" Falling serious again, he went on, "The pair of them grow anxious because I am not the mild hearth tender my father was. I have taken more land these last three years since his death than he did in an entire lifetime. And I am establishing a good trade with Less Britain and Gaul. The King likes it not that I am becoming a touch powerful in my part of the country." He glared across the room at Vortigern. "But if he thinks he can curb my rising position by yoking me under Brychan's rule, then he can damn well think again!"

Alarmed, Arthur looked hastily around. "Mithras, Gwynllyw! Keep your voice down if you intend to keep your bull head lodged on your neck!"

Gwynllyw compressed his lips, was tempted to make a scathing retort, but seeing sense laughed instead. "You're right!" He slapped Arthur's shoulder, turned the subject. "The horses arrived safe. Jesu, but Cunedda breeds fine stock!" Scanning the sea of faces, he asked, "Is he not here?"

"Gwynedd has cut itself from Vortigern completely since Etern's murder."

"That was a bad business."

A surge of bile rose in Arthur's throat. Aye, bad.

Gwynllyw failed to notice Arthur's sudden silence, for he was saying, "It was good fortune the day I met with you!" He was laughing, at ease, pleased to have met with an old friend and that other men admired his pretty young wife, as large as she was. "God in his wisdom smiled on us that day!"

Gwladys was not listening. She felt ill. She told herself the unease was due to the bulk of the child, thought the sickness was caused by the heat and noise of this room. When Arthur unexpectedly took her hand in his own, she squeaked and tried to jerk it away.

"I know not if God had a hand in the matter of our coming together," he was saying, "but by the Bull, I would not have missed seeing Brychan's face for an empire's fortune!"

Gwladys managed to retrieve her hand, put it in her lap. The fluttering had become a pounding gallop. She felt for the string of glass and jet beads hanging at her waist and, threading them through her fingers, silently recited the litany against the temptations of sin. Arthur's presence caused this turmoil—Arthur, and the thought of that never-forgotten afternoon by the river.

From the dais, Winifred observed the woman seated with the man she called husband, watched his preening attention and joyful laughter. He never laughed or seemed happy and content when in her company. She hated him. Hated his callous disregard of her and his frequent scathing remarks.

Hated wanting him so much.

Occasionally, alone in her bed for yet another night, Winifred wondered if she ought to take a lover, but come morning common sense always returned. What if there was a child? What if Arthur were to discover her infidelity? He would divorce her for certain, and was that not what he wanted? Legitimate grounds to be rid of her, to publicly cast her aside and keep all her dowry? Ah no! Divorce would be on her terms or not at all!

Curious, she beckoned her handmaid. "Find out who that woman with my husband might be."

The girl glanced across the hall. "I shall ask the servants, my lady."

A slave overheard, pricked up her ears. Moving innocently to Winifred's side she poured wine, said, "Forgive me, lady—she's Gwladys, daughter of Brychan."

Disregarding the girl's blatant forwardness, Winifred said, "The daughter stolen from under his nose?" She grasped the girl's wrist. "How do you know her?"

Masking her fright at the sudden painful hold the girl stammered, "I was a slave at her husband's stronghold."

Winifred watched Gwladys smiling at a tale Arthur was elaborately relating.

"She's very beautiful," the slave announced. "I remember we all said so when first we saw her. It's a shame she has a temper like a pregnant sow. She had me whipped for no reason and sold. That's how I come to be here."

Winifred digested the information, though she was not interested in the girl's petulance, beyond an idea it might prove useful. "Did my lord Arthur also think her beautiful?" she asked casually.

"Oh aye." The girl poured more wine. Seeing a chance to gain some small revenge, she grabbed at it—there might even be some form of reward! Freedom would taste very nice. She whispered, "I remember well the time he found her swimming naked in the river."

A muscle twitched in Winifred's cheek. She said calmly, as if uninterested, "Indeed? Where is it you work? The kitchens?"

The girl wiped her hands self-consciously on her filthy skirt, her heart racing. "Usually, lady, but we're all needed out here this night."

Winifred regarded her shrewdly. A pretty thing beneath the grime. Was it worth taking her spite seriously? "Would you rather serve as a handmaid?"

The girl's eyes lit up. She nodded eagerly.

Winifred beckoned her personal maid closer. "Find this wretch some suitable clothing, and make certain she takes a bath." To the girl, "We will talk again, later."

A glow of satisfaction warmed Winifred. Arthur thought he was so clever! Well, she had stumbled on something to turn that cocksure arrogance and, by God's truth, she intended to use it!

FOUR

W ET THROUGH, BOOTS AND LEGS PLASTERED WITH MUD, ARTHUR RETURNED from inspecting the out-wintering horses and went reluctantly straight to Vortigern's private chambers. Each time he was summoned he was forced to listen to a long litany of fresh complaints. At times he felt as though he were a child, being chastised by his tutor for failing yet again to write his Latin verbs correctly on the slate.

He was surprised to find Gwynllyw with the King. Glancing at the young man he was astonished to receive an icy stare of contempt in return.

Puzzled, Arthur inclined his head to Vortigern, the only concession of obedience the Pendragon would ever agree to make. "You sent for me?"

"By the express request of Gwynllyw, I did." Vortigern appraised Arthur's appearance and the trail of muddy footprints on the tiled floor. Said irritably, "Could you not change into clean garments before entering here?"

"I was ordered to attend you immediately."

Vortigern's lips thinned. Insolence!

Arthur added to the hostility by sauntering to a chair, hooking it closer with his toe, and sprawling in it, hands hanging over the arms, eye cocked between the King and Gwynllyw.

"You may sit," Vortigern said coldly. He turned to the other man. "Would you rather I informed the Pendragon of why he is here?"

Gwynllyw stepped menacingly towards Arthur, drawing his sword. "Let that pleasure be mine."

Arthur tilted the chair to its back legs, said with a laugh, "What in the Bull's name is this? Put your blade up, my friend!"

Gwynllyw's lip curled, hatred pouring from him. The tip of his sword hovered near Arthur's throat. "I am no friend of yours, Pendragon. Surely you are indeed your father's bastard!"

Vortigern pushed himself from his seat, walked towards Gwynllyw and nudged the blade aside with his arm. "Put the weapon away, it does not frighten the Pendragon. There will be time enough for bloodshed. Let us talk this thing over." He sauntered back to his chair.

Arthur let his own chair fall with a thud back to all four feet, stood abruptly. "Aye, and start talking quickly. I do not take kindly to a sword at my throat for a reason I know nothing of!"

Gwynllyw sheathed the thing, his hand hovering none the less over the hilt. He snarled. "You have dishonoured my wife Arthur Pendragon!"

For some moments Arthur could not reply. Stupefied, open-mouthed, he looked from one man's face to the other. Of all the reasons to be commanded before the King, threatened with a blade, and accused of whatever it was he was accused of he would not have thought it involved Gwladys! Plenty of other women, aye, but not Gwladys!

A string of thoughts came and went. Finally, thrusting his fingers through his sword belt he said, "I know not how you heard this lie, but lie it certainly is."

"You deny intercourse with my wife while I hunted?"

If Gwynllyw had not seemed so angry Arthur would have laughed in his face. "Of course I damn well deny it!"

Gwynllyw raged on, his voice husky with anger. "You also deny watching her swim? You remember that day, I presume? We left early, soon after sun-up; after a mile or two you said your horse was going lame and you elected to return to the Caer." His hand clasped tighter around his sword hilt. "If I had realised then what I know now!" He had the sword half out of the scabbard again, staying the action as Arthur lazily rested his hand on the weapon by his own side.

"Do you accuse me of taking the woman of a friend—and one who had been a bride of only a few days?"

Gwynllyw, almost pleadingly, searched Arthur's face for the truth. The idea of such a betrayal revolted him but Vortigern had insisted his source of information was reliable, and there were the rumours. Only whispers, but whispers murmured over often. Gwladys and Arthur and the river. Then there came the talk concerning the child. It had come quickly. Could he be certain he had the siring of it? And Gwladys? She seemed ill at ease, nervous and restless, turning from him in the intimacy of night. He had assumed it to be the burden of pregnancy but now he doubted. Could it be the guilt of carrying another's child—Arthur's child?

Vortigern had deliberately seated himself, always feeling at a disadvantage standing in Arthur's presence. God take the man, he was so annoyingly tall!

Accurately reading the fleeting signs of uncertainty on Gwynllyw's face the King interrupted. "We hear countless tales of your fondness for women, Arthur. Rumours reach my ears. It seems fathers—and husbands—lock their women-folk away when your turma is near."

Vortigern leant forward, rested an elbow on his knee; he was enjoying the Pendragon's discomfort. "Not," he added "from fear of the men—but from their leader. Your reputation, Pendragon, has not done you proud. I would suggest," he wagged a warning finger, "I command, you pay less attention to the whore and spend more nights with your wife!"

"Who is the most professional of whores!" Arthur snapped the reply without thinking.

Vortigern was on his feet and across the room in two strides, rage contorting his aged face. "Retract that or you will face my sword!"

Arthur stood his ground. "She was not so innocent when she came to me. Who is to say how innocent she is now?"

"You have no proof of this!"

Arthur smiled cynically. "Neither do you for Winifred's fidelity—or for Gwladys's lack of it." He turned to Gwynllyw. "I strongly deny the charge. Whom would you trust, myself or this lying tyrant? Has he said who so gener-ously revealed this absurd lie?"

Vortigern, still angry, reseated himself and said offhandedly, "You were seen with Gwladys on the river bank."

"Is that the accusation!" Arthur roared, hands on hips, head back. "I was seen with her! Of course I was seen with her! Eira was lame, I took him to the river to cool the inflammation; Gwladys was there also, she had been swimming. Know that she was dried, dressed, and about to leave for home when I arrived." A small lie, more a stretching of the truth. "We talked a while of Eira and the horses. All quite innocent, my friend." Arthur fixed a pleasant smile, deliberately refused to drop the affable term.

"You were seen holding her."

Arthur sighed, keeping patience. "I have already admitted to being with her, Gwynllyw! It clouded over swiftly if I remember correctly, and your wife had suddenly felt the cold. I helped her on with her cloak and sent her back to the Caer. I also seem to remember she was unwell that evening. Did she not say to you she must have caught a chill?"

Gwynllyw frowned. He did remember, quite clearly, for Gwladys had been ill during the night with sickness and sweating. "The next morning you rode out.

She was," he said, "far from well. The physician could not say what had caused the malady; he put it down to excitement over our marriage. Of course," he added in a low hiss, "it could equally well have been guilt!"

Arthur swung away in exasperation, hit the wall with his clenched fist. "It is for you to choose, Gwynllyw. There is no truth in this madness, and I shall willingly swear to that by whatever oath you ask."

Vortigern coughed, drawing their attention. "The truth may soon be revealed." His low laugh was a horrid grating sound, as if slate were being dragged over stone. He rose, ambled to a table to fetch wine. A few steps, and he regretted rising as pain spread, the undesired discomforts of old age. With a great effort he forced his body straight, attempted to disregard the searing ache from his hip.

"The child she bears may well resemble its father." He poured the wine, took a deep draught from the goblet. Wiping the residue from his lips, he turned back to Arthur, a malicious smile creasing his craggy face. "Unless your wife produces an heir, Arthur—which, given the present lack of intimacy between you, I fail to see occurring—you may be forced to admit Gwladys's child as yours. One of your bastards may have to carry the Dragon when I eventually decide to have you dispatched."

Arthur flew at the King, sword drawn, ready to strike. Gwynllyw and Vortigern reacted, the elder man more slowly, throwing the contents of the goblet clumsily at Arthur; Gwynllyw grappling Arthur's arm, shouting for him to hold.

Breathing heavily, Arthur backed off, began slowly sheathing his weapon. Vortigern smoothed his rumpled tunic, keeping excess alarm from showing in his face. He walked sedately to his chair, sat, stared unblinking at his son-by-law.

"Should you ever attempt such an action again, Pendragon," he said slowly, threateningly, "I shall have you flogged and torn limb from limb. Do you understand me, boy?"

Arthur thudded his sword in the scabbard, nostrils flaring. He returned Vortigern's snake-like stare through slit eyes. For a moment, Vortigern felt his heart lurch, his stomach turn over. He put it down to Arthur's sudden attack, was reluctant to admit fear.

"I understand you, Vortigern," Arthur said in a low voice. "I assure you there will be no next time. You have my word: should I have cause to draw my sword on you again, it will be the last action you ever see." He spun round on one heel. Ignoring the King and Gwynllyw, he strode from the room, slamming the door with a resounding crash.

Marching to his own quarters, he snarled viciously at servants who crossed his path, sending them scuttling for safety in the shadows. All the while his mind turned over the possibilities. Who had reported his encounter with Gwladys? His men were loyal, not one would willingly betray him. Unwillingly? He paused in mid-stride. He thought highly of Gwynllyw, had known his father, a good, trustworthy man, but had never met the son before last summer. How in the Bull's name could he accept these lies? He snorted scornfully. Easily! Vortigern, damn him, had been partly correct, for some did fear the coming of Arthur's cavalry. They were a wild, fierce lot, apt to get carried away when feeling the need to relax. Was this because the men followed their leader's example?

The Pendragon sighed, rubbing sweating palms over the nape of his neck. Happen they did. Lately he had sought escape in an excess of drink and women.

Gwynllyw must understand—must realise his tally of women did not, except in thought, include Gwladys. So he had made a try for her—happen he ought to admit to that, for the sake of truth. Ironic, he thought, the one time he had not lain with a woman he was accused of it!

Washed and clad in fresh clothing, he strode from his room and made for the one allotted to Gwynllyw. So blind was his desire to talk the matter through he marched straight into the chamber, barely pausing to knock.

He stood motionless, face drained of colour, frozen with embarrassment and incredulity at his own stupidity. It had not occurred to him Gwladys would also be using this same room. He never shared with Winifred.

Gwynilyw's wife stood in her undergarments. The maid squealed, hurrying to cover her mistress. Arthur made some hasty, futile apology; turned to leave, came face to face with Gwynllyw.

There was no sound or movement, then Arthur swallowed, reached a hand forward to explain. The calm shattered.

With a roar Gwynllyw thrust the hand aside, swung forward, driving his fist into Arthur's belly, following through with the other, slamming knuckles into his face. Arthur doubled at the first blow, fell at the second. The ladies screamed. Gwladys, grabbing the hasty covering, darted forward to kneel at Arthur's side.

"Why?" she asked, dabbing at the blood pouring from his nose.

Gwynllyw stared coldly at her. Out of spite, he kicked his boot twice into Arthur's ribs then turned on his heel and strode for the door.

She ran after him, catching at his sleeve, her clutched garment slipping to the floor. "What is it? What has happened?"

He drew back his hand, made to strike her, stopped himself. "Now I understand why you wish our first-born to be given to the Church! Because it is not mine! Do you take me for such a blind fool, woman?"

She looked blankly up at his contorted face. "I do not understand. Please, what has happened?"

"You ask me? Best ask your lover!"

The room reeled; Gwladys slid, legs buckling, to the floor. Her husband stared at her, spat out, "I have nothing further to say to you."

Arthur stumbled to his feet, clutching at the pain, but Gwynllyw had gone. Wiping away the blood as best he could, he turned to Gwladys. He tucked her fallen covering around her, tried to explain. "Your husband believes a gross lie. Some vicious tongue has spread a rumour that we were lovers—the child you carry is mine."

Her eyes flickered up to him, shifted away. He made to touch her, withdrew. Mithras! What to do? "You have been wronged, Gwladys; I promise all this shall be put to rights."

She said nothing, just sat staring. It was a punishment this, from God. A punishment for the sin of thought.

Arthur spread his arms wide, then let them drop. His ribs ached; there would be bruising when he stripped off his tunic. He left the room; there was nothing he could do here.

Fitful sleep for him that night encircled by grotesque faces. Gwladys naked before him, heavy with child, screaming. Gwynllyw slashing with bloodied sword; Vortigern watching with those red, snake eyes. Then a bed, a boy lying there frightened, a woman leaning over him, pinning him down, her head back. Laughing.

He woke drenched in sweat. He had not dreamt of Morgause for Mithras knew how long! His hand shook as he reached for wine, feeling sick, disgusted, and hopeless.

There had been others in the dream. Women's faces, women's voices, cackling like hags beneath the shadow of the full moon.

Winifred. Gwladys. He groaned, his head in his hands.

And then another. Her face lovely, her smile gentle and kind.

Gwenhwyfar.

Would he never forget her?

Not until past mid-morning did the answer hit him, as savage as the blows Gwynllyw had given. He was ploughing through ankle-deep mud beyond the stables when he halted, sending Cei bouncing off him.

"God's patience, Arthur!" Cei cursed, peered at him. "You have turned as white as a sun-bleached sheet! What ails you?"

"May she rot, the bitch!" Arthur said for answer and wading forward, headed for Vortigern's apartments. Cei shrugged, letting his friend and commander go. He knew better than to meddle in Arthur's business. He would find out what it was all about soon enough.

FIVE

ARTHUR BURST LIKE A CHARGING BULL INTO WINIFRED'S CHAMBER, SENDING A scatter of screaming women to their feet.

"Must a husband's attention to his wife be greeted by such hysteria?" he growled. He surveyed them for a few heartbeats, his eyes narrowing as he found what he had suspected.

"Get you all gone—except you." He grabbed at a red-haired girl, pulling her, none too gently, to his side.

"How dare you enter here in such a manner!" said Winifred, rising from the tapestry frame where she had been sewing. "My ladies will stay."

The women hovered, unsure which order to obey.

Arthur loosened his sword in its scabbard, saw their eyes flicker from Winifred to the door. "What I have to say is for your, and her," he shook the girl, "hearing only." He added as a threat, "I will cut off any ears that hear what they should not." He drew the sword an inch or so. Shrill screams and squawks of alarm as the women hurried away, the last one pulling the door shut behind her. Winifred compressed her lips. The fools—did they think he was serious?

"What is so important you must make a spectacle of yourself before my women?"

Dragging the girl with him Arthur moved to the tapestry, peered close. A Christian scene, almost finished.

"Pretty," he said, still smiling. "You are always, I have noticed, surrounded by pretty things, Winifred." He jerked the girl round to stand before him. "This one is the prettiest."

"Take your hand off Tangwen. You are hurting her."

"Tangwen? Is that your name, my pretty?" He ran his finger over her cheek, down her throat almost to the swell of her breast, his voice soft and sensuous. Then with an unexpected raw edge said, "I never bothered to ask before, did I?" He caught a loose strand of her red hair, curling it round his fingers. "I shall do more than hurt the bloody little liar!" He thrust her from him, throwing her to the floor, in the same movement caught up his short-bladed dagger. Tangwen screamed as he knelt over her and gripped her cheeks between the fingers of his left hand. "Shall I remove that wagging tongue of yours, Tangwen? Bitch! You deserve to have your throat cut!"

The girl squirmed, shook her head, pleading for mercy with her eyes. She shrieked as he dealt her a stinging blow.

"How dare you!" shouted Winifred, darting forward. "How dare you enter my chamber like a madman and attack my slave!" She clutched up the unfinished tapestry, flew at Arthur and hurled the thing down upon his back. The blow caused no harm, but Arthur released the girl.

Standing slowly, breathing hard, he glared at his wife. "How dare I?" he asked in a voice low and dangerously level. "You ask me that? You ask how I dare? Did you force this miserable wretch to tell you of what occurred at Gwynllyw's? Or did she blurt it out without realising how your warped, twisted little mind would use the information? It is unfortunate for you, wife, I recall where I have seen this slut before. I do not often remember the base-born whores I take, but her flame-coloured hair reminded me. That and tattle of a river and a lady swimming there."

Arthur dragged the snivelling girl to her feet. "I barely noticed you serving the other night. I suppose you were both counting on that, hoping I was too drunk to remember where and when I had you."

He thrust the girl at Winifred, causing her to fall against her mistress. Told in graphic detail of how he had coupled with the slave, leaving out no detail and enjoying every word of the telling.

"I have recounted things aright, have I not, Tangwen?" Arthur lunged forward, seized her by the shoulders, and shook her until she cried agreement. "I would hazard a guess she left that particular part out of the telling though, eh, Winifred?"

He struck his forehead with the palm of his hand. "Fool! Have I not also left a vital part out, Tangwen? What of the reason for you being at the river? What of you seeing me lying with the lady Gwladys?" He spun her round to face him, shaking her again. "What of it, girl? What of how I lay with the lady? A pretty tale. All of it lies!"

"'Twas not!" she screamed. "'Twas not all lies! I saw you kiss her!"

Winifred pressed her lips tighter together. Stupid girl.

Arthur spat, "You saw me kiss her. A parting kiss from one friend to another.

One chaste kiss was all you saw, was it not? Was it not!" She had not seen more—for if she knew Arthur had stood watching Gwladys bathing, had touched her, then for certain she would have told.

He slapped her again. "Answer me!"

Tears springing, she nodded.

"Speak up. You saw nothing save a parting kiss of friendship."

"Aye."

"Louder!"

"Aye!"

Arthur hurled the girl towards the door. She stumbled and he followed after her, hauled her up by the hair, opened the door and kicked her outside. "You will wait there." He pointed to the opposite wall. "Your mistress has no further use of you, but I do. May your god help you if you dare move so much as an inch!" He slammed the door, turned back to Winifred.

"Well," she said, applauding mockingly, "what an excellent performance! You burst in here, order my women out, beat one of them, then dismiss her from my service. You must visit me more often, husband, you are quite entertaining!"

Arthur remained silent, watching her through slit eyes, head slightly lowered. "It was a plausible tale, my dear," he said; "how unfortunate it failed. I grant you it almost succeeded, but if you wish to hurt me I suggest you do it direct, not by sinking your poisoned fangs into my comrades—or their pregnant wives."

Winifred laughed, retrieved some of her ladies' sewing that had fallen to the floor. "Is this also part of the entertainment—riddles?"

Arthur lunged, caught her to him. She gasped as his hand gripped her wrist. "You push your luck, woman! Luck has a nasty habit of running out when you need it most."

"I have no idea what you mean. If you are referring to those rumours concerning Gwladys's child, then I would suggest it is I who need the explanation!"

"Who told Vortigern? You? Tangwen would never have had the intelligence or courage to whisper such lies to the King."

Winifred plucked at his fingers. "You are hurting me," she said, pouting. "It is nothing to do with me—save for the insult of your bedding another woman." She struggled, kicked once at his shins, then kicked again, her anger overcoming her. She bit his arm, began to fight him with feet, teeth and free hand.

For a while he bore the blows, holding her away from him to stop her causing over-much damage, but soon tired of the senseless game. He smacked his fist into her face.

She staggered, head reeling, the flesh of her cheekbone already swollen and bruised. "You dare lay hands on me, Arthur Pendragon! You bastard!"

"I will do more than lay hands on you!" He felt no pity or guilt as he beat his wife with his belt across her arms and face. She screamed, huddled down on the floor, trying to protect herself from the flaying leather.

Breathing hard, disgusted with her and himself, Arthur flung the belt aside, turned his back on the sobbing woman. Humiliated, hurting, Winifred clasped her arms around herself. Her hand touched something cold at her waist. Her fingers curled round the small jewel-studded hilt of a dagger. She drew it cautiously, then, with anger searing as sure as the pain she sprang at Arthur's retreating back, the dagger scything down.

He recognised the death hiss of a blade through air and whirled, grasping her wrist with one hand, prising the light weapon from her clenched fingers with the other.

The jewels, diamonds and rubies, were set within walrus ivory. He had seen such a thing before—long ago. His voice very quiet, very dangerous, he asked, "Where did you get this?"

"I am not bound to answer your interrogation!"

He gave a sinister laugh. "Oh but you are. A wife is duty bound to her husband. How came you to be in possession of Gwenhwyfar's blade?"

Winifred looked him full in the eye, unflinching. "She gave it to me."

The Pendragon stood silent, memory flooding over him. Gwenhwyfar's hands deftly slitting fresh-caught fish; this blade glinting high, triumphant, as she taunted him and her brother Etern at mock battle. Her dagger, her mother's before that. "She would never part with such a personal treasure." Arthur returned Winifred's look, staring her down. "You stole it, didn't you?"

Winifred snatched at the dagger, screaming coarse abuse. Arthur flung it aside, sending it clattering harmlessly to the floor. She broke free of him and lunged desperately for the blade; his hand grabbed, missed, tore her gown, ripping the bodice. He kicked, sending the dagger spinning out of reach. She looked wildly around for some means of protection, backing away from his rage.

Arthur remained still, running his eyes over her partially revealed breasts. He leered at her, removing what remained of her clothing with his gaze. "I know a far more potent way of hurting your evil pride."

Furious at his implication, Winifred hurled whatever came to hand. Skillfully he knocked aside each missile—a vase, a chamber pot, a stool. Watching his chance, with the ease of a fighting man, he ducked in low and threw her to the ground. She tried to claw his face; he pinned her down, holding her between his knees and with one hand tore the remains of her gown from her. Unlacing his bracae, he entered her quickly, his satisfaction heightened by the burning outrage on her face.

She spat some word of abuse, furious with him, with herself, moaned as a sudden surge of pleasure shot through her body. She pushed herself from him, arching her back, drawing him deeper in as her arms encircled his shoulders, wanting more. Desperately wanting more.

He was kissing her now, his mouth covering hers, his hands on her breasts, stomach, then thighs.

Winifred gasped, twined her legs around him, her body jerking as she climaxed, and again as he came with her. Breathless, her body shuddering, she lay helpless beneath him, limbs spread, head back, panting.

When he moved, it was only to roll from her, spent. He lay there, eyes closed, breathing hard, sweating.

Winifred half sat up, reached a finger to tentatively wipe a drop of perspiration from his shoulder, instead licked it with her tongue. He did not move. Her tongue flicked at his throat, down over his chest, along the line of dark hair running to his navel. She changed to alternating kisses, moved lower.

When he was at last dressed he bent to take up Gwenhwyfar's dagger and pushed it through his sword belt. He sauntered to the door. Winifred remained flat on the floor, her body echoing the crescendo of sensations from their second coupling. Impulsively he strode back to her and seductively kissed her mouth, his tongue probing, lips insistent. His callused soldier's hand briefly fondled her white breast.

Her hand covered his, holding it there. "Come again to me soon, my lord."

He kissed her one last time, a light touch to her lips. "Only if I can find no better place to sheathe my sword."

She slapped his face with all the strength she could muster.

His laughter echoed along the corridors, mingling with her screamed abuse.

SIX

G WYNLLYW POURED HIMSELF ANOTHER LARGE MEASURE OF WINE, SWALLOWED the whole in one gulp, placed his tankard carefully before him. "I have been well played for the fool."

"Are we not all fools where women are concerned?" Arthur said, reaching across the wooden table to help himself to wine.

The tavern was crowded, men sat or stood, drinking, talking, and laughing, the place swirling with a variety of noises and smells. It had taken a while for Arthur to find his friend; a longer while, and four jugs of the place's best wine, to convince him of the truth.

Gwynllyw attempted a half-smile. The wine had gone to his head; he felt dizzy and ready for sleep. His speech came slurred. "What should I do now? How will I explain to Gwladys? Will she ever forgive me this madness?" He groaned and put his head in his hands.

Arthur tossed back his wine; he knew well what he would do, but how to advise Gwynllyw? "I would go straight to my lady's chamber, order her servants out, and bolt the door on them. I would then carry the wronged lady to her bed and make slow, passionate love to her." A grin broadened. "After, we would lie close a while, then I would do it all over again. And then..." Arthur paused. What then? He himself would make promises, vow his love, and leave her, immediately forgotten, and ride back to his men. "Then, I would order up the horses and go home. Sticking my cock up to Vortigern and Winifred, leaving the pair of them to rot in the dung-heap of their own lies."

Gwynllyw nodded agreement and stood up, swaying unsteadily. He held out his hand in friendship. "Sound advice. I will do that then."

Arthur watched him leave, tripping and stumbling from the tavern, weaving drunkenly through the door and up the street. Turning to a fifth jug, Arthur wondered whether he would make it to Gwladys's chamber, or be found lying drunk in the gutter come dawn's light.

★★★

Winifred groaned and pushed her maid aside sending the bowl of bloodied water splashing to the floor. She ached, she hurt. Every part of her body throbbed or screamed with pain.

She hated him, loathed the sight of him! How dare he do this to her? The bastard, the evil, brutal bastard.

Rising from the stool, she shuffled to the bed, winced as her maid again began salving her hurts, buried her head beneath a pillow as the tears came.

She wanted him dead—dead a hundred times over by a hundred sickening methods; but, oh dear God's love, she wanted him back!

Damn him! Damn, damn him! She would let him do it all over again, if only he would come back!

SEPTEMBER 454

SEVEN

EIRA SHIFTED WEIGHT FROM ONE HIND FOOT TO THE OTHER, EYES HALF SHUT in semi-sleep, his jaw resting heavy on Arthur's shoulder as his master absently stroked the soft pink velvet part between the horse's nostrils. With a deep sigh, the stallion drowsed in the hot sun.

Arthur was looking up the wooded slope watching the vaguely discernible shape of one of his men, carefully hidden within the dappled foliage. Somewhere behind a horse squealed, kicking out against the bite of a horsefly.

"Damn you!" Arthur hissed, turning towards the unwanted sound. Eira snorted, tossed his head, and backed a pace. "Keep your mount quiet!"

Red-faced, the rider calmed his horse, his eyes, in his deep embarrassment, looking everywhere except ahead and his commander's disapproval.

Then the lookout signalled. With the minimum of noise Arthur's turma of thirty or so men mounted and nudged forward in single file at a slow walk. The horses had come alert, were eager for action.

Arthur reached the end of the hollow and reined Eira back, the horse straining against the curbing bit with impatience. The lookout sat motionless, poised, one hand raised. Not daring to breathe, he willed the band of Saex cur-sons forward, just a few more paces... With a flourish, he dropped his hand.

The waiting was over!

A few of the Angli, to the fore of their band of fifty fighting men, yelled a startled warning as a rushing blur of colour and sound poured from the trees. Fleeting glimpses of pounding hooves, scything swords and thrusting spears. The Dragon, tubular shaped, glinting red and gold, writhed and tossed above the heads of yelling horsemen. The wind wailed through its hollow insides and screamed out through its tail of screaming ribbons, turning into a live thing, writhing and twisting and shrieking of death.

The Angli fought bravely while the sudden, swift slaughter lasted; the handful left alive dropped their weapons and fled back along the sun-dappled trackway, their eyes bulging with terror as Arthur's cavalry pursued them, picking off those who fell behind.

Sound drifted from the place of ambush, leaving only quiet. A fox slunk away from the disturbance, wrinkling his snout at the intrusive scent of human blood. Carrion birds gathered, gliding in on silent wings as if summoned by some faery spell; a few began to hop on ungainly legs to peck at the carnage of Anglian bodies strewn about the flattened grass.

With yells of excitement, Arthur encouraged his men forward, the thrill of the chase hot in his blood. Two scared Angli plunged down a weed-grown bank into the river, thrashing through rushing water, attempting to run against the current that pulled at weary legs.

Eira faltered at the crest of the low bank, ears flickering, hooves sensing the weakness of the ground. Arthur kicked him on, intending him to land out in midstream, but the horse's hind legs slipped as he thrust forward, his quarters dropping as he leapt. Somehow he twisted in mid-air, landed awkwardly, forelegs scrabbling for a firm hold. Spray spumed high as he went crashing down, taking his rider with him.

The horse panicked, thrashed the turbulent water, ears flat back, eyes rolling. He struggled, kicking with his hind legs, attempting to gain solid ground. Noise all round, shouts, neighing horses. Someone screaming.

A man was at the stallion's head—Cei, taking hold of the bridle, speaking calm words, gentling the trembling, snorting beast. At the sound of a familiar voice, the horse quietened; Cei persuaded him forward. With a heave, Eira lurched free of the water to stand head lowered, flanks heaving.

Cei, his own heart pounding, tossed the reins at someone and plunged back into the muddied water, running against the current, his face white.

Men equally anxious were already lifting Arthur, his blood turning the white river foam a grotesque pink.

Forgotten, the Angli ran on, offering aloud grateful thanks over and over to their own gods.

Merciful darkness had overtaken the Pendragon. He lay still as death as Cei bound the thigh tight, to splint broken bones and stem the bleeding. Men brought forward a hastily fashioned litter, lifted their leader as gently as they could and set their feet, minds numb, for camp.

EIGHT

CEI FOUND HIMSELF GRINNING FOOLISHLY WITH RELIEF AS ARTHUR YELLED an oath at the surgeon. "Mithras's life man!"

"I would not have believed I could be so pleased to hear your cursing!" Cei laughed, folding his arms and leaning against the wall.

"You will be hearing more if this oaf does not take more care!" Arthur grunted his reply, gritting his teeth as a fresh thrust of pain burst from his damaged right thigh.

The surgeon grinned back at Cei. "I prefer our commander unconscious. At least it made my work easier, and quieter." He frowned at Arthur. "If you were to be still, the pain would not be so intense."

"Be still? Balls, man, how can you expect that with you poking and prodding about as you are! Besides," he added curtly, "I have never been still."

The surgeon straightened, began rinsing his hands in the bowl of clean water Cei fetched from the far side of the small room. "So you will have something new to try. Horses crashing down upon their riders, then struggling to their feet, trampling a man's body as they do so, are apt to leave damage. You owe it to the blessing of Fortuna you escaped with your life."

Arthur fought hard to stop the screaming pain from reaching his lips. The past few days of semi-consciousness were a mindless mist of blinding red agony and grey-black, drifting, muttering sleep. The crashing fall, a distant haze of blurred memory. He recalled the ambush well enough, and the cheer that rang loud in his ears as the few remaining raiders took to their heels. Dimly he remembered urging Eira to jump that bank. The rest was a tangled muddle of choking water and thrashing hooves, shouting voices and screams of agony. His own, presumably.

Resigned to inactivity, he sighed. "How long before I can fight again?" It was a question that had been playing on his mind since morning. Now the incredible pain was showing signs of easing and the surgeon had ceased administering that bitter-tasting drink that always brought back a welcome escape, the questions were coming thick and fast. Some of them were not going to have pleasant answers.

Lovingly packing away the tools of his trade, the surgeon took a while to answer. He glanced at Cei, who raised his eyebrows.

"Fight, you say?" he said, stalling. Fight! By the holy God, all who loved and served the Pendragon had thought, as they dragged him muddied and bloody from that river, he would never walk again, if God in his wisdom granted him life. But fight!

"Well?" Arthur demanded, searching the older man's face. A good surgeon, this one, who had saved many a soldier's life—and wept over the many more he had lost. Arthur put his hand on the man's sleeve, his grip firm despite the weakness that shivered in his body. "I would prefer to know." He said it quietly, unsure whether he spoke truth.

Years with the armies had taught Marcus the army surgeon many skills. He could set bones, stitch wounds, pull spears, cut out arrow barbs. He considered himself one of the best in his profession, yet still he found it difficult to break hard news to brave soldiers or their remaining loved ones. It was not easy to tell of death, the losing of a limb, or an end to a way of life. How many had he had to tell that nothing lay ahead except bleak years of pain and disabled hardship? He drew in his breath and began to talk dispassionately, detached, telling the truth and telling it quickly.

"With time the bone and muscle should heal well enough to bear your weight. Time, patience, and good care should see you walking again. The thigh takes great stress and yours has been badly abused. Fighting needs the agility that comes from strength and stamina."

"Aye, well, you never were one to mince words!" Arthur said drily, easing himself into a more comfortable position. "What you are trying to tell me tact-fully," he smiled sardonically, "is that I may not fight again."

The man half saluted and made to leave. "To any other I would say, make plans for another life. But I knew your father, Arthur—I healed enough of his wounds—one near as serious as yours." His hands tightened on his medical bag. He had loved Uthr. Loved this, his son. "Battle killed him in the end. I could never expect him to forgo fighting, any more than I could expect him to stop pissing water." Then curtly, "You are much like your father." He saluted. "I will come again on the morrow."

Cei stood silent, observing Arthur's grey, stubbled face. At length he asked, "What do you intend to do?"

"Do?" Arthur replied, shifting slightly and instantly regretting it. "What would you do? Crawl into a hole somewhere and bury yourself along with your ambitions and plans?"

"Most would. But as the man said, you are Uthr's son. No hole would be deep enough for you. You would sit and fuss and fidget until the earth gave way and spewed you up again."

Arthur chuckled, then winced. "Mithras, Cei, when I am eventually in the thick of another skirmish remind me not to be so damned impulsive! Is there a way to fight without being hurt, I wonder?"

"Would there be much point?" Cei said, laughing. "It is the risk that brings the thrill."

"As for what I am going to do"—Arthur concentrated his thoughts—"I am leaving you, my second-in-command, in charge of the men, and I am going to lie here and bellow at all who enter. I am going to be the most tiresome, irritating patient."

Cei choked back laughter. "Well, that will certainly be a change of character!"

"And," Arthur added, rubbing his hand over the itching stubble, "I am going to have a shave!"

Days passed wearily, the outside thrum of routine barrack life blurring into a haze of time. This day as on any other, Arthur lay dozing, the difference being the rain had stopped and sunlight streamed through the open door of his quarters, lying hot on his face.

Cei entered quietly, but the movement disturbed the sleeper and he woke. Stretching cramped arms, he asked, "Back so soon? How did it go? A successful raid—I can tell it was!"

"Superb!" Cei walked swiftly to the bed and sat down, his face alight with excitement. "We swept down from cover as dawn broke—they never knew what hit them! You should have been there—the men fought so well; we have them at their peak. With more men and better horses we will be invincible!"

Arthur shrugged and uttered an explicit oath. "I ought to have been there. I am their leader, but I lie here doing damn all."

"Short of following by carried litter, there is not much for you to do about it, is there?" replied Cei, speaking plain. "It would be better for you if you were to return home to court. These barracks are no place for a restless spirit."

"Home? At Vortigern's court!" Arthur sneered, snorting with contempt. "Fight another round of endless bickering with my wife, you mean?" He made a derogatory noise and settled back against the pillows. "I have no home, save in Less Britain."

He sighed, his mind wandering to the villa estate where he was born and raised. To the calm, wide river where he swam and fished as a boy, the acres of vineyards stretching as far as the eye could see. He had spent his childhood there, yet it was not home. Home was a place where your woman waited with your children. Where unconditional love welcomed you to the warmth of the hearth.

Home was here. With his men.

"You ought to consider settling Winifred in your own holding, Arthur," Cei persisted. "In your own Caer, away from the influence of her mother, things would be better atween you. Especially now, with a child on the way."

Arthur shook his head, his lips puckered, nose wrinkling with distaste. "The last time I was with Winifred, a week or so before this," he pointed to his thigh, "I felt as though I had entered your Christian Hell. She demands so much of me, and there is nothing I care to give her save hard words. I cannot help it, I despise her. How can you give even a pretence of love when you hate someone enough to want her dead several times over?"

"For all that, she is your taken wife, Arthur."

"She is a scheming bitch. I cannot be kind to her. Besides, kind or unkind, it is the truth."

A disturbance outside stemmed any answer Arthur might have had.

A junior officer entered.

"Lord Pendragon, a messenger sent from Llwch."

"From Llwch in Londinium? Send him straight in!"

Arthur glanced at Cei, his eyebrow rising slightly. Llwch, a well-chosen, well-placed spy in Vortigern's household. His orders, to observe, listen, and glean information. A loyal man, Llwch.

A young man, grimed from his journey and with tired black smudges beneath his eyes, entered and saluted. His boots were muddied, even his tunic where the mire had splashed.

Arthur eyed him for a moment as he stood to attention, looking straight ahead. "You are, if I am not mistaken, Dafydd, son of Idris Ironfist. Have you eaten or taken drink?"

"Na, my lord. I have this minute ridden in."

"Seat yourself and tell me what news brings you so far so fast."

Cei crossed to the door and called for food while Dafydd, slightly hesitant, sank to a stool and smiled his thanks as Cei then poured a generous helping of wine. He gulped and wiped his lips, leaving a streak of white skin beneath the dirt.

"It is your wife, lord."

"What!" Arthur spluttered, spilling his own wine over himself and the bed covers. "Llwch has orders to send messages of urgent importance. By importance, man, I had matters of state in mind, not the petty grumblings of the sow I am wed to." Arthur hurled a pillow at the young man, who had come to his feet at his commander's shout and was again standing to attention. The pillow struck him, fell ignored to the floor.

"Her intention of running to Hengest is of no importance, my lord? You are not interested to hear the child she bears, if it be a boy, will be regarded as Saexborn to the people of the queen if it be brought to life at a Saex hearth?"

"Insolent whelp!" Arthur scowled at the messenger, held his hand out for the pillow to be returned. The lad retrieved it, placed it behind the Pendragon's back.

Wriggling himself comfortable, Arthur grumbled to himself. Said louder, "She would not dare birth a son of mine beneath a Saex roof!" His hand took hold of the pillow, hurled it at the far wall, and he swore as damaged muscles protested at the exertion. Cei was cleaning his nails with the tip of his dagger. He glanced up at the last words. "That is not a very kind thing to say."

"Can you be certain it is yours, Arthur?" asked Cei.

"She has been close watched. I am certain. Do you know more, lad?"

"Only that there is a smell of smoke in the wind, and growing rumbles of thunder from Hengest's direction. Your wife is taking full advantage of your"—the young man flicked an awkward glance at Arthur's bandaged leg—"incapacity."

"Well, let her go. I would be rid of her."

Dafydd said anxiously, "Sir, begging your pardon, if your wife sets foot on Saex soil you will lose control of her and the child. Llwch says, if it be a boy, he could one day become a powerful weapon against you—us."

Arthur waved the lad to silence. "We had all this talk when Rowena's boy, Vitolinus, was born. A sudden great fear that Hengest was going to sweep out of Tanatus—with fire and sword."

"Arthur," Cei broke in, "a child of yours, brought up in Saex hands, could make a dragon's den of mischief!" He whistled at the unpleasant prospect.

"I shall not acknowledge the boy."

"My lord," Dafydd urged, "forgive me, Saex ways are very different from

Roman. Princess Winifred, the mother, can declare her son's fathering. It will be enough for them."

Cei muffled a groan. "He is right, Arthur. Once Hengest has the boy, you will never again set eyes on him."

Arthur ran his fingers through his hair. It had grown longer of late, the ends touching his shoulders. He must have an inch or so trimmed off. "Oh, I would see him, have no doubt of that. Eventually he and I would meet somewhere across a battlefield." He glanced meaningfully at Cei, who sat chewing his bottom lip deep in thought.

"She must be diverted then," Cei said at length. Sourly Arthur grimaced, not relishing his own coming suggestion. "Happen it's time she was persuaded into her duty and paid a visit to her wounded husband."

Cei asked, "Vortigern has agreed to this visit to her grandsire, I assume, Dafydd?"

"He knows nought of it. This is the Queen and your wife's secret doing. We believe Hengest will soon rise against the King."

Arthur laughed suddenly, seeing a humorous side. He wagged a finger at Cei. "If I did not know better, my friend, I would swear this was some carefully hatched plan to rid yourselves of my presence here!"

Cei began to protest his innocence, but Arthur waved him down. "Na, you shall be rid of me—and my dear wife shall have the pleasure of my company instead. She obviously wishes to bear our child somewhere other than Vortigern's rotting palace in Londinium. Most sensible of her." He grinned, enjoying himself for the first time in weeks. "I doubt she will agree to my meddling with her arrangements though!"

NINE

"WHY AM I STILL WAITING?" WINIFRED, HER FOOTSTEPS TAPPING AS SHE stalked across the tessellated floor, snapped impatiently at a guard. "Why is my vessel not yet at the water gate? If it is not here soon, I shall forgo the river and ride to my grandsire!"

Her angry words sent her waiting ladies into a twitter of anxious protest. Irritated, she swept an ornamental vase from its pedestal, sending it crashing down to shatter into pieces. "Will no one discover what is causing this insufferable delay!"

She swung round, ready to vent her anger on her ladies, and found an insolently grinning British officer entering the chamber. He saluted and cheerfully apologised for the inconvenience.

"A merchant ship has shifted its load at the water gate, my lady, it will take hours to clear. We have arranged for a litter to take you to a wharf lower downriver where a ship awaits you." He pulled absently at the chinstrap of his helmet, added, "Only I would suggest you do not leave the palace at this moment, better to wait until the dawn tide."

"What!" Winifred's stare was murderous. "I have every intention of leaving now, on this coming tide."

"There is trouble, my lady—a rabble protesting over some minor incident at the palace gates. The King's guard is dealing with the matter, but the mood in Londinium is tinder dry."

Winifred glowered at him. "I am not afraid of a petty rabble, centurion."

He shrugged. "Na, my lady, I don't doubt it, but I would not advise venturing through the town in your condition."

"What does my father pay his guard for—to sit on their backsides all day or to protect the royal household? Are your men not capable of escorting me safely?"

The centurion sighed. "Quite capable, lady, I only thought..."

"You thought? You ignorant pig's muck, you have no brain to think with!" Winifred strode through the archway, her poise somewhat diminished by her pregnant bulk. She called, "I am ready to leave with this tide. Either you escort me or I find an alternative guard. Do I make myself clear?"

The centurion saluted and said, "Perfectly, my lady," adding under his breath, "Be glad to get rid of you."

Winifred was heading for the pillared colonnades which led to the palace main entrance. With a muttered curse the centurion hastily caught her up and barred her way.

"My lady, we must use a side entrance. The mob is dense to the front of the palace. My superior thought, should you still insist on departing, it would be best if you slipped away unnoticed." He indicated the direction.

She regarded him coldly. "Can this rabble not be contained? Are our soldiers so weak they cannot contend with a few scum?"

"There are pockets of fighting, lady, but the situation is well under control, We merely think of your safety," he glanced at her bulk, "and that of the child."

She nodded curtly, realising the sense of his words, but reluctant to give ground. She walked before him in silence, her ladies trotting and whispering behind.

Guards slammed their spears to attention as the group neared the side entrance and walked through into a narrow alleyway. There was rubbish strewn here, blown by the wind or dropped by unauthorised passers-by taking a short cut alongside the palace wall. A rat disappeared into a hole somewhere at the base of the wall.

The centurion handed Winifred into the waiting litter, made to draw the blinds. Winifred stared at him, her hand itching to wipe the silly insolent grin off his mouth.

"Your face is not familiar to me," she said peering close, suspicious. Her finger flicked the sash around his waist. "Yet you wear the colours of the King's guard."

"I am new to the honour of serving the King, lady, but I assure you I am not new to command. You will be safe under my protection."

Winifred was contemptuous. "Then if you are so sure of my safety we shall go directly to the wharf and I shall keep the blinds open. I prefer not to be hidden away."

"Na!" He spoke with authority. "I am certain of your safe conduct because we are not going direct to the wharf and because your litter *shall* be closed.

The rabble are protesting over the favouring of trade with the Jute kind—given your connection with these people and your destination it would not be wise for you to be seen at this moment." He took hold of the blinds with a firm hand, "We shall take a minor detour to ensure no one from the crowd suspects where we go. Then we shall head for your vessel. Best not to cause any undue antagonism."

"I will not travel so," Winifred insisted.

"My apologies, lady, but I have been given my orders."

"Who by?" she demanded, again probing.

The officer shrugged, astonished at her suspicion. "There is only one alternative to the King's guard," he said.

Winifred sucked in her breath.

The centurion looked over his shoulder to make sure no one observed or listened. He leant forward, on a pretence of drawing a cover over her and whispered, "The Queen takes great care in ensuring the right men follow her with loyalty and discretion."

Winifred's eyes rounded, her mouth forming a silent "oh!"

If the centurion was her mother's man, then surely he could be trusted? Satisfied, she pulled the blind shut.

Settling herself as the litter jolted forward, she smiled, contented. She was on her way; nothing would now go wrong! With the help of her grandsire she could achieve more with the birth of this babe than ever she had dared dream! She would hold the Pendragon by the throat—no, the nether regions would be more appropriate! You did not love me, husband, did not treat me well, so fear for the future!

She closed her eyes, her thoughts of Arthur. How foolish she had been to be so dazzled by him, to be so taken by his surface charm and appeal! Underneath that seductive smile lay an arrogant, self-opinionated louse. Happen she should have let that girl Gwenhwyfar have him. It would have been she who was now rejected and mistreated, she who had to suffer his whoring and drunkenness, his verbal and physical abuse.

The litter stopped; she heard gates opening and they moved on. She would soon hurl revenge in his face! But not until she felt the swell beneath the Jute ship that would carry her to safety could she breathe easy.

The journey was short and, apart from the distant roar of rioting crowds, uneventful. The litter ceased its lurching and Winifred parted the blinds to look out upon a small wharf some distance downriver away from the town. She stepped

out awkwardly. A flicker of alarm crossed her mind as she realised the ship bobbing gently on the slack water was British. That foolishly grinning centurion
took hold of her arm and led her firmly towards it.

"I was to travel under Jute sail," she protested, attempting to shake off
his hand.

"British or Saxon," he hastily corrected himself, "Jute, it makes little difference, you will reach your destination."

Winifred looked about her. Luggage was being unloaded from wagon to ship,
but there was no sign of her women. She asked their whereabouts.

"They are in safe hands," the centurion said, then, indicating the vessel, "Shall
we go aboard?"

Winifred frowned, reluctantly allowed herself to be escorted up the narrow
gangplank. He left her on deck with a polite excuse that he must see to the
loading of her possessions. The ship's captain, a squat, plump man, hovered at her
side and gestured graciously for her to follow him below.

"Welcome aboard, my lady, I trust you will have a pleasant voyage." He showed
her to a small but adequately private cabin situated near the stem.

"Send my women to me right away." Winifred gave her order as the captain made to leave her. He spoke no word, merely nodded his acquiescence.
Winifred prodded at the none too clean or comfortable bed squashed to one
side. Her women would have to sleep cramped on the floor; it would be no
hardship for them.

There was the expected noise and bustle of a ship about to make sail. She
ignored it as she lay silently alone. Her head ached and her ankles were uncomfortably swollen. She would close her eyes a moment. Just a moment.

It was with the first creak of movement that she pushed herself upright and
muttered a curse. The fool of a captain had forgotten her orders! She took her
cloak and swept up on deck—to see the riverbank dropping behind as the sail
began to fill and lift the ship into the ebbing tide.

Waiting for her was that damned centurion, still grinning. "Where are my
women?" she demanded.

"Safe," was all the reply she received.

Patience snapping, she snarled, "If you do not remove that inane smirk from
your face this instant, my hand will remove it for you!"

"Strike one of my officers, would you?"

Winifred froze, her face contorted with a mixture of rage, disbelief, and fear.
Involuntarily, her threatening hand, raised to wipe away that grin, went to her

own mouth. She pressed her teeth hard into her flesh to stop the scream. Slowly, she turned to face the speaker.

Men were setting down a litter. Arthur lay comfortably sprawled, eyes bright with triumph.

"You bastard!" she spat.

"And I am pleased to see you also, dear heart. You look well."

"Why are you here? What is this?" She was frightened, but masked it by an outpouring of rage.

"I heard you were anxious for somewhere safe to birth my son. Most commendable."

Her hand was on her throat; her fingers could feel the thump-thump of the pulse bounding in her neck. *Does he know?*

"We go to a place where my son will not be contaminated by any Saex disease."

How much does he know—or guess?

She flung at him, "I suppose you arranged that convenient uproar in Londinium also!"

He smiled. "It was not so difficult."

She raged then, for a while, stamping her foot, demanding the ship put about, return her ashore. Her protests fell on deaf ears. In desperation, she ran to the side, stretching her arms imploringly towards the land slipping so fast away. Briefly she considered jumping overboard and swimming for the shore.

Arthur read her thoughts. "I would not advise it, the distance is deceptive. It would be a tough swim for a man; a pregnant woman would not survive."

"I demand to know where we are going!"

"To my mother's."

Glaring, Winifred made to return below. Her husband's presence sickened her; if he saw, he would assume the nausea came from the ship's motion.

"Where are my women?" she asked for the second time, half turning back to him.

"I dismissed them. There are women aplenty to serve you at my mother's. I have arranged for a trusted female to serve you while at sea. I will send her to you." Arthur held up his hand to attract her attention, his expression ominous as he added, "I warn you, wife, to treat her well. Save you, she is the only female on board. Treat her badly and I may consider withdrawing her for my own use."

Her fury drained away and suddenly Winifred felt very tired, very alone. "Why do you hate me so, Arthur?" She took a faltering step. "I have done you no harm. I have given you wealth and pleasure in our bed. I have been a good, dutiful wife." She laid a hand on her swollen abdomen. "I bear your son, the next Pendragon."

Arthur's eyes flashed. "Would this be the same son you intended one day to use against me had Hengest been so foolish as to leave me alive?"

Jesu! He does know!

"No! Oh no, my lord!" Winifred waddled forward, knelt before him, her hands held out, pleading. "Who told you such a lie!"

"Contrition does not suit you. Suffice to say I know your planning." He took her chin between his fingers, studied her at close quarters. It occurred to him he had never really looked at her before, never cared to go beneath the facade. "What were you to gain from this, Winifred?"

Her body slumped, her shoulders dropping, head lolling defeated and dejected. All she could do now was save herself. If he also knew Hengest was preparing to rise and that she had intended to go with him, then it was her end. *Lie. Cover yourself with a lie!*

"I wanted you, Arthur." She lifted her eyes. "I only wanted your love. Was that so very much to ask?"

"So you seek a divorce. That makes sense." He flicked her chin aside, let her go.

"I love you."

"What a liar you are."

That was the whole trouble, the whole topsy-turvy reasoning behind this running away. She did not lie. By some cruel stroke of fate she did love him— loved him and wanted him, but only as her own, her very own, not to share with those others.

Hardness, a feint to hide behind. "Men and women snigger behind my back that my husband knows the tavern sluts better than his wife. Or that I can only please my husband when he is wine-soaked." Winifred pleaded again. "I do not understand. When you bed with me, we are so good together; we make love with an ecstasy that surely even the gods and goddesses of old would not have known. Is it so wrong for me to love you?" Change to defiance, "I intended to bargain with you, Arthur. Me for our son. For his return, you were to take the both of us. Both or neither." Challenging. "Put me where I belong as your respected wife and future queen, or have my son one day take your place."

He snorted with amusement. "You do not frighten me. Your father never has and you certainly never will."

"I will no longer be treated like some common piece of gutter muck! I am your wife; you will treat me with honour or forgo the knowing of your son."

"I can get other sons. When I overthrow your father I will get other sons." His narrowed eyes bored into hers, malicious, determined. "By another wife." He knew it would hurt, and he saw the involuntary flinch as his barb entered.

She flung a retort. "My father is old, has nothing left to face but the coming of death, but my grandsire shall never bow his head to you! He shall be king next, then we shall see who is the mightier!"

Arthur laughed. "Hengest? He could no more beat me in battle than he could piss on a forest fire to put out the flames. He is of small consequence." He clicked his fingers. "Escort the lady below. See she remains there."

"I need no escort." Winifred turned to make her own way, the bumping in her chest easing. He did not seem to know much beyond the outer fringes; that she was to have gone to Hengest for her well-being, not because of what was soon to come. Of that, relieved, she was certain. Certain enough to threaten, "You may have other sons, Pendragon, but remember this. Mine shall always be the first-born."

Arthur pulled a fur tighter about him. The evening chill on the river was becoming more penetrating. "How disappointed you will be should it be a girl."

Winifred ducked below, heard him add, "Or you may prove to be as worthless as your mother, breeding only the dead-born."

His love? Did she truly believe she wanted that? As of this moment, all she wanted was his death.

OCTOBER 454

TEN

G WENHWYFAR REINED IN HER MARE, CALLING TO THE BOY CANTERING AHEAD, and pointed with exaggerated movement to the ship making her way upriver. Bedwyr tugged his pony around, studying the vessel with his eyes narrowed against the bright sun.

He was much like his elder brother, Cei: brown-haired, brown-eyed, with the same jutting jawline. Gwenhwyfar assumed the sons favoured their dead mother, for they were nothing like their square-jowled father, Ectha.

"She's no ordinary trading ship!" he observed. "Where is she from, Gwen?" The glow of childhood shone in his face. Eleven, and all the confidence and enthusiasm of the Empire within him! He allowed Gwenhwyfar no time to answer, plunged on with, "From Britain, do you think? No Saex ship would dare flaunt such a bold red sail!" He screwed up his eyes, shielding them from the glare with his hand, trying to make out the pennant drooping at the masthead.

The ship was under oar now, coming slow around, but Bedwyr was losing interest. The waterway was always busy with traders and the like. He swung his pony inland, kicked him to a trot, and shouted a challenge at Gwenhwyfar to race.

Squeezing Seren forward, Gwenhwyfar trotted a few paces after him, her head swivelling to keep the ship in view. She hauled her mare to an abrupt halt, swung her to face the river, gaze intent. There was something about it—that red sail, or the carriage of her prow as she glided with the incoming tide?

A flurry of wind gathered in mid-channel, catching the lifeless pennant as the craft swung landward. Gwenhwyfar caught her breath. For a heartbeat she forgot the present; glimpsed, like a half-seen shadow, a memory of when she was a girl. She had been riding then, with a boy up on the hills. How long had it been now? How long since her flight into exile and, following her heels like death's shadow, news of Arthur's marriage? A lifetime, it seemed. Was it truly only a little more than a year? One long, lonely year.

Bedwyr was shouting for her to start the race. She waved acknowledgement, and pushed her mare into a canter, looking back over her shoulder just the once, for a final glance at the ship. Tear-blurred vision and the gentle sloping heath had hidden the span of river from view. She forced a brave smile for Bedwyr's benefit. "We had best get to old Gaius's," she said, "before his Juliana finishes her baking!"

Bedwyr whooped and thudded his heels into the pony's ribs, startling it forward into a plunging gallop. Gwenhwyfar let him win.

Gaius's farm was a favourite place to visit. A one-time cavalry officer of Rome settled now on his own few acres, he enjoyed the civilian life with his wife—who baked particularly wholesome barley-cakes. The elderly man greeted them with a friendly wave as they turned into the courtyard. Flinging himself from the pony, Bedwyr darted forward to give his friend a hug of greeting, the man embracing the lad in return. Juliana appeared, dusting flour from her hands. She swept Bedwyr to her, pleased to see him. His eagerness and high spirits eased the ache for her own two sons, killed long ago serving Rome.

She smiled an equally warm greeting at Gwenhwyfar. "You time your visit well, my dears—I have cakes ready to come from the oven. And a pot of sweet honey to spread on new-baked bread."

Bedwyr yelped with delight and sped off for the kitchen, his sandalled feet kicking up puffs of dust, Juliana plump and matronly in his wake.

"Do not get under foot!" Gwenhwyfar called.

Handing the horses to a slave, Gaius ushered Gwenhwyfar to the porch and, calling for refreshment, seated himself on a couch opposite his guest. He enjoyed a chance to talk and laugh—what better than to spend an afternoon with a pretty young woman who delighted in hearing the prattling of an old fool? Ah, if he were only many years younger, happen he could bring the smile back to her pale cheeks!

Gaius sipped his wine, nibbled his cheese, observing Gwenhwyfar with an indulgent smile. She had first come just over a year ago; walking quiet and ashen-faced beside young Bedwyr, a lad bursting with life and energy. Gaius had been instantly reminded of another such boy—young Arthur had helped to while away many an afternoon with talk of horses and soldiering. On that day, Gwenhwyfar had led her lame mare, seeking help. Gaius had welcomed her, tended the horse and offered to loan a remount.

They had come often after that, at first to inspect the mare's fetlock, later to enjoy the company of two elderly people. Juliana cooed and fussed over her visitors; Gaius, in his calm way, instilled much learning into the energetic young lad; together they brought a small flicker of happiness back to Gwenhwyfar. To Juliana, she was the daughter she had never birthed, a girl in need of a mother's guiding hand and unquestioning love. To Gaius she was a puzzle. Always quiet and soft-spoken, she would sit with Bedwyr listening to the tales Gaius told of his days with the Roman Cavalry, or help eagerly with the chores, never minding hard work. She could chop wood or reap corn as well as any man, was calm and gentle with an injured or frightened horse, and had a knack of soothing an irritable nanny goat or petulant ewe to stand a while for milking. She rarely spoke of her home. With the passing of time the old couple came to understand why. The speaking was too painful.

"Riding here," Gwenhwyfar said, "I thought of a particular day, years past. I was with my brother on the hills of Gwynedd." She stopped, remembering so clearly. Etern's grumpiness over her fat old pony, his joy on recognising that pennant. Etern. She would never see Etern again in this life.

Gwenhwyfar was like a tree, Gaius thought, a tree in winter. You knew it was a tree because there was a trunk and spreading branches; but it was not a tree, not until the spring, when leaves burst forth, shining green. Not until then did the thing of beauty come alive.

She looked at him shyly. "I so miss Gwynedd."

The man reached out, touched her hand. Her skin was cold.

She continued talking to ease the choking pressure building in her throat. How to explain the longing for a place? Mountains and streams. Restless sea. Mist, rain; sudden, dazzling sun. "Being away from Gwynedd is like parting from a lover gone to war. I remember the happy days when we walked and rode together, and hear the whisper of that special voice. I lie at night longing to be close to the one I love. To feel and smell that comforting nearness, warmth and strength enfolding me. But I am alone and my heart knows not when, if ever, we shall meet again."

Gaius refilled her cup, poured for himself. "Is it a place or a person you talk of?"

Gwenhwyfar started. "Oh, a place!" She busied herself with her wine, lifted her eyes with an apologetic smile. She could not lie to Gaius. "Both." She sighed. "The one I cannot go to. The other I cannot have."

"That is indeed love! Love is a piteous condition for which there is no cure!" Gaius said with a laugh.

She laughed with him, and Gaius noted, with the regrets of a man grown too old to do more than think and talk, how pretty she was when she laughed. Unexpectedly, as if it were of no matter, she said, "A ship has come from Britain."

"A special ship?" Gaius enquired, something in her offhand manner alerting him. This ship, then, was important.

Gwenhwyfar studied the cup she held. "Aye." It was good to talk to Gaius. His legs would no longer carry him far, his teeth were nearly all gone, and his hearing not so sharp, but for all that he would listen without a disapproving intake of breath at some private confession, unlike Ygrainne would do. Juliana had too sharp a sense of down-to-earth practicality, and Ceridwen, dear as she was, overmuch innocence for the sharing of despair. Besides, Ceridwen was caught in her own web of new-wedded bliss. She saw nought but sun and blue sky since the day Iawn took her as wife.

Gaius could not see so clear, but then Gaius did not see with his eyes alone. He was a man who saw hidden things with his heart, could see the shadowed movement beneath the surface of the pool, or the stars behind the clouds. A friend who cared enough to listen without the need to pass comment or judgement.

Gwenhwyfar said, "I feel I am the last leaf hanging on a tree at the end of autumn. Dangling there, alive still, but becoming shrivelled and dry. I do not know whether to stay clinging here or let go and get the waiting for death over with."

Gaius thought how strange that he had compared her to a tree also.

She looked at her hands clasping the pottery cup. Clean, manicured nails, smooth uncalled skin. In Gwynedd, her nails had always been jagged and short, her hands roughened from the continuous handling of horse and weapon. Here, she lived a life of Roman luxury. Pampered, tended like young spring vegetables, noblewomen of Rome did not groom their own mounts, or muck out stables or chop wood for the fire. Or fight. She put the cup slowly, carefully, on the table. "I can think only of dark times. The mother I never knew. Etern cruelly murdered. The reason why I am here, and the man I love, who is married to another." Her eyes filled with tears. Memories. So many black and bitter memories.

"Ygrainne talks constantly of God. Her righteous words follow me like a wolf in the night, stalking me, hunting me. I lie awake thinking, trying to sort my thoughts. She talks of the Hell we are condemned to in the next life unless we give our hearts to God in this. This place she talks of, I am already there!" She buried her face in her hands. "I am empty, I am nothing. I exist in a barren wasteland of endless days and longer nights. When I walk beside the river, I wonder if it would be better to drown quickly there, rather than slowly here."

Gaius wanted to speak, but held his tongue. To say something now might stop the girl from talking—and she needed to talk, needed someone to listen.

Gwenhwyfar looked up, her face a mask of grief, her eyes shadow-bruised. "I am frightened," she whispered. "Frightened of so many things."

"We all fear, child," the old man said, taking her hand between his own and holding it there, unobtrusive but comforting.

"I was managing," she said, "living from day to day, never thinking beyond the morrow. I shut out the past. The future also." She gave a shuddering breath. "Especially the future." For a moment she faltered. "Seeing that ship has brought back all the memories. The longing. The faces. Voices. Much has happened since I was forced to flee from Londinium. My life, the life of... others. Now," she looked again at her hands, "now I am frightened of facing what remains of today. Frightened of tomorrow and the day after. I knew this ship would come. Knew it would bring a day when I had to abandon pretence and face reality." Her tears fell freely, running down her cheeks. "I am so alone in this darkness, Gaius. There are people around me, many people, but I am alone. I must face this fear alone, but I cannot! I cannot! I want someone to reach down a hand, and pull me from this depth of despair, from these choking weeds. Anyone! Anyone to say, *I am here!*"

"Anyone?" Gaius waited.

She said nothing. He had listened well, not only to the words she had spoken; had listened more to those unspoken.

"Anyone, child?" he said again, his voice low and kind. "Or someone in particular? Someone aboard that ship?"

Through the tears she looked up sharp, startled.

Ah, thought Gaius, *I am right!* He reflected a while. He must say the correct thing here, wise words of comfort. "Memories are like battles, and battles can go one way or the other. You can stand and fight, no matter what pain runs from your wounds; or you can turn tail and run, knowing then the enemy will follow and without mercy hunt you down."

Gwenhwyfar sat silent. Her father's voice came to her, so clear she almost thought that if she were to turn, she would find him standing there behind her. She smiled through her tears. "It is as you say. I fear this ship, because of who is aboard. But most of all I fear what may happen because of his coming. I am not sure I can fight the problems he will bring, yet I am tired of running. My Da"—she wiped away the tears with her fingers—"my Da always said, *Fight fear, and fear will flee like mist before a rising wind.* But how do you fight a dream that has turned sour?"

"As you would any battle, with shield and sword raised, chin and heart high. You fight it, my dear, by looking it straight in the eye."

Impulsively, she leant forward and placed a quick, light kiss on the old man's cheek. "Thank you, Gaius. You have given me a small measure of courage."

Gwenhwyfar stood, gathering her light riding cloak around her. She felt cold, despite the warmth of the day. If she were to ride to battle, she had best go now. She called for Bedwyr, who came reluctantly, cheeks sticky with golden honey. She dabbed at them with the hem of her cloak and smiled indulgently. "I see you have been enjoying yourself! It is time to return home. Arthur has come."

ELEVEN

BEFORE THEY HAD RIDDEN MORE THAN TEN MINUTES, GWENHWYFAR regretted telling the boy of the ship's passenger. Bedwyr was in a flurry of excitement, all for racing home at a gallop. She could understand his pleasure but could not imitate it. The Pendragon was the boy's hero, his god almost. Gwenhwyfar remembered the excitement she and Etern had felt as they had hurried back to Caer Arfon; the thrill of recognising the Dragon pennant, of realising it was Uthr himself who had come to Gwynedd. Again the stab of pain.

She could not begrudge Bedwyr his pleasure as he rode, always a few paces ahead of her, his laughter echoing the joy remembered from her own childhood. She kept a tight rein on her own emotion, attempted to smile back at the boy as he chattered on.

He repeated once more every detail of the Nativity festival two years past when Arthur and Cei had come home after their first season of service with Vortigern. They had left as boys, and returned for those few brief weeks with feet well set on the road to manhood. Cei had been home since, but not Arthur.

Bedwyr relived those glorious weeks, his child's memory dwelling on the things that had been important to him personally. Presents, games, mock fights. Shared laughter and much happiness.

Gwenhwyfar let him chatter, murmuring occasional agreement at significant points. She had heard the same account many times over—he told his tale of that festival to any who cared listen. It had been hard for him to accept the going of Arthur and his brother when they had followed Cunedda's advice. Harder still to part with them again after their visit. Bedwyr longed to become a man— would the years never pass? Arthur had promised he could take ship and enter his ala of cavalry when he was older; he would ride his own horse, have his own sword. Would become one of Arthur's men!

Until then, he was left behind in Less Britain: a child anxiously waiting, alone and miserable.

Gwenhwyfar had brightened his dull life. Although quiet and subdued in the presence of his Aunt Ygrainne and his father, Gwenhwyfar had revealed a different side when they rode out alone. She was fun to be with, appreciated the ways of a child—a boy who nursed the wild ambitions of a young warrior. She could tell stories that made your heart soar as high as the clouds, tales of the old gods and brave battles. When he discovered she knew how to handle sword and shield, his worship of her became complete. If his cousin Arthur was his god, then Gwenhwyfar was surely his goddess.

For Gwenhwyfar, Bedwyr provided a welcome release from the behaviour expected of a lady. In the company of adults she conformed, was every inch the young, educated gentlewoman of noble birth, but when riding and fishing with Bedwyr, she relaxed and let her natural sparkle—though tarnished at the edges—shine through. And Bedwyr learnt from her. Learnt of Britain, of the Saex; the mountains of Gwynedd. The old ways and the past. He looked forward to his lessons with his fusty tutor after the coming of Gwenhwyfar, eager to surprise her with his own knowledge. They were good for each other, the lonely boy and the lost girl. Companions who supported each other.

As each stride took them nearer home, the feeling of fear gripped harder at Gwenhwyfar's belly, twisting tighter, colder. What should she expect? Was Arthur alone? Ah, was it not that question which stirred this running tide into a hundred, hundred eddies and whirlpools?

As if her thoughts had been spoken aloud, Bedwyr said suddenly, "I wonder if my cousin Arthur has brought his wife? Aunt Ygrainne was furious when she learnt of his marriage. To wed with the daughter of the man who had slain Uncle Uthr! Remember how she shrieked with rage for days after?" He whistled a short, catchy tune, added, "I expect Arthur had his reasons. I know he needed gold—he wrote me once he wanted to purchase horses for his men. I expect she was worth the taking for the extra wealth she would bring him. Mind," he prattled on, unaware of Gwenhwyfar's agonised silence, "I have heard some men do strange things, fall in love and such, pah!" He spat on the ground, a thing which would earn him a whipping were Ygrainne ever to see. "That's stuff for girls, not for war lords. Arthur thinks like a soldier, he has no time for soppy things like love!"

He spoke innocently, from a child's perspective. How could he know his words were burning like a red hot brand through Gwenhwyfar's heart?

She stammered out some brief answer. Swallowed the bile rising in her throat.

Arthur's marriage had caused a stir when the news had come, its ripples of gossip spreading wider afield than the villa. The town too had been shocked, speculation circulating for days, the consensus being that Arthur had wed the girl for her handsome dowry. Then the thing had become accepted and forgotten by family, friends, and town folk—but not by Gwenhwyfar; she could not accept or forget. She was to have been Arthur's wife, had given her pledge. She loved him and Arthur loved her—she rubbed a stray tear from her cheek—or so she had thought. What was it Bedwyr had just said? Arthur was a soldier, he would not dwell on idle things like love?

They halted on the crest of the vine-covered slope overlooking the villa. The courtyard below was bustling with servants unloading a wagon that sagged from the weight of baggage. The east wing of the building was a hive of activity. Behind wide-flung shutters, house servants scurried carrying clean linen and removing covers from furniture. Gwenhwyfar caught sight of Ygrainne hurrying past a first-floor window.

"I expect she is in a right bad humour," Bedwyr remarked, noticing her also. "My aunt dislikes unexpected visitors."

Or anything that upsets the flow of her dull, orderly life. Tactfully, Gwenhwyfar kept the thoughts to herself.

Ygrainne was a woman who was kindly to the sick, generous to the poor, but a woman devoid of warmth. Years of bitterness had deprived her of the glow that once had shone in her eyes. Her life was now devoted to God, leaving no room for anyone else.

Ygrainne never showed affection—not to her nephew Bedwyr, her brother-by-law his father, anyone. She had greeted Gwenhwyfar on the afternoon of her arrival cordially, accepting the girl's urgent need for sanctuary, providing it out of respect for Cunedda. They had kissed briefly, Ygrainne's lips cold and impersonal on Gwenhwyfar's cheek. That had been the first and only physical contact. Used to the warmth and spontaneous affection of brothers and father, Gwenhwyfar ached for the reassurance of fond hugs and sudden whirls of loving laughter.

From Ygrainne's attitude to Bedwyr, Gwenhwyfar could see how distance had grown between the woman and her only son, Arthur. Bedwyr was clothed, fed, educated, and disciplined. He had all a boy could wish for, save love. He had loved Arthur above all things. Desperate, both of them, for affection, it was no wonder Bedwyr and Gwenhwyfar became close friends. If Ygrainne noticed the shining love Bedwyr gave to Cunedda's daughter, she gave no sign of it.

Gwenhwyfar suspected the woman was relieved. With another to shoulder the responsibility of the boy her conscience was salved.

Yet Ygrainne was a fair woman. Short-tempered and impatient with incompetence, she was nevertheless quick to praise and reward hard work. Towards misdeeds by servants she was fair with punishment, never harsh or unjust. In the worship of her God, however, she was strict regarding rules and obedience, expected the same from her household.

Supervising the opening of the rarely used wing, Ygrainne sighed with intense irritation. She tucked a stray wisp of silvered hair back beneath her veil. How like her son to arrive like this, unannounced and unexpected! Not even an advance warning when the ship docked. He could have sent a messenger, but na, not him! He had waited aboard until the baggage was unloaded and travelled with the wagon. Did he do these things from lack of thought, or spite? Herself, she was not a vindictive person, not intentionally, but Arthur? She sighed a second time; somehow, his presence always managed to raise evil thoughts.

Ygrainne compressed her lips. He had generously stated as he entered the villa, it mattered not if his apartments in this wing were not aired. As if she could expect him to sleep on a bed with no linen, in an uncleaned room with stale air! He had waved aside her startled alarm at his arrival, saying to be home was reward enough! He was the bane of her life! Comfort might not matter to him, but he had brought his wife with him, what of her? How degrading to be caught in this state of disorder!

Ygrainne crossed herself, mumbled a short line of holy verse to stifle unbidden words of hatred. During His time on this earth Jesu had said love thine enemy. She fingered the gold crucifix hanging at her waist with the chain of keys dangling there, then closed her eyes in swift prayer. The words of the good Lord were so difficult to put into practice at times!

Ygrainne breathed deeply, turned to watch a servant spreading a sheet upon the bed. With a cry she darted forward and snatched it aside.

"Who laundered this? Look, here, look at this stain!" Pointing, Ygrainne indicated the offending mark, threw the sheet to the floor. "Fetch a clean one, girl—hurry! Think you Lady Winifred would not have noticed?" Damn her. Damn him!

She marched from the wing, her shoes tapping on the wooden floor. They were waiting in the living quarters, taking light refreshment.

Arthur was laughing as she entered, sharing some jest with Ectha. Ygrainne swept into the room. "We need more wine, brother-by-law," she said with stiff politeness. Ectha exchanged a suitably chastened look with Arthur, then fetched a new jug.

Bedwyr whooped loudly as he careered at a gallop down the sloping track. Gwenhwyfar hesitated. Impulsively she shouted, "I will be along soon! I have an errand!"

He heard; raised an arm, but did not stop. The pony's hooves sent a spray of gravel showering into the air as Bedwyr slithered to a halt and leapt from the saddle. Ygrainne appeared and ushered the boy inside. By the way her hand gripped his dust-encrusted tunic Gwenhwyfar guessed she was scolding him. She glanced at her own clothing. Skirt, cut and sewn to form loose riding bracae, which fell in modest folds when she was not mounted. It was a compromise; Ygrainne would not allow her to wear male gear even for riding. The ill-fitting tunic she wore hung baggy about her top half, and her favourite worn cloak was becoming grubby. The hem, she noted, was torn.

Mastering her mare's reluctance to turn away from stable and feed, she trotted back along the hill track. Gwenhwyfar did not want to return to the villa, but did not want to discard these friendly clothes for formal Roman dress. Nor have her hair bound and styled. Rebelliously she tugged at the braids coiled about her head, let the copper hair tumble loose and free.

She kicked Seren with her heels, lengthening the stride of a reluctant canter into a reckless gallop. The mare, resigned to the change of direction, responded eagerly, stretched her neck, and flew. They plunged through a copse, out and up on to the heath, where the wind stung Gwenhwyfar's eyes to tears. Hair and cloak billowed behind, streaming like some giant bird, exultant, escaping, for a brief while at least, the confines of a cage.

Blowing hard, Seren eventually began to slow, dropped to a walk. Gwenhwyfar loosened the reins, let her amble and snatch at mouthfuls of grass. Saliva dribbled green as Seren chewed round the iron bit, snatched for more grass. They had circled, were close by the banks of the Ligre river. The slow water was turning gold as the lowering sun coloured its surface. A few fishermen were beginning to make their way down to the estuary for their night's work. By first light, the market in town would be brimming with fresh-caught seafood. The last swifts darted above hunting insects, their high-pitched cries rising and falling with their whirling, flashing dance.

Gwenhwyfar wondered if the summer birds had left Gwynedd yet. Was the weather mild there also? Ygrainne would be angry with her for not returning with Bedwyr.

Some of her tears were not from the wind alone. She slid from the mare's back, burrowed her head into the black mane. How could she face him? How could she make polite conversation, entertain, and dine—sit alongside him? How, knowing all the while he was committed to a wife, and happen a child also by now?

She had thought the anger was gone, the desperate feeling of betrayal eased, but shards of broken dreams remained like shattered pieces of glass dropped on a marble floor. Self-pity had found time enough to weave a snare of despair and hopelessness; time to mix with an ample portion of jealousy, to breathe the sulphur fumes of hatred.

Gwenhwyfar remembered the details a young boy misses. Arthur's eyes. Shining hawk eyes that gleamed when he spoke of things dear to his heart. Eyes that darkened when something displeased him. Eyes that could see uninhibited into your heart and mind. His voice, his hair, his smell. How he bubbled with excitement, hurried to get things done, to get where he was going. Remembered a promise.

What was a promise anyway? Nought but words. Words spoken in childhood.

He must have known Cunedda had annulled that awful arranged marriage with Melwas. Surely he knew? Of course he did! The news would have been all across the country after her flight. There must have been one hell of a row, with Vortigern and Melwas powerless to do anything about it. So why had Arthur still married the bitch?

Even if there were reasons, rational, good reasons why he could not marry with Gwenhwyfar, need he have taken someone else quite so soon?

The sea crossing and those lonely, lost first weeks had been made bearable by her conviction someone would come—Arthur himself—to fetch her home, to promise her Melwas would never have her, that things would be all right. But no one came, save the traders with news of his marriage. Weeks slid by. Weeks turned to months, months to a year. Now he had come, but now it was too late. A year too late.

The remnants of hope had fluttered, ragged, in a gusting wind of passing time, were crumbled to dust.

She had no way of knowing the tide of events had run too swiftly for Arthur, that he too had been caught in the pull of a fast flooding current and was held there, adrift without any means of steering himself free. For Arthur, there seemed not even a remnant to guide him safe home.

Stroking the white star on the mare's forehead, Gwenhwyfar felt rising anger. How dare he come to taunt her like this! Did he think it amusing? Was he laughing at her? Well, she would soon strike that smile from his face!

Her green eyes had coloured storm dark. She brushed the tears from her cheeks, pinching the skin to hide the blotching. Vaulting into the saddle, she turned Seren for home.

As she crested the rise behind the villa another thought struck her with such force she almost reeled. She hauled Seren to a halt, the mare tossing her head and flattening her ears from the discomfort of a jabbing bit.

There had been no word from Britain for some weeks. Not even wild rumour; for all they knew, Vortigern could be rotting in his grave. Or this Saex bitch Winifred. Could she be dead? Many a woman died in childbirth. Death made no distinction between rich, poor, peasant, or princess. Had Arthur come because he had not forgotten; was here to take her home at last?

The seed of an idea was planted and germinated. It flourished and grew.

The mare required no urging with the smell of home in her nostrils. With each long stride of the horse's gallop, the visions increased. Arthur pacing angrily, demanding servants be sent to search for her. He would have banged through all the rooms, bellowing her name, marched to the stables—questioned Bedwyr. She would ride into the courtyard, he would run down the steps from the villa, swing her into his arms!

Gwenhwyfar trotted beneath the archway, through the open gate. Slid, breathless, from Seren her face glowing with anticipation. Where was he? A stable slave appeared. Not Arthur. Ygrainne hurried from the villa, her face creased with suppressed anger. Her words shrill.

"Gwenhwyfar! Where have you been? You are so untrustworthy, girl! My son has arrived with his wife. Make yourself presentable and see Lady Winifred is settled in her rooms. Lord in His Heaven knows what I shall do if the babe she carries comes early!"

For Gwenhwyfar, everything chilled to silence. She saw Ygrainne's lips moving, heard the words, but they held no meaning for her. Ygrainne stepped irritably forward, took her arm, and began to shake it. Gwenhwyfar stared numbly at Ygrainne's hand, watched it shake, heard her reprimand as if it came from a great distance. She stood unmoving, as if carved from stone.

With the rushing noise of a torrential waterfall sensation returned. Ygrainne's angry voice, the slave waiting to take the mare.

"This is as unexpected for me as it is for you, Gwenhwyfar," Ygrainne was saying; "Must you take all evening to think upon it? Give those reins to the slaves and get yourself cleaned and tidied." Ygrainne tutted, fingered Gwenhwyfar's straggling loose hair. "Look at you. You are like some beggar's brat, are not fit to be presented to my son and his wife!"

Habit led Gwenhwyfar to her room, changed her dress, washed her face, and combed her hair. The daily routine of washing and dressing. Her hands went through the motions, but her mind was blank, totally void of all thought.

Ceridwen appeared, chattering excitedly; she always looked radiant, Ceridwen. Clicking her tongue, she waved a slave forward to take up the task of washing off the dirt and sweat, and to tidy Gwenhwyfar's hair. Gwenhwyfar found herself perfumed and robed in fine garments; her hair styled. Her jewels were fastened in her ears, around her neck and wrists, pinned to her shoulder. Ceridwen talked of Arthur, his wife, the baggage they had brought, the pleasant surprise of their coming.

And all the while, four words crashed and echoed around in Gwenhwyfar's head. Four words heavy with meaning. The babe she carries.

Arthur was reclining on a couch with Bedwyr squatting beside him. The boy's face glowed. Eyes sparkling with pleasure, he plied him with one question after another, mostly about men and horses and the unrest of the Saex; battles, wounds, weapons. A hundred things. He did think to ask about Cei, was satisfied with a statement that his brother was well.

Seated opposite, Winifred sat erect and silent, lips pressed thin. Both she and Arthur looked up as Gwenhwyfar entered the room. Both pairs of eyes widened in naked surprise. For differing reasons.

Gwenhwyfar was obliged to greet them formally. She walked tall and serene to Arthur as Lord, first. He had risen, stood waiting, his face a blank mask. She sank into a deep reverence, dipping her head, refusing to meet his eyes. If he should look into her own eyes, he would know. Would know her body shook, her heart hammered, and he must not know that. He must not discover how easy it was to humiliate her.

"Gwenhwyfar! I did not know you were still here—I assumed you had returned to Gwynedd. When I last heard from your father he indicated he would be sending for you. That was," Arthur calculated rapidly, "sa, in the spring. Oh, get up." He reached out and took her hands, intending to help her to her feet. She lifted her head, looked at him with a clear challenge of angry defiance. He let her go, as if stung by a bee.

"I have heard of no such wish from Gwynedd." Gwenhwyfar was surprised, she had expected her voice to creak and squeak, but it came out calm. Quite regal.

"How are you?" he asked, his own voice neutral, formal, without warmth. "You look well, though thinner than when last I saw you."

Winifred's guttural accent interrupted. "Gwenhwyfar carried much puppy fat as I recall."

With a sweet smile, glad of the excuse to turn away from Arthur, Gwenhwyfar walked over to Winifred, dipped a second reverence. "Were we not all burdened by indulgence as children? It is for the woman grown to form a pleasing figure." Gwenhwyfar smiled, her eyes drawn to the bulge of Winifred's pregnancy. She bent forward to place a light kiss of greeting on each of Winifred's cold, artificially coloured cheeks.

Arthur's wife had not missed the barb in the reply. At this late stage of pregnancy she had no figure, did not need reminding of the ungainliness of her condition.

Arthur had seated himself, and indicated for Gwenhwyfar to do the same. She selected a stool placed well away from either of them. There was a moment's uneasy silence, broken as Arthur asked, "You are comfortable here, at the villa?"

"Thank you, yes. Your mother has made me most welcome." They spoke in elegant, formal Latin.

Bedwyr, silenced when Gwenhwyfar had entered, began his questioning again. Arthur laughed, rumpled his hair. "Lad, do you never stop?" Answered, as well as he could.

Gwenhwyfar was grateful for the boy's chatter.

As she had answered Arthur that last time, his eyes had sought hers—those hawk eyes, so hard to read unless you understood the mind that lay behind them. Something she had seen there unnerved her, shook the rigid self-control she was struggling to maintain. She had seen pain there, and a great sadness.

What was this Bedwyr was saying?

"Arthur has been wounded, Gwen. He was nearly killed, nearly lost his leg!" The boy was at her side now. "He has come home so we can help him grow strong again."

Arthur laughed, amused at the boy's exaggeration. "Nonsense! I was never that badly wounded—and I am quite strong already. I cannot ride for a while, that is all. Rather than idle away my days in some stuffy building I thought I would come and see how Ectha here is coping with the estate, and how much deeper my mother has committed herself to the Christ God."

Ectha laughed uncertainly, unsure whether Arthur jested or not. He felt uncomfortable in the young man's presence. By Roman law Arthur was the head of the family, not Ectha. Uthr had been husband to the eldest daughter, heiress to all her father owned; Uthr had taken the legal responsibility, had passed it to the son at his death. All the same, Uthr had taken little interest in the estate; Arthur even less so—was not even resident. The daily running of the place fell to Ectha.

Wounded? Gwenhwyfar had flicked an anxious glance at Arthur as Bedwyr had told the reason for his being here. Arthur had winced as he had risen to greet her, had put little weight on his leg when standing.

Bedwyr, not at all put out by his cousin's denial, went on to tell Gwenhwyfar the grim details, rather embellished. She listened, thankful she could be occupied with Bedwyr and not seem impolite to others in the room.

Arthur was talking to his mother. She had asked, "For how long, Arthur, do you intend to stay? You were somewhat vague upon your arrival."

"A while, Mother, that is all I can say, a while. I expect until the sea lanes reopen in the spring."

Ygrainne suppressed a groan. That long! He noted his mother's lack of enthusiasm. "You wish me gone from here before spring?" His voice was dry as he added sarcastically, "And I thought you would be so pleased to see me."

Irritated, she answered churlishly, "Of course I am. Your visits are rare. I wondered, merely, how long we could enjoy your company."

Under his breath, "Liar."

The room fell silent. Arthur beckoned a servant forward to refill his goblet with wine. He said after a moment, "I had a desire for my son to be born on my own, unquestionable territory. Pendragon land, not Saex."

Winifred smiled across at her husband, not missing his sarcasm. Outwardly her look was one of love and respect. "My husband is most thoughtful in these matters, Lady Ygrainne. We both desire the next Pendragon to be as great as his father and grandsire."

She accepted honey-sweetened fruit from a slave, said, her voice as sweet as the dish before her, "My lord husband was most upset his family were not with us to celebrate our wedding feast." She gazed fondly at Arthur. "Were you not, my dearest?" She lowered her voice slightly and said to Ygrainne, "Men can be such boys at times! He will never admit his true reason for bringing me here. Naturally he wishes to show the fruit of our happy union to his own people." She patted her swollen belly to emphasise her point, smiling all the while at

Arthur, daring him to contradict her. "In Britain," she added, "the Pendragon's banner is so eclipsed by that of my father."

She turned her sickly-sweet smile on Gwenhwyfar. "It is a pity you left Britain so hurriedly, my dear, for you too missed our wedding feast. It was a grand occasion! My husband was quite overcome with emotion, were you not, love?" She did not miss the flicker of anger in Arthur's eyes, nor the dullness in Gwenhwyfar's. "Our wedding night was, how shall I say, a fulfilment of joy for both of us. We are blissfully happy together."

Gwenhwyfar thought, *if she does not stop soon I will slap her.* Said, "I am pleased you are both content. The child will bring you future joy."

Winifred had been as startled as Arthur to discover Cunedda's daughter here at Ygrainne's villa. So this was where she had been hiding all these months! If her mother or father knew, they had never said. And Melwas? Vortigern had dismissed Gwenhwyfar's disappearance almost immediately, had more important problems to worry on. The fighting around the Angli settlements had flared again and there were reports of dissent in the north. Sulking, Melwas had taken himself off to his own Summer Land, had not been at court this past year. Did he know Gwenhwyfar was here? She must make sure he did.

More interesting had been Arthur's unguarded reaction as Gwenhwyfar had entered the room. His wife had caught the flicker of alarm and discomposure. That was not like Arthur; he was always in control, always mastered his expression. None could read his veiled thoughts, not through that lazy grin and those impenetrable eyes. But he had let the mask slip for a fleeting second. So, he still wanted Gwenhwyfar then?

Winifred had enticed Arthur, bedded with him; had begged her mother to find a way of securing this marriage—and she had, by some devious method. All that, because she had determined no one else would have Arthur, the best catch in the river. She had thought the past was dead.

Gwenhwyfar should have been betrothed to Melwas and then disappeared who knew or cared where. The past should have faded like the memory of yesterday's sunset.

The spark of jealousy, that had kindled when she had first realized Arthur wanted Gwenhwyfar, flared again into life. There was one satisfaction. It had shaken him, finding her here. And Arthur shaken was a rare sight worth the seeing! For the first time since she had found herself tricked on to his ship, Winifred felt a hint of pleasure. He, her arrogantly perfect husband, had made a mistake!

TWELVE

THE NIGHT WAS COLD. GWENHWYFAR LAY CURLED BENEATH HER SLEEPING fur listening to the sounds of darkness: an owl hunting; mice rustling; the wind from the distant sea tugging at autumn leaves. She glanced at the empty bed on the other side of the room, wished she still had Ceridwen's bright company during these long nights of loneliness.

Her cousin was happy in her marriage to Iawn; Gwenhwyfar did not begrudge her the contentment—how could she? Ceridwen was a sweet girl though a little too fanciful, oblivious to problems, seeing a good side to everything others thought bad.

Gwenhwyfar's hand touched a wrapped bundle beneath her pillow. The few letters that had come from Gwynedd, from her brothers Enniaun and Ceredig; one from her Da. She lay with her fingers touching the ribbon binding them, willed sleep to come.

Giving in, she pulled the bundle from its place of safety and padded across the floor to sit before the night lamp burning in the corner. She selected one letter at random, began to read. The words were faint in this dim light but she had read them often enough to need little illumination, knew every scrawled word by heart. It was one of Enniaun's. He wrote of a skirmish across the straits from Caer Arfon on the Isle of Mon, said the sea-wolves were having the worst of it. She selected another, this from Ceredig. He told of his first-born son, of his new own-held territory down the coast to the south of Gwynedd's borders. A third, received two weeks since, containing word of her own mare's foaling.

She dropped the letters in her lap, wishing Etern were alive. He would have written of the mountains, the colours of the trees, and the beauty of the horse herds being brought down from summer pasture.

Sitting in the silence of her room, Gwenhwyfar remembered past autumns. The early snows mantling Yr Wyddfa like an old woman's veil. The golds and browns and reds of the trees, leaves clinging like suckling babes to their mothers' breasts. The scent of wood-smoke and damp mountain earth. The kitchens at Caer Arfon alive with the bustle of preserving fruit and salting meat, the making of beer and wine. The cattle, those not to be slaughtered, gathered and, with the war-horses, divided among the outlying steadings for winter quartering. Each head of livestock carried a payment of corn, skins and spun wool for its good care. In this way the lord of Gwynedd saw to it his people were fed and adequately clothed throughout the winter months. For each animal returned fit and healthy, come spring, an extra payment was made. Cunedda's livestock were well tended and his people content.

The seasonal stocking of the storerooms was almost completed in Ygrainne's household also of course, but the excitement was lost here. No sharing of laughter as soft and hard fruits were picked; no giggling of servants and children as the huge vats of bubbling fruits were cooked and poured into storage jars. Here, the slaves and servants carried out their duties efficiently but with a dullness that would erase the brilliance of the sun.

Gwenhwyfar sighed, folded her letters. Samhain was approaching, the night when the dead returned. Despite Christianity, the festival survived. The religious ceremony had faded once there were no more Druid priests to officiate, but traditions were hard to break, particularly those linked with joyful festivity—or, as at Samhain, superstitious fear.

Ygrainne had scolded Gwenhwyfar when she mentioned the rite last autumn, impressing upon her that Christians followed Jesu and did not bow to the nonsense of pagan ceremony. Still, Gwenhwyfar had noted, with a smile, Ygrainne devoted herself to deeper prayer on Samhain eve, and Gwenhwyfar's was not the only bowl of milk placed before the threshold as a gift to any wandering spirits.

Bedwyr, with the children of neighbours and freeborn servants, had enjoyed playing the traditional games, although Ygrainne had frowned on those too. This year, remembering the fun, he was eagerly awaiting the close of the month, three weeks away. As a child at Caer Arfon Gwenhwyfar had looked forward with excitement to the festival, when they played and drank and feasted; when tales were told around the Hall fires of people from the past who might, even as the tales were being told, be creeping around the outer walls.

An owl hooted, long and low, an eerie, ghostly sound. Gwenhwyfar shivered, recalling the childhood thrill of being enjoyably terrified by the darkness of Samhain night. No doubt this year, as last, she would be expected to kneel in Ygrainne's cold stone chapel. Oh aye, Ygrainne said she did not believe in the nonsense of Samhain, but she did not rest easy on the night when the dead walked!

Gwenhwyfar caught her breath. Something moved by the shrubs bordering the ornamental garden beyond the window! For a heart-thudding moment she wondered if her thoughts had conjured up a spirit. She fought the panic down. Whatever it was, it had gone.

She relaxed, surprised to feel sweat trickling down her back and laughed at herself. Foolish to let her imagination run away with her. She reached for the small flagon of watered wine standing ready for night use. Half glancing at the gardens, not watching what she was doing, she tipped it over. By chance, Gwenhwyfar caught it before it crashed to the floor but wine gushed in a splashing fountain. She cursed.

Reaching for a shawl, Gwenhwyfar covered her shoulders and slid her feet into soft house shoes. Ygrainne would have insisted a house slave be wakened to clear up the mess, but Gwenhwyfar reckoned it quicker to fetch a cloth and do it herself. Why disturb those who slept for such a trivial task?

The kitchens were deserted and silent, a single night lamp casting a dim but adequate light. A lingering smell of the evening's meal pervaded.

Reaching for a beaker, Gwenhwyfar poured water for herself, drank thirstily, then searched for a cloth to wipe up the spillage in her room. She found something suitable, made her way back along the open colonnaded corridor running the entire length of the villa. Storerooms, kitchens, and dining room took up one wing, with servants' sleeping quarters above. The main living quarters formed the central block with the bath-house, Arthur's rooms and extra guest rooms on the third.

Something made her pause before turning to climb the narrow servants' stairs leading to the upper floor. She glanced at the two parallel rows of conifers forming a central aisle through the gravelled courtyard—and gasped. Someone, something, stood there with its back to her, gazing up at the cloud-veiled half-moon.

She must have made an audible noise for the shape turned.

"Who is there?" a voice called, low and wary.

"I could ask the same!" Gwenhwyfar countered, an edge of fear to her words. She stood motionless as a vague shadow walked forward, feet scrunching, oddly unbalanced on the gravel, a third noise clicking with the awkward pace.

The clouds parted and a thin radiance lit up the open space. Gwenhwyfar caught a brief glimpse of unmistakable features before the moon sailed again behind her shielding cover.

"What are you doing out here, Arthur?" she asked lightly, unsuccessfully masking a tremor.

"I could ask the same," he echoed.

Gwenhwyfar saw the reason for the third sound: he was leaning heavily on a crutch.

Climbing the five steps leading to the raised corridor, Arthur seated himself on the top one, stretching the injured limb before him. He sat quiet for a while, toying with the wooden crutch.

Gwenhwyfar hesitated, undecided between staying or going. She had made up her mind to leave when he said, "I truly did not expect you to be here, Gwen."

"As you can see, you expected wrong." The reply was curt.

He half looked round at her, standing there in her night shift with only a shawl around her shoulders. Her lovely hair tumbled as wild as he remembered; suited her better than that artificial, restricting style she had worn earlier. His initial shock at first sight of her had numbed him; it had taken all his wits and experience to master that sudden leap of panic.

He had known Cunedda had sent her here—it had been his own suggestion, for he knew the people of the town would not gossip and Gwenhwyfar would be safe with his mother. But Mithras, he had not expected her to have remained all this while!

He told himself again she was beyond his reach; he had tried to put her memory from him! Had succeeded, he thought, until she stood there before him, silent and thin and pale—more beautiful than ever he remembered. He had felt his whole being shake as he acknowledged her formal, distant greeting, stifled the longing to fold her in his arms, kiss her hair and eyes and lips—hold her close and safe.

Then he had glimpsed Winifred, his wife. Saw her hastily veiled gleam of triumph; realised he must never, ever, give way to his feelings before her, because, bitch that she was, she would destroy Gwenhwyfar as easily as crushing a butterfly.

Winifred was only too ready to sharpen her claws at his expense.

His voice cold, Arthur said, "I am eager to see my son come into the world. A grandchild may bridge the gap between myself and my mother."

Gwenhwyfar said nothing, looked beyond him to the scudding moon shadows. She had to ask. Had to know.

"Do you love her?"

He groaned, masked the sound by rubbing the persistent ache in his leg. "My wound is healing all too slowly. Often of a night it pains me. I find walking eases it." Then, "She is my wife, Gwenhwyfar."

"She is your wife, aye. Do you love her?" Gwenhwyfar stared at him, her hand clasped at her throat holding her shawl around her, a small protective barricade.

He rose unsteadily to his feet, the pain in his thigh and the grimace on his strained face genuine enough. He said again, "She is my wife, and Vortigern's daughter."

"She is the by-blow of a Saex bitch!"

"I repeat," low, a tinge of menace, "she is my wife. She carries my son."

Unable to help herself Gwenhwyfar flung a taunt at him. "The daughter takes after the mother. All Saex women are scheming whores—are you so sure it is yours?"

Despite his wound, Arthur moved quickly, grabbed her arm in a grasp so tight it hurt. In the morning, Gwenhwyfar would find an ugly bruise where his fingers had gripped.

The anger was genuine, but the direction of it false. He desperately wanted to see the end of the mare he was saddled with, but had no way of doing so save for her death. His pride would not let him show the chains which shackled him to her, so he lashed out in anger at the one he loved.

"I say for the final time, Winifred is my wife! I pleaded her hand," he snorted in self-disgust, "took her virginity in my bed. Through her may come an easy way of claiming the kingship. I have added benefits to my ambition—a wealthy woman for my bed to pleasure me, and a son soon to be born."

Gwenhwyfar laughed scornfully. "You sound so sincere I almost believe you."

"I have told no lie."

"Have you not?" she retorted. "Have you then forgotten our pledge the day your men cheered you as their lord?" Her eyes flashed in the dim light. "Have you so easily forgotten you asked me to be your queen, Arthur Pendragon?"

He turned away, limped a few paces, rested his hands on the waist-high railing. His stomach churned, he felt sick. His thigh throbbed abominably, his head also. Aye, he remembered. Remembered all too clearly!

Into the night he said, "We were children then."

She answered, "You asked my Da for my hand. You change allegiance as the tide turns."

He sucked in his breath and gritting his teeth, cursed silently. She knew then. He almost decided to drop this pretence, almost turned to her to admit all he truly felt, but na, how could he endanger her? He loved her too dearly to bring Winifred's spite down on her. Why in the name of Mithras had he come here?

He gripped the railing with his hands. "I asked for you because our marriage would have brought an unequivocal alliance with Gwynedd and easy access to your father's horses. Cunedda refused me, so I looked elsewhere for my wealth."

Gwenhwyfar stared at him, stunned. Was this the truth? Could she have been so blindly stupid? Had it all been lies, one long lie after another? She said simply, "I thought you loved me."

Arthur shut his eyes, tight, dug his nails into the wood of the railing. "Then you thought wrong." He did not want to hurt her; had to hurt her. "I tell all my women I love them. I suppose for the one night I am with them, I do give love. Come morning, I forget them."

Once, Gwenhwyfar had been kicked by her father's stallion. She had been eight years old, had foolishly walked behind the animal and paid the price. The blow had sent her spinning across the stable yard to crash into the opposite wall and lie screaming and crying as the pain shot up her leg. There were no bones broken, but she had nursed the bruising for weeks after. Strange, she had completely forgotten the incident until now. It was almost as if, again, she had walked where she ought not and been kicked for her stupidity.

Suddenly, she hated Arthur, hated him more than she would have thought possible. Without further word she turned her back on him and returned to her room. Dropping the cloth she had absently clutched in her hand, she crumpled to the floor. Sobs racked her body; great, bitter tears. Her heart, already these past months dangerously cracked, was shattered into a thousand tiny pieces.

DECEMBER 454

THIRTEEN

WINTER WAS PROVING BITTER AND MERCILESS, WITH A CRUEL WIND THAT blustered unceasingly, bending vegetation, man, and beast before it and whipping the river into flurries of restless agitation. Rain drizzled or soaked alternately; and tempers flared as easily as a spark to dry heath. Gwenhwyfar stayed as much as possible in the seclusion of her room, some days not leaving her bed until near noon. Her hair, if Ceridwen had not fussed, would have been left unwashed and uncombed. She dressed haphazardly, uncaring, for there seemed little point to anything, even life itself.

Iawn had gone with Arthur into Gaul. Ceridwen missed him terribly. She had tried to chirrup brightly at first but Gwenhwyfar's dull depression seemed catching.

Winifred had been left behind. Fortunately for the household, she had taken to her bed after the birthing of a sickly daughter. Quite the ugliest child Winifred had ever seen. It must be some jest, some horrendous joke that Arthur had played upon her, for she had been so certain she carried a son. This mewling and puking girl-child with sallow yellow skin and squinting, crossed eyes was surely not hers? She could not have borne this, this—thing! There was no grief when the creature died. Few expected a child born on the Dark Night of Samhain to live for long.

The days passed, turned to weeks, and they awaited Arthur's return, knew he would return some time before the Nativity.

Winifred waited, relieved the brat was gone. She wanted to go home! She waited for Arthur, hoping he would allow her to go, now there was no son to bind them.

Bedwyr, lonely and bored, awaited his cousin with excitement and expectation; Ygrainne, with the hope that spring would come early and Arthur would return to his men and take Winifred with him. Gwenhwyfar? She did not want his coming back.

He eventually arrived five days before the day of Christ's birth celebration, his coming throwing the household into renewed upheaval. To Ygrainne's intense annoyance he brought with him the eldest son of Aegidius, King of Gaul. Clutching her rosary of fine carved cedar, she sought the calm company of Father Simon, who tended the villa's small chapel.

"Feelings of alarm and anger are natural, my daughter," he said, setting a tender hand on her bowed head. "All God's children say and think careless things which come to mind in moments of weakness."

For the first and only time Ygrainne felt her belief waver. Did this man truly understand her feelings for this son of hers? She had been tending the hypocaust stokehole when Arthur had arrived. The brickwork had become worn and crumbled, the slaves too ignorant to use sense in the clearing of it, she had needed to supervise the work herself. How like Arthur to arrive at an inconvenient moment! With soot on her face and grime on her hands, she had to welcome Syagrius, a prince! Damn Arthur to Hell! He had made no apology, had sat his horse amid the bustle of armed escort and baggage as if everything was normal. Normal! She had met his eyes as he sat there unconcerned—and his look had frightened her.

The words of the priest's muttered blessing drifted past her. She knew those deep, dark eyes, the eyes of a man who had once loved her so. No, not Arthur's eyes, Uthr's. Tears slid down her pinched cheeks as the painful memories came— memories she had long since locked away under the protection of God's shield. She had loved Uthr, loved his tenacity for life, his determination to succeed. Loved him enough to follow him willingly to the edge of the earth. Uncomplaining, unflustered, heavy with child, she had faced those mountainous seas and an uncertain future for him, for Uthr. And Arthur had looked at her this afternoon with those same eyes, Uthr's eyes. But that look he had given her carried no love, no tenderness. Only loathing and contempt.

It had not been her fault! She had seen the sense in hiding her newborn son's identity, understood at the time of his birthing the threat of Vortigern, whose power spread wider in those days. Uthr was safe enough in exile but would he have remained safe if the tyrant had known of an heir? So she had agreed to the pretence of her son's death, sure in the knowledge it would only be for a while, until other sons came. But months stretched to years and there was no other son. She mourned that only one, the son she had never suckled or held; mourned, and accepted he was gone from her, to all purposes dead. Mourned, and turned to God for His wisdom and comfort. And Uthr had turned to Morgause.

Father Simon had fallen silent, his prayer ended. Ygrainne kissed the hem of his gown, left the chapel, and walked blindly into the settling night. She seated herself on a bench, pulling her cloak close against the harsh wind, looked towards the rear of the east wing, at the whitened plaster walls peeping through the darkness of the evergreens. Lamps had been lit, their glow filtering through the cracks of closed shutters. Uthr had never discovered that once, long, long ago, she had sat in this very spot and seen him through the open ground-floor window, loving with Morgause.

Sitting here, nursing her memories, Ygrainne realised Uthr had never questioned her turning to God for solace. He had been a demanding man, a man who took what he needed when he needed it. But he had never forced himself on her and, after the girl-children she bore also died, respected her not wanting him in her bed. Arthur hated her for the love she was unable to give, and Uthr had gone to Morgause for the necessities of manhood because he loved her, Ygrainne, so much. Both things so hard, so unbearably hard to accept.

They searched the villa for Ygrainne when she did not appear for the evening meal. Gwenhwyfar found her slumped, jaw slack and dribbling, beside the garden bench. Down Ygrainne's cheek tears glistened in frosted tracks.

FOURTEEN

Ectha sat numb with disbelief at the shock of Ygrainne's illness. He nursed an untouched goblet of wine between chilled hands, staring vacantly into space. Slave and servant crept about their duties, clearing the remains of a barely touched dinner, quietly awaiting further orders.

Gwenhwyfar was seated to the far side of the room, alone with her thoughts.

Syagrius cleared his throat, his voice loud in the stillness as he said, "I have instructed my servant to seek alternative lodgings in town on the morrow."

Arthur began to protest but Syagrius silenced him. "With your mother taken ill it would be inconceivable for me to intrude further."

Ectha summoned a weak smile. "The household has been put to no trouble. Gwenhwyfar is more than capable of running things, are you not, my dear?"

She nodded polite agreement, careful not to let her reluctance show. The acceptance of responsibility was as necessary as a warm mantle in winter, but she would wear it as heavy as she wore the weight of exile. Ectha assumed she would step into Ygrainne's place and organise the villa's daily needs with as much efficiency. She had not the heart, or conscience, to refuse him.

She said now, aware of her duties, "You are most welcome to stay; happen company would be a good diversion at this moment."

He smiled warmly, stood, and formally bowed. "I thank you, but arrangements are in hand. My business on behalf of my father will take but a short while." His smile widened as he stepped forward to take Gwenhwyfar's hand in his own, raised it to his lips. "I accepted Arthur's offer to stay here as an excuse to meet you, Lady Gwenhwyfar."

She blushed. He was no more than ten and five years, not even a man yet, with barely a need to shave those fine hairs more than once in the week. Yet here he was, with the self-assurance and expectation of full manhood.

His intimate gaze reflected all he implied, and more. Gwenhwyfar pulled tentatively to free her hand, but he held it firm.

"I must state," he said blithely, "Arthur did not speak the full truth of you."

She glanced briefly at Arthur who was sprawled along a couch frowning, interested of a sudden in his fingernails.

Syagrius had seated himself beside her on the couch, moved closer. She could feel his body, young and muscular, very intent, through the fine stuff of her gown. He still had hold of her hand.

"Arthur told me you were fair, but not that you were a Venus. I wished to see for myself the dazzling green eyes and spun copper hair he speaks of."

"Oh?" Gwenhwyfar was flustered. She tried again to release her hand, moving away as far as Syagrius would allow. "Has he then mentioned me? He has not spoken over many bad things about me, I trust?"

"Mentioned you?" Syagrius laughed, his fingers gripping tighter, his eyes never straying from her face. "He talks of no one else! Atween you and me," he dropped his voice, but deliberately not too low, "I believe he has a bit of a problem."

He looked shrewdly at Arthur who glowered back. "He has a wife whom he dislikes intensely. Assuredly a mistaken marriage."

Arthur laughed, the sound striking harsh behind its falsity. He swung his legs to the floor, limped to Syagrius's side, and placed a hand on his shoulder.

Gwenhwyfar took the opportunity to reclaim her own hand.

"My dear boy," Arthur said, forcing amusement. "How you do exaggerate! I mentioned my mother's guest but once. I doubt our dear Gwenhwyfar will take kindly to such obvious flirtation. By the Bull, how these unwhelped boys expect to shed innocence early these days!"

"I can assure you, friend," replied Syagrius, addressing Arthur but refusing to look away from Gwenhwyfar, "I shed my innocence of women many months past."

Gwenhwyfar, though, was bridling. "And why, Arthur Pendragon, would I not appreciate a man's flattery? I am a free woman of marriageable age, I have no tie of betrothal." She smiled radiantly at Syagrius. "And," she added pointedly, "I once said I intended to fly high. Who has a wingspan to rival the future king of Gaul?"

Syagrius raised his eyebrows quizzically, not quite understanding. "None, lady, even the Legions of the Eagles can no longer soar above my father's power and soon, my own." He grinned suddenly, aware something in the game had altered here, that Gwenhwyfar was no longer backing away from him, but responding to his courting! God's favour, he could scarcely believe his luck! Could she be interested in him? Well, why not? As she had said, she was a free woman, and he had to seek a suitable wife one day. But Gwenhwyfar? Dare he seriously try for her?

With a forced laugh, Arthur motioned their guest to his feet, steered him for the door. "We have been travelling since dawn, my lad, and the household seems as weary. It is time we retired to our beds." He gestured good night to Ectha and Ceridwen.

Syagrius, on the point of protesting, changed his mind as Arthur's elbow jabbed him sharply in the ribs. Sweeping a bow, he said to Gwenhwyfar, "It seems I am dismissed, Lady. I bid you a fond good night."

Boldly he returned across the room, tipped up her face with his fingers, and brushed her lips lightly with his own. His taste was pleasant, sweet, and soft. Lingering.

Stunned, Gwenhwyfar watched him leave, ushering an equally astonished Arthur before him. Heard him say, "Well do I understand your feeling for her now, Arthur! She is..." She heard no more, for the door had closed.

The room spun; she must see about watering the wine more on the morrow!

Well do I understand your feeling for her now, Arthur! Why had Syagrius said that? What had he meant? Confusion whirled with the dizziness of strong wine and tiredness. Arthur had ignored her, almost to the point of rudeness, and yet his hostility to Syagrius's boyish flirting was acute. Gwenhwyfar sighed—so many snarled tangles! Wearily, she pushed herself to her feet, telling the servants to seek their beds. "Come, Ectha, you must go to your bed also. A mild sleeping draught would do no harm," she advised.

Ectha's personal slave nodded his agreement. He noted her reddened, tired eyes. "I shall see to him, Lady. Such a draught would not come amiss for you also?"

Gwenhwyfar shook her head. "Na, but I thank you for your concern. Ectha," she had to shake the man slightly to gain his attention, "Father Simon is with Ygrainne; she is well tended."

Lost in his worry and shock, Ectha seemed dazed and confused. Gwenhwyfar smiled reassurance, said, "She is a strong woman and will be well in a few days. The physician said it was only a weakness of the spirit; a warning that she must ease on the way she pushes herself."

The blankness on Ectha's face remained. His slave placed his hands protectively on his master's shoulders. "He is most fond of his brother's wife. As we all are."

A shout of alarm followed immediate by a crash echoed through the house, coming from the far end of the open corridor outside. Gwenhwyfar ran, at her heels Ectha's slave and Ceridwen, followed by startled servants.

Arthur lay crumpled in a heap at the foot of the stairway. Syagrius stood at the top.

One hand extended, half afraid to touch the still form, Gwenhwyfar crouched beside Arthur. Was he dead?

Syagrius hurtled down the short but steep flight of stairs, squatted beside her. His face was chalk white. He spoke in short bursts, breath coming fast. "He was angry. I was teasing him. I meant no harm. He just slipped and fell. I did not touch him, I swear!"

"No one is saying you did," Gwenhwyfar replied calmly.

A sigh of relief swept through the group of peering servants as Arthur's eyes flickered open. He groaned, swore.

"Be still, do not try to move." Gwenhwyfar rested a hand on his arm.

He looked up at her, his face contorted with pain. "I have no bloody intention of moving, woman!" He was sweating profusely. When Gwenhwyfar touched his hand, the skin felt cold and clammy.

Ectha's slave sent someone scurrying for a blanket, another to fetch Cynan, Arthur's own servant. Ceridwen picked up her skirts, and shouting, ran for Iawn who appeared some moments later with three of Arthur's guard. "What has happened?" he panted.

"Arthur has fallen," Gwenhwyfar explained, allowing room for Iawn to examine his commander. When the leg was touched Arthur yelled. Iawn straightened, worried, and ran a hand through his fair hair. "Seems that leg has been damaged again. It has been bad all this while. Best send for the physician, my lady."

Gwenhwyfar herself groaned, leant back against the wall, closed her eyes a moment to let the world spin by. "He will not appreciate being sent for twice in one night."

"I need no physician so urgently he must leave his bed." Arthur's protest was made with eyes shut and held breath. "Get me to my room, I shall do well enough 'til morning. He is coming to see Ygrainne again then, is he not?"

Iawn and Gwenhwyfar, echoed by the servants, disagreed with the idea vehemently.

Teeth clamped, Arthur attempted to haul himself upright, pain tearing through the tortured muscles of his damaged thigh. "See, I am all right," he gasped. "I am in no urgent need of the physician."

"Very well." Realising his stubbornness would have it no other way, Gwenhwyfar gestured to four of the men to raise him. "Take him to my chamber—it is the nearest."

Syagrius watched them climb the stairs slowly. He stood stiffly against the wall, ashen-faced and silent. Gwenhwyfar laid her hand on his arm. "It was not your fault, accidents happen. Get to bed, there is nothing more you can do this night."

"What of his wife? Should she not know of this?"

"I doubt she is interested, but I shall send a servant to tell her."

"Gwenhwyfar." He caught her arm as she turned to go. "I know I was teasing earlier, with those things I said, but," he bit his lip, unsure what to say, "he thinks the world of you, but is too proud to admit it."

Gwenhwyfar smiled amicably. What did this boy know of things that had passed between herself and Arthur? "Get to bed," she said again, not unkindly.

Ceridwen held the door wide as they manoeuvred Arthur through and laid him on Gwenhwyfar's bed. Father Simon appeared, anxiously enquiring if there was anything he could do. Servants clustered in the doorway, twittering with concern.

Tired, irritated by their combined uselessness, Gwenhwyfar turned on them all. "The matter is in hand. I have all the help I require."

Cynan ran in, alarmed, his face shadowing; he was a trusted, reliable man, and Arthur thought highly of him. Efficiently he ushered spectators away, closed the door on them, and hurried to his master's side, where he began gently removing clothing.

"He ought have the physician," he said as he worked.

"So we all say, save your master," Gwenhwyfar retorted. "Ceridwen, can you fetch Livila? She may be old but her healing wisdom is great; Ygrainne has little faith in her, but she does well enough for the servants."

Cynan nodded his approval. "I hear she has skilful hands, enough to see us through this night at least."

Ceridwen touched Gwenhwyfar's arm. "Is there ought else I can do?" she asked.

"You can help by getting yourself to bed—and looking in or Bedwyr to see he sleeps sound. Go, get yourself to your husband."

With eight brothers, Gwenhwyfar had seen male nakedness often. She had seen Arthur, the boy, undressed many times in Gwynedd; how often had they swum naked in sea or river, or helped clean each other in Cunedda's small apology for a bathhouse? Seeing him lying vulnerable upon her own bed, holding out against the pain of Livila's administrations, Gwenhwyfar saw a different person, saw him for the first time as a man. Male genitalia meant little, no more than a stallion's equipment or a dog's. She had known from an early age what it was for, had seen males of a species mounting females. Watching now, tense, weary, frightened, and muddled, she found her eyes drawn repeatedly to his maleness, its significance starkly taunting.

He had a wife. Had lain with her, taken his pleasure with her, and given her his child. Why had he reacted to Syagrius? God's truth, but her head ached!

Livila demanded her attention, asking for light to be brought closer; she fetched another lamp and set it on a side table. How thin Arthur was, she realised with a start. Muscles slack against taut flesh, bones gaunt. It had not shown so starkly in his face.

As if reading her thoughts, Cynan said, "My Lord has lost much weight since the accident. He has fretted to be about his life, but this thigh is stubborn to mend."

Livila's worn teeth clicked in her slack jaw. "It be the way. Men will not rest or give damage time to heal. See here where this flesh be bruised? The muscle beneath be torn." She hissed as Arthur squirmed at her touch, face contorting in a fresh burst of pain. "Aye, lad, it hurts. You are fortunate, no further bones be broken, just unhealed muscles re-rattled." She regarded him solemnly through age wrinkled eyes. "The surgeon who tended you has worked well. The bone has mended clean, it be these muscles we must tend to now. With rest and my salves you will soon fetch as good as new."

Arthur saw the old woman through a haze of red agony, swore under his breath. Damn them all. Rest—how could he rest?

At some point during the early hours, utter exhaustion made seeing and doing automatic. Obediently Gwenhwyfar had held the lamp higher or lower, fetched, carried, passed bandages as Livila requested. The room and the people within were distant, fogged. Arthur had been given a sleeping draught, commanded by Livila's stern threats to swallow. As dawn approached he slept on. Cynan was curled on a pallet on the other side of the room, snoring gently. Livila had gone to her own given place,

The sky paled from black to the dull grey of a clouded winter's dawn. Numb, cramped, and exhausted almost beyond endurance, Gwenhwyfar slept where she had last sat, on a stool with head pillowed on her arms resting on the bed. She stirred, raised her head, found Arthur watching her. His skin glistened with sweat, his eyes burnt bright with fever, but at least he was conscious and aware.

"Did I ever tell you," he croaked, "you are so, very, very beautiful?"

"And did I ever tell you, Arthur Pendragon," she replied, wondering that she had enough energy to speak, "you are a bastard?"

Arthur smiled weakly and fumbled for her hand. "Frequently."

FIFTEEN

ROWENA'S SON WAS A GREEDY BOY, ALWAYS SUCKLING AT HER. NOW HIS FIRST birthday was well behind them and his teeth nearly all formed, she would need to consider his weaning.

Her father handed her a cloth to wipe the boy's mouth, said with a grunt of disapproval, "Your mother had a wet nurse to feed the childer."

Rowena smiled indulgently at her son as she sat him on her lap. Her mother had not lost the babies she had birthed. "Vitolinus is special, Father. I enjoy feeding him with my milk. Jute milk, not British watered muck."

Hengest laughed, took his grandson from her and seating himself, began bouncing the child on his lap.

"You will have him vomit, he has a full belly."

"Ah, but he likes it!" Hengest chuckled as the boy gurgled and demanded more.

"All the same," Rowena warned.

Reluctantly her father gave ground and, snuggling the boy in his arms, carried him to the cot, laid him down, and tenderly covered him. "Hush, my little son of Woden, go you to sleep so you may grow fine and strong like your grandfather."

Rowena indicated the slave might clear away the mess of feeding and changing a child, waited until the girl had left and she was alone with her father before saying, "I had a second letter from Winifred yesterday."

Hengest turned his head towards her, straightened himself from rocking the cradle. "Has she found enough sense to tell us of the Pendragon's movements?"

Rowena shook her head, took up her spindle. "She writes only of her unhappiness. She says the babe was a girl. It died." Rowena shook her head again sadly. Was death also to follow her grandchildren?

Hengest made no reply. Winifred had been a spoilt child; he had no time for her whining and demanding, nor for her constant changes of mind.

"She says Arthur has her close watched. Ygrainne's Roman priest managed to send this letter, as with the first, in secret," Rowena said.

Wrinkling his nose beneath the great bush of beard and moustache, Hengest resisted the urge to spit. Christians! Bah, weakling sentimentalists!

He wandered around the room, this semi-resplendent royal room. Bronzes, tapestries, fine furniture; none of it hid cracked ceiling and mould-spotted walls—or stopped the draughts. Woden's breath, but his wattle-built Hall was in better condition than this decaying Londinium palace!

"How much longer will Vortigern be?" he asked impatiently. "Considering he asked to see me, I am not pleased to wait like this."

Rowena vaguely flapped a hand. "I expect he has been delayed." Her hands had never returned to their former slimness; too many pregnancies had left them puffed and misshapen, the fingers slow to respond. Spinning and needlework were becoming difficult tasks for her lately. She set the spindle down, rubbed the ache in her knuckles. "He will come soon, Father. You heard, I assume, there was an attempt on his life a few days past?"

Folding his arms, Hengest nodded, frowning. "The man was caught and tortured, I hear, but would not reveal who hired him."

"You know nothing of it, I suppose?"

Affronted, Hengest put his hand to his chest. "I most certainly do not! Until I am strong enough to not give a sow's ear about who rules as king over the British, I prefer to follow the trail I know!" He found himself a seat, calmed his frayed temper. "Nay, it was not of my doing, daughter." He spread his hands over his thighs, rubbed them up and down the woollen cloth of his bracae. This place was so cold! "Aside, a man of mine would have succeeded."

Walking across the room, Rowena poured herself apple juice, added a herbal remedy to keep the pain of joint-ache at bay. Said, as she took a sip, "My husband is convinced the Pendragon was behind it."

"That drunken whore-user? He'd not be able to stab a pig on slaughter day!"

Rowena hesitated before answering, for her father had a low opinion of Arthur. He had argued savagely against Winifred marrying with him, and took pleasure in reminding Rowena of the objection whenever yet another trouble sent her daughter pleading for help. "I think you underestimate the Pendragon, Father," she said carefully.

"He is a boy playing at a man's game."

Rowena held her tongue. Then why were men clamouring to join his command? She said, "Winifred wants to come home, she asks me to organise a ship. Do you think if I were to write to Arthur he..."

Hengest erupted to his feet, stamped across to stand before her, fists on hips, legs spread. "Woden's Breath, Winifred is a woman grown and fully capable of seeing to her own concerns. She sowed the seeds and must now harvest the crop. The fact that only nettles have grown is her problem."

"But Father!"

"The Pendragon needs her wealth to keep his head from sinking below the stink of his own drunken vomit. He'd never allow her out from behind his shield—and frankly, I don't want her. She's useless. She deserves to belong to that cock-crowing whore-cub. They deserve each other." He turned away, reached for his cloak, and approaching the door, hand outstretched to open it, stopped surprised as it swung inward to reveal Vortigern standing there.

"A cock-crowing whore-cub?" he said drily, entering the room. "You can only be talking of the Pendragon. Where he is concerned, Hengest, I try to remember that such creatures have spurs and are bred to fight. They need to be kept secure until needed in the pit."

Vortigern shut the door and crossed the room to kiss Rowena's cheek, went next to peep at his sleeping son. "Unfortunately, one sure way to do so for this particular breed is to tether him by marriage to my daughter. I do not like having him so close, but life has a habit of kicking us in the balls, does it not?" He poured wine, sniffing suspiciously at the goblet before drinking.

Hengest said wryly, "You are wary of poison then?"

Vortigern shrugged, admitted, "I am even wary of my own shadow these days."

"Rowena says you think the Pendragon was behind this attempted murder?" Hengest said, accepting wine and resisting the temptation to also smell it for poison before drinking.

Vortigern glanced casually at the woman who had returned to her spinning. She made out she was the dutiful, loving wife, but he knew what she got up to and where her true interests lay! Rowena was her father's daughter first, her son's mother second, queen third, and loyal wife last. Vortigern seated himself more comfortably; the day had been long and tiring, and there was still much to do. How angry Rowena would be if she knew it was he who had made sure the Pendragon knew about Winifred fleeing to Hengest! He could not allow his daughter to go, any more than he would ever allow Rowena her freedom. The Pendragon had one good use. He saved Vortigern the bother of keeping an eye on Winifred.

"Do you know," Vortigern said into the silence, "how many of the Caesars were murdered by their own guard?"

Hengest shook his head.

Vortigern chuckled. "Neither do I in precise number, but too many, I am certain!"

Hengest laughed with him, the small moment of cold ice thawing slightly. They warily respected each other, these two men; respected each other's hold on power and authority, had no interest in the petty matter of like or dislike. Personal friendship lacked importance when running alongside survival. "It is a wise man who chooses his guard personally, and ensures they have reason to stay loyal."

Vortigern acknowledged the observation by raising his goblet, added, "Or by choosing those who have the better reason to keep him alive." He motioned for his guest to sit. "My eldest sons fight me. My son-by-law will rejoice at my death—the list goes on. My Council disagrees with me as a matter of course— were I pronounced a saint, Council would still disagree with my decisions." With an exasperated sigh he added, "It is a qualification for election, to disagree." He regarded Hengest thoughtfully, this bull-muscled Jute who needed only to sound his war horn to bring keels by the dozen across the sea. As he would, one day soon. "You have sure reason to keep me king," Vortigern said, pointing his finger knowingly at the man seated opposite him.

Hengest feigned innocence. "It is a matter of honour for a jute to serve his lord well!"

"Pig swill! It is a matter of tactics. You know I will grant you all I can in return for loyal service from your men. Few British are willing to remain so loyal to me now; I can turn nowhere but to you, and for that you can ask whatever price you seek. Were either of my two eldest sons to take power, or, God forbid," Vortigern shuddered, "the Pendragon, you would be kicked out of Londinium and the Isle of Tanatus as swift as would a dog jumping with fleas."

"Vortimer may hold sway over Council, I agree, but the others? I fear them not."

Vortigern leant forward, eyes slit, fierce. "Then you are not the wise commander I have taken you for all these years! The Pendragon playacts at his drinking and whoring, a leisurely pastime for him when there is nothing better to do. Give him a horse, a sword, and a turma of men, and he is a different man. Have you seen an adder basking in the sunshine, Hengest?" He waited for the man to nod. "Then you know full well how unwise it is to poke a serpent with a stick."

Hengest was not convinced. He finished his wine, stood. "This is all very interesting but I have many things to tend to. For what purpose did you ask me here? Surely not to talk of the Pendragon's nonexistent virtues!"

"I want your men, and only your men, as my personal and palace guard, at least until the coming of spring."

Hengest was shocked but held the surprise in check. Things were bad for Vortigern then! "If I agree, what is there for me?"

Smiling cynically the King answered, "Enough land to keep you and your people occupied until I am long dead and mouldered to dust. Probably enough to see you through until the coming of age of my youngest son here."

Hengest's eyebrows rose. "That is a lot of land."

"I need a lot of protecting."

SIXTEEN

WITHIN YGRAINNE'S CHRISTIAN HOUSEHOLD THE ROMAN SATURNALIA was celebrated as the Nativity. In the solemn little chapel Father Simon spoke the words of the Mass with feeling to his small congregation. Gwenhwyfar stood beside Ectha, dutifully murmuring her responses and accepting the holy communion of bread and wine.

Christianity had so neatly sidestepped the pagan practices, conveniently encompassing the old festivals, with suitable modification, into its own belief. Saturnalia for instance, a pagan festival of laughter and celebration and for the giving of gifts; reminiscent for the Christians of the gifts given to the infant Jesus.

Saturnalia, with the bringing of evergreens into the house as a reminder of the spring soon to come. Living green, bearing fruit amid the dark days of winter. As Mary bore Her Son during the darkness of sin. The pagan holly became the thorns placed on the head of the crucified Christ, its red berries the drops of blood on His forehead.

Mistletoe, the fruit of fertility adopted as a symbol of His birth. So Gwenhwyfar worshipped the birth of Jesu, and began, like so many, to forget the old ways.

Afterwards Father Simon accompanied the family back along the mud-slushed pathway to the villa, escorting Winifred. She was an unexpected presence. Out of courtesy, Gwenhwyfar, as acting headwoman, had invited her to share the family's day, explaining politely they celebrated the birth of Christ in a modest manner. To her surprise, Winifred had accepted eagerly.

Arthur's wife had entered the chapel, sinking into a low reverence before the altar, ostentatiously flourishing a glittering gold crucifix and bejewelled rosary. Father Simon had greeted her enthusiastically, delighted to see her.

Watching them Gwenhwyfar thought the two seemed well acquainted. At the first opportunity she questioned the servants, discovered Father

Simon had regularly attended the Lady Winifred while she had been confined with her illness following the birth, and death, of her child. Gwenhwyfar shrugged the matter aside; she cared little about Winifred or, for that matter, Father Simon.

Late afternoon. The sky was darkening with the threat of more sleet. Gwenhwyfar entered Arthur's chamber in search of Bedwyr. She laughed, the amusement spreading from full red lips to sparkling green eyes. He was seated beside Arthur, huddled beneath swathes of bed furs.

Arthur was expounding some greatly embellished tale of battle. "Is it so cold in here?" she asked, indicating the fur mound.

"It's damn nigh cold enough to freeze my essentials off!" replied Arthur, grinning impishly. "I sent Bedwyr to find someone to replenish the braziers, but it seems the household is too busy with seasonal festivities to bother about a wounded soldier cursed with the indignity of being bound to his bed."

Gwenhwyfar prodded at the nearest brazier, ignoring his petulance. "More charcoal is needed, I shall send someone to see to it. Bedwyr, the meal is all but ready, run along to wash and change."

He protested loudly.

"Suit yourself, stay with your cousin if you wish." Gwenhwyfar turned to leave the room, paused. "Except," she looked blandly at the two of them nestled cheerfully together, "if you choose to remain here, you will miss eating."

Aghast, the boy tumbled from the bed. Normally, he ate in the kitchens, only permitted to join the family for special occasions. He had no intention of missing a rare treat!

"Hold!" Arthur bellowed as the boy scuttered across the wooden floor of the first-floor chamber. He pointed to a chest which stood beneath one of the small casement windows. "Look in there, lad."

Bedwyr trotted to it, flung the lid wide, dived on two packages rolled in cloth.

"The largest is for you," Arthur said, added, "Bring the smallest to me please."

The boy did as he was asked, cradling his own prize in his arm, slipping the wrapped cloth from the concealed contents as Arthur relieved him of the smaller bundle. With a gasp of delight, Bedwyr brandished a sword, a real soldier's sword save for the blunt edging. "It will do you for now, lad. When you are a man grown, come to me and I shall replace it with one a little sharper."

Bedwyr ran to Arthur and hugged him, clamouring his thanks, eyes shining with pride and pleasure. Then he dashed from the room, eager to prepare for dinner and a chance to show his gift.

Gwenhwyfar closed the door, muffling the sound of his retreating, delighted whoops. "Your mother will not be pleased at your choice of gift. She has no wish for him to become a fighting man."

Arthur snorted contemptuously. "I am well aware she has plans to see him in some holy profession. If that is what he wishes, then that is his choice. But," he shoved the weight of heavy furs from his leg, "I may need every fighting man in a few years. I would rather have my cousin serving me, not God." Drolly, "And aside, it has harmed no holy man to have knowledge of wielding a sword. I have something for you. Come here."

She hesitated, a flutter of panic telling her to leave the room now. Heart beating, she stepped from the door, came to the side of his bed. He took her hand, gently but firmly, enclosing the soft whiteness within his own firm grasp.

"You are trembling?" he asked softly.

"You were right, this chamber is cold." She kept her eyes downcast, studying the bright pattern of the woven bed cover peeping beneath the furs.

"Are you afraid of me, Gwen?"

She looked up at that, meeting his brown eyes. They watched her intently, cutting through any pretence as easily as looking at the world through clear glass.

She answered truthfully, for few could lie to Arthur. "I am not afraid of you. I…" She halted, uncertain. She was not afraid, yet why did her heart beat so wildly? Why did the desire to run from the room overwhelm her?

He placed the package in her hand, curled her fingers round it. "For you."

She glanced from him to the parcel, frowning curiously, and tentatively unwrapped it. Across her palm lay a slender woman's dagger with carved ivory hilt set with jewels.

"How did you come by this?" she breathed, not daring to believe the happiness swelling within her.

Arthur shrugged carelessly. "Oh, I came across it."

"I never thought to see it again!" Her words came faintly, barely audible, so deep was her happiness at having her mother's dagger once again. A lump of emotion caught in her throat. She bit her lip, shook her head, willing herself not to cry like some immature child.

Arthur reached out and squeezed her hand. "I recognised it, knew it for what it was—I'd seen it often enough in Gwynedd, after all."

Was he still as she remembered him after all? He was older, battle wise, but, meeting his intense gaze, she recognised and welcomed with joy those qualities of understanding and empathy that had drawn them together as children.

"You do remember, then?" she asked cautiously, scarcely daring to hope for a reply. "You have not forgotten how it was."

He relaxed, the skin wrinkling with laughter lines at the corners of his suddenly caring, expressive eyes. Very quietly, he said, "I shall never forget, Cymraes fach. Never."

Gwenhwyfar had never thought to hear him call her by that name again. Shyly, she leant forward, placed a quick, light kiss on his cheek. A sound came from the door as it opened, followed by the rustle of a gown.

"I see you are recovering well, my husband."

Gwenhwyfar leapt away from the bed as if stung, her face flushing pink.

"Winifred, how nice of you to take the trouble to come and see me!" Arthur drawled.

"I have left my own bed only these past days, husband, plagued with a fever and other, women's, troubles." She swept past Gwenhwyfar, ignoring her. "But I have kept myself constantly informed of your well-being." Placing a sensuous kiss on her husband's lips, she sat on the bed, took his hand possessively in her own.

"I have been desolate," she said with convincing sorrow, "being so weak from the difficult birth and then the distress of the taking of one so young from us. And now this!" She patted his hand fondly, then dabbed at her eyes. "I so feared I should lose you also."

She settled herself the better beside him. "Thank God you are recovering and all my worry was for nought. Our child has gone, but there will be many chances for others." She bent forward and gave him a second, more lingering kiss.

The door closing broke her from the embrace to call, "Oh, Gwenhwyfar!"

Reluctant, Gwenhwyfar re-entered the room.

"My dear child." Winifred shifted slightly so as to look at her. "I must thank you for your kindness to my injured husband. I understand you have nursed him well." She clutched Arthur's hand between her own, tight against her breasts. "You have so many other duties in addition to this, what with Lady Ygrainne ill and the seasonal festivities." How sickly sweet that false smile of hers could be.

"Now I am well I can take some of the burden from your shoulders." Winifred turned back to Arthur, stroked hair from his eyes, an action he detested. "I shall take care of my dear husband now." A honey-sweet smile. Tainted with spite.

Gwenhwyfar dipped a slight reverence, said "It will please the household you are well enough to leave your room."

Arthur called, "Come back later, Gwen? I would be..." he paused, searching for the right words with Winifred listening, "pleased at your company."

Clutching her dagger between her hands, Gwenhwyfar nodded once, made to leave, heard: "The blatant cheek of that girl, my dearest! They all talk of how she oversteps her position, you know. I am surprised your mother stood for it."

Closing the door, Gwenhwyfar did not wait to hear Arthur's reply. If he had one.

JANUARY 455

SEVENTEEN

SITTING BY THE WINDOW OF ARTHUR'S CHAMBER, GWENHWYFAR STARED OUT at the black night and the curtain of rain. It fell so thickly she could barely see the courtyard below. "There will be flooding by morning," she said as a gust of wind battered heavy drops against the thick glass. She shivered.

"Come away from the window if you are cold," Arthur remarked, engrossed in the parchment he was reading.

"I am not cold," she retorted. All the same, she wandered over to a brazier, held her hands out to it.

"It must please you Winifred is now able to nurse you," she said, added to his derisive snort, "I had no idea she was so devout a Christian."

"Nor had I," he answered drily, letting the parchment roll up on itself. "It ought not surprise me though—she has wit enough to know where to place a safe footing. And," bitterly, "she is clever enough to snare the unsuspecting. Pay no heed to her, Gwen. I choose who I wish to have with me, not her."

Gwenhwyfar fingered the dagger sheathed safely at her side, its ivory handle proud against the wine red of her gown. She smiled to herself, recalling Winifred's glare of outrage when she had noticed it there.

It had happened while the family was being served with the second course of the celebrational dinner. The first course had been eaten with relish: olives, baked dormice sprinkled with honey and poppy seeds, spiced eggs, and honeyed wine. Ygrainne portrayed her home as a humble residence, but when guests were to be entertained her kitchens were found to be well supplied, and her cooks of excellent ability.

The servants had carried in roast sucking pig stuffed with pastry and honey and served with chicken livers, beets, and wholemeal bread. Iawn had noticed the dagger, remarked on its craftsmanship, and asked whence it had come.

Politely Gwenhwyfar had passed it to him, allowing him to inspect it more closely, saying, "It has been mine since my mother's death," adding, looking straight at Winifred, "And so it always shall be."

Gwenhwyfar had thought of relating the scene to Arthur in the days between, but decided against. He might think she was prodding to hear how he had come by it.

The Nativity gaiety, such as it had been, was past, and a few flurries of snow had given way to incessant rain battered by a north-easterly wind that gusted around the villa and found every crack and gap to scurry through. Spring seemed a long way ahead.

Arthur patted the bed. "Come sit beside me, I can barely see you in those shadows. It is not easy to hold a decent conversation by bellowing across the width of a room."

Timidly she came, sat perched on the edge like a bird ready for flight. She had been here in this room on four or five occasions since that evening when Winifred had swept in and underlined her position as Arthur's wife. Had come this evening at Arthur's express request because Winifred was safely tucked up in her apartment nursing another feverish head cold.

"How does your leg feel?" she asked, for want of anything better to say.

"Like a lead weight," he answered.

"Cynan tells me it heals well at last," she could not resist teasing, "now you are resting, as you were first ordered."

"Cynan talks too much," Arthur replied.

With no warning, he leant forward and took her wrist, holding it firmly, a little too tightly. "Be wary of Winifred, she has the tongue and bite of a viper."

Gwenhwyfar made a light-hearted attempt at parrying his sudden concern. "Then surely I ought not be in your bedchamber alone with you." She attempted to retrieve her arm, to pull away from him.

To her surprise he said, "Na, Cymraes, you ought not." He let her go, lay back against the pillows, a hand covering his eyes.

The pain of heartache gripped him as he said, "How can I lie here knowing you are moving around out there where I cannot see you? I want you to stay, talk a while." He let his hand drop, his face sagging with defeat. His eyes were closed.

For a moment, Gwenhwyfar hovered between staying where she was, perched on the edge of the bed, or leaving. Just as she decided to go, he opened his eyes, held his hand out for hers.

Hesitant, she gave it to him.

With his fingertips, he stroked the satin smoothness of her skin, turned her hand over to examine the palm. "Your hands were rough, with torn nails, in Gwynedd."

"Horses and weapons are not kind to hands."

"Nor to men's bones, it seems. Love of Mithras, Gwen, what can I do?"

Withdrawing her hand, folding her fingers together in her lap, she deliberately misunderstood.

"You can read, play board games with Bedwyr or tell him more of your outrageously exaggerated campaigns. There is plenty to amuse you while you rest." She got to her feet, fastidiously smoothing the place where she had sat.

He plucked irritably at the bed cover beneath his hand. "I do not want to be amused, Gwenhwyfar. I want you." There, he had said it.

A few strides would take her to the door. Her fingers could be on the handle, she could be away in two beats of the heart. So why, in all that was wise, did she remain standing here like a fool beside his bed?

She pretended not to have heard, but her voice came too shrill. "If you are bored, I could sing for you." It was a fine excuse; without waiting for a reply she whisked away, intending to fetch her harp from her own room, feeling hot colour burning her cheek.

Her chamber was quiet. She lit a single lamp that cast a flicker of shadow over the scant furniture. Gwenhwyfar opened the small chest standing at the foot of her bed, brought out a soft leather bag, slid from it her harp. It was a light instrument suited to a woman's touch. Her Da had thought to send it, knowing her love of the thing.

Kneeling beside the open chest, she laid it on her lap, strummed her fingers over the strings. It needed tuning. Her harp was a link with home. Home. Absently she plucked at the strings, tightening or loosening. Satisfied, she drew her fingers, gently, with a butterfly touch, rippling a whisper that vibrated with velvet sound.

She sang softly, her voice low, the words reflecting her despair, and her tears began to fall. Tears of surrender to the loss of hope, the ache stabbing like a war spear, her tears spilling like blood from the wound. Her head sank into her hands, and she sobbed.

Someone took the harp from her. Arms were about her shoulders, drawing her forward, enclosing her in a circle of loving protection. For a moment she clung, unaware, grateful for the solidness and the strength stopping her from sliding further into the cesspit of blackness that insatiably beckoned, that would not, would not leave her be. Her tears at last eased and, cried out, she slumped exhausted, her head against his shoulder. Still he held her tight, not letting go.

Her arms went around him pulling him to her, betraying her violent need to keep him close.

"I thought you had forgotten me, thought you felt nothing for me."

Arthur stroked the damp hair from her forehead, his hand cool; crooned to her loving and gentling. "I have never forgotten you, Cymraes. Feel for you more than ever you could imagine."

She believed him, knew he spoke the truth.

Self-conscious, Gwenhwyfar twitched her shoulders, shrugging herself free of his touch, and drew back from him a little. In the pouch hanging at her waist she found a cloth, blew her nose, rubbed fingers over puffed eyes.

With one finger under her chin he tilted her face up to him. What had he caused her? So much grief, so much pain and hopeless loss. If he stayed here with her in this chamber, how much more grief and pain would streak her beautiful, wonderful face with tears?

"I am in a web, and Winifred with her father sit in the middle like giant black spiders," he said.

"And you were lured into it like some unsuspecting fly?" The words burst from Gwenhwyfar before she could stop them. Her eyes flashed fire, the inner ring dark green around the gold-flecked iris. She stood, moved away from where he sat awkward on the floor.

With great calm Arthur shut the lid of the chest, used its solidity to haul himself upright. He sat on its closed lid, wincing at the pain coursing from his thigh. Blood of the Bull! Would this thing never stop throbbing? Folding the thin robe he wore tighter round his naked body, he said, "As you wish. I saw the web. Walked smack into it. Winifred was all you were not. That is why I wed her." He had his back to Gwenhwyfar. It was easier to talk truth that way, without the need to look at her.

"I agreed to the marriage when I thought you betrothed to Melwas. By the time you fled Britain, it was too late; I was already trapped, with no bolt-hole save for Vortigern to use as an excuse to make an end of me." He gave a wry smile, ducked his head to watch her over his shoulder. "And even for you, at that time my lovely, I had no wish to die." Using his hands as a brace, he sought a more comfortable seated position. "I had already taken Winifred to my bed, that night of the King's festival. But then, I suppose you knew that."

Gwenhwyfar shook her head. Wished he had not told her. She had no heart to hear the telling of detail.

"Ah well, no matter, you know now."

She stood beside the single lamp across the room, its feeble light trickling shadows over her face and body, glowing through the unruly copper wisps of hair that always refused to stay bound.

Strange, she had never studied a flame before now. The bob and dance of its yellow flicker calmed her chaotically spinning thoughts. How intricate its colours, how perfect its shape.

Keeping, with difficulty, the discomfort from showing, Arthur limped to her side. Standing deliberately close, he drew her to him. His lips closed over hers, a brief touch. She put out her hands, one on each side of his chest, pressed him, unconvincingly, from her.

"I don't want..."

"Are you afraid still?" he said, his voice low, searching.

"Na, but..."

"No buts, my Cymraes, no more buts, there is a time when it is best not to think, just do."

He kissed her again, more demanding, his tongue parting her lips, running along her teeth. His hands brushed across the smooth skin of her shoulders, bringing her nearer so that her body touched against his.

Suddenly afraid, the wheel spinning over fast, she pushed him away. "What of Winifred?"

Arthur released her, stood with head lowered, jaw set, fists clenched. What of Winifred? Ah, if only he knew the answer to that particular riddle! She, his wife, was beneath this same roof, was not some unbidden spirit of the imagination. Come dawn, she would still exist, not vanish with the morning mist. He felt no love for her. Felt nothing for her, not even hatred or contempt.

Why had he accepted her? Because she was everything his Gwenhwyfar was not. Sour against sweet, rough against smooth, loud against quiet. Deceit against truth, and hate against love.

"I care for you, Gwenhwyfar. I love you. Have always loved you."

Arthur reached for her hand, kissed the palm. There would be dangers, from Melwas, Vortigern, and Winifred. Great danger, death even, but what appeal had a safe life if it meant parting?

"At the first opportunity, I shall rid myself of her."

"Oh, Arthur, do you dwell so deeply in the land of faery dream?" She covered his hand with her own, her fingers curling within his. "You will never be rid of her."

They were standing close again; he could feel the contours of her body through his light robe.

"I will." His hand tightened around hers. Then he acknowledged, "Even if I cannot rid myself of her, she is nothing to me, a signed contract only. We were pledged with the vows of the Christian ceremony. I put more faith in the Old Ways."

He glanced at the warming glow of the charcoal brazier and gave a sudden smile. "This may not be your father's hearth, but it will suffice for our needs."

Shaking her head, bewildered, Gwenhwyfar let him lead her to it, stood where he placed her, opposite himself, the brazier between them, their hands clasped above its heat.

Two ways lay before her. She could step forward on to either path, but having once set foot to it there would be no turning back. One way began rough, with great jagged stones to be clambered over; beyond lay flat land, easy walking, but a country of endless emptiness. The other way was steep, with rocky outcrops and plunging valleys full of uncertainty and storm.

What to do? Which path to take? Her heart would surely break if she made him go, knowing he would never ever come back to her. But if she let him in, took him, what fears lay ahead then?

She knew what he was asking of her. Bid him be gone, or commit herself. To what? This desperate loneliness?

Of a sudden, sure of her path, she raised her head, said clear and confident the words of the Old Ways, the words spoken across a father's hearth at the binding together of a man and a woman.

"Your life is my life; your death, my death. I will follow where you lead, through water and fire, across earth and stone. My love for you shall burn until the very sun ceases to give us warmth and light; until the moon sinks behind the hills to rise no more. Your dreams are my dreams. Your destiny, my destiny. May the Mother of Earth bless our union."

He led her three times round the fire in the direction of the sun's path, then took her to him, a little breathless, not believing this was actually happening. *Mithras! Do not let me wake come morning to find this was all a dream!*

Gwenhwyfar stood trembling as he unfastened her shoulder brooches, let her gown fall. Beneath, she wore a tunic of fine linen. She raised her arms and he lifted it over her head, cast it aside. He fumbled slightly with the ties of her breast band, then let that too drop to the floor.

For a moment he stood looking at her, savouring her, his lips parted. She stepped to him, her firm young breasts and curved hips pressing timidly against his own responding body.

His thigh ached abominably, but then so did his need for her. He would have liked to lift her and carry her to the bed, but knew his limitations. Difficult enough to shuffle himself along! Instead, he steered her gently towards it, held his finger poised in the air a moment, went to the door and slid the bolt home.

Winifred was abed, but who knew with Winifred?

A catch of pain escaped as he came beside her, cast quickly aside as his nakedness touched hers. With pain forgotten, he took time to claim her for his own, the ache in his thigh subdued by the intensity of need. He wanted to take things slowly, patiently; she was to enjoy this, her first experience of his love.

EIGHTEEN

T HE OLD MAN STUMBLED THROUGH THE GREAT OAK DOORS INTO CUNEDDA'S Hall as evening was fading into the chill darkness of a winter's night. Tables clattered over, benches and stools scraped or tipped as men leapt to their feet, alarmed or concerned. Several ran to the man, propped his sagging and blood-ied body with their arms, then half carried, half dragged him towards Cunedda, who had risen from his seat and was striding down the length of the Hall.

"Who has done this?" he demanded of the old man. "Who dares attack and injure an elderly and respected man of Gwynedd?"

The wounded man grasped at Cunedda's woollen cloak, his gnarled and bruised fingers clutching tight. "Sea-raiders," he gasped, his breath coming in rasping pain from wheezing lungs. "They burnt our settlement, took the wom-en and children, our cattle." He coughed, blood frothing with the spittle. "They left me, a useless old man, for dead, but I came to you, came to get help."

"When?" Meriaun asked. "When did they come?"

The old man looked at him, squatting next to his grandsire and offering a cloth to stem the blood. "Night afore last." He took the cloth, put it to his bleed-ing scalp, and cast his eyes over the surrounding ring of faces, said to the shaking heads and muttered curses, "I came as quick as I could."

Cunedda sympathetically patted the man's shoulder. Old age and aching bones slowed a man so; aye, and that without injuries such as these! "You did well in the circumstances." He scanned the warriors gathered in his Hall, ques-tioning with gruff expression their thoughts and reactions. Nodded satisfied. "Sa," he said. "All we need do is find the nest-hole of their pitched camp and claim back what is ours."

The old man tried to laugh, coughed again, his lungs fired from age and injury. "Na, I have the knowing of that!"

Men leant closer, intrigued, interested.

"I came across them two, three miles further up the coast from my settlement." He gathered breath, the sound rasping in his throat. "I had to circle half a mile to avoid their set watch."

"Are you certain it was the same party?" Dunaut asked.

"Aye," Rumaun added, "There is many a camp this winter. The raiders come and stay. We have a summer ahead of us of nest-clearing."

"Oh, I'm sure," the man wheezed. "I stayed close long enough to recognise the women, and a raider with a great thatch of black hair. It were he who knocked me to the ground, splitting open my skull!"

Meriaun, Dunaut, Rumaun, and the other warriors looked at Cunedda. He only needed to say the word and they would be running for horse and spear! Cunedda watched the trail of leisurely blue smoke drifting up from the hearth fire, watched as it curled a while among the carved rafters before slipping away through the smoke hole into the darkness above. His knees pained him these cold winter days, his back ached and his eyes were not so sharp as they used to be. But for all that, the prospect of settling a score with these plagued sea-pirates was not unwelcome. He regarded the waiting men a moment, noted their eagerness, their edge of excitement. Winter was a dreary time, months of sitting around a fire telling tales, preparing for the new-coming season. Aye, it would be good to fetch up the horses. He grinned. "Let's go!"

The black hour before the coming of dawn lay quiet and still. No moon, but the bright patterns of winter stars glittered against a cold-frosted sky. The breath of the horses came in great clouds of steam, mingled with the heat of their sweating bodies. They were thick-coated this time of year, well protected against the bite of Eryri's sharp frosts and deep snows.

The Hibernian men were sleeping, huddled within oar and sail tents or beneath upturned keels. Their fires had died long since, but a bellyful of roasted ox and stolen ale, coupled with a captured woman, kept the worst of the winter chill away. The first few did not know the death that hit them, muffled by sleep and blankets as they were. The swords of Cunedda and his warriors sliced life and rousing screams with well-placed blows. Others had time to leap awake, fumble for weapons, make some small attempt at defence. None had chance to live, for Cunedda's fury was great and his revenge complete.

The killing was soon over and the several fires that burnt the sea-raiders' ships along with their mangled bodies and bloodied blankets rose thick and black to greet the lightening dawn sky.

Only there came no rejoicing from the sons of Cunedda. No cheering derision as Meriaun had set torch to the first pile of brushwood, flesh and bone. No happiness or carousel at victory. What joy was there in death? What pleasure came in the killing when their beloved Lion Lord, Cunedda, lay slain and growing cold beside the spilt blood of their enemies?

MARCH 455

NINETEEN

WINIFRED WATCHED ARTHUR AND GWENHWYFAR RIDE OUT, TROTTING beneath the arched gateway and kicking their horses into a steady canter beyond. The two sets of hooves left marked tracks through the dew-soaked grass, already tinted a lush green with spring growth. She glowered, knuckles gripping white against the wooden sill.

"To where do they ride?" She spoke the thought aloud, turned startled as a servant answered.

"Most times, to the farmstead of Gaius Justinian Maximus, lady."

Winifred's eyebrow rose. Gaius? She had heard Arthur talk of him. An old man who farmed his own land beyond the estate's boundary. She turned from the window, casually, as if only half interested. "How know you this?"

Fidelia blushed crimson, realising her impertinence at speaking out. She busied herself bundling up soiled bedlinen.

"Well?" Leaning against the wall, Winifred tapped her foot, expecting an answer. This girl knew something, and Winifred did not like others knowing things she did not.

If they had not been alone Fidelia would never have spoken, but Winifred's personal maid was elsewhere and the girl had long since discovered that you must seize an opportunity when the gods gave it.

She held the bundle of linen to her, hiding behind it as if it would give her protection. "I am friendly with a young man." She lifted her chin. She was no slave but a free woman, and entitled to make the acquaintance of a man of her choosing.

Irritably, Winifred fluttered her hand at her. What cared she for a servant's peasant life? "Your life is of no interest to me, girl."

Fidelia lowered her defence, put the bundle down on the bed, and walked the few bold steps to stand beside Winifred, eager to exchange gossip. "My man is a shepherd. He cares for the estate's flock up on the heath. He is often on our high ground, above Gaius's farm."

"Is he now?" Winifred smiled encouraging. "And he mentioned your master's presence at this farm of—Gaius, did you say?"

"Aye, my lady. He said he sees him there often, always with Lady Gwenhwyfar, sometimes with young Master Bedwyr also."

Winifred maintained her friendly smile while digesting the information with cold malice. "And what, child, do you suppose they do at this farmstead of Gaius Justinian Maximus?"

Fidelia chewed her lip, unsure what else to say, aware too late, she had already tattled over-much. She lifted her shoulders and hands. "They talk, lady, with the old man and his wife."

"Talk!" Winifred threw up her hands. "La, la, la! They ride that distance nigh on every day, to talk!"

The girl stepped back, alarmed at the burst of cynical laughter.

Winifred turned again to stare out the window, her arms folded tight. The two riders had gone. Thoughtfully she fiddled with a ring on her little finger. She turned back to smile at the girl.

"I assume you cannot yet marry with this shepherd of yours for lack of money?"

Fidelia inclined her head. He was a good man, kind and thoughtful, with passable features. A moderate lover, though she had been with better. She had lain with Arthur once, her first time that had been, several years past. For all it was before he had left to serve with Vortigern and before he had married Winifred, best not mention it!

Herding sheep was a fair living if you did not mind being poor. Were he to marry, her man would be given permission to build his own dwelling place where he could take his wife and raise his children. But sheep were demanding, silly, smelly creatures. Fidelia had no liking for them. Her man often spent days away with them, especially at lambing. Come spring, she barely saw him unless she cared to make the long walk up to the lambing pens. Once there, he had no time for her beyond a few exchanged words and a quick cuddle. Certainly no time for lovemaking. He had to keep a close eye on those stupid sheep. He would be gone soon now the ewes were heavy with lamb. One week more then he would be off, up to the pens with his lantern, his wolfskin cloak and his tom-eared dog.

Something worried Fidelia about their relationship. Though a good man, he would always be poor, his life always dreary. She did not relish either prospect.

Winifred held out the ring to her. "Take this as a token for your service, my faithful woman." She laughed at her play on the girl's given name, added, "I reward well those who serve me." She stared meaningfully at the girl who, understanding, took the ring.

Winifred dismissed her and went to her writing table. She must get a third letter to her mother! Her one anxiety now was if Hengest were to move before the coming of summer she would be trapped here with Arthur—and then she would not reckon much to her chances of remaining long on this earth! If only she had borne a living son—or carried another! Hah! What chance of that with the Gwynedd slut taking Arthur's attention!

"Talk!" she snorted, a stylus snapping between her fingers from over-hard pressure. "Is that the name they give for whoring in this God-cursed place?"

It took five days for Fidelia to discover more. Five days of walking with her man on the hills, of pretending to enjoy helping with those stinking sheep. Steering the conversation, probing and questioning, she found answers as hard to come by as wild strawberries in midwinter.

It was a dreary day. Low grey cloud drizzled rain, accompanied by gusting wind that rattled at the windows and crept through cracks under the doors.

Fidelia was combing Winifred's hair. There had been others around all morning, but at the first opportunity of privacy the girl said in a low voice, "I met with my man last evening, lady."

"What is that to me?" Winifred kept her tone indifferent, anxious not to push lest she push too far too soon. She had no intention of spoiling all this delicate work by rushing.

"He told me something of interest." Fidelia paused, the comb in her hand, eyeing the jewel casket standing on Winifred's table. That small ring the other day had fetched four gold pieces at market.

She had decided not to mention her little gain to her shepherd. Instead, had hidden the coins in a secret hole behind a half-rotten timber in one corner of her bedroom in the servants' quarters.

Casually Winifred pointed to her casket, ordered Fidelia to fetch it and made a pretence of selecting jewellery to wear for the day. "I swear I do not need all this." She held a brooch to her shoulder. "Look at this, I never wear the thing." She tossed it to the girl. "You have it."

Fidelia snatched the brooch up, put it deftly into the pouch at her waist, continued combing Winifred's hair. "My man said it was a curious thing how, when Lord Arthur and Lady Gwenhwyfar visit Gaius, the old man and his wife do not seem to entertain their company but go about the day as if no one were there."

Her mistress seemed pleased with the information; now she was started on this course she cared little that she was betraying the Pendragon. What had he given her? A quick tumble in the hay, a tossed bronze coin, and the need to seek old Livila to have the gotten babe removed. He had not laid eyes on her a second time, though she made it clear she was available. Fidelia would have liked to be mistress to Arthur, as Morgause had been to Uthr. The prospect would have offered a better life than that of a shepherd's wife.

For Gwenhwyfar, she felt a twinge of conscience. Gwenhwyfar had shown kindness, had given her a discarded tunic last summer. But the weight of gold eased the doubt considerably.

"When young Master Bedwyr accompanies them, my man says Gaius takes the boy with him to the fields or to tend the stock." Fidelia peeped through slant eyes, saving the best until last. "My lord and lady remain within the house, alone."

"I see." Winifred affected a puzzled, innocent face. "Why do you suppose that might be?"

With deft fingers, Fidelia began braiding Winifred's hair. "It is not my place to say, except..."

"Except what?"

The girl hesitated. If she said this next thing, she could be opening a box of trouble.

"Speak out, girl!"

The lid was lifted, she might as well open it wide. "I was about to say, why does any woman in love spend time alone with a man?"

"And you believe Lady Gwenhwyfar to be in love!" Winifred laughed, inwardly seething. How dare that Gwynedd bitch be so blatant! How dare she give the servants cause to gossip and twitter! Arthur was *her* man. She thought she had made that quite plain to the both of them. She said, incredulous, "Surely not?"

Fidelia finished the braid, twisted it neatly around Winifred's head, securing it with pins. "It is obvious, lady! From soon after the celebrations of the Nativity she has been a changed person. Gay and light-hearted, with a look of happiness about her. Why, I have never heard her sing so much. She used to mope about like a laundry day turned wet with sudden rain."

Winifred sat stone-faced, her hands clenched, nails digging into her palms. Anger threatened to burst from her tight throat. Bitch! This had been going on for some time—she ought to have suspected earlier! Winifred cursed herself; she had suspected, but thought they would not dare become lovers, not while she was in the same building! How could she have been so stupid and blind?

Arthur had come to her two or three times since he had been up and about on that lame leg of his. Said it was paining him still, gave that as the reason for not coming to her more often. She cursed herself inwardly again. Fool! She had mutely accepted his excuse for his apparent lack of appetite, welcomed it even, in view of her preoccupation with her own business. She had taken his word for truth. God's curse, when did Arthur ever speak truth?

So he was tumbling Gwenhwyfar? He would pay for making a fool of his wife; by God's grace, he would pay dearly!

But first she must play this thing through. No use to rave before this servant girl. She must seek to gain support and sympathy.

Winifred slumped forward, slithering off her stool to the floor with a little groan, her face crumpling in anguished disbelief. The effect was very good. Fidelia, with a squeak of alarm, dropped the hairpins and rushed to Winifred's side, placing a comforting arm around her heaving shoulders.

"Oh, my Lady! Do not weep, I beg you! We all know our men are deceitful. The Pendragon is so like his father in that way!"

Winifred clung to the girl, sobbing. Stammered, "My dear, sweet innocent child, you have no idea how I suffer at his hands!" She had judged her timing perfectly. Through tears, "I was forced into marriage with him. He took me, you see, took my maidenhood; seduced me with honeyed words and empty promises." Bitterly, "He wanted my dowry, my wealth, that was all, not me. What could I do? I wanted to tell my father it was rape, but who would listen to my word against the Pendragon?"

Fidelia was close to weeping also. Oh aye, she knew all about how the Pendragon could seduce a girl with sweet words and gentle hands!

Seating herself upon the stool Winifred patted the girl's hand. "How I envy you your choice of a simple, kind-hearted shepherd!"

Fidelia was caught and bound. She, a serving girl, was sharing intimate confidences with the King of Britain's daughter!

Winifred hurried on; she had her chance, she was not going to miss it. "He has beaten me, forced me to comply with his depraved ways." Winifred held the girl's hand tightly. "What harm have I ever caused him? I have been a loyal, faithful wife, while he has bedded others and openly shamed me! He keeps me here as a prisoner; has forbidden me to ride out, or go to town. I cannot write to my family or friends, am not allowed to communicate with any save those within this household and the good Father Simon. I am watched night and day by his guard."

Those last were true. Arthur had given specific orders that his wife was not to leave the villa's grounds, she was to be guarded at all times, and no letters written by her hand were to be sent. He did not know of the two already dispatched.

"Why should he do this to you? It is so inhuman!"

Winifred had taken a chance with the cultivation of this particular girl, assuming her to be willing to risk much for a few trinkets. But then Winifred was always shrewd. She pressed on. "He is inhuman. He is the vile spawn of a monster's loins." She placed both hands around the girl's. "All I wanted was to seek a divorce. He does not want me, has no care for me, but would he grant it? No. Instead he brings me, against my will, here. Keeps me as if I were some political hostage or a criminal to be locked away! I lie abed at night wondering whether I shall ever be free, whether I shall ever be allowed to speak with my mother again!" Winifred wept, her head bowed, buried in her hands. Said through great sobs, "And even whether I shall see the coming of a new day. I fear so much that he may decide to make an end of me!"

"Oh, Lady!" Fidelia tried to comfort her, put her arm around her mistress, held her close, rocking her like a child in need of love.

Winifred, her face hidden, let slip a smile. She had her! Hooked and landed. She grasped Fidelia's arms urgently, holding them tight. "I must get away! Get to the safety of my grandsire. Arthur cannot touch me there." She let the girl go and hugged herself, rocking backwards and forwards on the stool. "But how can I? I am not allowed to communicate with anyone beyond this villa. Arthur has forbidden it." She shook her head, sorrowful, dejected. "My parents do not even know whether I bore my child safely. Know not whether I live or die." Untrue, of course, but Winifred cared little for truth.

"Lady, that is a vile, wicked thing!"

Hooked, landed and gutted.

Fidelia knelt before her mistress. "What can I do to help? Tell me and I shall do as you ask!"

Scarcely able to contain her delight, Winifred shook her head, pathetic in her self-pity. "None can help me." Then a sudden idea. "Wait, there is something! If I could get a letter to my father! He will know what I must do!" She had decided against her mother this time. Two letters sent and no hint of a response to her pleading.

Crossing quickly to her writing desk, Winifred made a pretence of searching, found a small parchment scroll. "I wrote this some months past," she lied. "Arthur refused to allow its sending, though I openly showed it to him." She unrolled it. "It says nothing untoward, speaking only of our child's birth and taking, of my health. Nothing that should not be said. I end by asking the King to arrange for me to come home."

She thrust the parchment towards the girl and Fidelia made a pretence of scrutinising the neat lettering. It was upside down. As Winifred had expected, the girl could not read.

She was uncertain what she wanted to do, between seeing Arthur and Gwenhwyfar torn to pieces by horses, roasted alive on spits, or disembowelled slowly with a blunt-edged knife. Perhaps a taste of all three? Whatever death awaited those two, she must first get home!

She took the letter back, rolled it, and secured it. Safer not to place a seal. It was a pity she could not ask Father Simon to send another letter, but no, best to use the girl this time, though she seemed hesitant. Seeing her doubt Winifred opened the jewel casket again, placed a bracelet on the table. "Of course, such loyal friendship deserves reward."

Fidelia eyed the wonderful rubies and diamonds. If she sold it, she could ensure a life of considerable comfort; could do better than a shepherd for husband. Yet if she should be discovered it would be a whipping and dismissal from service—at the very least.

Casually, Winifred added a pair of earrings, said, coaxing, "These items are worth much gold, Fidelia. Think what you could do with gold coin!" She took a second bracelet. "This is to pay for the cost of carrying the letter; its value should exceed what is required. You shall, of course, keep any excess."

Winifred paused a moment, made to retrieve the items. "I ask too much of you."

Fidelia grabbed at Winifred's hand. "Lady, you do not! I shall see to it your letter is sent." She stowed the jewellery in her pouch, the parchment safe between her breasts, and scampered from the room.

Winifred went to the window. She smiled at the drizzle-wet hill sloping beyond, drummed her nails on the wood. "Make a fool of me, Arthur Pendragon? We shall see who laughs the louder!"

Soon, when her letter found its way safe, Vortigern would demand Arthur's recall; they would be going home and his little game of illicit love would be ended!

TWENTY

Juliana looked sideways at Gwenhwyfar, who sat with legs swinging on the edge of the kitchen table. Playfully slapped a hand creeping nearer the dough she was kneading. "You be too old, young miss, for sneaking bits from my baking!"

Gwenhwyfar laughed. "Never will I be too old!"

There was silence for a while. Gwenhwyfar began to hum a lilting melody; Juliana pounded her wheat bread. The grain had lasted well this winter, stored in the new granary Gaius had built last spring, she was thinking. She said, "And what will you do when his wife discovers all this?"

Gwenhwyfar ceased her tune.

"She will, you know. You cannot hide from it. One day you will have to face up to the fact he has a legal wife."

"He is to divorce her."

"Ah."

Silence again. Juliana pounded at her dough, flour covering her arms.

"What do you mean, ah?"

Patting the dough into shape, Juliana set it aside to rise, dusted her hands, wiped the table clean.

"Do you know why he married her in the first place, my dear?" she asked mildly.

"He was forced into it by Vortimer as a safeguard against her marriage to one of her own kind."

Juliana nodded. "I heard that rumour also."

Gwenhwyfar bridled, jumped from the table. "Are you suggesting Arthur has lied to me? That he took her willingly?"

"He was not *unwilling*, was he? He needed funds, child. Needed that fat dowry." At Gwenhwyfar's scowl, the woman placed her hands flat on the table, leant forward. "Lass, neither of you has stopped to consider this thing through."

"We have!"

Shaking her head, Juliana measured out fresh flour, began mixing ingredients for honeyed cakes. "The reasons of then, girl, still exist now. More so."

Gwenhwyfar snorted.

Juliana wagged a spoon at her. "Arthur can no more divorce Winifred now than he could refuse to take her as wife then. It made sense for him to marry with her. He must become king, and as Pendragon and husband to Vortigern's Saex born, he could take command of Britain *and* the Saex in one blow. There are many Saex who are not loyal to Hengest, those who were born and raised in Britain—as were their fathers. They are not loyal to Vortigern either, but the Pendragon? He is different, altogether different. And there are the practicalities. To become king, he needs her wealth; her title and her son to command the Saex. I say again, he cannot, will not divorce her."

Gwenhwyfar snorted louder. "What do you know of it?" She hoisted herself once more to sit on the table, folded her arms, sat hunched, hostile.

Juliana was vigorously stirring her mixture. "It does not take much of a brain to work out the obvious."

"They detest each other. They have no relationship, no feeling, nothing."

"Yet, I hear, he still visits her bed."

Eyes flashing, "You have good hearing then!"

"I have friends who are servants, child, and servants talk."

"He has not slept with her!"

"And I say he has!" Juliana beat harder at her mixture. "He is the Pendragon, girl. He needs a son."

"I shall give him one."

In exasperation, Juliana slammed her spoon down on the table. "You talk like an ignorant peasant! You are his mistress, nothing more." She took a handful of dough, began shaping round cakes between her plump red hands. "You will never be the mother of his heir. Winifred, for one, would never allow a bastard born of you to take precedence! La! I wish I had never allowed this thing to happen when it began! I ought have whipped the both of you and sent you away to Father Simon for the confession of your sins!"

"Then why didn't you?" Gwenhwyfar shouted her retort, then slumped, miserable.

Clicking her tongue, Juliana cleaned the sticky mixture from her hands, moved round the table and held her close as if she were a daughter.

"Why did I not? Because I would rather have you where you are safe, not doing this silly thing in some open field or hidden bush where any could watch. Arthur is like a son to me. I have watched him grow from boy to man. I am proud of him. But la," she cradled Gwenhwyfar to her, "I am not so proud of this mess."

Gwenhwyfar pulled a little away, close to tears. "Juliana, do not say such things! I have been so happy these past weeks."

"How long can happiness last? If Winifred should find out…"

"She will not."

"That, my dearest, is where you are wrong." Arthur stepped into the kitchen.

Dressed in rough-spun tunic and bracae, with a plain bronze buckle fastening the leather sword belt at his waist he looked like any soldier's son, except his air of authority and leadership belied any lesser rank than supreme commander. As Gwenhwyfar went to meet him, he encircled her slim waist with his arms, affectionately kissed the tip of her nose. "Winifred will find us out—I would wager she has already done so."

Gwenhwyfar nestled closer to Arthur's strength. "I am not afraid of her."

"Then you ought to be! She can cause much trouble should she decide to poke her stick in this ants' nest. And poking where she is not wanted is something my wife excels at."

Agreeing with him, Juliana added, "I would think twice, and once again before placing too much trust where that one is concerned." She slid her cakes into the oven. "Have you thought what is to happen," she asked, "when you return to Britain, Arthur?" She indicated his leg. "Your wound is well healed, God be praised, and the sea lanes are open again after the winter storms. How long before the army calls you back? What are you to do with your wife and mistress then, eh?"

Gwenhwyfar shuddered as a dark shadow passed over her. When Arthur goes? She had not thought of it, had not stopped to consider much at all beyond the here and now. She looked up with trust at his firm jawline, his long, straight nose and those piercing brown eyes, half concealed by the hair flopping over his face.

With conviction she said, "I am to go with you." When he did not reply, she said again, with more of a question, "I am to go with you?"

He wiped a hand around the previous night's growth of stubble he had not bothered removing that morning, perched his backside on the table where, before, she had sat, and held her at arm's length the better to see her.

"Only Winifred comes with me when I sail on the morrow."

Gwenhwyfar stared at him. Hearing the words, not comprehending.

"I have been meaning to tell you these past few days," he said, "but I did not want to spoil your happiness too soon."

Gwenhwyfar swung away to stand before him, hands clenched to her hips. "Spoil my happiness too soon? Like thunder out of a blue sky you sit there and calmly tell me you are going, not with me, but with her? I am to be discarded then? Dropped by the wayside like some worn cloak!"

"Cymraes, it is not as you think."

"Oh, is it not?" She stamped her foot. "How do you know what I think? I will tell you, shall I? I think you are a lying, deceitful, whoring bastard!" She fled from the kitchen, through the small but comfortable living space and beyond to the privacy of the bedchamber.

Arthur heard the door slam, looked helplessly at Juliana. "She had to know."

The woman matched his gaze. "Aye, she had to know. But not like that."

He flared up, more angry with himself than with Juliana. "How then? Tell her days since and destroy what small happiness she has had? Wait, and tell her tonight in front of the entire family?" He slammed the table with his fist, swore. Began again, calmer. "I apologise. You are, of course, right. I had not meant to tell her like that. I had intended to tell her later." He hung his head. "After our last time together."

Juliana touched his arm, recognising his pain. "You do love her, then?"

He groaned, swung away from the table, stood facing the wall, his hands resting above his head. "By all the gods there have ever been or ever will be, I love her." He leant his forehead against the whitewashed plaster.

His muffled voice did not hide the ache. "I have been ordered to return by Winifred's father to attend a meeting of Council with Hengest. There is to be a new treaty." He laughed wryly. "He mentioned his concern for my wife's welfare."

"Does he not have cause for such concern?" Juliana asked rather tartly.

Ignoring the sting, Arthur wandered to the table, brought a stool from beneath it and sat down with his chin resting on his hands. "She is a clever, cunning bitch. I would pay a high price to discover if she did manage to get a letter home, despite all my efforts to prevent it!"

"Father Simon?" said Juliana thoughtfully. "She has spent many an hour with him these past months. I know he is impressed by her devotion to the faith, and her generosity to the Church as a whole."

"You seem to know a lot about my estate's goings on, old woman," Arthur said cynically.

Juliana laughed, removed the cakes from the oven, their tantalizing aroma filling the kitchen.

"I go often to town and hear talk, and I am observant at Mass inside your mother's fine chapel on the Lord's day." She handed him a hot cake which he ate appreciatively. "Young Bedwyr chatters enough for me to know the inside workings of your villa backwards! Plus," she added, "I have heard nothing but praise of Winifred from the good father himself."

Arthur made a derisory noise. "Winifred, like her mother, can make a fine show of benevolence when it suits her."

"The light of God can move in mysterious ways, Arthur."

"I doubt," said Arthur, wiping crumbs from his lips, "even God would welcome that bitch into His kingdom. She is material more suited to the other place." He pointed downwards. "Father Simon is a man who sees good in every soul. He has begged and badgered me, these past weeks, to allow her more freedom. What does he know of politics? Does he not realise for the price of a gold ring she could be up and away, running to her Saex kin? I will not let her go where I cannot have her watched. Not while she still bears the title of wife."

With a quirk of her eyebrow Juliana added, "And of course, how could you allow her out while you are making so free with that one in there?" She nodded at the door, in the direction Gwenhwyfar had gone.

Arthur grinned, his eyes shining. "How could I indeed?"

"Has it occurred to you, lad, your wife might not want to be parted from you?"

Arthur coughed, spluttering crumbs. "What? Winifred? She wants me as much as a boil on the backside!"

Juliana persisted. "Are you so certain? Wife to the Pendragon is a title worth the having. I have heard she weeps for you at night when you do not go to her."

"Your ears are hearing the wrong tales." Arthur pushed himself away from the table and took another cake, Juliana swiping ineffectually at his hand. "During our short period of marriage I have made it my business to see through all Winifred's tricks and schemes. Her tears do not fool me one drip of rain water."

"Yet you still answer Vortigern's summons?"

"Until I am in a position to do otherwise I have no choice. If I step over far out of line, I could find myself in a worse position than my father did. I am biding my time. It will come."

He walked to the door, munching at the cake, spoke through a full mouth. "I am going to Gwenhwyfar."

"Be gentle with her."

TWENTY-ONE

G O AWAY!"
Arthur ignored Gwenhwyfar's muffled curse, sat on the bed beside her crumpled body. He cautiously rested a hand on her back. She shook it off. "I said go away."

"Not without talking first. I am sorry, I did not intend for things to be like this." He sighed. "Sorry" was such a hopelessly inadequate word. She remained face down, her arms curled around her head.

"Why?" She rolled over, sat up.

Arthur sighed again. What should he say? What could he say? "You know why."

"I do not!" she countered. "I have no idea why you are sailing for Britain on the morrow with your wife. I have no idea why you are taking her instead of me!" She swung her legs to the floor, moved away from the bed and the man sitting on it. She stormed around the small room, arms animatedly emphasising her words. "You are the Pendragon, rightful Lord of Dumnonia and the Summer Land; Lord of Less Britain. By all that is right, you ought be seated where Vortigern sits. You ought to be king." She laughed derisively, stabbed an accusing finger at him. "You? King? Ha! You cannot run your own life, let alone that of others! Vortigern barks and you jump! The Pendragon? What an empty title! Your father in the other world must be covering his head in shame." Her voice began to rise, shrill and tense. "You are nothing but Vortigern's puppet! Are no better than the rest of them who fawn and grovel at his feet!"

"Have you finished?"

"Na! All those lies about how you hate her, how she makes your life a misery. How you, you poor, poor man, were forced to marry her. Go on tell me, tell me again how you have no choice but to take her back with you. I dare you!" She spat the last words in his face.

His own anger rising he grasped her wrist. "You seem to have forgotten I have no power over the lands my father once held. He was exiled, remember? He lost those British rights. He died fighting trying to regain them, or have you forgotten that also? I have no wish to die for a hopeless cause that is lost before it is even begun!"

"So you admit to being a coward!"

Arthur came very close to losing his temper at that moment. He drew breath, swallowed hard, held it in check. "I value my own life and the lives of my men too highly to spill blood needlessly."

She still wanted to fight. "So claiming your rights is no longer necessary?"

"Gwenhwyfar, you are being deliberately obtuse. I have no love for Vortigern, nor his accursed daughter."

Gwenhwyfar interrupted, "Yet you share her bed!"

"Blood of Mithras! Once since the Nativity!" Lies came easy to Arthur. "I get no pleasure from her."

Gwenhwyfar spluttered with laughter. "I suppose the begetting of the daughter she bore you was no pleasure either? Or did you play God and produce a second virgin birth?"

"That is blasphemous!"

"My, all of a sudden you are a Christian!"

"Ah, my Cymraes, let us not quarrel," he said, his hands spread, pleading.

"That is all I am to you, Arthur. How Juliana and her husband must laugh. Arthur the Roman and his *Cymraes*, his native woman! His British whore!"

Arthur's temper snapped. It seemed such a little thing to push him over the edge but the name had been a special one to him since their childhood, the endearment signifying much more than a name between friends. Why, he could not say, it was just a thing that was. A link with childhood pleasure and vowed love. *Cymraes fach*, "little British woman," he had called her during those happy, sunny days in Gwynedd. He had dropped the "fach" unconsciously when he took her as his own.

Arthur's voice was quiet, almost menacing. "I thought the one I gave that title to was worthy of it." He added bitterly, "I thought she was far-sighted enough to realise the tangle of politics is a hard knot to unravel. Someone, I thought, who would be able to understand when my back is up against the wall. One who could share the pain of having to wait, and wait, and wait again until a move sure to win without being butchered can be made. I thought a *Cymraes* would know this. Obviously she does not." He turned to go. Angry at himself for being angry.

"But I am not your woman!" she screamed. "British born or no, do you not see that? Winifred is!"

With his back to her his hand on the door, he said, "Na, Gwenhwyfar, it is you who cannot see." He left, could not go back.

Juliana watched him ride away. If she saw the tears streaming down his face, she made no mention of it to her husband. Nor to the girl who lay across a bed, broken with grief, unaware of the new life growing within her.

TWENTY-TWO

LATE AFTERNOON, AND THE DRIZZLE OF THE PAST TWO DAYS HAD PASSED, leaving a leaden grey sky with low cloud that threatened more rain to come. Winifred wandered in the direction of the chapel. Father Simon, without seeing her, entered the squat building through the low door as she paused on the far side of the gateway. She glanced at her escort who nodded vaguely and settled himself on the grass growing alongside the wall. It was normal routine. Every afternoon Winifred went there to pray. Every afternoon the guard, a Christian himself, allowed this slight deviation from orders and let her enter the chapel without an escort. Save for the occasional presence of Father Simon, who was near-sighted in faith and vision, it was the only place outside her chamber where Winifred could sit unobserved. She paused in the porch before entering. The letter was to go with the noon tide, Fidelia had said, in trusted hands on a fast ship bound direct for Londinium.

The door was ajar. Winifred, her hand on the latch, was about to step inside when she heard the priest's voice saying, "Well, a stranger in my domain!"

Who was he talking to? Pushing at the door she stopped short as Arthur's voice answered. What was he doing here? She had watched him ride out again with that slut this morning, was not aware he had returned. She stood silent, ears alert, listening.

"My mother's chapel," Arthur stressed the ownership, "has few reasons to draw me here."

"Yet you come today?"

"Because today I have a reason. My wife comes here, I believe?"

Listening outside, Winifred bristled at the disgust in his voice. Had Arthur discovered the sending of her letter? A coldness congealed in the base of her stomach. She knew enough of Arthur to fear him. If he had read that letter she would certainly not see the dawn!

Inside, unaware of the listener beyond the door, the priest in his turn stressed ownership. "All are welcome in God's house."

Arthur did not miss the point but let it pass. He disliked Father Simon, he knew not why. He was a man who followed the ways of many of his kind, preaching the words of God, unflinching in his duties towards Christ, the sick and the poor. Arthur guessed his dislike stemmed from his mother, who worshipped the man almost to the point of blasphemy. He was her friend, mentor, confidant, and confessor, and she had thrust his words, God's words, down Arthur's throat so often in his boyhood that he was heartily sick of the three of them. The holy trinity? God, Ygrainne, and Father Simon!

As much as anything, it had been the need to escape their combined preaching that had persuaded him to take Cunedda's advice and leave, to gain experience under Vortigern's rein.

"Why does Winifred come here?" Arthur snapped the question, expecting an instant reply. Father Simon stared back at the young man before him. Noted the tired eyes, the sallow, drawn skin. The defiance shielding uncertainty.

Father Simon was given to trusting the promises of his small flock. He believed all could be saved and baptised to the true faith, with patience and understanding. He believed no man, woman, or child was wholly bad, merely ignorant of God's way. Some thought him a fool. Happen he was.

"Your wife," he answered, "comes here to pray for deliverance from this cruel prison you have immured her in."

Arthur laughed. "Is that what she has told you? Your eyes are veiled against deceit, Father."

"On the contrary my son, they are wide open." Father Simon seated himself. "My eyes tell me you are troubled, else why would you be here in Our Lord's house? My ears tell me you do not trust your wife. My heart tells me you are as imprisoned as she, and," he added, satisfied at knowing he was right, "my logic tells me all these things are connected."

"My wife," Arthur hissed, "is a liar and a cheat."

If he had meant to shock the priest, Father Simon showed no sign of it. He answered, "And are you not?"

Outside, Winifred almost laughed aloud. Well thrust!

The priest grew stern. "You exchanged the vows of marriage with her willingly."

"I did not. I was blind drunk."

"You consummated the marriage; she has since given you a child."

"She has given me pain and hatred."

"Which you have returned." Father Simon, refusing to be drawn placed a hand on the younger man's shoulder. "My son, can you not see what grief you have caused her? Taking her away from home against her will is distressing enough, but confining her and banning all communication with her family, is that not unreasonable?"

"Not when she plots against me; not when she intended to deprive me of my own child."

"But the child died. Your argument is invalid. Could it not be you keep your wife under guard because in your heart you do not wish to lose her? Because you have love for her?"

"What?" Arthur exclaimed sardonically. "Love that bitch!" He stood up and moved away, fingering the carvings along the top of his mother's high-backed chair.

"Then let her go."

"Are you judging me?" Arthur had the chair between them, hands still now, his stance daring the priest to answer.

Father Simon smiled benevolently, resting his hands on his knees. "It is our God who judges, not I."

"Your God, not mine," Arthur hurled back. "I follow the soldiers' god, Mithras."

"Mithras? Can the shed blood of his sacrificial white bull protect you more than the love of Christ?"

This persistent paganism was a constant thorn in the priest's side. The thorn festering with the knowing the son of Lady Ygrainne stubbornly refused to let go of the old and embrace the new. But then, Father Simon knew Arthur well. He had never been one to do as others advised. This Pendragon trod a lonely path.

Arthur backed down, raising his hands in surrender, walked around the chair and sat down, his leg hooked over the arm. "I have not come here for theological debate. I have come for your help."

Beyond the door, Winifred raised her eyebrows. Arthur—seeking help!

Inside, Arthur rubbed at sore eyes; he had not slept well these past nights. His thigh pained him often during the hours of darkness, and then there had been Vortigern's summons. He drew his cloak around him; it was chill inside these cold stone walls where no sunlight fell.

Rising from his seat, Father Simon walked to the altar, twitched a corner of the covering cloth straight. It was a beautiful thing of fine linen, stitched with care by Ygrainne.

"This night and the nights to follow Father, I ask for all the help I can get, from whatever God or gods are willing to give it."

"There is only the one true God. He can offer all the help you need if you would only bow to His will."

Arthur shook his head, unfolded himself from the discomfort of the hard-seated chair and began prowling around the small building—lightly touching carvings, moving a candle holder set in a niche, slightly to one side. The candle tipped, fell to the floor. "I am beyond saving. The help I speak of is not for me, not directly." He retrieved the thing, set it back in its place, said, "We have had our differences, Father but you are a good man with a kind heart. I ask if you will see to the well-being of Lady Gwenhwyfar. She will be in need of friends after I sail on the morrow."

Winifred froze, her eyes opening wide, her body tensing. Tomorrow! Leaving on the morrow! He could not possibly be intending to leave her here in this godforsaken place! She willed herself to be still, forced down the sudden urge to storm through the door and demand to be taken with him. To scream and scream. She must listen!

Father Simon sounded equally surprised. "Is this not rather sudden?"

"I received word of recall some days past." Arthur was now inspecting an embroidery hung at the back of the chapel. He recognised it as more of his mother's needlework, vaguely remembered her working on it. Aye, that blue bird swooping down—as a boy he had stood watching her fashion it. He remembered her needle flashing, fingers deft, the little bird appearing with each neat stitch like some work of magic. He would have been about five summers old.

Father Simon, clasping his hands together in an attitude of prayer said, "It may be indelicate of me to say this, but infidelity usually results in one party's extreme hurt."

Arthur's eyes narrowed. His silent response meaningful.

"And the Lady Winifred?" The priest's calm gaze ignored Arthur's hostility. "I would not see her the injured party. She is your wife." Sharp, judging, "The other woman is not."

Sidestepping the reprimand, Arthur ran his finger along a shelf, inspected the black smear of dust left on his finger. "Is there anything you need for this place? Salvers, gold plate?"

Father Simon folded his arms. Arthur always had been irritating, was forever ducking issues of importance as if he had not heard.

"Your lady mother is most generous with her gifts. We have all we need." He would not have the subject turned. "What of your lawful wife?"

"None the less," Arthur's hands were open, offering generosity, "I would be pleased to donate something. A chalice?" He strode towards the altar. A crucifix stood there and two silver candlesticks. "You do not have one. I shall see what I can obtain."

The priest inclined his head, his hands burrowing beneath the folds of his loose sleeves. "That would be most gracious of you. I thank you."

Almost an afterthought Arthur announced, "I am returning Winifred to Vortigern. I wish to divorce her and wed Gwenhwyfar."

Outside, Winifred caught her breath, relieved at first that she was to be taken home, then outraged as his meaning sank in.

Father Simon was slowly shaking his head, his lips pursed. "It is a sad day when solemn vows are broken."

Winifred's hands were clenching and unclenching, her eyes bulging. She mouthed silent curses, sending all the poxes and plagues possible to various parts of her husband's anatomy.

"I am to end soldiering." The Pendragon laughed ironically. "Who knows, when I am settled here on the estate I may even abandon Mithras. A farmer has small need of a soldier's god."

Father Simon did not laugh or smile. "It will be hard for you to give up such a life. Hard for your lady wife to be so cruelly set aside."

Almost to himself Arthur added, "Harder still to give up the hope of holding all Britain." Louder, "It will be no cruelty for Winifred. For once I am obliging her by giving her what she wants."

Ah, no! Winifred was thinking. *You will not get away with this! You will not discard me like some dried-up milk cow and exchange me for a wide-eyed heifer!*

Laying his hand on Arthur's arm, the priest asked with a frown, "You would renounce all for this one woman?"

"All of it." Arthur leant his hands on the altar, shoulders drooping. "Gwenhwyfar does not know of my plans—neither does Winifred."

Outside, Winifred sneered, mouthed *Ha! Do I not!*

"Gwenhwyfar believes I am deserting her, which is why I came to ask you to watch over her while I am gone. I would rather have my wife safely set aside before giving Gwenhwyfar what she deserves."

Oh, she will get what she deserves! Have no fear of that, my husband! In a fury Winifred retraced her steps from the chapel, marched back along the narrow path leading to the villa her guard scrambling to his feet, taken unawares. She slammed into her room and threw her cloak on the floor, screaming at scurrying servants to leave her.

So he was to abandon her! Was to take that whore as wife in her stead! Oh no, no, he would not! She would not let him. Forgotten now her desire for a divorce, her plans to be rid of him. Those things were all on her terms. Her terms, not his.

What angered her the most, made her teeth clench and her hand sweep phials and bottles from her table, were all those wasted hours. That soft treading and simpering, her forced smiles, her splendid charm. All winter she had striven to win confidences, gain sympathy. Father Simon, Fidelia, others. All that work to gain their trust, and a letter sent this very day to her father, all that and Arthur was leaving with her after all! Damn the man, damn him to hell!

She lifted a wooden box from the chest beneath the window. Inside, a phial, wrapped in soft velvet. As she uncovered it, green sparks gleamed as light caught the rough-made glass.

She lifted it held it up to the window, a malicious smile curving over her lips. "He will not have her. If he does not have me, he will not have her." She laughed, head back, mouth open. Laughed.

Reaching for the bowl of dried fruits beside her bed she sprinkled a few drops of the liquid, watched as it seeped through the wrinkled skins of dried dates and figs. Then she stoppered the bottle and returned it safe inside the box, wrapping it again in its protective cocoon of velvet. The lid shut, Winifred washed her hands in a bowl of water, dried them, called for Fidelia. One more task, one final trinket given.

During dinner, Winifred was unnaturally talkative, almost gay. As was Ygrainne, now recovering well from her illness, gaining strength by the day, colour returning to her cheeks.

Their last meal together. Both women were happy, eager for the departure. Both had expressed delight when Arthur informed them of the imminent return to Britain. Winifred had kissed him, holding him close. It gave her a sense of well-being, of gloating power to secretly know his plans.

Ygrainne felt relieved and relaxed now he was at last taking his leave. With God's blessing it would be a while before he returned!

Ectha asked the question Winifred had been burning to ask, but had thought better of. "Where is Gwenhwyfar this night? Does she know of your departure, my boy?"

Ygrainne answered for Arthur. "She was taken ill at the farm of Gaius Justinius Maximus. A message was sent. I shall send a litter for her on the morrow; it was too late to do so this evening." She sniffed. "Why she rides there so often, I know not. There is as much to do here on the estate as on some poor farm."

No one answered her.

Ectha took a further helping of roasted pig. "She is missing an excellently prepared meal."

Winifred smiled. No matter—one as well prepared awaited her.

Ceridwen sat silent on Gwenhwyfar's empty bed. Iawn, her husband, was staying in Gaul and, consequently, was wishing God speed to the men of Arthur's guard—which meant they were emptying many wineskins this night. He would not be abed until late.

She disliked retiring without him; she missed his comforting bulk, his strong arms protective around her. She patted the swelling bulge of her stomach. How proud he had been when she had told him of the coming child!

Her thoughts went to Gwenhwyfar. What a hopeless tangle she had got herself into. She would be so alone and miserable again now Arthur was going.

When the message had arrived from Gaius, Ceridwen was all for riding straight to be with her cousin, guessing at the reason for this sudden illness, but Ygrainne forbade it saying it would soon be dark, unsafe to ride. She could go on the morrow, with the litter.

Ceridwen padded on bare feet to the window, peered out at a star-peppered sky. She would away to her own bed. No use waiting for Iawn this night. Absently, she selected a handful of Gwenhwyfar's dried fruit from a table nearby, blew out the single lamp, and went to her own chamber, eating as she walked. Some of the fruit tasted bitter, she swallowed quickly, finished the handful, dusted sticky hands on her shawl, and went to bed.

Within two days, Ceridwen was dead.

APRIL 455

TWENTY-THREE

RETURNING, ARTHUR DISCOVERED, WAS LIKE BEING THROWN INTO A DEEP river and being swept along by the current unable to swim for shore or cry out for help. It was incredible so much could alter within so short a space of time.

It had not seemed so from a distance. The smoke from domestic fires drifting over red roofs, the glimpse of taller buildings beyond the solid bastions of the city wall—from this last curve of the river the city had seemed ordered and bustling in the midday sunshine. Ships were moored along the river frontage; the bridge ahead thronged with carts and men and cattle. With it all, the distant thrum of sound: voices, music, animals—donkey, cow, horse. The clatter of hooves, the rumble of wheels. Children shrieking, men and women shouting.

As he drew closer, he saw the smoke trails were less numerous than he had thought, the carts not so laden, and the city wall, and beyond it the roof tiles, were cracked and crumbling with great gaping holes here and there. And the ships were all Saex. Dozens of them. Trading ships with sails furled, some with cargo offloaded, others with barrels, baskets, and pots still aboard. Moored among them were flat-bottomed oared vessels, the largest Arthur reckoned to measure around sixty feet in length between the high curves of prow and stern. As his own ship slid by one of these great war monsters, lying like the rib-exposed carcass of some huge dead animal, he counted eleven rowing benches; calculated at least sixty men per ship.

He stood on deck, hands pressed against the rail, frowning. Why so many Saex? Where were the British craft and other coastal traders?

He peered astern. She was still there, although now hanging to leeward. The Saex craft had slipped her moorings down by the estuary signal station and had eased into the wake of his own vessel. She had kept her distance, but there was a distinct feeling of being herded like a lost sheep back to the fold. She was flying a banner depicting a white horse. Hengest's emblem.

Hengest. Warrior, leader. Hengest with his brother Horsa and his three keels rowed by fierce, loyal men had come, it seemed, a lifetime ago. Exiled from their Jute homeland, they had landed on British soil in search of ale for their horns, meat for their bellies, and blood for their swords. Had found all three under Vortigern's employment. Only now, the ale was running sour, the meat turned bad, and the blood? Aye, well, there was always plenty of blood for the taking.

By the number of moored ships, those three original keels had somewhat multiplied.

The following ship trailed Arthur almost to the bridge. There, before the current took her, she heeled aside, turning in a wide curve to make fast against the first of the Saex-crowded wharves.

The six oarsmen of Arthur's sailing vessel gave one last stroke, shipped their oars, and let the flow and their own momentum take them forward to the bridge and under the towering wooden structure, between two of its many piers. Arthur shut his eyes He was no sailor. Those rising stone pillars seemed to come close! Then they were through, shooting out the other side, the oars again dipping into the churning water that fought to make way between the barricades.

A few British ships were this side, gathered in a protective knot along the wharf at the mouth of the tributary river. His own ship back-paddled and swung in sluggishly, leaving the race of the river, heading for the palace water gate. She bumped against the oak planking. Mooring rope clasped in his hand, a crewman leapt ashore before she ducked outwards again, made her bow fast and ran to catch a second thrown rope astern.

Arthur did not wait for the plank to be lowered, jumped instead to firm ground and climbed the steps up to the palace two at a time, his simmering anger overriding the lurch and sway of sea swell. Two ragged guards at the gate, Saex, stared impassively as he strode past. Had the palace always seemed as shoddy and world-weary? Had it always been so in need of repair, or had he just not noticed?

Spring-grown weeds choked the cobbles, plaster had fallen away in great chunks, the exposed brickwork beneath beginning to crumble. His footsteps echoed under the entrance arch, unchallenged. He swung along corridors, up some steps, along more corridors and swept into Vortigern's outer chamber, where he came face to face with Melwas, Vortigern's sons Vortimer and Catigern, a British captain and, to his intense relief, Cei.

"What in the name of the Bull is happening here?" he thundered, removing his cloak and tossing it to a slave.

"You may well ask," Catigern drawled from where he sat sprawled across a couch like a swatted spider.

Cei had sprung forward the instant Arthur entered and greeted his cousin warmly, taking his hand, grasping it firmly. "You are quite recovered? I see you are, praise be to God—when I think of our fears some months past! Thank God they were proven false." He released Arthur's hand. "We expected you days since." Quietly he added, "Where in all Hell have you been? I have worried myself sick for your well being!"

"You alone, I presume," Arthur answered, ducking his head towards the glower of displeasure on Melwas's face.

Louder he said, "I had business to attend afore I came here." He steered Cei aside, said hastily, "I have been seeing to my divorce from Winifred. I have endowed her with the small parcel of land I hold along the south coast. That will suffice for her." He grinned with a devil-may-care gleam. "She has promised, with dark threats, to find lawyers to claim back her full dowry." He clapped a hand on Cei's shoulder. "I don't think she realises how irritatingly long these lawyers can take over domestic settlements!"

Vortimer crossed the room to clasp Arthur's hand. "It is as well you delayed no longer. Within a few weeks this place will be no more than an empty shell."

"It seems little more than that now!" Arthur said derisively. Then with caution asked, "Why?" There was an odd smell here somewhere. "What has been happening while I have been away? Why are there no British guards here or manning the signal stations? I saw no sign of life, save for Saex, the entire length of the Tamesis."

"A thousand whys and a thousand more to follow." Catigern was very drunk.

Cei poured Arthur some wine and part answered his question. "Vortigern has used only Hengest's men for some time now; he claims he can no longer trust his own breed."

Arthur took the wine and laughed. "It has taken him this long to discover it?"

Cei did not echo the humour. "Our men are camped a few miles from here." He pointed out their general direction beyond the north gate. "The King is withdrawing. Moving west to make Caer Leon his royal capital."

Arthur, the wine halfway to his lips, lowered the goblet in stunned disbelief.

Vortimer took up the telling from Cei. "The traders and merchantmen have not come to Londinium this spring. Nor will they the next. They say the Saex are too numerous along this eastern coast for safe trade."

"And from next month they will be taking over the sea lanes also," added the army captain, perched on the edge of a table.

When Arthur looked blankly from one to the other it was Melwas, surprisingly, who said, "My uncle proposes to cede the British Cantii territory to Hengest's overlordship."

"What?" Arthur spun round to face him, spilling his wine.

Melwas returned the hostile stare, dark eye to dark eye.

The door to Arthur's right was closed. Setting his goblet down with a decisive thud, spilling more of its contents, Arthur strode over to it.

"It is no use," said Vortimer, stepping in his path. "The King's mind is set. He will bring eternal peace, he says, between our two peoples this way."

"I thought he was supposed to have done that when he took Rowena as wife."

"A meeting between Council and Hengest's Eldermen to finalise the treaty is arranged—that is why so many Saex ships are gathering on the river. My father will not back down. There is nothing we can do."

"Damnation there isn't!"

Arthur thrust Vortimer aside, kicked the door open, and burst into Vortigern's private chamber, slamming the door shut behind him.

The King barely glanced up from the parchment he was reading. "I thought I heard your pleasant tone, son-by-law. Do come in."

"What do you mean by this?" Arthur shouted, coming to stand before Vortigern's table, his arms folded, his expression thunderous.

"Exactly the question I intended to put to you," said Vortigern unruffled. He searched among the pile before him on the table and tossed a parchment towards Arthur, who, glancing at it, recognised Winifred's neat hand. "I am none too happy with the way you have been treating my daughter."

Momentarily taken aback at the change of subject and with annoyance that the bitch had managed to get a letter through, Arthur stared at him. "I do not give a dog-turd about your daughter! What has she to do with this foolishness?" Angry, his hand swept the parchment aside, taking with it several other scrolls that rolled and bounced to the floor.

"She has much to do with it—she wrote it."

Arthur ignored the King's deliberate twisting of his meaning. "I will not allow you to so casually dispose of British land!"

Vortigern straightened some of the chaos Arthur had caused and laughed sourly. "*You* will not allow? Tch, tch, we are coming the high and mighty today!"

He sorted a muddle of written accounts into a neat pile. "Unfortunately for you, boy, I do care about my daughter. And," he added pointedly, "it is my kingdom to dispose of as I please, not yours."

"You will not give it away to Hengest!"

"Not even for an assurance of peace? I suggest you listen to facts before you start belly-aching."

"And I suggest you listen to sense, old man!" Arthur shouted.

Vortigern rolled another parchment, deliberately taking his time. He set it aside, reached for another. "Hengest has assured me he will be content to settle his people alongside those British who wish to remain in the Cantii land. They exchange one over-lord for another, that is all. It is no new thing, has been happening for centuries. The farmers care little what lord they pay taxes to, as long as they are left to farm in peace."

"And in return?" Arthur's voice was cold, hostile.

Vortigern sighed. This really was none of the Pendragon's business. A king did not have to justify himself. "Naturally he will pay land tenure to me in the form of grain and goods."

"Naturally," sarcastically. "Is that all?"

"What else need I ask for?"

"Hostages."

Vortigern leant back in his chair. "Hostages? My dear boy, Hengest is my father-by-law." Spelling facts out, "His daughter is my wife. Why would I have need of hostages?"

Arthur's eyes had narrowed to fierce slits. "You will do this over my dead body, Vortigern."

"That," the King replied with a chill smile, "I can arrange." His voice hardened. "I and Council make the decisions. Not you."

Arthur rested his hands on the table. "And I can hold the entire British army."

Vortigern laughed, attempting, unsuccessfully, to hide his unease. "I will take that as an idle boast, the sort boys crow after the taking of their first woman." He feigned contempt, well aware Arthur's threat was a distinct possibility. His manner changed, turned dark and ominous. "I do not like threats, nor do I like those who make them. The matter is closed."

He pushed his chair away from the table. "As for my daughter, I intend to ensure she receives a public apology for your disgusting behaviour, adequate financial compensation for her humiliating experience, and that from here on you bestow upon her the full duties of a husband."

Vortigern over-rode the response of verbal abuse by continuing with, "I would not like to hear any alternative view, boy. I would take any attempt by you to set aside my only daughter as a personal insult, would regard such an act as treason." He too leant his hands on the table. "Do I make myself quite clear, Pendragon?"

Winifred's pleading letter had annoyed Vortigern. He had allowed this marriage for two reasons: to keep a close eye on Arthur and to block him from making any other, more alienable marriage. Now in this sent letter the silly girl was begging him to seek a divorce for her? Ah no, he could not allow the Pendragon that freedom! "I assume she is disembarking from your ship? I wish to see her at once," he commanded.

"She is not here."

From his seat, his eyes never leaving Arthur's, Vortigern said, slow and deliberate, "You had best not have the nerve to inform me she remains a prisoner in Less Britain."

"She is in this country, safe from your clutches until such time as I see fit to return her to you. After I have completed the dissolving of our marriage, you can do what you want with her." Arthur was again standing with arms folded. "I'd send her to Hengest if I were you: her scolding tongue will drive him to fall on his own Saex sword." His hand shifted to the pommel of his sword. "You can have her back when I get what I want. All that I want."

The King linked his fingers across his stomach and tapped his thumbs together. "Which would be?"

Arthur hesitated, his carefully rehearsed words forgotten. He had intended to exchange Winifred for his freedom but this absurd treaty changed everything. Or was it an opportune excuse not to give up his command and his dreams?

On the voyage from Less Britain he had taken time to think, to sort the tide of fast-running emotion from sound sense. Would he survive a life of farming? What did he know of overseeing the estate, or of wine production? Nought! Ectha saw to all that. There would be nothing for Arthur to do save sit and watch a bulging belly gradually flop over his bracae belt. He was born to be a soldier, it was in his blood.

What of Gwenhwyfar? Would she think as well of him if he were to turn tail and abandon all he had dreamed of, worked towards? She had once said she would have only the best. To throw away the chance of securing the kingship would achieve nothing. Would she despise him, as much as he would despise himself? In all truth he did not think their love would hold, given such a bleak future as life on the estate under the shadow of Ygrainne. But there were alternatives. They could go to Gwynedd, he could fight from there. Or he could demand the return of his father's lands in exchange for Winifred's safe release.

On board ship he had tossed the ideas back and forth, regretting his confidence of rash intention with Father Simon. It had all seemed so reasonable there, with the raw wound of Gwenhwyfar's scalding tears stabbing his heart. He had sat morosely nursing one wine flask after another, drinking himself almost senseless as the ship battled her way through a heavy swell, hugging the safety of the coast, unable to put into the wind for fear of being smashed to pieces.

It had been Winifred who had cleared his mind. That first night, after a scant meal shared in the confines of the captain's quarters set aside as their own, she had confronted Arthur.

"Where are you taking me this time, husband?"

"Somewhere I can keep close watch on you while I negotiate our divorce."

She had not replied for some moments, then, to his surprise, said, "With my cooperation, you will not need to negotiate."

What was she up to now? he had wondered.

Winifred had smiled at him then, had taken his arm, kissed him lightly on the cheek. "I have been as miserable as you in this union," she had said, so sweetly. "I too wish it to end. On my terms."

He had nodded; that came as no surprise. "Which are?"

"We sort out our differences in private. Let it be seen our journey to Less Britain, the birth and sad death of our child, has united us. All I require is that I do not lose face." She had played with his hair, twisting the dark strands in her bejewelled fingers. "I wish to have my own, substantial estate and wealth, and for it to appear we are reconciled. In a few months' time, our divorce can come about as an amicable arrangement." Fiercer, "I will not be set aside or shamed, Arthur."

Winifred had rejoiced at his shrug of acceptance. "I suggest, husband," she had said, unlacing the thongs of his leather tunic, "we make the best of this unfortunate situation."

Like any male used to regular pleasure, he had great need of a woman's body, and strong wine, far from damping his urge, usually heightened it.

Each night of the tedious journey, made longer by the battle against an ill wind, they shared a bed. Gave, and received, pleasure. Holding his sleeping head to her breast through the hours of darkness, Winifred lay calculating the time of the month and praying for her womb to quicken. She had decided against divorce. Would not give him that freedom. It would be more satisfying to keep him chained, bound to her by neck and ankles. More amusing to watch as he grieved over his dead, high-born whore and watched as, week by week, she, Winifred, swelled with child.

Their ship had dropped anchor a short distance west along the coast from the fortified harbour of Portus Adumi. Sending men to obtain horses, Arthur had escorted his wife inland to the estate he had acquired the previous summer. She had ridden beside him, head high, smiling and proud. Triumphant.

His memory of Gwenhwyfar had been betrayed by his return to his wife, and Winifred's monthly course had not come! Her bleeding had always come on time before that wretched girl-child was born, and again since. There was no reason, save one, to expect this month to be different.

When this babe came, it would be a son. Within the turn of the month Arthur would know Gwenhwyfar was dead, that his wife was pregnant, and all hope of freedom was lost. She smiled broadly as they rode. Revenge had a taste as sweet as wild honey.

Arthur stood now, facing Vortigern, wondering whether to make his demands or wait. This treaty must be stopped. It would be the end of Southern Britain were so much to be given for so little. He was going to divorce Winifred, he was determined, and he had little doubt Winifred was equally adamant no divorce should take place. For months past she had wanted their parting; now she did not—but then Winifred was always perverse, wanting a thing only because it was her own idea, rejecting it if it was not.

Arthur had not been so blind drunk on board ship to not realize Winifred's submission was all sham, that she was thigh deep in some scheme of her own making.

The King grew tired of waiting for an answer. He said, "The contents of my daughter's letter proved very interesting. I have no doubt Cunedda's eldest son will be much angered to hear of your, shall we call it indiscretion, with his sister. Especially when he hears of the matter after it has been dragged through the alehouses and taverns. At least Cunedda's death has spared him the knowledge his precious Gwenhwyfar outshines any Messalina."

"You bastard!" Arthur had never known such overwhelming anger as that which took hold of him at that moment. He was filled with a blinding white rage at the vile comparison with one of Rome's most notorious whores.

He drew his sword. Action slowed to stillness for Vortigern. He had goaded too harshly, too soon, and realised it too late. Like all bullies, he had little courage.

Quick wits, coupled with a savage ruthlessness, had given him the position and reward he required. Blood and guts on the battlefield nauseated him beyond endurance. Facing Arthur's naked blade, he remembered suddenly the last time Arthur had drawn sword against him. Remembered Arthur's threat.

Arthur remembered too. It had been no idle threat and nor was this. As the blade whistled down, Vortigern felt a warm wetness trickle down the inside of his legs. He closed his eyes. Screamed.

The fatal slash of iron through flesh never came. He felt something touch his cheek, a hiss, a rush of air. Heard a scuffle, hard breathing, a clatter. Tentatively the King opened his eyes, put shaking fingers up to a wet stickiness below his left eye. Looked unbelievingly at the blood daubed on them.

The door stood wide, a group of horrified men gathered there.

Melwas, knowing Arthur's hatred of Vortigern, had deliberately placed himself within hearing on the far side of the door. The unmistakable venom in Arthur's raised voice and Vortigern's scream took him through to his king's aid, regardless of protocol.

"For once," Vortigern said drily, masking the fear that made his body tremble, "I will refrain from chastising you for the rudeness of your entrance, my nephew."

Melwas grinned, indicated with a jerk of his head for the captain, standing astonished with Vortimer and the others, to call for Jute guards. They came, seized Arthur from Melwas's hold, roughly dragging his arms behind his back. Melwas released his grip, bent to retrieve Arthur's sword from the floor, and placed it on the table before Vortigern.

The King shuddered, forced his eyes from the blade smeared with his own blood. He pointed with trembling fingers at the weapon.

"You shall pay for this outrage, Pendragon. The penalty for treason is death."

Melwas's hand was already drawing his own sword. "Let me finish him now!"

"Stay your hand!" Vortigern stood up, walked slowly round the edge of the table, stopped before Arthur, who stood mutely defiant between the two Saxons. "You will die, Pendragon—eventually. When I am ready to let you. When I have you on your knees, begging for me to release you from this life."

He turned sharply to Melwas. "I give this whore-son to you, nephew. I must know the whereabouts of my daughter. I am certain Arthur will be only too pleased to tell you."

Melwas saluted, a triumphant leer stretching his black-toothed mouth. He motioned the guards holding Arthur to follow, and led the way out.

Cei stepped forward, his hand on the hilt of his sword. Arthur shook his head warning his second-in-command to stand down. Muttered, "I was stupid enough to miss the bastard's throat."

The guards dragged Arthur away, marched him to the small block of prison cells set beneath the far walls of the palace, where Vortigern enjoyed providing his enemies with a lonely, agonising death.

By evening and the coming of the dark, Melwas took successful word to his uncle. Immediately, a fast jute ship was placed under his command, and by the coming of dawn he was heading for the fortress of Portus Adurni and an estate lying halfway between the port and the ancient Roman town of Venta Bulgarium.

TWENTY-FOUR

IN CONSIDERABLE DISCOMFORT FROM THE VICIOUS BEATING HE HAD ENDURED, Arthur huddled in the corner of a dank cell. The place was dim, although not altogether dark, for light from the distant guard's room crept through a wide gap under the bolted door. High up in the stone wall, a vent of a handspan's width gave on to the outside world. As dusk had settled, a small number of bats had descended from the eaves and flittered silently through the opening into the gathering darkness.

The long night passed slowly. His face, swollen and bloody, ached; pain stabbing at his side from fractured and bruised ribs made it difficult to sit or lie comfortably in the scatter of musty straw. More than the pain, he disliked the creeping fear that clawed at his stomach.

When they had brought him in here he had tried to ignore the sudden clutch of cold panic that, once it took hold, would not let go. He tried hard to conceal the dryness that came into his throat and the shaking that rattled his body. Melwas had laughed, highly amused at Arthur's ashen face, placing it as fear of what the guards were about to do.

The two of them had carried out their orders with alacrity and enthusiasm, while Melwas watched, leaning against the far wall, arms folded, eyes gleaming, and nostrils flaring from the pleasure. Fists and feet battered without mercy, until breathless, in pain, bruised and bloody, Arthur gave in and told of where he had taken Winifred.

Melwas took the surrender of information as a weakness. Arthur thought of it as common sense. Why suffer beyond endurance for something not important? For a while he had held out as a matter of principle, furious at Melwas's gloating, but had soon set principle aside in deference to thudding pain.

As a parting gesture Melwas had rammed his boot, twice, into Arthur's groin. He had walked away laughing, leaving Arthur semi-conscious and floating in a haze of red blood and dizzy blackness.

Sunlight streaking through the small vent illuminated swirling particles of dust that danced and spun in an unrehearsed pattern of intricate steps. Through the buzzing in his head, Arthur could hear the Saex guards talking, but understood little of their guttural language. He must learn some of the Saex tongue, he decided. If ever he got out of here,

The coming of day had eased the stifling fear of enclosed places a little, but not much. Arthur stared at the wooden door. The single shaft of sunlight ran straight as an arrow, from the vent to that door. He tried to look away, tried to set his mind to thinking on other things, but his eyes would be drawn back to those particles of dust swirling and tumbling down from the outside to the door. The door. The way out. The clutching desire was to run at it, beat on it, and kick at it. He would if only he could get up, if only his body did not ache so; if only his head would stop this giddy whirling. If his legs would stop their shaking.

He turned his back on the door, lay in an awkward heap keeping the weight off the side most injured. Inside he was screaming. He sat up, stared again at the door. His mouth would not open; fear had tightened his throat, clamped every muscle rigid. The walls were swaying, bearing down on him, collapsing.

Arthur fell forward, vomited, spewing until his stomach heaved empty. It did not help. Still the walls swam and closed in. He shut his eyes, held them tight closed. Beads of sweat stood out on his forehead, ran down his body, saturating a tunic already stained from sweat and blood. "Mithras," he groaned through clenched teeth, "by the love of the sacrificed Bull, please grant me death!"

TWENTY-FIVE

WHILE ARTHUR HUDDLED WITHIN HIS PRISON OF WALLS AND FEAR OF confinement, many miles to the south a storm-tossed ship ploughed her way through heaving seas.

Gwenhwyfar raised her head bleakly as Iawn stooped beneath the awning of oiled leather. His face, grey and hollowed from grief and stubbled from days of untended beard growth, bore a greenish tinge they all echoed, save for the hardiest members of the crew. Although even they had muttered prayers for deliverance to the new Christ and the old gods.

Struggling with the single flapping sail and the bucking oars, the Christians among the crew touched carved crucifixes dangling at their necks on leather thongs; pagan worshippers, a variety of talismans. This crossing of the channel between Gaul and Britain, these experienced Breton sailors agreed, was the worst within living memory.

It seemed to Gwenhwyfar, squatting beneath the rigged shelter to the stern of the stout little craft that her misery could not, surely, grow worse: until she looked up and saw the drawn tautness of Iawn's face.

"Tell me," she said wearily, resigned, knowing he was about to impart further bad news.

"We are apparently some distance off course. The steering board is barely operable and our captain doubts the mast will hold much further strain." Iawn lurched forward as the ship fell over a side wave, spray cascading across the deck.

"Gwenhwyfar's attempted smile did nothing to hide her despair. "Aside from that," she flapped her hand feigning indifference, "all is well?"

Grim, not echoing her false humour, Iawn hunkered down beside her, his broad shoulders hunched in his sodden cloak. "The captain has no choice but to run before the wind; there is no way of turning and heading back to where we should be making for."

"We are going in the wrong direction, then!" Gwenhwyfar pounded the sea-drenched deck beneath her with the palm of her hand. "We go east not west. Oh, Iawn, I want to go home!" She heard the childish whine in her voice, was powerless to prevent it. More than ever in her life Gwenhwyfar felt pushed to the edge of control. The despair of those long months cloistered within Ygrainne's suffocating hospitality, the news of her father's death and the agonising end of her much loved cousin, even the pain of Arthur's sudden departure were nothing to this! She longed for the security of Gwynedd's mountains, her brothers' solid protection. She was running away, running for a bolt-hole, but the holes when she reached them were blocked, so she had to turn around and run again, and keep running. Almost, with the misery of a churning stomach, thudding head, and tears that would not cease, Gwenhwyfar had forgotten why she was running. Best to forget. It was all too horrible to remember; but their faces continued to haunt her.

Iawn had not challenged her decision to leave Less Britain. Gwenhwyfar announced her intention the day after his wife had been laid to rest within the little cemetery beside the walls of Father Simon's chapel. Iawn had been numb, feeling nothing beyond disbelief at his loss. Even now, here on this god-forgotten ship, he expected to see his Ceridwen appear, face flushed with excitement over some incident of nature; the first butterfly; the first peep-peeping of fledglings in a nest; an arching rainbow; the wondrous colours of a glowing sunset. Ceridwen had delighted in all things of beauty, instilling the same appreciation in Gwenhwyfar and Iawn. Now she was dead, gone. Committed to the dark of the earth.

Na, Iawn had made no objection to running away.

Gwenhwyfar's grief was deeper, for she had the knowing of the sinister truth behind Ceridwen's death. Only Gwenhwyfar and Livila knew, and one other. The old woman had guessed at poison but who listened to the babbling of a feeble-minded servant? Certainly not the physician, who regarded Livila as a harmful witch and often said so to her face.

Ygrainne would be relieved when the tiresome old woman, the only member of the household who had refused to embrace the love of the Christ, relinquished her stubborn hold on life. Poisoned? What nonsense. Who would wish to poison Ceridwen?

Livila guessed and Gwenhwyfar knew. They had exchanged glances over Ceridwen's deathbed, seeing the truth in each other's eyes, sharing their awful knowledge.

Arthur had warned of Winifred—she could be dangerous, he had said. But she had made one mistake, one vital mistake. By not ensuring the poison reached its intended victim, by killing Ceridwen instead of Gwenhwyfar, the Saex bitch had dug herself a grave. Winifred would die; Gwenhwyfar, would see to it, one day, no matter how far in the future, when opportunity came. One day, Winifred would pay for Ceridwen in kind. There would be no gentle easing into the next life, a soft sigh of breath, a peaceful departure. Ah no, not for Winifred. She would face the horror of an appalling death.

Iawn did not know of the poison. Seeing his grief, feeling his pain, Gwenhwyfar could not tell him of it, had not the courage to tell him Ceridwen had died in her place. Enough of a wound in her own heart; she could not twist the knife in his. Some things were best left unsaid.

"I must reach Gwynedd!" she moaned now, desperate.

"Lady, we could all drown, assuming the ship were even capable of being turned." Iawn dropped his gaze, said, "For myself I have no fear of death, I have no wish to live without her." He shut his eyes, fighting back tears.

Gwenhwyfar reached for his cold hand, took it in her own, said nothing. What use words?

He struggled to compose himself. "My duty is to safeguard the Lord of Gwynedd's sister. I cannot risk your death, nor can I risk the ship's crew coming with me to meet my God."

Gwenhwyfar nodded. Of course he was right. "Where does our captain hope to put ashore?" she asked with a false bravado.

Iawn shrugged. "The first port he can reach. He dare not attempt to turn too soon or this storm will flatten us like barley before the scythe. We must run before it until such time as he can ease this floating coffin into a new course."

Gwenhwyfar smiled again and drew her damp blanket more tightly around her shoulders. "Then we must leave our fate to the gods."

Iawn managed an answering smile. "For all my faith in God, I would rather, at this moment, trust your life to the skill of our captain and his crew."

As the weather-shrouded southern tip of the Island of Vectis appeared in the distance against the murk of a dark sky, the swirling rain squalls had eased to a steady fall of drizzle and the wind had blown itself out of violent temper. With relief, and a hasty prayer to God, the captain manoeuvred his craft away from the tossing open sea and slid her into the calmer waters running between island and mainland.

As they churned into the sheltering straits, the gusting wind dropped and the crew cheered. Portus Adumi and safety lay ahead!

Huddled in the rain-sodden blanket, Gwenhwyfar shed its weight with relief and stepped out on deck, watching with interest as the ship made its way along the waterways, limping, tired and battered, but near enough in one piece. There was much laughter and jesting among the crew.

She was looking west, to the wide stretches of marsh running along the coast so missed another mast and its cross-chequered sail, moving swiftly out of port.

Someone in the crew raised a worried shout, pointed, his arm full out-thrust, head turned in alarm to the captain.

Gwenhwyfar swung round at his shout. She shielded her eyes, peered through the shadows of mist at the ghostly outline.

Another yell and the crew scattered, their relief melting into fear and disbelief as they hauled at the ragged sail and laid to the oars.

Confused, Gwenhwyfar watched their scurrying, listened to their cursing and swearing as they bullied the sluggish ship to respond.

Iawn ran to her, scooped her aside, manhandling her towards the stem hatchway that led to a dark stinking hold below decks. She fought free of him, demanded to know what was happening.

"That ship, lady."

"I am aware of it."

"It is Saex."

"It sails from a British harbour—happen it is one of Vortigern's mercenary fleet."

Irritated at her unusual stupidity, Iawn snapped a reply. "British ships do not fly the Saex flag. No merchantman of any nation would run close to such a ship. They are sea-wolves."

Rubbing her fingers across her forehead, trying to ease the persistent ache behind her temples, Gwenhwyfar struggled to think clearly. The stress of this voyage and the whirling confusion of the past days fogged her mind as deftly as the haze beyond the bows masked the outline of that ship, now altering course and heading fast straight for them.

The captain roared orders but the weary crew, not needing them, had already swung into defensive action. The mate passed close by Iawn, running to take a bow position. He tossed half order, half advice in his clipped accent. "Get woman below, open deck no place for her."

He said no more, running to tend his own salvation as best he could. Once that ship closed, it would be every man for himself. No matter who she was, few of the crew would put Gwenhwyfar's safety above their own. It was the risk you took with the sea; you faced storm and sickness alone. And Saex sea-wolves.

Iawn was worried. He thought furiously of the best course of action, understanding the almost hopeless situation. This was a merchant ship, a trader, not a warship, its only weapons his own and the daggers the crew carried. Against a Saex ship! God, do not think like that! If he could hide Gwenhwyfar, she might be overlooked. He glanced at the land, a good mile distant. Could she swim if he were to drop her overboard?

Gwenhwyfar read his thoughts. "I am not that strong a swimmer, Iawn. I have little desire to drown."

"It may be a preferable option." He opened the hatch cover, indicated she was to climb down.

"And if you are thinking," she said firmly, "that I am going to scuttle into some foul corner and cower like a trapped rat, then you can think again."

Iawn opened his mouth to protest, read her determination. He had seen that same look on Cunedda's face. He nodded, drew his sword, ran a thumb along its fine double edge. "Then we had best prepare ourselves for a fight."

Gwenhwyfar nodded back at him, one brief nod. All of a sudden her headache was gone; she felt alive and eager. Throwing her cumbersome cloak from her shoulders, heedless of the steady rain, she gathered her skirts and drew the back hem forward between her legs. Tucking it up through her belt, she pulled the leather tighter about her waist to form a crude pair of bracae to allow unhampered movement. A sailor scurried by and she grabbed at his woollen cap, plucking it from his head.

He turned with a snarled curse, biting the scathing words back as he saw who the thief was; shrugged good-naturedly as Gwenhwyfar produced a small bronze coin from the pouch at her hip and threw it to him.

He tossed the coin in the air, caught it, then with his thumb flipped it over the side of the ship. "Gods'll be wantin' that. Best t'pay for me way to the next world now while I 'ave the chance. I'll 'ave little need for money soon I'm thinking." He made to walk off, turned back with a toothless grin. "Have no need for me cap either."

Gwenhwyfar had plaited and bound her hair in Roman fashion before leaving Less Britain. Most of the pins were lost now, great hanks of hair straggling loose and unkempt during the rough weather. She curled the hanging loops on top of her head, pulled the cap tight down, tucked away a few stray wisps.

"Not so obvious a woman now?" she queried.

Iawn grunted.

The Saex were gaining rapid ground. What chance had they, a lame deer running against a young wolf? Gwenhwyfar waited, alert, shoulders back, chin lifted. Beside her, Iawn.

"Stay beside or behind me, whatever happens," he ordered.

Waiting, watching, as the Saex ship beat relentlessly nearer, her legs braced against the pitch and roll of the wooden deck, Gwenhwyfar thought of everything and nothing. Voices, half-forgotten phrases; faces, drifting and passing. Memories and dreams mingling with regrets and hopes.

She could see details of the Saex rigging; see the cross-woven strips running through the sail giving it that chequered pattern. See the dull glint of drawn weapons and the hands clutching grappling hooks held at the ready. Faces, as the two ships came together, the Saex vessel ramming her heavy reinforced bow into the fragile sides of the trader.

Gwenhwyfar stood in the stern, flanked by Iawn, a boy, the captain's slave, no older than ten years, and, surprisingly, the mate.

A great cry went up. Attack from the Saex, yells of defiance from the trader. The sea-wolves boarded, leaping the gap between the two ships, others throwing their hooks, bringing the ship around, alongside. As the two hulls crashed together, more leapt, savage in their eagerness to kill and plunder. Two of the crew were dispatched immediate, others putting up a fight as more and more Saex poured aboard.

For a moment, while she still had a brief second in which to think, Gwenhwyfar wished she had obeyed Iawn and hidden herself away down below. She stood trembling a little behind him, feeling the tight knot of fear binding in her belly. She had seen men killed before, knew the flood of blood and choking cry of death, but those had been deaths on her father's orders, executions, punishments. She had seen the wounded return from war with limbs shattered or removed, faces misshapen, bodies hacked, eyes gouged out, noses split. Death hovering, like gulls over a catch of fish. This was different. This was cold, bloody, and happening for real.

Her stomach clamped tighter, a gasp escaping her lips as she looked up and saw. She felt sick. Standing on the Saex deck, legs spread, fists on hips, and laughing as he watched the merciless slaughter stood Melwas.

Gwenhwyfar clutched at Iawn, shrinking behind her protector, but Melwas looked directly at her, their eyes meeting across the two decks.

His nostrils flared and he gave a wide, lazy grin. The wind caught his cloak, spreading it like wings behind him. He looked like some bird of prey hovering, waiting the right moment to plunge down and sink its talons into a defenceless victim.

He folded his arms, waited. He had recognised her, knew who she was.

Something made Gwenhwyfar glance up at the low-hanging sky; she caught sight of a ragged fluttering at the masthead.

How stupid of them! There, for all who cared to see, flying alongside the Less Britain pennant, proudly proclaiming the ship's passenger, rain-sodden but clear enough to distinguish, the Lion banner of Gwynedd.

The Saex were upon them now, this valiant little group in the stem. Iawn and the mate struck forward. With his sword, Iawn took off an arm, the mate with his thinner and shorter sailor's blade plunging into the fight, hacked through flesh and bone.

Others came on, relentless. The boy had sunk to the deck, curled himself in a tight ball, moaning in terror. He never saw the blade that slit him almost in two.

An instinct for survival stirred Gwenhwyfar—that and remembered voices of brothers and father, shouting, bullying, never letting up on those days of weapon training. *Go, Gwenhwyfar! Thrust, go for the belly, throw your body weight behind your dagger—light on your feet, girl—light, I said! GO!*

She lunged with her dagger, screaming the Gwynedd war cry, drawing bright blood from an opponent's severed artery as her weapon scythed through a thigh.

The mate went down. He struggled to regain his footing; a blade pierced his throat. It took a while for his life blood and spittle to gurgle from the wound, spouting foul redness over wooden deck and leather boots.

Iawn fought savagely, using sword, shield, and body with skill; fighting with strength and wit. It was useless. He pushed Gwenhwyfar with his elbow towards the rail. "Jump!" he screamed, eyes as ferocious as the order, turning his head for her to catch his words.

A sword, raised high, glimmered bright against the leaden sky some trick of light reflecting off its shining blade. This was no ordinary Saex sword, but a thing of finer work, crafted, surely, by the hands of faery folk? Gwenhwyfar's line of sight flickered to it as Iawn shouted, taking in every detail of its fascinating, deadly beauty. A sword made for a king's hand.

Iawn saw it also, hesitated, caught off guard by the massive brute wielding such a fine weapon. The blade slashed down, whistling as it cut through wet air.

It sliced through Iawn's helmet, through scalp, bone and brain. Blood and matter spewing out, drenching everything. Gwenhwyfar screamed. A hand grabbed at the cap on her head and her bright copper hair tumbled free. The huge Saex, lowering his wondrous sword, stared, momentarily astonished at his lucky catch, then said something in his guttural tongue to his companions who laughed.

Gwenhwyfar flew at him, biting, scratching, and kicking. All her Da's training clean forgotten. The man guffawed louder, lifted her off her feet with one hand. She saw a blade glint and fall. Blood gushed into her eyes and then came darkness.

TWENTY-SIX

GWENHWYFAR CLAWED HER WAY TO CONSCIOUSNESS THROUGH A SWIMMING haze of pain. Her arms felt numb, her body cold and drained. It was a battle to open her eyes; when she managed it she looked straight into the bloodied, vacant stare of Iawn's eyeballs, wide in his severed head. She vomited where she lay in her crumpled, bound heap.

Her arms were tethered behind her, ankles roped together. Wriggling, ignoring the protests of aching muscles, Gwenhwyfar managed to turn herself from the gruesome trophy dangling from the mast. A drizzle of rain pattered on her upturned face, its coolness reviving her thrumming senses. The ship was moving fast, running before a lee wind, skimming through troughs of rail-high waves. It would have been a fine ship, had it not been Saex. Sickness swelled in her throat again. She closed her eyes. Still they remained, Iawn's blank, staring eyes and the crunch of metal slicing through bone and sinew, severing head from neck. Her stomach heaved. She fought hard against bile and tears. Failed against both.

Reluctantly she opened her eyes again; the sky moved near then far, rising and falling as the ship breasted the waves. On the edge of her field of vision, woollen bracae tucked into deer-hide boots, braced in a wide stance against the roll of the sea.

"You have not had a pleasant journey."

Melwas.

"So you attack and slaughter your own kind openly now? Has the hidden sliding of a knife into gut lost its amusement?" She was not looking at him, but knew he shrugged, uncaring.

"My men require payment. If they can claim it themselves from gained plunder, then so much the better." He squatted then, so she could see his face. "Aside, I would be a fool to miss the opportunity of claiming what is rightfully mine."

"You forfeited any rights when you murdered my brother!"

He leered at her, showing blackened, gapped teeth. Sa, she still had fight left in her. "You have not forgotten me, then?"

Gwenhwyfar's hatred was manifest. "Gwynedd never forgets."

"Yet your father conveniently forgot our betrothal when he spirited you away." He grabbed her hair, his hand lashing out, fingers curling in its length. "I will not be made to look the fool."

"You make yourself a fool."

He struck her for that, once, across the cheek. A dribble of blood oozed from her lip, mixing with the trail of dried blood from the wound made by that Saex sword pommel striking her on the temple.

"More of a fool!" she added, refusing to be cowed. "Only fools threaten Gwynedd."

He struck her again, harder. "Gwynedd will bow the knee to me. I intend to make a start with your submission."

Gwenhwyfar regarded him unflinching. "I am not afraid of you, Melwas the fool. My brothers are stronger."

He walked away, tossed over his shoulder, "But your brothers are not here, are they?"

As the ship rounded the chalk cliffs of Dubris, the wind and rain ceased at last, though a grey sea still rolled beneath oppressive, greyer skies.

Gwenhwyfar recalled little of the horrendous, cramped voyage. Melwas did not bother her again, nor did the Saex, busy about ship's business. They sailed up the coast, darkness well settled long before the crew lowered the mast and took to the oars. Rowing steadily, they sent the vessel skimming into the Tamesis estuary, their low-chanted song keeping rhythm, the reflection of steering lamps bobbing on calmer water. The tide would turn soon and carry them forward, up river.

The pitching and rolling eased once they joined the calm of the river, and finally Gwenhwyfar fell asleep. She must have slept for a long while, for dawn was well past when the ship bumped the shore, jolting her awake.

She recognised the wharf of the water gate at Londinium. Two Saex, one the man who had killed and beheaded Iawn, hauled her to her feet, releasing her ankles but not her bound wrists. He wore her dagger, tucked proud beside his wondrous sword. They marched her forward, her numb limbs shaking, and she stumbled as they dragged her down the plank to shore and up worn steps into the palace.

Saex kind were everywhere. She did not see one British guard the whole length of the debris-choked pathways and dusty corridors between the wharf and the chamber to which they took her. But then that was to be expected. Melwas would not risk her meeting with a possible sympathiser.

They cut the rope binding her, threw her to the bed, and left, talking in their language which to her ears, sounded as pig-like grunts. A key turned in the lock and the bored scrape of feet indicated men moving to stand easy outside.

So, she was a prisoner then.

Gwenhwyfar looked about her for some vague hope of escape. The room was small, with the bare essentials of furnishings. A bed, a chest, a table. There was one window, narrow and rectangular, unshuttered. Thin though she was, she doubted she would be able to squeeze through. Even if she could, there would be a considerable drop beyond. She attempted to open the casement, but the iron lever was rusted and refused to move. Rubbing away grime and dust with her fingers, she peered through a single pane of the thick glass, wondering if it were possible to smash a way through.

She started and whirled around as a woman entered. A British slave bearing water in a jug and a platter of food.

"I am Gwenhwyfar of Gwynedd. Melwas is holding me prisoner." Gwenhwyfar emphasised her voice to that of command. Slaves were expected to obey. "I need get word to my brother. There will be a manumission for you if you help me."

The woman did not even glance up, but placed the items on the table, turned away, and left. Gwenhwyfar hurled the platter at the closing door.

She fumed for a while, uttering all the obscenities she knew, cursing the slave and cursing her daughter's daughters. Exhausted of oaths, she realised her hunger and devoured the provisions, sitting cross-legged before the closed door picking crumbs from the wooden floor. She drank some water. Appetite and thirst satisfied, she set about her appearance.

Stripping herself of boots, torn gown, and sodden under-garments, all stinking of vomit and blood, she kicked the things away from her and washed as best she could in what water remained in the pitcher.

She stood naked and shivering, reluctant to creep into the bed where it would be warm, although she was tempted. Twitching the top fur covering aside, she discovered coarse linen beneath. She stripped the bedding, fashioned a crude wrap-round linen garment, and added the fur as a cloak. Then she sat on the floor at the far side of the room, opposite the door, her back to the wall, and waited.

TWENTY-SEVEN

VORTIGERN WAS A CREATURE OF HABIT. HE LIKED HIS BED, LIKED EVEN MORE the seclusion and peace his bedchamber offered. A place in which to deliberate and plan ahead; a quiet, undisturbed cocoon where he could think upon the day past and the day to come. This morning, the evening's Gathering occupied his thoughts. It should prove interesting, amusing even, to observe Hengest and his clamour of jute Elders and Thegns sitting opposite a sullen-faced Roman Council. Things looked set fair for a promising event! A few knots to be untangled; whispers to be dropped in ears, promises or threats to be made—ah, that was the irritating thing. Vortigern wriggled his shoulders deeper into the comfort of his pillows. There were those few who were still mumbling their misgivings about this unconditional giving of land to Hengest. He cracked his fingers, delighting in the pleasant nastiness of the sound. They would come to his way of thinking; that, or be subtly reminded of debts or taxes yet to be paid.

A discrete tap on the door interrupted his thoughts. He growled an answer, beamed a smile as Melwas entered. "Ah, nephew, come in! A good voyage?"

"A very good voyage!" Melwas replied with an expressive sweep of his hands. Seating himself at Vortigern's bidding, he took wine from a slave, drank thirstily.

"You found my daughter?" Vortigern asked, motioning for another pillow to be placed behind his shoulders.

The question must be answered, but Melwas hesitated.

Astute, the King caught the pause, frowned suspiciously across the room at his sister's son. "I trust Winifred is in good health?"

Melwas nodded eagerly. That he could answer. "She is very well." He added, "We encountered a Breton trading ship as we sailed out from Adurni."

Vortigern grunted as he pummelled at a lump in the stuffing of the pillow, hardly listening.

"We took it."

Absently the King said, "Good, good."

"The haul paid the crew well."

"Even better." Vortigern was not to be sidetracked. "What is it you are not telling me about my daughter?" He snorted in disgust. "I assume she was disgruntled that I have forbidden her divorce from Arthur. She always was one to want her own way." He fixed Melwas with his small, sharp eyes. "Is she still planning to plot against me with Rowena? The pair of them have dangled fingers in the forbidden honeypot for years."

Melwas's laugh at Vortigern's thin pretence of humour was a little overdone.

"Is there more?" Vortigern had a niggling feeling the pleasing day he was looking forward to was about to turn sour.

Melwas toyed with the remainder of his drink. "This is an excellent wine. Greek, is it not? Uncle, it is good to be back in your service again!" He looked sheepishly at the floor. "I was an ass to stay away so long."

"You are often an ass, nephew. You let anger rule your better sense. Be that as it may, I know you well enough to see there is something you are not telling me."

The younger man shifted on his stool, fidgeting uneasily. "As I said, Winifred is well. She sends her devotion to you and is, as you ordered, under escort to Caer Gloui."

Vortigern was not satisfied; there was something more here. He said, "It will be easier to keep a close eye on her alongside her mother and young brother, Vitolinus." Did not add that his villa of Caer Gloui had high, secure walls and a dependable British guard. And that it was many safe miles distant from Hengest.

Melwas raised an eyebrow at the King's revelation. This was unexpected. "You have sent the Queen and your son west also?"

Vortigern chuckled. "She was most annoyed. My two clucking hens can sit in their roost and share their impotent scheming! I do not intend to take Hengest's word of fealty unquestioned, Melwas. Rowena is too ambitious, particularly now she has a son to dandle on her knee. She would like to reign as regent in his name, her and her father between them." He laid a finger on his nose. "It has been done before, you know: mother kills father for infant son to rule." He nodded his head slowly, deep in thought, adding, "This night I finalise my greatest treaty and pay Hengest off into the bargain. I thought it best to have his daughter and grandchilder safe beyond his grasp, just in case there were any bright ideas hatched atween them." He wagged a solemn finger. "You do not quieten a chained dog by parading a bitch on heat before him."

So, Melwas had learned something this day he had not known! "You do not trust Rowena, then?"

Vortigern laughed. "Trust her? Trust a woman—a wife? I would as soon trust a starving beggar to ignore a bannock of bread cooling on the kitchen sill!"

"She is a hostage then, against Hengest?"

The King stretched and yawned, threw the bedclothes aside and beckoned his slave forward to dress him. "She is my dearest wife, Melwas, but also a most convenient weapon to level at Hengest's heart. He dotes upon his daughter and her infant son." His voice became muffled as his head disappeared beneath a garment. "All his kind have this close affinity with kindred." He resurfaced, stood as the slave tied lacings. "It is the same with these tribal British—owing this, that, and the other. Loyalty to kin! Pah, can't see the reasoning of it myself."

Raising the last of his wine in salute, Melwas gestured agreement. The King would not see the loyalty of brother to brother, father to son, would he? Vortigern, as a young man, had murdered his own elder brother and his father to gain power, and was often close to doing the same with his grown sons.

Dressed, waving the slave away, Vortigern returned to the subject of his daughter. "So Winifred is well, but… ?"

"But, my Lord?"

"What is amiss?"

Puffing out his cheeks Melwas spread his hands wide. "She refused to leave the estate where I found her. The Pendragon has apparently signed the land over to her. She demanded to know where he was and, when I told her, insisted he be set free."

"God's truth!" Vortigern turned to his nephew in amazed surprise. Was the girl totally mad? "What is she playing at? I receive a letter begging my help in securing an immediate divorce—and now she is pleading for the bloody man's life!" He paced a few steps, then turned to Melwas again. "What ails her?" He scowled. "Has she decided to back the Pendragon?" Vortigern kicked at the side of a chair. "There is some scheme for the Pendragon to ally with Hengest against me, eh?"

Melwas brought a sealed document from his pouch, held it a moment in his hand. It would be betraying the trust of his cousin to pass it over but his loyalty was to the King! "She paid one of my men to deliver this to Arthur—she thought her gold was enough to keep the thing secret." He half grinned. "My men know better than to go against me."

Vortigern took it, looked with distaste at the small roll of parchment. "You know what is in this?"

Melwas spread his hands, affronted. "My lord King, it is addressed to Arthur!" His grin widened. "Of course I know what is in it!"

Pursing his lips, Vortigern broke the seal, noting with a nod of approval how well Melwas had patched his own breaking of it. He read grimly.

"So, after the agreement of this treaty, Hengest is plotting with Rowena to murder me?" He tossed the parchment aside. "I knew that months ago."

"Aye, but do you not find it interesting that Winifred is warning Arthur, and is offering to help him to do away with her mother and brother? With you dead, the country in turmoil, and Rowena out of the way—the path would be clear for the Pendragon."

Vortigern glowered and sat down in his comfortable high-backed chair. "So my daughter aims to become queen!" His eyes shone wickedly. "What ambitious kin I have!" The smile snapped off. "You managed to persuade her to Caer Gloui?"

"Eventually. She agreed when I promised to secure the Pendragon's release." Melwas grinned. "Unfortunate that I arrived back too late to stay his execution."

Vortigern's smile returned, his lips curling over toothless gaps. "Most unfortunate."

"In light of this," Melwas indicated the letter, "is it wise to have your daughter so near your wife?"

"Oh aye. They will be under close guard. Aside," Vortigern cackled with amusement, "happen the one will do away with the other and save me the task." He regarded Melwas shrewdly, added, "I assume you would enjoy disposing of Arthur?"

Melwas stood up. "It would be my pleasure."

Aye, Melwas took much enjoyment from the suffering of others. He was an evil breed, which was why Vortigern liked him. His nephew had the stomach for these "unpleasant" duties, unlike his two sons who complained and whined if such-and-such a thing was not right in God's sight.

"The Pendragon is where you left him. I thought a few days to sit and shiver and dwell upon his circumstances would be of use to his over-large sense of cock-sureness." Vortigern rubbed his hands together, delighted. The day was looking good again! "The Pendragons have been a boil on my backside over long. It is time the nuisance was lanced." He looked at Melwas. "He is to be dispatched with no undue attention. See to it this night. Minds shall be on this Gathering."

Melwas agreed, began making to excuse himself, but Vortigern lifted a hand to stay his going. "I would suggest a Saex blade would be best. It may be prudent to lay blame at the hand of our, er, friends."

A nod of agreement. Melwas walked to the door, stopped, said with a half turn to the King, "That Breton ship."

Vortigern had gone to a table, was busying himself with some papers. "What of it?"

"I took payment for myself also."

Ah, Vortigern thought, there is more to tell, then! "In what form?"

"A woman."

The King's eyebrows shot up. "They use female sailors in Less Britain now, do they?" He warmed to the thought. "What a superb idea. A sure way to enliven the dullest sea voyage."

Used to his uncle's lewd humour, Melwas explained further. "She was a passenger. We had no trouble finishing her bodyguard."

There it was again, a vinegar-sour threat to darken this sunny day, a sudden feeling his nephew was about to tell him something he was not going to like. "Go on."

Uncertain whether it was wise to continue, Melwas was forced to plunge on. The old man was sure to find out sooner rather than later—best say now. "She was mine anyway, I have simply claimed my own."

His voice lowering to an unpleasant growl, Vortigern said, "Go on."

"The passenger was Gwenhwyfar of Gwynedd."

The fool! Vortigern took three strides across the room, was before Melwas. "If a war comes because of this, you fight it alone!"

"Cunedda agreed betrothal!"

"Cunedda is dead. I remind you he claimed the right of blood feud. Until it is settled the claim passes as inheritance from father to son."

Vortigern laughed suddenly, his mood swinging away from ill-humour. Cunedda's sons would be furious! He slapped Melwas on the shoulder. "Good luck to you, lad. If you can hold her, then she is yours." He held a finger up in warning. "Just remember, this is between you and Gwynedd. I will have nought of it."

Pleased, relieved, Melwas said, "Then I have your permission to take her as wife?"

"Wife?" Vortigern was astonished. "Why do you want her as wife? Na, lad, keep her as mistress." He noticed Melwas's glower of displeasure, slapped his shoulder again. "Have it as you will! But take my advice, do not bother with formalities, at least not straight away. Take her as your woman now. Once she is in your bed and breeding, Gwynedd will be gagged, unable to shout over loud."

His nephew grinned by way of reply. "Exactly what I had in mind." He bowed, anxious to put words into action but Vortigern stayed him.

"Your lusting must wait awhile, lad; I have duties for you, details of this evening's work. Let me break my fast—meet me within the hour."

Melwas saluted, headed whistling for the kitchens to satisfy his growling belly. What a day! The end of the Pendragon and the taking of Gwenhwyfar! He sang a few bars of a Jute war song as he waited for the slaves to serve him.

TWENTY-EIGHT

USK. GWENHWYFAR HEARD THE STAMP OF FEET AND THUD OF SPEARS AS guards stood rapidly to attention. This was it then. He was coming. She stood, clutching the fur around her, stubbornly not allowing the fear to show as Melwas entered. He brought two slaves, the woman who had come earlier and a boy. Melwas threw a blue gown on the bed, noting the stripped linen. He sat beside the gown, ignoring Gwenhwyfar, allowing the boy to pull off his boots.

The woman shambled about the room, lighting the lamps and candles. Melwas stood, the boy removed his leather and iron-studded war gear. "When I have done with you," he said, talking to Gwenhwyfar but not looking at her, "you will dress yourself as befits a woman of mine."

Standing in undertunic and bracae, Melwas picked up a boot, hurled it at the slave woman, striking her in the small of the back. She spun to face him, afraid. He gestured impatiently for her to leave, kicked at the boy, indicating he should also go. The boy scooped up his master's body armour, retrieved the thrown boot, and scuttled out behind the woman.

"A loyal slave, that woman," Melwas mused, approaching Gwenhwyfar. "But damned useless at times, on account of her being as deaf as stone."

Gwenhwyfar was able to master a blank expression. So that was why she had been ignored! The woman had not heard her! Ach, let Melwas taunt, it would get him nowhere.

He stood, arms folded, observing her makeshift robe, then he reached out to finger the untidy hair cascading around her shoulders.

"It is a pity I cannot show you off at the feasting this night. Ah, well. I will savour you for myself." He wrinkled his nose at the distasteful smell which clung to her. "Should have had you bathed," he muttered.

He attempted to kiss her but she pulled away. Melwas let her go a few steps, then lunged forward, grabbing her hair and pulling her back. He kissed her on the mouth, holding her firmly to him, with a free hand, felt inside the fur, took her breast, fondling the nipple as his mouth bruised hers.

"I have spoken with Vortigern," Melwas said, his face close to hers; "he has acknowledged my claim to you." His hand fondling beneath the fur pulled at the linen sheet; it fell to the floor. Struggling, Gwenhwyfar kicked at him with bare feet. With her hands, she clung to the fur, clasping it around herself.

He held her all the tighter, ignoring her flailing legs. His pawing hand moved down over her stomach, brushed her inner thigh, his fingers groping upwards and she brought her knee up, slammed it into his groin. He slumped, grimacing, let her go.

Gwenhwyfar fled for the door, but he was quicker, catching the trailing end of her covering, pulling it sharply, tripping her. She fell heavily and lay winded.

"As of this day you are my woman." He stood over her, spoke with dark menace. She did not answer; he did not expect her to.

Slowly, taunting, he removed his woollen shirt, revealing a muscled, hair-covered chest. He unhitched the leather belt at his waist, let the bracae fall, stepped out of them, and stood naked. His intention, with his manhood rapidly swelling, obvious. Clasping her wrist, he hauled her upright, held her, crushing her mouth with his.

During the long day Gwenhwyfar had thought and planned. She had intended to fight, if necessary kill herself before submitting, but now it was happening, brave ideals slid away. Was that not what he wanted—for her to scream and beg for mercy?

His broad soldier's hand smashed her cheek, tearing the already bruised and tender skin. He wanted her to cower away, wanted to master and break her.

Gwenhwyfar remained still, silent, staring back at him. He found it unnerving looking into those green eyes that shone with calm defiance. Angered, he knocked her down and tore the fur from her, expecting her to shrink away or fight.

She lay motionless on the floor as he knelt astride her, pushed her legs apart and thrust himself into her, his impatience making him finish quickly and without much satisfaction. He withdrew almost at once, rage reddening his face. Yelling his fury he stood, beating and kicking her, shouting. "You bitch, you damned, heathen, whoring bitch!"

Gwenhwyfar laughed up at him, aware she had won. She made no attempt to ward off the blows, she just lay there laughing.

"Who took you first?" he bellowed, kicking his foot into her ribs. "Who claimed your maidenhood? What bastard was it?"

"Arthur," she mocked, her body shaking, teeth chattering. "Arthur. He is a fine lover."

Melwas's hands were at her throat, squeezing, choking her. Panic, already close to the surface, almost peaked, but Gwenhwyfar forced herself to think clear and calm. *Relax. Let the body go limp, submit to his rage.* She placed her hands on his, in a feint to prise the gripping fingers away, then moved quickly and precisely. Raising her hands, she slashed at his eyes with a woman's shaped nails. At the same instant she jerked her knee up, ramming home into his genitalia. With her hip, she thrust his pain-doubled body aside and, rolling clear, sprang to her feet. She grabbed for the water jug and smashed it over his head.

Crouching, holding the remaining broken shard before her as a weapon, she waited a long minute, but he lay unmoving.

Snatching up the gown he had brought, Gwenhwyfar ran to the door, opened it, and, throwing it wide, ducked low into the lithe, swift movement of a forward roll.

The guard, one of Hengest's mercenary Jutes, had been dozing, not expecting Melwas to emerge for some while yet. His momentary hesitation, combined with her unexpected manoeuvre, gave Gwenhwyfar the precious time she needed. She jabbed the jagged, broken edge of the jug at his face, ripping through his eye.

He yelled in pain and surprise and dropped his spear.

Catching it before it touched the floor, Gwenhwyfar drove the iron tip through his chest, paused only to remove a dagger from his belt. She took to her heels, clothing clutched against her nakedness, thankful she had some knowledge of the complexities of the palace corridors.

She almost ran straight into a further group of Jute nobles making their way to join the noise of Vortigern's great Council chamber. Changing direction along a side corridor, Gwenhwyfar found herself by a door leading to the gardens. Creeping into the shadows, she squatted, gaining breath and time to think.

Melwas was not dead, would be after her all too soon. The fine drizzle was soaking her hair and clinging uncomfortably to her naked skin. She shivered, her sweating body rapidly cooling. Tugging the woolen Saxon dress over her head, she found two brooches pinned to secure the shoulders. The jewellery, doubtless valuable, was, to her British eyes, vile and repugnant, but would have to suffice for now. She fastened them quickly, then huddled into the shadows to plan her next move.

These gardens formed a square bordered by guest chambers opposite; the

King's private apartments to the north and on this east side. Along the fourth ranged the administrative offices. Over them, on the first floor, brooded the council chamber and the banqueting hall where Vortigern held his rare but magnificent feasts. Lights blazed from every window.

The private apartments lay behind her. Beneath the centre of the illuminated first floor of the public rooms lay an archway leading out to the palace, flanked, she could see, by Hengest's men, standing in knots talking and laughing. The torches beneath the archway and glow from the windows lit up their drooping moustaches, rough skins, and fierce eyes.

Opposite, through another central arch between the guest apartments, were domestic buildings and, beyond those, the lower gardens leading down to the water gate. Would that, too, be guarded? Why so many of these Saex, so many lights and moving shadows beyond the windows? She could hear the distant hum of voices, the bark of male laughter. Melwas had talked of a feast. What was happening?

She eased forward, keeping low, wriggling on her belly where necessary, making full use of the concealing shadows from low walls, shrubs, and hedges. Clearing the arch, running for the darker hiding places, she found herself in the domestic quarters. The unmistakable aroma of horses assailed her; urine, dung, hay. Few men were about here. She peered cautiously into the first barn, slid inside, and, ducking under a rail, settled herself beneath the manger at the far end of the stall. The occupant, a wise-eyed bay of good quality, snorted and snuffed suspiciously at her. Losing interest, he returned to his hay.

Warmth, and the steady munch of horses eating, was relaxing and soothing. Gwenhwyfar ached, every bone and muscle felt battered. Her right eye was barely open, her eyelid and cheek bruised. She hurt dreadfully where he had so roughly penetrated her.

Gwenhwyfar laid both hands on her belly, wondering. She had thought of this thing often during the long days at sea. Was the sickness all from the swell of the tide? The need to speak with a woman had been desperate, but impossible. But did she need confirmation? Her bleeding had not come, surely she needed no other sign? One thing to be thankful for, she had known before this night that she carried Arthur's child, had known days before Melwas took her.

She trembled again as she remembered him. His grotesque form as he knelt over her, his leer of triumph as he had entered her. Gwenhwyfar closed her eyes, felt the ground beneath her spinning.

She wanted to sleep, to find oblivion, but she could not, she was not safe here. At any moment Melwas and his Saex dogs might come searching. She managed to get to her feet, clung to the horse with his soft warmth and un-yielding strength. Friendly, he nuzzled her, welcoming the company. Gently, she pulled one of his brown ears as a parting gesture and slipped back into the night.

From here she had no idea which way to go. Noticing a pile of discarded sacking, she selected a suitable length and fastened it around her shoulders, using one of the gaudy Saxon brooches to secure it. She stole in the direction of the kitchens, hoping to blend in with scurrying servants and slaves. No one paid her any attention; she must look as shabby and dirty as any of them if her legs and feet were anything to go by.

A mule cart was making to leave by the narrow service gate. Taking her chance, Gwenhwyfar ran and, resting a hand on the back, walked behind the vehicle for all the world as if she belonged to the carter.

He never noticed her, being busy at the heads of the mules, and the guard at the gate did not glance her way. She was out!

Think quickly! The eastern area of the city, once a wealthy district, she knew to be almost derelict. It had been abandoned during the last plague to sweep through Londinium and no one had come back to claim property—happen they were no longer alive, or had no inclination to return. She ducked down a small side street between palace walls and shops, and ran silently on bare feet keeping to the shadows, ever watchful. Once, at a street intersection, she almost ran into a group of drunken Saex. Gwenhwyfar hid in a doorway, her heart pounding, and let them weave past. She was more careful after that.

The rain fell steadily. She was sodden, cold, and so very tired. With a sob of relief, found a building she remembered. She had walked through this obsolete corner of Londinium one afternoon, attempting to escape the palace confines and Winifred's tedium. How long ago was that? It seemed like centuries past.

This particular house she remembered well. It was large and had obviously belonged to someone of great importance. She had asked various people at the palace but no one seemed to know or care who its owner had been.

Apart from broken windows and its partly fallen roof, it looked habitable from the outside. She squeezed past the door, which leaned askew from one hinge, and picked her way carefully through weeds and debris. Something scrunched under her feet, a sharp pain shot through her right sole. She muffled a cry and slumped against the wall, hunkering amongst the scatter of sharp-edged, broken roof tiles.

At least it was sheltered here, and away from the noise of the streets. In the distance she heard drunken men singing, and, further away, shouting. Nothing more.

TWENTY-NINE

G WENHWYFAR MUST HAVE SLEPT, FOR A SOUND STARTLED HER AWAKE. SHE groaned; her body felt as though it were being torn very slowly into pieces. The shouting she had heard earlier, before drifting asleep, was now louder, more persistent, and definable. Shouts and cries. Frightened screams. Footsteps ran by, fairly close, nailed boots rapping along the cobbled road leading to the nearest city gate. More followed; a crowd of people panting as they ran, someone among them sobbing; the cry of a baby.

Clinging to the solidity of the wall, Gwenhwyfar pulled herself upright, wincing as her cut foot touched the ground. Staying within the shadows, she limped cautiously to a broken window and peeped out. As she bent forward, the sacking around her shoulders caught on something sharp and ripped. The brooch tumbled to the floor; she heard the chink as it fell, made no move to retrieve it. Let it lie among the shards of roof tiles for someone else to find! Ugly thing.

She could see nothing beyond the fallen building between herself and the road, except a vague blur of hurried movement. As quietly as she could, given the darkness and the rubble on the floor, Gwenhwyfar crept from the house, curiosity drawing her back in the direction of the palace, from where the confused sounds of distress came.

She reached the main roadway and found herself looking at a panic-stricken crowd flooding past. Men and women, mothers with babies in their arms, others with frightened children clutching at their skirts. Slaves and servants mingled with the free, all of them pushing and clawing their way forward, desperate to reach the gateways out of the city, to get to the open marshes and fields beyond, to head for the distant spread of woodland.

Wild, drunken Saex were herding them, swinging forward into the terrified crush of people, slaughtering any they caught hold of, man, woman, or child. Maiming and laughing.

Two came close to Gwenhwyfar's sheltered hiding place, engrossed in kicking some ragged thing before their feet. It struck against the wall a few paces before her, rolled away, and was trampled and swept forward by other feet. The Saex, swearing and cursing at the loss of their plaything, reeled drunkenly after it.

Sickness choked Gwenhwyfar as she recognised the thing. A child's open-mouthed severed head.

Trembling, she retraced her steps along the alley, back into the sheltered, quiet darkness of the squalid, mostly untenanted buildings. At a movement to her left, she squeezed herself into a doorway, through the door hanging by its rusted hinges. Four Saex reeled from a corner wine shop, its frontage broken down by the industry of their axes. One carried an unstoppered amphora, its contents spilling out; the others, shouting with laughter, dragged a luckless slave girl. She was screaming, pleading for help that would not come. She kicked one of the brutes, who swore and threw her to the ground.

His companions cheered as he unfastened his bracae.

Gwenhwyfar crouched, buried her head, hands pressed tight to her ears. She did not want to see or hear, but she could not blot out the sounds and movement as the four of them took swaggering turns at the girl. Her screams rose with the first two, then faltered. After the fourth, fell silent after one last, shrill sound.

The Saex lurched away, gulping their wine, searching for fresh sport. Eventually they met with a group of British soldiers who dispatched the barbarians as dispassionately as they had slit the girl open.

Gwenhwyfar hesitated, unsure which way to go. To the palace, or back into the derelict quarter?

Footsteps, the sound of boots moving nearer. A group of men, shadows only, at the intersection of alleys slightly to the left. Gwenhwyfar drew back into her safe place, flattening herself against the wall, her breath held.

She had ready the dagger she had stolen from the guard outside Melwas's room. One man stopped, bent over the body of the murdered girl.

He swore vehemently. Ripping the helmet off his head, he wiped his hand over an ashen face.

"What in God's name is happening here?" he asked rhetorically.

Gwenhwyfar closed her eyes for a joyous moment of thankful prayer, then ran forward, sobbing with relief, tears pouring down her cheeks. "Cei! Cei!"

The man swung up, saw the running figure, stood alert with sword raised; glimpsed a face barely recognisable beneath blood and bruise.

"Gwenhwyfar! What are you doing here?" She was in the safety of his arms, leaning against him.

On his barked orders, a protective wedge of men formed instantly around their commander and the young woman clinging to him. Cei managed to make a little sense out of her confused torrent of words, and using his brain, added two and two and came up, more or less rightly, with a tally of four.

"Melwas is back?" he asked urgently, holding her from him. When she nodded, he swore a heathen oath. "Do you know where he is now?"

She shook her head.

One of the men, as grey-faced as his commander, said, "Let us pray to God we are not too late for Arthur."

Gwenhwyfar's heart lurched. She put a hand to her mouth. "Arthur?" she cried. "He is here?"

"Vortigern has him under arrest," said Cei. He was looking up and down the alley as he spoke.

Gwenhwyfar felt her legs go weak, and as she crumpled Cei eased her to the ground, wrapped his own cloak around her.

She came round almost immediately in a state of great distress. "I did not know Arthur was here," she muttered. "What have I done?" She clutched at Cei's hand, her nails digging deep into the flesh. "Melwas—does he know Arthur is here?"

"It was Melwas who escorted him to the cells some days since." The soldiers' peering, anxious faces blurred before her. The words of her taunt at Melwas echoed like some evil chant. "Arthur!" she scrambled to her feet, pushing Cei aside, her pain forgotten. "He is in danger!" She was desperate to make them understand!

"Aye, we know, that is why we are here, a last attempt to free him."

"Na, you could not know. Melwas, I told him—I..." Oh, they would not understand!

Cei was holding her arm tight, keeping her close, steering her forward at a trot now as they neared the palace. Her foot stabbed, her legs and arms and ribs screamed with each breath, each movement of muscle, but she did not care, cared for nothing save running with Cei to find Arthur!

They entered through the same service gate she had left by, save there were no guards there now. They could hear screaming and the smell of blood and fear hung heavy in the air.

Cei would have preferred not to be encumbered by a woman, but what choice had he? Leave her—amid this madness of death and destruction?

They waited within the palace walls to assess their next move, then ran to the rear of the kitchens. The screaming was louder here. "Why leave it so long before helping him?" Gwenhwyfar panted.

Cei glanced at her. "I have been pleading with Vortigern all this while—tonight I gave up only to find the city crawling with Saex. They are like carrion come to pick over the dead." He nodded back towards the city. "Particularly in that direction. I have lost three of my men getting this far."

They ran behind the height of a woodpile, paused for breath. The noise and stench reminded Gwenhwyfar of animal slaughter pens.

The kitchen door was flung wide, casting a beam of light across the courtyard. A woman lurched out, bleeding profusely from a near severed arm. She came close, screamed as one of Cei's soldiers caught her and dragged her into the shadows. They bound her arm, gave her drink from a leather flask; took some while to calm her.

"What is happening?" Cei had to repeat the question over and over.

All he could get at first were the words, "Saex" and "killing." Then, as she calmed, "The Saex have killed all at the King's Gather! Now they slaughter servants and slaves also!" Cei looked at his men, stunned. But then, was it so hard to believe?

"It had to happen," one man said.

Another said, "A mad dog eventually turns to bite his master's hand."

They left the dying woman, tucking her for her safety deep behind the pile, then made their way slowly forward, dodging between buildings, killing those Saxons who reeled into their path, ignoring bodies strewn at their feet.

Breathless, they reached Vortigern's cells, a stone-built building at the farthest easterly corner of the perimeter walls.

Cei ordered two men to stay outside, told Gwenhwyfar to remain with them.

"I will not stay out here, with this." She indicated the small rectangular courtyard and three bodies. Two men, one woman with her skirts thrown over her head, blood that had trickled down her thighs, drying.

He did not like it, but said, "Follow, then. Stay well back."

She nodded, entering the narrow corridor into the building cautiously behind the men, feeling the comfort of the stolen dagger gripped tight in her hand. Cei motioned for silence. They heard Melwas's voice ahead and his malicious laugh, followed by the sound of blows.

Cei's eyes narrowed and he stepped forward, his sword waving before him. They came to a corner and peered round, Gwenhwyfar shouldering her way through the men.

Two Saex guards stood in an open doorway ahead. From beyond, Melwas's voice.

"I was ordered to kill you, and so I shall. Slowly and with pain, Pendragon. When they find you come morning they will think you were just another victim of these murdering barbarians. Make a fool of me, would you? I think not." Melwas struck again—then felt, rather than heard, a movement behind him.

He turned, gasped, as he saw two things. The guards falling dead, blood gushing from throats slashed open, and Cei lunging forward.

For all his weight, Melwas moved swiftly, parrying the blow with the handle of his whip. They grappled. Melwas kicked out, sent Cei sprawling.

He raised the whip, intending to strike Cei, but the blow never fell. Melwas slumped forward, blood trickling from his open, surprised mouth.

Gwenhwyfar stared at the dagger in her hand, at the warm slime of blood sliding down the blade, staining her clenched fingers.

One of Cei's men ran forward and slashed through the ropes binding the Pendragon; another knelt over Cei, who lay dazed.

With great effort, gasping from pain and lack of breath, Arthur pulled himself upright, stumbled to Gwenhwyfar.

"You look as I feel," he croaked.

With a sob, she flung the weapon away and herself into his arms. He let her stay there, let her cry for a while, stroking her hair, murmuring soothing words, wincing as jolts of pain shot through his own hurts.

She tried to speak once, but he shushed her quiet. "I know what happened, my Cymraes. He bragged of it to me." The bastard, every detail.

"You do not understand," she sobbed, catching her breath. "I told him it was you who first had me; I did not know you were here!"

The full impact of her mocking words to Melwas struck her. "He was going to kill you because we were lovers!" Her voice rose, hysterical.

Arthur tried to calm her, holding her close, holding her tight, though it hurt; kissing her with difficulty through his own swollen lips. "He was here to do that anyway. Vortigern had given the order for it to be done this night, while all were occupied with this Gathering of treaty."

His head jerked up as Cei clambered to his feet, snorting, "Not treaty: massacre. The Saex have turned, made their move. Hengest picked the time and place well."

Arthur cursed obscenely. "There have been some happenings this night which will not be easily forgotten."

One of the men left on guard outside ran in. He saluted when he saw Arthur, carefully avoiding looking directly at the more obvious hurts on his body.

"Sir, a few of the palace buildings have been fired and Lord Vortimer has at last arrived with soldiers—some of them our lads. They say Hengest's rabble are too far gone with wine and blood-lust to put up much more of a fight. Most are taking to their ships."

Cei nodded curtly. "Detail four men to escort Lady Gwenhwyfar and the Pendragon to safety."

Arthur interrupted. "Hold that order, soldier! Four men to escort the lady, and someone to find me clothing of whatever sort, and suitable weapons; quickly!"

The soldier saluted smartly and ran off at the double. Cei began to protest. "You are in no fit state to fight!"

"On the contrary, I have never been fitter!" More gently, "Anger does wonders for the healing of hurts, Cei." As he talked, Arthur rubbed at Gwenhwyfar's arms, attempting to ease the trembling chill. Her eyes, hollow in sunken sockets, gazed at the spreading dark patch on Melwas's cloak between the shoulder blades. She shuddered.

"Let us leave here," Arthur said, indicating the body. "She has seen enough horror for one day." He added in lower tones, "And I'd not be sorry to leave."

"Like as not to see many more before dawn," Cei muttered, taking one last look around as they made their way outside.

Arthur gulped mouthfuls of sweet air, grateful that few had seen his conditions of imprisonment or noticed the haunted look in his eyes. Melwas had treated him brutally, but the beatings and floggings had been nothing compared to the enclosing darkness. He swallowed hard, fighting the remnant of his childhood phobia, unsure how he had survived the clutching terror of these past days. But survive it he had. He was here, in the air, living and breathing.

Clothing appeared, a Saxon tunic, bracae, and short sword. Arthur made a noise of disgust but dressed without further protest. Even Saex weave was preferable to bare skin.

"Lady Gwenhwyfar must be taken clear, then we will see to our business." He clapped Cei's shoulder, grinning. Fresh air and freedom coursed through him. He felt little of the swelling or bruising, nor the spiteful pull of lash marks across his back. Tomorrow would be time enough to wince and allow the shakes of fear to run their course.

He beckoned a man to him. "What is the situation beyond the palace walls?"

"None too good, Sir. Part of the city is burning—what they cannot loot they fire. The river is crammed with their ships. Little hope for the poor beggars who live out there, even with us now here."

Arthur scowled. The picture, although for a soldier a familiar enough one, saddened him. "This could be the end of Londinium. Plague; trade diminishing down the years to a dribble; and now this? Love of the Bull, Cei, did he not realise this would happen?"

"Vortigern? I think not. He hoped ceding the Cantii territory would be enough for Hengest."

Arthur buckled on the sword belt, nodded in the direction of the stables. "We shall use the horses. I will not let good stock go to waste."

It took a while to bridle the stabled mounts, for the smell of blood and smoke and the crackle of flames made them uneasy and restless. Five were hastily saddled and four men mounted, leading the reins of the spare mounts. Arthur helped Gwenhwyfar on to the fifth. She winced as she seated herself, and patted the fidgeting horse, feeling a tingle of comfort on realising it was that same bay she had met earlier.

Arthur gripped her thigh, smiled up at her. "My men will escort you through the city—the Saex are on the run by the sound of it. You should get through safe. Stay within the mass of horses, none shall touch you there. Once clear, go to our camp, rest there. I will join you as soon as I can." Whenever that would be!

He stepped away and slapped a hand on the horse's rump, sending it springing forward. The others surged round and they set off at a canter, hurtling beneath the archway, through the gates, and out into the streets. Drunken groups of remaining Saex sprang aside with cries of alarm as the hooves came trampling. The horses gathered speed, galloping now, ears laid flat, nostrils flaring in a frenzy to escape the smells and sounds of surrounding fear.

The west gate loomed ahead, watch-towers standing empty, unmanned and shrouded in smoke and flame. The great gate stood wide, but a group of Hengest's men stood ground before them, waving their arms and shouting. The leading horses, already terrified, baulked. One reared, throwing his rider. In an instant, the Saex were on them.

THIRTY

Londinium was finished. Not even on a battlefield had Arthur seen such carnage.

Dressed in uniform now, after an hour's snatched sleep and some welcome hot food in his belly, he stalked through the smoking remains of the city. He poked at bodies with his toe, his frown of anger deepening.

They had found Gwenhwyfar's escort, their bodies horribly cut to pieces and hung like dead rats on the city gate. Four men, no woman.

Arthur stopped by a naked female. Her body bulged with pregnancy, her eyes staring, mouth open, her screams frozen in death. He wondered if they had mutilated her before or after they had killed her. How many had taken her? She was little more than Gwenhwyfar's age. He groaned, turned aside, and was violently sick.

The three men behind respectfully turned their gaze away from his grey, beard-stubbled face.

Arthur walked on, one of the men stepped to his side said with quiet sympathy, "We will find her, Sir. We will."

Arthur looked at him, glanced meaningfully back at the girl's body. "I am not entirely sure I want to."

They entered the palace grounds. More bodies, more blood. To the left, the prison cells. Arthur made to turn to the right, thought again, headed left.

"Search over there," he ordered, pointing away from the cells, "I have a task of my own to do."

It took him an eternity to step through the doorway from dull sunlight into musty darkness. Heart hammering, sweat trickling down his back he eased forward along the internal corridor.

Melwas lay there, none having bothered with him. It was a petty thing to do but when he had finished Arthur felt an immense satisfaction of revenge. His only regret, the body was long dead. Punishment for rape should be dealt to the living.

He stood upright, wiped the soiled blade of his dagger on Melwas's cloak, and left, hurrying from the oppressive place.

Arthur was not a religious man. Save for his faith in the soldiers' god, Mithras, he used appropriate gods as and when he required them. At this moment, he welcomed the belief of a world beyond, praying that the humiliation he had caused to Melwas's manhood would reach the spirit and plunge it into internal suffering.

The body was discovered some few days later by a Romano-British woman searching for food and safe shelter. She fled at the brief glimpse of a man's mutilated body, his private parts hacked off and stuffed into his mouth. Telling others of the scene, she would add, "*Wicked are these Saex! Barbarian wicked.*"

For Arthur, it had been small recompense, but Gwenhwyfar would appreciate the gesture. If he ever got to tell her. He bit his lip. She was not within the city, that much was certain, and she had not reached the camp. If Hengest's Saex had her, there was only one way to barter for her return. Exchange her for Rowena or Winifred.

Rejoining them, Arthur growled at his men to follow. Cei was making his way across the bloodied courtyard from the direction of the great hall.

"Leave all this," Arthur bellowed as the man came closer. "We ride to Caer Gloui."

Cei chewed his lip, staring bleakly at the surrounding heaps of bodies. He sighed. So much death, so much more to come. "Vortimer wishes to speak with you."

Arthur repeated an oath, ordered his men to get the horses ready.

"Has Vortigern been found?" he asked as he walked with Cei.

"Vortimer has him, I do not give much for his chances of survival should anyone lay hands on him. The British are shouting for his head—and other parts."

"A shame they did not do so before now. Ah, Vortimer!" Arthur stepped through charred timbers into what remained of the great council hall. The bodies of those murdered had been removed, but the bloodstains pooling the tessellated floor remained. One relief was that many elders and nobles had deliberately stayed away from Vortigern's call to this Gathering of Council as a protest. Those who sided with the King or sought favour were the unfortunates. Some, Arthur privately mused, they were well rid of!

The King's eldest son, Vortimer, looked up, haggard, from a parchment he was reading. Behind him his brother Catigern stared warily at Arthur. It was no secret that one day the Pendragon would make a bid for the kingship. The brothers, it seemed, were pooling their strength against him. Today the door to power stood wide open, but together they barred entrance with spears crossed. It would not be this day the Pendragon took command.

Arthur perched himself on the edge of a charred bench. "This was bound to happen eventually. No soldier, Saex or British, will fight unpaid without strong cause. There must be a reward at the end. Our men fight for their homeland, women, and children. What is there for the Saex? They fight in Vortigern's army for no quarrel of their own. If they are not given what they ask it must be expected that one day they will take it." He halted. Neither of the old king's sons answered.

Arthur went on, "They were hired as mercenaries to swell the army so Vortigern could hold sway over counter claimants to the throne—against men like my father. They are no different from countless other such troops employed by Rome in this country and others." Silence from Vortimer and Catigern. Arthur finished with a slight shrug of one shoulder. "They were not paid. Were given nothing, save empty promises. The Saex were never to be content with only the occasional tossed bone."

He thumped the bench, then lurched to his feet. "Do not look at me as if it were I who caused all this! As I hear things, Council voted against Vortigern, refused to cede the land as payment. Hengest intended to take what he wanted with or without permission." He gestured at the mess. Shouting almost, he concluded, "If I were in Hengest's boots, like as not I would do the same!"

Catigern stepped forward at that. "A pretty speech, Pendragon. It sounds to my ears almost as though you back Hengest. Are you in league with him, then— you and your bitch wife?"

Arthur refused to take the bait, not wishing to become involved in argument. He needed to be gone. "Na, man, grant me more sense than that! I am pointing out Hengest's view. A leader's view."

About to make some hot reply, Catigern was silenced by his elder brother who asked, "You deny all knowledge that Hengest was intending to rebel?"

"Beyond personal speculation, aye." Arthur was becoming suspicious. "What is all this?"

"You deny plotting to murder our father; that your wife was to help you?"

"Of course I bloody deny it! Blood of Mithras, I have been in the cells facing death myself for the Bull knows how many days!"

Catigern sneered, "A place of convenient safety."

Never having liked Catigern much Arthur thought it best to ignore him, to talk instead direct to Vortimer. "What has my wife to do with this? Ex-wife. I have applied for legal divorce."

Vortimer tapped the parchment he had been reading on his palm. "That is not what she says, not in this letter."

"What letter?" Arthur held out his hand for it.

Vortimer hesitated, then passed it over, saying, "I found it among my father's papers."

Arthur scanned the words quickly, tossed the thing back to Vortimer. "I have not seen it before. What she says is rubbish. I will take the kingdom if I get a chance—you know that—but not with her, not on her plotting. I say again, I am to divorce her and marry with Gwenhwyfar." He brought his head forward, his eyes narrowing, said menacingly, "May I remind you both whose idea it was I marry Winifred in the first place? I did not want her then. I do not want her now."

Catigern growled, "Yet you were at my father's throat the other day."

Arthur sneered at him. "When am I not? I usually have good cause. Come to that, when are you not?"

Vortimer released a long sigh. "We had to be certain, Arthur—you do see?"

He did not, but again, he let the matter pass.

Vortimer tore the parchment in half and half again, let the pieces fall to the floor. "Council, for right or wrong, condemned the giving of land as payment for service. Vortigern gambled and lost and the Saex responded with murder. It is in my mind Hengest knew full well he would not get what he wanted so easily and used the occasion as his chance to strike. As you rightly say, Arthur, now he will try to take whatever else he wants. While we are in disarray, he will step in with Rowena and the boy."

"So what do you intend to do? I assume you have taken command?"

Disliking the tone of Arthur's question, Catigern pushed himself further forward to defend his brother. "He intends to regroup the army—our army, British men. We will make a stand against Hengest. A wise decision, do you not think, Pendragon? Or is this a chance for you to seize command?"

Arthur laughed, amused at the hostility. "Aye, it is." Turning his back on Catigern he stood beside Vortimer.

"I have already said, I know nothing of this plot between my wife or Rowena and their Saex kin. I am not sorry to see Vortigern fall—we share the same sentiment there." He winced at the stiffness in his limbs. "If I were foolish enough to dispute leadership with you at this moment, Vortimer, what few fighting men we possess would be obliged to take up arms against each other. Many would rally to my Dragon, but as many would go to your Red Boar. Would that not be playing into Hengest's hands?"

He turned his head, his eyes piercing Catigern. "Hengest knows Vortigern's fall will re-open the dispute of leadership." He directed his attention back to Vortimer, held out his hand in friendship. His knuckles and fingers were blood-ied, bruised, and swollen where Melwas had repeatedly stamped into the flesh.

"For all your brother's taunts, Vortimer, I can wait a short while longer."

Vortimer visibly relaxed, accepted Arthur's hand. "I am relieved to hear it. I would not wish to give the order to, er, detain you, should your plans not be, shall we say, beneficial?"

Arthur smiled lazily. "Yet I noticed neither you nor friend Catigern here at-tempted to secure my release from your father and cousin's pleasures? It would have suited you to be rid of me at the expense of someone else's conscience."

Vortimer began to protest, but Arthur lifted a hand to silence him. "In your position I would have done the same." Though, he thought, with more ef-ficiency, no wasting time with sadistic pleasures. Arthur would have had them instantly hanged.

"While you show sense, Vortimer," Arthur grimaced as he stretched the ache from his shoulders, "I will buckle myself to your orders." He paused, regarding Britain's new king. "For a price."

"Which is?"

"My father's West Country lands. Dumnonia and the Summer Land must return to my overlordship; and custody of Rowena, her son Vitolinus, and Winifred."

Vortimer frowned. "Melwas is lord of the Summer Land, and Meirchion gov-ernor of Dumnonia. Were I to say take them, I would have two men up in arms against me."

"Melwas is dead."

Vortimer raised an eyebrow. "You are certain?"

Arthur seated himself again, regretted it as fire shot across his buttocks, up his back, and through his shoulders. Riding was going to be an agony.

"I can show you his body."

A smile formed on Vortimer's lips. "One less problem to deal with then."

Arthur said, "And Meirchion is a worm who slithers from rock to rock. He allied with Vortigern against my father. It is only a matter of time before I kill him also, for all he is cousin to my father."

"I would rather you delayed in the slaughter of too many men you hold in dislike, Arthur. Enough died here last night; if you add to the tally, I will be hard pressed to form a Council."

Saying nothing, Arthur simply regarded Vortimer, his silence making his intention all the clearer. He would have the West returned. Legally given, or in his own way.

"I freely grant you the Summer Land. But Dumnonia with it? That would make you a powerful man, Pendragon."

"With or without the land, Vortimer, I am close to being that. If I wanted, I could hold most of the army. With men at my back I can take all I want, without waiting for you to give it."

This was true. Vortimer puffed out his cheeks. "May I suggest a compromise? Meirchion has no male heir and is growing old. Persuade him you are to be that heir."

"I have your word you will recognise such an agreement when the man dies?"

"If I in turn have your sworn fealty to me, then sa, it shall be so." Vortimer regarded Arthur sternly. He knew the position. The Pendragon was not yet strong enough to make his claim, but give him a few more men to command, more campaigns and experience under his belt, and the situation would change. To hold the entire West Country, as his father once had, would give him command over those needed men and bring in the wealth to attract and finance others. This cavalry idea of his, for instance, would be a viable concern were Arthur to have the finances those territories would bring, and would provide the grazing land for the breeding, rearing, and keeping of horses.

"I have already agreed to fight alongside you," Arthur said, heaving himself upright, stifling a groan. "In as much as fighting the Saex anyway. More, I cannot guarantee."

Vortimer walked a few paces, considering.

Catigern had been silent, but now he went to his brother, spoke in a low tone. Arthur caught a few not over-complimentary words.

Vortimer replied sharply, ushered Catigern aside. Arthur was no fool and he was a good soldier—too good. There was every possibility the bulk of the straggling British army would decide to follow the Pendragon today, would not wait for the morrow.

Arthur said, with a good humour that emphasised his intent, "I will have the land, Vortimer. It was my father's and his father's before him. It is mine by right. Vortigern stole it. I am taking it back."

"By agreeing I give away a substantial portion of revenue."

"Which is why Vortigern took it in the first place to parcel out to his lapdogs. Your father had control over all but Gwynedd and the wild lands to the north." Arthur shrugged, made as if to leave. "Keep your legacy whole then, Vortimer. If you can."

"Hold!" the new King called, raising his hands. "I do not have the ambitions of Vortigern. I am a soldier, not a king or emperor. As long as we can achieve the same aim—to hold these barbarians from our shores—then I am content. Have your land."

"But brother…" Catigern blurted disagreement. He had hoped for the same package Arthur was claiming. Vortimer was giving Arthur the position of second-in-command!

"Na, Catigern!" Vortimer rounded on his brother. "I have no hope of holding this kingdom together. Vortigern tried and failed. Let Arthur have what is his, and good luck to him."

He clasped Arthur's hand, "Understand it is yours to see to, though. Do not come bleating to me when you find Meirchion is not willing to submit to you."

"Oh, he will submit," Arthur said confidently.

Vortimer had no reason to doubt him, fully expected to receive word the Governor of Dumnonia had met with some "accidental" death ere many moons waned. So be it—the matter was not his problem.

"The women and the boy?" Arthur asked.

"The boy is too young. I will not have him harmed."

Catigern, already angry with his brother's decision, burst out, "You cannot let him remain free! God's truth, why not hang your sword up now!"

"Hold your tongue!" Vortimer roared. "I am King. I say what is to be! I have no intention of letting the half-Saex boy loose, but nor will I have him harmed. I command you, Pendragon, to see him placed in close custody somewhere safe."

Arthur nodded. He could accept that, for now. "And Rowena?"

"Rowena is to be executed on a charge of treason."

Arthur thought briefly before answering. It would give him great pleasure to comply, but, "Is that wise? Will it not antagonise Hengest?"

"I care not what Hengest thinks of my decisions. She is evil and I would have an end to her."

"What of Vortigern?" Arthur queried, letting the subject rest a moment. "Someone said he was not killed?"

Vortimer's answer was hard as stone. "They left him alive. Hengest, apparently, would not order the death of his daughter's husband." He added sarcastically, "Kin, you see."

Catigern spat. "Vortigern ought to hang alongside Rowena!"

His brother indicated a bundle huddled in a far corner. "I agree, but there is nothing left worth hanging."

Puzzled, Arthur crossed the hall, tore away a layer of what he had taken to be piled rags. He drew in his breath sharply as he gazed on a crumpled, pathetic old man, slavering at the mouth, whimpering and mumbling feebly.

Vortigern. The translucent skin drawn tight over his bones gave his face the look of a skeleton's mask. He fumbled for the protective covering Arthur had pulled aside and withdrew into its shielding darkness, eyes staring, seeing the red blood gushing, hearing men and women shrieking. His world had collapsed and his mind had fled.

Vortimer stood at Arthur's shoulder, regarding the sorry shell of his father. "He will not trouble us again. He ought to die, but it would be as pointless as murdering a child."

Arthur did not agree, but held his council.

Vortimer asked, "Can I trust you to see to Rowena's end?"

Arthur looked wearily at the man, his King. "I cannot say. I thought to exchange her for Gwenhwyfar, should she be held captive."

"Is that likely?" Vortimer placed a sympathetic hand on Arthur's arm, aware of her disappearance. "When we have defeated these barbarians, when they are on the run, they will not be in any position to bargain. I promise you, Arthur, when Hengest capitulates before me you can demand from him what you will. For now, I must have Rowena dead, if only for my own satisfaction. She defiled the memory of my mother and she must pay for it. I would that I could personally string her up, but I have an army to bring together. I ask again, Arthur—can I trust you?"

Arthur thought on it. Were he to go seeking Rowena he would be conveniently absent from the army. With no Pendragon to rally to, those men who had small liking for Vortigern's progeny would follow Vortimer through lack of choice. He ran a hand through his hair. He would like a bath, but idle luxury must wait. It had been a rash idea, this one of exchange, clutching at frayed rope. Leave it.

Vortimer added, seeing Arthur's doubt, "You must face the facts, man. If they do have Gwenhwyfar, then what is left of her will not be worth taking back. For you, she is dead, Arthur. Dead."

"She is alive, of that I am certain." Arthur held his hand out to seal their agreement. "Very well, you have my word Rowena will hang for treason. So too, shall Winifred."

Vortimer shrugged, uncaring. "Do what you will with her, she is your wife. You know where to find them?"

"Aye, Melwas insisted on informing me. At Vortigern's summer villa outside Caer Gloui."

After he had gone, Catigern, bitter at his brother's ruling said, "You are a fool to trust the Pendragon. I am your brother; I should hold the honour of high command, not he."

Vortimer was standing close to where his bundled father lay. He nudged the heap of rags with his toe and the thing shifted, crabbing across the floor.

"If you think you could hold higher command than the Pendragon, then it is you who are the fool, Catigern."

MAY 455

THIRTY-ONE

I^T HAD RAINED, ON AND OFF, FOR MOST OF THAT SPRING. THE RIVERS were running swollen, crops lay rotten and blackened, and mud oozed thick, clinging and stinking. The low ground between the Hafren and Caer Gloui was continuously soggy underfoot, squelching beneath boots, seeping into dwelling places and old people's bones. The river would burst its banks soon if the rain did not cease. There was little anyone could do, save wait, watch, and pray.

Arthur rode into the Caer two days after the beginning of the month. He hated this town—and more, hated its inhabitants.

"They are like those eastern birds Aegidius of Gaul has strutting around his palace grounds," he said to Cei, riding at his side. "Peacocks, birds stuffed fat with their own importance."

"This is a rich area," Cei answered neutrally.

"What has wealth to do with it?" Arthur snorted his contempt. "Not all rich men are crinkle-nosed asses!"

Cei laughed. "Most are! Even you!"

Arthur blustered indignation and Cei laughed the louder. "You are so sure of your own convictions you will never tolerate other people's views!"

"That is not true!"

"Na?"

"Na. I listen to some people."

Cei roared delight. "Only those who agree with you! Take these townsfolk. You know but a handful of them, yet you judge all by those few. There may be one or two pleasant families living hereabouts."

Straight-faced, Arthur nodded towards a man who was approaching, hitching one trailing end of a worn toga from the mired road.

"Think you this may be one of the two, Cei?"

The man shook his fist. "You are not thinking to ride through this town with that rabble in attendance!" He was shouting, red-faced, pointing at the sixty mounted men of Arthur's two turmae.

Arthur halted Eira, swung round in his saddle, and regarded the men behind him, as if he were surprised to find them there. He scratched the stubbled beard on his face and sniffed loudly. "I am not thinking of it, old man." He nudged his horse forward at a walk, his men following.

Cheeks scarlet, the elderly man stepped in front of the stallion, causing Eira to toss his head and lay his ears back. Arthur eased a hand down the rain-soaked neck.

"I will not tolerate unlawful gangs of, of..." the man blustered, seeking an appropriate word, "of heathen Vandals entering this town!"

Arthur half grinned at Cei. "Not even one or two."

Cei chuckled.

"There is nothing amusing about this!" The man's voice was rising. "You army people are all the same, think you own the place! Unless you have come to help shore the river banks against flood, get you gone!" He waved his arm about, setting the horses dancing.

Arthur had heard enough. "In the first place, my men are not a rabble. They are a trained, disciplined cavalry unit. Secondly, we have ridden many miles in this incessant rain. We are cold, wet, hungry, and tired. My men and their horses require shelter."

"Then seek it outside the town!"

"There are inns aplenty within. And third," Arthur leant forward, across his stallion's neck, said emphatically, "I am not thinking of riding through, I *am* riding through."

He spurred his horse forward, the animal responding to the pressure of heel and leg, shouldering the obstructing man aside.

The two turmae rode solemnly past, not daring to let the laughter inside them show, leaving the man shaking his fist and spluttering apoplectic oaths.

The inns welcomed them with pleasure, grateful for custom. Travellers were few and far between this wet weather.

After seeing men and animals well settled, Cei and Arthur retreated to a quiet corner of their chosen quarters, welcomed the steaming bowls of broth placed before them.

"I rather think you ought not have angered the old man."

Arthur sucked broth from his bowl. "Daft old dung-heap."

"Na, you will not be famed for being a leader with tact," Cei grinned.

"Tactics, not tact, interest me more." Mopping up the last of his broth with a chunk of bread, Arthur pushed away the empty bowl and reached for wine. "They annoy me, people like him. First to complain, first to belly-ache and whine. Last to *do* anything. How many give a toss about what is happening east of here? How many give a damn about Vortigern's failed, blundering policies and this mess we are mired in?"

Cei wiped spillage from his lips. The broth had been good. "More than we would give credit for. The Hibernian raid heavily along the coasts." Cei signalled to the innkeeper for a refill. "These people are as aware as we are of the dangers in losing control."

"Oh aye, they are aware. As you say, sea-wolves come along the coast looking for land ripe for the taking. Go fight the Saex, keep them from our doorstep, they say. Yet when it comes to paying the army or hosting us for a night, Caer Gloui and such towns are of a sudden safe within their walls, have their own militias and weapons. The army is not needed. Not wanted. Go away! Fah!" He spat into the fire, sending up a hiss of sparks.

The innkeeper's daughter brought the broth and a second jug of wine, good quality stuff set aside for men of rank and means. Her liquid dark eyes met with Arthur's. She blushed, lowered her gaze.

"The bathhouse is available should you require its use," she said shyly, not meeting his eyes. Arthur's line of sight flickered to her rounded bosom; glanced at a figure who sat hunched and dozing, his clothes steaming, before the heat of the fire.

"Gladly would I accept such an offer," Arthur indicated Cynan, "but my servant is asleep. He is a faithful lad and I have not the inclination to disturb him." Rubbish. What were servants for? The girl blushed a second time, said quietly, "I am sure I can arrange an alternative attendant, my Lord."

Arthur grinned at that, pushed the bench from him as he stood. "Then lead on, girl!" He winked at Cei, who stretched, laughing.

"No tact," Cei said. "Open and obvious!"

THIRTY-TWO

S HAVED, CLEAN, AND RELAXED FROM A NIGHT OF PLEASURE AND SLEEP, ARTHUR entered Vortigern's private residence sited beside a curve of the Hafren two miles beyond the west gate of the Caer. It was still raining and the river, Arthur noted absently, was already lapping against the outer wall. He was not surprised to find Winifred and her mother expecting him.

Winifred ran to Arthur as he drew rein, skittering out from under the portico, her veil tossed carelessly over her head, feeble protection against the pouring rain. She embraced him, kissed him, her mouth lingering on his, her fingers delicately touching the remaining bruises on his skin. Letting him know she wanted him, had missed him.

He did not brush her aside, but then neither did he return the embrace and kiss. The opposite of her desire; let her know he did not want her, did not miss her.

Clinging to his arm, Winifred walked inside with him, staying close, her body brushing against his, heedless of his wet clothing.

Slaves bustled forward to take wet cloaks, offer wine, and remove boots. Arthur shed his cloak, drank down a goblet of wine, kept his boots.

"Did you receive my letter? I had to take great care lest Melwas discover it—or Mother. She was plotting with grandfather. I had to warn you, dearest." Winifred spoke breathlessly, in a whisper, fearing her mother might discover her betrayal. Rowena was not one to cross, not even for her daughter. "Thank God you are safe through it!"

Winifred pressed herself against him, resting her head on his chest, her arms tight around his waist. Of all the stupid, pathetic things, she meant it, actually meant it! "When we heard of," she swallowed, "of what happened, I was so afeared you too had been killed." She smiled up at him, loving him. *God alone knows why*, she thought. "I was so relieved to hear you were come to Caer Gloui. I have been kept here at my father's command, not allowed to leave. Have you come to take me home?"

Arthur had not answered, had walked away from her into the living quarters to where Rowena was waiting.

Winifred trotted to keep pace with him. "I risked much to warn you into stopping my father holding that Gathering, or at least for you to act well on it." She broke into a sudden broad smile. "But you did! You did act! Oh, Arthur, I knew I could be of help. I knew by betraying Mother and Hengest, I could open the way for you to claim your title!" She linked arms with him, prattled on about Melwas coming for her at the estate, forcing her to leave. "The brute was so rough and insolent. I managed to bribe one of his men to take the letter—I had fears my father would not let you free, but I thought, as my husband, he would be honour-bound to release you."

Arthur stopped dead, plucked her hand free of his arm. "Shut up, you stupid woman."

For a moment, Winifred was taken aback. Her face began to crumple, her lip quiver, but he was not watching, had walked on. She took several deep breaths, followed him, excuses formulating. *He is tired and wet through; he is king now, has much on his mind.* Gleefully, thought, *with Arthur king, I am queen!*

"I have heard rumours." Rowena reclined along a couch, dressed richly, one hand resting lightly on the head-rest. She inclined her head as Arthur entered, said, "Are they true?"

"If you are asking is it true that your father's wolf pack has shrugged itself free from the leash, then aye, it is true."

If she was pleased, her face gave nothing away. "And my husband?"

"He matters no more. Vortimer has the kingdom now."

Winifred had entered a little behind Arthur. She ran to his side. "What? But you are the Pendragon. You are to be king!"

"I am content for Vortimer to rule."

"No!" Winifred stamped her foot. "I warned you of this uprising so you could be there to step in!" Too late, her hand covered her mouth, head swivelling towards her mother.

Rowena's eyes had narrowed. What was this! Her daughter turned betrayer? She had no opportunity to question, for Arthur was speaking to his wife.

"You are so fond of me then, Winifred? Yet a few months past you were prepared to flee to the Saex, keep my child from me, and make plea for divorce. You must love me well!"

Her arms twined around his waist. "I do! I was so confused and scared for the child then, I thought you were close to death—and," she pointed accusingly at her mother, "and she made me do it!"

Rowena sat composed. "I? Nonsense, daughter! You begged for my help, said you could not abide the foul-mouthed, slime-trailed man you were forced to call husband." Only a woman such as Rowena could remain so pleasantly smiling while delivering insults.

Beneath the calm exterior she was furious. So! Winifred had turned against her, was sidling up to this posturing braggart, Pendragon! Was after being queen herself, no doubt. Beyond that, she was angry with Vortigern for sending her to this accursed place. How dare he usher her off like some scolded child! Then, she was angry with her father for taking action while she was unable to reach a place of safety. She had expressly said in her last communication she needed to be there when he struck, to claim the status of king for Vitolinus. And she was angry with Arthur for being who he was.

She talked smoothly, hiding her rage. "It was you who talked of divorce and of ending your marriage, not I."

Winifred had always known her mother was a bitch, had seen her tongue lashing a variety of unfortunates. Until now, the sting had never been aimed at her. Well, she was her mother's daughter, had watched and learnt and copied. Winifred could be just as much the bitch!

"Because you put the idea in my mind! You ought not have trusted me, Mother. I know all the details of that planned murder! She forced me to run, Arthur, threatened me and our child—and you. She said she would have you murdered if I did not do her bidding."

Clinging to him, Winifred implored Arthur to believe her. "It was God's providence you rescued me. I am your loyal wife, I will serve you well as queen."

Rowena broke in quickly. "My son is named heir. If Vortimer is calling himself king I, as regent, shall have him arrested on a charge of treason."

Arthur smiled, strolled to a couch, and seated himself, placing his muddied boots on the fabric coverings. "Vortimer is the first-born son—and is not tainted by Saex blood. You and your kind are no longer wanted here."

"Without my father's help, these shores would be harassed tenfold from what they are now!" Rowena's composure was weakening. "My father's people kept to their side of the bargain; it is you British who have lied and cheated and stolen from us. Add to that, my brother fought well against the northern uprising, or have you forgotten?"

"Na, lady, I have not forgotten how your brother, on your husband's orders, murdered Typiaunan, eldest son to Cunedda of Gwynedd." Arthur spoke quietly, his disgust intense. "It seems cold blooded murder sits well on Saex shoulders."

"My father sought just payment. Council has brought this destruction!"

"Have you finished?" Arthur growled. "It was your Saex who hid their daggers. The British were unarmed. Most were old men. Helpless, defenceless old men. What brave people you are! Thank you, Winifred," his mocking, pleasant smile lingered on his wife; "I will have wine."

She glowered—she was no servant to order about! None the less, she fetched and poured wine.

He drank, belched, wiped his mouth, and swung his legs from the couch. "You talked of treason." He went to stand before Rowena, one hand resting on his sword. "You are under arrest. I am here to hang you."

Rowena turned white, her hand, gold and silver bangles jingling, flying to her throat. "But I am the Queen."

"No longer. You are Hengest's daughter and you are to die. Here and now."

Rowena thought fast. She must gain time. "What of my son?"

"What of him?" Arthur examined a bowl of dried fruits, took a selected handful, stood chewing. He wondered how long Vortimer would last. The man was too soft; you needed an iron stomach to survive in this game.

He went to the closed door, opened it. Beyond were two of his own guard. "You have a choice, Rowena. Die now, quietly, or on the morrow after my men have enjoyed you."

"You have no right!"

Winifred saw a chance. She simpered up to Arthur, took his hand between hers, held it to her breast.

"The Pendragon has every right."

Arthur patted her holding hands with his free one, smiled down at her. "You, wife, will be keeping your mother company."

"What!" Winifred paled, tried to pull away, but he held her fast. Gwenhwyfar had told him of Ceridwen, briefly, a few hurried words as the horses had been saddled. Enough.

"But I sent you warning, I tried to help you I…"

Arthur could be so cold behind that safe, deceptive smile. "I never received such a letter. I know nothing of it. I have seen the evidence to assume you to be in league with Rowena here, so you are to die also, my sweet." With one hand he stroked her cheek, seductively gentle. "You are no use to me alive. Your death will bring me all your wealth and solve the need for those messy little divorce settlements and such."

She should have known he would turn on her! Why had she bothered to try and help him? Why had she not, instead, paid Melwas to run him through? "If you plan to marry with your Gwynedd whore, you will be disappointed, husband. She is dead."

Arthur stared at her, his smile sudden gone. How did she know?

Winifred saw the anguish course through him, realised, with jealousy, the deep love he felt for Gwenhwyfar. Inside she glowed with triumph. With her gone he would still need her as wife.

Dry mouthed Arthur demanded, "Who told you this?"

She was still standing close, but he had let her go. She took his hand in hers again, pressed it to her cheek, thinking quickly of a plausible answer. "From Caer Leon. Messengers are searching for you—they assumed you would be at the King's new seat of administration. When they found you were not there they stopped here, naturally, knowing I was here. I sent them on to Londinium."

"Messengers?" This smelt like a rotting carcass. "What messengers?"

Her cheeks were flushed, her breath coming a little too quickly.

"Why," she said, "messengers from your mother. That last night, Gwenhwyfar was detained ill with that elderly farming couple, remember? It seems she was more ill than anyone suspected. She died." In a sympathetic voice, she added, "I am so sorry. I assumed they had found you, assumed you knew. I know how fond you were of her."

Arthur swung his hand, his fist smashing into her face. Winifred screamed and fell, blood pouring from a broken nose.

"You lying bitch! I have seen Gwenhwyfar this past week in Londinium!"

Bear's breath, no! Winifred lay crumpled on the floor, blood gushing. What had gone wrong? She had poisoned her. Gwenhwyfar was surely dead!

He was calling for guards. They were coming into the room, spears and swords at the ready.

Rowena, ignoring her daughter, had risen from her couch. "I am no fool, Arthur."

"That, I grant, is true," he hissed.

"I accept I have lost, I am to die. May I take a few moments to bid farewell to my son and make preparations to meet my God in privacy?"

"Na, you may not."

Rowena tried again, polite, calm. Thinking. *Damn you, you bastard, may you rot in Hell!*

"As a Christian, you cannot forbid me my prayers, Pendragon."

"Has your daughter never informed you? I care little for religion. I find it convenient to change faiths as the whim takes me. As you seem to do."

"We are true Christians, as well you know!" Winifred retorted through the veil held to her face to stem the blood,

"Do not talk to me, bitch!" Arthur shouted at her. "You are nothing to me, nothing except a discarded vessel where I once emptied my need."

She knelt on the floor, fingers bloodied. "Can I be blamed for loving you?"

"Love? You know not the meaning of the word!"

"Do I not? I have given you love in your bed, I have borne you one child, believe I carry another. I love you, husband—why else would I write you warning? What more can I do to prove myself? Our son, when he is born, will bear witness for me!"

Arthur did not hear, not wanting to listen. He beckoned the guard. "Take them away."

"With respect, Sir, many among us are followers of Christ. We acknowledge the need for these ladies to hang, but you must in turn acknowledge their need to make peace with our Lord."

Arthur roared his anger, came within a handspan of striking the man. "Are you challenging my authority, you insolent pat of cow dung?"

Cei strolled in almost casually, as if it were only by chance he was passing, whispered in Arthur's ear.

Arthur cursed, kicked at the table sending fruit and bowl clattering to the floor. "Very well. A few moments only; have them close watched!"

Cei spoke quickly to the guard who saluted and ushered the women from the room, Rowena composed, Winifred weeping. "You realise she is playing for time, Cei? She will be hatching some means of escape."

"Your men will follow you to the edge of this earth, Arthur, but not if you deny them our God."

"I deny them nothing, so long as it does not interfere with me. And this interferes, Cei!"

"Reject Christ if you will, but walk that dark path alone!" Cei flung the words at him and marched from the room, following in the wake of the group heading across the atrium for the private chapel. He called to a servant. "Summon the priest, and fetch the boy!"

Furious, Arthur stormed to the outer courtyard where some of his men had already flung two ropes over the boughs of a sturdy tree growing close to the perimeter wall. "Will this be sufficient, lord?"

"It will have to be. Curse this rain—will it never cease?" Arthur kicked at the tree trunk, leapt back in alarm as the thing moved. His eye strayed to the wall and he stood, fascinated, as the cracks, hitherto unnoticed, spread and divided. Water trickled through the brickwork.

A low rumble grew in volume from the far side. Slowly the wall crumpled and water began pouring through. The river, swollen to bursting point by the rain, was suddenly gushing into this quiet paved area, sweeping debris, shrubs, and men with it.

Arthur and two others grabbed at the dangling ropes, hauling themselves into the branches of the tree, which creaked and swayed, but held.

They watched in disbelief as the flood waters burst through into the villa, ripping timbers and brickwork apart as if they were parchment.

Everywhere was river. There was no wall now, no ordered garden. Trees, dragged up by the roots, clawed grotesquely through its churning waters. A dead sheep swirled by; a cat, yowling, clung arch-backed to what looked like a house-rafter. On the far side of where the wall had once stood the distant town of Caer Gloui seemed like an island within a boiling turmoil. An apple bobbing in a pond.

Arthur could only guess at the panic down there within those fine buildings.

Then he saw something which made him shout out and attempt to leave his safe perch.

Two women, one with a child clutched in her arms, scrambled over the fallen masonry of the villa's small chapel, floundering through knee-deep water. They reached higher ground, ran for the shelter of the woods.

Arthur shouted, waved his arms, trying desperately to alert his men who struggled, dazed and confused, among the debris and could not hear his voice above the roaring waters. Swearing all the oaths he knew, he tried again to let himself down into the swirl of muddied water below. He gasped at its coldness and strength. For a wild moment he struggled to retain his balance, gained a footing, thrust forward against the current to higher ground where the men were gathering.

He scrambled out of the flow of flood water, chest heaving, clothing sodden, muscles aching. Too many hurts had battered his body of late! A soldier put a hand under his arm, hauled him up.

Mithras! Arthur looked at the anxious faces crowding round, at six men, beyond where the wall had once been, clinging to the reins of frightened horses. Thank the gods they had left the animals out there to graze, had not taken them into the stables! Other men were thrashing about in the water. Arthur reached out a helping hand to Cei.

When those who had survived were safe, gaining their breath, stunned and wet through, Arthur peered again to where he had last seen the fleeing women.

There was no sign of Winifred, Rowena, or the boy Vitolinus.

Several explicit oaths flurried through Arthur's mind.

AUGUST 455

THIRTY-THREE

They sat, cross-legged, nursing sword or bow; or stood leaning on war ribboned spears. Silent, or whispering. No loud sound. Waiting.

On the far side of the ford, another army waited for the order to move forward. Hengest, slightly apart, stood with several of his thegns, his brother and his son. He stood, legs widespread, fists on hips, surveying the wide river crossing that stretched away before him. A dull sky overhead. The sun well risen behind the thick covering of cloud, promised little warmth this day. It would rain before long.

He sucked his lip, scratched at the red beard covering his chin. Ah, it felt good to stand ready before his men, holding them in check, anticipating that tumultuous roar of release.

Men close to him watched their leader, eager and expectant. Those further down the line glancing often at the White Horse banner, waiting for it to dip to signal the advance.

Hengest was resplendently dressed on this, his day of supreme victory. His helmet was decorated at the apex of the skull with a gold effigy of a boar, the whole thing a milky greenish-grey in the misty half light, the colouring coming from plates of split horn placed between the silvered iron frame. His red cloak, covering chainmail shirt, lifted in the wind.

He shifted his right hand to the hilt of his sword, which hung from a baldric fastened across his chest with an ornate gold and garnet buckle. The pommel felt good in his hand, warm, vibrant and alive.

Behind him, his battle slave caressed two spears taller than himself and with them, a huge iron-studded shield.

When victory came there would be reward for all, slave and warrior alike. Men waited. The Jutes, their fair hair braided on each side of their faces and a tail of hair hanging from the crown, stood with oval shields resting on the ground and short swords at the ready, waiting.

One man, dressed as richly as Hengest, stepped forward. He too had a red beard and hair, a stout frame, muscular legs, and a warrior's stem face. They were much alike, these two brothers.

"Is it not time?" he asked.

Hengest nodded once, turned and took shield and spears from the slave. "Ja, my brother, I think it is time!"

They came like a rush of wind sighing across a field of sun ripe barley. Swift, not silent, an indefinable whisper; a soft shush of distant noise.

There were so many of them! The front ranks seemed static at first, barely making headway down the hill flanking the river. Bobbing heads, lifted spears, waving standards, all coming on at a steady walk.

Their voices and war horns, tossed by a following wind, reached the waiting Romano-British. No single words, just a composite sound of nearing death.

Arrows from the British bowmen hissed across the water. Their deadly flight would be seen to blacken the sky, were any man fool enough to look upward.

They were close enough now, the Saex, to show individual faces; mouths open in battle cry, eyes wide, blue, green, or brown against white. They came relentlessly down the hill to the bank of the river as if impervious to the hail of spears and arrows sent to main and kill by the British. Where one man fell, another stepped into his place.

The water churned white foam as men began to wade. Mud mixing with blood. Those who fell, dead or still alive, stayed down, trampled underfoot. Men began to fight hand to hand; sword clashing on sword, spears thrusting into soft flesh. Where weapons were dropped or lack of space rendered them useless, they used their hands, teeth and feet. Wrestling, grappling. Battle, and the scream of death.

Seated astride Eira Arthur waited, taut and furious, watching the carnage at the ford spread below his vantage point of this raised ground.

His men, ranged behind him, stroked their horses' sweating necks, curbing them back. The tension for rider and beast as tight as a strung bow.

Vortimer was wrong! His plan sound in theory, but in practice monumentally wrong.

Their infantry stood firm at the ford, refusing to give ground, denying Hengest's Jutes access across the river. But for how long? An hour? Two? Then what? It was not sufficient to hold this crossing, they must push forward, take it in decisive victory and put an end to this thing before it grew into something more.

A half wing of Hengest's Saex broke away, swung along their right-hand bank, moving off at a steady jog trot. Ducking low through scrub, they avoided those few arrows or spears that sailed across the dividing water.

Arthur had been ordered to wait, to hold hard in case the line failed and the enemy managed to break across the Horse Ford. It was the one place wide and firm enough for herded cattle or horses, ridden or driven, to cross. Other places up and down river afforded access to single riders or men on foot, but the Horse Ford was a drovers' way. An essential crossing to hold, for either side.

Cei pointed with his spear at the disappearing Saxons, said, "If they find a way over downstream and close behind us, we are finished."

Arthur remained silent: no point in answering the obvious.

"The marshes may hold them back," Cei added unconvincingly, "but they are canny with the ways of water, and there are paths of firm ground aplenty for men in single file on foot down that way."

"Vortimer knows," Arthur hissed. "Do you not think I told him of this when I argued against our position? Would he listen? Mithras, what a mess!"

The rain drizzled, puddling underfoot so that in places it was difficult to tell rain-sodden earth from river marsh.

Arthur dared not take the horses too far down river; the ground was too soft, too treacherous. Yet could he allow a free path for these Saex to creep through?

He signalled a rider forward, spoke briefly, sent him galloping to where Vortimer and his brother, with the infantry reserve, watched the battle below. Within moments the rider returned with a second mounted man, Catigern himself.

"My brother the King does not wish you to leave your position, Pendragon."

"I don't give a fart what he wishes! There is a sizeable force wading across the river down there." Arthur pointed through the murk. "It is an even wager they will negotiate that marshland. If they are not stopped they will come up behind us. How else does your brother," sarcastic, "the King, intend to block their path if he will not allow my cavalry to see to it?"

"The ground is not firm for horse! Jesu, we had the selfsame argument yester-eve!" Catigern waved an irate hand towards the battle. "Our men are holding up well, Hengest cannot cross. A bit more of a push and we may be able to thrust them back."

Patience went. "Well! Well? Bull's blood, man, another half hour and our men will be done in! Thrust back? Soon they will not be able to stand on their legs! If Vortimer cannot see it is time to bring the cavalry into play and get this thing finished, then he has no right to lead us!"

"Are you challenging my brother?"

It took many deep breaths for Arthur to stop himself bellowing "Aye!" He managed a controlled "I want to do something useful with my men, not be left sitting here like brooding hens."

He gathered the reins, edged Eira forward, smiling at Catigern. "Tell your brother, the King, in my opinion it is essential we ride to protect our rear." The smile went. "If he does not like my opinion, then he can go to his Christian God's Hell!"

Arthur kicked the stallion into a hand canter, his men following without question.

Catigern cursed, shouted impotent orders to hold position, knowing even if Arthur's men heard they would not obey. He wheeled, galloped back to his brother where he spoke brief word, and gathering to him the waiting infantry reserves, took them to join the wavering ranks of weary soldiers at the ford.

The day was a disaster. Mid-afternoon, and Hengest pulled his flagging men back. Too weary to follow, the British let them go, knowing this to be a breathing space only, for men to bind their wounds, clean bloodstained weapons and regain their breath—until another day.

Neither side had won. Both had lost. Neither side held control of the ford; both sides lost many and many a brave warrior.

Hengest took one last look across the rain-sodden plain below him before he entered the shelter of the trees. Beside him his son Aesc stood as sober faced as his father. Four thegns carried a dead man, his red beard bloodied from the wound that had split his face open from temple to jaw. Aesc plodded after them into the woodland.

"I will be back for your stinking Weleas blood!" Hengest shouted, holding the stained blade of his sword before him. "I promise you this, by the name of my dead brother, slain this day at Agealesthrep!"

He followed the bier, his legs and arms as heavy as his heart. There would be another fight, another day, but not yet. Now was the time to bury the dead and to mourn. Now was the time to send for more keels, to grow and gather in strength, ready for that day.

Vortimer and Arthur were arguing. Had they not been so tired they might have come to blows; as it was, their words were bitter enough.

"You disobeyed me, boy!" Vortimer shouted.

"I saved many from certain death!" Arthur yelled back. "The Saex were well-nigh across those marshes—as I said they would be. What was I to do? Sit astride my horse and welcome them forward?" He swept a hand before him, bowed slightly. "Feel free, Saex, come up behind, stab us in the back like you did in Londinium! Let the son be as bloody stupid as the father!"

It was then that Vortimer almost struck the Pendragon. Instead, he shouted, "And how many horses did you lose in that bog? Ten? Twenty? Forty?"

"I lost ten and seven. Compared with losing the whole of the army, a small price to pay."

Vortimer, stopping himself from thrusting his knuckles into the Pendragon's teeth, said, "I was about to send the infantry reserve there. Infantry could have handled the situation. Instead, Catigern had to lead them where you ought have gone."

Arthur exploded into anger. "Infantry could not have moved fast enough—you left things too late! Catigern did right by moving the reserve to the ford!"

"Where cavalry would have performed a better job—and happen would have left my brother alive!"

"Ah, so that's it?" Arthur thrust his face into Vortimer's with contempt. "The truth. You hold me responsible for Catigern's death!"

Cei, ill at ease at this quarrelling, interrupted, holding an arm between his King and Arthur. "No one is to blame for anything. We all know battle decisions have to be made in a hair's breadth of time. Some go well, others do not. That is war. Many a good man has lost his life this day. Many more are with us to fight again."

Other officers present stood shuffling and feeling embarrassed, hoping not to get involved; the Pendragon's temper was too volatile, this new King untried.

Arthur had heard enough. He strode for the open tent flap and ducked through, tossing out as he went, "Unless the cavalry is used to its full potential, Vortimer, I am no longer with you."

Cei, uncertain, made to call him back. Vortimer, sighing heavily, seated himself. God's truth, he was tired! He said, "Let him go, Cei; he is in a hot temper, but he will cool. He has more need of us than we of him; he will be back tail tucked atween his legs before long." He managed a weak smile. "Only do not tell him I said so."

Cei regarded the man. He liked Vortimer and admired him for his dedication to country and duty. Yet Vortimer was no longer a young man. His face, this evening, looked more like a skeleton's mask than anything human; his hands, Cei noted, were shaking.

The day had gone badly. Had Hengest's brother not fallen and the wind, consequently, been taken out of Saex sails it might have gone worse. Defeat had been uncomfortably close.

Cei saluted, turned from the tent. He respected Vortimer, acknowledged him as king, but he had been wrong in this. Very wrong. And Arthur right.

Vortimer knew it too, knew it for himself and from the expressions of those officers waiting for orders. It was Arthur they needed, Arthur with his knack of knowing what to do and where to do it—and doing it well. Closing his eyes, Vortimer let his head and shoulders sag. He had a sad, but relieved feeling that he was not going to be king for long.

Cei caught Arthur up, touched his arm. "I was told earlier there is someone you ought to see among the wounded."

"There are many I ought to see, Cei. My men, those who fought bravely this day; boys, old men who will never fight again. Then I ought to see those few Saex prisoners we took. And the horses." He put his own hand on Cei's arm. "Not now, Cei, later."

Cei was insistent. "I was told this thing before Vortimer summoned us. You ought to see this one."

Arthur shook off Cei's restraining arm. "I am tired and I am hungry. Has Llwch questioned those prisoners?"

"Aye, they know nothing of Gwenhwyfar." Cei stepped in front of his cousin, blocking his path. "I say again, you ought to see this man."

Arthur was not listening. "I have small hope of finding her after all this while. Easier to seek a thread in a hay meadow."

Cei again, louder, "Will you listen to me!"

"Who is it, then? Why the urgency?"

"Osmail."

"Osmail? Cunedda's Osmail? Gwenhwyfar's eldest brother Osmail?"

"Aye to all three."

"What in the name of the Bull is he doing here?" A sudden thought: "Happen he knows of Gwenhwyfar's whereabouts! A ransom demand gone to Gwynedd?" As he spoke, Arthur was hurrying to the hospital tent erected on the outskirts of the camp. He ran most of the way.

He thrust back the entrance flap, and stood aside to allow exit for two men removing a corpse. Arthur looked, did not recognise the dead man. A bearer said, "We will have many like this come morning."

Osmail lay near the back, what remained of his leg swathed in fresh bandaging, already soaked through. He had no colour, save for a tinge of blue around the lips.

Arthur touched him gently. The man roused briefly, managed a weak smile of pleased recognition. His eyes rolled white, then the life spirit sighed from him. Osmail was dead.

Arthur's head slumped forward. Suddenly he wanted to weep. "Are none of his brothers here?" he asked, cursing that he had not come earlier.

"None," Cei replied. "I asked a few questions; he joined us yester-eve, rode alone. None knew why. None asked."

Arthur bent to examine the small pile of belongings beside the dead man. Boots, helmet, bloodied cloak. A leather pouch. In it, a scrap of parchment. Eyebrows raised, Arthur read aloud:

"*Branwen. Understand why I did this thing. I must make peace with myself before I can do so with my God and my father's spirit. You are safe with the Holy Sisters of the Virgin; the gold I left in your keeping will suffice to keep you in comfort. I write this, knowing you will receive it should death be my path on the morrow. I ask you to forgive me, and pray for my departed soul.*" Arthur screwed up his eyes at the scrawled writing. "What in damnation is this all about?"

Cei took it, reread it. "No doubt his wife will know."

"Where did he fight?"

"No idea. Someone pointed him out to me when I was searching for our own wounded, said you would wish to know one of Cunedda's brood was here."

Arthur rolled the parchment. "Which someone?"

Cei grinned. "Someone else I believe you would be interested in meeting."

"A day for surprises, eh?" Arthur grinned back. "Well, where is he?"

"I am here!"

Arthur spun round at the voice, saw a man vaguely familiar, a few years his senior.

"You are?"

The man laughed good natured, held his hand out in greeting. "I am named for your grandfather, Ambrosius Aurelianus. My brother—your father—and my friends call me by my British given name."

Arthur started forward, delighted, to embrace the man, his uncle. "Emrys! I ought to have known you! What brings you here?" They clapped each other on the shoulder. "Are you not needed to defend your own coastland?"

A shadow crept across Emrys's face. "There is nothing left to defend. We were raided, some months past. My wife and daughter are dead. An all too familiar story."

"Sea-wolves?"

"Saex pirates, aye. They came, took what they could carry, slaughtered what they could not. They left me for dead. With God's protection they missed my son, hidden by the quick thought of a slave."

"You came alone to fight with Vortimer, then?"

"Your cousin Geraint is here also. He has two sons born, did you know?"

Arthur was guiding his uncle from the tent, talking animatedly. A soldier's arm plucked at his tunic as he passed.

"Glewlwyd! What? Wounded?" Arthur hunkered down, concerned, beside one of the bravest of his turmae.

"Nothing serious, my Lord—a sword slash, 'twill heal." The man nodded a respectful greeting at Cei and the other man he did not know, said to Arthur, "We did well—could have done much better had we been used right."

Arthur patted his shoulder affably. "And we shall be used right the next time we fight, I promise you. I have finished with simpering in the shade alongside those who have not the stamina to stand in the full sun."

Beaming, Glewlwyd attempted to rise from his bed. Arthur playfully pushed him back. "Take your time to heal sound first, man. You are no use to me in pieces!"

With his two companions Arthur left the hospital, the idea planted so long ago in his mind ripe at last, ready for the harvesting.

As they walked Emrys talked of everyday things; poor crop yields, raiders, his family. His young son.

Arthur, not listening, deep in thought, suddenly stopped him. "Vortimer has not the ability to lead us and I will not follow a blind man into darkness. I am going to make the break. Now. I intend to gather men to me, fetch up those horses Gwynedd has ready, and gather more from my restored lands to the west. But I need the backing of prominent men. Are you with me, Emrys?"

A man hailed him, coming up behind saying, "After this day's bungling I am, Pendragon, for certain!"

Arthur spun to greet Geraint, son to one of Uthr's sisters, with warmth and pleasure. They had met on occasion as boys, had liked each other's company. Geraint greeted Cei, but acknowledged Emrys, Arthur noted with interest, with distinct reservation.

The four men strolled to Arthur's tent in search of food and wine as Arthur outlined his ideas. He could barely contain himself at the knowledge that at last his ambition was becoming some solid thing, hovering just beyond his grasp. The years of waiting were almost over.

But where to start that first push to send the stone rolling downhill? It needed one stone only to gather speed, taking up rocks and boulders, shrubs and trees as it went. Rolling faster and faster, becoming an unstoppable landslide. One stone.

While they were eating, huddled around the dim glow of a single brazier, the conversation turned for a while to lighter topics.

Geraint, mentioning his infant twin sons went on to say, "My wife had a liking to show them off to her family; we were visiting there when we heard of the Londinium massacre. We were on the road home when Vortimer made his call to arms. I had not the time to escort them safe home, so have left them with the Holy Sisters of the Virgin at Yns Witrin."

Arthur started in surprise, fingers hurriedly feeling for a rolled parchment tucked in his belt. "Twice today have I heard of these Sisters!" He slapped a meat-greased hand on his thigh. "That settles one nagging thought, then! We ride to Dumnonia to persuade Vortigern's placed governor that he is now to swear allegiance to the Dragon, and on the way we call at Yns Witrin to see your lads, Geraint," he raised his goblet in salute, "and Osmail's widow."

Things were looking hopeful. Happen Branwen knew something about Gwenhwyfar.

Geraint yodelled his delight. Cei handed round more meat. Emrys, embarrassed, cleared his throat.

"I will not be with you."

Silence.

Arthur laughed. "You do not have to ride if you have no wish for the exercise, Uncle! Go gather your son and meet us at our rallying place in Gwynedd."

Emrys twiddled a chicken bone between his fingers. "I meant I will not back you in this fight for a royal torque, Arthur." He looked at his nephew with no trace of embarrassment. "For the same reason that I would not back your father. I do not hold with kings. We are of Rome, we have an Emperor. We are a province of Rome and should look to her for guidance and protection."

For a moment Arthur sat silent, astounded. Was the man serious? When Emrys said nothing more, Arthur realised he was.

"Rome cannot help us. We have been abandoned to our own fate," he said.

"I disagree. We are temporarily left to our own devices but Rome will recover from her trials, you will see. Some few seasons from now the Emperor will gather his armies and come to our aid. He will not be pleased to see another claiming his title." Emrys placed the bone to burn on the brazier, got to his feet. "For all that, I wish you well, Arthur."

With narrowed eyes Arthur observed, "Yet you fought this day under a king."

"As, should your bid be successful, I may one day fight under you. I recognise the need for a leader, a man to command while Rome sorts her troubles, though I would wish that leader had not reverted to an abandoned tribal title, but that's as may be. Through temporary need I must recognise a king, whoever he is, but I will not become involved in civil fighting over who is to be that king. Again, I wish you well." He was gone, stepping from the tent into the wet night.

Geraint and Arthur looked at each other incredulously. Geraint shrugged, poured himself more wine. "Living in the past, that one," he said.

Arthur laughed, tore with relish into his meat, reached also for the wine. "I remember Uthr saying his brother Emrys had an odd way of thinking. They never saw eye to eye on anything. I always put it down to the years between them, but happen it is more than that. Fool of a man! Rome will not be back. Eh, Cei? You are quiet this night. What say you?"

Cei stretched, tossed his sucked bone into the flames, finished his wine and stood. "I say it is time I checked the men and horses." He walked from the tent, saying over his shoulder as he left, "But you ought know, for the most part, I agree with Emrys."

THIRTY-FOUR

GWENHWYFAR KNEW SOMETHING WAS TO HAPPEN. NOT PRECISELY WHEN, but soon, very soon. It was an odd feeling this, something inside niggling like an image vaguely remembered after a waking dream. For the past week she had climbed the Tor each morning, settled herself close by the largest standing stone on the summit, and watched. For what, she did not know, just watched.

It was not a Christian place, this Tor; the Holy Sisters did not like her walking here. Yns Witrin it was called, the Glass Isle. Even in the driest of summers there was always water spread around the foot of this conical hill—sodden places, marsh oozing underfoot, pitted with deeper bog that could trap and drown the unwary. Come winter, or after weeks of rain such as this year had brought, the low flat levels became a plain of dotted lakes and running channels. The brooding height of the Tor reflected in those vast, mirroring waters. An imaged island as delicately translucent and brittle as glass.

Shrouded in morning mist and with its ancient miz-maze path winding back and forth in ritual pattern up the steep slopes, the Tor squatted over a cluster of little hills, like a matriarch presiding over her mixed brood sheltering within the fall of her shadow.

It might not be Christian, but it was a revered and mystical place. A sanctum of the Old Ways, of the Mother Goddess and Avallach, God of the Underworld. She danced on the buttercup-spotted or frost-rimed grass, He slept beneath, in his domain of Avalon within the darkness of the hollow hill, waiting for the souls of the dead to find their way by night down the passages into the Other World.

Once, there had been many who served the Goddess; now the young women went to the Christian Mother. Daughters learnt the litany of the Holy Church, not the ancient learning of a Goddess who was sliding into obscurity. Only three priestesses were left down there at the base of the Tor, their poor dwelling houses built along the shore of the water.

Theirs was an ancient, once elite, clan. The Ladies, they were called, women of the Goddess. With the passing of the three, the Goddess would be gone from the Tor. Forgotten.

Drawn to this richly spiritual place, Christian people had settled their community among the cluster of hills set on the flat of the Summer Land. They had built their little chapel and crude dwellings; set up their market place and expanded as each year more came. The chapel became a church, the dwelling houses merging together into cloistered orders where men and women could live and work alongside God and Christ. Traders arrived. Farmers brought their produce and cattle to the market and prospered; a tavern flourished to provide bed and food for weary travelers who came to worship at the wondrous-built church, or seek healing or learning from the holy men and woman. Under the Christ God the Glass Isle thrived.

It may have been very pagan, this Tor that hovered above the mist of a damp spring or autumn morning, or floated on a flood plain of glistening, sky-bright water, but Yns Witrin possessed a pull of awe and inspiration. A place where it was easy to listen to the voice of your God. Within the spirit of the Tor, you could see through the shaded windows of your own soul.

And the Tor was a place of the Mother. Whether she were the old Goddess or the Virgin Mother of Christ, she was still the Mother. Gwenhwyfar had been safe here under her protective wing, was calmed and becoming healed of fear and the disgrace of an unwanted and uninvited invasion of her body. Rape carried a powerful backlash of wretchedness.

To her, this quiet hill was a patient, contented place away from the dark, crowding shadows of horror. A place for the female. A sanctuary where time drifted with the moon cycle and where the earth beneath your feet understood the pain of labour and the joy of birth.

Have other women stood here, where I stand on this wind-teased summit? she wondered. *Watching as I watch, waiting as I wait, for their child to be born or their menfolk to come back from war?*

Probably. The Tor was a guardian shield for women. It was said children were conceived or borne with ease and safety up here. Women's natural troubles were healed. The Tor, a buffer against the harsh reality of life out there in the bad lands.

It seemed so long ago, so far away, that rain-drenched night in Londinium. Yet it haunted her, clinging like stale perfume. Sickly and repulsive.

She had a vague recollection of how she came to be here. She remembered the shouting and a clash of weapons; fearful desperate faces. Pounding hooves, sobbing breath—her own? Frightened horses bolting. Her arms clinging exhausted to a bay horse, muscles locked, unable to let go until he shuddered, eventually, to a halt.

Gwenhwyfar had no idea how far that wild flight had taken her or to where she was taken. Knew only that her body ached and head throbbed. She was unaware of the jagged slash across her forehead, barely recalled the swinging hilt of a sword on a rocking boat that had caused it. The scab had long since peeled itching away, the scar beneath fading white against darker skin.

The Holy Sisters said she had ranted delirious in fever for several days.

Had an inner sense guided her to them? Or had it been the wandering bay horse with a rider slumped across his withers who had trotted to other horses, eager for company? Whatever, the six women making their way to join the Sisters of Yns Witrin had taken her to their wagon, tended and cared for her. Unsure who she was or where she had come from, and unwilling to delay their journey, they had decided to take her with them.

In her dazed state, Gwenhwyfar had raised no objection.

The gentle Sisters fluttered round her, enfolding her in the safe seclusion of their nest, clucking and cooing, thanking the wisdom of the Virgin for guiding a daughter to safety. Gwenhwyfar let their attentions wash like healing balm over her muddled mind, having no energy or inclination to contradict them, relieved and thankful that the Goddess—under whatever guise—had brought her here, once strength and sense began to return, to idle among these gentle women of peace.

Once, she had visited the Ladies, going across the spread of the lake to their huddle of meagre dwellings at the base of the Tor. The two she had met had welcomed her, were as kind as the Sisters, but—and this surprised Gwenhwyfar—could offer her no more comfort than the Christian community. Strange, it was the quiet, simple lives of the Holy Sisters that provided the inner peace she craved.

The Ladies were brash and gaudy—their bangles jangling at their wrists, the vivid-bright tunics, the startling blue tattooed in writhing swirls on face and arms. Inside the squat building they took her to a heavy, mind-numbing aroma muddled her mind even more and left her disorientated and distant. They were kind, concerned, and eager to help, but Gwenhwyfar sat with them tense and stiff, like a doll carved of wood.

And something else she realised as she punted the little boat back across the lake: they seemed to be living a pretence. A theatre play. Women dressed up as the Goddess's Ladies, raising their hands to the sky and calling with shrieks and cries for the Mother to hear and help. Not that it had been like that; there had been no wailing or moaning, but the intoned prayer had jarred with a stilted rhythm which had grated and pierced the ears instead of relaxing and pacifying the spirit as did the chanting of the Sisters.

Gwenhwyfar would walk on the Tor, but she never went back to the Ladies at the Lake.

The Sisters led a life of rigid routine revolving around daily chores and prayer. Their speech was quiet but not without laughter; indeed, they laughed often, sharing the many pleasures of their God's created world of happiness and beauty. In the Sisters' chapel or about their duties, they would often sing, chanting their praising rhythms to the glory of God. A comforting sound.

One other reason kept Gwenhwyfar away from the Ladies. Morgause was one of them. She was the third Lady.

After leaving the Ladies on that one visit, Gwenhwyfar had walked down the sloping path, through the clusters of alder and willow, and had met with her, coming up from the lakeside.

They had not exchanged words, merely stood, the one eyeing the other, stone faced, critical. Morgause was dressed as a Lady of the Goddess, her golden hair loose with the blue-painted patterns tattooed on her cheeks, forehead and bare arms. In comparison, Gwenhwyfar, with cloak clutched tight to her breast, was pale, frightened, and tired.

This was the Lady they talked of then, down in the market place and in the tavern; the women with clacking disapproval, the men with shared winks and nudging elbows. She had wondered, Gwenhwyfar, meeting with the two Ladies, what there was in them for the men to be so excited over. They were old, shrivel-skinned, claw-fingered women with creased, toothless smiles.

Her Holy Sisters were virtuous, pledged to serve God, not a man's lusting. The Ladies welcomed the pleasure a man could give. Though what pleasures could be shared with those two crones Gwenhwyfar could not imagine. Not until she stood before Morgause. As young and perfectly beautiful as ever.

She had dipped her head and stood aside to allow Gwenhwyfar to pass, hon-our-bound to a guest of the Goddess. Gwenhwyfar had murmured her thanks and hurried by, barely noticing the child, darker skinned but with the same golden hair, tucked behind Morgause's flame-coloured skirts.

The wind lifted Gwenhwyfar's loose hair; she liked letting it flow unbound up here on the Tor, it added a sense of abandoned freedom. She would have liked to cast aside her clothing too, run naked over the short, springy turf. But that would shock the dear Sisters too much, and besides she did not have the courage to prance about in the open birthclad.

Overhead, a screech of swifts darted, swooping and diving, their calls shrill but wildly exciting. She watched them pass, clapped her hands at their breathtaking aerobatics. As quickly as they had appeared, they were gone, skimming down the side of the Tor and away.

Gwenhwyfar closed her eyes and breathed in deep, holding the heady scent of morning-damp air, releasing it slowly. Thank God today the rain had ceased! Gwenhwyfar smiled, felt the babe within her kick at her belly.

That was one thing she was grateful for. One solid thing that had given her strength to defeat the evil sense of dirt that Melwas's stench had left on her. The child she carried was too large, too well formed, to have been put there by him. She placed her hand on the bulge, felt another hefty kick. "Ah, babe, you are anxious to see your Da? Soon, will I send for him and he will come for us; soon."

"Talking to yourself? They oft-times say it is a madness sign."

Gwenhwyfar swivelled, startled. Morgause leant against another of the standing stones, her arms folded, expression mocking. The child was with her again, a pretty girl for all the grubbiness of skin, hair, and dress—and the startling sign of fear that surged, naked, in her wide, dark eyes.

Gwenhwyfar had seen similar eyes somewhere before. Where?

"Happen it is best to talk with yourself if you know the answers make sense." Gwenhwyfar spoke to the woman pleasantly; the Tor did not lend itself to bad moods and sour answers. "Aside," she said with a smile, "I talk to my child."

"Ah, your child." Morgause seated herself on the grass a few feet from Gwenhwyfar, querying with her hand and a raised eyebrow whether Gwenhwyfar minded. It was not for Gwenhwyfar to say—the Tor belonged to all.

Morgause leant her head back, letting the warmth of a sudden burst of sun shine on her face. To the grey-blue sky she said, "Why are you here, Gwenhwyfar of Gwynedd?"

"I could ask the same of you."

Smiling at the neat answer, Morgause indicated Gwenhwyfar's swollen belly and said, "Except I can guess your reason. Now the great Cunedda has gone you fear Gwynedd might throw you out for breeding a fatherless bastard?"

She liked hurting, Morgause, enjoyed the pleasure of another's pain, would poke and stab at vulnerable places and watch her victim squirm under her torture. Animals, children, unprotected adults—few were safe from torment at Morgause's hand. If she had intended to hurt Gwenhwyfar with this one, though, she failed. Gwenhwyfar had long accepted her father's death—liked it not, but accepted it. And her brothers would not reject her when she became ready to contact them.

Morgause sat forward, hugging her knees. "As I recall, Cunedda had a fondness for fatherless bastards."

Gwenhwyfar did not miss the inference, said with a lifted eyebrow, "He had a father, though, didn't he—Arthur?"

Several thoughts wandered through Morgause's mind: Uthr, and his son; the love she held for the one, the hatred for the other. The son should have been hers. If she had borne Uthr a son, then... then what? Would Uthr still be alive, would she now be queen? The thread of Fate would never weave so smooth a pattern. Even had she borne a son, Uthr would still be dead, she would still have come here to seek shelter with the Ladies, become one of them. It suited her to be here. For now, until the time came to move on.

"So," she said to Gwenhwyfar, pleasantly, "you come to the kingdom of Avallach and the garden of the Goddess to bide your time before dropping your child."

"I come to share the peace of the Holy Sisters."

"Hah!" Morgause snorted with amusement. "That pathetic bunch of nanny-goats! What would they know of bastard brats? It is in my mind you hide away here lest your brothers discover your condition. You ought to have had it aborted." Morgause ran her hands across her own flat belly. "We of the Goddess know how to keep a womb empty." She giggled, a crude sound full of suggestive pleasure. "Though men try hard to fill it." Scornfully she added, "I doubt your Sisters know anything of such matters. Would scream rape should a man dare catch a glimpse of an ankle beneath that drab garb they encase themselves in."

"The nuns are good, kind women—do not mock them."

"What, all of them? Even that other one from Gwynedd? Branwen." Morgause was massaging her toes, wriggling each one between her fingers.

Gwenhwyfar answered affably, "I see little of her, she has private lodgings." Thought, *thank all God's goodness!*

The little girl had wandered some way off, was absorbed in picking daisies and threading them into a joined chain.

Gwenhwyfar had no wish to talk to, or of, Branwen. Disagreeable woman! She said instead, "She is a pretty child, your daughter."

"What makes you assume she is my daughter?" Morgause laughed.

Cocking her head to one side, Gwenhwyfar watched the little girl. She was dressed in a rough-spun tunic, sleeveless, reaching a little below her knees. A shabby bandage was bound about her right hand. There were bruises, Gwenhwyfar noticed, on her arms and legs. A lot of angry bruises, but then children were always falling and hurting themselves.

"I say it because twice now I have seen her trotting at your heels and because, although she has not your delicate skin, she is very like you." And someone else?

Lifting her shoulders, Morgause made light of it. "So she is mine. The Goddess smiles that she has another to follow her path." She gathered up her skirt, folding the cloth back to her thighs, and stretched her bare legs to the sun. She threw Gwenhwyfar a sly sidelong look; eyeing her bulge, assessing how far the babe had grown. "Who is the father? Or can you not name him for fear of decrying his wife?"

Gwenhwyfar replied, indifferent to the taunting, "I have no intention of fighting with you, Morgause. It is no business of yours to know. I could as well ask who fathered your girl." She added with a twist of returned spite, "Or do you not know?"

Morgause watched the child a moment through slit eyes. A stupid girl who answered questions in a mumble and had downcast eyes, a runny nose, a bottom lip that trembled most of the time, and clumsy hands that dropped everything. She still wetted the bedding. Punishment seemed to have no effect, even though it was becoming more severe.

Take this morning. The idiot child had spilt scalding porridge all over Morgause's gown. She had immediately plunged the girl's hand into water boiling in the cooking pot; doubted whether even that punishment would have any effect. The child would be as clumsy some other time, some other way. A tiresome, disappointing weed of a brat.

With a sigh, "She is nothing like her father." Morgause scratched at an itch along her inner thigh and lay back, her hands tucked behind her head. "It is as well he does not know of her. He would be disappointed."

"I think my man will be pleased with mine."

Morgause learnt much from that. The father, whoever he was, knew nothing of the coming child. Also, Gwenhwyfar was not certain of him. She took that to mean there had been some passing affair, torrid meetings of a night, a sharing of lust, and now the man had gone. Back to his wife? Probably. It usually went that way.

"That is just as well," Morgause said, climbing to her feet and straightening her skirt. The sun was becoming blanketed by a thick bank of cloud. It was darkening in the west, more rain coming. It was time she went. She looked north across the flood plain, north to where, somewhere, the Goddess was still held in awe, where this Christian God had trod no lasting footprint. The Ladies were revered in the far north, were welcomed. A gifted Lady could soar high among the Picti people. Could, if canny, fly as high as a queen.

Aye, it was time she went from Yns Witrin.

In passing she said with unexpected good intention, "The Goddess has a place for girl-children should yours be born female. She does not need to know a father's name, would welcome yours to her bosom."

"As would the Christian Virgin."

The kindness disappeared. "Hah! That is not how I heard it." Brushing at a grass stain Morgause came to stand before Gwenhwyfar. "You would fare better under the Goddess; she is in need of new servants."

So that was why Morgause was being so friendly this day! Gwenhwyfar had wondered. She held her tongue, for Morgause spoke the truth of it. The nuns were kind-hearted, well-meaning, and loving, but a few had tutted and mumbled over her condition.

When Gwenhwyfar first came, there had been guarded questions, met with a polite silence. They knew her name, that was all, but of her parentage, her home, and the father of the child Gwenhwyfar had said nothing.

All that had changed several days past when Branwen and Osmail arrived. This was a small community where word, especially scandal, spread faster than a winter flood, and Branwen had within a day made it her business to give full detail of Gwenhwyfar's history. But, not even Branwen could discover who had fathered the child.

Was that something moving out there on the plain?

He was dead of course, Osmail. He would never have survived a battle, she knew it as surely as that distant muddle of movement was forming into a turma of horse.

She had entered the community chapel one afternoon and had seen a man sitting there. "*Osmail? Osmail!*" She had dropped the gathered flowers intended for the altar and run to him, throwing her arms about him, tears of joy and laughter mingling with his own. He had come, he said, to leave Branwen and his sons with the Sisters while he rode to join Vortimer, driven by some crazed need to prove he was his brothers' equal. Proving nothing, Gwenhwyfar had retorted, except that he was a fool and could die as easily as anyone else. But he had gone all the same, riding out the next morning.

One other part of their conversation came back to her as she sat in the cloud-patched sunshine up here on the wind-whispered Tor. "*They are searching for you,*" he had said. "*Our brothers and Arthur.*"

She had deliberately not informed anyone of her whereabouts. That they would be suffering pain she realised, but it would be a short, soon mended hurt. Her own hurt, for the time being, came more important. She was not ready for the harassment of the outside world, was not ready for the sympathy and swamping affection that, however well intentioned, would drown her severely cracked spirit. The Sisters gave her those things, but in a distant, impersonal way.

"*Soon,*" she had promised Osmail, "*I will send a messenger soon. When I am ready to take up my cloak and go out into the world again; but for now I need time for my wounds to heal, here within the peace and privacy of Yns Witrin.*"

And suddenly she received the welcome knowing that "soon" had come. She was ready to turn aside from tranquillity and face reality.

"I must be getting back," Gwenhwyfar said, rising to her feet. She took a few paces down the slope, stopped to say, "I shall tell the Pendragon when I see him that you are here, Morgause."

Morgause laughed, hands on hips, head tossed back. "So he may avoid the place? Do not bother yourself, I am leaving. I need somewhere more," She smiled. Wicked, Morgause's smile could be. "Beneficial."

She watched Gwenhwyfar go; watched, too, the horsemen for that knot of clouded shapes was definitely horsemen. The girl had come up, was standing a few inches from her mother.

"I met with Gwenhwyfar when I had the Pendragon," Morgause said to the wind. "Not this Pendragon, I speak of the father." She clasped her arms about herself. The wind was growing chill. "He was a man worth the having." She looked down at the child who stood wide-eyed with fear, thumb stuck in her mouth. A patch had spread on her skirt where she had wet herself.

"Love of the Mother!" Morgause snarled. "Uthr was worth the having, but by the pleasure he gave, were you?"

THIRTY-FIVE

Tired horses, steaming from a fine spatter of rain on hot coats, filled the rutted courtyard of the small tavern built alongside the outer wall of the Holy Sisters' compound. The keeper welcomed the arrivals graciously, if somewhat doubtfully, making rapid calculations for sleeping arrangements.

Cei slapped him on the back, almost toppling the little man. "No panic, we stay but the one night to rest horse and man."

Two men had remained mounted, the officer in charge and another man—a civilian, for all he was dressed in war gear. They talked briefly but earnestly out beyond the arched gateway.

It had surprised Arthur that Emrys had joined them after all—although, as he had been quick to explain, only to ride as far as Yns Witrin. "I have a fancy to reside a while with the holy Brothers." Put out by Emrys's rebuff, Arthur had said he could suit himself what he did. They had ridden in silence for the first few miles.

Emrys was saying he did not care to stay at the tavern with Arthur and his men, was all for seeking a more suitable bed within the Brothers' monastery, away to the left of the road.

Arthur took that as another slight. Said, "Go where you will, Uncle. It is nothing to me where you sleep." Thought, *We do not need your solemn face casting disapproval on our drinking and whoring this night.*

He swung Eira aside, intending to trot into the courtyard—halted. For a long, long, moment he sat there staring up the muddied lane, unable to take in what he was looking at.

Gwenhwyfar had walked slowly back, taking her time to amble down the slope of the Tor, coming the long way round to avoid the Lady's lake. Then she had stopped to drink from the women's water of the spring. It was good water, red-tinged, bubbling from the ground even in the hottest of summers, so she was told. It was healing water, folk said, and indeed she always felt a surge of energy after drinking there, no matter how tired she had been before.

Then it had started raining; a fine, warm drizzle. She had walked on along the narrow track, stopping to listen to a bird trilling a bursting chorus of glorious sound. Stooped to peer, fascinated, at a webbed nest of new-hatched spiders, the little things weaving their way from the massed clump of siblings, climbing hesitantly out along leaf stems and grass stalks—a minute, busy little world. Further on, a beetle lay in her path, its legs waving frantically in the air as it struggled to right itself.

She flipped it over, watched as it scuttled away, shiny black. She could hear voices ahead, and horses. The rain was falling harder now. She had no wish to meet with riders, not yet, so she ducked her head against the wet and walked a little faster, aiming for the rear door into the Sisters' garden.

Suddenly Arthur was off Eira's back and running up the lane.

She looked up, faltered, her veil slipping back from wet hair.

His arms swept around her, lifted her off her feet, swinging her round and around. Then he put her down, gazed at her, still unbelieving, thinking this was some dream; he would wake any moment and find her gone. Finally, almost choking with happiness and relief, he kissed her.

He was aware, as his breathing calmed and his heart eased its wild hammering, of men gathered down the lane, faces grinning, voices raising a cheer. Cei had come up behind, was saying with a broad grin, "Can we expect a more amenable mood now, lad?"

Emrys too had wandered up the lane, was regarding the woman in Arthur's arms with interest. He had heard of Gwenhwyfar ferch Cunedda, from sources other than Arthur.

They were very different, Emrys and his brother Uthr. Eldest and youngest, with fifteen years between them. Emrys had been a babe in his mother's womb when their father died, was a child when Uthr fled into exile. He was no soldier, Emrys, had lived a quiet life of learning, of books and study. With his elder siblings gone about their own lives and his father dead, he was left in the care of his mother. A good, pious woman who brought up her last son in the way she had been taught; to honour God and Rome, the one almost blending with the other—but then her father had come from Rome, was the son of a Senator. He had served a while as Duke of Britain, governor of the entire north—until Rome had recalled the legions and he had gone marching away with them. Emrys's mother had stayed in Britain, with her husband.

Emrys had met Cunedda and disliked him for all the reasons his elder brother had liked the man. Cunedda was ambitious, had a liking for war, was brash and lewd and cherished a love for an independent Britain and a return to the Tribe. Uthr and Cunedda were glad to see the back of Rome. Emrys had never trusted Cunedda, nor Uthr. And Arthur was too much his father's son. Did this daughter too take after her father?

He stepped forward to greet her. Recoiled, for as Arthur let her go her cloak flapped open, revealing her swollen figure. "My God, she carries a child!" The shocked exclamation left Emrys's lips before he could halt it.

No one spoke.

It had not occurred to Gwenhwyfar to wonder how Arthur would react to the discovery. She had always assumed he would be pleased, but seeing Emrys's horrified disapproval she was suddenly afraid.

Arthur must have seen the panic scuttle across her face, for he took her hand in his, said to Cei, "Settle the men and horses and escort my uncle to his chosen lodging. I have unfinished business to attend." He slid his arm around Gwenhwyfar, drew her close to his side, clearly dismissing his audience.

To her he said, "Where can we talk?"

She indicated an open doorway in the convent wall through which herb and vegetable gardens were visible. He led her there, shut the door, looked about. Beneath a drooping willow he saw a crude bench, took her to it, and seated her. Standing over her, he gathered his thoughts.

They both spoke at once. "Gwenhwyfar..."

"Arthur..."

Laughed.

"Let me speak, Cymraes."

She bent her head, her hands folded in her lap. He was not going to want her now—now she bore a child which only her word said was his.

Arthur had not dared to hope he would find her again, and now he had did not know what to say. This child she carried—he had gone over and over all the things that could have happened to her these past weeks, had not thought of this one possibility. It must be his. Wasn't she too far advanced for it to be Melwas's— or had there been someone else? Mithras, how to ask without giving offence? Ask—he had to. He started clumsily.

"I did not expect you to be with child."

"I did not expect to be with child. It is a thing that seems to happen when two people lie together." Her answer came out harsh, too flippant.

"Na, I meant," He fumbled for words, decided to leave it a moment. "Winifred has gone. I know not where, nor do I particularly care. She may be drowned or have reached her mother's people—I hope the former. Either way, officially, legally documented, she is no longer my wife."

He sat beside her, sharing his cloak, covering her shoulders with its ample width. Awkwardly he took her hand in his own, found it cold to the touch. "I have much to do, Gwenhwyfar. Vortigern is no more and Vortimer is unfit to lead. It is almost time for me to take the kingdom as my own." He glanced apprehensively into her green eyes, watched, fascinated, the swirl of gold at the centre. "For the next months, years, I must gather all I can to me, will have to fight those who stand in my way." He studied her hands. Slender fingers, smooth skin. "I would that there might be a loving woman at my side." He brought her hand to his lips, kissed it. "I have a thousand dreams spinning in my head, Cymraes. I need desperately to share them with a woman who has the heart to see them with me."

Wistfully she answered, "We had so many dreams as children. Where do they go when we grow? Are they swallowed up by the mundane things of everyday life? Or do we lose them, leave them behind us in the dust, for new children to find and take up?"

"My dream is still with me, Gwenhwyfar. Unaltered, save that I may have tidied up the ragged edges along the way of growing up. Come with me, as my wife."

She looked into his eyes. Few could read Arthur's thoughts; few were allowed to see beyond those veiling outer shutters that kept the inner feelings safe hidden. Gwenhwyfar alone could see into his heart, see as clear as if looking into a clear pool. Her free hand went up to his cheek, caressing, a delicate touch. He was unshaven, the prickle of stubble sharp on her palm. He smelt of horse and leather, rain and sweat. His wet hair was stuck against his forehead and hanging limp about his neck.

"I recall you making a promise to me once, Gwenhwyfar, close by Gwynedd's sacred Stone. You vowed your sons to me."

She smiled at that. "You remember, then?"

"I would not forget it."

"This son I bear you shall be the first of many."

Tentatively Arthur stretched out a hand to touch her bulk. "It is mine, then?" He asked it hesitant, afraid of hearing the wrong answer.

Gwenhwyfar pressed his hand down firmer. He jumped, astonished as a tremor jerked at his palm.

"Would a babe acknowledge any man other than his Da?" she said for answer.

He stroked a finger lovingly down her cheek. She was thin, pale, needed feeding and loving. There were things he had to ask, had to know.

"I know what..." He paused. He meant to say "Melwas," but found he could not say that name aloud. "What he did to you. Cei, others, have guessed it. This child—you are sure it is... ?"

She bit back the threatening tears, knew what he was thinking. And if he thought it, what of others? "Am I sure it is not his? Na, it is not, it is yours." She attempted to swallow her tears.

Arthur was content. Nodded his acceptance, slowly, with deliberation. He held both her hands in his, rubbed their cold fingers. "Even if it had not been mine, I would still ask you to be my legal wife, Gwenhwyfar."

"Even though I carried his child?"

Arthur scowled, had to admit, "I want you for certain. The child? In truth, were I not satisfied it was mine, then na, I would not accept it."

Scarcely breathing she asked, "And are you satisfied?"

He said simply, truthfully, "Aye."

Gwenhwyfar kissed his eyes, his cheek, then his lips, held him to her, savouring his nearness, his firm responding hold. The nightmare had passed; she was awake and it was a beautiful day. The rain dripped through the leaves, pattered on her closed eyelids. Who cared about the rain? For Gwenhwyfar, the sun shone.

A great sigh left her, her head lying on his shoulder, his hand rubbing her back. She said, "Even the simplest of men can see with their eyes and count on their fingers. This child was begun well before Melwas raped me."

She lifted her head, surprised at herself. The word had just come out, of its own accord. Not once since that first halting telling to Arthur had she spoken of the thing—not to herself, not to the Sisters or the Ladies. But now she had said it, and suddenly it was not so hideously frightening any more. She laughed, kissed Arthur again, revelled in his return kiss.

She said, smiling radiantly, "Your son and I have waited so patiently for this day." She tapped his chin with her finger. "We do not intend to be parted from you again."

He laughed, jumped up, lifted her to stand on the seat his arms encircling her broad waist. "Pregnancy suits you well," he observed.

"Mud and sweat," she replied, wrinkling her nose, "do not do the same for you!"

"Well that, woman, I am afraid, is a thing you need grow used to!" He gathered her to him, holding her weight easily in his arms. "Which way this church I have heard so much reverent talk about?"

She dipped her head, puzzled, towards the east. "Over there, why?"

"You will see." Arthur carried her from the gardens and up the muddied lane, bellowing for Cei, who came running.

"Get you to that church—fetch Emrys and Geraint." Arthur shifted Gwenhwyfar to a more comfortable position, kept on walking. "And any other who would care to witness my marriage. Oh, and fetch me someone fitting to hear our vows—no poxed insignificant novice Brother, mind. Find a priest or something."

There was much shouting and running. Yns Witrin, normally a quiet, sleepy place, was suddenly filled with noise and activity. Sisters came bustling and twittering; Brothers, with less gaiety but as much curiosity. A Bishop came trotting from his quarters, solemn eyed, a little flustered. He did not have much occasion to solemnise marriage vows in a community of nuns and brethren.

"A Christian wedding!" Arthur declared, setting Gwenhwyfar down before the church door. "So none may doubt or counter my claim on my queen!"

Geraint, with his wife, hurried up and slapped Arthur on the back, pleased his cousin had found his lost love. He embraced Gwenhwyfar, kissed her, and handed her to his wife who, smiling, welcomed her as kin. Arthur's men, too, were crowding round, delighted. There would be a few days of relaxation now, and some good drinking and enjoyment ahead too if they were lucky! Aside, many knew Gwenhwyfar, remembered her quick wit and knowledge of horses. She was a woman well liked and accepted by Arthur's men.

Then it was Emrys's turn. He had come to the church in a flurry of unease. He took Arthur aside while some of the Sisters and Geraint's wife were twining hastily gathered flowers in Gwenhwyfar's unruly hair.

"My boy, it is my duty as your Uncle, to ask if you are certain of this thing you do."

Thumbs hooked through his belt Arthur took a step back from his father's brother and regarded him through narrowed eyes, head cocked—for all the world like someone listening intently.

Encouraged, Emrys rested a hand on Arthur's shoulder, meaning to draw him a little away from the crowd. Resolute, Arthur stayed put.

"She is of good birth, I grant, Arthur, but—well, lad, I must be blunt—I think you are acting hastily. This child—it is not seemly for you to marry with her while she carries it. There will be talk, speculation." Emrys cleared his throat, realising belatedly this was not going well after all. "Let her have the child and, whether it be boy or girl, give it to some holy house for rearing where it will serve good by being with God but will also be soon forgotten, and then take her as wife. It is my advice, lad. Sound advice."

Gwenhwyfar had come up behind him. Arthur looked over Emrys's shoulder at her, said, "What say you to my uncle's advice, Gwenhwyfar?"

Her cloak had been gathered around her against the damp and cold, but now Gwenhwyfar tossed it back and walked proudly to Arthur's side, showing her swollen figure for all to see. She threaded her arm through his.

"I think that to advise our next king to set aside his first-born heir is most unwise. I might almost think, my Lord," she addressed Arthur but looked with open challenge at Emrys. "any who would give such advice must have his own reasons. Happen he does not welcome a son born to the Pendragon because he has an eye on a royal torque for himself? There were many who were privately glad when Uthr was slain, not expecting a son to come after him."

A single, curt incline of his head saw Arthur agree with her. He took Gwenhwyfar's hand, began to walk with her inside the church. He halted on the threshold. "There are those who, for whatever reason, did not back my father when he took his chance to rid this country of tyranny and greed. There will be those who, for the same reasons, will not back me. I will say this to those men. I give not a damn whether you pledge me your sword or not. I will be king, and my son," he laid his hand on Gwenhwyfar's stomach, "*my* son, will be king after me."

He looked with challenging defiance at Emrys. Uthr had never liked his younger brother, had said once—and Arthur remembered this from childhood, "*A young man who spends more time with his books and on his knees before God is a man I would trust to hear my confession or to give spiritual guidance. But I would not trust such a man to guard my back with a sword. Book learning can make a man think he knows many things; book learning serves no purpose when you are faced with the blood red death of an enemy.*"

"You serve your conscience as best you will, Uncle Emrys. I have already taken Gwenhwyfar as mine in the manner of the Old Way; I now take her in the Christian way. I am happy with that. If you are not, well then, that is for you to grieve over, not I."

The Pendragon, polite, nodded dismissal to his uncle and took Gwenhwyfar inside the church. Emrys did not follow.

A small girl had wandered unnoticed into the crowded church. She had never seen inside a Christian building before, was awed by its dazzling whiteness and the gleam of gold arrayed on the altar. It was a wonderful place. She watched from a secretive corner, enthralled as Arthur and Gwenhwyfar exchanged their vows. Felt the laughter and happiness that soared in this peaceful little building.

When Arthur led his bride from the church, he saw her and smiled. Impulsively he tossed a small bronze coin at her. She made to catch it, missed, her face puckering at the humiliation of her clumsiness before this great crowd. Arthur stooped, picked it up, placed it in her hand, curling his fingers around hers. "Do not cry, little one, I will not have tears this day." Then he was gone, and all the dazzling people with him.

No one had ever smiled or spoken to her in kindness before. She had never known laughter, happiness, or love. Her only companions were slaps and bruises, tears, and fear of her mother's temper and violent hatred.

Morgaine was always to remember Arthur for his kindness. Remember and love him for it, although she knew her mother would be angered, and probably beat her were she to know of it. For Morgause hated Arthur, wanted him dead. Morgaine knew that because her mother had said so, not an hour since.

DECEMBER 455

THIRTY-SIX

C AER ARFON SEEMED NO DIFFERENT. THE SOLID TIMBER PALISADE ROSE formidable from the sea wall, the Lion flag of Gwynedd fluttered lazily against a backcloth of bracken-browned, snow-shawled mountains. Gulls wheeled and cried, the sea beat its restless pulse of incoming, outgoing tide. It all seemed much as Gwenhwyfar had left it.

Sliding an arm around her broad waist, Arthur pointed to the nearing wharf. "We are here. I promised you your son should be born in Gwynedd."

"*Our* son," she corrected amiably, settling her weight against him. She filled her lungs with the sea air of home, closed her eyes, savouring the fresh tang of salt. Her husband's pleasing nearness.

They had been at sea two days; their first chance of private conversation and close contact. The ship boasted one bed, which had become Gwenhwyfar's, and Arthur had curled with his men under blankets on deck, when he had found time for sleep. Most of the journey he had passed in deep discussion with the captain, taking a keen interest in the mysteries of navigation and handling the craft. Never one for idling, he took the opportunity to learn and appreciate new skills, absorbing the ways of the sea with an eagerness matched by the crew's willing patience to explain.

Wind and weather had remained calm, but the sea had been heavy, the small coast-hugging craft wallowing in the swell like a bloated whale. Gwenhwyfar had sailed or paddled boats almost since before she could walk, was used to the sea but perhaps because of her bulk and her anxiety to get home, this journey had been nothing but sickness swamping her belly. She rested the back of her head against Arthur's shoulder. In a little while she would be walking on firm ground—thank the gods!

The babe was causing her discomfort. Its head was low down, pressing on birth canal and bladder, hard in the pit of her womb when she sat or walked. The necessity to relieve herself frequently was irritating. Her only comfort was

the ungainliness of advanced pregnancy would soon be over—this voyage home
to Gwynedd was left late for peace of mind.

Then, too, the foetid odours of that unpleasant stronghold they had come
from still clung. Savouring the fresh air, she said, "I thought we would be en-
tombed with Meirchion in Dumnonia for ever."

Arthur laughed. "He was rather tedious." Leaning over the rail, he studied
the foaming water swirling against the hull. "A hesitant man," he said, "unsure
where to lay his wager until the winner becomes a certainty. It took a while for
him to decide which way to bend, with me or Vortimer."

"He knows you for what you are then, husband."

Arthur looked at her suspiciously. "What do you mean?"

"That your fingers are itching to bleed each wealthy man dry. Meirchion and
my brother to head the list."

"Certainly not!"

"Certainly so! In Enniaun's case you want every ounce of horseflesh he owns
for next to nothing in return." She relented, her smile twitching into laughter. She twined her arm through his when she realised he had taken her seriously. "I am teasing!" She sighed, placed a light kiss on his cheek. He was so
quick to take offence these days; living on a knife edge, sinking often into a
brooding silence.

He did not answer her, was watching the shore coming nearer.

Gwenhwyfar pulled a little away from him, leant her arms on the rail as he
did, looked out over the tossing grey sky. The Caer ahead was growing larger—
another five, ten minutes and they would be there. Could she never say the right
thing to Arthur? If being king meant constant bickering, then she would rather
he decided on a more agreeable role. Gods, if she were ever queen, would she
have to visit other such places as Meirchion's stink of a stronghold?

She shuddered at the recollection of the place, her features wrinkling into
a grimace of distaste. An ordeal was not the whole of it! "Almost eight days
was I cloistered with that odious wife of his!" she said to the sea. "Phew, God
knows when she last bathed!" Gwenhwyfar scratched her head, still feeling the
itch of parasites; numerous washings in salt water scooped by the bucketful had
seen them gone, she hoped. "I shall scream if I find any fleas from that place
on me!"

Arthur whistled through his teeth, his quick anger forgotten. He held her, the
embrace awkward because of her size.

"You are complaining? I had Meirchion himself! Did he ever cease eating? I think I did not see him once without some form of food clasped in his greasy paw. Chewing all the time he ducked and swerved, talking of everything under the sun but the reason why I was there! When I did finally manage to get in a word about the holding of land, he went off on a separate path about the whys and wherefores of his right to possess it because of his service to Vortigern! Service? Fah! Grovelling, I call it. Like a pig at the trough." Arthur spat over the side.

"Poor Meirchion," Gwenhwyfar said, finding some little pity. "After all these years when he thought himself secure, you arrive unannounced, tell him you are now lord, and demand his allegiance." She laughed. "He did stop eating, Arthur, I saw him. For a full minute he stopped chewing as we entered—his jaw hung open like a hooked fish!"

"I did not demand! And he was not that surprised to see me, knew well I would come one day."

"We were in danger, Arthur. Had he a named heir, Meirchion would have had us murdered before the sun set on the day we arrived."

The ship was slowing, the square blue sail flapping as the men hauled it down from the central mast. Others sat waiting, poised to dip oars into the churning sea.

"If he had such an heir I would have approached the matter differently." Arthur gazed outwards. There were people gathering on the shore. "I chose the path I took because Meirchion is a superstitious man; he would not harm an unborn child."

Gwenhwyfar moved away, standing squarely behind him, hands on hips. She had just realised! "You took me as security, didn't you? Did it not occur to you that you might be goading Meirchion beyond endurance? There are ways of achieving what you need. Openly declaring war if he refused to do as you say is not very diplomatic!"

"What was I to do then?" He turned, rising to her anger. "*Meirchion, I care not whether you side with me or Vortimer now his useless father is destroyed. Please, suit yourself; use my rightful inheritance of land, wealth, and men against me!* I assumed you had more sense, wife!"

"As I assumed you did!" she shouted back at him.

The ship bucked as the oars dipped and pulled, banking the craft sharply to the steer-board side. Misbalanced, Gwenhwyfar lurched forward, caught by Arthur who lunged swiftly to avert a fall. He held her a moment, then kissed her.

"Remove that pout of displeasure," he said. "You are right. As you usually are."

He braced her weight against his own body, steadying her against the manoeuvring craft. "I was full aware of the danger to you and the child, but I had to take the gamble. I need Meirchion's willing agreement to back me, and I needed you for protection."

Gwenhwyfar opened her mouth to protest, but he stopped her words with a second kiss.

"For all his blustering, he understood the position as well as I, Cymraes. Since the day your Da declared me as Uthr's heir, Meirchion has known he could lose all—so could I—if war broke out between us. Yet I could not risk complacency. I had to enforce the threat of aggression, or gain nothing from him."

"And knowing you were going to threaten, you walked us openly into his lair?"

Arthur grinned, kissed the tip of her nose. "Guessing Meirchion would chance fighting me, but never your kin. You were my pass to safe keeping."

"You took a great risk, Arthur."

"My whole future is a risk, love. Our future."

Gwenhwyfar looked earnestly up at the man before her. Arthur stood several handspans above her own height—a tall man, as his father had been. Dark-haired with those piercing hawk eyes. "You will keep the promise you made him?" she asked, suddenly unsure and afraid of this callousness she had not seen in him before.

Vaguely he answered, "Happen."

Alarmed, she responded quickly. "Arthur, you must! You promised he could hold those lands until his death!"

"You are overprotective of Vortigern's former friends all of a sudden? A moment since, you were condemning him as an odious parasite! That is politics: setting one loyalty against another to gain the upper hand. How else am I to gain support? Men must learn to see me as more powerful and more dangerous than Vortimer. How think you your brother Enniaun survives as Prince of Gwynedd?"

She kicked his boot, not hard, but enough to show displeasure. "Because he keeps promises."

Arthur's mouth twitched. "Not many of them, Cymraes—and only the ones that serve his purpose. I pledged Meirchion's security—and I intend to honour that pledge, so long as it suits me and he keeps his word. The winner, love, is the man who can smile and promise the sun and moon, knowing he has only mountain mist to give."

Placing his hands on her shoulders, he turned her round to face the shore rushing to meet them. "If Meirchion remains loyal then I shall leave well alone. That I can promise."

Rich-clad people stood to the forefront of the crowd gathered at the wharf-side. Gwenhwyfar sighted two brothers who still remained at the Caer, the twins Rumaun and Dunaut. With them, various nephews, nieces, and cousins. The dark-haired young woman beside her brother Enniaun she guessed to be his wife, Teleri, a princess of the northern Picti people.

A wave of unexpected alarm swept through her. She had been away so long. So many things had changed; she had changed. She clung to Arthur's arm, trembling slightly, whether from excitement or fear she could not tell. A little of both?

"How can I face them?" she asked.

Shrewdly Arthur replied, "As boldly as I face the Lion's son in his den."

The ship bumped, ropes were flung, caught by eager hands. A plank was run out. Gwenhwyfar found herself engulfed in enthusiastic greetings and tears of welcome. She could not control her own brimming eyes, clung to her eldest living brother smiling, laughing, and crying all at once; her emotions tumbling together like fleeting rain showers on a bright sunny day.

Teleri touched Gwenhwyfar's cheek with her own, not quite a kiss, an uncertain greeting, more polite than friendly.

Rumaun pushed forward before the two women could exchange further conversation, swept his sister to him with a yell of delight. "How round you are, Gwen!" He poked gently at her protruding bulk, added, "I trust there is only one in there!" He winked at his twin brother and they all laughed, Gwenhwyfar saying, "One is quite sufficient! Do you not agree, Teleri?"

Off guard, the woman muttered a shy and embarrassed reply.

Enniaun held his wife fondly at his side, smiling down at her.

"You have another niece!" he told Gwenhwyfar. "A bonny lass. She will be a good playmate for your child as they grow!"

A sharp retort almost left Gwenhwyfar's lips. Her child would play with no daughter of this Picti crab! She bit it back—that was unfair. "Happen she will," she said.

Teleri trailed silently behind as they walked up the incline to the Hall. She was a shy person, awkward and often clumsy in her eagerness to please. She tried so hard to do the right thing, aware the Picti were resented here in Gwynedd, usually ended by making herself look a fool. Gwenhwyfar's coming worried her. She had heard so much about her husband's sister—how could she survive beneath such an eclipsing sun?

Seeing Enniaun's easy laughter with Gwenhwyfar, Teleri felt a stab of sharp envy. For all the kindness shown her, she still felt like an outsider. Head down, hands clasped tight together, she followed at the rear of the crowd of happy people, wishing Gwenhwyfar had not come, would go soon.

At the doorway to the Hall servants and slaves waited, eager to give greetings. Gwenhwyfar embraced some of them, a special hug for Brenna who was as old as the hills and as dependable.

Teleri took up the cup of welcome and carried it in both hands towards the Pendragon.

The confusion and jostling was great. People were pushing forward, reaching out hands in greeting. Hounds milled about, barking, tails wagging. One, a great brindle, a favourite of Enniaun's, launched himself at his master. Annoyed, he kicked him aside and the dog tumbled, yelping to fall awkwardly against Teleri. She was of small height and build, like a sparrow she seemed. The enormous dog knocked her off balance and she stumbled to her knees, spilling red wine over herself and those gathered at the threshold. Some laughed; more grumbled.

Arthur had assessed her at first sight. He always had an eye for a pretty girl, and found this one's slight form and shyness attractive. Had she not been wife to Enniaun, well, who knew how much more he might have decided to learn of her? He stepped forward, gallantly helping her to her feet. He kept hold of her hand, grasping it tightly in his own as he swept his eyes over her, raising a deep flush on her face.

She felt disconcertingly naked before his gaze, knowing his look for what it was, a measuring of the body beneath her gown. The wine, where it clung to her bodice, highlighted the round curve of her breast.

"You need spill only a token gesture to appease the gods." His voice was as smooth as the rich wine.

Teleri met his eyes and felt her legs begin to shake. He lifted her hand and kissed the white skin. She withdrew it sharply and mopped ineffectually at her sodden dress, attempting to conceal her embarrassment.

Someone hastily refilled the cup and handed it to Arthur to drink first. He gave his blessing on the household then spilt the customary small drop on the floor, adding to the accidental spillage.

Unexpectedly Gwenhwyfar remembered another such cup, when Cunedda had returned after Uthr's death. She could see herself there again, a leggy girl

with cherry buds for breasts, scrawny and impatient for the excitement of womanhood. How young she had been!

Arthur handed the golden cup to her. For a moment she held it between both
hands, staring into the dark pool of liquid. She had not expected Enniaun's wife
to be quite so young and pretty. Nor had she missed that look of keen interest
from Arthur. Beside Teleri Gwenhwyfar felt an ungainly lump with swollen feet
and puffed ankles, waddling like a land-bound duck.

How does he see me, she wondered. As I was in Less Britain, a girl breathless for
his loving, living in the dream days of sunshine? Or as I am now—irritable, often
crying for no reason, with sharp words always on my tongue?

"Welcome home, sister," her brother was saying, his voice distant among her
thoughts. *Home,* Gwenhwyfar thought with a start. She looked about her, at the
Hall stretching wide and grand beneath soaring rafters, at the happy faces and
welcoming smiles. Family, friends.

Caer Arfon had been the only home she had known. There were other, more
modest strongholds scattered throughout this vast territory of Gwynedd, some
in which they lived for months at a time, depending on the season, the avail-
ability of game, and the pressing calls of justice and law. None were "home," save
Caer Arfon.

Gwenhwyfar sipped the wine. For so long had she wanted this, to come back
to Caer Arfon. Now she was here, she found the pink glow had faded, leaving
only smudged grey edges. With startling clarity, she realized the truth. Now her
Da was gone, and she had Arthur for her own and a child coming, Caer Arfon
was no longer her home.

She swallowed a gulp of wine and its strength burnt her throat with a stinging
warmth, sending her head spinning a moment, leaving her thoughts suddenly
settled and clear. She had never wanted to be headwoman here; that status belonged to Teleri, the new prince's wife.

Caer Arfon was the place of childhood and those days were gone, for she was
a woman grown with a child restless to be born. Straightening her shoulders,
Gwenhwyfar tipped the remaining liquid to the floor. A hard lesson to learn, but
there could be no going back, only forward.

They were waiting, feet shuffling, some coughing, impatient. Those memories of childhood were distant but there all the same, and the future lay ahead
with who knew what changes? Well, so must it be!

Gwenhwyfar looked at Arthur eye to eye, gave him a dazzling smile which
he returned from his heart. It shone from him, a radiance, every part of his body

smiling his pride in her and love for her. She placed her hand confidently in his and stepped across the pool of wine lying on the threshold.

She was coming to Caer Arfon, not as daughter of Gwynedd but as wife to the Pendragon and mother to his child. She had outfaced the dark dreams and set aside the shadows that lurked among the haunting echoes of fear.

THIRTY-SEVEN

A FROSTED NIGHT, WITH A CRISP SCENT IN THE AIR AND A SHARP BITE TO cheeks and fingers. The white touch of winter was beginning to shoulder aside the mellow golds and reds of autumn. Gwenhwyfar stood gazing at the snow-tipped mountains, rising silent-shadowed against a star-scattered sky. Old friends, the mountains.

In the Hall, heat from crowding people and glowing fires had flushed her face, wine and food warming her from within. She shivered, pulled her cloak tighter. The cold had soon chased away that drowsy, complacent glow, filling her nose and lungs with brittle wakefulness. The mountains would always be there, and the stars. The river still ran into the sea, and the tide washed against the shore. Reliable, dependable things.

The Stone stood before her, a black pillar pointing like a finger up towards the four corner stars of Orion and the brilliance that was the eye of his faithful hound following at heel. Gwenhwyfar walked forward, boots crunching on the white, spangled ground. Her hand touched the cold hardness of the Stone, her fingers caressing its familiar rough surface. How many other clear nights such as this had she stood here to set free confused thought?

What scenes the spirit of this carved rock must have witnessed! Warriors gathered for a hosting, hopes and hearts edging as high as Yr Wyddfa as they honed an edge to their weapons, talking among themselves, confessing fears or boasting bravado. Daily comings and goings to and from the Hall. Spring lambs, born calves; summer harvest; autumn gather and slaughter; winter cold. The pledging of loyalties and swearing of oaths. Arthur had stood here as a boy, when he became Pendragon. Uthr, before he left to meet his death. Osmail, Etern. Her father.

A step crunched on the frost-hardened ground. "Gwenhwyfar?"

Without turning she said, "The mountains are so ageless, Enniaun."

He came up beside her, his eyes lifting towards the hills. "With the coming and passing of seasons they wear different cloaks, but it is good to know beneath those mantles of green, brown, or white they remain as always. They were here when we were born, will be here when we die. 'Tis a sobering thought." He seated himself beside the Stone, his back leaning against it. Tipped his head to watch the stars.

"They shone as bright two nights past, for Samhain. We lit a fire to welcome our Da and brothers, should their spirits decide to come," he said.

"I thought you might."

"It is a pity you were not here."

"It is a pity they are dead."

Enniaun stretched his legs, shuffled himself more comfortable. "We must all die, sister."

She rounded on him. "That we must, but do we need to walk into death's embrace? Da ought not have gone; he was not so young, nor so agile."

Enniaun lifted his hands, palm open. "Nor was he in his dotage and crippled. His was the death every warrior seeks, Gwen. Triumphant in battle, not suffering age or the bone ache, not waiting for death to remember you."

An owl glided silent above the thatch of the Hall, his wings ghost white under the light of the stars. Gwenhwyfar watched his passing, said, "I thought I had accepted their deaths. But now I am here, where I can see and hear and smell them, the ache of grief has returned."

"It never leaves, not with someone we love. Their presence burns too vivid in our memories. Happen that is as it should be, for otherwise we would too easy forget."

Gwenhwyfar squatted beside her brother, shifted herself close for warmth. He draped the swirled length of his cloak around her shoulders.

"So much has changed," she said.

"Change has to come for life to struggle forward. We none of us can ever stand still." He smiled, took his sister's hand between his own. "We are not the mountains or stars, sweetheart. Would we not grow bored waiting for nothing to happen?"

She smiled at that and squeezed his hand. "Bored, aye, but much safer."

He thought a moment, rubbing the cold of her hands with his fingers. "I heard a story once. A man was told by a wise woman in five days he was going to be crushed to death. Well, at first he didn't believe her, but as the fifth day approached he began to get nervous. Come the dawn, he was so frightened he decided to stay all the day in his bed."

"And so he cheated the wise woman's prediction?"

Enniaun laughed. "Na. The roof fell in on top of him."

Gwenhwyfar swiped at her brother's head with the back of her hand. "Idiot," she said, but she was laughing, the black mood lifting.

"Did he die easy, my Da? No one ever wrote me the full details, only that he had been killed."

"I was not here either. I was away to the north agreeing trade and alliance with old Necthan." He sighed, clasping his hands together. "Had I been here, then happen Da would not have gone." He hung his head, said quietly, "I mourn him too, sister, for I have had to replace him, and no one can ever fill that vast emptiness left by the Lion Lord Cunedda."

For a while and a while they sat together, silent, watching the stars tread their endless dance, until Gwenhwyfar at last said, "It is forgetting that troubles me. So desperately am I trying not to forget Da's face, Etern's laugh, or even Osmail's scowl. But they are all slipping away, fading as a rainbow does after its brief shine of glory. And then, the things I so need to wipe from my mind—Melwas, and what he did to me, Ceridwen's death of agony, Iawn... all those horrid things, not one tiny detail, not one, will leave me."

"They will, Gwen. When your child is born you will have new things to think on. Change, you see." Enniaun kissed her cheek then stood, stamping his feet and clapping his hands to his sides. "I tell you one thing that must change— me out here for me in there!" He laughed as he nodded up the hill towards the Hall. "Are you coming?"

She stood also, stretching an ache from the pit of her back. "I am tired. I think I will go to my bed."

Giving his sister an affectionate hug, Enniaun began to walk away, but stopped and faced her again as she called out, "I believe, brother, that lion cubs are often as strong as their sire, the lion."

He grinned. "I have heard that also." About to resume his walk back to the Hall, he halted again, said into the darkness, "I can tell you one other thing, Gwen. Our father's death shall be avenged. I have vowed to rid Gwynedd of all the poxed sea raiders who have taken it upon themselves to dirty our soil." He looked at her across the few feet separating them, his expression so reminiscent of his father's. "And that vow shall not change until it is completed."

THIRTY-EIGHT

THE COMPLEX OF BUILDINGS BEHIND THE HALL BECKONED CHEERFULLY; servants had lit night torches which burnt in friendly welcome. Caer Arfon had always seemed grand to Gwenhwyfar as a child, but then she had seen nothing else save her Da's other strongholds, all smaller than this one. For the first time she saw it for what it was, a hotch-potch mixture of Brythonic and Roman. Thatched roofs among slate, daub and timber walls running alongside stone built. Round, traditional dwelling places and the family's impressively Roman chambers. All this, ranged around a rectangular chieftain's Hall. Compared to Ygrainne's grand villa the buildings, even those in the Roman style, were primitive.

Gwenhwyfar paused before entering her chamber, aware that never again would she share a room with chattering girls. Her position of wife, especially wife to the Pendragon, afforded her the luxury of privacy, but with that came solitude and loneliness. She swung away from the door, headed instead for the darkness of the walled garden.

So many memories, bad and good. So much truth to be faced. She walked slowly, head bent, lost within her own world of thought. The sound had been there, but remained unnoticed until it ceased abruptly with a stifled exclamation.

Gwenhwyfar's head snapped up. "Who is there?" Servants up to some mischief? No answer. There was no moon and the stars gave little light here in the shadows. She said again, commanding, "I know you are there. My Lord Enniaun will not tolerate illicit coupling within his private grounds—get you gone!"

A vague movement, a rustle, like wind rummaging through fallen leaves. Then silence. Angrily Gwenhwyfar strode forward, gasped as a single cowled shape appeared before her. A woman. The star silvered light fell on her face—Teleri.

Gwenhwyfar was about to say something harsh, but compassion stopped her. Instead, "You are shivering, have you no thicker cloak? Here, take mine." She unpinned the brooch at her left shoulder and swung the woollen garment from her. Teleri hunched herself into the warmth, stumbled a thank you through chattering teeth.

"Why are you out here?" Gwenhwyfar asked.

"The garden is a good place to be alone," Teleri answered, with a catch of despair in her voice. Standing so much closer now Gwenhwyfar could see the tracks of tears on her cheeks. She took Teleri's hand impulsively in her own.

"You and I, Teleri, are two lost souls, weeping for everything and nothing!"

Taken aback, all Teleri could think to say was, "I thank you for the cloak."

The misjudged dislike Gwenhwyfar had felt for her brother's wife evaporated as she saw her for what she was, a lonely girl far from home. Someone lost and afraid.

Gwenhwyfar could understand that.

"We are strangers you and I, Teleri. We should not be, for we are both women of Gwynedd."

"You may be, not I. I am an alliance, a surety between a husband and a father."

Gwenhwyfar was staggered by the desolation in her voice. "Are you not happy here?" she asked. "Does my brother not treat you well? Enniaun loves you, he has said so." Gwenhwyfar was concerned. Her family would treat any deserving woman with respect—especially one brought as wife. Even to Branwen they had shown politeness, however grudgingly. She said confidently, "My brother would not keep a wife against her will—for all the alliances offered."

Teleri bit her lip, aching to talk, to free herself of the unbearable loneliness. She must take this chance to speak out, the opportunity might never come again.

"It is not that I am unhappy. My husband treats me well, as do his brothers and their wives." She added with a show of courage, "Though I am glad I never had cause to meet with the one they call Branwen." Staggered at her impertinence she said hastily, "It was with sorrow that I learnt of Osmail's death. I pray often for his soul."

Gwenhwyfar smiled and slid her arm through Teleri's, inviting her to walk. "That is kind—thank you. The whole stronghold was relieved when Branwen passed beneath the gate!"

Teleri's brow creased. "Then you were not friends with her?"

"Friends! By Heaven I was not! I nearly fainted with horror when I met her again at Yns Witrin!" Gwenhwyfar laughed.

Teleri laughed with her, a strange sound to her own ear, for she had rarely laughed these past months. Suddenly she was talking, with an urgent need to spill her heart. "I can do no right! Everything I touch I break, every word I say is wrong. I am clumsy in action and tongue. Your brothers think me a fool."

"They do not! Dunaut told me this very evening of his liking for you, said you were unsure of yourself but you made Enniaun happy."

A glow of cheerfulness warmed Teleri. She said breathlessly, amazed at her sudden ability to talk, "I am one of two and twenty daughters produced from five wives. My father made it known he had no hope of arranging good marriages for more than the favoured few. My mother was British, a Christian. When she died I found solace within the small community of holy sisters, where I began learning the language of herbs and healing remedies. My sisters were not the kindest of girls."

"You did not want to become one of God's women?"

Teleri paused, glanced at the heavy gold and sapphire ring on her finger, her marriage band. "Somehow that dedicated life seemed so, so…"

"Dreary?"

Teleri smiled shyly. "I had no choice, you see. I hoped that if my healing proved useful my father would look on me with more favour." Teleri lifted her hands. "It did not, but it did unite me with Enniaun. He spent a while with us, negotiating agreements of trade and alliance with my father, and fell badly on a hunting trip. I was summoned to see what I could do. I must have been of use, for within the month I found myself married and on my way south to Gwynedd."

Gwenhwyfar whistled. "As quick as that! He was surely taken with you."

Teleri shrugged, spoke as she saw the truth. "It was for my healing. He has little love for a fumbling birdbrain."

"Nonsense. I have seen how he looks at you, heard the fondness in his voice when he speaks of you and his daughter. Which reminds me—I have yet to meet her."

Impulsively taking the other woman's hand, Gwenhwyfar ran forward—an awkward shuffle rather than a run because of her bulk. "Come, you shall introduce us now!"

"But she is sleeping."

"We need not wake her."

Teleri was running too, laughing, overwhelmed at the pleasure coursing through her. She had dreaded Gwenhwyfar's home coming, dreaded facing such an incredible person. Her own sisters were harsh, vain creatures who constantly sneered and jibed at her, sapping her confidence and courage, and Teleri had expected Gwenhwyfar to be the same. Although the night was dark, it seemed to her the sun had burst from behind storm clouds. Gwenhwyfar was not contemptuous, was not aloof. Apart from the baby daughter she cherished, for the first time in her life Teleri had discovered a friend.

Hand in hand, they scudded breathlessly across the gravel courtyard. Abruptly, Gwenhwyfar stopped, pleasure fleeing from her face. Her thighs felt wet, sticky, and a gush of water splashed from her, spreading on the ground at her feet. She cried out in alarm, frightened and embarrassed. Teleri darted to her side, uttering reassuring, calm words.

"It is only the waters of the womb that have broken. It is quite normal—it happened to me. Your bairn wants to come!" The younger girl, confident in her knowledge, guided the elder one forward, calling for assistance. Servants appeared. One ran for old Brenna who came bustling from the kitchens.

Within the security of her own chamber, cleaned and reclothed in her night shift, Gwenhwyfar felt a little foolish. There was no pain, no momentous thing happening to her body; just a dull ache in her lower back, and her thighs were cramped, uncomfortable, but no more than the usual feeling that accompanied the start of her monthly flow. Then it came, a tightening of muscles, like cramp or the urgent need to relieve oneself of a constipated stool. It heightened and Gwenhwyfar bit her lip to stop the trembling. As suddenly, it passed.

Teleri grinned. "It gets worse!"

"If you are to be a friend," Gwenhwyfar retorted, "I would rather you did not tell me such things."

Mares, bitches, sheep, sows, slaves, and servants birthed often enough, she reflected. But all the same, the screams of women who had a difficult time clung obstinately to her mind. "Is it very bad?" she asked.

Teleri gestured for Brenna to answer. She was ageing now, this old freed slave, but kindness was as much a part of her face as wrinkles and creases. Brenna had made life tolerable for Teleri.

"For some 'tis easy, some hard," the old woman said, crossing the room to take Gwenhwyfar's hand in her own. "We are in the hands of God."

Gwenhwyfar winced. "I would rather put my faith in Our Lady. What does a male god know of birthing?" She caught her breath. "That one was stronger."

"They will get so. By this time on the morrow we shall know if you carry boy or girl."

"That is exactly as you told me, Brenna!" Teleri exclaimed. Through the shudder of another contraction Gwenhwyfar said, "I must meet my niece another day, it seems."

When another pain came, Brenna placed her gnarled hand on Gwenhwyfar's abdomen, counting softly to herself. She peered at the birth canal, probing gently with her fingers, and grunted, satisfied. She snorted as Gwenhwyfar remarked, "Birth is not overdignified."

"For that matter," the woman replied with a laugh, "neither is conceiving!" She gestured for Gwenhwyfar to cover herself. 'Twill be some while yet. Babies come in their own time, we can do nothing to hurry them from their bed."

There was a commotion outside. Arthur burst in, thrusting aside a group of household servants. "Have you no work to attend!" he barked, slamming the door in their startled faces. He strode over to Gwenhwyfar, saying anxiously, "I was told you were taken ill!"

Gwenhwyfar shook her head. "Na, husband, not ill."

"Fools!" Brenna snapped, stumping from the room. "Can I never trust another to take a message correctly?" She was gone, her voice chiding, grumbling. Teleri made to leave also.

Gwenhwyfar said quickly, "Do not go. Stay with me."

"If you wish it, I shall be glad to help." Teleri felt a vast surge of happiness at that. She smoothed the expensive material of her gown, said, "Let me change into clothing more suited." She smiled shyly at Arthur. "Something plain is more appropriate."

Arthur waited until she had gone. "My son is coming, then?"

"So it seems." Gwenhwyfar narrowed her eyes. "You must not tease Teleri."

"Tease her? Would I do that?"

"Aye, you would." She was going to say more, let it drop as a fresh wave of contractions rippled through her.

"Arthur," she whispered, holding him tight, welcoming the strength of his arms, "I am frightened."

"Of what? Birth occurs every day."

Gwenhwyfar flared at his tactless remark, plunging away from his embrace. "Does that make it easier or safer? You men desire the pleasure, want the sons—but forget the hardship we endure to provide both!"

"The pleasure is yours also," he answered. The last thing he wanted was an argument, but, by the Bull, Gwenhwyfar was touchy these days! The slightest innocent remark and she was off, galloping in full stride. It was getting so that he was reluctant to remark on anything, important or trivial.

"Is it?" The words were out before she could swallow them.

Arthur sat silent on the bed, staring at the wall ahead, not at her. "I assumed it was," he said after a while. "I am sorry I do not please you."

Kneeling on the bed covers, Gwenhwyfar shuffled forward. She touched his shoulder. "I did not mean it to sound like that."

"How did you mean it, then?" He shrugged her aside, churlish.

"In Less Britain it was..." She fumbled for the right words. "Before, I wanted you and needed you. I enjoyed our lovemaking, it was good. It is just that," she did not know how to say her thoughts. "You must not expect too much of me too soon! I cannot comfortably give you my body with a child so large within me!"

Gwenhwyfar masked the pain of a contraction, her hand pressing tight against her abdomen. The pains were growing stronger, more frequent. She moved from the bed and walked across the room. Her back ached terribly; her legs felt unsteady. Reaching for the wall, she turned to him, hands spread in appeal. "I love you. I always have and I always shall. All I ask from you is time to come to terms with what has happened to me. Is that too much for you to give?"

Another strong contraction shuddered through her. She gasped, clutched quickly at the back of a chair.

Arthur sat motionless, watching her. He too was frightened. He loved Gwenhwyfar, but fear dried his throat, numbed his senses, shook his legs. Fear. He knew all too well how many women died giving birth or from complications after. If it should happen to Gwenhwyfar...

He steeled himself, forced himself to stand behind her. He placed his hands on her shoulders, gasped as she jerked away.

"Leave me alone!" she snarled, almost running from him, across the room.

"I cannot do a damn thing right for you lately, can I?" He stood a moment, head drooping, arms slack at his side. "I love you, Cymraes."

The contraction passed, but fear of what lay ahead and thoughts of what crowded behind made Gwenhwyfar say, "Love! Men use women for their own gain. Use and abuse! By the Mother, you shall not misuse me!"

Proud men are reluctant to give ground, and Arthur did not know how to show himself with shield down. For too many years of miserable childhood he had hidden behind a defence of bland indifference where women were concerned. The wall was too strong to breach with one blow, although for

Gwenhwyfar, it was crushing, slowly, coming down. But not this night. Fear bound the mortar tight.

He knew he ought to give support and encouragement, desperately wanted to. Why then did he bellow, "I shall use you as my woman and my wife, in my way!"

Was it so surprising she screamed, "Get out! Get away from me!" Her shrill voice could be heard clear across the courtyard. Brenna, supervising the moving of the birthing chair and sundry other items, picked up her skirts and trundled at a hobbling run back to the chamber. Reaching the door, she reeled as Arthur swung blindly past her.

Gwenhwyfar was huddled on the floor, the pains coming sharper, lasting longer. Teleri appeared. With a puzzled glance over her shoulder at Arthur's retreating form, she asked, "Is all well?"

Cradling Gwenhwyfar, Brenna persuaded her to rise, to walk, as her labour swept on. She nodded at the door. "Shut the Caer out, lass. We will manage better without the world peering in."

THIRTY-NINE

RUMAUN FOUND ARTHUR IN THE EARLY MORNING HOURS. WITH A SKIN OF wine, he sat curled in one corner of his stallion's stall, half buried by bracken bedding. Eira snorted as Gwenhwyfar's brother squeezed past his rump. The horse was settled now and eating contentedly, although it had taken some hours for the shivering to cease, for Eira disliked the sea. Arthur would have preferred to ride to Gwynedd from the south but Gwenhwyfar had wanted to get home. It was quicker by sea.

Rumaun patted the beast, giving reassurance, called to Arthur. "Are you sleeping?"

Arthur grunted, opened one eye, shut it again. "Na."

Settling himself with a tired sigh, Rumaun pushed the horse's inquisitive muzzle aside, reached for the wineskin. Tipping it to his lips, enquired, "Is there any left?" He scowled as only a few drops trickled from it, and threw the empty thing down. "We have been searching for you. Did you not hear us calling?"

If he had, Arthur gave no indication. He remained hunched, arms clasped around himself, chin tucked low, eyes firmly closed.

Determined, Rumaun continued. "The babe has come. Mother and son are fine. She had a quick time of it. Like her mother, she births her sons well." He faltered. What more should he say? As most of the Caer, he was aware of the harsh words exchanged between his sister and her husband. He said, "Women react in peculiar ways when carrying a child, and Gwenhwyfar has always been one for a sudden storm, though they blow themselves out. You must not take her words to heart." Rumaun trailed off as a tear trickled from beneath Arthur's closed lashes.

Emotion was rarely suppressed by a warrior. Any man would weep for the death of a lord or a beloved son, wife, brother, or friend, and none thought the worse of him for showing honest feelings. Yet this was no death. Where the reason to mourn?

He grasped Arthur's forearm. "Gwen is well, Arthur, believe me. Tired, Brenna says, but well."

A great breath of relief juddered from the Pendragon, "Mithras be praised—thank God!"

Rumaun hid a smile at Arthur's mixture of faiths, but aye, he agreed.

Arthur opened his eyes and stared blankly out of dilated pupils. "I have let her down." He drew a hand over the extensive stubble on his chin. "Not for the first time either. Damn this pride of mine!" He slammed his fist into the wall, causing Eira to snort and toss his head. "I have to keep proving myself, showing how good I am! All the while knowing I live a lie!" He laughed bitterly. "And Gwenhwyfar is the only woman with courage enough to tell me the truth to my face."

Rumaun nodded. "Aye, she's never been one to mince words."

A pause, then Rumaun said, "Problems look their darkest in the early hours, especially with a head pounding from over-much wine." He stood up, stretched, and brushed stable bedding from his bracae. "Brenna says you can go and see your son and wife."

Arthur toyed with the edge of his cloak, pulling the hem through his fingers. He did not answer.

Rumaun's patience was running thin; it had been a long night. "In the name of God, man—put this black mood from you!"

Arthur raised troubled eyes. "Does Gwenhwyfar wish to see me? Can she forgive me?"

"What is there to forgive?" Rumaun headed for the stable door. "A quarrel? We all have those. I can understand your anxiety for her safe delivery—but that is past." He opened the door, pushing Eira, who had walked behind him, back. "However, I would suggest no woman would forgive a husband for not coming with all haste to take up his son."

Arthur took his meaning and grinned agreement. "Aye, you say right." He stood, easing the stiffness from shoulders and back, and shoved Eira's rump aside. He put his hand on his brother-by-law's shoulder. "I had best make my peace with her, then."

He strode from the stables whistling, leaving Rumaun standing confused. God's truth, he hoped his sister understood the man better than he did!

The Pendragon found his wife drowsing, a wrapped bundle cradled in her arms. Brenna ceased her tidying and smiled as he crept through the door.

"You have a fine family. A strong wife and a healthy son."

He took a step within the doorway, saying nothing, fiddling with the gold buckle of the baldric slung across his chest. The hilt of his sword hanging at his left hip chinked against the metalwork on his leather gear as he shifted weight from one foot to the other.

Carrying a bundle of soiled linen, Brenna patted his arm maternally as she passed by him to leave. "Give her time, lad—and yourself." Noting the dark shadows beneath bloodshot eyes, added, "There is more to a marriage than the lust of coupling. Two people can only live as one when each is prepared to give and receive trust and understanding. Above that lies respect. Without respect for how the other feels, no marriage is worthwhile."

She placed her weathered old hand over his. "My eyes have seen many a problem come and go 'tween man and woman. My ears hear of plenty more. Put your trust in Gwenhwyfar and believe in yourself." Her fingers squeezed his and she left.

"Do you intend to stand there 'til dawn breaks?" Gwenhwyfar asked, her eyes closed. She opened them and smiled radiantly at him.

"I thought you were sleeping," he said in a half-whisper, stepping closer to the bed.

"I was. Brenna's talking roused me." She tenderly peeled back the baby's wrap, revealing a wrinkled pink face and button nose. Arthur sat carefully beside his wife, staring in amazed pride at the tiny thing in her arms.

"I have never seen so new born a babe," he admitted.

The bundle hiccuped, opened his eyes, squinted at the vague, blurred shape of his Da. He was warm, his belly was full of his mother's milk, and he was content with this world.

Arthur tentatively reached forward. As he touched the small hand, minute fingers curled around one of his own and gripped with astonishing strength. Arthur gasped, impressed. His eyes met Gwenhwyfar's, a grin broadening on his awed face. "He is perfect."

"Of course he is!" she laughed. "Is he not made from us?" She held the child out to him and when he hesitated, placed the bundle firmly in his arms. For a moment, Arthur fumbled, afraid to harm or drop this fragile being. Gwenhwyfar guided his hands beneath the baby's bottom and head, settling a secure but gentle hold.

"He must have a name," Arthur declared, touching the softness of his son's cheek with a loving finger.

"That he must. A name fitting for a prince and heir to the Pendragon."

Arthur glanced at Gwenhwyfar. She looked tired. Her hair tumbled loose, uncombed and free, as he liked it best. His son's hair was dark.

"I was thinking of Llacheu," he offered.

Gwenhwyfar rolled the name round in her mind. "'Tis a fine name, a British name for a British prince." Teasing, "You have thought some time on it?"

Arthur crimsoned, admitted, "Aye!" He leant forward, awkward with the child in his arms, to kiss her cheek.

Gwenhwyfar pointed to the reed-woven cradle. "He shall be safe in there."

Carefully, mindful of the head, Arthur lowered his son and covered him with the blanket, tucking it firm around the tiny body. He sat silent for a while, unable to take his gaze from the sleeping child. It was a beautiful thing, new life, especially when the new life was your son.

"Ah, Cymraes, I have been a stupid ass. These past hours I have sat alone with my sins, convincing myself everything that could go wrong with the birth would do so." He bowed his head. "I thought I was to lose you and I would forever live with the knowledge we had parted with sour words, as enemies."

Gwenhwyfar, throat tight, held out her arms to him, cradled her husband as lovingly as she had held the child. "I could never be your enemy. I dislike your ideas sometimes, but beyond that I love you." She sought for a way to explain it. "My love for you is like the full moon, sailing high and clear and bright. Only, occasionally a cloud drifts across hiding her from sight. We cannot see her, all light has gone, yet we know for certain she is still there, waiting for the wind to blow the cloud away. My love for you is like that—always there but sometimes hidden. Do not dwell on words spoken in anger." She laughed. "Most women hate their menfolk during labour."

His arms tightened about her waist, clinging urgently. He held her, his head buried against her full breasts. Already a scent of baby clung to her. "I was afraid. Of what, I am not certain—anything and everything. Afraid of losing you, afraid of not having your love." He sat up and took her face between his hands, searching her eyes, a soft, muted green, that reflected their love and happiness.

"I use women—as you said. I have twisted myself into the habit of taking what I want before they take from me. Morgause began it, all those years ago." It was difficult for him to admit the truth, to allow another into the privacy of his well-shielded fears.

Briefly Gwenhwyfar wondered whether to tell him Morgause was with the Ladies at Yns Witrin and had a daughter. To what point? It would open old wounds—best he knew nothing more of her.

"She frightened me." He shrugged, feigning casualness. "I shut that fear from me, buried myself behind a rampart and wall determined never to feel shame and terror again." His voice filled with hatred, as he added, "I would kill her if ever I met with her again." No idle threat, he meant it.

As well, Gwenhwyfar thought, *not to have said anything of her.*

Touching his cheek with the tips of her fingers, she traced the drawn lines of fatigue, said softly, "Do I frighten you?"

Arthur caught her head, brought it up to his lips, kissed each finger, then the palm. "You more than any. In a different way. Others, I have taken as I willed with no thought save for myself. I needed to dominate them, show I was not scared of their feminine power. Whores care not how they are treated as long as they receive payment, and Winifred, I think, enjoyed it that way. But you," he placed tender kisses on her eyes, cheeks and lips. "You frighten me because I am so scared I might lose you." He faltered, embarrassed at talking of these deep-running feelings. "I know it is because of what Melwas did that you are unable to respond to my touch, but still I tell myself it might not be the reason. And that one there," he indicated the sleeping child, "I was jealous of him. He kept me from your bed." He stayed the words of protest that were forming with another, longer kiss. "But I am proud of him now he is here."

She responded by returning the kiss with a passion she had forgotten existed. "Do you love me, Arthur?"

"Need you ask that of me?"

"I need."

"Then aye, I love you. I have never loved any other than you. Nor have I had love in return, for the sake of love alone. I fear the slender thread that binds us will snap. That I have sawn through it." He added something more. "You are more than my wife, you are my Cymraes. You are one alone, special, a single bright star shining in the blackness."

"Then why talk of a slender thread, husband? For myself, I am bound to you by a chain of iron. Unbendable, unbreakable. Even death shall not free my soul from yours."

He lay back, resting his head on the pillow, and snuggled close to her warmth, surrendering to the tiredness that hammered persistently behind his aching forehead.

Gwenhwyfar held him lightly, thinking on his words. "I know of the conflict within you, dear heart, but I too have such a battle to wage. Happen together we can conquer this war which is tearing at us. Given enough patience."

She tilted her head to see his face more clearly, realised his breathing had slowed, shallowed.

Brenna entered the room some while later. Gwenhwyfar put her finger to her lips, whispered, "My two men sleep."

APRIL 456

FORTY

MARCHING WAS NEVER A VERY APPEALING PART OF ARMY LIFE. MARCHING with full equipment in the pouring rain, and leading a perfectly rideable horse, could bring some men close to mutiny. Except, the Pendragon was putting himself through the same punishing routine, and the men were wanting to become part of his elite Artoriani. Arthur had made things quite clear to them at the outset: "*If you are not fit, if you cannot stand the pace, then get you back to Vortimer's soft-bellied lizards.*"

Throughout the winter men had drifted to Gwynedd in groups of three and four, singly, or brother with brother to join Arthur. From Dyfed, fifty young men had braved the first heavy snow to set their spears beneath his banner. The warming of spring saw more coming, the groups larger, the men eager. With those who had left Vortimer with Arthur, they had enough to form a full ala quingenaria. Five hundred enthusiastic men, striving to become the fittest, best-disciplined and most admired troops since the Roman Eagles had lifted the standards for which they were named, and taken sail back to Rome.

Arthur was determined to have them the best. These men, and those who would follow when the name of the Artoriani came familiar to everyone's lips. He saw a day, in the not too distant future, when every young man who could sit a horse would seek to join his cavalry. But that day was not yet here, and until then he had to prove himself—and his men. So they drilled and they marched, they practised their fighting skills. On horseback, on foot. In pairs, as a group, as a turma of thirty men. And together as an ala.

Arthur wiped rain from his nose and hefted the shield slung across his shoulders. As commander, he did not need to carry full equipment, but the muscles of horses and men had to be tightened and there was no better way than trotting ten miles over rough terrain carrying a full pack. He glanced behind at his men, walking with heads ducked, some with arms resting over their horses' necks. Three miles to home. On the morrow they would practice again with spear throwing. Mounted, dismounted, from a walk, trot, and canter. Already he had his men able to do most things at any pace. The jest around the campfires at night was that by the time Arthur had finished with them, they would be able to piss into a bucket at fifty paces while riding at full gallop.

He would let them mount up soon. The horses had not required the rest, but the men needed the additional exercise. Walking in this regular, steady-paced rhythm with his hand resting lightly on Eira's sodden neck, Arthur's mind began to drift—easy in safe territory where there was no need to watch for an enemy's approach.

Several letters had arrived three days back. Most had been routine correspondence that came with any position of command. Two had not.

From Vortimer word that Vortigern was dead. He had fallen, hit his head on a step, and never again opened his eyes. Whether he had in truth fallen or was pushed, Arthur had no particular care; the man was gone, leave it at that. With the news, a plea for the Pendragon to return with all possible speed. Arthur would have ignored it, let the fool drown in the ruin of his own making, except Vortimer had not asked, had not ordered, but had begged. "*I will need every able man, Arthur, and you with your following are more able than most. I beg for your help, on your terms, Pendragon. Your terms.*"

It was tempting. Very tempting.

And then there was the second letter. From Winifred.

Arthur halted Eira, signalled for the men to mount. Settling himself in the saddle, his thighs sliding neatly under the curve of the two pommel horns, he waited for the men to make ready, then moved off at a trot. Dusk would be falling soon and he had had enough of this damned rain. Enough of trailing through these mountains, too. Training was all very well, but occasionally there came a need for more. For the real thing.

He would go back to Vortimer, as the man said, on his own terms, and he would sort out this latest problem with his ex-wife. Gwenhwyfar would not like either of his decisions, but then she would not need to know of the second thing, would she?

Plunging his stallion into the foaming race of a river, Arthur gasped as its coldness hit his feet and legs, even through the warmth of grass-stuffed leather boots. After all, he reasoned, Winifred can do no harm now, and this son of hers means nothing to me, or Gwenhwyfar.

But if that was true, why did he feel this chum of dread in the pit of his stomach?

MAY 456

FORTY-ONE

WINIFRED'S SON HAD BEEN BORN A LUSTY, HEALTHY BOY. WITH THE COMING of spring, he reached six months and he was crawling, gurgling and as chubby as a fatted ox.

Winifred adored him.

Sitting across the room, watching the man she insisted on calling husband drink his wine, she realised two important things. She loved Arthur and, though he had never seen their son, he detested their child.

"So," she said breaking the uneasy silence, "you have gathered almost a quarter of the men loyal to my half-brother to your side."

"I am as loyal to Vortimer as ever. It is just that some men prefer to ride behind my Dragon rather than his Boar."

"While awaiting the chance for the dragon to slay the boar, aye, I suppose you would be."

Arthur drained his goblet and stood up. "I agreed to see you, Winifred, against my better judgement. I expected to be insulted but not accused of treason. Say what you wanted me to hear and let me be gone."

Winifred too stood. She lifted the wine jug from the table beside her and crossed to refill Arthur's goblet. "Sit, husband, let us not quarrel." She gestured towards the couch, smiled as she perched next to him, her skirts not quite touching his leg.

"I understand Vortimer intends to stand against Hengest some time soon, make a valiant attempt to send him back across the sea."

Arthur laughed and moved along the couch away from the over close proximity of his ex-wife. "Did you arrange to meet with me just to discover the intentions of the King? Sorry, Winifred, find yourself another tattle-tale."

She kept the smile pinned firm to her lips. He was as irritating as ever! "I asked to talk with you to discuss our son's needs, husband. I am merely attempting to make polite conversation."

Laughing all the louder, Arthur reclined back, his legs and arms sprawled haphazard. "I believe you, Winifred, truly I do." He shook his head, still laughing, and sipped his drink. This wine was strong. He usually took more water with it, but he'd not lose face before this black-clad scheming bitch. All the same, he had best keep a clear head, which would not be easy the way Winifred kept topping up his goblet.

He touched her robe with one finger. "Why this drab garb? It looks most tragic, but does little to flatter your colouring."

Her eyes sparked slightly, flattered, she inclined her head. "I wear it in mourning for my father, and also because the Holy Christian Sisters tend to wear such clothing. However, I thank you for the compliment."

He grunted. "It was not meant as one."

Winifred was not to be rebuffed. She took his hand in her own, replied, "All the same, it sounded as one."

Withdrawing from her touch, Arthur plumped a cushion more comfortable behind his back. "And since when, Winifred, have you been a Holy Sister?"

Not missing the sarcasm she decided to answer truthfully. "Since the day you abandoned me to widowhood." Arthur grunted again, unimpressed. "I have founded a women's cloister on the edge of my estate; they have granted me the honour of conferring me as Abbess." Ignoring a third snort of derision, she continued, "In fact I am here at Verulamium to meet with Bishop Patricius to discuss where to found another such house."

"Patricius? Was he not the fat fool who married us?"

Winifred ignored the insult. "I thought it most fortuitous you were also here."

Arthur bit back a retort. Nothing about Winifred was ever by chance. She was a schemer, like her mother—too much like her mother. He had never trusted either of them and was not about to alter strong-founded opinions just because Winifred professed to be enshrined in the Christian faith. She could be wailing to Woden on the morrow if it suited her.

In fact, this afternoon's meeting had taken Winifred a lot of arranging. She had to speak with Arthur direct, but had to wade through a mire of past misunderstandings and prejudices to do so. The use of the Church would prove costly but, as she had succeeded in seeing Arthur, it would be worthwhile.

Now all she had to do was convince him of her loyalty and get him to acknowledge his son as his heir. Not that she needed formal acceptance, but why climb over the rocks if there was firm sand to walk upon?

"You knew I had sent letters from Less Britain, didn't you?" she said.

Letters? Arthur carefully controlled his expression, sipped at his wine. One letter he knew of—but letters, plural? "Naturally," he lied.

Winifred smiled to herself. So-o he had not known! "Then, as you also know, I pleaded with my mother to send help, to bring me home. It took a while, Arthur, for me to realise she had no need of me, not since she had a son to take my place." She put her hand over his. "A son, Arthur, who may one day become king, can mean so very much to a woman."

He did not answer, nor, Winifred noted, did he this time remove his hand.

"That time at Caer Gloui, my mother left me struggling against the water swirling around our legs, left me to drown. She cared only to save her son." Glancing sideways at Arthur: "You know she and my young brother are with Hengest?"

Arthur nodded. He knew.

Winifred shifted closer, her thigh pressing against his, fingers closing tighter around his hand. "When you slay Hengest, I ask you to slit Rowena's treacherous throat also."

Drily Arthur observed, "This request would have nothing to do with each of you vying for your own son to become king of the British?"

Winifred laughed, playfully squeezed his thigh. "Nothing at all."

Deliberately, Arthur retrieved his hand and moved his leg away from hers. He sat forward, twisting his head to look at her. "I already have a son to follow me. He is named Llacheu ap Arthur and his blood is pure British with no taint of Saex poison." He rose and tipped the wine on the floor, then opening his fingers he let the goblet fall, trod on the shattered glass.

Placing his hands on the couch on either side of her, he leant close, his lips almost brushing hers. "You have your entire dowry returned, the estate near Portus Adumi, and your freedom to do what you will, within reason. Go raise your son to be a farmer or a priest and keep him well out of my way, Winifred." He kissed her, a parting touch of mockery that sealed his threatened meaning. "If you do not, he will be nought but dust mouldering in a grave."

She did not move away from him, sat completely still, but her voice trembled as she questioned, "You would not slaughter your own son?"

Arthur walked from her and crossed to the door, lifting his cloak from a stool as he passed. "I would not advise you to put me to the test."

For a long while Winifred sat staring at the door he had closed behind him. She had turned from her mother's people to ensure her son became Arthur's heir. That the father would not accept the boy came as no surprise, but she had wanted to try, wanted at least to try. She stood, ignoring the shards of crushed glass crunching beneath her boot among the puddle wine. Cerdic would one day be king, Llacheu or no Llacheu. Winifred smiled to herself as she left the room by a second door. Preferably no Llacheu.

JULY 456

FORTY-TWO

JULY. THE SUN HUNG AGAINST A CLOUDLESS BLUE SKY, RIVERS WHICH RAN AS torrents in winter had dwindled to the trickle of streams, and even the mountains of Eryri seemed to sag beneath the heat. The coast had become too dry, the hot wind blowing sand into eyes, nose, and throat; beaches stank of rotting seaweed and dead fish and birds. Enniaun moved his household to an inland stronghold where the mountains and valleys funnelled a cooling breeze.

Gwenhwyfar was helping to work the horses. She enjoyed the young stock, admired their natural reluctance for discipline, tempered by an eagerness to please. She was lunging a colt, setting him circling her on a long halter rope. His dark mane fell in a cascade from a proud neck and he carried his tail high as was the way with his ancestors, the desert-bred horses. His coat, the smudged charcoal colour of a youngster, would not turn white until maturity. Gwenhwyfar had especial pride in this one, a son of Cunedda's best stallion and her own mare Tan. A big colt, fast and powerful but with the manners and affability of a riding gelding. She called him Hasta, the Latin for Spear.

At the start he had fussed and cavorted, refusing to drop his head, bend his spine, and flex his hocks beneath him, but he had soon given in to Gwenhwyfar's insistence on a relaxed swinging stride. His ears flicked at the sound of her encouraging voice as he went through the paces of walk, trot, and canter, his head tossing and tail swishing against the irritation of flies.

As he worked she was pleased to observe that already his body was supple and compliant, his muscles strengthening. Soon it would be time to turn him out in the horse runs, to rest and grow into that last strength of maturity. By next spring he would be ready to wear bit and saddle, take a light rider. As he paced round her, she thought on next summer's work. To sit astride him, ease him into leg and hand commands, taking him through each stage of learning gradually and with sympathetic patience. By the time he was a four-year-old he would be ready to start the serious work of becoming a warhorse. It took many years to raise and train mounts for use in battle. There were no short cuts, no making do. When a man's life might depend on his horse's instant response, there could not be.

Other young horses were being put through their lessons at practical distances around the training ground. To one side of Hasta, a three-year-old chestnut was misbehaving, rearing against the restraint of a bit, refusing to go forward.

Gwenhwyfar clucked to her colt, urging him on, talked to him, steadying his extending, excited pace. The chestnut suddenly plunged backwards into Hasta, sending the younger and smaller grey, crashing down. Hooves thrashed for a moment, kicking up dust, then Hasta was on his feet again, his off-hind leg trailing as blood dripped, spotting the dry ground.

Gwenhwyfar swore, hastily wound in the long rein and soothed the frightened young horse as best she could. Men came running, slowing their pace as they neared. Enniaun pushed his way through the gathering crowd. "I saw what happened," he said frowning. "This is the third time this week that chestnut has caused trouble. How is your youngster?" This last to Gwenhwyfar, who was bending over the wounded hind leg.

"Superficial, the blood makes it look worse. He'll be lame some while though." She cursed inwardly, said aloud, "He was making fine progress too."

Peering at the cut hock, Enniaun agreed with her diagnosis. Straightening up, he studied the chestnut. "We will geld that one—he'll make a fine riding horse but he has not the sense for a war mount." He signaled someone to remove the offender and as the crowd drifted away, walked with Gwenhwyfar, leading Hasta, across the training ring to the stables.

"You have worked hard with this colt."

Gwenhwyfar patted the horse's neck. "He is for Arthur. Eira serves well but is ageing. Besides, when Arthur brings his cavalry together he will need more than one reliable mount."

"Will he be ready?"

For a moment Gwenhwyfar was uncertain whether her brother referred to the horse or Arthur. Either way the answer came the same. "He will be ready when the time comes."

They reached the stable yard, dry in this weather, normally squelching in ankle-deep mud. Gwenhwyfar tied the halter rope to an iron ring in the wall and fetched water, calling for a slave to bring linen, taking her time to thoroughly wash and clean the wound. Enniaun stood at the horse's head, playing with ears and forelock, watching his sister's experienced hands.

Arthur would be calling for the rest of his men soon, and those horses that were ready. Rubbing the grey's forehead, Enniaun was suddenly reminded of his father. Cunedda had promised the Pendragon all the horses he needed, but Enniaun was not the horseman his father had been. And there were the coasts that needed cleansing of Hibernian scum and Council to attend and—oh the list was endless!

"I cannot supply all Arthur's needs, Gwen."

She finished, patted the animal's rump, and straightened, pushing sweat-damp hair from her forehead with her arm. A smear of blood smudged her cheek. "He knows that, does not expect you to." She led the horse to the nearest stable, fetched hay, watched him settle to eat, resting the weight from the injured leg. "It is not so essential now he has control of the entire West Country and the pick of the horses. All we need is the time to train them, and the men to ride them."

"Men will come. As for time, there is never enough of that." Enniaun was squinting through the glare of sunlight towards the gate arch. Riders were coming in. He did not recognise the horses, nor, as they came nearer, the riders themselves. He began to brush the dust off his tunic and step forward. Gwenhwyfar glanced up as he ceased talking, watched the riders with a frown of curiosity. If she hadn't known better she would swear that was... Blood of Mithras, it was! Winifred!

Fortunate that Gwenhwyfar had an excuse to escape, dirty as she was from her own and horse sweat and blood. She exchanged polite greetings and departed as soon as she could for the security of privacy. This stronghold was not so grand as Caer Arfon, smaller and more restricted with not a Roman building in sight, but for all that the wattle-built round-house was comfortable and private.

Gwenhwyfar found she was shaking as she entered Enniaun's Hall, as evening descended deliciously cool. A thousand thousand questions skittered through her mind as she made her way through the throng of men pushing to seat themselves for the day's meal. Questions that needed answers. Why was Winifred here? And why was she travelling with Bishop Patricius?

Gwenhwyfar had noticed Winifred's black clothing, the white veil. So she had become a Holy Sister. That at least explained why she rode with the bishop. But why here to Gwynedd? To stir trouble, for sure—there could be no other reason.

It came as a surprise, and rather disconcerting, to see Winifred's polite and demure—almost humble—behaviour. She served the bishop herself with food and drink brought in by the slaves, and served Enniaun, although, Gwenhwyfar realised with amusement, the humility did not extend to serving others of the family, notably herself.

In accordance with custom, Enniaun could not ask their business until his guests were fed and rested. The waiting passed in an agony of impatience; by the time the slaves at last began to clear away the trestle tables and remains of the meal, Gwenhwyfar was almost squirming in her seat.

The bishop drank his wine slowly, asked for a refill, then excused himself for the latrine. At last he settled himself and the Hall grew quiet. "Lord Enniaun," he began, "I come with the Lady Pendragon"—there came several sharp intakes of breath, that was Gwenhwyfar's title—"to plead for land to be given to God."

Enniaun's brows had drawn together, but he answered pleasantly, "Much of my land is already given to God. We have several chapels here in Gwynedd."

"Chapels, but no holy house. Dyfed has a cloister, as does your brother's land of Ceredigion. My Lady here"—Patricius indicated Winifred—"has ridden with me these many weeks past to find a suitable place in her father's Powys."

Winifred had been sitting silent, head bowed, hands in her lap. At this she looked up and added, "I needed to create something of God for my father's lost soul. A holy building would come near to providing penance for him, but two such places would ensure he rested in peace."

Several nodded their heads in agreement.

"And you thought to found somewhere in Gwynedd?" Enniaun asked with curt politeness.

Winifred was about to reply, but the bishop silenced her.

"It was my suggestion, Lord Enniaun, for Gwynedd is the only British-held land that has not fully embraced God. An oversight which saddens my heart. My Lady Pendragon has offered to set the matter straight."

Gwenhwyfar was saying nothing, staring with growing rage at this pompous fat man and the arrogant scheming woman seated beside him. Enniaun could not agree to this—this absurdity! But to her horror he was nodding his head, offering his hand. No! This must not be! She leapt to her feet, slamming the table with the palm of her hand, the noise bursting like a thunderclap around the confined space of the Hall.

"I will not allow this! A Saex whore's bitch founding a holy house in our Gwynedd—and in Vortigern's name? It was her father who slew Uthr, my husband's father…"

Winifred stared coldly at Gwenhwyfar and interrupted with a shrill cry.

"Under God's law a man can have but one wife. I am the Pendragon's wife, the mother of his son."

Gwenhwyfar turned pale. She stood a moment, rocking, then sat heavily, the room spinning. Son? She said son. Winifred had a son by Arthur?

"Yes, I have a son, Gwenhwyfar." Winifred's voice shot like a spear into Gwenhwyfar's numbed mind. "Born later by a few weeks to yours, but mine was conceived in wedlock to my husband. My husband, Gwenhwyfar, the one I have never accepted the order of divorce from. The one recognised by Holy Church." She bent low, said into Gwenhwyfar's ear, "I have made appeal to his grace the Pope, Gwenhwyfar. I am a respected woman of the Church, you a pagan slut. It is my son he will declare legitimate, not yours! My son who will become the next Pendragon, the next king."

She would have said more, kicked harder while Gwenhwyfar was down, but Meriaun burst forward, stood with hands planted on the table, a snarl of contempt etched on his face. "I challenge you on this decision, Enniaun. I will have no house, however holy, built by the kin of the man who ordered the brutal murder of my father."

At his words, the Hall erupted in an uproar of assent. Men and women came to their feet and moved towards the high table, growling and muttering. Enniaun was standing, appealing for calm; some heard and faltered, most ignored him, surging round Winifred, Vortigern's daughter.

It was only the bishop, lumbering to his feet and thrusting her behind him, who saved Winifred from the mob. Enniaun leapt forward, physically pushing the angry crowd back. "I call for peace!" he was yelling. "Peace! Calm yourselves."

His urgent words got through. The anger subsided, bubbling beneath the surface—better than the raging torrent of a moment before.

Enniaun patted the air with his spread hands, calming them further. "Be seated, all of you. Let us talk of this thing in a civilised manner."

Gwenhwyfar was shaking. Civilised? Winifred, the bitch who had murdered Ceridwen… but then the fight went out of her. There was no proof, only a suspicion. And it was not Winifred who had caused the death of her kin, but her father. Winifred was innocent of the charges. The bishop was talking, she realised, stating the laws of the Holy Church and the Pope in Rome. If Cunedda had been here he would have kicked the man's fat backside from here to Dyfed, but her Da was not here; Enniaun was Prince of Gwynedd, and Enniaun was a devout follower of Christ.

FORTY-THREE

SIX DAYS GWENHWYFAR ENDURED WINIFRED'S PRESENCE, SIX DAYS OF HER gloating and patronising insults. Six long days of clenched fists and fingers that itched to take up a dagger and cut her accursed throat. And then the messenger from Arthur arrived.

He galloped into the Caer, his mount labouring with lathered neck and frothing mouth. The rider slithered from the saddle, his knees buckling with exhaustion. Someone fetched him water and he drank in great gulps, gasped, "Urgent word for Lord Enniaun!"

A brief letter, bearing Arthur's seal but written in a strange hand, struck Gwenhwyfar with dread. If it was addressed to her brother, then surely it carried bad news? She watched, fingers clutching her tunic as he broke the Dragon seal, watched with held breath as he read quickly, muttering the written words.

Gwenhwyfar thought, *Is Arthur hurt? Dead?*

Winifred swished into the Hall, Bishop Patricius puffing like a lapdog at her heels. "A message from the Pendragon?" she demanded. "For me? May I have it?"

Enniaun ignored her, read through to the end, though there was little to read. He lifted his head, said to the gathering crowd, "Hengest has made his move; he has met with Vortimer near the ford of the river Crae, way beyond his designated territory. They outnumbered our British. Three to one." He gave the communication to Gwenhwyfar, hovering ill at ease at his shoulder, let her read for herself. Absently, she passed it to Winifred, who scanned the writing quickly "This is not Arthur's hand," she said.

No one bothered answering her. What mattered if it were Arthur's hand or not? The writing would not alter the facts. Arthur's hurriedly dictated words, written by a clerk in a precise, neat hand, told that he and his men, stationed to the north of Londinium, had ridden swiftly to give Vortimer aid but arrived too late. The stilted words conveyed little of the destruction they had found, the bare facts only, two short paragraphs that could not hope to match the indecent slaughter.

Arthur sent word of the killing and asked for Enniaun to send south those men and horses that were ready. He would await them at Caer Leon.

"I have taken command, Enniaun, and I intend to finish this thing with Hengest. I need to complete my Artoriani."

The Pendragon had been too sickened to say more. How could words describe the death of good men? When he arrived, too late, at the Crae ford, bodies were strewn across a churned battlefield, the ravens already gathered, gorging on the corpses and flapping around the broken standard of Vortimer's Boar.

Fighting the nausea that heaved within him, Arthur found what remained of the King. Hanging from a cracked and blood-stained banner's shaft, he found Vortimer's head, one eye already gone, the other dangling from pecked sinew. As for the rest of him, there was no way of knowing which stripped and mutilated body had once been a king.

Arthur had sunk to his knees and spewed the revulsion from him. The stench. Men, taken prisoner and grouped together with their hands bound, had been tortured and butchered, their ribs torn open, insides ripped out.

With Vortimer dead, the sons of Vortigern were no more—aside from one Saex-born cur, the boy Vitolinus.

Standing, staring bleakly at the grotesque remains of men he had known, Arthur realised that leadership was his for the taking. Why then did he weep? For this waste of men? For the sorrowing wives and fatherless children? It should not have happened. Not like this.

At the edge of the stench and vileness, hearing his men retching and coughing as they gathered the dead, Arthur had dictated his matter-of-fact letter. He spoke the words dull and flat, a toneless, distanced account of fact.

Dismissed, the clerk hurried away to seek a messenger, glad to escape. Arthur stayed, watching as his men began to bury the mutilated corpses.

AUGUST 456

FORTY-FOUR

MERIAUN, TYPIAUNAN'S SON, WAS TO TAKE THE HORSES TO ARTHUR. IN NO uncertain terms, he told Enniaun what he thought of his deal to parcel out Gwynedd land to the greed of the Church and the lying daughter of a murdering bastard. Told his dead father's brother he would join with the Pendragon and return no more to Gwynedd. Enniaun let him go, knowing a man's passionate temper often cooled given time.

What Enniaun did not expect, nor Winifred, was that Gwenhwyfar took herself and her son with him. They arranged it secret between them, she and Meriaun. Winifred might have the power of the Church behind her plea for her son, but Gwenhwyfar was now Arthur's wife, and no God-kneeling Saex was going to over-shadow Llacheu! A son may be named heir, may be first-born, second-born, bastard born, if the army did not want him as king when the time came to claim the title, then king he would not be. The sure way to get an army to shout loud for their chosen man was for them to know that man. Oh aye, Gwenhwyfar would go to Arthur, and take her son with her! Winifred could claim what she liked, but Llacheu would grow and learn and live with Arthur's men. It was him they would choose when the time came for another Pendragon! Llacheu, not this rat-spawned Cerdic.

They left Caer Arfon, heading south along the coast where safety lay in their own land and Ceredig's adjoining holding. Two women, a young boy, two hundred men, and three times as many horses. There came no trouble those first few days, aside from a kicking match between two stallions and another with a bruised sole. The horses settled well after the initial excitement, walking steady, with heads down, ears lopping, and tails swishing.

The weather held fine. Warm days with a pleasant breeze. From Ceredig's borders they had turned south-east, making for the welcome of Builth, but those friendly lands were behind them now, with the hostile ranges of plunging valleys and lonely hills rising ahead. The desolate land of the wolf.

At least these open hills gave scant cover for raiders. Trees and thickets hid men only too well—and they knew there were men following them. The Watchers, they called them, for want of a better description. Watchers keeping pace, never showing themselves, two, happen three men.

Little clues and gut feelings told Gwenhwyfar and the men they were keeping pace a steady mile or so behind. That prickling sensation on the back of the neck, the knowing that eyes were on you. The thought that if you turned round quick someone would be there—but when you did, there was nothing save a swaying branch or waving grass and a blurred shadow.

Once at night they heard the whinny of a horse, hastily muffled. Come dawn, Gwenhwyfar sent a scout to ride in a sweeping half-circle behind them. He found the remains of a fire, with flattened grass where men had lain, and horse droppings. A second dawn, a signalling whistle carried clearly.

Shadows unobserved, like midnight wraiths, always following. Their presence unsettling, unnerving. Sometimes dropping further back, never coming nearer, always there. Watching.

When the heavy woodland at last fell behind, Gwenhwyfar and the men breathed relief for this open country. Nowhere now for their unwanted companions to hide. Let them show themselves or be gone!

Around the night-time fires talk of who they might be had taken many meandering turns. The favoured theory was that they were men of Builth, ensuring the travellers came and went in peace. The new-claimed petty kingdom was friendly with Gwynedd, but friendship was too uncertain to trust wholehearted. Horses such as these would be a fine prize indeed for an ambitious young man who had elevated himself to the tribal title of king. But they had passed into the open hills, out beyond Builth's borders, and no attack had come. The tingling along the spine and hair rising along the collar faded under the expanse of blue sky rolling along the hilltops. Men relaxed. The Watchers, whoever they were, seemed to have gone.

Such was life—one problem exchanged for another. Before them lay uncertain territory, the first swelling hills of Brychan's borders over to their right. He was a man who blew with the wind. He could be friendly, but was just as capable of falling into an unexpected rage. Add to that, he had no liking for Arthur; he might take pleasure in stealing his horses.

Not far ahead lay the Usk valley, and from there it was downhill to Caer Leon and Arthur. Easy riding, except for these outlying hills of Brychan's.

Gwenhwyfar, riding loose-limbed and relaxed on her mare, ran her hand through the hair falling down her back. She had not bound it, not caring to take time over neatness. It was clean, washed early that morning in the cool waters of a stream—who cared for women's braiding? Not she!

She burst suddenly into song, a jaunty tune with a marching rhythm. Her nephew Meriaun, riding close behind, joined in, his rich baritone blending well with her light soprano. Men began to add their voices—and their own, soldiers' words.

The weather was still holding, and they had not far to go. By tomorrow nightfall Gwenhwyfar would be with Arthur. The day was good. The sun shone, and all was well.

Three worries had been constant. The first was wolves, for though it was mid-summer these hills and valleys were their hunting grounds. Their mournful cries could be heard at night, echoing among the hills. Men turned uneasily in their blankets, one ear cocked for a wolf-bark that sounded over-near. Their rank scent sometimes blew downwind, stirring horses into restless unease. Wolves were always a beast to be minded.

Raiders, too, prowled as skulking packs. Sea-wolves—human kin to the grey-coated kind—were no danger this far inland, but Brychan had come as a raider and settled, claiming land for his own, swallowing more and more, like a voracious cuckoo in a sparrow's nest. And there could be others—these Watchers? Many a man resented Gwynedd's influence and power. Others disliked the Pendragon, remembering Uthr his father. Any petty chief could be tempted, when the gift dangled promisingly enough.

The third worry, the threat of bad weather.

The last two, of course, came together.

By late afternoon, clouds lumbered in from the west, a great bulk of grey hanging above the hills like a gathering army. Distant grumbles of thunder warned of a storm, and the air fell sickly hot and sullen, lying heavy on sweating man and beast. Horses flicked their ears uneasily, sensing the change, bunching together, a few kicking or snapping.

Scouts returned with word of a sheltered valley ahead; it was agreed to make early camp, sit the storm out. It was a risk to stay so close to Brychan's land, but risks had to be weighed.

They reached the valley as the first stinging raindrops beat against flesh and hide. The horses eased to a halt, tucked their tails, and turned sodden rumps into the wind. One or two younger beasts jumped nervously as the thunder rolled across a black sky but, eager for grazing, they settled soon enough.

Tents were hastily erected. Small hope of a fire this night! Gwenhwyfar saw Llacheu and his nurse, Enid, into the dryness of their quarters, paused before ducking out beneath the flap. She said, with a proud smile, "My son has travelled well."

"Aye, he likes horseback!" Enid replied.

Gwenhwyfar laughed. "The next night he cuts a tooth and keeps us awake, happen we should cuddle him close on the back of a horse to ease him to sleep!"

Smiling, Gwenhwyfar pulled her cloak tight around her and ducked out into the squalling rain. Head lowered, she ran towards the commanding officer's tent. They would all be eager to complete the evening's discussion of progress and the morrow's plans.

The second watch of the night. Gwenhwyfar rode among the grazing horses, sitting easy in the saddle but alert. She did not need to ride watch, but she enjoyed it, insisted she took her turn. Even in such foul weather.

Head bent against the rain, Gwenhwyfar saw a rider slither from his horse. She cursed aloud and turned the chestnut she rode—Caradog had been drunk over often this trip! More than his share of the strong barley beer the pack ponies carried had passed down his throat. The decurion had lashed him twice already with thong and tongue. There would not be a third time.

With a caustic remark ready, Gwenhwyfar cantered over to his prone body, expecting him to rise unsteadily, grinning foolishly at her approach, some quick excuse on his tongue.

An arrow lay buried in his chest, the shaft still quivering.

Swinging her horse aside, Gwenhwyfar shouted a warning, her voice snatched by the wind. Another arrow! She heard its hiss, felt the jolt as it thudded into the soft muscles of her left bicep.

She thought fast. Ramming her heels into the horse's ribs, she galloped forward, barging into a group of grazing animals. They tossed their heads, snorting, as she pulled the chestnut round on his hocks and brought him to a slithering halt. Here, amid the cover of other horses, she drew her sword. Raising the blade high, she swung it above her head, screaming the war cry of Gwynedd.

Other men of the watch had already seen and heard the danger; three of their number lay dead. The alarm sounded in camp. Men began to tumble from their tents, cursing, sleep instantly gone, weapons drawn, eager for action.

Those mounted swung into a gallop, streaking to meet the enemy, spears poised, ready to throw at a sighted target.

Gwenhwyfar, galloping hard, shouted for them to pull up, wait for others before attacking. Useless to fight at half-strength in a higgle-piggle of disorder. An officer joined her, an older, experienced soldier. His face contorted with rage, he brought the flat of his sword blade slamming down on the back of any man he could reach, yelling and yelling at them to turn back, wait for the command.

There was no choice—blood was up. Gwenhwyfar rode with them.

Visibility was poor. Rain came in gusting squalls blown by a veering wind. Lightning illuminated the valley, sending dark waiting figures hunched beneath cloaks scurrying into cover. A few let a hail of arrows fly, their hurried aim falling short, blown aside.

Arthur's men, mostly young lads, untried, newly trained, had seen them. Twenty, thirty men? Brychan's? Or had the Watchers at last gathered strength and emerged from hiding? Time enough to discover names and faces later; there was a more urgent need at this moment—staying alive.

The infant Artoriani moved forward, the mounted men well ahead, leaving those on foot to run fast, make their way best they could. Some were still clad only in under-tunics, dragging on leather fighting gear as they ran.

On the hillside, the attackers rose to meet them with an ululation of expected victory. By their dress and weaponry they were Hibernian settlers—Brychan's men. They closed, riders flinging themselves from horseback to fight sword to sword, shield to shield, unable to fight mounted on rain-sodden sloping ground in the dark.

Gwenhwyfar was among the men, furious at their lack of discipline, their "strike first think later" impulsiveness. Little she could do about it now, but later... She came up with the decurion. His eyes bulged, and he was snarling like a wounded dog-wolf. He shouted something to her, and though she did not catch the words she guessed their meaning. What had become of the rigorous training; the day-by-day monotony of drill, drill, and more drill? She exchanged blows with one of Brychan's men, striking two-handed with her sword, ripping its blade through his thigh, dodging herself to avoid a similar thrust. Cursed at the stupidity of these raw young men.

A weird dance was stepped in the darkness, men fighting hand to hand, killing or falling wounded beneath lashing rain and rolling thunder. Another man came before Gwenhwyfar, his face leering, lit up ghostly pale by a lightning flash. His foot slipped, the sole of his boot slithering over wet grass. She took advantage, driving her blade up, through his belly. She had to push his body from her sword with her foot, swearing as fluently as any soldier when the blade sucked out, spewing steaming intestines over her feet.

Turning aside, her breath coming in gasps, Gwenhwyfar glanced quickly with another flash of lightning at the horses grazing in the valley below. Only a few, younger colts mostly, were fidgeting, ears flicking, legs stamping. They had been trained with infinite care for Arthur. She snorted—so had the men, but they had so easily forgotten! Just as well the horses had not! The roar and clash of fighting and the scent of blood ought to now come as natural to them as a cock's crow and the smell of dung. Patience had paid off; those hours of mock battles, the quiet calming of nervous horses as cattle were slaughtered before them, the nauseating stench of offal strewn around the paddocks! Gwenhwyfar had time for a quick smile. Her Da had known a thing or two about the training of horses!

The tents away to the left caught her eye. Figures were running, illuminated momentarily, sharp and white against the blackness. Damned fools! Stupid, stupid idiots! They had all turned out, running fit to burst into the attack; not one man left to guard the camp!

A thought hit her like an axe through her skull. She screamed as she ran, slithering on the wet grass of the slope. "Llacheu!"

The horses had remained where they had been left—another insistence of Cunedda's training. A man must be able to count on his horse to stand when he dismounted, intentionally or otherwise, for an unseated cavalryman could lose his life while blundering around the battlefield in search of his mount.

Slipping for some way on her backside, Gwenhwyfar scrambled to her feet, ran to the nearest horse, seized the reins and vaulted into the saddle. Barely settled, she hauled his head round and raced to her son.

Thunder cracked overhead, smothering Enid's terrified screams as a man dragged her by the hair away from the tent. He was admiring his prize, did not see the single blow that severed his head in a neat stroke, sending it rolling grotesquely down the incline, thick lips still grinning.

Gwenhwyfar pounded on past, her sword red with the man's blood. Enid, released, flung her skirt over her head and crouched shrieking. Gwenhwyfar swung her horse round and came back, heeling him forward, hooves flinging up great clumps of sodden, muddied turf, to meet a second man.

Realising his danger, the man dropped his bundle of loot and grabbed at Enid, holding her before him as a shield. He stood ready, half crouched, sword raised, lips parted, watching as Gwenhwyfar galloped closer, his mind registering with amusement it was a woman riding at him.

In Hibernia, the home he had left many years since to settle this new territory with Brychan, some women were known to fight as fearsomely as men. He was surprised at this woman, though. The British men were soft-bellied; the women, Roman spawn, pampered creatures fit only for bedding.

Not this one, it seemed!

Gwenhwyfar's sword whistled down. He thrust it aside with his own; let Enid go with a kick to her buttocks that sent her sprawling on her face, and followed through by reaching up and grabbing Gwenhwyfar's arm, pulling her from the horse.

She rolled, half winded, her hand clasped white-knuckled around the pommel of her weapon. She had forgotten the arrow embedded in her arm. The shaft broke with the fall, but she did not feel the jolt or the sudden spurt of blood.

He saw it though, a dark stain spreading against her tunic. Saw also she was slight, rather on the thin side, not muscled and hardened like the fighting women of his homeland. He grinned. Soft and flabby with fat, or bone-thin wraiths, these British women were nothing more than a husband's lap-pet!

Gwenhwyfar was doubly enraged from the attack and the disobedience of the men, and now this! The strength of a mother protecting her young possessed her. Who dared confront the lioness with cubs nearby? No one in his right mind— but then this man was unaware of the child in the tent. And Gwenhwyfar was unaware of his unknowing.

He taunted her with his sword tip, making mock thrusts, circling around, playing, noticing other things by now. Interesting things, like her pretty face and the promising figure half hidden beneath her leather jerkin. Shapely hips and thighs, a narrow waist. He decided not to kill her but to take her for his own.

Gwenhwyfar saw the intention clear in his eyes. His beard-shadowed chin, square jaw and leer of anticipation reminded her, with a shudder of fear, of another man. Melwas.

They circled, the woman crouching low, her sword ready, body light and balanced, her eyes locked to his; the man amused, eager, willing to play this little game, sure of his superiority.

He moved quickly, spinning as he leapt so that he lunged to the right but attacking to the left towards her wounded arm—and realised his mistake. She had seen it, seen his feint in the flicker of his eyes.

The eyes, her father had taught her. *Watch the eyes, they move to where the blade means to pass.*

Overconfidence fled from him as his sword, neatly caught by hers, arched through empty air to embed itself in the turf some yards away. He backed off, laughing, masking astonishment, angry at himself for being so easily fooled. A dagger flashed into his hand as he lunged again. Light on her feet, Gwenhwyfar skipped aside, but he had expected her reaction this time. Darting forward, he knocked her off balance with his foot, sending her staggering almost to her knees. She recovered quickly, but not quick enough.

Seizing her right wrist, his grip intentionally painful, he dragged her arm up and back, forcing her to drop her weapon. He shook her arm, the pain ripping along muscles, sending the sword falling into the mud. Triumphant, he held her firm, pulled her body to him.

Gwenhwyfar made herself go limp, struggling against an inner voice of panic telling her to fight and kick, to get away. She breathed slowly, deeply, repeating the rules of defence in her mind: *Think. Plan. Fight him and he will fight you. Take him off guard; relax. Play dead.*

He laughed again, triumphant, mouth open showing broken teeth. He grasped Gwenhwyfar's copper-gold hair. Forcing her head back, he bent to kiss her.

She gagged at the rank stench of his unwashed body. He said something in his own tongue which Gwenhwyfar did not understand, but could guess at the meaning. As his mouth closed over hers, her fingers encircled the head of the dagger sheathed at her waist.

His chuckle of pleasure was cut short in a vomiting gurgle, blood and froth issuing from his mouth. He staggered, clutching at the weapon driven deep into his lungs, staring bulge-eyed. Gwenhwyfar stood panting, her teeth bared and her eyes narrow slits. The she-wolf and her kill.

A third man had watched from the shelter of the tent opening, his laughter as his companion had bent to kiss the woman fading into open-mouthed astonishment as the man had sunk to his knees and slowly toppled to lie flat-faced and still in the mud.

Furious, he ran at Gwenhwyfar, shouting, an axe raised above his head. Gwenhwyfar whirled to him, aware too late she had no weapons. She lunged for her sword, lying where it had fallen, knew she would not reach it.

Something stopped him. He stumbled a few paces, fell forward, his body inert, blood gushing from his split skull. Enid stood behind him, too afraid to scream. A mallet used to drive the wooden tent-pegs home dangled from her hand, a dark patch, with pieces of clinging white bone and matted hair, staining its solid square head.

Gwenhwyfar snarled, a wild, primitive noise. She had her sword now, used it to hack and chop at the man she had fought, slashing at his face, hands, and vitals. Blood was on her clothes and skin, had gutted into the mud, forming a black, stinking pool.

Hands clawed at her, pulling her away. She thrust them aside, striking out with her sword when they refused to leave her be, its blade whistling through the air. Someone swore and let go, then came again, trying to hold her, shouting her name.

"Gwenhwyfar! Gwenhwyfar, leave it! Leave it, he is dead! It's over!"

A voice, a man she knew. His words sank in as she heard what he was saying. Feebly, trembling, she again pushed his hands aside, but her strength had evaporated, leaving behind a sagging weariness.

"Llacheu?" she asked, the need to cry suddenly overwhelming.

They knelt on the ground, the man holding her, his arms strong, so comforting and gentle. She shut her eyes, rested her forehead on his chest.

He looked enquiringly at Enid, who was hovering, uncertain, fingers twisting the folds of her skirt.

"He is safe," she gasped, still breathless and shaking. "I bundled him, still sleeping, beneath clothing. They were not here long enough to find him."

"Hear that? He is unharmed."

Gwenhwyfar nodded, gulped hot tears.

"Blood of the Bull, Gwenhwyfar!" Arthur roared suddenly, his hands on her shoulders shaking her, his brows creasing into deep furrows of fury. "If you ever, ever put yourself or my son in such danger again, by Mithras I'll... I'll..." He hauled her forward and held her to him, cradling her head; finished lamely, "I know not what I would do."

She was sobbing. "Meriaun said you would be cross with me for coming without your sending." She spoke through chattering teeth, her voice muffled against his chest.

"Cross!" Arthur held her away from him, his hands again on her shoulders. She hung her head, afraid to meet his blazing eyes. "Cross? I am bloody livid!" He shook her with each word, then he was clasping her to him again, rocking her back and forth, smothering her face with kisses, stroking her rain-drenched hair.

"The Bull, Cymraes, but I am also proud of you!" He was laughing, and crying too. Trembling from fear, relief, and pleasure. "Damned proud of you, you foolish, irresponsible, beautiful, beautiful woman!"

FORTY-FIVE

S HE HAD NOT WANTED TO SLEEP. HER WOUND, TENDED AND DRESSED AND a bitter-tasting liquid persuaded down her throat, coupled with being tucked warm beneath dry blankets, let drowsiness creep in unbidden. She could hear shouted orders, the bustle of more tents being erected, and the neighing of horses. She snuggled deeper, content. Slept.

It was quite dark when she drifted awake; the lamps were out. The sound of spattering rain had ceased and all was quiet. What had woken her? An arm slid around her waist, cold feet touched her warm legs. She shivered. "I did not intend to wake you," Arthur said.

Gwenhwyfar nestled into his arms, burrowing her head into his shoulder. "I am glad you did. I tried to stay awake for you. I think," she smiled up at him, though neither could see in the blackness, "I think something was put in my drink."

He cuddled her closer. "It was."

"I was tricked!" she protested, tickling his ribs with her fingers, causing him to squirm. As he tickled her back his hand touched the swell of a breast beneath her night shift and he ceased the teasing. His lips brushed hers, half expecting her to stiffen and pull away, the rise of pleasure all the more acute when she did not. He lay back, still holding her, settling his head on the rolled-blanket pillow.

Into the blackness she said, "Your coming upon us was no accident, was it, Arthur?"

"You have been watched since leaving Ceredig's land."

Gwenhwyfar caught her breath. "The Watchers! You?"

"Watchers?" Arthur snorted with amusement. "I sent men to keep a close eye on you." He chuckled at her start of indignation, laid a finger on her lips to silence her. "I know what you are about to squawk. They had my orders to stay out of sight."

She pouted. "Why? You made us uneasy for no reason."

"Why?" He jerked half upright. "Enniaun sent a galloper to tell me you were coming with the horses—Mithras, I was furious! Though whether I was angrier with you, or with him for allowing it, I know not. My wife," he paused to lean over and kiss her, "my wife and son are more precious to me than damned horses!"

"I came because of our son!" She too sat up, lying back grudgingly as Arthur pulled her down with him below the warmth of the blankets.

"I know it, Meriaun has told me."

Gwenhwyfar snuggled closer to Arthur, twining her arms around him, tucking her feet under his legs. Drowsy, she must have dozed a minute, for he was near asleep when she realised he had not answered her question. She kicked him. He only grunted so she kicked him again, harder.

"Arthur! Why did you set men to spy on us?"

Through a yawn he answered, "Because it occurred to me, once I had calmed down enough to look at the thing rationally, these newly trained men might not need a wet-nurse." He moved his hand more comfortably around her waist, "but I was not prepared to entrust raw soldiers with the safety of my wife and son." He did not add the shambles of this night had proved him right. "We were riding to meet you when—what did you call my men? Watchers? Warned us a raiding party from Brychan's rat nest was abroad. We came up as fast as we could." His voice turned cold. "Just as well we did." He said no more. The entire valley had cringed at his explosion of rage, once he had been assured his wife slept. One out of every ten men, selected by drawing a short blade of grass, lay buried in shallow graves this night, bludgeoned to death by their disgraced comrades. A serious thing to disobey orders, to take matters into their own hands or desert their post—to leave a camp undefended.

Arthur demanded strict discipline; each man was to work with the other as a team, one welded body. Punishment needed to be severe, for men's lives could be put at risk by those who recklessly disobeyed orders; haphazard enthusiasm left themselves and their comrades open to death. The lesson of Arthur's wrath had sunk in. It was the first and last time men of the Artoriani so disgraced themselves.

To cover his sudden silence, Arthur said to Gwenhwyfar, "Brychan will think twice about harassing what is mine in future. He will not be pleased at the gift I have sent him."

Gwenhwyfar made no comment. She guessed his meaning, cared little for details.

He was right. Brychan bellowed and cursed for days after his men found a heap of dismembered bodies flung some yards inside his border.

"How is the arm?" Arthur asked, changing the uneasy subject.

"It aches." Shyly she added, "But not as much as I ache for you. We have been apart too long a while."

Thinking of several pert answers, Arthur cast them aside. Instead he brought her closer to kiss her, savouring the delight of her taste, smell, and feel. He stroked the inside of her bare arm, mindful of her wound; moving on to her neck and face, enjoying her softness. He broke away as Gwenhwyfar buried her head in his shoulder and, clasping him tight, said urgently, "I was so afraid when I learnt of Winifred's son. I still am."

Holding her with one hand, Arthur stroked her hair with the other.

She lifted her head and said determined, "I will fight for my son, Arthur. I realise to you they are both sons, but Llacheu is mine and he is a Briton, not some half-Saex—"

He placed his lips over hers, silencing her. "Winifred was born a bitch and shall die a bitch, Cymraes. I also intend to fight for our son, for I have no illusions about the power a Saex cur may try to wield. Especially not one raised by her hand."

He spoke so vehemently Gwenhwyfar moved a little away from him. This was a side of him that frightened her. Arthur angered was a man to be avoided. She knew the punishment the men had faced, knew Arthur would have watched its execution dispassionately. She thrust such thoughts aside. Arthur was a soldier; there was no room for soft words and a gentle touch on the battlefield, or from a king who intended to demand discipline and respect.

Taking her hand and kissing the tip of each finger one by one, he whispered, "For this night, can we forget the harsh realities? I know a place where there is only pleasure and love. I'll take you there, if you want me to."

"Is that a promise?"

"Aye."

A rare thing for Arthur, he kept his promise.

APRIL 457

FORTY-SIX

A MOOD OF GUARDED ANTICIPATION BREATHED THROUGH CAMP, BLENDING WITH AN unspoken expectancy. Some who were there, sitting around campfires or curling under blankets to snatch a few hours' precious sleep, remembered the carnage they had encountered when Vortimer had been so horribly slain. They nursed mixed feelings of revenge and fear. All of them felt the prickling of fear for the coming of dawn, and battle.

Few of those huddled men denied that by the morrow's setting sun they too could be the victims of Hengest's thirst for British blood.

Only one man instilled courage.

Arthur, son of Uthr Pendragon, toured the camp as dusk fell, pausing to talk or laugh with men who idled away the last remnants of the day. Exchanging a jest with one man, admiring another's new spear, asking after the healed lameness of another's horse. Small things, intimacies, making each man feel as though he were a personal friend. Arthur had made it his business to know the names and characters of all his mounted Artoriani, to know some small thing of each and every one of his nine hundred cavalrymen.

The march from the fortifications at Durobrivae had been an anxious one; the awareness of hidden shadows and the constant edge of alertness had been wearing. They were in hostile territory, pushing resolutely deeper into Hengest's claimed kingdom, advancing along the sweeping heights of the northern downs which commanded a view over thick forest, grassy plain, and river meadows that mingled with the salt-crusted coast.

Scouts had routed several set ambushes, vain attempts at harrying Arthur's mounted army. Even so, some ten and three of their cavalry had been seriously wounded from Saex spears. Three more were dead. Arthur considered the toll a light one, less than he expected. His men knew full well these attacks were designed to slow them down, to annoy and irritate, like flies constantly buzzing. Tactics aimed at goading them further on, to walk into the spider's sticky web. Arthur had complied, had pushed forward with his cavalry, ever watchful, aware the way back could be closing despite the vigilance of a rear guard of infantry.

Before returning to his own tent, Arthur walked to the edge of the rise to stand quiet, surveying the darkening land below. Cei and Gwenhwyfar's nephew Meriaun came up behind and stood flanking him. Three men watching and thinking their own thoughts.

The first few stars were showing, glimmering like diamonds between drifting clouds. A heady smell of damp earth hung in the air. Rain was coming. A man who ate, slept, lived, fought, and died under the open sky, interpreted the signs, could read the approaching weather with as much ease as the literate read words written on a parchment.

Cei broke the silence. "We have ridden many miles for this."

For answer, Arthur swept his hand across the horizon, to the clearings and farms scattered below. His finger came to a halt, indicated the walled town nestling in the hollow a mile away.

"There are a few people, Romano-British people, left in that town, which was once a thriving centre of trade and wealth. Look at it now. In this light you cannot see clearly, but I know 'tis nothing but shacks and crumbling buildings occupied by a handful of die-hard, stubborn folk who refuse to be intimidated." He let his arm fall to his side. "This Cantii territory has always been the first prize. 'They came to plunder and make war... and later to settle down to till the soil.' Caesar, before the birth of the Christ, wrote that. Only he was not describing the Saex kind; he wrote of the people we now defend, people who, even before Rome invaded, came themselves from across the sea and settled here. They called themselves Belgae, a tribe soon to be lost amid the enveloping nationality of Romano-British." He glanced at his companions, took a slow breath. "Names and tribes, even loyalties, change, but still the land of Cantii is the prize."

"A prize to be won or lost."

"Or given."

Cei frowned at Arthur's soft-spoken reply. "Given?"

"A prize won must be held. A prize lost must be fought for another time, to save pride. A prize given, exchanged, can be the settling of an amicable arrangement. Vortigern had the right of it there, though he gave for the wrong reasons, to barter time, to save face, and demanded nought in return."

Meriaun too had been studying the evening sweep of land dotted with homesteads. Good grazing land for cattle, rich soil for crops and fruit orchards. He said, with a curl to his lip, as if he were talking of some unpleasant waste product, "Many down there are of Saex descent."

Arthur answered swiftly with heat. "Their blood may be Saex but their hearts are Roman. As I said, names and tribes change. Those settlers are the children's children of men who fought to defend Rome's empire; men who garrisoned the Shore Forts, who kept pirates from breaching the curtain wall. They have earned their right to our land, earned a right to pledge loyalty to Britain, to be one with us."

Cei snorted. "And for how long shall that pledge survive? Already they are welcoming Hengest, allowing him his absurd whim of leadership, paying tribute to him!"

"Do you blame them? They are farmers, the families of veterans, old servicemen no longer active. The *grandfathers* down there fought for Rome. Not the fathers, not the sons. All they want is to plough and sow and harvest in peace. As long as they have peace they care little who oversees them. It happened before, when the Belgae came from across the sea a handful of years before Caesar. They settled, eventually dominated. Life went on. The Cantii mixed with the Belgae, became one. Then Rome came, settled, dominated. Life went on, the people became one. Romano-British. Romano-Saex."

"What you are trying to say, my foster brother," Cei cut in with a hint of irritation, "is that eventually these Saex swine will dominate?"

Arthur, standing with his weight on his sound leg, considered a reply. His left hand rested against the reassuring feel of his sword. The evening had darkened. The distant outer edges of the great Forest-Where-No-One-Lives was darker still, black against blackening sky. A dog-fox barked, answered by the yip of his vixen. An owl drifted from a tree to their right, flapped its wings once and gave a piercing cry. Arthur's thigh, injured it seemed, aeons past, ached. It always ached when rain was coming.

Into the gathering cloak of darkness he said, "For the Cantii the Saex will dominate. Who can hold back the tide or command a thunder cloud to roll aside?" He lifted his shoulders, shrugged. "'Tis no use scowling, the both of you. 'Tis so. Hengest knows it, I know it." He jerked his head back at the camp. "Most of those men know it. I should imagine the settlers on their farms down there know it also, and accept the inevitable."

"Then why, in God's name," snapped Cei, exasperated, "are we here?"

Arthur grinned, his face lighting with a glint of enthusiasm. "Because, for the prize to be given, it first has to be won!"

Cei flung up his arms. "Holy Jesu, Arthur, you could ride rings round the Great Henge and not get dizzy!"

FORTY-SEVEN

GWENHWYFAR PROPPED HERSELF UP ON ONE ELBOW. THE PALLET WAS NOT uncomfortable, but the night air was cold and the flickering lamps denied her sleep. She watched her husband, sitting at the table studying written reports and rough-drawn maps. His face was crinkled with tiredness, eyes hollowed but burning with a brightness of determination that belied the restlessness of his fingers, twitching at the corner of the map he held.

"Come to bed."

Arthur answered without looking up. "Na, sleep would not come."

"Without trying, how do you know?" she replied simply. She gathered a rough-woven blanket around her and padded barefoot across to stand behind him, regarding the map. She pointed to the marks he had made. "This is where you intend to make for, before dawn light?"

He nodded. "I know Hengest waits at Rutupiae. Here." He pointed to the Shore Fort on the mainland across the narrow channel beside the isle of Tanatus. "Rutupiae was built by the first Romans to set foot on these shores, Cymraes. Their bridgehead. When the Emperor Claudius came in the wake of the victorious soldiers, he landed there and proclaimed Britain as his."

Looking thoughtful at the ink marks on the spread parchment, Gwenhwyfar began absently kneading the taut muscles of her husband's shoulders. He arched himself into the feel of her fingers and closed his eyes a moment.

"I have no doubt Hengest is familiar with that knowledge also. The great white monument to Claudius no longer stands, but it is the legend, the spirit of Rutupiae, that counts. It is Britain's gateway. By drawing his army up within sight of those walls Hengest is proclaiming what is his, just as Claudius did." His eyes snapped open, his hand caught hers and pulled her round to sit across his lap. "Except when Rome came, they were the mightier power—and we still carry that legacy of Rome. Hengest does not. I wish you had remained at Durobrivae with Llacheu."

Looping her arms around his neck, Gwenhwyfar kissed the tip of his nose. "Liar. You wish I had remained with him at Caer Leon."

Arthur laughed, kissed her with a warmth that betrayed his need. "Part of me, the sensible part, should have ordered you to stay in safety. The male part of me demands otherwise."

She nestled closer to him. His hands slid beneath the heavy blanket, feeling the soft excitement of her skin.

"The male part of you, eh?" she said, hiding her amusement. Her hands ran over his back, sending a shiver down his spine. Then she was touching his thigh, her fingers moving to a more intimate area of his body. She giggled; his response had been immediate. "Do you refer to this part of you, by chance?"

For reply Arthur scooped her up in his arms and carried her over to their bed. Still silent, he stripped with haste, tossing tunic, boots, and bracae aside.

Their lovemaking was fervent, leaving them breathless, skin prickling with sweat and hearts pounding. Arthur sought the blankets and cradled his wife close, her head resting on his shoulder, her copper hair tumbling over his chest. He twisted a strand of it about his fingers, toying with its silkiness.

"How do you keep this mane of yours so soft?" he asked.

"By keeping it clean and rinsing it with herbal infusions—camomile, things like that."

He brought the strand up to his nose, savoured the fresh, clean smell. "Is that what gives it such a perfume? One of the things I have always remembered about you, Cymraes, is your hair." He ran his fingers through its lush thickness, tugging gently at a tangle. "I can remember the sun shining on it when you were a girl, remember seeing it whirl about you as you rode or ran." He kissed the end of the strand and then kissed her, a bruising possessive kiss which rekindled his desire.

Gwenhwyfar laughed as he began caressing her body with less urgency this time, content to savour her scent and feel. "And you did not wish to come to bed?"

Arthur lay quiet afterwards, sleep eluding him as he had known it would. Gwenhwyfar, a look of satisfied contentment on her face, slept peacefully, her hand entwined in his. He lay watching her as her lashes flickered and her mouth twitched into a smile. He wondered of what she was dreaming. For all the delights his body had received, he knew he was taking a dreadful risk. Like his men, he was well aware they could be marching into a trap. One that might not hold a bolthole. And he had allowed Gwenhwyfar to enter it with him.

He placed a butterfly's touch of a kiss on her forehead. Her clasping hand tightened and she turned in her sleep to snuggle nearer, her body moulding compatibly with his own. What could he have done? Chained her to the wall at Durobrivae? Ordered the rearguard posted there to confine her in the cells? No other method would have kept her there! Gwenhwyfar had stated she would ride with him. He had begun to realise her statements were not to be taken lightly, were fact.

Cei had argued heatedly against the wisdom of having her with them, yet even he could not deny her determination, and had been forced to admit grudgingly that, contrary to expectation, the men loved her presence.

Gwenhwyfar had felt rather disgusted when she discovered they thought of her almost as a mascot, but had wit enough to use their amusement to her advantage, turning it rapidly into respect. Word had spread of her ability to fight and defend herself. Arthur's mounted Artoriani admired her courage. The casual infantry—farmers, traders, men, and boys who had responded to Arthur's call to arms—would tell of Gwenhwyfar, riding beautiful at the Pendragon's side.

Arthur had not been slow either to judge the mood of his men. He noted how in subtle ways they paid homage to Gwenhwyfar, saw too they watched over her. The men were like loyal hounds, fiercely protective, and Arthur knew full well there were few men in camp, dozing the light sleep of the alert soldier, who would not willingly lay down their life for him and his lady.

Watching her in the dim light cast by the remaining lamp, he was suddenly anxious. She was safe while his men were able to provide a guard, but what of the morrow? What if the years of his planning and scheming should not come to fruition? Who would defend her against Hengest if he and his men lay dead on the battlefield? Was it fair of him to ask these men not only to die for their leader, but for his reckless wife also?

The questions echoed in the night. He did sleep, a restless, haunted sleep where his horsemen thundered across a dark plain, to drown in a river of blood. And a woman stood alone on a windswept hill, a small child huddled at her side while the war drums and horns of the enemy ringed her round, coming ever closer.

FORTY-EIGHT

ARTHUR WAS ALREADY UP AND DRESSING WHEN GWENHWYFAR STIRRED AND opened her eyes.

"Is it time?" she asked, rubbing bleary sleep from her.

"Aye. 'Tis a few hours before dawn rises. We should have plenty of time. With Fortuna on our side we shall catch the whore-sons shitting with their bracae round their ankles!"

Meriaun called out, peered hesitant through the tent flap. Arthur beckoned him in, Cei following at his heels. The two men briefly nodded to Gwenhwyfar, who gathered a blanket close for modesty. Arthur winked at her, receiving a brilliant smile in return. "Is all well?" he asked Cei.

"Rhys returned half of an hour since. He said the Saex were sleeping like babes."

"Then let us hope, like children, they sleep sound."

Outside the tent there was movement. Men rising, hastening to the makeshift latrine ditch to relieve themselves or eating a frugal breakfast. A distant shuffle from horses being lightly watered and fed. There was a distant air of solemnity, not the usual bustle and excitement of troops preparing for what could be their last day in this world. It was the manner of death after failure which instilled an influence of mute unease, not the fear of an approaching battle. That, and the awareness this battle was different. It would mark the beginning, or the end, of Arthur's bid to become Britain's Supreme Leader, their unequivocal king.

Gwenhwyfar dressed quickly once the three men had gone. She began to braid her hair but her fingers shook. Until this moment, she had not regretted the decision to leave Enid behind at Durobrivae with the boy. She told herself not to be foolish, to stay calm and not worry—her husband would survive. Sensible advice, which she did not take. Abandoning the braids, she left her hair loose, ducked from the tent.

The air was fresh, washed clean by the rain that had fallen earlier in the night. It had ceased an hour since, leaving the sky vaulted bright with speckled stars.

Her boots scuffed the clinging wetness from the grass as she walked to where the men were assembling, beyond the rows of leather tents.

Arthur watched her approach, felt his stomach knot with wanting at the sight of her. A cheer, muted, in awareness of possible danger, swelled as he held out his hand to her and brought her to him in an embrace. No soldier watching would deny he would give anything to be in Arthur's position, to feel that lithe, beautiful body against his own; but then, no soldier would ever allow another to take advantage of their lady.

Grinning, Arthur leapt atop a small hillock which raised him about four feet higher than his men. He helped Gwenhwyfar up to stand beside him, his arm encircling her waist.

"You are putting on weight, my lass," he said cheerfully as they waited for their audience to settle.

Gwenhwyfar made some flippant answer, turned the subject back to the waiting men. Her heart steadied as Arthur began to talk, in a low but carrying voice.

By the Mother! If he should suspect she was carrying another child he would be furious! It had taken all her cunning, all her wits, to accompany him to Durobrivae, let alone this far! As it was, she knew she would have to face his anger when he learnt she had deliberately flouted danger in such a condition. It would make not the slightest difference she was but a few months gone and that the babe was threatened with no more danger than the rest of them. Men were so stubbornly protective in these matters.

Arthur spoke only briefly. He emphasised the necessity for caution, for as little noise as was physically possible. "We have men posted; we are as sure as we can be that not one of Hengest's scouts will take word to him." He gestured, and an older, experienced soldier dressed in simple tunic and bracae, but wearing a magnificent wolfskin cloak, stepped forward. He carried something in his hand. "Mabon brought a trophy back with him when he came in a short while since."

The man called Mabon, who had fought with Uthr and now served the son, lifted the thing he held. None had doubted Arthur had spoken the truth, but the sight of an enemy scout's head, still dripping fresh blood, well proved the point.

Eira was brought up, stamping and snorting, a light excited sweat darkening his arched neck. Arthur swung easily into the saddle and nudged the horse forward, thought again. He reined the animal back, leant from the saddle, and scooped Gwenhwyfar up to his level. She laughed, grabbing hold of Eira's long mane for support. Arthur kissed her and swung her back down to firm ground.

She cried, "Take care, my Lord! Bring me back a trophy!"

"I will. Hengest."

FORTY-NINE

THE FAINT STIR OF DAWN WAS FLARING OVER A FLAT, DARK SEA AS ARTHUR'S men spread out in wide formation behind him. Through the previous months they had trained together; tedious hours of endless drill. Practising, always practising, until Arthur was satisfied they knew the movements like the backs of their own hands; recognised each given command; responded immediate and with deadly accuracy.

Arthur's cavalry was a team, a formidable fighting force, their ranks swelled now to nine hundred elite mounted men. The Artoriani. But he needed more. He needed twice nine hundred to maintain his supreme force, and they would come once he had proved his cavalry could be used to mount the main offensive with local militia infantry as rearguard, archers, and reserve. Aye, from the morrow they would come.

He looked behind him. Rank upon rank of tossing manes, silvered helmets. and waving, bright-coloured banners. Red turma, green, blue and yellow. It was unheard of in Britain, this formation. Normally, the cavalry was placed in reserve or on a wing, never in the centre.

As the sky lightened from slate grey to dusky pink, Arthur ran the tip of his tongue nervously over dry lips. Sa, the last report had been true enough. Hengest was no untried fool. If Arthur had not been expected, the Saxon leader had at least anticipated his arrival. A mile distant, straddled before the massive walls of the disused Roman fortress of Rutupiae like a swarming nest of ants, waited Hengest and his Saex army.

Arthur looked towards Meriaun, who commanded the left wing. Meriaun swung his sword in the air, the blade flashing in the strengthening light. Then he looked to the other wing, the right, usually the most important. Often the commander took this wing. Men were trained to fight with weapons in the right hand, leaving the left, the shield side, as the defensive one, a fact exploited in battle by pressure from this right wing. Cei held the command.

There was a loud crash as Cei's men brought spears or swords across their shields in a staccato burst of sound. Echoing their example, this declaration for Arthur, came the clash of arms from Meriaun's wing, and from the centre under Arthur. For this day, for this battle, the centre was all important and the Pendragon would have it for his own.

Arthur's grin was a broad beam of triumphant pleasure. The sun was rising, and it was to be a glorious day!

Slowly, so slowly that at first it seemed they barely moved, Arthur led his men forward.

Hengest had chosen the ground and had the advantage. He had the wind behind him, and his back to the dazzling glare of the rising sun. The Saex were advancing too, a mass of swaying bodies, bobbing heads and fluttering banners. The steady thump, thump of spear or sword beating against shields in a regular rhythm. The singsong voice of the war chant whipped forward by the salt scented wind from the sea. Individual calls lost, the sound as one, a wordless moan from a baying beast.

Behind him, Arthur's own men sat their mounts silently, saving their breath for when it would be needed. Disciplined, steady, covering the ground between the two armies at a held walk. He could hear the ripple of hooves swathing through the fetlock high grass; hear the toss and jangle of horses' bridles, the creak of leather, and the metallic clink of weapons. It was an eerie sensation, this voiceless progress. Arthur turned, half expecting to see a ghost army ranged behind him, mist figures silent in the rising dawn. He gasped, realised Hengest had made his first mistake.

The sun had risen higher. Its glow lit the sky with a brilliant glare, a blazing flood of gold pouring down upon the morning, the rays striking like bursting flames upon British spear tips and silvered helmets, gold cloak pins, bronze buckles of baldrics, and belts and harness. Every metal object on man and horse reflected the sudden burst of brilliant light, emitting a corona of radiance around the entire mass of Arthur's men. To him, at their head, the spectacle was breathtaking, as if the hand of the soldiers' god Mithras was cupping them. How then must it look to Hengest!

Arthur bellowed at the signallers, "I want enough noise to awaken the dead!" It was not as he had originally ordered. Remain silent until we are closer, he had said, but he had also warned that orders could change rapidly. This was where the drill came in. *Obey my orders*. Each man listened to the signal notes of the curled bronze trumpets. The instruments blared the command, and were obeyed.

The blast of responding shouts was tumultuous. Arthur yelled a second order, shrewdly gauging the closing distance between the two armies. The bowmen had been expecting it, and at the first sequence of notes from the horns their bows were lifted, aimed and loosed. A thousand, thousand arrows flew, the scream of their flight shrilling through the air. Arthur's army rode steady on, their yells increasing, their arrows falling like a stormy rain of death.

The Saex army wavered, staggered. From a ranked, silent mass, the army before them suddenly took on an ethereal appearance. One minute shaded, a seething, hustled group of darkness, split only by the dim colours of banners and the occasional glint of weapons. The next, a blazing radiance of light with a bestial howl which spat deadly tipped venom. Man after man at the fore of the vast Saex army fell as arrows from the British bowmen found their mark. Hengest saw the doubt, the uncertainty and fear, cursed and swore at his men, bullying, threatening, trying desperately to reinstall lost courage.

Arthur seized his chance. His hand flew up. Bowmen, their arrows spent, dropped back, the space they left instantly occupied by the waiting cavalry.

Like a burst dam, the Saex swarmed forward, daunted by the army ahead but more afeared of their own leader's wrath. With courage renewed they hurtled towards the British. Arthur's two wings increased pace to a jogtrot outpacing the centre, who held back at a steady walk.

The Saex launched their spears, the weapons humming through the air, many finding their mark. Artoriani launched their own volley with the pilum, much favoured by the legionaries of Rome, a well balanced spear with heavy shaft and light iron tip. Some inflicted wounds, but most thudded, seemingly harmless, into Saex shields. The thin, soft neck of the thing bent and caught, so it became impossible to remove and throw back—rendering a shield useless by its dragging weight.

The second volley of spears from the British bit home. Heavier weapons this time, with more intention of maiming. The paced jog increased to a hand canter, one horse's shoulder against another, shields held before the rider, swords ready. When one fell another from behind lengthened pace and took his place. No gaps, no stragglers. Within these last few yards of the enemy, Cei and Meriaun took the right and left wing into the charge. Full gallop, plunging into the soft mass of men, shouting the war cry. The wings of both armies came together. Fighting was at close quarters now, mounted men against foot, the discipline of tight formation against the Saex fighting individually, each man for himself.

Hengest's Saex were thrown off balance by this onrush from the two British wings coming in on them from each side. Their centre was left exposed, helpless to aid comrades in desperate situations at the sides, aware Arthur's centre had yet to attack.

Already uncertain and apprehensive, the Saex found themselves suddenly faced with a new, overwhelming onrush of trampling hooves and slashing swords as Arthur yelled the order to move forward, his men responding instant into a gallop. The urge to drop their weapons and run spread rapidly among the faltering Saex. Some, at the rear, hearing the confusion and panic, did run, pushing their way back through the men behind. Within moments, they realised with horror that the British wings, pressing from each side, had driven their own wings inward to tangle with the centre, crippling rear movement and thrusting the Saex forward deeper into Arthur's charge. As space to manoeuvre decreased, their faltering became fear, and the fear became panic.

It was the horses which were so terrifying. Great beasts with bared teeth and trampling hooves. Hengest's men tried their best to fight the riders of these creatures, slashing with short swords and jabbing with spears, but the situation was desperate, hopeless. For each horse or rider that fell, another took his place, and another.

Arthur, after the first thrill of exhilaration from the charge, settled to a steady blow-by-blow thrust. The Saex swarmed, many falling and becoming trampled by shod hooves. Faces—nameless, bearded faces with flaxen hair braided and tailed—rose and fell before him. Arthur felt something stab at his thigh, a glancing blow from one of the Saex's short swords which did no damage through the thickness of his padded bracae. He swung Eira round, the horse rising on to his hind legs, thrashing with his forefeet. His nearside hoof struck bone, split a skull wide. The unfortunate man clutched his head as blood spurted, then fell dead. Eira, unsteadied, slipped, righted himself in a flurry of thrashing legs, but not before one of Hengest's personal guard saw and took advantage.

The man was big, built like an ox, with muscled biceps, sturdy torso and thick, bulging thighs. He lunged at Arthur with his shield, the heavy bronze boss slamming into the Pendragon's shoulder. Arthur could not dodge the blow; his left arm suddenly felt numb and his useless fingers dropped his own shield. He reeled and, as Eira scrambled upright, lost his balance and tumbled from the saddle. He squirmed, landed somehow on his feet, facing this formidable giant.

It was as if there was no one else on the battlefield, just himself and this one, massive built Saex. They circled, eyeing each other, assessing the other's worth, taking note of build and balance, of height and sword reach.

Arthur was at a disadvantage through the loss of his shield, but then he was the lighter man, the less blown. And his men were winning, there was no doubt of that. His gaze flickered to the man's sword, no ordinary thing, a weapon of unequalled craftsmanship. The Saex revered their weapons, believing them to possess magical powers. For all their barbarism, Arthur admired their craftsmanship.

The numbness was easing from his shoulder, leaving a dull ache, but he had the use of his fingers again. He shuffled his torso, balancing his weight evenly, light on the balls of his feet. With both hands he gripped his own sword—a well-forged thing with a gilded hilt of bronze and silver, but not comparable with that of his opponent. Arthur suddenly desired that sword. Was going to have it.

The Pendragon's lips parted in a slow smile, widened into a fearsome look of determination, What was it he had said about prizes being won? This was one prize he would enjoy gaining! He watched the Saxon's eyes, narrow slits of brilliant blue, scowling from beneath the headpiece of the warrior's silver-etched helmet. Two men, well matched.

As the Saex lunged, Arthur parried with his own sword. Sparks spat from the clash of iron. He followed through with a forceful thrust and they exchanged blows, neither giving ground, neither doing damage.

First blood to the Saex. His sword cut to the side in a feint which Arthur turned, but the Saxon's weapon was superior. It slid the length of the British blade, the honed edge slicing into the padding of the sleeve which covered Arthur's lower arm. The fabric ripped, dark blood welling with the frayed material, staining the white linen. The Saxon plunged forward, taking the advantage.

The ground beneath their feet was slippery from the night's rain and grass churned now into mud, reddening with spilt blood. Arthur swore, attacked with renewed fervour. As he struck forward, the Saxon whirled aside and Arthur spun with him, but his foot tangled with someone fighting behind, sending him tumbling to his knees.

The Saxon lifted his sword high, ready, triumphant, to smash down with the death blow. Arthur squirmed, brought his sword point up, ramming it awkwardly, praying it would make contact with flesh not mail.

With a bellow, the Saxon brought his sword down, the blade thudding into the soil a hair's breadth from Arthur's helmet, the great man toppling forward with it. Arthur kicked out, deflecting the body from falling across his own as it fell face forward, the weight driving the Pendragon's thrust sword deeper through the abdomen.

Breathing hard, Arthur rolled the dead man over, and realised he would have difficulty removing his weapon, so deeply was it embedded. He saw a glint of gold from a small jewelled dagger in the Saex's belt. As his fingers curled round the lightweight hilt, he felt the movement of air behind him. Arthur whirled, striking with the dagger, plunging it into the throat of a Saxon whose axe was plunging downwards.

Sweat trickled down Arthur's back. He swallowed, the clutch of death over close for comfort. He wiped the blade on his sleeve, started as he recognised the decorative jewelling. He knew this thing, this light, slim-bladed weapon! A woman's dagger, but obviously prized for its quality and beauty. How in the name of Mithras had that ox got hold of Gwenhwyfar's treasured dagger? The riddle must wait. Arthur thrust the weapon into his own belt and bent to re-trieve the Saxon sword.

As his hand clasped the hilt, he felt a surge of pleasure course through his body, a tingle of excitement, a sparkle of wonder. This sword was magnificent! Eyes alight, he struck at a Saxon to his left who had a British soldier down, at his mercy. The blade sliced clean through flesh and sinew, severing the warrior's head with a single blow. The reprieved victim scrambled to his feet, gabbling his thanks. Arthur turned to grapple with another of Hengest's sagging army, the sword in his hand seeming to possess a life of its own as it hewed and slashed and killed. A sword for a king. And Arthur would be king!

He saw Eira, wild eyed, close to panic without the reassurance of his rider but, for all that, standing still. Arthur grabbed the reins, ran his hand soothingly down the stallion's neck, and mounted quickly. With the familiar guidance from voice and legs, the horse calmed, plunging forward at the given signal towards Hengest's swaying White Horse banner.

Hengest was fighting for his life. He recognised defeat, knew as only a matter of moments before his army threw down their weapons and fled. He looked anxiously around for Aethal, his friend and honoured warrior. Aethal was spe-cial, a brave man, husband to one of his daughters. For a while, he had com-manded the fool king Vortigern's personal guard of Saex warriors, ostensibly serving alongside the nephew, Melwas, but in truth there to carry word between Hengest and his eldest daughter, Rowena.

Aethal had become separated and Hengest found himself alarmed. If it were known the mighty warrior, Aethal, had fallen, his men would never hold!

A rider was bearing down on them, cleaving his way through the close hand-to-hand fighting. The man wore a scaled hauberk, with a crimson cloak swirling from his shoulders. Hengest could not discern the face beneath the protection of the helmet, but the poise, audacity, and charisma were as telling as any recognisable features.

When Hengest saw the sword Arthur wielded, his hopes died. Aethal's sword. The sword forged by the god Weyland near the crystal waters of Freya and endowed, by that same Lady, with powers of strength and endurance. No man who held that sword could be slain, it was said, save by the cunning and strength of a dragon.

Hengest groaned, let his own sword fall slack in his hand. So, the legend was true! Aethal had boasted he could best any fire-tongued beast, dared such a monster to come within range of his blade. They had all laughed, listening to his talk while gathered around Hengest's hearth, proud of Aethal and his strength, amused he had fooled Vortigern and Melwas into believing him their servant. Yet none of them had realised the hidden danger and mocking truth. It was no beast that rose superior, but a man. The Pendragon.

Hengest's Jutes had seen Arthur, recognised that flashing sword. Abandoning their weapons, demoralised, faced with the reality of defeat, they began to flee. As they ran, the cavalry surged after them, cutting them down. The tide had swept out, turning the low land between island and mainland into treacherous mudflats divided by a narrow navigable channel. A few men, weighing the risk of stinking mud or death by British sword, ran out into it, to find their feet stuck, their legs dragged down into its sucking depths. In years to come, the protruding sand bars hastened the silting up of the channel, trapped the land, which as centuries passed became reclaimed, turning Tanatus from island to promontory. A stretch of coast that would, for all time, remember the coming and defeat of Hengest.

FIFTY

THE ROAR FROM THE ELATED MEN ECHOED OVER THE FLAT LANDS OF THE coast. The great cry was caught by the sea wind and tossed up to the scudding clouds and screaming gulls. As Arthur walked forward, dressed in parade armour with his beautiful wife at his side, the men of Britain let their jubilation explode. Victory was theirs, and they had the right to shout their loudest acclaim!

At Rutupiae all that remained of the splendid monument of triumph dedicated to the Emperor and god Claudius was its battered square base. Guarded well and displayed for all to see, Hengest stood atop its rough surface chained like a common slave. Left weary and thirsty, itching from the dust and sweat of battle, he watched Arthur approach, waited for the order of death that was surely to come. He did not mind the dying, only the manner of its making. It was nothing less than he expected, the losers were to suffer. It could as easily have been the other way around.

One thought occurred to him as he stood, head held proud, giving no sign of fear. It could have been Winifred walking there with the Pendragon. He ought to have tried the harder to secure her place as future queen, but then he had made a grave error the day he misjudged this son of Uthr. Hengest gave a grunt of self-mocking laughter. Had he not been warned to keep a wary eye beneath Arthur's masking cloak of drunken whoring? What was it he had once said of the Pendragon? *A boy playing a man's game.* The mistake of all men, they forgot to watch the sons growing, realising too late that the young buck had become the antlered stag.

Arthur reached the makeshift dais, leapt up, and, taking her hand, helped his wife climb after him. For a moment Gwenhwyfar stared at Hengest, chained there in the centre of the massive block of white stone. She started as his unflinching eyes met with hers. That haughty gaze, how like Winifred's! Diamond-hard eyes, showing nothing beyond the ceaseless plotting and calculation of gain. He was beaten but not deterred, even seemed slightly amused.

Gwenhwyfar clung tight to her husband's arm, directed her attention to the clamouring men. Hengest had shown plainly the thought behind those eyes. *I do not fear, for Cerdic, boy of my blood, is yet to come!*

Arthur raised his hand for silence, the roar of acclaim fading slowly, reluctantly. Men crowded close, shoulder to shoulder, eager faces lifted to hear the words of the Pendragon. Many had waited a long time for this day's kingmaking.

When he could be heard, Arthur took a step forward, cast his wide smile over the sea of faces. "You have done well, my brothers," he called. "Very well! Let none say the men of Arthur lack for courage and strength! From this day, our enemies shall fear our name and tremble before our war cry!" He let them shout and cheer a while before drawing the sword from his side, lifting it so all might see its fine wonder. "I took this sword from a Saex I killed. I cannot form my tongue around the Saex name it bears, but in our British speech, its calling would be Caliburn." He let the men have a good, long, admiring look at its perfection. They were listening to him intently, hanging on his every word, barely a sound issuing from their lips.

"It is said by the Saex this sword has qualities of none other and it has a story behind its being. One day a man, a young warrior, was walking beside a lake. He came across a boat and paddled to the centre of that lake. There he waited until the sun and the moon had chased each other twice across the sky. And then, as dawn's finger touched the glass surface of the sleeping lake, the waters parted and a Lady arose from beneath. A beautiful woman, a goddess. She held a sword—a sword that could only have been forged on the anvil of a god. She charged this mortal to take the weapon into the world of men and to wield it until such time as the man it was made for came to take it by trial of strength. A man who was destined to be the greatest of all kings. 'That man,' this goddess said, 'shall be a king above all kings; a man supreme, who will make the dark light, and turn the blood of war into the calm waters of peace.'"

Arthur laid the blade across his open palms, studied its superb, delicate workmanship, felt the fineness of its being against his skin. He had won his sword; now, had to win the men, his army, had to use his wits and get them to kneel without question. There would be arguments about the way he intended to do things, bitter disagreement from the Church and men such as his uncle Emrys, who fervently believed that Rome would soon return. He must ensure the support of this army, these ordinary men who would fight unquestioning for what he, the supreme king, decided. With them behind him, the opposition could shout to the four winds, for all the good it would do them.

"That was a story from long past and it was a tale woven by Saxons, yet here I stand before you with this sword in my hand. I fought for it and by greater strength took it for my own. Am I not, then, your King?"

They answered with spears hoisted, swords crashing against shields, and voices proclaiming for Arthur. "Pendragon! Pendragon! Pendragon!" Arthur sheathed the sword, held both his hands high, quietening them.

"Na!" he countered. "The cry shall not be for me. My cavalry are the Artoriani, but the rest of you, the foot, the militia guard, and the medics; all you farriers, scouts, and harness makers, shield bearers and grooms. You farmers with your scythes, and tradesmen with club or staff. The hunters with your spears. Professional soldiers or laymen—all of you are from this day of victory the defenders of our country. My army. You need, and shall have, some special name, some special title to wield in battle, a cry that reminds us and our enemies we fight together for our families, for our women and children, those born and those yet to come!" He paused while a new burst of cheering rang out, then went on, shouting to be heard. "We need something unique, something that is not just for me, your king, but for us all!"

He took Gwenhwyfar's hand, brought her forward, the evening sunlight flashing against the precious stones of the royal torque at her throat and the circlet of gold crowning her braided hair. Gold twining with copper. "Many of you know the term of endearment by which I call my woman. Cymraes. My Lady Gwenhwyfar can trace her ancestry back to beyond the coming of Rome, to the deeper tribal blood of Britain." He took breath. Men were listening, nodding. This they knew.

"I speak to you in Latin, the tongue of the Empire because our fathers and fathers' fathers did so. Today, despite our Roman laws and our Roman speech, we think of ourselves not as Roman but as British. Bound together, we are the Cymry, fellow native-born countrymen. This, then, shall be our call, my countrymen. We shall cry 'Cymry'!"

They took up the challenge eagerly, and swept it straight into their hearts, as he had known they would.

"Cymry!" They shouted it over and over until it drowned the sound of the incoming tide and the shrill cries of the gulls. "Cymry!"

The war cry of Arthur Pendragon. The King.

AUTHOR'S NOTE

THERE IS VERY LITTLE EVIDENCE FOR WHAT REALLY HAPPENED IN THE hundred years or so between the going of the Romans and the dominance of Britain by the Anglo-Saxons, the English. There is a period of myth and romance, a Dark Age where knowledge has been forgotten and replaced by stories. As time has passed, these tales have become more and more distorted; events and characters exaggerated or invented. We have a few, challengeable facts and even fewer names, the best-known being Arthur and his wife Guinevere or, as I call her, Gwenhwyfar.

Whether Arthur was real or a character of fiction is not certain. We do know fifth century Britain was in turmoil, and that someone had the strength to apply organisation to the chaos. If it was not "Arthur" there is no other legendary character to fit the gap.

My *Pendragon's Banner* trilogy is my personal view of those Dark Ages. I am not an historian; I speak no Welsh or Latin. I am not expressing fact, merely what might have been. The dates are my own interpretation, gleaned from a hotch-potch of muddled theories and chronologies. They may not tally with those proposed by the professional historian, but as virtually no date of this period can be established as absolute fact, I feel I can justify my theories.

Some few situations and people in my story are indeed fact. Vortigern lived, although this now commonly used name may then have been a title meaning something like "overlord." Hengest probably existed, as did Cerdic. Emrys, who fleetingly appears in Book One, is better known by his Roman name, Ambrosius Aurelianus. He did exist. Exactly when and where is open to question, but possibly in the south. Usually he is placed before Arthur, but to my mind this is not logical, and so in this trilogy he comes after. You will discover how and why in Book Two, Pendragon's Banner, and in particular in Book Three, Shadow of the King. Cunedda and his sons are acclaimed as the founders of the Gwynedd dynasty, leading down to Llewelyn, Prince of Wales, who died fighting against Edward I of England, who then plundered Wales for his own. It is told Cunedda migrated into Gwynedd from the territory of the Votadini, which ran from modern Edinburgh down into Northumbria. Why and how and when we do not know, except, if it is true, it must have been after Rome had abandoned Britain to look to her own defence and before the firm hold of settled Anglo-Saxons. Some time, therefore, in the early fifth century.

I invented Gwenhwyfar as Cunedda's daughter because I wanted to include him in my story. Imagine my delight when, on searching through some early genealogies (which admittedly are extremely unreliable), I discovered he did have a daughter called Gwen! In all probability she was not Gwenhwyfar, wife to Arthur—but the wonderful thing about this period of history for a writer of fiction is that "probably" cannot be proven as "unlikely"! Any writer on these unknown Dark Ages has a free rein of imagination—although I have tried my best to keep that rein curbed within the margin of at least the plausible. For any errors, I apologise, or claim poetic licence!

As for Arthur, no one knows if he was real. A few scattered poems and early Welsh bardic tales were adopted by the twelfth century Normans who were responsible for the stories we know so well today. The knights, chivalrous deeds, and the Round Table belong to this later period, as did the fictitious invention of Lancelot, his adultery with Gwenhwyfar, and Merlin the wizard. You will not find them in my tale.

Early references to Arthur do not portray him as a chivalric, benevolent king—the opposite in fact. A down-to-earth, ruthless war leader. This, then, is my Arthur. There are no court niceties in *The Kingmaking*. Legend tells of Gwenhwyfar's abduction and rape by Melwas, and of the pagan women at Glastonbury. I am not the first person to suggest Arthur may have married a daughter of Vortigern and that Cerdic may have been his son. The tale of Gwynllyw and Gwladys's flight from her father is also an old one, complete with Arthur playing dice and lusting after her, and Cei's outraged reprimand.

For places and personal names I have often had to invent my own, or used a mixture of Latin, Welsh, and English. The language my characters use would also have been one of the three tongues. On the whole, I assume Arthur and Gwenhwyfar would be talking in British (Welsh). I have, through necessity, taken one or two liberties with my use of Welsh, for which I apologise. When Arthur first gives Gwenhwyfar her "nickname" he would probably have said something like "fy nghymraes fach i" ("My little Welsh woman"), which is unfortunately too ponderous for those of us who struggle with Welsh pronunciation. I have therefore settled for the more familiar "Cymraes."

Some terms are blatantly out of context with the period, but I have used them because they are more familiar in meaning to our modern times. For instance, "witch." Correctly, perhaps, I should have used "hag," but this conjures up a picture of a bent old crone, which is not the description I wanted. It is uncertain how soon after the going of Rome the term "king" became used. Emerging leaders at this time were perhaps war lords, overlords, or supreme commanders, but I have used "king" because it conveys a consistent meaning in our modern tongue. The terms and traditions surrounding dowries and a man's heir may also, technically, be slightly out of place, but again I stress this is primarily a novel, not a factual record.

The skirmish along the Devil's Dyke in Cambridgeshire is embroidered by my own fancy, for it is not certain when this, and similar earthworks cutting at right angles across the ancient Icknield Way, were first constructed. Some archaeologists and historians place them any time from the Roman period to as late as the seventh century. I feel the Devil's Dyke is neither Saxon nor Roman but an earlier, Celtic boundary. It seems logical that it formed a man-built "gateway" between the natural defences of the Ouse and the Stour, dense woodland and impassable marsh. The only unprotected area into the ancient kingdom of the Iceni was the seven and one-half miles intersected by the ridge along which ran the Way. Iceni artefacts have been found to the north of the Dyke, but few to the south. Therefore I believe the Devil's Dyke would already have been around four hundred years old at the time when, in my tale, Arthur was grumbling about Vortigern's incompetence.

The story of Arthur taking his sword from the stone and thus becoming king is a familiar one. It has been suggested however, that during Medieval times there was a translation error of "from a stone" (*ex saxo*) with "from a Saxon" (*ex saxone*). Clerks were occasionally in the habit of dropping the "n" and putting a stroke above the next letter (*ex saxo*) which could account for the discrepancy. Alternatively, the stone could be a reference to the sacred stones of the tribal British. Excalibur, the well known sword of legend given to Arthur by the Lady of the Lake, is often confused with the one from the stone. In my story, or perhaps in this instance, Arthur's, the two have been combined.

There were indeed battles at Agealesthrep (Aylesford, Kent) and Crecganford (Crayford, Kent), though the dates are not precise. The Cantii territory does seem to have been settled at an early date. Cantii had become Kent; the name Canterbury still echoes its British inheritance.

I have used the Arabian type horse for Arthur's mounts for no reason except I like the breed. There have been many horse bones found on Roman sites that are very similar to this distinctive horse, so my whim is not entirely fanciful—and no one is certain just how or when the Arabian features were first bred into the sturdy Welsh breed of today's ponies. I like to think this was Cunedda's doing!

It is thought there really was a massacre of Vortigern's Council; Gloucester (Caer Gloui) is renowned for flooding; and archaeologists found a Saxon broach among the broken Roman roof tiles in Londinium…

Helen Hollick
2009

Read on for a preview of Book Two in
the Pendragon's Banner trilogy by Helen Hollick.

PENDRAGON'S
BANNER

OCTOBER 459

ONE

WITH AN EXHAUSTED GRUNT OF EFFORT ARTHUR, THE PENDRAGON, RAISED his sword and with a deep intake of breath brought it down through the full force of weight and momentum into the skull of an Anglian thegn. Another battle. Arthur was four and twenty years of age, had been proclaimed Supreme King over Greater and Less Britain three years past by the army of the British—and had been fighting to keep the royal torque secure around his neck ever since.

The man crumpled, instantly dead. Arthur wrenched his blade from shattered bone and tissue with a sucking squelch, a sickening sound, one he would never grow used to. Oh, the harpers told of the glories of battle, the victory, the brave daring and skill—but they never told of the stench that assaulted your nostrils, bringing choking vomit to your throat. Nor of the screams that scalded your ears, nor the blood that clung foul and sticky and slippery to hands and fingers or spattered face and clothing.

He turned, anxious, aware that a cavalryman was vulnerable on the ground. His stallion was somewhere to the left, a hind leg injured. The horses. Hah! No harper, no matter how skilled, could ever describe the sound of a horse scream-ing its death agony. There was no glory in battle, only the great relief that you were still alive when it was all over.

Sword ready to strike again, Arthur found with a jolt of surprise there was no one before him, no one to fight. Eyebrows raised, breathless, he watched the final scenes of fighting with the dispassionate indifference of an uninvolved spectator. No more slopping and wading through these muddied, sucking wa-ter-meadows; the Angli were finished, beaten. The rebellion, this snatching of British land that was not theirs for the taking, was over.

The Anglian leader, Icel, had wanted to be more than a petty chieftain over a scatter of huddled, backwater settlements, and that wanting had plunged deep—deep enough for him to unite the English warbands. Fighting against the British had been sporadic at first, skirmishes, night raids, and isolated killings. Arthur had not been King, then, when Icel began making a nuisance of himself, but when the Pendragon bested Hengest the Saxon, away down to the south of Londinium, the army of Britain had acclaimed him as Supreme. And Icel sent word across the sea for his kinsmen to come with the next spring, to come and fight this new-made King of the British who rode at the head of an elite cavalry force; to come and fight, for surely the victory over such a war-lord would be worth the winning! The damn thing had grumbled on through the roll of seasons ever since.

Those Anglians able to run or walk or crawl were escaping, running away to die or survive within the safe, enveloping darkness of fastcoming evening. It was over. After all these long, weary months, over. Until the next uprush of the Saex-kind tried for the taking of more land, or some upstart son of a British chieftain fancied for himself the command of supreme rule.

With slow-expelled breath, the Pendragon lowered his sword and unbuckled the straps of his helmet, let them dangle free, his face stinging from the release of the tight, chaffing leather. He was tired. By the Bull of Mithras, was he tired! Arthur stabbed his sword-blade into the churned grass and sank to his knees. His fingers clasped the sword's pommel as he dropped his forehead to rest on his hands, conscious suddenly of the great weariness in his arms and legs and across his neck and shoulders. It had been a long day, a long season. He was bone tired of fighting and this stink of death. He had a wife, two sons born, another child on the way; he needed to be with them, to be establishing a secure stronghold fit for a king and his queen; to be making laws and passing judgements—raising his sons to follow after him. A king needed sons. Llacheu would reach his fourth birthday next month... Arthur had hardly seen his growing; the occasional few days, a passing week. He needed Gwenhwyfar, but she was to the north more than a day's ride away at Lindum Colonia, uncomfortable in her bulk of child-bearing. Love of Mithras, let it be a third son!

Movement. Arthur opened his eyes but did not lift his head. Two booted feet appeared in his lowered line of vision, the leather scratched and spotted with the staining of blood. He would recognise those fine-made boots anywhere; the intricate patterning around the heel, the paler inlet of doe-hide. He looked up with a spreading grin of triumph into his cousin and second-in-command's face. Cei, wiping sweat and the spatter of other men's blood from his cheeks, grinned back, his teeth gleaming white behind the darkness of his stubble-bearded face. For a while and a while the two men stood, grinning at each other like inane moon-calves.

"That is it then," Arthur said, climbing slowly to his feet and pulling his sword from the ground. It felt heavy to his hand now, now that the fighting was done. "Happen we can think about going home to our women and families."

Cei shrugged a non-committal answer. If God was willing they could go home soon. When the dead were buried and the wounded tended. When the submissions were concluded, hostages taken, and the King's supremacy over these Saex scum endorsed. When the grumbling and muttering from the British, discontent with Arthur's objectives were silenced. Aye, happen then, they could.

Arthur bent to wipe his blade against the tunic of a dead Anglian lying face down in the blood-puddled, muddied grass. He gazed at the man's back a moment, with his foot turned over the body. A boy, not a man, with only the faint shadow of hair on chin and upper lip. A boy who had listened to the harper's tales of battle and had felt his heart quicken for the excitement and honour. A boy, who knew nothing of the reality of this goddamned mess! Sons were needed to fight with their fathers. And to die alongside them. The harpers ought sing of that! Sing of the cruelty of losing a beloved son; the pain of wounds that were beyond healing. Arthur sighed. So many sons and fathers dead. So much spilt blood.

He pulled the spear that had killed the boy from the body. Said with regret, "We ought to live together in peace, Cei. Angli, Jute, and Saxon in peace aside us British. Surely there is enough land for us all to build our dwelling places, enough grass to graze our cattle?"

He bent to close the boy's staring, frightened eyes. "Why must strength be shown by the blade of a sword? Why not through discussion and wise talk?"

A voice answered from behind, the accent guttural, the words formed in hesitant Latin. "Because you and I were born to different ideas and beliefs, my Lord King. Differences breed mistrust and suspicions, which spread like weeds in a neglected cornfield. Fear—and greed—grows unchecked until eventually it rots into swollen lies and black untruths. Overspills onto a battlefield."

Arthur remained squatting over the dead boy, wiped his hand across his face, fingers firm against nose, across cheeks, down to the stubble on his chin. Wiped away this seeping mood of bleak depression. He jerked upright, turning with the same movement to clap his hand to the newcomer's shoulder, announced with a smile as broad as a furrowing sow's belly, "But you and I, Winta of the Humbrenses, you and I think different!"

The answering smile was as friendly, as astute. "If we did not my Lord, then would I fight beneath your Dragon against English kinsmen?"

Sliding his arm full around the man's shoulders, Arthur began to steer the tall, fair-haired man towards the northern end of the battlefield, to where, beyond a clump of wind-moulded trees, the British had set their camp. To where soon, the prisoners would be herded and forced to kneel before a British king.

"Some of us," Arthur said, walking with long strides, keeping Winta close by the grip of his hand on the man's arm, "have found enough sight and wisdom to see beyond the differences, to learn of them with interest and intelligence. Some of us," he patted the man's shoulder for good measure, "are astute enough to go into the fields and hoe the weeds. We, my friend, prefer to see the gold of ripening corn."

Arthur halted, beckoned his cousin to walk at his other side. "Some weeds though, can be cultivated, used for good purpose. Can they not, Cei?"

Cei was scowling slightly, saying nothing. To his mind all weeds ought to be pulled up and burnt. He shrugged non-committed. He disliked—no—mistrust-ed Winta, a petty lord over a scattering of Saex settlements along the southern shore of the Abus river. Weeds were weeds, whatever their brilliance of flower or healing use. Angli? Jute? Ally, enemy?

Saex were Saex, whatever their given title and declared promises!

READING GROUP GUIDE

In May, 450 A. D., Uthr Pendragon returns to Britain from exile with his war host, his brother's supposedly illegitimate son, Arthur, and his mistress Morgause. Given the antagonism between Morgause and Arthur, was it wise of Uthr to bring them both along? Seeing Uthr's behavior, which of them does he care for more? What effect do you think Morgause's treatment of Arthur has on him later in life?

Uthr and his host land at Caer Arfon in Gwynedd to join forces with his long-time friend Cunedda, the Lion Lord. They are full partners in their purpose to regain Uthr's lost lands from Vortigern and reinstate Uthr as Supreme King. Yet while Uthr was exiled, Cunedda built Gwynedd from a wasteland to a prospering kingdom. In Cunedda's place, would you have felt resentment at helping someone else gain supreme kingship? Would you have felt resentment at the adoration your people held for another lord?

Initially, Gwenhwyfar feels jealous at the quickly made and close friendship between Arthur and her closest brother, Etern. Then, Gwenhwyfar bears witness to Morgause's hateful treatment of Arthur, and Arthur in turn frees Gwen from the chapel where Branwen has her locked up. Their relationship changes from an uneasy and bickering truce to one of respect and great liking. Have you had personal relationships change from a negative extreme to a positive one? After initial dislike, were you able to trust that person? Become friends with him or her? Fall in love?

Understanding the great danger to him, when Arthur is born his parents let everyone believe that their child has died and that Arthur is the illegitimate child of a serving girl. Everyone treats him as such until his true parentage is revealed after Uthr Pendragon's death. As a parent, would you have been able to give your child up to be raised by strangers, even if you knew it was in the child's best interest? Would you be able to love the child, like Uthr, or do you think you would turn away, like Ygrainne?

Branwen always treats Gwenhwyfar very harshly. Consider Branwen's motivation. Is she well-meaning but overzealous, or is she malicious? Is Branwen testing her husband's loyalty to her? Is she seeking Cunedda's approval and recognition? Does she think Gwenhwyfar is growing up too free-spirited for a girl, needing discipline to prevent this behavior into adulthood? According to the values of the time, is she right?

After Uthr's death, Cunedda advises a young Arthur to seek service with their arch-enemy, Vortigern. Do you think that this was good advice given the circumstances? Arthur complies and goes to serve Vortigern—what does that say about Arthur's personality? Would you be able to work for the man who had killed your father, even if it would bring about his eventual downfall?

After Vortigern defeats Cunedda and Uthr's war band, Cunedda discovers that the Christian priest at Caer Arfon had betrayed them to Vortigern, leading to the burning of the church. Cunedda and his family believe in the Old Ways, but as Christians, Cunedda's oldest living son, Osmail, and his wife, Branwen, angrily leave Gwynedd. Do you feel the people of Gwynedd were justified in burning the church? Is it significant to you that they burned a church as opposed to any other building?

In order to save the people of Gwynedd, Cunedda agrees to Vortigern's demand that Gwenhwyfar wed Melwas, one of Vortigern's allies and therefore an enemy of Gwynedd. If you were in Cunedda's position, would you have been able to sacrifice the happiness of someone you loved in order to save the lives of many people? This makes Cunedda a good ruler, certainly, but is he a good father? Cunedda never feels right about this commitment. Do you think he made the right decision in waiting so long to tell Gwenhwyfar? In what ways does Cunedda try to make up for the burden he has placed on his daughter?

Arthur is portrayed for a good portion of the novel as a man with hard edges and a strategic mind for battle. He is also an unrelenting womanizer. In Arthurian legend, Arthur is described as a gentle, kind ruler. Were you surprised at this portrayal of Arthur? Did it change your opinion of him?

Arthur agrees to marry Winifred, daughter of Vortigern and his Saxon wife Rowena. Why does Arthur marry Winifred? How would things have been different if Arthur had never married Winifred?

After finding out that Winifred was carrying his child, Arthur decides to take her to the home of his mother Ygrainne, in Less Britain to give birth as he does not want the child born in Saxon territory. Knowing that he had already sent Gwenhwyfar to Ygrainne, do you think it was wise of Arthur to take his wife there? Considering the circumstances, how would you have felt in Gwenhwyfar's position? In Winifred's?

Gwenhwyfar's dagger, inherited from her mother, frequently changes hands by force, trickery, or gift (going to Rowena, Winifred, and Arthur to name a few) before it finally returns to Gwenhwyfar. What do you think the dagger symbolizes?

Arthur first marries Winifred in a Christian ceremony. Then, while in Less Britain, he marries Gwenhwyfar in the Old Way. Which ceremony do you believe was more valid? Arthur marries Gwenhwyfar again in a Christian ceremony at Yns Witrin. Does this legitimize their union even if the first ceremony did not?

If Winifred never accepted Arthur's petition for divorce, was he really free to marry again?

Claustrophobia is Arthur's weakness. How does this affect him as a leader? In what ways, if any, does he compensate or overcompensate for it?

It is divulged that Morgause, Uthr's former mistress and Arthur's former tormentor, is also at Yns Witrin at the time of Arthur and Gwenhwyfar's marriage with a daughter named Morgaine. She had told Arthur earlier that she never let any of her female children live. Why do you think this one was different? Or was she perhaps not telling the truth?

Gwenhwyfar gives birth to her and Arthur's son, Llacheu, at Caer Arfon. When Arthur goes south to Caer Leon to finish off Hengest, Gwenhwyfar secretly goes as well—and takes Llacheu with her. Gwenhwyfar reasons that if the army saw Llacheu they would accept him as heir if need be. Do you think he is safer with Gwenhwyfar and Arthur at Caer Leon, or would Llacheu have been safer at Caer Afron? Who or what is Gwenhwyfar most concerned with when she brings Llacheu to the battlefield? Llacheu? Arthur? Herself? The country they are trying to liberate?

Set in 450 A.D., the way of life in the novel, including character's opinions, interactions, and priorities, seems very different than our modern way of life. Do you believe the way of life back then is actually very different from today? In what ways are things similar?

Winning the title of Supreme King is not easy. Arthur had to be a ruthless warlord in order to gain, and then keep, his position as Supreme King. In your opinion, did the ends justify the means? Do you think another path could have won Arthur his kingship?

ABOUT THE AUTHOR

Helen Hollick lives in London, England with her husband, daughter, and a variety of pets, which include several horses, cats, and two dogs. She has two major interests: Roman/Saxon Britain and the Golden Age of Piracy—the early eighteenth century. Her particular pleasure is researching the facts behind the small glimpses of history and bringing the characters behind those facts to full and glorious life. She has an Honours Diploma in Early Medieval History and is co-scriptwriter for the movie project *1066*.

For up-to-date information you are invited to visit: www.helenhollick.net.